LaVyrle
Spencer
Three Complete Novels

LaVyrle Spencer

Three Complete Novels

The Hellion

Separate Beds

Hummingbird

WINGS BOOKS
NEW YORK
AVENEL, NEW JERSEY

This 1997 edition is published by Wings Books,
a division of Random House Value Publishing, Inc.,
201 East 50th Street, New York, New York, 10022,
by arrangement with Random House Reference & Information Publishing.

Wings Books and colophon are trademarks of
Random House Value Publishing, Inc.

Random House
New York • Toronto • London • Sydney • Auckland
http: / / www.randomhouse.com/

Book design by Clair Moritz

Typeset and printed in the United States of America

Library of Congress Cataloging-in-Publication Data
Spencer, LaVyrle.
    Three complete novels / LaVyrle Spencer.
    p.   cm.
    Contents: The hellion—Separate beds—Hummingbird.
    ISBN 0-517-06017-5
    1. Love stories, American.   I. Title.
    PS3569.P4534A6   1991   91-17657
    813'.54—dc20   CIP

20 19 18 17 16

Contents

The Hellion

To
Charles and Aline Spencer
whom I love so dearly

Chapter 1

IT WAS WELL known around Russellville, Alabama, that Tommy Lee Gentry drove like a rebellious seventeen-year-old, drank like a parolee fresh out, and whored like a lumberjack at the first spring thaw. He owned a four-wheel-drive Blazer for his hunting trips, a sixteen-foot runabout for his fishing trips, and a white Cadillac El Dorado to impress the town in general. He was rarely seen driving any of them without an open beer or an on-the-rocks glass in his hand, more often than not with one arm around some carmine-lipped floozy from up Muscle Shoals way, his left hand dangling limply over the steering wheel and a burning cigarette clamped between his strong white teeth.

And all this in a county that was dry and strongly southern Baptist.

He'll kill himself one day, they all said, and one of his whores right along with him!

On that mellow February afternoon, Tommy Lee was living up to the town's expectations of him, all except for the tinted blonde he was currently seeing. After the news he'd just heard, he had some thinking to do, and he couldn't do it with Bitsy under his arm.

The El Dorado rolled beneath him like a woman just short of climax, and without removing his glowering brown eyes from the road he reached across the front seat, found another can of beer, and popped its top. As he tipped it up, his shaded glasses caught the reflection of pine trees whizzing past at the side of the road he knew by rote. He scarcely looked as if he was aware of the wheel beneath his hand, or the tires spinning beneath the heavy automobile.

From his office on Jackson Avenue to his house on Cedar Creek Lake it was precisely 9.8 miles, and he knew every one of them as intimately as he knew a woman's body. Unconsciously he avoided the rough spots, driving on the left when it suited him, straddling the center line for stretches of a half-mile or more at a time to avoid the ruts and ridges that put rattles into his status symbol. Blindly he reached into his breast pocket, withdrew a pack of ciga-

5

rettes, tipped one out, and lipped it straight from the wrapper. Lifting his hips, he found the lighter in his trouser pocket and squinted above its flame before drawing deep, then taking another pull of beer.

Rachel. Staring at the white center streaks as the car chewed them up, he remembered her face. *Rachel.*

She's a widow now.

He could make this lousy run in nine minutes flat, and had done it on occasion in eight and a half. Today, by God, he'd do it in eight. The pines looked as if they were poured now, one into the next. Beneath his hand he felt a slight tremor in the wheel, but stared fixedly, guiding the car with a single index finger—still cold from the beer—while taking another draw on the cigarette. He glanced at the speedometer. The damn thing had a high of only eighty-five, and the needle quivered between the two digits. He took a sharp right curve with a heavy braking and the long complaint of rubber squealing on tar. Ahead twisted a second curve. He tested his mettle by negotiating it with the beer can cutting off half his vision. On the straightaway again he smiled. *Good job, Tommy Lee. You still got it, boy.* When he hit a sharp left and gave up blacktop for gravel he lost her in a skid, braking sharply and swearing under his breath. But his heart didn't even lurch. Why the hell should it lurch? If a man had really lived, he didn't have to be scared of dying.

And Tommy Lee had really lived.

The car came out of the skid as he cranked sharply on the wheel, ignoring the fact that his driving idiosyncrasies made no sense at all—avoiding jars on the tar, then beating the hell out of the car on these gravel washboards. He reached the turnoff into his place, depressed the button for the power window, and tossed the dead soldier into the underbrush. Thirty seconds later when he careened to a halt in his circular driveway, he nearly stood the car on its hood ornament.

He laughed aloud, raising his face at a sharp angle. Then he fell silent, staring out the windshield at his front door. *Rachel Talmadge.* He hooked his thumbs loosely over the top of the steering wheel, and as he rested his forehead on them his eyes sank closed. *Hollis,* he reminded himself. *Her name is Rachel Hollis now, and you'd best remember it, boy.*

He left the key in the ignition and walked unsteadily toward the house. Nobody within a radius of a hundred miles would steal Tommy Lee's cars, not the way he drove them.

His front door was unlocked. If anybody wanted anything, let them come in and take it. Hell, if it came down to that, all they had to do was ask, and Tommy Lee would deliver it!

His bloodshot eyes traveled across the shadowed room—richness everywhere, enough for three wives and some left to spare, he thought. If there was one thing Tommy Lee knew how to do it was live. And if there were two things he knew how to do it was to live rich. Making money was child's play. Always had been.

His house showed it. He'd hired an architect from Memphis to design the contemporary structure that fell just short of being futuristic. Outside it was wrapped diagonally in rough-sawn cedar, and its steeply canting roof sections were shingled, in cedar shakes. It appeared as an asymmetrical study in geometrics, a staggered cluster of unexpectedly pleasing sections reaching high, then higher, then higher still toward the Alabama sky from between the pines and broadleaves of the surrounding wooded shoreline. A railed catwalk stretched from the driveway to the double front doors, which were glossy black and windowless. Above them a single outsized hexagonal window looked out over the landward side of the property.

Crazy boy, half the town had said when they'd seen the house going up five years ago, after his *third* divorce. Crazy boy, buildin' a house with no windows that looks like three Cracker Jack boxes got caught in a paper cutter.

But the crazy boy now took three loose-kneed bounds up into the living room of a house that had more windows than most. All the windows, however, faced the lake or were tucked coyly amid the junctures of wall and stair to give unexpected splashes of light that surprised when come upon by the first-time visitor.

There wasn't a curtain in the place. Instead, the endless windows were clothed with blue sky and plants potted in glazed earthenware tubs of browns and blues. But the plants looked lifeless and drooping, many with curled, brown leaves that showed how the landlord watered them: with an occasional ice cube dumped from a cocktail glass.

Tommy Lee stopped beside a sickly looking shoulder-high schefflera and stared through a sheet of glass at a lake that wasn't there. *Damn,* he thought, *I wish it would hurry and rise.* Pushing back his leather sports coat, he threaded his hands in his pockets and stared out disconsolately.

If I could get in my boat and open it up, I could drive her *out of my mind.*

But the Bear Creek Water Control System and the Tennessee Valley Authority controlled the flooding of the 900-square-mile Bear Creek Watershed System on which Tommy Lee lived, so Cedar Creek Lake wasn't really a lake at all but the backwash of man's whims, controlled by a series of four dams and reservoirs. And right now, man's whims dictated that Tommy Lee look out over nothing but lake bottom exposed to the sunset sky, a flat, muddy expanse of sticks, stones, and logs with nothing but a damp spring-fed creek running up the middle of what would be the deepest channel of the lake in midsummer.

Turning from the depressing sight, Tommy Lee faced another that did little to cheer him. The waning sun spilled across plush navy-blue carpet, revealing a three-week collection of lint and ashes. It exposed glass-topped tables, which should have been lustrous but were filmed with dust and blighted by rings from sweating glasses, long dried. Twenty-dollar ashtrays whose blue and brown ceramic artistry had been carefully chosen by an interior decorator were buried beneath a stale collection of dead butts. Clothes were strewn along the back of a sprawling sand-hued conversation pit, which faced a limestone fireplace.

Tommy Lee stood, staring, for a full minute. Then he swiped up a yellow cotton-knit shirt, whipping it off the back of the sofa. Damn them! Damn them all! He sliced the air with the shirt as if driving a golf ball, then his hand fell still and his chin dropped disconsolately to his chest. He rubbed his eyes, opened them, and mechanically dropped the shirt onto the floor.

Hungry. That's what he was. Should've had a steak in town, but food had been the last thing on his mind after hearing the news.

He leaned against the back of the sofa and pulled off his loafers, then padded in stocking feet around the fireplace to a deep, narrow kitchen. At the lake end of the room a table and chairs of chrome and cane sat in the embrasure of corner windows. The tabletop was dusty and held a motley assortment of articles: several days' mail, a jar of instant coffee, a cup holding pitch-black dregs, a fingernail clipper and, oddly out of context, a spool of thread. On the opposite side of the room the countertops were bare of all but an electric blender, a coffee maker, and a sea of dirty glasses.

Tommy Lee draped an elbow over the open refrigerator door, tugging at his tie while studying a can of tomato juice with thickened red showing at the triangular tears in its top. He contemplated it for long minutes, trying to remember when he'd opened it. Sighing, he reached for it, swirled the contents, took a mouthful, then lunged to the sink to spit it out. He backhanded his mouth, turned on the water full force, and searched for a clean glass. Finding none, he lowered his mouth to the running stream, rinsed, and spit again. Turning, he found the refrigerator door still open, slapped it shut so hard the appliance rocked, then stared at it.

"Goddamn," he whispered, still staring, disassociated again from all around him. In time he moved back to the living room, where his stocking feet halted at the yellow shirt he'd dropped earlier. He studied it until it became a blurred puddle, and the silence roared around his ears. The sun was warm on his back as he dropped his chin to his chest, slipped his fingers beneath his glasses to press his eye sockets. Suddenly he snapped backward and roared at the ceiling, *"Where is everybody!"*

But, of course, nobody was expected. Only Tommy Lee. And he was home.

The funeral was held on a flawless golden day, the Alabama sky a clear blue bowl overhead. Tommy Lee Gentry was the last to arrive at Franklin Memory Gardens, pulling the white Cadillac up behind the long line of vehicles, then quietly slipping into the outer fringe of mourners circling the grave.

He picked out Rachel immediately, studying her back as she clung to her daddy's arm while from all around came the sound of soft weeping.

Rachel. My Rachel. I'm still here . . . waiting.

It had been twenty-four years since he'd been this close to her. He'd been a boy then, green and seventeen, and though he was no boy now, even at forty-one being in her presence made him feel like one again, uncertain and vulnerable.

After all these years, all these mistakes, the sensation swept back with unkind intensity.

A pain lanced his heart as he studied her; she had grown so thin. But there were appealing changes, too, ones he'd intrinsically sensed happening through the years, living in the same town as they did. She had acquired style, a thin-boned chic that had perhaps looked healthy until the last half-year had turned it nearly emaciated. Even so, the pearl-gray fabric of her designer dress draped upon her shoulders with a look of understated elegance few could manage, given that thinness. Unlike his own, her hair had gained a reprieve from grayness. It was still as rich as black-belt loam, and equally as dark. She wore it shorter now, but with an elegant flair that spoke of costly professional attention. Watching her, Tommy Lee felt the old familiar ache in his heart.

* * *

Rachel Hollis stared at a spray of white roses bound by an enormous satin bow with gilt letters on its streamers. Beneath the bouquet, the polished bronze of the coffin caught the afternoon sun and sent it scintillating along a gleaming crease in the metal, like a white laser. A lone mockingbird perched on a nearby headstone, running through its repertoire. A soft breeze, scented with camellia, caught a streamer and sent it tapping against the coffin cover: Beloved Son and Husband.

But Rachel shut it all out, all the draining ordeal of the past two years, clinging to her daddy's arm until some faint movement of his elbow brought her back to the present. The service was over. Hands squeezed hers, cheeks were pressed to hers, murmured condolences were offered, and finally the mourners drifted toward their cars. Everett's steadying hand turned her toward the waiting black limousine.

Suddenly his fingers tightened on her elbow as he demanded in a vehement undertone, "What's *he* doing here?"

Rachel lifted mournful eyes and for the first time saw the man standing some fifteen feet away. Her feet became rooted and her heart seemed to come alive.

Tommy Lee. Oh, God, Tommy Lee, you came.

She felt herself blanch, and she became slightly lightheaded. Her father's thumb dug into her elbow, ordering her to turn and leave, but her body remained riveted, eyes drawn to the man who studied her from such a short distance away. After twenty-four years of avoiding each other at every possible turn, there he was. Deliberately.

Like characters in a ballet they stood poised, gazes fixed, seeing nothing beyond each other.

She could make out his eyes only partially. He now wore glasses, the rimless type with only a strip of gold winking across his eyebrows. The shaded brown lenses hid his upper eyelids and left only enough iris visible to intrigue. Beneath a rich brown leather sports coat the oyster-colored collar of an expensive shirt had been drawn up tightly by a raw-silk tie.

"Rachel, come," her father commanded sternly. "We have to go." He might as well have ordered a stone carving to move. Rachel's body had gone stiff, captivated by Tommy Lee as he slowly, deliberately crossed the space between them. She held her breath and felt her heart knocking out a warning.

He didn't stop until he was so close she had to raise her chin to meet his gaze.

"Hello, Rachel." His voice was deeper, gruffer than she remembered, and his eyes held a sadness reaching far beyond sympathy. She didn't realize she had pulled away from her father until Tommy Lee captured her icy hand in both of his, squeezing slowly, slowly, but too tightly for the handclasp to be merely consoling. She felt a tremor in his fingers, became aware of how much thicker they were, how much fuller his palms. They were a man's hands now, and it struck Rachel that in the intervening years he'd grown perhaps two inches taller.

But there were other changes, too. He had grown heavy. Even his stylishly tailored sports coat couldn't quite conceal the extra weight at his midsection, and his constricting collar pressed a bulge of skin upward, revealing the fact that his neck had lost much of its firmness. There were deep grooves running from his handsome nose to his well-remembered lips, and lines of dissipation about his eyes. His coloring was not the healthy brown of their youth but tinged with a telltale undertone of pink. Apparently all they said about him was true.

"Hello, Tommy Lee," she answered at last, trying to keep her voice steady.

Of course they'd seen each other many times over the passing years. It was unavoidable in a town the size of Russellville. But never this close. Always, one of them had crossed the street or become politely engaged in conversation with some passerby when the other approached.

But now their eyes clung . . . for longer than was prudent. Suddenly Tommy Lee became aware of Everett Talmadge's scowl and dropped Rachel's hand reluctantly.

"Sir," he greeted with a curt nod.

"Gentry," Talmadge acknowledged coldly. The animosity between them was palpable and made Tommy Lee take a single step back. Still, he could not resist returning his attention to Rachel for a moment longer.

"I hope you don't mind that I came, Rachel. I heard the news and wanted to offer my condolences personally."

"Of course I don't mind. We . . ." She glanced guardedly at her father and amended, "I'm so glad you did. Thank you, Tommy Lee." The name sounded ill-suited now that the boy had become a man, yet the years had schooled her till she could think of him by no other.

"I didn't know Owen personally, but everyone around town says he was a wonderful man. I'm sorry. If there's anything I can do . . ."

The tears brightened Rachel's deep brown eyes, making them gleam and appear larger, childlike in their threat of full-scale weeping. He reached for her hand again. "Rachel, I shouldn't have come," he said hoarsely.

She felt her control slipping and her heart thrusting heavily in her breast. A blink brought the tears pooling as she rose on tiptoe to press her cheek briefly to his. "No . . . no, I'm glad you did. Thank you, Tommy Lee." Then she spun around, linked her arm through her father's, and strode hastily toward the waiting black limousine.

Her scent seemed to linger at his jaw as his eyes followed the car along a row of bare forsythias, around a bend, until it was obscured by a line of gnarled cedars. He sighed, hung his head and stared at the toe of one shiny Italian loafer, then removed his glasses and wearily rubbed his eyes. But her face remained, revived.

What good are regrets? Almost angrily he replaced his glasses, reached for his cigarettes, and lit up with the unconscious motions of the seasoned smoker.

The mockingbird was still singing. The click of the lighter was the only other sound in the deserted stillness. The smell of roses became cloying, and his nostrils flared, drawing in a diaphanous line of gray to obliterate the floral scent. Absently he studied the silver-spindled branches of a nearby crepe myrtle bush. Its leafless limbs appeared pearlescent, like the color of Rachel's mourning dress. Drawing on the cigarette, he turned back toward the coffin of her husband.

Owen Hollis. What had her life been like with him? Had she been happy? Had he been good to her? What had she suffered during Hollis's bout with cancer? Why had they never had children? And, above all, had she ever told her husband about Tommy Lee Gentry?

He swung toward the only other stone in the Talmadge plot: Eulice, Rachel's mother, dead four years now. He hooked a shoe on the polished curve of marble, braced an elbow on his knee and squinted as the smoke drifted up, unheeded. *Why did you do it, Eulice? You and that husband of yours . . . and my own mother and father?*

He took one last deep drag, but the taste of the cigarette had grown acrid, so he withdrew it from his lips and with a fillip sent it spiraling through the air.

I never should have come here today. What the hell good did it do? He dragged his foot from the tombstone, slipped his hands into his trouser pockets, and turned sadly toward the car.

Nothing is changed. Nothing.

Rachel had been running on sheer willpower for days now, months—for two years, actually, ever since Owen had learned he had cancer. Though she'd kept herself from breaking down during the graveside ceremony, she was perilously near it as the black limousine pulled up before the house on Cotako Street where she'd grown up.

Stepping from the car, she raised her eyes to the familiar beige limestone on the double-gabled structure. The entry and portico were fronted by a deep overhang behind wide limestone arches that supported the arm of the house holding her upstairs bedroom. The diamond-shaped framework of the small casement windows matched the diamond pattern of the dark shingles. Her mother's narcissus still bloomed gaily out front, and the azalea and holly bushes were carefully tended, though by a gardener these days. The same English ivy climbed the side chimney. The same cedars flanked the north side of the house. And the same sweetgum tree dropped its spiked artillery on the highpitched roof and sent it rolling earthward. How many times had she and Tommy Lee, barefoot, stepped on those sweetgum balls and gone howling to one of their mothers in pain? Either mother. Whichever one happened to be nearby. In those days it hadn't mattered—the families were so close.

Unable to resist, Rachel glanced next door, but the view of the Gentry house was almost completely obscured by the high boxwood hedge that had been allowed to grow along the property line, untrimmed, for twenty-four years now.

Tommy Lee. But he wasn't there. He hadn't set foot on the place for years. As if he'd been watching, Everett took her elbow to guide her up the sidewalk, discouraging her from dwelling on the past.

Inside, the funeral party was gathered. Voices hummed and the scent of expensive cigars drifted above that of fresh-brewed coffee. The faces were those of people Rachel had known all her life: the town's elite. Half were close to her age, the other half closer to her father's.

When she'd weathered what seemed like hours of well-meant condolences until she felt she could stand no more, she slipped upstairs to her old bedroom. It was tucked beneath the gables, its ceiling following the roof peaks, creating a pair of cozy niches. The walls were papered with the same pink daisies she'd chosen at age thirteen. Her hand trailed over the flowers as she recalled that she had brought Tommy Lee up here to show him, the minute the paper was hung. That was in the days when they'd felt free to spend brief, innocent minutes in each other's bedrooms, where they'd often played as toddlers.

The bed was a girl's, a four-poster with a canopy of airy white eyelet to match the tiered spread and the tiebacks at the recessed windows. Though the room was cleared of mementos, the fixtures remained as they'd been years ago, dredging up memories of the days when her mother was alive and everybody on both sides of the boxwood hedge was happy.

At the south window Rachel held back the folds of white eyelet, studying the house where Gaines and Lily Gentry still lived. It was brought clearly to view from this high vantage point several feet above the hedge.

The shared history of the Talmadges and the Gentrys went back even further than Rachel's memory allowed. But what she couldn't remember was kept alive in old photo albums her father could never quite bring himself to throw away.

The two couples had settled into these houses as young up-and-coming pillars of the community. The men had played golf, the women tennis, and together they'd made up a foursome at bridge. Then, in the same year, both Lily and Eulice had become pregnant. They'd compared their discomforts and hopes and, together with their husbands, the names they'd chosen even before their babies were born.

Rachel and Tommy Lee came into the world only two months apart. Side by side they'd had their diapers changed, been plunked into the same playpen while their mothers drank coffee, and into the same backyard splash pool—naked—while their mothers sipped iced tea and talked about their children's future. When one of the youngsters inadvertently hurt the other with a careless toss of a toy, the mothers taught them to kiss and make it better, and sat back to watch their offsprings' rotund bodies grow healthy and vigorous.

At six, Rachel and Tommy Lee had toddled bravely, hand in hand, up Cotako Street Hill to begin first grade at College Avenue Elementary. In second grade they'd lost their front teeth simultaneously, and in third Tommy Lee, while trying to string a tin-can telephone between his bedroom window and Rachel's, had broken his arm falling out of the pecan tree that intervened between the two houses.

Both dark, brown-eyed beauties, blessed with good health and sunny dispositions, Tommy Lee and Rachel had grown up knowing the pride of their parents' eyes each time they achieved the next plateau of maturity, and sensing their parents' approval as they ran off together to whatever pursuit called them at any given age.

The memories struck Rachel like an assault—so many of them.

Her eyes dropped to the hedge. From above, it was clearly visible where the single boxwood had been left unplanted to create a walk-through between the two yards. Not even twenty-four years had disguised its original intent; it seemed to be waiting for one of them to breach it and cross again into the neighboring yard.

She'd been reminiscing for long minutes, her head leaning against the window frame when Callie Mae found her there.

"Miss Rachel?"

At the sound of the familiar voice, Rachel turned to find wide arms waiting to gather her in and tears glittering in the kind eyes.

"Callie Mae." The black woman was shaped like a wrecking ball, her skin the color of sorghum syrup, and she smelled of the kitchen, as she always had. "Oh, Callie Mae." For a moment the two women comforted each other; then Callie Mae drew back, holding Rachel's arms tightly in her broad hands.

"What you doin' up here, hidin' away?"

Rachel sniffed and ran a hand beneath her eyes. "Exactly that, hiding away."

"Your daddy lookin' for you."

"I just needed to come up here for a while. To think."

Callie Mae's eyes roved to the window briefly. " 'Bout Mr. Owen?"

Rachel turned aside guiltily. "Yes. Among other things."

"I seen you standin' there lookin' across the yards. Can about imagine what *other things.*" But there was no note of scolding in the older woman's voice. Instead it was reflective and sad. "Don't seem right they don't come and pay their respects on a day like this. But then it's the second time somebody died in this family and they was too stubborn to do what they knew was right."

"It's not only them. It's Daddy, too."

"Yes. Stubborn fools."

For a moment Rachel tried to repress the words, but in the end could not hold them back.

"Tommy Lee came to the cemetery today."

Callie Mae silently rolled her eyes, folded her hands, and said, "Halleluja." Then she caught Rachel's chin with one imperious finger, forcing it up while she noted, "So *that's* why you're cryin'."

Callie Mae had been the Talmadges's maid when Rachel and Tommy Lee were growing up, and in the years since Eulice's death had divided that duty between Rachel's house and Everett's. There were no secrets kept from Callie Mae.

"Partly."

Again Rachel was wrapped in a motherly hug. "Well, you go ahead, get it all out o' your system. You just cry it out, then you'll feel better. And when you're done, you come down to the kitchen." She backed away and smiled down at the woman she would always look upon as a girl no matter how adult and refined she'd become. "Got your favorite down there, cream cheese pound cake."

That at last brought a wan smile to Rachel's face. Food was Callie Mae's panacea for all the troubles in this world.

"Not today, Callie Mae. I just don't think I could hold anything down."

"Hmph! You nothin' but skin and bones, Miss Rachel. It's time you started eatin' right again." She turned toward the door with a sigh. "Well, time I got back down there."

When she was gone, Rachel listened to the sound of voices from below. Lord, she was so tired. If she waited a few more minutes, maybe the last of them would leave.

She crossed to the bed, tested the mattress with five fingertips, and fell across the white eyelet spread with an arm thrown above her head. She closed her eyes and for a moment was fourteen again, a blushing fourteen, lying in bed quaking with disbelief because Tommy Lee Gentry had just kissed her in the break of the boxwood hedge. For the first time—*really* kissed her. Then his eyes had widened with wonder and he'd walked backwards to his side of the yard while she'd stood staring, amazed, for several heart-thumping seconds before spinning to her own yard and racing, as if a ghost were chasing her, up the stairs to this room, to this bed, to flop on her back and stare at the white canopy in the moonlight and feel herself begin to change from girl to woman.

Rachel rolled to her back, eyes closed, soul shot with guilt for dredging up dreams of Tommy Lee within hours after burying her husband. Where were the memories of Owen? Did nineteen years of happy marriage count for nothing? She thought of their childless house, and emptiness clawed upward through her body. If only there were children—someone to comfort her now, to help her through the days ahead. Instead, Rachel faced the dismal prospect of returning to the empty house alone.

"Oh, here you are, Rachel."

At the sound of Everett's voice, Rachel coiled off the bed as if caught perpetrating an indecent act upon it.

"Daddy . . . I'm sorry. I must have drifted off."

"Marshall was looking for you."

"Oh. I'll go down in a minute. I just needed to get away."

Everett's eyes slowly circled the room. "Finding you here in your room this way . . . it brings back memories of when you were a girl and your mother was alive." Absently he wandered to the south window, drew back the curtain and gazed at the view beyond. "Times were so happy then." As if suddenly realizing what he'd been staring at, he dropped the curtain. "I wonder if I'll ever stop missing her."

You could have friends, she thought. *Two more than you've got. Two who meant so much to both of you at one time.* She glanced at the top of the Gentry house beyond her father's shoulder, then at his back. It was slightly stooped now—funny, she'd never noticed it before. But then, the weight of guilt rested heavily; it was bound to weigh him down in time.

But he was still her father, and in spite of everything she loved him. At times when she remembered, when she thought of all she'd missed, she found it possible to hate him. But he was human, had needs, perhaps even regrets, though these he never revealed.

Very quietly she asked, "Do you ever see them?"

His shoulders stiffened. "Drop it, Rachel." But his stern tone only forced her on.

"I've heard that Tommy Lee doesn't talk to them anymore."

"I wouldn't know. And it's none of my business."

You made it your business twenty-four years ago, Daddy, she thought. But aloud she only observed in the quietest of voices, "I was looking at the hedge you and Gaines Gentry planted all those years ago. You can still see the break where—"

"Rachel!" he barked, swinging around. "I fail to understand how you can be preoccupied with thoughts like that on a day when you've just buried Owen."

She flushed, standing before him with fingers clasping and unclasping against her stomach. Guilt came creeping over her, and she upbraided herself for speaking of the Gentrys today of all days. She studied Everett's face, noting how gray and shaken he was. "I'm sorry, Daddy. Owen's death has been terrible for you, hasn't it?" It was an odd question from a widow, but they both knew her relationship with Owen had been staid, comfortable at best, and the past six months had been hell for her. His death had come as somewhat of a relief, so Rachel had her guilt, too.

"I had such plans for him," Everett sighed, prowling the room, avoiding his daughter's eyes.

"I know you did." Owen had been his hope, the son he'd never had, his right hand in business. But Everett's shoulders lifted in a fortifying sigh, and he turned again to his daughter.

"I guess we'd better go back down. I left the Hollises there, visiting with Marshall."

"Yes, I guess we'd better." But she wondered how she'd tolerate any more of Pearl Hollis's noisy weeping, or Frank Hollis's dolorous looks, which seemed to say, if only Owen had had children.

But children, like boxwood hedges, were never mentioned; both were taboo subjects in this house.

Downstairs Marshall True was waiting, gallant and accommodating as always. "Rachel dear, I was worried about you." He came forward quickly, reaching for her hands. She gripped his fingers, relying upon him once again for emotional support, while Marshall's kind gray eyes rested upon hers reassuringly. "Whenever you're ready I'll take you home."

An hour later, as the two of them rode toward Rachel's house in Marshall's car, she slumped back against the seat with a sigh. His understanding eyes moved to her, then back to the street. "I know the feeling well. I remember when Joan died, how difficult it was to dream up responses to all the well-meaning phrases friends came up with."

Rachel closed her eyes. "Am I ungrateful, Marshall? I don't mean to be."

"No, dear, I don't think so. Just tired. Tired of it all, and glad it's over."

She rolled her head to look at him and asked quietly, "Am I really allowed to be glad it's over?"

"You shouldn't have to ask that question of me, of all people."

She smiled wanly, remembering how Marshall had seen them through the worst of it, cheering Owen through the depressions, bolstering Rachel's courage when bleakness threatened to beat her down, remaining steadfast until the end, just as they had done for him when his wife had died four years ago.

"But I feel so guilty because I . . . I'm relieved he's gone."

"That's natural, when the death has been lingering."

Was there another person in the world who always knew the precise thing to say, at the precise time it was needed, the way he did?

"Thank you, Marshall. I simply don't know what I'd have done without you."

He pulled up in Rachel's driveway and reached for her hand. "Well, perhaps we're even, then. You and Owen were the only ones who saved me from breaking down after Joan died. And I intend to hang around and do the same for you." As if to illustrate, he turned off the engine and solicitously came around to open her door. "Now, what's this I hear about you taking a trip?"

"Oh, so Daddy told you."

"Yes. St. Thomas, he said. I think it's a wise idea." They went in the front door of a house that could only have been described as gracious. Rachel led the way through a slate-floored entry, which came alight beneath a brass and crystal chandelier. Then she switched on a lamp in a living room decorated in ice blue and touches of apricot. A quilted floral sofa was fronted by a pair of bun-footed Victorian chairs, the grouping centered around a marble-topped table holding five blue candles on five gold candlesticks of staggered heights, a pair of brass giraffes, and a brandy snifter filled with potpourri. Every piece of furniture in the room looked as if it had just been purchased that day. The regal tiebacks on the windows were hung so perfectly they might have been advertisements for an interior decorator. The carpeting was so lush their footsteps left imprints in its ice-blue nap.

And the house smelled delicious. Rachel not only scented it with crystal snifters of potpourri, but left tiny open cedar boxes of crushed rose petals on end tables, hung pomander balls in her closets, tucked stems of herbs into gold cricket boxes in the bathrooms, and hid delicate organdy sachet pillows of Flora Danica fragrance amid her personal garments in the bureau drawers.

That lavish touch was repeated in the careful selection of each item in each room. It was the home of a woman accustomed to luxury.

Marshall studied Rachel as she stood in the middle of the painfully neat living room, rubbing her arms.

"You know, Rachel, you don't have to worry about money. The check from Owen's life insurance policy should be here by the time you get back."

Marshall was an insurance broker, and he had seen to protecting both Rachel and Owen with adequate coverage years ago. Also, he was that kind of man—careful, a long-range planner, one who did things at their appointed time and kept life's business affairs in impeccable order. He would, he had assured both her and Owen before Owen died, keep an eye on Rachel's affairs and be there to advise whenever she felt she needed him. Having made the promise, he was certain to keep it.

"I'll drop by now and then to make sure things are working okay —the pool cleaner and the air conditioner. You know how things have a way of breaking down when you're gone," he offered. That was Marshall, all right. He kept everything of his own in sterling condition, from his clothing to his grass, and it was often joked about in their social circle that when and if he sold his property, he'd come back to reprimand anyone who dared let it fall into disrepair.

Rachel fondly placed her hands on his forearms. "You don't have to worry about me, Marshall. I can take care of myself."

"I know you can. But I promised Owen."

"But the furnace won't break down, and the pool will keep filtering, and . . . and . . ." Suddenly Rachel was immensely glad to have Marshall there, a living, breathing entity who knew how dreadful it would have been for her to face the empty house alone at this moment.

She bit her lower lip to keep it from trembling, but tears spilled, nonetheless. "Oh, Marshall . . . oh, God . . ." Her chest felt crushed as he took her into his arms, gently, consolingly. "Oh, thank you for coming home with me. I didn't know how I was going to face it alone."

"You don't have to thank me. You know that." His voice was gruff against her hair. "I loved him, too."

"I'll . . . I'll be all right in a minute."

"Take it from me, dear, you won't be. Not in a minute, or a week, or even a month. But whenever you need somebody, all you have to do is call, and I'll be right here."

Before he left, Marshall walked through the house to make sure everything was safe and sound. Watching his tall form walk away, she thought, Whatever *would* I do without him? He was as steady as Gibraltar, as dependable as taxes, and as sensible as rain. Owen said before he died, "You know, Rachel, you can rely upon Marshall for anything."

She had wondered at the time if Owen was hinting that he himself might choose Marshall for her . . . if and when. But Marshall wasn't that sort. Not steady-as-you-go, polite, socially adept Marshall. He was simply the kindest man she knew, and one with whom she'd shared the most devastating of human experiences not once, but twice.

But when he was gone, she still faced the desolation of going to bed alone. The house seemed eerie, especially the bedroom she and Owen had shared. When she'd donned her nightgown, she crept instead to one of the guest bedrooms across the hall, lying stiffly upon the strange-feeling mattress in the dark—unmoving, for a long time. Rachel had been propelled from one necessity to the next for so long, putting off the awesome need to cry. But there was little else she could have done, with no children to take over the burdens. It was the thought of children that did it at last. The dam cracked, then buckled, and when her tears came, they struck with the force of a tidal wave. She gripped the sheets, twisting in despair, sobbing pitifully into the dark. The racking sound of those sobs, coming back to her own ears, only made her cry the harder.

She cried for all the pain Owen had suffered, and for her own powerlessness to help him. She cried for the dream-filled girl she'd once been, and the disillusioned woman she now was. She cried because for almost two decades she'd been married to a man with whom she'd had a comfortably staid marriage when what she'd wanted was occasional tumult. She cried because in one split second she had looked up at a man's face across a quiet graveyard, and that tumult had sprung within her when it was her husband who should have caused it to surface all these years. She cried because it seemed a sin to admit such a thing to herself on the very night of his funeral.

And when her body was aching with loss and desolation, she cried for Owen's child, which she'd never conceived.

And for Tommy Lee's child, which she had.

Chapter 2

ON THE FOURTH morning following the funeral, Tommy Lee found little to smile about. He awakened sprawled on the sofa, still wearing a tweed sports coat, trousers, and tie, a foul taste in his mouth, and a head beating like a voodoo drum. Gingerly he rolled over, sat up, and nursed his tender head.

Upstairs things were a little better. The sun was already up behind the dogwoods and cedars and came cascading into his east bedroom and bath, bringing the sounds of spring birds from the trees.

Naked, he brushed his teeth, then straightened to study his reflection in the generous mirror above the vanity. His conclusion was the same as ever. *You got to lose some weight, boy. You got to slow down with the women and spend a little time on healthier activities.*

But somehow he never did. Somehow the beer was always too cold to refuse, and the women too warm. Life had its compensations.

But out of the blue came the thought of Rachel, svelte and graceful, not an ebony hair out of place, smelling sweet, still beautiful. What would she think if she saw him this way?

Angrily he spit, drew a mouthful of water and tilted his head back while rinsing, spit again, but avoided looking in the mirror while he tossed his wet toothbrush onto the vanity top and flicked on the radio. From its speaker, WWWR announced it had been serving Franklin County and Northwest Alabama since 1949. Then a strong female voice musically advised Tommy Lee to "Blame It on Love."

The hiss of the shower cut her off in mid-word.

For three days he'd resisted the urge to drive past Rachel's store, but when he arrived in town later that morning he gave in, passing his own office and continuing north along Jackson Avenue, the main drag of town, until he came abreast of a small dress shop on the left. Above the door hung a crisp sign bearing a distinctive stylized lily and the word "Panache." He recalled when she'd first opened the place, ten years ago, that he'd looked up the word to find it meant "dashing elegance." At the time he'd been amused. Russellville, Alabama—population 10,000—seemed ill-chosen as a town to be availed of dashing elegance. Nonetheless, she'd brought a touch of it here. Above and beyond this, Rachel was an astute businesswoman. The store had succeeded, then thrived.

Poised, well dressed, genteel, she'd set a fine example for the ladies of the town. By now, every woman in Russellville knew who Rachel Hollis was. She was the pretty one, the soft-spoken one, the one in the Evan Picone suits and the Vidal Sassoon nail polish, the one who gave something from her store to every fund raiser, attended the First Baptist Church on Jackson Avenue, drove a sedate four-door sedan, had her hair done regularly in Florence, and lived in an elegant home on the east edge of town. She was the wife of that nice young man who worked at the bank with Rachel's daddy. She was Everett Talmadge's daughter.

As Tommy Lee drove past Panache, he saw Verda McElroy approach the front door and open up for the day. For a moment he thought she'd turn and see the white Cadillac cruising past, and he breathed a sigh of relief when

Verda brushed inside and closed the door without turning around. He drove two blocks farther, swung over to Washington and returned to his own office at the south end of Jackson.

He drew up before a small brick building with white shutters, the home of TLG Enterprises, Ltd. Tommy Lee really didn't need an office; he could easily have run his business affairs out of his home. But renting the building got him out of the empty house and gave him somewhere to go during the day. It also provided a place for Liz Scroggins to answer the phone and carry on the secretarial duties he required.

Liz was thirty-five and divorced, and one of the few women who'd ever sent out signals Tommy Lee had ignored. Oh, she'd never sent them overtly, probably never even realized she'd sent them at all, for Liz was a perfect lady. She was a looker, all right, but too damn good a worker to risk losing at the end of a messy affair. So Tommy Lee always got his poon tangin' someplace else.

He gave her a smile as he sauntered in and stopped before her desk. Though he drove like a wild man, he never appeared to be in a hurry when on foot.

"Well, good mornin', Liz."

"Mornin', Mr. Gentry."

"Don't you look like a li'l azalea blossom today." His eyes scanned her neat pink dress and he saw her blush.

"You say that every morning, I swear."

He laughed, unaware of the inborn Southern charm he exuded as he idled before her desk. "Well, then, it must be true." He did, in fact, admire the way Liz dressed, never in slacks, her golden hair always freshly fluffed and curled, her makeup conscientiously applied. There were times when he thought it was a shame she was his secretary. "I'm expecting some quotes from Hensley in the mail today. Let me know when they come in."

She nodded and leafed through three written messages, handing them across the desk, one at a time. "Muldecott called from the Florence Bank. A Mr. Trudeau called from Sheffield Engineering." Liz kept her eyes carefully downcast as she slipped the last message across to him. "And your daughter called and asked to have you call her as soon as you got in."

As he took the yellow slip of paper, Tommy Lee's eyebrows drew into a frown. "Thank you, Liz." Already he was moving toward his private office. The door was rarely closed between the two rooms, and he left it open now as he picked up the phone and dialed Muscle Shoals.

"Hiya, baby, it's Daddy."

"Ohhh, Daddy, you'll never guess what's come up. Marianne Wills is having this pool party and I've been invited, but Mother refuses to let me go because there are gonna be boys there, too. She says I'm too young, but everybody I know is going, Daddy, and they're all fourteen, the same as me. Will you talk to her and get her to change her mind?"

"Baby, you know your mother won't change her mind because of anything I say."

"Pleeease, Daddy."

Tommy Lee rocked forward in his chair and wearily rubbed his forehead. "Beth, if I take your side it'll only make things worse. You and your mother will just have to fight it out."

"That's all we ever *do* is fight!"

"I know, I know . . ."

There followed a brief silence, then Beth's voice again, softer, more pleading. "Daddy, I hate it here. Why can't I come and live with you?"

"We've been over that a hundred times before."

"But, Daddy, she——"

"Your mother won't allow it, Beth. You know that."

Beth's voice suddenly turned accusing. "You don't want me. You don't want me any more than she does!"

Pain knifed through Tommy Lee's heart. "That's not true, Beth. You know I'd have you with me in a minute if I could." He knew Beth was manipulating him again, but the pain was real, nevertheless. As he always did, he sought an antidote. "Listen, honey, just in case she breaks down and lets you go to the party after all, how would you like a brand-new bathing suit?"

"Really, Daddy?" By the quick brightness in his daughter's voice it was apparent to Tommy Lee that he was only adding to her problem by trying to buy her off, but he felt helpless, and the offer of a new suit eased his guilt. "There'll be a nice crisp fifty-dollar bill in the mail tomorrow. Now, will you try to make peace with your mother, and don't buck every decision she makes?"

"I'll try, Daddy, but she's——"

"She's doing the best she can, baby. Try to remember that."

Why did I defend Nancy? he wondered after he'd hung up. *She's a nagging bitch and Beth has done well to live with her for this long.*

Liz appeared in his doorway, leaned one arm against it, and studied him with a sympathetic expression on her face. "You know you shouldn't send her the fifty dollars again, don't you?"

He turned from the window, his unsmiling face masking a thousand hidden emotions. "I know. Don't nag me, Liz."

"If I don't, who will? My ex-husband pulls that on me, and for days after the boys visit him, I'm the bad guy around home. Nothing I can do or say is right. The boys keep saying, but Daddy does this, and Daddy lets us do that. Sometimes I want to tell them, If you want to go live with your father, *go.*"

He sighed. "Maybe I wish that's what Nancy would say."

"Do you?" she asked quietly. A man with your lifestyle—her expression seemed to say—what would you do with a fourteen-year-old daughter?

"That house is so big and so damn empty it echoes."

She assessed him silently for several seconds before adding softly, "When you're in it alone."

Surprisingly enough, Tommy Lee had the grace to blush. His relationship with Liz was unlike any he shared with any other women. They were aware of each other's availability, and a fine sexual tension hummed between them at moments like this. Yet they both understood that if it ever snapped, she'd lose the best job she'd ever had—and the friendship of a man whose life-style she should abhor, but for whom she instead felt a great deal of pity, because she could see beyond the ceaseless chasing to the loneliness it masked.

Liz pulled away from the door frame. "You wanted me to remind you that you were going to meet at eleven this morning with the people from the city about the zoning regulations on that apartment complex." The tension eased and they became merely boss and employee again.

"Thanks, Liz."

He watched her pink dress disappear around the corner and wondered what he lacked that he couldn't marry some nice woman like her and settle down companionably and work toward building a home with some permanent love in it, and think about approaching old age. Wasn't one woman enough for him?

His eyes swayed back to the window. Across the street and half a block away he could see the corner of the First State Bank of Russellville, the one Rachel's daddy ran, the one Tommy Lee shunned in favor of taking his business to the town of Florence, twenty-three miles away. He lit a cigarette without even realizing he was doing it, then sat mulling.

Staring at the bank, he thought, *One woman* would *have been enough for me. But only one.*

On his way to the eleven o'clock meeting at City Hall, Tommy Lee slowed the Cadillac to a crawl as he passed Panache, but nobody was about. When he emerged from the meeting with the assurance that the zoning restrictions had been lifted and the plans for the new apartment complex could go forward undeterred, he paused at the curb beside his car to light a cigarette and glance southward along the street. From here he could see the sign above the door of her store. A woman came out. Tommy Lee squinted, but from this distance couldn't tell if it was she or not. He sprinted around the car, hurriedly backed out, and made an illegal U-turn in the middle of Jackson Avenue, keeping his eyes riveted on the figure walking along the sidewalk ahead of him. He slowed as he pulled abreast, but even before he passed the woman, he realized it wasn't Rachel.

You damn fool, Gentry, you're acting the age of your own daughter! But the disappointment left him feeling deflated.

Back at the office, when he'd exchanged necessary messages with Liz, he went inside, flung the building-code regulations on his desk, then moved to the window behind it.

Again he studied the bank, a burning cigarette hooked in the curve of a finger, forgotten. The smoke curled up and he took a deep drag while his eyes remained fixed on the building a half-block away. Then he anchored the cigarette between his teeth, crossed to the door, and closed it.

Liz looked up in surprise, frowned, but decided it was none of her business.

Tommy Lee reached for a ballpoint pen and wrote the telephone number on a yellow legal pad—he knew it by heart. He stared at it through the smoke that drifted up past his nostrils. His heart seemed to have dropped into his guts. His palms were sweaty and his spine hurt. After a full minute, he thrust the pen onto the desktop and wilted back into his chair, trying to calm his breathing. *Come on, Gentry, what're you scared of? How many women have you called in your life? How many have refused you?*

He reached for the phone, but instead his hand veered to the pen. He grabbed it and wrote the number again. Twelve times he wrote it . . . in the same spot . . . until it was pressed into eight sheets of the tablet.

The cigarette had burned low and he stubbed it out absently, reached for the phone, and actually picked up the receiver this time. But after five seconds he slammed it down without dialing, then ran four shaky fingers through his gray-black hair. Lord a'mighty, he hadn't faced anything this nerve-racking in years.

He grabbed the phone and punched out the numbers too quickly to give himself a chance to change his mind.

"Good afternoon, Panache."

Dammit, why couldn't *she* have answered?

"Is Ra—Is Mrs. Hollis there?"

"I'm sorry, she's not. Can I help you?"

"No, thank you. I'll try again later."

He slammed the phone down as if it had bitten him. Then he sat with his face in his palms, shaking so hard his elbows rattled against the desktop. He dropped his forearms flat against the blotter, head drooped, while he sucked in huge gulps of air. Then his palms pressed his cheeks again and eight fingertips dug into his eyes beneath his glasses. *You're insane, Gentry. Plumb nuts. What the hell would you have said if she'd answered?*

But after two hours he felt less crazy and decided to give it another try. He went through the same ritual again, only this time he made sure he had a cigarette lit when he dialed, to steady himself.

"Good afternoon, Panache."

Goddammit, doesn't Verda ever go home? "Is Mrs. Hollis there?"

"No, I'm sorry. I don't expect her in today. Is there anything I can do?"

"No, thank you. I'll call again tomorrow."

"Can I tell her—"

Tommy Lee slammed down the receiver in frustration. *No, you can't tell her anything! Just get the hell home so she'll have to answer her own damn phones!*

When Tommy Lee lurched from his chair and flung the door open, Liz's head snapped up. But he only stormed past, throwing over his shoulder, "I won't be in till morning." A moment later tires squealed outside, and she shook her head.

Tommy Lee Gentry was a land developer. He knew every acre of every section of land within a radius of fifty miles around Russellville. He'd owned the land on which Owen Hollis had built his house, had subdivided it into lots, contracted for the installation of improvements, then resold the lots to the builder who'd eventually put up the brick house where Rachel and Owen had lived. It was on the eastern edge of town in a hilly, wooded area called Village Square Addition, but there was nothing square about it. The streets curved and curled around the natural undulations of the land, making it highly desirable property lacking the dreary severity of rigidly perpendicular streets.

Hollis had done right by her, if the house was any indication. It was a rambling U-shaped thing of peach-colored brick, hugging a swimming pool in its two outstretched arms. It had a hip roof that deeply overhung arched fanlight windows trimmed with eave-to-earth Wedgwood-blue shutters. At the base of each window an azalea bush formed a precisely carved mound, while between them the warm brick walls sported espaliered Virginia creepers, trained into faultless Belgian fence designs by a weekly gardener. At each corner and beside the center door, Chinese holly bushes stood guard while the shaded yard bore lush magnolias and live oaks, with not a fallen leaf to be seen anywhere. On either side of the house a high box-cut podocarpus hedge blocked out the sight of the backyard, overlapping at one point to create a hidden entrance, like that around a tennis court.

Tommy Lee knew the exact summer they'd had the pool put in. He'd been up at City Hall looking through some files when he'd come upon their application for a pool permit. As he approached the house now, he wondered if she might possibly have taken the day off and what she'd say if he simply presented himself at her door unannounced.

But in the end, he chickened out. *Use your head, Gentry. She's only been a widow for a week.*

He drove on by, made a U-turn in a circle at the end of her street, then left the area with a long lingering study of her house on his way out.

Once on the main road again, he angrily loosened his tie. *Damn.* He'd had such good intentions of trying to make it through one night without any liquor. But he needed a drink worse than ever. Stinkin' dry Baptist county! He'd have to make the run up to Colbert County to buy his booze tonight.

He bought enough to get him through the weekend without having to make the trip again. Then he stopped and ate a fat filet mignon with all the trimmings, and hit the road again armed with an after-dinner drink in a plastic glass. He passed his office by rote, checking it cursorily before heading home. He timed his run, tossed out the empty glass just before the last turn, as usual, and pulled up before his black front doors showing a record time of eight minutes.

He gave a roaring rebel yell to celebrate.

But a minute later, when he entered the house, his jubilant mood vanished. The place was just as silent as ever, and just as disorderly. Even more so, for more garments had been added to the collection strewn across the sofa. *I should clean it up. But for whom?*

Instead, he mixed himself a double Manhattan in the hope that he'd get good and loose so that when he picked up the phone and dialed her number it wouldn't shake him in the least.

But his hand still trembled. His palm still sweat. And after seventeen rings it dawned on him that Rachel wasn't home.

Nor was she at Panache the next day when he called, or any of the days following that. But finally Verda McElroy disclosed that she'd gone to St. Thomas for two weeks, putting Tommy Lee out of his misery temporarily.

Rachel's father had been waiting at the Golden Triangle Airport, but even with him beside her, the house seemed eerie when she walked into it.

"Should I make us some tea?" she asked hopefully.

"It keeps me awake. I'd better not."

"Anything else?"

"Nothing. I'll carry your bags into the back, but it's late. I'm afraid I can't stay."

When he was gone, Rachel wandered listlessly from room to room, realizing that the trip to St. Thomas had only been a respite that delayed her acceptance of Owen's irreversible absence. Standing in the doorway of their bedroom, she chafed her arms, shivering. Her nostrils narrowed. The room still seemed to smell of sickness. Perhaps it was only an illusion, but Owen had spent so much of his last months here and had slipped into death right there on the bed in the middle of the night while she lay beside him.

Again she shivered. Then she was besieged by guilt for dwelling more on the unpleasant memories created in this room than on the pleasant.

When the phone rang, she jumped and pressed a hand to her heart, then stared at the instrument on the bedside table. It rang again and she hurried to answer it, sure it must be Marshall.

"Hello."

But the low, masculine voice was not Marshall's. "Hello, Rachel."

"Hello," she repeated, hoping for a clue from his inflection.

"How are you?" Still she couldn't identify the caller and had a sudden wary prickling along her spine—might it be one of those obscene callers who preyed on new widows?

"Who is this?" she asked icily.

"It's Tommy Lee."

For a second she wished it had been only an obscene call. She wrapped her free hand around the mouthpiece and sank back onto the edge of the bed, her throat suddenly tight and dry.

"Tommy Lee . . . I . . ." *I what? I went away to mourn my husband's death and thought more of you than I did of him?* "I certainly wasn't expecting it to be you."

"Oh? Who were you expecting?"

"I . . . nobody." After a breathless pause, she repeated, "Nobody."

"You've been gone."

"Yes, to St. Thomas."

"And how was St. Thomas?"

Her voice was falsely bright. "Oh, lovely. Lovely! March is their dryest month. No rain, and highs in the eighties." But once the weather report was finished she fell silent, that silence greeted by a matching one from the other end of the line. The strain grew between them until Rachel felt it between her shoulder blades. When her voice came again it was low and subdued. "I didn't expect to see you at the funeral."

Again there followed a long pause, as if he was measuring his reply. When it came, it was as tightly controlled as hers. "I didn't expect to be there."

"You shouldn't have come, Tommy Lee."

"I know that now."

"I don't mean to sound ungrateful." She swallowed, eyes closed, both hands gripping the phone. "It *did* mean a lot to me to see you there."

A full fifteen seconds of silence followed, then, "Rachel, I want to talk to you." His voice sounded tightly controlled, and she could hear his raspy breathing now.

"I'm here."

"No, not on the phone. I want to see you."

The very idea brought fresh pain to Rachel, laced with a hint of panic. "What good would it do?"

"I don't know. I . . ." He sighed deeply. "Don't you think it's time?"

She hugged her ribs tightly with one hand, bending forward slightly. "Tommy Lee, listen to me. It would be a mistake. What's done is done and there's no use reviving old regrets. We're different now. You . . . I don't . . ." But she was stammering, voicing hollow words, unable to reason very well. "Please, Tommy Lee, don't call me anymore. I have enough to deal with as it is right now." She hadn't realized tears had been welling in her eyes until they slipped over and darkened two spots on her skirt. Staring at them, she wasn't sure if they were for Owen or Tommy Lee.

"Rachel, I'm sorry." He sounded as if his lips were touching the mouthpiece of the phone. "Look, I didn't mean to upset you. I just called to see how you're doing and let you know I've been thinking about you . . . and . . ."

"Tommy Lee, I . . . I have to go now."

They listened to each other breathe for endless seconds.

"Sure," he said at last, but it came out so softly she could scarcely hear the word.

"Good-bye, Tommy Lee." She waited, but he neither said good-bye nor hung up. Finally she replaced the receiver with utmost care, as if not to disturb it again. Huddled on the edge of the bed, she hugged herself harder, squeezing her eyes closed, rocking forward and back, seeking to blot out the loneliness that always stemmed from thoughts of what could have been. She saw Tommy Lee again as he'd looked at the cemetery. Older, so much older, just as she was. She fought against recalling the facts she'd gleaned about him over the years, the events of his life that had aged him, those that had brought him happiness, wealth, sadness, hope.

You've got to stop thinking about him. Think of anything else . . . anything at all. The bedroom! If the bedroom is difficult for you to face, have it redecorated. Think of colors, textures, furniture . . . anything but Tommy Lee Gentry.

But in the end, as she wandered off to sleep in a guest bedroom again, the memory of his face and his voice on the phone was her lullaby.

It was busy at Panache the following day. Spring had arrived and the seasonal fashion change brought a flurry of shoppers. Verda had managed beautifully while Rachel was gone. Sales had been good. New stock had come in. Rachel was tagging a shipment of swimwear when Verda remembered, "Oh! Some man kept calling for you while you were gone."

Rachel's head snapped up. "Who?"

"I don't know. He wouldn't give his name, but I'd recognize his voice if he called again."

A premonition of dread struck Rachel. Could it have been Tommy Lee? The last thing she needed was to have Verda aware that he had called. With his reputation, eyebrows would rise in no time.

"Did he say what he wanted?"

"No, just kept saying he'd call back, and I finally told him you'd gone to St. Thomas and would be back today."

So he'd known when she'd get back. That's why his phone call had come immediately upon her return. That meant last night's call hadn't been impetuous, as she'd hoped. But she'd made it clear she didn't want to see him or talk to him again. Surely Tommy Lee wouldn't force the issue.

He didn't. For two weeks.

But during the third, after suffering sleepless nights and haunted days, he knew he could put it off no longer—he had to see her.

He left the office at the end of a balmy spring day and made the run home in the usual nine minutes, bounded into the house and began stripping off his jacket before he hit the stairs to the living room. If he'd been planning to see Bitsy tonight he would have been whistling. But as it was, he found his mouth dry, so he washed a glass from the kitchen sink and mixed himself a martini to carry with him upstairs to the bathroom.

In the shower he thought of Rachel, becoming conscious once again of the twenty-five pounds he should lose. When he'd finished shaving, he paused in the act of patting after-shave on the slack skin about his jaws, scowling into the mirror. Brushing his hair, he wished he'd used something to cover the gray, but it was too late now. He recalled the ducktail he'd worn all those years ago when he and Rachel were teenagers. And she'd worn a long black ponytail, and sometimes a high-placed doughnut circled by a ring of tiny flowers to match her blouse or skirt. Lord, she'd come a long way since then. Her stylishness alone made Tommy Lee quaver. So when he dressed, he chose carefully: an expensive pair of trousers in oatmeal beige; a coordinating belt with a shining gold buckle; a blue-on-blue dress shirt; and a summer slubbed-silk sports coat the color of a coconut shell. He debated about a tie, decided against it, and, as he slipped his billfold into his back pocket and studied his reflection in the full-length mirror, decided this was the best he could do. But when he drained the last of his martini and clapped the glass on the dresser, his hand was shaking. He was scared to death.

Rachel's house looked closed up and forbidding as he pulled the Cadillac up to the curb and glanced at the arched windows. Yes, it was a beautiful house, he thought, continuing to study it as he slowly got out and slammed the car door. The click of his hard heels on the concrete walk sang out like rifle shots. The front door was windowless, painted Wedgwood blue to match the shutters. Facing it, he quailed again, but adjusted his shirt collar, drew a deep breath, and pressed the doorbell. Inside it chimed softly while he waited, his heart clamoring and a thousand insecurities making his stomach jump. Unconsciously he ran a hand over the crown of his head, then half turned toward the street, hoping to appear nonchalant.

But at the first click of the latch, he swung back eagerly. The door opened and all the rehearsed greetings fled his mind. The hundreds of yesterdays came back with a nostalgic tug—how many times had he appeared at her door, invited or uninvited?

She was more beautiful now than she'd been at seventeen, and her loveliness struck him like a blow, made him stand speechless far too long, taking her in.

She wore soft lavender tapered trousers with tiny-heeled shoes to match. Her lilac silk blouse had long sleeves and buttoned up the front to a classic open collar that revealed the tips of her collarbones and a fine gold chain holding a gilded giraffe suspended at the hollow of her throat. At her waist was a thin gold belt that made no pretense of holding up her slacks, but only accentuated the flatness of her stomach and the delicacy of her hipbones. She paused with one palm on the edge of the door, the other on the jamb, her sleeves softly draping, brown eyes startled yet somber.

When he could breathe again, he said, "Hello, Rachel."

She sucked in a surprised breath while her face took on a look of utter vulnerability. He wondered if she always wore soft rose-colored lipstick when she was home alone at night.

"Hello, Tommy Lee," she said at last. Her voice was quiet in the evening shadows and held a tinge of nervousness. She stood unmoving, guarding the entry to her house, while the smell of it drifted out to him—floral and tangy and woodsy all at once. Or maybe the smell came from her—he couldn't tell.

"Could I come in?"

Her expression grew troubled while she deliberated. Her glance flickered to his white Cadillac at the curb and he could read her hesitancy quite clearly— suppose someone she knew saw the car there? Still, he held his ground, waiting. At last, almost wearily, she let her hand slip from the edge of the door and stepped back.

"For a minute."

He moved inside then turned to watch a graceful hand with long painted fingernails—the same shade she wore on her lips—press the door closed while her head dipped forward as if she were arming herself to turn around and face him. The back of her short black hair seemed to spring into natural waves that no amount of professional attention could quite subdue. When she turned to face him she slipped her hands into her trouser pockets and drew her shoulders high, emphasizing the thinness of her frame as the blouse draped more dramatically, scarcely rounding over the vague swell of her tiny breasts. For a moment, as their eyes met, neither of them knew what to say, but finally Rachel, with her exquisite sense of correctness, invited, "Would you like to come in and sit down?"

She led the way into the elegant living room whose fanlight windows he'd viewed many times from outside. The room's pastel colors were as tasteful and proper as those of Rachel's clothing and skin. The lamps were lit; and she waved him toward a quilted sofa, then took a seat on a small chair directly facing him, a marble-topped table between them. She crossed her knees, curved her hands over the front edge of the chair seat, and leaned forward, again with her shoulders drawn up in that off-putting way.

She wasn't going to make this easy for him.

So, all right, he'd play it her way.

"It's been a long time since I was in a Talmadge house."

"My name is Hollis now."

"Yes, I seem to remember that at regular intervals."

"I asked you not to come."

"I tried not to, but it just didn't work. I had to see you."

"Why?"

"To satisfy a long curiosity."

"About what?"

His eyes dropped to the pair of rich brass giraffes on the table between them. "About how life has treated you." His glance continued idly about the room, and when it came back to her his voice softened. "About how he treated you."

"As you can see, both life and he treated me just fine." She settled back in her chair, letting a hand fall casually on the far side of her crossed knees, wrist up.

No, she wasn't going to make this easy for him. But suddenly he realized she was just as scared as he; in spite of the loose-flung wrist, the nonchalant pose, she was undeniably tense. And she meant to keep him contained in this showplace of a living room that looked as if not one hour's worth of *living* had ever been done in it.

"Yes, so I see. You seem to have everything." He glanced left, then right. "Except an ashtray."

He enjoyed making her move. When she did, he could watch her covertly. As she walked the length of the room toward the dining room beyond, he noted again her thinness, but it was classy, not brittle. He'd never before known a woman who wore lavender shoes. On Bitsy they would have looked like a whore's shoes. He watched them as Rachel opened an étagère, withdrew an ashtray, then softly closed the glass door. Returning, she placed the heavy crystal piece on the table, resumed her seat, then watched as he reached inside his sports coat and drew out a pack of cigarettes. When he unexpectedly looked up at her, she dropped her eyes to the toe of her shoes, only to see his hand appear, extending the red and white package with one cigarette half cocked.

She met his eyes nervously. "No, thank you, I quit years ago."

"Ah, I should have guessed."

He lipped the cigarette straight from the pack—a memory from the past— and she saw that his mouth had not changed at all. The evidence of aging that marked the rest of his face had not reached his lips. They were crisply etched, generous, as beguiling as ever. When he suddenly stood, her heart leapt. But he only fished for a lighter in his trouser pocket, then sat on the edge of the sofa again while she watched him light up. He scowled as the smoke lifted, then threw back his head on a heavy exhalation as he slipped the lighter into his breast pocket. At last the ritual was through, and he rested with his hands pressed butt to butt between widespread knees, the cigarette seemingly forgotten in his fingers. He studied her until it took great effort for Rachel to keep from begging him not to.

"So, Rachel, where do we start?"

His question startled her, though she tried hard not to let it show.

"I think you know the answer to that as well as I do. We don't start."

"Then maybe I should have asked, where do we end?"

"We ended years ago, Tommy Lee. I really don't know why you've come here."

He glanced around. "I wanted to see your house from the inside for once. It's a beautiful house, what I can see of it. Owen must have worked out fine with your daddy."

A faint blush heated her chin and cheeks. "Yes, he did. He worked his way up to vice-president at the bank."

"Yes, I know," he said softly.

"Yes, I suppose you do. There's probably very little we don't know about each other."

"There's no such thing as a secret in a town this size, that's for sure."

She shot him a sharp glance, but he was studying his cigarette, and when he raised his gaze she hurriedly dropped hers. "I understand you live out on the lake now."

"Yes, ma'am," he drawled with a touch of irony. "Got a big house out there." He chuckled quietly. "Folks called me crazy when I built it, but now they drive by in their boats and stare at it, and I think a few of them actually like it."

She couldn't help smiling for a moment, but she knew all the other things they said about him, too.

"Do you enjoy being . . . unconventional?"

"Unconventional?" He glanced up with a crooked, sad smile. "Why, I'm as conventional as the next one. What you're meaning to ask is if I enjoy being the hell-raiser they say I am, isn't it, Rachel?"

"You said it, Tommy Lee. I didn't."

He seemed to consider the question a long time, all the while studying her closely. When he answered, he sounded resigned. "No, I don't enjoy it much. But it kills time."

Rachel bristled. "Is that what you consider three marriages and three divorces—killing time?"

He flicked his ashes into the crystal ashtray and answered as if to himself, "Well, it was killing anyway. But then we all can't be lucky like you and end up with a marriage made in heaven, now, can we?"

"You've grown cynical over the years."

"Hell, yes. Wouldn't you if you tried three times and failed?" She glanced aside as if appalled by his admission. "Does it bother you, Rachel, the fact that I've been married all those times? Is that why you're so tense?"

Her eyes snapped angrily. "I'm tense because I've just been through two grueling years watching my husband die of cancer. It would make anybody tense." She jumped to her feet and he followed, catching her elbow above the marble-topped table.

"Rachel honey, I'm sorry."

She carefully withdrew her arm. "I'm not your Rachel-honey anymore, and I begin to see what it is people object to about you, Tommy Lee. You had no business coming here like this so soon after Owen's death, and especially after I asked you not to."

Their eyes clashed for long seconds. Then she turned her back and walked to one of the arched windows, where she stood staring out at the fading twilight. He leaned down, studying her back while he stubbed out his cigarette. Then he crossed to stand behind her. He caught her scent again, the Rachel-scent, the lingering of fine, costly powder caught in her clothing and on her skin, and it created a maelstrom in his senses.

"I didn't come here to upset you, Rachel. Not at all. But my life is in a hell of a mess and I don't think it's going to get straightened out until I can talk to you about what happened." He touched her shoulder, making sure he didn't touch too hard. "Rachel, turn around. I've been thinking of this day for . . . for years. And now you turn away. Please, Rachel."

She dropped her chin, sighed, then turned very slowly, allowing him to look at her at close range while similarly studying him. They were strangers, yet they knew each other well. Their past was best forgotten, yet it never would be. Time should have kindly seen to it that they no longer appealed to each other, yet they did.

"Jesus, you're more beautiful than ever. Did you know that?"

One of them had to be sensible. She carefully hid the pleasure brought about by his words and replied, "I'm forty-one years old, and I'm told constantly that I'm too thin. And the last two years, the last six months in particular, have put road maps on my face. It's not Rachel Hollis you think is beautiful, but Rachel Talmadge, the girl I stopped being twenty-four years ago. She's the one you came here to find."

"No. I didn't come here looking for her, only to talk about her and find out where she went and why. And why I never heard from her afterward."

Her eyes closed and he saw the flawless violet makeup tremble on her lids while he battled the urge to draw her into his arms, hold her close, and comfort her. And himself. But if he touched her, he knew she'd flee. Her deep brown eyes opened again and she asked quaveringly, "Why, Tommy Lee? Why now?"

"Because I couldn't wait another year. I've wasted too many already."

"But Owen—"

"Owen is gone. That's why I came."

She made a move as if to turn away, but he blocked her with his shoulder. "Rachel, I'm sorry if my timing is bad. I'm sorry if I haven't given you the proper time to mourn him, but I've put this off until I can't anymore. I'm forty-one, too, Rachel. Please understand."

She was afraid she was beginning to understand all too well. What he seemed to be saying was too shattering to contemplate this soon after Owen's death. He shouldn't even be here in her house, with his distinctive car parked out front where anyone and everyone could see it. Nor should he be broaching the subject that had been carefully avoided since they were seventeen years old.

"I want to know what happened to you, Rachel."

She met his eyes squarely and challenged, "Ask your parents, Tommy Lee. They were in it with Daddy and Mama."

"I asked them years ago, but they would never tell me anything. Then after just so long, I stopped asking altogether. It's been years since I've talked to them."

"I know that, too." Impulsively she reached out to touch his arm, understanding fully what the estrangement must have cost all of them. "When will you decide you've made them suffer enough?"

"Never!" he spit out, and spun away, for her nearness brought too intense an ache. "Just as they've made me suffer all these years. I guess I'm not as . . . as magnanimous as you are, Rachel. I can't forgive them and be their loving son again, like you forgave your parents."

The bitter feelings she'd had the day of the funeral, while gazing out the bedroom window, came back again, rife and fresh. It was rare that she let them take precedence, but they did now, and when they'd lodged like a thorn in her heart, she asked, "Don't you think there are times when I feel bitter? When I still blame them? There are times when I have to guard myself against . . . against hating them for what they did to us." Once the truth was spoken, Rachel realized how heavy its burden had been all these years. She'd never said it aloud before, but then, there was nobody but Tommy Lee to whom she could have.

He turned, and as their eyes met and held, it struck them both that they'd suffered many of the same things over the years, in spite of the different roads their lives had taken.

"You, Rachel?" he asked, as if unable to believe it of her. She nodded, dropping her eyes to the fingers laced over her stomach. "But you and your daddy have always stood by each other. You seem so close."

"On the surface. But there are undercurrents."

Once again Tommy Lee felt a compelling urge to touch her. Instead, he backed away a step. "This room makes me uncomfortable, Rachel. Could we sit at your kitchen table or somewhere else?"

She hadn't expected him to stay that long. Still, looking up at him now, wondering many things about the man whose eyes she could only half make out behind the glasses, she realized that talking about everything—at last—was something they owed each other.

Chapter 3

SHE LED THE way through a pair of white louvred café doors into a shining kitchen decorated in white with splashes of geranium red. The room constituted one arm of the house and had a wall of sliding glass doors that overlooked the pool. Unlike Tommy Lee's kitchen, this one hadn't a thing out of place. The white countertops and appliances gleamed. The polished vinyl floor shone. The walls were cheerfully splattered with that same geranium color, which was repeated in a set of pots hanging on a wall beside the stove and a teakettle sitting on one burner.

Rachel touched a wall switch and a tulip-shaped lamp of white wicker came alight above a small white pedestal table flanked by a pair of bentwood ice-cream chairs situated smack in front of the windows.

"Sit down, Tommy Lee. Can I get you something to drink?"

"Yes, whatever you're having."

She moved to the refrigerator, and he to stand before the wide expanse of glass. In the shadows he could make out the brick-walled backyard, the stretch of pool reflecting a newly risen moon, and an assortment of tables and chaise lounges. The house curled around to his right, hugging the pool between the glass wall of what he guessed to be a family room, leading at a right angle off the kitchen, and the bedroom wing, straight across the water. The entire view was nothing short of sumptuous.

"You really meant it when you said he'd been good to you. This is even nicer than I always imagined it to be."

The butcher knife paused over the lime Rachel was slicing. "Than you imagined?"

He glanced over his shoulder. "I used to own this land, you know. I was the original developer who subdivided it, had the improvements put in, then sold the lots. Cauley built this house, didn't he?"

"Yes, he did."

"And I saw your application for a pool permit when I was up at City Hall that spring you put it in. I always wondered what it looked like back here behind that hedge."

Rachel felt disquieted to realize Tommy Lee had kept such close track of the personal plateaus in her life with Owen.

"You've driven past often?"

She felt his eyes measuring her, though she couldn't see beyond the top half of the brown lenses. His voice was subdued as he answered, "You've never been far from my mind, Rachel." They stared at each other for a pulsating moment, then he added, "Not even when I was married."

Flustered, she turned to reach into an upper cabinet for two thick amber glasses. From an ice dispenser on the refrigerator door came the clunk and chink of cubes falling into the tumblers. His eyes followed each movement of her slim back, the shift of her silk blouse and the pull of the lavender trousers across her spine as she reached, bent, opened a chilled bottle of carbonated water, dropped lime wedges into the glasses and filled them.

She turned with the sparkling drinks in her hands and said composedly, "Let's sit down."

Despite her outward calm, Rachel knew a sudden reluctance to approach him. A dangerous flutter of physical awareness now hummed in her stomach. How silly. They were not at all the same people. She was thin and gaunt, and he was graying and too heavy, and beneath the unkind light she saw again the lines of dissipation that reiterated the truth about his life-style.

He took the iced drink from her hand, and without removing his eyes from her, pulled out her chair, waited for her to sit, then took the chair across from her. She felt his eyes intensely lingering and dropped her own to the white Formica tabletop, where a poppy-red mat held a thriving green sprengeri plant in a toadstool planter. But even without looking she knew he studied her unwaveringly, and it set her midsection trembling. Between them the old compelling magnetism tugged and seemed to draw her to him against her will.

After a full minute's silence he asked, very quietly, "So . . . where did you go, Rachel?"

Her eyes, dark and wide, lifted to his, but they focused on her own reflection in his glasses.

"They sent me to a private school in Michigan."

"In *Michigan?*"

"Yes."

"They were going to make damn sure I couldn't find you, weren't they?" He took a perfunctory sip from his glass, grimaced, and set it aside.

"They talked it over, all four of them, and decided to tell everyone here the truth—that I'd gone off to finish high school in an exclusive high-priced private school up north. No excuses. No questions. Given my daddy's bank account, nobody thought a thing of it."

"Michigan," he ruminated, staring at his glass. "How often I wondered." The room was utterly silent. Rachel waited, suspended in dread anticipation for the question she knew would come next. He lifted his eyes to hers, and his voice held an audible tremor as he asked softly, "And did you have the baby there?"

She wanted to tear her eyes away from his, but could not. How many years had she forced herself never to imagine this moment happening? Now it was here, and her emotions exploded with a force for which she wasn't prepared.

"Yes," she whispered.

He swallowed. His lips opened, but no sound came out. After several seconds he finally managed, in a strangled voice, the question that had haunted him through three marriages and the driven time since, "What was it?"

"A girl," came the nearly inaudible answer.

He jerked his glasses off, and they hung over the table edge from his lifeless fingers while he rubbed his eyes as if to stroke away the pain. He sucked in a great gulp of air. His shoulders heaved once, then sagged again. The room was as silent as they had been to each other over the intervening years.

The old hurt rushed back, sharpened by nostalgia.

He opened his eyes, stared at her delicate hand resting on the tabletop. His heavy hand moved the few inches to hers and enclosed it loosely while he watched his thumb rubbing across her knuckles. It was not at all the way he'd imagined touching her again, if he ever got the chance.

Rachel's fingers tightened. "Oh, Tommy Lee, they said you'd be told. They shouldn't have kept it from you."

He continued staring at their hands. She still wore her wedding ring on her left hand, while his held a gold florentine band with a cluster of seven large diamonds. With his thumb he drew circles around her engagement diamond, and went on tiredly. "They did. My daddy called me into his office at the lumberyard one day that spring and said you'd had the baby and that it was a girl. But somehow I always wanted to hear it from you."

Rachel's heart softened, as did her voice. "She was born April nineteenth."

Their eyes met and held. Their child's birthday would fall very shortly. Neither Rachel nor Tommy Lee could help wondering what that day would be like if they were husband and wife and she their acknowledged daughter.

"You never wrote," he mourned.

"Yes, I did. Many times. A couple I sent, but most I just threw away. I knew they wouldn't let you find out where I was. They were very powerful, you know. Once they got us to agree that adoption was the only solution, they simply"—she shrugged sadly—"took over."

"I've asked myself a thousand times why we went along with it."

"We were weaned knowing that college was meant to be part of our lives. Given their age and experience, it was easy for them to make us see the sense in what they said. We were so . . . immature, malleable. What could we do against all that superior reasoning they gave us?"

"And so they sent you to Michigan."

"Yes."

"I've never been there. What's it like?"

What is hell like? she thought, gazing at him. To a seventeen-year-old, torn away from the boy she loved, hell could be Michigan. But of course she dared not answer that way.

"It's cold," she replied quietly, "and very lonely."

The skin about his eyes seemed drawn and pale. "I was lonely, too. I used to dream that I'd be walking down the street someday and there you'd be just like always."

They were still holding hands, and she couldn't find the inner resources to pull away.

"They kept me there until you were safely tucked away at Auburn. I got my high school diploma in Michigan that July, then entered the University of Alabama."

"You went to Alabama, I went to Auburn, just as they'd always planned for us." His sad smile was aimed at the ring with which he continued to toy. She dropped her eyes to it and laughed once, a sad little sound.

"Their alma maters."

His pained eyes moved to hers. "While the baby went on to new parents."

She lifted her eyes and nodded silently.

"Do you know who got her? What kind of people they are?"

Oh, God, she thought, *can I go through all this again? Must we dredge up old regrets and form new recriminations for what can never be changed?* But he waited, and he deserved to know the little she'd been told.

"They're both Baptist, and college graduates. They had one other adopted daughter three years older, and they live somewhere in the Flint area."

"That's all? That's all you know?"

"Yes. They didn't tell you much in those days."

"Not even her name?"

For the first time self-consciousness struck Rachel. She withdrew her hand and picked up her glass, lifting it to her lips. "Oh, Tommy Lee, what does it matter now?"

With one finger he pushed down on the rim of her glass, preventing her from taking a drink. "It matters, Rachel. It matters."

She didn't want to tell him. She didn't want him to impose new meanings on a decision made years ago by a mixed-up girl scarcely past adolescence. But, again, he had a right to know.

She lowered her glass, drew a deep breath, and admitted, "They let me name her."

"And?"

Even before she answered, she felt a full-body flush, but there was no escaping the truth. "I named her Beth."

His shoulders recoiled against the back of the chair as if he'd taken a load of buckshot, and his shocked face blanched. "Oh, Jesus," he whispered, and jerked from his seat to stand with both palms flat against the glass door as if doing vertical push-ups. "Rachel, I need something a little stronger right now than lime water. Have you got anything else in the house?"

The proof of his habits came as a disappointment, but she supposed this catharsis was adequate reason for needing a drink. She rose from her chair and found her knees shaky as she moved into the family room.

"We never kept much around the house, but Owen had a couple of bottles somewhere in here."

As her voice trailed away, Tommy Lee pressed against the glass, then, realizing what he was doing, snapped back and stared at his own palm prints on the spotless surface. He turned to follow Rachel, scarcely noticing the plush sofas and built-in shelves of the room she had entered. He was trying to blot out the picture of her on a delivery table, giving birth to their daughter, then naming her Beth.

Rachel was squatting before a low set of doors on the far wall. She reached into the cupboard, withdrew a bottle, read its label, and reiterated, "I'm afraid we don't have much of a selection."

His voice sounded just behind her shoulder.

"Anything you've got. That's fine."

"It's scotch."

"It'll do, Rachel. I'm not fussy."

"I don't know anything about mixing drinks." From over her shoulder the bottle was taken out of her hands.

"I do." She swung around and stood watching as he returned to the kitchen, obviously in a hurry. When she reentered the room he was pouring the lime water down the drain. Then he replaced it with straight scotch, added no more than a splash of tap water, stirred it with his finger, and swung to face her, leaning his hips against the edge of the sink while taking a long drink. Lowering the glass, he noted, "You disapprove."

She turned her back on him and said tightly, "Who am I to approve or disapprove of your life-style?"

"Still, you do," he reaffirmed. Her shoulders were stiff and she stared at the sliding glass door as if studying something in the dark pool. "I needed it to get through this . . . this emotional wringer, okay?" He crossed his ankles and draped his empty hand over the cabinet edge in a calculatedly casual pose, though his legs trembled. "Why did you name her Beth?" he asked, so quietly that shivers ran up Rachel's neck.

They were both vividly remembering the many nights they'd lain in each other's arms in a dark parked car, sexually sated, planning their future and the names of their children. Beth. Their first daughter would be Beth, they had agreed. As she remembered it now, Rachel's skin tingled.

In the glass doors he saw her full reflection. Her arms were now tightly crossed over her ribs.

When Rachel's answer came, her voice was far from steady. "I . . . we . . . I was seventeen, and still in love with you, and I know it was a foolish thing to do, but it seemed a way to bind us to her, even though we had to give her away."

He took another long pull and considered at length before admitting hoarsely, "I have another daughter named Beth."

"Yes, I know." Against the fallen night he watched her face, eyes tightly closed, mouth gaping as if fighting for breath.

He lowered his brows. "You know, Rachel?"

"The announcements of all your children's births were in the *Franklin County Times.* You have a nineteen-year-old son named Michael and a seventeen-year-old named Doyle, and a fourteen-year-old daughter named . . . named Beth."

A sharp stab of exhilaration lifted his ribs. "So I'm not the only one who kept tabs."

She ignored his remark and stood as before, tightly wrapped in trembling arms.

"Rachel . . ." He'd resisted touching her as long as he could. He crossed the room and laid a palm on her shoulder, but she flinched away. Rebuffed, he dropped the hand. "Turn around and look at me."

"No. This is difficult enough as it is." She didn't want him to see her face when she asked the next question, even though they both knew the answer, both remembered those sweet shared secrets in a dark car. Her voice was scarcely more than a whisper as she asked, "Why did you name your daughter Beth?"

He touched her again, and this time she obeyed his silent command, turning very slowly, her arms still locked across her ribs. He stood close, but dropped his hand from her. "Do you want the truth or do you want a lie?" he asked.

"I wouldn't ask if I didn't want the truth."

His glasses still lay on the table, and she could see his eyes clearly now, the pale webbing at the corners, drawn lines angling away from his lower lids. But the irises and lashes were the same clear dark brown of the Tommy Lee she'd known and loved back then. With his eyes fixed on hers, he answered, "Because I was twenty-seven years old and still in love with you."

She felt the shock waves undulate through her body and she turned safely away, dropping tiredly to her chair once again. "Oh, Tommy Lee, how can you say such a thing?"

"So you'd rather have had the lie."

"But you were married to somebody else." It made her feel guilty in some obscure way.

He laughed ruefully. "Yes, one of the three."

"You say that as if you didn't love any of them."

"There were times when I thought I did." Suddenly he wilted, ran a hand through his hair and breathed, "Hell, I don't know." He reached into his breast pocket, came up with a cigarette and lighter, and dipped his head as the two joined. When the cigarette was burning, Tommy Lee poured a fresh drink without asking Rachel's permission, disappeared into the living room, and returned with the crystal ashtray, then took up his post with hips and hands braced against the edge of the counter.

When her eyes again confronted him, there was a hint of censure about her puckered brows. "Tommy Lee, how can you be so . . . so blithe about it? You conceived children with two different women. How could you have done that if you weren't sure you loved them?"

He took a long, thoughtful drag, then a long, thoughtful drink. "Who knows why children are conceived?" he asked ruminatively, then admitted, "I can't really say there ever was much discussion about whether or not Rosamond and I should have had the two boys. What else do you do when you've graduated from college? You find some girl to marry and settle down with, and babies just naturally follow."

"You mean you . . . you never wanted them?" She sounded shocked.

"Maybe we never *should* have wanted them. Roz and I . . ." He studied his smoking cigarette with a faraway expression in his eyes. "We got married for all the wrong reasons. Maybe subconsciously we thought that having the boys would pull us together. But it didn't. It was a poor excuse, and the boys are the ones who paid for it." He studied his crossed ankles as he ended quietly, "They're both sorry."

"Sorry?"

He looked up. "Rebellious, troublemakers, in and out of scrapes with school, the law, you name it. Not exactly all-American boys."

"Oh, Tommy Lee, I'm so sorry."

He half turned, stubbing out his cigarette. "Yeah, well, don't be. It was Roz's fault and mine, not yours. Maybe if we'd loved each other more we would have been better parents and raised better kids. I don't know."

"And they live with her?"

He nodded. "In Mobile."

"Do you ever see them?"

"As little as possible. When we're in the same room you can see the sparks in the air."

"Do they write to you?"

He lifted sad eyes to her. "When they need money. Then good ol' dad gets a letter."

Her heart melted with pity. He looked lonely and defeated, and she wondered if losing a child the way he had wasn't more devastating than giving one up for adoption.

"And what about . . . Beth?" The name was difficult for Rachel to say.

He smiled ruefully, shook his head, then crossed to take the chair opposite Rachel, dropped an ankle over a knee, and drew circles on the white Formica with the bottom of his glass. "Beth is hovering on the brink. I'm not sure yet which way she'll go. She and her mother don't get along and I'm out of the picture."

"You had her with your second wife."

It struck Tommy Lee that Rachel had kept close tabs, indeed, but for the moment he answered her non-question by going on, "Yes, my second wife, Nancy. Do you know why I married Nancy?" His glass made dull murmurs on the tabletop. When she looked from it to his face, she found his eyes on the giraffe at her throat. They moved up and locked with hers as he admitted quietly, "Because the first time I saw her, she reminded me of you. Her hair was the same color as yours, and her mouth was a lot the same. And when she laughed, there was always that little half-hiccup at the end, just like you do."

The pause that followed was anything but comfortable for Rachel. She was embarrassed, yet flattered, and her heart seemed to thump in double time while she couldn't think of a single sensible thing to say. She was thankful when he went on. "But before we were married a year I realized she was nothing at all like you. She's a vicious bitch. I married her because I was lonely, and on the rebound from another marriage. That—granted—wasn't so hot, but at least it was company. I needed the sound of another human voice at the end of the day, and somebody across the supper table. So I married Nancy."

She could well imagine his loneliness at the time, for by then he'd cut himself off from his parents.

"And your third wife, Sue Ann?" she prompted.

He flexed his shoulders against the back of the chair, glanced out at the night, chuckled ruefully and shook his head. "What a joke. The whole damn town knows why I married Sue Ann Higgenbotham." He swallowed the last of his drink, set the glass down and crossed his forearms on the table, meeting her eyes directly. "I think most people refer to it as male menopause."

She smiled at his candor but recalled her mortification upon reading of his third marriage to a woman fifteen years his junior, and one known for her licentious relationships with countless older men around town. She recalled the snickers and raised eyebrows, and the way she'd always reacted to them with a quick defensive anger. How many times had she bitten back a quick defense of Tommy Lee? She experienced again the quick flash of anger she'd felt toward him then for making himself vulnerable to speculation and gossip.

"But did you have to choose someone that much younger than yourself? And a girl like *that?*"

"Why, Rachel," he noted, grinning, "do I detect a spot of temper?"

She colored slightly, but unloaded her convoluted feelings at last. "I used to get so angry with you for . . . for cheapening yourself that way. There were times when I wanted to smack you in the head and ask you just what in the world you were trying to prove! And you realize, don't you, that you left *me* open to questioning, with all your antics. People remembered that we were practically born and raised together, and they'd come up to me and ask the most embarrassing questions, as if *I* still kept tabs on you."

"Apparently you did."

"Don't get smug, and stop trying to evade the issue. I asked you why in the world you got tangled up with somebody like Sue Ann Higgenbotham."

"Chasing after my own youth, I guess. Trying to find it with somebody who was as young as I wished I was."

"But you *were* young." She leaned forward earnestly. "You were only thirty-five, Tommy Lee."

Again her recordkeeping struck him, but he made no issue of it. "Rachel, I've felt old since I was twenty-one, fresh out of college, marrying some woman because it was the acceptable thing to do."

"That was different. She was your own age, and you were starting out together. With Sue Ann I always had the feeling you were throwing her in your parents' faces."

"How could I throw her in their faces when we weren't even talking to each other?"

"You know what I mean. Flaunting her, choosing the worst woman the town had to offer. They were just as aware of what a mess you were making of your life as everyone else in Russellville. Through the years I've often felt you came back to do it under their noses just to humiliate them."

He pondered, studying her steady eyes. "Maybe I did. God, I don't know. You as much as admitted there were times when you had the urge to get even with your parents, too."

"Yes. Times. But I wasn't raised that way, Tommy Lee, and neither were you. I realize they were as fallible as anybody else. They made their decision because they loved me and thought it was best for me."

There was a stern edge to his voice and his brows drew downward. "But it wasn't, Rachel, was it?"

Her heart thundered heavily as she met Tommy Lee's eyes and wondered if her own disillusionment showed as openly as his. "My life with Owen was very good," she argued, perhaps a little too quickly.

Tommy Lee's eyes swept around the room, returned to her before he asked very simply, "But where are the children, Rachel?"

Her polished lips fell open and a pained expression etched her eyes. Beneath the draping silk blouse he saw her breasts heave up once, as if she were struggling for control. He was terribly sorry to do this to her, but what she'd suffered—if she had—was important to him.

She dropped her eyes to her empty glass and admitted quietly, "We were never able to have any."

"Why?"

Their eyes met, delved deeply, and he saw fissures of vulnerability within the woman who always appeared so carefully in control. She pondered the advisability of revealing the truth to the man who'd fathered the only child she'd ever been able to have, but somehow it seemed right that he should know. Her lips trembled, paused in shaping the first word, but finally she got it out. "I . . . I was allergic to Owen's sperm."

He couldn't have looked more surprised if she'd slugged him. His jaw dropped and he tried to speak, but nothing came out. Though she was hidden by the table from the waist down, his eyes dropped to the point where her stomach must be, then as he realized where he was gazing, they flew back to her face again. But his own face was a mask of regret.

"Ironic, isn't it?" Rachel added. "But it's true."

"I've never heard of such a thing," he blurted out.

Her face was slightly pale, his growing increasingly pink as she went on, chafing her crossed arms as they rested on the table edge. "It's not all that uncommon. It seems my body had an excessive sensitivity to his semen, and put up what they called an immunologic reaction to it. I actually created antibodies that prevented the sperm from reaching the egg to fertilize it."

He was stunned by the queer twist of fate that had made her pregnant at a time in her life when she didn't want to be, but had prevented pregnancy during the years when it was what she must have most desired. Yet she stated it all with apparent clinical coolness while he sat before her, greatly discomfited by the personal revelation. Still, something forced him to go on.

"Couldn't anything be done about it?"

"Believe me, we tried. I visited gynecologists as far away as Rush Medical Center in Chicago. Different doctors said it could be treated in a number of ways, but none of them had a history of success. I took drugs, but some of them had unpleasant side effects. We even tried artificial insemination—something to do with bypassing the cervix and going directly to the womb—but that didn't work, either. In some women the antibodies disappear by themselves after a while, but I wasn't so lucky. More than one doctor felt that reducing my exposure to the sperm would reduce the sensitivity and the antibodies would disappear, or at least decrease enough so that I could conceive. We tried long periods of no contact, but when we resumed, there still was no pregnancy."

He drew a hand down his face, covering his mouth for a moment while studying her solemnly. Then he took one of her hands in both of his. "Rachel, I'm so sorry."

She met his empathetic eyes and saw how uneasy he was with the intimate subject, after all. She was disquieted, too, but forced herself to maintain a poised exterior. "It's all right. I've learned to live with it."

"But, Rachel, our ba—"

"Don't say it!" she warned, raising both palms, closing her eyes momentarily.

But he didn't need to say it, for the awful truth scintillated between them as their gazes met again. Together they had conceived the only child she was likely to have, and their parents had decreed that it be taken from her and given to strangers in Flint, Michigan. He felt devastated for her and curiously guilty, as if he'd unwittingly slighted her in some way.

At last he said shakily, "It should have been me you were allergic to."

She reached across the table and pressed her fingertips to his lips. "Shh." She'd thought the same thing countless times. *What if . . . what if . . . ?* But it was shattering to hear him put her thoughts into words.

He grasped her hand and lowered it to the table. "God, Rachel, I feel so guilty. Me with three kids and my life so loused up not one of them is with me. It makes me realize I should have worked harder at being a better father, tried to make them shape up and make something of themselves." The expression about his lips grew soft and his eyes roved her face lovingly. "You'd have been so good at that. You'd have been a good mother, the kind who turns out successes."

"Maybe so. But it's too late to think about it, isn't it?"

Yes, he thought sadly, *it's probably too late.* The room grew quiet. She picked up their glasses and took them to the sink and he knew he should leave. But there were so many more questions he wanted to ask, and their time together had been too short. Walking away from her would be more difficult than ever, especially after the intimate discussion that had him feeling closer to her than he had in years. But he picked up his glasses from the table, slipped them on and crossed to stand behind her.

She felt his presence at her shoulder, but forced herself to remain as she was, staring out a black window over the sink. The words she forced herself to say were more difficult than she'd ever imagined they could be.

"I'm very tired, Tommy Lee. I think it's time—"

"You don't have to say any more, Rachel. I'm on my way out. Thank you for the drinks."

"You're welcome."

Neither of them moved. He studied the back of her neat black hair and a diagonal wrinkle on her violet blouse where it had been pressed against the chair. She smelled so good, so feminine.

"Rachel," came his strained voice, "I'd like to see you again."

She gripped the edge of the sink. "No," she replied shakily, "I don't think so."

"Why?"

"Because it's too painful."

"We could work on that, couldn't we?"

"Could we?"

"Once all the skeletons are out of the attic, we'll feel better."

"If tonight is any indication, I don't think so."

"I didn't mean to hurt you by coming here, you know that, don't you?" He turned her by an elbow, but she stared at his top button instead of his appealing eyes. "Rachel, I'm sorry. I wish I could make it all up to you. You're the one who deserved three more babies, not me."

Her throat constricted suddenly. "Shh . . . don't. In spite of what I've told you tonight, Owen and I were happy. We really were. We were compatible, we had money, success. That was enough. Children aren't every-thing, you know."

Beneath his fingers her elbow trembled, but she wisely drew it from his grasp. He gazed down at the top of her head, but she refused to look up. "Could I take you to dinner some night and we'll talk about more pleasant things?"

And start all over again? she thought. But there was no starting over, only picking up from where they were. The load they had to carry was too heavy, and they had changed so much. Too much for things to work out between them.

"I'm sorry—the answer is no."

"Just dinner—"

But she knew he wanted more than dinner. "No. I'm not in the market for dinner, or dates, or . . . or . . ."

"All right. I won't push it." He turned and she followed him through the dining and living rooms to the entry. She opened the door and stood back, but he made no move to exit, standing instead with both hands buried in his trouser pockets, staring at his shoes. When at last he lifted his head, the question in his eyes could not be concealed by the tinted lenses. What he wanted tingled in the air between them. One hand came out of his pocket and he reached up to lift the tiny gold giraffe on a single fingertip. He leaned closer . . . but the scent of scotch came with him, reminding her of the changes that could not be denied.

She pressed her hands to his chest and turned aside. "Don't, Tommy Lee," she whispered.

His head was half bent toward the kiss. It remained that way while his eyes swam over her and he absently fingered the giraffe. Then he dropped it against her skin. "You're right. It was a stupid idea."

Her heart was thrumming crazily. Beneath his shirt she felt his doing the same. For a moment she was tempted, for old times' sake, but common sense prevailed and she withdrew to take up her pose as doorkeeper, outwardly poised, unruffled, one hundred percent a lady. He backed off politely, leaving her feeling vaguely disappointed and oddly guilty—it had been years since she'd had occasion to deny a man a kiss, and it was no less embarrassing now than it had been as a teenager. But she forced her eyes to meet his, and knew beyond a doubt that saying no was best for both of them.

"Good night, Rachel," he said, stepping out.

"Good-bye, Tommy Lee."

At her choice of farewell words he turned, gave her a last lingering look, then spun away. She watched him until he was halfway down the sidewalk, heading for his Cadillac. Then she closed the door, leaned her forehead against it, and fought the tears.

Chapter 4

DURING THE DAYS that followed, Rachel tried to put Tommy Lee out of her mind. Her father and Marshall helped tremendously. Everett had taken to popping in unexpectedly in the evenings, and Marshall, whose two daughters were already grown and married, found it easy to do the same. On her three days a week at Rachel's house, Callie Mae always stayed until Rachel got home in the late afternoon. She would cast a droll eye on Rachel's slim profile, remind her there was a chocolate pie—or some such calorie-filled delight—in the refrigerator, then chastise, "If you don't put some meat on them bones, you gonna quit castin' a shadow, Miss Rachel."

Rachel would smile and tease, "You won't rest until I'm wearing a size sixteen, will you, Callie Mae?"

But Rachel's appetite remained paltry, and eating alone seemed to decrease it even more. But if Rachel often passed up Callie Mae's offerings, Marshall never did. He came often, to share a meal, to check on Rachel, or to "get her out of the house," as he put it. Having shared many of the same friends for years, it seemed quite natural that together they'd round out a table at bridge, attend backyard barbecues or an occasional movie, and even go shopping for the new furnishings for the master bedroom, which Rachel had decided to have redecorated.

Owen's life insurance had come through, and Marshall solemnly delivered the check shortly after Rachel's return from St. Thomas, then, together with Everett, mapped out the investment plan they deemed most prudent.

The three of them fell into the habit of driving up to one of the nicer clubs in Florence for dinner each Friday night, and though Rachel was most often grateful for their company, there were times when she felt smothered by them. Marshall was very much like Owen in many ways—quiet, steady, sensible, but, to her dismay, a bore. She grew tired of listening to him talk about his chief pastime—taking meticulous care of his yard. And of her father talking about his chief pastime—money and its management. Often when she was with them she found herself withholding sighs: Bermuda grass, investments, azalea bushes, interest rates, annuities, pruning, IRA accounts . . . The two of them droned on about the same dull subjects while Rachel grew listless.

But whenever they were not there Rachel found herself wishing she had children. How different these days would be if she could return home each day to the sound of their voices in the house, perhaps the blare of a stereo from one of the bedrooms, the clatter of a tennis racket being dropped in the middle of the kitchen floor, even the sound of adolescent bickering. She could imagine one of them coming to her, complaining, "Mother, will you tell him—" Or *her* . . .

Don't think about Beth. Don't think about her father.

But every time she walked into the newly decorated bedroom, she thought of Tommy Lee. The room had been repapered with an airy yellow and white bamboo design, and the furniture was pristine white wicker—fresh, bright, a breath of springtime brought inside. Colorful silk flowers adorned a miniature dressing table, above which hung a wicker-framed mirror. The bed was strewn with the whitest, ruffliest spread she could buy, and piled high with yellow and white throw pillows. She'd dappled the room with potted palms and pothos, and changed the scents in the closet and drawers to a brisk herbal that complemented the new look. It was the bedroom of a fifteen-year-old girl now, as bright and different as Rachel could make it. But when she viewed it, she often thought with silent chagrin, "Is this my 'Sue Ann Higgenbotham'?"

And at night, when she lay with the new woven wood shades lifted clear of the sliding glass door, she studied the reflection of the moon on the surface of the pool and took stock of her life, the void, the boredom that was becoming oppressive. She wondered if she would simply drift into her fifties, then her sixties, accepting Marshall's and her father's company as her social mainstay, because the town was small and offered little more.

But it offered one other whom she could not erase from her mind.

She pictured him as he'd looked the night he'd come to the house, wearing the new glasses that made him seem half a stranger, knowing in her heart that he was scarcely a stranger. She remembered the pain in his eyes as he'd told of his failed marriages and his lasting feelings for her. She recalled his lips, as familiar as they'd been years ago, and found herself wishing she had kissed him again, then felt guilty for making such a wish when Owen had been gone such a short time. But Owen's illness had depleted him so rapidly during the last half-year that their sexual relationship had been nonexistent. While he was alive, she'd been too preoccupied with concern for him to rue the lack, but now, alone in bed at night, memories of Tommy Lee and the past came crowding back, leaving her restless and unsatisfied.

Thank heavens she had the store to fill her days. She loved it and was tremendously proud of its success. It had taken ten years to endow the business with its current éclat—a Dun & Bradstreet rating of over $100,000 a year —and almost as long to acquire the eclectic fittings that made the setting at once genteel and warmly welcoming. Oddly enough, Panache was the antithesis of Rachel's house, where each item had its place and where neatness reigned.

The front door boasted a stained-glass window she had found at an auction. Apple-green carpeting created a soothing backdrop for well-chosen touches of pink in the accoutrements.

An elegant French provincial sofa of shell-pink velvet sat before the front bay window, surrounded by hanging ferns. At the rear of the store a tall French armoire spread mirrored doors wide, its illuminated interior highlighting the current display of Giorgio Sant'Angelos and Gloria Betkers draped artistically over the gaping doors and tilting from willow hangers.

At one rear corner was the fitting room: nothing more than a length of fringed French moiré, again in pink, shirred on a circular brass rod. Inside was a delicate wicker chair that matched the chest just outside, where a mountainous burst of spruce-green eucalyptus exploded from a fat-bellied pot in bleeding shades of rose. The spicy fragrance blended with that of herbal soaps, bath salts, and sachets displayed in an open curved-glass curio cabinet and the central display of Flora Danica fragrances.

The opposite rear corner housed Rachel's prized Louis XIV kneehole desk and matching chair with its gilded legs and rose damask seat. There was only one rectangular showcase in sight, and that housed jewelry and scarves in the center of the store. Otherwise, clothing was displayed hither and thither: on an antique butterfly table, hanging from the doe-foot supports of an oval shaving mirror, strewn with an artful eye on the graduated shelves of a what-not, and slipping from the drawers of a provincial lowboy with graceful acan-thus-leaf pulls. Around the walls, dresses hung on charming brass extenders, alternating with the array of wall decor that brought the green-and-white trellised paper to life: miniature Renoir prints, framed cross-stitch embroidery, sprigs of feathergrass bound with green and pink ribbons, toadstools and unicorns on knick-knack shelves, decoupage fancies and gold-beaded neck ropes. The handmade crafts interspersed with couturier labels lent Panache that look of artful clutter only the most talented can successfully achieve. And the store managed to reflect its owner: cool, elegant, tasteful, and always, always fragrant.

Rachel's workdays followed a routine: up at seven, open at nine, paperwork at her corner desk in between helping customers, post office at eleven, lunch at twelve-thirty—usually a piece of fruit or a carton of yogurt at her desk while perusing *Women's Wear Daily.* The afternoons were slightly more varied: dust the furniture, water the ferns, steam the wrinkles from any newly arrived garments, tag incoming merchandise, straighten the stacks, rehang the tried-ons, then, at exactly quarter to four, walk down to the bank with the day's deposit before returning to the shop to help Verda close up for the day.

Given this regimentation, the biyearly clothing markets presented an invit-ing change of routine for Rachel. It was on a Wednesday in early April, when she and Verda were discussing the upcoming market in Dallas, that the phone rang on Rachel's desk. Verda, who happened to be standing right beside the desk, automatically picked it up. A moment later, wide-eyed, she covered the mouthpiece with her palm and announced in a stage whisper, "It's for you! It's him!"

Rachel's head snapped up. "Who?"

Verda's eyebrows nearly touched her hairline. "It's the one who kept calling you while you were gone to St. Thomas. The one who'd never give his name."

Rachel's stomach did a somersault, but she gave away none of the trepida-tion she felt as Verda handed over the phone, then stood listening, making no effort to appear as if she weren't.

"Hello?"

He needn't have given his name; this time she recognized the voice. There followed a long pause, and then Tommy Lee's voice came again. "I've been thinking about you."

With Verda right there, Rachel measured her reply carefully. "Is there something you wanted?"

"Yes. I wanted to know if you'd like to come out and see the lake rise. The dam's been opened for two months, and the water level's finally coming up at my end of the lake."

"I'm really sorry, but I won't have time."

"How do you know? I haven't told you when yet."

Verda now had her ear cocked like a robin listening for a worm. Unable to dream up an evasive reply, Rachel was forced to ask, "When?"

"Friday afternoon. I thought we could drive out together after we're both finished with work."

It sounded so much more appealing than dinner with her father and Marshall, but she quelled the urge to accept. "I'm sorry. I have plans for that night."

"I don't believe you, but that's okay. I'll try another time."

"That won't be necessary, T—" She caught herself just short of pronouncing his name.

"I know. But I'll try just the same." Then he ended softly, "Bye, Rachel."

"Good-bye."

Verda followed every motion as Rachel hung up the phone and slipped her large, squarish reading glasses back on her nose.

"Well, who was it?" the clerk asked point-blank.

Rachel managed to exude an air of total indifference as she relaxed against the chair with one slim wrist draped over its rim. "Oh, just someone I knew years ago who heard of Owen's death and wanted to express his sympathies."

"That's not what it sounded like to me. It sounded like somebody asking you out on a date."

"A date?" Rachel pushed her glasses low and peered at Verda over their rims, hoping she didn't look as shaken as she was by the sound of his voice. "A date? With a widow of less than two months? Don't be silly, Verda." Then she returned to her study of the calendar and the market announcement. "I'll make my flight reservations this afternoon." The subject of the phone call was set aside while they discussed the upcoming trip.

But that afternoon when Rachel made her three forty-five walk to the bank, Tommy Lee was standing in the doorway of his office building as she passed on the opposite side of the street. When she saw him, her navy-blue high heels came to an abrupt halt and she clutched the zippered bank pouch more tightly against her ribs. She'd been passing his office for ten years, and the few times he'd happened to come out while she was directly across the street he'd moved to his car with no indication of having seen her.

He raised a palm now, silently. While she acknowledged it with a silent nod, she mentally calculated how many people up and down Jackson Avenue might have witnessed the exchange. Then she hurried on, breathing freely only when she reached the comparative safety of the bank lobby. From inside, she turned to see if he was still there. He was, studying the bank steps, his expression unreadable from this distance. He found a cigarette, lit it, tossed his head back in that masculine way she sometimes pictured when she thought of him—late at night when she couldn't sleep—and turned, then disappeared into his office.

Rachel spun around, her eyes zeroing in on her father's glass-walled office. He was sitting behind his desk, watching her with a disapproving look on his face. Had he seen Tommy Lee? A disquieting memory came back to her at that moment. She'd heard it said that when Tommy Lee graduated from college and returned to Russellville to set up his business, he had come to the bank to apply for a small-business loan, and her father had personally seen to it that Tommy Lee's application was turned down. Odd that the recollection had come back after all these years.

Her father watched her like an eagle as she turned toward the teller's window to make her daily deposit. She felt his eyes auguring into her shoulder blades and became angry that he should still have a modicum of control over her where Tommy Lee was concerned.

But when her business was completed, she squared her shoulders, put on a false bright smile, and clicked into his glass office, seeking to confirm their Friday night date so she wouldn't feel tempted to take Tommy Lee up on his invitation after all.

"Hi, Daddy. Are we still on for Friday night?"

"Of course. Just as usual."

But Friday night sounded more lackluster than ever. Stepping back onto the sidewalk to make her return walk to Panache, Rachel glanced immediately to the red-brick building half a block away. But Tommy Lee had not come back. His car was parked out front, though, and she had the disturbing feeling he was watching her through the window.

The following day Rachel was folding some silk scarves at the jewelry display case when she absently glanced up to see the tail end of a white Cadillac cruising by at a sloth's speed. Her heart seemed to slam into her throat and she snapped a glance at Verda. But Verda was busy with a customer and hadn't noticed.

Tommy Lee Gentry, don't you dare!

If only he drove some mundane mid-size car in everybody's blue! But everyone in town could count the times he cruised past in that Cadillac. And if he started making a habit of it, what would she do?

Before two days were up she understood . . . he'd started to make a habit of it. How many times had she glanced up to see the car easing along the street at far less than the thirty-mile-an-hour speed limit? Adolescent tactics! Yet each time she saw it her heart fluttered and she felt hot and weak.

On Friday when she stepped out of the bank with the empty pouch in her hand, she again came up short. There he was, on her side of the street, visiting casually with three other businessmen as if they'd just *happened* to meet on the sidewalk. The quartet broke up just as Rachel stepped abreast of them. Tommy Lee turned and fell into step beside her quite naturally.

"Well, hello, Mrs. Hollis."

"Hello, Tommy Lee."

"You're looking exceptionally pretty today."

She walked a little faster and kept her voice low. "Tommy Lee, what on earth are you trying to prove, waiting to ambush me on the street? And who do you think you're fooling, calling me Mrs. Hollis when everyone in town knows we grew up on Cotako Street side by side!"

He grinned down charmingly. "Sorry, then. Hello, *Rachel,* you're looking exceptionally pretty today."

Good Lord, how long had it been since she'd blushed? But it was impossible to be unaffected by his nearness, his compliments. "Tommy Lee, stop it! And stop driving past my store at five miles an hour ten times a day!"

"Today I only drove past six times. Can I see you sometime this weekend?"

"No, I have plans."

"I don't believe you, Rachel. And if you don't want me to grab your elbow and drag you to a stop you'd better do it yourself and act as if you're giving me a civil time-of-day." They were directly across the street from his office now, and Rachel obediently halted, then lifted her flustered eyes to his. "Who are you going to see tonight?" Tommy Lee demanded, standing before her with both hands in his trouser pockets, shirtsleeves rolled to mid-forearm and tie loosened over an open top button. Looking up at him gave her that strange familiar feeling in the pit of her stomach, just like years ago when he'd stop her this way in the halls at school. It struck her that he was handsomer than either Owen or Marshall, though the thought appeared out of nowhere to rankle her.

"My daddy. He's taking me to dinner in Florence."

"Oh." He scowled, glanced toward the bank and thrust his lips out in a peculiarly attractive fashion.

"Yes. Oh. I can hardly tell him I'm sorry but I'm breaking our date to go out with Tommy Lee Gentry, can I?"

"What about tomorrow? The water's up enough that we could go out on the boat."

It sounded absolutely wonderful. "Tomorrow I'm working. I gave Verda the day off."

"Sunday, then."

"Sunday I'm going to church. You remember church, don't you, Tommy Lee? That big red-brick building down there on the corner where you used to go?" It was as close to snide as Rachel had ever come as she pointed to the First Baptist, several blocks away. But the more she was exposed to him, the harder she had to fight to remind herself that he wasn't exactly parlor fare anymore.

"Sunday afternoon?"

She sighed heavily and looked slightly crestfallen. "I'm sorry, Tommy Lee. I can't see you. Please don't ask me again."

Their eyes locked for several electric seconds; then Rachel resolutely turned and continued down the street.

That night over supper she was distracted and forlorn. Everett and Marshall carried on a dull conversation about how investment institutions were slowly usurping the bank's role as chief money holder for many private individuals. While Everett expounded on the droll subject, Rachel tried to keep her mind off Tommy Lee, but he slipped into her thoughts time and again. *I could have been with him at this very moment.* She wondered what his house was like, and if he'd invited someone else to go boating and, if so, who she was. She recalled the sun sparkling off the dark hair on his arms below his rolled-up sleeves, and the inviting shadow cast on his throat by the loosened collar and tie. She imagined another woman enjoying his company and shivered with a sudden inexplicable wave of jealousy.

Later that evening when Marshall saw her home he seemed worried about her.

"You seem rather blue tonight, Rachel," he noted as they stood in the entry, preparatory to his leaving.

"Blue?" She tried to put on a gay expression, but failed. "No, just tired. It's been a long week."

There came into Marshall's eyes a look she'd never seen there before, and as he took her gently into his arms she sensed a difference in the pressure of his hands on her back.

No, not Marshall, she thought in a panic.

But as he leaned back to look into her face, she saw a flicker of emotion that went beyond fraternal care. "You've been doing great. Pushing ahead, getting on with life. I'm very proud of you, you know." He touched her cheek and she wanted to shrink back, wary of allowing him to think for a moment that she wanted any kind of relationship with him other than the one she had. He bent his head to touch his lips to her cheek. She was already searching for the proper words to fend him off when he straightened, gave her arms a platonic squeeze, and said good night.

For some reason the experience with Marshall made her wonder how she would have reacted had it been Tommy Lee who'd given her such ardent glances and pulled her into his arms that way.

Dangerous thought! She promised herself she'd stop dwelling on Tommy Lee this way, and the next time she saw him, she'd walk straight on by with nothing more than a polite hello.

But the next time she saw him she *couldn't* walk away. It was the following Friday at four-thirty. Verda was running the vacuum cleaner over the carpet prior to closing, and Rachel was seated at her desk, putting away the empty bank pouch.

The door opened, Rachel looked up and froze.

He was dressed in an open-collared black sport shirt topped by a gray sports coat a shade lighter than his trousers. His hair was tousled by the wind, and as he closed the door his eyes were already seeking her out.

Her stomach went fluttery and she felt fifteen again. *This time I'll end up saying yes.*

The vacuum cleaner wheezed into silence and Verda greeted him. "Well, howdy, Tommy Lee. Now, what in the world are you doing in a place like this?"

He carefully avoided glancing Rachel's way and sauntered farther into the store with a charming smile for Verda. "I need to buy a present for someone."

"Well, now, I'm sure as eternity not going to ask who it's for. I might not like the answer."

He laughed and looked down at the rectangular glass showcase in the center of the store, studying the accessories arranged there, fingering silk scarves, poring over a basket of earrings. Rachel sat watching him, her pulse hammering out a warning in her throat, but he scarcely gave her a glance. Momentarily, Verda spoke up again. "Y'all just take your time looking while I finish up this floor. If there's anything you like, maybe Rachel can help you."

He looked up as if only now realizing Rachel was there. "Oh, hello, Mrs. Hollis. Never been in your store before." He glanced around, drummed four fingertips on top of the glass cabinet. "It's very nice. Classy." His eyes returned to her and he flashed a quick smile. "Smells good, too."

It smelled of Rachel. It was no particular scent and all scents lingering together in a potent mixture that spoke of things delicate and feminine. Her eyes dropped to the desktop and she busied herself writing something, sitting at a chair almost as delicate as she, her legs crossed and the hem of a melon-colored skirt riding just above the knee. In the cleft of her white embroidered collar lay a collection of chunky coral and brown beads.

Her eyes met his again as the vacuum cleaner cut off the possibility of further talk, but he noted the quick rise and fall of her breasts and the tendons of her right wrist standing out boldly as she clutched the fountain pen. Who but Rachel still used a fountain pen? he wondered. Then he dropped his eyes again to the jewelry counter and she turned away. Covertly he glanced up from time to time to see if the pen moved over the paper, but it was held poised while Rachel's back remained stiff, her head dropped forward.

It struck Verda then who belonged to the voice on the phone, and the vacuum stopped moving, though the brushes still whirred against the carpet. She glanced up sharply at Tommy Lee Gentry, then at Rachel. But Tommy Lee was flicking through the earrings, and Rachel wasn't paying him the least attention.

Rachel wasn't paying him the least attention?

Since when did Rachel ignore a customer? But Verda turned back to her task, deciding to stretch it out as long as possible, to see what Rachel would do.

After some minutes he signaled and she rose to help him. Verda turned off the machine, fussed around putting away things left in the fitting room, and listened.

"Those little red ones," he was saying.

"These?"

"Yes, ma'am."

"These are for pierced ears. Does she have pierced ears?"

"Well, now, I'm not sure I ever noticed," he drawled.

"Most women do these days."

"If she doesn't, could I bring them back?"

"I'm sorry, pierced aren't returnable. State law."

"Oh. Well, it's only nine dollars. If hers aren't pierced, maybe she'll have a friend."

Rachel was incensed, and having a hard time hiding it. How dare he come in here and buy baubles for his tootsies! The shop had grown incredibly quiet. Rachel was aware of it, and of Verda coiling up the vacuum cord and of Tommy Lee studying her own trembling hands as they removed the red button earrings from the case and began scraping the gummed label from the back of the card with a perfect long peach-painted nail.

"Do you want them wrapped?" Rachel asked, braving a glance at his face to throw Verda off balance. *See how unaffected I am by him?* But the moment she raised her eyes, she realized her mistake. Once their gazes met she felt heated and uncomfortable and angry all over again.

"You do that here?"

"Yes. It's a customer service. No charge." The words were difficult for Rachel to say, given the fact that she wanted to sling the red earrings in his face. It angered her further to realize that she couldn't help wondering who they were for. But then, according to the gossips, he had innumerable female friends to whom he might offer such a gift. Rachel's fingers were still shaking as she placed the jewelry in a small apple-green box, wrapped it in green paper, and placed a pink lace bow on the cover.

Tommy Lee had wandered to the armoire and stood studying a midnight-blue slip displayed there with matching bikini panties and a scanty brassiere. He reached out to finger the lace edging at the hem of the slip, and as he moved, his face became visible in the mirror. He looked up, caught Rachel studying him, and had the audacity to smile! She waggled the box in the air.

Immediately he turned. "All wrapped?"

"Yes. That'll be nine dollars and sixty-three cents."

"Do you take Visa?"

"Yes, Visa will be fine."

The two of them moved toward the end of the glass case, where an enormous brass cash register reared its curlicued head. Tommy Lee extracted a card from his wallet and she dropped her eyes; there was something masculinely attractive about a man pushing back his jacket to reach for a wallet. Throughout the exchanging of the card and while she ran it through the imprinter and he signed it, Rachel searched her mind for one of the countless inanities she usually exchanged with a customer at a time like this, but came up with none. She watched his dark hand scrawl a signature while the expensive diamond ring flashed, and again she wondered who the woman was, and damned him for coming here and putting her through this.

"There you go." Smiling, he handed her the pen.

Verda pushed the vacuum cleaner off into the back room just then, and the moment she disappeared through the doorway, Tommy Lee bent across the counter and whispered, "Do you work tomorrow?"

"No . . ." Then, realizing her mistake, Rachel amended, "Yes."

"Want to go water ski—" The ping of the ancient cash register bell cut off the rest of his question and the drawer sprang out at the same moment Tommy Lee reached across the counter and grabbed Rachel's wrist.

"Rachel, come out to the house, please." His mouth looked intense and sincere.

How dare he come here and do this to her! Verify the fact that there were other women in his life while inviting her to become one of them!

"No!" Her eyes veered toward the back room. "Please, Tommy Lee . . ."

From the rear of the building came the scrape and thump of Verda putting away the machine. Rachel's wrist strained against his hold.

"Sunday?" he asked quickly, his fingers tightening.

Her startled eyes held both anger and an undeniably tempted look, so he hurried on. "Beth will be there, so we wouldn't be alone. I want you to meet her."

Verda's footsteps were coming back and he was forced to drop Rachel's wrist. When the clerk emerged from the doorway Tommy Lee was putting his credit card away and Rachel was dropping the gift into a tiny floral paper sack.

"Thank you for stopping in," she said cheerfully, handing him his purchase. "And have a nice weekend."

Tommy Lee carefully wiped his feelings from his face and brought forth a lazy smile. "Y'all do the same, Mrs. Hollis, and you, too, Verda."

He nodded to the clerk, who called out the customary "Y'all come back." Then he strolled from the store without a backward glance.

The moment the door closed behind him, Verda propped a hand on her hip, raised one eyebrow, and said, "Mrs. Hollis?" Her shrewd eyes homed in on Rachel. "What's going on?"

"Going on?" Rachel busied herself arranging the scarves on top of the showcase. "Nothing's going on, Verda. Whatever in the world do you mean?"

"I suddenly put a name with the voice on the phone. It's his. Tommy Lee Gentry." She peered closely at Rachel. "He been pestering you?"

"Oh, for heaven's sake, Verda, don't be silly. What would Tommy Lee Gentry be doing pestering me?"

"What does Tommy Lee Gentry do pestering half the women of this town?" She glanced toward the door. "Which one of his doxies do you reckon those earrings were for?"

The question shot a flash of cold through Rachel. She wanted to cringe and defend him simultaneously. Why should she care about his indiscretions or what the town thought of him because of them? Yet the fact remained that she did. She always had.

"Do you want to stand there wondering about it all weekend, or would you rather lock up and go home?" Rachel forced an amused smile to her lips, as if she, too, were curious about the woman whose ears would be decorated with the red beads.

"You sure it wasn't him?" Verda couldn't resist asking one more time, scrunching up her eyes and studying Rachel closely.

"Tommy Lee Gentry?" Rachel turned away casually, heading for the light switch by the armoire. "I swear, Verda, if I have to put up with any more ridiculous questions from you I'll begin to wonder if I've given you enough time off lately." Rachel's low laugh followed, and Verda gave up.

"Oh, all right, but I could've sworn it was him when he walked in here and started talking."

Duplicity was not Rachel's long suit. When she'd locked up and was on her way home, safely away from Verda's inquisitive eyes, she pulled over to the curb along a tree-shaded street, crossed her wrists on the steering wheel, and dropped her forehead on them.

Rachel Hollis, get the man out of your mind. See what people think of him? And just what do you think they'd be saying about you if you were seen with Tommy Lee Gentry when Owen is scarcely cold in his grave?

But it hurt, having to lie about Tommy Lee. She felt she was injuring him more, yet what else could she have done with Verda all ears and eyes? But she remembered his wind-whipped hair, his fingers on her arm, the soft invitation in his voice as he leaned across the counter. And his lips . . . those lips that hadn't changed a bit in all these years. And she thought of the empty house, superimposed on images of herself in a boat, or on water skis, or riding off somewhere beside him in the white Cadillac to have dinner.

But then, remembering how many others had done those same things—and more—with Tommy Lee, she shook his image from her mind and continued home to the waiting, silent house.

Chapter 5

BY BY SUNDAY afternoon the house had grown too silent, too oppressive. It was spring, and Alabama had embarked upon that time of color and rebirth.

Blossoms were exploding everywhere: azaleas in shades of red and pink, dogwoods in white, wisteria in violet, and redbuds like a purple haze limning the countryside. Was there a time of year that tugged at the heartstrings more than this? That drew memories out of hiding and made them even more poignant in recollection than they'd been in reality?

Rachel lay in the backyard while bees buzzed in the blossoming pyracantha bushes bordering the high brick wall. She moved restlessly on the chaise lounge, closing her eyes against the sun and the loneliness, but seeing dancing pictures on her closed eyelids. Pictures of Tommy Lee past and Tommy Lee present. She rolled to her stomach, trying to shut them out, but they persisted even as she searched for a distracting sound to take away the memory of his voice, inviting, "Come out to the house . . . please." But there was nothing so silent as a small-town Sunday afternoon.

When she could tolerate it no longer she flung herself up and marched into the house, driving her fingers through her twenty-five-dollar hairdo, realizing that stubbornness was a poor substitute for company. *Don't think about whether it's wise or not—for once, just go with your heart.*

She bathed, applied fresh makeup, dabbed scent behind her ears, and dressed in a sporty knit pink and gray striped top with matching skirt, both of which snapped up the front. She slipped her bare feet into white thong sandals, debated about what bathing suit to take, and decided to stop at the store and pick out a new one.

The store was different on Sundays—empty and shadowed. The display lights were off, the silence oddly disquieting, and Rachel had the strange feeling she was being given this pause as a last chance to come to her senses. But today spring controlled her senses. Almost defiantly, she stepped to the bathing suit rack. She flipped past the array of bikinis, which were for the most part too revealing for her taste, but cast a disdainful eye on the one-piecers, which seemed sexless and dull. In the end she chose a modest two-piece design of shimmering gold with a diagonal bar of red slicing from left hip to right breast, interrupted by a band of naked skin. Assessing herself in the full-length mirror, she tugged the waist up securely and checked to make sure it fully covered the scar on her stomach, then turned to view her back. *Lord, Callie Mae is right. If I don't gain some weight this thing will fall right off me.*

She turned full front to the mirror again, and her dark eyes appeared uncertain. Standing with her fingertips resting on her stomach, she thought she could feel nerves jumping inside.

He said his daughter will be there, so what can happen when you'll be chaperoned by a fourteen-year-old?

The suit had a matching cover-up of luxurious velour that reversed the design and colors, sporting a diagonal bar of gold on red. Its elasticized waist closed with a single gold catch, leaving provocative glimpses of the bathing suit and her bare midriff showing above and below the closure. But, considering her shape, Rachel hardly felt provocative, and decided the outfit would do. She stripped it off, packed it in her straw bag, and dressed in her street clothes again, then locked the store and bounded to her car before she could change her mind.

The drive out to Cedar Creek Lake was beautiful. She took old Belgreen

Road, which wound through the hills west of town, curving through pine forest and past areas where orange peaks of overburden from long ago strip-mining created a stunning contrast against the lush greenery surrounding it. The old limestone quarries gave over to glimpses of the TVA transmission towers, which were responsible for changing the area so much. Nestled in the foothills of the Appalachian Mountains, Franklin County rolled and undulated, presenting unexpected vistas: blue-hazed hills and endless rolling forests that abounded with wildlife. Even the hated kudzu vine was beautiful now, carpet-thick in the ditches, blossoming in purple. Beneath the hickories and turkey oaks flashed an occasional cloud of white dogwood. The road straightened, then doglegged, angled uphill and down, but she knew the route as if she'd driven it every day. Somehow she'd never forgotten where his house was, once it was pointed out to her.

His driveway twisted through a stretch of some five acres of untainted wildwood before arching around in a loop that brought her to his front door. She turned off the engine, then peered up at the house, feeling a knot tighten her stomach. Slowly she opened her door and stood for a long time in its lee while staring over the roof of the car at the sheer clifflike stretch of diagonal cedar siding, the irregular roofline, the ebony doors and railed ramp. She removed her sunglasses and studied further. How odd—the place seemed familiar. Yet this was the closest to it she'd ever been. The smell of the woods was rich and fecund. She lifted her gaze to the heavens—cedars and sassafras trees and one venerable magnolia at least 150 years old.

Drawing a deep, shaky breath, Rachel slammed the car door, slipped her glasses on, and made her feet move toward the wooden ramp.

She came up into a deep entry in which were ensconced two redwood tubs of boxwood badly in need of watering, and glanced up at the only window facing this side, the large hexagon above the doors. A faint memory shivered through her. *Don't be silly,* she thought. *How can you remember something you've never seen?* Then she quickly rang the bell before she could lose her courage.

Two minutes passed and nothing happened—except that Rachel became aware of a tiny pain at the back of her head—tension. *He's probably out on the lake with his daughter.* She rang again and felt a trickle of sweat drizzle down the center of her back while the seconds ticked past and a woodpecker thwacked away someplace in the trees behind her.

Suddenly the door was jerked open and there stood Tommy Lee, looking as if he was recovering from a four-day drunk and wishing he'd died instead. His hair was tousled, his face grizzled by an unkempt beard, shirt dangling limp and wrinkled and unbuttoned. The knees of his jeans were rumpled and his feet were bare. He stood staring at her as if she were a reincarnation.

"Rachel, my God, you came!"

"Yes. You invited me, remember?"

"But I never thought you would." Unconsciously, he closed a single button at the waist of the shirt, which only emphasized its hapless condition.

"The house was driving me crazy, it was so quiet. And the lake sounded good."

He remained in the open doorway as if too surprised to orient himself. She felt the rush of conditioned air cooling the fronts of her legs and wondered how long he intended to stand gaping at her. "Am I intruding?" she asked, tilting her head slightly.

Abruptly he jerked awake. "Oh . . . no. No!" He stepped back. "Not at all. I was asleep. Come in." He finger-combed his hair while she cautiously entered. When the door closed she found herself in an enormous entry and peered up at a contemporary brass and smoked-glass light fixture hanging before the hexagonal window from a height of eighteen feet. She removed her sunglasses and glanced at what she could see of the rest of the place from here: a lot of wood, windows, and staggered levels. The house was silent as a tomb as Rachel's gaze made a circle and came back to him. Their eyes met. Tommy Lee's hand still rested on the fancy doorknob. He flashed her a self-conscious smile, which she returned with a quavering one of her own, then dropped her eyes to the floor only to encounter the bare feet she recognized from all those carefree days of swimming at City Park. His second toes were longer than the big toes, and his feet were shaded now with dark hair. Quickly she glanced up at the living room, which overhung the entry.

"Come in." He gestured her ahead of him, up six steps into a room that looked worse than its owner, if possible. Dirty glasses, full ashtrays, and clothes littered the furniture. The carpet, though dense, hadn't been touched by a vacuum cleaner in weeks, and the hundreds of dollars' worth of potted plants along the glass wall were drooping, drying up, and dusty. Newspapers were scattered over the vast expanse of sofa, which turned two corners and seemed to sprawl forever, its mother lode of ottomans creating a veritable sea of cushions before a glorious fireplace. Glancing at the array of flotsam, Rachel wondered how Tommy Lee could possibly manage to look so neat in public when his entire wardrobe seemed to be flung around his living room.

She glanced back uncertainly and stopped in her tracks.

"I wasn't expecting company," he explained, and moved around her to scrape an armful of garments off the back of the sofa.

"You told me your daughter was coming for the weekend."

"Yes, she was, but at the last minute her mother decided not to let her." His eyes dropped to the shirts in his hands, then wandered off with a dismal expression to some distant point across the lake. "I was going to come home Friday night and get everything in shape before Beth got here, but when she called to say she wasn't coming it seemed pointless."

Somehow she believed him, that he hadn't invented Beth's visit to lure her here with a false sense of security. His eyes swung back to Rachel and he seemed to make a conscious effort to put away his troubled thoughts. "But even though she's not here, I'd still like you to stay."

In this? she thought. The place smelled like an unaired saloon—stale smoke, used filters and alcoholic dregs, and even if she could find a spot to sit on that davenport, there wasn't a single place to do so without putting her feet up. Furthermore, she didn't want to be next after the woman with the red earrings.

Sensing that she was close to having a change of heart, he hurriedly moved around the room, leaning over the back of the sofa to sweep up newspapers, socks, and neckties. "Just give me a few minutes and I'll run upstairs and grab a quick shower, okay?" He straightened with his arms full and appealed, "Now, don't go away, okay?"

She shook her head and dredged up a faint smile while he gazed at her hopefully, backing away. Then he turned and with a flash of shirttail, bounded up a stairway and out of sight.

She looked around, reluctant to sit down on anything, though the room was luxurious at its core. She moved around the corners of the U-shaped sofa, studying the dirty glasses, the dried rings where others had been, the dust caught and held in gray overlapping circles, the empty matchbooks and full ashtrays. Coming to one glass that was still sweating, she reached down and touched it. It was still cold. She held it to her nose and sniffed. Gin, diluted by melted ice. She set it down distastefully and dropped her eyes to the sofa. The picture was clear: a depressed alcoholic, lying in an inert sprawl, sipping away his lonely weekend while the cobwebs collected around him, and his mind and body grew dissipated.

It had been a mistake to come here.

She turned her back on the living room and moved toward the end of the fireplace wall where the dining area was announced by caned chairs surrounding a fruitwood table. Empty containers from take-out food lay amid his unopened mail, a half-eaten bag of cheese curls, and an open jar of peanuts. *He doesn't eat right,* she thought, and the realization saddened her as she gazed at two cold french fries and a blob of dried-up ketchup. A fingernail clipper lay beside them, and the sight of it rent her heart as she pictured him here at the table, clipping his nails in silence, then eating his supper alone.

She turned to glance at the working end of the kitchen, but the cabinets held only dirty glasses and an array of booze bottles, all partly empty. Again she closed her eyes, wishing she had sensibly stayed away.

She sat on one of the cane and chrome chairs and turned her eyes to the lake, to something that was pleasant and clean and told no tales. From overhead came the sound of the shower, then in a few minutes the buzz of an electric razor, and in record time Tommy Lee's footsteps thumped down the stairs.

At first he thought she'd left, for the living room was empty, and as he raced through it his heart seemed to stop. But then he caught sight of her at the kitchen table and his shoulders slumped with relief. How many years had he pictured Rachel here? The sight of her with her tanned legs crossed, a white sandal hanging from her toes, a delicate elbow resting on the table edge, seemed too good to be true.

"I'm sorry I kept you waiting, Rachel."

"I've been enjoying the view."

He looked down his chest. "I dressed for the water. I wasn't sure what you wanted to do."

He wore white swimming trunks and a matching terry-cloth cover-up snapped at the waist, revealing a V of skin with far more hair than he'd had on his chest the last time she'd seen it—and some of it glinting silver in the light from the long windows. His hair was neatly combed and, from this angle, as thick as it had been in high school. But as he approached she made out the wiry texture of the gray at his temples and was surprised to find it not altogether unpleasing.

She forced her eyes away. "I brought a bathing suit. It's in the car. But I . . . I expected Beth to be coming along."

Her reluctance was so obvious that he felt obliged to give her a choice. "Do you want to put it on?"

No, she thought, *not anymore. Not since walking in here and realizing your life-style is precisely what it's purported to be, and nothing I want to become involved with.*

"I'll run out and get it for you," he offered with boyish eagerness. And seeing how much it meant to him to have her here, she relented.

"No, I'll go."

She felt his eyes follow her as she arose and crossed the living room, moved down the steps and outside. When the door closed behind her, she tipped her head back against it and sucked in a long breath. Tears stung her eyes. *Oh, Tommy Lee . . . Tommy Lee. We can never go back.* Her nostrils flared and she opened her eyes to see the tips of the trees blurred as she contemplated the loneliness she had just witnessed. *What am I doing?* she wondered as she made her way to the car and reached inside for a wide-mouthed straw tote bag. But something made her retrace her steps up the ramp to the shiny black doors.

He had put away the pile of newspapers while she was gone, and she caught him carrying dirty ashtrays and glasses to the kitchen. Their eyes met, then swerved apart.

"You can use the guest bedroom upstairs at the first landing."

Her footsteps were muffled by the deep pile of the indigo carpeting. Against the white walls and natural wood, it was stunning. At the first landing an unexpected window cranny looked out over a steeply canting roof, and a potted fig tree drooped before it. She peered around a doorway into a beautifully decorated bedroom done in eggshell, muted blue, and brown, its double bed covered with a geometric quilted spread whose design continued in a mountain of throw pillows, then up the wall between two long, narrow windows decorated with nothing but a pair of mobiles.

The tiny metal sailfish circled slowly as she stepped inside the room and surveyed a baretopped Danish dresser and chest of drawers with natural waxed wood finish, costly lamps, and a large framed photo of a pair of well-used toe shoes with their ribbons worn and sides misshapen.

Beth's room—she must be a dancer.

For a moment his Beth and their Beth melded into one, and she had the awesome feeling that she was stepping into her own daughter's room, and again that feeling that she'd been here before. But she shook herself and crossed to a far doorway that led into a lovely bathroom with blue fixtures and a shower curtain of the same design as that of the bedspread. Lush blue towels hung from the towel bars, but as she moved closer she saw that their folds bore a line of dust. At the foot of the tub another window looked out over the roof and the shimmering lake beyond. Over the tub hung a dead ivy.

What a beautiful house, she thought, glancing once more around the bedroom and bath. But their stark, unused look contained a message as poignant as that of the abject disorder downstairs.

It was a house that cried out for life.

She tried to put the thought from her mind as she changed into her swimsuit. But when she was slipping it on, she confronted the cesarean-section scar on her stomach, realizing afresh what an irony it was that the birth of her and

Tommy Lee's baby had left a permanent mark as a reminder that their child was the only one she'd ever have. She tugged the waistband into place and told herself to stop thinking senseless things about the past. But again, when the halter was tied behind her neck, Rachel studied her reflection in the mirror, then cupped both breasts, pushing them high, dismayed to see that even by doing this she could create no cleavage. It was impossible not to remember that at sixteen she had been fuller-breasted than now, or to imagine that Tommy Lee would not notice.

Her distraught eyes scolded those in the mirror. You foolish middle-aged woman, what are you doing? You shouldn't even be here in the first place, and you're looking for cleavage? She dropped her hands and covered herself with the beach jacket, glanced disparagingly at the glimpse of skin still revealed above and below, sighed, grabbed her towel, slipped on her thongs again, and left the room.

In the hall she paused and glanced at the carpeted stairs that continued up two more levels with windows and potted plants announcing each floor. Steps, handrailings, and white walls rose to the various levels of the house, which had appeared so tall from outside. Tommy Lee's bedroom must be up there. And it must have as stunning a view as that from an aerie.

It struck her then why she'd sensed a feeling of déjà vu about the house, and her head snapped back as she stared up the steps, trying to calculate where the chimney flue would rise up through the walls if the master bedroom had a fireplace . . . a deck overlooking the lake. It struck her like lightning. *My God, it's our house! The one we planned together when we were starry-eyed teenagers!* For a moment she felt dizzy, and her stomach seemed to tilt. *No, you must be wrong, Rachel.* But a quick mental assessment of the rooms below confirmed it. This was their dream house. It had just taken her some time to recognize it beneath the clutter and loneliness. She returned to the lower level feeling shaken, and though she thought she'd approached soundlessly, Tommy Lee's voice called, "I'm out here, Rachel."

She found him in the kitchen, a black towel slung over his shoulder as he hunkered down before the open refrigerator packing a cooler. When she rounded the corner he lifted his eyes to her, dropped them slowly down her tanned legs, swallowed in a way that made his Adam's apple move, then returned his attention to the refrigerator. "What would you like to drink? I've got beer, rum, vod—"

"Do you have limes?"

He looked up again. "Sure. Gin and tonic with a twist of lime?"

"Just plain tap water with a twist of lime will be fine."

He went on piling cold beer into the red and white cooler, and as she counted the cans, she wondered how many he intended to take. From the crisper he took two limes, dropped them into the cooler, and asked, "Perrier water okay?"

She nodded and several small bottles joined the cans. Then he snapped the cooler shut and stood up.

"Ready?"

She forced a smile and he gestured toward the door, following her to slide the heavy glass panel aside and allow her to step through before him. They crossed a slatted redwood deck, moved down steps to a grassy stretch of lawn and on toward a dock where a black and white speedboat waited beneath a yellow canopy. He tossed his towel on a seat, then presented a palm to help her board. To ignore it would have made more of an issue than to touch him. His fingers clamped hers tightly as she stepped down and the boat rocked. Though the contact was brief, it left a residue of awareness that Rachel tried to put from her mind.

"Sit there." He pointed to the front passenger seat, then busied himself freeing both bow and stern lines before leaping down to join her. She was extremely conscious of his long bare legs and feet, peppered with dark hair, and of the casual way his glance washed over her as he squeezed through the small opening between the seats, his thigh nearly brushing her shoulder, before he settled himself behind the wheel with the cooler close at hand and inserted the key in the ignition.

The touch of a button brought the soft buzz of the motor being lowered, then the inboard growled to life, followed by the swish of water purling against the hull. The lake was as calm as a glass of water, and as the boat got under way it skimmed the surface with scarcely a vibration. He eased the throttle forward and Rachel's hair lifted, then flurried back. Instinctively she raised her nose into the air, sniffing, feeling life flowing back into her veins as she dangled an arm above the water.

Tommy Lee turned to watch her as her eyes closed and she nosed the wind. Lord a'mighty, had there ever been a woman as perfect? She'd been a knock-out in high school, but age had only refined her fragile beauty. She had weathered the years so much more gracefully than he had. And she'd achieved a reputation of highest regard in both her personal life and her business, while he had become merely déclassé. It seemed quite unbelievable that she was here with him at last, for in spite of all his dreams, he'd never really believed it would happen.

Rachel hung her head back, felt the cool droplets spray her fingertips, heard the snick of a lighter, then caught the faint drift of cigarette smoke. Even with her eyes closed, she knew he was studying her.

The boat suddenly thrust forward with a jerk that lifted its nose above the water and snapped Rachel's head farther back. Her eyes flew open and she shot a look at Tommy Lee.

He had a cigarette clamped between china-white teeth while his broad teasing smile shone devilishly. Left hand on the wheel, right on the throttle, he studied her with a challenge in his glinting eyes.

"Let's cool off." The words were distorted around the filter as he spoke, but they gave him a rakish appeal much as he'd had in those days when they'd roared off, carefree, in his '57 Chevy.

A tiny smirk appeared at the corners of Rachel's mouth. "You always did like speed."

"Always!" he shouted above the wind, while she herself became exhilarated by it as the boat gained momentum then leveled off with the fluttering wind pressing against her ears, lifting and swirling her hair.

It was wonderful! Releasing! She turned to him and shouted to be heard above the motor and the thump of the hull bouncing on the water. "I can remember my daddy saying to you, 'Now, drive carefully, and don't speed.' Then we'd get one block away from the houses and fly like the wind."

He laughed, throwing his head back while taking the cigarette out of his mouth as an ash flew backward. "I still love it!" he shouted.

"So I've heard!"

His eyes returned to hers and they measured each other silently. Then he shouted, "Do you want me to slow down?"

By now the minute ripples on the surface of the water had become nothing more than a blur as the rumbling inboard propelled them forward like a dynamo. She pushed the whipping hair back from her temple with the palm of one hand and yelled, "No, it feels wonderful. I think it's exactly what I needed."

But he couldn't hear her and leaned across the aisle, lowering his ear.

She leaned close enough to smell fresh after-shave. "I said, it feels wonderful! I think it's exactly what I needed!"

He straightened, smiled wider, and warned, "Hang on!" Then he anchored the cigarette between his teeth, dropped his hand to the throttle, and pushed it full forward. Their hair whipped like flags; their jackets billowed like sails. Their bodies jiggled as they rocketed toward a vanishing point on the far horizon, wrapped in the ebullient sensation of near-flight.

Tommy Lee cramped the wheel and suddenly Rachel was high above him, the water spuming wide from the hull, churning out a rabid wake behind them. She laughed and he tossed an appreciative glance her way, then spun the wheel in the opposite direction. She made an owl face at him and pressed a hand to her stomach while rolling her eyes. His answering laugh sounded faintly above the roar of the wind in her ears and the thrumming cylinders. Then they were snaking right and left, right and left, lifting and falling until Rachel felt giddy. Again she laughed, feeling gay and unfettered for the first time in months, letting the reckless ride take her deliciously off kilter. But finally she reached out and squeezed Tommy Lee's forearm, shaking her head, pressing a hand to her stomach once more. He straightened the wheel but left the speed where it was until Rachel finally reached out and covered his hand on the throttle with her own, drawing back both until the boat quieted and slowed and drifted in the abrupt lift of its own backwash.

In the sudden quiet their combined laughter drifted above the lake. As if directed by a baton, they stilled simultaneously and found themselves gazing at each other. At that moment Rachel realized her hand still rested on his, the pads of her fingers contouring his knuckles, and she withdrew it as casually as possible, but not before his eyes fell to the sight of their joined hands on the throttle, then came back to her face.

"It's nice to hear you laugh again," he said.

"It's been a long time since I have. It feels good."

She thought for a moment he was going to touch her; the look in his eyes said he was thinking about it. But then, abruptly, he twisted around to fetch himself a beer from the cooler.

"Want one?" He popped the top and tossed it over his shoulder into the water.

"No, thank you." She bit back the reprimand about littering the lake with pop-tops and told herself it was none of her business. She was only spending one afternoon with him. "Just lime water."

He wedged the can between his legs, tight against his swim trunks, while twisting to reach for the cooler again. Realizing her gaze had followed the can of beer, she turned sharply to study the water beyond her side of the boat until a cold touch on her arm announced the lime water.

They cruised the lake, too aware of each other, yet maintaining a cautious distance at all times. She counted the cigarettes he smoked, the butts he threw into the lake, the beers he downed. When he'd begun his third, she moved restlessly and suggested, "Why don't we swim?" thinking that if he was swimming he couldn't be drinking.

"Anything you say," he complied. "Anyplace in particular?"

"You know the lake better than I do."

"All right. Hang on." His latest cigarette butt went the way of the others, and again the boat shot forward at hair-pulling speed until a few minutes later Tommy Lee throttled down and killed the engine completely.

Rachel glanced around quizzically. "Here?" she asked. They were in an inlet with trees all around, but it was a long swim to shore in any given direction, and there wasn't a soul in sight.

"You want to go somewhere else?"

"I thought we'd go to one of the beaches."

"With all those people? You really want to?"

She turned to find his shaded lenses facing her, but couldn't make out his eyes behind them. "No . . . no, this is fine."

"Okay, I'll drop anchor." At the touch of his finger, an electric buzz accompanied the soft *shrrr* of the anchor line paying out. Silence followed, vast upon the sunny stretch of the blue water with its canopy of matching sky. The sun beat down and shimmered while Tommy Lee downed the last of his beer, fished a Styrofoam floatboard from beneath the foredeck, tossed it over the side, leaned down again, and came up with a lightweight ladder.

"You first." He waved Rachel aft, and she slipped between their two seats toward the stern of the boat, then turned to find him bending to hang the ladder on the side. Straightening, he was already yanking at the single snap at his waist, and a minute later the terry-cloth jacket lay on the seat and Rachel found herself confronted with the entire stretch of his bare chest, mesmerized by the dense Y of pewter gray while it struck her again how much more masculine a man is at forty than at sixteen.

Guiltily she turned her back while releasing the hook at her waist and removing her cover-up. She found it difficult to confront the changes wrought upon them by the years, not only her thinness but his heaviness.

"Last one in buys two bucks' worth of gas," he said quietly.

She looked back over her shoulder, then turned to find him with a nostalgic look on his face. Years ago, when they'd crowded into somebody's car with a gang of kids and driven out to City Park to swim, that had always been the challenge. Nobody had money then, and how happy they'd all been. Now they both had all the money they needed . . .

She searched for something to say, anything that would lift the heavy weight of remembrance and bear her back to the present. But the past created a tremendous gravity between them, and she sensed him deliberately training his eyes above her shoulders. She knew what control it took to keep them there, because it was equally hard for her to keep her eyes above his waist.

Attempting to sever the skein of sexuality that seemed suddenly to bind them, she quipped, "If I were you I'd take my glasses off before I issued any challenges." Then with a deft movement she was over the side, diving neatly into the deep, cool sanctuary of Cedar Creek Lake. She heard the muffled surge of his body following, then opened her eyes to bubbles and blueness, kicking toward the surface while Tommy Lee was still on his way down. Emerging, she skinned her hands down her face, then saw his head pop up six feet away.

He swung around, tossing his head sharply, sending droplets flying in a glistening arc from his hair.

"Waugh! That's a shock!" he bellowed.

"But much better," she added. "Now I can see your eyes at last."

"I didn't know you wanted to or I'd have taken my glasses off an hour ago."

"They're very attractive, but it's hard to tell what a person's thinking when you can't see his eyes. Can you see without them?"

"Enough to know where I'm going. Come on."

He struck off at an energetic crawl while she followed at the carefully paced stroke of a well-tuned swimmer. In no time at all she met him coming back, puffing. She chuckled and continued on a leisurely turn around the boat, passing him once, twice, then three times while he floated on the miniature surfboard. His arms were crossed upon it, feet drifting idly as she came around for the fourth time and joined him.

"You're back." He smiled.

Rachel dipped below the surface, emerged nose first, her hair seal-slick, and crossed her arms on the opposite end of the four-foot board.

"Yes, I'm back." She propped her chin on her crossed wrists. "You didn't last very long."

"I'm all out of shape."

"You shouldn't be. Not with the lake right here. You should be swimming every day."

"It looks like you do."

"Just about."

"It shows. Rachel, you look great."

The water washed over the surfboard and she swished it lazily with one hand, her chin still propped on the other. "I told you. I'm too thin."

"Not to suit me." His eyes without glasses were extremely sparkly, almost beautiful with a wealth of deep brown lashes shot with droplets of glittering water. With his chin on a fist, he reached out his free hand to swish the water along the surface of the board, missing her fingers by a mere inch. "Do you remember when I used to see if my hands could span your waist?"

She watched his hand brushing near hers. "Mmm . . . in those days I'd have been ecstatic if they had. But now, when they probably could, it would only point out that I'm shriveling up."

Tommy Lee laughed, his teeth white against his dark-skinned face. "Shriveling up? You're a long way from shriveled up, Rachel. I'd say you're in your prime."

"My prime," she said thoughtfully. "That's a palliative offered to people in their forties who don't want to be. I feel shriveled up, after the last two years."

His hand stilled and his expression turned concerned. "Was it bad, Rachel, going through all that with Owen?"

She shrugged and the motion brought a wave of cool water between her arms and the board. "At the time you don't stop to wonder if it's hard. You just do what you have to do, carry on from day to day. Toward the end, when his pain got worse . . ." She stopped, mesmerized by the stunning brown eyes studying her across the floatboard. "I didn't come out here to talk about that. I came to forget it."

His cool, wet fingers captured and held hers loosely. "I'm sorry you had to go through that, Rachel. When I heard he had cancer and how bad it got, I wanted to call you a hundred times, just to say I was thinking of you and ask if you needed anything—if I could help you in any way. But I figured your daddy was there with you, and what was there I could do for you anyway?"

Rachel blinked, focusing wide eyes on his. "You did? You really did? It's an odd feeling to think you were following the events of my life all those years."

"But you knew what was going on in mine, too."

"Only what I read in the papers and what people told me. I didn't go driving past your house."

His fingers were warm as he continued holding hers. His thumb moved along her knuckles, then circled her diamond before he went on reflectively. "Funny how people who remember we used to date never missed a chance to tell me what was going on in your life. Sometimes I wanted to tell them to keep their damn mouths shut, keep all their social tidbits to themselves. I didn't want to know how happy and successful you were becoming with Owen. Other times I fed off it. And, naturally, I'd drive past your house and wonder."

Rachel's heart lilted. He was much more honest than she. There were times when she'd experienced some of the same feelings, only she was reluctant to admit it. "Wonder?" she prompted now.

"If he knew about us."

For a moment she didn't answer, thinking of the scar on her stomach that could hardly have been hidden from a husband.

"Did he, Rachel?" Tommy Lee asked softly.

"He knew I'd had the baby, but he didn't know whose it was."

"Wasn't he curious?"

"We made a pact early in our marriage that the issue would never come up again, once we'd talked it out."

"It says a lot about a man that he can live with a question like that unanswered and never let it come between you."

She wasn't about to tell him that it *had* been between them, always. They might not have talked about it, but there had been hundreds of times when she'd caught Owen studying her across a room, and she'd known instinctively what he was thinking.

Tommy Lee's eyes pierced her across the speckled blue surface dividing them. "If you had been my wife all that time, I'd have gone crazy wondering."

"From the things you told me the night you talked about your wives, I would have said you weren't a jealous man."

His fingers pulled her hand closer to his chin and he said raggedly, "They weren't you, Rachel."

"Don't," she breathed, trying to pull her hand away. But he held it fast.

"Don't? Don't for how long? Until you really are shriveled up? Until your debt to Owen is paid—whatever it might be? Until you decide to take off his rings?" His hand squeezed so hard the rings dug into her skin. "How long do you intend to wear them, Rachel?"

Her heart was racing faster than before. "I don't know. It's . . . it's too soon."

"Is it? Let's see." Without warning, Tommy Lee gave the float board a push that sent it sideways, and in one swift kick brought himself only inches from Rachel's nose. Her heart hadn't time to crack out a warning before one powerful hand circled her neck and scooped her close. He kissed her once, a hard, impromptu meeting of two water-slicked mouths while the wavelets lapped at their chins, accentuating how warm their lips were. During the brief contact their legs instinctively moved to keep them afloat, and the sleek texture of skin on skin brought shivery sensations.

The kiss ended and somehow they were each hanging onto the float board with one hand. Rachel's surprised lips dropped open as Tommy Lee pulled back, staring into her eyes. Her hair coiled around his fingers like a silken tether while he moved a thumb just behind her ear. Water beaded on his dark, spiky lashes and gleamed on his cheeks. They stared at each other, breathing hard, for several stunned seconds. Then Tommy Lee's hand drifted from her neck down one slick shoulder, and beneath the water his calf slid between her knees, then was gone. "Come on." He smiled. "Let's play." And with a twisting sideways dive, he disappeared beneath the surface.

It had been an elementary kiss. His tongue hadn't even touched her; yet she was trembling inside and felt hot and threatened and enticingly sexual. Needing to cool off, Rachel, too, did a surface dive, then took several enormous breast strokes underwater, hoping to come up a safe distance from him.

When she nosed into the daylight again he was trying to get to his feet on the surfboard—with little success. From behind, she watched him battle it, wondering how many women he'd kissed in all these years, and if his reputation had women chasing him, or if he did all the chasing. In particular, she wondered about the woman to whom he'd given the red earrings.

"What did you do that for?" she shouted, treading water.

"What'd I do?" The surfboard rocked and bucked him off. Immediately he began trying to master it again, giving it all his attention.

"You kissed me, Gentry, and you know it!"

"You call that a kiss? Hell, that was barely a nibble. I've learned a little more than that since we were teenagers."

"I'll just bet you have. And with how many different women?"

"I lost count years ago."

"And you have no compunction about admitting it, do you?"

"None whatsoever, because you could become my last if you wanted to."

He had one knee on the board, his backside pointing her way as he struggled to make it to his feet. With several deft strokes she swam up behind him, hollered, "Not on your life, you no-account Lothario!" and gaily tipped him over.

Instead of bobbing up, he caught her ankles and hauled her under. She grabbed enough air to survive, but felt as if her lungs would explode as they struggled. His teeth nibbled the arch of one foot and his chin tickled it while she writhed and fought, needing to laugh. Their antics stirred up a froth of bubbles in the silent blue depths until at last she coiled around and pinched his nipple hard. He released her and they shot to the surface like geysers, both of them gasping and laughing, hair slicked down and gleaming.

"Ouch, damn you!" he scolded, rubbing the wounded spot.

"Good enough for you! You nearly drowned me, pulling me under like that."

"I just wanted to find out if you were still ticklish."

"Now you know, so leave me alone," she spouted in mock indignation, striking out for the ladder with him right behind her.

"In all the same old spots?" he teased as she lunged up onto the first rung, streaming water into his face. He caught her around the waist and hauled her back down with an enormous splash. Again they became a tangle of arms and legs and slithery skin as his hands snaked along her ribs and his arms circled her playfully. But in the midst of the skirmish they suddenly fell still, staring at each other with a gripping sense of rediscovery while the only sound was that of water lapping against the boat. One of Tommy Lee's hands held a ladder rung, the other arm circled her waist, and her hands quite naturally had fallen against his chest where the wet hair felt as elusive as mercury. Their eyes remained fixed upon each other, taking in gleaming skin, tangled hair, dripping faces, and rapt expressions. Their drifting thighs brushed. A drop of water slipped down Rachel's cheek and his eyes followed till it fell over her lip and the pink tip of her tongue curled up to sip it away. "Oh, Rachel," he breathed softly, spreading his palm wide and warm on her cool, sleek back, drawing her infinitesimally closer . . . closer . . .

But she pressed a palm to his chest and turned aside. "Please," she begged breathlessly, "don't kiss me again, Tommy Lee. Please."

Beneath the water their limbs brushed again, washed by the current they'd stirred up. His thighs were silicon-sleek and distractingly inviting. His gaze covered her face and she knew it beseeched her for more than she'd come here to give. At the small of her back his hand caressed the bare skin, then slid up between her shoulder blades.

"Are you sure you mean that?"

"Be sensible, Tommy Lee."

"I've never been sensible in forty-one years. Why should I start now?"

And though she, too, would have welcomed an excuse to toss sense aside for a brief time with him, she realized she had the power to wound him terribly. "Listen, I came out here today because I was very lonely and I . . . I needed someone. But I never meant for this to happen. Honestly I didn't, Tommy Lee."

His eyes traveled across her face, as if memorizing each feature. "If you needed me, only to make you laugh for one afternoon, that's a start."

A start of what? she wondered, but realized if she continued seeing him the answer would be understood. Yet he *had* made her laugh, for the first time in months. And in the end, he'd made her forget Owen and the cares that had besieged her for so long. And though his kiss had been startling, and not unwelcome, much of the excitement had been generated by nostalgia and by the fact that he was socially off limits to a woman like her.

"I'm starved," he said, with an abrupt swing of mood and a crooked smile. "What do you say to some catfish and hush puppies?"

"You still go wild for catfish and hush puppies?"

He grinned, squeezed her waist once, and answered in one of his favorite catch phrases from long ago, "You betchum, Red Ryder." And once again Rachel was laughing, charmed by the Tommy Lee she'd known so long ago. And, oh, he could be so charming. It was no wonder the ladies like him.

Chapter 6

THEY WENT TO Catfish Corner, a tin-roofed shanty out in the country at the intersection of two county roads off the Huntsville Highway. They took his car, and he drove it exactly the way they all said he did—too fast, too carelessly, and always with that everlasting cigarette crooked through one finger. Yet Rachel felt safe with him.

At Catfish Corner the crowd was mostly black, friendly, and vocal. "Hey, Tommy Lee!" someone shouted as soon as they entered the smoky, low-ceilinged room. "Been wonderin' when we'd see y'all around these parts again. C'mon over, boy, and bring yer lady with ya!"

Tommy Lee waved at the gregarious black man whose backside was twice as wide as the red plastic seat of the bar stool, but he took Rachel's elbow and guided her to a table instead. "If it's all the same to you, Eugene, I'm gonna keep my lady away from a sweet talker like you. No sense takin' chances."

A chorus of laughter went up from the group at the bar, while Tommy Lee directed Rachel to a vintage kitchen set with chrome legs and gray-marbled plastic seats amid a group of others much like it. He pulled out her chair, then seated himself across from her. Beside the table a crude window tilted outward, hinged at the top and propped open with a stick of wood. The trees pressed close to the building and insects worried themselves against the screen. A potted candle in a red glass snifter sent flickering light up to join that from the neon beer signs around the bar and the weak splashes of color from bare gold bulbs overhead.

When they were seated, Tommy Lee grinned teasingly. "Well, there's one thing you can't accuse me of, and that's trying to impress a lady with atmosphere. I brought you here because Big Sam fries the meanest catfish this side of the Mason-Dixon Line. And I don't know about you, but I worked up an appetite swimming."

Rachel studied the handwritten menu to cover her disappointment with his choice of restaurant. "Mmm . . . me, too." But she felt she needn't put catfish in her mouth to taste it—the smell was everywhere, mixed with a strong odor of onions and grease.

"Rachel?"

She met his eyes and found him still grinning, one shoulder pitched lower than the other as he leaned back against the chair. "Don't judge until you've eaten, okay?"

Before she could answer, a buxom woman appeared, her breasts the size of cantaloupes, earrings the size of handcuffs. She laid her hand familiarly on Tommy Lee's shoulder. "Well, I declare, if it isn't the most handsome honky to put foot in Catfish Corner since the last time he was here. What you mean by stayin' scarce all this time?" And she shamelessly leaned over and kissed Tommy Lee full on the lips.

Rachel watched, shocked, as his hand rested on her hip while her breasts brushed his chest. She checked to see if others were watching, but just then the man behind the rectangular window dividing the main room from the kitchen bellowed, "Hey, Daisy, you leave off kissin' the customers so's they can order catfish, you hear?"

Everyone at the bar laughed, and Daisy slowly raised her head, cocked a wrist on one hip, and toyed with the hair above Tommy Lee's ear. Her eyes appeared hooded and sultry as she looked down into his smiling face and drawled, "We want him to come back, now, don't we?"

Rachel was horrified. Never in her life had she seen a white man kiss a black woman, yet Tommy Lee did it with obvious relish. When Daisy finally disengaged herself, he belatedly reminded her, "I've got a lady with me tonight, Daisy. Meet Rachel."

Daisy turned laconically, still with one hand on her hip, the other cocked at the wrist. "Don't pay no never-mind to me, honey. I been kissin' your man since before there was catfish in that creek outside. He's like a son to me."

Tommy Lee gave her a nudge and ordered, "Get out of here, Daisy, and bring us two orders of the usual, and a glass of lime water for the lady."

"Lime water! What you think we runnin' here, a fruit stand?"

"Just ice water then. Now, scat."

She turned away with a chuckle and sauntered off while Rachel watched her bulging backside wriggle in tight cerise pants. When her eyes returned to Tommy Lee, she found him smirking at her.

"Just like a son, huh?" she repeated dryly, cocking an eyebrow.

"That's right."

Rachel pulled a hard paper napkin from a metal dispenser, held it between two fingers, and cocked her wrist while handing it to him. "I think you'd better wipe that shiny purple lipstick off . . . *son*. We wouldn't want it to get in your food and poison you."

Tommy Lee laughed while rubbing the garish lipstick off his mouth. "Don't think anything of Daisy. She's Big Sam's wife—that was him hollering through the porthole from the kitchen."

"His wife!" Rachel was shocked at the familiarity the woman had just displayed under her husband's nose.

"She kisses all the customers that way. And every time she does, Big Sam hollers through the kitchen window, and everybody at the bar laughs on cue. That's how it is out here. We're all friends."

But Rachel couldn't help harboring reservations about his choice of friends.

During their wait for the meal, Tommy Lee had two drinks, then another while they ate. The food was exceptional, and served in such sumptuous portions that Rachel barely put a dent in hers. Tommy Lee eyed her plate and asked, "You all done?" At her nod he inquired, "Mind if I clean up the rest?"

While he did, she thought about his eating habits, probably fasting all day, living on alcohol and ice, then feeding on fatty foods in periodic spurts of excess. It was no wonder his physique had suffered. After some consideration she asked, "When was the last time you ate a decent meal?"

He glanced from his plate to her and back again.

"Oh, I didn't mean including this one," she said. "It's delicious, really. I just have a feeling your diet is rather slapdash."

He only shrugged, wiped his mouth, and lifted his eyes to find her studying him contemplatively. "You don't like it here, do you?"

"Oh, the food was wonderful!" she replied brightly, but coloring.

"You don't have to say it. I know what you're thinking. But I wanted you to know where I've been, who my friends are . . . no secrets."

"Why?"

"Just so you'll know. I find people like these far more genuine than the bigots in town." He tossed his napkin onto his plate. "The country club set— you can have 'em."

Just then a small black boy bounded up to the table and flung himself across Tommy Lee's lap. He looked to be no more than seven years old, had a front tooth missing, and wore a stretched-out T-shirt with a picture of Darth Vader on the back.

"Hey, Tommy Lee, Tommy Lee, where you been, huh? Been savin' them rocks like you said to, so you'n me can show Darla she ain't so hot! Got *a-a-a-ll* these." He dumped a double fistful of rocks on the tabletop. "See? They just as flat as pee on a plate."

Tommy Lee's face lit up with laughter, ending with a grin as he gently scolded the youngster, "Hey, hey, mustn't talk like that around a lady." He roughed the child's hair and asked, "Where have you been hiding?"

"Mama, she wouldn't let me come out till you was done eatin'." The boy reached up to loop an elbow around Tommy Lee's neck. "You reckon we can make eleven?" He beamed into the man's face with excitement and obvious hero worship.

With one arm coiled around the little boy's waist, Tommy Lee looked across at Rachel and explained, "Darrel and I are trying to find the perfect stone that'll skip eleven times. So far the best we've done is nine. But his sister, Darla, claims she's done ten."

"She ain't done no ten—I know she ain't! She lyin!" spouted Darrel. "And besides, lookit these what I found."

Tommy Lee sifted through the collection of prize stones, nudging them around the table while his dark wavy head bent near the much smaller one of black close-cropped curls. "Whoa! This one looks like a prize!" Tommy Lee held it aloft.

"Can we go out and try it now?"

Tommy Lee smiled down at the boy. "Reckon it's too dark to see tonight."

"You come back on Sunday? Then we c'n show Darla? Please, Tommy Lee?"

"Today's Sunday," he reminded the child.

"But I mean *next* Sunday, like we used to. And you can stay for dinner after church and we can all play ball and—"

"Come to think of it, I do have next Sunday free. You tell Darla she'd better be ready to put her money where her mouth is." He affectionately swatted the boy's backside and watched him barrel off toward the kitchen. "He's Sam and Daisy's boy. A bundle of dynamite." At last he dragged his eyes back to Rachel, who wore a slightly amazed expression. "Something wrong, Rachel?"

"No . . ." Rachel sat up straighter. "No." But after adding it all up she queried, "You come out here and go to church with them on Sundays?"

He deliberated silently for some time and finally answered, "Sometimes. They've got a nice little white clapboard church out in the pines about a mile from here. Well, you know what those little Baptist country churches are like. Peaceful. I prefer it to the brick one downtown."

She studied him silently for a while. Then it all came clear.

"Your surrogate family, Tommy Lee?" she questioned softly.

He reached for a cigarette, took some time to light it and blow out a cloud of smoke, then studied her thoughtfully before answering, "I guess you might say that."

Rachel's heart wrenched with pity. He had children of his own; yet he came out here to play ball and skip pebbles. He had a church of his own; yet he came out here to attend theirs. He had parents of his own; yet he shunned them, though it obviously cost him much to do so. She pictured Gaines and Lily Gentry. Did they long for their son while he gave his affection to a black family who ran a catfish restaurant by Bear Creek? How terribly they all must be hurting. Suddenly she wanted that hurt mended, for everyone's sake.

"Tommy Lee, why don't you go see your mama and daddy?"

He carefully ironed all expression from his face and snorted through his nose.

"They're getting old," she reminded him. "If I can forgive, why can't you?"

But again they were interrupted. "Beg pardon, ma'am." It was Big Sam, standing beside their table with four green bills in his hand. "Tommy Lee, got the next installment for you on that loan." He proudly peeled off and laid down four five-dollar bills, counting carefully. "Five, ten, fifteen, twenty dollars." He beamed at Tommy Lee. "You write that in your book like always?"

"You bet, Sam. And how's the dishwasher running?"

"Runnin' slick as a skinned eel, Tommy Lee. And Daisy, she comes around snugglin' the end of a hot day like this, just thankin' me for not havin' to wash them dishes by hand like she used to."

Tommy Lee laughed, reached for a napkin, and wrote something on it, then handed it back to Big Sam. Sam glanced at it, then looked up. "It say the same like it always say?"

"Yessir. Received of Samuel Davis twenty dollars on dishwasher loan. And I put the date there."

"Good." Big Sam pocketed the napkin carefully in the breast patch of his sweat-soaked shirt, then patted it. "See you next Sunday. Darrel say you comin' to dinner. You bring the lady if you want to."

"Thank you, Sam. That's up to her. This is Rachel, a girl I used to go to high school with."

Sam bowed from the waist three times. "Miss Rachel, how was the catfish and pups?"

"The best I've ever eaten," she replied truthfully, warming to the big man who hovered self-consciously beside the table.

"Got to get back to the kitchen. Y'all come back. Tommy Lee, you bring Miss Rachel back, you hear?"

"I'll do that, Sam. And would you fix me one for the road?"

"I sure will. Comin' right up."

When they were alone again Tommy Lee reached for the check as if to leave, but she covered his hand on the tabletop. "You lent him money to buy a dishwasher for this place?"

His eyes remained carefully noncommittal as they met hers. "He tried to get it in town, but the bank took one look at this tin heap and decided he didn't have either enough collateral or enough education to merit approval of the loan."

Neither of them had to say that as president of the bank, her father was its chief loan officer. Their eyes held while the knowledge flashed between them.

"But how much money can a dishwasher cost?"

"Six hundred dollars," he answered, rising from his chair, dropping enough bills on the table that Rachel didn't have to count them to realize they included a more than generous tip.

"Six hundred dollars? And he pays you back twenty dollars at a time?"

"When he can. Sometimes it's five, sometimes ten. He must've had a good week. Should we go?"

She was still trying to digest what she had just learned about her father and about Tommy Lee, as the latter stepped politely behind her chair. On his way out, he picked up a drink from the bar. It had been mixed in a plastic tumbler, which he lifted in a good-bye salute as he opened the door for Rachel.

Outside it was black. The soles of their shoes crunched on the gravel as they made their way to the car, which was parked beneath the thick overhanging branches of a catalpa tree, nosing against the high bank of Bear Creek, which snuffled along through the darkness. The sound of hundreds of crickets undulated through the night while the scent of the damp creek bank rose up to meet the dust of the dry gravel lot.

After Tommy Lee had politely seen her to her side of the car she watched him in the glow of the overhead light as he slipped behind the wheel, his face introspective now and grim. She found herself evaluating this side of him, which nobody around Russellville saw. The interior of the car went black and she heard the key slip into the ignition. She reached out to touch his warm, bare arm—and immediately felt the muscles tense.

"I'm sorry, Tommy Lee," she said softly. "You were right. I was judging them. I had no right."

"I suppose it's inevitable that you and I do that occasionally —judge people. We are, after all, our parents' children. But I try my damnedest not to anymore."

"Meaning I'm like my father in a lot of ways. Is that what you're saying?"

"It's been so many years, Rachel, I really have no way of knowing that. But I hope not."

"He's not altogether bad, Tommy Lee, no matter what you think."

"Probably not. But he'd never take the time to make a run out here and order a platter of catfish to see what the place staked its future on, and to see how damn hard Sam and Daisy work, and that they're the most honest people on the face of the earth."

"Tell me something," she said, curious, but at the same time sure of what the answer would be even before she asked. "Do you charge them interest?"

But Tommy Lee mistook her reason for asking. She was every bit Everett Talmadge's daughter, he thought, and it rankled that he couldn't help loving her.

With a flick of his wrist he started the engine. "Rachel, do you have to be told what it does to me when you lay your hand on my arm that way?" She jerked her hand away and clasped it in her lap. He gave one humorless chuckle and said coldly, "That's what I thought," then threw the car into reverse and peeled out of the lot, spraying gravel twenty feet behind. When he straightened the wheel the car fishtailed, and Rachel released a quiet cry of fright. By the faint dash lights she saw him glance her way, then let up on the gas until they'd slowed to a nearly reasonable speed. But as he studied the path of the headlights, which cut a golden cone through the narrow opening between the close-pressing trees, he added offhandedly, "Don't worry. If there's anyone in this world I'd never want to hurt, it's you."

Her head snapped around and her heart lifted. All day long he'd been doing that to her, making her emotions vacillate until she was utterly confused about her feelings for him. He had two distinctly different sides, and she was attracted to the one and repelled by the other. Back at Catfish Corner she'd found herself drawn to a Tommy Lee who was both virtuous and vulnerable. But here she was, another in a long string of women, riding along with the Tommy Lee who'd had more than his share to drink, who was even now sipping something that smelled of pine needles while he wheeled nervelessly down a dark country road, brooding. A man who hadn't the emotional where-withal to bind the frayed edges of his life and make something more than a financial success of it. A man who was a three-time loser at marriage and had rightfully gained one of the most unsavory reputations in the county.

Rachel dropped her head back against the seat, letting her eyes sink shut, while wondering for the hundredth time that day what she was doing here. She heard him light a cigarette, and then they rode in silence, locked in their own thoughts.

Just before they reached the turnoff into his place, he lowered the window and slung his empty glass out into the weeds. Rachel sighed and straightened in her seat, looking away. His car negotiated the twists and turns of his driveway, and when he pulled up behind Rachel's car and killed the engine, all was silent.

He propped an elbow on the open windowsill, gripped the edge of the roof and stared straight ahead while Rachel sat hugging herself. Outside the night sounds buzzed and chucked and the smell of cedar was thick. Tommy Lee took a last drag from his cigarette, then set it spiraling in a red-tailed whorl before expelling a last breath of smoke that clearly told of emotional exhaustion. Almost angrily he reached for his door handle and lurched out. She followed suit, and they met near her car, both apprehensive and wary.

"Thank you for everything, Tommy Lee."

Though it was very dark she sensed how tense he was, standing with feet apart, hands buried in his back pockets, keeping a safe distance from her.

"Will you come again, Rachel?" he asked tightly.

"I . . . I don't know. It probably isn't such a good idea."

He released a rush of breath and ran an exasperated hand through his hair. "So you're going to put me through it all again. Is that what you're saying?"

"I never meant to *put you through* anything. You say it as if I'm guilty of some gross social misdemeanor, Tommy Lee!"

"I don't know about social misdemeanors, but I do know about feelings." Suddenly he captured her upper arms and brought her to her toes. "Goddammit, Rachel, I love you. I've never stopped loving you, don't you know that by now? Did you think you could sashay into my life for one afternoon, then sashay out again as if you'd done no damage?"

Her heart raced at his touch, but she was frightened by the mere fact that it did.

"I didn't know I was under any obligation when I came out here."

"Oh, didn't you?" he bit out, almost nose to nose with her. "So you thought you'd just toy around with good old Tommy Lee for a few hours, see how far you could push him. Do I count so little to you?"

"You're not being fair, Tommy Lee. That's not why I came out here and you know it."

"I don't know anything, least of all why I can't get you out from under my skin." His fingers tightened, and her heart clamored harder.

"Let me go. There's too much in our past to . . . to . . ." But she stammered to a halt and his voice turned a shade softer, silkier.

"To what, Rachel? To start it again? That thing that's been on both of our minds all day long?" Already he was drawing her close. "This . . ."

His open lips came down on hers with a soft, firm pressure, and immediately his tongue came seeking.

"Don't!" She twisted her head to one side and pushed on his chest.

"Why?"

"Because everything is different now. I'm different, you're different, our life-styles are totally incompatible."

His mouth followed her jaw as she arched fiercely away from him. "I can change. I will . . . for you, if—"

"I said, don't! It won't work and we'll end up hurting each other." She tried to twist free, but his hold was too sure and his fingers dug into her arms.

"I would be anything you wanted me to be, don't you know that, Rachel? If it meant having you back again . . . Rachel, please . . ." His hands cradled her head and drew her once again nearly onto tiptoe for a deep, thorough kiss. But as his questing tongue entered her mouth, it brought the aftertaste of gin. Angrily she pushed him away and stepped back.

"Don't you dare kiss me with your sixth drink of the night still foul on your lips!"

"Oh, so you've been counting?"

"Yes, I've been counting. All across the lake in the boat and tonight through supper *and* on the ride home!"

He loomed before her but made no further move to touch her while she stood with fists clenched, angry that he couldn't see what he was doing with his life.

"I can stop drinking any day I want," he stated belligerently. "Just give me a reason to!"

She ran a hand through her hair and twisted aside. "Oh, Tommy Lee, you fool. Don't you see, nobody can give you that reason but yourself? And it isn't just the drinking. It's the way you live. In that . . ." She flapped a palm toward the house. "That beautiful, sad, unkempt mansion where you sleep on your dirty laundry!"

His shoulders wilted slightly. "Rachel, I didn't know you were coming or—"

"It shouldn't have made a difference. For God's sake, Tommy Lee, you weren't raised in squalor. How can you live that way? And don't blame it on our parents! It's not our parents who ruined your life, it's you! You've become content to just . . . just drink yourself into oblivion and . . . and *atrophy!* But it's not too late to do something about it if you really want to. You could start by going in there and cleaning up that place, or if you don't want to clean it up yourself, at least hire some help to do it for you. And while you're at it, make it somebody who'll cook you something besides greasy fattening foods!"

He stiffened and pulled back while she felt heartless for striking at his most vulnerable spot. But if she didn't try to make him see the light, who would?

His voice was tight with suppressed anger as he invited caustically, "Well, don't quit now. You're on a roll."

At his words she felt a rich, roiling rage that he had so blithely profaned both the body and spirit of the Tommy Lee she had once loved and been so proud of.

"All right, you asked for it," she shouted, and pointed into the woods. "Go walk back a mile down that road and pick up the litter you threw out the car window, and stop throwing your trash in the lake." Her hand fell to her side and her fists bunched. "And stop driving by my dress shop fifteen times a day and coming in to buy red earrings for your women!" She was nearly in tears as she finished.

"Anything else?" he snapped.

Her lips were trembling and she knew in a moment she'd be crying. It was terrible, finding herself falling in love with him again while admitting a thousand reasons not to be.

"Yes! And water your plants!"

He did a silent double take. *"What?"* His head jutted forward and his face scrunched up.

She felt foolish for having brought up such a picayune grievance, which had nothing whatever to do with anything, and to make matters worse, the tears were beginning to flood her throat and eyes. She spun away from him and began to pace. "Oh, don't you see, Tommy Lee, we've grown so different than we used to be. All the time I'm with you I find myself wondering what people's reaction would be if they knew." She faced him and spread her palms helplessly. "All right, so I'm a snob, but I can't help it. I'm . . . you've changed so much. . . . You . . . you're—" She pressed her lips tightly against her teeth and turned away, not wanting to hurt him any further.

"I'm what?" He stalked her, his voice coming from just behind her shoulder. "That whoring, drinking, fast-driving no-good son of a bitch our parents made me into when they forced you and me apart and made us give up our baby? Do you think that's what I want to be, Rachel?" She was suddenly whirled around, and she found him bending above her, gripping her arms again. "Do you think I don't know what the whole town calls me? That *hellion,* Tommy Lee Gentry." She tried to escape his hands, but he jerked her erect before him. "But you know something, Rachel? I don't give a damn about what they think or say. All I care about is you. Why do you think I didn't take you to some classy restaurant in Florence tonight? Why do you think I asked you out on my boat instead of someplace in town where we could be seen? Do you think I don't know how shocked the residents of Russellville would be if they saw the prim and proper Widow Hollis in the company of that hell-raiser Tommy Lee Gentry? But I can change, Rachel. You just watch me. Because no matter how you try to hide it, there's still something between us. I could see it in your eyes today when you didn't think I was looking. I could see you wondering if it would be as good as it used to be, and if we could make it over the hundred and one hurdles we'd have to face if we decided to go public and announce to the world that we were going to pick up where we never should have left off twenty-four years—"

"You're wrong. You—"

"Shut up, Rachel, and get it into your head that you're not done with me yet. Not by a long shot. We *will* pick up again, only it won't be where we left off because we've both learned a lot since then—about life and about what to do in the back seat of a car."

"Let me go, Tommy Lee! I don't want—"

"I said shut up, Rachel, because you're going to be kissed whether you like it or not, and I'll be back to get the rest later—daddies or no daddies!"

He hauled her up against him, took a handful of her hair to tip her head back, and crushed his mouth to hers while his tongue writhed against her tightly sealed lips, trying to force them open. Her heart thrust mightily against his chest as she wedged an elbow between them, gripping his shirt while the heel of one hand bored into his chest. But he was powerful in his anger, and she was as defenseless as a doll in his arms. He felt her muscles strain and quiver while she fought him, but his arms and tongue were relentless until the ferocity of his kiss gradually mellowed. And only then did she slowly, cautiously begin to relax against him, allowing herself to feel what it might be possible for them to have again. The silken circles he drew over her lips at last unlocked them, and her body rose up slightly to accommodate his, while the hand clasping his shirt rested easy, just short of caressing. Somewhere in the depths of her mind it registered again that he'd grown taller, for her head tilted sharply back. His chest was fuller beneath her palm. And he'd learned a thorough and sensual technique of kissing that soon raised responses, as his tongue explored the interior of her mouth while one hand prowled beneath her elbow to boldly caress her breast.

But the contact had scarcely begun before Tommy Lee abruptly pushed Rachel away, spun around, and stalked to his car. He yanked the door open and threw himself into the driver's seat, then slammed the door with uncontrolled vehemence. The engine was already gunning before Tommy Lee realized he wasn't going anywhere.

Rachel stood where he'd left her—trembling, angry, aroused. Suddenly the engine died and the car door was flung open again. It slammed into the night stillness and he faced her with that same hulking stance he'd presented earlier.

"Well, what're you still doing here?" He took a single ominous step her way. "Git! If you know what's good for you, Rachel, you git!"

She turned and ran for her car, her heart raising a furor in her body. And this time it was Rachel who tore all the way back to town.

Chapter 7

THE REFORM OF Tommy Lee Gentry began in earnest the very next day. He arose earlier than usual, put on a pair of shorts that were too tight around the waist, and went for a jog down his curving driveway as the sun sent splinters of pure morning through the leaves. But he scarcely noticed. He was absolutely miserable—sweating, side-aching, leg-cramping miserable. He hadn't gone fifty yards before he had to stop, lean against a tree, and pant. *Fifty yards! Lord a'mighty, in high school the coach sent us ten times around the track!* He made it to the end of the driveway with six stops, then had to walk back to the house, clutching his left side. The waistband of the shorts was nearly slicing through his skin by now. He kicked them off with a foul curse and ran down to the lake buck naked, dived off the end of the dock, and found out why they call it a belly flop.

Cursing again, he determinedly plowed through the water in a formless crawl, the muscles of his arms and legs aching from yesterday's unaccustomed workout. *With the lake right here, you should swim every day, Tommy Lee.* Remembering Rachel's words he forced his arms through the water and thought, *I'll show you, Rachel!*

Dammit, he loved that woman, and he'd get into shape even if it took a full year of this misery to do it! But as he slogged from the water after a torturous four-minute swim, panting so hard his throat hurt, checking his bright red stinging belly, he wasn't too sure he didn't dislike her intensely.

Back in the house he dressed in faded blue jeans and called Liz Scroggins to say he wouldn't be in till later, then faced the horrendous job of housecleaning. Standing at the edge of the living room, he grimaced, cursed again, and attacked the job like a belligerent child whose allowance has been withheld pending an improvement in cooperation and attitude.

All through that wretched morning, while he forced his sore muscles to do tasks they abhorred, while he suffered a hunger such as he hadn't known in years, while he returned time and again to his empty refrigerator searching for nourishment that wasn't there, Gentry ranted. He worked for hours, then took a break to search again for something to give him sustenance, but all he could find was beer, hard liquor, and limes. He drank a glass of despicably bitter lime water, picturing Rachel's skinny little ribs, and puckered up his face, then cursed again while vowing, *Damn you, Rachel Hollis, you'll kiss me next time without a fight.*

But the housecleaning was scarcely half done. Thinking of all there was yet to do he slammed several cupboard doors hard enough to break the filaments in the light bulbs, then gave up, strode out to the car and drove to Catfish Corner.

"Daisy!" he bellowed, slamming through the deserted bar area toward the living quarters in the rear. "Where the hell are you?"

Daisy's smiling face appeared around the corner. "Uh-oh, what I done now?" she teased.

"Daisy, I need two things, and I need 'em fast. A maid who can cook and something to eat that hasn't got any calories in it!"

Daisy fed him some summer squash that nearly gagged him, then called her sister-in-law, who called her married daughter, who called her first cousin by marriage, who said, sure thing, she'd be happy to work for Mr. Gentry, but taking a job for a holy terror like him was kind of risky, so she wanted two hundred a week, the first week in advance, and a room of her own—after all she wasn't made of money and didn't have a car, so how was she supposed to get back and forth to that no-man's-land of his? She'd live *in* or she wouldn't do it at all. And she wanted Saturdays and Sundays off, and a ride back to town so she could spend them with her family and could attend her own Baptist church, then she'd need a ride back out to the country no earlier than 9:00 P.M. on Sunday night to give her plenty of visiting time.

Daisy stood with one hand on her hip, dangling the receiver over her shoulder, smirking across the kitchen at Tommy Lee while on the other side of the room Sam smiled behind his hand. "What should I tell her?"

"If she can cook better than you, tell her yes, I'll meet her outrageous demands, but if she ever puts summer squash in front of me she's fired on the spot!" He glared at Daisy and added for good measure, "And ask her what the hell ever happened to slavery!"

Daisy moved her shoulders saucily, but her face was all innocence while she spoke to Georgine in an exaggerated Uncle Remus accent. "Mr. Gentry, he say yes, two hunnerd a week is nuttin', and if he too busy entertainin' his ladies to carry you home, you jiss plan on fetchin' yoself in one o' his big fancy cars. He says he *know* how all us black folk like big fancy Cadillac cars."

Tommy Lee came half out of his chair. "Daisy!" he roared. "A simple yes will do!"

Before the day was out Georgine was installed in Tommy Lee's house. She was given a pretty little guest bedroom and the keys to the Blazer so she could drive into town and stock the cupboard shelves properly. That night when Tommy Lee sat down to supper he demanded to know what the hell she'd spent a hundred and twenty dollars on when all he found on his plate was turnip greens and a piece of broiled, butterless fish that'd leave a medium-size cat howling for seconds!

Georgine replied with a wordless pursing of her lips as she whipped her apron off and headed determinedly for the front door. Tommy Lee was forced to plead with her to stay, though when he bit into the tasteless fish he had no idea why he'd bothered.

Later that evening he wanted a martini so badly he went up to his bedroom, where Georgine couldn't see him, and tried to do push-ups to take his mind off the drink—only to find out he couldn't do push-ups anymore. When in the hell had *that* happened? He sat in a dejected heap on the floor, staring at his traitorous biceps and hating them. He'd been intending to call Rachel that night and apologize for treating her so roughly and for telling her to shut up, but after the failure of his body to perform, he was too angry with both himself and her to pick up the phone.

He ended the night starved, thirsty, and suffering through twelve of the most painful sit-ups he'd ever performed in his life.

On Tuesday he called Panache, but Verda claimed Rachel wasn't in. "Humph!" he snorted, and slammed down the receiver with typical dieter's temper.

On Wednesday he managed the downward stroke of a push-up, but after quivering in the suspended state for thirty seconds, still could not push himself back up. He called Panache again, and this time, when he was told she wasn't in, barked, "Well, how the hell can she run a business when she's never there!" Then he hung up again.

On Thursday he made it to the end of the driveway without stopping. But when he got there he threw up. None of his calls to Rachel's house turned up an answer and Tommy Lee raged inwardly. How dare she ignore him when he was suffering like a blue bitch—and all for her!

On Friday his arms ached from the pair of six-pound "executive dumbbells" he'd bought the day before and had overused in an effort to strengthen his traitorous biceps, which would only push him up once. His stomach growled constantly, and every time it did, he pictured a plate of Big Sam's catfish and hush puppies. And tried phoning Rachel again. And got angrier. And finally stalked into Panache to confront her personally only to find her out, and himself forced to buy another pair of earrings as an excuse for having come in.

Meanwhile, Rachel was spending a long tiring week in Dallas at the Trade Mart, meeting with the representatives of the various clothing manufacturers at appointed times, trying to determine what would sell and what wouldn't next fall. "Going to market" was always harrowing. A poor decision was costly, and since her merchandise turnover was limited, it was imperative her choices be prudent. Nor could she buy in quantity. In a small town no woman wanted to confront her newest designer dress walking toward her on another woman.

Discounts were discussed, haggling done, the autumn line of garments viewed.

Dallas was hot and dry and very lonely. At night she returned to her hotel room to think about Tommy Lee and try not to cry. She remembered the evidence of his abject loneliness and her heart broke for him. That house—oh, Lord, that house. It was a monument to what they'd once had, and thinking of it again stirred her in a heart-wrenching way. What kind of devotion drove a man to build a house for a woman who was married to someone else? And what woman could see it, recognize it, and not be moved by it?

She thought of him living in that beautiful place, dreaming his dreams while years rolled on and made him older, more lax about the direction his life was taking . . . and the tears gathered in her throat. Had he really been waiting for her to be free again? Unbelievably, it seemed to be true.

The house itself gave evidence to that fact.

She remembered them returning to it after their swim, and how he'd paused on the stairs above her on his way to his room to change. He'd looked back down and said, "You can't imagine how many times I've dreamed of you being here in my house, looking exactly the way you do right now." She had clasped the door frame and stood gazing up at him, feeling again the magnetic appeal he still had for her. It was one of the rare uncomplicated moments she'd experienced that day. She'd held all extraneous circumstances in abeyance and had allowed herself to admit that she still had—probably would always have—deep feelings for him.

It had been on the tip of her tongue to tell him she recognized "their house," but if she had, she wasn't sure she could have kept from asking to see the bedroom. And that would have been a mistake.

For the longer she was with him, the more her thoughts wandered in that direction. How odd that in spite of his flaws, in spite of all the other women he'd known, she still looked upon him as *her* Tommy Lee. And when she thought that way she felt prickly and decidedly female.

Lying sleepless, huddled in a lonely bed in a Texas hotel room, thinking of Tommy Lee, she again felt the sensations creep along her skin. It did little good to remind herself of his bad reputation, for it held an odd attraction all its own. He was forbidden, thus tempting. She supposed with all the practice he'd had, he was a superb lover by now.

Shouldn't that repel rather than entice her?

She tossed restlessly, trying to put him from her mind. But her body was exerting demands of its own that had gone unsatisfied for months and months. She thought of his kiss, of their bare limbs brushing silkily beneath the water, and knew again the sweet yearning of arousal.

But in the end she was forced to ask herself the question that was weighing more and more heavily on her mind as the days passed. Was she attracted to Tommy Lee as he was today or as he was remembered by a lonely, childless middle-aged woman who'd been spending altogether too much time lately dwelling on the past?

Rachel returned to Russellville on Saturday, exhausted and in a bad mood, only to learn that *he* had called more than once during the week, and that Tommy Lee Gentry had been in yesterday to buy another pair of earrings. Hot pink ones this time.

And once again her anger flared. How dare he tread a second time on the hallowed ground of her business world? And to buy hot-pink earrings yet! The look in Verda's eyes stated very clearly that she knew Tommy Lee and the caller were one and the same man. In an effort to escape those speculative looks and to cool her own anger, Rachel went for a shampoo and styling by her own Selma. It felt marvelous to have the Texas dust washed away by competent hands that knew her hair better than the strange beautician in the Dallas hotel.

In the late afternoon she carefully arranged herself on an inflated plastic raft, making certain her meticulous hairdo stayed dry, trailing only one foot in the water as she closed her eyes and drifted lazily, shutting out all thought.

She was dozing peacefully when an angry voice brought her head up sharply off the raft.

"You don't believe in answering bells, do you!"

The buyer of hot-pink earrings! She pushed her sunglasses down on her nose and scowled over the frames at the last person in the world she wanted to see. He stood with his hands on his hips, pushing back the jacket of a tailored suit, while above his white shirt and tie he wore a bulldoggish expression.

"How did you get in here?"

"I walked through the damn hedge, that's how. After standing at your front door ringing the bell for five minutes."

She lowered the glasses and lay back as if he wasn't there. "The air conditioning is on. I didn't hear the bell through the sliding glass doors."

"And what about the thirty-seven phone calls you didn't answer? Were you out here floating on your air mattress *all week?*"

Let him think what he would. She didn't reply.

"Rachel, dammit, how do you get off ignoring a person who's trying to get in touch with you?"

She dipped a hand into the water and spread it on her chest while he watched and felt his stomach begin to hurt more than any hunger pains had caused it to ache during the past week.

"Rachel, talk to me, dammit!"

"I didn't invite you here. Please leave."

"Go to hell, Rachel," he said with the coolest tone he'd displayed since arriving. "Are you going to Catfish Corner with me tomorrow?" But the invitation was issued with all the warmth of a general ordering his troops to open fire.

She peered at him over her glasses for a moment and found him standing as before, like an angry samurai. "Catfish Corner?"

"Sam invited you, too, you may recall." She fell back, eyes closed behind the sunglasses, not a hair out of place, and every rib showing while Tommy Lee glared at her and recalled the past week of aching muscles and abstinence, all for her. And now she refused to open her eyes and glance at the results. He'd lost five pounds, and was as proud as if it were fifty! He wanted her to notice, dammit!

When she calmly went on ignoring him, his anger freshened. "Rachel, I was trying to call you all week to tell you I was sorry for acting like a caveman last Sunday, and for all the things I said."

She didn't flinch.

"Dammit, Rachel, will you come out of that pool and talk to me?"

"I just got here."

"Rachel, you smug, supercilious . . . socialite! I'm trying to apologize to you, dammit!"

"Do you know how many times you've said dammit since you got here?" This time she scooped the water onto her midriff. The lazy movement was like a wave of a matador's cape before a bull. Tommy Lee glared at her for a long minute, then the expression on his face turned fox-like while he methodically slipped off one loafer, then the other, calmly removed his billfold from his pocket, and descended the steps into the pool. As he struck out in a crawl he noticed that it didn't even hurt him to swim anymore. He was already experiencing a jubilant feeling of accomplishment as he reached the raft and unceremoniously tipped it over.

Rachel went sprawling onto her belly while she let out a surprised squawk, accompanied by an ungainly thrashing of arms and legs. The shriek was severed as her head went under, sending up a series of bubbly glugs. She emerged coughing, hair straggling into her eyes, water streaming into her mouth, while she blindly reached for the raft and began swearing a blue streak.

Some of the more choice words that fell from her tongue made Tommy Lee's eyebrows shoot up in gleeful surprise as he struggled toward the shallow end followed by the doused Widow Hollis. Finally she pushed her hair back, snorted the water from her nose, and glared at him. "You . . . you damn crazy no-'count redneck jackass! I could kill you!" Tommy Lee reared back and laughed uproariously. She slammed her fists into the water and yelled, "Go on, laugh, you damn hyena!" Then she rolled her eyes upward and wailed, "Ohhhh, my hair!" and clasped her head in despair. "I just paid twenty-five dollars to have it done and look at it now!"

But he was still roaring with laughter, standing in water up to his armpits, his tie floating on the surface and a two-hundred-and-fifty-dollar suit puffing out around his body.

"Get out of here!" she screamed. "Get out of my swimming pool!"

When he could talk again he perused her with an insufferable grin on his face. "The last time I made you that mad was when we were about thirteen years old and I asked you if you'd started your period yet and you slapped my face and told me to grow up, then went off bawling and said you hated me and would hate me to my dying day. And it wasn't a year later I was kissing you crazy, and you loved every minute of it."

Rachel stood outraged, watching him turn and slog toward the steps, blissfully unconcerned about his expensive clothes.

"You're a despicable, crude . . . yokel!" she shouted at his back, ramming her hands onto her hips, shaking with anger.

He only tipped his head back and laughed again while mounting the steps, then turned and pointed at her cheeks. "Your mascara's running, Rachel."

Angrier than ever, she shouted, "You're exactly what they call you, you hellion! And I can't for the life of me see what all those stupid women find to chase after!"

He took one warning step back into the pool, grinning wickedly. "You want me to show you, Rachel?"

"You just stay away from me, you egomaniac!"

He gave her an assessing glance and shrugged uninterestedly. "No, I guess I won't. But maybe if you'd put a little meat on those bones I might give it some thought."

"And maybe if you took a little meat off yours, I'd let you!" she retaliated.

His expression soured. He crossed the patio, then leaned sideways from the waist with practiced nonchalance, plucked up his billfold, extracted some bills and dropped them on the patio table. "Twenty-five dollars, you say? Here, have your hair done again. It was worth every cent."

Then Tommy Lee calmly picked up his shoes and disappeared, leaving a sputtering Rachel behind to pound the surface of the water and promise herself she'd never speak to him again.

Rachel was so incensed that tears of frustration stung her eyes. She stormed into the house mopping her ruined hair and vehemently denying all the tender thoughts she'd had in Dallas.

Of all the nerve! Were there actually women who put up with treatment like that and came back for more? And he hadn't been content to tip her into the pool, he'd implied that she was skinny . . . *skinny!* She stepped before a mirror, scrutinized her reflection . . . and burst into tears. Lord, she was so mixed up about him. He *had* been trying to apologize, and the least she could have done was accept his apology gracefully. She thought about his anger, the names he had flung at her. All right, so she was a . . . a smug, supercilious socialite. But she couldn't help it. She'd been raised to believe that one's public image was important. Did he think she should blithely open her door to him one day, then ring up his hot-pink earrings the next?

On Monday a package arrived for her at Panache. She opened it to find an electric blow dryer and a note: "Learn to fix your hair yourself so you can be prepared for the unexpected."

She raged inwardly and swore she'd have him put under lock and key if he kept pestering her this way. Then she wrapped the hair dryer and mailed it back to him with a note saying, "You'll need this to dry your suits when you stumble into the next woman's pool."

The following week Rachel got home one day to find an enormous bouquet of white roses and leather-leaf fern on the dining room table. The card read, "I'm sorry, Rachel. I found out you were in Dallas. And you're not too skinny. Please have dinner with me Friday night at my house. We'll be well chaperoned this time."

So what was he doing now, going around town asking people questions about her comings and goings?

Callie Mae watched Rachel's face closely as she read the message. She noted the scowl, then the dismissing look Rachel gave the flowers before tossing the card down and never looking at it again.

"Mighty pretty flowers," Callie Mae remarked. "Expensive, too." But her curiosity was not to be satisfied. Neither Rachel nor the card gave any clue as to who they were from.

Tommy Lee waited several days for her to answer his invitation but soon realized she wasn't going to.

He tried to run the disappointment out of his system. By now he could jog to the end of the driveway and back with no trouble at all, and as the days passed he worked himself up to four miles a day. He ran to the beat of her name—Rachel, Rachel, Rachel. Every day he swam, too, and worked with the weights and did sit-ups. His muscles tautened, his stomach began to flatten, and even his chin grew firmer. The exercise, coupled with Georgine's parsimonious cooking, soon gave his skin a healthy elasticity that seemed to dissolve the webs from about his eyes.

But it mattered little, for Rachel had neither answered his invitation nor thanked him for the flowers. Weeks passed and he stopped driving past Panache, hoping it would help evict her from his thoughts. But nothing helped. Nothing.

There were times when he grew righteously angry, thinking, *The world is full of women, why do I waste my time mooning over one who keeps saying no? There are plenty of nice women in the world, and how do I know one of them wouldn't please me just as much as Rachel? Hell, I haven't been with a really decent woman in years!*

He was in precisely such a mood one day as he stepped to the doorway between his office and Liz's, glancing up to ask her about an invoice he was holding. But she was on the phone so he stood for a moment, waiting for her to finish the conversation.

She had a pleasant way about her when doing business on the phone. She never got upset or impatient, and she laughed readily, as she did now, at something being said on the other end of the line. She lifted her eyes to Tommy Lee and gave him an I'll-be-done-in-a-minute signal.

He stood listening and watching while she concluded the conversation, realizing once again how attractive she was. Her blond hair was shorter now for the summer and she wore a fresh butter-yellow suit as tasteful and attractive as anything Rachel might wear. Come to think of it, she was a lot like Rachel. She was nice, decent, and infinitely respectable. She dressed and acted like a lady at all times, was poised, efficient, and friendly. No matter what his own mood, hers remained cheerful—and he realized he'd been grouchy more often than not lately.

Liz hung up the phone and said, "Sorry. What can I do for you?"

And out of the clear blue sky, Tommy Lee answered, "You can go out to dinner with me tonight."

Liz's eyebrows rose in surprise. "To dinner!"

"Well, it's about time, isn't it? You've worked for me six years and I've never even treated you to a night out. And you deserve it. I've been a regular bear lately. I don't know how you put up with me."

She laughed and replied, "Come to think of it, you have."

"Does that mean yes?"

"I'm sorry. The boys will be home and I probably can't find a baby-sitter on such short notice."

"How about your parents?" He saw her waver momentarily and pushed his advantage. "Come on. Help me celebrate—I've lost over half the weight I've set out to lose."

"And you want to celebrate by putting some of it back on? A real friend would say absolutely not."

"I'll pick you up at seven—what do you say?" She chuckled and was already turning toward her typewriter as she gave in. "Oh, all right, but if you don't let me get back to work I'll still be here at seven."

They had a delightful meal at a Mexican restaurant in Florence, and afterward talked all the way back to Russellville. Their years of working closely with each other put them very much at ease, and they found themselves readily able to converse on a variety of subjects, laughing at Liz's amusing anecdotes about her boys, discussing the personalities of various people Tommy Lee did business with, and reaching back into their ample store of high school and college stories to come up with the most outrageous pranks they had pulled in their youth.

When they reached Liz's house he walked her to the door, their spirit still bright, feeling relaxed and easy with each other.

"Thank you so much, Mr. Gentry. The dinner was delicious and I had a wonderful time."

"That goes double for me, but you could drop the formalities and call me Tommy Lee."

"It wouldn't seem right to call my boss Tommy Lee."

"But tonight I'm not your boss . . . just a friend, okay?"

"Well, in any case, good night, and thank you again." She was already turning away toward the door when he captured her arm and swung her back to face him.

"Hey, not so fast there."

"Tomorrow's a workday and I wouldn't want to be late," she replied perkily. "The boss might get upset."

"I guarantee he won't."

Though she gave the expected chuckle, he sensed a change in her the moment he touched her. The smile fell away and she dropped her eyes. Her arm was soft and bare, and she wore a familiar cologne whose scent he readily associated with her after having smelled it all these years around the office. He realized again that much of his attraction for her stemmed from the fact that she was every inch a lady, the kind who very naturally commanded a man's respect, the kind who probably didn't do this kind of thing often or lightly.

We've both wondered for a long time, he thought. *So let's find out.*

Her blue eyes closed and her pink lips opened as he dropped his mouth over hers in a soft, undemanding kiss. She was honest enough to allow herself to sample him—just as he sampled her—before pressing a hand to his chest and backing away.

"No, I don't think so," she answered quietly, as if he'd asked her a question.

He raised his head in surprise. "You don't think what?"

"This isn't really what you want."

"It isn't?" He was baffled by her unusual response to the kiss—very different from what he'd expected.

She shook her head. "Uh-uh. I know you've wondered, and I'll admit I have, too. But what you really want is someone else, I think."

He was still smitten by surprise as he asked, out of curiosity, "Who?"

"Rachel Hollis."

Oddly enough, he didn't even think of denying it. "How did you know?"

"How did I know? I've worked for you for six years. On more than one occasion, I've watched your eyes follow her when she walked along the street to the bank. There's a certain way a man looks at a woman that tells it all, and you can't even watch her pass by without giving yourself away."

He'd never realized it showed. He felt rather like a schoolboy caught cheating on a test.

"I've also seen you talking to her on the street lately. When you come back into the office afterward, you're a bundle of frustration."

Tommy Lee hung his head and tried to think of something to reply.

"Oh, don't look so guilty, all right? It was high time you and I did what we just did, just to get it out of our systems and clear the air. But I'm only a substitute, and I'd rather be a good secretary than a poor substitute."

"I never realized before how perceptive you are, Liz."

She crossed her arms and leaned back against the wall. "Do you want to talk about it? I've got a willing ear."

So, to his surprise, he ended up telling her nearly the whole saga of Tommy Lee Gentry and Rachel Talmadge Hollis. It felt wonderful to discuss it with someone who was impartial, who neither made demands of him nor judged him.

When the story ended, she asked him matter-of-factly, "Well, you aren't going to give up now, are you?"

He was slightly taken aback by the question. "I don't want to, but she seems dead set against seeing me."

"Do you think she loves you?"

Why should it be so difficult to answer that simple question? He'd asked it of himself countless times and had always come up with the same answer, the one that made him wonder at Rachel's stubbornness. Answering Liz now, he felt rather timid.

"Yes. Sometimes . . . yes."

"Well, then . . . she's scared, don't you see? And she's got a perfect right to be. Why, look at your record! What woman would willingly take on a man with a record like that? You've got to assure her you mean it when you say you've changed. But whatever you do, don't give up on her. If she loves you, believe me, it's the last thing she wants."

"It is?" The idea was stunning. Women were strange birds. Why did they do one thing when they wanted to do another?

"Take my word for it."

He carried the idea away with him, and it stayed on his mind throughout that sleepless night. The following day he thought about it again, and wondered how he could show her he had changed and was so much happier with the new Tommy Lee that he wouldn't dream of backsliding. That afternoon he was jogging past the end of his driveway when he stopped and eyed the kudzu vine tangled across the ditch. He pondered for some time before finally picking up three rocks and flinging them in, to clear the area of snakes. Then he forced his way through the thick vines to the place where he always used to toss his empties.

As he moved through the ditch, he grew amazed. *Lord o'mercy, did I drink all this?*

He picked up a can, tossed it up absently, and caught it. Then his eyes narrowed and he stared off into the distance. *All right, Rachel, I'll try one more time.*

The following day Rachel came home from work to find a huge black plastic trash bag on her front step, bound at the top by an outsized red satin bow. She approached it cautiously, surveyed its lumpy exterior, touched it with a toe, and heard a metallic clink. Gingerly she untied the bow, peered inside, and found it filled with aluminum beer cans. She also found a note: "All right, Rachel, you win. I'm cleaning up my act. What else do I have to do to get you to say yes?"

What the hair dryer and flowers had failed to do, the sack of beer cans accomplished. Rachel pressed four fingertips to her lips and burst into tears. *Oh, Tommy Lee, you crazy, off-beat, irresistible hellion, can't you see it would never work?*

Callie Mae was immediately concerned to find a tearful Rachel dragging a huge black bag into the house.

"Why, Miss Rachel, what's wrong?"

"Everything!" The bag sent out a mysterious sound as Rachel dropped it and dissolved into tears on Callie Mae's shoulder.

A sympathetic hand patted the back of Rachel's head. "Now, you just tell Callie Mae everything."

"I c-can't."

" 'Course you can. You want to start with what's in that bag that set you off?"

"Oh, C-Callie Mae," she wailed, "it's a g-gift from Tommy Lee."

Over Rachel's shoulder Callie Mae gave the bag a second look. "So that's it."

Rachel drew back and mopped her eyes, still sniffling. "He won't stop p-pestering me, and I . . . we . . ." Her words trailed off and ended with a woeful look of misery and renewed weeping.

"You don't have to explain nothin' to Callie Mae. I see how it is with you two. I always seen."

"How it is between us two is impossible." Rachel threw her hands out and began pacing agitatedly.

Callie Mae pursed her mouth and grunted, "Hmph." Then she asked, "You mind if I take a look at what he brung you?" Rachel shook her head and Callie Mae opened the sack and peered inside. "Well, now, what do you know about that!" she exclaimed softly, then asked, "He the one sent you them flowers, too?" Rachel nodded while Callie Mae noted her crestfallen expression. "Jus' *when* he call you skinny?"

"Don't you go getting that . . . that *look* in your eye, because it isn't going to work. He isn't going to sweet-talk me into making a fool of myself. Not with a philanderer like him."

Callie Mae crossed her hands against her stomach and affected a sober, judgmental expression. "Yup, he's a wild one, that Tommy Lee."

Rachel paced. "And he couldn't make a single one of his marriages work."

"Nope. He sure couldn't."

"And he hasn't gone to church in years." It wasn't exactly true, but it felt reassuring to heap blame on him.

"At least ten, fifteen."

"And he still drives like a maniac."

"He's one crazy white boy, for sure."

"And you should see the way he lives." Rachel threw up her hands. "Why, his house looks like a pigpen!" Suddenly she came to a halt, looked up, and felt herself color.

Callie Mae cocked an eyebrow and said, "Oh?" But she wiped all expression off her face and busied herself unnecessarily dusting a table with her apron while advising softly, "And you mustn't forget, there's the fact that Mr. Owen, he's only been gone a few months. And your daddy would have a conniption fit if he was to find out Tommy Lee been nosin' around his daughter again. And o' course we all know what the Good Book says about honorin' fathers, no matter if they're right or wrong. But there couldn't be no question about your daddy bein' right. After all, he's got one o' the best heads in this county. Why, he runs that bank over there like them Yankees run the war— merciless. You know he always gonna end up winnin', and though he don't always smile a lot, people got respect for him, and there's them that say he's a mite cold and calculatin' at times, but he seems to get along just fine without a lot o' friends since your mama died. Yes, ma'am, your daddy, he's one smart man, got the respect of everybody in this county. And folks say you're turnin' out just like him. You want I should put this sack of junk out for the garbage man to pick up tomorrow?" Callie Mae looked up innocently, holding the sack of beer cans now.

Rachel glanced from the sack to Callie Mae's face, then back again, trying to think of a reply. But she was too shaken to know what to say, and finally Callie Mae trudged off through the house, dragging Tommy Lee's offering with her while mumbling something about it being worthless and wondering what that crazy white boy was thinking to drop such trash on people's front steps!

Rachel remained where Callie Mae had left her, round-eyed and stunned, digesting what the woman had just said, quite horrified at the thought that she might be turning out just like her father. Was she really all those things? Merciless? Cold? A person who'd rather have the town's respect than smile a lot? She swallowed convulsively, closed her eyes, and bit her trembling lip, wanting to deny it.

But that made two people now who'd told her the same thing, for hadn't Tommy Lee called her a smug, supercilious socialite?

And if it wasn't true, why was she crying?

⟶ Chapter 8

TO RACHEL'S UTTER surprise, Tommy Lee showed up at church the following Sunday morning. He was standing on the steps when she arrived, and she realized her mistake the moment her feet stopped moving. Their eyes met, and her first thought was that he had new glasses, styled like the old ones, except that these had clear lenses through which she could clearly see him taking in her white and brown linen dress and matching spectator pumps.

She felt herself blush but could not tear her eyes away from him. He looked magnificent! His skin was brown and healthy looking, and he appeared thinner, dressed in a pale blue suit with a rich navy shirt. The midmorning sun caught the black and silver strands of his hair and threw chips of gold off his tie clasp and the rims of his glasses while a light breeze lifted the end of his tie and gently turned it back, then settled it into place again.

She wasn't certain how long she stood staring before becoming aware of the girl at his side. She was tall and lanky with dark shoulder-length hair, and from the way she took his arm and gazed up at him, there was no question she adored him. Just then the breeze furled the girl's hair and blew it back from her temple, and as Rachel caught sight of the red button earrings, her heart sank.

Oh, no, she thought, *not again. This one's young enough to be his daughter.*

Just then the girl turned, revealing Lily's cupid's-bow mouth and brown eyes that might easily have belonged to Tommy Lee himself at age fourteen. Rachel stared, transfixed, feeling her composure slip as she confronted the girl who, had circumstances been different, might have been her own daughter. Her eyes were helplessly drawn to Tommy Lee again, and they stood like a pair of marble statues. *Move!* she told her feet. *Half the town is watching you gape at him, including his daughter and your own father!* For in that horrifying moment Rachel realized Everett had joined her, after parking the car, and stood watching the silent tableau with growing disapproval.

Beth's eyes flashed from her father to the pretty dark-haired woman and back again. Then, to Rachel's relief, Tommy Lee gave a silent nod and moved away with her.

Beside her Everett said stiffly, "Rachel, for God's sake, people are staring."

To her horror, she glanced around to find it was true. Several pairs of curious eyes had taken in the scene, but as Rachel looked up, they all quickly glanced away.

The church service seemed interminable. It took a great deal of self-restraint for Rachel to face front for a full ten minutes before checking behind her under the guise of picking up a hymnal from the seat. Just as she'd suspected, Tommy Lee and Beth were only a few pews back. Surreptitiously she glanced at her father, but he was facing front with a stern, forbidding expression on his face. When she opened the hymnal, the print seemed to blur, and she was terribly conscious of Tommy Lee's eyes boring into her back. In a panic, she wondered where Gaines and Lily Gentry were sitting. Were they watching him watch her? Undoubtedly they were as shocked as she was to see him here this morning. After countless years of absence, he couldn't possibly attend without being conspicuous.

When the service ended and everyone flooded the center aisle, she picked him out from behind by the thinning hair at the crown of his head. Odd how the sight of it lent him a certain vulnerability; she felt guilty to be studying it. And a little sad.

Outside, she witnessed the stunned reactions parade across the faces of Tommy Lee's parents as they paused to watch their son and granddaughter leaving the church behind them. Gaines Gentry's hand went to Lily's elbow, and her free hand covered her lips while their eyes followed Tommy Lee's progress until he became aware of them and halted in mid-stride, pulling Beth up short, too. Rachel sensed the girl's momentary confusion, and the yearning among the other three. But then Tommy Lee nodded brusquely and headed toward his car with long-legged steps, already lighting a cigarette as Beth trailed along beside him.

Everett drove Rachel home in stony silence, but the moment they were inside he confronted her directly, his face rigid and darkened by a scowl. "What's going on between you and Gentry?"

She spun to face him angrily. "Nothing!"

"Nothing?" He snorted. "I wasn't born yesterday, Rachel. If nothing's going on, then tell me what was all that about on the church steps?"

"All what? I didn't even speak to the man!"

"You didn't have to, to set the whole town talking."

Suddenly Callie Mae's words came back, and Rachel stiffened her spine. "The town, the town! That's always your first concern, isn't it, Daddy? What the town might be saying! What business is it of theirs anyway?"

"Rachel, are you forgetting what you have made of yourself? You're one of Russellville's leading citizens. You're a businesswoman whose reputation must—"

"Oh, for heaven's sake, Daddy, stop." She pressed one hand to her forehead and turned away. "I don't want to hear it."

He whirled her around by an arm. "Well, you're going to! I will *not* have you seeing Tommy Lee Gentry. Is that understood?"

For a moment she was a girl again, hearing those same words, experiencing the same eruption of anger she'd felt then. It swirled up in a red haze, bringing with it the rage and rebellion she'd been unable to display then, when she could do nothing but bend to his will. But she no longer had to buckle under to her father's demands. She clamped her jaw in defiance, her face took on a belligerent expression, and there came a sweeping sense of a release in rebelling against him at last.

"I'm not seventeen anymore. By what right do you tell me whom I can and cannot see?"

"You're still my daughter. When a daughter behaves irresponsibly, what else is a father supposed to do?"

"You could try letting me make my own choices," she returned brittlely. "I'm forty-one. Wouldn't you say it's time?"

His face took on an apoplectic hue as he shouted, pointing toward the church, "And *that's* the choice you propose to make?"

"Suppose I did, would that be so terrible?"

"For God's sake, Rachel, Owen is scarcely dead in his grave and you're taking up with a . . . a hellion like Gentry?"

"Tell me," she said, narrowing her eyes. "Exactly what do you think made him that way?"

"That's not the point!"

"Oh, and what is?"

"The point is, I will not have you spoiling your reputation by being seen with the most notorious skirt chaser this county's ever seen!"

She was every inch her father's daughter as she returned coolly, "And if I choose to see him?"

"So you *are* seeing him!"

She studied him levelly for some time before asking quietly, "What are you so scared of, Daddy?"

He let his shoulders wilt, blew out an exasperated breath, and gestured appealingly. "Rachel, for heaven's sake, he's been married three times, he drinks like a fish, and he—"

"No, Daddy," she interrupted, shaking her head slowly. "That's not it at all and we both know it. You're afraid that if I start seeing Tommy Lee again you may be forced to come face to face with your own guilt."

"*My* guilt!" He was enraged now, gesturing angrily. "You disgraced us with him once. Wasn't that enough?"

Again she shook her head, saddened by his inability to bend, to recognize his own fault in creating some of the wounds that had gone unhealed all these years.

"No, Daddy, we didn't disgrace you. You disgraced us. By sending me away and treating me as if what we'd done was unforgivable. To us it wasn't. To us it wasn't sordid or . . . or immoral. We loved each other!"

Again he gestured with an upturned palm. "Rachel, we did what we thought was best for all."

"Did you?" she asked softly, sadly. "Then tell me why you and the Gentrys never talked to each other again."

The room grew hushed and neither of them moved a muscle. Everett's face slowly grayed while Rachel stood firm, facing him squarely. Then suddenly he lurched around her, heading for the door. She grabbed his arm, begging, "Daddy, could we talk about it? Please?"

But Everett jerked free and proclaimed angrily, "There is nothing to talk about!" then slammed out the door leaving her feeling hopeless and sad and wondering if it would ever be possible to untangle the webs of the past.

Why did I goad him? Why didn't I just come right out and say that there really is nothing between Tommy Lee and me?

The answer was simple. There would always be something between them, no matter how hard she fought it. And it seemed only a matter of time before it would all come to a head.

Rachel was still blue later that day when Marshall stopped by after his usual Sunday afternoon visit to his daughter's. She answered the bell to find him standing on her step with slumped shoulders and a dejected face.

"Why, Marshall, what's wrong?"

"Carolyn and I had a fight."

"A fight!"

Rachel might have chuckled; in a way it was amusing to think of the mild-mannered Marshall fighting with anybody. But she could see he was truly down in the dumps even before he added, "And furthermore, I hate the idea of facing the empty house. Want to take a ride?"

It was so rare to find Marshall in low spirits that Rachel wouldn't have dreamed of refusing. Especially not after all the times *he'd* cheered *her* up.

"Why not? I haven't been exactly on top of the world myself today."

He drove as if he didn't care where he was going, and they ended up near the small town of Phil Campbell about ten miles south of Russellville. When he turned in at the entrance of the Dismal Gardens, Rachel teased, "The Dismals? On an evening when I'm supposed to be cheering you up?"

Marshall smiled distractedly. "Apropos, isn't it?" Then he glanced out the window. "I haven't been out here in years. Have you?"

"No, not since I was a child."

"Care to take a walk through?"

"Why not?"

They parked, and Marshall paid their admission as they entered the gardens through a little country museum house, then stepped down into a rocky depression surrounded by house-size boulders that created the gateway to the park. They wandered through the waning afternoon, companionably silent, letting the surroundings ease their troubles.

Unlike their name, the Dismal Gardens were stunningly beautiful, a refreshing breath of untainted nature in a setting left untouched by man since the canyon and its surrounding woods and caves had been inhabited by the Paleo Indians 10,000 years before. The gardens took their name from the dismalites, tiny incandescent worms that lived in the moss on the rock cliffs and shone like stars at night.

As Rachel and Marshall entered the park, the sun was still above the cliffs, and they followed a clear tumbling river into shaded coolness where the air was thick with the fecund smell of moss and leaf mold. They explored stunning rock formations with such names as Pulpit Rock, the Grotto, and Fat Man's Misery.

It was peaceful here, restorative. A pileated woodpecker flashed through the forest in a wink of red. Wild hydrangea vines clung to the high walls where trailing arbutus sprouted magically from the face of sheer rock. Farther along they came to Phantom Falls, a tiny opening no more than ten feet in diameter. Inside, they stopped and lifted their faces toward the small circle of sky overhead, listening to the roar of water echoing mysteriously through the depression, though the falls themselves were some 250 feet downstream.

When Rachel dropped her eyes, she found Marshall studying her with an odd look on his face. She laughed nervously and moved along the trail, calling back, "Well, come on, slowpoke, get a move on!"

The expression changed to a sheepish grin as he followed at her heels. But when they reached Rainbow Falls, she again sensed his gaze on her as if he was puzzling something out. She lifted her eyes to the twin rainbows high overhead, which were caught by the sunlight that couldn't reach into the shady depths where they stood. She feared he hadn't invited her here for anything as simple as a breath of fresh air. In a moment her suspicions were verified as he spoke in a serious tone.

"Rachel, I heard something today that's rather disturbing."

"Oh?" She dropped her eyes to find he'd been studying her intently, but immediately he glanced at his feet.

"It . . . well, it could be a rumor. You know how small towns are."

"Gossip, you mean?"

His eyes met hers again. "I hope so." He suddenly captured her hand and tugged her toward a large boulder. "Let's sit down." When they were seated side by side he dropped her hand, seemed to struggle for the right words, and finally lifted his gaze to hers, asking, "Rachel, have you been seeing Tommy Lee Gentry?"

With unexpected swiftness her blood came to life and her heart started banging. "What do you mean, have I been *seeing* him?"

"His car has been seen at your house."

Frantically she searched for an answer. "Tommy Lee and I are old friends," she answered vaguely.

"That doesn't answer my question." He swallowed and continued. "Friends or no friends, you know what kind of man he is."

She suddenly grew incensed with people pointing their fingers at Tommy Lee when they knew so little about what drove him. "Oh? And what kind of man is he, Marshall?" Rachel surprised even herself with her brusque tone.

He jumped off the rock, presenting his back to her while jamming his hands into his pockets. "Oh, come on, Rachel. He's got women from one end of this county to the other, and nobody would put it past him to try to move in fast on a new widow."

Growing angrier by the moment, Rachel questioned, "Did my father put you up to this?"

Marshall swung around to face her again. "Your father? Why, no! I heard the rumor, that's all, and I wanted an answer straight from you."

It suddenly dawned on Rachel that this was what Marshall and his daughter had argued about, and for the first time ever she grew more angry with them for gossiping than with Tommy Lee for making himself vulnerable to their gossip. But just then Marshall came close and reached for her hand again. "Rachel, don't get angry with me. Please. That's the last thing I wanted."

At his apologetic look she softened. "You don't have to worry about me, Marshall. I have a very level head on my shoulders."

"Yes, I know you do. But even so . . ." His words trailed off and she saw how upset he was, which was terribly unlike Marshall, who was always very low key and unruffled. "Rachel, may I speak frankly with you?"

Though something warned her she might not like what he had to say, she could only respond, "Why, of course, Marshall. What else are friends for?"

He solemnly studied their joined hands. "I wasn't going to say anything for some months yet, but after what I heard today, I realize I can't put this off." He swallowed nervously and his eyes flicked briefly to hers, then away again. "Rachel, I know that for the last half-year or more you and Owen had no ah . . ." Marshall nervously cleared his throat. "No . . . sexual relationship. He talked to me about it because he was very depressed over it. He was . . . well, worried about you." She felt her face grow hot and resisted the urge to yank her hand from his. "You're normal and healthy . . . and at this point in your life, extremely vulnerable."

Though her face was now fully flooded with crimson, she said pointedly, "To a man like Tommy Lee, you mean?"

Now it was Marshall's turn to color. "Yes." He cleared his throat and swallowed again. "Rachel, at the risk of sounding calculating, I'll admit to you that I've been thinking for weeks about taking care of you since Owen died, of marrying you as soon as a decent length of time had passed."

"Marrying me!" Rachel tried to retract her hands, but he held them firmly, meeting her brown eyes squarely at last.

"Does it come as such a surprise, Rachel? Surely you've guessed that I began loving you long before I had the right to say so."

"But, Marshall, I—"

"I know. I know. I'm not the debonair type, not the kind with flash and style like Gentry. But I love you, Rachel, and I'd be good to you."

Oh, there was no doubt in her mind about that. But . . . Marshall? Marshall with his sober sensibilities, his nondescript brown hair, and wing-tip shoes? She looked at him and tried to imagine spending the rest of her life watching him putter and prune his yard on Saturdays, then on Sundays going off to visit his married children. And in between, she could listen to him and her father discuss interest rates and twenty-pay-life plans. He was gazing at her pleadingly now, and she had to think of something fast.

"But, Marshall, Owen's been gone such a short time, and I . . . I . . ." It had always been embarrassing for Rachel to turn down even so much as a kiss. This was devastating. Marshall was gazing at her as if he wanted to gift-wrap those two rainbows and lay them at her feet!

"I had no intention of asking you so soon," he went on nervously. "I told you that. But when I heard the rumors, I got scared."

"Oh, Marshall . . ." she said softly, moved in spite of herself because he was so sincere and flustered.

"I guess I took you by surprise, didn't I?" He hung his head quite boyishly while fidgeting idly with her hands. "I thought you knew all along how I felt about you. There have been times when I've felt rather disloyal to Owen because of my premature feelings for you. Times when I'd leave your house and go home alone and think about . . ." He lifted his eyes to hers and drew her gently to her feet. His Adam's apple lurched and his face looked pained as he took her into his arms, gazing adoringly into her face. "Oh, Rachel, I've never even kissed you."

His warm, open lips were something of a shock, simply because they belonged to Marshall—old, reliable Marshall. His tongue parted her lips, and when it touched hers she struggled not to recoil. But kissing Marshall seemed unholy and about as exciting as kissing a brother.

To Rachel's dismay, his hands dropped lower on her back and he pulled her flush against him, revealing the fact that he was fully aroused. Rachel's heart hammered in shock while the kiss grew more ardent and she wondered how to get out of this without hurting him more than he deserved. She wedged her hands between them and turned her face aside. "No . . . please."

He was breathing laboriously when the kiss ended. Then he transferred his lips to her jaw and ran his hands more demandingly along her hips and spine. "Rachel, darling, I love you. I have for so long."

"But I—" Why should it be so impossibly hard to come right out and say she didn't love him? Instead she softened it by saying, "No, Marshall, it's too soon."

He was surprisingly strong as he forced her head around and held it immobile while covering her mouth with his once again. Rachel began to stiffen and was about to rear back and stop him before he went any further. But she found his protestations of love flattering. Some devilish gremlin tempted her to find out just how far he'd go, and whether her reactions would be as quick and fiery as they'd been to Tommy Lee, so she relaxed in his arms and let his tongue stroke the inside of her mouth.

When he felt her acquiesce, his hand swept up her ribs and captured a breast, caressing it while his tongue delved between her lips with growing fervor. She waited for that magical surge of sexual reaction, but when her nipple puckered and hardened she felt mildly repulsed. Marshall's tongue felt alien within her mouth. His body seemed too long and bony. His hands only made her wish they belonged to another man. All that came were thoughts of Tommy Lee, and how his kisses and touches had set off a series of involuntary responses that had left her shaken and wanting more when he'd turned her loose. Marshall made a soft throaty sound, feeling the distended nipple through her thin summer dress. But when his hips began thrusting against her she realized she was only leading him on fruitlessly, and gently pushed him away.

"Stop, Marshall!" His breathing was agitated and his eyes bright with desire while hers remained as calm as if she'd just awakened from a nap. He cupped her jaws and she had to force herself not to recoil.

"Please, Rachel, I realize you're alone as much as I am, that you have needs, just as I do. If you aren't ready for marriage yet but you need a man in your life, for God's sake, don't turn to one like Gentry."

Good heavens, he was suggesting an affair! Horrified, she stepped back and gaped at him. "I . . . I'm sorry, Marshall, but I . . . I just don't feel that way about you. We've been friends too long to become lovers."

"I thought you needed—"

"Well, you thought wrong." She turned away, growing angrier by the minute that he should point his finger at Tommy Lee, then propose a liaison to serve his own purposes. At least Tommy Lee was no hypocrite.

"Rachel, I'm sorry. I didn't mean to insult you."

She turned to confront a very pink-cheeked Marshall. "Should I be honored, Marshall, that you've suggested having an affair with me right after lecturing me on the inadvisability of having one with Tommy Lee Gentry? Right after practically accusing me of having one with him! What makes you that much better than him?"

Red to the roots of his hair now, Marshall stammered, "Rachel, I didn't mean . . . please don't misunderstand—"

"Oh, I understand perfectly, and frankly, I'm rather dismayed."

"Please, dear, d-don't let this c-come between us. We can still be friends."

But Rachel was reasonably certain the last five minutes had put a strain on their friendship that would never ease. She was also sure that half the town already had her paired up with Tommy Lee Gentry, so why was she fighting it?

The ride home seemed endless. The few attempts at conversation dwindled into a silence that became more and more uncomfortable as the minutes passed. Sometimes Rachel sensed Marshall's eyes on her, but she found it difficult to confront them now.

When he pulled up in her driveway she quickly said, "Thank you for the ride, Marshall," then jumped out before he could turn off the engine. She leaned down to look at him through the open window. "I've changed my mind about Wednesday night. All things considered, I think it's best if you find someone else to be your fourth at bridge."

"Rachel, wait!"

But she was already heading for the house at a half-run.

Inside, she leaned back against the door and breathed a sigh of relief, waiting for her stomach to stop quivering. How acutely embarrassing. And, in a way, how sad. Dear friends were treasures not to be valued lightly, but how could she ever face Marshall again?

She wandered through the quiet house, pausing in the kitchen to stare out at the pool, recalling Tommy Lee sitting at the table, confessing that he'd never stopped caring, while she gave him no encouragement whatsoever. She meditated on Callie Mae's caustic assessment of the direction her life was taking. Was she really cold, merciless? She didn't want to be. She wanted warmth in her life just like any woman. But in Marshall's arms she'd felt nothing. Only with Tommy Lee did she come alive. Even when she was angry with him she felt exhilarated. And wasn't she the one who had so recently admitted to herself that what she'd wanted in her life was occasional tumult? Like being overturned in a swimming pool by a crazy fool who waded in in a dress suit? Then having him send her a blow dryer with a note implying that any woman worth her salt should fix her own hair? And why hadn't he told her the earrings were for Beth?

Rachel glanced at the phone and her heart accelerated at the very thought of hearing his voice. She recalled her father's stern order that she not see Tommy Lee again and asked herself if the reason she wanted to was simply to demonstrate her own headstrong independence. But it was something more, something deeper, a compulsion that simply could not be denied any longer.

She picked up the receiver with a trembling hand, wondering while she listened to the electronic beeps and rings if he might possibly have another woman with him, and how to open this conversation, which had her heart pounding even before it began.

He answered in an uninterested grunt, "Yeah, Gentry here."

The breath seemed to catch in her throat; then she closed her eyes and replied quietly, "Hollis here."

"Rachel?" The way he said it made her imagine him slowly rolling his back away from a chair in disbelief.

"Yes."

A long silence passed before he said again, "Rachel . . . ?" More softly this time, as if his world had suddenly come aright.

It took great effort to keep her voice steady. "I've received three curious gifts in the past several weeks. You wouldn't know anything about them, would you?"

"Me? Nuh-uh." But in spite of his levity there was an unmistakable quaver in his voice.

She smiled, picturing his dark teasing eyes. "None of the cards were signed."

"What kind of guy would send a card without signing it?"

She heard the snick of the lighter, then the soft rush of breath as he exhaled, and she pictured him stretching across a sofa or bed to reach for an ashtray.

"That's what I'd like to find out."

"So, what'd he send you?"

"A blow dryer, a dozen roses, and a sack of beer cans." But suddenly she dropped the game and her voice turned gentle as she held the receiver in both hands. "Thank you for the roses, Tommy Lee. They were lovely." She sensed once more how pleasantly shocked he was by her phone call and how careful he was being about what he said. She herself felt shaken as she tried to think of a proper comment regarding the beer cans, but being unsure if their cryptic message meant what she thought it did, she safely avoided the subject.

"Listen, Rachel, I acted like a damned idiot, tipping you over in the pool that way and carrying on like a Neanderthal. It'd be my own damn fault if you really meant it when you said you wanted to kill me."

"I do," she replied wistfully, suddenly feeling like crying. Then she added softly, "Sometimes."

Neither of them spoke for several electrified seconds, and she wondered again what his bedroom looked like, and if that's where he was, and if he'd been asleep when she called.

"You invited me to dinner on Friday night, but you didn't say which Friday. Am I too late to accept the invitation?"

His voice sounded forced and slightly breathless. "Oh, Lord, do you mean it, Rachel?"

"If you still want me to come."

"Want you to come!" He laughed ruefully. "God, it's all I've thought about for weeks and weeks. This Friday?"

Something in the question sounded tentative. "Oh, are . . . are you busy?"

"No . . . no!" She relaxed her shoulders, not realizing how much she'd tightened up at the thought that he might have other plans. "And this time we *will* be chaperoned. That's a guarantee."

She wasn't sure whether to be disappointed or not.

"Your daughter?" she asked.

"No."

"But that *was* Beth with you at church, wasn't it?"

"Yes, things went sour between her and her mother, so she's living with me now."

Rachel's heart felt a surge of joy for him, but he went on quickly, "We'll talk more about it when I see you. Now, about Friday night—"

"But if it's not Beth who'll be chaperoning us, who is it?"

He chuckled and replied indignantly, "A dragon named Georgine. I hired her to keep house for me. But I've been tempted at least three times a day to tell her to ride her broom back to where she came from."

"You hired a housekeeper?" Rachel's mouth fell open in surprise.

"That's right. Isn't that what you told me to do? One who could cook me low-calorie meals?"

"But I . . ." She felt chagrined at having been so outspoken, then having her criticism acted upon so spontaneously. "Tommy Lee, I'm sorry too, for the things I said to you that day in the pool. I called you some terrible names and—"

"But you were right!" he interrupted. "There've been a lot of changes around here. You'll be surprised when you see them. And Georgine will be cooking for us Friday night."

She thought about his trimmer profile when she'd seen him at church, and about the message in the beer cans, and felt her heart lift with hope.

"What time shall I come out?"

"Rachel, I . . ." She heard him pull in a deep breath and sensed a boyish hesitation that seemed totally out of character for a man with a reputation like his. "Listen, I'd like to pick you up at your house, all proper this time." He chuckled nervously, then added, "I promise I won't dunk you or manhandle you or do anything that's not thoroughly polite. I'd be there at six-thirty."

She remembered the other time she'd opened the door to find him on her step, and what a shock it had been. What a thrilling shock. But to get dressed and wait for him as she had years ago . . . Rachel closed her eyes for a second and felt a thrill of girlish anticipation at the thought.

"All right. Six-thirty."

"Six-thirty," he repeated.

Then a full ten seconds passed while neither of them said anything more. Finally Rachel put in a wistful "Well . . ."

He cleared his throat and repeated in a more businesslike voice, "Six-thirty."

She laughed nervously and reiterated for the fourth time, "Six-thirty. Well, good-bye, then."

"Bye, Rachel."

When Rachel hung up the phone her face lit with an ear-to-ear smile; then she clasped her hands on top of her head and spun in a circle.

When Tommy Lee hung up the phone he sat on the edge of the bed with his elbows on his shaky knees, covering his face with both hands. He sat for a long time with his pulse racing, listening to his breath beat against his palms. *My God, she said yes! Incredible! She really said yes!* Then Tommy Lee frowned at the floor.

No kissing, no touching, no cussing, Gentry, you hear? Show her you can be the gentleman she deserves.

He fell back, arms thrown wide, eyes closed, imagining. After ten minutes of pure bliss, he leapt to the floor and did thirty push-ups in record time—and all with a smile on his face.

Chapter 9

IT WAS A golden August evening with scarcely a wisp of breeze stirring. The week seemed to have crawled by with slothlike slowness while Rachel agonized over what to wear, what to say, how to act. Just like that first date with Tommy Lee after he'd kissed her in the break of the boxwoods years ago.

It was strange to feel girlish at her age when she thought she'd given up giddiness years ago. But she actually had butterflies in her stomach, doubts about whether the gold earrings might have been better than the silver, and misgivings about the dress she'd chosen.

But it was too late to change now. The white Cadillac was already pulling up beneath the magnolia, and she drew back from the window, feeling pulses beating through her body in the places they had no business beating, as she watched Tommy Lee slowly get out of the car, then pause to look up at the house a moment before finally slamming the door. He buttoned his suit jacket, glanced down at his stomach, then unbuttoned the jacket and slipped a hand down his carefully knotted tie like a schoolboy at his first recital.

Rachel touched her lips, smiling. *Why, he's as nervous as I am!* Her smile grew wider. Imagine that, the Hellion of Franklin County getting all unstrung over walking to a woman's door!

She watched him come up the walk, assessing his new honed profile, and the hand dropped from her lips to her skittering heart. The bell rang. Her eyes closed for a moment while she savored the wild anticipation. Then she smoothed her skirt unnecessarily and moved to open the door.

And couldn't think of a single word to say.

They stared at each other with a breathless hush of appreciation, standing as still as the long shadows across the yard, feeling the awesome tug of nostalgia and the even greater one of reality. She had caught him smoothing his tie again, and his hand remained half hidden inside the suit jacket at waist level, unmoving now. At closer range she saw things she'd only glimpsed on the church steps. The puff of skin was gone from above his tight, crisp collar. The jowls had disappeared, leaving the skin about his jaws looking healthy and resilient. His eyes seemed clearer, the pockets of loose flesh gone from beneath them. And his coloring had changed from drinker's pink to runner's bronze.

After what seemed like aeons, he finally dropped his hand to his side and breathed "Hi."

"Hi," she managed, though the word seemed to stick in her throat and came out in a queer falsetto. Her eyes swept him from shoulders to toes and she blurted out, "You look wonderful!" Then she felt herself blush.

With a lift of his chin he laughed, and the sound relieved some of the tension. "Thank you, but I think you stole my line. You look"—his appreciative gaze scanned her, missing nothing—"absolutely perfect. Prettier than when you were sixteen."

"Well . . ." She flapped her hands stupidly and stepped back. "Come in. I'll get my purse." *Rachel Hollis, act your age! You're gawking and blushing like an adolescent in the throes of hormone change!*

He watched her walk away—slim hips moving with scarcely a sway, narrow shoulders bare beneath delicate spaghetti straps that emphasized her fragility. Her shoes were very high heeled and backless and made a soft slapping sound against her heels as she went. Her muted blue floral-print dress was elasticized at the waist and just above her breasts, and there appeared to be nothing beneath it except her body. Tommy Lee's bones seemed to turn to jelly as he watched her bare shoulders disappear. She was, plainly and simply, the most desirable woman he'd ever known. How ever would he make it through the evening without touching her?

In no time at all she was back, holding a tiny white purse, a shawl caught in the crook of a wrist. Several feet before him she stopped, glanced up uncertainly, and gave a fluttery half-smile, then dropped her eyes to study the clasp of her purse as she toyed with it. "After being married all these years I'm afraid I'm out of practice in the art of dating. I feel inept and awkward."

He studied her for a moment, then a grin lifted one corner of his lips. "Awkward? You, Rachel?" He chuckled and moved toward the entry. "You haven't been awkward since you lost your baby fat at . . . let's see, when was it? About thirteen?" He cocked his head as he opened the door. "Fourteen?"

She swept past him with mock imperiousness, scolding, "Thomas Gentry, I never had baby fat!"

He couldn't resist slipping a hand to her waist as they moved toward the car. "Oh, yes, you did. I've got pictures to prove it."

"What pictures?" His hand sent shivers along her arms and raised the fine hairs of her spine, as did the sight of his car, freshly washed and waxed for the occasion. As he leaned forward to open the car door for her, she caught the scent of sandalwood and spice in his after-shave.

"I've got pictures of us as far back as when we used to go bathing together in a plastic pool. Remind me to show 'em to you sometime."

She knew which pictures he referred to and felt uncharacteristically ruffled and shy at the thought of the snapshots of their two plump, naked baby bodies side by side. But the subject was cut off as he slammed the door and rounded the hood of the car. She watched him pause to light a cigarette before getting in beside her, bringing the sharply pleasant tang of freshly lit tobacco with him.

The interior of the car was immaculate, and the man at its wheel the essence of companionability as they drove out to his place without once exceeding the speed limit. When they approached the spot where he'd flung out his plastic glass the last time she was riding with him, she leaned forward to peer around him at the woods and ditch. Then she gave him an impish grin.

"Mmm . . . not tossing your glasses out into the weeds anymore?"

He only swung his eyes her way, gave a lazy smile, then carefully tamped out his cigarette, dropped the butt into the ashtray, and closed it. She noted each improvement in manners with an uplift of the heart.

"Do you know, you're the first man who ever gave me a bag of beer cans?"

"And you're the first woman who ever chewed me out and gave me a lecture on demon rum." They smiled at each other, remembering that night.

The car swayed through the curving woodsy drive, and when they pulled to a stop, he ordered, "Wait here," then got out with a bounding movement and appeared at her door to open it. They took the wooden ramp side by side, not touching, then he solicitously opened an ebony door to let Rachel precede him into the house. Music was playing softly, and a delicious aroma wafted through the air. He touched her elbow lightly and gestured toward the stairs leading up to the living room, calling, "Georgine?"

In the next moment Rachel was standing in the spotless room and his new maid was rounding the corner from the kitchen.

"Rachel, this is Georgine, who's been given the task of keeping me from perdition. Georgine, this is Rachel Hollis, a girl I went to school with."

Georgine tipped a small bow. "I know Mrs. Hollis . . . You run the dress store in town." Then she turned to Tommy Lee, informing him he'd had a call from someone named Bitsy who said she wanted him to call back. Finally, she asked, "Are you ready for your drinks now?"

"Drinks" proved to be a delicious concoction of pineapple juice and coconut cream, served in narrow stemmed glasses with fresh pineapple chunks and cherries on thin skewers. Rachel sipped hers, tasted no alcohol, and raised her eyebrows. "Mmm . . . delicious." She wondered if his drink was plain or spiked, but didn't ask, only glanced around the living room to find the plants had been trimmed of drying leaves, washed, and sprayed with leaf polish. The tables gleamed and the carpet hadn't one dot of lint or ash on it. Under Georgine's care the lavish room had truly come to life.

"How about taking our drinks out on the deck?" he suggested, and pulled the door open, then followed her out. The sun was hovering an hour's ride above the western rim of the lake, sending a highway of shimmering gold straight at them across the water. Overhead a pair of gulls caught the sun on their wings and squawked their tuneless call. It was warm, peaceful, and private. Rachel rested her glass on the railing, then leaned her hips against it, squinting into the bright reflection. "This place is really beautiful."

She watched him find and light a cigarette. Odd how the simple motions held a new attraction for her as he tilted his jaw, flicked a thumb on the wheel of the lighter, and scowled through the cloud of smoke. He threw his head back, exhaling, turned abruptly, and caught her watching him intently.

Immediately she looked at the lake.

"You like it?"

"Yes, very much. Who could help but like it?"

He turned his back to the view and perched a buttock on the rail, one knee riding wide and the suit jacket gaping open as he swiveled toward her. "I built it for you," he said matter-of-factly.

Her eyes flew to his, and they stared at each other for an endless moment. His new untinted glasses left the expression in his brown eyes open for study, and she saw there a grave sincerity that rocked her senses. Gone were the days when she wanted to turn away from his probing gaze. Now she wanted to immerse herself in it. He looked so different. Younger. Less worry-lined. Head-turningly handsome. She stood riveted before him while he made no move whatever to touch her, yet she felt touched in a wholly wonderful way. She became acutely conscious of his masculine pose, the tailored beige jacket having fallen aside to reveal expertly cut brown trousers stretched between his cocked hips.

At last she found her voice. "Yes I know. I recognized it the moment I walked into it."

"Did you?" His voice was gently gruff.

"It was unmistakable."

"And what did you think?"

Again she gazed out over the lake. "That I was married to Owen when you built it."

"So you were." He lifted his glass, watched her over the rim as he took a drink, then dropped the hand to his knee.

"Oh, Tommy Lee, whatever were you thinking, to do a thing like that?" Her eyes were troubled, and the corners of her mouth tipped down as she turned toward him.

He remained silent for a long time, studying the contents of his glass while swirling it distractedly, bumping it against his kneecap. Then he captured her brown eyes with his own and spoke softly. "Remember how we used to dream about it?"

"Yes, I remember. But that was . . . years ago."

He went on as if she hadn't spoken, glancing lazily over his left shoulder at the lake. "It's right where we always said we'd like to live." She felt his eyes move back to study her profile. "And it has all the windows you said you wanted, and all the natural wood I said I wanted." He drew deeply on the cigarette. "And the master bedroom with enormous walk-in closets made of cedar, and the view of the lake, and the fireplace for winter, and the sliding doors and deck for summer." He pointed above their heads with the tip of the cigarette. "That set of steps leads directly down from the bedroom, right to the lake for midnight swims."

Rachel's heart was thundering and her lips dropped open as she resisted the urge to look up at the deck cantilevered over their heads. My God, he remembered everything. She recalled walking in here the first time, noting his choices, adding them up, and wondering what the bedroom looked like. Why should it come as such a shock to know it, too, was designed from secrets whispered in the dark more than two decades ago?

The sliding door rolled back and Georgine asked, "Would you like your salads out here?" At the far end of the deck stood an umbrella table and four cushioned chairs.

"No, thank you, Georgine, we'll come inside." Tommy Lee eased his leg off the rail. "Rachel?" He swept a hand toward the door, and she let her eyes meet his. But they skittered away again from the impact.

The table was simply but elegantly set with thick slubbed linen placemats and matching blue napkins in ivory rings, a centerpiece of blue and brown, and a pair of ink-blue candles, already lit. When Tommy Lee had solicitously settled Rachel into her chair, he took the one directly opposite, reached for his napkin, and glanced up to find their view of each other blocked by the tall tapers. Without a word, he leaned over to push the centerpiece and candles aside, smiled, and settled back into his chair, saying, "There . . . that's better."

She busied herself removing her napkin from its ring, but felt tingly in the ensuing silence, and even more unnerved when she looked up to find him relaxedly lounging in his chair, studying her bemusement with a look of total appreciation.

The salad was made of crabmeat, endive, and water chestnuts and was served without wine. Scrambling about in her mind for a subject of conversation, Rachel finally asked, "So . . . did you and Darrel make ten?"

His head went back as he laughed, and the movement gave him a look of renewed youth that caught at Rachel's heart.

"Yes, we made ten, and tied Darla. Now the fight is on for eleven."

Their eyes met. Rachel felt a rich closeness to him in that moment as they spoke of things linking them to more than this night. But when the subject died, she sensed him in little hurry to pick up the strings of another. He seemed content to sit there in silence, studying her while the fork trembled in her hand.

When she could stand it no longer she finally insisted, "What are you *looking* at?"

A grin tugged at his cheek. "You. Trying to get my fill."

"Well, you're embarrassing me."

"Sorry, I didn't mean to." But still he didn't look away. "I'm trying to grasp the fact that you're really here at last, sitting at my table across from me. Incredible . . ."

She didn't know what to say, so she fiddled with the hem of her napkin.

"You know, Rachel, through the years I watched you maturing, and sometimes I'd grow angry with you. I'd want to call you and say, why don't you wither up or get gray or haggard! But instead you just grew more and more beautiful as the years passed."

She braced an elbow on the table, dropped her forehead onto her knuckles, and shook her head. "Keep that up and I'll have to leave."

"Is that a blush I see?" he teased, cocking his head as if to see behind her hand.

She propped her chin on the hand and presented him with a tight-lipped grin. "What do you think? I told you, I'm out of practice."

He laughed, sending a flash of white teeth through the growing shadows. "Ah, I love it."

"Could we please change the subject, Mr. Gentry?"

"As you please. Pick one."

She clasped her hands in her lap and said softly, "Beth."

"Which one?" he asked.

She felt herself color again as she answered quietly, "Your Beth. You said she's living with you."

He cleared his throat and sat up straighter in his chair. "Yes, for two weeks now, but she's gone off with some kids to the movies. She met a bunch down at the beach the first week, and already she's saying she wants to register for school here."

"You must be ecstatic."

"I am." His expression sobered slightly. "But it takes some adjusting."

"I imagine it does. What . . . how . . . ?" Rachel became discomfited and waved an apologetic palm. "I guess it's none of my business."

"Of course it is." He leaned his elbows on the table edge and met her eyes directly. "Nancy and Beth haven't gotten along well at all for a couple of years now. Nancy is what you might call an overprotective mother, unwilling to let her birdling out of the nest for the first time. They have terrible fights, and the result of the last one was that Beth ran away from home. She was gone for three days, and when we found her it was decided it'd be best if she tried living with me for a while. And so it seems, I've been granted a second chance to be a father."

"You mean she might stay? Indefinitely?"

"If things work out right. If she's happier here. If I can keep her on the straight and narrow."

Her dark eyes lifted to his. "And can you?" she asked in a near whisper.

He studied her with a loving expression in his eyes. "At this moment, Rachel, I feel as if there's nothing in this world I can't do."

The elation caused by his words lasted through the main course, which was beef Stroganoff. He ate his without any rice, and uncomplainingly drank lime water without so much as a grimace. The wine or champagne she'd expected was nowhere in evidence.

He talked some more about Beth, asked Rachel's advice on buying school clothes, which led to a discussion about her own store. She entertained him with humorous tales of the idiosyncrasies of her various customers, then asked him about his development corporation.

They ran out of things to talk about and found themselves staring at each other. Out of the blue Rachel blurted, "I like your new glasses much better than the old ones."

He grinned, but remained as before, bracing his jaw on one hand. "Oh, do you?" And she knew without being told that he'd changed them because of her.

She felt color washing upward and knew a sense of expanding sexual awareness between them. She dropped her eyes to the banana cream pie on her plate, but they wandered from it to his coffee cup and the cigarette crooked in dark tapered fingers that toyed with the cup handle while his unwavering gaze rested on her.

"Aren't you having any dessert?" she asked, letting her eyes skip up to his.

He answered simply, "No, not tonight."

And suddenly she realized how serious he was about his reform, and that he had not undertaken it solely because of Beth coming back to live with him. She, Rachel, had laid down parameters and he was striving to fit himself into them. And it was working. A rush of blood thrummed through her body, bringing again that sensual pounding deep in her vitals. As untamed as their longing for each other had been when they were teenagers, it seemed insipid compared to this mature reaction she was feeling for him. Yet he lounged in his chair with all the indolence of a sated maharaja, studying her closely while she fidgeted with the cloth of her skirt and grew hotter beneath his scrutiny.

Then Georgine took away their dessert plates and said if there wasn't anything more she was going to bed, and the gentle bump of her footsteps sounded up the carpeted stairs before all was still.

"She lives here, too?" Rachel asked, wide-eyed.

Tommy Lee fingered the rim of his coffee cup while studying her through the smoke that lifted between them. "Yes, in one of the guest rooms."

"Oh." So, he could no longer bring his women to that sprawling sofa.

"Weekdays," he added, then snuffed out his cigarette.

"Oh," she said again inanely, and wondered if he would ever try to get her onto that sofa with him. She thanked her lucky stars it couldn't possibly happen tonight with Georgine asleep upstairs and Beth probably due back any minute.

"Would you like to take your coffee into the living room?" he asked, as if reading her mind and deciding to tease her.

Rachel twitched and her eyes grew rounder. "Oh . . ." She glanced skittishly at a corner of the sofa visible beyond the fireplace. "All right," she added belatedly, but missed the grin on Tommy Lee's face as he watched her peruse the field of ottomans fit for a harem.

But he pushed the ottomans back, and they took separate places on the sofa with a decorous space between them, and he was everything he'd promised to be: the perfect gentleman.

And Rachel was the slightest bit disappointed.

They headed back to town before Beth returned home, and all the way Tommy Lee smoked continuously, the only indication that he might be as tense as she. He had kept his promise all evening, never saying or doing anything untoward. By now it was driving her crazy. She turned to study his face, illuminated by the pale dash lights, which reflected from his lenses and lit his knuckles on the wheel. He glanced her way. Her eyes veered out the side window, then closed on the thought that it had been years and years since she had become this aroused by merely looking at a man.

There could be no question that the most sensible way to end the evening would be with a graceful, polite parting. But being sensible was far from her mind, as she was sure it was from Tommy Lee's. There was no denying he was tempting, so tempting that these hours with him had been a study in control.

They were wheeling slowly through the city streets when Rachel drew a deep breath to ask, "Tommy Lee, who is Bitsy?"

It was some time before he answered, "Bitsy is a woman I was seeing."

"Was?" Afraid to look at him, she trained her eyes on the path of the headlights.

"Yes, *was.* She keeps calling and suggesting that we get together again, but I seem to have lost my taste for other women lately." He drew deeply on his cigarette before going on. "There's no use denying it, Rachel—there've been a lot of them. I suppose that bothers you."

It did. It made her mentally step back a pace when she wanted to move nearer. But beneath her reservation a disturbing tingle of jealousy made her reply defensively, "Should it?"

"Does it?" he shot back.

The moment sizzled with their acute absorption in each other as their eyes met and clashed; then she forced hers toward the windshield again. "Yes, it does. But it's more a disappointment than anything else."

"I didn't know I had the power to disappoint you."

"Well, you do."

"Why?"

"Because." She searched for a way to express it. "Because we were children together, good friends even before we became lovers, and I wanted you to remain that . . . that hero you'd always been for me. When rumors spread about you and yet another woman, I used to get so . . . so *angry* with you, I'd want to rap you on the skull and knock some sense into your head!" He laughed again and immediately she scolded, "Don't you dare laugh. You don't know what you put me through. Somehow I always ended up in a position of having to either defend or blame, and I didn't want to do either."

He grinned her way beguilingly. "And which did you do?"

She turned a snooty nose in the air. "None of your business."

"All right. Fair enough. So, what about Marshall True?"

Her head snapped around. "M-Marshall?" Her face burned at the memory of her last confrontation with Marshall.

"The town has the two of you linked together. Surely you know that."

"I'm not seeing Marshall anymore."

"Oh?" His eyes flashed over her, but she looked straight ahead.

"Marshall made a pass at me that I didn't like at all."

"You don't like it when a man makes a pass at you?" he questioned quietly.

She picked at her purse catch with a thumbnail. "I didn't like it when *Marshall* made a pass at me."

Just at that moment they reached Rachel's house and he drew up at the curb beneath the deep, shielding branches of the magnolia, eased the car into neutral, and turned on the parking lights, then sat back smoking. "I take that to mean you never had an affair while you were married to Owen."

She was shocked by his words, appalled that he might even think her capable of such a thing. "No, never!"

"Not even at the end?" Again she flushed at the realization that he, too, had guessed the extent to which Owen's illness had incapacitated him.

"No, I could never have handled the guilt."

"And what about now?" he asked.

"Now?" Her eyes flew to his dimly lit profile, the crisp knot of his tie, the crisper outline of his lips, chin, and nose. "Are you one of those widows who would feel disloyal to her husband's memory if she had sex with another man?"

The warning rockets went off in Rachel's body. How many times had she asked herself the same question and come up with no answer? Twenty years with the same man had left her feeling shaky and doubtful about considering another. Yet she knew that when Tommy Lee made his move, she would not turn him away. And there was no doubt he was about to make it. She held her breath, waiting for him to turn off the engine and draw her into his arms, but instead he strung an arm along the back of the seat, half turning to her to say, "Rachel, I can't thank you enough for tonight."

Disappointment made her stomach go hollow as she realized he'd been sitting there waiting for his cue, which she had not given. Maybe it was best this way. Her common sense knew a thousand reasons why she should hurry to the house and let him drive away, but her heart knew as many more for wanting him to stay. His company was pleasurable . . . and he'd changed. So much. But would the changes last? At that moment it ceased to matter, and she groped for a means to keep him with her a while longer.

"But I should be thanking you."

"No . . . no," he said quietly. But still he sat politely on his side of the seat while her heart hammered crazily.

"Tommy Lee, I . . ." Did he really intend to say good night without even kissing her?

"You what?"

She didn't know what she was going to say next until the words fell from her mouth. "Why didn't you tell me the earrings were for Beth?"

"You wanted to believe the worst about me."

"I did?"

"Of course. That would have made it much easier for you to deny what you were feeling."

"And what *am* I feeling?"

"You tell me."

But she really didn't know. There was this powerful attraction, but at the same time she feared his wildness, his reputation, the very real possibility of his backsliding.

So she asked, "Did you get the new glasses because you knew I didn't like the old ones?"

His hand rested very near her shoulder. "Absolutely," he answered in a voice as soft as the fall of a dogwood petal.

Her eyes dropped to his lapel. "And your suit is new, isn't it?"

He, too, glanced down at his chest. "I'm afraid it is. I had to buy it to replace a perfectly good one I ruined in your pool." They laughed quietly, then fell still again, feeling the tension grow.

"And you've been . . ." She was suddenly afraid to broach the delicate issue.

"I've been what?"

"You've been dieting."

"High time, wouldn't you say?"

She had saved the most delicate issue for last. "And how long has it been since you stopped drinking?"

His hand left the back of the seat and fished for a cigarette. "Six weeks," he answered, leaning forward to push in the dash lighter, leaving his arm extended while waiting for it.

She added it all up, as she'd been adding it up all evening, and her heart melted. She laid her hand on his crisp jacket sleeve. "Oh, Tommy Lee, that's wonderful."

His eyes flashed to the spot where she touched him, then quickly away. "You made me see I was on a fast train to nowhere. I decided it was time to change tracks."

The lighter popped out, and she dropped her hand from his arm while the tip of the cigarette took fire. The idling engine was making her more nervous by the second, and she sensed his impatience to get away if the evening was going to end here with a simple good night.

Suddenly his face took on a hard expression as he studied the glowing coal of his cigarette and asked, "Rachel, why did you come tonight?"

She was so surprised at his change of mood that she didn't know what to answer. She only stared at him, big-eyed.

"You wanted to check me out, find out if I really meant it when I said I could change. But what does it mean to you that I have?"

"Mean . . . ? I-I'm not sure what you—"

"Let me put it this way, then. Just because I've changed, I can't expect that I'll stand a chance with you. That's how it is, right, Rachel?"

"No! No, that's not it!" But it was. In spite of the sexual awareness she felt, she was afraid of people finding out she was spending time with him, afraid of the way he played romantic leapfrog, afraid that they were attracted to each other more by the tug of yesteryear than of today.

"Oh, isn't it? You've already told me you're not a woman who has affairs, and it would be stretching the imagination to believe you wanted anything permanent. So if I kiss you, if I start something, where does that leave me except hurt?"

He studied her intently now, waiting for some response. She felt like a hypocrite, wanting him sexually, yet unable to deny that she wouldn't want the town to find out. He turned to face her, crooking a knee on the seat and draping an elbow between the headrests. She was reminded of his similar pose on the deck railing earlier and pictured his trousers drawn tight, his jacket fallen open. With the hand that held the cigarette, he lifted a strand of her hair and let it fall. "It's all right, Rachel. You don't have to say it."

She closed her eyes and let the sensation of his touch thread down through her limbs and bring goose pimples as the hair dropped from his fingertips time and again. A thought filtered through—something about too much water over the dam—but it felt so good to be touched again, even in so casual a fashion. From above her head the smoke curled, filling her nostrils, while he played with her hair and made her shiver. At last she opened her eyes and found him watching her carefully.

"But still I can't resist you," he said throatily. "You know that."

All was still. Their eyes clung and questioned while intensity spun between them. *He's right,* she thought sadly, *you could hurt him so badly.*

"We have so much working against us," she said, in a soft, pained voice.

"Do we?"

She was hazily aware of his arm rising over her head, and of the way he reached toward the ashtray to tamp out the cigarette while studying her over his shoulder. Then he turned to her again, and one strong hand closed about the back of her neck.

"Come here, Rachel," came his thick-throated appeal.

He drew her halfway across the seat, meeting her there with the kiss she'd been afraid would happen, afraid wouldn't. His lips were open, soft, and suckling, covering hers in a first exploratory hello-again that made her heart carom. The tip of his tongue drew persuasive lines along the seam of her lips, and she could no more have kept them closed against him than she could have stilled the wild thrum of her heart. Their tongues met—a sleek, hesitant greeting filled with uncertainty.

When they drew apart, their eyes shone like flinders of glass as they studied each other in the faint greenish-white light. He tucked a strand of hair behind her ear. "Now tell me," he ordered softly. "What do we have working against us?"

It was difficult for Rachel to reason, with her pulses racing this way. She forced herself to ease back to her own side of the seat, but the moment she did he took up the sensual fingering of her hair again. She shivered, came to her senses, and shrugged away. "Don't do that, Tommy Lee," she demanded sensibly, forcing herself to evaluate the situation rationally. He was justified in asking her exactly why she was here and what she wanted from him.

"Sorry," he said, letting go of her hair. "A minute ago I thought you were enjoying it."

"A minute ago I was, but I shouldn't have been."

"What are you afraid of, Rachel?"

"The same things you are. You . . . me . . . the past . . . the future."

"Broad answers. Could you narrow them down?"

She sighed and looked away from him in the hope that she would be able to think more clearly. "Oh, Tommy Lee, you're so . . . so practiced!" She made an irritated gesture with her hands.

"Practiced!"

"Yes, practiced. I have the distinct feeling you've done it all, said it all a thousand times before. Do you blame me for being put off by the thought of all those others?"

"All right," he snapped, "so I'm not a fumbling schoolboy anymore. Is that what you want?"

"I don't know," she said miserably, propping her forehead on her knuckles. "I'm so mixed up."

"I told you before, Rachel. Those other women were only substitutes."

"And when you say things like that it only makes me wonder if you give this standard line to every one of us."

He tensed; then the lines of his face hardened, and he removed his arm from the back of the seat. "I don't have a standard line," he stated angrily.

"You wanted me to tell you what we had working against us, so there it is —part of it—and I'm not sure I can ever get past it."

He studied her profile for a full minute, then went on with stern reproof in every word. "Let me tell you something, Rachel. When you first came home from college, you wore your hair down to your shoulder blades, and you had a saucy little red shiny-looking coat that barely reached past your butt, and the day you were married it was sixty-seven degrees and raining. You honeymooned in Greece, came back, and lived in a rented house at fourteen hundred Oak Street, and your phone number was 555-6891. You went to work for the Chamber of Commerce during the time when your hair was screwed up in Afro ringlets, and you wore a more sedate gray cloth coat that fall—that was when you had the maroon Chevy Nova, the one that kid sideswiped that time when you hit your head on the windshield and had to have stitches in your scalp—let's see . . ." With seemingly clinical detachment he clasped her head in both hands and explored her hairline with his thumbs. "I forget which side it's on, but I know it's right here someplace . . ."

She chuckled and pulled away. "Oh, Tommy Lee, you're impossible."

"Do you want me to tell you about the cinnamon-colored suede suit that really knocked my socks off when I first saw you walking by in it? Or the grand opening of your store, held on September fif—"

She cut him off with four fingers on his lips. "No, you don't have to tell me any more," she answered meekly.

He kissed her fingertips, then pressed them to his lapel before declaring in a soft, sincere tone, "I don't have a line where you're concerned, Rachel."

"I'm sorry I said that. I really am."

"But I don't know what you want from me. What is it, Rachel?" His hand gripped hers harder. His eyes, so close now, held a vulnerability he made no effort to hide.

"I don't know," she said. "Sometimes the thought of you scares me. You're so . . . so . . ."

"When I kissed you, you weren't scared."

"When you kissed me you caught me with my guard down."

His eyes dropped to her lips. He smoothed the back of her hand, and even through his stiff lapel she could feel the strong, fast thud of his heart. "You're afraid I'll use you and move on, is that it?"

"That's part of it."

"And the other part?"

She looked into his eyes with a sad realization that there were no guarantees in this world. "That I'll use you and move on," she admitted, then continued softly. "There are still feelings between us, I won't deny it. But why? Simply because we were denied the right to each other once a long time ago? And if and when we've explored those feelings, what then? Please understand, Tommy Lee, I don't want to hurt you, but it's becoming clearer all the time how easily that could happen."

"Suppose I'm willing to take the risk?"

The longer she sat with her hand over his clamoring heart, the more willing she herself was becoming. She withdrew her hand and searched for more reasons to stop this folly.

"There's something else." Her lips dropped open and the tip of her tongue came out to wet them. "People say things about widows . . . unkind things." She swallowed and felt herself beginning to blush, recalling Marshall's readiness to become her lover, and his reasons for believing she needed one. And though she'd be the first to admit he'd been right, Rachel was chagrined when she faced the fact. Finally she blurted out, "I don't want to be thought of as a . . . a sex-starved widow. But I—I—" She stammered to a halt, feeling tears sting her eyes, hating this confusion, which was so foreign to her.

"You what? Say it. Don't be afraid," he prompted.

I suddenly find you more than I bargained for. I want to feel your arms around me, your mouth on mine, your hands on my body. I want to feel alive again, desired, loved. But I'm so afraid to let it happen with you.

"I'm afraid to," she said shakily.

He reached out to touch her cheek, reading in her eyes the unmistakable tug of carnality against which she fought. "Poor Rachel, so mixed up, wanting one thing, telling herself she wants another."

He studied her thoroughly, puzzling out this new, uncertain Rachel. Then he smiled, leaned close, and grazed her jaw with his lips. "So, what'll it be?" he murmured teasingly. "Wanna neck a little bit and see how it feels?"

She laughed unexpectedly, feeling the tension ease. And he kissed her neck with a fleeting touch that could scarcely be felt. But his scent was in her nostrils, smoky, mixed with the remnants of his shaving lotion and the starchy smell of new fabric from his suit. Her eyelids drifted closed, and his nearness sent the blood roaring to her ears.

"Mmm . . ." she murmured softly while he worked his way toward her earlobe and worried it gently with his teeth.

"Nice?" he murmured in return.

"Mmm . . ." It was more than nice. It was heady, enticing. "Tommy Lee," she whispered, "why did you leave the car running?"

He drew back to study her eyes, his arms forming an open harbor for her to sail into if she chose, one resting on the wheel, the other on the seat but not touching her. "If you want it off, turn it off yourself."

And so here it was—the choice. If she shut the car off there would be no turning back. If she didn't she had the feeling she'd regret it forever.

Her hand trembled as it reached toward the keys that dangled from the ignition on a silver chain. They chinked softly; then the car fell silent. Neither of them moved for a long, tense moment. At last, with his eyes rapt upon her, he reached through the steering wheel and shifted the car into park, felt for the light switch and brought darkness descending about their heads. His hand rose slowly to his temple, and with a twist of his head the glasses came off and he laid them on the dash. In slow motion, his hand closed about her neck, urging her near until she tilted toward him. For the space of several thundering heartbeats they hovered with their lips an inch apart.

"I don't want an affair," she claimed in a shaken whisper, but she needed very much to be kissed and caressed again.

"I know." His lips brushed hers in a kiss as tentative as the first one shared years ago in the break of a boxwood hedge. Her right hand came up to rest shyly against his chest, while his shifted to her hair, his long fingers threading through it.

They backed apart slightly, gauging each other's reactions and the dangers of carrying this to its limits. Those dangers were many and very, very real. But the great force of sexuality pressed down upon them, lying in their vitals with a heavy anguish of longing while their heartbeats scudded like thunder before a summer storm.

"Tommy Lee . . . we're crazy," she whispered.

"No," came his whispered reply. "We deserve this. We paid for it long ago."

Chapter 10

THEY MOVED WITH one accord, tipping their heads until their lips met again in tremulous reunion, sweeping them back in memory to the time of sweet innocence, when only bright dreams lay ahead.

Rachel's fingertips moved from his lapel to his shirtfront, and felt the skin warm through the cotton as his breath came with a celerity that matched her own. Their heads swayed in a lovers' choreography, seeking a firmer fit of mouth upon mouth. His hand flattened on her warm, bare back, drawing her nearer as his tongue slipped between her silken lips, bringing the taste of tobacco and some long-remembered essence as individual as a fingerprint. A sound rose in his throat—the end of the bitter, a rebirth of the sweet—and came a second time while his tongue scribed ever-widening circles over her eager mouth.

Ardor flared. Intimacy beckoned.

"Rachel . . . Rachel," he murmured, the name slurred between their hungering mouths. And as the kiss grew greedier he reached up to loosen his tie, then settled more firmly against her, slipping a hand to her ribs as he pressed her shoulders against the resilient leather seat.

The kiss swept them with the realization of how easily sensuality had been revived between them, and the pleasure they still found in each other. They experimented, recalling how it had been in the past—a scrape of teeth against a soft inner lip, a gentle bite, an interchange of tongues in the most secret recesses of their open, willing mouths, a suckling that seemed to tug deep within. Rachel's body shimmered in response. It had been so long . . . so long. His body pressing hers was vital, resilient, healthy. Her breasts peaked and yearned for the warmth of his hands.

But the kiss ended and he backed away to look down into her face. "Rachel," he whispered in wonder. "I can't believe it. After all these years." He wrapped her in two tight arms, her chin catching on his shoulder as he rocked her in jubilant celebration. "God, I can't believe it."

She smiled against his jaw and hugged him back. "I can't either."

Abruptly he backed away, but his eyes held embers as he ordered gruffly, "Turn around." Deftly he manipulated her, twisting her about until she was cradled in his lap, and in the same sweeping motion he returned his mouth to hers. Sealed beneath his lips she felt herself settled against his chest while a hand swept down to draw her knees up onto the seat. Then he leaned back into his corner and stretched his legs out toward the passenger door.

And it felt like coming home—birdling to nest, cub to den, Rachel to Tommy Lee. How warm and secure and familiar was this spot she'd known uncountable times before. And, ah, how their bodies fit together. So natural, with her arms twined about him until their joined breasts left space for nothing more between them than the paired heartbeats. He shifted a hip, raised one knee to buttress her spine and buttock while kissing her in a remembered way that brought welcome sensations sizzling through her body.

She had thought the years would have created obstacles to interfere, to present warnings. But instead, she felt only impatience. This was right. This was where she belonged.

She reveled in the feeling, exploring the back of his neck, sliding her long nails into his midnight-black hair while his hands played over her back and his tongue blandished, coaxed, and sent shivers scattering along her skin.

When he finally lifted his head their hearts were beating crazily. Rachel's limbs felt weighted. Her eyes drifted open to find his mouth still close, his palm lazily stirring the fabric on the side of her breast.

"How many times do you think we lay like this in my car?"

But she couldn't even guess. She could only recall the grand and terrible temptation of those days when they'd gone only so far but restrained themselves at the last moment. It had been heaven. It had been hell.

"Too many to remember. A hundred . . . two hundred . . . more."

"Do you remember the last time?" His hand made patterns that threatened to cup her breast but never did, bringing back the sharp thrill of the forbidden.

"No, I don't remember."

"It was the night when we'd driven up to Muscle Shoals to a dance, and you were wearing a flared skirt with green squares on it, and you could hardly get it buttoned anymore because you were pregnant."

She lay back comfortably in the crook of his arm, feeling again the seductive sense of security—how painless it was to talk about the past, wrapped in his arms this way. She touched his lower lip tenderly. It was puffed and moist from kissing. "You remember everything."

"Yes," he confirmed softly. "Where you're concerned, I remember everything. The smell of your skin, the exact brown of your eyes, the texture of your hair . . ."

In that moment it was incredibly easy to love him, and she wondered how she would find the strength to turn the tide of their desire. His head dropped and he crushed her close while lowering his open lips toward hers. The past melded with the present to bring a desire more potent than any they'd known in their youth. Their tongues imitated the act they'd shared in the days when they were raring and insatiable, and they felt again the supreme urgency they'd thought themselves able to curb.

His hand slipped around her to cover one tiny breast at last, working the

sleek cloth over her aroused nipple. She writhed in complementary circles, rising toward his touch, making a faint mewling sound in her throat. Beneath her she felt his tumescence, sheathed tightly but straining warmly through his trousers as she moved restlessly upon it. His hips began thrusting, and she instinctively drew common sense back into its rightful place, pressing a restraining hand against his chest.

Immediately his body stilled. He drew a tortured breath and buried his face in the fragrant curve of her neck. "I swore I wouldn't rush you . . . but it's damned hard."

She was breathless, floating, realizing how naive she'd been to think she could tread such a tightrope again without falling. Had she thought being forty-one instead of sixteen was adequate insurance against desire? Her voice shook as she answered, "And I swore I'd be sensible and settle for a few kisses." She laughed tightly, ending with the familiar little hiccup he had never forgotten. Then she surged up, holding him tightly, pressing her forehead into the inviting hollow below his jaw. "But you guessed right. It's been a long time since I've done anything like this, and the last time was with a man who was ill and unable to dredge up the fire I needed." She held him possessively and said through clenched teeth, "But you feel so good, so healthy. It's terribly hard to stop."

His hand caressed her breast, then slipped down one buttock and stroked it deftly before moving to the warm hollow behind her knee.

"Why should we stop?"

"Because it's the most sensible thing to do. Because I've only been a widow for a few months. Because our motives may be strictly carnal. Because if we start something it could get to be a habit," she recited in a rush against his neck, willing herself to believe it.

"I believe, Rachel"—he kissed her eyelid—"it's already started"—and her nose—"and out of our hands."

When his mouth opened hotly over hers she found herself clinging, kissing him back with nothing held in reserve. His hand caressed her hip, then sought her flat stomach before moving in one unerring swipe to cup the yearning warmth between her legs, pressing her skirt against the damp curve of femininity, tracing arousing circles on her flesh until she murmured inarticulately into his mouth.

"We have to stop . . ." she tried to say, but the words were muffled beneath his lips.

"You feel so good . . . so tiny . . . just as I remember. . . ."

"It's too tempting."

"Just like the old days."

His hands moved over her freely while she lay across his lap, her heart pounding so hard it seemed to make the magnolia leaves tremble above them. His fingers curved—contouring, pressing, stirring, kindling, while she lifted and drifted, thinking, *Just a little more, just a little . . .*

Then her dress rustled up and his hand sent fire-flashes dancing up her thighs and stomach as he sought naked skin.

When he reached her waist she stopped him.

His head rose. His eyes questioned.

"Don't, Tommy Lee . . . please," she whispered urgently. To her surprise, he immediately complied, but took up the idle rhythm through her clothing again.

"Rachel, remember the first time?" he whispered.

"Yes. It was out by the quarries, and I was very scared."

"So was I."

"You were? I never knew that before. You seemed so confident, as if you knew everything about it."

"I didn't know any more than you did." He bit her lower lip, adding persuasively, "But I've learned some new things since then."

She chuckled throatily. "So have I. Like how disastrous it would be to get caught like this if a policeman came by in a prowl car and shone his spotlight on us."

He laughed softly, caressing her stomach. "It wouldn't be the first time, would it?"

"No, but it would be a lot more embarrassing at our age. Why don't we take a walk and cool off?"

"So you're teasing again, Rachel?" he questioned, but without rancor.

"Again?"

"Yes, again."

"When have I ever teased you?"

"You teased me plenty back then, before you finally let me make love to you."

"Oh, back then. Well . . . I was scared I'd get pregnant. And besides, it was forbidden."

"And what about now? Is that what's holding you back?"

She considered for a moment, then ran the tip of an index finger along his lips. The nail skimmed his teeth until they opened and suckled the fingertip, then clamped down lightly upon it. "Will you understand if I say maybe that's partly true? You're that . . . that naughty Tommy Lee Gentry," she whispered. "And there's something inside every woman that's drawn to a bad boy. I'll admit I'm shamelessly attracted to the forbidden side of you. But no matter how many times I analyze it, there's still a part of you that's *my* Tommy Lee, the one who gave me my first kiss in the break of the boxwood hedge. That's the Tommy Lee who keeps crowding my mind when I can't sleep at night."

"You mean I've kept you awake, too?"

"Ceaselessly. Thinking about what we're doing now. Which is why one of us needs to be sensible and get us out of this car so we can cool off."

He sighed as if put upon, but obediently released her and pushed her up. "All right. A walk it is," he obliged, then opened the door and got out, watching her slide beneath the wheel, hair tousled, lips swollen, dress twisted at the waist. When the door slammed he dropped his hands to her hips and adjusted the disheveled dress until it hung properly again. "What an untidy little mess you are," he teased. Automatically she reached up to smooth her hair. "No, don't. Leave it." He pulled her hands down. "I love it that way. You look like you used to after we'd been out parking. Not a trace of lipstick left on your mouth, and your lips all red and puffy." He caressed them lightly with a thumb, weakening her resolve again. And when his hips pressed her back against the car, she looped her arms around his neck, unable to stop herself from inviting his warm kiss or the capture of her breasts in his wide palms.

After several tempting minutes, she drew away and reminded him shakily, "I thought we were going to take a walk and cool off."

"Yes, dammit, we were." He draped a wrist over her shoulder and she entwined her fingers with his, their joined hands bumping her collarbone with each step. They ambled aimlessly along the darkened street, talking of their past. He told of the dreams he'd had of coming back to Russellville after college and succeeding in business, of achieving that success but finding it hollow as relationship after relationship failed and he had no one to share it with. She confessed how badly she'd wanted a child to replace the one they'd lost, and of the slow death of that dream, and how devastated she was to learn she could not conceive again. They walked then in silence, nothing but the night chorus of crickets and peepers accompanying their lazy footsteps along the somnolent avenue where shadows were deep. They returned at last to her familiar magnolia, crossed the night-damp grass, which wet her nylons through her open-toed shoes, then passed beneath a hickory tree, blacker than black, and wandered thoughtlessly toward her backyard. They moved beyond the soft hum of the filtering equipment. Then all was silent but for the burble of water circulating somewhere in the pool, and their own matched, lazy footsteps clicking on concrete.

It was very late, and they were both tired, but unwilling to call an end to the night as they stopped, Rachel with her back to Tommy Lee and his hands resting on her shoulders. They looked up at the myriad lights burning across the night sky. The moon was at its apex, a lopsided blue-white smile amid the winking eyes of the stars. From the dew-laden juniper bushes along the brick wall came the thick scent of evergreen, and somewhere crickets sang in unison.

Tommy Lee turned Rachel to face him, leaving his palms in an undemanding parenthesis about her neck. He drew a shaky breath but spoke with uncommon steadiness.

"I told you this once in anger, but that's no way to say it—I love you, Rachel. There. I've wanted to tell you for so many, many years."

"Oh, Tommy Lee . . ."

She found herself near tears. *What am I going to do with this man? How long can I fight him?* Her arms circled his neck and she kissed his left cheek, then his right, wondering if she loved him, too, in the way he loved her. But to say so without being sure would be cheating them both. She meant her kisses to express affection without commitment, but when she would have backed away he suddenly pulled her flush against him, lifting her on tiptoe, matching her curves to his. Tongues, hips, and hands soon began taking an active part in the kiss, and by the time it ended, both Rachel and Tommy Lee were breathing as if winded.

"Rachel, this is silly. You want it, too. Let me come in with you."

She managed to shake her head and back away.

He studied her for a moment, wondering just what it would take to make her break down. "All right, have it your way. We'll cool off again." Then, calm as you please, he began removing his suit jacket. Her first impression was to giggle, but when she realized his intent, she grabbed his lapels.

"Oh, no, you don't, not in the pool!"

"Why not in the pool?"

"Because that's the oldest ploy in the history of seduction, and I'm not about to fall for it."

He nuzzled her ear. "Come on, Rachel, it could be fun."

"And dangerous."

"Have you ever done it before? Shucked down in the dark and gone in with nothing on?"

"No, and I'm not going to start now."

Suddenly there came a snap as he whipped off his tie. "Mind if I do?"

"And what do you expect me to do? Stand here and watch?"

"Mmm . . . it could be interesting." He leaned close and bit her earlobe.

"You haven't changed a bit!"

He chuckled and moved away toward the pale shadow of the patio table, and before her astonished eyes he went on undressing, slipping off his shoes, then hanging his jacket neatly on the back of a chair before reaching for his belt.

"Tommy Lee, don't you dare!"

"Ain't no damn way I'm ruining another suit." She watched in utter helplessness as his trousers came off and were laid across the table, followed by his socks. Panic and excitement turned her skin hot.

"If you take off one more stitch, I swear I'll go in the house and lock the door and call the police to tell them there's a naked man using my pool without permission."

Her threats bounced off him like the moon's reflection from the surface of the pool. His fingers lazily worked their way down his shirt buttons, and she sensed him grinning at her out of the deep shadows. She had a flashing thought about the wisdom of occasional tumult, but if Tommy Lee continued what he was doing, it would be more tumult than was advisable. He'd already half shrugged out of the shirt when she appealed in a desperate voice, "Please . . . please, don't."

He stopped in mid-motion and flipped his palms up. "Okay, you win. I'll leave the rest on." But he casually removed the cigarettes from his shirt pocket and set them aside, then strode lazily toward her. As he advanced she sensed the feral gleam in his eye and retreated.

"Tommy Lee . . ." she warned.

But he kept coming, deliberately, unrelentingly.

"You're the one who said you wanted to cool off."

"Tommy Lee, you wouldn't."

"Oh, wouldn't I?" He was a mere foot in front of her when she reached out a hand to fend him off. In the blue-white smile of the moon she saw his devilish grin a second before he lunged.

"Tommy Lee Gentry, don't you dare!" she squealed, but he clasped her beneath her knees and armpits and headed for the steps of the pool.

"Kick your shoes off, Rachel, if you don't want them to get wet."

"Gentry, you hellion, put me down!" She was still squirming as his feet splashed into the water.

"The choice was yours—with our clothes on, you insisted." The water touched Rachel's derriere. Her hips bucked, and she squealed and grabbed his neck. "Mmm . . . nice. Do that again," he teased, lowering her again until the water soaked six more inches of underwear and her toes went under.

"My shoes!" Her knees straightened like a switchblade, sending a spray of droplets scintillating across the surface of the pool.

"Too late now. You should have taken them off when you had a chance."

Down she went again, deeper this time, until the water's cold fingers slipped between her thighs. A shudder pelted across her skin, bringing a chuckle from Tommy Lee as he nuzzled her neck. Then he licked her skin with his warm tongue while bobbing her lower and lower and lower into the water.

"The chlorine's going to ruin my dress," she insisted, but with waning urgency.

Against her neck he mumbled, "Send me a bill."

She stopped fighting him then, hanging suspended and helpless in his tight grip, feeling the water lick up and down her thighs with a faint suction and slap each time she was drawn free, then plunged beneath the surface. The shivers were steady now. Goose bumps sprouted up and down her arms and across her bare shoulders. Her breasts—dry though they were—had puckered up like a pair of gum drops.

"Tommy Lee, you're crazy . . . crazy." But the words came out in a breathless murmur as her knees relaxed and her shoes trailed in the water.

"I know—crazy white boy who builds crazy houses, and dreams crazy dreams, doing crazy things because he's got his woman in his arms at last and he doesn't want to let her go."

He kissed her fiercely, the contact so warm when contrasted against the cool seeking water swashing between her thighs. Her arms twined about his neck as she went pliant and welcomed his probing tongue, which sent a new, different set of shivers up her spine. He started nipping her—sharp, enticing tugs between teeth that knew exactly how hard to bite, and where.

"Crazy . . ." she whispered, letting her head loll back.

Her eyelids slid closed and the water seemed to grow warmer as Tommy Lee turned them both in a circle. One of her shoes drifted free and sank somewhere in the water. But she no longer cared. Riding weightlessly in his arms, she felt the cool caress of the night water slithering along her skin. It pressed the wet nylon tight against her calves, then shimmied along her thighs to make the dress cling, then unfurl as he reversed directions.

The scent of her—woman and perfume—drifted through the night, released from garments and skin by the water. She opened her hands on his tensile shoulder blades, then drew back to meet his eyes, which reflected the moon and a wealth of desire. He came to a halt, his shirttail drifting in a pinwheel on the surface of the water.

His voice was gravelly, intense. "I want to make love to you. I want to do all the things we were too ignorant to know how to do back then. For twenty-four years I've wanted it."

His head blotted out the moon and his lips were summer-warm as they opened over hers. She kissed him back with delight, which swiftly changed to impatience, seeking out each changing texture and mood of his mouth as it demanded more, then less, then more again. The wrist beneath her knees slipped away and the water bore her weight for a moment before she was drifting down, down, until her toes settled on something stationary and she found herself standing waist deep in water, fully dressed, kissing Tommy Lee Gentry, their bodies coalescing, half dry, half wet, but all aroused.

He gripped her hips, drew circles on them with his own, swaying, kissing, losing his balance and righting himself again as the water nudged them. His hands slipped deeper, cupping her buttocks, holding her securely as he rocked against her. The next moment she flinched and gasped as he brought both palms up, dripping, and clamped them over her breasts. Her nipples cinched tighter as the wet fabric clung, but soon the warmth of his palms eased through as he teased, caressed, heated. His hands rose to skim the straps from her shoulders, drawing the flimsy dress down to her waist.

Then his open mouth possessed her breasts, one and then the other, and her head fell back, eyelids closing, blocking out the moon. He dipped lower, and the shocking sensation of heat and cold sent renewed shivers through her limbs as the water lapped near his lips. She drove her fingers through his hair and clasped his head tightly against her stomach.

"Oh, Tommy Lee . . . it was inevitable, wasn't it?"

He straightened, and their eyes met in a moment of surrender. She slipped her hands inside his shirt, spreading it wide to kiss his chest, his collarbone, his neck, his chin. His mouth. Ah, his warm, long-denied mouth. Her hands rode his shoulders, divesting him of the garment, which soon lay adrift upon the water. Moments later it was joined by her dress and a brief scrap of white they had together shimmied from his loins. Her pantyhose came next, followed by an even tinier scrap of white as he grasped her beneath the arms and held her buoyant while she kicked free of her panties. Before the garments drifted to the surface, Rachel's legs were clamped tightly around Tommy Lee's waist.

He waded toward the steps, his mouth communing with hers, then laid her down on the concrete, still warm from the day's sun, her feet trailing in the water, while he rested on one hip beside her. The moon shimmered along her wet limbs like a rich silver garment while his hand followed its path, relearning the curves of breast, stomach, thigh, and mons.

"Rachel," he managed throatily, "I've loved you since we were fourteen years old—maybe even before that. There were times when I thought I'd die without getting the chance to tell you again."

She raised her arms in welcome and he came to her, pressing his length to hers as she caressed his back and buttocks, whispering, "Oh, Tommy Lee, none of us can ever quite get over our first love, can we? And you were that for me. I loved you so much . . . so much. And some of that love has always stayed with me, no matter who either of us was married to or what was going on in our lives." She felt him shudder and gently pushed him back to delve the dark mystery of his eyes. "I feel it still, and it grows stronger each time I see you." This was the supreme surprise, that she should at last recognize the love lying fallow within her heart, untouched, untarnished all these years, and be so eager for it to be nurtured and brought to bloom again.

A stab of wonder pierced his heart, and she saw it in his eyes, realizing fully what this moment meant to him. And she was suddenly filled with the need to give him back a thousandfold all the happiness he had missed in life.

She kissed his eyelids, held his face in both hands. "When I saw you tonight, walking to the door . . . this feeling started then. You looked so devastatingly wonderful to me, as if the past twenty-four years had never happened." She praised his sleek shape with the brush of her hands and felt him shudder.

He kissed her eyelids, uttered her name in a pained murmur, and returned to her mouth with an impatience he found reflected there. "Ah, sweet woman, the things I want to do to you . . . things I was too green to know about then. Do you realize that I've given you a baby but never a climax?"

"Mmm . . ." Yes, she realized it only too well, had thought of it often, especially during these last months along. "Please feel free . . ."

Their exchange sent a fresh current of sensuality rippling through Rachel's limbs. As his hands reacquainted themselves with her body, time spiraled in reverse, taking her back to that first nubile exploration, when he'd initiated her into the rites of sexuality. Once again he brought her the thrill of anticipation, then the even greater thrill of sensation as he touched the inner Rachel, whose secrets could no longer be withheld.

Her palm gathered the moisture from his back, transferred it to his belly, and closed about his flesh, still chill from the water, but quickly warming beneath her touch. He groaned, and the wasted years fell away. He twisted low, following the moonbeams down her wet breasts, sipping the dampness from them with his warm tongue, dipping into the shallow navel where more water pooled, like dew in the chalice of a flower. He kissed the glistening hair at the juncture of her legs, where droplets still clung, bringing again to her lips the mewling sound. And only the heaven-borne stars and the guardian moon stood witness as he moved lower, inundating her with rapture.

And when they hovered at the pinnacle, their bodies taut and trembling, he turned again to press his length to hers, then paused on the brink of entering to vow, "I love you, Rachel Talmadge," unconsciously slipping back to the name he'd planned to change to his own when first they'd loved this way, aeons ago.

She touched his face with great tenderness while savoring this wondrous exchange about to happen.

"And I love you, Tommy Lee Gentry," she whispered with tears in her eyes.

Then the hurts of the past were lifted away as he thrust deep and fell into the rhythmic pulsing that made their bodies leap and flow. Soon the cry that shuddered from her throat was joined by his deep growl of release.

And in this world of false starts and misgivings, they knew at last where they belonged.

Chapter 11

THEY HAD DIPPED into the pool and rinsed each other off, to emerge dripping and shivering. "Show me your bedroom. I'm tired of concrete."

She laughed and reached for his hand. "This way." And so simply was it decided he would stay the night.

The air had chilled their skin, bringing goose bumps and puckers as they ran for the house, two laughing specters with slapping feet. Inside, all was midnight shadows as they groped their way down a hall and found a linen closet, exchanging intermittent kisses, then swipes of thirsty towels. They paused for a heartier kiss, damp skin sealed by the residue of water warming between them, sending out a sharp smack as they drew apart.

He touched her face lovingly. "The bedroom," he reminded her, and again she led the way.

She stopped in the center of a darkened room where the only thing visible was the moon's silver reflection lilting across the surface of the pool beyond a set of sliding glass doors.

"Is this the room you shared with Owen?"

"Yes, but everything in it is brand-new."

He glanced at the shadowy bed. "Everything?"

"Yes." She turned into his arms. "Even me."

Their kiss was brief, but welling with rebirth. "So turn on the light and let me see." Immediately he sensed her reluctance, even before she spoke.

"But it's nothing special, just yellow carpet and wicker and bamb—"

He covered her lips with an index finger. "Turn on the light, Rachel," he commanded quietly.

She thought of her thinness, and the breasts that were so minuscule they hardly showed when she was dressed, and of course the scar on her stomach.

"But . . . but why?"

"Because we're not children anymore." His palms bracketed her neck, thumbs lightly pushing on her jaw. His voice became even softer. "Because I've made love to you more times than I can remember, but I've never seen you naked." Timidity intruded and she tried to drop her chin, only to have his thumbs press it upward unrelentingly. He kissed the corner of her mouth, whispering, "Please, Rachel. I'm forty-one, too, and I have my insecurities just like you do. But turn it on anyway . . . for me."

She crossed the room with the faint brushing of bare feet on carpet and clicked on a low bedside light, pausing with her hand beneath the shade to glance back over her shoulder, her eyes wide, dark, and exquisitely beautiful. At last she turned to face him.

The two of them studied each other. Tommy Lee's towel was draped about his neck. Rachel's was clutched against her stomach. His eyes traveled a slow path from her brown irises to her pink toenails, then back up. Hers moved lingeringly from parted lips to strong brown feet, then returned to rest within the rich, waiting depths of his gaze. How amazing that they should never before have seen each other this way. In her eyes he was unutterably perfect. The marks of age became only testimony she cherished.

"You have much more hair on your chest than you used to," she noted shakily.

"And most of it's gray."

"Gilding," she praised softly. Her heart lifted expectantly as he slowly moved toward her, sliding the towel from about his neck with singular lack of haste. He ran it down the shallow ravine between her breasts, where beads of moisture caught the light and sent it radiating like polished chips of amber. Their eyes clung while the towel skimmed her naked back. "You're beautiful, Rachel. Perfect. Too perfect for this world." Then Tommy Lee dropped to one knee and meticulously dried her legs. When he arose, his eyes locked with hers as he drew the towel from her fingers and tossed it aside with his own.

He stepped back. His eyes slid down her exposed body, but when they reached her stomach, the dark brows curled and he flashed her a questioning look.

"Rachel, what's this?" Automatically he reached out.

Automatically she shielded the scar. "Nothing . . . nothing."

He clasped her wrists and drew them to her hips, searching first her stomach, then her eyes again. "You had the baby by cesarean?"

"It doesn't matter," she reassured him.

"Doesn't matter?" He made a throaty sound as with one swipe he lifted Rachel and placed her diagonally across the bed, bending over her. Gingerly he touched the pale scar. "Everything about you matters. That's what this is from, isn't it?"

Tears shimmered on her eyelids, and her heart eased with the blessed relief of sharing it with him at last, after all these years. "They said I was too small to deliver it naturally."

His eyes seemed unable to pull away from the telltale line running from just below her navel into the black pubic hair. He traced it with four curious fingertips. Then his eyes darkened, glittered, and filled with the past as he opened a hand wide upon her stomach and uttered thickly, "Our baby . . . God, she was our baby. Think of the waste. . . ."

His voice broke, and suddenly he bent to caress Rachel's stomach with his face, placing warm lips at the spot where the scar disappeared into the dark triangle, breathing on her while wondering at all she'd gone through because of the seed he'd planted within her, letting the hurt rush back and take him one last time.

He felt a sting behind his eyelids and slipped both arms around her hips, cradling his cheek against her warm stomach. "Rachel, I wanted to marry you so badly, and keep her. I wanted to take care of you and have other babies with you, and watch them grow, and get old with you."

It had taken Rachel years to get beyond self-pity and regret, but at the sound of Tommy Lee's emotional outpouring, sensing how close he was to tears, her own eyes blurred. "I know, darling, I know." She rolled to her side, coiling about his head and shoulders, caressing his warm skull while they let the anguished past in to be cleansed.

"What did she look like?"

She closed her eyes, remembering.

"She had a perfect cap of dark, dark hair, just like yours. . . ." Her fingers knew again that hair, finding it crisp now at his temples, while she rued each wasted year that had grayed him and thinned her and kept them from knowing these changes daily. "And gray eyes in a face with the tiniest, most perfect mouth I'd ever seen. I only got to hold her once."

"Rachel . . . Rachel . . ." His tortured words were muffled against her, and she saw again the rosebud mouth of the child they had created together, while the pain billowed within them both. "Our baby . . ." he murmured—a prayer now. "I wanted her . . . took you both away from me . . . my Rachel . . . all these years . . ."

They had only one means of solace to offer each other, and as his mouth, hands, and body moved over her in recompense, her heart cried and sang at once. Their lovemaking was fierce this time, an attempt to dissolve a past that could never be dissolved, for when they came together in cataclysm, that past bound them more surely than vows.

The bedside clock read 3:18. The lamp glowed softly on two dark heads and across the yellow and white bamboo-designed sheets that covered Rachel's breasts as she lay tucked in the shelter of Tommy Lee's arm. He was propped against a cache of ruffled pillows, smoking, her temple pressed to his slow-thudding heart.

"And what happens now, Rachel?" he asked, staring at the surface of the pool beyond the open shades.

"I don't know."

He took a deep, thoughtful drag, and she heard the air enter his lungs beneath her ear. "Then I'll tell you. You marry me, the way you should have twenty-four years ago."

Her fingers stopped combing the coarse hair on his chest. How simple things became in the throes of passion; how complex upon reconsideration.

"Oh, Tommy Lee, how can I marry you?"

"Do you mean, what would people say?" His voice held a honed edge as he rested a wrist across an updrawn knee.

What *would* people say? She had pushed the question aside all night, but now it pressed for an answer. "Owen's only been dead for a few months."

"And the fact still remains that I've had three wives and a stable of lovers the whole county knows about, and I've spent a hell of a lot of years drinking like there was no tomorrow, and you're scared it set a pattern I can't break, is that right?"

She tried to sit up, but he held her fast. "Rachel, don't run away. Did you think I kept after you for nothing more than a roll in the hay, and now that I've had it I'll let you walk out of my life again?"

"I didn't think that, I just—" *Just what? Needed my sexual thirst slaked? Wanted to see if I could still bring Tommy Lee Gentry to heel? Am I so shallow that I'd use him, then toss him aside, knowing all along how vulnerable he is where I'm concerned?* Slowly she pushed herself up. He let her go this time, watching her naked back curl and the side of one breast slip into view as she doubled her arms across her updrawn knees.

"You just what, Rachel?" His voice sounded brittle, hurt already.

Miserably she dropped her forehead onto her arms and shrugged.

"You don't have much faith in my reformation, do you?"

She felt small and guilty while silently admitting the truth.

"Well, you would if you could crawl inside my body and know what I've felt for you all these years. Without you nothing and nobody mattered. Now everything is possible. Don't you understand, Rachel? Even *I* matter now."

She lifted her head and stared at the wall, torn by his words. "We have to be honest with ourselves. Are you sure we aren't just . . . just searching for our lost youth in each other?"

He studied her naked rump, the delicate shadow disappearing down its center, the sheet caught in the fold of her hip. He drew deeply on his cigarette, forced his eyes away from her so he could think more clearly. "I can't answer for you, but I know how it is for me. If it had happened overnight I might suspect that was true. But I told you before, it's been going on for twenty-four years, every time I'd see you on the street or in your car or going into your daddy's bank."

At the mention of her daddy, Rachel's head swung around and their eyes clashed momentarily before she turned away again. He worked the edges of his teeth together, then studied the glowing tip of the cigarette while drawing circles with it on the bottom of the ashtray. "You're still scared of him, aren't you, Rachel?" he asked quietly.

Was she? She didn't want to think so, but she couldn't deny how much she hated the thought of all the strife there was bound to be if her father found out about tonight. And there was a facet of her misgivings that Rachel had been afraid to examine too closely up until now, because she didn't want to believe it might be true. But she could hold it inside no longer.

"By marrying me, you 'd show them all, wouldn't you, Tommy Lee? You'd have your revenge for what they forced us to do all those years ago?" It was a thorn that had pricked each time he'd called, each time she'd seen him over the past several months. No, she didn't want to believe it, but wasn't it possible?

"Is that what you think, Rachel? That I'm only using you to get back at them?"

She covered her face with both hands and shook her head until her hair fluttered. "Oh, God, I don't know what to think. All of this would be so much simpler if you'd made your peace with your parents, and if they'd made their peace with mine. But everything's so . . . so complicated!"

His warm palm caressed her back, sending shivers around her ribs to the tips of her breasts. "There are some things I can't change. But those that I can, I have. I love you, Rachel . . . for yourself, and for no other reason. And that's why I want to marry you. You've got to believe that. You're the only thing I ever wanted . . . not other women, not . . . not liquor and fast cars and shiny boats and—" He broke off and dropped his head back wearily, letting his eyes slip closed and swallowing noisily. "Oh, God, Rachel, I'm so tired of being that way. I need you in my life to give me some peace at last."

A sob escaped her throat as she whirled and flung herself into his arms. He caressed her head, embracing her with a strength close to fury, shutting his eyes against the thought of facing more Rachel-less years, now that he'd come this close.

"Oh, Tommy Lee, I'm so mixed up. Sometimes I don't think *I* deserve *you.* You've been more faithful to me than a husband in a lot of ways, no matter how many women you've known."

"There haven't been any others since the day of Owen's funeral. Nobody but you, Rachel. I love you so much . . . do you really think I'd blow it all now that I stand a chance of having both you and Beth in my life again?"

There came a time when trust had to take its rightful place in a relationship. He *had* changed. Dramatically. And if he thought the changes were permanent, her belief in him could be all he'd need to make it true. She thought about all he'd said that first night he'd come to her house, the years of misery he'd suffered. She thought about the house he'd built, the hope that had spawned such a task—and there wasn't a doubt in her mind that he loved her. So wasn't it time she began believing in the wonders love could work?

His voice rumbled quietly beneath her ear again. "You said you love me. Is that true, Rachel?"

"Yes . . ." She squeezed him mightily. "Oh, God, yes. I'm falling in love with you harder than the first time, and it's the scariest thing I've ever gone through in my life."

"Then we'll have to face some things . . . some people But it'll work out, you'll see," he promised, then set the ashtray on the bedside table and settled back against the pillows, cradling her again, catching his chin on top of her head. She let his confidence imbue her, and lay in his protective embrace while peace settled over them like a soothing palm.

The minutes slipped by, and his hand moved absently in her hair. "You know," he murmured, "she's old enough to have kids of her own already. Do you realize that? Somewhere in Michigan we might have grandchildren."

She chuckled tiredly against him. "Oh, Tommy Lee, I don't think I'm ready to be a grandma yet. I surely don't feel like one tonight."

He jiggled her a time or two and grinned down lovingly. "You sure's hell didn't act like one. Grandmas are supposed to bake gingerbread cookies and go to sewing circles."

"Remind me to join when I grow tired of this."

She felt his chest lift with silent chuckles. Again his fingers sifted idly through her hair. "Have you ever thought about trying to find our Beth?"

"Yes, I've thought about it. But never for long. It would be too hard to see her, possibly even talk to her, then walk away. And what good would it do? She has parents to love. If she learned about us it could be devastating for her, too. Does it bother you?"

He shrugged. "No, not like it used to. Especially since my other Beth has come to live with me."

They lay silent for some minutes, then Tommy Lee said the most startling thing.

"Rachel, suppose you're pregnant right now."

She snapped back and gaped into his dark, amused eyes. "But . . . but I can't be pregnant now!"

"Why not? You're only forty-one, and you're not on any kind of birth control." His brow wrinkled. "Are you?"

"But I'm allergic to sperm!"

"You were allergic to Owen's sperm, not mine. If we had one baby, why isn't it possible for us to have another?"

Suddenly Rachel burst out laughing. "Tommy Lee, you're crazy!"

He smiled crookedly. "Maybe. But it's fun thinking about it . . . 'cause then we'd have to get married." He settled her back where she'd been before. "Imagine the expressions on our parents' faces when we walked up those church steps together, and you pregnant out to here." His hand caressed her abdomen, and they laughed together, imagining it. Then Rachel fell serious.

"Forty-one is too old to become parents."

"Who says?"

"I do, for one." But her heart lurched at the thought, gave a little kick of independence, and left her feeling slightly giddy.

"I know I wasn't much of a father, but I always thought that if it had been you and me together I'd have been so much better at it, loving you the way I did. They say a child's security stems from the love of its parents for each other, so think about it, okay?" He reached out to snap off the light and knocked a few pillows onto the floor, then curled her tightly against his body. "With or without a pregnancy, we're both getting a second chance with Beth."

What a stunning and beautiful thought. Mulling it over, Rachel fell asleep.

They awakened to a butterscotch sun streaming through the bedroom. Tommy Lee stretched and quivered magnificently, then opened his eyes to find Rachel beside him, watching.

"Hi." He grinned with half his mouth.

"Hi." She thought he looked wonderful with his hair tousled and whiskers beginning to show.

"What're you grinning at?"

"What're *you* grinning at?"

"Rachel Talmadge, all messed up."

"Yeah, well, look who messed her."

"Tell me, Miss Talmadge, what do you think about morners?"

"I always kinda liked them myself. Tell me, Mr. Gentry, what do you think about morners?"

"They rate right up there with nooners and afternooners."

"In that case I don't suppose you'd care to indulge with a messed-up woman who just *might* be a grandma."

He reached out lazily and ran a knuckle across her lips. "Ohh, Grandma, what nice lips you have."

"The better to kiss you, my dear." And she made a pretense of gnawing his knuckle.

His hand moved down to cup one small breast.

"Ohh, Grandma, what nice breasts you have."

She gyrated the breast against his palm. "The better to entice you, my dear."

He came up slowly and turned her to her back while running a hand down to explore her sweet mysteries. "Ohh, Grandma, you ain't like no other grandma I ever come across in the woods."

She smiled and indulged in some sensuous writhing that felt positively wonderful. She nuzzled the silver hair on the side of his head, then bit his ear and asked seductively, "Isn't this the story where somebody's always eating up somebody else?"

"Oh, nasty, nasty Grandma," he said against her lips, then lowered his open mouth to her breast as they set about ushering in the morning properly.

A half-hour later Rachel was dressed in a floor-length robe of pink satin and coffee was perking as she wrung out Tommy Lee's shirt in the laundry basin.

"Rachel, can I use your brush?" he called from the bathroom.

"Sure. It's in the top left drawer of the vanity."

She heard the drawer open, tossed the shirt into the dryer and turned it on, then stepped into the kitchen.

When the rush of running water stopped at the far end of the house, she called, "Help yourself to towels." Then she cocked her head and asked, "Do you like bacon?"

"I love it, but it's fattening!" he called back.

She smiled as she laid several thick strips on the hot griddle. The bacon was sizzling and the buttons of the shirt were ticking noisily against the tumbling dryer, so she didn't hear the front door opening.

She wasn't aware of Everett's presence in the house until she turned the corner into the family room with a glass of juice in her hand.

At the sight of her father she came up short and her stomach seemed to tilt. He was standing in the middle of the family room, staring at the surface of the pool, where miscellaneous pieces of clothes were caught in the skimmer. Her eyes darted outside to find even her shoes visible, lying in the aquamarine depths of the shallow end. Everett's stormy gaze moved from the pool to scan her pink wrapper, pausing for the briefest second on the fabric shimmering unmistakably over bare nipples.

"Daddy," she gulped.

"I came to have coffee with you before you left for the store," he said acidly. But just at that moment Tommy Lee stepped out of the bathroom and entered the room from the opposite direction, dressed in nothing but trousers, toweling his wet hair. When his face emerged from beneath the towel he stopped dead in his tracks.

The suffocating moment seemed to stretch forever while Everett fired angry glances from one to the other and nobody said a word. His face turned stony while Rachel's began to redden.

"Well, well," he drawled after several interminable seconds. "What have we here?" Tommy Lee glanced helplessly at Rachel while Everett went on silkily. "But I guess it's obvious what we have here. The county's most notorious whoremonger, preying on one of its most vulnerable widows."

Tommy Lee and Rachel both spoke at once.

"Now just a minute!"

"Daddy, it's not that way!"

Everett pierced his daughter with malevolent eyes and pointed an outraged finger. "You shut up, girlie, I'll get to you later!" Then he spun on Gentry. "How dare you set foot in my daughter's house!"

"I didn't realize I had to ask permission to see a forty-one-year-old woman."

"*See?*" Talmadge hissed. "It appears you did more than *see* her! It isn't enough that you have every two-bit whore between here and Montogmery? Do you have to drag my daughter down with you?"

Tommy Lee's hands tightened into fists on the ends of the towel. "Your daughter is a lady, and my being here doesn't change that."

"Oh, doesn't it? I wonder if her neighbors agree with you!"

Suddenly Rachel came to life. "Daddy, stop it."

He whirled on her again. "Have you no respect for yourself, or for Owen? He hasn't been gone for—"

"Don't keep throwing Owen up in my face. I married him and gave you the kind of son-in-law you wanted, and I stuck with the marriage, no matter how dull and disastrous it was. But I will not keep revering a dead man at the cost of my own happiness!"

"No, instead you cheapen yourself with trash like him!" Everett thumbed over his shoulder, and Tommy Lee had all he could take. He stalked across the room and whirled Talmadge around by an elbow.

"I'm getting mighty damn sick of you thinking you can control our lives, so get this through your head." He nudged Talmadge in the chest with two strong fingers that set him back a step. "You're all through interfering!"

"Not when she's about to make the same mistake twice, I'm not!"

Tommy Lee's face was grim, his fists clenched at his sides while blue veins bulged up the length of his bare arms. "The mistake wasn't hers, it was yours! But you just can't admit it, can you, Talmadge? You took something away from her that you had no right taking away, and the disaster was doubled when you found out it could never be replaced. And now here I am, back in her life, bringing it all back for you to face. That's what you're fighting against!"

Talmadge's face was mottled and his jowls shook. "I love my daughter, but I won't stand—"

"Love her! Hah!" Tommy Lee glared, jamming his fists onto his hips. "If you love her you've got a damned strange way of showing it. You don't give a damn what she's feeling. All you care about is protecting yourself from having to admit that the decision you made twenty-four years ago made more people miserable than you'd care to count!"

"Don't go laying the blame on me, Gentry. You screwed up your life all by yourself. You didn't need any help from me!"

Exasperated, Tommy Lee rammed four fingers through his damp hair and shook his head. "How blind can you be, man? How long are you going to keep fighting what's right before your eyes? Rachel and I never should have been forced apart—never! We tried to tell you that twenty-four years ago, but you and my mama and daddy knew so much better than Rachel and me what was good for us, didn't you?"

"And if I hadn't, where would she have ended up? Married to a drunkard who couldn't be satisfied with one woman."

"She was the only one I ever wanted, and you know it," Tommy Lee growled dangerously.

"Well, you finally got her, didn't you? And you made sure the whole town knew it by leaving your car in front of her house all night long!"

Suddenly Rachel intervened. "What about me? You talk as if I had no choice in the matter. Daddy, I asked him here. I did *not* ask you. I should think, since you saw the car, you would have had the common decency to respect my privacy."

"Don't you go preaching to me about common decency, missy! Not when I walk in here and find your clothes floating on the top of the pool and him half naked at eight o'clock in the morning!"

"That's exactly what you did! You walked right in as if it were your God-given right. Well, it's not. I'm all grown up now, Daddy, and this is my house, and you have no right to walk into it unannounced and give me a lecture on how to live my life!"

Her fists were clenched, and the tendons in her neck stood out. Everett raised a hand in appeal. "Rachel, for God's sake, don't you care what people think?"

"No, not anymore. I've lived my whole life according to some nebulous code that you pushed down my throat. But there's no room in that code for mitigating circumstances, is there? Tommy Lee has changed. I've changed." She pressed her hands against her chest and leaned toward him supplicatingly. "Why can't you see that?"

"All I see is a daughter I have to be ashamed of. Lord, girl, I protected you from gossip all these years. What do you suppose it does to me to see you take up with him again?"

"Daddy, please, for once, could you think about my feelings instead of your own? Would you ask yourself *why* I'm with him again?"

His face grew hard and he pierced Tommy Lee with a venomous gaze that passed from his naked chest to his bare toes. "I believe that's altogether too obvious."

Rachel moved a step nearer Tommy Lee until her shoulder blades touched his chest. "No. You're seeing only what you want to see. Your own stubbornness is making you blind. Daddy, I love him. Can't you accept that and let us all try to forget the past?"

Everett's face turned scornful. "Love him! For God's sake, girl, don't delude yourself because I caught you red-handed."

Tommy Lee's hands came up to rest on Rachel's shoulders as he stated, "It's you who are deluding yourself, Talmadge. I have a feeling it's the only way you could have lived with the decision you made all those years ago."

The sight of Tommy Lee's hands resting possessively on Rachel's shoulders made Everett cringe. "Marshall would have—"

"No, Daddy." Rachel's eyes closed for a long moment, as if in finality. "You've chosen all the men for me you're ever going to. Marshall is a carbon body of Owen, and though it's taken me some soul-searching to admit it, Owen was not the kind of man I needed to make me happy. This time I'm doing the picking," she ended prophetically.

Her voice softened to an appealing note. "Daddy, Tommy Lee has asked me to marry him. If I do, will we have to fight you every step of the way, just like before? Would you do that to us . . . again?"

Everett's shock was complete. He gaped from Rachel to the man behind her, and to his daughter again. "You can't mean it. Rachel, you've never had a vindictive bone in your body, but if you're doing this just to get back at me for—"

"No, Daddy. I told you. I love him." On her shoulders, Tommy Lee's hands tightened reassuringly.

Everett sensed himself losing ground and blustered, "You love some . . . some teenage fantasy. But we're talking about real life here. We're talking about a man with three ex-wives!"

To Tommy Lee's surprise, she smiled and squeezed his fingers, which still rested on her collarbone. "Then I'd better watch my p's and q's, hadn't I?"

Everett was stupefied. "Rachel, for the love of God—"

But she calmly stepped forward and cut him off. "Daddy, as I said earlier, I didn't invite you here." She led the way toward the foyer without turning to see if he followed, but when she reached it, he was right on her heels, hoping to talk some sense into her. He didn't get the chance. She opened the door and stood waiting for him to walk through it. "In the future when you come to see me, I'd appreciate your knocking before you come in."

When she had closed the door behind his angrily stalking form, she turned to find Tommy Lee waiting in the archway. He opened his arms and she walked into them and clung, her cheek pressed against the silky hair on his chest, and his arms circling her shoulder tenaciously. "Darling, I'm so sorry," he said gruffly.

She was trembling uncontrollably as she shook her head against his chest. "No, it's not your fault. Oh, Tommy Lee, how could he just . . . just come in here like that and start shouting at you?"

He rubbed her shoulder and kissed the top of her hair. "He's desperate, Rachel. He's clung to his self-righteousness for a long time. Imagine how frightening it is to a man like him to have to admit he was wrong."

"But he's so bullheaded! Would it hurt him for once to say, okay, Rachel, go ahead and love Tommy Lee, and be happy?"

Tommy Lee's warm palm rubbed her spine. "Did you ever stop to think that maybe he's a little jealous, too? He's had you to himself for quite a while."

She pulled back and gaped up at him in surprise. "Jealous? But he was never jealous of Owen or . . . or Marshall."

"He didn't need to be. He could control them."

She sighed wearily and fell against him. "Oh, I'm so tired of it all. All I want is for everyone to see how foolish all this hostility has been, and settle it once and for all so we can get on with our lives." He folded her close to him again and rocked her gently. After several minutes she murmured plaintively, "Oh, Tommy Lee, remember how it used to be? When we were young and our mothers would be having iced tea on the lawn and you and I would come charging out of the house with our tennis rackets? They'd smile and wave, and tell us to have a good time. I've often wondered, if my mother had lived, would it have made a difference? She was so different from Daddy."

She heard Tommy Lee swallow against her temple. "They were like second parents to me."

She rubbed her hands along his back, feeling his steady heartbeat against her breast, wondering again if love was powerful enough to overcome such long-standing enmities. Loving him, even marrying him, would never be enough. Until the hostilities were over, the two of them could never know complete serenity.

"Tommy Lee?"

"Hm?"

"I want to make a bargain with you."

He drew back, tilting his head to see her face. "A bargain?"

She looked up with eloquent brown eyes, hoping what she was doing was right.

"A bargain."

"What kind of bargain?"

"You . . . you still want to marry me?"

He released a breathy, rueful laugh that said it all, and she went on, fixing him with her steady eyes. "I'll promise to marry you if you'll promise to go see your mama and daddy and make peace with them."

She felt him begin to stiffen and quickly framed his jaws with both hands, holding him where he was. "Please, hear me out. When you pull away and get that look on your face you remind me of Daddy. In your own way you're as stubborn as he is, don't you see?"

Tommy Lee didn't appreciate being compared to Everett. He gave an ironic sniff, but she forced him to listen to reason.

"The only way it'll work for us is if we make every attempt at forgiving," she went on. "You've just said my daddy is frightened of admitting he's been wrong all these years. Well, aren't you, too? So where do we start putting an end to it all?" When he tried to pull away again she held him, continuing persuasively, "Oh, Tommy Lee, I saw the look on your mama's face—and your daddy's, too—when they saw you walk up those church steps last Sunday. They love you and they miss you terribly, and whether you want to admit it or not, you miss them, too. You're their only son, and Beth is their granddaughter. Isn't it time you became a family again?"

Beneath her palms she felt his tense muscles and quivering nerves, and made small, soothing circles with her thumbs on his cheeks. "I want to tell you something that I've never told you before," she said in an equally soothing voice, studying his deep, dark eyes. "Your mother and father were against sending me away. My mother told me before she died. She was never happy with the estrangement between the two couples, but there was little she could do, given my father's stubbornness. He's very strong-willed, and he talked your parents and my mother into agreeing with him about giving the baby up for adoption. I spent years blaming all of them equally, but it was really my father who forced the issue. If I can forgive him, can't you forgive your parents, too?"

She could see his defenses weakening and rushed on. "I'll help you. I'll go with you if you want. You and I together have a chance to show them how to forgive. Maybe . . . just maybe, if we take the first step, they'll follow suit." She smiled at the idea. "Imagine it—we could set off a whole chain reaction."

But Tommy Lee remained unconvinced. "You're so idealistic. What if they throw me out?"

Behind his words she sensed a vulnerability that touched her heart. "They won't. You know they won't. All it'll take is for one of you to make the first move."

"And you really think if we can patch things up with them they'll suddenly soften toward Everett?"

"It's worth a chance, isn't it?"

"And what about this newest fracas? Are you forgetting you just threw your daddy out of your house? I'd say that leaves you and him with some patching up of your own to do."

She dropped her hands from his face, but captured the two ends of the towel that hung around his neck. "We've fought before. But in the end we always seem to realize that we're the only family left. You leave him up to me for the time being. When he sees me happily married to you, he's bound to soften." She smiled up at him. "There's something you have to realize about my daddy. Underneath all that bluster he has a grudging respect for anybody who'll stand up to him." She tugged on the towel and drew him down for a short kiss. "So what do you say?"

"You drive a hard bargain, Rachel."

Suddenly she saw through the idealist's eyes he accused her of having and slipped her hands beneath the towel, locking her fingers behind his neck while meeting his brown eyes intensely. "I want it to be the way it used to be."

"It'll never be the way it used to be."

"It could be better." She squeezed his neck for emphasis. "It *could* be . . . you know it could. You, me, your parents, my father . . . and Beth. What about her? You're cheating her out of her own grandparents by carrying this grudge."

"I know." He sighed wearily and drew her into his arms, resting his chin on top of her head. "I know."

"Grandparents can be a wonderful influence on young people, and vice versa. And besides"—she kissed his Adam's apple—"I thought I was the woman you'd do anything in the world for."

Somewhere in the house, bacon was burning and the buttons of a shirt sang out against the metal tumbler of a dryer. Tommy Lee folded Rachel against his heart and buried his face in the flower-scented skin of her neck, realizing that if things went right he had within his grasp the chance of gaining back everything he'd once had taken from him.

Rachel was very wise, knowing even better than he how badly his old wounds needed to be cauterized. "You'll really do it, Rachel? You'll marry me?" he asked hoarsely.

"Don't you think it's time?" came her trembling reply.

He drew back to look into her dark eyes, and his own traversed her face, cataloging it feature by feature while his thumbs brushed the crests of her cheekbones. Her lips were slightly parted, her hair in disarray, and the expression in her eyes was one he'd dreamed of seeing there during the endless years when nothing and no one else could quite fill the empty spot in his heart.

"Oh, Rachel . . . my Rachel." He dropped his forehead against hers, letting his eyes sink shut, capturing the essence of the moment to carry within him as a talisman during the days ahead. "How I love you."

She swallowed back the tears in her throat. "I love you, too . . . so much."

Then their mouths were joined and emotions billowed. They clung together in an ardent kiss, pressing their bodies close, hands wandering impatiently now that the decision was made.

Abruptly Tommy Lee drew back, holding her head with both hands. "When?" Without giving her time to answer, he rushed on, "Right away, as soon as we can get a license and find somebody to do it. I want us to have a honeymoon, so you'll have to make arrangements at the store, and afterward . . . which house do you want to live at? I'd live here if you asked me to, but . . . oh, Rachel, say you'll move into my house on the lake. God, it'll be like a dream—"

"Hold on." She couldn't resist chuckling at his impetuousness. "Aren't you forgetting something?"

He frowned in puzzlement. "What?"

"Beth. Shouldn't I meet her first? Don't you think we should get her approval, since she's going to be part of the family, too?"

"Oh, Beth." He wrapped Rachel loosely in his arms and rocked her. "Beth is going to love you."

He said it with such thoughtless conviction there seemed no other way it could be.

Chapter 12

THE EXPRESSION ON his daughter's face when Tommy Lee walked into his house less than an hour later warned him trouble lay ahead.

"Where *were* you all night?" She stood with both hands stuffed into the tight pockets of her blue jeans, a scowl on her face.

"Oh!" He came up short, searching for a reply. "Did you wait up for me?"

"Hardly. That's what *parents* usually do. Georgine wanted to leave for home, and when you weren't getting up and weren't getting up she sent me in to wake you, but your bed wasn't even slept in."

Tommy Lee was saved from replying when Georgine came around the corner with her purse in her hand, her lips drawn up tight and a disapproving tilt to her chin.

"We already had breakfast *and* cleaned up the dishes *and* called town to say I'd be gettin' there late!"

"I'm sorry, Georgine. If you're ready I'll take you now."

"If I'm ready . . . hmph." She snorted past him on her way to the door, and Tommy Lee asked himself for the hundredth time why he put up with her insubordination. He truly disliked the woman, but now that Beth was here, he needed her more than ever.

"You wanna ride along, honey?" he invited Beth.

"No," she pouted, crossing her arms stubbornly.

"You sure? We could talk."

"I'm sure."

But he could see the hurt in her eyes. "Back in half an hour and we'll spend the day doing whatever you want to, okay, sugar?"

For a minute the stubborn expression remained on her chin, but at last she nodded.

In the car Georgine sat as if she had spine trouble, her mouth as sour-looking as if she'd just bitten into a kumquat.

"Georgine, I'm sorry I wasn't here to get you into town right away this morning."

"Ain't me you should be sayin' you're sorry to; it's your daughter. Impressionable young girl like that—what she gonna think?"

Tommy Lee imagined she'd think exactly what she was thinking, but he wasn't going to admit it to Georgine. He hadn't given a thought to Beth last night and realized too late the import of his having been out all night, especially given Beth's age. He was not accustomed to having restrictions put on his freedom, but Georgine was right. He certainly hadn't set a good example.

When he got back home he found Beth in the kitchen stirring something at the stove. Her hair fell down the center of her back in a single French braid, and even from behind he could see the first curves of maturity already beginning to sculpt her body. She had a waist now, and gently swelling hips tapering into long legs. She had fought with her mother over a boy after Nancy caught the two of them kissing, which had started the whole fiasco that finally led to Beth's running away and ending up here.

The eternal taboo on sex, he thought ruefully, going back for a moment to when he and Rachel had been the same age Beth was now. He stood for a long minute with his hands in his trouser pockets, studying her, wondering how to handle the delicate situation. He could tell from the way her head was drooped that she was upset with him and maybe a little shy about facing him.

"Still mad at me, huh?" he asked quietly.

She shrugged, but still didn't turn around.

"You don't even want to talk to me?"

Again came the sheepish shrug. He couldn't help smiling—so young, so idealistic. He moved up behind her and cupped a hand around the side of her neck.

"I'm sorry, baby. I've got no excuses."

She stared into the kettle and kept stirring. "After the show I brought the kids back here to meet you, and you weren't even home."

"I said I'm sorry. It won't happen again, and that's a promise."

"Where *were* you?"

This time it was his turn to withhold an answer. In spite of the fact that he'd planned to tell Beth about Rachel immediately, he was reluctant now, for fear it might cast a shadow over his daughter's impression of the woman he loved.

"You were with a woman, weren't you?"

"Beth, I'm forty-one years old."

At last she turned and lifted accusing eyes to his. "I know who it was. It was that one on the church steps, wasn't it?"

For a moment their eyes clashed; then Tommy Lee sighed and held her by both shoulders. "What makes you say that?"

"I could *see* how you were looking at her, Daddy. I'm not exactly a *child.*"

"Her name is Rachel, and the first thing I want you to understand is that I love her."

"Mother always said you liked other women too much and that's why she got divorced from you."

"Beth, I'm not going to argue with you about your mother. It's pointless."

Suddenly tears brimmed on Beth's eyelids. "But I don't understand . . . She got mad at me when all I did was kiss a boy. But you . . . well, you . . . you stayed out all night. You mean it's not okay when you're fourteen, but it's perfectly all right when you're forty-one?"

Tommy Lee didn't know how to answer. There could be no double standard, and to claim there was would be hypocritical. He had wanted a second chance at being a father. Now here it was, and he was finding out exactly how difficult fatherhood could be.

"No, sweetheart," he admitted, "I'm not saying that. I'm saying that at forty-one a person is better equipped to handle the consequences of his actions. But your mother is wrong about one thing. There's no reason to feel guilty for kissing boys when you're fourteen years old. As a matter of fact, that's exactly how old I was when I started kissing girls, and you know who the first one was?"

She shook her head, mesmerized by the sudden turn of the conversation.

He smiled, looking down into her pretty brown eyes, the freckles on her cheeks, her generous bowed lips, which were very much like his. "It was Rachel Talmadge—that was her name then."

"You've known her that long?"

"Uh-huh. Since we were kids."

But instead of impressing Beth, the fact made her stiffen and pull away. Puzzled, Tommy Lee watched her turn toward the stove again, and the momentary rapport between them was broken.

"I made you grits and sausage while you were gone, since Georgine didn't hold breakfast for you."

He watched her get a plate and spoon grits onto it, then move to the sink to fill the kettle with water, and he was suddenly weary, wondering how to deal with her jealousy. She stabbed three sausage links and added them to the plate, switched off the burners and turned expectantly with her offering in her hands, and Tommy Lee thought, *Lord, will the way ever be smooth for Rachel and me?*

"You don't like talking 'bout Rachel, do you?" he asked.

Her tone was defensive as she blurted out, "I wish Mother had been your first girlfriend. Then maybe you'd still be married to her."

And after that it seemed best to drop the subject of Rachel for the time being until things smoothed over a little bit.

During the weekend Beth displayed an increasing possessiveness about her father. Though he admitted he was again being manipulated by a female smart enough to realize he felt guilty and to use that guilt to get what she wanted, he went along readily with her plan for him to take her shopping for school clothes in Muscle Shoals. The following morning when they glimpsed Rachel on the church steps, Beth commandeered Tommy Lee's arm and maneuvered him inside before he got a chance to talk to her. The remainder of that day was devoted to taking Beth's new friends waterskiing, and when the afternoon finally ended, Tommy Lee wanted nothing so badly as to see Rachel for a couple of hours, having thought of nothing but her for two solid days. But when he casually mentioned that he thought he'd drive into town to pick up some things from his office to glance through at home, Beth immediately said she'd ride along with him.

Finally, late Sunday night, Tommy Lee escaped to his room so he could call Rachel. At the sound of her hello a sharp upthrusting stab of love pressed beneath his heart and suddenly everything seemed right again.

"I've missed you," he breathed, closing his eyes, lying flat on his back across the bed.

"And I've missed you. I looked for you all day today."

"I'm sorry I couldn't make it, but it appears we have one problem I hadn't counted on."

"It's Beth, isn't it?"

He rubbed the corners of his eyes. "God, is it ever. She acts as if she doesn't want me out of her sight for a minute. She wasn't exactly happy to see me getting home in the middle of Saturday morning and wanted to know where I'd been."

"Did you tell her?"

"She guessed." He scowled at the ceiling.

"She guessed? . . . But how?"

"She called you 'the woman on the church steps.' "

"Ahh . . . of course."

"Was I that obvious when I looked at you?"

Rachel's soft laugh came over the wire. "Was I?" He pictured her as she'd been Friday night, soft, pliant, smelling sweeter than anything nature had ever conjured up. He felt his body nudging toward arousal at the mental images.

"All I've thought about since walking out of your house is you. While I was chauffeuring Beth all over Muscle Shoals, and driving a speedboat full of shrieking teenagers, I wanted to be only one place."

"Where?" she murmured in a soft, seductive voice. It was not the words that mattered, rather the subtle nuances of two lovers infatuated with the mere act of listening to each other breathe.

"In your bed. In you."

Her breath again seemed to brush his ear. "Tommy Lee, I want to see you tonight. Can't you come over?"

"I'm tempted, darlin', but if I did I'd never come back home, and I promised Beth I'd be spending nights here from now on."

She sighed in disappointment, and he pictured her curling into a ball in the middle of her bed. "When will I see you again?"

"Tomorrow afternoon. I'll pick you up as soon as you close the store."

"I'll have my own car there. Meet me at the house instead."

"Do you think we can hang in there till then?"

"I don't know. We have a lot of lost time to make up for, don't we?"

His voice held a tremor as he declared, "But we will, babe, we will."

"I can't wait. Can you stay for supper tomorrow?"

No matter how much he wanted to, he answered, "I'm afraid not. Beth's got something special planned for the two of us. She's doing the cooking."

"Well, next time, then."

"Next time for sure." Tommy Lee stifled a yawn—he hadn't had much sleep all weekend. "Rachel, I'm exhausted. I've been on the water all day."

But she wasn't ready to give him up yet. "Are you in the bedroom?" she asked.

"Yes, staring at the ceiling and picturing you as you were Friday night."

"*Our* bedroom?" she inquired softly.

"Yes . . . *our* bedroom."

"What's it like?"

"It's carpeted in blue to match the lake. The whole west wall is glass, and it's the only room in the house with draperies—they're the color of the sand on the beach. There's a king-size bed with a spread that's striped and kind of soft."

"What's it made of?"

"Made of?" He rolled his head to check it out, smiling at the questions women came up with. "Hell, I don't know. It's got stitches all over it."

"It's quilted, you mean?"

"I guess so."

"Well, if I'm going to sleep there I have to know these things. Go on. Tell me more."

As teenagers, late at night after curfew, they used to talk on the phone like this—lazy inanities, unimportant chatter meant to do nothing more than delay the inevitable good-bye. Tommy Lee smiled, assessed the room, and imagined her entering it for the first time. "Across from the foot of the bed is a fireplace smaller than the one downstairs and with an arched opening. And do you remember once years and years ago when you told me you liked rocking chairs?"

"No, did I?"

"Well, there are two of them, big fat things covered with some kind of fuzzy blue stuff, one on either side of the fireplace. There's a walk-in closet big enough to put your whole store into." She chuckled appreciatively and he went on. "And beside the closet door is a valet chair with nothing on it at all right now. Everything's neatly put away."

There wasn't even a hint of laughter as she sighed. "Oh, Tommy Lee, I love you. I can't wait to live there with you."

At her confession his heart cracked like a flag in high wind, and he experienced the renewed wonder of dreams coming true.

"Tell me again, Rachel—I still have trouble believing it."

"I love you," she whispered.

He closed his eyes, absently running his free hand over the quilted spread as if it were her skin. "I want us to get married as soon as possible."

"I do, too. Did you tell Beth we want to?"

His eyes opened to study the ceiling again, and the hand that had been stroking the spread rested with its wrist against his forehead. "No, not yet."

"So she really is upset about the other night?"

"I'm afraid so."

"I should have thought of her. How selfish of me to keep you here overnight."

"You'd have played hell trying to get me to leave—don't you know that?" She laughed, but the sound was slightly strained. He drew a deep breath and went on, "Don't worry about Beth. I'll tell her soon. Then I want the two of you to meet. Properly. Out here at the house where we're all going to make it as a family. We are, Rachel, I swear it," he pledged intensely. Then, as if sealing a vow, he added prophetically, "Tommy Lee and Rachel and Beth."

"I'll hang on to that thought," she promised. "And I'll see you tomorrow at five."

The clock seemed to crawl as the following afternoon waned. Just before closing, Rachel stepped into the washroom to check her hair, dust her cheeks with blusher, touch a wisp of scent to her throat, and apply fresh rosy gloss to her lips.

In fifteen minutes I'll be with him again.

Her heart felt borne aloft by a bevy of butterflies. Life was a constant surprise. Who ever would have said one week ago that she would be experiencing this resurgent zest that lit her eyes, put a lilt in her step, and made her press a hand to her heart, as if to hold it captive within her body? And all this at the mere thought of Tommy Lee Gentry.

It was uncanny how one could revert to self-indulgent daydreaming when smitten by love, no matter what one's age. All day long she'd been wondering what he'd be wearing, what he'd say when he first saw her, fantasizing about their first kiss, making love, and following it up with an intimate talk, snuggled close in a nest of pillows.

His Blazer was in the driveway when she pulled around the corner and depressed the activator for the automatic garage door. He got out and stood with his hands on his hips, watching her drive past him into the garage. He was dressed in tight tan jeans, white leather tennis shoes and a sporty baby-blue pullover with a V-neck. The first thing he said was "Come here." He had opened her car door and was waiting to haul her into his arms even before she captured her purse from the seat. They stood in the wedge of the open car door, her arms clinging to his neck, her breasts buried against his hard chest, kissing recklessly, murmuring in the wordless, insatiable way of lovers who'd thought this moment would never come.

His tongue was hot and insistent as it roved the contours of her mouth, and hers brought an answering urgency as it tasted and tantalized. His hands spread wide, covering her back with demanding caresses before dropping low to ride her hips, then the curve of her buttocks as their bodies pressed together in anticipation, then swayed from side to side in an age-old message of accord.

Their heads slanted, changing directions as their mouths remained locked, open and impatient. His hand cupped her breast and hers found his naked back, slipping beneath the ribbed waistband of his sweater onto the warm flesh. His thumb rubbed her nipple and she shivered and thrust her tongue more forcefully into his mouth. She ran her hands over the back pockets of his jeans, drawing him as close as possible, holding him as he'd held her a moment ago.

When at last the initial rush of possessiveness had been accommodated, they drew apart, found each other's eyes, then clung again, rapturously.

"My God, did you ever think it could be this way again?" he asked breathlessly.

"Never! I've felt like a teenager all day!"

Again he backed away to look into her radiant eyes. "You, too?"

She smiled and nodded a little sheepishly. Then they were laughing and holding hands as he impatiently hauled her after him toward the back door. He flung it wide and tugged her inside behind him, both of them giddy, giggly, and slightly flushed . . . and came up short at the sight of Callie Mae, spreading chocolate frosting on a pan of brownies.

The older woman swung around, her eyes flew wide, and she gave a chortle of amusement. "Well, I declare, if it ain't that nasty li'l Tommy Lee Gentry, used to come snitchin' my cookies just before suppertime."

Tommy Lee and Rachel gaped at the maid, then at each other, then burst out laughing again before Tommy Lee lunged across the room to give the woman a bone-crushing hug. "Callie Mae, you crusty old despot—damn, it's good to see you!"

She backed off to adore him with glistening eyes while his hands pressed her thick waist.

"Lord, Lord, but ain't you a sight for these tired old eyes—you and Miss Rachel, come a-laughin' in the way you used to." A tear plumped on her eyelid as she hugged him again, and Rachel looked on with glowing eyes. Suddenly Callie Mae pulled back and her heavy pink lips took on a scolding pout. "Been wonderin' when the two o' you would come to your senses."

Tommy Lee cocked one eyebrow and suppressed a grin. "Oh, you have, have you?"

She turned back to her brownies, giving an indignant sniff, while Tommy Lee's and Rachel's eyes met and shared an instant of powerful nostalgia. Memories tumbled back, of another time, another kitchen, two sun-drenched children scampering in to the gruff but loving maid who, like them, never questioned their rightful place together. Washed now in Callie Mae's benediction—the first, after facing so much opposition—they felt hopeful and ebullient. It was like stepping into a scene in which the action had been frozen twenty-four years ago and had been waiting all that time for them to walk on stage and bring about a happy conclusion.

Tommy Lee looped an arm around Callie Mae's shoulders and turned his attention toward the counter. "What're you cookin' up there, darlin'?"

"Why, just one o' your favorites. My prize-winnin' chocolate brownies with plenty of pecans, just how you like 'em."

"Whoo-ee!" He licked his lips. "Them's mighty hard to resist." Tommy Lee pointedly checked his watch, then let a grin crawl up one corner of his mouth. "And besides, it's a whole hour before supper." He snatched the spatula from Callie Mae's fingers and dug a bar from the corner of the pan, lifting it to lick an icicle of fresh frosting that oozed over the edge.

Callie Mae laughed, gave him a playful swat, and nodded in Rachel's direction. "You wanna do something, you git *her* to eat brownies. She's the one needs 'em!"

Tommy Lee turned around, smiling.

Rachel chuckled and said to him, "See what I've been putting up with all these years?"

"Mmm . . . Callie Mae is kind of mouthy, all right. She might not work out after all."

"She might not. On the other hand, I *am* rather used to her outspokenness. And you'll have to admit, she *is* a pretty decent cook."

Tommy Lee swallowed his mouthful of brownie and shrugged indifferently. "Yeah, these are all right, I guess."

"All right?" Callie Mae exploded, swinging around with her hands on her hips.

Tommy Lee took another nonchalant bite, grinned at Rachel, and asked teasingly, "Think we should tell her?" He wandered over and held the brownie to her lips.

She took a nibble, grinned, and returned conspiratorially, "I don't know. What do you think? Should we?"

"Tell me what?" Callie Mae insisted.

Rachel took a bigger bite of brownie and the frosting fell in a string down her lip. She reached up to swipe at it, but Tommy Lee waylaid her hand, then

held the wrist while leaning forward to lick the frosting off. Without removing his eyes from Rachel's, he smiled and answered Callie Mae, "Might be a new job opening up for you."

"A new . . . ?" But Callie Mae's lips fell open and her eyes sparkled with speculation as she watched Tommy Lee lean down and place a lingering kiss on Rachel's uplifted mouth, the brownie all but forgotten in his fingertips.

He lifted his head lazily, and still gazing into Rachel's eyes, added, "Out at my place."

Callie Mae's beaming eyes rested on the two she'd loved for so long, as Rachel rose up to brush Tommy Lee's lips once more, then added dreamily, "Working for both of us."

Callie Mae rolled her eyes heavenward, threw her hands wide, and exclaimed, "Lord o' mercy . . . at last!" She watched them kiss again, and when they drew apart, they seemed to have forgotten anyone else in the room. "Hmph!" Callie Mae snorted. "I can see there ain't no need for me to hang around here no longer. Act like I don't count for nothin' . . ." She grumbled on in mock reprimand while whipping off her apron. "Person ain't never done teachin' children their manners . . . fine thing, bein' ignored." She threw open a pantry door, hung up the apron with a flourish, and swept up her purse. She was still muttering as the door slammed behind her.

At the sound, the pair in the kitchen seemed to come awake. They glanced at the door, then at each other, and laughed while Rachel flung her arms about Tommy Lee's neck.

"Everyone will know now," she said.

"Do you care?" he asked against her hair.

"No. All I care about is you . . . us. I missed you so much."

"I missed you, too . . . every minute."

Their mouths met again eagerly as he reached out blindly to set the brownie on the counter. His fingers were coated with chocolate, and when he lifted his hands to impatiently lick off a thumb she captured the hand and carried it from his pursed lips to her own, meticulously laving each finger, slipping it into her mouth with sensual slowness, aroused by the salt-sweet taste of him, by the heavy, hooded look that overtook his eyes as he watched. When the fingers were clean she ran her tongue down the palm of his hand and bit its heel, while his relaxed fingertips rested on her closed eyes. She kissed his wrist, the metal band of his watch warm beneath her lips, then moved beyond it to the soft warm skin of his inner elbow.

Suddenly he pulled her head to his chest, groaning softly, and beneath her ear she heard his pounding heart as his fingers plowed through her hair to contour her skull and cradle her head possessively.

She felt an outpouring of love, far too powerful to be voiced. And as she raised her eyes to his, she saw it returned a thousandfold. They stood close, caught in the shaft of late-afternoon sun melting through the window. It glinted off the golden rim of his glasses, scintillated from her open lips, gilded the gray above his ears. Had they loved this fully at sixteen? Perhaps it had seemed so then. But in this moment as they stood bound together by feelings so profound as to be voiceless, their lorn love of long ago seemed paltry by comparison.

She reached both hands up to slip off his glasses and set them beside the brownie on the counter. His hands clasped her jaws as his mouth descended —open, hungry, purposeful. Her answering lunge and lift were all he needed before his fingers trembled over buttons, hooks, and zippers, and they knew again the swift swelling of sexual appetite, appeasing it with little thought of time or place. In moments they stood among scattered articles of clothing, pressing their naked bodies together, exulting. He lifted her to his waist and her legs twined about his hips, the vacant core of her femininity seeking only one restitution: to be filled by him. The contact was sleek, immediate, and restorative as their bodies reunited and their arms clenched possessively.

He perched her on the edge of the counter, and the sun burned warm on her shoulders as his lean hands parenthesized her hips. Dark eyes captured and held hers. Lips parted. Breath mingled. The movement began.

And in moments Rachel and Tommy Lee shared that glorious outpouring of body and soul found only by the very lucky—by those who bring unquestioning love to the act. When their matched cries echoed through the kitchen, she held his head to her breast and sighed in repletion.

His shoulders were damp—she brushed the sheen from them.

His heartbeat was uneven—she pressed a palm to it.

His eyelids were closed—she kissed them.

And in the end he stayed for a late, late supper.

Chapter 13

A WEEK PASSED, during which Rachel and Tommy Lee had only stolen hours together whenever possible, but "stealing" time left them dissatisfied and impatient. Only one thing happened that brought them smiles. Tommy Lee had to make an unexpected overnight trip, and before leaving town he stalked, unannounced, into Panache, crossed straight to Rachel, and dropped a heedless kiss on her mouth. "Hello, darling. I've got to fly to Atlanta and I won't be back till tomorrow. Thought I'd better let you know before I left."

Verda stood taking it all in, her jaw hanging slack.

"Atlanta?"

"Uh-huh. I'm on my way to the airport now." Oddly enough, Rachel didn't even consider subterfuge. She merely removed her reading glasses, left her desk, and followed his impatient figure to the door.

"Business?" she asked.

"Yes. Some land I've been thinking about buying that somebody else has suddenly taken an interest in. I'd rather not go right now, but it can't be helped. If anything comes up, you can reach me at the Sheraton. Okay?" He was already reaching for the doorknob.

"Okay. Have a safe trip. I'll see you when you get back."

Distractedly he dropped a parting kiss on her mouth while she held the door open, and then he left in a rush.

When he called her, late that night, she casually mentioned, "You threw Verda into major shock when you came sashaying into the shop that way and kissed me."

His laughter came across the wire. Then he asked, "What'd she say?"

Now it was Rachel's turn to laugh. "Are you sure you want to know?"

"Of course. You've piqued my interest."

"She said, 'I thought he wasn't pesterin' you!' "

When his second round of laughter died, Tommy Lee asked teasingly, "Am I pesterin' you, Rachel?"

"You bet. Please hurry home so we can get on with it."

But their bit of mirth at Verda's expense was the only lighthearted escape they shared during those days when intimacy was denied them. He returned the following evening straight to her arms as if he'd been gone a fortnight. They shared a quick and frenzied reunion. Then he tore himself away, declaring he *had* to get home and spend some time with Beth, especially since he had missed the supper she'd painstakingly prepared for him several nights earlier plus several others, and had found little time to devote to her since.

"I'm sorry, Rachel. I'd like to stay longer, but I'd better go home and try to smooth the waters."

"You don't have to apologize, darling. I understand. But don't you think it would be better if you introduced the two of us so that she can see I'm not trying to snatch her father and lure him away from her?"

He smiled and squeezed her arms. "You're right."

But she could see he was apprehensive about it. "When?"

He drew a deep breath and seemed to pluck an answer from the air before he could change his mind. "This weekend. When the dragon isn't around."

But one day before the weekend, the shop door opened and Rachel glanced up to find three teenage girls entering. Since her merchandise was targeted chiefly at mature middle-income women, girls of this age rarely shopped at Panache. She smiled a welcome. Then her heart seemed to pause in trepidation as she recognized Beth as one of the three, though Beth didn't give Rachel so much as a glance.

She had a pretty little face, and Tommy Lee's mouth, but her attractiveness was spoiled by a smug expression as she sauntered into the store with her giddy friends. They were obviously in one of those abhorrent adolescent moods that can seize a band of normally polite teenage girls and change them into rude little minxes who delight in disdaining anything smacking of middle-aged maturity.

They were a little too loud and disruptively brash as they invaded the store, plucking at this item and that, dropping them in distaste and making faces at one another that sent them into spasms of laughter.

"Hello, girls, can I help you?"

One of the trio hooked her thumbs in the rear pockets of her jeans and answered while she chewed gum exaggeratedly, "Naw, just checkin' things out. Gotta buy somethin' for my grandmaw." Then she made some inside comment to the other two that sent them into giggles as they sashayed toward a rack of autumn dresses. More rude giggling started as one of them plucked a hanger down and held the dress against her.

"Well, look as long as you like, and let me know if there's anything I can show you."

"Sure, lady," their spokesman said, then turned away, adding something under her breath that brought snickers to her friends and a flush of anger to Rachel's cheeks.

It was Verda's day off, so Rachel was alone in the store, sitting at her desk in the corner, working on invoices. She slipped her reading glasses back onto her nose, pretending to go back to what she was doing, but stingingly aware that Beth Gentry had still not even glanced her way.

The girls worked their way through the store systematically, while Rachel carefully ignored them, wondering whether to get up and politely introduce herself to Beth. But before she could decide, the other two moved to the French armoire where they tried on a wide-brimmed felt hat, leaving Beth to pore over the jewelry at the center counter. Rachel wrote her name on a check, inserted it into an envelope, and licked it shut. Finally she gave in to the urge and raised her eyes, only to have the blood seem to drop to her toes.

The deep-set eyes of Beth Gentry were fixed upon her in unconcealed dislike, issuing a hard, cold challenge that said, "Hands off my father." And while skewering Rachel with that unmistakable message, Beth blatantly slipped a silver bangle bracelet over her wrist. Rachel's eyes dropped to it, and her lips opened to protest as she instinctively began to leave her chair. But she froze, her hands still braced on the edge of the desk, and glanced up at Beth again to find the undisguised defiance still sizzling at her. It was obvious Beth considered her a rival for her father's attention.

Rachel remained poised, tense and shocked, her mind racing with indecision, while she and Beth raced off in a pivotal moment that would undoubtedly dictate the tone of their future relationship.

There was scarcely time to think. Rachel's reaction happened within seconds, though it seemed hours that she hovered with Beth's defiant eyes locked on her own. Then Rachel relaxed her shoulders, dropped her hands from the desk, and sat back in her chair while Beth lowered her wrist, shook the bracelet into place and let a victorious grin slip to the corner of her mouth. Without removing her eyes from Rachel, she called, "Come on, you guys, there's nothing in this place even your grandma would want." Then, with an imperious toss of the shoulder, she swung around and led the way out the door.

Rachel sat stunned.

What should I do?

It's too late now. You made your choice and she won.

She threw her glasses off, leaned her elbows on the desk, and covered her face. The nerves in her stomach were trembling. She was angry and depressed and upset. Did the whole world have to defy her and Tommy Lee? Was there some unholy force working to thwart their happiness, no matter how hard they tried to achieve it? What had she done that was so terrible? *What?* She had fallen in love with a man and was willing to make room in her life for his daughter, share him with her, and try to make a family. But how was that possible now?

She threw herself back in the chair and whammed a fist on the desktop — something totally out of character for Rachel.

Damn that girl.

Couldn't she see how little happiness her father had had in his life? Couldn't she understand how her jealousy was distressing him?

Rachel lurched from her chair, slipped her hands into the front slash pockets of her tailored skirt, and stood at the front window, staring out unseeingly.

So what do I do now? Tell him? Add this to the burden he's already carrying? Give Beth Gentry the opportunity to deny having stolen the bracelet and turn the situation to her advantage by declaring that *Rachel* was jealous of *her*? Could a girl of fourteen be that devious? Given what she'd just done, the question seemed ludicrous. Tommy Lee had said she was hovering on the brink. Rachel's reaction to this incident could be the nudge that pushed her over or the tug that drew her back. Rachel dropped her chin to her chest, staring at her shoe as she pivoted the heel against the carpet, feeling inept and out of her league. Such a tender, malleable thing, the teenager psyche —and being childless, she didn't know the first thing about molding it. The wrong decision could be disastrous for all concerned.

Lord help me, what should I do?

She turned around and was staring dejectedly at the jewelry counter when the answer suddenly came.

Rachel dressed with utmost care that Sunday morning for church. She chose a tasteful shirtwaist dress of periwinkle-blue voile, matching pumps, and a delicately feminine straw hat with a floppy brim that cast dappled shadows over her forehead and made her appear younger. She added a single strand of pearls, a dash of scent, and sighed hopefully as she gave a last glance in the mirror.

She had called her father and asked him if she could ride with him to church, deciding that if he could be stubborn, so could she. He hadn't called or come over since the day of the confrontation with Tommy Lee, and she'd made up her mind if she had to do battle, she might as well take on all the opposing forces at once.

When Everett's car drew up, she grabbed her purse and hurried out, meeting him halfway up the walk. His hands were in his trouser pockets and he came to an abrupt halt as she slammed the front door and approached with a bounce in her step.

"Hi, Daddy," she said brightly, tipping her head up to plunk a quick kiss on his cheek before airily continuing past him.

He scowled after her without returning her greeting, and after a brief hesitation she heard his footsteps follow. Without turning around, she said, "Thank you for picking me up. Tommy Lee would have, but he's running a little late this morning. His daughter is living with him now, and you know how poky we women can be. I'll meet her after church and ride out to their house with them, so you won't have to haul me back home."

As she opened the car door she heard Everett's footsteps come to a halt behind her, but she blithely climbed in and slammed the door.

In a moment he joined her, and she could see peripherally that he gave her a disapproving glance as he started the engine. She had him stymied and she knew it. He might have been expecting her to maintain a stoical silence, as he had, or to vehemently argue her cause. But the one thing he hadn't been expecting was her gay mien and her openly filling him in on what was going on between her and Tommy Lee. She hurried on while she had her father buffaloed.

"I'm terribly nervous . . . do I look all right?" She flipped her palms up and glanced down at her dress, then went on brightly. "Meeting a man's children is a bit unnerving, and of course I want to create a good impression, since we'll all be living together in the near future. She's already started school here and Tommy Lee says she's blending in beautifully. She's made some friends already and doesn't seem to want to go back to live with her mother."

She saw her father's mouth drop open in surprise and rushed on before he could say anything. "You saw her with Tommy Lee on the church steps several weeks ago, the one with the long, dark hair and that unmistakable Gentry mouth. She's a pretty little thing, don't you think? But every time I look at her I want to teach her how to put on her makeup properly—you know how girls of that age tend to overdress, almost like playing grown-up when they're first turned loose." She flipped the visor down, checked her lipstick in the mirror, and smiled. "Ah, well, at least it'll give us some common ground to talk about. Lord, I hope so—I'll need something to break the ice with her." Up went the visor with a snap. "So tell me, Daddy, how've you been?"

She felt positively winded after that mouthful, and her heart was pattering animatedly, but she turned to her father with a disarming smile, as if she greeted him this way every Sunday morning.

"Rachel, what in heaven's name has gotten into you?"

She leaned across the seat and pecked him on the cheek again, knocking her hat brim askew and giving a little laugh as she shot a hand up to hold it on. "I'm happy, that's all. Isn't everybody when they fall in love?"

He snorted and cast her a doubtful glance from the corner of his eye.

"Oh, Daddy, don't be such a cynic."

"You're makin' the mistake of your life. A skunk doesn't change its stripes."

But again she threw him a curve. "Would you like to meet Beth, since she's going to be your granddaughter?"

He gripped the wheel and blared, "I most certainly would not!"

She pulled away with a mock show of defense. "Okay, okay . . . maybe it is best if you wait until she's learned to accept me first."

By the time they reached church Rachel was weak from putting on her act all the way, but she crooked a hand through her father's elbow and kept her step spry as they moved directly inside and found their pew.

The moment she sat down she felt the tension between her shoulder blades and wilted slightly. The worst was yet to come, and she wondered if she was a good enough actress to pull it off when she faced Beth Gentry an hour from now. She had chosen the time and place for its very public aspect. What could Beth Gentry do with half the town milling about, witnessing their first meeting?

When the service ended she studied Tommy Lee's face as they converged in the middle of the crowd, and for a moment she forgot the young woman at his elbow and felt only the thrill of seeing him again.

"Hello, Rachel." His dark eyes adored her while he extended a hand.

"Hello, Tommy Lee." His palm was warm and large as it surrounded hers momentarily, and she smiled up at him.

"I'd like you to meet my daughter Beth."

Rachel transferred her smile to the girl and offered her hand as benignly as if they'd never laid eyes on each other before.

"Hello, Beth. I've certainly heard a lot about you."

Color crept up Beth's cheeks and her mouth hung open in surprise as she let Rachel shake her hand.

"H-h'lo."

Still holding her hand, Rachel smiled up at Tommy Lee. "Why, she's a beauty, just as you said." Again she directed her comment to the girl. "You have your grandpa Gentry's eyes, but your grandma's mouth." And at last she dropped Beth's hand and tipped her head up to Tommy Lee again. "But then, so does your daddy."

He smiled and took her elbow, then did the same to Beth. "What do you say we stop somewhere for breakfast?"

"I'd love to. I'm famished." Rachel poked her head forward to peer around Tommy Lee. "How about you, Beth?"

From his far side came a grunt.

At the car Rachel slipped into the back seat, leaving Beth to share the front with her daddy, feeling thankful that Tommy Lee didn't make an issue of it.

Throughout the meal Rachel tried by action and word to make it clear she had no intention of usurping Beth's place in Tommy Lee's life, but the girl remained sullen and untalkative, speaking only when asked a question.

Over coffee Rachel produced from her handbag a miniature apple-green box with a pink bow and offered it to Beth. "Here . . . a little something from my store, since your daddy told me how much you like them."

Beth shot a puzzled glance from Tommy Lee to Rachel to the box, then up at Rachel again. Obviously, she was as dumbfounded by Rachel's actions as Everett had been earlier. Rachel could read the question sizzling through Beth's mind as clearly as if it had been spoken: *You mean she didn't tell my daddy what I did?*

"Y-you brought a present for *me?*"

Rachel nodded, set the box on the tabletop, and nudged it toward Beth. "Uh-huh. Just something little."

"B-but . . ." Again her eyes dropped to the gift, and Rachel saw how flustered Beth had become.

"Go ahead . . . open it."

Beside Beth, Tommy Lee braced a jaw on one palm and smiled, watching her. Her eyes darted up to his, then quickly away as she hesitantly reached for the box. She removed the bow and drew the protective cotton aside to reveal a pair of tiny silver loop earrings, their Florentine finish a perfect match for the bangle bracelet.

At the sight of them, Beth's face flushed brightly and she trained her eyes downward, refusing to lift them to Rachel again.

"Thank you," she mumbled.

"When I was your age girls weren't allowed to wear earrings. How silly, huh? I remember fighting with my mother over every new thing I wanted to try—makeup, nylons, high heels."

Tommy Lee shifted his gaze to Rachel across the table. "With good reason. I remember the first time you broke out in lipstick. It was the color of a matador's cape, and you had it uneven on the top, and painted too far down in the corners. I can remember thinking—yuck!"

Rachel laughed, her eyes sparkling up at him. "Yuck? You were thinking *yuck* when I thought I was stunning enough for the silver screen?"

"At the time I liked you better in grubby jeans, climbing the pecan tree with your hair all full of twigs."

"Remember that time you fell out of it?" She leaned forward and rested her elbows on the table.

"Do I ever. I wore a cast for the rest of the summer."

"And we never did get that tin-can telephone strung between our bedrooms, did we?"

Tommy Lee chuckled. "Uh-uh. Instead we were forced to use the real one and drive our parents crazy."

Rachel was conscious of Beth, looking on and listening with piqued interest. She gave her a quick glance. "Your daddy was a devil. Do you know what he used to do?" She again fixed her grin up at the man across the table, and beneath it rubbed his trouser leg with her shoe. "He had this old purse and he stuffed it full of play money, tied a string to its handle, and laid it out in the middle of the street in the dark of night. Then he'd hide in the bushes, hold on to the other end of the string and wait for some unsuspecting driver to come rolling along and spy the purse in his headlights. But, of course, by the time the car had jerked to a stop, or backed up, and the driver got out to investigate, the treasure had disappeared from sight!"

Tommy Lee laughed. "God, I'd forgotten about that. The old purse-on-the-string trick. Remember the time we pulled it on old man Mullins? I thought that old dude was gonna commit himself by the time he finally gave up."

"I wasn't with you when you duped old man Mullins. Once was enough for me, lying out in the weeds with the worms and snails and getting bitten up by insects, all for such nonsense."

Though their reminiscing had intrigued Beth, she took no part in the conversation, nor did she show any enthusiasm during the remainder of the day. They spent it at Tommy Lee's house, and though time and again Rachel tried to draw Beth out, she was unsuccessful. Beth's reticence remained between them, intractable.

By the time Tommy Lee drove Rachel back into town, she had a pounding headache. She sighed and fell back against the car seat.

"I don't think it worked," she said. "She's totally belligerent."

Tommy Lee drew on his cigarette, scowled and brooded. *"Dammit,* she was a rude little snot!"

Rachel reached over and brushed his arm. "We have to give her time to get used to me."

"I'm sorry, Rachel."

"It's not your fault. And don't give up yet. We'll try again."

"I just don't understand her!" He thumped the steering wheel. "How could she sit there scowling at you all day long? Didn't she realize how rude that was?"

"She was making her point, darling. I'm a threat to her—or haven't you heard? Women of all ages are infamous for being possessive about their men. She'll get over it, but we have to be patient."

But Tommy Lee had wasted too many years to wax patient when the woman he loved had agreed to marry him and the greatest stumbling block seemed to be his petulant teenage daughter.

When he returned home and walked into his house it was as if a different personality had stepped into Beth's body. This one was smiling and gay and filled with chatter.

"Hi. Fixed us a snack—hot fudge sundaes with pecans. Should I scoop you out one now?"

He threw his car keys onto the table and swung to face her, suddenly upset with her constant attempts to win him over by playing the surrogate housewife. "I'm on a diet. I'll pass."

She stood in the middle of the room holding a dish of chocolate-covered ice cream, licking the back of the spoon. At his curt reply she looked up innocently. "Oh. Well . . . should I slice you some fruit then?"

"Beth, I don't need mothering, all right? And I have a housekeeper, so you don't need to constantly try to please me with all this . . . this domestic subterfuge! What I want you for is to be my daughter."

"Well!" she huffed. "I thought I *was.*"

"Then start acting like one and stop acting like a jealous brat!"

Her face soured. "I can see *she's* been working on you."

"*She* has a name!" Tommy Lee's face reddened with anger and he hooked his thumbs on his hips. "It's Rachel, and I'd appreciate it if you'd afford her the common courtesy of using it when she's here! And the last thing in the world she'd think of doing is *working on me,* as you put it. She was totally willing to excuse your unforgivable rudeness to her today." He tapped his chest. "But I'm not!"

"When she's with you, you forget that I'm even in the room!"

"That's not true and you know it."

"Oh, isn't it? All day long the two of you blabbed on and on about all that junk from when you were kids and left me out."

"And what did you do when she asked you about your dancing, and about school? You grunted a one-word answer and turned a cold shoulder on her. How do you think that made her feel when she was trying her best to be friendly?"

Beth's face was a mask of hatred. "I will *never* be her friend. *Never!* Because she's the one . . . I know she's the one. I found that box of pictures and I know!"

Tommy Lee's brows curved into a frown. "What pictures? What are you talking about?"

She pointed to a distant spot in the house. "All those pictures of you and her, from the time you were babies, naked in a plastic wading pool, riding your tricycles together, and all the way up through high school. You've got more pictures of her than you do of Mother!"

"Beth, we grew up together. You knew that."

"Yes, I knew that." There were tears on Beth's cheeks now. "Mother told me there was someone in your past who made you go through three wives, but none of them could ever measure up to her. She didn't know who it was, but I do! And if it wasn't for your precious Rachel things would have turned out different for me. I'd have a . . . a mother *and* a father like other kids, and . . . and—"

Suddenly Beth threw her dish and spoon on the floor and spun from the room, sobbing.

"Beth, wait!"

"Go to your precious Rachel! Go!" she screamed, slamming up the stairs.

Tommy Lee's heart thundered as he stood in indecision. Should he go to Beth and allay her fears, assure her he'd never leave her as he had her mother? For that was her greatest fear, it was plain. Years of living with a single parent —and a bitter one at that—had left Beth insecure and grasping.

Tommy Lee sighed and dropped to a chair, leaning forward and rubbing his eyes behind his glasses.

Complications. The need for love, that all-powerful drive experienced by everyone—would it work against him all his life?

He considered going upstairs and telling Beth the entire story about Rachel and himself, but she was only fourteen years old. She had her whole sexual life ahead of her. A story like that might leave her with any number of false impressions—that he condoned sex at sixteen, that Rachel was a "bad girl" when she was young, that she was indeed responsible for Nancy's bitterness.

Lord, what went through the minds of fourteen-year-old girls? He didn't know. He'd never had one before. If he told her the whole truth, would it soften his daughter or add to the problem? And to tell it was to include, by necessity, his own estrangement from his parents. Surely she would question him about that. He had promised Rachel he'd make an attempt at reconciliation, but stepping up to that house, then inside it, after all these years, was going to be even more difficult than dealing with Beth.

Gentry, how did you get into this emotional mess?

Disconsolate, he held his head in both hands and stared at the floor between his feet. Then with a weary sigh he unfolded himself and went to clean up the bowl of ice cream. It had left a stain on the carpet, and he supposed he should have hauled Beth back to pick up the mess herself, instead of allowing her to throw a tantrum and get away with it.

How does a guy learn to be a father?

Hunkered down on one knee in the middle of the living-room floor, a dishcloth dangling from his fingers, he dropped his elbow and forehead onto the upraised knee and fought the urge to cry.

Chapter 14

FALL MOVED ON with no perceptible changes in the attitudes of either Beth or Everett. In October Rachel listed her house with a realtor, believing the decisive move would force her father to accept the idea of her upcoming marriage, but he remained unyielding. The few times Rachel confronted Beth at Tommy Lee's house the girl was chilly and aloof, escaping to her room as soon as possible.

In November the realtor found a buyer for Rachel's house, and with that enormous obstacle overcome, she and Tommy Lee set the wedding date for the Saturday following Thanksgiving. But as the holiday approached, they still had not overcome the other obstacles that were casting shadows over their future together. And they both wanted very much to begin their married life without clouds hanging over their heads. They had done all they could to give the two time to accept the idea of their marriage, yet neither had.

And so, they agreed, it was time for an ultimatum.

The November wind was chilly, catching at Tommy Lee's trouser legs as he strode purposefully from his office, crossed Jackson Avenue, and covered the distance to the First State Bank of Russellville. He flung the door open, marched inside, and stopped before the receptionist, who looked up with a cheery smile.

"I want to see Everett Talmadge."

"If you'll have a seat over there, I'll ring him."

Tommy Lee was too agitated to have a seat. He stood, his feet widespread, before the receptionist's desk, eyes riveted on the glass cubicle that was clearly visible in the far corner of the bank. He saw Talmadge reach for his phone; then the receptionist spoke.

"There's someone here to see you." Talmadge appeared to be distractedly scanning something on his desk when the woman answered his unheard question. "It's Tommy Lee Gentry."

Talmadge's head came up with a jerk and his eyes met Gentry's across the width of the business floor. His lips moved again and the receptionist asked Tommy Lee, "What is this in regard to?"

Still staring at the bank president, Gentry replied, "Tell him I want to make a deposit."

The women pivoted the mouthpiece below her chin. "But depos—"

"Just tell him!" Tommy Lee interrupted.

Obediently she brought the phone to her lips. "He says he'd like to make a deposit, sir."

Even from this distance, Tommy Lee could see the belligerent expression overtake Talmadge's face before his mouth worked again.

"Deposits are made at the teller windows, Mr. Gentry," came the relayed message.

"I'll make this one personally with the president," Tommy Lee informed her, then added impatiently, "Never mind. I can see he's not busy. I'll just go right in."

"But, Mr. Gentry—"

Tommy Lee was halfway across the room before the woman could rise from her chair. He opened the door without knocking to find Talmadge already on his feet, then slammed it with a resolute thud that shook the glass walls. He dropped a portfolio in the middle of the desk with a slap, then confronted his foe head-on.

"It'll take more than a timid receptionist to keep me out this time, Talmadge."

"There's a whole row of tellers out there. Any one of them can open an account for you."

"You'd like that, wouldn't you? But you're not getting off that easy, not this time! We're going to have this thing out once and for all—you and me." Tommy Lee planted his hands on his hips while his face took on a stubborn look to match any Everett Talmadge had ever exuded.

"I don't want or need your money in my bank, Gentry."

"This isn't about money and you know it—but my money's going to be here whether you like it or not. I'm sick and tired of driving up to Florence to do my banking, just because you had a burr on your ass twenty years ago and decided you'd show me who was boss. Well, I've proved myself, financially — without your help. I ran a quarter of a million through that damn Florence bank last year, and I've just closed my accounts there, so get used to the fact that you'll have to face my success along with a few other things."

"Gentry, I can have you thrown out of here!"

Tommy Lee bent over the edge of the desk, demanding, "And exactly what would that settle? Throw me out—go ahead!" He straightened and flung a hand in the air. "But you can't throw me out of your daughter's life, so isn't it time we both tried to live with the fact and reach some kind of compromise . . . for her sake?"

Talmadge only glared, standing stiffly with his brow beetled and his hands knotted into fists.

"I love your daughter and she loves me, and all the feuding in the world isn't going to change that fact."

Talmadge emitted a disdainful sniff and eyed Gentry askance while moving with calculated laziness around his desk chair. He stood behind it rolling a pencil up and down between his palms. "Been seein' any of the local trollops lately, Gentry?" he asked unctuously.

Tommy Lee resisted the urge to settle his fist in the middle of the old man's face as he went on resolutely, "I've asked her to marry me and she's agreed. Now, we'd like to do it with your blessing, but if not—so be it. We've been fighting the whole damn world, it seems—you, my daughter, even each other at times—but we're done waiting. We're going to be married next Saturday."

Talmadge's eyes remained cold. "For how long?"

Tommy Lee swallowed his pride and said stiffly, "I'll admit, my past is far from spotless, but I don't feel compelled to justify it to you as long as Rachel trusts me enough to marry me, and she does."

Talmadge flung the pencil onto the desktop. "Rachel's got a bad case of conscience because of this affair she's been carryin' on with you—it's badly colored her judgment."

Tommy Lee ground his back teeth together and met the insolent eyes directly, softening his tone slightly. "Can we quit butting heads for just five minutes and talk about what really matters?"

"And what matters more than Rachel's happiness?"

Tommy Lee braced his hands on his hips and studied the man before him, wondering how a person came to be so pugnacious and bullheaded. "All right, I'll say it straight out. Rachel had our illegitimate baby, and we gave her away against our wishes. I'll admit I've carried a grudge over that for years, but

Rachel and I have both learned to live with it, and we're willing to put it in the past if you are."

Talmadge's face took fire, and he turned away. It was the first time Tommy Lee had ever seen the man come up short of words, but still there remained that damnable stony pride.

The younger man gestured in appeal at the back that was turned against him. "Can't you see what you're doing to her? She doesn't want to have to choose between us, but if you keep fighting me, I can't guarantee she won't. And if she chooses, it'll be me—then what will you have gained?"

Talmadge said nothing, so Tommy Lee tried one last time. "What do you say we bury the hatchet and at least make an attempt to grin and bear each other?"

"And you'd have your revenge at last, wouldn't you?"

Tommy Lee bit back a sharp retort, sighed, and dropped his chin to stare absently at a granite pen holder on top of Talmadge's desk. It was just like the stubborn old fool who owned it—cold, unfeeling granite.

He looked up at Talmadge's back. "I'm going to make your daughter happy, in spite of what you think. She wanted me to tell you she's found a buyer for her house. We'll be living out at my place on the lake, and Callie Mae has agreed to come to work for us, just as she has for Rachel. When and if you finally decide to—" Tommy Lee shook his head, realizing the man would probably never soften. "Well . . . you're welcome there any time." Tommy Lee sighed, slowly picked up his portfolio from the desk, and added quietly, "I'll see one of the tellers on my way out."

Crossing the main floor of the bank to a teller's window, Tommy Lee did not see Talmadge draw the draperies, sealing himself into his cocoon of loneliness. Nor did he see Talmadge fall wearily into his desk chair, prop his elbows on the desk, and drop his face into shaking hands while guilt besieged him and he wondered how he could ever face Rachel and Tommy Lee as husband and wife after the years and years—not to mention the child—he'd stolen from them.

Rachel drew her car up before the Russellville High School only minutes before the bell signaled the end of the day. She slipped on a pair of warm gloves, stepped into the windy afternoon, and after slamming the car door behind her, crossed the street to the row of school buses waiting with their engines running.

Three times she asked, "Does this bus go out old Belgreen Road?" before she found the right one.

When the students came pouring out of the building she studied their faces, waiting beside the door of the bus with her coat collar turned up, holding it together at the neck until she finally caught sight of Beth approaching with one of the girls who'd come into the store with her. The girl spied Rachel first, came up short, and poked Beth in the ribs.

"Hey, Beth . . . somebody waiting for ya."

Beth glanced up at her friend, then followed the direction of her eyes, and planted her feet.

Her companion immediately swerved away from her. "Listen, Beth, I'll see ya around, okay?" she said, and disappeared into the stream of moving bodies.

Beth dropped her eyes to the ground and moved toward the door of the bus as if to pass Rachel without a word.

Rachel calmly stepped in her way. "You won't be riding the bus today."

Defiant brown eyes snapped up. "Oh, yeah?"

Rachel raised one sardonic eyebrow and replied coolly, "Oh, yeah. Unless you want me to make a scene in front of all your new friends by attempting to drag you off bodily to my car. I imagine they'd find it quite amusing, don't you?"

Beth considered a moment, gave a one-shouldered shrug and trudged around the hood of the bus, leaving Rachel to follow. They crossed the street, climbed into the car, and drove off with Beth slumped down in the seat in a typical pose of adolescent rebellion.

Rachel's opening question straightened Beth's spine perceptibly and brought her halfway out of her slouch.

"Have you ever been in love, Beth?" There came no answer, but Rachel didn't need one to see she had captured Beth's attention fully. Nor did Rachel forget for one moment that she was speaking to a girl whose mother had been outraged by an innocent teenage kiss. "What's the matter?" She gave Beth a half-glance, then returned her eyes to the windshield. "Somebody give you the idea that you couldn't possibly feel such an adult emotion at fourteen?" Rachel let a ghost of a smile tip up one corner of her mouth, knowing her passenger eyed her keenly. "Don't let 'em fool you. I fell in love at fourteen — well, let's be conservative and make it fifteen. After all, it was a long time ago and I could be off by a year or so."

Rachel flicked on the left-turn signal, looked over her shoulder, and changed lanes, then kept her eyes on her driving. "I fell in love with your daddy, and—wonder of wonders—he fell right back. It came as something of a surprise after all the years we'd known each other. Of course, we've told you a little about those years, but I wanted to show you something. You don't mind going for a little ride before I take you home, do you?"

Rachel glanced at Beth to find herself being covertly studied, but immediately the dark eyes darted toward the front—obviously the girl was trying to decide what to make of all this. The car turned onto Cotako Street, and Rachel drew up at the curb in front of the two familiar houses. She let the engine idle, rested an arm along the back of the seat, and pointed. "This is the house where your daddy grew up, and where your grandpa and grandma Gentry still live. And that . . . is where I grew up, and where my daddy still lives. See that window up there?" Beth's head swerved. "That was my bedroom window, and this one was your daddy's. Remember when we told you the story about the tin-can telephone we tried to rig up between our rooms? Well, I just wanted you to see how close we really lived.

"We were just children when our daddies planted this row of boxwoods here, but about halfway down they left one bush out, and that's where we all used to cut through between the two houses. If you look really close you can still see the spot."

Rachel put the car in gear, pulled away, and headed up the hill while Beth craned her neck for a last glimpse of the houses. "I remember the day we started first grade. Your daddy and I walked bravely up this hill to school, holding hands. I don't know who was more scared—him or me." She chuckled softly, remembering. They arrived at the top of the hill and she glanced across to the red-brick building and the adjacent playground, noting that Beth did the same. "Once he got himself into big trouble and ended up in the principal's office for punching Dorsey Atwater during recess because Dorsey said something nasty about me—funny, I don't even remember now what it was."

The reminiscing went on as Rachel drove to City Park and circled the small lake surrounded by pole fences, scattered hardwoods, and yuccas. A trio of geese drifted on the water, but otherwise the area was deserted. She passed a small building housing a snack bar and canoe rental, and a swimming pool, closed for the season. "Ah, the hours we spent out here. There was no pool, in those days, but we lived in the lake. Whole summers, with all the friends we'd grown up with."

As she drove on down Waterloo Road, which led through the park, Rachel recalled the many nights she and Tommy Lee had parked out here, and had a moment's pause to hope telling Beth was the right thing to do. So far she hadn't said a word, and it was difficult to gauge the impact—if any—her words were having on the girl.

"I guess you might say this is where we fell in love." They left the park behind and headed for the country. "As I told you, we weren't much older than you when we discovered it. We used to park down by the lake and talk about getting married." Rachel let a smile linger on her lips. "We'd pick out names for our future children, and make up stories about the house we wanted to have—it'd have lots of windows and natural wood, and it would face a lake and have fireplaces and be carpeted in blue—oh, you know how it is when you're making up fairy tales."

Rachel adjusted her hands on the wheel and went on. "Anyway, our parents always seemed happy that we were dating each other, but then when I was sixteen . . . I found out I was pregnant." She saw Beth's head snap around to stare at her, but carefully kept her eyes on the road. "Tommy Lee and I were scared at first, but after talking it over we decided there was nothing to be scared about. After all, we were in love, and by the time the baby was born we'd be seventeen and there'd be just a little of our senior year left in high school, and somehow he'd manage to finish, and so would I. So we decided to get married.

"But when we told our parents the news we found that they had other ideas." Rachel drew a deep breath, but kept carefully unemotional in her recital. "They talked it over and decided that the best thing to do would be to send me away to have the baby, and so I ended up in Michigan."

Rachel didn't need to turn her head to know she had captivated Beth's full attention now. She added quietly, "But they wouldn't tell your daddy where I was.

"Things were much different then, and when the baby was born I had little to say about it. The decision had been made by all four parents that she would be given up for adoption, and she was.

"But I did have a say about one thing. They let me name her, and I quite naturally chose the name your daddy and I had dreamed about for a girl . . . I named her Beth."

There was a sharp indrawn breath, but Rachel trained her eyes straight forward and resisted turning to Beth as she continued with her story.

"The decision about giving up the baby caused a tremendous backlash of guilt and remorse. Our parents could never quite face each other again, and it's been years and years since they've talked to each other. And Tommy Lee . . . he blamed his mama and daddy, and though he's been married to several women, he could never seem to find happiness with any of them. I had a . . . a good marriage, but my husband and I could never have any children, and that complicated matters between myself and my parents, though it wasn't their fault—they had no way of knowing how things would turn out at the time they made the decision about the adoption.

"Well, it's been a muddle for years. Your daddy and I avoided each other as much as possible until . . . well, until my husband died. It had been twenty-four years, but when we saw each other again . . ." Rachel spread her hands and let them fall back to the steering wheel, giving a short helpless smile. "It might have been easier for all concerned if we hadn't gotten together again, but what we felt for each other was too strong. We could no more have fought it than . . ." She chanced a peak at Beth and found her sober, listening attentively. "Well, love is a strange thing. It always seems to have its own way."

They approached the turn onto Tommy Lee's property, and Rachel added plaintively, "It can hurt a lot. But it can heal, too."

The car came to a halt in the curved drive before the cedar house with its glossy black doors. When the engine stilled, it left an immense silence between the two passengers. The November wind tilted the tips of the trees, and beyond the house the lake was gone again, drained away until spring dictated its return. The oaks now bore rusty leaves, and the hickories had gone to husk. Autumn . . . with Thanksgiving imminent. If things went right there could be so very, very much to be thankful for.

Rachel looked across at Beth to find her staring at her thumbnails, which were locked together. Beth blinked hard, then looked out her window. When she spoke, her voice was barely above a whisper. "This was the house you planned, wasn't it?"

Softly Rachel answered, " Yes, Beth, it was."

"And he named me Beth, too."

Rachel wisely remained silent.

"Did you ever see her again—that other Beth?"

"No, but it doesn't matter anymore."

"Except that she's my half sister." She turned tear-filled eyes to Rachel, adding, "And they're my grandparents."

"I know," Rachel replied sadly. "And I'm working on that. I believe, in time, everything will come out right. Your daddy is as stubborn as all the rest of them in his own way. But he's promised to do his best to set things right before our wedding." Rachel could see she had given Beth a lot to digest in such a brief time. "Your daddy and I thought you were old enough to know, but he asked me to tell you because . . . well, he was a little self-conscious about parts of it." Rachel touched Beth's shoulder. "Oh, Beth, dear, please try to understand him. He's been through so much pain and he loves you so very, very much."

The huge, brimming tears spilled onto Beth's cheeks as she tried valiantly not to cry.

"I don't want to take him away from you, don't you see? I want to share him with you, just as he wants to share you with me. You're not the same Beth we lost, and I would never substitute you for her in my mind, but . . . but doesn't it seem prophetic that you both have the same name . . . as if you were given to us as our last chance to have a daughter to love?" Beth's lower lip trembled and she clamped it between her teeth while Rachel appealed tenderly, "And I would very much like the chance to get to love you, Beth."

In a sweeping motion Beth threw herself into Rachel's arms. "Oh, Rachel, I'm . . . s-so sorry," she sobbed. "I didn't know."

Rachel felt tears sting her own nose and eyes. "Of course you didn't."

"M-my mother used to . . . to say terrible things about how Daddy couldn't forget his 'precious teenage lover,' and I t-took her side. I hated you because I thought if it w-wasn't for you . . . well, you know."

Beth retreated from Rachel's arms, hung her head, and self-consciously wiped her eyes.

"Yes, I know. You've been very mixed up about where I would fit into your affections, but please believe me—I would never try to take your mother's place. She'll always be your true mother." Rachel reached up to tip Beth's chin and meet her tear-filled gaze. "But you and I could be friends, couldn't we?" Beth swallowed, and her lips quivered as Rachel went on in a softly appealing voice. "Your daddy made a lot of mistakes along the way, Beth, but all he was really trying to do was be happy. It hurt him terribly to lose his children. He felt guilty and inadequate as a father and as a husband. But now you've brought him the chance to try again."

Beth swallowed hard and admitted, "I was such a br-brat."

Rachel laughed shakily and touched the silky bangs that had gotten messed. "I wish I could disagree with you, but I'm afraid you had me thinking the same thing for a while."

"Do you think he'll ever forgive me?"

Rachel smiled and hugged Beth hard, then leaned back to look into her eyes. "Believe me, there'll be nothing to forgive if you'll only give us your blessing for our wedding Saturday."

"I'll do more than that. Maybe—" But suddenly she stopped.

Rachel ducked her head as if to peer up into Beth's downturned face. "Maybe . . . ?" she encouraged.

Beth looked up hopefully. "Well, I was thinking, maybe I could be your maid of honor, or whatever you call it."

"My attendant?" Rachel returned, surprised. "You'd really want to?"

Again Beth shrugged sheepishly. "I think you deserve it after the hard time I've given you." Then she dropped her eyes self-consciously. "You never even told him what I did in your store, did you?"

"What good would it have done? That was something between you and me, and I wanted to try to work it out without having him worry about it."

Beth looked up, and suddenly a light seemed to brighten her eyes. "Wait here!" she ordered, and jumped out of the car, then slammed the door and ran toward the house. Puzzled, Rachel did as ordered.

When Beth returned, she stuffed the silver bangle bracelet into Rachel's hands. "Here. Put it back in the showcase where it belongs."

"Oh, Beth, it's only worth—"

"No! Take it back and sell it!" Then in a more subdued tone she added, "I've never been able to make myself wear the dumb thing anyway."

Rachel tucked the bracelet into her purse. "Okay, back to the store it goes. And in the future, if you want to argue about your father, what do you say we do it honorably, straight to each other's faces?"

"Argue? B-but . . ."

"You don't think we're going to live together in one house, three adults—" Rachel considered Beth before amending, "Well . . . *almost* three adults, and never disagree, do you? Your daddy and I have a lot to learn about being parents, but if there's one thing this family is going to do, it's talk things out. I've had all I can take of stubborn people who hold grudges for years and years and refuse to talk them out."

Beth smiled at Rachel for the first time ever. "All right. At the first thing you do that I don't like, I promise to get on your case."

Rachel laughed, too, and a tremendous weight seemed to have been lifted from her heart.

"Since we've agreed to talk things over there's something I should ask you. Would you be terribly disappointed if we let Georgine go? I'm afraid your daddy and she don't get along too well."

Beth made a face. "Georgine's a crab."

Rachel chortled, then put in, "I probably shouldn't say so, but your daddy agrees wholeheartedly. We have someone in mind to replace her. Callie Mae worked for my family when I was a girl. Your daddy and I were the light of her life, and we've promised her she can come and work for us as soon as we're married."

"You mean, she knows everything?"

"Everything. Including the fact that she'll have another teenager to coddle."

Beth's eyes lit up and another broken piece seemed to fall into place.

"Oh, Rachel, I think . . . well, it seems like . . ." Beth seemed unable to voice all her newfound feelings, and finally blurted out, "Well, all of a sudden, I just can't wait!"

And as the two shared a last embrace, their newfound amity seemed a portent of peace ahead.

Tommy Lee and Rachel had decided to go together to visit Gaines and Lily Gentry. Verda was already winding up the cord of the vacuum cleaner when Tommy Lee stepped through the door of Panache. He had come straight from work and wore a brown tweed sports coat and tie beneath a crisp oyster-colored trench coat, its collar turned up. The wind had messed his hair, and as he closed the door and turned, he combed it back with his fingers.

Watching, Rachel marveled again at the powerful swell of emotions his appearance never ceased to create in her breast. It was more than just the missed years—oh, they were part of it—but there was pride in how much he'd changed, exhilaration in the thought of their future, and a vibrant sexuality that scintillated between them each time they encountered each other.

Seeing him, that first glimpse as he entered a room, rounded a corner, opened a door as he had just now, brought the most astounding response. Her heart accelerated as it had long ago, and she felt warm and knew her cheeks grew pink each time his eyes sought her out as they did now across the scented shop.

"All ready, darling?" he asked, crossing to her, touching his lips briefly to hers.

"Almost. We're just closing up." She moved to the armoire and switched off its light, then to her desk to tamp some papers into a neat pile and push the chair beneath the kneehole.

Verda looked on benevolently—by now she had grown used to Tommy Lee coming in this way. There was a new glow about Rachel since she'd been seeing him, and he was looking sexier than ever, though today he wore a distant, worried expression.

Verda offered, "You two go on. I'll lock up."

Rachel flashed her a grateful smile. "Thanks, Verda. See you tomorrow."

It was a drive of only minutes from the store to Cotako Street. As they pulled up before the Gentry house, Tommy Lee was silent and introspective. He smoked his cigarette voraciously, though Rachel was quite sure he didn't even realize he had it between his fingers. She reached over and brushed the back of his hand.

"Are you sure you want me to come in with you?"

The hand turned over and his fingers gripped hers. "Yes. Please. I need you."

"You're sure you wouldn't rather talk to them alone?"

But the pressure on her fingers told her how tense he was, how much he relied upon her for moral support. She leaned over to kiss his cheek and said, "All right, then, let's get it over with."

It felt awkward, standing on the front step waiting for someone to answer the bell—after all, they'd scampered at will into and out of this house for years. Tommy Lee stood with his hands buried in his coat pockets, his collar still turned up, his expression grave as he stared at the black metal mailbox beside the door. The wind lifted his coattail and slapped it back across his thigh, and Rachel placed her hand on his sleeve to squeeze his arm reassuringly.

The door opened and there stood Lily, gaping as if they were ghosts, holding the edge of the door and not moving a muscle.

Finally Tommy Lee said, "Hello, Mother."

His words seemed to shake her out of her trance. Her lips opened and her eyes skipped from Tommy Lee to Rachel and back, but though her throat worked, no sound came out. So Rachel added, "Hello, Lily."

At last Lily found her voice. "H-hello," she said, though it was not more than a weak, breathless squeak.

"We wondered if we could talk to you and Daddy."

"Wh-why, of course. Come in. Come in." Suddenly she was all action and smiling solicitousness, stepping back and waving them in with fluttery, nervous gestures. "Well, my gracious, what a surprise this is. I was just . . . Come, sit. Where did he . . . Gaines?" she finally called, glancing around as if she'd misplaced him.

"Lily, where are my slippers?" came his voice from upstairs.

Lily flapped her hands. "Oh, that man, forever losing something. Just . . . Would it . . . Excuse me just a minute." She went to the bottom of the stairs and called up, "Gaines, we have company. Leave your shoes on."

"Company? Who?"

"Come see," she answered.

A moment later Gaines Gentry appeared at the foot of the stairs, and when he saw who stood across the room he stopped dead in his tracks. His eyes zeroed in on Tommy Lee, held for some time before shifting to Rachel momentarily, then settling on his son again. Disbelief registered on his face. His cheeks began turning an electric pink, and finally his feet started moving.

"Well, this is a surprise."

"Hello, Daddy. I hope we're not interrupting your dinner," Tommy Lee began.

"No . . . no!" Gaines responded eagerly. "We hadn't started yet. Your mother was just setting the table." He stood near enough to touch, but both he and Tommy Lee refrained from reaching out to each other. Rachel sensed his breathlessness and noted a trembling in his hand as he patted his shirtfront and repeated, "Well, this is *quite* a surprise. Tommy Lee." And as if just now remembering himself, Gaines turned to include his other visitor. "And Rachel, too."

"Hello, Gaines."

Tommy Lee cleared his throat. "We'd like to talk to both of you if you have a minute."

"Why, sure, sure . . . let's sit down. Lily, is there any coffee?" he rambled nervously.

"No," Tommy Lee interjected. "No coffee for us. We'll only be a minute."

"Well, sit down anyway. Can I take your coats?"

The whole thing was starting out just as Rachel had suspected it would, with everyone walking on eggshells. Gaines's face was so bright by now he looked in danger of having a stroke, and Lily wore a porcelain smile that made it quite impossible to look her in the eye. Finally they were all perched, Gaines and Lily on overstuffed armchairs, Tommy Lee on a davenport beside Rachel, the only one to lean back with any semblance of composure.

Silence fell for several uncomfortable seconds. Then Tommy Lee cleared his throat, rested his elbows on his knees, and chafed his hands together, studying the floor between his feet, finally glancing up to ask, "So, how have you both been?"

"Fine!" they replied together, then glanced at each other sheepishly while the room grew tingly with tension.

"Me, too. I ah . . . live out on the lake now."

"Yes, we heard."

"My daughter lives with me."

"Your daughter!" Lily said, as if surprised.

"Yes, the one you've seen with me at church."

"Oh, yes, of course. My, but she's pretty."

Tommy Lee allowed himself to smile, raising his eyes to Rachel as if for fortification. "Rachel says she looks like you." Lily grew fluttery again, and

Tommy Lee cleared his throat and lurched to his feet, then began pacing nervously.

"We, ah . . . Rachel and I have been seeing quite a bit of each other since her husband died."

"We were so sorry to hear the news, Rachel. Such a young man."

"Yes . . . well . . ." Rachel searched for something to say to cover the awkward moment. "Tommy Lee has helped me tremendously to get over Owen's death."

She lifted her face to Tommy Lee, and their eyes met and held as he added, "And Rachel has helped me, too. I've been managing, with her help, to get my life back on track." He drew a prolonged breath, and she offered a smile of reassurance to force him on. "I was running pretty wild there for a quite a few years . . . thought I had the world by the tail, but actually I was on a self-destruction course. Rachel made me realize that." Still their eyes communicated as he added more softly, "Rachel's made me see a lot of things."

Gaines and Lily observed the tender expression passing between the two and dropped their eyes to the carpet, but their son suddenly seemed to draw himself back to the present, squaring his shoulders and facing the two seated on the matched chairs.

"You see, it's because of her that I'm here. She and I . . . we're . . ." Tommy Lee's troubled eyes wavered from his mother to his father. Then he swung around, took two jerky steps toward the fireplace, shoved one hand through his hair, and mumbled, "Oh, hell." Finally he spun to face them once more, and when at last he said what he'd come to say, it came out all in a rush. "Rachel and I are going to get married this Saturday, but before she would agree to it she made me promise to come here and settle things with you, so here we are."

Not a sound adulterated the silence. From the kitchen came the smell of supper cooking, while in the living room four uncertain people faced one another, each waiting for the next one to say something.

Lily was the first to respond. She pulled her lips together long enough to breathe, "Married?" Her eyes were enormous as she looked up at her towering son, who stood with his hands buried in his coat pockets, a defensive scowl on his face.

"Yes, married. We thought you should know."

Lily's face was pale as parchment, and she touched her heart and looked to her husband for a reply, but he was as surprised as she. Though they had seen Rachel and Tommy Lee exchanging hellos on the church steps, they had no idea the two had been seeing so much of each other.

Tommy Lee crossed to his mother's chair and hunkered down before it, taking her hand. "I love her more than I could ever begin to tell her. I've never stopped loving her. Having her in my life again has given me the strength to turn it around in the nick of time. But she's very wise, more so than any of us three . . ." His eyes moved to a stunned Gaines, then back to Lily. "She realized that a lot of what was wrong with my life stemmed from the bitterness I felt toward you two. And I want it over. Over and done with." Then he ended softly, "Don't you?"

The look they exchanged was poignant as Lily's eyes filled with tears. "Oh, Tommy Lee, I've prayed for years to hear you say that."

"Why didn't one of *you* say it?" he asked, a shadow of hurt in his tone.

Her eyes dropped to their joined hands. "Stubbornness, I guess. Pride." She looked up into her son's eyes and added quietly, "Guilt."

Still holding his mother's hand he turned his head to include his father as he said, "Rachel and I want an end to all that. It's over. She and I have a second chance and that's all that matters now. Beth will be living with us, and—don't you see? It's almost as if Providence decided in our favor after all these years. She's not the same Beth we lost, but that doesn't matter. Isn't it time we all put that incident behind us? God knows I'm as guilty of keeping old wounds from healing as anybody. But now there's going to be Rachel . . . and me . . . and Beth. I . . . I'm anxious for you to meet her."

"Our . . . our granddaughter." Lily's face had all but collapsed with emotion. She struggled to hold back the tears, but they coursed down her cheeks.

Tommy Lee smiled crookedly and teased, "Well, it's nothing to cry about, Mama."

And at last they could restrain themselves no longer. Lily threw her arms around Tommy Lee's neck and he fell to his knees beside her chair, hauling her roughly against him. Looking on, Gaines stood and took a halting step toward them, and Rachel could tell by the expression on his face that he was having difficulty restraining his own tears.

When mother and son drew apart, Tommy Lee looked up to find his father hovering nearby. Slowly he straightened and the two confronted each other with a gravity that was palpable, while the eternal moment lengthened. Then they pitched roughly together and slapped each other's shoulders.

"Son . . ." Gaines choked.

Tommy Lee's eyes were closed, his throat working convulsively against his father's shoulder.

They backed apart, laughing self-consciously. Then Tommy Lee was striding toward Rachel, reaching for her hand to pull her to her feet and include her in the celebration. She went from Lily's arms to Gaines's, accepting and giving embraces with a residue of self-consciousness still making the scene very strained.

"We all have a lot of time to make up for," Lily offered.

It seemed to Rachel that Lily had shrunk over the years, and it made her realize how old their parents were getting. Yes, there was much to make up for. Lily tried several times to say something before finally managing to complete the thought.

"Would you . . . Thursday is . . . Well, I was just thinking, if you . . . haven't made any other plans, Thursday is Thanksgiving, and it seems we have a lot to be thankful for this year. Would you care to join us for dinner? And bring Beth, too?"

The eagerness shone in her eyes. Tommy Lee and Rachel both saw it there before exchanging a silent glance. Actually, they'd made plans for Rachel to spend the day with Tommy Lee and Beth at the lake house. But now she answered for all three of them.

"We'd love to. Is that okay with you, Tommy Lee?"

"Uh . . . oh, of course!"

The look of delight that came over Lily Gentry's face was radiant while

Gaines patted his shirtfront and rocked back on his heels, smiling and nodding.

Tommy Lee and Rachel left minutes later amid more stilted farewell pats and hugs. When they were walking to the car, Tommy Lee asked, "So what about that turkey we bought, and the plan to move your stuff out to my house after dinner Thursday?"

"We'll leave the turkey in the freezer and move my things at midnight if we have to. As your mother said, we have a lot to be thankful for this year, and it will be auspicious to begin all together at a Thanksgiving table."

As Tommy Lee opened the car door for her he added, "Just about all together."

She glanced over her shoulder. The pecan tree was bare of nuts now, and beyond it the break in the boxwood hedge was merely a shadow. The sweet-gum tree had dropped all its balls, too—everything looked wintry and cold. She lifted her eyes to the house beyond the hedge and thought of how wintry and cold its lone resident must be. *Daddy,* she thought, and her heart ached with pity for a man so steeped in pride he would remain in self-imposed exile rather than bend.

"We'd better go, Rachel," Tommy Lee said softly.

She looked up at him beseechingly. "Do you suppose he'll ever change?"

"It would take a miracle, I think."

As they drove away, Rachel's eyes lingered sadly on the dim light in her father's living-room window.

Chapter 15

THANKSGIVING DAWNED GRAY and misty, but Gaines had a cheery fire already ablaze in the hearth when Tommy Lee, Rachel, and Beth arrived at the Gentry home. The aroma of roasting turkey filled the place, and there was a sense of true welcome as the three stepped inside. Gaines and Lily were smiling and jovial, and though it was easy to see the excitement shining from their eyes, upon meeting Beth there was a first cautious reserve. To Rachel and Tommy Lee's delight, it was Beth who put it to rout.

With the offhand congeniality that can sprout from teenagers at the most unexpected yet opportune times, Beth assessed the two eager faces, grinned over her shoulder at Tommy Lee, who stood behind her, and commented, "You're right, Daddy, I do look like them."

The laughter that followed broke the ice, and within half an hour of their arrival they were all immersed in photo albums filled with pictures of Tommy Lee and Rachel, and for each picture there was a story. Beth listened raptly, laughing at the photographs of her father as a skinny teenager who appeared to be all bones and hair, and at Rachel in a ponytail and spit curls. Lily proved to have a marvelous talent for storytelling, relating tales even Rachel had forgotten.

Gaines served hot cranberry drinks and soon Lily excused herself to tend to things in the kitchen. Rachel offered her hand, and as they left the living room Lily turned back to suggest, "Tommy Lee, why don't you take Beth upstairs and show her your old room?"

"Oh, yes, Daddy, please?" Beth pleaded.

And so it was that with everyone occupied, Gaines found himself alone. He sat before the fire, sipping his hot drink, staring at the flames and reliving the years, the happy memories revived by the photographs and stories.

Of course, there had been pictures of Everett and Eulice, and these, too, he admitted, had brought their share of nostalgia. A golden flame leaped and licked while he stared at it, unseeing.

Who was it that got stubborn first . . . me or Everett? he wondered. So long ago . . . it was hard to remember. *The kids went away and all the happiness seemed to go out of our lives. We were ashamed of what we'd done, and every time we faced each other we faced our own shame, and so it was easier to simply stop facing each other.*

Gaines sighed, took an absent sip of his drink, listened to the sounds of the women getting things ready in the kitchen, an occasional spurt of laughter from overhead, and pictured Everett all alone in that empty house.

Everett, you and I have been a pair of mule-headed old fools, and it's time one of us did something about it.

He set his glass on the coffee table, sighed weightily, and went to the coat closet under the stairs to find his warm maroon sweater. After buttoning it from neck to hip, he slipped out the side door, closed it behind himself, and paused to look across the lifeless grass to the stone house beyond. He rolled the thick collar of the sweater up around his neck, stuck his hands into its pockets, and studied his feet as he made his way toward the familiar break in the hedge. There he stopped and took a moment to survey the opening —so much narrower now but still not quite obliterated. It appeared to have been waiting all these years for one of them to breach it again and lay the past to rest. He ducked low, pushed a branch aside, and crossed to the other side.

Front door or back? But a chill drizzle was falling, and the back door was closer. He climbed the steps, opened a squeaking screen and door, and moved with echoing footsteps across the wooden floor of the porch to a closed door that led—he knew—into the back hall just beside the kitchen.

He knocked, stuffed his hands into his sweater pockets again, and waited.

An interminable time seemed to pass while Gaines pondered the probability that nobody ever came to Everett's back door anymore. He had just raised his knuckles to rap harder when the latch clicked and the door wheezed open with a grating of old swollen wood.

When Everett saw who was on his back porch his face became a mask of concealed surprise. He seemed unable to move and obviously didn't know what to say. The two men studied each other for several long, silent seconds while time spun backwards to a day when they, like their children, had freely moved within the scope of each other's everyday lives. They had missed a lot of shared good times in the last twenty-four years, and as their eyes met and held, they both realized it. Then the wind blew in through the screen, sending a shiver up Gaines's spine, and he took the bit between his teeth to state, "I think it's high time you and I had a talk, Everett. Can I come in?"

The turkey was on a carving board and the stuffing had been scooped into a serving bowl. Bustling trips were being made back and forth between the kitchen and the dining room, and Lily called again, "Gaines?" She scowled and fussed. "Now, where is that man?"

Tommy Lee and Beth breezed into the kitchen. "Can we help?"

"Yes, carry that bird to the table and find your daddy. It's time he started carving it."

Board and bird disappeared through the doorway in the hands of Tommy Lee and were followed by vegetable bowls and gravy boats carried by the women. They were attempting to make room on the linen-covered table for the last of the dishes when the side door slammed and Gaines appeared in the dining room doorway.

"Set a place for one more, Mother. Look who's here."

Rachel was leaning over the table with a tureen of steaming sweet potatoes in her hands when Gaines stepped aside to reveal a slightly sheepish-looking Everett behind him. He hung back, his hands in his pockets, while Rachel stared, dumbfounded, then suddenly dropped the tureen and squealed, "Ouch!" as she pressed a burned palm to her thigh.

Somebody said, "Rachel, are you all right?" But she didn't hear. Her attention was riveted on the man in the doorway. His eyes found her, and he gave a trembling smile that at last sent her moving around the table.

Even before she reached him, both hands were extended, and as he clasped them, she felt a tremor in his flesh.

"Daddy . . ." she said. Then she was in his arms.

"Baby . . ." he murmured against her ear, holding her as if she'd been lost and just now found.

Her heart felt as if it could not be contained within her breast; it threatened to swell and burst with its burden of joy.

"Oh, Daddy, you're here."

She backed off and lost herself for a brief emotional moment in his uncertain eyes, then spun to bestow a hug of equal fervor on Gaines. "Thank you . . . oh, thank you," she whispered, kissing his florid cheek.

Then she returned to her father, and took his elbow to draw him into the room. She found tears in her eyes as she watched him pick out his hostess, nod, and murmur, "Lily."

"Welcome, Everett," Lily greeted, coming forward to offer her hands much as Rachel had done a moment ago. And when she'd stepped back, Everett's eyes came to rest on Tommy Lee. Again he nodded stiffly, and though it was a stilted beginning, it was a beginning nevertheless.

"I don't believe you've met Tommy Lee's daughter, Beth," Rachel put in, to fill the awkward moment.

"Hello, Beth."

"Hi." Beth smiled.

Rachel's eyes met Tommy Lee's, and she didn't stop to question the awesome need that suddenly propelled her—she only knew she had to press herself against his chest, feel his arms around her shoulders, her heart beating vibrantly against his, while celebrating this moment for which they'd both waited so long.

He seemed to understand it, though, for when she came to him he held her tightly, his cheek against her hair, his chest solid and warm.

"I have everything I want now," Rachel whispered in his ear.

"So do I," came Tommy Lee's answer, while together they shared the overwhelming sense of true thanksgiving.

They were married two days later in the parsonage of the First Baptist Church. It would have been asking too much too soon to expect Everett to be present. And anyway, Tommy Lee and Rachel wanted to keep the celebration as private as possible, so they decided the only witnesses they'd invite would be Beth and Sam and Daisy Davis.

After the ceremony Sam drove Beth to her grandpa and grandma Gentry's, where she would spend the remainder of the weekend, which was all the honeymoon Tommy Lee and Rachel were to have at present. It was the busiest season of the year in the retail business and impossible for Rachel to leave before Christmas. But as soon as the holiday rush ended, the Gentrys and their daughter were planning a family cruise together. Rachel didn't mind putting off the trip. There was really only one place she wanted to be on her wedding night. . . .

The Cadillac pulled to a stop near the venerable 150-year-old magnolia tree in Tommy Lee's front yard. The key was switched off, and the chain swung silently from the ignition. Tommy Lee slipped his arm around Rachel's shoulders and drew her against his hip.

"Mrs. Gentry . . . we're home."

"Yes . . . at last."

He kissed her ear, then pressed his lips warmly against it while they both gazed at the house for a minute.

"It was a long road, getting here," he said quietly, the words stirring the hair at her temple.

"But we made it."

"Yes, we made it. Would you care to go inside and see what's in store for you for the rest of your life?"

She turned to brush a thistledown kiss on his lips. "I thought you'd never ask."

They smiled—brown eyes into brown eyes—with a look that spoke of unending love. Then Tommy Lee got out of the car and waited while she slipped under the steering wheel and joined him. With their arms around each other they strolled slowly across the gravel drive and up the wooden ramp to the twin doors leading to the home they'd planned when they were too young to realize all it would entail to build and take possession of it.

He pulled open one shining black door, swung her up into his arms, and said against her lips, "This time we do everything according to the book— right?"

"Right," she agreed, looping her arms around his neck.

Inside, he did an about-face, and Rachel kicked the door shut with a delicate mauve high heel. He mounted the stairs with her in his arms, all the way

to the top level of the house, where he finally halted in the middle of a blue bedroom with a fireplace, a balcony, and a view of the lake.

Setting her on her feet, he reached immediately for the single button at the waist of her mauve wool suit jacket. "Once upon a time," he began, "there was a little girl named Rachel who lived next door to a boy named Tommy Lee. Right from the beginning he had eyes for her—from the day they first sat together in their birthday suits in a little plastic swimming pool."

"In their birthday suits? Tsk, tsk, tsk." Rachel played along as he turned her around and took the jacket from her shoulders, then tossed it onto a chair before swinging her to face him again, pulling the waist of an ivory silk blouse out of her skirt.

"Uh-huh. That's when it all started, I believe. Then, when they were about seven, eight years old, he had second thoughts—you see, the girl of his dreams lost *all* of her front teeth. Oh, she was quite a sight then! Nothing at all like the little doll he'd always known." The wrinkled tails of her blouse hung free, and he raised his hands to the top button and worked downward at a leisurely pace that matched his story.

"But things got even worse. She got freckles, and a shape like a bean pole, and he didn't know what in the world she was going to turn into. But along about this time he started thinking that even though she wasn't much to look at, she wasn't so bad to have around. After all, she was just like one of the boys—liked to climb trees, punch, wrestle, build tree forts. Yup, he decided, this tomboy was for him!"

Rachel's face was bright with suppressed laughter while her husband grinned into her eyes, lazily reached for one ivory cuff, and unbuttoned it without ever dropping his eyes.

"But you'll never guess what happened," Tommy Lee went on, while she docilely offered him the other cuff, her amused eyes locked with his. "One day, out of the clear blue sky, he looked at her and did a double take. Lord a'mighty"—the blouse flew toward the chair, missed, and slithered to the floor —"she'd grown up."

Rachel was growing warm and tingly at his leisurely seduction, but he took his own sweet time with the story. "Her tousled hair was all combed neatly and pulled into this cute little corkscrew of a ponytail. . . ." He drew her hair back from her temples and held it tightly somewhere behind her head. "And the freckles seemed to dissolve into peaches and cream"—he dropped her hair, brushed a knuckle over her cheek—"and she started wearing lipstick"— he touched her lips—"and he began to be fascinated by it, and by her mouth. Until one day he decided to kiss her, just to see what it'd feel like." He leaned forward lazily and brushed his lips to hers, breathing warmly against her mouth after the kiss ended. "It felt absolutely wonderful. He decided he wanted more of that." And Tommy Lee took more, slipping his tongue into Rachel's mouth with a sinuous invitation she immediately answered. Her heart beat crazily, just as it had that first time. But all too soon he drew back and the story continued.

"It was about that time that she started getting curves." His hands clasped her shoulders, kneading them gently while she went loose and malleable and let his motions rock her on her feet. "A waist"—his hand slid down over her arms and clasped her waist—"and hips. . . ." His hands dropped lower.

"And pretty soon she gave up blue denims for skirts and sweaters, and that's when he realized she not only had a waist and hips, but breasts, too."

His hands rode up her silky slip to cup both lace-bound breasts, thrusting them sharply upward while finding their points with his thumbs, drawing circles that sent rippling sensations through Rachel's limbs. When her nipples were hard and erect, he drew back only far enough to bestow that lazy grin on her. "And the first time he touched them he knew it wasn't going to end there."

He released her breasts and freed the button at her waist. "They learned a lot together, these two." The zipper snicked open and the skirt fell to the floor.

As Rachel stepped out of it, she reached for his suit jacket and forced it back over his shoulders. "It must have been scary," she said, "all those firsts." His jacket joined hers on the chair and she reached for the knot of his tie.

"Yes, it was. But by this time they realized they'd fallen in love, and there was no way they could stop themselves."

His tie slipped free and she went to work on his shirt buttons. "And . . . ?" she prompted.

"And so one day he got brave and undressed her in the back seat of his Chevy." Rachel's slip slid up her body, covered her face, and disappeared over her head as she raised her willing arms in the air.

Standing before him, half undressed, her heart doing a wild dance in her breast, she asked innocently, "And did she undress him?"

"No, she was too scared."

Rachel raised sultry eyes to his, letting her fingertips flutter over his shirtfront.

"Dumb girl . . . there's nothing to it," she murmured against his lips, before removing his glasses, setting them carefully aside, then turning her attention to his shirt, which she skillfully slipped off to caress his naked back.

She felt his hands at the catch of her bra. "Mmm, I see . . . nothing to it." And a moment later it, too, was gone.

Their warm skin touched, her breasts flattened against the silvered hair on his chest, and suddenly the game fell away.

"Oh, Rachel . . . remember how it was?" he uttered against her lips.

"Yes," she breathed. "Just like now . . . we couldn't hold back . . . and then we couldn't get enough."

"And I'll never get enough of you . . . never," he vowed, covering her face with kisses, then stepping back, the better to see her eyes while clasping her head in his wide hands. He drew her up on tiptoe, placed one hard kiss on her mouth, then deftly slipped the last of her clothing down her legs, stood, and reached for his belt. But she brushed his hands aside and took over the welcome task, divesting him of trousers, briefs, stockings, and shoes, dropping to one knee before him, then pausing on her way back up to kiss his hard thigh, his staff of masculinity, his stomach, his chest, the soft hollow of his throat. Joining her fingers behind his neck, she kissed his mouth last, lingering there longest while gently rolling from side to side, catching him high against her belly before stepping back to view him in his entirety.

"You are"—reaching to claim him, she searched for an adequate word—"resplendent."

He laughed indulgently, with a quick flash of even, white teeth, then stood back, running his palms from her armpits to her hips.

"Am I really?"

"Mmm-hmm."

"Funny thing . . . you are, too." They gazed the length of each other's bodies, experiencing a subtle difference this time—they were husband and wife now; they belonged to each other. They touched . . . and trembled a little. Glanced up . . . and laughed softly. Glanced down . . . and fell silent.

They touched more freely. His bare foot covered hers. His naked knee lifted to separate her silken thighs, then pressed high and hard against her eager flesh. She drew her hands up the backs of his thighs, clutching him close, holding him for a long, appreciative moment while contemplating the fact that she need never say good-bye to him again.

"Sometimes when I remember, I get greedy. I want the years we lost."

"Shh . . . don't," he whispered gruffly. "Only remember the good. Like the first time I kissed you here . . ." His hands again captured her breasts and he bent his head, rubbing soft closed lips back and forth across a turgid nipple while fondling the other. "You were exquisite . . . you still are."

In one swift motion he slipped his hands beneath her arms and fell back onto the bed, taking her with him and lifting her high while his mouth opened and sought her flesh. When his lips surrounded and stroked her breast, she breathed a throaty moan, arching sharply, head tipped back and eyes closed, letting herself be overcome by sensation.

He took her other breast in his mouth, biting lightly, washing it with wet warmth, then suckling it in a way that started her body rocking upon his. His legs fell open, creating a lee where her body fit precisely while he took up a matching rhythm.

His arms trembled as he drew her higher, sliding her body along his until she straddled him, and he pressed his mouth to her flat stomach. And yet he forced her higher, murmuring unintelligible phrases while turning to brush his lips against the soft skin of her inner thigh, the warm secret hollow above it, then the core of her femininity. With his mouth still claiming intimate possession he rolled them onto their sides, nuzzling, stroking, bringing wordless replies to her lips.

Her body moved in lissome accommodation while heat radiated through her limbs and the blood quickened in her veins. Then with a sudden call, she forced his head back and withdrew.

"Stop." Her voice trembled as she looked down at him, her fingers threaded through the hair at his temple. "Together . . . the first time should be together."

"The first time," he repeated. His eyes closed as if in benediction, and he kissed her stomach one last time before drawing himself up until he was gazing into her lambent eyes. "The first time as Mr. and Mrs. Gentry."

Her eager hands sought his flesh, coddled it, inciting his hips to seek hers as she rolled to her back, drawing him atop her.

"Come into me, Tommy Lee . . . where you belong."

She lifted . . . he lunged . . . and nature's choreography took over.

"Where I've always belonged."

Marriage . . . the blending of souls that lent meaning to the blending of bodies. Though each time had had a magic all its own, no other had matched the poignancy of this. Holding nothing in reserve they gave themselves freely. He was powerful and tensile as he drove within; she limber and lithe while lifting to receive. His arms quaked and his head hung low while the thrusts grew mightier. She gasped at the brink of climax, driving her head back sharply, lifting her shoulders in the timeless gesture of appeal.

Together they hovered on that awesome brink while savoring the coming cataclysm, and when it shuddered through them, they called out aloud, clinging together until the final ease.

The afternoon sun splashed through the wide glass doors, throwing dappled patterns on the blue carpet beneath a leafy schefflera plant. The fireplace awaited its first fire. Beside it, two cozy chairs invited years and years of contentment, while beside Rachel rested a man who promised occasional tumult.

She chuckled and he lifted his head to find her eyes closed as the sound rippled from her throat.

"What's so funny?"

She opened her eyes, smiled a very satisfied smile, and twisted a strand of his hair around her finger. "Nothing. I'm just so incredibly happy. I really do have everything I want."

He tucked her head beneath his chin, sighing with equal satisfaction.

"I love you, Tommy Lee."

He kissed her forehead and nestled her close once more. "And I love you, Rachel."

She snuggled against him, toying with the hair on his chest while dreaming of their future. Suddenly she pulled back, reminding him, "You never did finish telling me that story. So what ever became of the girl and boy?"

"Oh, let's see . . ." He pondered silently, absently caressing her naked spine. "She turned into a successful businesswoman, selling ladies' wear and showing all the women in town what *panache* means, and he became a thin, dashing, handsome, irresist—"

"You can skip the unimportant stuff," she teased. "The love story—how did it turn out?"

"Why, he married her, of course."

"Mmm . . ." she mused. "He married her after all."

"And carried her off to his beautiful castle on the shores of Cedar Creek Lake, and when she saw it, she knew it was where she'd always wanted to spend her life."

"And did she?" Rachel smiled up at Tommy Lee.

He kissed the tip of her nose. "Forever and ever. You see . . . they somehow managed to live happily ever after."

She closed her eyes, feeling his steady heartbeat against her temple, the soft brush of his palm on her back. Then Rachel Gentry tucked herself close to Tommy Lee, and together they sighed with satisfaction over the final chapter of a love story begun many years before.

Separate Beds

*With love
to my husband, Dan,
the best thing that ever happened
in my life*

Chapter 1

CIRCUMSTANCES BEING WHAT they were, it was ironic that Catherine Anderson knew little more of Clay Forrester than his name. He must be rich, she thought, scanning the foyer, which revealed quite clearly how well-off the Forrester family was.

The deep side of the expansive entry opened into a sprawling formal living room of pale yellows and muted golds. Above was a great crystal chandelier. Behind her, a stairway climbed dramatically to the second story. She was faced by double doors, a console table whose cabriole legs touched the parquet as lightly as a ballerina's toes and a brass accent lamp reflected by a gilt-framed mirror. Beside her stood an immense brass pitcher bursting with an abundance of overpoweringly fragrant dried eucalyptus.

The pungent stuff was beginning to make her sick.

She turned her eyes to the massive carved oak entry doors. The knobs weren't shaped like any she'd ever seen. Instead, they were curved and swirled like the handles of fine cutlery. Acidly Catherine wondered how much handles like those must cost, to say nothing of the pretentious bench on which she'd been left. It was lush brown velvet, armless, tufted—the kind of absurd extravagance afforded by only the very rich.

Yes, the entire foyer was a work of art and of opulence. Everything in it fit . . . except Catherine Anderson.

The girl was attractive enough, her apricot skin and weather-streaked blond hair having a fresh, vital look. Her features bore the strikingly appealing symmetry often found in those of Scandinavian ancestry—the straight nose and fine nostrils; shapely, bowed lips and blue eyes beneath arched brows of pleasing contour.

It was her clothing that gave her away. She wore a pair of heather colored slacks and shirt that spoke of brighter days long gone. They were homemade and of poor fabric. Her trench coat was limp, frayed at hem and cuff. Her brown wedgies were made of artificial stuff, worn at the heels and curled at the toes.

Yet her clean, wind-blown appearance and fresh complexion saved Catherine from looking disreputable. That, and the proud mien with which she carried herself.

Even that was slipping now, the longer she sat here. For Catherine realized she'd been left like a naughty child about to be reprimanded, which actually wasn't far from the truth.

With a resigned sigh, she dropped her head back against the wall. Vaguely she wondered if people like the Forresters would object to a girl like her laying her head against their elegant wallpaper, supposed they would, so defiantly kept it there. Her eyes slid shut, blotting out the lush elegance, unable to blot out the angry voices from the study: her father's, harsh and accusing, followed by the constrained, angry reply of Mr. Forrester.

Why do I stay? she wondered.

But she knew the answer; her neck still hurt from the pressure of her father's fingers. And, of course, there was her mother to consider. She was in there, too, along with the luckless Forresters, and—rich or not—they had done nothing to deserve a madman like her father. It had never been Catherine's intention to let this happen. She still remembered the shocked expressions of both Mr. and Mrs. Forrester when her father had barged in upon their pastoral evening with his bald accusations. They had at first attempted civility, suggesting that they all sit down in the study and talk this over. But within moments they understood what they were up against when Herb Anderson pointed at the bench and bellowed at his daughter, "Just plant your little ass right there, girlie, and don't move it or I'll beat the livin' hell outa you!"

No, the Forresters had done nothing to deserve a madman like Herb Anderson.

Suddenly the front door opened, letting in a gust of leaf-scented autumn air and a man whose clothing looked like the interior decorator had planned it to blend with the foyer. He was a tapestry of earth tones: camel-colored trousers of soft wool, European-cut, sharply creased, falling to a stylish break upon brown cordovan loafers; sport jacket of subdued rust and camel plaid, flowing over his shoulders like soft caramel over ice cream; a softer shade of rust repeated in the lamb's wool sweater beneath; an off-white collar left casually open to foil a narrow gold chain around his neck. Even nature, it seemed, had cooperated in creating his color scheme, for his skin bore the remains of a deep summer tan, and his hair was a burnished red-gold.

He was whistling as he breezed in, unaware of Catherine who sat partially shielded by the eucalyptus. She flattened her back against the stair wall, taking advantage of her sparse camouflage, watching as he crossed to the console table and glanced through what must have been the daily mail, still whistling softly. She caught a glimpse of his classically handsome face in the mirror, its straight nose, long cheeks and sculpted eyebrows. They might have been cast in bronze, so flawless and firm were their lines. But his mouth—ah, it was too perfect, too mobile, too memorable to be anything but flesh and blood.

Unaware of her presence, he shrugged off the stylish sport coat, caught it negligently in the crook of one wrist and bounded up the stairs two at a time.

Catherine wilted against the wall.

But she stiffened again as the study door burst open and Mr. Forrester stood framed against the bookshelves within, his slate-gray eyes submerged below craggy brows with a formidable expression, his anger scarcely held in check. He wasted not so much as a glance at the girl on the bench.

"Clay!" The invincible tone stopped the younger man's ascent.

"Sir?"

The voice was the same as Catherine remembered, though the formal word of address surprised her. She was not used to hearing fathers called *sir.*

"I think you had better step into the study." Then Mr. Forrester himself did so, leaving the door open as yet another command.

Had the circumstances been different, Catherine might have felt sorry for Clay Forrester. His whistling had disappeared. All she heard now was the soft shush of his footsteps coming back down the stairs.

She squeezed her ribcage with both arms, fighting the unexpected flood of panic. Don't let him see me! she thought. Let him walk right past and not turn around! Yet common sense told her she could not escape him indefinitely. Sooner or later he'd know she was here.

He reappeared around the newel post, shrugging once again into his sport coat, telling her even more about his relationship with his father.

Her heart beat in the high hollow of her throat and she held her breath, the stain of embarrassment now coloring her cheeks. He stepped to the mirror, checked his collar and his hair. To Catherine, for the briefest moment he seemed vulnerable, being watched from behind that way, unaware of her presence or of what awaited him in the study. But she reminded herself he was not only rich, he was degenerate; he deserved what was coming.

He moved then and her image became visible in the mirror. His eyes registered surprise, then he turned to face her momentarily.

"Oh, hi," he greeted her. "I didn't see you hiding back there."

She was suddenly conscious of the frightful thud of her heart, but she carefully kept her face placid, giving him no more than a silent, wide-eyed nod. Never having planned to lay eyes on him again, she was not prepared for this.

"Excuse me," he added politely, as he might have to any of the clients who often waited there to do business with his father. Then he turned toward the study.

From within came his father's command. "Shut the door, Clay!"

Her eyes slid closed.

He doesn't remember me, Catherine thought. The admission made her suddenly, inexplicably want to cry, though it made no sense at all when she'd hoped he'd walk right past like a stranger, and that was precisely what he'd done.

Well, she berated herself, that *is* what you wanted, *isn't it?* She summoned up anger as an antidote to the tears which Catherine Anderson never allowed herself to shed. To feel them threatening—and here, of all places!—was unspeakable. Weaklings cried! Weaklings and fools!

But Catherine Anderson was neither weakling nor fool. The circumstances might appear otherwise just now, but in twenty-four hours everything would be far different.

From behind the study door Clay Forrester's voice exploded, "Who!" and her eyes came open.

He doesn't remember me, she thought again, resigning herself to the fact once and for all, straightening her shoulders, telling herself not to let it matter.

The study door flew open, and she affected a relaxed and unconcerned air as Clay Forrester confronted her framed in that doorway, much as his father had before. His eyes—gray, too—impaled her. His scowl immediately told her he didn't believe a word of it! But she noted with satisfaction that his hair now looked finger-combed. Pushing back both front panels of his sport coat, hands on hips, he challenged her with those angry eyes. He scanned her summarily, allowed his glance to float down to her stomach, then back up, noting her detached air.

She suffered the insolent way his gaze roved downward—like a slap in the face—and retaliated by pointedly studying his full, lower lip, which she remembered quite well, considering the brevity of their association and the time that had lapsed since. But, knowing virtually nothing about him, Catherine decided she'd best take care in dealing with him, so she carefully remained silent beneath his scrutiny.

"Catherine?" he asked at last. She expected to see his breath, the word was so cold.

"Hello, Clay," she replied levelly, maintaining that false air of aloofness.

Clay Forrester watched her rise, slim and seemingly assured. Almost haughty, he thought, but certainly not scared . . . and hardly supplicating!

"You belong in here too," he stated tersely, holding that implacable stance while she gave him one extended look which she hoped appeared cool. Then she walked past him into the study. Antagonism emanated from him. She could nearly smell it as she passed so close in front of him.

The room was like a storybook setting: pre-supper fire burning on the grate, stem glasses half full upon polished tables, book-lined walls, an original Terry Redlin wildlife oil on the wall behind a leather loveseat, soft carpeting underfoot. Masculine, yet warm, everything about the room spoke of an interrupted coziness, which was precisely why Herb Anderson had chosen this time of day to make his appearance, when he figured all the Forresters would be home. His exact words had been, "I'll get them rich sons-a-bitches when they're all holed up together in that fancy brick mansion, wearin' all them family jewels, and we'll see who does the paying for this!"

The contrast between Clay's parents and Catherine's was almost laughable. Mrs. Forrester was ensconced in a wing chair at one side of the fireplace. She was shaken, yet extremely proper, feet crossed at the ankles. Her clothing was impeccable and up-to-date, her hair done in a tasteful coiffure which made her features appear youthfully regal. Upon her shapely hands glittered the magnitude of gems Herb Anderson derided.

Ada Anderson, in the matching chair on the opposite side of the fireplace, picked at a slub of her bargain basement coat, keeping her eyes downcast. Her hair was mousy, her shape dumpy. Upon her hand was only a thin gold band whose apple blossom design was worn smooth from years of hard work.

Mr. Forrester, double-vested in well-tailored business gray, stood behind a morocco-topped desk that held several leatherbound books in a pair of jade bookends worth as much as the entire Anderson collection of living room furniture.

Then there was her father, decked out in a red nylon jacket boasting the words *Warpo's Bar* on its back. Catherine avoided looking at the bulging beer belly, the bloated face, the ever-present expression of cynicism that perpetually claimed the world was out to beat Herb Anderson out of something, when actually it was the other way around.

Catherine stopped beside her mother's chair, conscious that Clay had stopped behind her. She kept a shoulder turned away from him, choosing instead to face his father, easily the most formidable person in the room. Even his position behind the desk was strategically chosen to connote command. Understanding this, she chose to confront him on her feet. Her own father might swear and carry on like a drunken sailor, but this other stern adversary was by far the greater threat. Catherine sensed the man's total control, sensed, too, that should she face him with a hint of challenge on her face it would be the worst possible mistake. He was the kind of man who knew how to deal with hostility and defiance, thus she carefully kept them from her countenance.

"My son doesn't seem to remember you, does he?" His voice was like the first edge of November's ice on a Minnesota lake—cold, sharp, thin, dangerous.

"No, he doesn't," Catherine replied, looking at him squarely.

"Do you remember her?" the father snapped at his son, daring it to be true.

"No," answered Clay, raising Catherine's ire not because she wanted to be remembered, but because it was a lie. She hadn't really expected the truth out of him anyway, had she?—not once she'd suspected he had enough money to back up any lies he chose to tell. Still, his answer rankled. She turned to find him nearer than was comfortable and accosted him with blue eyes that rivaled the frost in his father's.

Liar! Her eyes seemed to shout, while he smugly perused her features, then cast a glance over her blond hair and saw the fire create sundogs on it, dancing behind her that way. And suddenly he recalled it backlit by fireworks.

Oh, he remembered her all right. . . . Now he remembered her! But he cautiously kept it from showing in his face.

"What the hell is this, a frame-up?" he accused.

"I'm afraid it isn't, and you know it," Catherine replied, wondering how long she could maintain this feigned calm.

But then Herb Anderson jumped in, yelping and pointing. "Your goddam right it isn't, lover boy, so just don't think—"

"You're in my home," Mr. Forrester interrupted explosively, "and if you want this . . . this *discussion* to continue, you will control yourself while you are here!" There was an undeniable note of sarcasm in the word *discussion;* it was obvious Herb Anderson didn't know the meaning of the word.

"Just get busy and make lover boy here own up, or, so help me, I'll squeeze the truth outa him like I done outa her."

Something slimy seemed to crawl through Clay's innards. He glanced sharply at the girl but she remained composed, her eyes now on the desk top where whitened knuckles were depressing lustrous leather.

"You will remain rational, *sir,* or you and your wife will leave at once and take your daughter with you!" Forrester ordered.

But Anderson had been waiting all his life for his ship to come in, and this . . . by God! . . . was it! He turned to confront Clay nose to nose.

"Let's hear it, lover boy," he sneered. "Let's hear you say you never laid eyes on her before, and I'll make you the sorriest lookin' mess you ever seen in your life. And when I'm done, sonny, I'll sue your old man for every goddam penny he's got. Rich bastard like you, think just because you got a few bucks your kind can go around screwing everything in skirts. Well, not this time, not this time!" He shook his fist under Clay's nose. "You're gonna pay up this time or I'll be hollering rape so fast it'll make you wish you was a fag!"

Mortified, Catherine knew it was useless to argue. Her father had been drinking all day, getting primed for this. She'd seen it coming but could do nothing about it.

"Clay, do you know this woman?" his father demanded grimly, pointedly ignoring Anderson.

Before Clay could reply, Herb Anderson pushed his face near his daughter's and sneered, "Tell him, girlie . . . tell him it was lover boy here knocked you up!" Instinctively Catherine drew away from the disgusting smell of his breath, but he reached out and grabbed her cheeks and rasped, "You tell him, sister, if you know what's good for you."

Clay stepped between the two. "Now, wait a minute! Take your hands off her! She's already pointed the finger at me or you wouldn't be here." Then, more quietly, he added, "I said I don't know her, but I remember her."

Catherine flashed him a warning look. Actually, the last thing she wanted from Clay Forrester was noble self-sacrifice.

"There! You see!" Anderson made a motion like he'd slapped a trump card on the desk top. Mrs. Forrester's face quivered. Her husband's showed the first sign of defeat as his lips fell open.

"You're admitting that this woman's child is yours?" Claiborne Forrester exclaimed disbelievingly.

"I'm not admitting any such thing. I simply said I remember her."

"From when?" Claiborne insisted.

"This summer."

"This summer, when? What month?"

"I think it was July."

"You *think* it was July! Hadn't you better do more than *think?*"

"It was."

A look of gloating turned Herb Anderson's face more detestable than ever.

"July what?" Claiborne pressed on, facing the calamity head-on, in spite of his growing dread.

"July fourth."

"And what happened on July fourth?"

Catherine held her breath again, embarrassment for Clay making her acutely uncomfortable now.

"We went on a blind date."

The room grew church-silent. Catherine sensed everyone counting off two and a half months since then.

Claiborne's chin hardened, his jaw protruded. "And?"

Only the soft hiss of the fire spoke while Clay considered, his eyes briefly lighting on Catherine. "And I absolutely refuse to answer another question until Catherine and I speak alone," he ended, surprising her.

"You, Clay Forrester, will answer my question here and now!" his father exploded, rapping a fist on the desk top in frustration. "Did you or did you not have relations with this woman on July Fourth?"

"With all due respect, Father, that is none of your business," Clay said in a tightly controlled voice.

Mrs. Forrester put a trembling hand to her lips, beseeching her son with carefully made-up eyes to deny it all here and now.

"You say this is none of my business when this man threatens to bring a paternity suit against you, and to ruin your reputation along with mine in this city?"

"You've taught me well enough that a man makes his own reputation. As far as you're concerned, I don't think there's anything to worry about."

"Clay, all I want is the truth. If the answer is no, then for God's sake, quit protecting the girl and say no. If it's yes, admit it and let's get it over with."

"I refuse to answer until she and I can talk privately. Obviously we were both left out of any earlier discussion. After we've had a chance to talk, I'll give you my answer." He gestured to Catherine, motioning her to follow, but she was too stunned to move. This was one turn of events that was totally unexpected!

"Now, wait just one goddam minute there, sonny!" Herb Anderson hissed. "You ain't gonna go skipping out on me and leaving me lookin' like some jackass don't know which end is up! I know *exactly* what your game is! You take her outa here and pay her off with some measly couple o' hundred bucks and shut her up and your problem is solved, huh?"

"Let's go." Clay made a move to pass Anderson.

"I said, hold on!" Anderson stuck his pudgy fingertips in Clay's chest.

"Get out of my way." Some grim note of warning made Anderson comply. Clay strode toward the door, curtly advising Catherine, "You'd better come along with me if you know what's good for you."

She walked toward Clay like a puppet, even while her father continued his tirade at their backs. "Don't you get no ideas about givin' her the money to get rid of the kid either, you hear me! And just see to it you keep your hands offa her, lover boy. She better not have no more complaints or I'll have the law down on you before the night is out!"

Face scorching, insides trembling, Catherine followed Clay into the foyer. She assumed he would lead her to another room of the house, but instead he stalked to the front door, flung it wide and ordered, "Let's take a ride." It took her off-guard and rooted her to the parquet, quite involuntarily. Realizing she hadn't followed, he turned. "We've got some talking to do, and I'll be damned if I'll do it in the same house with all of our parents."

Still she hesitated, her blue eyes wide, mistrusting. "I'd rather stay here or go for a walk or something." Not even the blazing color in her cheeks softened him. Her hesitation only made Clay more unyielding.

"I'm not giving you an alternative," he stated unequivocally, then turned on his heel. From the library came the sound of her father's voice, badgering the Forresters further. Seeing no alternative, she finally followed Clay outside.

Chapter 2

A SILVER CORVETTE was parked now in the horseshoe-shaped driveway behind her family's sedan. Without waiting, Clay yanked a door open and got in, then sat glaring straight ahead while she tried to quickly measure the risk of going for a ride with him. After all, she knew nothing about him. Did he have a temper like her father? Was he capable of violence when cornered this way? What would he do to keep her from making trouble in his life?

He glanced back to find her looking balefully over her shoulder at the front door as if help would step through it at any moment.

"Come on, let's get this over with." His choice of words did little to reassure her.

"I—I really don't care to go for a ride," she stammered.

"Don't tell me you're afraid of me!" he taunted with a dry laugh. "It's a little late for that, isn't it?" He started the engine without taking his insolent eyes off her. She moved at last, only to realize, once she was in the car, that there was one eventuality she hadn't considered. He'd kill them both before this was over! He drove like a maniac, throwing the car into gear and careening down the brick driveway while manicured shrubbery blurred past the windows. At the road, he scarcely braked, changing gears with a screech and a lurch, then tearing at breakneck speed through a maze of streets that were unfamiliar to her. He slammed his hand against a cassette that hung in the tape deck, sending throbbing rock music through the car. She couldn't do anything about his driving but she reached over and lowered the volume. He angled her a sidelong glance, then stepped a little harder on the gas. Obstinately she wedged herself into her seat and tried to ignore his childish antics, deciding to let him get it out of his system.

He steered one-handed, just to show her he could.

She sat cross-legged, just to show him she could.

They sailed around corners, up curving hills, past strange street signs until Catherine was totally lost. He took a sharp right-hand curve, gunned his way into a sharper left, flew between two stone gate markers onto gravel where they fishtailed before climbing into a pocket of wooded land. The headlights flew across a sign: PARK HOURS 10:00 A.M. to—but the lights moved too fast for Catherine to catch the rest. At the top of the last incline they broke onto a parking lot surrounded on all sides by trees. He stopped the car much as he'd driven it—too fast! She was forced to break her forward pitch with a hand on the dash or sail through the windshield!

But still she stubbornly refused to comment or to look at him.

Satisfied, anyway, that he'd managed to budge her from that damn uppity cross-kneed pose, he cut the engine and turned to her. But he remained silent, studying her dim profile, knowing it made her uncomfortable, which suited his purpose.

"All right," Clay said at last in the driest of tones, "what kind of game are you playing?"

"I wish it were a game. Unfortunately, it's very real."

He snorted. "That I don't doubt one bit. I want to know why you're trying to pin the blame on me."

"I understood your reluctance to answer with our parents present, but here, between just the two of us, there's no further need to play dumb. Not when we both know the truth."

"And just what the hell *is* the truth?"

"The truth is that I'm pregnant and you're the father."

"I'm the father!" He was in a high state of temper now, but she found his shouting preferable to his driving.

"You sound slightly outraged," she said levelly, giving him a sideways glance.

"*Outraged* isn't the word for me right now! Did you really think I'd fall for that kangaroo court back there?" He thumbed over his shoulder.

"No," she answered. "I thought you'd flatly deny ever having laid eyes on me and that would be the end of that. We would go our separate ways and take up our lives where we'd left off."

Her unruffled detachment took some of the wind from his sails. "It's beginning to look like I should have."

"I'd survive," she said tonelessly.

Baffled, he thought, she's an odd one, so composed, almost cold, unconcerned. "If you can survive without me, tell me why you created that scene in the first place."

"I didn't; my father did."

"I suppose it was entirely his idea to storm our house tonight."

"That's right."

"You had nothing to do with it," he added sarcastically.

At last Catherine grew upset, losing her determination to remain unruffled. She whirled sideways in her seat and let him have it. "Before you say one more thing in that . . . that damnably accusing voice of yours, I want you to know that I don't want *one damn thing from you! Not one!*"

"Then why are you here, picking the flesh from my bones?"

"Your *flesh,* Mr. Forrester?" she parried. "Your flesh is the last thing I want!"

He pointedly ignored her double entendre. "Do you expect me to believe that after all the accusations that have been hurled at me tonight?"

"Believe what you will," she said, resigned again, turning away. "I don't want anything but to be left alone."

"Then why did you come?" When she only remained silent, he insisted again, "Why!"

Obstinately she remained mute. She wanted neither his sympathy nor his money nor his name. All she wanted was for tomorrow to hurry and get here.

Antagonized by her stubborn indifference, he grabbed her shoulder roughly. "Listen, lady, I didn't—"

She jerked her shoulder, trying to free it from his grasp. "My name is Catherine," she hissed.

"I know what your name is!"

"It took you some time to remember it, though, didn't it?"

"And what is that supposed to mean?"

"Let go of my shoulder, Mr. Forrester, you're hurting me."

He dropped his hand, but his voice zeroed in, slightly sing-songy now. "Oh,

I get it. The lady is feeling abused because I didn't recognize her right off the bat, is that it?"

She denied him an answer, but felt herself blushing in the darkness.

"Do I sense a little contradiction there? Either you want recognition from me or you don't. Now which is it?"

"I repeat, I don't want anything from you except to be taken home."

"When I take you back, it'll be when I'm satisfied about what I'm being threatened with."

"Then you can take me back now. I'm not threatening anything."

"Your mere presence in my home was a threat. Now let's get on with what you want for a payoff . . . that is, if you're really pregnant."

The thought had never occurred to her that he'd doubt it.

"Oh, I'm pregnant all right, make no mistake about that."

"Oh, I don't intend to," he said pointedly. "I don't intend to. I mean to make damn sure that baby is *not* mine."

"Are you saying you really do *not* remember having sexual intercourse with me last Fourth of July?" Then she added in a satirically sugary tone, "You'll notice I do not mistakenly call it making love, like so many fools are prone to do."

The dark hid the eyebrow he cocked in her direction, but it couldn't hide the cocky tone of his voice. "Of course, I remember. What does that prove? There could have been a dozen others."

She'd been expecting this sooner or later, but she wasn't expecting the anger it evoked, the way she simply had to fight back, no matter how degrading it was to have to. "How dare you say such a thing when you know perfectly well there weren't!"

"Now you're the one who sounds outraged. Promiscuous females have to be prepared to be doubted. After all, there's no way to prove paternity."

"No proof is necessary when it's the first time!" She smoldered, wondering why she wasted her breath on him. Without warning the overhead light came on. In its beam, Clay Forrester looked like she'd just thrown ice water on him.

"What!" he exclaimed, genuinely stunned.

"Turn that thing off," she ordered, turning her face sharply away.

"Like hell I will. Look at me." Something had changed in his voice, but it made it even more impossible to face him.

The view outside the window was totally black but she studied it as if for answers. Suddenly a hand grabbed her cheeks, the fingers sinking into them as he forced her to look at him. She glared into his surprised face as if she hated every feature of it, gritting her teeth because she didn't.

"What are you saying?" Intense gray eyes allowed her no escape. She was torn by the wish to have him know nothing of her and the equally strong wish to let him know everything. He was, after all, the father of the child she carried.

He stared into her imprisoned face, wanting to deny her words, but unable to. He tried to remember last July fourth more clearly, but they'd had too much wine that night.

"You're hurting me again," she said quietly, making him realize he still held her cheeks imprisoned in his grasp.

He dropped his hand, continuing to study her. She had a face that wasn't

too easy to forget: shapely, narrow nose; long cheeks dusted with a suggestion
of freckles; blue eyes trying hard not to blink, meeting him squarely now
within long, sandy lashes. Her mouth was sullen, but memory flashed him a
picture of it smiling. Her hair was shoulder-length, blond on blond, tabby-
streaked, its bangs feathered back but falling in alluring wisps onto her forehead. It curled hither and thither around her long neck. She had a tall, thin
frame. He suspected, although he could not clearly remember, she was shaped
the way he liked his women shaped: long-limbed, hollow-hipped and not
overly breasty.

Like Jill, he thought.

Sobered at the thought of Jill, he again fell to trying to remember what had
passed between himself and this woman.

"I . . ." Catherine began, then asked with less acid in her voice, "will you
turn out that light?"

"I think I have a right to see you during this sticky conversation we're
having."

She had no choice but to be studied like a printout from a lie-detector test.
She tolerated it as long as she could before turning away, asking, "You don't
remember, do you?"

"Parts of it, I do, but not all."

"You struck me as a man of experience, one who'd know a virgin every
time."

"If you're asking me how often I do things like that, it's none of your
business."

"I agree. It's none of my business . . . but I wasn't asking. I was only
defending myself, which I had no intention of doing in the first place. You are
the one who seemed to be asking how often *I'd* done things like that, and no
girl likes to be called promiscuous. I only wanted to point out that it was
undeniably my first time. I assumed you'd have known it."

"Like I said, my memory is a little fuzzy. Suppose I believe you—there
could have been others after me."

That brought her anger back in full force. "I have no intention of sitting
here and being insulted by you any further!" she spit out. Then she opened the
door and got out. He wasn't far behind her, but she stalked off into the dark,
her shoes crunching gravel, gone before he could storm around to the other
side of the car.

"Get back here!" he shouted into the dark, his hands on his hips.

"Go to hell!" she yelled from somewhere down the road.

"Just where do you think you're going?"

But she just kept on walking. He broke into a run, following her shadowy
form, angered more than he could say by her stony insistence that she wanted
nothing from him.

She felt his hand grab her arm and swing her around in the dark. "Dammit,
Catherine, get back to the car!" he warned.

"And do what!" she exclaimed, turning to face him, fists clenched at her
sides, "Sit and listen to you call me the equivalent of a whore? I've taken that
kind of abuse from my father, but I certainly don't have to sit still and take it
from you!"

"All right, I'm sorry, but what do you expect a man to say when he's confronted with an accusation like yours?"

"I can't answer your question, not being a man myself. But I thought a—a worldly stud like you would know the truth, that's all!"

"I'm no worldly stud, so knock it off!"

"All right, so we're even."

They stood in the dark, unmoving combatants. She wondered if he could be as experienced as he'd seemed that night and yet not recognize the fact of her virginity. He, meanwhile, wondered if a girl of her age could possibly have remained a virgin all that time. He guessed her to be twenty or so. But in this day and age, twenty was old, sexually. Again he strove to remember anything about that night, how she'd acted, if she'd been in pain, if she'd resisted. All he knew for sure was that if she *had* resisted in any way or asked him to stop, he would have. Wine or no wine, he was no rapist!

Giving up, he said cajolingly, "You must have done all right. I never knew the difference."

His chauvinistic remark riled her so swiftly she lost good sense and swung on him, giving him a good one with her knuckles in the middle of his breastbone.

Caught off-guard, he gasped and stumbled one surprised step backward. "Ouch, that hurt, goddammit!"

"Oh, that's rich! That's so rich I could throw up! *I* must have done all right! Why, you insufferable egotistical goat! Telling me *I* must have done all right when you're the one who can't even remember clearly!"

Nursing his bruised chest, he muttered, "Christ, are you always like this?"

"I don't know. This is a first for me. How do your pregnant girl friends usually react?"

Wary now, he was careful not to touch her. "What do you say we stop trading insults, okay? Let's just forget our sexual histories and own up to the fact that we went out on a blind date and gave each other a little refreshment for the night, and take it from there. You say you were a virgin, but you can't prove it by me."

"The dates will bear it out. The baby is due on the sixth of April. That's the only other proof I have that it was you."

"Pardon me if I seem dense, but since you claim you don't want anything from me, why are you trying so hard to convince me?"

"I'm not . . . I . . . at least I wasn't until you questioned me about there being others. It was a point of self-defense and nothing more." Then, realizing she was beginning to sound more and more entreating, she muttered, "Oh, why do I waste my breath on you!" And she turned down the road again, leaving him with the diminishing sound of her footsteps.

He let her go this time and stood there with one hand on his hip in the dark, thinking to himself that she was the singularly most irritating woman he'd ever met. It was all the more frustrating to think he'd made love to a wasp like that! Then, with a rueful grin, he corrected himself, making it, had "sexual intercourse" with a wasp like that. He listened to her footsteps fading away, thinking, Good riddance, lady! But in the end he couldn't let her go.

"Catherine, don't be an ass!" he admonished, hurting her ego further as she hotfooted it down the gravel road. "You're at least three miles from my house, and God-knows-how-many miles from yours. Get back up here!"

The fragrant night resounded with her response: "Up yours, Clay Forrester!"

He cursed, returned to his car and twisted the key so violently it should have broken off in the ignition. The headlights flashed on, arced around, and the Corvette went roaring down the hill, picking out Catherine's belligerent back as she continued to stalk. He roared past her, spraying dust and gravel.

About fifty feet in front of Catherine, at the bottom of the hill, the brake lights flashed on, followed by the interior light as Clay got out again and stood leaning an elbow on top of the open door, waiting. She would have ignored him, but he wouldn't allow it. When she was abreast of him, a hand shot out and detained her. "Get in, you little spitfire," he ordered. "I'm not leaving you out here whether I want to or not. Not at this hour of the night!"

The light from the car limned her angry face as she thrust her lower lip out, beetling her brows in curled distaste. "I must have been crazy to come to your house in the first place. I should have known no good would come of it."

"Then why did you?" he insisted, holding her easily by a forearm, but well enough away so she couldn't punch him again.

"Because I didn't think your parents deserved the likes of my old man. I actually thought by going along with him I could save them from some unpleasantness they didn't deserve."

"Do you expect me to believe that?"

"I don't care what you believe, Clay Forrester! Let go of my arm, dammit!" She yanked herself free, then whirled like a bantam rooster, unable to keep explanations mute. "You've gotten a dose of my old man. It doesn't take very long to get the drift of how he operates. He's mean and vindictive and lazy, and an alcoholic to boot. He'll stop at nothing to get whatever he can out of either you or your parents. I think he's stark, raving mad to go shoving his way into your house the way he did, badgering your family."

"And what does he expect to get out of it?"

Catherine debated, decided she had nothing to lose by being frank. "A free ride."

She could tell he was surprised, for he studied her in the vague light cast from the car, then exclaimed, "You admit that?"

"Of course I admit it. It'd take a fool not to see what he's up to. He smelled money, which he's never had enough of, and it brought out his every greedy instinct. He thinks he can use this situation to make life a little easier on himself. I don't kid myself one bit that it's my reputation he's concerned about. He can harp all he wants about his little girl's loss of innocence and her ruined future. But it's really his own future he's looking out for. He wants to feather his bed till it's as soft as he thinks yours is. I don't really think he believes for one minute he can get you to marry me. I don't even think he *wants* you to. He'd rather have your guilt money, and he'll do everything in his power to get it. I warn you, he's a dangerous man. You see, he believes his ship just came in."

"And none of those thoughts entered your head?"

"I didn't know you from Adam last July. How could I possibly have smelled money?"

"Your cousin, Bobbi, lined us up. She's Stu's girl, and Stu is an old friend of mine. It follows."

She threw her hands up and paced agitatedly back and forth. "Oh, sure! First I ran a financial check on you, then got myself lined up with you on the *perfect* night to get pregnant, then I seduced you and sent my father in after the pickings." She snorted derisively. "Don't flatter yourself, Forrester! It may surprise you to learn that not every girl who finds herself pregnant wants to marry the man. I made one mistake last July, but that doesn't mean I'm going to make a second by forcing you to marry me."

"If you're innocent, tell me just how in the hell your old man knew who to come to. Somebody pointed him in my direction."

"I did not *point!*"

"Then how did he choose me to come after?"

She suddenly clammed up, turned her back on him and walked around the car, saying, "I believe I will take a ride home after all." And she got in.

He got in, too, leaving one foot out on the gravel so the light would remain on while he grilled her.

"Don't avoid the issue," he demanded. "How?"

"I did *not* give him your name. I refused to tell him anything!"

"I don't believe you. How did he find out then?" Clay saw how she worried her lower lip between her teeth, refusing to look at him.

Catherine willed her mouth to stop forming explanations for his benefit, but she was not the cunning woman he thought, and it galled her to be accused this way.

"How?" he repeated, waiting.

Her nostrils flared, she stared straight out over the dash, but finally divulged, "I keep a diary." Her tone was quieter and her eyelids flickered slightly.

"You what?"

"You heard me," she said to the window on her side.

"Yes, I heard, but I'm not sure I understand. You mean he found it?" It was beginning to dawn on Clay just what kind of unscrupulous bastard her father really was.

"Leave me alone. I've already said more than I wanted to."

"There's a lot at stake here. I deserve to know the truth if that baby is really mine. Now answer me. Did he find it?"

"Not exactly."

"What then?"

She sighed, laid her head back against the seat but continued staring out the window away from him. Then from the side he saw her eyelids slide shut wearily, almost resignedly. Her voice lost much of its agitation.

"Listen, none of this has anything to do with you. Leave it be. What he is and what he did was never supposed to enter into it. I only wanted to keep your parents from paying his demands. That's why I came along."

"Don't change the subject, Catherine. He found the diary and found my name, right?"

She swallowed. "Right," she whispered.

"How did he find it?"

"Oh, for God's sake, Clay, I've kept a diary since I was in pinafores! He knew it was there someplace. He didn't just *find* it, he ripped my room apart until he found the evidence he was always accusing me of. You wanted the truth, there it is."

Something coiled in Clay's gut. His voice softened. "Didn't anybody try to stop him?"

"I wasn't there. My mother wouldn't try to stop him if she could. She's scared of her own shadow, to say nothing of him. You don't know my old man. There's no stopping him when he gets something in his head. The man's insane."

Clay pulled his foot inside and slammed the car door. He sat brooding, putting it all together, then cradled the steering wheel in both arms, clasping a wrist behind it. At last he looked back over his shoulder at her. "I'm almost afraid to ask . . . what was in it?"

"Everything."

With a small moan he lowered his forehead to the steering wheel. "Oh, God . . ."

"Yes," she repeated quietly. "Oh, God . . ."

"I take it you remembered that night more clearly than I did?" he asked, embarrassed now himself.

"I'm no different than any other girl. It was my first time. I'm afraid I was quite explicit about my feelings and the events of that night."

The silence lengthened and Catherine's composure slipped. It was far more disconcerting having him even remotely sympathetic than having him angry. After some time he sank back against his seat, shuddering a sigh, leaning an elbow high on the window ledge and rolling his face aside to knead the bridge of his nose. The long, strained silence became painted with provocative images that flickered through their minds until at last Clay forced his thoughts back to the present and the unpleasant aspect of her father's threats.

"So he wants reparation."

"Exactly, but whatever he says, whatever he threatens, you must not meet his demands. Don't pay him anything!" she said with sudden passion.

"Listen, it's not just up to me anymore. He's brought my father into this, and my father is . . . my father is the most exasperatingly honest man I've ever known. Either he'll force me to pay, or he'll pay whatever your father demands before this thing is over."

"No!" she exclaimed with an intensity that brought her near to clutching his arm. "You must not!"

"Listen, I don't understand you. You've spent the night convincing me you're carrying my baby. Now you beg me not to pay your father anything. Why?"

"Because my father is the scum of the earth!" Her words were as sharp as knives, but the knives were double-edged, for the words she was forced to utter cut her deeply. "Because I've hated him for as long as I can remember, and if it's the last thing I do, I want to make sure he doesn't cash in on any good luck due to me. He's been waiting for years for something like this to happen. Now that it has, it almost thrills me to be responsible for his coming so close, then foiling him!"

Suddenly Clay prickled with awareness. "What do you mean, if it's the last thing you do?"

She managed a sardonic laugh. "Oh, don't trouble yourself, Mr. Forrester, supposing for a minute I'd commit suicide over this. That would hardly foil him anyway."

"How then?"

"Depriving him of the payoff money will be quite enough. You don't know him or you'd realize what I mean. It'll almost be worth every time he—" But she stopped just short of being carried away by the hate she felt, by the memories she had no intention of revealing.

Clay again began rubbing the bridge of his nose, fighting against getting involved with her past any more than necessary. But the vindictiveness she displayed, the abusive way the man had treated her and spoken to her, the accusations she said her father undeservedly made to her—it was the classic picture of a physically violent man. But to involve himself in sympathy for this woman would be a mistake. Yet even while Clay refused to allow himself to delve any further into her past, what he knew of it was already festering in the dark silence while he grew upset over being embroiled in this fiasco in the first place. It was all so damn unnecessary, he thought. Pinching the bridge of his nose, Clay found he was now beginning to develop a headache.

He boosted himself up and outlined the wheel with his arms again. "How old are you?" he asked, out of the blue.

"What possible difference does that make?"

"How old!" he repeated, more forcefully.

"Nineteen."

He emitted a single sound, half-laugh, half-grunt. "Nineteen years old and she didn't have the sense to take some precautions," he said to the ceiling.

"Me!" she yelped. A quick, smoking anger assaulted her, making her shout louder than necessary in the close confines of the car. "Why didn't *you?* You were the one who had all the experience in these matters!"

"I wasn't planning on anything that night," he said, still disgusted.

"Well, neither was I!"

"A girl with any sense at all doesn't go around looking for sex without being prepared."

"I was not looking for sex!"

"Ha! Nineteen and a virgin and she claims she's not looking for it!"

"You conceited bastard, you think—" she began, but he cut her off.

"Conceit's got nothing to do with it," he ground out, nose to nose with her now across the narrow space, "you just don't randomly go out on the make without some kind of contraceptive!"

"Why?" she shouted. "Why me? Because I'm the woman? Why not you? What was the matter with you thinking ahead a little bit, an experienced stud like you?"

"That's the second time you've called me a stud, lady, and I don't like it!"

"And that's the second time you've called me *lady,* and I don't like it either, not the way you say it!"

"We're getting off the subject, which was your neglect."

"I believe the subject was *your* neglect."

"The woman usually takes care of precautions. Naturally, I assumed—"

"Usually!" she croaked, throwing her hands in the air, then flopping back exaggeratedly, talking to the ceiling. "And *he* calls *me* promiscuous!"

"Now just a minute—"

But this time she interrupted him. "I told you, it was my first time. I wouldn't even have known how to use a contraceptive!"

"Don't hand me that! This isn't Victorian England! All you'd have had to do was open the phone book to find out how and where to learn. Or hadn't you heard—women have come of age? Only most of them prove it by showing a little common sense with their first fling. If you'd have done the same, we wouldn't be in this mess."

"What good are all these recriminations? I told you, it happened, that's all."

"It sure as hell did, and it was just my luck that it happened with an ignorant girl who doesn't know the meaning of the words *birth control.*"

"Listen, *Mister* Forrester, I don't have to sit here and be preached to by you! You're equally as guilty as I am, only you're blaming me because it's easier than blaming yourself. It's bad enough I have to tolerate your inquisition without defending myself against ignorance! It took two of us, you know!"

"Okay, okay, just relax. Maybe I came down a little heavy on you, but this could have been avoided so easily."

"Well, it wasn't. That's a fact of life we have to live with."

"Clever choice of words," he muttered.

"Listen, would you mind? Just take me home. I'm tired and I don't want to sit here arguing anymore."

"Well, what about the baby—what are you going to do with it?"

"It's none of your business."

He bit the corner of his lip and asked quickly, before he lost his nerve, "Would you take money for an abortion?"

Her preliminary silence nearly made her reply redundant. "Oh, you'd like that, wouldn't you? Then your conscience would be clear. No, I wouldn't take money for any abortion!"

Long before she finished, he felt like a confirmed pervert.

"All right, all right, sorry I asked." He couldn't tell yet if he was worried or relieved by her answer. He sighed. "Well, what are we going to do about your father?"

"You're so smart, you figure it out." Catherine knew that after tomorrow, when Herb Anderson's pregnant little trump card disappeared, his ship would lose the wind from its sails. But she was damned if she'd tell Clay Forrester that. Let him stew in his own juices!

"I can't," he was saying almost contritely, "and I'm not that smart and I'm sorry I called you ignorant and I'm sorry I called you promiscuous and I shouldn't have gone flying off the handle like that, but what man wouldn't lose his temper?"

"You might be justified if I were making demands, but I'm not. I'm not holding a gun to your head or forcing you to do anything. But neither am I going to sip from your tarnished silver spoon," she ended sarcastically.

"And what is that supposed to mean?"

"It means that maybe my father was right to resent you because you're rich. It means that I resent your thinking you can sweep it all under the rug by an offer of a quick abortion. I'd have respected you more if you'd never suggested it."

"It's legal now, you know."

"And it's also murder."

"There are conflicting views on that too."

"And obviously yours and mine conflict."

"Then you plan to keep the baby?"

"That's none of your business."

"If it's my baby, it's my business."

"Wrong," she said with finality, the single word stating clearly that it was useless for him to try to get anything more from her. The silence waged war with Clay's conscience while he sat disconsolately cradling the wheel. When next he spoke, the words told more truth than either of them had expected.

"Listen, I don't want that kid raised in the same house with your father."

You could have heard a leaf drop from the blackened branches that drooped above the road. Then Catherine's voice came quietly into the dark.

"Well, well, well . . ."

For answer he started the engine, threw the car into gear and tried to drive away his frustration. Brooding, he drove again one-handed, allowing the car just enough excessive speed, but not too much. She leaned back, silently watching the arch of trees spin backward above the headlights, losing all sense of direction, shutting out thoughts momentarily. The car slowed, turned, nosed along the street where he lived.

"Do you think your parents might still be here?"

"I have no idea. A madman like him just might be."

"It looks like they've gone," he said, rolling past, finding no sedan in the driveway.

"You'll just have to take me home then," she said, then added while turning her face toward her window, ". . . so sorry to put you out."

He came to a halt at a stop sign and sat waiting with feigned patience. When she only continued staring stubbornly out that window he was forced to ask, "Well, which way?"

Under the blue-white glance of the streetlight she noted the effrontery of his insolent pose: one wrist draped over the wheel, one shoulder slightly slumped toward his door.

"You really don't remember anything about that night, do you?"

"I remember what I *want* to remember. *You* remember that."

"Fair enough," she agreed, then settled her expression into one of indifference and gave him a street address and brief directions on how to reach it.

The ride from Edina to North Minneapolis took some twenty minutes—long, increasingly uncomfortable minutes during which their angers diminished at approximately the same rate as the speed of Clay's driving. With verbal combat forsaken, there was only the sound of the car purring its way through the somnolent city with an occasional streetlight intruding its pale, passing glimpse into their moving world. Within the confines of that world an uninvited intimacy settled, like an unwanted guest whose presence forces politeness upon his host and hostess. The silence grew rife with unsaid things —fears, dreads, worries. Each could not be more anxious to part and be rid of this tension between them, yet for both a final separation seemed too abrupt. As Clay turned a last corner onto her street the car was nearly crawling.

"Whi . . ." His voice cracked and he cleared his throat. "Which house?"

"The third on the right."

The car rolled to a stop at the curb, and Clay shifted into neutral with deliberate slowness, then adjusted some button till only the parking lights remained on. She was free to flee now, but, curiously, remained where she was.

Clay hunched his shoulders and arms about the wheel in the way with which she was already growing familiar. He turned his eyes to the darkened house, then to her.

"You gonna be all right?" he asked.

"Yeah. What about you?"

"God, I don't know." He laid back and closed his eyes. Catherine watched the pronounced movement of his Adam's apple rising and falling.

"Well . . ." She put her hand on the door handle.

"Won't you even tell me what your plans are?"

"No. Only that I've made them."

"But what about your father?"

"Soon I'll be gone. I'll tell you that much. I'm his little ace-in-the-hole, and with me gone he'll have nothing to threaten you with."

"I wasn't thinking about me when I asked that, I was thinking about you going in there now."

"Don't say it . . . please."

"But he—"

"And don't ask any questions, okay?"

"He forced you to come to the house tonight, didn't he?" His voice was strained.

"I said, no more questions, Mr. Forrester," she said in a distractingly gentle tone.

"I feel like hell, you know, letting you go this way."

"Well, that makes two of us."

The vague light from the dashboard cast their eyes in shadow, but somehow the intensity conveyed itself. She looked sharply away from his face, for she would not be haunted by the conscience-stricken look she saw there. She opened her door and the overhead light came on and he reached out to stop her. Silence fell while the heat of his hold burned through the arm of her coat. She pulled, slowly, steadily, inexorably away from him, turning, straining toward the door. But her neck arched sideways, revealing under the mellow light three purple bruises strung there in a row, each a finger's width apart. Before she could prevent it, the backs of Clay's fingers glided over the spot and she cringed, lowering her jaw into her collarbone.

"Don't!" Her eyes were wide, fierce, defiant.

In a strident voice, Clay asked, "He did that, didn't he?"

Denial would have been useless, admission folly. All she could do was avoid answering.

"Don't you dare say anything sympathetic or sentimental," she warned him. "I couldn't take it right now."

"Catherine . . ." But he didn't know what to say, and he couldn't sit here restraining her any longer. He didn't want to be involved in her life, yet he was. They both knew it. How could she get out of this car and carry his child away into some hazy future without both of them realizing how fully he was already involved in her life?

"Could I give you some money anyway?" he asked, almost in a whisper.

"No . . . please . . . I want nothing of you, whether you believe it or not."

By now he believed it.

"Will you get in touch with me if you change your mind?"

"I won't." She raised her elbow, pulling it by inches out of his fingers until he no longer commanded her.

"Good luck," he said, his eyes on hers.

"Yeah, you too."

Then he leaned over to push her door open, the back of his arm faintly brushing against her stomach, sending goosebumps shimmying through her, radiating outward from the spot.

Quickly she stepped out onto the sidewalk.

"Hey, wait a minute . . ." He leaned across the seat, peered up at her with a curiously sad expression about his eyes and mouth. "I—what's your last name again, Catherine?"

His question swept her with the insane urge to cry, an urge she'd felt earlier in the foyer when he'd failed to recognize her.

"Anderson. It's Anderson. So common it's easy to forget."

Then she turned and ran into the house.

But when she was gone, Clay Forrester folded the arms of his expensively tailored sport coat over the wheel of his expensive sports car, laid his well-groomed head upon them, knowing he would never forget her name as long as he lived.

Chapter 3

THE ONLY LIGHT burning on the lower level was the lamp on the console table. Reaching for it, Clay caught his reflection in the mirror. A troubled frown stared back at him. *Catherine Anderson,* he thought, *Catherine Anderson.* Not liking what he saw, he quickly snapped the light off.

Upstairs the door to his parents' bedroom suite was ajar, casting a pyramid of brightness into the hall. He stopped, arms akimbo, staring at the floor in the way he was wont to do when troubled, wondering what to say.

"Clay? We heard you get home. Come in." His father moved into the open door. From the shadows Clay studied him, his heavy velour jacket shaped like a short kimono over his trousers. The older man's hair lay in soft silver waves around his healthy face. Momentarily Clay had the desire to grasp his father's neck and bury his face in the silver waves, feel that tanned cheek against his own as when he was a child and came running in for a morning hug.

"I didn't mean to keep you and Mother up."

"We'd be up in any case. Come in."

The ivory carpeting swallowed his slippered steps as Clay followed, to find his mother, wearing an ecru Eve Stillman dressing gown, her feet tucked up into the corner of a powder blue chair of watered silk.

It was like stepping back twenty years. Coming and going in their separate adult pursuits, they had little occasion to cross each other's paths except when dressed in street clothes. Gone now were the impeccable suits, high heels and jewelry from the woman curled protectively into the corner of that chair. Clay again experienced the strange sensation he'd had in the hall. He wanted to bury his head in her lap and be her little boy again.

But her face stopped him.

"We were having a glass of white wine to soothe the frayed nerves," his father said, crossing to fill his glass from a crystal decanter while Clay took the chair that matched his mother's. "Would you like one?"

"No, none for me." Sardonically he thought, wine, tricky wine.

"Clay, we assume nothing. Not yet," his father began. "We are still waiting for your answer."

Clay looked at his mother's anxious face, at that guardian-like pose which cried out that she didn't want to learn what might be true. His father stood, swirling the wine around and around in his glass, staring at it, waiting.

"It looks like Catherine is right," Clay confessed, unable to tear his eyes away from his mother's shifting expression, her widening eyes which gaped momentarily before seeking her husband's. But Claiborne studied the expression on his son's face.

"Are you sure it's yours?" Claiborne asked forthrightly.

Clay worked his hands against each other, leaning forward, studying the floor. "It seems so."

Stunned, Angela expressed what both she and her husband had been thinking for the past several hours. "Oh, Clay, you didn't even know her today. How can it possibly be true?"

"I only met her once, that's why I didn't recognize her at first."

"Once was apparently quite enough!" Claiborne interjected caustically.

"I deserve that, I know."

But suddenly Claiborne Forrester, father, became Claiborne Forrester, counselor. Silently he took up pacing for a moment, then stopped directly before his son, brandishing his wineglass as he often brandished a finger at a client too quick to admit his guilt. "Clay, I want you to make damn sure you are the man responsible before we take this thing one step further, do you understand?"

Clay sighed, stood up and ran four lean fingers through his hair. "Father, I appreciate your solicitude, and . . . believe me . . . when I first found out why she was here, I was just as surprised as you. That's why I took her out for a ride. I thought maybe she was just some kind of gold digger trying to stake a claim on me, but it seems she isn't. Catherine doesn't want a thing from me, or from you, for that matter."

"Then why did she come here?"

"She claims it was all her father's idea."

"What! And you believe her?"

"Whether I believe her or not, she doesn't want one red cent from me."

His mother said hopefully, "Maybe she's had a sudden attack of conscience for blaming you unjustly."

"Mother," Clay sighed, gazing down at her. How defenseless she looked with her makeup cleansed off this way. It broke his heart to hurt her. He crossed to her chair, reached down to take both of her hands. "Mother, I won't make much of a lawyer if I can't cross-examine a witness any better than that, will I?" he asked gently. "If I could honestly say the baby's not mine, I would. But I can't say that. I'm reasonably sure it is."

Her startled eyes pleaded with her son's. "But, Clay, you don't know anything about this girl. How can you be sure? There could . . ." Her lips quivered. "Could have been others."

He squeezed the backs of her hands, looked into her despairing eyes, then spoke in the softest of tones. "Mother, she was a virgin. The dates match up."

Angela wanted to cry out, "Why, Clay, why?" But she knew it would do no good. He, too, was hurting now—she could see it in his eyes—so she only returned the pressure of his hands. But without warning, two tears slid down her cheeks, not only for herself, but for him, as well. She tugged at his hands, reaching to pull him down and kneel as she held him.

He felt a keen, sharp pain at having disappointed her, a deep welling love at her reaction.

"Oh, Clay," she said when she could speak once more, "if only you were six years old this would be so much easier. I could just punish you and send you to your room."

He smiled a little sadly. "If I were six, you wouldn't have to."

Her own wistful smile trembled and was gone. "Don't humor me, Clay. I'm deeply disappointed in you. Give me your hanky." He fished it out of his pocket. "I thought I taught you"—she dabbed her eyes, groping for a graceful phrase—"respect for women."

"You did, you both did." Abruptly Clay stood, plunged his hands in his trouser pockets and turned away. "But for God's sake, I'm twenty-five years old. Did you really think I'd never had anything to do with women at my age?"

"A mother doesn't think about it one way or the other."

"I'd be abnormal if I were pure as the driven snow. Why, you and Father were married already by the time he was twenty-five."

"Exactly," Claiborne interjected. "We were responsible enough to put things into their proper perspective. I married your mother first, no matter what my baser instincts advised me while we dated."

"I suppose you'll preach me a sermon if I say things are different now."

"You bet I will. Clay, how could you let a thing like this happen on a *blind date,* and with a girl like that! It might be understandable if you were engaged to the girl or had been seeing her for a while. If you . . . if you loved her. But don't stand there and ask me to condone your indiscriminate sex, because I will not!"

"I didn't expect you to."

"You should have had more sense!" the older man blustered, pacing feverishly.

"At the time sense didn't enter into it," Clay said dryly, and across the room Claiborne's eyes blazed.

"That goes without saying, since you obviously hadn't enough wits to see that she didn't get pregnant out of it!"

"Claiborne!"

"Well, dammit, Angela, he's an adult who *has* used the brains of a child to let a thing like this happen. I expect a man of twenty-five to display twenty-five years' worth of common sense!"

"We each assumed the other had taken precautions," Clay explained tiredly.

"Assumed! Assumed! Yes, you've assumed yourself right into the hands of that obnoxious, money-hungry father of hers with your stupidity! The man is a raving idiot, but a shrewd one. He has every intention of taking us to the cleaners!"

Clay couldn't deny it; even Catherine had said it was true.

"You're not liable for my actions."

"No, I'm not. But do you think reasoning like that is common to a man like Anderson? He wants restitution made for his little girl's seduction and he won't rest till it's made to suit the figure he has in mind."

"Did he mention how much he wants?" Clay asked, afraid to hear the answer.

"He didn't have to. I can tell his mind works best with big, round numbers. And Clay, something else has come up that bears consideration." The glance he gave his wife told their son it was something Angela, too, knew about. "I've been approached by members of a local caucus to consider running for county attorney. I hadn't mentioned it to you because I thought it best to wait until you'd passed your bar exams and become part of the firm. But frankly it's something your mother and I have been considering quite seriously. I don't have to tell you how detrimental a little muckraking can be to a potential candidate. It won't matter to the voters who the source is."

"Catherine said she has her plans made, although she won't tell me what they are. But once she leaves home, he won't have a leg to stand on as far as a paternity suit is concerned. She refuses to be a part of his scheme."

"Quit fooling yourself, Clay. You're almost a lawyer, and I am one. We both know that a paternity suit is one of the hardest nuts in the bucket to crack. It's not the outcome of a suit I'm worried about, it's the reverberations it can stir up. And there's one more issue we haven't touched on yet." He looked down into his glass, then into Clay's eyes. "Even if the man does decide to back down and cease his demands, there is a moral obligation here that you cannot deny. If you do, I will be far, far more disappointed in you than I am right now."

Clay's head came up with a jerk. "You aren't saying you expect me to marry her, are you?"

His father studied him, dissatisfaction written on every line, every plane of his face. "I don't know, Clay, I don't know. All I know is that I have attempted by both example and word to teach you the value of honesty. Is it honest for you to leave the woman high and dry?"

"Yes, if it's what she wants."

"Clay, the woman is probably scared senseless right now. She's caught between a stranger she doesn't even know and that raving lunatic of a father. Don't you think she deserves every bit of cooperation she can get from you?"

"You've said it for me. I'm a stranger to her. Do you think she would want to marry a stranger?"

"She could do worse. In spite of the thoughtlessness and insensibility you've displayed recently, I don't think you're a hopeless case."

"I would be if I married her. Jesus, I don't even like the girl."

"In the first place, don't use profanity before your mother, and in the second, let's stop calling her a girl. She's a full-grown woman, as is entirely obvious. As a woman, she should be willing to listen to reason."

"I don't understand what you're driving at. You can see what kind of a family she comes from. Her father is a lunatic; her mother is browbeaten; look at the way they dress, where they come from. That's obviously not the kind of family you'd like me to marry into, yet you stand there talking as if you want me to ask her."

"You should have considered her background before you got her pregnant, Clay."

"How could I when I didn't even know her then?"

Claiborne Forrester had the innate sense of timing peculiar to every successful lawyer, and he used the elongated moment of silence now to speak dramatically before he cinched his case. "Exactly. Which, rather than exonerate you, as you think the fact should, creates—in my estimation —an even greater responsibility toward her and the child. You acted without a thought for the repercussions. Even now you seem to have forgotten there *is* a child involved here, and that it's yours."

"It's hers!"

His father's jaw hardened and his eyes iced over. "When did you turn so callous, Clay?"

"Tonight when I walked in here and the buzzards swooped down."

"Stop this, you two," Angela demanded in her quiet way, rising from her chair. "Neither one of you is making sense, and you'll regret this later if you go on. Clay, your father is right. You do have a moral obligation to that woman. Whether or not it extends to asking her to marry you is something none of us should try to decide tonight." Crossing to her husband she laid a hand on his chest. "Darling, we all need to think about this. Clay has said the girl doesn't want to be married. He's said she's refused his offer of money. Let's let the two of them settle it between them after everyone has cooled down a little bit."

"Angela, I think our son needs—"

She placed her fingers on his lips. "Claiborne, you're running on emotions now, and you've told me countless times that a good lawyer must not do that. Let's not discuss it anymore at the moment."

He looked into her eyes, which were luminous with emotion. They were large, lovely oval eyes of warm hazel which needed none of the artifice she used daily to enhance them. Claiborne Forrester, at age fifty-nine, loved them as much now devoid of makeup as he had when he was twenty, and she'd used it to woo him. He covered the hand which lay on his chest. There was no need for him to answer. He bowed to her judgment, giving her a reaffirmation of his love with a gentle pressure of his warm palm.

Watching them thus, Clay felt again the security which emanated from them, which had emanated from them as long as he could remember. What he saw before him was what he wanted in his life with a woman. He wanted to duplicate the love and trust shining from his parents' eyes when they looked at one another. He did not want to marry a girl whose last name he'd forgotten, whose home had been fraught with the antithesis of the love he'd grown up with.

His mother turned, and behind her, his father's hands rested upon her shoulders. Together they looked at their son.

"Your mother is right. Let's sleep on it, Clay. Things have a way of becoming clearer with time. It lends perspective."

"I hope so." Clay's hands hung disconsolately in his pockets.

To Angela he looked like an overgrown boy in that scolded pose, his hair far from neat. Intuition told her what he was struggling with, and wisely she waited for him to get it out.

"I'm so damn sorry," Clay choked, and only then did she open her arms to him. Over her shoulder he sought his father's eyes, and in a moment the arms of the velour robe were there to rub his shoulders in brief reassurance.

"We love you, Clay, no matter what," Angela reminded him.

Claiborne added, "The proof of it may seem curious at this time, but as the saying goes, love is not always kind." Then, placing his hands once again on Angela's shoulders, he said, "Good night, son."

Leaving the two of them, Clay knew they would remain allied on whatever stand they took; they always did. He had no wish to play them one against the other, though his mother seemed the far more tractable. Their unity of purpose had created such a great part of Clay's childhood security, anything else would have been out of character now. He could not help but wonder what kind of parenting team he and the volatile Catherine Anderson would make. He shuddered to think of it.

Angela Forrester lay with her stomach nestled tightly against her husband's curled back, one hand under her pillow, the other inside his pajamas.

"Darling?" she whispered.

"Hmm?" he answered, fast enough to tell her he hadn't been asleep either.

The words seemed to stick in Angela's throat. "You don't think that girl will go and have—have an abortion, do you?"

"I've been lying here wondering the same thing, Angela. I don't know."

"Oh, Claiborne . . . our grandchild," she whispered, pressing her lips against his naked back, her eyelids sliding shut, her mind filling with comparisons—how it had been when she first fell in love with this man, how elated they'd been when she became pregnant with Clay. Tears sprang to Angela's eyes.

"I know, Angie, I know," Claiborne soothed, reaching behind to pull her body more securely against his. After a long, thoughtful silence he turned over, taking her in his arms. "I'd pay anyone any amount of money if it meant preventing an abortion, you know that, Angie."

"I kn . . . I know, darling, I know," she said against his chest, strengthened by his familiar caress.

"I had to make Clay face up to his responsibilities, though."

"I know that too." But the knowing didn't make it less painful.

"Good, then get some sleep."

"How can I sleep when I—I close my eyes and see that odious man pointing his finger and threatening her. Oh, God, he's ruthless, Claiborne, anyone can see that. He'll never let that girl get away while he thinks she's the key to our money."

"The money's nothing, Angie, it's nothing," he said fiercely.

"I know. It's the girl I'm thinking of and the fact that it's Clay's child. Suppose she takes it back home to the same house with that—that vile man. He's violent. He's the kind—"

In the darkness he kissed her and felt her cheeks were wet. "Angie, Angie, don't," he whispered.

"But it's our grandchild," she repeated near his ear.

"We have to have some faith in Clay."

"But the way he talked tonight . . ."

"He's reacting like any man would. In the light of day let's hope he sees his obligations more clearly."

Angela rolled onto her back, wiped her eyes with the sheet and calmed herself as best she could. After all, this was not some reprobate they were talking about. It was their son.

"He'll do the right thing, darling; he's just like you in so many ways."

Claiborne kissed his wife's cheek. "I love you, Angie." Then he rolled her onto her side and backed her up against him again, settling a hand upon her breast. Her hand crept behind to cradle the reassuring warmth inside his pajamas. And thus they drew strength from each other in the long hour before sleep eased their worries.

It took practiced skill to outwit the caginess of Herb Anderson. He had the sixth sense that inexplicably thrives in alcoholics, that uncanny intuition which can make the hazy brain suddenly work with alarming clarity. The next morning Catherine carefully maintained her customary routine, knowing any small change would trigger his suspicion. She was standing at the kitchen sink eating a fresh orange when Herb came shuffling into the room. The fruit quenched some new taste she'd developed lately, but it seemed to amuse him wickedly.

"Suckin' on your oranges again, huh?" he grated from the doorway. "Lotta good that'll do ya. If you wanna suck something, go suck up to old man Forrester and see if you can get something outa him. What the hell's the matter with you anyway? The way you stood there like some goddam lump last night—we won't get nothin' outa Forrester that way!"

"Don't start in on me again. I told you I'd go with you but I won't back your threats. I have to go to school now."

"You ain't goin' anyplace till you tell me what you got outa lover boy last night!"

"Daddy, don't! Just don't. I don't want to go through it again."

"Well, we're gonna go through it, soon as I have me a coffee roy-al, so just stand where you are, girlie. Where the hell's your mother? Does a man have to make his own damn coffee around this dump?"

"She's gone to work already. Make your own coffee."

He rubbed the side of his coarse hand across the corner of a lip. Catherine could hear the rasp of whiskers clear across the room.

"Got a little uppity since you talked to lover boy, huh?" He chuckled. She no longer tried to stop him from using the term lover boy. It pleased him immensely when she did. He came to the sink and started slamming parts of an aluminum coffeepot around, dumping the grounds out, leaving them to stain the sink, wiping his hands on his stretched-out T-shirt. She stepped back as the stream of water hit the grounds and some came flying her way. He chuckled again. She leaned over the sink sideways, continuing to eat the pieces of quartered orange. But, at close range, he smelled. It made her stomach lurch.

"Well, you gonna spit it out or you gonna stand there suckin' those oranges all morning? What'd lover boy have to say for himself?"

She crossed to the garbage can beside the ancient, chipped porcelain stove, ostensibly to throw away the orange peel; actually she could not stand being so near the man.

"He doesn't want to marry me any more than I want to marry him. I told you he wouldn't."

"You *told* me! Hah! You *told* me nothin', slut! I had to search my own goddam house for any fact I wanted! If I wouldn't've had enough brains to go lookin' I still wouldn't know who your lover boy is! And if you think I'm gonna let him get off scot-free, well, sister, you better think again!" Then he fell to mumbling in the repetitive way she'd learned to despise. "Told me . . . she told me, ha! She told me goddam nothin' . . ."

"I'm going to school," she said resignedly, turning toward the doorway.

"You just keep your smart little ass where it is!"

She stopped with her back to him, sighed, waited for him to finish his tirade so she could pretend to go to classes and he'd leave the house in his usual, aimless way.

"Now I wanna know what the hell he means to do about this mess he got you in!" She heard the exaggerated slam as the coffeepot hit the stove burner.

"Daddy, I have to go to school."

Whining, mimicking, he repeated, *"Daddy, I have to go to school,"* and finished by roaring, "You wanna go to school, you answer me first! What's he intend to do about gettin' you knocked up!"

"He offered me money," she answered, truthfully enough.

"Well, that's more like it! How much?"

How much, how much, how much! she thought frantically, pulling a figure out of the air. "Five thousand dollars."

"Five thousand dollars!" he exploded. "He'll have to do better than that to see the end of me! My ship just come in and he wants to pay me off with a measly five thousand bucks? One o' them diamonds in the old lady's rings was worth ten times as much."

Slowly Catherine turned to face him. "Cash," she said, pleased with the greedy light that responded in his eyes, promising herself to remember it and laugh when she was gone. He pondered, scratching his stomach.

"What'd you tell him?" His face wore that sly weasel's expression she despised. It meant the wheels were turning; he was scheming again about the best way to get something for nothing.

"I told him you'd probably be calling his father."

"Now that's the first smart thing you said since I come in here!"

"You'll call him anyway, so why should I have lied to him? But I haven't changed my mind. You can try bleeding him all you want, but I won't have any part of it, just remember that." This too was her long-taken stand. Should she suddenly veer from it he would undoubtedly become wary.

"Sister, you ain't got the brains God gave a damn chicken!" he blasted, yanking a dirty towel off the cabinet top, then slapping the edge of the sink with it. But she'd long grown inured to his insults; she stood resignedly in the face of them, letting his spate run its course. "You not only ain't got enough brains to keep yourself from gettin' knocked up, you don't know when your ship's come in! Ain't I told you it's come in here?"

The term sickened her, she'd heard it so often, for it was part of his grand self-delusion. "Yes, Daddy, you've told me . . . a thousand times," she said sarcastically before adding firmly, "But I don't want his money. I'm making plans. I can get along without it."

"Plans," he scoffed, "what kind of plans? Don't think you're gonna sponge offa me and raise that little bastard around here 'cause I ain't raisin' his brat! I ain't made outa money, you know!"

"Don't worry, I won't ask you for a thing."

"You bet your boots you won't, sister, because you're gonna call up lover boy there and tell him to fork over!" He pointed a finger at her nose.

"To whom? You or me?"

"Just don't get smart with me, sister! I been waiting for my ship to come in one helluva long time!" She almost cringed again at the hated expression. He'd built his pipe dreams upon it for so long that he was no longer aware of how often he used the term, nor the shallowness of character it only served to emphasize.

"I know," she commented dryly, but again he missed the sarcasm.

"And this here is it!" He jammed a dirty finger at the floor as if a pot of gold were there on the cracked, green linoleum.

"Your coffee is going to boil over. Turn the burner down."

He studied the pot unseeingly while the lid lifted with each perk and the man remained unaware of the hiss and smell of burnt grounds. The girl who looked on felt a sudden despair at the changelessness of the man and her situation in this household. Almost as if he'd forgotten her, he now conspired with the coffeepot, leaning the heels of his hands upon the edge of the stove, mumbling the litany Herb Anderson repeated with increasing fervor as the years crept up on him. "Yessir . . . a long time, and I deserve it, by God."

"I'm going. I have to catch my bus."

He came out of his reverie, looked over his shoulder with a sour expression. "Yeah, go. But just be ready to put the screws to old Forrester again tonight. Five thousand ain't a piss in a hurricane to a rich son-of-a-bitch like him."

When she was gone, Herb leaned over the sink and took up whispering to himself. He often whispered to himself. He told Herb that the world was out to get Herb, and Herb deserved better, by God, and Herb was gonna get it! And no uppity little slut was gonna ace him out of his rightful due! She had her mother's whorish blood, that one did. Didn't he always say so? And didn't she prove him right at last, getting knocked up that way? Just goes to show, things come out even in the end. Yessir. Catherine owed him—Ada owed him —hell, the whole damn country owed him, if it come down to that.

He poured himself another coffee royal to stop the shakes.

Goddam shakes, he thought, they're Ada's fault too! But after his third drink he was as still as a frog eyeing a fly. He held out his hand to verify the fact. Feeling better, he chuckled to think how clever he was, making sure old man Forrester wouldn't want any Andersons tied to his highfalutin' bloodlines! By the end of the week Forester'd pay, and pay good to see no wedding took place between his high-class son and no knocked-up Catherine Anderson from the wrong side of the tracks.

It took Herb until nearly noon to get his fill of coffee royals and amble from the house in search of his imminent ship.

From the corner grocery store Catherine watched her father leave, hurriedly called her cousin, Bobbi Schumaker, then returned to the house to pack. Like Catherine, Bobbi was in her first year at the University of Minnesota, but she loved living with her family. Her home, so different from Catherine's, had been a haven for Catherine during her growing-up years, for the two girls had been best friends and allies since infancy. They kept no secrets from each other.

Bumping along an hour later in Bobbi's little yellow Beetle, Catherine felt relieved to have escaped the house at last.

"So, how'd it go?" Bobbi glanced askance through oversize tortoiseshell glasses.

"Last night or this morning?"

"Both."

"Don't ask." Catherine rested her head back tiredly and shut her eyes.

"That bad, huh?"

"I don't think the Forresters could believe it when the old man barged in there. God, you should have seen that house; it was really something."

"Did they offer to pay the bills?"

"Clay did," Catherine admitted.

"I told you he would."

"And I told you I'd refuse."

Bobbi's mouth puckered. "Why do you have to be so almighty stubborn? It's his baby too!"

"I told you, I don't want him to have any kind of hold on me whatsoever. If he pays, he might think he has some say in things."

"But the economics of it doesn't make sense! You can use every cent you can get. How do you think you're going to pay for second semester?"

"Just like I'm paying for the first." Catherine's lips took on that determined look Bobbi knew so well. "I've still got the typewriter and sewing machine."

"And he's got his father's millions," Bobbi retorted dryly.

"Oh, come on, Bobbi, they're not quite that rich, and you know it."

"Stu says they're rolling in it. They have enough that a few measly thousands wouldn't tip the scales."

Catherine sat up straighter, her chin stubbornly thrust out. "Bobbi, I don't want to argue. I've had enough of it this morning as it is."

"Sweet old Uncle Herb on the warpath again, huh?" Bobbi questioned, with saccharine dislike. Catherine nodded. "Well, this is it; you won't have to put up with it after this." When Catherine remained despondent, Bobbi's voice brightened. "I know what you're thinking, Cath, but don't! Your mother made her choices years ago, and it's her problem to live with them or solve them."

"He's going to be in a rage when he find out I'm gone, and she'll be there for him to take it out on." Catherine stared morosely out the window.

"Don't think about it. Consider yourself lucky you're getting out. If this hadn't happened, you'd have stayed forever to protect her. And don't forget, I'll get my mother to drop in there tonight so yours won't be alone with him. Listen, Cath . . . you're getting out,that's the important thing." She slanted a brown-eyed glance at her cousin before admitting with a grin, "You know, for that I'm not totally ungrateful to Clay Forrester."

"Bobbi!" Catherine's blue eyes held a faint gleam of humorous scolding.

"Well, I'm not." Bobbi's palms came up, then gripped the wheel again. "I mean, what the heck."

"You promised not to tell Clay, and don't forget it!" Catherine admonished.

"Don't worry—he won't find out from me, even if I think you should have your bricks counted. Half the girls on campus would give their eyeteeth to exploit the situation you've landed in and you get a case of pride instead!"

"Horizons is free. I'll be all right." Again Catherine resignedly looked out the window.

"But I want you to be more than just all right, Cath. Don't you see, I feel responsible?" Bobbi reached to touch her cousin's arm, and their eyes met again.

"Well, you're not. How many times do I have to repeat it?"

"But I introduced you to Clay Forrester."

"But that's all you did, Bobbi. Beyond that, the choices were my own."

They had argued the point many times. It always left Bobbi a little morose and crestfallen. Quietly, she said, "He's going to ask, you know."

"You'll just have to tell a white lie and say you don't know where I am."

"I don't like it." Bobbie's mouth showed a little stubbornness of its own.

"I don't like leaving my mother there either, but that's life, as you're so fond of saying."

"Just make sure you keep that in mind when you're tempted to give in and get in touch with her to see how she's doing."

"That's the part of it I don't like . . . making her think I'm running across the country. She'll worry herself sick."

"For a while she might, but the postcards will convince her you're doing okay and they'll keep your old man away from the university. There's no way he'll suspect you're still in town. Once the baby is born, you can see your mother again."

Catherine turned pleading eyes to her cousin. "But you'll call and check on her and let me know if . . . if she's okay, won't you?"

"I told you I would, now just relax, and remember . . . once she realizes you've had the nerve to pack up and leave him, she might just find some nerve of her own."

"I doubt it. Something holds her there . . . something I don't understand."

"Don't try to figure out the world and its problems, Cath. You've got enough of your own."

From the moment Catherine had first seen Horizons she'd felt at peace in it. It was one of those turn-of-the-century monstrosities with seemingly far too many rooms for a single family's needs. It had a vast wraparound porch, unscreened, festooned now with macrame pieces created by the various inhabitants who'd come and gone from the house. A few of the plants in the hangers looked peaked, as if they, too, had been touched by a late September frost like the maples that lined the boulevard. Inside, there was a wide entry hall, separated from the living room by a colonnade painted a yellowed ivory color. The stairway that led off the left end of the foyer took two turns, at two landings, on its way up. A rich, old, heavy handrail with spooled rails spoke of grander days. Beyond the colonnade spread the living room and dining room, like a sunny, comfortable cavern. Colored light filtered through old leaded glass, splashing across the living room like strokes of an artist's brush: amethyst, garnet, sapphire and emerald falling through the elegant old floral design as it had for eighty years and more. Wide baseboards and hip-high wainscoting had been miraculously preserved. The room was furnished with an overstuffed davenport and chairs of mismatched designs that somehow seemed more proper than the most carefully planned grouping would have been. There were tables with worn edges, but of homey design. The only incongruity present seemed to be the television set, which was off now as Catherine and Bobbi stood in the front hall watching three girls clean the room. One was on her knees sorting magazines, one was pushing a vacuum cleaner and another was dusting the tables. Beyond the far archway, a little girl bent over a dining room table that could have easily seated the entire Minnesota Viking team. Chairs of every nameable style and shape circled the table, and so did the little girl, slapping at each seat with her dishcloth. She straightened up then and placed a hand on her waist, fingers extending around to the small of her back, stretching backward. Staring, Catherine was abashed when the girl turned around to reveal a popping, full-blown stomach. The child was no more than five feet tall and hadn't even developed breasts yet. She might have been thirteen years old or so, but was at least eight months pregnant.

A glorious smile broke out on her face when she saw Catherine and Bobbi. "Hey, you guys, turn that thing off. We've got company!" she yelled toward the living room.

The vacuum cleaner sighed into silence. The magazine girl got up from her knees; the one who'd been dusting threw the cloth over her shoulder, and they all came toward the colonnade at once.

"Hi, my name's Marie. You looking for Mrs. Tollefson?" said the girl who looked like her name: very French, with tiny bones, pert, dark eyes, a wispy haircut and piquant face that Catherine immediately thought of as darling.

"Yes, I'm Catherine and this is Bobbi."

"Welcome," Marie said, extending her hand immediately, first to one then to the other. "Which one of you is staying?"

"I am. Bobbi's my cousin; she brought me here."

"Meet the others. This is Vicky." Vicky had a plain, long face whose only redeeming feature was the bright cornflower blue of her eyes. "And Grover." Grover looked as if she should have learned better grooming habits in junior high home ec class; her hair was stringy, nails bitten, clothes unkempt. "And that's our mascot, Little Bit, playing catch with the dishcloth over there. Hey, come on over, Little Bit."

They were all in various stages of pregnancy, but what surprised Catherine was how very young they all looked. Up close, Little Bit looked even younger than before. Marie seemed to be the oldest of the four, perhaps sixteen or seventeen, but the others, Catherine was sure, were not older than fifteen. Amazingly, they all seemed cheerful, greeting Catherine with warm, genuine smiles. She had little chance to dwell on ages, for Marie took the lead, saying, "Welcome then. I'll see if I can hunt up Tolly for you. She's around here someplace. Have you seen her, Little Bit?"

"I think she's in her office."

"Great. Follow me, you guys." While they trailed after Marie, she informed them, "Like I said, Little Bit's our mascot around her. Her real name's Dulcie, but there's not much to her than a little bit, so that's what we call her. Mrs. Tollefson's a good egg. We all call her Tolly. As soon as we talk to her we'll get you settled. Hey, have you guys had your lunch yet?"

Whatever Bobbi's preconceived notions had been about this place, none of them fit. The four girls she'd met so far exuded such an air of goodwill and sorority that she felt quite Victorian at what she'd expected. They all seemed happy and industrious and helpful. Following the bouncy Marie down a hall that led to the rear of the house, Bobbi began feeling better and better about leaving Catherine here. They came to a small room tucked beneath what must have been the servants' stairway at one time. It was as comfortable as the living room, only more crowded. It housed a large desk and bookshelves, and a patchwork sofa in shades of rust and orange that gave a homespun feeling to the room. Shutters were thrown back to let the noon light flood in upon an enormous fern which hung above the desk. Behind the desk a woman was searching through the depths of an open drawer.

"Hey, d'you lose something again, Tolly?" Marie asked.

"Nothing important. It'll show up. It's just my fountain pen. Last time Francie borrowed it she hid it in this bottom drawer. I guess I'll just have to wait until she decides to tell me where it is this time."

"Hey, Tolly, we got company." The woman's gray head popped up, her face appearing for the first time from behind stacks of books. It was a flat, plain middle-aged face with smile lines at the corners of its eyes and bracketing its mouth.

"Oh, glory be, why didn't you say so?" Smiling, she said, "Well, Catherine, I wasn't expecting you quite this early or I would have told the girls to watch out for you and bring your things in. Did anyone get your suitcases yet?"

"We'll take care of it while you talk to her," Marie offered, "if Bobbi'll show us where the car is." But before they left, Marie said to Mrs. Tollefson, "I'll be her sister."

"Wonderful!" the woman exclaimed. "I take it you two have already met, so I'll dispense with introductions. Catherine, we usually have one of the established girls help each new girl, show her where things are, tell her how we arrange work schedules, what time meals are served, things like that."

"We call it being sisters," Marie added. "How'd you like to take me on?"

"I . . ." Catherine felt rather swamped by the goodwill which she had not quite expected, at least not in such immediate displays. Sensing her hesitancy, Marie reached out and took Catherine's hand for a moment. "Listen, we've all been through this first day. Everyone needs a little moral support, not only today, but on lots of days when things get you down. That's why we have sisters here. I rely on you, you rely on me. After awhile you'll find out this is really almost a terrific place to be, right, Tolly?" she chirped to Mrs. Tollefson, who seemed totally accustomed to such scenes. She wasn't in the least surprised to see Marie holding Catherine's hand that way. Catherine, who had not held the hand of another female since she'd given up jump rope and hopscotch, was far more uneasy than anyone in the room.

"Right," answered Mrs. Tollefson. "You've been lucky, Catherine, to be adopted by Marie. She's one of our friendliest residents."

Dropping Catherine's hand, flapping a palm at Mrs. Tollefson, Marie chided, "Oh, yeah, you say that about every single one of us here. Come on, Bobbi, let's get Catherine's stuff up to her room."

When they were gone, Mrs. Tollefson laughed softly and sank into her desk chair. "Oh, that Marie, she's a ball of fire, that one. You'll like her, I think. Sit down, Catherine, sit down."

"Do they all call you Tolly?"

The woman was carelessly dressed and exuded a friendly warmth that made Catherine think she ought to be wearing a cobbler's apron. Instead she wore a pair of maroon jacquard-knit slacks of definitely dated style, and a nondescript white nylon shell beneath an aged cardigan sweater that had long ago lost it shape to that of Mrs. Tollefson's rotund breasts and heavy upper arms. Altogether, Esther Tollefson was a most unstylish woman, but what she lacked in fashion, she made up in cordiality.

"No, not all of them," she answered now. "Some of them call me Tolly. Some call me 'Hey-you,' and some avoid calling me anything. Others don't stay long enough to learn my name. But they are few and far between. Some think of me as a warden, but most of them consider me a friend. I hope you will too."

Catherine nodded, unsure of what to say.

"I sense that you're self-conscious, Catherine, but there is no need to feel that way here. Here you will deal with keeping yourself and your baby as healthy as possible. You'll deal with making decisions about what to do with your life after the baby is born. You will meet young women who have all come here for the same reason as you have: to have a baby that is being born out of wedlock. We do not force you into roles here, Catherine, nor do we place labels on you or on the decisions you will make. But we do hope you'll spend time considering your future and where to pick up after you leave Horizons. We will need a little intake information for our records. Anything you answer will, of course, remain completely confidential. Your privacy will be strictly protected. Do you understand that, Catherine?"

"Yes, but I may as well tell you immediately that I don't want my parents to know where I am."

"They don't have to. That's entirely up to you."

"The rest of the information . . ." Catherine paused, looking down at the manila card, looking for a blank that said "Father's name" or "Baby's father" or something like that. She found no such thing.

"There is no coercion here of any kind. Fill out only what you want to for now. If, as time goes by, you wish to add additional information—well, the card will be here. These first few days we want you to concentrate chiefly on gaining your equilibrium, so to speak. Decisions about the future can be made in due time. You'll find that talking with all the girls will help very much. Each of them has a different outlook. There may be some fresh ideas that will help you immensely. My best advice is to remain open to the support that they may want to give. Don't shut them out, because they may be asking for your support when it appears they are giving you theirs. It won't take you long to find out what I mean."

"Are they all as friendly as the ones I've met so far?"

"Certainly not. We have those who are bitter and withdrawn. With those we try all the harder. We have—as you'll soon see—one girl whose rebellion at her situation has taken on the form of kleptomania. There is no punishment here of any kind, not even for stealing fountain pens. You'll meet Francie soon, I'm sure. If she steals something of yours please let me know. I'm sure she will, right off the bat, just to test your reaction. The best thing to do is to offer her some compliment or suggest doing something for her or ask her advice about something. It always makes her return whatever it is she's stolen."

"I'll remember that when I meet her."

"Good. Well, Catherine, as I said before, during the first few days we want you to relax, gain your composure again and get to know the others. I think I hear the girls coming in now. They'll find some lunch for you and show you your room."

Marie appeared in the doorway just then.

"All set?"

"All set," Mrs. Tollefson replied. "Feed this girl if she's hungry, then introduce her around."

"Aye-aye!" Marie saluted. "C'mon, Catherine. This way to the kitchen."

Some thirty minutes later Catherine walked out to the car with Bobbi. They stopped, and Bobbi turned to look back at the house.

"I don't know what I expected, but it wasn't anything like this."

"Anything's better than home," Catherine said with a definite chill in her voice. Bobbi saw the defensive veneer which always seemed to glaze Catherine's eyes when she made comments such as this. A mixture of pity and relief welled up in Bobbi—pity because her cousin's home life had been so painfully devoid of the love to which every child has a right, relief because Horizons seemed as good a haven as possible under these circumstances. Perhaps here Catherine might at last have, if not love, at least a measure of peace.

"I feel . . . well, better about leaving you here, Cath."

The introspective look faded from Catherine's face as she turned to her cousin. The brilliant autumn sun burned down through the balmy afternoon, and for a moment neither of them spoke.

"And I feel good being left here—honest," Catherine assured her. But that guilty look which Catherine had seen so often lately in Bobbi's expression was back again.

"Don't you dare think it," Catherine scolded gently.

"I can't help it," Bobbi answered, thrusting her hands into her jeans pockets and kicking at a fallen leaf. "If I hadn't lined you up with him—"

"Bobbi, cut it out. Just promise you won't tell anyone where I am."

Bobbi looked up, unsmiling, her shoulders hunched up, hands still strung up in those pockets. "I promise," she said quietly, then added, "Promise you'll call if you need anything at all?"

"Promise."

There hung between the two girls an intimate silence while each of them thought about that blind date last July, their many shared confidences of girlhood leading to this greatest shared secret of all. For a moment Bobbi thought maybe this time Catherine would make the move first.

But Catherine Anderson found touching a difficult thing to do. And so she hovered, waiting, until at last Bobbi plunged forward to give her the affectionate squeeze Catherine needed so badly. In a life where love was a foreign thing, Catherine's feelings for this vibrant, bubbly cousin came as close as any to that emotion. And so, the hug she returned told a wealth of things, although she herself remained dry-eyed while tears gathered in Bobbi's throat before she backed away.

"Take it easy, huh?" Bobbi managed, her hands jammed once again in her pockets while she backed away.

"Yeah, for sure . . . and thanks, huh?"

And only when Bobbi spun and headed for the car, getting in and driving off without another backward glance did Catherine admit that she felt like crying. But she didn't. She didn't. Still, she came closer than she had since, at age eleven, she'd promised herself never to allow that weakness again.

Chapter 4

IT WAS TWENTY-FOUR hours since Herb Anderson had appeared at the Forrester home with his threats and accusations, twenty-four hours during which Clay had slept little and found it quite impossible to concentrate on the evolution of the law as affected by the McGrath vs. Hardy Case he was currently analyzing in Torts II.

Angela heard the car door slam and moved toward the desk where Claiborne sat in his swivel chair. "He's home, darling. Are you quite sure about what we've decided?"

"As sure as it's possible to be, under the circumstances."

"Very well, but must you confront him seated there like some oracle behind your desk? Let's wait for him on the loveseat."

When Clay came to the study door he looked haggard. He stood in the doorway scarcely aware of the comfortable fire within the cozy room. He was too occupied with the strain upon his parents' faces.

"Come in, Clay," Angela invited, "let's talk."

"I've had a hell of a day." He came in and sank down wearily on the coffee table with his back to them, slumping forward and kneading the back of his neck. "How about you two?"

"Likewise," his father said. "We spent the afternoon out at the Arboretum talking. It's quiet out there at this time of year after the picnickers have gone. Conducive to thinking."

"I might as well have stayed home for all I accomplished today. She was on my mind all day long."

"And?"

"It's no different than last night. I just want to forget she exists."

"But can you do that, Clay?"

"I can try."

"Clay," his mother's concerned voice began, "there's one possibility we did not discuss last night, although I'm sure it entered all our minds, and that is that she might possibly get an abortion. Forgive me for sounding like a grandmother, but the thought of it is utterly sickening to me."

"You might as well know, we talked about it," Clay admitted.

Angela felt a quiver begin in her stomach and travel up to her throat. "You —you did?"

"I offered her money, which she refused."

"Oh, Clay." The soft, disappointed swoon in her tone told Clay how it hurt her to hear the truth.

"Mother, I was testing her. I'm not sure what I'd have said if she had agreed." But then Clay swung around on the shiny table to face his parents. "Oh, hell, what's the use of denying it? At the time it seemed like an easy solution."

"Clay," Angela said, as near to scolding as she'd been in years, "I fail to see how your feelings for that child as its father can be any less than ours as its grandparents. How could you think of—of denying it life, or of spending the rest of your own wondering where and who the child is?"

"Mother, don't you think I've thought the same things all day long?"

"Yet you don't propose to do anything about it?" Angela asked.

"I don't know what to do, I'm just mixed up . . . I . . . oh, hell." His shoulders slumped further.

"What your mother is trying to make you see is that your responsibility is to make sure the child is provided for, and that its future is made secure. She speaks for both of us. It's our grandchild. We'd like to know its life will be the best possible, under the circumstances."

"Are you saying you want me to ask that girl to marry me?"

"What we want, Clay, has been superceded by your thoughtless actions. What we want is what we've always wanted for you, an education, a career, a happy life—"

"And you think I'd have those things married to a woman I don't love?" Suddenly Clay rose and walked to a window, glanced absently at the gathering dusk outside, then turned to confront them again. "I've never said it before, not in so many words, but I want the kind of relationship you two have. I want a wife I can be proud of, someone of my own class, if it comes down to that, whose ambitions match mine, who is bright and . . . and loving, and who wants what I want out of life. Someone like Jill."

"Ah . . . Jill," Angela said with an arched eyebrow, then leaned forward intently, her petite elbow on her gracefully crossed knees. "Yes, I think it's time you considered Jill. Where was Jill when all of this happened?"

"We'd had a fight, that's all."

"Oh, you had a fight." Angela settled back again, her casualness belying the seriousness of the subject. "And so you took out Catherine to—to get even with Jill, or for whatever reason, and by doing so, wronged not one woman, but two. Clay, how could you!"

"Mother, you've always liked Jill far better than any of the other girls I've gone with."

"Yes, I have; both your father and I admire her immensely. But at the moment I feel your responsibility to Catherine Anderson is far greater than that to Jill. Besides, I haven't the slightest doubt that if you'd wanted to marry Jill you'd have asked her years ago."

"We've talked about it more than once, but the timing just wasn't right. I wanted to get school behind me and pass my bar exam first."

"Speaking of which, I should like to point out a few facts you may have overlooked," Claiborne said, rising from the loveseat and taking what Clay knew was his "counsel for the plaintiff" stance: both feet flat on the floor, jaw and one shoulder jutting toward the accused. "That father of hers could make more trouble for you than you might think. You are aware that your bar examinations are less than a year off, and that the State Board of Law Examiners goes to some lengths to establish that any person making application be of good moral character. Up to this point I've never given it a second thought regarding you, but I've done nothing but consider it today. Clay, something like this could be enough for them to deny you the right to take your boards! When you apply, you'll be asked for affidavits respecting your habits and general reputation, and they are fully within their rights to demand you to furnish a character investigation report to the National Bar Examiners. Do you realize that?"

The expression on Clay's face made an answer unnecessary.

"Clay, it only takes one dyed-in-the-wool conservative who still sees abortion as immoral, regardless of its legal ramifications, or who believes that siring a bastard is cause enough to doubt your moral character, and it could be the death knell to your legal career. You have less than a year left. Do you want it all to go for nothing?" Claiborne moved to his desk, touched a pen distractedly, then sought Clay's eyes. "There is a minor concern which I cannot help but inject here. As an alumnus at the university, I'm a member of the Partnership in Excellence and The Board of Visitors. I enjoy those positions and they speak well for me. They are prestigious and would undoubtedly be an asset, if I decide to run for county attorney. I should like no slur on the Forrester name, whether it be on yours or mine. And if I do run, I am counting on you to continue my established practice during my term. Of course, we all realize what is at stake here." Claiborne dropped the pen on the desk for effect. It was implicit: he was threatening to exclude Clay from the family firm, upon which Clay had always built his plans for the future.

Claiborne steepled his fingertips, looked over them at his son and finished, with further innuendo, "Your decision, Clay, will affect all of us."

At that moment Herbert Anderson was stalking back and forth across Catherine's deserted bedroom like a caged cat.

"Goddam that girl; I'll break every bone in her body if she ain't with Forrester talking money right this minute! Talk about gratitude, that's gratitude for you!" He landed a vicious kick on a drawer that gaped at him with nothing but newspaper lining its bottom. The kick left a black scuff mark beside those he'd already put there.

From the doorway Ada stammered in a quaking voice, "Wh-where do you sup—suppose she'd of gone, Herb?"

"Well, how the hell am I supposed to know!" he yelled. "She don't tell me one damn thing about her comings and goings. If she did, she wouldn't of got herself knocked up in the first place 'cause I'd of made goddam sure she'd of known something about that lover boy of hers before she went out and got herself diddled by him!"

"Maybe—maybe he took her in after all."

"He took her in all right, and she's got a belly full of his brat to prove it!" Stalking to the telephone, he elbowed Ada rudely aside, continuing his tirade as he dialed. "Damn girl ain't got the sense God gave a cluck hen if she's not with Forrester. Wouldn't know what her ship looked like if it run her down and sliced her in half! Them Forresters was my ticket, goddammit! My ticket! Damn her hide if she run off on me and . . ."

Just then Clay picked up his ringing phone, and Anderson bawled into the mouthpiece, "Where the hell is my daughter, lover boy!" The three Forresters were still in the study discussing the situation. Claiborne and Angela didn't need to hear the far end of the conversation to know what was being said.

"She's not here." There were long pauses between Clay's responses. "I don't know . . . I haven't seen her since I dropped her off at home last night . . . Now listen to me, Anderson! I told her then that if she wanted money, I'd be happy to give it to her, but she refused. I don't know what more you expect of me . . . That's harassment, Anderson, and it's punishable by law! . . . I'm willing to talk to your daughter but I have no intention of dealing with a small-time con artist like you. I'll say it one more time, Anderson, leave us alone! It will take no more than a call from your daughter, and financial aid will be in her hand before the day is out, but as for you, I wouldn't give you the directions to a soup line if you were dying of starvation! Do I make myself clear! . . . Fine! Bring them! She's nowhere in this house. If she were, I'd be happy to put her on the phone right now . . . Yes, your concern is very touching . . . I have no idea . . ." There followed a longer pause during which Clay pulled the receiver away from his ear while the muffled anger of Herb Anderson crackled through the wire. When Clay hung up, it was with equal portions of anger and worry.

"Well, it seems she's disappeared," he said, dropping down into his father's desk chair.

"So I gathered," Claiborne replied.

"The man is a lunatic."

"I agree. And he's not going to stop with one abusive phone call. Do you concur?"

"How should I know?" Clay jumped up again, paced across the room and stopped to sigh at the ceiling. "He threatened at least four various felonies during the course of the conversation."

"Have you any idea where the girl might have gone?" his father asked.

"None. All she would say was that she had plans. I had no idea she intended to disappear this fast."

"Do you know any of her friends?"

"Only her cousin Bobbi, the girl Stu's been dating."

"My suggestion is, you see if she knows where Catherine is, and the sooner the better. I have an idea we haven't heard the last from Anderson. I want him stopped before any word of this leaks out."

Meanwhile, in Omaha, Nebraska, the sister of a student in Bobbi Schumaker's Psych I class dropped a letter in a U.S. mail depository. It was written in Catherine Anderson's clean, distinctive hand and addressed to Ada, telling her not to worry.

The following evening the Forresters were at dinner, the table set tastefully with white damask linens, bronze-colored mums and burning tapers. Inella, the maid, had just served the chicken Kiev and returned to the kitchen when the doorbell rang. With a sigh she went to answer it. She had no more than turned the handle when the door was smacked back against the wall with a violent shove, flying out of Inella's surprised fingers.

A guttural voice rasped, "Where the hell is he!"

Too shocked to attempt forestalling him, she only gaped while the man used an elbow to thrust her aside. She landed against the side of the stairs, overturning the brass pitcher of eucalyptus. Before she could right herself, the words Warpo's Bar were disappearing into the living room, trailed by a string of filth that made Inella's ears ring worse than the thud her head had just suffered.

"I told you I'd get you, lover boy, and I'm here to do it!" Herb Anderson shouted, surprising the trio at the dining room table.

Angela's hand was poised halfway to her mouth. Claiborne dropped his napkin and Clay began getting to his feet. But halfway there he was caught in the chin by a set of crusty knuckles whistling through the candlelit room without warning. His head snapped back and the sickening sound of the fist landing on her son's face made Angela scream and grope for her husband's help. Clay reeled backward, taking his chair with him to the floor while the red nylon jacket dove after him. Before Claiborne could reach Anderson's poised arm, it cracked downward again in a second punishing blow. From the doorway Inella screamed, then covered her mouth with her hands.

"My God, call the police!" cried Angela. "Hurry!"

Inella spun from the room.

Claiborne got Anderson's arm, avoiding the swings which continued falling seemingly in every direction at once. He managed to catch the crook of Anderson's elbow, spinning the heavy man in a circle. Anderson's backside struck the edge of the table, sending crystal wine goblets, water glasses and candleholders teetering. The tablecloth caught on fire as candle wax sprayed across it, but Angela was embroiled in attempting to subdue the madman along with her husband. Clay got to his feet, bleeding, stunned, but not too stunned to throw his weight into a fist that settled satisfyingly into Anderson's paunch. The air whoofed from Anderson, and he doubled over, clutching himself, while Angela grabbed a handful of his hair and yanked as hard as she could. She was crying, even as she held the detestable hair in a painful tug. Clay stood like a crazed man himself, the look on his face pure fury as he pinned one of Anderson's arms behind his back and leaned a knee across the words on the back of the red nylon jacket. The fire on the tabletop grew, but just then a sobbing Inella ran back into the room, tipped the bouquet of chrysanthemums over to douse the flames, then stood clutching her knuckles against her lips while tears streamed down her cheeks.

"The police are coming."

"Oh, God, make them hurry," Angela prayed.

The shock of the attack was sinking in as the three Forresters looked at each other across the subdued man. Angela saw the cut on Clay's jaw, another above his right eye.

"Clay, are you all right?"

"I'm okay . . . Dad, how about you?"

"I'll get you rich sons-a-bitches!" Anderson was still vowing, his face now pressed into the yellow carpet. "Goddammit! Let go o' my hair!"

Angela only pulled harder.

Outside, sirens grew closer and Inella fled from the room to the front door, which was still yawning open. Blue uniforms sped through the house behind the maid, who was shaking uncontrollably now.

Anderson was cuffed quickly and forced to remain on the dining room floor, all the while spewing threats and oaths at the Forrester family in general. The smell of burned linens permeated the room. The officers saw the charred tablecloth, the overturned dishes and the flowers strewn across the table and onto the floor.

"Is anybody hurt?"

Everyone turned to look at Angela first, as at last she flung herself into her husband's arms, crying.

"Angie, are you hurt?" he asked concernedly, but she only shook her head, leaving it buried in his chest.

"Do you know this man?" an officer asked.

"We've only met him once, day before yesterday."

"What happened here tonight?"

"He forced his way in and accosted my son while we were having dinner."

"What's you name, Bud?" This to Anderson, who was now kneeling on the floor.

"You ask *them* what my name is, so they'll never forget it!" He jerked his head viciously in Clay's direction. "Ask lover boy there who I am. I'm the father of the girl he knocked up, that's who!"

"Do you want to press charges, sir?" an officer asked Claiborne.

"What about me?" Anderson whined. "I got some charges need pressin' here if anybody does. That son-of-a-bitch—"

"Take him to the squad car, Larry. You'll get your chance to answer later, Anderson, after we read you your rights."

He was pulled to his feet and pushed ahead of the officer to the front door. Outside the flashing scarlet light was still circling, the radio crackling a dispatcher's voice. Anderson was locked in the caged backseat to rain accusations on the entire Forrester family only to be ignored by the officer who calmly sat up front, writing on his clipboard.

Shortly before supper the following day, the hall phone at Horizons rang. Someone shouted through the house, "Phone call . . . Anderson!"

Running downstairs, Catherine knew it could only be Bobbi, and she was anxious for word about her mother.

"Hello?"

"Cath, have you read the paper today?"

"No, I had classes. I didn't have time."

"Well, you'd better."

Catherine had a sudden, horrible premonition that her fears had become reality, that Herb Anderson had taken it all out on his wife.

"Is Mom—"

"No, no . . . she's all right. It's Clay. Your old man busted into his house last night and laid one on him."

"What!"

"I'm not kidding, Cath. He pushed his way in there and popped him. The police came and hauled sweet old Uncle Herb off to jail."

"Oh, no." Catherine's fingertips covered her lips.

"Just thought you'd want to know."

There was a hesitation, then, "Is—is Clay hurt?"

"I don't know. The article didn't say. You can read it for yourself. It's on page eight-B of the morning *Trib.*"

"Have you talked to my mother?"

"Yeah, she's okay. I talked to her last night, must have been while your dad was in Edina beating up Clay. She almost sounded happy that you were gone. I told her not to worry because you were safe and that she'd be hearing from you."

"Is she—"

"She's okay, Cat, I said she's okay. Just stay where you are and don't let this change your mind, huh? Clay can take care of himself, and a night in jail might even mellow out your old man."

Before she ended the conversation, Bobbi added a fact that she'd earlier decided not to tell Catherine, then had decided to tell after all.

"Clay called me and asked if I knew where you are. I lied."

The line buzzed voicelessly for a moment, then Catherine said quietly, "Thanks, kiddo."

Catherine found the article in the *Minneapolis Tribune* and read it several times, trying to picture the scene her father had created. Although she hadn't seen the dining room of the Forrester house, she could well imagine a luxurious setting there and what it must have been like when her father burst in. Clay Forrester's face welled up before her, his gray eyes, handsome jawline, and then her old man's fist ramming into it. Guilt welled up unwanted. She heard Clay's voice as he'd asked her to accept his money, and somehow knew that if she'd accepted it he would not have been assaulted by her old man. She knew, too, that her running away had thwarted Herb Anderson's plans for getting rich quick and had been further cause for him to turn his rage on Clay. At least Herb's volatile anger had been diverted away from Ada, but Catherine's conscience plagued her mercilessly until she assuaged it with the thought that, after all, the elder Mr. Forrester was an attorney and could easily prosecute his son's assailant, which would be no more than Herb deserved. The thought brought a short smile to Catherine's lips.

Bobbi wasn't surprised to answer the door the next day and find Clay Forrester there.

He said without preamble, "I've got to talk to you. Can we take a ride?"

"Sure, but it won't do any good."

"You know where she is, don't you?"

"Maybe I do, maybe I don't. Who wants to know, her old man?"

"I do."

"You're a day late and a dollar short, Clay."

"Listen, could we go somewhere and have a cup of coffee?"

She studied him a moment, shrugged, and answered, "Let me get my sweater."

The Corvette was at the curb. She eyed it appreciatively and wondered again at Catherine's foolishness in not exploiting the situation, if only financially. Watching Clay round the front fender, Bobbi couldn't help thinking that if she were in Catherine's shoes she herself might not mind exploiting Clay Forrester in more ways than one.

They drove to a small restaurant called Green's where they ordered coffee, then sat avoiding each other's eyes until it came. Clay hunched over his cup, looking totally distraught. His jawline had been altered and a bandage rode his right eyebrow.

"That's a nice little shiner you've got there, Clay." She eyed it and he scowled.

"This thing is getting out of hand, Bobbi."

"Her old man's always been out of hand. How do you like him?"

Clay sipped his coffee and looked at her over the rim of the cup. "Not exactly my idea of a model father-in-law," he said.

"So what do you want with Catherine?"

"Listen, there are things involved here which I don't care to get into. But, for starters, I want her to take some money from me so her old man will leave me alone. He's not going to stop until he's seen green, and I'll be damned if I'll lay it in his hand. All I want her to do is to accept money for the hospital bills or her keep or whatever. Do you know where she is?"

"What if I do?" There was an unmistakable note of challenge in her attitude. He studied her a moment, then leaned back, toying with his cup handle.

"Maybe I deserved to get knocked around a little bit, is that what you're thinking?"

"Maybe I was. I love her."

"Did she tell you I offered to pay my dues, financially?"

"She also told me you offered her money for an abortion." When he remained silent Bobbi went on. "Supposing she's off having one right now?" Bobbi studied his face carefully and found the reaction she wanted: dread. She added sardonically, "Is your conscience bothering you, Clay?"

"You're damn right it is. If you think the only reason I want to see her is to get Anderson off my back, you're wrong." He closed his eyes and squeezed the bridge of his nose briefly, then muttered, "Lord, I can't get her off my mind."

Bobbi studied him as she sipped. The black eye and bruised jaw Uncle Herb had doled out could not disguise Clay Forrester's handsomeness nor the worried expression about his eyes. Something in Bobbi softened.

"I don't know why I feel compelled to tell you, but she's okay. She's got her plans all made and she's carrying through with them. Catherine's a strong person."

"I realized that the other night when I talked to her. Most girls in her position would come at a man with palms up, but not her."

"She's had it hard. She knows how to get by without any help from anybody."

"But still you won't tell me where she is?" He turned appealing eyes to her, making it extremely difficult for Bobbi to answer as she had to.

"That's right. I gave my word."

"All right. I won't try to force you to break it, but will you do just this much for me? Will you tell Catherine that if she needs anything—anything at all—to let me know? Tell her I'd like to talk to her, that it's important, and ask her if she'd call me at home tomorrow night. That way neither one of you will have to give away her whereabouts."

"I'll give her the message, but I don't think she'll call.She's stubborn . . . almost as stubborn as her old man."

Clay looked down into his cup. "Listen, she's"—He swallowed, looked up again with an expression of worry etched upon his eyebrows—"She's not having an abortion, is she?"

"No, she's not."

His shoulders seemed to wilt with relief.

That night when Catherine answered the phone, Bobbi opened by saying, "Clay came to see me."

Catherine's hand stopped where it was upon her scalp, combing her hair back from her face. Her heart seemed to stop with it. "You didn't tell him anything, did you?"

"No, I just complimented him on his shiner. Your dad really meant business!"

It took great effort for Catherine to resist asking if Clay was really all right. She affected a businesslike tone, asking, "He didn't come to show you his battle scars, I'm sure. What did he want?"

"To know where you are. He wants to talk to you."

"About what?"

"Well, what do you suppose? Cath, he's not so bad. He didn't even complain about getting beaten up. He seems genuinely worried about your welfare and wants to make some arrangements for paying for the baby, that's all."

"Bully for him!" Catherine exclaimed, casting an anxious glance down the hall to make sure no one was within earshot.

"Okay, okay! All I am is the messenger. He wants you to call him at his house tonight."

The line grew silent. The picture of his house came back all too clearly to Catherine. His house with its comfortable luxury, its fire burning at dusk, his parents in their finery, Clay walking in whistling with his hair the color of autumn. A weakness threatened Catherine, but she resisted it.

"Cath, did you hear me?"

"I heard."

"But you're not going to call him?"

"No."

"But he said he's got something he has to talk over with you." A rather persuasive tone came into Bobbi's voice then. "Listen, Cat, he kind of threw me. I thought he'd try to wheedle your whereabouts out of me, but he didn't. He said if you'd call him, neither one of us would have to give away any secrets."

"Very upstanding," Catherine said tightly, haunted even further by the remembered look of concern on Clay's face as she got out of his car.

"This might sound disloyal, but I'm beginning to think he is."

"What, upstanding?"

"Well, is it so unbelievable? He really seems . . . well, concerned. He isn't acting at all like I thought he would. I find myself wondering what Stu would do if he found himself in Clay's situation. I think he might have left town by now. Listen, why don't you give Clay a chance?"

"I can't. I don't want his concern and I'm not going to call him. It wouldn't do any good."

"He said I should tell you if there's anything you need, just say so, and you've got the money for it."

"I know. He told me that before. I told him I don't want anything from him."

"Cath, are you sure you're doing the smart thing?"

"Bobbi . . . please."

"Well, heck, he's loaded. Why not take a little of it off his hands?"

"Now you sound like my old man!"

"Okay, Cath, it's your baby. I did what he asked; I gave you the message. Call him at his place tonight. From there on out it's up to you. So how's the place?"

"It's really not bad, you know?" Then, fighting off thoughts of Clay Forrester, Catherine added, "It has no men, so that's a plus right there."

The voice at the other end became pleading. "Hey, don't get that way, Cath. Not all men are like your father. Clay Forrester, for instance, is about as far from your father as a man could get."

"Bobbi, I get the distinct impression that you're changing sides."

"I'm not changing sides. But I'm getting a better view of both sides, caught in the middle like I am. I'm always on your side, but I can't help it if I think you should at least call the guy."

"Like hell I will! I don't want Clay Forrester or his money!"

"All right, all right! Enough! I'm not going to waste any more time arguing with you about it, because I know you when you get your mind made up."

Absorbed as she was in her conversation with Bobbi, Catherine was unaware that three girls had gone into the kitchen for a snack, and from there any telephone conversation could be easily heard. When she hung up, she headed back for her room, more rattled than she'd care to admit by what Bobbi had said. It would be so easy to give in, to accept money from Clay, or to solicit his moral support during the difficult months ahead, but should she rely on him in any way she feared he would have a hold on her, on the decisions about her future which must still be made. It would be better to stay here where life was better than that which she'd left. At Horizons there was no censure, for everyone here was in the same boat.

Or so they thought.

Chapter 5

THE TENSION AROUND the Forrester home grew as Catherine's whereabouts remained unknown. Angela walked around with a drawn expression about her mouth, and often Clay found her eyes upon him with such a hurt expression that he carried its memory with him to the law school building each day. His concentration was further thwarted by the fact that Herb Anderson was released after twenty-four hours without a formal charge made against him. The necessity to let him go scot-free rankled mercilessly, not only on Clay but on his father. They knew the law, knew they could pin Anderson to the wall for what he'd done. To be unable to do so only raised the pitch of their taut nerves.

Once Anderson was free, he became more self-righteous than ever. He smiled in self-satisfaction all the way home while he thought, I got them sons-a-bitches where I want them and I ain't lettin' go till they come through with the greenbacks!

When Herb got home, Ada was standing in the living room with her coat still on, reading a postcard. She looked up, startled to see him coming in the door.

"Why, Herb, you're out."

"Goddam right I'm out. Them Forresters know what's good for 'em, that's why I'm out. Where's the girl?" His eyes were bloodshot, his knuckles still taped, the bandages dirty now. He already had the rank stench of gin on his breath.

"She's all right, Herb," Ada offered timorously, holding out the card. "Look, she's in Omaha with a friend who—"

"Omaha!" The word rattled the windows as Herb reeled and smacked the postcard out of his wife's hand. She cowered, watching with huge eyes as he teetered and stooped to pick up the card off the floor. He gaped at the handwriting to make sure it was Catherine's. He swiped the soiled bandage across the eyes that always wore a film of water over their ochred whites. When his vision cleared, he studied the card again, then whispered, "Them rich sons-abitchin' whorin' no-good bastards are gonna pay for this! Nobody makes a horse's ass outa Herb Anderson and gets away with it!" Then he shoved past Ada as if she weren't there, heading out again.

She collapsed into a chair with a shudder of relief.

At Horizons, Francie got even with a few of life's injustices by stealing a bottle of Charlie perfume from the top of Catherine Anderson's dresser.

At the University of Minnesota one of those very injustices was at that moment folding her exquisite, thoroughbred legs into Clay Forrester's Corvette.

"You're late," Jill Magnusson scolded, placing one gleaming fingernail on the door to prevent Clay from closing it, at the same time turning upon him a stunning smile that had cost her father approximately two thousand dollars in orthodontia. Jill was a beauty, and a member of the elite sorority Kappa Alpha Pheta, whose members were loosely referred to as the "Phetas," known down through the years as the rich girls' sorority at the U of M.

"Busy day," Clay answered, suddenly piqued by her method of holding them up. He was too distracted to be charmed by those supple limbs right now. He slammed the door and walked around to his side. The engine purred as they pulled away from the curb.

"I need to stop by the photo lab to check on some pictures for a research project." Jill was more than a superficial appearance; she was majoring in aviation electronics and had every intention of designing the first jet shuttle between the earth and moon. With career goals set high she wasn't the least bit interested in getting married yet. She and Clay understood each other well.

But tonight he was unusually testy. "I'm late and you're the one who's going to stop at the photo lab on our way to the party!" Clay snapped, laying a thin line of rubber as the car peeled away.

"My, aren't we touchy tonight."

"Jill, I told you I wanted to stay home and study. You're the one who insisted we go to this party. You'll forgive me if I dislike playing escort service on the way."

"Fine. Forget the lab. I can pick the photos up myself tomorrow."

Gearing down at a stop sign, he screeched to a halt, throwing Jill forcefully forward.

"What in the world is the matter with you!" she exclaimed.

"I'm not in a party mood, that's all."

"Obviously," she said dryly. "Then forget the photo lab and the party too."

"You dragged me out to this damn party, now we're going!"

"Clay Forrester, don't you speak to me in that tone of voice. If you didn't want to go with me you could have said so. You said you had a case to study this weekend. There's a vast difference between the two."

He threw the car into gear and screamed down University Avenue toward the heart of the campus, zinging in and out between other cars, intentionally laying rubber with every shift of the gears.

"You're driving like a maniac," she said coolly, her auburn hair swinging with the erratic motions of his lane changes.

"I'm feeling like one."

"Then please let me out. I'm not."

"I'll let you out at the goddam party," he said, knowing he was being despicable but unable to help it.

"Since when have you taken to insouciant cursing?"

"Since approximately six P.M. four nights ago," he said.

"Clay, for heaven's sake slow down before you get us both killed, or at the very least get yourself a walloping ticket. The campus police are thick tonight. There's a concert at Northrup."

Ahead at an intersection he could see a cop patrolling traffic, so he slowed down.

"Have you been drinking, Clay?"

"Not yet!" he snapped.

"You're going to?"

"If I'm smart, maybe."

Jill studied his profile, the firm jaw, the tight expression about his usually sensual mouth. "I don't think I know this Clay Forrester," she said softly.

"Nope, you don't." He glared straight ahead, curling his lower lip over his upper, waiting for the cop to flag the traffic through the intersection. "Neither do I."

"It sounds serious," she ventured.

Instead of replying, he hung his right wrist over the steering wheel and continued to glare at the cop, that lip still curled up with contempt at something.

"Wanna talk about it?" she asked in what she hoped was a coercive voice. She waited, dropping her head slightly forward so her hair fell like a rust curtain beyond her cheek.

He looked at her at last, thinking, God but she's beautiful. Poised, intelligent, passionate, even a little cunning. He liked that in her. Liked even more the fact that she never tried to hide it. She often teased him that she could get him to do anything she wanted, simply by using her long-limbed body. Most of the time she was right.

"What would you say if I admitted that I'm afraid to talk to you about it?"

"For starters I'd say the admission has added some common sense to your driving habits."

He had indeed begun driving more sensibly. He reached over and rubbed the back of her hand. "Do you really want to go to the party?"

"Yes. I have this gorgeous new lambswool sweater and this magnificent matching skirt and you haven't even noticed. If you won't compliment me, I'd like to find someone who will."

"All right, you got it," he said, swinging left, heading for the Alcorn Apartments, where the party was in full swing when they arrived. Inside it was a maze of voices and music, too many bodies packed into too little space. The Alcorn was a converted gingerbread house with bays, nooks and pantries, the kind of place easily gotten lost in if playing hide-and-seek. The furniture throughout the first-floor apartment was positively decimated, but nobody cared because nobody seemed to own it. Jill led the way through the press of people, taking Clay's hand, tugging him to the kitchen where the bar was set up on a dilapidated porcelain-topped table, the kind that went out with World War II. A guy named Eddie was tending bar.

"Hey, Jill, Clay, how's it going? What'll you have?"

"Clay wants to get smashed tonight, Eddie. Why don't you give him a little help?"

In no time Eddie extended a drink that was supposed to be mixed; it was the color of weak coffee. Clay took one sip and knew three like this would knock him smack off his feet. If he really wanted to get smashed, it wouldn't take long. Jill accepted a much weaker drink. She was too intelligent to get drunk. He'd never seen her have more than one or two cocktails in an evening.

He teased her now. "Why don't you come down one notch and show you're at least as human as me and have a couple of strong drinks tonight? Then when we go to bed you'll be as uninhibited as I intend to be."

Jill laughed and swung her waist-length hair back behind a well-turned shoulder.

"If you want to get roaring drunk go right ahead. Don't expect me to abet it by being equally as stupid."

He raised a sardonic eyebrow to Eddie. "The lady thinks I'm stupid." Then he mumbled into his drink, "If she only knew the half."

In the crush of bodies and the assault of noise Jill didn't quite hear what Clay said, but he was troubled tonight, not acting like himself. "I don't know what's gotten into you tonight, but whatever it is, I don't like it."

"You'd like it even less if you knew."

Just then somebody came by and bumped Jill from behind, spilling a splash of her drink on her new sweater at the fullest part of her left breast.

"Oh, damn!" she exclaimed, sucking in her stomach, searching in her purse for a Kleenex. "Have you got a hanky, Clay?"

He reached for his hind pocket. "That's the second time this week that a lady has needed my hanky. Here, let me help you with that, mademoiselle." He grabbed Jill by the hand, found a vacant corner beside the refrigerator and pushed her into it. With the hanky he began dabbing at the spot where the liquor had already darkened the sweater. But an odd, troubled look overtook his face. His motions stilled, and his eyes found hers. Then he grabbed hanky, sweater, breast and all and flattened himself against her long, lithe body, kissing her with a sudden fierceness that startled her. Fondling her breast, controlling her mouth, he pressed her into the corner where the refrigerator met the wall. She thought he'd lost his mind. This was not the Clay she knew, not at all. Something was more wrong than she'd guessed.

"Stop it, stop it! What's the matter with you!" she gasped, breaking away from his kiss, trying to push his hand from her breast.

"I need you tonight, Jill, that's all. Let's go someplace and leave this noisy bunch."

"I've never seen you like this, Clay. For God's sake let go of my breast!"

Abruptly he released her, backed up a step, put the guilty hand in his trouser pocket and stared at the floor. "Forget it," he said, "just forget it." He raised his drink and took an abusive swallow.

"You're going to get sick if you continue at this pace."

"Good!"

"All right, I'll go with you, but to make sense, not sex, agreed?"

He looked at her absently.

"Whatever it is that's bothering you, let's talk it out."

"Fine," he said, taking her glass almost viciously and depositing it and his back on the table which was littered with dozens of others. Without another word he grabbed Jill's wrist and started pushing his way through the mob.

When they were halfway to the door someone yelled, "Hey, Clay, hold up!" Turning, he saw Stu Glass's ruddy face making its way toward him, both hands raised above the press of elbows, trying to keep from spilling a pair of drinks. Over his shoulder Stu shouted, "Follow me close, honey; I want to talk to Clay a minute."

"The two couples converged in the milling crowd. "Hey, Clay, you leaving already?"

"Hey, Stu, whaddya say?"

"Haven't seen you around all week. Dad wanted to know if you and your father decided about partridge hunting next weekend yet."

The two fell to discussing hunting plans, leaving Bobbi and Jill to exchange small talk. They knew each other only slightly, through their relation with the men, but now, for the first time, Bobbi studied Jill Magnusson more assessingly than ever before. She took in Jill's expensive wine-colored sweater and skirt, that angel's face of hers, and the negligent way Clay Forrester's arm looped around her waist while he went on talking to Stu. If ever two people were made for each other it was these two, thought Bobbi. Jill, with her burnished skin, her cover-girl's features and that glorious mane of hair, and Clay with his sun-drenched good looks, flawless taste in clothing to match the girl's, and both of them blessed with self-assurance, wealthy families and preordained success.

It struck Bobbi quite suddenly that Catherine was positively out of her class with a man like Clay. He belonged with the kind of girl he was with now. How futile it was to wish she'd used better judgment last Fourth of July, yet, observing Clay and Jill together, Bobbi felt a sting of deep regret.

All the while Clay talked with Stu he was aware of Bobbi. When at last someone from the crowd bumped through and took Jill momentarily away from his side, and Stu along with her, he got his chance.

"Hi, Bobbi."

"Hi, Clay."

The two eyed each other a little warily.

"What's new with you?"

"Same old thing."

Damn her, thought Clay, she's going to make me ask it. He threw a quick eye at Jill, who stood near enough to overhear anything being said.

"Have you heard anything from your cousin lately?"

"Yeah, just today, as a matter of fact."

"How's everything?"

"The same."

Clay's eyes shifted away and back again. "I never got that call."

"I gave her the message."

"Could you please ask her again?"

"She's not interested."

Someone from the crowd jostled his way behind Bobbi, pushing her forcibly closer to Clay. He used the opportunity to insist, "There've been some serious repercussions. I've got to talk to her!"

But just then Jill recaptured Clay, running her painted nails up his arm in a familiar way, taking his elbow in her own. There are people in this world who have things just a bit too good, thought Bobbi, and others who never get a break. Just to even the scales a little bit, some cunning gremlin inside Bobbi made her call after the couple, "I'll tell Catherine you said hello, Clay!"

He turned and burned her with a look that seemed to say he'd like to throw a hex on her. But he replied civilly, "Give her my best."

When Jill and Clay had disappeared, Stu asked, "What was that all about?"

"Oh, nothing. We lined Clay up with my cousin Catherine last summer one time, remember?"

"We did? Oh yeah, that's right, we did." Then, shrugging, he took her elbow and said, "Come on, let's go freshen our drinks."

Clay and Jill decided to drive out to the Interlachen Country Club, a place where both of their parents belonged and where they'd been coming for as long as they could remember, to play golf or eat Sunday brunch. The dining room was half empty, left now to those members who stayed to dance on the small parquet floor to the music of a trio that played old standards. They were seated at a table situated in the lee of corner windows overlooking the golf course, which was lit by single lights strewn along the fairways. The dapples of brightness created a jewelled view from this vantage point in the high, glass-walled room. The course boasted fifty different species of trees. Were it high noon, they'd be seeing every warm color of the spectrum across the expanse below, but now, night having settled over the acres of trees and manicured grass, it looked like something from a fairy tale, the trees shimmering silhouettes against the strategically placed lights.

For some minutes after they were seated, Clay continued staring out at the view below while Jill swirled her wine in its lengthy stem glass. When she'd waited as long as she intended to wait, Jill forced the issue.

"And who is Catherine?" Even a question such as this reflected Jill's breeding, for her voice grew neither accusing nor harpyish. It flowed instead like the amber liquid around the sides of her glass.

After a moment's consideration Clay answered, "Bobbi's cousin."

Raising the stem glass to her lips, Jill hummed, "Mmm . . ." then added, "Has she got something to do with this sour mood of yours?"

But Clay seemed far removed again, pensive.

"What's so interesting out there in the dark?"

He turned to her with a sigh, rested his elbows on the linen tabletop and kneaded his eyes with the heels of his hands. Then, leaving his eyes covered, he grunted dejectedly, so she could scarcely hear, "Damn."

"You might as well talk about it, Clay. If it's about this . . . *Catherine,* I think I deserve to know. It is, isn't it?"

His troubled eyes appeared once again, gazing at her, but instead of answering her question, he asked one of his own. "Do you love me, Jill?"

"I don't think that's the subject of this discussion."

"Answer me anyway."

"Why?"

"Because I've been wondering lately . . . a lot. Do you?"

"Could be. I don't know for sure."

"I've been asking myself the same question about you too. I don't know for sure if I love you either, but it's a very good possibility."

"That's a little too clinical to be romantic, Clay." She laughed softly, sending the lights shimmering off her sparkling lips.

"Yeah, I've been in a clinical mood this week—you know, dissecting things?" He gave her a brief rueful smile.

"Dissecting our relationship?"

He nodded, studied the weave of the tablecloth, then raised his eyes to study Jill's flawless face, her hair gleaming beneath the subdued lights of a massive chandelier. Her long fingers with tapered nails glistening as she absently fondled her footed glass, her grace as she relaxed back into her chair, one arm draped limply on its armrest. Jill was like a ten-karat diamond: she belonged in this setting just as surely as Catherine Anderson did not. To bring Catherine Anderson here would be like setting a rhinestone in gold filigree. But Jill . . . ah, Jill, he thought, how she dazzles.

"You're so damn beautiful it's absurd," Clay said, a curiously painful note in his voice.

"Thanks. Somehow it doesn't mean as much tonight as if you'd said it just that way, with just that tone of voice, with just that particular look in your eyes, say . . . a week ago, or, say, four days ago?"

He had no reply.

"Say before the subject of Catherine Whoever-she-is intruded?"

Clay only chewed his lower lip in a way with which she was utterly familiar.

"I can wait all night for you to spill it out, whatever it is. I'm not the one who has studying to do this weekend."

"Neither do I," Clay admitted. "I used that as an excuse because I didn't want to see you tonight."

"So that's why you pounced on me like a parolee fresh out of prison?"

He laughed softly, admiring her cool, unruffled presence. "No, that was self-flagellation."

"For?"

"For last July fourth."

A light dawned in Jill's head. She remembered quite distinctly the fight they'd had back then.

"Who was she? Catherine?" Jill asked softly.

"Exactly."

"And?"

"And she's pregnant."

Jill's poise was commendable. She drew in a deep, swift breath, her perfect nostrils flaring into slight imperfection during the length of it. The cords in her neck became momentarily taut before relaxing once more as her eyes and Clay's locked, searching. Then she gracefully braced an elbow on the tabletop and lowered her forehead onto the back of her hand.

Into the silence, a waiter intruded.

"Miss Magnusson, Mr. Forrester, can I get you anything else?"

Clay looked up, distracted. "No, thank you, Scott. We're fine."

When Scott had drifted discreetly away, Jill raised her head and asked, "Is she the reason for the shiner, which I have so graciously avoided mentioning all night?"

He nodded. "Her father." He took a drink, gazed out at the lights below again.

"I'll forgo the obvious question," Jill said, with a hint of asperity creeping into her tone, "realizing you wouldn't have told me unless the situation were clearly defined and you're certain it is yours. Are you going to marry her?"

This time it was Clay's turn to draw a ragged breath. He sat with ankle crossed over knee, one elbow slung on the edge of the table. To look at him, at the careless pose, at the classic cut of his tailored clothes, his handsome profile, one would not have guessed the slightest thing to be amiss. But inside he was a knot of nerves.

"You haven't clearly answered whether or not you love me." Slowly Clay drew his eyes back to hers, suffering now nearly as much as he could see she was.

"No, I haven't, have I?"

"Is it"—Clay searched for the correct word—"superfluous now?"

"I think so, yes, I think so."

Each of their eyes dropped down to their drinks; each of them experienced a touching sense of loss at her words.

"I don't know if I'm going to marry her or not. I'm getting a lot of pressure."

"From her parents?"

He only laughed ruefully. "Oh, Jill, that's so incredibly funny. Too bad you'll never know how incredibly funny that is."

"Sure," Jill retorted caustically, "Ha—ha—ha . . . aren't I funny, though."

He reached for her hand on the tabletop. "Jill, it was a thing that happened. You and I had had that big fight the night before. Stu and Bobbi lined me up with this cousin of Bobbi's . . . Hell, I don't know."

"And you got her pregnant because you wanted to set up housekeeping with me and I refused to leave Pheta House. How chivalrous!" She yanked her hand free.

"I expected you to be bitter. I deserve it. The whole miserable thing is a lousy mistake. The girl's father is a raving lunatic, and believe me, neither the girl nor I want anything to do with each other. But there are, shall we say, extenuating circumstances that may force me to ask her to marry me."

"Oh, she'll be overjoyed that you *have to!* What girl wouldn't be!"

He sighed, thought in exasperation, Women! "I'm being pressured in more ways than one."

"What's the matter, has your father threatened to deny you a place in the family practice?"

"You're very astute, Jill, but then I never did take you for a dumb redhead."

"Oh, don't humor me; not at a time like this."

"It's not only my father. Mother walks around looking like she's just been whipped, and to complicate matters Catherine's old man is threatening to get vocal about it. If that happens, my admission to the bar is in jeopardy. And to complicate matters even worse, Catherine has run away from home."

"Do you know where she is?"

"No, but Bobbi does."

"So you could reach her if you wanted to?"

"I think so."

"But you don't want to?"

He drew a great sighing breath and only shook his head forlornly. Then he reached for her hand again across the corner of the table. "Jill, I don't have much time to waste. All the devils of hell seem to be riding on my back right now. I'm sorry if I have to lay one of them on yours, and I'm sorry, too, if the occasion isn't what it should be at a time like this, but I want to know your feelings about me. I want to know if, at some time in our future, when all of this is straightened out, when I've completed law school and gotten my life back in working order, would you ever consider marrying me?"

Her composure slipped a notch and she cast her eyes aside as they grew too glisteny. But they were drawn back to his familiar, lovable face, of which she knew every feature so intimately. In a choked voice she answered, "Damn you, Clay Forrester. I should slap your Adonis's face."

But the softness of her words told him how very hurt she was.

"Jill, you know me. You know what I'd have planned for us if this hadn't interfered. I'd never have asked you this way, at a time like this, if I'd had the choice."

"Oh, Clay, my heart is—is . . . falling in little pieces down to the pit of my stomach. What do you expect me to say?"

"Say what you feel, Jill." He rubbed a thumb lightly across the back of her hand while she covered his face, hair and body with her eyes, letting her hand remain passively in his.

"You asked me too late, Clay."

Pained moments spun by while the piano player tinkled some old tune and a few dancers moved across the floor. At last he picked up Jill's hand, turned it over and kissed its palm. Returning his gaze to her face he whispered, "God, you're beautiful."

She swallowed. "God, you are too. That's our trouble. We're too beautiful. People see only the facade, not the pain, the faults, the human failings that don't show."

"Jill, I'm sorry I hurt you. I do love you, you know."

"I don't think you'd better bank on me, Clay."

"Do you forgive me for asking?"

"No, don't ask me to do that."

"It mattered to me, Jill. Your answer mattered a lot."

She slowly pulled her hand free of his and picked up her purse.

"Jill, I'll let you know what comes of it."

"Yeah, you do that. And I'll let you know when my space shuttle leaves for the moon."

This time it happened so fast that Clay saw nothing. He stepped out of the Corvette in the driveway and a husky shadow slinked swiftly from behind the bulk of a pyramidal arborvitae. Clay was yanked roughly around, slammed against the fender of the car just as a meaty fist smashed into his stomach, leaving no mark, breaking no bones, only cracking the wind from him viciously as he doubled over and dropped to his knees on the ground.

Through his pain he heard a grating voice informing, "That was from

Anderson. The girl's run off to Omaha." Then heavy, running footsteps disappeared into the night.

When Bobbi called the following evening, she sounded breathless. "I ran into him at a party last night, Cat. He asked about you again and said to tell you it's really important. He had to talk to you."

"What good would it do? I'm not marrying him and I don't need his money!"

"Oh, jeez! You're so obstinate! What harm can it do, for heaven's sake!"

But Marie passed along the hall just then and Catherine turned her face toward the wall, couching the mouthpiece furtively. But from the knowing glance Marie had flashed her way, Catherine suspected she'd heard the last remark. Quietly she said into the phone, "I want him to think I've left town."

Bobbi's voice suddenly became critical, scolding. "If you want to know what I think, I think you owe him that much. I don't think it's enough for you to insist that *you* don't need a single thing from Clay Forrester. Maybe he needs something from you. Have you considered that?"

Dead silence at Bobbi's end of the line for a long moment.

Catherine hadn't considered that before. She clasped the receiver tightly and pressed it against her ear so hard her head began to hurt. Suddenly it tired her immensely, having to think about Clay Forrester at all. Her emotions were strung out to the limit, and her own problems were more than she wanted to handle without taking on Clay Forrester's too. She sighed and dropped her forehead against the wall.

Bobbi's voice came through again, but very calmly and quietly. "I think he's in some kind of big trouble over this, Cath. I don't know exactly what because he wouldn't say. All he said was something about serious repercussions."

"Don't!" Catherine begged, her eyelids sliding shut wearily. "J-just don't, okay? I don't want to hear it! I can't take on any of his troubles. I have all I can do to handle my own."

Again there followed a lengthy silence before Bobbi made one last observation which was to gnaw at Catherine's conscience mercilessly in the hours and days to come: "Cath . . . whether you want to admit it or not, I think they're one and the same."

Chapter 6

THE WIDE BLUE curve of the Mississippi River glinted beneath the autumn sky as it cut a swath through the campus of the University of Minnesota, dividing it into East Bank and West Bank. The more heavily wooded East Bank wore the school colors, maroon and gold. Homecoming was approaching, and it seemed almost as if the grounds had festooned themselves for the event. Stately old maples wore ruddy tones in startling contrast with the fiery elms. Constant activity churned along Union and Church Streets as home-coming preparations advanced. On the lawns students soaked up summer's warm leftovers. Pedestrians dawdled, waiting for buses in the shaded circle before Jones Hall. Bicycle wheels sighed through tumbled leaves. Ornamental stone parapets adorned gracious old frat houses down along University Avenue, their retaining walls, steps and balconies draped with idlers, slung there like lazing lizards. And everywhere couples kissed, heads bare to the afternoon sun.

Passing a kissing couple now, Catherine looked quickly away. Somehow the sight of them made the books ride a little more heavily upon her hip. At times lately, leaning to lift those books, twinges caught her side in newly strange places.

Clay, too, was often disarmed by the sight of a young man and woman kissing. Striding down The Mall now, he observed an embrace in progress and his thought strayed to Catherine Anderson. Pulling his eyes to the students moving along the sidewalk ahead of him, he thought the girl with the leaf-gold hair could almost be her. He studied her back while it disappeared and reappeared around others who came between them. But it was only his preoccupation with her lately that made him look twice at every blond head in a crowd.

Still, the hair was the right color and the right length. But Clay realized he could easily be mistaken, for he'd never seen her in broad daylight before.

Dammit, Forrester, get her out of your head! That's not her and you know it!

But as he watched the tall form with its straight shoulders, it swayless hips, the books riding against one of them, a queer feeling made his stomach go weightless. He wanted to call her name but knew it couldn't be Catherine. Hadn't he gotten the message loud and clear? She'd run off to Omaha.

Deliberately Clay glanced across the street to free his eyes and mind from delusions. But it was no good. Momentarily he found himself scanning the crowd more intently, seeking out the blue sweater with blond hair trailing down its back. She was gone! Absurd, but a hot flash of panic clutched Clay, making him break into a trot. He caught sight of her once more, farther ahead, and breathed easier, but continued following. Long stride, he thought. Long legs. Could it be? Suddenly the girl crooked an arm and stroked the hair away from her neck as if she were hot. Clay skipped around a group of people, studying the long legs, the erect carriage of her shoulders, remembering her air of haughtiness and defensiveness. She came to a street and hesitated for a passing car, then glanced aside to check traffic before crossing. As she stepped from the curb, her profile was clearly defined for a fraction of a second.

Clay's heart seemed to hit his throat and he broke into a run.

"Catherine?" he called, keeping his eyes riveted on her, shouldering his way, bumping people, mechanically excusing himself, running on. "Catherine?"

She evidently did not hear, only kept walking on, the sound of traffic grown heavier as a bus pulled away from the sidewalk. He was short-winded by the time he caught up with her and swung her around by an elbow. Her books tumbled from her hip and her hair flew across her mouth and stuck to her lipstick.

"Hey, what—" she began, instinctively bending toward the books. But through the veil of hair she looked up to find Clay Forrester glowering down at her, his chest heaving, his mouth open in surprise.

Catherine's heart cracked against the walls of her chest while the sight of him made tremors dance through her stomach.

"Catherine? What are you doing here?" He reached again for her elbow and drew her up. She only stared, trying to conquer the urge to run while her heart palpitated wildly and the books lay forgotten on the sidewalk. "Do you mean you've been here all the time, right here going to school?" he asked in astonishment, still grasping her elbow as if afraid she'd vanish.

Clay could see she was stunned. Her lips parted and the look in her eyes told him she felt cornered and would surely run again. He felt the sweater slipping out of his fingers.

"Catherine, why didn't you call?" Her hair was still stuck to her lipstick. Her breath coming through billowed it out and in. Then she bent to pick up her books while he belatedly leaned to do the same. She plucked them away from his fingers and turned to escape him and the countless complications which he could mean to her.

"Catherine, wait!"

"Leave me alone," she flung over her shoulder, trying not to look as if she were running from him, running just the same.

"I've got to talk with you."

She kept half running half walking away, Clay a few steps behind her.

"Why didn't you call?"

"Dammit! How did you find me?"

"Will you stop, for God's sake!"

"I'm late! Leave me alone!"

He kept up with her, stride for stride, very easily now, while Catherine's side started aching and she pressed her free hand against it.

"Didn't you get my message from Bobbi?"

But the blond hair only swung from side to side on that proud neck as she hurried on. Irritated because she refused to stop, he grabbed her arm once again, forcing her to do his bidding. "I'm getting tired of playing Keystone Cops with you! *Will you stop!*"

The books stayed on her hip this time but she tossed her head belligerently, a yearling colt defying the bridle. She stood there glaring at him while he restrained her. When at last it seemed she wouldn't bolt, he dropped his hand.

"I gave Bobbi the message to have you call me. Did she tell you?"

Instead of answering his question, she berated herself. "This is the one thing I couldn't control, chancing running into you somewhere. I thought this campus was big enough for the two of us. I'd appreciate it if you'd keep it to yourself that I'm here."

"And I'd appreciate it if you'd give me the opportunity to explain a few things and work something out with you."

"We did all the talking we needed the last time we were together. I told you, my plans are made and you don't have to worry about me."

Curious passers-by eyed them, wondering what they were arguing about.

"Listen, we're making a spectacle here. Will you come with me someplace quiet so we can talk?"

"I said I'm in a hurry."

"And I'm in a fat lot of trouble! Will you just give me two minutes and stand still?" He'd never seen anyone so defiant in his life. It was more than just his parents' ultimatum driving him now. This had come down to a contest of wills as she strode away up The Mall with him just behind her shoulder again.

"Leave me alone," she demanded.

"There's nothing I'd like better, but my parents don't see it that way."

"Pity."

He grabbed the back of her sweater this time, and she nearly walked out of it before realizing why it wasn't coming along with her.

"Give me a time, an anonymous phone number, anything, so I can get in touch with you and I'll leave you alone until then."

She yanked her sweater free and spun to face him defiantly. "I've already told you, I made one mistake and it was a dilly. But my life isn't ruined as long as I don't consider it ruined. I know where I'm going, what I'm going to do when I get there, and I don't want you involved in any way whatsoever."

"Are you too proud to take anything from me?"

"You can call it pride if you want. I prefer to call it good sense. I don't want you having any kind of hold over me."

"Suppose I have the solution to our problems, and it would leave neither of us indebted to the other?"

But she only eyed him acidly. "I've solved my problems. If you still have some, it's not my fault."

People were looking at them curiously again, and Clay became incensed at her stubborn refusal to listen to reason. Before she knew what was happening, he'd clamped an arm around her waist and propelled her off the sidewalk toward an old, enormous elm. She found herself thrust against it, her ears flanked by both of his palms, which leaned against the bark.

"Something else has come up," he informed her, his face no more than two inches from hers. "Seems your father's been making trouble."

She swallowed, pressing her head back, glancing first into his eyes, then aside, afraid of the determination she saw so clearly at this close range.

"I heard about that and I'm sorry," she conceded. "I really thought he'd give up when I left."

"For Omaha?" he asked sarcastically.

Her startled eyes flew to his. "How did you learn that?" She noted the remnant of a cut above his eyebrow and wondered if her father had put it there. He glowered, holding her prisoner so that all she could see was either his face or a bronze-colored sweater smack in front of her eyes. She stared at the sweater.

"Never mind. Your father is making threats, and those threats could mean the end of my law career. Something's got to be done about it. I find the idea of paying him off as distasteful as you do. Now, can we work on a reasonable alternative?"

Catherine's eyes slid shut; she was unable to think quickly enough. "Listen, I've got to go now, honest. But I'll call you tonight. We can talk about it then."

Something told him not to trust her, but he couldn't stand there restraining her indefinitely. All he could do was let her go for the time being. He knew he could find out easily where she lived, now that he knew she was a student here. As he watched her walk away he waited to see if she'd turn around to check if he was tailing her. She didn't. She entered Jones Hall and disappeared, and guessing that her patience was probably greater than his, he turned back, heading for the car.

The following day Catherine met Mrs. Tollefson in the office with its patchwork sofa and fern. Thinking Tolly would forge ahead into the subject Catherine most dreaded, Catherine was surprised when instead the matronly woman only chatted about school and asked how Catherine was getting along now that she'd settled into Horizons. When Catherine told her she was attending college on a small study grant and supplementing it by doing typing and sewing, Mrs. Tollefson noted, "You have a lot of ambition, Catherine."

"Yes, but I'll be the first to admit it's self-serving. I want something better out of life than what I've had."

Mrs. Tollefson ruminated. "College, then, is your ticket to a better life."

"Yes, it was going to be my final escape."

"Was?" Mrs. Tollefson paused. "Why do you speak in the past tense?"

Catherine's eyes opened a little wider. "I didn't do it consciously."

"But you feel you're being forced to drop out of school?"

A brief, wry laugh escaped Catherine. "Under the circumstances, who wouldn't?"

A gentle expression complemented Tolly's soft voice. "Perhaps we need to talk about that, about where you've come from, where you are, where you're going."

Catherine sighed, dropped her head back tiredly. "I don't know where I'm going anymore. I did once, but I'm not sure if I'll get there now."

"You're speaking about this baby as an obstacle."

"Yes, one I haven't wanted to make decisions about."

"Perhaps decisions will come easier once we look at all your options." Mrs. Tollefson's voice would be suited well to the reading of poetry. "I think we need to explore where your baby fits into your plans."

Oh, God, here it comes. Catherine sank deeper into the cushions of the sofa, wishing it would take her down, down, into its depth forever.

"How far along are you, Catherine?"

"Three months."

"So you've had some time to think about it already?" The kind woman watched the cords stand out in Catherine's neck as the girl swallowed, and her eyes remained closed.

"Not enough. I—I have trouble thinking about it at all. I keep pushing it to the back of my mind, thinking someone will come along and make the decision for me."

"But you know that won't happen. You knew that when you came to Horizons. From the moment you chose not to abort, you knew a further decision was in the offing."

Childlike now, Catherine sat forward, arguing, "But I want them both, college and the baby. I don't want to give up either one!"

"Then let's discuss that angle. Do you think you're strong enough to be a full-time mother and a full-time student?"

For the first time Catherine bridled. "Well, how should I know!" She flung her hands out, then subsided with a sheepish look. "I—I'm sorry."

Mrs. Tollefson only smiled. "It's okay. It's fine and healthy to be angry. Why shouldn't you be? You just started putting your life on track when along came this major complication. Who wouldn't be angry?"

"Okay, I admit it. I'm—I'm mad!"

"At whom?"

A puzzled expression curled Catherine's blond eyebrows. "At whom?" But Mrs. Tollefson only sat patiently, waiting for Catherine to come up with the answer. "At—at me?" Catherine asked skeptically in a tiny voice.

"And?"

"And . . ." Catherine swallowed. It was extremely hard to say. "And the baby's father."

"Anybody else?"

"Who else is there?"

It grew quiet for a long moment, then the older woman suggested, "The baby?"

"The baby?" Catherine looked aghast. "It's not his fault!"

"Of course it's not. But I thought you might be angry with him just the same, maybe for making you think about giving up school, or at the very least, for slowing you down."

"I'm not that kind of person."

"Maybe not now, but if your child prevents you from completing your college education, what then?"

"You're assuming I can't do both?" Catherine was growing frustrated while Mrs. Tollefson remained calm, unflappable.

"Not at all. I'm being realistic though. I'm saying it will be tough. Eighty percent of the women who become pregnant before age seventeen never complete high school. That statistic goes up with college-age women who must handle heavy tuition costs."

"There are day-care centers," Catherine noted defensively.

"Which don't accept a child until he is toilet-trained. Did you know that?"

"You're really laying it on heavy, aren't you?" Catherine accused.

"These are facts," continued the counselor. "And since you're not the kind to go man-hunting as a solution to your problem, shall we explore another option?"

"Say it," Catherine challenged tightly.

"Adoption."

To Catherine the word was as depressing as a funeral dirge, yet Mrs. Tollefson went on. "We should explore it as a very reasonable, very available answer to your dilemma. As hard as it may be for you to consider adoption—and I can see how it upsets you by the expression on your face—it may be the best route for you and the child in the long run." Mrs. Tollefson's voice droned on, relating the success of adopted children until Catherine jumped to her feet and turned her back.

"I don't want to hear it!" She clutched one hand with the other. "It's so—so cold-blooded! Childless couples! Adoptive parents! Those terms are—" She swung again to face Mrs. Tollefson. "Don't you understand? It would be like feeding my baby to the vultures!"

Even as she said it, Catherine knew her exclamation was unjust. But guilt and fear were strong within her. At last she turned away and said in a small voice, "I'm sorry."

"You're reacting naturally. I expected it all." The understanding woman allowed Catherine to regain composure, but it was her responsibility to delineate all choices clearly; thus, she went on.

Catherine again listened to the facts—adopted children tend to develop to their fullest potential; adopted children are as well- or better-adjusted as many children who live with their birthparents; child abuse is almost nonexistent in adoptive families; parents who adopt are generally in an above-average income bracket; the adopted child runs a better chance of graduating from college than if parented by an unwed mother.

A great vise seemed to tighten, thread by thread, at Catherine's temples. She dropped to the sofa, her head falling back as an overwhelming weariness pervaded her.

"You're telling me to give it up," she said to a shimmering reflection on the ceiling.

Mrs. Tollefson let the old guilt-laden term pass for the moment. "No . . . no, I'm not. I'm here to help you decide what is best for your welfare, and ultimately, for the child's. If I fail to make you aware of all eventualities, of all avenues open to you, and of all that may close, I am not doing my job thoroughly."

"How much time would I have to decide?" The question was a near whisper.

"Catherine, we try not to work with time limits here, which sounds ironic when each young woman is here for a limited time. But no decision should be made till the baby is born and you've regained your equilibrium."

Catherine considered this, then her concerns came tumbling out in an emotional potpourri. "Would that really happen? Would I resent the baby because he slowed me down? I only want to make a decent life for him so he won't have to live in the kind of home I had to live in. I set out to get a college education to make sure of that, only to find out, if I pursue it, I may defeat my purpose. I know what you said is true, and it would be hard. But a baby should have love, and I don't think anybody could love it as much as a real mother. Even if money is a problem, it seems like copping out to give the baby away because of the expense."

"Catherine." Mrs. Tollefson leaned forward, caring deeply, her face showing it. "You continue to use the term *give away,* as if you own the child and are rejecting him. Instead, think of adoption as perhaps a better alternative to parenting the child yourself."

Catherine's large blue eyes seemed to stare right through the woman before her. Finally she blinked and asked, "Have you ever seen anyone make it? With a baby, I mean?"

"All the way through college? Single parent? No, not that I can remember, but that's not to say you can't be the first."

"I could get . . ." She thought of Clay Forrester's offer of money. "No, I couldn't." Then she sighed. "It almost makes me look stupid for passing up an abortion, doesn't it?"

"No, not at all," the kind voice reassured.

Again Catherine sighed, blinked slowly and turned her eyes to the blue sky beyond the window. Her voice took on a rather dreamlike quality. "You know," she mused, "there's no feeling there yet. I mean the baby hasn't moved or anything. Sometimes I find it hard to believe it's in there, like maybe somebody's just pulling this big joke on me." She paused, then almost whispered, "Freshman hazing . . ." But when she looked at Tolly again, there was true sadness in her face, and the realization that this was no hazing at all. "If I'm already feeling so protective when there's not even any evidence of life yet, what will I feel when he moves and kicks and rolls around?"

Mrs. Tollefson had no answers.

"Do you know, they say a baby has hiccups before it's born."

The room remained still again, flooded with late sunshine and emotion while Catherine dealt with possible eventualities. At last she asked, "If I decided to give him up—" A raised index finger stopped her. "Okay, if I decide on adoption as the best route, could I see him first?"

"We encourage it, Catherine. We've found that mothers who do not see their children suffer a tremendous guilt complex which affects them the rest of their lives." Then, studying Catherine's face carefully, Mrs. Tollefson posed a question it was necessary to ask. "Catherine, since he has not been mentioned so far, and since I do not see his name on the card, I must ask if the child's father should be a consideration in all of this."

The blond young woman rose abruptly and snapped, "Absolutely not!"

And had her attitude not changed so quickly, Mrs. Tollefson might have believed Catherine.

The records office of the U of M refused to give out Catherine's home address, thus it took Clay three days to spot her again, crossing the sprawling granite plaza before Northrup Auditorium. He followed at a discreet distance as she cut between buildings, following the maze of sidewalks until finally at Fifteenth Avenue she turned northward. He kept sight of her blue sweater with the blond hair swaying upon it until she turned into an old street of homes that had been stately in their younger day, but hovered now behind massive boulevard trees in a somewhat seedy reflection of the grandeur they once knew. She entered a gargantuan yellow brick three-story with an enormous wraparound porch. The house had no marking other than a number, but while Clay stood wondering a very pregnant woman came out and stood on a chair to water a hanging fern. He might not have thought anything of it if he hadn't suddenly realized, as she turned, that she was not a woman, but was, instead, a young girl of perhaps fourteen. As she raised up on tiptoe to fetch down the plant, the sight of her swollen stomach triggered Clay's suspicion. He looked again for a sign, but there was none, nothing to indicate it was one of those homes where girls went to wait out their pregnancies. But when the girl returned inside, Clay wrote down the house number and headed back toward the campus to make some phone calls.

By the time Catherine had been at Horizons a week and a half she found herself accepted without question and knew her first taste of sorority. Because so many of the girls were in their young teens they looked up to Catherine, who, as a college student, seemed to them much more worldly. They saw her leaving each day to pursue an outside life while they themselves had forfeited theirs for the duration of the stay, and their admiration grew. Because Catherine owned a sewing machine which was often in demand, her room came to be the gathering place. Here she heard their stories: Little Bit was thirteen and wasn't sure who was the father of her baby; plain-faced Vicky was sixteen and didn't talk about the father of hers; Marie, age seventeen, spoke amiably about her Joe, and said they still planned to get married as soon as he graduated from high school; the unkempt Grover said the father of her baby was the captain of her high school football team and had taken her out on a bet with a bunch of his team members. There were some residents of Horizons who cautiously avoided getting too close to anyone, others who brazenly swore they'd get even with the boy responsible, but the majority of the girls seemed not only resigned to living here, but enjoyed it. Especially nights like this when, all together, a group was working on a pair of nightgowns for Little Bit to wear during her hospital stay, which wasn't far off.

By now Catherine was accustomed to the banter at times like these; it was a combination of teasing and gaunt truths.

"Someday I'm gonna find this guy and he's gonna have hair like . . ."

"Don't tell me. Let me guess—hair like Rex Smith."

"What's the matter with Rex Smith?"

"Nothing. We've just heard the story before and how he's just going to *know* you're the woman he was made for."

"Listen, kiddo, don't forget to tell him somebody else thought the same thing before him." Laughter followed.

"I want to be married like Ali McGraw in *Love Story* . . . you know, make up my own words and stuff."

"Fat chance."

"Fat chance? Did somebody say *fat* chance?"

"Hey, I'm not always going to be shaped like a pear."

"I want to go to school and learn to be one of those ladies who cleans teeth. The kind of job where you nestle the guy's head in your lap so you can move in close and throw your charms at him."

Laughter again.

"I'm never gonna get married. Men aren't worth it."

"Hey, they're not all bad."

"Naw, only ninety-nine percent of 'em!"

"Yeah, but it's that other one percent that's worth looking for."

"When I was little and my folks were still together, I used to look at this picture of them on their wedding day. It used to sit in their bedroom on the cedar chest. Her dress was silk and there were little pearls on top of her veil and it trailed way around the floor in front. If I ever get married, I'd like to wear that dress . . . 'cept I think she threw it away."

"Wanna know something funny?"

"What?"

"When Ma got married she was pregnant . . . with me."

"Yeah?"

"Yeah. But she didn't seem to remember it when I told her I wanted to get married."

And so the talk went. And somebody always suggested going down to the kitchen for fruit. Tonight it was Marie who won the honors. She waddled downstairs and was passing the hall phone when it rang.

"Phone call . . . Anderson!"

When Catherine came to pick it up, Marie was leaning a shoulder against the wall, a curious half-smile on her face.

"Hi, Bobbi," she answered, glancing at Marie.

"Guess again," came the deep voice over the line.

The blood dropped from Catherine's face. She sucked in a quick breath of surprise and remained motionless for a moment, gripping the phone, before the color seeped back up her neck again.

"Don't tell me. You followed me." Marie continued toward the kitchen then, but she'd heard all she needed to hear.

"That's right. It took me three days, but I did it."

"Why? What do you want from me?"

"Do you realize how ironic it sounds to have *you* asking *me* that question?"

"Why are you *hounding* me?"

"I have a business proposition for you."

"No, thank you."

"Don't you even want to hear it?"

"I've been propositioned—so to speak—by you once already. Once was enough."

"You really don't play fair, do you?"

"What do you want!"

"I don't want to talk about it on the phone. Are you free tomorrow night?"

"I already told you—"

"Spare me the repetition," he interrupted. "I didn't want to put it this way but you leave me no choice. I'm coming to get you tomorrow night at seven o'clock. If you won't come out and talk to me, I'll tell your father where to find you."

"How dare you!" Her face grew intense with rage.

"It's important, so don't put me to the test, Catherine. I don't want to do it, but I will if I have to. I have a feeling he might have ways to get you to listen to reason."

She felt cornered, lost, hopeless. Why was he doing this to her? Why, now when she'd at last found a place where she was happy, couldn't her life be peaceful? Bitterly, she replied, "You're not leaving me much choice, are you?"

The line was silent for a moment before his voice came again, slightly softer, slightly more understanding. "Catherine, I tried to get you to listen to me the other day. I said I didn't want to put it that—"

She hung up on him, frustrated beyond endurance. She stood a moment, trying to collect herself before going back upstairs. The phone rang again. She clamped her jaw so hard that her teeth hurt, put a hand on the receiver, felt it vibrate again, picked it up and snapped, "What do you want this time!"

"Seven o'clock," he ordered authoritatively. "Be ready or your father finds out!"

Then he hung up on her.

"Something wrong?" Marie asked from the kitchen doorway.

Catherine jumped, placing a hand on her throat. "I didn't know you were still there."

"I wasn't. Not for very long anyway. I just heard the last little bit. Was it anyone important?"

Distractedly, Catherine studied Marie, small, dark, her doll's face an image of perfection, wondering what Marie would do if Joe had just called wanting to talk to her tomorrow night at seven.

"No, nobody important."

"It was him, wasn't it?"

"Who?"

"The father of your baby."

Catherine's face turned red.

"No use denying it," Marie went on, "I can tell."

Catherine only glared at her and turned away.

"Well, you didn't see the color of your face or the look in your eyes when you picked up that phone and heard his voice."

Catherine spun around, exclaiming, "I have no look in my eyes for Clay Forrester!"

Marie crossed her arms, grinned and raised one eyebrow. "Is that his name, Clay Forrester?"

Infuriated with herself, Catherine spluttered, "It—it doesn't matter what his name is. I have no look in my eyes for him."

"But you can't help it." Marie shrugged as if it were a foregone conclusion.

"Oh, come on," Catherine said in exasperation.

"Once you've been in this place you realize that no girl who comes here is immune to the man who's the other half of the reason she's here. How could she be?"

Although Catherine wanted to deny it, she could not. It was true that when she'd heard Clay Forrester's voice something had gone all barmy in the pit of her stomach. She'd grown shivery and hot all at once, light-headed and flustered. How could I! she berated herself silently. How could I react so to the mere voice of a man who—two months after the fact!—forgot that he'd ever had sexual intercourse with me?

Chapter 7

THE MINUTE SHE came home from classes the following afternoon, Catherine knew something was up. The atmosphere was charged, the girls giddy, giggly. Everyone turned suddenly helpful, advising her to go upstairs and get her studying done right away, not to worry about setting the table—Vicky would do it for her. Someone suggested she do her nails and Marie suggested, "Hey, Catherine, how about if I blow-dry your hair? I'm pretty good at it, you know."

"I did it this morning, thanks."

Behind her back Marie made an exasperated gesture, followed by a rash of questions about whether or not Catherine had ever worn purple eyeshadow. Apricot blush? White lipliner? By the time she went down to supper Catherine accosted the crew with a sly look on her face. "All right, you guys, I know what you're up to. Marie's been talking, hasn't she? But this is *not* a date, so don't misconstrue it as one. Yes, someone's coming for me, but I'm going exactly as I am." There stood Catherine, confronting the whole dining room full of critical faces, dressed in faded blue jeans and an outsize flannel shirt, looking like she should be slopping hogs.

"In that!" Marie fairly choked.

"There's nothing wrong with this."

"Maybe not for a game of touch football."

"Why should I primp? I told you, it's *not* a date."

"The word is out, Catherine," Grover proclaimed. "We all know it's *him!*"

Marie, without question the group leader, put a hand on her hip and sing-songed, "Not a date, huh? What'sa matter, Catherine, is he old and feeble or something? Hasn't he got any hair on his legs?"

They all started laughing, Catherine included. Someone else picked up the teasing, carrying it forward. "Maybe he's got body odor! Or halitosis. No, I know! Ringworm! Who'd want to dress up for a guy with ringworm?" By now they were circling Catherine as if she were a maypole. "I know, I bet he's married." But what had started out to be funny suddenly angered Catherine, who saw the girls as a pack of feral animals, nipping at her, closing in for the final attack.

"Nope, I know he's not married," Marie informed the group. "It's got to be something else."

"A priest then, a man of the cloth. Oh, shame, shame, Catherine."

"I thought you were my friends!" she exclaimed, confused and hurt.

"We are. All we want to do is see you dolled up for your fella."

"He's not my fella!"

"You bet he's not, and he won't be either if you don't get out of those everyday rags and paint your nails."

"I am not painting my nails for Clay Forrester. He can go to hell, and so can all of you!" Catherine broke from the circle and ran upstairs.

But she was not allowed to sulk, for momentarily Marie appeared, leaning against the door frame. "Tolly doesn't allow anybody to skip meals around here, so you'd better get back down there. The girls were just having a little fun. They're all quite a bit younger than you, you know, but you're the one who's acting childish by coming up here and sulking."

Catherine threw a derisive glance at her roommate. "I'll be back down," she said coldly, "but tell the girls to lay off! It's nobody's business how I dress."

Supper was an uncomfortable affair for Catherine, but the rest carried on as if nothing had happened. She sat stonily, her nerves as taut as fiddlestrings.

"Pass the strawberry jam," Marie requested, eyeballing a silent message to Vicky, on Catherine's left, then to Grover, who was refilling milk glasses. When Grover reached Catherine, she made sure a cold splat of milk landed in the angry girl's lap. Catherine's chair screeched back, but she only glared silently at Grover.

Marie's voice was as smooth as melted butter. "Why, Grover, can't you be more careful?"

Grover set down the milk carton, grabbed some napkins and made a show of swabbing the wet leg of Catherine's jeans. Titters started around the table as Catherine viciously yanked the napkins away and said icily, "It's okay, forget it."

But as she leaned forward to pull her chair back up to the table, a hand shot out from her left, bearing a biscuit, oozing jam. The sticky strawberries caught Catherine on the left temple, smearing into her hair, ear and eyebrow.

"Oh, my, look what I've done," Vicky said innocently.

Catherine leaped up, anger bubbling uncontrollably. "What kind of conspiracy is this! What have I done to make you all so hateful?"

Just then Marie, their ringleader, arose, wearing her piquant smile and came to put her arms around Catherine. "We only want to help." Catherine stood in the circle of Marie's unwanted hug, holding herself stiff.

"Well, you have a strange way of showing it."

But just then Marie drew back with a false gasp, and Catherine felt something warm and cloying plastering her shirt against her back where Marie's arm had been.

"Now I've really done it. I got gravy on your shirt, Catherine." Then with a sly glance at all her coconspirators, Marie suggested, "We'll just have to see what we can do about it, won't we, girls?" And standing back, hands on hips, the shorter girl surveyed Catherine critically. "Have you ever seen such a mess in your life?"

Catherine, dumbfounded, only now began to suspect the method behind their madness as smiles bloomed all around the table. One by one they passed her on their way upstairs, each offering something.

"You really should wash your hair. I have a bottle of strawberry shampoo."

"And I have some yummy Village Bath Oil you can borrow."

"I haven't done my laundry yet. If you'll leave your jeans and shirt in the hall, I'll throw them in with my stuff."

"Institution soap is the pits. I'll leave mine in the bathroom."

Marie swiped a finger across Catherine's temple, then sucked the jam from it. "Yuck! I guess we'll have to give you a fresh hairdo after all."

"For heaven's sake, get her upstairs and do something with that jam, Marie!"

Marie winked at Catherine, reached out a small hand, waiting. In the moment before she placed her own in it to be led upstairs, Catherine felt a lump lodge in her throat, a curious, new growing thing, a learning thing, a trusting thing. But before she quite decided how to deal with it, she was in their hands.

Many times during the next hour Catherine raised her eyes to Marie's in the mirror, understanding now, feeling warmed and grateful because they cared— they all cared so very much. "You're crazy, you know," she laughed, "you're all a little bit crazy. It's not even a date."

"By the time we get done, it will be," Marie deemed.

The pile of makeup that appeared would have put Cleopatra to shame. With gratitude but reservation, Catherine accepted pedicure, manicure, coiffure, jewelry, even lacy underwear, all offered with the best and most optimistic intentions. After holding her dress while she slipped it on, the stubby Marie stood on top of one of the beds to fasten a gold chain around Catherine's neck.

"Hey, when you gonna grow up, Marie?" someone quipped.

"Hadn't you noticed?" she rubbed her belly. "I'm growing daily, only in the wrong direction." Laughter followed, but subdued now, almost reverent, while Catherine stood in their midst, looking unbelievably lovely.

"Go on, have a look," Marie prompted, nudging Catherine's shoulder.

Catherine walked to the mirror, fully expecting to see a Kewpie doll looking back at her. But she was stunned at the surprisingly lovely woman reflected there. Her hair was glowing, flowing back from her face as if its golden streaks were blowing in the wind. The makeup had been done tastefully, giving her cheeks a delicate, hollow look, her blue eyes a new luminous size and glitter. The gloss on her lips reflected a bead of light, as if she'd just passed her tongue along them and left them provocatively wet. Small gold hoops at her ears complimented the shadowed length of her neck and emphasized her delicate jawline, while the loop of gold around her neck drew her eyes downward to the open collar of the soft, blue wool shirtwaist with its long sleeves and front closure. The collar stood up in back, flared open in front, leaving a bit of exposed skin above the highest button.

Without conscious thought, Catherine lifted a manicured fingertip and touched the hollow of her right cheek, the hollow she'd never been aware of before. Her own sober eyes stared back at her approvingly, but with a new worry in them.

My God, she thought, what will Clay Forrester think?

Behind her the girls observed the telling movement of her fingers upon her own cheek, the hand that rested briefly upon her pulsing heart as if to say, "Can it be?" And while the silent group stared, a frowsy, brown-haired fifteen-year-old with tortoiseshell glasses came forward. In the mirror, Catherine saw her coming and fought to control emotions that bubbled up and threatened. She did not want to be their hope. She did not want Clay Forrester to think she'd done all this for him. But while the hopelessly plain Francie came forward, Catherine knew that for this one evening she was doomed to play the role these girls so desperately needed her to play.

Francie, who had never spoken a word to Catherine before, came forward, bearing a bottle of Charlie perfume.

"Here," she said, "I stole this from you."

Catherine turned to take the bottle, smiling into Francie's eyes, which held no more sparkle than cold dishwater. "I have a couple of different kinds. Why don't you keep it?" But as Francie extended the bottle, Catherine could see the girl's hand tremble.

"But this one must be your favorite. It's the most used up."

Francie's eyes impaled her, wavering neither right nor left. Then Catherine smiled and took the bottle and sprayed herself lightly behind her ears and upon her wrists. When she finished she said, "You're right, Francie, it is my favorite, but why don't you put it on your dresser and when I want it, I'll just come in and take a squirt."

"Really?" Had Catherine been a movie star who suddenly stepped off the screen to materialize before Francie in flesh and blood, the girl could not have been more awed.

This is ridiculous, thought Catherine. I'm not Cinderella. I'm not what they want me to be. But something stung her eyelids as she pushed the bottle of perfume more firmly into Francie's hands, undone by the look in the younger girl's eyes.

Marie, still standing on the bed, broke the tension by quipping, "I think this is what's called a pregnant silence."

So Catherine was saved from tears, and Francie was saved from shame, and everyone laughed and began drifting from the room until Catherine was left alone with Marie. Impulsively she gave the shorter girl a hug.

"Mutt and Jeff, aren't we?" Marie joked.

"I don't know what to say. I misjudged all of you earlier. I'm sorry."

"Hey," Marie reached to fix a certain curl at the side of Catherine's cheek, "we laid it on a little heavy. We understand."

"So do I . . . now."

"You're going for all of us, Cath."

"I know, I know."

"Just hear him out, okay?"

"But he's not coming to ask me to marry him. We already—"

"Just hear him out, that's all. Give the girls a little something to hope for. Pretend for them that it's real. Promise? Just for one night?"

"Okay, Marie," Catherine agreed, "for all of you. But what happens to their hopes when it doesn't come to anything?"

"You don't seem to realize that this is a first for them. Just give them something to talk about when he comes to the door. Be nice. Make them dream a little bit tonight."

Marie wondered how any man could resist a woman as beautiful as Catherine. Being short herself she naturally admired Catherine's height. Being dark, she admired her blondness. Being bubbly, she admired her reserve. Being round-faced, she admired the long elegance of Catherine's face. Catherine was everything that Marie was not. Perhaps that's why they felt so strangely drawn to each other.

"Hey, Cath," Marie said, "you're a knockout."

"No, I'm not. You just want me to be."

"This guy must be something to have a girl like you."

But just then someone hollered from downstairs, "Hey, what kind of car has he got?"

Knowing before she answered that her response was certain to raise a hullabaloo, Catherine mentally grimaced, then called, "A silver Corvette."

Marie looked like she'd swallowed a live crayfish. "A what!"

"You heard right."

"And you're resisting him! No wonder you look pained."

I do not look pained! thought Catherine. I *do not.*

From downstairs issued a noisy mingling of catcalls, wolf howls, whistles, and out-and-out girlish squeals, followed by violent shushing.

"Too bad you have to miss the talk after you leave," Marie giggled, smirking. "It'll be something tonight. Come on, Cleopatra, your barge has arrived."

Standing at the top of the stairs Catherine told herself this was not Cleopatra's barge nor high school prom nor Cinderella's ball. But as she clutched her knotted stomach, a little ache of expectation created a quiver there. A damning rush of blood crept up the V of exposed skin behind the blue collar. She could feel it as it rose and heated her cheeks.

This is insane, she told herself. The girls put ridiculous fancies in your head with all their giddy teenage fussing. So your nails are cinnamon and your hair is terrific and you're powdered and perfumed. But none of it is your doing, none of it is because a silver Corvette is coming to pick you up with Clay Forrester behind the wheel. So close your glistening lips, Catherine Anderson, and act like you're breathing normally and don't make more of an ass of yourself than you're already going to seem when he walks in that door and sees you!

Suddenly all the commotion stopped downstairs. Then footsteps ran in every direction and the silence that followed was ridiculous! Somebody, thankfully, got to the stereo and turned it on just as the doorbell rang.

Upstairs, Catherine felt a trembling begin somewhere down low in her groin and silently cursed every girl in this place for what they were forcing her to do. Down below she heard his voice and she closed her eyes, steadying herself.

"Is Catherine Anderson here?"

Suddenly Catherine wished she were a snail and could crawl inside her shell. Vicky's voice—utterly innocent, utterly faky—came clearly. "Just a minute, I'll see."

I'll see? thought Catherine, rolling her eyes behind closed lids. Oh, Lord!

"Catherine?" Vicky called up the stairs.

Behind her Marie whispered, "A silver Corvette, huh? Git going," and gave her a nudge.

The stairs came up to meet her high heels, and the clicks sounded like gunshots in her ears. In a last panic she thought, I should have washed off the perfume and blotted that glossy lipstick. Damn you, damn you, damn you! What am I doing?

The town idiot would not have been fooled by the obvious lack of activity downstairs. The staged poses, the casually lounging bodies, strategically placed so that each girl could see into the hall from their vantage points in the living room, the Scrabble board on the dining room table with not a wooden letter on it, and every eye in the place trained on Clay Forrester who stood by the colonnade as if framed for display and purchase.

It might not have been so bad if he hadn't dressed up, too, but he had. He was wearing a gray Continental-cut suit that made him look like an ad for some high-priced Canadian whiskey. Catherine set her eyes on the top of his wine-colored tie; it was knotted so perfectly that it stood away from his neck like a crisp, new hangman's noose. She let her gaze move up to the pale blue collar that cinched him just below the Adam's apple, where the bronze tan began.

"Hello," he said as casually as possible, considering that the change in her that made him feel like her old man's goon had only now smashed him in the stomach.

Oh, Christ! thought Clay Forrester. Oh, sweet Christ!

"Hello," she returned, trying to make the word as cool as a cucumber sandwich. But it came out wilted by the scorching heat of her face.

Her eyes were different, he thought, and her hair, and she was wearing an understated dress worthy of a travel ad in *The New Yorker*. Looking at her face again he saw that she was blushing. *Blushing.*

Catherine saw Clay's Adam's apple move like it was trying to dislodge a fishbone stuck in his throat. She bravely looked him in the face, knowing full well that her own was scarlet, silently warning him not to give away any hint of either surprise or approval. *Please!* But one glance told her it was too late. He, too, was red to the collar. To his credit, he acted as refined as his grooming, all except for one quick glance down at her stomach, followed by a quicker one at the crowd of gawking faces in the living room and dining room.

"Do you have a coat?"

Oh, God, she thought, October and I leave my coat upstairs!

"I left it up—"

But of all the girls, Marie finally did the right thing. She came down at an ungainly half-gallop, bringing the coat. "Here it is." And without any sign of ill ease, thrust out a hand toward Clay. "Hi, I'm Marie. Don't keep her out too late, okay?"

"Hi. I'm Clay and I won't." He smiled for the first time, shaking her hand firmly.

Jumping Jehoshaphat! thought Marie, he looks good enough to eat! And that smile. Look at that smile!

So when Catherine reached for her coat, Marie handed it instead to Clay. Correctly trained young swain that he was, he did the proper thing, and Catherine gratefully faced the door as he slipped the coat over her shoulders.

"Have a good time," Marie said.

"Good night," Catherine wished them all.

Like a kindergarten class, they all said in unison, "Good night."

Wanting to disappear into thin air, she reached for the doorknob, but Clay's hand shot around her, forcing her to allow him to open it for her or contest his gallantry before the girls. Catherine dropped her hand and moved out into the blessedly cool October night that touched her scorching skin in sweet relief. But still from behind them, Clay and Catherine could feel the eyes that peered out of every front window of the house.

Following her to the car, Clay caught the smell of a pleasant scent threading from her, heard the tap of high heels on the sidewalk, saw in the beam from the porch light the back of her artfully arranged hair. And although he hadn't intended to, he walked first to her side of the car and opened her door, conscious yet of all those curious eyes, his mind half on them, half on the long legs Catherine pulled into the car.

Indoors, a chorus of giddy sighs went swooning.

Within the car, the atmosphere was so tense and silent even the low rumble of the engine was welcome as Clay turned the key. Carefully, Catherine kept her eyes off him—something about a man and his car and the things he does when he gets into it, moving to start it, touching things on the dash, folding himself into the seat, the way the shoulder of a suit coat ridges high as he reaches for the mirror, disarming things that are too peculiarly masculine for comfort. She kept her eyes straight ahead.

"Where do you want to go?"

She looked at him at last. "Listen, I'm sorry about that in there. They . . . well, they . . ."

"It's all right. Where do you want to go?"

"It's not all right. I don't want you to get the wrong impression."

"I think the windows still have eyes." There was a touch of amusement in his tone as he waited, seemingly at ease now with his hands on the familiar wheel.

"Anywhere . . . I don't care. I thought we'd just go ride and sit somewhere in the car and talk like we did the other time."

The car moved away from the curb and she felt his quick assessing glance and knew he was adding up the dress, the hair, the makeup, the high heels. She wanted to die all over again. Go for a ride, indeed, she could hear him thinking.

"Do you drink?" he asked, taking his eyes back to the street.

She shot him a look, remembering last summer and that wine. "I can take it or leave it. Most of the time I leave it."

He thought of her father and thought he knew why.

"I know of a quiet place where the music doesn't start up till nine. It should be uncrowded this early and we can have a drink there while we talk, okay?"

"Fine," she agreed.

He pulled out onto Washington Avenue, heading toward downtown, across the Mississippi River. The silence grew uncomfortable so he reached, found a tape, engaged it in the deck, all without taking his eyes from the road. It was the same kind of music as before, too pulsing for her taste, too lacking in subtlety and musicality. Just a bunch of noise, she thought disparagingly. Once again she reached over and turned the volume down.

"You don't like disco?"

"No."

"Then you never tried dancing it?"

"No. If I danced anything it would be ballet, but I never had the chance to take lessons. But people used to say I'd make a good ballet dancer." She realized she was rambling on to hide her nervousness.

He sensed it, too, and replied simply, "They were probably right." He recalled where the level of her hair had matched his eyebrows.

She considered telling him that her father's beer and whiskey had sopped up all the spare money that might have meant ballet lessons, but it was too personal a comment. She wanted to avoid delving into personalities at all costs.

"Are all those girls back there pregnant?" he asked.

"Yes."

They stopped for a red light and Clay's face took on an unearthly tint as he looked at her. "But they're all so young."

"I'm the oldest one there."

She could sense his amazement, and suddenly she was chattering as fast as if this were a debate she wanted to win. "Listen, they won't believe this isn't a date. They *want* it to be a date. They want it so badly *they* did all of this to me. We were at supper and . . ." And the whole story came tumbling out, all about how they messed her up, then fixed her up as if she were a high priestess. "And I couldn't make them understand they were wrong," Catherine ended. "And it was awful . . . and wonderful . . . and pathetic."

So that's why, he thought. "Don't worry about it, okay? I understand."

"No! No! I don't think you do. I don't think you possibly can! They're making me their—their emissary!" She threw her palms up hopelessly, and related the tale about Francie and the perfume and how she was forced to put it on.

"So you smell terrific and you don't want to?"

"Don't be funny. You know what I'm trying to say. What could I do besides use the perfume, with a kleptomaniac looking at me with big eyes, begging me to make something in her life okay?"

"You did the right thing."

"I did what I had to do. But I wanted you to know it was out of my hands. When you arrived I wanted to die because I thought you'd think I—I had designs on you."

By now they'd pulled into a parking lot where a neon sign identified the place as The Mullion. Clay killed the motor, turned to her and said, "All right, I admit it was pretty uncomfortable there for a minute, but just so their efforts won't have been for nothing, you can tell them I said you looked fantastic."

"That's not what I was fishing for, don't you understand!"

"Yes, I do. But if you make anything more of it by being so insistent, I'll think you really do have designs on me." Already Clay knew the signs warning of her approaching anger. So, quickly he got out, slammed the door and came to open hers.

And though she simmered from his last comment, she couldn't help wondering, as they crossed the parking lot, why he'd worn that expensive suit.

Chapter 8

THE MULLION TOOK its name from the series of leaded bay windows facing east across the river. Clay touched Catherine's elbow, leading her to a table placed within a deepset bay which afforded semi-privacy, surrounded on three sides as it was by leaded glass and the night beyond. He reached for her coat, but she held it on like armor, sitting down before he could pull her chair out for her.

He sat down opposite, asking, "What will you have to drink?" He noticed how she now removed her coat by herself and let it fall back over the chair.

"Something soft."

"Wine?" he suggested. "White?" It was disconcerting that he remembered she preferred white to red. But then, in the early part of the evening on their one and only date, they'd been quite sober, sober enough for him to remember such a thing.

"No, softer. Orange juice—unadulterated."

He let his gaze drift to her stomach momentarily before looking back up to find her expression unreadable.

"They encourage the drinking of fruit juice there," she said, enlightening him.

Their eyes met, his rather sheepish, she thought, and she quickly looked away at the lights of automobiles threading their way across the Washington Avenue bridge, creating bleeding, golden shimmers in the water's reflection. Clay surprised Catherine by ordering two unadulterated orange juices. She braved a glance at him, but quickly shifted her eyes away. She couldn't help wondering if the baby would look like him.

"I want to know your plans," he began, then added pointedly, "first."

"First?" She met his eyes. "First before what?"

"Before I tell you why I brought you here."

"My plans should be obvious. I'm living in a home for unwed mothers."

"Don't be obtuse, Catherine. Don't make me eke every answer out of you again. You know what I'm asking. I want to know what you're planning to do with the baby after it's born."

Her face hardened. "Oh, no, not you too."

"What do you mean, not me too?"

"Just that every time I turn around lately somebody wants to know what I plan to do with the baby."

"Who else?"

She considered telling him it was none of his business, but knew it was. "Mrs. Tollefson, the director of Horizons. She says her job is not to find babies for the babyless, but any way you slice it, that's what she does."

"Are you planning to give it away, then?"

"I don't consider that anyone's business but my own."

"Meaning, you're having trouble coming to a decision?"

"Meaning, I don't want you to be part of that decision."

"Why?"

"Because you're not."

"I'm the father."

"You're the sire," she said, impaling him with a stabbing look that matched her words. "There is a big difference."

"Funny," he said in some strangely colorless voice, "but it doesn't seem to make any difference when I think of it."

"Are you saying you're suffering a fit of conscience?"

"That baby's mine. I can't just wipe it off the slate, even if I want to."

"I knew this would happen if I saw you. That's why I didn't want to. I don't want any pressure from you to either keep the baby or give it away. The responsibility is mine. Anyway, what happened to the man who offered me money for an abortion?"

"You may recall that I was under a bit of duress at the time. It was a quick reaction. Whether or not I'd have wanted you to go through with it, I don't know. Maybe I just wanted to know what kind of person you are."

"Well, I'm afraid I can't enlighten you, because I don't know what I'm going to do yet."

"Good," he said, surprising her.

The waitress arrived just then with two tall, skinny glasses of orange juice on the rocks.

Clay reached into an interior breast pocket, and Catherine automatically reached for her purse. But before she could retrieve her wallet Clay had laid a five-dollar bill on the tray.

"I want to pay for my own."

"You're too late."

The sight of his money being taken away unnerved her.

"I don't want . . ." But it was hard for her to explain what she didn't want.

"You don't want me buying orange juice for my baby?"

She stared at him, unblinking, trying to figure out her motives. "Something like that."

"The cost of a glass of orange juice doesn't constitute a lifelong debt."

"Skip it, okay? I feel you're infringing on me and I don't like it, that's all. Taking me out, buying me drinks. Just don't think it changes anything."

"All right, I won't. But I'll reiterate something that does. Your father."

"Have you told him—" she began accusingly.

"No, I haven't. He doesn't have any idea you're here. He thinks you're out in Omaha someplace. But he's been making a nuisance of himself in more ways than one, only he's sly enough to stop just short of getting pinned for anything. Now he's taken to sending his—shall we call them—emissaries around to the house occasionally to remind us that he's still waiting for a payoff."

"I thought he came himself."

"That was only the first time. There've been others."

"Oh, Cl—" She stopped herself from uttering his name, began again. "I—I'm sorry. What can we do about it?"

He was very much his lawyer-father's son as he leaned toward her, outlining the situation, his eyes intense, his expression grave. "I am a third-year law student, Catherine. I've worked very hard to get where I am, and I intend to graduate and be admitted to the bar this summer. Unfortunately, I also have to prove I'm morally upstanding. If your father continues his vendetta and it gets to the Board of Examiners that I've fathered a bastard, it could have serious repercussions. That's why we haven't pressed charges against your father so far. And while it has not been stated explicitly, it has been implied that even should I pass and be accepted to the bar, my father may deny me a place in the family practice if I've shirked my responsibility to you. Meanwhile, my mother walks around the house looking like I've just kicked her in a broken leg. Your father wants money. You want your whereabouts to remain unknown. People are pressuring you to give up the baby. A bunch of pregnant teenage girls see you as their hope for the future. What do you think we can do about it?"

The glass stopped halfway to her open, gleaming lips. "Now just a min—"

"Before you get angry, hear me out."

"Not if you say what I think you're going to say."

"It's a business proposition."

"I don't want to hear it."

Her face became highly colored and her hand shook. She turned her cheek sharply away, not quite hiding it behind a hand.

"Drink your orange juice, Catherine. Maybe it will cool you down and make you listen to reason. I propose that you marry me and we'll—"

"You're crazy!" she snapped, dumbfounded.

"Maybe," he said coolly, "maybe not."

She tried to push her chair back but he deftly hooked one foot around its leg, guessing she was preparing to bolt.

"You're really one for running out on unpleasantness, aren't you?"

"You're mad! Sitting there suggesting that we get married! Get your foot off my chair."

"Sit down," he ordered. "You're making a spectacle again."

A quick perusal told her he was right.

"Are you adult enough to sit here and discuss this levelheadedly, Catherine? There are at least a dozen sensible reasons for us to get married. If you'll give me a chance, I'll delineate them, starting with your father . . ."

That, above all, made her ease back into her chair.

"Are you saying he's caused you to get beaten up more than once?"

"Never mind. The point is, I'm beginning to understand why you vowed never to see him benefit from this situation. He's not exactly what I'd call ideal father-in-law material, but I'd take him as a temporary one rather than give him what he wants. If you and I marry, he'll be forced to give up his harassment. And even if the Board of Examiners somehow learns that a baby is due, it won't throw a shadow on my reputation if you and I are already married. I know now that what you said is true—your father is not really interested in your welfare as much as he is in his own. But my parents are.

"I feel like a juvenile delinquent every time my mother throws those censuring looks at me. And for some ungodly reason, my father is right in there with her. They're feeling . . ." He glanced up briefly, then down at his glass ". . . they're feeling like grandparents, reacting as such. They want to keep the baby in the family. They've taken a stand they won't back down from. And as for me, I won't bore you with my emotional state. Suffice it to say that it bothers me immeasurably to think of the baby being given up for adoption."

"I didn't say I was going to."

"No, you didn't. But what will you do if you keep it? Live on welfare in some roach-infested apartment house someplace? Give up school?" Again he leaned both forearms on the table, accosting her with his too-handsome, Nordic features set in an expression of worry. "I'm not asking you to consider marrying me without getting something out of it. When I saw you crossing the campus the other day, I couldn't believe my eyes. I didn't know you were a student there. What are you using for money?"

She didn't answer; she didn't need to for him to know finances were tight for her.

"It's going to take you some time to get through, isn't it? Even without the baby?"

Again, no answer.

"Suppose . . . just suppose we marry, agreeing in advance that it will be only until I finish school and take my bar exams. Your father will leave both of us alone; you'll be able to keep the baby; I'll be able to get my *juris doctor;* I'll be taken into my father's practice. When that happens you'll have your turn, and I'll pay for your schooling and for the child's support. That's my proposition. From now until July, that's all. And six months after that we'll have our divorce. I can easily handle it, and it is far less damaging to a career than a bastard child."

"And who keeps the baby?"

"You do," he answered without hesitation. "But at least I won't lose track of him and I'll see to it that neither he nor you ever has any financial worries. You can keep the baby and finish school too. What could be more sensible?"

"And what can be more dishonest?"

A look of exasperation crossed his face, but she knew that rankled, for he sat back in his chair and studied the lights across the river in a distracted fashion. She went on.

"You told me once that your father is the most exasperatingly honest person you know. What will he and your mother think when they learn their son has deceived them?"

"Why do they have to learn? If we do it, you'll have to agree never to tell them."

"Oh," she tossed out casually, knowing her remark was barbed, "so you don't want them to know you're a liar."

"I'm not a liar, Catherine. For God's sake, be reasonable." But he ran his fingers through his perfect hair and came forward on his chair again. "I'd like to finish law school and become part of my father's business. Is that so awful? That's the way we've always planned it to be, only now he seems to have lost reason."

She mused a while, then toyed with her glass. "You never had to worry about your ship coming in, did you?"

"And you resent that?"

"Yes, I suppose in a way I do."

"Enough to reject my offer?"

"I don't think I could do it."

"Why?" He leaned forward entreatingly.

"It would require acting talent that I don't possess."

"Not for long. About a year."

"At the risk of sounding hypocritical, I have to say it: your parents seem like decent and honest people and it would not settle well with me to hoodwink them just to make things easier for myself."

"All right, I admit it. It's not honest, and that bothers me too. I'm not in the habit of lying to them, no matter what you might think. But I don't think they're being totally honest, either, by taking the stand they've taken. They're forcing me to own up to my responsibilities, and I am. But, like you, I have a certain kind of life mapped out for myself, and I don't want to give it up because of this."

"There simply is no way I would marry someone I don't love. I've had a bellyful of living in a house where two people hated each other."

"I'm not asking you to love me. All I want is for you to think sensibly about the benefits we'd both derive from the arrangement. Let's backtrack a minute and consider one question which still needs answering. Do you want to give the baby up for adoption?"

He was leaning toward her now quite beseechingly. She studied the glass within his long, lean fingers, unwilling to look into his eyes for fear he might convince her of something she did not want.

"That's not fair and you know it," she spoke in a strained voice, "not after what I told you about the girls and my conversation with Mrs. Tollefson."

He sensed her weakening and pressed on. "None of this is, is it? I'm no different than you, Catherine, no matter what you might think. I don't want that baby living with strangers, wondering for the rest of my life where he is, what he is, who he is. I'd like to at least know that he's with you, and that he's got everything he needs. Is that such a bad bargain?"

Like a recording she repeated what Mrs. Tollefson had said, hoping to shore up her defenses. "It's a well-known fact that adopted children are exceptionally bright, happy and successful."

"Who told you that, your social worker?"

Her eyes flashed to his. How easily he can read me, she thought. The waitress approached, and without asking Catherine, Clay signaled to order two more orange juices, more to get rid of the interference than because he was thirsty. He watched the top of Catherine's hair as she toyed with her glass. "Could you really give it up?" he asked softly.

"I don't know," she admitted raggedly.

"My mother was decimated when she found out you were gone. I never saw her cry in my life, but then I did. She didn't have to mention the word abortion more than once for me to know it was on her mind night and day. I guess I learned some things about my parents and myself since this thing happened."

"It's so dishonest," she said lamely. Then after long silence, she asked, "When are the bar exams?" She could not quite believe what she was asking.

"I don't know the exact date yet, but sometime in July."

She rested her forehead against her hand, as if unutterably tired of everything.

Suddenly he felt obliged to reassure her so he reached for her arm, which lay disconsolately on the tabletop. She didn't even try to resist the small squeeze he gave it.

"Think it over," he said quietly.

"I don't want to marry you, Clay," she said, raising her sad, beautiful eyes to him, a pinched expression about their corners.

"I know. I'm not expecting it to be a regular marriage, with all the obligations. Only as a means to what we both want."

"And you'd start divorce proceedings immediately after the exams and you wouldn't use some clever tricks to get the baby away from me?"

"I would treat you fairly, Catherine. I give you my word."

"Would we live together?" Her eyelids flickered; she looked aside.

"In the same place, but not together. It would be necessary for my family to think we were married in more than name only."

"I feel utterly exhausted," she admitted.

Some musicians filed in, turned on some dim stage lights and began tuning up their guitars.

"There's not much more to be said tonight"—Clay fiddled with the table edge a moment—"only that I'd keep out of your way if you marry me. I know you don't like me, so I won't push anything like that."

"I don't dislike you, Clay. I hardly know you."

"I've given you plenty of good reason though, haven't I? I've gotten you pregnant, offered you abortion money, and now I'm suggesting a scheme to get us out of it."

"And am I so lily-white?" she asked. "I'm actually thinking it over."

"You'll consider it then?"

"You don't have to ask. Against my better judgment, I already am."

They drove back to Horizons in silence. As he pulled the car to a stop at the curb, Clay said, "I could come and pick you up at the same time tomorrow night."

"Why don't you just call?"

"There are too many inquisitive ears around here."

She knew he was right, and though it was difficult for her to be with Clay, neither did she want to give him her answer with an audience around the corner. "Okay, I'll be ready."

He let the engine run, got out and came around to open her door, but by the time he got there she was already stepping out of the car. He politely closed the door for her.

"You don't have to do all these things, you know, like opening doors and pulling out chairs. I don't expect it."

"If I didn't, would it make you feel better?" They walked toward the porch steps.

"I mean, you don't have to pretend it's *that* real."

"Force of habit," he said.

Under the garish light of the porch she at last dared to look directly into his face.

"Clay." She tested the word fully upon her tongue. "I know you've gone with a girl named Jill Magnusson for a long time." Catherine struggled to find a way to say what was on her mind, but found she couldn't say it.

He stood still as a statue, his expression void, unreadable. Then he reached for the screen door, opened it and said, "You'd better go in now."

He turned on a heel, took the steps in one leap and ran to the car. As she watched the tail lights disappear up the street she felt, for the first time in her pregnancy, like throwing up.

Chapter 9

THE FOLLOWING DAY was one of those flawless Indian summer days in Minnesota which are like an assault on the senses. The warmth returned, dormant flies reawakened, the sky was deep azure, and the campus crimson and gold was vivid as autumn color peaked. It was October; new match-ups had been made, and to Catherine it seemed the entire population of the University moved in pairs. She found herself captivated by the sight of a male and a female hand with their fingers entwined, swinging between two pairs of hips. Without her consent her mind formed a picture of Clay Forrester's clean, lean hands on the wheel, and she wiped her damp palm on her thigh. She passed a couple kissing in the entrance to Tate Lab. The boy had his hand inside the girl's jacket just above her back waistline. Unable to tear her eyes away, Catherine watched his hand emerge from under the garment, then pass along the girl's ribs as the two parted, went their separate ways. She remembered Clay's words, *not a regular marriage with all the obligations,* and though that's what she, too, insisted it must be, there were goosebumps on her flesh. In the late afternoon, on her way home, she spotted a couple sitting on the grass Indian style, face-to-face, studying. Without taking his eyes from his book, the boy absently ran his hand up inside the girl's pantleg to her knee. And something female prickled down low inside of Catherine.

But I'm pregnant, she thought, and Clay Forrester doesn't love me. Still, that didn't make the prickly longing disappear.

Back at Horizons Catherine carefully changed clothes, though casually enough so as not to appear seductive. But when her makeup was complete, she looked closely in the mirror. Why had she reconstructed last night's careful shadings and highlights? Subtle mauve shadow above her eyes, a faint hint of peach below them, sandy brown mascara, apricot cheeks, glistening cinnamon lips to match her nails. She told herself it had nothing to do with Clay Forrester's proposal.

Turning from the dresser, Catherine found Francie waiting hesitantly in the doorway, wearing the first suggestion of a smile Catherine had seen upon her face. In silence, Francie extended the bottle of Charlie.

Catherine forced a bright smile of her own. "Why, thank you, I was just coming to get it." The perfume followed the makeup, and a moment later Marie came in to say Clay had arrived.

When Catherine came downstairs, there was a first awkward moment while they each scanned the other's clothes and faces, that too-meaningful assessment making her heart thud heavily.

He was wearing navy blue trousers this time, stylishly pleated, and a V-neck sweater of pale blue lamb's wool. Beneath was an open collar, short tips clearly stating it was this season's style. He wore a simple gold chain around his neck, and it seemed to accent the golden hue of his skin. Admitting how utterly in vogue Clay always dressed, and how it pleased her, Catherine wondered for the hundredth time that day if she were doing the right thing.

There was a feeling of unreality about walking out before him, passing through the door he held open, feeling him behind her shoulder as they took the porch steps and walked toward the car. She battled to submerge the feelings of familiarity which were already cropping up: the way he leaned sideways from the hip when he opened her car door, the hug of the bucket seat as she slid in, the sound of his footsteps coming around the car, his own peculiar movements as he settled into his seat. Then once again the smell of his shaving lotion in the confined space, and all of those thrice-noticed motions of a man and his car: already she knew just in which order he would do them, wrist over wheel as he started the engine, the unnecessary touch on the rearview mirror, the single shrug and forward jut of his head as he made himself comfortable, the way he left his hand on the stick of the floor shift as the Corvette pulled away from the curb. He was driving sensibly tonight. Instead of the tape deck, the radio was on this time, softly, voices proclaiming musically that they were tuned to KS-ninety-five. Then, without warning, The Lettermen began singing, "Well, I think I'm going out of my head . . ." And Clay just drove. And Catherine just sat. Each of them wanting to reach over and turn the song off. Neither of them daring. Lights coming, going, flashing, waning while the car moved through the mellow Indian summer night, its engine cooing along on a note as rich as any coming from The Lettermen, whose song finally reached its medley stage and wove its way into words that were even worse: "You're just too good to be true . . . can't take my eyes off of you . . ."

Catherine thought she would do anything for some wildly pulsating disco! But she found she could not give credence to the meaningful words coming from the radio, so she braved it out until the song ended. When it had, Clay asked her a single question.

"Did the girls do all that to you tonight?"

But with the suggestive song ended, she'd regained control of her senses. There was no reason to lie. "No."

He gave her a sidelong look, then tended to his driving again.

She somehow guessed where they would go. She needn't know the exact route to be sure of the destination. He drove as if it were predetermined, out onto the Interstate, under the tunnel and west on Wayzata Boulevard to Highway 100, then south toward Edina. Again the unwanted feeling of familiarity crept over her. She had a sudden desperate hope that she might be wrong, that he'd choose to drive to some other place, thus avoiding the establishment of further familiarities. But he did not.

The wooded trail wound up into the park, taking them to the same secluded spot as that first night. He stopped at the top of the gravel road and switched off the engine but left the radio playing softly. Outside it was full dark, but the vague light from the dash illuminated his profile as he entwined his fingers behind the steering wheel and distractedly tapped a thumb upon it in time to the music.

Panic clawed its way up her throat.

At last he turned, propping his left elbow on top of the wheel. "Have you . . . have you thought about it any more or decided anything?"

"Yes." The lone syllable sounded strained.

"Yes, you've thought about it, or yes, you'll marry me?"

"Yes, I'll marry you," she clarified, with no hint of joy in her voice. She answered instead with a throb of regret tumbling her stomach. She wished he would not study her so and wondered if he was feeling as hollow as she was at that moment. She wanted to get out of the car and run down the gravel hill again. But where would she run? To what?

"Then we might as well work out a few details as soon as possible."

His businesslike tone thrust her back to reality.

"I suppose you don't want to waste any time?"

"Considering you're three months pregnant already, no I don't. I don't suppose you do either?"

"N-no," she lied, dropping her eyes to her lap.

A short, nervous laugh escaped him. "What do you know about weddings?"

"Nothing." She gazed at him helplessly.

"Neither do I. Are you willing to go and talk to my parents?"

"Now?" She hadn't expected it so soon.

"I thought we might."

"I'd rather not." In the dim light she looked panic-stricken.

"Well, what do you want to do then, elope?"

"I hadn't given it much thought."

"I'd like to go talk to them. Do you mind?"

What else could she do? "We'll have to face them sooner or later, I guess."

"Listen, Catherine, they're not ogres. I'm sure they'll help us."

"I have no illusions about what they must think of me and of my family. They can't be martyrs enough to be willing to forget all that my father has done. Can you blame me for being less than anxious to face them?"

"No."

They sat there thinking about it for a while. But neither of them knew the first thing about planning a wedding of any kind.

"My mother will know what to do."

"Yeah, like throw me out."

"You don't know her, Catherine. She's going to be happy."

"Sure," she replied sullenly.

"Well, relieved then."

But still they sat, aware of the sharp contrast between what *was* happening and what *should be* happening at a time like this.

Finally Catherine sighed. "Well, let's get it over with then."

Clay started the car abruptly. He took them back down the twisting streets, through the rolling neighborhoods of elegant lawns whose breadth spoke of estates rather than lots. She heard the unfamiliar sound of tires on cobblestone as they swept up the curve and stopped before that massive pair of front doors she had once studied so critically from inside. They cowed her now, but she made up her mind not to let it show.

Following Catherine to the house, Clay found himself thinking of Jill Magnusson, and how it should be her going with him to speak to his parents.

The foyer assaulted Catherine with memories of the last time she'd been here: the way Clay had come breezing in and the scene that had followed. She found herself before the mirror, glanced quickly away from his regarding eyes and stopped her hand from touching a wisp of hair that was out of place. Disarmingly, he read her thoughts.

"You look fine. . . . Come on." And he took her elbow.

Angela looked up as they approached the study door. The sight of them stirred her warmest blood, made it race crazily at their unexpected arrival. They were like a pair of sun-children, both of them blond, tall and strikingly beautiful. Nobody had to tell Angela Forrester how beautiful a child of theirs would be.

"Are we interrupting anything?" Clay asked. His father glanced up from something he'd been working on at his desk. Everything in the room marked time for that interminable moment while they all allowed the surprise to run its course. Then Angela unwound her ankles in slow motion and removed a pair of reading glasses. Claiborne rose, halfway at first, as if stunned. He and Angela stared at Catherine, and she felt the blood whipping up her neck and fought the urge to duck behind Clay.

At last he spoke. "I think it's time you all met properly. Mother, Father, this is Catherine Anderson. Catherine, my parents."

And yet, for a painful moment more, the room remained a Still Life With Parents and Children.

Then Angela moved. "Hello, Catherine," she said, reaching out a flawless, jeweled hand.

Immediately Catherine sensed that Angela Forrester, like the girls at Horizons, was an ally. This woman wants me to marry her son, she thought, amazed.

But when Claiborne Forrester emerged from around his desk, it was with a less-welcoming mien, although he extended his hand and greeted Catherine, also. But where Angela's touch had been a warm peace offering, there exuded from her husband a coolness much the same as the other time Catherine had been in this room.

"So you found her, Clay," the older man noted unnecessarily.

"Yes, several days ago."

Angela and Claiborne looked at each other, then quickly away.

"Several days ago. Well . . . ." But the word dangled there, leaving everything awkward again. "We're glad you've changed your mind and come back to talk things over a little more sensibly. Our first meeting was, well, shall we say, less than ideal."

"Father, could we forego the obvious recrim—"

"No, it's all right," Catherine interrupted.

"I think we'd all better sit down." Angela motioned toward the loveseat where she'd been sitting. "Catherine, please." Clay followed and sat down beside her. His parents took the chairs beside the fireplace.

Although her stomach was twitching, Catherine spoke calmly. "We thought it best to come and talk to you immediately."

The eagle's frown was there upon Mr. Forrester's face, just as Catherine remembered it.

"Under the circumstances, I should certainly think so," the man said.

Clay edged forward as if to respond, but Catherine hurried to speak first. "Mr. Forrester, I understand that my father has been here more than just once. I want to apologize for his behavior, both the night I was with him and any other times when I wasn't. I know how irrational he can be."

Claiborne grudgingly found himself admiring the girl's directness. "I assume Clay has told you we have refrained from pressing charges."

"Yes, he has. I'm sorry that's what you decided. I can only say I had nothing to do with his actions and hope you'll believe me."

Again Claiborne felt an unwanted twitch of admiration at the girl's straightforward manner. "We, of course, know that Clay offered you money, and that you refused his offer. Have you changed your mind?"

"I haven't come here asking for money. Clay told me you haven't paid my father anything he demanded, but I'm not here pleading his case, if that's what you think. I never intended for any of it to happen. That night I came here I had already made plans to run away from home and make it look like I was headed across the country where he couldn't catch up with me. I thought when I was gone he'd leave you alone. If any of it could have been avoided by my staying, I'm sorry."

"I make no pretense of liking your father or of excusing him, but I must admit I'm relieved Clay found you so this mess can get straightened out once and for all. I'm afraid we've all been rather anxious and have been upset with Clay's behavior."

"Yes, he told me."

Claiborne quirked an eyebrow at his son. "Seems you and Clay have been doing a lot of talking lately."

"Yes, we have."

Whatever Clay had expected, it wasn't Catherine's cool control. He was pleasantly surprised by the way she was handling his father. If there was one thing Claiborne Forrester admired it was spunk, and she was displaying an inordinate amount of it.

"Have you come to any conclusions?" Claiborne pressed on.

"I think that's for Clay to answer."

"He didn't bother to tell us that he'd found you, you know."

"I made him promise he wouldn't. I'm living in a home for unwed mothers and didn't care to have my whereabouts known."

"Because of your father?"

"Yes, among other reasons."

"Such as?"

"Such as your son's money, Mr. Forrester, and the pressure it could exert on me."

"Pressure? He offered you money, which you refused to accept. Is that what you call pressure?"

"Yes. Isn't it?"

"Are you upbraiding me, Miss Anderson?"

"Are *you* upbraiding *me,* Mr. Forrester?"

The room crackled almost electrically for a moment before Claiborne admitted in a less accusing voice, "You surprise me. I hadn't expected your . . . detachment."

"I'm not at all detached. I've been through two very hellish weeks. I've been making decisions that haven't been easy."

"So have my wife and I, and—I dare say—Clay."

"Yes, he told me about your—I dare say—ultimatum."

"Call it what you will. I don't doubt that Clay represented it to you in anything but its true light. We were grossly disappointed in the lack of good judgment he showed and took steps to see that he not only own up to his responsibilities, but that he not ruin his chances for the future."

Angela Forrester sat forward then on the edge of her chair, legs crossed, leaning a delicate elbow on one knee. "Catherine," she said, her voice the first emotional one in the room, "please understand that I—we have all been utterly distraught about your welfare and that of the child. I was so afraid you'd gone off to have an abortion anyway, in spite of what you told Clay."

Catherine could not help angling a quick glance at Clay, surprised that he'd told them he'd suggested abortion.

"They know everything that we talked about that night," he confirmed.

"You're surprised, Catherine?" Angela asked. "That Clay told us the truth or that we . . . rather . . . forced the issue?"

"At both, I guess."

"Catherine, we knew you were here against your wishes the first time. Believe me, Clay's father and I have asked ourselves countless times what is the right thing to do. We coerced Clay into bringing you back here, so are we any less guilty of force than your father?"

"My father is a man who doesn't know how to reason, or rather, who won't. Please don't think that I'm anything like him. I . . ." Catherine looked down at her lap, her first outward show of her inner turmoil. "I intensely dislike my father." Then she confronted Claiborne's eyes again, continuing. "You may as well know that part of the reason I am here now is to see that he doesn't bleed you for a single red cent, and that my reasons have little to do with altruism."

Claiborne rose, crossed back to his desk and seated himself behind it. He picked up a letter opener and began toying with it. "You're a very direct young woman."

Angela could tell this pleased her husband. While the girl's directness put her off somewhat, she was moved to sympathy by a daughter harboring such strong negative emotions for a father. The girl, it was obvious, was defensive about it, too, which meant she was hurt by it. All of this touched the mother in Angela.

"Does that bother you?" Catherine was asking.

"No, no, not at all," Claiborne blustered, ruffled that someone else controlled the conversational reins which he was accustomed to controlling.

Again Catherine dropped her eyes to her lap. "Well, anyway, I don't have to live in the same house with him anymore."

Again Angela experienced a twinge of pity; her eyes met her husband's and went to Clay, who was studying Catherine's profile.

Clay dropped his hand from the back of the loveseat onto the back of Catherine's neck, to the spot where he'd once detected the evidence of her father's abuse. Startled, she met his eyes, burned by the heat of his hand through her hair. Then the heat disappeared and Clay looked toward his father. "Catherine left home and arranged for her father to think she was running across the country so that she could continue school without being hassled by him."

Surprised, Claiborne asked, "You're a student?"

"Yes, at the university."

Again Clay spoke. "It goes without saying that she'd have a tough time of it with the baby. I managed to convince her that it was sensible to let me help with finances." He allowed a moment to pass silently before capturing Catherine's hand, pressing it onto his knee in a way she found embarrassingly familiar. "Catherine and I have talked everything over. Tonight I asked her to marry me and she accepted."

Angela carefully kept the pain from showing in her face, but her throat worked convulsively. The letter opener slipped from Claiborne's fingers and clattered onto the desktop. He then rested one elbow on each side of it and covered his face with both hands.

"We've agreed that it's best this way," Clay said quietly, and his father's eyes emerged from behind his fingertips just in time to see Catherine slip her hand cautiously off Clay's knee.

What have I done? thought Claiborne.

Angela murmured, "I'm so relieved," and wondered if she really was.

Claiborne could not help asking, "Are you sure?"

Catherine felt Clay's eyes pulling her own to his face. He gave her a secretive look which could easily be misinterpreted by his parents. Then he rested an elbow on the back of the sofa and laid a hand on her shoulder nearest his chest. "Catherine's friends and I have managed to convince her," he said, with just enough implied intimacy to give them the fully wrong impression.

Catherine felt her face redden.

Angela and Claiborne witnessed their son's eyes caressing the young woman's face, and their own startled eyes met. How could this possibly have happened so quickly? Yet they each remembered that the two had been intimate once; apparently there was some basis for attraction. Everything about Clay's attitude suggested it, and the girl's blush confirmed it. But sensing that Catherine was displeased with the way Clay allowed his appetites to show, Angela moved toward them, offering congratulations. Claiborne rose and came to clasp their hands. When he held his son's hand firmly within both of his, he said honestly, "We're proud of your decision, Clay."

But there was an undeniably painful mixture of eagerness and disappointment permeating the room. Feeling it, Catherine thought this must be how a thief felt while casing victims who were also friends.

It was some time later that the issue of the wedding came up as Angela asked, unassumingly, "Do you want your father and I in on the arrangements?"

"Of course," Clay answered without hesitation. "Catherine and I don't know the first thing about planning a wedding."

"Why not have the wedding here?" Angela asked most unexpectedly.

It was immediately apparent Catherine had not thought that far ahead. Angela placed a hand on her arm apologetically. "Oh, forgive me, have I been too assuming? From the things you've said about your father I thought perhaps . . ." But her words trailed away, leaving an uncomfortable void. She realized she'd put her foot in her mouth, something Angela Forrester rarely did.

Catherine attempted to ease the tension by affecting a wan laugh. "No, no, it's all right. You're probably right. My father wouldn't be inclined to lay out money when it was his intention all along to realize a profit from this situation."

"But I've embarrassed you, Catherine, and that was not my intention. I don't mean to usurp your parents' place, but I want you to understand that Clay's father and I would be more than happy to give both of you whatever you want in the way of a wedding. I simply don't want you to think we would stint you on anything. Clay is our only son—please understand, Catherine. This will happen only once. As his parents, we'd love to indulge in our dreams of a perfect wedding celebration. If you'd . . . well, if you'd both agree to have the service here at the house, we'd be utterly happy, wouldn't we, darling?"

Claiborne, looking rather lost and beleaguered, could only concur. But, goddammit, he thought. It should have been Jill. *It should have been Jill!* "What Angela says is true. We certainly are not strapped, and we'd be happy to foot the bill."

"I don't know yet," Catherine said, floundering in this new possibility that she hadn't considered.

"Mother, we haven't had a chance to talk about it yet," Clay explained.

Angela chose her words carefully, hoping that Clay would understand there were social obligations that people of their position must fulfill.

"I see no reason for either of you to feel you must sneak off like two chastised children. A marriage should be treated as a celebration. I . . . Catherine, I can see that I *have* embarrassed you, but please take our offer in the light it is intended. We can very easily afford to pay for a small affair here. Call it selfish, if you want to. Clay is our only son, you must understand."

"Mother, Catherine and I will talk it over and let you know."

To Clay, she said, "There are so many people who would be disappointed if you eloped—not the least of whom are your father and me. I'd like the family and a few close friends anyway. You know how your grandparents would be hurt if they were eliminated. And I'm sure Catherine will want her family."

But neither Clay nor Catherine knew what the other's feelings were on the subject.

"Well"—Angela straightened her shoulders—"enough said. I've been rather premature, I realize, but whatever you decide, I know we can implement your plans."

"Thank you, Mrs. Forrester. We'll have to talk it over."

Again an awkward silence fell, and as if suddenly inspired, Claiborne clapped his hands with mock joviality, suggesting a glass of wine to honor the occasion.

Clay immediately seconded the motion, going to find an untapped bottle while Claiborne fetched four crystal goblets.

A glass of white wine of excellent vintage was placed in Catherine's hands. Momentarily the goblet blotted out Clay's face before its rim touched her lips, and above it she telegraphed Clay a message which he, thankfully, understood. The toast done, he took Catherine's glass from her hand and set it, along with his own, on the table.

"Catherine and I will see you . . . when, Catherine?" He looked to her. "Tomorrow night?"

So fast! she thought, things are moving so fast! But she found herself agreeing to tomorrow night.

Preparing to leave, Catherine tried to thank Angela, but Angela's eyes were unmistakably dewy as she said, "Things will work out." The diamonds upon her hands flashed as she made a gesture of command with the wineglass. "Go now," she finished, "and we'll see you tomorrow."

As she left the room where Claiborne and Angela stood with their arms around each other's waists, Catherine found herself comparing them to her own parents and admitted that the Forresters did not deserve to be deceived.

They were the "rich sons-a-bitches" her father had despised, whom she'd nearly caught herself despising. But she saw them now only as a mother and father who wanted nothing but the best for their son. Leaving their house Catherine thought, I'm no better than my father.

Chapter 10

OUTSIDE IT HAD turned colder, and a spiritless rain had begun. The heater, not yet warmed up, breathed clammy air onto Catherine's legs as she girded her knees with both hands to keep from shivering.

Headed back to Horizons, Clay asked peremptorily, "Well, what do you think?"

"I have a feeling this thing is going to get out of hand right before our very eyes. I never thought your mother would come up with such a suggestion."

"I didn't either, but I guess I didn't have time to think. Still, it's better than the whole church thing with a thousand guests, isn't it?"

"I don't know what I expected, but it wasn't grandpas and grandmas." Somehow Clay Forrester seemed too chic to have grandparents hidden somewhere in the woodwork.

"I didn't evolve from a splitting cell, you know," he said, attempting to inject a little humor into the otherwise humorless situation.

"Right now I almost wish you had. Me too."

"Don't you have any grandparents?"

"No, they're all dead. But if I did, I think I'd burn an effigy on their front lawn to protest their having an offspring like my dad. Clay, I will not have that man at our wedding, no matter what."

"Well, it wouldn't hurt my feelings not to invite him, but how can you leave him out and still have your mother? Is that what you're suggesting?"

"I don't know what I'm suggesting. This whole idea of a—a real *ceremony* is . . . well, it's preposterous! My old man would get pickled and become obnoxious as usual and the whole scene would be worse than any so far. Either that, or he'd go around telling all the guests how his ship just came in!"

"Well, I don't see how we can avoid him."

"*Clay!*" she said in an I-don't-believe-this tone of voice.

"What? What does that mean—*Clay?*" He repeated her exact tone of disbelief.

"You really want to go along with this whole shindig, don't you? I mean, you think we should let your mother go through with all the preparations and the expense of a real wedding, and let them believe it's for keeps?"

"If she wants to do it, let her do it. She's in her glory when she's organizing what she calls her 'little social events,' so let her organize one. Who's it going to hurt?"

"Me! I feel like a felon already, planning what we're planning. I don't want to haze your parents any more than necessary."

"Catherine, I think you have to put things into perspective. The whole occasion will probably cost less than one of the rings on my mother's hands. So why not let her have her fun?"

"Because it's dishonest," she said stubbornly.

He grew a little irritated. "That fact is already established, so what's the difference how we go about it as long as we're going to go about it anyway?"

"Can't we just go off to some justice of the peace or something?"

"We can if that's what you really want. But I think it would only hurt my parents more. I don't know about yours—your mother anyway—but I doubt that she'd be too disappointed to see you getting married with a show of my parents' support. That's really what it boils down to, you know. My parents have chosen to accept our marriage and want it known that they do. Isn't that what weddings are all about?"

"No. Most weddings are about a lifelong commitment between a man and a woman."

But Clay sensed something more behind Catherine's refusal. "You wouldn't like any *vile ostentation* on your account, is that it? Especially if the bill was picked up by the despicable rich you've been cultured to hate so much?"

At the beginning that had been part of it, but no longer. "Okay, I'll admit it, I've been prejudiced by my father's prejudices against the rich. And, yes, I've had preformed notions about what your family would be like, but your parents are not bearing them out."

Clay worked the edges of his teeth together, noting that she did not include him in her summary of findings. "You mean you like them?"

But Catherine had decided that liking them was a pitfall she would do well to guard against.

"I respect them," she answered truthfully, "and that in itself is something new for me."

"Well, then, couldn't you respect their wishes and go along with my mother?"

Catherine sighed heavily. "Lord, I don't know. I'm not very good at any of this. I don't think I ever should have agreed to it."

"Catherine, whatever you might think, my mother is not a manipulator. She does try to do things in the accepted fashion, and I haven't mentioned it before, but I know that part of the reason for a reception of some kind is political. It may not have been mentioned, but business etiquette requires invitations to occasions such as these for certain long-established associates who have become more than just business connections down through the years. Some of them are close personal friends of my parents by now. I'm sorry if that lays an extra burden on you, but that's the way it is."

"Why didn't you tell me this when you first suggested the scheme?"

"Frankly, I didn't think of it then."

She groaned softly. "Oh, this gets worse all the time."

"If you ask Mother to scale it down, I'm sure she will. But I guarantee that whatever she has a hand in will be handled with taste and efficiency. Would that be so hard to accept?"

"I . . . it scares me, that's all. I don't know anything about . . . society weddings."

"She does. Let her guide you. I have a feeling the two of you could work well together, once you get to know each other."

Again Catherine felt cornered, this time by Clay's obvious wish to please his parents, even if it meant a wedding that was larger than prudent. And again as she remembered his light touches, the looks of implied intimacy, she decided to take up the subject now so that he clearly understood her stand on the matter.

"That was quite a performance you put on back there, and totally unnecessary. I'm sure your parents aren't that gullible."

"You may have thought it unnecessary; I didn't."

"Well, spare me in the future, please. It's bad enough as it is."

"I wanted as few questions as possible, that's all. And I think it worked."

"You have no conscience whatsoever, do you?"

"We've been over this once before, so let's not go over it again. I don't like it any more than you do, but I'm going through with it, okay? If I have to touch you now and then to make it convincing, I'm sorry."

"Well, that wasn't part of our agreement."

"Are you that insecure that a touch on the shoulder threatens you?"

She would not grace him with an answer to such nonsense. But when she sat silently stewing for some time, he added, "Just forget it. It didn't mean anything, it was only an act."

Only an act, Catherine thought. Only an act.

It was warm in the car as Catherine sighed, leaned back in the comfortable seat and let the whisper of rain beneath the tires hypnotize her. The purring syllable of the engine, the faint vibration of the road, the gentle sway now and then as they rounded a curve or changed lanes—she let it engulf her in a place halfway between sleep and wakefulness, halfway between worry and security. The swoop of the windshield wipers mesmerized her and she drifted away, playing the game of pretend, as she and Bobbi had done so often in childhood. What happened to the girl who romanticized stories in her diary all her growing years? What happened to those dreams that had been an escape hatch then? What would it be like if this wedding were not some trumped-up scheme? What if it were real, and she and Clay both wanted it?

There was a bouquet of sweet-scented flowers in her hands as she drifted through a crowd of people with radiant smiles. She wore a stunning white gown with a skirt so voluminous it filled the width of the stairway from banister to wall. The diaphanous veil on her head tumbled around her, following like an aureole as she passed a table spread with lace and laid with silver, and another that bore an eruption of gifts which scarcely took her notice as she searched the throng for the eyes she knew so well. Bobbi was there, kissing her cheek, crying a little bit from happiness. But again the search for gray eyes and she found them and they smiled. He waited for her to reach him, and when she had she knew peace and fulfillment. Rice flew, and the bouquet flew, straight into Bobbi's upraised hands, and Bobbi tossed her a kiss that said, "See? It happened just like we pretended, you first, then me." And mother's face was in the crowd, eased of worry, because Cathy had picked the right man. Then she and the very right, very gray-eyed man were sailing through the door toward a honeymoon, a honeylife, and it was real . . . real . . . real . . .

Catherine's head leaned at a fallen angle upon the seat of the car. Clay leaned near her, shaking her elbow gently. "Hey, Catherine, wake up." The dash lights picked out a series of golden needlepoints from the tips of her eyelashes which formed a dim fan of shadows across her cheek and nose. Her hair was messed up on one side, caught against the car seat and billowed out in disarray around her ear. He noticed for the first time that the ear was pierced. She wore a tiny silver stud in it. Her lips had fallen relaxed, all of their earlier gloss now gone. The very tip of her tongue showed between her teeth. The tendons of her neck were highlighted, creating intimate shadows behind them. The faint, inviting scent of her perfume still clung there.

How defenseless she looks, thought Clay, all wilted sideways, with her usual air of aloofness erased. She was a beautiful girl this way, but when she awoke he knew her stern facade would quickly return, and with it the cold overtones that Clay already disliked so intensely. He wondered if he might not learn to love her if her personality were as warm and sweet as the look of her right now. His eyes moved down to her lap. One hand was still lightly closed around a clutch purse, the other lay against her low abdomen. Behind that hand his child thrived. He let the thought carry him. He considered what he wanted out of life and wondered what she wanted out of hers. The hand in her lap twitched and he studied it, thinking how easily she could have had an abortion. Momentarily he wished she had, then again, was relieved she hadn't. He wondered what the baby would look like. He wondered if it would be a boy or a girl. He wondered if it were a mistake, this wedding idea. He felt a momentary tenderness toward her because of the life she carried, and decided no, it was no mistake; his child deserved a better start in life than he, Clay, had given it so far. He wished, oh, how he wished, that things were different, that this girl were different, so he could love her. He realized he still held her arm, just above the elbow. He could feel her pliant flesh, her body heat through her coat sleeve.

"Catherine, wake up," he repeated softly.

Her eyelashes lifted and her tongue glanced across her lips. Her head rolled upright, and her eyelids shut once more.

"You fell asleep," he said, close to her, that hand still resting on her forearm.

"Mmmm . . ." Catherine murmured, resisting wakefulness a little longer. She stretched without stretching, using only her shoulders. She was aware of his touch, and she pretended for a minute longer, knowing now that he was very near, even though her eyes were still closed.

"You were supposed to be thinking things over instead of sleeping." But his voice was devoid of criticism, holding instead a note of warmth. She opened her eyes to find him a hovering shadow before her, his features eclipsed, for he'd slung one elbow over the wheel and half-turned her way.

"Sorry. I seem to do that so easily lately. The doctor said it was natural though."

Her words created an intimacy that lightly lifted Clay's stomach, coming as they did upon the heels of his thoughts about the baby. He had never considered the personal changes going on inside her body before, nor the way they affected her day-to-day routine. It struck him that he was responsible for many changes she was undergoing, of which he was totally unaware.

"It's okay. I really don't mind."

It was the first time they ever had spoken unguardedly to each other. Her defenses were down, drowsy as she was.

"I was pretending," she confided.

"Pretending what?"

"Not really pretending, but remembering how Bobbi and I used to sit for hours and plan our weddings and make gowns out of dishtowels and safety pins, and veils from old curtains. Then we'd write it all in our diaries, all our glorious fantasies."

"And what did you write?"

"Oh, all the usual things. Girlish dreams."

"*Lohengrin* and trailing veils?"

She laughed softly in her throat and shrugged.

"You never said that before. If you wanted all those things, why did you argue earlier?"

"Because the traditional things will only be empty and depressing if all they do is create a front for what's missing."

"Hearts and flowers?"

She had never seen him this mellow before. Again she wondered what it would be like with him if this were real. "Don't mistake my meaning if I say yes."

He moved away slightly, squaring himself in the seat. "I won't. Do you assume that men don't want the same things?"

"I never thought about what men want."

"Would it surprise you to learn that I've recently done some wishing of my own?"

Yes, she thought, yes, it would. Have I robbed you of your dreams? She stole a glance at his profile. It was a very appealing profile, one she had looked at directly very few times. It wore an amenable expression now.

"Did you?" she asked at last, unable to stop the question.

"A little, yes. Mostly hindsight, you know."

She tried for an understanding note as she observed, "You really don't like being a disappointment to your parents in any way, do you?"

"No."

She didn't want to seem prying, yet she had to know—it had been bothering her for so long. She took a careful breath, held it, and finally asked softly, looking down at her lap, "This other girl you've been going with . . . Jill . . . she's the one they hoped you'd marry, isn't she?"

He turned, saw the way she idled her fingers back and forth across her purse, staring down. She looked up and their eyes met.

"Maybe. I don't know." But he squared his shoulders and studied the lights on the dashboard again. A muscle in Catherine's stomach set up a light twitching. A little trail of guilt went weaseling its way upward.

"Maybe they'll get their wish when this is all over," she said.

"No, it'll never happen now."

They'd talked about it, then, Clay and Jill. Maybe this wedding would be his only chance to be feted in the recognized style. He seemed to be admitting that it bothered him. But just as Catherine came to that conclusion he spoke.

"You make the choice about the wedding, and whatever you want, it'll be okay with me. Mother will just have to accept it, that's all. But she'll be making plans in her head, so I'd like to tell her your decision as soon as possible."

"It's your wedding, too, Clay," she said quietly, undone by what she'd guessed about his feelings.

"Weddings are mostly women's doings. You make the arrangements."

"I . . . th-thank you."

"You know, it seems like every time I drop you off here, it's to give you a limited time to come to some monumental decision."

"But I've got plenty of helpers inside to help me with this one."

He chuckled. "A whole houseful of pregnant, unmarried teenagers. I can imagine how unbiased their advice will be. They're probably still pinning curtains on their heads for veils."

Catherine thought of how utterly close to the truth he was. The rain pattered on the roof, the windows had steamed up. It was warm and insular in the car, and for a minute, Catherine did not want to get out, back to reality again.

"Whatever you decide is okay, huh?" he said. "And don't let those kids talk you into anything."

He reached for his door handle, but she quickly insisted that he stay in the car. She could make it to the house just fine. When she reached to open her door, he stopped her by saying, "Catherine?"

She turned.

"It's been . . . well, I was going to say fun, but maybe I should just say better. It's been better, talking without arguing. I think we needed this."

"I think we did too."

But, getting out of his car, running to the house, Catherine knew she lied. She didn't need this at all, not at all. Oh, God, she was beginning to like Clay Forrester.

Marie was still awake, waiting, when Catherine came inside, and though she hadn't intended to, Catherine found herself admitting, "I'm going to marry Clay Forrester."

Pandemonium broke loose! Marie leaped up, hit the light switch, bounded to the center of her bed and bugled, *"Wake up everybody! Catherine's getting married!"* In no time at all the place was a madhouse—everybody whooping, rejoicing, jumping and hugging.

Mrs. Tollefson called from the bottom of the stairs, "What's going on up there?" and joined the fracas to congratulate Catherine, then offered to make cocoa for everyone.

It took an hour for things to settle down, but during that time some of the girls' undaunted enthusiasm crept into Catherine. Maybe it began while they hugged her and—for the first time—she found herself unreservedly hugging back. They seemed to have given her some indefinable gift, and even now, lying in bed, wide awake, she was not sure what it was.

Marie's voice came quietly from across the way. "Hey, you asleep?"

"No."

"Give me your hand, huh?"

Catherine reached and in the dark her fingers were grasped by Marie's. There was silence then, but Catherine knew Marie, the always gay, always cheery Marie, was crying.

Chapter 11

THE FOLLOWING AFTERNOON Clay called before Catherine got home and left a message saying his mother had invited her out to the house for dinner, so would Catherine please not eat at Horizons? He'd be there to pick her up around six-thirty.

Speculation ran rampant among the Horizons' residents, who swarmed all over Catherine as she came in the door. When she admitted she was going there to make wedding plans, wide eyes gaped at her from every angle. "You mean they want a *real* wedding . . . *the Real McCoy!*"

The Real McCoy, it seemed, was exactly what Angela Forrester had in mind. From the moment Catherine put herself into Angela's hands, she sensed what Angela had called an "intimate affair" was destined to be an extravaganza.

Yet it was hard to resist the charming Angela, with her laugh like the song inside a Swiss music box and her constant striving to put Catherine at ease and her unaffected touches, especially for Claiborne. From the first Catherine noted how the two touched, lovingly, without conscious thought, as her parents never had, and how Angela always called him *darling* and he called her *dear.* "Isn't it wonderful, darling, we'll have a wedding here after all," Angela fairly sang.

Though the details made Catherine's head swim, she drifted along with Angela's irresistible tide of plans for caterer, florist, photographer, even engraved invitations.

There were times during the following days when Claiborne thought his wife guilty of bulldozing. But Catherine gave Angie full sway. Sometimes he met the girl's eyes and read in them a hint of helplessness. Maybe it was this, and the fact that she understood what the wedding meant to Angie, which began to make Claiborne look at the girl differently.

The subject of the guest list was the first at which Catherine assertively gainsaid Angela by refusing to have Herb Anderson included.

"But, Catherine, he's your father."

"I won't have him here," Catherine stated vehemently, and stuck to it. The Forresters were surprised when Catherine said she wanted her brother Steve to give her away. They hadn't known she had a brother stationed at Nellis Air Force Base in Las Vegas.

In her turn, Catherine was surprised at Angela's lack of compunction in inviting the residents of Horizons.

Catherine stammered, "B-but they're all pregnant."

Angela only laughed and inquired charmingly, "Are they too big to fit in my house?" That issue settled, Angela suggested Catherine call her brother immediately, using the phone in the study.

Catherine sat in the deep leather desk chair. Dialing, waiting for the phone to ring, she felt the empty longing which always overtook her at thoughts of Steve. She thought of the photographs he'd sent over the last six years, of how, during that time, he'd grown from a lean boy into a full-grown man, and she'd missed it all.

A crisp voice answered her ring. "Staff Sergeant Steven Anderson here."

"S-Steve?" she asked, a little breathlessly.

"Yes?" A brief hesitation, then, "Who's—Cathy? Babe, is that you?"

"Yes, it's me. But nobody's called me babe for a long time."

"Cathy, where are you?" he inquired with undisguised eagerness.

She glanced around the shadowed, private study, knowing Steve wouldn't believe it if she described her whereabouts fully. "I'm in Minnesota."

"Is anything wrong?"

"No, nothing. I just wanted to call instead of writing." Phone calls were costly and rare; Catherine reminded herself to thank Mr. and Mrs. Forrester.

"It's so good to hear your voice. How are you?"

"Me?" She was close to tears. "Oh, I'm . . . why, I'm in clover."

"Hey, you sound a little shaky. Are you sure nothing's wrong?"

"No, no. I just have some news that couldn't wait."

"Yeah? Well, out with it."

"I'm getting married." As she said the words Catherine smiled.

"What! A skinny, flat-chested sack of bones like you?"

She laughed shakily. "I'm not anymore. You haven't seen me for a long time."

"I got your graduation picture so I know you're telling the truth. Hey, congratulations. And you're in college now too. Lots of changes, huh?"

"Yeah . . . lots." Her eyes dropped to the rich leather of the desk top.

"So when's the big day?"

"Soon. November fifteenth, in fact."

"But that's only a couple weeks away!"

"Three. Can you make it home?" Catherine held her breath, waiting.

The line hummed momentarily before he repeated skeptically, "Home?"

She said pleadingly, "You wouldn't have to stay at the house, Steve." When he didn't reply, she asked, "Is there any chance of you getting here?"

"What about the old man?" A coldness had crept into Steve's voice.

"He won't be there, I promise you. Only Mom and Aunt Ella and Uncle Frank and Bobbi, of course."

"Listen, I'll try like hell. How are they all? How's Mom?"

"The same. Nothing much has changed."

"She's still living with him, huh?"

"Yes, still." She rested her forehead on her knuckles a moment, then picked up the letter opener from Claiborne's desk and began toying with it. "I gave up trying to convince her to leave him, Steve. He's the same as he ever was, but she's too scared of him to make a move. You know how he is."

"Cathy, maybe if I come back there the two of us together can get her to see some sense."

"Maybe . . . I don't know. Nothing's any different, Steve. You might as well know that. I don't think she'll ever admit how she hates him."

Steve injected a false brightness into his voice. "Listen, Cathy, don't worry about it, okay? I mean, this is your time to be happy, okay? So, tell me about your husband-to-be. What's his name, what's he like?"

The question disconcerted Catherine who had never tried to put Clay into a nutshell. Her first instinct was to answer, "He's rich." But she was startled to learn there was much which mattered more. "Well . . ." She leaned back in the tilting desk chair and considered. "His name is Clay Forrester. He's twenty-five, and in his last year of law school at the U of M. Then he plans to go into practice with his father. He's . . . well . . . smart, polite, well-dressed, and not too hard on the eyes." She smiled a little at this admission. "And he has a very proper family, no brothers and sisters, but his father and mother, who want to have the wedding at their house. I'm at their house now."

"Where do they live, in the old neighborhood?"

"No." Catherine tapped the letter opener against the tip of her nose, leaning back and looking at the ceiling. "In Edina."

There was an expressive pause, then, "Well, well . . . what do y' know about that? My kid sister marrying into Old Establishment. How did you manage that, babe?"

"I-I'm afraid I managed that by becoming slightly pregnant."

"Preg—oh, well, it . . . it was none of my business. I didn't mean to—"

"No need to sound so embarrassed, Steve. You'd find out sooner or later anyway."

"I'll bet the old man had plenty to say about that, huh?"

"Don't mention it."

"Have they met him yet, the Forresters?"

Catherine recalled the small scar that still showed above Clay's eyebrow. "I'm afraid so."

"I suppose the old man thinks his ship came in this time, huh?"

"Your memory is right on target. It's been hell around here. I moved out of the house to get away from him."

"I can just imagine what he was like."

"Hey, listen, he's *not* coming to the wedding, understand? I won't have him there. I don't owe him a thing! This is one time in my life that the choice is mine, and I intend to exercise it!"

"What about Mom?"

"I haven't told her yet, but she's next. I don't know if she'll budge without him. You know how she is."

"Tell her I'll do my best to be there and take her, maybe that way she'll go."

"When will you know for sure if you can get leave?"

"In a few days. I'll put in for it right away."

"Steve?"

"Yeah?"

Catherine came forward on her chair, blinking dangerously fast, her lips compressed with emotion until at last she stammered, "I—I want you here . . . s-so bad." She dropped the letter opener, spanned her forehead with her hand, fighting tears.

"Hey, babe, are you crying? What's the matter? Cathy?"

"N-no, I'm not crying. I n-never cry. We agreed to give that up long ago, remember? It's just so damn good to hear your voice and I miss you. After six years I st-still miss you. You were the only good thing around that place."

After a long, intense silence Steve said shakily, "Listen, babe, I'll make it. One way or another, I'll make it. That's a promise."

"Hey, listen, I've got to go. I mean, I don't want to run up the phone bill here any more than I have to." She gave him the number at Horizons.

Just before they hung up, he said, "God, I'm happy for you. And tell Mom hi, and tell Clay Forrester thanks, huh?"

Catherine wilted back against the high leather chair; her eyes slipped closed and she rode the swells of memory. She and Steve, childhood allies, sharing promises of never-ending support. Steve, a freckle-nosed boy of thirteen, standing up to Herb for her, regardless of his fear of the man. Steve and Cathy, children, huddling together, waiting to see who the old man's wrath would be turned on this time; Cathy's tears when it was Steve's turn to take a licking; Steve's tears when it was Cathy's; their trembling, tearless terror when it was their mother's turn; their mute agony of helplessness. But as long as they had each other they could bear it. But then came the day Steve left, the day he was old enough. She relived again her dread sense of desertion when he was so quickly gone for good. She felt again the desolation of being the one left behind in that house where there was only hatred and fear.

"Catherine?"

Her eyes flew open at Clay's soft question. She sprang forward as if he'd caught her rifling the desk drawers. He stood in the doorway, one hand in the pocket of his trousers as if he'd been studying her for some time. He came into the dim room, and she spun to face the shuttered window as two tears scraped down to her lashes and she covertly wiped them away.

"Couldn't you reach him?"

"Y-yes, I reached him."

"Then what's wrong?"

"Nothing. He's going to put in for leave immediately."

"Then why are you upset?"

"I'm not." But she could barely get the two words out. She was uneasy knowing Clay studied her silently. His tone, when at last he spoke, was concerned and gentle.

"Do you want to talk about it, Catherine?"

"No," she answered stiffly, wanting nothing so much as to turn to him and spill out all the hurtful memories of the past, to exorcize them at last. But she found she could not, especially not to Clay Forrester, when he was only passing through her life.

Clay studied her back, recognizing the defensive stance, squared shoulders and proud set of head. How unapproachable she could make herself when she wanted to. Still, he wondered, if he crossed the short distance of the room and touched her shoulders, what would she do? For a moment he was tempted to try it, sensing her utter aloneness in whatever it was she was suffering. But before he could move, she spoke.

"Clay, I'd like to make my own dress for the wedding. I'd like to provide at least that much."

"Have I given you the impression I'll object to anything?" He couldn't help but wonder what had brought on this abrupt defensiveness again. She turned to face him.

"No, you haven't, you've been more than compromising. I only want to make sure I don't shame you before your guests in a homemade dress."

She saw questions flit through his eyes, knew he was puzzled, but how could she explain to him her need to lash out sometimes, when she didn't fully understand it herself? What was she challenging? His place in society? His safe, secure, loved upbringing? Or the fact that he'd caught her with her defenses down a moment ago?

"You don't need my permission," he said quietly, and she suddenly felt sheepish. "Do you need any money to buy things for it?"

She felt the red creep up her neck. "No. I have some saved for next quarter's tuition I won't be needing."

Now it was his turn to feel slightly uncomfortable.

Although the days before the wedding were interrupted by these emotional point counterpoints, on the whole, Clay and Catherine grew increasingly comfortable with each other. There were even times when their moods were undeniably gay, like the following night when they called Bobbi and Stu to ask them to be attendants at the wedding. Clay had settled comfortably on the loveseat in the Forrester study, to eavesdrop, he admitted. Dialing the phone, Catherine grinned, glanced up and couldn't resist revealing, "Bobbi considers you quite a catch, you know." He only smirked, stretched out comfortably with both hands locked behind his head and settled down to listen to one side of the conversation.

"Hi, this is Catherine . . . No, everything's just fine . . . No, I'm not . . . as a matter of fact, I'm out at Clay's house . . . Yes, Clay Forrester"—The corners of Clay's mouth tipped up amusedly—"Well, he brought me out to have supper with his parents"—Catherine's eyes met his—"what do you think I'm doing? . . . Yes, a few times . . . He ran into me on campus and followed me there . . . You might call it that . . . No, he's been very polite, nothing like that"—Catherine wanted to wipe the smirk off Clay's face—"Bobbi, prepare yourself, you're in for a shock. Clay and I have decided to get married and I want you to be my maid of honor"—Catherine covered the mouthpiece, made silly eyes at Clay and let Bobbi rave on a moment—"Well, I am, I mean, I called as soon as we decided . . . Stu . . . Yes, he just talked to him . . . Steve is going to try to make it home, too . . . In three weeks, on the fifteenth . . . I know, I know, we'll have to find a dress for you . . . Listen, I'll talk to you tomorrow. I just wanted to let you know right away."

When Catherine hung up, her eyes met Clay's, and they both burst out laughing.

"That must have been quite a jolt to old Bobbi, huh?" He sat as before, amusement painted all over his face.

"Well, you heard her, didn't you?" Catherine's expression was perhaps a little bedeviling.

"And after all her efforts to keep your whereabouts a secret," he mocked.

"Did you have to sit there smirking all through my conversation?"

"Well, you sat there smirking through mine." He noted she was still doing so.

"Yes, but guys react differently than girls."

He arose lazily, sauntered toward Catherine and pressed his palms to the desk top, leaning forward as he teased, "Just getting to know my . . . bride, is all. See how she works under pressure." His gray eyes sparkled into hers.

He had never called her his bride before. It conjured up intimacy and made secret shivers tiptoe down Catherine's spine. She turned the chair aside, slid to her feet and pressed her blouse against her still-flat stomach, looking down at it. "Give me six months or so and you'll see precisely how I work under pressure."

Then she gave him one of her first genuine smiles. He thought if she'd be this way more often, the coming months could be enjoyable for both of them.

Catherine's adamant refusal to have her father at the wedding left Angela in a quandary. There was only one way she could think of to see that Herb Anderson was tidily out of the way the day of the wedding. When she tactfully brought it up to Claiborne, he reluctantly admitted the idea had been on his mind too. There was no guarantee it would work. Three weeks was a very short time; there was no assurance the case could be fitted on the docket that soon; there was no guarantee Anderson would be found guilty or be given a sentence.

But just to tip the scales, Claiborne hired the finest criminal lawyer in the twin cities. If Leon Harkness couldn't do the trick, no lawyer could.

Chapter 12

ADA ANDERSON WORKED the day shift at the Munsingwear plant on Lyndale Avenue on the north side of Minneapolis. She had worked there so long the place and its surrounding area no longer affected her. Its utilitarian setting in a dismal commercial zone, its clattery workrooms and changelessness were what she'd come to expect. But Catherine, getting off the city bus, looking up at the building, was hit by a wave of desolation at the thought of how long her mother had labored there, sewing pockets onto T-shirts and waistbands onto briefs. The factory had always depressed Catherine, but it was the only place she could talk to her mother and be sure she wouldn't run the risk of bumping into the old man.

Ada came scuffing out of the noisy, lint-strewn room with a look of fear on her simple face, put there by the fact that her supervisor had called her away from her machine to see a visitor—something highly unusual in this place. The moment Ada saw Catherine the fear disappeared, to be replaced by a smile with more seams than Ada Anderson had stitched in her sixteen years in this place.

"Why, Catherine," Ada said in that tired, surprised way.

"Hello, Mom."

"Why, I thought you was gone someplace out west."

"No, Mom, I've been in the city all the time. I just didn't want Daddy to know I was here."

"He's been awful mad about you running off."

Catherine would have welcomed a hug, but there was none, only her mother's tired acceptance of the way things were.

"Did he . . . has he taken it out on you, Mom?"

"No. Just on the bottle. Hasn't been sober a day since you left."

"Mom, is there somewhere we can sit down?"

"I don't know, honey, I don't get a break yet for another thirty minutes or so."

"How about the lunchroom?"

"Well, there's always the girls in there, and they got big ears, if y'know what I mean."

"Could we at least get away from the noise? Out on the stairway maybe?"

"Just a minute, I'll ask."

Something cracked in Catherine, some fissure of irritation at her mother's spinelessness. Not even here, after sixteen years, not even given the situation which should mean so much to her, could she simply take command and step away for a while.

"For heaven's sake, Mother. You mean you have to ask for five minutes away from your machine?"

Ada touched her chin in a feeble, troubled way, making Catherine instantly sorry for attacking her for something Ada was perhaps helpless to change in herself. Quickly Catherine touched her mother's arm. "Ask then, go ahead. I'll wait."

When they were out on the steps and the noise became a muffled clatter behind them, it somehow seemed an appropriate background for this worn woman who looked fifteen years older than she was. Catherine suddenly thought of it as a song of lament for the defeated. A surge of tenderness overtook her.

"Come on, Mom, let's just sit down here, okay? What'd you do to your finger?" There was a bandage on Ada's right index finger.

"Wasn't nothing much. I ran it under the machine last week. You'd think I'd've had more sense after all this time. They said I had to have a tetanus shot, though, and that was worse than this."

Catherine wondered if her running away, then, had distracted her mother that much. "I didn't mean to make you worry, Mom. I just didn't know how to keep Daddy off my back. I thought he'd track me down at college and start making trouble for me again and for the Forresters. I thought that if he thought I was gone where he couldn't find me, he'd let it go. But he didn't."

"I tried to tell him he'd best let up, Catherine. I tried to tell him. 'Herb,' I says, 'you can't go badgerin' people like them Forresters. They ain't gonna put up with it.' But he went there and he beat up that young man and spent the night in jail. He started drinkin' worse than ever after that, and now he walks around whisperin' to himself about how he's gonna get them to pay up. It scares me. You know how he is. I says to him, 'Herb, you're gonna make yourself sick if you keep this up.' "

"Mom, he is sick. Don't you understand that by now?"

"Don't say that, honey . . . don't say things like that." The fear was back in Ada's eyes. She glanced skittishly away. "He's bound to slack off pretty soon."

"Pretty soon? Mom, you've been saying that for as long as I can remember. Why do you put up with it?"

"There's nothing else I can do."

"You could leave," Catherine said softly.

Again Ada's eyes did what Catherine expected. They grew fearful and twitchy. "Why, where would I go, honey? He wouldn't let me go nowheres."

"I'll help you any way I can. I told you I'd find out what needs to be done to get help for him. There are places, Mom, right here in the city, that could help him."

"No, no," Ada insisted in her pathetically fierce way, "that wouldn't do any good. He'd just come out and be worse than ever. I know Herb."

Catherine thought of the Johnson Institute right at their fingertips, where help could be had for a phone call. But she gave up the argument which was, by now, as shopworn as Ada herself, defeated once again by her mother's self-inflicted blindness.

"Listen, Mom, I have some good news."

"Some good news?" Even when her eyes registered hope they looked sad.

"I'm not exactly sure how it happened, but I'm going to marry Clay Forrester."

Catherine held both of her mother's hands, rubbing her thumbs across the shiny surfaces where the skin seemed so thin the veins looked exposed. The expression on Ada's face visibly brightened.

"You're going to marry him, honey?"

Catherine nodded her head. Her mother at last squeezed her hands.

"Marry that handsome young man who said he didn't know you? How can that be?"

"I've been seeing him, Mom, and I've been back to his house several times and have talked with his parents and they're really quite nice. They've been very understanding and helpful. Can you believe it, Mom? I'm going to have a real wedding in that beautiful house of theirs."

"A real wedding?" Ada touched Catherine's cheek while her own eyes turned glossy. "Why, honey . . ." Again she squeezed Catherine's hand. "So that's where you run off to, to that young man of yours. Well, isn't that something."

"No, Mom, I've been living out near the campus, and I've made lots of new friends, and I've seen Bobbi, and she's been letting me know how you've been all along."

"You don't have to worry about me, honey. You know I always end up on my feet. But you, look at you, ain't you something. A real wedding." Ada reached into her pocket and found a tissue and dabbed at her rheumy eyes. "Listen, honey, I got a little money saved, not much, but—"

"Shh, Mom. You don't have to worry about paying for anything. It's all taken care of."

"But you're my baby, my own little girl. It should be me that—"

"Mother, the Forresters want to take care of it, honest. I could have eloped if I'd wanted to, but Mrs. Forrester . . . well, she's really on our side, Mom. I've never met anyone like her."

"Oh, she's a fine lady all right."

"Mom, I want you there at the wedding."

Startled eyes were raised to meet Catherine's. "Oh, no, honey, why, I would never fit in that place. I couldn't."

"Listen, Mom. Steve's coming."

Surprise held Ada's tongue a moment before she repeated disbelievingly, "Steve?" Her eyes turned alight with that inextinguishable flicker of mother-love. "You talked to Steve?"

"Yes, and he's going to try to come home."

"Come home?"

Together they counted back six years.

"Yes, Mom. And he said to tell you he'll take you to the wedding with him. That's what I came to tell you."

"Steve . . . coming home?" But at the thought Ada raised those tentative fingers to her lips again. "Oh, but there'll be trouble. Herb and Steve . . ." Her eyes dropped down to her lap.

"Daddy's never going to know. Steve and you are coming to the wedding, but not Daddy." Determinedly Catherine squeezed her mother's hands.

"But I don't see how."

"Please, Mom, please listen. You can tell him you're going to play Saturday bingo like you do sometimes. I want you at my wedding, but you can see that if he came too, it would only mean trouble, can't you?"

"But he'll know, honey, he'll guess. You know how he is."

"He won't know if you don't tell him, not if you just walk out like you're meeting Mrs. Murphy for bingo like you've done a hundred Saturdays before."

"But he's got that sixth sense. He's always had it."

"Mama, Steve's not coming to the house, you know that, don't you? He swore when he left that he'd never set foot in it again, and he hasn't changed his mind. If you want to see Steve, you'll have to see him at my wedding."

"Is he all right?"

"He's just fine. He sounded really happy and asked how you are and said to give you his love."

"Steve's twenty-two now." Ada's mind seemed to drift away into the racket of the machines from the workroom. The rhythmic clack and thump accompanied her lost thoughts while she hovered on the steps with her knees almost touching her daughter's. The lines of fatigue on her face could not be smoothed, but as she reached back in time, thoughts of her son placed some new determination in the network of wrinkles about her lips. When she raised her eyes to Catherine again, she said, "Twyla's got a bolt of blue knit in the remnant room'd make me a pretty nice dress. I get it at employee's discount, you know."

"Oh, do you mean it, Mom?" Catherine smiled.

"I want to see Steve, and I want to see my little girl's wedding. Why, stitching up a dress ain't nothing to me after all the years I put in here."

"Thank you." Impulsively Catherine leaned forward to hug her mother briefly around the thin shoulders.

"I'd best get back now, or my daily quota will be low."

Catherine nodded.

"I won't say a word to Herb this time, you'll see."

"Good. And I'll let you know if Steve calls again."

Ada braced hands to knees as she creaked to her feet. "I'm glad you come, honey. I didn't like to think of you off acrosst the country someplace like Steve." She climbed two stairs, then turned around, looking down at Catherine.

"Is it gonna be the kind with flowers and cake and a white dress for you?"

"Yes, Mom, it is."

"Well, feature that," Ada said thoughtfully. Then she stopped to do so, with the expression of wonder growing grander by the minute upon her time-worn features. "Just feature that," she repeated, as if to herself.

And for the first time, Catherine was fully, totally, one hundred percent happy that she'd gone along with all of Angela Forrester's wishes.

The invitations were ice-blue, embossed with rich, ivory letters of finest English Roundhand that pirouetted across the marbled parchment like the steps of a dancer. As she lifted a card from the box, it crackled like the dancer's crinoline beneath Catherine's fingers. She touched a raised character, ran her fingertips lightly along a line, as the blind read braille. The ascenders and descenders formed graceful swirls that rose up to meet her searching touch.

You can feel these words, Catherine thought, you can feel them.

Awe-filled, she studied the invitation, not quite accustomed yet to everything that was happening so fast. The words read in that formal lexicon peculiar to occasions that mark the steppingstones of life:

CATHERINE MARIE ANDERSON
AND
CLAY ELGIN FORRESTER
INVITE YOU TO SHARE IN THEIR JOY
AS THEY CELEBRATE
THE SOLEMNIZATION OF THEIR MARRIAGE VOWS
AT SEVEN P.M. ON NOVEMBER FIFTEENTH
AT THE HOME OF CLAIBORNE AND ANGELA FORRESTER
NUMBER SEVENTY NINE
HIGHVIEW PLACE
EDINA, MINNESOTA

Again, Catherine grazed the words with her fingertips. But with a woeful sense of yearning she thought, yes, the words can be felt, but it is not enough to feel only with the fingertips.

Chapter 13

BY NOW CATHERINE and Clay could meet in the front hall of Horizons and display a friendly familiarity that lacked the edginess of those first couple of meetings. Catherine invariably found herself scanning his clothing, invariably, too, found herself pleased by what greeted her. Likewise, Clay found himself approving of her appearance. Her clothes were neat, if unostentatious, and she wore them well. He watched for a first sign of roundness on her, but so far none was showing.

"Hi," he said now, while his eyes performed that first perusal which she'd come to expect. "How are you holding up?"

She struck a pose. "How does it look like I'm holding up?"

He glanced once again over the plum wool dress, loose-belted, trimmed with top-stitched pockets at hip and chest.

"Looks like you're doing fine. Nice dress."

She dropped her pose, wondering if she'd done that on purpose to wrest a compliment from him. She found his approval pleasing. But since that night she'd fallen asleep on the way home, they had each made a conscious effort to be nicer to each other.

"Thank you."

"You're going to meet my grandparents tonight."

By now she could manage to be less alarmed at such announcements. Still, this one made her slightly apprehensive.

"Do I have to?"

"They come with the package, I'm afraid."

Her eyes moved down his length. "The package, as usual, is wrapped to perfection." And so it was, in bone-colored, pleated trousers and a complementary Harris Tweed sportcoat with suede elbow patches.

It was the first compliment she'd ever paid him. He smiled, suddenly warm inside.

"Thanks, glad you approve. Now let's hope my grandparents do."

"The way you put that sounds forbidding."

"No, not really. But then, I've known them all my life. My Grandmother Forrester is a crusty old gal though. You'll see what I mean."

Just then Little Bit came downstairs, stopped and hung over the banister halfway down. "Hi, Clay!"

"Hi, Little Bit. Is it okay if I take her for a while?" he asked, teasingly.

"Why don't you take me instead tonight?" Little Bit swooned farther over the railing. The girls had given up trying to hide their fascination with Clay.

But at that minute Marie came down the steps. "Who's taking you where? Oh, hi, Clay."

"Do something with that child, will you, before she drops on her head and gives birth to a dimwit?"

Marie laughed and slapped Little Bit lightly on the rump as she passed behind her. They both came the rest of the way downstairs.

"Where you off to tonight?" Marie asked, eyeing them appreciatively.

"To my house."

"Yeah? What's the occasion this time?"

"Another one of the seven tortures. Grandparents, I'm afraid."

Marie raised an eyebrow, took Little Bit's hand to tug her off toward the kitchen while giving Catherine one last conspiratorial glance over the shoulder. "Lucky thing you decided to wear your newest creation, huh, Cath?"

Clay looked the dress over a second time, with greater interest.

"We do have nimble fingers, don't we?" he asked, and without winking, gave the impression he had.

"Yes, we do. Of necessity." And Catherine laid a hand lightly upon her stomach. Smiling with Clay, she felt a little happy, a little venturesome.

Something had changed between them. The lurking sense of anger and entrapment had begun to wane. They treated each other civilly, and occasional spurts of repartee such as this were becoming more frequent.

By the time Clay turned into his parents' driveway full dark had fallen. The headlights picked out the herringbone design of red bricks while upon them the tires hummed the note that by now Catherine unconsciously listened for.

The yard was dressed for winter. Leaves were but memories, while tree trunks were swathed in white leggings. The shrubs had hunched their shoulders and pulled mulch-quilts up beneath their chins. An occasional pyramidal bush was laced into winter bindings like an Indian papoose.

The house was lit from within and without. Catherine glanced at the twin carriage lanterns on either side of the front door, then down at the tips of her high heels as she approached the house. Her pocketed hands hugged her coat close as she tried to keep her growing apprehension from getting the best of her. Without warning, from behind, Clay's fingers circled her neck, closing lightly in a warm grip.

"Hey, wait, I have to talk to you before we go in."

At his touch, she instantly turned, surprised. He left both hands on her shoulders with his thumbs pressing her coat collar against each side of her windpipe. Catherine needn't say it for him to be reminded that she'd rather not be touched this way.

"Sorry," he said, immediately raising his palms.

"What is it?"

"Just a technicality." Gingerly he inserted a single index finger into her coat sleeve, tugging until the hand came out of her coat pocket. "There's no ring on this." Her bare hand dangled out of the sleeve. While he looked at it, the fingers suddenly clenched protectively, shutting the thumb inside.

"Grandmothers tend to become suspicious when they don't see what they expect to see," he noted wryly.

"And what do they expect to see?"

"This."

Still holding her coat sleeve, he lifted his other hand to reveal a jeweled ring riding the first knuckle of his little finger. In the meager light from the carriage lanterns it wasn't at first evident exactly what it looked like. Clay wiggled the finger a little and the gems glittered. Catherine's eyes were drawn to it as if he were a hypnotist using it to mesmerize her. Her mouth went dry.

It's so big! she thought, horrified. "Do I have to?"

He commanded her hand, sliding the ring onto the proper finger. "I'm afraid so. It's family tradition. You'll be the fourth generation to wear it."

With the ring not quite on, she gripped his fingers, stopping them, feeling the ring cut into her.

"This game is going too far," she whispered.

"The significance of a ring is in the mind of its wearer, Catherine, not in the fact that it's on a hand."

"But how can I wear this with three generations behind it?"

"Just pretend you got it in a box of Cracker Jacks," he said unconcernedly, completing the adornment of her third finger, pushing the ring all the way on. Then he dropped her cold fingers.

"Clay, this ring is worth thousands of dollars. You know it and I know it, and it is not right that I'm wearing it."

"But you'll have to anyway. If it helps to relieve your mind, remember that the Forrester side of the family made a business of gems before my father broke the tradition and went into law. Grandmother Forrester still owns a thriving business, which she refused to relinquish when Grandfather died. There are hundreds more where this came from."

"But not with this one's significance."

"So, humor an old lady." Clay smiled and shrugged.

She had no choice. Neither did she have a choice when, in the entry after he'd taken her coat, Clay returned and laced his hand half around her neck in that careless way of his. That was how they entered the living room, with him affectionately herding her along and Catherine doing her best to keep resilient under his touch.

They approached first a withered little pair of people who were dressed formally and sat side by side on a velveteen sofa. The man wore a black suit and looked like an aged orchestra conductor. The woman, in mauve lace, wore a little twinkling smile that looked as if she'd donned it seventy years ago and hadn't taken it off since. Approaching the pair, Catherine felt Clay's hand slide down her back, linger at her waist, then depart as he bent to take the woman's cheeks in both hands and plop a direct, noisy kiss on her mouth.

"Hi, sweetheart," he said irreverently. Catherine could have sworn the old girl actually blushed as she looked up at Clay. Then she twinkled as she shook a crooked, arthritic finger at him—her only greeting.

"Hello, sonny," the grandfather greeted him. "You get your grandma more excited with that word than I can anymore." Clay's hearty laugh swept the two.

"So, Granddad, are you jealous?" He put an arm around the shoulders of the bald man who might have been stepping up to a podium with his aging slump. To Catherine's surprise, the two embraced unabashedly, chuckling together.

"I want you both to meet Catherine." Clay turned back, reached out a palm and drew her forward. "Catherine, this is Grandma and Grandpa Elgin, better known around here as Sophie and Granddad."

"Hello," Catherine said, smiling easily, squeezing each parchment hand in turn. Sophie's and Granddad's smiles were so alike it was like seeing double.

Then Clay captured her elbow, turning her toward a woman who sat with a matriarchal air in a high-backed chair that need not be a throne to bespeak the woman's regal mien. The feeling was there. It permeated the very air about her. It was evident in her bearing, her facial expression, the faultless blue-white waves that crested her head, the shrewd eyes, the glitter flashing from her fingers and the glacial assessment she gave Catherine.

Before Clay could speak, the woman pierced him with an arch, amused look.

"Don't try those flirtatious tactics with me, young man. I'm not the blushing fool your Grandmother Sophie might be."

"Never, Grandmother," assured Clay, wearing a devilish grin as he lifted one of her bejeweled hands and bent over it quite correctly. He made as if to kiss its blue-veined back, but at the last minute, turned it over and kissed the base of her thumb.

Catherine found herself amused at these cat-and-mouse goings-on. The old lady's mouth pursed to keep from smiling outright.

"I've brought Catherine to meet you," Clay said, dropping the hand, but not the half-smile. Again he urged Catherine near with a slight touch on her elbow. "Catherine, this is my Grandmother Forrester. I never call her by her first name for some reason."

"Mrs. Forrester," Catherine repeated, while her hand disappeared within all those flashing gems.

"My grandson is a precocious young upstart. You'd do well to watch your p's and q's around him, young lady."

"I intend to, Ma'am," Catherine rejoined, wondering what the old lady would think if she knew the extent to which p's and q's would need to be watched in the months ahead.

Mrs. Forrester raised an ivory-headed cane and tapped Catherine's shoulder lightly, perusing her with gray irises from beneath one straight eyebrow and one that was cocked in an aristocratic arc.

"I like that. I might have answered in just that way myself." She rested the cane on the floor again, crossed her hands upon the ivory elephant with its sapphire eyes, and angled a bemused expression again at her grandson, asking, "Where did you find this perceptive young lady?"

Clay moved a hand lingeringly up and down the inner side of Catherine's elbow while he searched her face and answered his grandmother. "I didn't. She found me." Then his hand trailed down, enclosing hers. Elizabeth Forrester's eyes followed it and registered the way the girl's fingers failed to clasp Clay's. The pair turned toward Claiborne and Angela who were pouring port and making room on a marble-topped table for the silver tray of canapés which Inella carried in at that moment.

Clay had a greeting for Inella too. He dropped a hand on her shoulder as she leaned to set down the tray. "And what kind of epicurean delights have you dreamed up tonight, Inella? Don't you know Father's been concerned about his waistline?"

Everyone laughed.

"Epicurean delights," scoffed the pleased maid. "Where do you dream up such stuff?" She left, smiling. There followed a full-fledged hug between Clay and his mother and a clasp of hands with his father.

Catherine had never seen so much touching in her life. Nor had she seen Clay in this element before, warm, humorous, obviously loved and loving everyone in the place. The scene gripped her with something akin to envy, yet deep in some part of her, Catherine was slightly intimidated. But she could not pull away as the next warm touch fell her way and Angela's cheek pressed against her own while Claiborne—thankfully—only smiled on, and gave her a friendly verbal greeting.

"Young woman, sit here," ordered Elizabeth Forrester imperiously.

Catherine could do nothing but perch on a loveseat at a right angle to Elizabeth Forrester's chair. She was actually grateful when Clay sat down beside her. His presence somehow made her feel fortified. Elizabeth Forrester's shrewd eagle-eyes assessed Catherine, probing like a laser while she made what appeared on the surface to be inconsequential conversation.

"Catherine . . ." she mused, "what a quaint and lovely name. Not clever and will-o-the-wisp like so many of today's insubstantial titles. I dare say there are many I'd be thoroughly ashamed to be plagued with. You and I, however, have each been preceded in name by an English queen, you know. My given name is Elizabeth."

Catherine wondered if she were being given permission to use the name or being tested to see if she were so presumptuous. Assuming the latter, Catherine consciously used the more formal mode of address.

"I believe, Mrs. Forrester, that the name Elizabeth means 'consecrated to God.' "

The regal eyebrow raised a notch. The girl is astute, thought Elizabeth Forrester. "Ah, so it does, so it does. Catherine . . . is that with a *C* or a *K?*"

"With a *C.*"

"From the Greek then, meaning 'pure.' "

Catherine's stomach did somersaults. Does she *know* or does she *want* to know, Catherine wondered, making a great effort to appear unruffled.

The matriarch observed, "So, you are the one who will carry the Forrester name forward."

Catherine's stomach tightened further. But Clay, whom she didn't know whether to damn or to thank, nestled closely beside her with his thigh against the length of her own, meeting his grandmother's probe directly.

"Yes, she is. But not without some persuasion. I think Catherine was a little put off by me at first. Something to do with our having different stations in life, which I had trouble convincing her didn't matter one damn bit."

My God, thought Catherine, he's actually challenging the old girl!

Understanding that challenge very clearly, Elizabeth Forrester only chided. "In my day, your grandfather didn't pronounce vulgarities in my ear."

Clay only grinned, sparring expertly. "Oh, Grandmother, you're sterling, pure sterling. But this is not your day, and a man can get by with a little more." But then, feeling the muscle of Catherine's leg grow rigid, he dulcified his remark by adding, *"Damn* is hardly considered a vulgarity anymore, not even a crudity."

She merely cocked the eyebrow again.

"Father," Clay said, "bring your mother a glass of port. She's being testy tonight and you know how port always mellows her. Catherine, do you like port?"

"I don't know."

Elizabeth Forrester missed not a word.

"White wine then?" her grandson suggested. The girl's reaction was curious. She attempted to move her thigh away from his. Unconcerned, he arose without waiting for an answer and went to get the wine.

"How long have you known Clay?" his Grandma Sophie asked then, leaning forward with birdlike tentativeness.

"We met this summer."

"Angela says you are sewing your own dress for the wedding."

"Yes, but I have lots of help," Catherine answered, realizing too late that she'd left herself open for further questioning.

"Why, how nice. I never could sew a stitch, could I, Angela? Is your mother helping you?" Sophie's manner of speech was exactly the opposite of her counterpart's. Where Elizabeth Forrester was audacious and quizzing, this woman was shy and unassuming. Still, her innocent line of questioning made Catherine again feel boxed into a corner.

"No, some friends of mine are helping me with the dress. I do some sewing to help out with college expenses."

"My, Clay didn't tell us you're in college."

He came to her rescue then, returning with a stem glass of imported German liebfraumilch. As Catherine reached for it, the gems in her ring glittered like the lead crystal glass which held the wine. Before she sipped, she changed hands, resting her left, knuckles-down on her lap.

"Yes, she is. She's a clever girl too. She made the dress she's wearing tonight, Grandma. She's very good with her hands, isn't she?"

Catherine almost choked. Quickly she added, "I also type theses and manuscripts."

"You do? My, my," Grandma Sophie remarked inanely.

"You see, Grandma, now I won't have to pay to have my papers typed this year. That's really why I'm marrying her." He grinned mischievously and laid his hand along the back of the loveseat as he said it, making Sophie's eyes soften in approval.

"Mother," Angela put in, "Clay is up to his usual teasing again. Don't pay any attention to him."

The talk moved on, interspersed with the nibbling of crab-stuffed *petits choux* and marinated mushroom caps. Clay relaxed beside Catherine, his knees lolling wide so there was the ever-present intrusion of his thigh against hers. He kept up the small talk, asked once, close to Catherine's ear, if she didn't like the crab, confirmed that's what it was she was eating, murmured just loud enough that the elder Mrs. Forrester overheard him tell his fiancé there were lots of things he'd teach her to like. He bantered with Elizabeth, teased Sophie, agreed to play racquetball with his father one evening soon, and through it all, managed to act as if he doted on Catherine.

By the time they went to dinner, she was nearly undone. She wasn't used to sitting so close to him, nor being wooed in so obvious a manner for the benefit of others. At the table it went on, for Clay was seated directly beside her, and now and then during the meal he rested his elbow on the back of her chair and spoke trumped-up confidences into her ear in a highly convincing way. He could laugh just softly enough, glance at her just beguilingly enough to make his grandmothers smile at each other over their salmon steaks a la Inella. But long before the meal ended either the steaks or Clay or both had caused Catherine's stomach to begin to churn. Add to that the fact that Elizabeth

Forrester brought up the ring, and Catherine wondered if she'd make it through the meal.

"I see Angela has given you the radiant. How wonderful, Angela, to see it on Catherine's hand. What does your family think of it, dear?"

Catherine forced herself to continue cutting a cheese-encrusted Irish potato.

"They haven't seen it yet," she answered truthfully, learning the game quickly, determined not to give the hawk-eyed woman an edge.

"It looks beautiful on such long, slim fingers, don't you think so, Clay?"

Clay picked up Catherine's hand, took the fork from it, kissed it, replaced the fork, and said, "Beautiful."

"Would you like to prick my grandson with that fork, Catherine, just to let a little of that self-satisfied hot air out of him? Your fondling seems to distract Catherine from her eating, Clay."

But it was as much the ring as everything else that was distracting Catherine.

Clay only laughed and delved into his food again. "Grandmother, I think I detect a note of testiness again. Nobody told you you had to pass the ring on to Mother. Would you like it back?"

"Don't be cheeky, Clay. As your bride, Catherine should and will wear the ring. Your grandfather would be thrilled to distraction if he could see it on a girl as beautiful as she."

"I give up. For once you've left me speechless because you're right."

Elizabeth Forrester was left to wonder if her suspicion was correct. The boy seemed incapable of stopping himself from fawning over the girl. Well, time would tell, soon enough.

In the car on the way home Catherine laid her head back against the seat, struggling with each passing mile to control her roiling insides. But halfway there Catherine ordered, "Stop the car!"

Clay turned to find her eyes closed, one hand convulsively gripping the console.

"What is it?"

"Stop the car . . . *please.*"

But they were on the freeway where controlled accesses made it difficult to stop.

"Hey, are you all right?"

"I have to throw up."

An exit ramp beckoned and he pulled over, careened halfway up, drove the car completely over the curb and onto the shoulderless area of grass, then slammed on the brakes. Immediately Catherine rolled out her side of the car. He heard her retching, then she gasped and spit.

Sweat broke out under Clay's armpits. Across his chest the skin grew tight and hot, and saliva pooled beneath his own tongue as if he were the nauseated one. He got out, unsure of what to do, saw her huddled over, her hair hanging down over her cheeks.

"Catherine, are you all right?"

"Do you have a tissue?" she asked shakily.

He came up behind her, reached in his hip pocket and extracted his handkerchief. He handed it to her and took her elbow to lead her a few steps aside.

"This . . . is your . . . han . . . hanky. I can't use . . . your hanky." Her ordeal had left her fighting for breath.

"Christ, use it . . . anything. Are you okay now?"

"I don't know." She gulped air like a person coming up for the second time. "Don't you have any tissues?"

"Catherine, this is no time to be polite. Use the damn hanky."

In spite of her wretchedness, it suddenly dawned on Catherine that Clay Forrester swore when he was scared. She swabbed the inside of her mouth with his clean-tasting handkerchief.

"Does this happen often?" His voice was shaky, concerned, and he left a solicitous hand on her arm.

She shook her head, waiting yet, unsure if there was more.

"I thought it only happened in the mornings."

"I think it was the fish and the grandmothers." She tried to laugh a little, but didn't quite succeed, so instead sucked in the starlight.

"Cat, I'm sorry. I didn't know it would be that hard on you or I wouldn't have added to it."

She heard mostly the word *Cat*. God, no, she thought, don't let him call me that. Not that!

"Do you want to go back to the car?" he asked, at a loss, feeling protective toward her, yet utterly useless.

"I think I'll stay here in the air awhile longer. I still feel funny." She refolded the hanky and wiped her forehead with it. He reached to push aside a strand of hair that had caught on her cheek.

"Are you going to keep this up when we're married?" There was a smile in his question, an attempt to make her feel better.

"If I do, I'll wash the hankies for you. I don't know, it's never happened before. I'm sorry if I embarrassed you."

"You didn't embarrass me. I just got scared, that's all. I don't know much about handling retching girls."

"Well, live and learn, huh?"

He smiled, waiting for her to gain her equilibrium again. She ran a shaky hand over her forehead and down one temple. Her stomach was calming down, but Clay's continued touch as he held her arm was unsettling. Wisely, she extricated herself from it.

"Clay, your grandmother Forrester knows." Catherine's voice shook.

"So what?"

"How can you say that when she's so . . . so . . . ."

"So what? Dictatorial? She's really not, you know. She loved you, couldn't you tell that?"

"Loved me? . . . *Me?*"

"She's a shrewd old devil, and there's not much she misses. I had no notion of trying to deceive her tonight. Yes, she knows, but she's given you her stamp of approval anyway."

"She chose an odd way to show it."

"People have their ways, Catherine. Hers are . . . well, different from those of Mother's parents, but, believe me, if she hadn't approved, she would never have said what she did about the ring."

"So the ring was a test—that's why you made me wear it tonight?"

"I guess in a way it was. But it's tradition too. They all know that there's no way I'd be taking a bride without putting it on her finger. That was understood before I was ever born."

"Clay, I was . . . well, scared. It was more than just the ring and the way your grandmother quizzed me. I have to be told when I'm eating crabmeat that it's crab and I don't know port wine from a fishing port and I don't know that pink diamonds are called radiants and—"

His unconcerned laughter interrupted her. "A radiant is a cut, not a color, but what does it matter? You foiled the old girl, Catherine, don't you know that? You foiled her by letting her guess the truth and having her approve of you anyway. Why feel scared about that?"

"Because around your family I'm out of my league. I'm like a . . . like a rhinestone among diamonds, can't you see that?"

"You have a surprising lack of confidence lurking behind that composed exterior you usually display. Why do you insist on putting yourself down?"

"I know my place, that's all, and it isn't in the Forrester family."

"It is as long as I say it is, and nobody's going to contest it."

"Clay, we're making a mistake."

"The only mistake made tonight was when you ate Inella's salmon." He touched her shoulder. "Do you think you've finished with your revenge on her?"

She couldn't help smiling. "What *is* it with you that you can be so casual about all this?"

"Catherine, it's only temporary. I made up my mind to enjoy what I can of it, and not to let the rest bother me, that's all. And I'm even learning in the process, so there."

"Learning?"

"Like you said . . . how to handle a pregnant lady." He turned her toward the car. "Come on, I think you're okay now. Get in and I'll drive like a good boy."

Farther down the road, Clay began talking about Sophie and Granddad, reminiscing about them, and the stories he told made Catherine understand where Angela got all her loving ways. Riding with Clay, listening to stories about his youth, she found herself enjoying his company fully.

She laughed once, saying, "I had all I could to keep from bursting out laughing when Granddad called you 'sonny.'" She turned a skeptical grin toward Clay and repeated, *"Sonny?"*

Clay himself laughed. "Well, I guess that's how he'll always think of me. You know, I really love that old dude. When I was little, he used to take me to see the ore boats on Lake Superior. Just him and me. Once he took me up on the train, because he said trains would soon be gone, and I shouldn't miss the chance to ride on one while I could. Saturday afternoons he'd take me to see Disney movies, to museums, all kinds of places. And I'd go to the ballet with both Granddad and Sophie."

"The ballet?" She was genuinely surprised.

"Uh-huh."

"How lucky."

"You've never been to one?"

"No, only dreamed about it."

"I assumed you had, from what you said once about being a ballerina."

"No, you assumed wrong," and for the first time Catherine opened up a portion of her secret regret to him. Not much, but a little—an important little. Like wiping off a tiny peek-through from a dirt-filmed window, she gave him a first glimpse of what was inside. "My dad drank a lot, so there was never any money for the ballet."

Suddenly afraid she should not have said it, she waited for Clay's reaction. She did not want him to think she was eliciting his sympathy. She could feel his gaze on her for a moment before his words made her heart dance against her ribcage.

"There is now," was all he said.

Chapter 14

THE SHORT TRIO of weeks before the wedding, coupled with the countless necessary arrangements, saw Catherine and Clay together almost as much as they were apart. The thing Catherine feared most began to happen: she grew familiar with Clay. She began expecting things before they happened—to have her car door opened, her coat held, her fast food paid for. Personal things about Clay intruded too—the way he always took time to kid the girls at Horizons before snatching Catherine away again; the continuing sense of closeness he displayed with his family; the endless touching about which none of them felt inhibited; his laugh. He laughed easily, she discovered, and seemed to accept what was happening far more readily than Catherine herself was able to.

She grew familiar with the incidental things: the way his eyes were drawn to the vapor trails of jets; the way he removed the pickles from his hamburgers but added extra ketchup; the fact that most of his clothes were brown, that he was slightly color-blind between browns and greens and sometimes mistakenly chose socks of the wrong color. She came to know his wardrobe and the scent of him that lingered in his car, until one evening when it changed it came as a shock that she'd even detected the change. She learned which of his tapes were favorites, then the particular songs on those tapes that were even more favored.

Then one day he offered her the use of his car to complete all her errands. Her wide blue eyes flew from the keys, dangling off his index finger, to his grinning eyes.

She was speechless.

"What the hell, it's only a car," he said offhandedly.

But it wasn't! Not to Clay. He took care of it the way a trainer takes care of a Kentucky Derby winner and with equally as much pride. His trusting her to drive it was another stitch in the seam of familiarity binding Clay and Catherine even closer. She saw all this clearly as she stared at the keys. To accept them was to break down another of the barriers between them, this barrier so much more significant than any which had fallen before, for it had delineated their separate rights. Accepting the keys would only meld the two, which was something Catherine sought to avoid.

Yet she took the keys anyway, tempted by the luxury they represented, the freedom, the thrill, telling herself, "One time . . . just this once . . . because there's so much running to do, and it'll be so much easier by car than by bus."

Driving the Corvette, she felt she had usurped Clay's world, the car was so much a part of him. There was a sense of willful intrusion that made her heart race when she placed her hands on the wheel in the precise spot where his usually rested. The feel of her flesh on *his* spot was decidedly intimate, so she quickly reverted to the more cavalier pose with one wrist draped indolently over the wheel, put the machine in motion and turned on the radio, experiencing a heady jolt of freedom when the music poured from the speakers. She even used the horn once, unnecessarily, and laughed aloud at her precociousness. She adjusted the rearview mirror, amazed at how suddenly exotic Minneapolis, Minnesota, looked when viewed in reverse from a white leather bucket seat inside a sleek, silver bullet.

She watched men's heads snap around and women's faces affect expressions of disdain, and allowed herself to feel temporarily superior. She smiled at drivers of other cars while sitting at stop signs. The Corvette was superficial, ostentatious, and somebody else's. But she didn't care. She smiled anyway.

And she took first Marie, then Bobbie, out shopping in it.

And for one day—one magic day—Catherine allowed herself to pretend it was all real. And somehow, for that one day, it was. For that single day Catherine had a taste of the full flush of joy wedding preparations can bring.

The making of Catherine's wedding dress became a "family project" with almost every girl at Horizons sharing the work in some way. Then one day before the gown was finished Little Bit had her baby. It was a girl, but they all knew Little Bit had long ago made the decision for adoption, so nobody spoke much about the baby. When they visited Little Bit in the hospital they spoke of the wedding, the gown, even the Corvette ride. But on the shelf by her bed there was only an ice-blue wedding invitation where there should have been baby cards too.

After that Catherine sensed a new wistfulness when the girls touched her wedding gown. They vied for the right to zip it up the back when Catherine fit it on, touching it with a reverence she found heartbreaking. It was a lovely creation of ivory velvet, with wrist-length sleeves, an Empire waist and a miniature train. The front bodice was gathered at the shoulder and on up the high, tight neck, and draped in soft swags from shoulder to shoulder. Studying her reflection, Catherine could not help wondering what the months ahead would bring.

The plans for Catherine and Clay's immediate future came down to more personal things. They had to think about a place to live and furnishings for it. Once again the fairy-tale aura pervaded as Clay announced his father owned various properties around the twin cities and there were at least three different ones unoccupied. Would Catherine like to look at them?

He took her to a complex of town houses in the suburb of Golden Valley.

Catherine stood back, watching Clay fit the key into the lock with an odd thrill of expectation. The door swung open and she stepped inside, hearing the door close behind her. She stood in the foyer of a split-level house. It was disconcertingly silent. Before her, chocolate-carpeted stairs led up one level and down one. Clay touched her arm and she jumped. They walked up the steps, unspeaking, to be greeted by a great open expanse of space which ended in sliding glass doors on the far side of the living room. To her left was a kitchen, to her right the steps leading to the sleeping level. She hadn't expected such luxury, such newness.

"Oh, Clay," was all Catherine said, sweeping the living room with her eyes.

"I know what you're thinking."

"But I'm right. It's too much."

"Don't you like it? We can look at others."

She swung to face him in the middle of the bright, vast room. "I can't live in this with you. It would be like cheating on my income tax."

"Okay, let's go. Where else do you have in mind?"

"Wait a minute." She reached out to detain him, for he'd turned impatiently toward the foyer. "I'm not the only one who has a say."

He paused, but she could tell his teeth were clenched.

"Clay, what are we going to fill all this up with?"

"Furniture, but it won't be *filled*. We'll just get what we need."

"Just . . . *get?*"

"Well, we'll go out and buy it, dammit! We have to have furniture, and that's the usual way of getting it." It was unlike him to speak in such a brittle manner. She could tell that he was disappointed and not a little angry.

"You want it, don't you?"

"I've always liked this place, but it doesn't matter. There are others."

"Yes, so you said before." She paused, met his displeased eyes and said quietly, "Show me the rest of it."

She followed him up the short flight of stairs. He switched on a light and a spacious bathroom was revealed. It had a long vanity, topped with gold-veined black marble, sporting two sinks and a mirror the size of a bedsheet. The fixtures were almond-colored, and the walls papered in a bold geometric of beige and brown with touches of silver foil adding a richness for which she was not prepared. She quickly glanced from the vanity stool to the shower stall—separate from the tub—with its opaque glass walls.

"Any of the paper can be changed," he said.

"That won't be necessary. I can see why you like it as it is—all these browns."

He switched off the light and she followed him to a small bedroom on the opposite side of the hall. Here again was a room papered in brown and tan geometric, very masculine, evidently decorated as a den or study.

Silently they moved on to the other bedroom. It was massive and could easily have been divided into two rooms. It, too, was papered in shades of brown, but this time a cool, restful dusty-blue had been added. Clay walked over and opened a door, revealing a generous walk-in closet with built-in drawers, shoe shelves and luggage racks up above.

"Clay, how much is this going to cost anyway?"

"What difference does it make?"

"I . . . we . . . it just does, that's all."

"I can afford it."

"That's not the point and you know it."

"What is the point then, Catherine?"

But for answer, her eyes slid to the spot where the bed so obviously belonged. His eyes did the same, then they quickly looked away from each other. She turned from the room and abruptly went back downstairs to check the kitchen.

It was compact, efficient, had a dishwasher, disposal, side-by-side refrigerator-freezer, glossy flooring of rich vinyl, almond-colored appliances—everything. She thought of the kitchen at home, of her father slinging coffee grounds in the sink without bothering to wash them down, of the dirty dishes that were forever piled in the sink unless she herself washed them.

Catherine thought about what it would be like working in this clean kitchen with its gleaming appliances, its wood-grained Formica countertops. She turned to eye the peninsula and imagined a pair of stools on the other side of it —a cozy, informal eating spot. She pictured Clay sitting there in the morning, drinking coffee while she fried eggs. But she'd never been with him early in the morning and didn't know if he liked coffee, or fried eggs. And furthermore, she had no business imagining such things in such a wishful way.

"Catherine?"

She jumped and whirled to find him leaning in the doorway, one elbow braced high against it. He was dressed in a rust-colored corduroy jacket with a matching vest beneath. The way he stood, the jacket flared away from his body creating inviting shadows around his torso. It struck her again how flawless his appearance was, how his trousers never seemed to wrinkle, his hair never to be out of place. She felt her mouth go dry and wondered what she was letting herself in for.

"There's only a week left," he said sensibly.

"I know." She turned toward the stove, walked over and switched on the light above it because it gave her a reason to turn her back to him and because she'd been wondering if he drank coffee in the morning and because she'd been thinking of the shadows within his corduroy jacket.

"If it's what you want, Clay, we'll take it. I know the colors suit you."

"Do you want to look at something else?" He was no longer angry, not at all. Instead his voice was mellow.

"I love this, Clay. I just don't think that we . . . that I . . . ."

"Deserve it?" he finished as she faltered.

"Something like that."

"Would it make things more fair if we lived in a hovel someplace, is that what you think?"

"Yes!" She spun to face him. "No . . . oh, God, I don't know. This is more than I ever imagined I'd live in, that's all. I'm trying very hard not to be overcome."

He smiled, raised his other hand so both were now braced against the door frame above his head, then he shook his head at the vinyl floor.

"You know, sometimes I don't believe you."

"Well, sometimes I don't believe you either." She threw her hands wide, indicating the whole place in one gesture. "Now furniture too!"

"I said we'd only get the necessities."

"But I'm fast learning what you consider *necessities.*"

"Well, I'll do my damnedest to hunt up some stick furniture if it'll make you happy. And I'll string some thongs from the bedroom wall and haul in a fresh load of straw for on top of them. How's that?"

His face wore the most engaging grin; it was irresistible.

He was teasing her. Standing there leaning against their future kitchen doorway looking good enough to serve for dinner, Clay Forrester was teasing. His laughter started as a soft bubble of mirth deep in his throat, but when it erupted into full, uninhibited sound, all she could do was laugh back.

He chose an enormously long davenport because, he said, his mother drove him nuts with all her loveseats that a man couldn't even stretch out on. And two armchairs of tweed, and a pecan coffee table and end tables, and a lamp that cost as much as one of the chairs, although Catherine could not convince him this was utterly spendthrift and silly. He said he liked it, expensive or not, and that was that. They chose two stools for the kitchen peninsula, but Catherine adamantly refused to furnish the formal dining room. They really wouldn't need it, she said. She won on that point, but the bedroom set she said was "good enough" wasn't good enough for Clay. He picked out one that cost nearly double that of her choice, and a triple dresser *and* a chest of drawers, which she said were unnecessary because the closet had built-in drawers.

They were standing in the aisle arguing about nightstands and lamps when their salesman returned to them.

"But why do we need more lamps? There are ceiling fixtures; that's good enough."

"Because I like to read in bed!" Clay exclaimed.

The salesman began to clear his throat, thought better of it, and withdrew discreetly to let them argue it out. But Catherine knew he'd overheard Clay's last comment and was left beetfaced, feeling like a complete fool, standing there in the aisle of a furniture store arguing with a fiancé who exclaimed he liked to *read* in bed!

Things started happening so fast.

Steve called to say he'd be arriving on Thursday, the thirteenth.

Ada called to say she'd finished making her dress.

The store called to make arrangement for delivery of the furniture.

Bobbi called to say the Magnussons would definitely be at the wedding.

The doctor's office called to say Catherine's blood count was low.

Angela called and apologetically explained that Claiborne had pressed charges against Herb Anderson and successfully managed to have him convicted to ninety days in the workhouse for assault and battery.

And then one evening Catherine walked into Horizons to find a surprise bridal shower awaiting her, and not only were all the girls there, but seated side by side on the sofa were her mother and Angela. And Catherine, giving in to what is each bride's right, covered her face with both hands and burst into tears for the first time since this whole charade began.

Chapter 15

WHEN CLAY CAME to pick up Catherine and take her to meet Steve's plane, she was totally unprepared for the sight that greeted her. She stopped stupidly, dead in her tracks!

Clay was dressed in faded denims and a faded blue flannel shirt beneath a disreputable-looking old letter jacket that would have been shaped like Clay even had his body not been inside it. It was the kind of possession taken for granted. The jacket hung open haphazardly, limp from age, its pocket edges worn bare, its zipper long since grown useless. The rough clothes gave Clay a rugged look, flattering in its unexpectedness, disarming because it brought back memories of the first time Catherine had ever seen him. Oh, he was neater that night, but he'd been dressed in faded Levi's jeans and a tennis shirt.

Catherine stood transfixed while Clay, oblivious to her reaction, only greeted her with, "Hi, I brought the Bronco. I thought we'd be more comfortable in it." He'd already turned toward the door before realizing she wasn't following, so turned back to her. "What's the matter? Oh, should I have dressed up more? I was waxing the Corvette in the garage and forgot about the time . . . sorry."

"No—no, it's okay . . . You look . . ." But she didn't finish, just gaped at him.

"What?"

"I don't know—different."

"You've seen me in jeans before."

Yes, she certainly had, but she didn't think he remembered.

She moved, at last, out the door with him.

At the curb was the vehicle she remembered from last July, some kind of man's toy with high bench seats and plenty of windows all around, and room for hunting equipment in the rear. She stopped walking as if she'd run up against a barbed wire fence.

"I thought we'd be a little crowded in the Corvette with your brother's gear and the three of us." Clay caught her elbow, propelling her forward. She began shivering; it was bitter for November—easy to blame her shakes on the weather. Clay moved ahead to open the door of the Bronco, but looked back again impatiently to find her eyeing him in a curious manner.

Catherine stood there, swallowing, fighting the overwhelming surge of familiarity—those jeans, and the old jacket, his hair that—for once—wasn't quite tidy. His collar was turned up, and as he stood waiting, his breath formed a white cloud. His nose was a little bit red, and he shivered, then hunched his shoulders.

"Hurry up," he said with a small smile. "Get in or you'll be scolding me for being late."

"Is this your father's?"

"Yeah."

He took his hand off the icy handle and buried it in his other pocket. Without thinking, she dropped her eyes to the zipper of his jeans, staring at the way the old, faded spots undulated between patches of deeper blue. Her eyes darted to his face, discovering that he'd been watching her. And suddenly the color of his cheeks matched his nose.

Appalled at herself, she climbed hurriedly into the seat and let him slam the door shut.

Neither of them said a word all the way out to the Air Force Reserve Base in Bloomington. Catherine stared out the side window, damning herself for letting memory play upon her this way. Clay drove, seeing over and over again the way her eyes had dropped to his zipper, recalling now the reason why. Women, he realized, placed greater importance on memories than men do. Until that happened back there he hadn't given a thought to the Bronco or his blue jeans, or the fact that he'd used them both last Fourth of July.

Clay did not touch her as they walked to the correct building. The stab of self-consciousness was again too concentrated.

A tall, strapping blond man, dressed in civvies, turned from his conversation with a uniformed desk clerk at the sound of their approach. He glanced up and hesitated. Then his mouth fell open, he smiled, and he started running toward the tall blond girl who, also, had broken into a run. They met like thwarted lovers and it came as something of a surprise to Clay, seeing for the first time a genuine display of affection from Catherine. There was a near greediness in the way her fingers dug into the back of her brother's jacket, a hungry desperation as their eyes closed while they clasped each other tightly and swallowed tears. Clay stood back uneasily, not wanting to watch them, unable not to. Steve swung Catherine off her feet, whirled her around, repeating an endearment which struck Clay as ill-suited, yet touched him all the same.

"Babe . . . oh, God, babe, is it really you?"

Her lips quivered and she clung. She could say little more than his name, backing away, spanning his tan cheeks with her palms, looking into his changed face, then at the breadth of his shoulders, then lunging into his arms again, burying herself, unable to restrain her tears now that she'd seen his.

To Clay it was a revelation. He watched Catherine's face, recalling this same expression on it that night after the long-distance call.

Finally Steve pulled back and said, "If that's Clay over there, I think we're making him uncomfortable." He tucked Catherine securely beneath his armpit, and she circled his torso with both arms while the two men shook hands.

Catherine's smile was unreserved. Her hold upon Steve was possessive. For Clay, it created an odd momentary twinge of jealousy, soon lost in the inanities of introductions, the first assessment of man to man.

"So you're the one she told me about." Steve's grip was solid, winning.

"So you're the one she told *me* about."

Clay reached for the duffel bag, and the three walked down the corridor and across the parking lot, Catherine and Steve catching up with bits of news about each other and the family. He squeezed her extra hard once and laughed. "Will you look at my baby sister. What happened to your cowlicks and pimples?" There followed another impulsive hug, then they clambered into the Bronco.

"Where to?"

"I made reservations downtown."

"But, Steve, we won't even get a chance to talk!" wailed Catherine.

"Listen, you two, why don't I drive out past the house and you can drop me off and Steve can take the Bronco?"

"Oh, Clay, really?" Catherine's blue eyes radiated appreciation.

"We've got more cars at home than we need."

Steve leaned around Catherine. "That's damn nice of you, man."

"Think nothing of it. I can't leave my future brother-in-law stranded in a downtown hotel, can I?"

Steve smiled.

"Then it's settled."

Catherine and Steve talked all the way out to the Forrester's. When they arrived, Steve took in the sprawling house, cobbled drive, extensive lawns, and said, "Well, well."

Catherine couldn't help the tiny thrill of pride, realizing how the house must appear to Steve for the first time. "This is where the wedding's going to be."

"Babe, I'm happy for you."

Clay pulled up, shifted into neutral, but he'd only dropped one leg out when Catherine laid a hand on his arm.

"Clay?"

He looked back over his shoulder at the touch on his sleeve.

"I don't know what to say."

Neither did he just then. He only looked at her, at the pleasant, warm expression she had willingly displayed toward him. She was so different today; he'd never seen her like this before. This, he thought, is how I've always wondered if she could be.

"Thank you," she said sincerely.

"It's okay. Like I said, we've got more cars around here than we know what to do with."

"Just the same—thanks." She moved impulsively toward him and brushed her cheek briefly against his, not quite kissing it, not quite missing, while he hung half in the seat, half out.

"You two have a good talk. But make sure you get some sleep, huh?"

"Promise."

"I'll see you tomorrow night then."

She nodded.

He lowered his voice and pleased her immeasurably by saying, "I think I like him."

Her only answer was the same genuine smile that he was already enjoying. Then Clay swung out, found Steve standing there waiting, and said, "Time enough for you to meet my folks tomorrow. I know you and Catherine are anxious to be alone."

"Listen, man . . ." Steve extended a hand. There followed a prolonged grip, then, "Thanks a lot." Steve then glanced up at the house and back once again at Clay. His tone changed, then he added quietly, ". . . for both of us."

There was an instantaneous sense of rapport between Clay and Steve, the inexplicable thing that happens only rarely when strangers meet. It had nothing to do with Catherine or her relationship to either of them. Neither had it anything to do with gratitude. It was simply there: some compelling invitation coursing between the clasped hands. "Here," it seemed to say, "is a man I feel good with."

Odd, thought Clay, but of all Catherine's family, this is the first person I've felt drawn to, and that includes Catherine herself.

He'd been expecting someone like Catherine's father, some harsh, forbidding younger version of Herb Anderson. Instead, he found a genuine smile, intelligent eyes, and a face much like Catherine's, only warmer. He thought perhaps the years away from home had given Steve Anderson the ability to smile at life again, which Catherine could not yet readily do. In her brother's face, Clay found the possibility of what Catherine could be, should she ever stop carrying that chip on her shoulder and that shield of armor over her emotions. Perhaps, after all, Clay liked Steve because he alone seemed able to move Catherine, to make her feel, and make it show.

When the noon break came and Ada Anderson left her machine, there was a sparkle of life in her eyes that had been missing for years. The skin about them was as corrugated as ever, but the eyes themselves were alive with expectancy. Her usual lifeless shuffle was replaced by a brisk step. Ada had even put a touch of lipstick on.

"Ada?"

She turned at the sound of her supervisor's voice, impatient to be out the door.

"I'm kind of in a hurry, Gladys. My boy is home, you know."

"Yes, I know. I checked on your output and the week's been good. The whole line had a good week, as a matter of fact. Why don't you just take the rest of the afternoon off, Ada?"

Ada stopped fussing with her coat collar. "Why, Gladys, do you mean it?"

"Of course I do. It's not every day a boy comes home from the Air Force."

Ada smiled, slid the handle of her vinyl purse onto her arm, casting one eye at the door, then back at Gladys Merkins.

"That's awful nice of you, and if you ever get in a bind when the girls get behind on their quotas, I'll put in extra."

"Get going, Ada. The quotas we'll worry about some other time."

"Thanks a lot, Gladys."

Gladys Merkins watched Ada hurry out the door, wondering how a person becomes so downtrodden, so stolid and unassuming that she doesn't even ask for a day off when she hasn't seen her son for six years. If word hadn't been passed around the shop, Gladys herself wouldn't have known. It did her heart good to see the pitiful woman with a smile on her face for once.

Outside, Ada scanned the street, clutching her coat at her throat where her heart beat in wild expectancy. The wind caught at the hem of the garment, lifting it, tugging at Ada's gray-streaked hair. She scanned the ugly street uncertainly. It sported only cold brick structures of commerce, and noisy truck traffic that never seemed to cease. Chain link fences were decorated with weathered paper scraps. There was the ever-present smell of exhaust fumes. Huddled against the wind, Ada looked like a deserted scrap of refuse herself.

But then a vehicle careened past and swerved to an abrupt halt beside the curb. A young man burst from it, forgetting to shut the door, waving, smiling, running, calling, "Mom! . . . Mom!" And the little scrap of refuse was transformed into vibrant life. Ada ran, her arms outstretched, her face tear-streaked. As her arms clung at last to her son's neck she wondered how it could possibly be him, so big, so broad, so real at last.

"Oh, Mom . . . Jesus . . . Mom."

"Steve, Steve, let me go so I can look at you."

He did, but then he saw her better too.

She appeared infinitely older, sadder. He could only hug her again, guilty because he knew some of that age, some of that sadness had been caused by his leaving. She was crying, but he saw past the tears to a much more profound sorrow, hopeful that somehow he could help erase it before he had to leave her once more.

"Come on, Mom, Cathy's in the car and we're all going out for lunch."

Chapter 16

IT WAS CATHERINE'S wedding day, the last day she would share with the girls at Horizons. So she allowed their suffocating attentions, feeling at times like she was smothering in their overcaring midst. The expressions on their faces—those doe-eyed looks—were etched on her conscience; she thought they would be her penance forever, long after she gave up her place as Mrs. Clay Forrester. The saga she had brought to Horizons would remain legend within its walls, rivaling any Hans Christian Andersen tale. But its ending, which none of them yet knew, would be her own private hair shirt.

She swallowed the knowledge of it while the girls played "wedding day" with her, dressing her up as they had their dolls as children, humming *Lohengrin* as they had for their dolls, pretending that the doll was themselves.

For Catherine it was an ordeal. Keeping the smile on her lips, the lilt in her voice, the eagerness in her pose became a task of sheer love. She realized it as the last hour neared—that she loved, genuinely loved, so many of these girls.

She sat before a mirror, her face flushed, and framed by an appealing aureole of soft blond curls, slung high and held by a winter gardenia set in baby's breath, trailing a thin white ribbon down the back. They had bought her a garter and were putting it on her calf, laughing, making silly jokes. Catherine was dressed in the sexiest undergarments she'd ever owned. Her mother had bought them from the employees' store at Munsingwear, surprising everyone at the shower. The bra was an incidental thing, plunging low in front, molding Catherine's lower breasts in lotus-shaped satin fingers that curved up to the crests of her nipples, barely covering them. Exquisite satin briefs, trimmed in peekaboo lace, left a strip of skin nearly exposed up each hip. The slip was beautiful enough to be an evening gown. It followed closely the low décolletage of the bra, flowing and clinging to her thighs and the perceptible bulge of her tummy. She placed her hands on it now, looking at the garter, at all the faces around her. Her eyes filled. She took a deep breath, fluttered a fingertip beneath her lashes, knowing the girls' eyes followed the twinkle of the diamond.

"Come on, you guys, don't!" she said, laughing shakily, quite close to breaking down completely. "Don't look so happy for me. It should be every single one of you, not me!" She widened her eyes to make room for the tears.

"Don't you dare cry, Catherine Anderson!" Marie scolded. "Not after all the work that's gone into that makeup. If you get one single tear on it, we're all going to disown you."

Another fragile, borderline laugh, and Catherine sputtered, "Oh, no, you won't. You can't disown me any more than I can disown you. Not anymore. We're all in this together."

But Catherine compressed her lips. A tear had its own way, hovered, then splashed over the edge of her lashes, and she laughed shakily, flapped her hands and demanded a tissue.

Somebody quipped, "Hey, Anderson, dry up, or else!"

It relieved the tension. The makeup passed inspection, and somebody brought the plain dress Catherine would wear in the car, her gown, carefully sheathed in plastic, her purse and the small bag she'd packed.

"Have you got your perfume in there?"

"Yes, thank you for reminding me, Francie."

"How about your Dramamine pills?"

"Dramamine pills?"

"You'll need them for flying high."

"Clay's the one that'll need them when he gets a load of that underwear!"

"Be careful of the gardenia when you get in the car now."

"Your brother is here, he just pulled up!"

They thronged downstairs. Steve was at the door. He carried Catherine's things outside, came back for a second load and for her.

Then there was nothing left to do but go. It was so hard to do, suddenly, to turn away from all the warmth and love. Mrs. Tollefson was there, hovering near the colonnade, then coming forward to be the voice of the entire group.

"Catherine, we're all so happy for you. I think you've made every girl here into something more than she used to be. Right, girls?" Catherine was hugged against Mrs. Tollefson quite roughly. She pinched her eyes shut.

"Listen . . . I—I love you all." As she said it, she experienced an explosive force of emotion. Those words, so unfamiliar to her tongue, created an expansiveness like she'd never felt before. She knew it twenty-five-fold, for at that moment it was true. She loved each woman crowded around her and suddenly wanted more than anything to stay among them, to let their hands pull her back into the security of their fold.

But that phase of her life was over. She was swept out into the November afternoon where a fine snow was falling, glittering onto her hair like stardust. The skies were pale, with smudges of gray clouds lying low, shedding their enchanting burden into Catherine's wedding day. With eyes now dry, Catherine watched their progress through the city, in a sort of enhanced state of clarity. Bare trees stood out in crisp distinction, blacker than black when wet by the snow. The snow had a pristine smell of newness, as each first snow does. It tantalized her, falling like petals strewn before the bride, touching everything with white. She stared out the window, sighed, closed her eyes, told her heart to beat right. But it beat all the more erratically as she envisioned the Forrester house, the guests who would soon be arriving, and Bobbi and Stu on their way, and somewhere, waiting . . . Clay.

Clay.

Oh, Clay, she thought, what have we done? How can all of this be happening? Me riding toward you with a velvet gown on the seat behind me and this diamond on my finger? And all those starry-eyed looks burning into my soul from the house I've just left? And your father and mother and grandparents all waiting to welcome me into your family? And guests coming, bringing gifts, and-—

"Stop the car!"

"What?" Steve exclaimed, surprised.

"Stop the car. I can't go through with this."

He pulled over, watching his sister drop her face into her hands. He slid across the seat and gathered her into his arms.

"What is it, babe?"

"Oh, Steve, what should I do?"

"Shh, come on now. Don't start crying, not today. It's just the last-minute jitters. But, really, babe, I don't think you should have the slightest qualms." He lifted her chin, making her look at him. "Cathy, if I could handpick a brother-in-law, I'd probably pick Clay Forrester, from what I've seen so far. And if I could handpick a family to trust you to, it would probably be his. You're going to be loved and taken care of for the rest of your life, and I couldn't be happier with who's going to be doing it."

"That's just it. It's not for the rest of my life."

"But—"

"Clay and I are being married under duress. We've agreed to divorce as soon as the baby has a name and he's passed his bar exams and entered his father's business."

Steve sat back, absorbing this news. His brows gathered into a scowl.

"Don't look at me that way! And don't ask me how this mess got started because right now I don't think I could even explain it to myself. I only know I feel like the biggest fraud on the face of the earth, and I don't think I can go through with it. I thought I could but I can't."

Steve slid back behind the wheel and stared at the wipers that slapped disconsolately across the windshield. His eyes seemed focused on nothing. "You mean none of them know?"

"Oh, Steve, I shouldn't have told you, but I had to get it off my chest."

"Well, now that you have, you're going to listen to what I have to say. You *should* feel like a swindler. It's a damn rotten trick you're playing on some damn fine people; at least I think they are. And since you obviously do, also, you haven't got any choice but to go through with it. If you back out now, you're going to embarrass them even further than our illustrious father already has. They've been more than fair to you, Catherine. They've been supportive and decent and, in case you've forgotten, quite lavish with their money. Frankly, the things I've learned about the Forrester family have boggled my mind. I find myself wondering how I'd have accepted the situation if I were in their position and faced with the bizarre set of circumstances they've been faced with. It takes some pretty big people to be as accepting as they've been. I think you owe it to them not only to go through with this marriage, but to make a helluva stab at making it work afterward.

"Furthermore, if I were faced with the opportunity, like you are, I think I'd do my damnedest not to let a man like Clay slip out of my fingers as easily as you intend to."

"But, Steve, you don't understand. We don't love each other."

"You're carrying something that says you'd better, by God, try to!"

She'd never seen Steve so upset with her before. She, too, raised her voice. "I don't want to have to *try* to love my husband. I just *want* to!"

"Listen, you're talking to old Steve here." He tapped his chest. "I know how stubborn you can be, and if you set your mind to something you'll stick with it, come hell or high water. And what you're telling me is that you aren't going to try to make this marriage work, right?"

"You make it sound like it's all my idea. It's not. We agreed to start the divorce in July."

"Yeah, and you wait and see how far your agreement goes when he gets a load of his own kid in some hospital nursery."

Catherine's heart flew to her throat. "He promised the baby will be mine. He won't fight for it."

"Yeah, sure." His hands hung on the wheel. He stared unseeingly. "The baby goes with you, you go your way, he goes his. What the hell kind of agreement is that to make?" He looked down at his thumbs.

"You're angry with me."

"Yes, I am."

"I don't blame you, I guess."

He felt robbed, robbed of all the elation he'd held for her, angry that she'd stolen it from him. Frustrated, he slammed the butts of both hands against the steering wheel.

"I like him, goddammit!" he blustered. "I felt so damn happy for you, ending up with a guy like him." Then he stared a long time out his side window.

"Steve." She slid over and touched his shoulder. "Oh, Steve, I'm sorry. I've hurt so many people already, and hardly any of them know yet that they've been hurt. You're the only one, and look how you feel. And when Mom finds out, and his folks, well, you can see why I don't think we should go through with it."

"You back out now and you'll break Mom's heart. She thinks you're set for life, and she'll never have to worry about you living like she's done, with that —that . . ."

"I know."

"Well, Christ! She's waiting at home right now in her homemade dress, probably all nervous about it, and—Hell, you know how she gets. She's actually, honest-to-God happy, or as close to happy as I've ever seen her, with the old man gone and your future set. Don't do it to her, Cathy."

"But what about me?"

"You started it, all those people heading for your wedding, all the preparations made, and you ask 'What about me?' I think you'd better think it over and consider what happens if you back out now. Count the number of people involved."

"I have! Every day I have! Facing all those pregnant teenagers at Horizons while they treated me like I was Snow White and they were dwarves, stitching on my wedding dress all starry-eyed. Do you think that's been easy?"

He sat stiff and silent. She slid back to her own side. The snow fell in flat plops while she stared at it unseeingly. Finally she quoted, as if to herself, "Oh, what a tangled web we weave, when first we practice to deceive."

The silence was broken only by the sweep of the windshield wipers, which were still slapping away. Catherine spoke to the snow. "I had no idea at the beginning how many lives would be touched by this wedding. It seemed like a decision that would mainly affect Clay and I and the baby. But things got out of hand somehow. Angela said he's their only son and wanted to have at least a few of the family—an intimate little affair she called it. And then all the girls at Horizons got into it, helping me make the dress. Then Mom sees me heading for what she thinks is the good life. Clay's grandparents even gave me their approval, to say nothing of the family jewels." She turned to Steve at last. "And you, my God, it even brought you home. Do you know what it means to me to have you here, and how I hated telling you the truth? I'm getting in deeper than I wanted though. Steve, please understand."

"I understand what it would do to a lot of people if you say no at the eleventh hour."

"And even after what I told you, you think I should go through with it?"

"I don't know . . . What a mess." But then he turned to her with a look of appeal on his face. "Cathy, couldn't you try to give it a chance?"

"You mean, me and Clay?"

"Yes, you and Clay. What are your feelings for him?"

That was a tough one; she thought for a minute before answering. "I honestly don't know. He's . . . well, he's able to accept all of this far more easily than I can. And the funny thing is, once he got over the first shock, he never blamed me in any way. I mean, most men would be throwing it up to a woman all the time how their plans were ruined. But he's not that way. He says he's going to make the best of it, takes me out and introduces me to his family just as if I'm his real choice, gives me this huge old ring that's been in the family forever, and treats me like a lady. Yet, at the same time, I know it's all a hoax. He does very well at keeping his family from suspecting it though. They've accepted me surprisingly well. The trouble is, Steve, I think I'm accepting them too. Oh, Steve . . . it's awful . . . I . . . don't you think I realize all those things you felt about them? They're genuinely good and loving people, and I'm drawn to them; I like them. But it's dangerous for me, don't you see? I'm to be a part of them, yet I'm not. Giving them up in a few months will be tougher than leaving Horizons was today."

"All this time you've talked about his family, but you still haven't answered my question about Clay."

"How can I? The truth is I don't know him as well as you think I do."

"Well, it's obvious you were attracted to him once."

"But it's not . . ." She paused, looked away. "I met him on a blind date. He was going with another girl at the time, and they'd had a fight or something."

"So what?"

"So it was a one-night stand, that's what."

"Are you saying he loves someone else?"

"He never mentions her."

"Hey"—Steve's voice was as gentle as his touch upon her arm—"babe, I don't know what to say, except, maybe—just maybe—Clay is worth fighting for."

"Steve, you above all people should understand that I don't want a marriage like Mom and Dad's. If there's one thing I learned in that house it's that I will not merely *survive* a marriage; I want to *live.*"

"Hey, give it a chance. Had you considered that you kind of fell into the pot here and could come out smelling like a rose?"

She couldn't help smiling. "If it'll put your mind at ease, the baby will be taken care of for the rest of his life. That's part of the arrangement. After Clay graduates, he'll help me with tuition so I can go back to school."

"So the deal is made, huh? I guess we both know you can't back out of it now, don't we?"

She sighed. "You're right. I can't, and I knew it all the time, even when I told you to stop the car."

He studied her a moment before saying, "You know, little sister, I'll give you odds you won't come out of this feeling quite as platonic about him as you claim to be now. How much you wanna bet?"

"That's wishful thinking and you know it. And I'm going to be late for my own wedding if you don't get this thing into gear."

"Okay." He shifted into drive and they pulled back into traffic.

After a few minutes she touched his arm and smiled at Steve. "Thanks for letting me unload on you. I feel better now."

He winked at her. "You really are a babe, in lots of ways," he said, covering her hand with his own, hoping Clay Forrester recognized that fact.

Chapter 17

THE WINDOWS OF THE Forrester home were all ablaze, throwing oblique patches of gold across the snow of early evening. Each of the front columns was festooned with an enormous arrangement of Indian corn, scarlet leaves and bearded wheat with nutmeg-colored ribbons trailing streamers that drifted in a meek breeze. Snow settled softly upon the scene and Catherine gave a soft exclamation of surprise at the liveried attendant who was sweeping the cobbled walk.

She could see that Angela's expert hand had done its work and wondered what other surprises awaited her inside. Catherine fought against the overwhelming sensation of coming home. She fought, too, against the both terrible and wonderful sense of expectation. Surely this incredible day was not happening. Yet the scent of gardenia was real. And the diamond on her hand was so large she couldn't draw her glove over it. Summoning common sense did little good. The flutter of excitement persisted, disquieting, reducing Catherine to nervous jitters.

Then the attendant was smiling, opening the door, while Catherine fought the crazy sensation that she was debarking from a coach-and-four.

The foyer door opened upon yet another dreamlike setting: bronze and yellow flowerbursts threaded with ribbons, cascading from the spooled stair rail at evenly spaced intervals. Angela appeared with Ada in tow, sweeping Catherine into a hurried hug, whispering conspiratorially, "Hurry on up. We don't want you to be seen here."

"But, Steve—" Catherine strained to glance over her shoulder, dismayed at being whisked through the tantalizing foyer without being allowed to dote upon it. Angela's laughter tinkled into the softly glowing space as if she understood Catherine's reluctance to be swept through so hastily.

"Don't worry about Steve. He knows what to do."

The floral impressions had to be left behind momentarily. Yet a last look behind her gave Catherine the sight of two white-capped maids peeking over the banister for one forbidden glimpse of the bride.

Insanity continued as Catherine was ushered into a stunningly appropriate bedroom, trimmed in pink flounced ruffles and floor-length priscillas. It was carpeted, too, in palest pink, and furnished with a glorious brass bed and free-standing cheval mirror, ruffled pillows, and a girlish look that seemed the counterpart to Angela's giddiness.

When the door closed behind them, Angela immediately captured both of Catherine's hands. "Forgive an old-fashioned mother her whims, my dear, but I didn't want to run the risk of your meeting Clay somewhere in the hall." Angela squeezed the damp palms. "You look lovely, Catherine, so lovely. Are you excited?"

"I . . . yes . . . it . . ." She glanced at the door. "All those flowers down there . . . and a doorman!"

"Isn't it exciting? I can't think of another affair I've had more fun arranging. I believe I'm a little breathless, as well. Can I tell you a secret?" She smiled conspiratorially again, then turned to include Ada in the secret. "So is Clay."

The idea seemed preposterous, yet Catherine asked, "He is?"

"Ah! He's been driving us crazy all day, worrying if there was enough champagne and if the flowers would arrive on time and if we'd forgotten Aunt Gertie's family on the guest list. He's been the typical bridegroom, which pleases me immensely." Then Angela breezily commandeered Ada. "Now we'll leave you alone for a minute. I want to show your mother the cake and gifts. You'll find everything you need in the bath there, and if you don't find it, let one of the maids know. Come on, Ada. I think we deserve a little glass of sherry to calm our mothers' nerves."

But before they could leave, a maid opened the door and ushered in a breathless Bobbi, with a plastic clothing carrier over her arm. There followed a flurry of kisses and greetings and hanging up of gowns, and exclamations over all the subdued activity going on downstairs.

"We'll see you later, Catherine." Angela waved two fingers and took Ada away, but not before warning, "Now remember, you're not to leave this room until I come for you."

"Don't worry," Bobbi promised. "I'll see that she doesn't."

Left alone, Catherine and Bobbi had only to look at each other to burst into matching grins and hug each other again, before Bobbi exclaimed, "Have you seen what's going on down there!"

Catherine, panicked afresh, placed a hand on her hammering heart and pleaded, "Don't tell me. I'm giddy enough as it is. This is all so unbelievable!"

Whatever Catherine had expected this evening to be, she had not in her wildest dreams believed it would turn out like the make-believe weddings she and Bobbi had conjured up during childhood. Yet it seemed to be. Each of the girls realized it as they stood in the feminine bedroom, exchanging inanities, occasionally giggling. A maid knocked to ask if their dresses needed any last-minute pressing. They sent her away and went into the bathroom to check each other's hair, giving a last swish of hair spray, then laughing into each other's eyes in the huge mirror. Another knock sounded and produced a maid with two large boxes containing their bouquets.

They laid them on the bed and looked at the unopened, white containers.

"You first," Catherine said, clasping her hands beneath her chin.

"Oh, no, not this time. We're not eight-year-olds pretending anymore. You first!"

"Let's open them together then."

They did. Bobbi's held a quaint basket of bronze mums and apricot roses, with streamers of pale ribbon falling from its handle. Catherine stood back, quite unable to reach for the stunning spray of white gardenia, baby's breath, and apricot roses nestled in their transparent bag with dewy beads of moisture clinging inside. Bobbi watched her press her hands to her cheeks, then close her eyes momentarily, open them once again to remain stock-still, staring at the blossoms. So Bobbi leaned down, removed the pearl-headed pin and lifted the huge spray from its wrapper, releasing the heady fragrance of gardenia and roses into the room. She pinned one of the gardenias into Catherine's hair. Still, Catherine seemed unable to move.

"Oh, Cath, they're beautiful."

Bobbi lifted the bouquet and at last Catherine moved, wordlessly plunging her face into the nosegay. Looking up again across the flowers, she stammered, "I—I don't deserve all this."

Bobbi's voice was soft with emotion. "Of course you do. It's exactly what we dreamed about, Cath. One of us has made it, and everything turned out even better than make-believe."

"Don't say that."

"Don't dissect it, Cath, just enjoy every precious minute of it."

"But you don't know—"

"I know. Believe me, I do. I know that you have doubts about the way you and Clay got started, but don't think about them tonight. Think of the good side, okay?"

"You wanted me to marry Clay all along, didn't you, Bobbi?"

"I wanted something good for you and if it's Clay Forrester, then, yes, I wanted it."

"I think you've always been a little soft on him yourself."

"Maybe I have. Maybe not, I don't know. I only know if it were me standing there holding that bouquet, I'd be ecstatic instead of depressed."

"I'm not depressed, really I'm not. It's just more than I bargained for, and it's all so sudden."

"And so you doubt and question? Catherine, for once—just for once—in your godforsaken life, will you accept a little manna from heaven? You're so used to living in hell that a little heaven scares you. Come on, now, smile! And tell yourself that he asked you to marry him because he wanted to. It's going to work. Clay is one of the nicest men I know, but if you tell Stu I said so, I'll kill you."

At last Catherine smiled, but she was affected more than she cared to admit by Bobbi's opinion of Clay.

"Now, come on, let's get your dress on."

They stripped off its protective plastic, looked at each other meaningfully once again, recalling all those childhood games, all that make-believe. But the luxurious velvet was real. Bobbi lifted it high while Catherine raised her arms. When she was halfway into it a sound—suspiciously like a harp—came from below.

"What's that?" Bobbi cocked an ear.

"I can't hear in here," came the muffled voice from inside the dress.

"Oh, here, get your ears out of there!"

When Catherine emerged, they posed like robins listening for worms. They looked at each other in disbelief.

"It sounds like a harp!"

"A harp?"

"Well, doesn't it?"

They both listened again.

"My God, it does!"

"Could there really be a harp in this house?"

"Apparently so."

"Leave it to Angela."

Then they both burst into laughter and finished drawing the dress over Catherine's arms. By now she was shaking visibly. Her palms were damp but she dared not wipe them on the velvet.

"Bobbi, I'm scared stiff."

"Why? You're the main attraction and you look it. Be proud!"

Bobbi zipped and buttoned busily, then walked around behind Catherine and extended the miniature train onto the pink carpet. Catherine caught a glimpse of herself in the mirror, pressed her hands to her tummy and asked, "Do I show a lot?"

Bobbi slapped her cousin's hands down, scolding, "Oh, for heaven's sake, will you *please!*" Then she had an inspiration; she handed over the bouquet. "If you must worry about it, hide behind this."

Catherine struck a prim pose that made them both laugh again, but now the sounds from downstairs were definitely steadier, the hum of voices intermingling with the mellow tones of the music.

The door opened and this time it was Inella who stood there with a tiny, foil-wrapped box.

"Why, don't you look lovely, Miss Catherine," the maid said with a wide smile. "Your groom gave me the honor of delivering this." She extended the box. Catherine only gaped, then reached out a tentative hand, withdrew it, then finally took the gift.

"What is it?"

"Why, I'm sure I don't know, Miss. Why don't you open it and see?"

Catherine turned wide eyes to Bobbi.

"Inella's right, open it! I'm dying to see!"

"But what if it's something—" She stopped just short of saying "expensive." The box was too small to be anything but jewelry. It lay in her hand accusingly while she wondered with a sinking feeling why Clay had done this to her. Again her eyes sought Bobbi's, then Inella's. Quickly she stripped away the foil and found a small, velveteen ring box. Her heart was hammering, her throat went suddenly dry. She lifted the lid. Inside no jewels glittered, no rings twinkled. Instead, couched in the velvet slot was a brass key. No message, no clues. Catherine breathed again.

"What's it for?"

"Why, I'm afraid I couldn't guess, Miss Catherine."

"But—"

A knock sounded and Angela came in. As the door opened, the gentle swell of voices told that the crowd was growing below.

"It's nearly time," announced Angela.

"Look." Catherine held up the key. "It's from Clay. Do you know what it's for?"

"I'm afraid I haven't any idea. You'll have to wait until after the ceremony and ask him."

Catherine tucked the key away in her garter where it seemed to burn warmly against her leg.

"Is Mother okay?"

"Yes, dear, don't worry. She's already in her place."

Inella ventured a tidy kiss on Catherine's cheek, then said, "You do look radiant, Miss Catherine." Then she was gone to attend to her duties below.

Again Bobbi picked up Catherine's bouquet, handed it to her and gave a last caress on the cheek, and stood awaiting her signal. The door swung open and Catherine watched Angela meet Claiborne in the upstairs hall. There was a brief smile from him, a last hovering look from her before they left Catherine's range of vision. Next came Stu, in a lush tuxedo of rich spice-brown, with an abundance of starched, apricot-colored ruffles springing from his chest below a high, stiff collar and bow tie. Stu grinned in at Catherine, and she attempted a quavering smile in return before Bobbi moved out into the hall and headed for the stairs.

And then came Steve. Her beloved Steve, looking so handsome in a tuxedo of his own, holding out both hands to her as if inviting her to a minuet. He wore a smile that melted her heart, that washed away their earlier disagreement. Catherine knew she must move forward, but her feet refused. Steve, sensing her thoughts, stepped gallantly to the bedroom doorway, bowed from the waist and extended an elbow. Suddenly she realized that people below were awaiting them and were more than likely gazing up the steps.

She felt the tug of the train upon the carpet, Steve's firm arm beneath her hand and the pressure of her heart thudding high against her ribcage. From below came a collective "Oooh . . ." as she stepped to the head of the stairs.

A sudden intimidation gripped her as the raised sea of faces swam into view. But Steve, sensing her hesitation, closed his free hand over hers, urging her down the first step. She was dimly aware of candles washing everything with a mellow glow. They were everywhere: in wall sconces, upon shelves and tables, gleaming and twinkling from the floral sprays attached to the railing and from within the study where an overflow of guests watched. A path emerged as she and Steve rounded the newel post and glided toward the living room. Catherine had a fleeting memory of the first time she'd been in this foyer, sitting on the velvet bench now hidden behind the multitude of guests. How apprehensive she'd been then, yet this was not really so different. Her stomach was in knots. She moved in hypnotic fashion toward the living room doorway, toward Clay. From somewhere an electronic keyboard had joined the harp in a simple Chopin prelude. And everywhere, everywhere, there was the aura of candleglow, all gold and amber and warm and serene. The smell of flowers mingled with the waxen scent of candle smoke while Catherine drifted through the throng of guests, quite unaware of their great number, of their admiring gazes, or of how, for many of them, the sight of her brought back quicksilver memories of their own breathless walk down the aisle. The living room doorway captured her every thought; the idea of Clay waiting on the other side of it sent her heart flitting and her stomach shaking.

She had a dim impression of her mother waiting in a semicircle of countenances that faced her from the bay window, of space emerging as people rustled back to clear the way. But then all others were forgotten as Catherine's eyes fell upon Clay. He stood in the classic groom's pose, hands clasped before him, feet spraddled, face unsmiling and a bit tense. She had thought to avoid his eyes, but hers had a will of their own. As if he had materialized at the whim of some talented spinner of fairy tales, both he and the setting were too perfect.

Lord help me, thought Catherine, as their eyes met. Lord help me.

He waited, his hair like ripe wheat with the sun setting over it. A tall sconce of countless candles turned his skin to amber, reflecting from the deep apricot ruffles that only added to his masculinity. He wore a vested tuxedo of rich cinnamon, a sternly tied bow tie which suddenly bobbed up, then settled back in place at his first sight of her. His eyes—in that flawless face—widened, and she caught the nearly imperceptible movement as he began locking and unlocking his left knee. Then, just before she lost his glance, his hands dropped to his sides and he wet his lips. Blessedly, he then became only an impression at her side. But she knew he turned to gaze once more at her flushed cheek while the organ and harp faded into only a murmurous background.

"Dearly beloved . . ."

The charade began. Things became surrealistic to Catherine. She was a child again, playing wedding with Bobbi, walking across a lawn dressed in dishtowels and curtains, carrying a bouquet of dandelions. Pretending she was back there took away the sting of guilt at what she was doing.

"Who gives this woman?"

"I do, her brother."

Reality returned and with it Clay's arm, taking the place of Steve's. It was solid, but surprising, for minute tremors scuttled there, felt but not seen.

This time I wanna be the bride.

But, you're always the bride!

No, I ain't! You were the bride last time!

Aw, come on, don't cry. Okay, but next time I get to wear the curtain on my head!

From her left, Bobbi smiled, while sweet, naive memories came whirling back. The minister spoke; he had a mellifluous voice and could manage to sound as if what he said were being spoken solely to her and Clay. Catherine trained her eyes on the minister's lips, concentrating hard on the words as he reminded those about to be joined of the importance of patience, love and faithfulness. Some muscle tensed into a knot beneath Catherine's hand, was forcibly relaxed, then twitched again. She realized that the minister had asked all the married couples present to join their hands and renew their wedding vows silently along with the bride and groom. Silently Catherine pleaded, No! No! What you're witnessing is a sham! Don't base your reaffirmation of love on something that is meaningless!

She escaped once again into the play days of yesteryear.

When you get married, what kinda man are you gonna marry?

Rich.

Oh, Bobbi, honestly, is that all you think about?

Well, what kind you gonna marry?

One who likes to be with me so much he comes straight home instead of stopping at bars. And he's always gonna be nice to me.

The minister asked them to turn and face each other and hold hands. The profusion of gardenias and roses was given into Bobbi's hands. During the exchange their childhood fantasies were reflected within a glance the two exchanged.

Then Catherine's hands were clasped firmly in Clay's brown, strong fingers, and she felt dampness on his palms and on her own. The minister's voice droned on, far away, and Catherine was suddenly afraid to look Clay full in the face.

I'm gonna marry a man who looks just like Rock Hudson.

Not me. I like blond hair and stormy eyes.

My God, thought Catherine now, did I really say that?

She raised her eyes to blond hair, to gray, sober eyes that wore an expression of sincerity as they probed hers for the benefit of their guests. His face was limned by flickering candlelight which accented the straight nose, long cheeks and sensitive lips which were parted slightly, but somber. An errant pulsebeat showed just above his high, tight, apricot-colored collar and the stern bow tie. His manner was faultless, convincing. It created havoc within Catherine.

A man who is nice to me. Blond hair and stormy eyes. One who is rich.

Phrases from the past resounded through the chambers of Catherine's heart, filling it with remorse unlike any she'd suffered before. But those who looked on couldn't guess the turmoil within her, for she paralleled Clay's superb act, searching his eyes as he searched hers, while the pressure on her knuckles grew to sweet agony.

What are we doing? she wanted to cry. Do you know what you do to me with those eyes of yours? What do I do to myself by clenching your too-strong fingers this way, by pretending to idolize your too-perfect face? Don't you recognize the pain of a girl whose youthful dreams painted this very illusion, time and time again, who escaped into scenes just such as this when reality threatened? Don't you understand that I honestly believed those dreams would come true one day? If you do, release my hands, release my eyes, but above all keep my heart free of you. You are too flawless and this is too close to the real thing and I have suffered long enough for the lack of love. Please, Clay, turn away before it's too late. You are a temporary illusion and I must not, must not get lost in it.

But she was trapped in a farce of her own making, for Clay did not turn away, nor release her eyes, nor her hands. Her palms felt seared, her heart felt blistered. And for a moment she knew the cruel bite of wishfulness.

At last she dragged her eyes downward. Then Stu stepped forward, drawing a ring from his pocket. She extended her trembling fingers and Clay slid a diamond-studded band halfway on and held it hovering there.

"I, Clay, take thee, Catherine . . ."

While his deep voice spoke the words, Catherine's cheated heart wanted suddenly for this to mean something. But this was only a fantasy. Her thoughts tumbled on while Clay completed the ring's journey to its nesting place beside the heirloom already there.

She was startled then to find a ring placed in her palm—Angela had thought of everything—and her eyes fled once more to Clay's. Another prop for the play? hers asked. But perhaps he had chosen it himself, not Angela. Obediently she dropped her gaze and adorned his finger with the wide, gold unstudded florentine band.

"I, Catherine, take thee, Clay . . ." Her unsteady voice was threatened by shredded nerves, lost dreams and the awful need to cry.

But still there was more to be endured as they turned once again full-face to the blurred minister's garb. Hazily Catherine heard him pronounce them man and wife. Then the cleric smiled benevolently and sealed Catherine's and Clay's joined hands with both of his own.

"May your lives together be long and happy," he wished simply, never suspecting what the words did to Catherine's already strained emotions. She stared at the wavering sight of all their hands together, quite numb now. Then the minister's hands disappeared and his voice poured out softly for the last time. "And now you may seal your vows with your first kiss as Mr. and Mrs. Clay Forrester."

Shattered already, Catherine didn't know what to do. She felt as if she aged years in the mere moment while Clay took the lead, turning toward her with every misty eye in the house upon them. She lifted her face; the breath caught in her throat. She expected no more than a faint brush of lips, but instead his face loomed near, those gray eyes were lost in closeness, and she found herself enfolded in Clay's arms, gently forced against the starched ruffles of his elegant shirtfront, besieged by soft, slightly opened lips which were far, far too compelling. Haunting memories came flooding back.

No, Clay, don't! she longed to cry. But he did. He kissed her fully. And in that moment of first contact she sensed his apology, but found herself unable to forgive him for the convincing job he was doing.

He released her then, to the accompaniment of a collective murmur, and his breath touched her nose as he stepped back and looked into her startled eyes.

There followed the kind of smile she'd been waiting for since childhood, sweeping Clay's face as if the moment were genuine, and she was forced to return one equally as bright. Then Clay tucked her hand possessively within his arm and turned her to face their guests.

She wore the pasted-on smile until it held its own. She was beleaguered by hugs, kisses and congratulations, starting with Stu, who unabashedly kissed her hard on the mouth. Next came Steve, holding her a little too long, a little too protectively, rocking a little while he squeezed her and whispered "Chin up" in her ear.

"Oh, Steve," she allowed herself to say, knowing that he alone understood.

"Shh, babe, you're both doing fine. I wish you could see how you look together."

Clay's father appeared, held her by the upper arms and welcomed her to the family with a generous hug and a direct kiss—the first kiss from him ever. Over his shoulder she saw Clay with his arms wrapped around Ada. Grandma and Grandpa Elgin gave her elfin pats and smiles, and Elizabeth Forrester bestowed upon her a regal kiss for each cheek and a tap of her cane upon the right shoulder, as if she were being knighted.

"You are a beautiful young woman. I shall expect beautiful children from you," the old eagle stated sagaciously before turning away as if the matter were settled. Then Catherine was passed around like a dish of divinity, tasted by many mouths until she was actually quite grateful to be returned at last to Clay—until he pleased every guest there by voluntarily giving them what they waited for!

He swooped down, smiling boldly, and grasped Catherine firmly around her ribs, then picked her cleanly up off the floor until she hung suspended like a marionette. Indeed, she had no more choice than a marionette whose strings are controlled by the puppeteer. She could only submit to Clay's lips while the gardenias were wrapped so far around his neck that her nose was buried in them. She closed her eyes, spinning like a leaf in a whirlwind, intoxicated by the overpowering fragrance of the waxy flowers, by the awful sense that this was real, pretending momentarily that it was. The instant he touched her lips, Catherine felt the almost automatic reach of Clay's tongue toward her own, then her own surprised tongue arching in hesitation, not quite knowing what to do with itself. Then Clay's withdrawing politely again. She was faintly aware that the crowd had burst into applause but allowed herself to become mesmerized by the sensation that the world was twirling crazily. With her eyes closed and her arms around her husband's neck she endured an endless kiss while he slowly turned them both in a circle. But the kiss had grown long —difficult to find a place for a tongue in the midst of such a kiss if it does not take its natural course—until at its end, his tongue again touched hers, then, elusive as quicksilver, was gone.

But the crowd saw nothing more than a groom turning his bride in a slow circle in the middle of a candlelit room, kissing, rejoicing in the accepted fashion. They knew nothing of the elusive tongue-dance which accompanied the embrace.

Catherine came out from behind her gardenias with scarlet cheeks, which added to everyone's delight except her own. But then she was grateful to Clay for the convincing ploy, for when she turned from his arms it was to find a string of familiar faces with sparkling eyes that had just witnessed the entire scenario with awe-struck rapture. For the first time Catherine didn't need to act. Her elation was genuine as she flew to greet Marie, then Francie, and Grover and Vicky too!

Having them there made it nearly perfect. Catherine was touched by the sight of the usually unkempt Grover with her hair all shining and curled like Catherine had never seen it before. And Vicky, who had miraculously managed to let her nails grow beyond the tips of her finger and had polished them the most horrendous shade of blood-red. And Francie, smelling of Charlie perfume. Marie, tiny and petite in spite of how close she was to her due date. Marie, the sprite, the matchmaker, who had first taught Catherine to accept the contact of a caring hand. How many times had they touched hands since?

Clay arrived at Catherine's side again, encircling her waist loosely, then pulling her against his hip with a smiling expression she knew was for the girls.

"Isn't she something?" Francie demanded. And obligingly Clay tightened his grip, spread his hand upon Catherine's ribs and dropped a loving kiss on the corner of her eye.

"Yes, she's something, my bride." Catherine refused to look up at Clay. His fingers rode perilously close to her breast.

"What do you think of our dress?" Marie asked.

Again he moved the hand, caressing the velvet appreciatively, answering, "Gorgeous," then continuing to play their game by asking, "Who's going to wear it next?"

"Well, that depends on which one of us can snag a guy like you. Hey, why don'tcha let go of her and let us have our turns?"

Deftly Marie divided Clay from his bride while he gave Catherine the required Help!-what-can-I-do look, then threw his all into a tremendous kiss for the tiny Marie. Now it was Clay's turn to be passed around like a sweet. Catherine could only look on, smiling in spite of herself. He kissed them all, giving them a taste of what they wished was theirs. He returned to his bride only when they'd tasted their fill, some of them for a little too long, some with too-rapt expressions as their kiss ended.

But for his understanding, Catherine was again grateful to Clay.

They moved through the crowd again, Catherine at last realizing it was far, far larger than Angela had hinted it would be. Not only the girls from Horizons, but business associates, family friends and numerous relatives had been impetuously added to the invitation list. Angela's "intimate little affair" had blossomed into a full-blown social event of the season.

Chapter 18

SHE AND CLAY were ensconced in the study to sign the marriage certificate under the gaze of the minister. They gave away no more than shaky fingers, then the photographer was there, popping his bulbs at their hands posed upon the document, then upon Catherine's bouquet, then herding them back into the living room to pose in the bay window with the other members of the wedding party. Throughout all this Catherine succeeded in being spontaneous and gay, as brides are expected to be. Bright repartee fell from her lips and from Clay's while they touched again and again until it became automatic, this reaching for each other's waists. And somehow Catherine found herself beginning to enjoy it.

Upon the dining room table a fountain of champagne cascaded. Clay and Catherine were buffeted there to catch their glasses full and sip around each other's love-knotted arms while the cameras again recorded the moment for posterity. The gentlemen guests posed around Catherine's gartered leg. She caught Clay's eye—was it twinkling?—above the glass of champagne he sipped. Next she posed on the stairway, where she tossed her bouquet over the banister. It was caught by a young girl Catherine didn't recognize.

Small tables appeared, set up with smooth efficiency by a host of hired waiters. Angela managed to oversee the dinner arrangements with silent skill while giving the impression that she'd never left her guests' sides nor swayed her attentions away from them.

Angela's know-how brought off a masterpiece of coordination. By the time Catherine was seated beside Clay at the head table, her admiration for his mother had grown immensely. It took more than money, Catherine realized, to achieve what Angela had here tonight.

The guests were served elegant plates of chicken breast stuffed with Minnesota's rare and delectable wild rice, garnished by crisp broccoli and spiced peach halves. The plates were as delightful to look at as they were to dip into. But what was most appreciated was the almost slick transition from reception rooms to dining hall. The entire festivity was proving to be a stunning success. Gratified, Catherine leaned around Clay to tell Angela so. But she only waved a nonchalant hand and assured Catherine the joy had been hers, she'd have felt cheated to do less and every minute had been worth it. Then she squeezed Catherine's hand.

It was in the middle of the meal that Catherine remembered the key. "Clay, I got your gift. Inella brought it upstairs before the ceremony, but I don't know what it's for."

"Guess."

She was afraid to. The whole evening was already overwhelming.

"The town house?" she ventured, but there was too much noise. Clay leaned down, his ear directly in front of her lips.

"What?"

"The town house, I said."

He straightened, smiled teasingly and only shook his head. She saw his lips move, but there was such a tinkling clangor going on that she couldn't hear him either. Now she lowered her ear to his lips, but while she was thus posed,

306

straining to hear his reply, she became aware that all voices in the room had stopped and only the demanding sound of spoons striking wineglasses filled the air.

Startled, she looked up to find every eye waiting. Then she realized Clay's hand rested on the back of her neck. It slid away and he smilingly began getting to his feet. Realization dawned, but still she hesitated, linen napkin forgotten in one hand, fork in the other, unprepared for yet another assault on her senses.

Clay stepped behind her chair, leaned near her ear. "Apparently they're not going to let us off with a couple of quick kisses that half of them didn't see."

Quick kiss, she thought, was that last what he calls a *quick* kiss?

It was an old custom, one on which Catherine hadn't reckoned. The first kiss had been part of the ceremony. The second had taken her by surprise. But this one—this one was something altogether different. This was the one where plenty of schmaltz was expected.

From behind her came the innocent invitation, "Mrs. Forrester?" But Catherine suspected that could she see his face she'd find one eyebrow cocked up saucily, along with the corners of his mouth. She had no choice, so she gave the expected nervous laugh and got to her feet. There was no evading the issue this time as Clay gave her a regular Valentino job. Oh, he laid it on with aplomb! He pinned both of her arms at her sides, bent his head sideways and her slightly backward until she thought they'd both land on the floor. Her hands spread wide, finding nothing to hold onto but the taut fabric across his back. And while his tongue plundered the inside of her mouth in no uncertain terms, everyone in the room whistled and hooted and tapped their glasses all the more noisily until Catherine thought she would die of agony or ecstasy or a combination of the two. She died of neither. Instead, she found some welcome reserve of humor. He released her, straightened, and laughed into her eyes for the benefit of their guests, holding her loosely now about the waist with his hips resting against her own.

"Ah, Valentino, I'm sure," she said with a smile.

"They love it," he rejoined above the burst of applause. If anyone cared to read lips, Catherine was sure it would appear that Clay had said, "I love it." He held her a moment longer in that relaxed and familiar slackness. From the far reaches of the room it appeared they were the typically starstruck nuptial pair. He even rocked her sideways once, then plunged forward again to whisper in her ear, "Sorry."

Catherine's stomach felt at that moment like she'd eaten too much of Inella's salmon again. But before she could dwell on it, the photographer was there, demanding that they pose, feeding each other from filled forks. It was disconcerting, watching Clay's mouth open to receive food, holding the pose like a statuette, watching the glistening tip of his tongue which had only a moment ago unabashedly invaded her own.

The meal progressed, but Catherine couldn't eat another bite. Clay poured more champagne into her glass and she dove into it like a sailor from a burning ship. It made her head light and fuzzy and she warned herself to be careful. It was confusing stuff.

But before the bubbles cleared from her eyes, the glasses were ringing out again and Clay was standing up, taking her by the upper arm. This time it was easier, better, the wine having gone to her head somewhat, and her inhibitions sagged shamelessly while Clay gave her a kiss the likes of which turned her spine to aspic.

What the heck, the bride thought, give them what they want and forget it. And so she threw a little more of her heart into it—to say nothing of her tongue, which found a readily receptive mate within Clay's mouth. She even emoted a little, plopping her hand on top of her head as if holding it on, quite tickled by her own ingenuity.

The kiss ended. Clay laughed into her eyes. "Good job, Mrs. Forrester."

"Not bad yourself, Mr. Forrester." But she was all too aware of the way his hips again nudged her own through the velvet gown and the way her slightly bubbled tummy intruded upon the spot where his crisp tuxedo jacket hung open. "But I think you'd better stop filling my glass."

"Now why would I want to do a thing like that?" He smirked cutely, raising an eyebrow suggestively. His hands skimmed lightly downward to rest upon her hips. She wondered if it were her imagination or had he pressed himself momentarily closer? But then she decided it was her imagination. After all, he was performing—just as she was—for the benefit of all the tinkling glass-tappers out there.

The cake was wheeled in on a glass cart. It was a towering creation of fluted columns and doves with ribbons threaded through their confectionary beaks, and it raised a chorus of aah's that gratified Angela. Clay's and Catherine's hands were trained upon the knife handle with its voluminous white satin bow. Flashbulbs exploded, the knife sliced through the cake, and the bride was instructed to feed her groom, this time from her fingertips. But he not only took the cake, he lipped the frosting from her knuckle while, above it, his gray eyes crinkled at the corners. Naughty sensations tingled their way down to Catherine's toes and her eyes swerved swiftly aside.

"Mmm . . . sweet stuff," he said this time.

"Bad for your teeth," she smiled up at him, ". . . and rumored to cause hyperactivity."

He reared back and laughed wholeheartedly and once again they sat down.

"Let's have one of the groom feeding the bride," the photographer suggested, zooming in on his quarry.

"How many more must we take?" Catherine asked, flustered now, but not entirely disliking the game.

"I'll be neat," Clay promised in an aside. But that same devilish crinkle tugged at the corners of his mouth and eyes. He lifted a morsel of cake and she took it, tasted sugar, swallowed, then found him still standing there with an index finger frosted and waiting.

With a smile as sweet as any confection she said, "This is getting bawdy." But all she could do was suck the end of his finger, finding it slightly salty too.

"Our guests find it amusing."

"You, Mr. Forrester, are unforgivably salty." But at that moment she caught Elizabeth Forrester's bright, knowing gaze snapping down the table at them, and she wondered what the old girl suspected.

The moment turned serious when Claiborne rose to give Catherine his official welcome. He came around the table and gave her a hug and a kiss and his approval for all to see. She sensed sobriety returning to Clay as he leaned an elbow on the table's edge and absently brushed an index finger across his lip, watching. Then he rose and shook hands with his father. Applause followed as Clay sat back down. The whole thing had been appallingly earnest on Claiborne's part, and as their eyes met, both Catherine and Clay realized it.

"On second thought, you'd better pour me another glass," she said, "and smile. Your grandmother Forrester is watching every move we make."

"Then this is for her, and for Mother and Father," Clay said, and reached a finger to tip her chin up and placed the lightest kiss upon her lips. Then he reached for the champagne bottle. But his smile and gay mood did not return.

The meal ended and dancing began. Catherine met more of Clay's relatives and spent the appropriate amount of time with each. Then she found time to move off by herself and seek out her mother, and Uncle Frank and Aunt Ella. The evening was moving inexorably toward its close, and with each passing minute Catherine's apprehension grew.

Standing with Bobbi in the living room, Catherine caught sight of Clay out in the foyer. He stood with a remarkably beautiful girl whose auburn hair trailed down to the middle of her back. She cradled a champagne glass as if she were born with it in her hand. She smiled up at Clay, gyrated her head as if to toss her hair back. But it fell alluringly across her cheek. Then the girl circled Clay's neck with the arm bearing the stem glass, raising her lips to his and kissing him differently than any of the starry-eyed girls from Horizons had. Catherine observed the somber look upon Clay's face as he spoke to the girl, dropping his eyes to the floor, then raising them to her face again with a look of apology etching his every feature. Catherine would have been lying to herself had she not admitted that the touch he gave the girl's upper arm was a caress. He spoke into her eyes, rubbed that arm, then gave it a lingering squeeze before he bent to drop an unhurried kiss upon the crest of one flawless, high-boned cheek.

Quickly Catherine turned her back. But the picture rankled until something pinched at her throat and made it hard to swallow the champagne she lifted to her lips.

"Who is that girl out there with Clay?"

Bobbi glanced toward the foyer and her smile immediately faded.

"It's her, isn't it?" Catherine questioned. "It's Jill Magnusson."

Bobbi turned her back on the couple too quickly. "Yes, it is. So what?"

"Nothing."

But try as she might, Catherine could not resist looking their way again to find Clay now relaxed, one hand in his trouser pocket while Jill threaded her arm through his and rested her breast leisurely against his biceps. She was the kind of girl who could get by with a touch like that. Her sophistication made it look chic instead of shabby. An older man had joined them now and Jill Magnusson laughed, leaned sideways without relinquishing her claim on Clay and gave the older man a swift kiss on the side of his mouth.

"And who's he?" Catherine asked, carefully keeping the ice from her tone.

"That's Jill's father."

There was a sick and empty feeling settling in the pit of Catherine's stomach. She wished she hadn't witnessed Jill leaning casually against Clay in the presence of her own father, nor her obvious lack of unease at kissing Clay with an arm looped around his neck. But Catherine was in for a further surprise, for even as she looked on, Elizabeth Forrester approached the group and it was immediately apparent that Jill Magnusson was as comfortable with the old eagle as she was with the champagne glass and Catherine's new husband. The unapproachable old woman didn't daunt Jill one bit. The brunette actually linked her remaining arm through Elizabeth's, laughing gracefully at whatever Clay's grandmother said. Then—unbelievably—the old eagle laughed too.

And Catherine finally turned away.

At that moment Clay's eyes drifted up, found Bobbi observing the quartet, and immediately he withdrew his hand from his pocket, excused himself and crossed toward her and Catherine.

"Jill and her parents were just leaving," he explained. It became apparent as soon as the words left his mouth that explanations should not have been necessary. They had not been for the other guests who'd already departed.

"Somehow it seems that Catherine was not introduced to the Magnussons."

"Oh . . . I'm sorry, Catherine. I should have seen to it." He glanced uncertainly from Catherine to the front door. But it was opening. Angela and Mrs. Magnusson were touching cheeks fondly while the two men shook hands, and Jill gave a long, last look across the expanse that separated her from Clay. Then they were gone.

"Catherine . . ." Clay began, but realizing Bobbi was still there, said, "Excuse us, will you, Bobbi?" He took Catherine's elbow and moved her beyond earshot. "I think it's time we left."

Certainly, now that Jill Magnusson is gone, thought Catherine. "But shouldn't we thank your parents first?"

"I've done that already. Now we're expected to simply slip away unnoticed."

"But what about the gifts?" She was grasping at straws and she knew it.

"They'll be left here. We're not expected to thank anyone for them tonight. We're only supposed to disappear while they're busy."

"Mom will be wondering . . ." she began lamely, looking around.

"Will she?" Clay could see how nervous Catherine had suddenly become. "Steve is with her. He'll see that she gets home okay."

Catherine saw Ada in happy conversation with Bobbi's parents and Steve. Catherine raised her glass to her lips, but found it empty. Then Clay removed it from her lifeless fingers, saying, "Slip upstairs and get your coat and I'll meet you by the side door. And don't forget the key."

Once more in the pink bedroom, Catherine at last allowed her shoulders to sag. She plopped down on the edge of the gay little bed, then leaned back and let her eyelids close wearily. She wished this were her own room, that she could snuggle in and awaken in the morning to find that no wedding had taken place after all. Absently she picked up a small pillow, toyed with the ruffled edge, staring until the design on it seemed to wriggle. She blinked, tossed the pillow aside and went to stand before the cheval mirror. She pressed her dress against her lower abdomen, visually measuring. She raised her eyes and stared at the reflected face, wondering how it could be so pink when she felt so bloodless. From the depths of the silvered glass, blue eyes watched her fingertips touch one cheek, then flutter down uncertainly to her lips. Her brows wore a troubled look as she assessed her own reflection and found countless imperfections in it.

"Jill Magnusson," she whispered. Then she turned and flung her coat loosely about her shoulders.

Outside the world wore that semi-dark glow of the first snow of the season, glittering almost as if from within. The night sky looked as though someone had spilled milk across it, obscuring the moon behind a film of white. But as if a droplet slipped off now and then, an occasional snowflake drifted down. The lights from the windows twinkled playfully upon the white frosting, and the leafless limbs of the trees looked warm now beneath their blankets. The air was brittle, though, brittle enough to freeze the tender petals of the gardenia forgotten in Catherine's hair.

Catherine clutched her coat beneath her chin, raised her face and sucked in the taste of the cold. Revitalized, she hurried through the shadows to the end of the house near the garages. It was quiet. Not even the hum of distant traffic intruded, and she savored it, trying to make it calm her.

"Sorry it took so long."

She jumped at the sound of Clay's voice and clutched her coat tighter. He materialized out of the darkness, a tall shadow with its coat collar turned up. "I got caught by a few well-wishers and couldn't get away."

"It's okay." But she drew her mouth down within the protective folds of her coat.

"Here, you're freezing." He touched her back, steered her toward a strange, dark car that waited there. Even in the blackness she could see that it had streamers trailing from it. He opened the driver's side door.

"Have you got the key?" he asked.

"The key?" she asked dumbly.

"Yes, the key." He smiled with only one side of his mouth. "I'll drive tonight, but after this, it's yours."

"M-mine?" she stammered, uncertain of which to look to for verification, the car or his face.

"Happy wedding day, Catherine," he said simply.

"The key was for this?"

"I thought you'd like a wagon, for groceries and things like that."

"But, Clay . . ." She was shivering worse now, the tremors quite pronounced in spite of the way she hugged herself into the coat.

"Have you got the key?"

"Clay, this isn't fair," she pleaded.

"All's fair in love and war."

"But this is not love or war. How can I just . . . just say 'Thank you, Mr. Forrester' and drive off in a brand new car as if I have every right to it?"

"Don't you?"

"No! It's too much and you know it."

"The Corvette isn't exactly a family car," he reasoned. "We'd have trouble getting even the wedding gifts to the town house in it."

"Well, fine, then, trade it in or—or borrow the Bronco again, but don't hand me the world on a platter that I feel guilty to eat from."

His hand dropped from the car door; his voice sounded slightly piqued.

"It's a gift. Why do you have to make so much of it? I can afford it, and it will make our lives infinitely easier to have two cars. Besides, Tom Magnusson owns an auto dealership and we get great deals from him on all the cars we buy."

Common sense returned with a cold swipe. "Well, in that case, thank you."

Catherine got in and slid across to the passenger side. He got behind the wheel to find her leg angled across the transmission hump, her skirt pulled up. She produced the key from within her garter and handed it to him.

It was warm in his palm.

He seemed a little ill at ease as he started the engine, but let it idle. He adjusted the heater, cleared his throat. "Catherine, I don't know how to say this, but it seems we each got a key tonight. I got one too."

"From whom?"

"From Mother and Father."

She waited, trembling inside.

"It's for the honeymoon suite at the Regency."

She made a sound like air going out of a balloon, then moaned, "Oh, God."

"Yes, oh, God," he agreed, then laughed nervously.

"What are we going to do?" she asked.

"What do you want to do?"

"I want to go to the town house."

"And let the Regency phone tomorrow and ask why the bride and groom didn't show up?"

She sat silent, shaking.

"Catherine?"

"Well, couldn't we . . . couldn't we just"—she swallowed—"check in and leave again and go to the town house, maybe leave the key for them to find in the morning?"

"Do you want me to go back into the house and pick up a load of gifts and hope we find some sheets and blankets when we open them?"

He was right; they were trapped.

"Catherine, this is adolescent. We've just gotten married and we've agreed to spend the next several months living together. You realize that we're going to bump into each other now and then during that time, don't you?"

"Yes, but not in any honeymoon suite at the Regency." Still she knew that before the night was out they'd have put the lie to her words.

"Catherine, what the hell did you expect me to do, stuff the keys back into my father's hand and say 'Use them yourselves'?"

There was no point in arguing. They sat there thinking until finally Clay put the car in reverse, and backed away from the shadow of the garage.

"Clay, I don't have my suitcase!" she gulped.

"It's in the back with mine," he said, while the doorman grew small behind them, his arms folded and his collar turned up.

They drove along in silence, Catherine still gripping her coat although the car had long since grown warm. The smell of new, hot oil mingled with that of new vinyl. With each mile Catherine grew tighter.

Finally she said, "Why does it seem like everything important that happens between us happens in one of your cars?"

"It's one of the few places we've ever been alone."

"Well, your parents sure took care of that, didn't they?"

With an abrupt swerve he pulled to the side of the road, skidded to a halt and craned to look back over his shoulder.

She perked alert. "Now what?"

He was already turning around. "You want to go to the town house, okay, we'll go to the town house," he snapped.

She clutched his arm. "Don't," she pleaded. "Don't, not tonight."

He brooded silently, tense now too.

"I was wrong, okay?" she conceded. "Just don't drive crazy—not tonight. I know they meant well to get the room for us, and you're right. What difference does it make where we sleep?" she dropped her hand from his arm. "Please try to understand, though. It's been a nerve-wracking night. I'm not used to lavishness."

"Maybe you better get used to it, because they never do anything halfway."

He drove on more sensibly now.

"How much do you imagine it cost them to arrange all that?"

"Don't let it bother you. Mother loved it all. I've told you before, she's in her element planning things like that. Couldn't you tell how she was enjoying her success?"

"Is that supposed to ease my conscience?" she asked.

"Catherine, are we going to go through this every time we get something from them? Why do you constantly berate yourself? Had it occurred to you that maybe you're not the only one benefiting from our arrangement? It may surprise you to learn that I'm actually quite happy to be moving away from home. I should have done it years ago, but it was easier to stay where I was. It's not exactly a hardship being coddled and taken care of. But I'm tired of living with them. I'm glad to be getting out. I wonder if they aren't equally relieved to have me leave at last.

"And as for my parents—don't think they didn't get something out of that production number. Did you see my father's face when he was brandishing his champagne glass? Did you see Mother when she was directing waiters around, watching while everything slipped into place like greased gears? They get high off social success, so just think of it as another autumn gala thrown by the Forresters. They throw one quite like it several times a year anyway.

"What I'm trying to say is, that it's their style. Giving us the night at the Regency is what their friends expect them to do, plus—"

"Plus what?" She shot him a look.

"Plus, giving us the right start gives them a false sense of security. It helps them believe everything will turn out right between us."

"And you don't feel guilty to accept any of it?"

"Yes, dammit!" he burst out. "But I'm not going to go out and buy a hair shirt over it, all right?"

His belligerence surprised her, for he'd been mellow for days. They arrived at the Regency in strained silence. Catherine made a move toward her door handle and Clay ordered, "Wait here until I get the suitcases out."

He walked around the car, yanking the crepe paper streamers off. His breath formed a pale pink cloud, refracting the glow from the colorful hotel sign and the lights at the entry. He opened the tailgate, and she heard the muffled swish as he tossed the streamers in.

When he opened her door and she'd stepped out, he reached for her arm. "Catherine, I'm sorry I yelled. I'm nervous too."

She studied his odd-colored visage in the neon night, but she could find nothing to reply.

Chapter 19

THE PORTER FLOURISHED his hand toward the room and Catherine followed it with her eyes. It felt as though she were couched in a Wedgwood teacup. The room was elegant and tasteful, decorated exclusively in oyster white and Wedgwood blue. The cool blue walls were trimmed with pearly moldings done in beadwork, arranged in rectangles with a carved acanthus centered in each. The design was repeated on two sets of double doors which led to closet and bath. Elegant white silk draperies were crowned by an ornate swagged valance while alabaster French Provincial furniture contrasted soothingly with the room's plush blue carpeting. Besides the enormous bed there was a pleasant grouping of furniture: a pair of chairs and coffee table of Louis XVI persuasion, with graceful cabriole legs and oval, marble tops. On the table sat a profuse bouquet of white roses whose scent was thick in the air.

When the door closed, leaving them alone, Catherine approached the flowers, found the tiny green envelope and turned questioningly to Clay.

"I don't know, open it," he said.

The card read simply, "All our love, Mother and Dad."

"It's from your parents." She extended the card, then sidled a safe distance away while he read it.

"Nice," he murmured, and stuck the card back into the roses. He pushed back his jacket and scanned the room with hands akimbo. "Nice," he repeated.

"More than nice," she seconded, "more like smashing."

Upon the triple dresser was a basket of fruit and a silver loving cup bearing a green glass bottle. Clay walked over, lifted the bottle, read the label, set it back down, then turned, tugging the knot from his bow tie and unfastening a single button of his shirt. Her eyes flew off in another direction. She walked over and gave a careful peek into the depths of the darkened bathroom.

"Can I hang up your coat for you?" he asked.

She looked surprised to find it still crumpled between her wrist and hip. "Oh—oh, sure."

He came to reach for her garment and again she retreated a step.

"Don't be skittish," he said laconically, "I'm only going to hang up your coat."

"I'm not skittish. I just don't know what to do with myself, that's all."

He opened the closet doors, spoke at the tinging hangers inside.

"I'd call that skittish. Maybe a glass of champagne would help. Do you want one?" He hung up his tux jacket too.

"I don't think so." But she wandered back to the dresser anyway and looked over the bottle and the basket. "Who is the fruit from?"

"The management. You want some? How about a last pear of the season?" A tan hand reached around her and hefted one.

"No, no pears either. I'm not hungry."

As she drifted away he tossed the fruit in the air once, twice, then forgot it in his hand, studying her.

"No champagne, no fruit, so what would you like to do to pass the time away?"

She looked up blankly, standing there in the middle of the room as if afraid to come into contact with any article in it. He sighed, dropped the pear back into the basket and moved to carry their suitcases across to the bed.

"Well, we're here, so we might as well make the best of it."

He stalked to the bathroom door, flicked on the light, then turned, gesturing toward it.

"Would you like to be first?"

And the next thing Catherine knew, she was laughing! It started as a silent flutter in her throat and before she could control it, it erupted and she had both hands over her mouth before she flung them wide and continued laughing to the ceiling. At last she looked across to find Clay—the corners of his eyes crinkled now—still waiting just outside the bathroom doorway.

"Come on, hey, wife, I'm trying to be gallant and it's getting tougher by the minute."

And suddenly the tension was relieved.

"Oh, Clay, if your father could see us, I think he'd demand his money back. Are we really in the honeymoon suite of the Regency?"

"I think so." Gamely, he looked around, checking.

"And did you just sign our names in the register as Mr. and Mrs. Clay Forrester?"

"I think so."

She looked up as if appealing to the heavens. "Help, I'm floundering."

"You should do that more often, you know?" He smiled her way.

"Do what, flounder?" She chuckled and made a hapless motion.

"No, laugh. Or even smile. I was beginning to think you were going to wear your stiff face all night long."

"Do I have a stiff face?" It looked mobile and amazed as she asked.

"Stiff might not be the right word. Deadpan is probably more accurate. Yes, deadpan. You put it on like armor at times."

"I do?"

"Mostly when we're alone."

"So you'd like it if I smiled more?"

He shrugged. "Yeah, I guess I would. I like smilers. I guess I'm used to being around them."

"I'll try to remember." She glanced toward the window, then back at him. "Clay, what you said down there in the car, well, I'm sorry, too." Her face had turned suddenly serious, contrite.

"No, it was me who got short with you. My timing really stunk."

"No, listen, it was partly my fault too. I don't want us to fight all the time we're married. I've been around it all my life and now I simply want . . . well, *peace* between us. I know this sounds silly, but it feels better already, just admitting that we're nervous, instead of the way we were acting on the way over here. I want you to know that I'll try to do my part to maintain some kind of status quo."

"Good. Me too. We're stuck with each other for better or for worse, so let's make the better of it instead of the worse."

She smiled a little. "Agreed. So . . . me first, huh?"

They both looked at the bathroom door.

"Yup."

What the heck, she thought, it's only a regular old bathroom, right? And I'm choking in this dress, right? And dying to get comfortable, right?

But once inside the bathroom she was too aware of his presence just outside. She turned on the faucet to cover any personal sounds. She kept glancing furtively at the doors. She confronted herself in the mirror, moving close to analyze her reflection until her breath beaded on the glass.

"Mrs. Clay Forrester, huh?" she asked her reflection. "Well, don't go getting ideas. He told you once you don't play around without paying for it, and he was right. So put on your nightie and go out there and clamber into bed with him, and if you're uncomfortable doing it, you've got nobody to blame but yourself."

Her fingers trembled as she undressed. She stared herself down with too-wide eyes as she removed her velvet wedding gown, then the slip and that ridiculously minuscule bra. Her breasts were weightier now, the nipples broad and florid. At their sudden release, dull twinges of ache flowed through them —not pain exactly, but something akin to it—and she closed her eyes and cupped one in each hand, squeezing and lifting in that way which lately could abate those unexpected throes. Once the pangs were gone came the relief of being unbound. She watched herself scratch the red marks where her bra had bitten too tightly at the top of her ribs, then her stomach, which felt like the head of a drum and itched mercilessly now as the skin began stretching.

Unbidden the thought came that the man who waited on the other side of the door had created these changes in her body.

She shook off the thought, brushed her teeth, ran warm water and soaped a cloth. But just as she was about to scrub off her makeup, it struck her that her face had many shortcomings which would be emphasized without the makeup, so she left it on.

She threw up her arms and a yellow nightgown drifted down like a parachute in the wind, followed by a matching peignoir. Her hands slowed, tying the cover-up at her throat. It was so obviously new. Would he mistake her reason for wearing such frillery? Should she march out there and announce that Ada had bought it at the company store at an employee's discount and had given it to her for a shower gift?

Through the peignoir her new girth was disguised, and she soothed the front, thoughts skittering from one to another. She was putting off opening the door and she knew it. She closed her eyes and swallowed . . . and swallowed again . . . and felt a hidden tremor deep within her stomach.

Suddenly the memory of Jill Magnusson was there in full color behind her eyelids and Catherine knew beyond a doubt that had it been Jill here getting ready to join Clay, there would be no schoolgirl shyness.

She supposed Clay was wishing right now she *were* Jill Magnusson. A hint of self-pity threatened, but she barred it. She remembered that last, long look of regret on Jill's face as she looked back across the room at Clay before walking out the door.

At last Catherine admitted, I carry his child. But it should be her, not me.

The door was soundless. Clay stood with his back to her, gazing down into her open suitcase, his tie forgotten in one hand, toothbrush in the other.

"Your turn," she said quietly, expecting him to jump guiltily. Instead he looked over his shoulder and smiled. His eyes made one quick trip down and up the yellow peignoir.

"Feel better?"

He had pulled his shirttails out of his trousers. Her eyes went down to them like metal shavings to a magnet, to the network of wrinkles pressed into the fabric by his skin. Then farther down, to his stocking feet.

"Much."

They exchanged places and Clay moved into the bathroom, leaving the door open while he only brushed his teeth. In the suitcase, Catherine found a corner of her diary showing beneath the neatly folded clothing there. She tucked it away and closed the suitcase with a snap.

"Are you tired?" he asked, coming back from the bathroom.

"Not a bit."

"Do you mind if I break into that champagne then?"

"No, go ahead. It might help after all."

When his back was turned, she tugged at the top of her neckline; it was far from seductive, but not quite demure. His shoulders flexed and twisted as he worked away at the cork, and the wrinkles on the rear tails of his shirt did incredible things to her stomach, hanging free that way, shifting against his buttocks with each movement. The cork exploded and he swung the bottle over the loving cup.

"Here," he said, coming back with bottle in one hand, glasses in the other. She held the glasses while he poured. But his shirt was unbuttoned all the way now, exposing a thin band of skin a slightly deeper shade than the fabric itself. She dragged her eyes back to the champagne glasses, to the tan, long-fingered hand that reached out to reclaim one.

"To your happiness," he said simply, in his Clay-like, polite, usual way, while she wondered just what would make her happy right now.

"And to yours."

They drank, standing there in the middle of the room. There was a lump in her throat, she realized, as she swallowed the golden liquid. She looked down into her glass.

"Clay, I don't want either of us to pretend this is something it isn't." Rattled now, she put a palm to her forehead and swung away. "Oh, God."

"Come on, Catherine, let's sit down."

He led the way, set the bottle on the table beside the roses and strung himself out on a chair, lying low against its back, legs outstretched, ankles crossed, while she curled up opposite. He had a glimpse of her bare feet before she tucked them up beneath her in the corner of her chair. Together they raised their glasses, eyeing each other as they drank.

"I suppose maybe we're setting out to get drunk," she mused.

"Maybe we are."

"That doesn't make much sense, does it?"

"Not a lick."

"It won't change a thing."

"Nuh-uh."

"Then why are we doing it?"

"Because it'll make crawling into bed easier."

"Let's talk about something else."

"Whatever you say."

She fiddled with her glass, then sat back, drawing circles with it upon her turned knee. Finally she asked, "You know what was the hardest?" Across the table, he was looking very relaxed.

"Hmm-mmm." His eyes were closed.

"Your father's official welcome at the dinner table. I was very touched by it."

Clay's eyes drifted open, studied her a moment before he observed, "You know, I think my father likes you."

With a fingertip she toyed with the bubbles on the surface of her drink. "He still scares me in so many ways."

"I suppose to a stranger he seems formidable. Both he and Granдmother Forrester have an air about them that seems rather officious and puts people on their guard at first. But when you get to know them, you realize they're not that way at all."

"I don't intend to get to know them."

"Why?"

She raised expressionless eyes to his, then dropped them as she answered, "In the long run that'd be best."

"Why?"

His head lolled sideways, yet she suspected his catlike pose was not all real. She considered evading the issue, then decided against it. She leaned to take one rose from the bouquet and held it before her upper lip.

"Because I might learn to like them after all."

He seemed to be mulling that over, but he only tipped his glass again, then shut his eyes.

"Do you know what your Grandmother Forrester said to me tonight?"

"What?"

"She said, 'You are a beautiful bride. I shall expect beautiful children from you,' as if it was an official edict and she'd brook no ugly grandchildren spawned with her name."

Clay laughed appreciatively, his eyes again scrutinizing Catherine from behind half-closed lids. "Grandmother's usually right—and you were, you know."

"Was?" she asked, puzzled.

"A beautiful bride."

Immediately Catherine hid behind the rose again, became engrossed in studying the depths between its petals.

"I didn't know if I should say it or not, but—dammit, why not?—you were a knockout tonight."

"I wasn't fishing for a compliment."

"You make a habit of that, you know?"

"Of what?"

"Of withdrawing from any show of approval I make toward you. I knew before I said that that you'd turn defensive and reject it."

"I didn't reject it, did I?"

"You didn't accept it either. All I said was that you were a beautiful bride. Does that threaten you?"

"I—I don't know what you mean."

"Forget it then."

"No, you brought it up, let's finish it. Why should I feel threatened?"

"You're the one who's supposed to answer that question."

"But I'm not *threatened* in the least." She swished her rose through the air offhandedly. "You were a terrific-looking groom. There, see? Does that sound like I feel threatened by you?"

But her very tone was defensive. It reminded him of a child who, taking up a dare, says, "See? I'm not either afraid to walk up and ring Crazy Gertie's doorbell," then rings it and runs to beat hell.

"Hey, what do you think," he said in a bantering tone, "are we supposed to thank each other or what?"

That at last drew a smile from her. She relaxed a little as if maybe the wine were now making her sleepy.

"Do you know what your mother said to me?" Clay asked.

"What?"

He mused silently, as if deciding whether or not to tell her. Abruptly he leaned forward and occupied himself with refilling his glass. "She said, 'Catherine used to play wedding when she and Bobbi were little girls. That's all those two would play, always arguing about who'd be the bride.'" Then he lounged back again, propped an elbow on the arm of the chair, rested his temple against two fingers and asked lazily, "Did you?"

"What does it matter?"

"I was only wondering, that's all."

"Well, don't wonder. It doesn't matter."

"Doesn't it?"

But abruptly she changed the subject. "One of your uncles mentioned that you usually go hunting at this time of year but that you haven't had much chance this year because of the wedding interruptions."

"It must've been Uncle Arnold."

"Don't change the subject."

"Did I change the subject?"

"You can go, you know, anytime you want."

"Thank you, I will."

"I mean, we're not *bound* to each other, and nothing has to change. We can still go our separate ways, keep our friends, just like before."

"Great. Agreed, Stu and I will hunt all we want."

"I wasn't really thinking about Stu."

"Oh?" He quirked an eyebrow.

"I was talking about her."

"Her? Who?"

"Jill."

Clay's eyes turned to gray iron, then he jumped up, stalked to the dresser and clapped his glass down hard. "What has Jill got to do with it?"

"I saw you standing in the foyer together. I saw the two of you kissing. I include her when I say you're not bound to me in any way."

He swung around, scowling. "Listen, our families have been friends for years. We've been—" He stopped himself before he could say *lovers.* "I've known her since we were kids. And furthermore, her father was right there in front of us, and so was Grandmother Forrester, for God's sake."

"Clay"—Catherine's voice was like eiderdown—"I said it's all right."

He glared at her silently, then swung toward his suitcase, shrugging his shirt off as he went, flinging it carelessly across the foot of the bed before disappearing behind the bathroom door.

When Clay returned, Catherine was sitting on the far edge of the bed with her back to him. The wilted gardenia lay discarded on the bedside table while she brushed her hair. His eyes traveled across the white satin sheets to the robe lying on the foot of the bed, to the back of her pale yellow nightgown, to the brush moving rhythmically. Without a word, he doubled his pillow over and lay down with both hands behind his head. The brush stilled. He heard her thumbnail flicking across its bristles, followed by a clack as she laid the thing down. She reached for the lamp and the room went black. The mattress shifted; the covers over his chest were pulled slightly in her direction. He had no doubt that if he reached out, he'd find her back curled against him.

Their breathing seemed amplified. Sightlessness created such intimacy. Clay lay so rigid that his shoulders began to hurt. Catherine huddled like a snail, involute, acutely aware of him behind her. She thought she could hear her eyelids scraping on her dry eyeballs with each blink. She shivered and pinioned the satin sheet tightly between her jaw and shoulder.

A rustle, barely audible, and she sensed his eyes boring into her back—invisible though it was.

"Catherine," came his voice, "you really have a low opinion of me, don't you?"

"Don't sound so wounded. There's no reason to be. Just to keep the record straight—it should have been her who was the bride today. Do you think I don't know that? Do you think I couldn't tell how she *belongs?* I felt like a square peg in a round hole. And seeing you and her together brought me back to reality. I was becoming rather swept off my feet by all the lavish trappings around me. I'll answer your question now. Yes, I did used to play wedding with Bobbi when we were kids. I'm an old pro at weddings, so this time I found myself really getting into the act. But I'm not pretending anymore. I see things for what they really are, okay?"

Goddammit, thought Clay, I should thank her for giving me permission, but instead it makes me angry. Goddammit, I shouldn't feel like I have to be faithful to a wife, but I do.

Catherine felt the bed bounce as he tossed onto his side and punched his pillow.

Somewhere outside a jet went over, its faraway whine and whistle ebbing off into oblivion. The bed was very large; neither of them had much sensation of sharing it physically, except for the sound of their breathing, far away from each other and in opposite directions. But the animosity between them was a much more palpable presence. It seemed like hours had gone by and Catherine thought Clay had gone to sleep. But then he flung himself onto his back again so abruptly she was sure he'd been wide awake all this time. She was stiff and cramped from staying in her tight curl for so long, but she refused to budge. Her shoulder got a cramp and she had to relax it. The sheet slipped off, and at last giving up, she eased onto her back.

"Are we going to get in each other's hair this way every time bedtime arrives?" he asked coldly.

"I didn't mean to get into your hair."

"Like hell you didn't. Let's at least be honest about it. You meant to bring a third party into bed with us and you succeeded very well. But just remember, if she's here it's at your request, not mine."

"Then why do you sound so angry?"

"Because it's playing havoc with my sleep. If I have to go through this for the next year, I'll be a burned-out wreck."

"So what do you think I'll be?"

Against his will, as he lay brooding, Clay had been resurrecting pictures of Catherine at the ceremony. The way she looked when she'd come around the living room doorway, when they spoke their vows, when she'd discovered all the girls from Horizons there, when he'd kissed her. He remembered the feel of her slightly rounded stomach against his. This was the damnedest thing he'd ever been through, going to bed with a woman and not touching her. All the more absurd because for the first time it'd be legal, and here he lay on his own side of the bed. Dammit, he thought, I should've watched the champagne. Champagne made him horny.

He finally concluded that they were being quite childish about all this. They were husband and wife, they'd been through some decidedly sexual teasing during the course of the evening and were now trying to deny what it was that was keeping them both awake.

What the hell, he thought, things couldn't be worse. "Catherine, do you want to try it again, with no strings attached? Maybe then we can get some sleep."

The muscles in her lower abdomen cinched up tight and set to quivering. She shrank to her side of the bed, turning her back on him again.

"The wine has gone to your head" was all she said.

"Well, what the hell, you can't blame a guy for trying."

She felt like her chest bones might burst and fly into a thousand pieces. Angry with herself for wishing the night to be more than it was, angry with him for his suggestion, she wondered what exquisite torture it would be to turn to him and take him up on his invitation.

But she remained as she was, curled into herself. In the long hours before sleep she wondered over and over again if he had any pajamas on.

Chapter 20

CATHERINE WAS AWAKENED by the sound of draperies opening. She sat up as if a hundred-and-twenty-piece band had struck up a Sousa march beside her bed. Clay stood in the flood of sunlight, laughing.

"Do you always wake up like that?"

She squinted and blinked, then flopped backward like an old rag doll, covering her eyes with a forearm.

"Oh God, so you *did* have pajamas on."

He laughed again, free and easy, and turned toward the view of the awakening city washed in pink and gold below them.

"Does that mean 'good morning'?"

"That means I wasted a perfectly good night worrying about a dumb thing like whether or not you were wearing pajamas."

"Next time just ask."

Suddenly she was pulling herself off the bed, and running for the bathroom door which thwacked shut behind her.

"Don't listen!" she ordered.

Clay leaned an elbow against the window frame, chuckling to himself, thinking of the unexpected charms of married life.

She came out looking sheepish and went immediately for her cover-up.

"I'm sorry if I was a little abrupt about that, but this little feller in here has made some sudden changes and that's one of them. I'm still not used to it."

"Does this confidence mean you're not mad at me anymore?"

"Was I mad at you? I don't seem to remember." She busied herself doing up the front of the garment.

"Yeah," he said, moving away from the window, "I made some underhanded suggestion and you got huffy."

"Forget it. Let's be friends. I don't like fighting much, even with you."

He confronted her now, barechested, giving her hair the once-over so that she started combing it with her fingers.

"Listen," she explained, "I'm not at my best in the morning."

"Who is?" he returned, rubbing his jaw. Then he turned toward a suitcase and rummaged inside it, beginning to whistle softly through his teeth. Mornings she was used to her mother scuffling around the house with an air of martyrdom and tiredness as if the day were ending rather than beginning. And the old man, with his belching and scratching, drinking coffee royals and muttering imprecations under his breath.

But this was something new: a man who whistled before breakfast.

He stopped on his way to the bathroom, holding a leather case of toilet articles.

"What do you say we get dressed and find some breakfast, then go out to the house and pick up the gifts."

"I'm starved. I never did finish my dinner last night."

"And you're not the only one who's hungry?" He dropped his gaze briefly to her stomach. She was contouring it with both hands.

"No, I'm not."

"Then let me buy you both breakfast."

She colored and turned away, realizing she liked the morning Clay.

When the shower was splattering away she dropped down onto the bed again, fell back supine in the sun, thinking of how different Clay seemed this morning. She even enjoyed his teasing. She heard the bar of soap drop, then a muffled exclamation, then light whistling again. She remembered him turning from that window with those coolielike pajamas hanging so tentatively low on his hips, and the thin line of red-gold hair sparkling its way down the center of his stomach. She groaned and rolled over and cradled her face in the L of an arm and the sun crept over her in warm fingers of gold and she fell asleep, waiting there that way, as pregnant women are prone to do.

He came into the bedroom wearing pajama bottoms and a towel slung around his neck. He smiled at the sight that greeted him. She lay there sprawled luxuriously and he studied the way the yellow fabric followed the contours of her shoulders, back, buttocks, the one knee drawn up, the other with its bare foot dangling over the edge of the bed.

In daylight, he decided, she was much more amiable. He'd enjoyed their little repartee upon waking.

He looked around, spied the roses, nabbed one and began tickling the sole of her foot with it. The toes curled tight, then the foot rotated on the ankle irritably. Then it kicked him in the knee and she laughed into the bedclothes.

"Cut it out," she scolded, "I told you I'm not at my best in the morning. I have an ugly disposition until almost noon."

"And here I was thinking how nice you were before."

"I'm a bear."

"What are you doing here? You're supposed to be getting ready for breakfast."

She looked at him with one cheek and an eye lost in the blankets.

"I was just catching a catnap."

"A catnap—when you just got up?"

"Well, it's your fault."

"Oh, yeah? What'd I do now?"

"Dunce. Pregnant ladies tend to sleep a lot, I told you that before." She reached backward and waggled her fingers. "Gimme."

He put the rose in her hand, and she sniffed it—one deep, long exaggerated pull—then rolled over and said to the ceiling, "Morning has broken." And without another word went to bathe and dress.

Catherine could see that her greatest adversary was normalcy. Clay, being well-adjusted, intended to forge ahead as if their marriage were ordinary. But she, herself, was constantly on guard against the compelling gravity of the commonplace. That first day gave her glimpses of what life with Clay could be like if things were different.

They arrived at the Forresters' through the high sun of the November afternoon which had melted away all but a few hints of last night's snows. The doorman was gone now—it was just an ordinary house again. Squirrels, much the color of the lawns, chittered and chased, still on the search for winter stores. A nuthatch darted from one of the festoons beside the door where it had been dining on bearded wheat.

And as it always could, the home welcomed.

They caught Claiborne and Angela nestled together on the loveseat like a pair of mated mallards while the Minnesota Vikings radiated from the screen. There were the inevitable touches of greeting, in which Catherine was now included. They opened most of the gifts together—the four of them—with time out for instant replays, and for teasing Catherine about her ignorance of the game. Sitting on fat pillows on the floor, Catherine and Clay laughed over a grotesque cookie jar that looked like it belonged in a Swahili kitchen instead of an American town house. And she learned that Clay's favorite cookies were chocolate chip. They opened a waffle iron and she learned that he preferred pancakes. Halftime highlights came on and she learned he disliked the Chicago Bears. Angela made sandwiches and Claiborne said, "Here, open this one next," with a surprising giddiness, now that the game was over.

And amid a mound of used wrappings Catherine felt herself being sucked into the security of this family.

In the late afternoon they piled their loot into the cars and drove to the place they'd now call home. She met Clay at the door and watched as he set down his load and bent to put the key in the lock. Her arms were full of gift boxes overflowing with excelsior, and she peered around, watching him pocket the key.

The door swung open and before she knew what was happening he had turned and deftly scooped up the whole works—wife, excelsior, boxes and all.

"Clay!"

"I know, I know. Put me down, right?"

But she only laughed while he floundered, acting like his legs had turned to rubber, and collapsed onto the steps with her in his lap.

"In the movies somehow the wife never has a paunch," he teased, leaning his elbows back on the steps behind them.

She scowled, called him a very nasty name, then felt herself being pushed from his lap. "Get off me, paunchy."

The apartment lay steeped in late afternoon dusk, silent, waiting. As they stood surveying the living room, it seemed to beckon with the intimacy of a lover about to shed her clothes: new furniture, still wearing tags and dust wrappers, waited—stacked, leaning, unassembled. Lamps with their bases encased in padding lay upon the davenport while their shades waited on the floor in plastic sleeves. Barstools and tables stood about. Pieces of bed frame lay beside the mattress and the box spring leaned against the wall. Boxes and suitcases which they'd brought earlier were stacked on the counter, strewn about the room.

The moment held a poignance that took away their laughter and made them wistful for a moment. It all seemed so ironically like the real thing. The reflection of sunset slipped its lavender fingers through the broad expanse of glass, lending an unearthly glow to the place. Catherine felt Clay's hands on her shoulders. She turned to find him startlingly close behind her, his jaw almost colliding with her temple as she swung around.

"Your coat?" he said. She thought there was a tortured expression about his mouth, wondered if he were thinking of Jill Magnusson. But—just that quick —he removed it and in its place was a grin.

They changed into blue jeans and sweatshirts and set to work—she in the kitchen, he in the living room. Again the air of normalcy returned. For Catherine it was like playing house, working away in this place that seemed too good to be true, packing away wedding gifts in the cupboards, listening to the sounds of Clay shoving furniture around. As they worked, evening spun in, and at times she allowed the line between reality and fantasy to blur.

"Come and tell me where you want the davenport," Clay called. She got up from her knees and went to ponder with him, and they arranged the room together.

And once she went laughing, asking, "What in the world do you suppose this thing is?" displaying some odd piece of steel that might have been either sculpture or a meat grinder. They laughingly agreed that it must be a sculpture of a meat grinder and relegated it to a hidden spot behind the tissue box on top of the refrigerator.

And dusk was deep when he appeared in the kitchen, asking, "Are there any lightbulbs anywhere?"

"Shove that box over here; I think it's stuff from the shower."

They found bulbs. A few moments later, still on her knees, she saw lamplight appear over the peninsula of cabinets from the direction of the living room, and smiled when she heard him say, "There, that's more like it."

She'd finished most of the kitchen unpacking and was lining the linen closet shelves as he passed through the hall, carrying pieces of clanging bed rail.

"Watch the wall!" she warned . . . too late. The bed rail dug into the door frame. He shrugged and disappeared with his burden. Next he came through with the headboard, then with a toolbox from his trunk. She began unpacking linens, listening to the sounds coming from the bedroom. She was hanging up new towels in the bathroom when he called, "Catherine, can you come here a minute?"

He was on his knees, trying to hold the headboard and bed rails at right angles while he tightened nuts and bolts—and having one hell of a time.

"Hold that up, will you?"

His hair was messed and curling across his forehead while he concentrated on his work. Holding the metal rails, she felt the vibrations wriggle their way to her palms as he plied the screwdriver.

He finished, and the thing was a square. He put the cross-slats in and stood up, saying, "I'll need a little help getting the mattress up the stairs."

"Sure," she said, uncomfortable now.

On their way up the steps with their ungainly cargo, Clay warned, "Now, just guide it, don't lift it."

She wanted to say, don't be solicitous, but bit her tongue.

And then the bed was a bed, and the room grew quiet. They looked across the short expanse—his hair all ascatter and hers slipping free of the combs with which she'd carelessly slung it behind her ears. He had sweat rings beneath his arms and she had a dust smudge on the end of her right breast. His eyes dropped down to it fleetingly.

"There," he announced, "you can take over from here, okay?"

The new, bare mattress made them both uneasy.

"Sure," she said with affected brightness, "what color sheets would you like? We've got pink with big white daisies or beige with brown stripes or—"

"It doesn't matter," he interrupted, leaning to pick up a screwdriver and drop it in the toolbox. "Make it up to suit yourself. I'll be sleeping out on the davenport."

Catherine was brushing her palms off against one another, and they suddenly fell still. Then he swung from the room. She stood a moment, staring at nothing, then she kicked their brand new box spring and left a black shoe mark on it. She stared at the mark, hands in her jeans pockets. She apologized to the box spring, then took back the apology, then spun and dropped down onto the edge of the unmade bed, suddenly feeling like crying. From the living room came the sound of some bluesy music with soft piano and a husky female voice as he started up the stereo. Finally she quit her moping and made up the bed with crisp, fresh sheets, then decided to put her clothing into the new dresser drawers. She stopped with her hands full of sweaters, and called, "Clay?"

But apparently he couldn't hear her above the music.

She padded silently down the carpeted hall, down the few steps to the living room and found him standing, cowboylike, feet astraddle, thumbs hooked up in his rear pockets, staring out the sliding glass doors.

"Clay?"

He started and looked around. "What?"

"Is it okay if I take the dresser and you take the chest of drawers?"

"Sure," he said tonelessly, "whatever you want." Then he turned back to the window.

The inside of the dresser drawers smelled of new, spicy wood. Everything in the place was so spanking, so untouched, so different from what Catherine was used to. She was struck again with a sense of unreality, simply because of the inanity of what she was doing. But when Catherine considered where she was and what lay around her, she felt as if she were usurping someone else's rightful place, and again the image of Jill popped up.

The sound of a drawer opening brought her from her reverie, and she glanced over her shoulder to find Clay also putting his things away. They moved about the bedroom, doing their separate chores, silent except for an occasional *excuse me* when their proximities warranted. She snapped on the closet light to find he'd brought his hanging clothes over sometime during the week. All his sport coats hung neatly spaced, shirts squarely centered on their hangers, pantlegs meticulously flush and creased. She'd somehow imagined that Inella took care of his clothing, kept it flawless and groomed, and was surprised to find such neat precision all his doing.

The scent he wore lingered in the enclosure, much as it did in his car. She snapped out the light again and turned with her handful of hangers.

"I guess I'll take the closet in the other bedroom if it's okay with you."

"I can push my stuff closer together."

"No, no, it's okay. The other closet's empty anyway."

When she disappeared into the room across the hall, he stared into the drawer he'd been filling in the bureau—contemplating.

A short time later their paths crossed in the living room. Clay was occupied putting away his tapes.

"Listen, are you hungry?" Catherine asked. "We didn't have supper or anything." It was nearly ten P.M.

"Yeah, a little." He continued his sorting, never glancing up.

"Oh, well . . . gee," she stammered, "there's nothing here. We could—"

"Just forget it then. I'm really not very hungry."

"No, we could go out and get a hamburger or something."

He looked up at her stomach. "Oh, you're probably hungry."

"I'm okay."

He sighed, dropped a tape back into the cardboard box where it clacked before the room fell silent. He stared at it, kneeling there with the heels of his hands on his thighs, then shook his head in slow motion. "Aren't we even going to eat together?"

"You're the one who said first you were hungry, then you weren't."

He looked up at her squarely. "Do you want a hamburger?"

She rubbed her stomach with a timorous smile. "Yes, I'm starved."

"Then what do you say we stop playing cat and mouse and go out and get one."

"Okay."

"Let's leave the rest of this stuff for tomorrow night."

"Gladly, and tomorrow I'll get some groceries in the house."

And with that everything seemed better.

The illusion lasted till bedtime. Then, again, they walked on eggshells.

Coming in after their late supper she hurried to remove her coat before he could help her, afraid lest he should inadvertently touch her. He followed her to the living room.

"Feel better?" he asked.

"Yes, I didn't know how hungry I was. We did a lot of work today."

Then they couldn't think of anything else to say. Clay began an exaggerated stretch, twisting at the waist with his elbows in the air.

Panic hit her and made her stomach twitch. Should she simply exit or offer to make up his bed or what?

They both spoke at once.

"Well, we have to get up—"

"Should I get your—"

She flapped her hands nervously, gestured for him to speak, but he gestured for her to speak at the same time.

"I'll get your bedding," she got out.

"Just show me where it is and I'll do it myself."

She avoided his eyes, led the way up the steps to the linen closet. When she started to reach up high he hurriedly offered, "Here, I'll get them down."

He moved too quickly and bumped into her back before she could move aside. He nearly pulled the comforter down on her head. She plucked a package of sheets and another of pillowcases from the shelves and put them on top of the comforter in his arms.

"I saved the brown and beige ones for you."

Their eyes met briefly above the bedding.

"Thanks."

"I'll get your pillow." She fled to do so.

But they had only two pillows, which were both on the king-size bed, already encased in pink-flowered pillow slips. There was some sticky hesitancy as she returned with one, saying she guessed he wouldn't need that other pillowcase she'd given him. And then everything went wrong at once because he reached to take her pillow and the comforter tipped sideways and the plastic-wrapped packages slipped off the top and she lunged to try to catch them and somehow their fingers touched and the whole pile of bedding ended up on the floor at their feet.

He knelt down quickly and began gathering it up while she scuttled back to the security of the bedroom, shut the door and was about to begin changing into her nightgown when he came back for his pajamas. He knocked politely, and she let him pass before her to go in and get them, then shut the door again as he left.

By the time she donned her nightgown her stomach was in knots.

She sat down on the end of the bed, waiting for him to go in and use the bathroom first. But apparently he was sitting downstairs waiting for her to do the same thing. Naturally, they both decided to make the move at once. She was halfway down the hall and he was halfway up the steps when they spied each other headed in the same direction. Catherine's feet turned to stone, but Clay had the presence of mind to simply turn around and retreat. Afterward she closed herself into the bedroom again, climbed into the vast bed and lay there listening to the sounds that the walls couldn't quite hide, picturing Clay in those pajama bottoms as he'd been that morning. The toilet flushed, the water ran, she heard him spit after brushing his teeth.

In the bathroom, Clay studied her wet washcloth hanging on the towel rack, then opened the medicine chest to find her wet toothbrush inside. He laid his next to it, then picked up a bottle of prenatal vitamins, studied its label thoughtfully and returned it to the shelf.

She heard the bathroom light snap off, then he knocked gently on her door. "Catherine?"

Heart clamoring, she answered, "What?"

"What time do you usually get up?"

"Six-thirty."

"Did you set an alarm?"

"No, I haven't got one."

"I'll wake you at six-thirty then."

"Thank you."

She stared at the hole in the dark where the door would be if she could see it.

"Good night then," he said at last.

"Good night."

He put on a tape and the sound of the music filtered through the dark, through her closed door while she tried to erase all thought from her mind and find sleep.

She was still wide awake when the tape finally stopped.

And a long time later when she heard Clay get up in the dark and get a drink of water in the kitchen.

Chapter 21

THE WAY THEY did things the first time usually set the precedent for their routine. Clay used the bathroom first in the mornings; she used it first in the evenings. He got dressed in their bedroom while she was showering, then she got dressed while he put his bedding away. He left the house first, so he opened the garage door; she left second and closed it.

Before leaving that Monday morning he asked, "What time will you get home?"

"Around two-thirty."

"I'll be later by an hour or so, but if you wait I'll go grocery shopping with you."

She couldn't conceal her surprise—it was the last thing she'd expect him to want them to do together. Crisp and combed, he stood in the foyer looking up the steps at her. He put a hand on the doorknob, smiled briefly, raised his free hand and said, "Well, have a good day."

"You too."

When he was gone, she studied the door, remembering his smile, the little wave of good-bye. Juxtaposed against it came the memory of her father, scratching his belly, roaring, "Where the goddam hell is Ada? Does a man hafta make his own coffee around this dump?"

Catherine couldn't forget it all the way to school in her own car, which she kept expecting to turn back into a pumpkin.

It was an odd place to begin falling in love—in the middle of the supermarket —but that's precisely where it began for Catherine. She was still boggled by the fact that he'd come along. Again she tried to picture her father doing the same, but it was too ludicrous to ponder. She was even further dumbfounded by the silliness that sprang up between her and Clay. It had started out with the two of them learning each other's tastes, but had ended on a note of hilarity which would undoubtedly have seemed humorless to anybody else.

"Do you like fruit?" Clay asked.

"Oranges, I crave oranges lately."

"Then we shall have oranges!" he proclaimed dramatically, holding a bag aloft.

"Hey, check how much they cost first."

"It doesn't matter. These look good."

"Of course they look good," she scolded, looking at the price, "you've chosen the most expensive ones in the place."

But when she would have replaced them with cheaper ones, he waggled a finger at her and clucked, "Tut-tut!" Price was no object, he said, when he bought food. And she dropped the oranges back in the cart.

At the dairy case she reached for margarine.

"What are you going to use that for?"

"What do you think, not for a hot oil treatment for my hair."

"And not to feed to me," he said, grinning, and took the margarine from her hands. "I like real butter."

"But it's three times as much!" she exclaimed. Then she reclaimed her margarine and put his butter back in the case.

He immediately switched the two around again.

"Butter is three times as fattening too," she informed him, "and I *do* have an imminent weight problem to consider." He made an affected sideward bow, then put her margarine in the cart next to his butter as they moved on.

She spied a two-gallon jar of ketchup up ahead, and when Clay's back was turned she picked up the ungainly thing and came waddling over with it clutched against her outthrust stomach.

"Here," she puffed, "this should hold you till next week."

He turned around and burst out laughing, then quickly relieved her of the enormous container.

"Hey, what're you trying to do, squash my kid?"

"I know how you like ketchup on your hamburgers," she said innocently. By now they were both laughing.

They wandered along behind their mountain of food, and at the frozen foods she chose orange juice and he, pineapple juice. They took turns laying them in the cart like poker players revealing their next cards.

She played a frozen pumpkin pie.

He played apple.

She drew corn.

He drew spinach.

"What's that?" she asked disgustedly.

"Spinach."

"Spinach! Yuck!"

"What's the matter with spinach? I love it!"

"I hate it. I'd as soon eat scabs!"

He perused the bags and boxes in the display case with a searching attitude. "Mmm, sorry, no scabs for sale here."

By the time they reached the meat counter they were no longer laughing, they were giggling, and people were beginning to stare.

"Do you like Swiss steak?" she asked.

"I love it. Do you like meat loaf?"

"I love it!"

"Well, I hate it. Don't you dare subject me to meat loaf!"

Warming to the game, she just had to trail her fingers threateningly over the packages of hamburger. He eyed her warningly out of the corner of his eye — a buccaneer daring her to challenge his orders.

She picked up the hamburger, weighing it on her palm a time or two, plotting the insidious deed.

"Oh, yeah, lady?" He made his voice silky. "Just try it." He grinned evilly, raking her with his pirate's eyes until she stealthily slipped it back where it had come from.

Next he turned on her, ordering autocratically, "You'd better like pork chops!" He took up a challenging stance, at a right angle to the meat counter, feet apart, one hand on a package of chops, the other on the nonexistent scabbard at his belt. The tile of the floor might very well have been the deck of his windjammer.

"Or else what?" she fairly growled, trying to keep a straight face.

He grew cocky, raised one eyebrow. "Or else"—a quick glance to the side, a hint of a smile before he snatched up a different package and brandished it at her—"we eat liver."

She hooked both thumbs up in her waist, ambled nearer, looked directly into his swashbuckler's handsome, brown face and rasped, "Suits me fine, bucko, I eats my liver rawww!"

He tilted a sardonic brow at the liver.

"More'n likely doesn't know how to cook it."

"The plague take you, I do!"

A twitch pulled at the corners of his lips. He tried to get the words out without snickering, but couldn't quite make it.

"Lucky for you, woman, be . . . cause . . . I . . . don't."

And then the two of them were dissolved in giggles again.

Where Catherine's comic instinct had come from she couldn't guess. She'd never suspected she harbored it. But she warmed to it, found herself lifted in a new, spontaneous way by their levity. Somehow Clay—who she had to admit was charming as a swashbuckler—had given her a glimpse of him that she liked. And a glimpse of herself which she liked, as well. Such bouts of good humor sprang up between them more often after that. She was surprised to find Clay not only humorous, but complaisant and even-tempered. It was the first time in her life that she lived free of the threat of erupting tempers. It was an eye-opener to Catherine to learn it was possible to live in such harmony with a male of the species.

The town house, too, wove its charm about Catherine. At times she would come up short in the middle of some mundane chore and would mentally pinch herself as a reminder not to get too used to it. She would load the dishwasher—or worse yet, watch Clay load it—and remember that in a few short months this would all be snatched away from her. He shared the housework with a singular lack of compunction which surprised Catherine. Maybe it started the night he hooked up the washer and dryer. Together they read the new manuals and figured out the machine settings and loaded the washer with their first bundle of dirty clothes and from then on a load was thrown in by whoever happened to have the time.

She returned home one time to find him vacuuming the living room—the new blankets were linty. She stopped in amazement, a smile on her face. He caught sight of her and turned off the machine.

"Hi, what's the smile for?"

"I was just trying to feature my old man doing that like you do."

"Is this supposed to threaten my masculinity or something?"

Her smile was very genuine now.

"Quite the opposite."

Then she turned and left him and the vacuum wheezed on again while he wondered what she meant.

It was inevitable that they be bound closer by inconsequential things. A telephone was installed and their number was listed under the name, Forrester, Clay. A grocery list was established on a corner of the cabinet, and on it mingled their needs and their likes. She bought herself a tape by The Lettermen and played it on his stereo, knowing full well it would not always be available for her to use. Mail began arriving, addressed to Mr. and Mrs.

Clay Forrester. He ran out of shampoo and borrowed hers, and from then on
they ended up buying her brand because he liked it better. Sometimes they
even used the same washcloth.

But every night, out came the spare blankets, and he made up his bed on the
davenport, put on a tape, and they lay in their separate darks listening to his
favorite one night, hers the next.

But by now she had grown to expect that last tape of the day, and left her
bedroom door open, the better to hear it.

Thanksgiving came and it was disturbingly wonderful for Catherine. Angela
had included both Steve and Ada in her invitation, plus all of Clay's grandparents and a few assorted aunts, uncles and cousins. It was the first time in six
years that Catherine, Ada and Steve had celebrated a holiday together, and
Catherine found herself awash in gratitude to the Forresters for this opportunity. It was a day steeped in tradition. There were warm cheeks meeting cold,
cozy fires, laughter drifting up through the house from the game room below,
a table veritably sagging beneath its burden of holiday foods, and of course
Angela's magical touch was everywhere. There were bronze football mums
laced with bittersweet in the center of the table, flanked by crystal candelabra
upon imported Belgian linen. Seated at dinner, Catherine swallowed back the
sickening sense of future loss and strove to enjoy the day. Her mother was
truly coming out of her shell, smiling and visiting. And it was crazy the way
Steve and Clay took to each other. They spent much of the meal badgering
each other about a rematch at pool as soon as the meal was over, but with the
best of spirits.

How the Forresters take this for granted, thought Catherine, gazing around
the circle of faces, listening to the happy chatter, soothed and sated as much
by their goodwill as by their food. What happened to my notions about the
wicked rich? she wondered. But just then her eyes met Claiborne's. She found
a disturbing gentleness there, as if he read her thoughts, and she quickly
looked away lest she be drawn to him further.

In the afternoon Catherine received her first lesson in how to shoot pool. Was
it accidental or intentional, the way Clay crowded his body close behind her as
he leaned to show her how to extend her left hand onto the green velvet,
crossing her hip with his right arm, his hard brown hand gripping hers on the
cue?

"Let it slide through your hand," he instructed into her ear, sawing back
and forth while his sleeve brushed across her hip. He smelled good and he was
warm. There was something decidedly provocative about it all. But then he
backed away and it was men against women in a round robin that pitted Clay
and Steve against Catherine and a teenage cousin named Marcy. But in no
time it was obvious the sides were uneven, so Catherine played with Steve as
her partner, and they whipped the other two in short order. Steve, it seemed,
had been dubbed "Minnesota Skinny" during the hundreds of hours spent at
pool tables during basic training and the years since. Eventually pool was
preempted by football, and Catherine found herself snuggled into a comfortable cushion between Clay and Steve. During replays Catherine received her

second lesson on the sport, explained succinctly by Clay, who slouched comfortably and rolled his head toward her during his comments.

At the door Claiborne and Angela bade them good-bye, and while Claiborne held her coat, Angela asked, "How are you feeling?"

She raised her eyes to twin expressions of concern, surprised to be asked in so point-blank a way about her pregnancy. This was the first time since before the wedding that anybody had brought it up.

"Pudgy," she answered with a half smile.

"Well, you're looking wonderful," Claiborne assured her.

"Yes, and don't let female vanity get you down," added Angela. "It's only temporary, you know."

On the drive home Catherine recalled their solicitous attitudes, the concern behind their simple comments, threatened by that concern more than she cared to admit.

"You're quiet tonight," Clay noted.

"I was thinking."

"About what?"

She was silent a moment, then sighed. "The whole day—what it was like. How all of your family seems to take it for granted . . . I mean, I've never had a Thanksgiving like this before."

"Like what? It was just an ordinary Thanksgiving."

"Oh, Clay, you really don't see, do you?"

"See what?"

No, he didn't see, and she doubted that he ever would, but she made a stab at comparison. "Where I came from, holidays were only excuses for the old man to get a little drunker than usual. By mealtime he'd be crocked, whether we were at home or going to Uncle Frank's. I don't ever remember a holiday that wasn't spoiled by his drinking. There was always so much tension, everybody trying to make things merry in spite of him. I used to wish . . ." But her voice trailed away. She found she could not say what it was she'd wished for, because it would seem guileful to say that she wished for a day like she'd had today.

"I'm sorry," he said softly. Then he reached over and squeezed her neck gently. "Don't let bad memories ruin your day, okay?"

"Your father was very nice to me today."

"Your mother was very nice to me."

"Clay, I . . ." But once again she stopped, uncertain of how to voice her growing trepidation. Catherine didn't think he'd understand that Thanksgiving had been just too, too nice.

"What?"

"Nothing."

But that *nothing* was a great big lump of something, something good and alive and growing which would—she was sure—be bittersweet in the end.

It was shortly after that when Clay came home one evening with a four-pound bag of popcorn.

"Four pounds!" she exclaimed.

"Well, I'm awfully fond of the stuff."

"You must be," she laughed, and flung the bag at him, nearly doubling him over.

That night they were sitting on the davenport studying with a bowl between them when Catherine suddenly dropped a handful of popcorn back into the bowl. Her eyes grew startled and the book fell from her fingers.

"Clay!" she whispered.

He sat forward, alarmed. "What's the matter?"

"Oh, God . . ." she whispered, clutching her stomach.

"What's the matter, Catherine?" He eased nearer, concern etched across his eyebrows.

She closed her eyes. "Ohhh . . ." she breathed while he wondered if she had written the doctor's number down where he could find it fast.

"For God's sake, what is it?"

"Something . . . something . . ." Her eyes remained closed while sweat suddenly broke out across his chest. Her eyes opened and a tremulous smile played at the corners of her mouth. "Something moved in there."

His eyes shot down to her stomach. Catherine held it like she was getting ready to try a two-hand set shot with it. Now he held his breath.

"There it goes again," she reported, her eyes closing as if in ecstasy. "Once more . . . once more . . . please," she whispered invocatively.

"Is it still moving?" he whispered.

"Yes . . . no! . . . wait!"

"Can I feel?"

"I don't know. Wait, there it is again—no, it's gone."

His hand advanced and retreated several times through all this.

"There it is again."

She made room for one of his hands on the gentle mound beside her own. They sat there mesmerized for a long, long time. Nothing happened. Her eyes drifted up to his. The warmth of his hand seeped through to her flesh, but the flutter within remained stilled.

"I can't feel anything." He felt cheated.

"It's all done, I think."

"There, what was that?"

"No, that wasn't it, that was probably only my own heartbeat."

"Oh." But he didn't take his hand away. It lay there warmly next to hers while he asked, "What did it feel like?"

"I don't know. Like—like when you're holding a kitten and you can feel it purr through its fur, only it lasted just a moment each time."

Clay's face felt hot. His scalp prickled. He still cupped her stomach with a hand which stubbornly wasn't going to move away without feeling *some* thing!

It's good to touch her, he thought.

"Clay, nothing's going to happen anymore, I don't think."

"Oh." Disappointed, he slid his hand from her. But where it had been, there were five buttery smudges on her green cotton blouse.

"You've marked me," she joked, stretching out the shirt by its hem, suddenly too aware of how good his hand had felt.

He caught a glimpse of a zipper that wasn't completely zipped, a snap which wasn't snapped.

"Yes, for life," he said on a light note, but he had the sudden urge to kiss her, she looked so expectant and crestfallen at the brevity of the sensation. "Promise me you'll let me feel it next time it happens?"

But she didn't promise. Instead, she moved a safe distance away, then muttered something about getting the butter out before it set permanently and headed in the direction of the laundry.

When she returned, she was wearing a pink duster and fuzzy booties, and he had great trouble concentrating on his studying after she resumed her place on the other side of the popcorn bowl.

By now Catherine well knew how Clay enjoyed his morning coffee at the counter. He was there at his usual place, reading the morning paper a few days later when she appeared from upstairs. He blew on his coffee, took a sip, looked up over his paper, and his lips fell from the rim of the cup which hovered, forgotten, in midair.

"Well, well, well . . . lookit here," he crooned.

She pinkened, got suddenly very busy plopping a piece of bread in the toaster with her back to him.

"Turn around so I can see."

"It's just a maternity top," she said to the toaster, looking at her reflection in it.

"Then why so shy?"

"I'm not shy, for heaven's sake!" She swung around. "I just feel conspicuous, that's all."

"Why? You look cute in it."

"Cute," she muttered disparagingly, "like Dumbo the elephant."

"Well, it's got to be more comfortable than going around with your zippers open and your snaps flapping." Again she colored. "Well, I couldn't help but notice the other night when I was feeling your tummy."

"I kept thinking of facing your grandmother in maternity clothes and putting it off as long as possible."

He put down his paper and came around the peninsula to pour another cup of coffee. "Nature will have its way, and not even Elizabeth Forrester can stop it. Don't frown so, Catherine."

She turned to butter her toast. "I don't want to think about facing her for the first time wearing these."

On an impulse he moved close behind her and touched his lips to the back of her hair, his cup still in his hand. "That probably won't be until Christmas, so stop worrying."

Facing the cabinets, she was unsure of what it was she'd felt on the back of her head, and then, without warning, he slipped an arm around her middle and spread his fingers wide on her stomach.

"Is there any more activity going on in there?" he asked.

From behind, he saw her jaws stop moving. She swallowed a mouthful of toast as though it were having some difficulty going down.

"Don't touch me, Clay," she warned, low, intense, fierce, not moving a muscle. His hand stiffened, the room seemed to crackle.

"Why? You're my w—"

"I can't stand it!" she snapped, slapping the toast down on the counter. "I can't stand it!"

He felt the blood surge to his head, stung by her unexpected outburst.

"Well, I beg your goddam puritanical pardon!"

He clapped his cup down vehemently, and stormed out of the room, out of the house, without so much as a good-bye.

When the door slammed, Catherine leaned over, braced her elbows on the countertop and buried her face in both hands. She wanted to call, Come back, come back! Don't believe me, Clay. I need touching so badly. Come back and make me let you touch me, even if I argue. Smile at me and wish me your sweet-tempered good-bye like always. I need you so badly, Clay. Coddle me, comfort me, touch me, touch me, touch me. Only, make it all mean something, Clay.

She had a miserable day that day.

She made supper and waited. And waited. And waited. But he didn't come. She finally ate alone, staring at his empty stool beside her, the food like cardboard in her mouth. She ate very little.

She put on one of his favorite tapes, just for some racket in the place, but that was worse. She felt more miserable than ever, for it only brought back the memory of his slamming out the door as he had. She put on one of her favorites, but naturally, it soon rolled around to the same old song which always reminded her of him: "You're Just Too Good To Be True." That made her more miserable than ever, so she chose to wait in silence. At eleven o'clock she gave up and went to bed.

She woke up at two A.M. and crept down the dark hall and checked the living room. In the blackness it was hard to see. She felt her way to the davenport with her feet, reached out a careful hand only to find that there was no bedding there, no Clay.

Finally, at five she fell asleep only to be awakened an hour and a half later by the alarm. Catherine knew before she went downstairs that he wouldn't be there.

Chapter 22

SCHOOL WAS AN exercise in futility that day. Catherine sat through her classes like a zombie, seeing little, hearing less. All she saw was Clay's hand on her stomach the night when they'd been eating popcorn. All she heard was his voice, "Can I feel?" She remembered his eyes, those eyes she'd grown to know so well, with a brand new look, wide-gray, excited. "I can't feel anything, Catherine. What did it feel like?"

Her insides trembled at the thought of his staying away all night. She'd have to call his parents if he wasn't home when she got there. Sick at the thought that he might not come home tonight either, she delayed going there herself. She stopped at Horizons after classes for a visit with the girls. Only, she learned that Marie had gone into labor around ten o'clock that morning and they were all waiting for news from the hospital. Without a second thought, Catherine drove to Metro Medical Center and obtained permission to wait in the father's waiting room. By the time news came, it was nine o'clock. She was not allowed to see Marie, for they had taken her directly to the recovery room, so Catherine finally headed for home.

When she got there, the living room light was on. At the sight of it she felt her heartbeat go wild and racy. Catherine opened the door to silence. Slowly she hung up her coat, and even more slowly ascended the stairs. Just inside the living room Clay was standing like an outraged samurai. His shirt hung open and wrinkled, his beard was a smudge across his cheeks, his hair was unkempt and his face bore the ravages of a sleepless night.

"Where the hell were you!" he roared.

"At the hospital."

His anger swooshed away, leaving him with that gut-hollow feeling as after an elevator drops too fast. He looked at her stomach.

"Is something wrong?"

"Marie just had a six-and-a-half-pound baby girl." She turned on her heel, heading upstairs, but found herself swung around roughly by an elbow.

Madder than ever at having been duped into thinking something was wrong with Catherine, he barked, "Well, you could have called, you know!"

"Me!" she yelled back. "I could have called! What about you!"

"I'm the one that got thrown out, remember?"

"I did not throw you out!"

"Well, you sure as hell didn't make me feel anxious to come back."

"The choice was yours, Mister Forrester, and I'm sure you didn't suffer out in the cold."

"No, I sure as hell didn't."

"Did she let you paw her nice flat stomach all night long?"

"What's it to you? You gave me permission to paw anything I want of hers, didn't you?"

"That's right," she hissed, "anything you want!"

"Catherine, let's not get into it, okay? I'm beat and I—"

"Oh, you're beat! Poor baby. I didn't get two hours sleep last night worrying that you drove it out of your system until you cracked up the Corvette someplace and all the while you were with her and now you come home crying that you're tired? Spare me."

"I never said I was with her. You assumed that."

"I don't give a tinker's damn if you were with her or not. If it'll keep you off my back, fine! Spend all the time you want with Jill Magnusson. Only do me the courtesy of reminding me not to cook supper for you on your nights out, all right?"

"And who do you think cooked supper for you tonight?"

Her eyes slid to the kitchen. Sure enough, there was evidence of a neglected meal all over the place. Catherine didn't know what to say.

He raged on. "Just what do you suppose I thought when you didn't show up to eat it?"

"I know what you didn't think—that I was out someplace with an old boyfriend!"

He ran a hand through his hair, as if searching for control, then turned away.

"You'd better call your mother; she's worried sick."

"My mother? How did she get into this?"

"I couldn't think of anyplace else you'd be, so I called her place."

"Oh, fine, just fine! I didn't call *your* mother to check up on you!"

"Well, maybe you should have 'cause I was there."

He stomped across the living room and plunked down on the davenport. "Lord," he said to the windows, "I don't know what got into you yesterday morning. All I did was touch you, Cat. That's all I did. Was that so bad? I mean, what do you think it makes a man feel like to be treated that way?" He got to his feet and started pacing back and forth. "I mean, I've been living like a goddam monk! Don't look! Don't touch! Watch what you say! Sleeping on this davenport like some eunuch! This setup just isn't natural!"

"Whose idea was it in the first place?"

"All right, granted, it was mine, but be reasonable, huh?"

Her voice grew taunting. "What am I to you, Clay? Another conquest? Is that what you're after? Another notch on your"—she glanced insolently at his crotch—"whatever it is you notch? I should think you could do better than one banged-up, big bellied loser like me. Listen, I plan to come out of this marriage with fewer scars than I had going in, and to do that I need to keep you away from me, do you understand? Just stay away!"

Suddenly Clay stormed across the room, grabbed one of her wrists and, in his fury, flung his other hand wide, exclaiming, "Damnit, Catherine, I'm your husband!"

Instinctively she yanked free of him, covering her head with both hands, hunkering down, waiting for the blow to fall.

At the sight of her, dropped low in that crouch, the anger fell from him to be replaced by pity, which hurt—hurt worse than the thought that she could not stand being touched by him.

He dropped to one knee beside her.

"Cat," he said hoarsely, "God, Cat, I wasn't going to hit you."

But still she cowered on her knees, sunken in some fear too big for him to fully comprehend. He reached out a hand to soothe her hair. "Hey, come on, honey, it's Clay. I'd never hit you, don't you know that?" He thought she was crying, for her body quivered terribly. She needs to cry, he thought, she needed it weeks ago. He watched her knotted fists dig into the nape of her neck. He touched her arms. "Come on, Cat." He gentled, saying, "It's only a silly fight, and it's over, huh?" He brushed back a strand of hair that fell like a golden waterfall covering her face. He leaned down to try to see around it, but she clutched her head and bounced on her haunches as if demented. Fear tore through his gut. His heart felt swollen to twice its size.

"Cat, I'm sorry. Come on, don't . . . Nobody's going to hurt you, Cat. Please, honey, I'm sorry . . ." Sobs collected in his throat. "Let me help you to bed, okay?" Something switched her back to reality. She raised her head at last, just enough to see him with one eye around that veil of gold. With infinite tenderness he promised, "I won't touch you. I just want to help you to bed; come on." The tears he expected to see were not there. She unfolded herself finally, tossed back her hair and eyed him suspiciously. Her face wore a protective mask of expressionlessness.

"I can do it." Her voice was too controlled. "I don't need your help."

With measured movements, she rose and left the room, left him kneeling there in the middle of it with a knot of emptiness inside him.

After that Catherine spent her evenings in the spare room. She either sewed maternity clothes or did typing jobs on a card table she'd set up in there. When she had studying to do, it, too, was done in the spare bedroom. Like a hermit crab, she crawled off into her shell.

After several nights of her incessant typing, Clay came to the bedroom doorway, stood there studying her back, wondering how to approach her.

"You're doing a lot of typing lately. Your professors laying on a heavy load or something?"

She didn't even turn around. "I got a couple of jobs typing term papers."

"If you needed money, why didn't you say so?" he asked impatiently.

"I want my typing to stay good."

"But you've got enough to do keeping up with your classes and things around the house without taking on more."

At last she looked over her shoulder. "I thought we agreed not to interfere with each other's private lives."

His mouth drew into a straight, hard line, then she turned back to her work.

The following evening when she was again seated at the typewriter, she heard the door slam. Her fingers fell still, hovering over the keys while she listened. Finally she got up and checked the living room and kitchen to find him gone. She sighed and returned to the spare room.

But there was undeniably a lonely feeling about the place, knowing he wasn't out there.

He got home around ten, offering no explanation of where he'd been, getting no questions from Catherine. After that, he would leave occasionally that way, preferring not to face her indifference, or the isolation of the living room with the sound of the clattering typewriter or sewing machine coming from upstairs.

One evening he surprised her by returning home earlier than usual, coming into her hideout with his jacket still on. He dropped a checkbook on the cardtable and she glanced up questioningly. He leaned from one hip a little, hands in his jacket pockets, only his eyes and hair picking up a faint reflection from the gooseneck lamp pointed down at the table.

"What's that?" she asked.

He eyed her from the shadows. "I ran out of blank checks and had to have some new ones printed."

She looked down at the black plastic folder, opened it and found her name imprinted beside his on the top check.

"We had a deal," said Clay. "I'd support you."

She stared at the paired names on the blue rectangle, reminded of their wedding invitations, for some reason. She looked up but his features were inscrutable above her.

"But not forever," she said. "I'll need money next summer and recommendations from satisfied customers. I want to take these jobs."

He shifted feet, leaned on the opposite hip. His voice was slightly hard. "And I want you back out in that living room in the evenings."

"I've got work to do, Clay." And she turned back to her typewriter, making the keys fly. He left the checkbook where it was and strode angrily from the room.

After he was gone, she leaned her elbows on the machine and rested her face in her palms, confused by him, afraid—so afraid—of allowing her feelings for him to sway her. She thought of the coming summer, the separation that was inevitable, and sternly began typing again.

The spare bedroom soon became cluttered with her things: piles of blank paper and manuscripts lying in heaps on the floor beside patterns and fabric scraps. Textbooks, a tote bag, her schoolwork.

Christmas break arrived and she spent most of it holed up, typing, while he spent most of his time in the law library at the university, which was open seven days a week, twenty-four hours a day.

He arrived home one evening just before supper, tired of the austere law library and its dry books and rigid silence. He hung up his coat while cocking an ear toward the spare room. But everything was silent; the clack of the typewriter was disturbingly absent. He wandered upstairs, glanced into the cluttered room only to find it dark. He hurried downstairs again, to find a note.

"Bad news this time. Grover's baby born early. Going to Horizons. Back late." It was signed simply "C."

The house seemed like a tomb, silent and lifeless without her. He made himself a sandwich and wandered to the sliding glass doors to stand looking out at the snow while eating. He wished they'd have a Christmas tree, but she expressed no desire to buy one. She said they had no ornaments anyway. He thought about her cold withdrawal from him, wondered how a person could insulate herself from feeling as she did, and why. He was used to living in an environment where people conversed at the end of the day, sat and shared some talk with their dinner, sometimes watched television or read books in the same room, companionable even in silence. He missed his mother and father's house very much, picturing the enormous Christmas tree that was an annual fixture, the fires, the aunts and uncles dropping in, the gifts, the decorations which his mother lavished upon the house. For the first time ever, he wished Christmas would hurry up and get past.

He took his sandwich and wandered idly upstairs to change into a jogging suit to lounge around in. He stopped at the doorway of the dark workroom, took another bite of the sandwich, wandered in and snapped on the gooseneck lamp. He touched the keys of the typewriter, read a few words from the paper she'd left in the platen and glanced over the papers that covered the top of the crowded table.

Suddenly he stopped chewing, arrested by the dark corner of a book that was peeking from beneath a stack of papers. He licked off his fingers, slid the book out to reveal a half-filled page of Catherine's handwriting.

"Clay went out again tonight . . ." it began. He pushed the book back and hid it as it had been, took another healthy bite of tuna salad and stared at the corner of the book. It lured him, peeking out that way. Slowly he set his plate

down, licked some mayonnaise from a finger again, drawn by that volume.
Finally he gave in and laid the diary across the typewriter platen.

"Clay went out again tonight but didn't stay out quite as late as last time. I
try not to wonder where he goes, but somehow I do. It always seems lonesome
here without him but it's best not to get used to having him around. Today he
mentioned buying a Christmas tree, but no matter how bad I want one, too,
what's the use? It's just another tradition to break next year. He wore his
brown corduroy jacket today, the one he wore the time—"

There she had stopped.

He dropped down into her chair, still staring at the words, feeling great
guilt at having read them, but rereading them just the same. He pictured her
sitting here, holed up in this room away from him, writing her secret feelings
instead of talking about them with him. Again and again he read the words,
"He wore his brown corduroy jacket today, the one he wore the time—" and
wondered what she'd have written had she completed the thought. She never
mentioned anything about his clothes. He'd never thought before that she
even was aware of what he wore. Yet this . . .

He closed his eyes, remembering how she had said she couldn't stand to
have him touch her. He opened them again and read, "He wore his brown
corduroy jacket today, the one he wore the time—" Was it a pleasant memory
she attached to the brown jacket? He remembered the fight they'd had over
Jill. He reread, "It always seems so lonesome here without him."

Before he could do something foolish he rose, buried the book they way
he'd found it, snapped off her light and went down and turned on the television. All this very abruptly. He sat through three commercials and one act of
a show he didn't recognize before going back upstairs and pulling the diary
out again. He told himself that this was different, that *he* was different, that he
wasn't out to use anything he read against her.

She had used up so many pages last Fourth of July that he didn't waste time
counting them.

"Today was a day of discovery.

"For once we were going to be all together and have a family picnic out at
Lake Independence. As usual, Daddy got blind drunk and ruined everything.
Mom and I had the picnic all packed when she changed her mind and called
Uncle Frank to say we wouldn't be coming. One thing led to another, and
Daddy accused Mom of making him the family scapegoat when all he'd had
was a couple shots. Ha! He started in on her and I stepped in, so he aimed his
attack at me, calling me the usual, only it was worse this time because I was
wearing my bathing suit, all ready to take off for the lake. I took it as long as I
could, but finally retreated to my room to contemplate Life's Injustices.

"Bobbi called in the late afternoon and said she and Stu were going to
Powderhorn to watch fireworks and how would I like to come along with a
friend of Stu's. If it hadn't been such a miserable day, I might not have gone.
But it was, and I did, and now I'm not sure if I should have.

"His name was Clay Forrester, and when I first met him I'm afraid I made
an absolute fool of myself by staring. What a face! What hair! What everything! His eyes were gray and he seemed a little brooding at first, but as the
night went on, he smiled more. His eyebrows are not exactly the same. The

left one quirks up a little more and gives him a teasing look at times. His chin has the suggestion of a dimple. His hair was the color of autumn leaves—not the reds, not the yellows, but the ones in between, like some maples, maybe.

"When Stu introduced us, Clay was just standing there with his thumbs hooked in his jeans pockets and all he said was Hi and smiled and just like that my heart hit my throat. I wondered if he could tell.

"What happened was insane. I'm not sure if I believe it yet. We walked around Powderhorn with this huge jug of wine, taking turns sipping, and waiting for full dark. I remember that we laughed a lot. Bobbi and Stu were ahead of us, holding hands, and sometimes Clay's shoulder bumped mine and shivers went up my arm. By the time the fireworks started, we were all nearly as high as they were!

"It turned out there were blankets in the truck and pretty soon Bobbi and Stu disappeared with one of them. I remember just the way Clay stood there with the bottle of wine in one hand and the handle of the truck door in the other. He asked if I wanted to sit in the truck and watch the fireworks or use the other blanket. I still can't believe I really answered, 'Let's use the blanket' but I did.

"We sat down under a huge tree with lacy black branches, and Clay pulled the cork out of the wine bottle with his teeth and spit it high in the air and we both laughed. I remember thinking how different it felt, getting drunk, when you were the one doing it instead of watching somebody else.

"He was leaning on one elbow, stretched-out-like on the blanket, resting the bottle on the ground between us when he leaned over and put an arm around my neck and pulled me over to kiss me the first time, and somehow my breast came up against his hand and the neck of that bottle. 'Fireworks,' he whispered in my ear afterward. He put his hand under my hair and held me there, moving the back of his hand and the top of the bottle against me. I guess I said 'Yeah' or something, just to see what'd happen. What happened was that he said 'Come here' and put his other arm around me, wine and all, and pulled me over there beside him and stretched out. I went willingly, remembering the names that Daddy had called me that morning, thinking to myself that maybe I'd prove him right.

"Clay took his time. He was some kind of a kisser. I've kissed boys before but this was different. And I've been pulled tight against guys before, but somehow they always were panting and clumsy and overeager and I was repelled. I waited for that to happen again, but it didn't. Instead, when I stretched out beside Clay, he gave me all the time I needed to make up my mind. I had it made up long before he pressed himself against me. I could feel the wine bottle bump against my back, cold through my shirt compared to his tongue, warm in my mouth. Lazy, it was at first, lazy and slow. I remember the feeling of his teeth against my own tongue, and the taste of wine in both of our mouths together. I remember him using his lips to urge me to open my mouth wider, then the feel of his tongue exploring me made me go all barmy and warmy. Funny thing was, while he did it, he loosened his hold on me and I found myself lying there drifting into submission more from his lack of force than the presence of it. At last he nudged himself away and collapsed onto his back with a wrist over his eyes. He was still holding onto the wine bottle with the heel of it against the ground, rocking it back and forth.

"He said something like 'Whew, you're good at that.' Did I say 'So are you' or not? I don't remember. I only know I felt all loose and woozy, and by then my heart was pounding between my legs and both of us were breathing so hard you could hear it above the boom of the fireworks.

"I think it was me who said I needed more wine, and I think it was him who said he needed less. Anyway, we both laughed then and when the wine bottle was corked up again and not hindering him, he pulled me over half on top of him and this time the kisses were harder and hotter and wetter and both of our bodies were doing a lot of talking. He rolled me onto my back, lying half across me and I remember thinking how secure it felt to have somebody hold me that way. It seemed to take away the hurt of the awful things Daddy was always yelling at me. It was like coming home ought to feel, or like Christmas, or like all the best scenes from all the best movies all rolled into one. He flattened me with the length of his body and began moving, moving, moving against my hips, kissing me all over my face. Once he broke away and groaned, 'Oh, God,' but I wouldn't let him go. I pulled him back on top of me and made him not stop. Maybe if I hadn't done that, things would have eased up a little. But by that time I didn't want them to ease up.

" 'Hey, listen, I think we're both a little drunk,' he finally said, and rolled off of me. But I found the wine bottle and said, 'Not yet.' Then I took a mouthful of wine and leaned over and kissed him and when his mouth opened, I let the wine drizzle into it. He took the bottle and sat up and filled his mouth, pushed me onto my back again and did what I'd just done to him. The wine was warm from the inside of his mouth. When I swallowed it, he bathed my lips with his tongue, running it over them like a mother cat washes her kitten. And before I knew what was happening, he ran his tongue down my jaw and laced his fingers through my hair and forced my head back. Then I felt the neck of the bottle against my own neck and the cool trickle of the wine as he poured it in the hollow of my arched throat.

"Crazy! I thought. We're crazy! But I felt like my pores were alive for the first time ever while he lapped the wine from my neck, then he moved up to continue kissing me under my jaw, intentionally touching me nowhere else, I think.

"I remember the pulsing happening in my body in places where I wished he'd pour the wine and cool me off. But I knew pouring the wine wouldn't really cool me off, and anyway, I didn't want to be cooled. When his tongue left me again, my hand groped for the wine bottle and he played along, letting me take my turn at drinking from him. I made him lie on his side and we were both giggling terribly while I tried to pour wine into his ear and he said, 'What are you doing?' and I said, 'Deafening you' and he said, 'What?' and I said, 'Deafening you!' and he said, 'What?' again, louder and louder and we were laughing and I was taking wine from his ear with the tip of my tongue. Only most of it had gone running down behind it and into the soft hair at the back of his neck and I followed it and we laughed and laughed.

"When it was his turn again, he teased me by pretending to consider for a long, long time, and finally he rolled me onto my stomach and said, 'Pick your hips up off the blanket a little.' I did and felt him pull my shirttails out of my jeans. Next I felt the wine run into the hollow of my spine before he slipped his arm under me and held me up a little while taking the wine off my back. And always we were laughing, laughing, even when he lay down on top of me and started kissing the back of my neck, using his hips from behind to tease me, while I pleaded breathlessness with his weight on top of me that way.

"My turn next, and there was only one place I could think of—if you could call it thinking by that time, my mind was so fuzzy. We were kissing when I pushed him onto his back again. Then I sat up and boldly unbuttoned his shirt and—like he'd done to me—pulled it out of his jeans. I poured my turn into the shallow valley between his ribs, and tried to lap it up before it ran down to his stomach, but of course I couldn't and we started giggling foolishly, getting hotter all the time, avoiding the final confrontation with this silliness we'd somehow cooked up together. I've read about different kinds of foreplay before, but this one beat anything I'd ever read about.

"Next it was his turn, and suddenly the giggling stopped. He unbuttoned my blouse in the flashes from the fireworks, and without uttering a word, poured wine in my navel, and ever so slowly pushed the cork into the bottle and threw it far away onto the grass someplace. He leaned over and no sooner had I felt his tongue on my stomach than he got both arms around my hips some way, and we rolled back and forth with his face against my stomach, and one of his hands swept up and down from the small of my back to the back of my thighs, and I knew what would happen if I didn't stop him, so I reached down to pull at his shoulders, but he rolled over and pinned the bottom half of me down, kissing his way around the waist of my jeans. Then he tried to open the snap with his teeth. Finally I managed to make him come up and join me, stretched out again. But my blouse was opened and he had my bra off before his lips got to mine. Again we were flattened against each other and his skin felt so good against mine. He ground himself against me and I ground right back. He raised his knee and pressed it high between my legs and I clung to him, to the very, very good and right feeling of being close that way to another human being.

"He had a way of moving his hands over my breasts that made me forget all the names Daddy had ever called me, that made me feel utterly right to lie there beneath his touch, letting his knee ride hard and high between my thighs, letting him pull one of my legs over his hip until we were as close to joined as it's possible to be when you're both still wearing jeans.

"Once he whispered, 'Hey, listen, are you sure you want to do this?' and something about him not usually doing this with strangers and I think I stopped his words with my mouth and then his hand plunged down into the back of my jeans and I gave him every permission with the movement of my body. Names Daddy had called me came teasing, but somehow they didn't apply. I wanted that closeness, needed it like nothing I had ever needed in my life. And when Clay zipped down my zipper and tucked the backs of his fingers against my bare skin, I sucked in my stomach to make it easier for him. His hand moved down and I closed my eyes and lay there pretending that at last somebody loved me. Who was I at that minute? Was I some heroine from a forgotten childhood film or was I myself, the me that had gone without affection all her life? I think maybe I was a little of each, for I knew a treasured feeling that could only happen in the movies. At least, I'd always believed it only happened in the movies, yet here it was, happening to me. I felt like all nineteen years of my life had been pointed to this moment, to this man who was showing me that there was more than hate in this world, there was love too. He called me Cat then. 'Ah, Cat,' he said, 'you feel good' and I was sure that he could feel me throbbing, touching the inside of me that way, and I wanted to say to him that I'd never felt that way before, not ever, not even close. But I didn't. I only closed my eyes and let everything in me swim toward his touch until my body thrust against his hand of its own accord, and I knew my mouth hung slack but could not seem to close it. I seemed to forget how to kiss even, but lay there beneath his kiss nearly unaware of it, for its adequacy seemed to pale compared to the sensations that wanted completion in the lower half of my body. And the wine led my hands to search his hard hips, feeling them pull away, giving me consent, freedom, space.

"The heat of him was a surprise and I felt awkward and graceful, both at once, knowing this was what I was expected to do, yet unsure of how to go about it. At my touch he grunted, pressed closer against my hand, moved sinuously. 'Go ahead, Cat,' he said in my ear and his breath on my neck was equally as hot as the beating of his blood through denim.

"I did it, in slow motion, I think, fearing with every opening tooth of his zipper that somehow my father would know what I was doing. Then I put him from my mind. No, that's not true. I didn't have to put him from it, because thoughts of him and everything else fled when I touched Clay Forrester for the first time. Whatever I had expected, I had not expected such heat. Neither had I expected the silkiness. But he was both hot and silky and I had enough sanity about me to marvel at the fluid way he could move, his thrust and ebb making me feel the experienced one holding his flesh in my hands, when I feared being naive and inexpert.

"When I used to imagine making love, I always thought it must be awkward and clumsy. First times are bound to be, I thought. But it wasn't. Instead, it was easy and as graceful as any dance. When he came into me, he called me Cat again, plunging deep while little of the discomfort I'd been led to expect happened. I learned that my body had had some hidden knowledge all along that my mind had not, for it undulated and surprised me and pleased Clay (I think) and it really was like the ballet, each movement so in tune with the other. It was effortless and natural and rhythmic, and would be beautiful to watch, I thought later. But when we were soaring everything came clear, and I suddenly knew why I was doing it. I was doing it to get even with Daddy, and maybe even Mom.

"In the middle of it all, my muscles suddenly lost motion and I only clung to Clay and let him finish without me. I wanted to cry out loud, 'Why didn't you love me? Why didn't you hug me? Why did you make me do this? You see, it's not so hard to touch, to be tender. Look, a total stranger can show me all this, why couldn't you? I didn't want much, just a smile, a hug, a kiss sometime to know you approved of me.' I wanted to cry then but made myself not. And maybe I hung onto Clay too tight, but that's all. I'll show them! I'll show them all!"

The room was a circle of dark around the lightblot shining over the cluttered tabletop. The words on the page became hazy and Clay's hand shook as he replaced the diary where he'd found it. He propped his elbows on the type-

writer and pressed his lips against his folded hands. His eyes closed. He tried
to gulp down the lump in his throat but it stubbornly remained. He dropped
his face into his palms, picturing a father reading that from his daughter.
Further, he tried to conceive of a father so devoid of emotion as to fail to
respond to such a cry for love. His mind wandered back to the evening he'd
first learned that Catherine expected his child. Vividly he recalled her stubborn refusal to ask anything of him, and for the first time he thought he
understood. He thought he understood, too, why she had done such a convincing job during the wedding and reception. *I'll show them! I'll show them
all!* He felt a new and oppressive weight of responsibility that he'd not known
until now. He recalled her aversion to being touched, her defensiveness, and
realized why it was so necessary for her to build such a barrier around herself.
He pictured her face the few times he'd seen it genuinely happy, knowing now
the reasons for her quicksilver changes and why she had been striving so hard
to remain independent of him.

His elbows hurt. He realized he'd been sitting for a long time with them
digging into the sharp edges of the typewriter. He opened his eyes and the
light hurt them. Listlessly he rose and turned off the lamp, wandered into the
bedroom and fell on the bed. He lay there with his mind reeling and groping,
waiting for her return.

Clay heard her come in, sat up, wondering how to treat her, an odd sensation,
for now his concern was with her, not with himself. When he came downstairs, she was sitting with her coat still on, her head laid back against the
davenport, eyelids closed but quivering.

"Hi," he said, stopping way across the room from her.

"Hi," she said, without opening her eyes.

"Something wrong?" The lamplight shone on her windstrewn hair. She
hugged her coat very tightly around herself and turned the collar up around
her jaw.

"The baby died."

Without another word he crossed the room, sat down on the arm of the
davenport and put a hand on top of her hair. She allowed it but said nothing,
showed no signs of the heartbreak and fear that bubbled inside her. He moved
his hand, rubbing in warm circles upon her hair, then smoothing it down in
wordless communion with her. She swallowed convulsively. He wanted desperately to kneel down before her and bury his head in her lap and press his
face to her stomach. Instead, he only whispered, "I'm sorry."

"They said its l-lungs were underdeveloped, that wh-when a baby comes
early there's always a ch-chance of . . ." But her sentence went unfinished.
Her eyes opened wider than normal, focused on the ceiling and he waited for
only a single sob, but it never came. He tightened his fingers gently on the
back of her neck—an invitation to avail herself of him in whatever way she
needed. He could tell how she needed to be held and comforted but she
overcame it and sprang up, away from his touch, jerking her coat off almost
angrily.

He stopped the coat while it drooped yet over her shoulder blades, grasping
her upper arms from behind, expecting her to yank free of his touch. But she
didn't. Her head sagged forward as if her neck had suddenly gone limp.

"It doesn't mean ours is in danger," he assured her. "Don't let it upset you, Catherine."

Now she yanked free and spun. "Don't let it upset me! What do you think I am? How can I not let it upset me when I've just seen Grover crying for a baby she never wanted! Do you know how she got pregnant? Well, let me tell you. She was suckered into a date with a high school jock who did it on a dare because she was such a troll! That's how! And she thought she hated the thing growing inside her and now it's dead and she cried like she wished she had died too. And you say 'don't let it upset you?' I don't understand h-how this w-world got s-so . . . screwed up . . ."

He moved suddenly before he could change his mind, before she could run from him again or hide her need behind more of her anger. He wrapped both arms around her and gripped her fiercely. He cradled the back of her head and forced it into the hollow of his neck and made her stay that way, their muscles quivering, straining until at last she gave in and he felt her arms cling to his back. More like combatants than lovers, they clung. Her nails dug into his sweater as she gripped it. Then he felt her fists thumping against the small of his back in desperation, although she wasn't trying to escape him anymore. Just those pitiful thumps, growing weaker and weaker while he waited.

"Catherine," he whispered, "you don't have to be so strong all the time."

"Oh, God, Clay, it was a boy. I saw him in the incubator. He was so beautiful and fragile."

"I know, I know."

"Her mom and dad wouldn't come. Clay, they wouldn't come!" A fist hit his back again.

Let her cry, he thought. If only she'd cry at last. "But your mom's going to come and so is mine."

"What are you trying to do to me?" She suddenly started pushing, palms against his chest, almost thrashing.

"Catherine, trust me."

"No, no! Let me go! This is hard enough without you mixing me all up even worse."

Then she ran up the stairs, taking with her all her years of bottled-up hurt. But now he knew that gentleness would work. It would take time, but eventually, it would work.

Chapter 23

IT BEGAN SNOWING shortly after noon on Christmas Eve day. It came down like diamond dust, in light, puffy featherflakes. By evening the earth looked clean-white. The sky bore a soft luminescence, lit from below by the lights of the city reflecting off the snow.

Catherine wore a new homemade jumper of mellow rust wool, with a tie

that cinched it loosely beneath her breasts. She had decided to meet Elizabeth Forrester head-on this time. Yet, approaching the front door, some of Catherine's aplomb quavered at the thought of the grand dame eyeing her popping stomach for the first time.

"Do you think she's here yet?" she asked Clay timorously, while he paused with his hand on the door latch.

"I'm sure she is. Just do like I said, face her squarely. She admires that."

The smile she managed nearly faded as they entered, for Elizabeth Forrester was advancing upon them from the height of the open stairway. Her cane led the way, but it had a surprising tuft of Christmas greenery tied about its handle with a red ribbon.

"Well, it's about time, children!" she scolded imperiously.

"Merry Christmas, Grandmother," Clay greeted, taking her arm as she approached the lowest step.

"Yes, I'm given to understand that it certainly is. I can help myself down the steps, if you please. If you want to pamper someone, I understand that your wife is in the way of a woman who needs pampering. Is that so, my dear?" She turned her hawk-eyes on Catherine.

"Hardly. I'm as healthy as a horse," replied the girl, removing her coat into Clay's hands, revealing the maternity dress.

About Elizabeth Forrester's lips a thin smile threatened, and the eyes that pointedly refrained from dropping to Catherine's abdomen glittered like the jewels upon her fingers. Then she cocked a brow at her grandson.

"You know, I like this young woman's style. Not unlike my own, I might add." The ivory-headed cane pecked twice at Catherine's stomach while the matriarch passed on her decree. "As I've said once before, I shall most assuredly expect him to be beautiful, not to mention bright. Merry Christmas, my dear." She bestowed a cheek to Catherine's, miming a kiss which did not quite land, then exited to the living room in her usual grand style to leave Catherine gaping at Clay.

"That's all?" she whispered, wide-eyed.

"All?" he smiled. "Beautiful *and* bright? That's a pretty big order."

A smile began about the corners of Catherine's eyes. "But what if *she* is only *cute* and of *average intelligence?*"

Clay looked shocked. "You wouldn't dare!"

"No, I don't suppose I would, would I?"

Their smiles lingered for a long moment, the encounter with Elizabeth Forrester somehow already forgotten. Gazing up at Clay, at the smile upon his firm cheeks, his charmingly handsome mouth, and that brow that curled provocatively over his left eye, Catherine found her self-restraint slipping. She realized she'd been standing there with her eyes in his for some time, and thought, It's this house. What is it that happens to me when I'm in this house with him? Breaking the spell, Catherine swept her glance around the magnificent foyer, searching for something to say.

"I think this place deserves to have its gentlemen arrive in capes tonight, and its ladies with fur muffs, with sleighs outside and nickering horses."

"Yes, Mother's been having fun, as usual."

Then they turned to join the others.

If the house exuded cordiality at other times of the year, it had a special spell at Christmas. Pine swags looped their way up the banister, their pungent aroma a heady greeting to all, while red candles sprang from freshly cut holly branches on tables everywhere. The pine scent mingled with that of smoke from the blazing fireplaces and cooking aromas from the kitchen. Within the study, hurricane lanterns couched blazing candles on the mantel, while a childish rendition of "Deck the Halls" came from the piano in the living room. There, within the bay window, stood a tree of enormous size, a proud old balsam with traditional multicolored lights that cast their rainbows across the walls and faces there and were redoubled in gilded swags of tinsel garland that threaded the balsam's limbs. It bore so many dazzling ornaments that its green arms fairly drooped. A mountain of gifts—foiled, beribboned, sprigged with greens—cascaded around the foot of the tree. Upon the longest living room wall was an outsized wreath of nuts, garnished with a red velvet bow whose streamers were caught within the beaks of gilded partridges which hung on either side of the wreath. Everywhere there was the buzz and babble of happy voices, and above them came the laugh of Angela, who'd been ladling eggnog in the dining room, looking like some delicate little Christmas ornament herself in a pale lavender lounging outfit of soft velour, her tiny silver slippers matching the thin belt at her waist and the fine chains around her neck.

"Catherine, darling," she greeted, immediately leaving her task and crossing to them, "and Clay!" Her melodious voice carried its usual note of welcome, but Clay affected an injured expression.

"You know, it used to be 'Clay-darling' first and then 'Catherine-darling,' but I seem to have been upstaged."

Angela gave him a scolding pout, but nevertheless kissed Catherine first, then him, flush on the mouth.

"There. Is that what you were waiting for, standing there so innocently?"

She quirked an eyebrow at the archway above his head, which held a kissing ball of mistletoe. "As if you didn't know," teased Angela, "it's there every year."

Clay quickly ducked aside, playing the beleaguered male while Angela only laughed and bore Catherine away toward the eggnog where Claiborne now turned with a warm greeting.

The doorbell kept ringing until the laughter and voices were doubled. Left momentarily alone, Catherine scanned the ceiling to find the place peppered with mistletoe. Someone approached to congratulate her on her pregnancy, and she tried to forget about mistletoe. But everybody else was using it to great advantage, and it made for a gay mood. Catherine assiduously avoided it.

The food was served buffet style, crowned by real English plum pudding that arrived steaming from the kitchen. That was when Granddad Elgin caught Inella under the mistletoe in the kitchen doorway as she fussily gave orders not to touch the pudding until she returned with the warmed dessert plates. Catherine laughed to herself, standing nearby with a cup of coffee in her hand. It was delightful and so unexpected to see little birdlike Granddad Elgin kissing the maid in the kitchen doorway. Catherine felt someone behind her and glanced over her shoulder to find Clay there. He raised his eyebrows, then his eyes, to a spot over her head.

"Better watch out. Granddad Elgin will get you next," he said.

She quickly scuttled from beneath the mistletoe. "I wouldn't have suspected it of your Granddad," she said smilingly.

"Things get a little crazy around here at Christmastime. It's always this way."

"They certainly do," Clay's father said, approaching just then. "Do you mind, Young Mister Forrester, if Old Mister Forrester kisses your wife while she's standing in that advantageous spot?"

Catherine wasn't under the greens anymore; still, she looked up and backed up a step. "I wasn't—"

"Not at all, Mr. Forrester."

Claiborne captured her for a hearty kiss, then stepped back, squeezing her biceps, looking into her face.

"You're lovelier than usual tonight, my dear." He put one arm around her shoulders, his other around Clay's. He looked first into one face, then into the other. "I don't think I remember a happier Christmas."

"I think a little of the glow might be from you spiking the eggnog," Clay teased his father.

"A little, not all though."

Catherine and Clay found a corner to sit in and eat their plum pudding, but she only dabbled at hers. It seemed they had little to say to each other, although time and again she felt Clay's eyes on her.

Soon Angela rounded everyone up and took her place at the piano to accompany the younger children who piped carols off-key until the entire group ended with "Silent Night." Claiborne stood behind Angela as she played, with his hands on her shoulders, singing robustly. When the last note finished, she kissed one of his hands.

"You weren't singing," Clay said behind Catherine.

"I'm a little inhibited, I guess."

He was close enough to smell her hair. He thought of what he'd read in her diary. He'd been wanting her ever since. "People will be leaving now. I'll help them find their coats."

"And I'll start picking up glasses. I'm sure Inella is tired."

It was after midnight. Clay and Catherine had ushered the last straggler out the door, for somehow Angela and Claiborne had disappeared. The entry was dim, pine-scented and private. With slow steps, Catherine radiated toward the living room and the soft glow of tree lights. Clay was just behind her, where it seemed he'd hovered more and more as the night moved on. His hands were in his pockets. She ran her fingers through her hair, brushing it behind an ear as they ambled thoughtlessly toward the archway.

But there Catherine stopped, warned by a movement in the shadows at the far end of the dining room. Claiborne and Angela stood there, wrapped in each other's arms, kissing in an impassioned way in which Catherine did not think people of their age kissed. Claiborne had a dishtowel slung over his shoulder and Angela was shoeless. His hand moved over Angela's back, then stroked her side and moved to her breast. Quickly Catherine turned away, feeling like an intruder, for the two were certainly unaware of her presence across the wide, dimly lit rooms. But as she turned discreetly to withdraw, she bumped into Clay, who, instead of retreating, only placed a single finger over his lips, then raised it to point at the mistletoe above their heads. His hair and face and shirt were illuminated in the muted hues of Christmas, all red, blue, green and yellow, and he looked as inviting as the gifts beneath the tree. His eyes, too, reflected the glow of the tree lights as with a single finger he traced the line of Catherine's jaw, burning its path to the hollow beneath her lower lip. Her startled eyes widened and the breath clawed its way into her throat. She laid a hand against his light-dappled shirt, meaning to hold him off, but he captured it, along with her other, and carried them around his neck.

"My turn," he whispered.

Then he lowered his lips to hers, caught them opened in surprise, expecting the struggle to begin. But it didn't. He knew he did not play fair, catching her while his parents were right there doing the same thing. But it had been on his mind all night, and playing fair was the farthest thing from his mind as he delved into the silken depths of her mouth. Their warm tongues touched. He plied her with singular lack of insistence, remembering what she had written about such things, inviting rather than plundering, with a luxuriant slowness. He felt fingers curve around the back of his collar and stilled his tongue— waiting, waiting, with his hold still merely a suggestion upon her body. Then a single fingertip found the skin of his neck and gently he tightened the arm about her waist.

Her body had grown since their wedding. It had blossomed into a captivating fullness that now held their hips apart. But he ran a hand possessively up and down her back, wishing that now the baby would kick—just once—so he could know the feel of it against his loins.

Reluctantly he ended the kiss.

"Merry Christmas," he whispered, near her face.

"Merry Christmas," she whispered back, her lips so close he felt the whisper of breath from her words. The room was utterly still. A needle dropped from the Christmas tree, making an audible ping as they gazed into each other's eyes. Then their lips were willing and warm and seeking again and her stomach was pressed lightly against him. She wished this could go on forever, but the very wish reminded her that it couldn't, wouldn't, and she withdrew. But when she would have been turned loose he instead entwined his fingers loosely behind her back, leaning away, swiveling lazily back and forth with her, smiling down at her hair, her lips and her breasts, which were undeniably growing.

She knew she should insist on being turned loose, but he was tempting, tender this way, handsome with his face limned by the low lights, his hair colored like fire. They turned their faces to look at the Christmas tree. Contented for the moment, she let him pull her lightly near him until her temple rested on his jaw. And from the shadows, the pale faces of Angela and Claiborne—in a like embrace—watched the younger couple, and Claiborne wordlessly tightened his embrace.

"I have a marvelous idea," Angela said softly.

Catherine started slightly, but when she would have pulled away, Clay prevented it.

"Why don't the two of you spend the night and that way we'll be able to creep down in the wee hours in our nighties and robes just like we've always done."

Clay felt Catherine stiffen.

"Fine by me," he said, rocking her as before, the picture of a satisfied spouse.

"But I don't have my nightie," she said, alarmed.

"I'm sure I can find one for you, and we must have a spare toothbrush around here someplace. You could stay in the pink room."

Catherine groped for excuses, came up with one. "But we have to pick up Mother on our way over tomorrow morning anyway."

"Oh, that's right."

Clay's heart fell.

"Well," Angela mused, "it was a good idea anyway. But you two make sure you get here bright and early."

At home, Clay took his sweet old time about dragging out his own bedding and using the bathroom. He hovered around the upstairs hall, leaning against her doorway, watching while she slipped off her earrings and shoes, "Want a glass of soda or something?" he asked.

"No, I'm stuffed."

"I'm not very tired, are you?"

"I'm beat."

He unbuttoned his shirt. "I guess that's to be expected, huh?"

"Yes, the heavier I get the less zip I have."

"How much longer are you planning to stay in school? Shouldn't you be quitting pretty soon?" He finally decided to come into the bedroom, passing close behind her to stand beside the chest of drawers and empty his pockets.

"I can go as long as I want."

"How long is that?"

"A while yet, maybe till the end of second semester."

He watched her moving around the room, knew she was making motions at inconsequential things to look like she was busy. He wandered to the closet door, idle himself, leaning against the door frame and watching while she opened a dresser drawer. Her fair hair swayed forward over her shoulder as she leaned to retrieve something from inside. The skin across his chest felt as tight as a piano string. His heart beat upon it like a velvet hammer. His voice, when he spoke, was a deep, resonant note, softly struck.

"How long can a pregnant woman safely have intercourse?"

Catherine's hands fell still. Her head jerked up and she met his eyes in the mirror. The muscles of her groin involuntarily tightened, as did her hands upon the garments she'd been needlessly straightening in that drawer. Clay didn't move a muscle, just lounged there against that door frame with a hand strung negligently in his trouser pocket and a thin strip of golden-haired skin showing behind his open shirt. His expression was unreadable as she struggled to think of a reply.

"I want to, you know," he said, in that same hushed tone that raised every hair along the base of her spine. "And since you're already pregnant, what else could happen? I mean, if it's safe for you, of course." But she only stared at him. "I've been wanting to for weeks, and I've told you in every possible way except in words. Tonight when we were kissing under that mistletoe I decided I'd tell you. You're a very desirable wife, did you know that, Catherine?"

At last she found her voice, trembling though it was. "I'm a very pregnant wife."

"Ah, but that doesn't detract from your desirability in the least. Particularly since it's my baby you're carrying."

"Don't say any more, Clay," she warned.

"Don't be afraid of me, Catherine. I'm not going to force the issue. It's entirely up to you."

"I'm not afraid of you, and the answer is no." Suddenly she found what she was looking for in that drawer and slammed it shut.

"Why?"

She kept her back to him, looking down at something on the dresser top, but in the mirror he could see how she pressed herself against the edge of it, clutching some blue filmy thing in her hand.

"Why are you doing this tonight when it's been such a perfect day?"

"I told you, I'd like to go to bed with you. Would it be dangerous?"

"The subject never came up at the doctor's."

"Well, why don't you bring it up next time you're there?"

"There's no point in it."

"Isn't there?"

The silence that followed was as pregnant as the woman leaning against the dresser. Then Clay's voice became convincing.

"I'm tired of sleeping out there on that davenport when there's a luxurious king-size bed in here and a perfectly good, warm woman to snuggle up to. And I think she'd enjoy it, too, if she'd let herself. What do you say, Catherine, it's Christmas."

"Don't, Clay. You promised."

"I'm breaking my promise," he said, bringing his shoulder away from that door frame in slow-motion.

"Clay," she said warningly, turning to face him.

"How can you kiss that way and not get turned on, will you tell me that?"

"Stay away from me."

"I've been staying away. All it does is make me need it all the more." He advanced halfway across the room.

"I am not going to bed with you, so you can just forget it!"

"Convince me," he said low, still advancing.

"Do you know what your problem is? It's your ego. You simply can't believe I can live with you and not give in to your deadly charms, can you?"

In a voice like velvet he accused, "Cat, you're a goddam liar. You're forgetting I'm the one that was kissing you earlier. What's the harm in it? After all, it's legal, if it comes down to that—all signed, sealed and documented by the preacher. What are you afraid of?"

He was no more than an arm's length in front of her now, his gray eyes warmer than she'd ever seen them. Unconsciously she covered her widening girth with both hands.

"Why do you do that? Why do you try to hide from me? Always keeping me at a distance, avoiding even being in the same room with me. Why can't you be like you were earlier tonight more often? Why don't you talk to me, tell me how you're feeling, even complain about something? I need some human contact, Cat. I'm not used to living this insular life."

"Don't call me Cat!"

"Why? Tell me why."

"No." She would have turned away, but his arm stopped her.

"Don't turn away from me. Talk to me."

"Oh, Clay, please. It's been the most wonderful night. Please don't ruin it now. I'm tired, and happier than I've been for the longest time; at least I was until you started this. Can't we pretend the kiss never happened and be friends?"

He wanted to put voice to the root of her problem, to say to her that making love with him would not make her the slut her father told her she was. But she wasn't ready for it yet, and furthermore, it was a truth she must discover for herself. He knew if he forced her before she recognized that truth, the damage would be irreparable.

"If you mean it, and you're genuinely going to be friendly toward me from now on, that's a start. But don't expect me to forget that kiss ever happened, and don't expect me to believe that you'll forget it either."

"It's that house. Something about that house. I feel different when I go there, and somehow I do crazy things."

"Like letting your husband kiss you under the mistletoe?"

She was struggling with emotions she could not control, wanting him, afraid of the heartbreak he could cause her in the end. He reached out one brown hand, capturing the back of her neck, pulling her a little nearer, though she stiffly resisted.

"You are afraid of me, Catherine. But you don't have to be. When and if . . . the decision will be yours."

Then he kissed her lightly on the mouth, still holding her with that single hand on her tight neck muscles.

"Good night, Cat," he whispered, and was gone.

Her determination to resist Clay was further weakened when on Christmas morning she opened up a small package from him and found two tickets to *Swan Lake,* coming up at Northrup Auditorium in late January. She read the words on the tickets and raised her eyes, but he was tearing into a gift from his mother, so Catherine leaned over and touched his arm softly. He looked up.

"You remembered," she said, with the warmth expanding in her chest. "I . . . well, thank you, Clay. I'm sorry I have no gift for you."

"I haven't been to a ballet in a long time," he said.

The moment grew complicated by the looks in their eyes, then she broke the tension by teasing, "Who says you're invited?"

But next Catherine bestowed one of her rare smiles.

Chapter 24

DURING THE FOLLOWING week, Clay invited Catherine to go shopping with him. He needed something to wear on New Year's Eve, which they'd agreed to spend with Claiborne and Angela at the country club. But Catherine declined, believing it best to avoid such little domestic sallies.

Clay came home one night with a pair of plastic-sheathed garment bags, and tossed one casually across the back of a living room chair. "Here, I thought we both ought to have something new."

"You bought something for *me?*" she asked from the kitchen.

"Sure. You were stubborn so I had to. It's quite formal at the club—kind of a tradition."

Then he bounded up the stairs with his hanger. She wiped her hands on a dishcloth and walked around the peninsula with her eyes riveted on the dress bag.

When Clay came back, she was standing with the dress aloft, holding the black crepe skirt like an opened fan.

"Clay, you shouldn't have."

"Do you like it?"

"Well, yes, but it's so impractical. I'll probably only wear it once."

"I want you looking just as classy as every other woman there."

"But I'm not. I've never owned a dress like this in my life. I'll feel funny." She looked momentarily crestfallen, but he could tell how much she liked it.

"Listen, Catherine, you're my wife, and you have as much right to be at the club as anyone else. Understand?"

"Yes, but—"

"*Yes, but* nothing. All I'm worried about is if the thing will fit. It's a first for me, you know—buying a maternity dress."

She couldn't help chuckling. "What did you do, go in the store and say 'Gimme a dress that's, say, four ax-handles around?'"

He rubbed his chin, measuring her visually. "No, I figured more like five."

She scarcely looked at him as she laughed; she had eyes for nothing but the dress.

"I'll look like a circus tent, but I love it . . . really."

"You're awfully touchy about losing your shape. Isn't it time you accept it? I have."

"It's easy for a man to say when he doesn't have to face getting blown up like some dirigible and having to lose the extra pounds afterward. If I'm not careful, no man will look twice at me next summer."

As soon as Catherine said it she felt him bristle. His good humor fled as Clay remarked, "Oh, so you plan to go husband-hunting then?"

"I didn't mean it that way. But I certainly don't intend this marriage to mean the end of my love life."

For Clay the pleasure of giving her the dress suddenly dissolved, leaving him feeling angry, his ego stung. It irritated him that she could make a comment like that while she wouldn't even let him lay a hand on her. He'd given her the best home she'd ever had, all the things he could think of to make her life easy. He'd taken on his share of the housework, given her the

355

freedom to come and go and to do her abominable typing—which irked him no end and made him want to drop the damn typewriter off the balcony. And he'd been more than patient with her, even when he wanted more attention than she gave. And how did she repay him? By being cold and standoffish, then bemoaning the fact that no man would look twice at her if she didn't preserve her shape? What the hell was she trying to do to him anyway?

While they were getting ready to go out on New Year's Eve, Clay was as stony as he'd been during the three days since he brought the dress home. Catherine had learned how lonely it felt to be the one on the receiving end of such treatment.

She put the finishing touches on her hair. Just then Clay came in the bedroom to rummage through his jewelry box for a tie pin. From behind, he was tantalizingly thin and tapered in the new smoky-blue suit with its trim cut and double vents at the rear.

Clay swung around to find her studying him.

"I'm almost ready. Excuse me," he said, edging around her briskly.

"I see that. Is that your new suit?"

He didn't answer, just moved to the mirror to insert the needle of the pin through a new striped tie.

"You always manage to look like an ad in *The New Yorker,*" she tried.

"Thank you," he replied icily.

"And the dress fits, see?"

"Good."

She was stung by his indifference. "Clay, you've hardly talked to me at all this week. What's wrong now?"

"If you don't understand it, I'm not going to waste my breath explaining."

She knew very well what was wrong, but it was hard for her to apologize.

He dropped the back clasp of the tie pin and muttered, "Damn."

"Clay, I know I act ungrateful sometimes, but I'm not. And you and I had an agreement before we got married."

"Oh, sure! So why are you in here offering me compliments? Why do I suddenly merit applause for how I dress?"

"Because it's true, that's all."

"Catherine, don't, okay? I don't know how to handle you anymore. You've walked around me like I was some cigar-store Indian for weeks now. And when you finally decide to start talking to me, it's to tell me you're worried you might gain too much weight so it'll be tough when you go on the make again. How do you think that makes me feel when you practically start shopping for chastity belts every time I try anything with you?"

"Oh, for heaven's sake, what's the matter with you, anyway!"

"You want to know what's the matter with me?" he barked, whirling on her, accosting her face-to-face. "What's the matter with me is the same damn thing that was the matter with me last week and the week before that and the week before that. I'm horny! That's what's the matter with me! You want the truth, lady? There it is in a nutshell! So don't come sashaying in here after all this time and suddenly start fawning over my looks, which are the same as when you married me! You know what you are?"

She had never seen Clay this angry. His face was suffused with color; the veins above his collar stood out boldly.

"You, Mrs. Forrester are a——" But even as angry as he was he couldn't say it.

"What!" she yelled. "Finish it! Say it!"

But he got control of himself and turned away, tugging at his lapels and adjusting the knot of his tie.

"My mother raised me to speak with respect around females, so I'll refrain from using the four-letter prefix to the word____teaser."

"How dare you, you bastard!"

He gave her an insolent look in the mirror. "Take a look at what happens to you after a few days of being ignored. You come in here with your cute little compliments, just enough to keep me swimming after the bait, huh? Do you know how many times you've warmed up to me just enough to keep me interested? I won't bother to recount them because you'd deny it anyway. But it's the truth. You've accused me of being the one exploiting you to boost my ego, but I believe the shoe's on the other foot."

"That's not true! I've never led you on!"

"Catherine, at least I've been honest about it, starting with our wedding night. I've come right out and said that I wanted to make love to you. But do you know what you do? You skirt the issue, you skitter away, then allow me close enough only when it suits you. Your problem is you want to forget you're a woman but you can't. You like being pursued, but on the other hand, you're afraid if you break down and allow yourself to be made love to, you'll be what your father always accused you of being. What you don't realize is, that makes you as sick as your old man!"

"You bastard," she growled, low in her throat.

"Go ahead, call me names so you don't have to face yourself."

"You said, 'no sex,' when you asked me to marry you."

"You got it. I've decided not to harass you anymore. You want to sleep in your big bed alone, fine. But let's end this sweet little charade we play in between bedtimes, okay? I won't press you for attention, and you won't give me cute little compliments you don't mean, huh? Let's just keep out of each other's way until July, like we agreed."

There was nothing in the world she wanted to do less than go to the club that night. Things became even less tolerable when, shortly after they arrived, so did Jill Magnusson, along with her date and her family.

Clay put on a devoted-husband act, timing his repeated returns to Catherine's side very assiduously all night long, making sure she had whatever drink she wanted, making sure introductions were made where necessary, making sure she was never left at the table alone when every other woman was dancing. Around his parents Clay was the epitome of husbandly courtesies, but Catherine lost track of how many times he danced with Jill. At two minutes before midnight Clay was dancing with his wife, but when the band broke into "Auld Lang Syne" and he kissed her, it was the most impersonal, tongueless kiss she'd ever had. Furthermore, he had artfully maneuvered them near enough to Jill and her partner that it appeared quite natural when they were the first couple to exchange partners. Catherine found herself pressed

into the arms of a stocky, black-haired man who solicitously refrained from embracing the pregnant lady too tightly. But while she and the dark man kissed, her eyes were open, watching Clay and Jill sending a silent message into each other's eyes—long and tenuous—before enfolding each other in a painfully familiar fashion. Clay's hands caressed Jill's bare back, his fingers spread seductively so that his little finger hooked beneath a red spaghetti strap, traveled up Jill's shoulder blade and disappeared beneath her cascading hair. Catherine dropped her eyes only to see Clay's hips pressed provocatively against Jill's. The couple broke apart momentarily, then Jill laughed and half-turned to Clay as she captured him again. Now Catherine could see Jill's long fingernails glittering through Clay's hair. Unable to drag her eyes away, Catherine watched as their mouths opened wide upon each other and could see a movement at Clay's cheek as his tongue danced into Jill's mouth.

Then, thankfully, Stu was there to claim a kiss from Catherine. But he could see the way she fought the intimidating rush of tears and whispered, "Don't think anything of it, kiddo, okay? We've all been kissing each other Happy New Year since we were too young to know what it meant."

Then Stu smoothly parted Clay and Jill and moved in for a kiss. But Catherine noticed when Stu kissed Jill there was none of that open-mouthed business, nor did she run her glistening nails through *his* hair.

Before one o'clock arrived, Jill and Clay were both mysteriously missing. Nobody seemed to notice except Catherine, who checked the clock at least twenty times during the twenty minutes they were gone. When they returned, they entered carefully from opposite doors. But Clay's tie had been loosened and she could tell he'd freshly run a comb through his hair.

Dreary January settled in, bringing snow and cold and little to cheer anyone. Clay began leaving the house in the evenings again, although he never stayed out overnight. He and Catherine withdrew into their polite roles of roommates, and nothing more. The spirited teasing they'd once shared seemed gone forever, and the consideration Clay had once shown Catherine disappeared with New Year's Eve. When they were at home at the same time, they rarely ate together, avoided even passing each other in the hall. With Herb still in the workhouse, Catherine visited her mother more often, raising no objection in Clay when she'd return home later than he. The night before the ballet she reminded him of it, but without looking up from his book he suggested she take Bobbi or her mother because he wouldn't be free to go with her. Catherine took Bobbi, but somehow the ballet had lost its appeal.

Clay spent the night of the ballet at home. Occasionally his thoughts meandered to Catherine, remembering her pleasure at receiving the tickets. He'd thought back then that it would be fun to take her to see her first performance. Most of the time when he was alone he tried not to think of her at all, but tonight it was hard, knowing where she was. There had been times during the past month when, if she would have offered even the slightest warming toward him, he might have reneged and dropped the uncaring front behind which he'd been posing. But he'd been hurt by her rebuffs too many times to approach her again. A man could stand being turned away only to a point before withdrawing a safe distance, or—better yet—going where he knew he'd find a positive response.

When Catherine came home, Clay was drowsing in the living room with a book on his lap. He yawned, sat up and ran a hand through his hair. It had been a long time since they'd said anything civil to each other. He thought, maybe . . .

"How was it?" he inquired.

She glanced over his tousled hair, wondering why he bothered to make it appear as if he'd been home all night when she hadn't the slightest doubt whom he'd been with. She kept her voice intentionally expressionless as she replied, "I didn't like the way you could hear the dancers' feet echoing on the floor every time they landed."

Clay withdrew further into his protective shield.

February came, bringing gray days that thwarted even the most blithe spirits. Catherine decided to stay in school until the semester ended in mid-March, but the chore became harder and harder as she grew heavier and more listless.

And in the town house in Golden Valley not even the briefest word was spoken between husband and wife.

Chapter 25

THE DAY THEY released Herb Anderson from the Hennepin County Workhouse, the Chenook winds were blowing elsewhere in the country, but in Minnesota the cold leaden skies matched Anderson's temperament. Gusty winds lapped at his ankles, whipping their icy tongues along the frozen slush beside the road as he walked. It was hard going without overshoes. Time and again his slick soles skittered on the uneven wayside and he swore under his breath. He hitchhiked his way into Minneapolis, finding the city as dismal as the highway had been, malcontent under the dirty blanket of late-winter ice that bore the remnants of the road crews' seasonal efforts at sanding and salting.

It was late afternoon, everybody scurrying with their chins pulled low into coat collars, scarcely looking up. Herb was forced to take a city bus to the old neighborhood, and even on it, the cold seeped in. He rode with arms crossed tight, staring out the window with unsmiling eyes.

Jesus, a drink sounds good. Kept me dry all these months, thinking they finally got old Herb. Hah, just who in the hell do they think they are, taking away a man's free will? I can dry out any damn time I want to. Didn't I always say I could! Well, I did it, by God, just like I said I could. But what gave them sons-a-bitches the right to force it on me? When I get to Haley's I'll show them sons-a-bitches that Herb Anderson quits drinkin' when Herb Anderson's good and ready, and not one day sooner!

At Haley's Bar the usual old crowd was there, picking up glasses instead of their kids.

"Well, look who's here! Been keepin' a stool warm for ya, Herb."

All of his cronies moved aside to make room, slapping him on the shoulder, settin' 'em up.

"First one's on me, huh? Hey, Georgie, bring Herb here a taste of what he's been missin'!"

Ah, this is what a man needs, thought Herb. Friends who talk your language.

The feel of the varnished bar was like balm beneath his elbows. The smoky, neon haze around the jukebox burned his unaccustomed eyes wonderfully. The blaring medley of good ole country songs about wronged loves and foiled hearts made the wounds bleed like ulcers, self-opened. Herb raised another shot and downed it, then squeezed the shot glass and reveled in being the center of attention.

And all the while the alcohol did its dirty work; all the outrage that life had handed Herb Anderson came doubling back.

Ada tensed, placed trembling fingers to her lips at the sound of someone fumbling at the door. It was locked, but there came the click of a key. Then the door was flung wide and Herb wavered before her.

"Well, well, well, if it isn't Ada, keeping the home fires burning," he observed thickly.

"Why, Herb," she exclaimed in her timid way, "you're out."

"Goddam right I am, no thanks to you."

"Why, Herb, you should've told me you were coming home."

"So you coulda had lover boy here to keep me out?"

"Shut the door, Herb, it's cold."

He eyed the door sullenly. "You think it's cold in here, you oughta try prison a while." He swung wide and slapped hard at the door, which cracked against the frame and bounced back open. Ada edged around him and shut it again. He watched her suspiciously, weaving slightly, hanging onto the front edges of his jacket with both hands.

"H-how are you, Herb?"

He continued to glower at her with sallow eyes. "What the hell do you care, Ada? Where was your concern in November? Man expects his wife to stand behind him at a time like that."

"They told me I didn't need to come, Herb, and Steve was home."

"So I heard. Bet the bunch of you got together and saw to it I wouldn't even see my own kid, didn't you!"

"He was just here for a little while."

"Ada, he's my only goddam kid, and I got rights!"

She dropped her eyes and fidgeted with a button on her duster.

"You know what a man thinks about in prison, Ada?"

"It wasn't prison, it was just the workh—"

"It was the same as a prison and you know it!" he roared.

Ada began to turn away, but he caught one thin arm and swung her around to face him. "Why the hell'd you do it to me? Why!" The blast of his breath made Ada turn her face sharply away but he caught a fistful of her duster and lifted her to her toes, an inch from his mouth. "Who was he? I deserve to know after all these years."

"Please, Herb." She plucked at his knotted fist but he only clenched the cotton all the tighter.

"Who! I sat in that stinkin' hole and made up my mind I'd get it out of you once and for all."

"It don't matter. I stayed with you, didn't I?"

"You stayed because I'd've found you and your lover boy and killed you both, and you knew it!" He suddenly thrust her away and she fell sprawling upon the sofa behind her. "Just like I'd like to kill that slut of a daughter you spawned while I was off fighting the goddam Vietcong! How could you do a thing like that? How! Everybody looks at you and me together and I can read their minds. Poor little Ada, living with that no-'count bum, Herb! You had 'em all fooled, all these years with your little mouse-in-the-corner act. But not me, not me! I never forgot, not for one minute, what you done to me while I was good enough to go out and fight your war for you. Every time I look at that blond hair and that bastard face of hers I remember, and I swore long ago I'd get even with the pair of you one day. And finally I get my chance when the little slut gets herself knocked up by that rich son-of-a-bitch, and I figger for once in his life Old Herb is gonna get paid back for what he put up with all those years. And do you know how sweet it was to think it was comin' straight from the hand of one who owed it to me—that whorin' no-good who's just like her mother?" Herb was weaving, his eyes bright with rage. "You owed it to me, Ada! You both owed it to me! But what did you do? You saw to it that I ended up empty-handed again, didn't you!"

"I never—"

"Shut up!" he barked, pointing a finger straight at her nose, "Shut up!" He towered over her, leaning dangerously near. "You had this comin' for nineteen years, Ada. Nineteen years I looked at your bastard and seen my own flesh and blood turned against me by the two of you till he finally run away from home. Then when he comes back the first time, you side with them and let them railroad me into prison. And just to twist the knife in the wound, you marry her off to my meal ticket. Goddamit, Ada, I had to read about the wedding in a *newspaper*. You kept me away on purpose, and I never even got to see Steve!"

"I didn't have nothing to do with—"

But Ada's cowering body was jerked to its feet.

"Don't lie to me, slut! I took nineteen years of your lies, and what does it get me but prison!"

He reeled back and swung the first blow to the side of Ada's head, sending it twirling while she fought to cover her face.

"You was on their side all the time, always siding against me!"

The next blow fell on her jaw and dropped Ada to the floor.

"That was my ship comin' in and you knew it!"

A savage kick raised Ada and dropped her back onto the floor.

Incensed now beyond reason, Herb Anderson's injustices fed upon themselves. The hate that had been too shallowly submerged for so long erupted in a wild red rage that found vent upon the hapless Ada. The alcohol lent its beastly hand in raising the man's temper and fists until the deed he'd begun

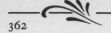
lay senseless and broken on the floor before him. He stared at the huddled heap, wiped a trickle of sputum from the side of his mouth, then tasted her blood on his knuckles and ran from the house, then from the neighborhood, and the next day from the town, then the state.

Catherine was typing when the phone rang downstairs. A moment later she heard Clay's footsteps pelting up the stairs, then his voice behind her.

"Catherine?"

He watched as she raised an elbow and kneaded the back of her neck.

"Cat?" he said gently.

The word—that above all others—made her suddenly swing around to find apprehension written on Clay's face.

"What is it?"

"That was Mrs. Sullivan, your mother's neighbor."

"Mother?" She half-rose from her chair. "What's wrong?"

Clay saw the lines of fright that suddenly pinched up her face. Instinctively he moved to her and laid a hand on her shoulder. "Your mother is in the hospital. They want us to come right away."

"But what's wrong?"

"Come on, we'll talk about it on the way."

"Clay, tell me!"

"Catherine, don't panic, okay?" He took her hand and led her hurriedly through the house. "It's not good for you in your condition. Here, put your coat on and I'll back the car out."

She nearly tore his jacket sleeve off stopping him. "Don't coddle me, Clay. Tell me what's wrong."

He covered her hand, squeezed it so hard that he curled it up. "Cat, your father is out of the workhouse. He got drunk and went home that way."

"Oh, no," she wailed from behind her fingertips.

Fear trickled through Clay, but not for her mother, for her.

"Come on, we'd better hurry, Cat," he said gently.

For the first time ever Catherine was grateful for Clay's penchant for speed. He drove the Corvette with the grim determination of an Indy-500 racer, taking curves and lane-changes in robotlike fashion, taking his sight from the road only long enough to assure himself Catherine was still all right. She sat huddled and shivering, reaching out to clasp the dashboard occasionally, eyes riveted straight ahead. Once they arrived at the hospital, she was out of the car like a shot, and Clay had to jog to catch up with her. When they reached the emergency ward, Catherine broke away from Clay, surging toward the broad-beamed woman who immediately rose from a chair and came forward with outstretched hands.

"Cathy, I'm so sorry."

"How is she, Mrs. Sullivan?"

The woman's eyes immediately sought Clay's. He nodded.

"The doctors are still with her. I don't know yet. Oh, girl, what that man done to her . . ." And Mrs. Sullivan dissolved into tears. Clay's first thought was for Catherine, and he urged her into a chair while Mrs. Sullivan whimpered into a limp handkerchief. He stood before the pair, clutching Catherine's icy hand in his.

"She—she made it to the phone to call me," choked Mrs. Sullivan. "I don't know how, though."

Clay felt utterly helpless. He could do nothing but take the chair next to Catherine's and hold her hand while she stared with glazed eyes at the other pieces of cold, uncomfortable furniture across the room. Finally a nurse approached, saying the doctor would talk to them now. Clay restrained Catherine, pulling on her hand.

"Maybe I should go."

"No!" she insisted, yanking her hand out of his. "She's my mother. I'll go."

"Not alone then."

The doctor introduced himself, shook their hands and glanced at Catherine's roundness.

"Mrs. Forrester, your mother is in no danger of dying, do you understand?"

"Yes." But Catherine's eyes were locked on the door behind which her mother lay.

"She has been badly beaten and has a very bruised face. She's been sedated so there's really no point in your seeing her. Perhaps tomorrow would be just as well."

"She insists," Clay said.

The doctor took a deep breath and sighed.

"Very well, but before you go in I must warn you that she is not a pretty sight. I want you to be prepared for that. In your condition, shock won't help you at all. Don't be frightened by the amount of equipment—it looks far more complicated than it is. Your mother has suffered a fractured nasal septum, which is why her nose appears to be pushed to one side. She also has two fractured ribs. They compromised the breathing so a tracheotomy had to be performed, and she has a tube projecting from her throat. The respirator machine looks alarming, but is only helping her breath temporarily. She'll soon be doing it on her own again. She has a nasal-gastric tube, a prophylaxis, to empty the stomach and prevent vomiting, and of course we are giving her some IV's, a little plasma.

"Now, do you still think you want to go inside?" He found himself wishing the girl would spare herself the sight. But she nodded, so the doctor was given one of the unpalatable tasks that sometimes made him ask himself why he'd chosen this profession.

The woman on the bed did not even remotely resemble Ada. Her nose was flattened. Her forehead was grotesque with bulging, strawberrylike welts. The cracked lips were puffed beyond recognition and showed telltale marks of blood. Tubes seemed to be stitched into her everywhere, leading to inverted bottles above the bed, a plastic sack hanging beside the mattress, and the respirator which created the only sound in the room with its bellowslike mechanism breathing steadily. A blood-pressure cuff circled her arm, its cords connected to a computer which gave a constant digital printout of vital signs. In contrast to her puffed face, the rest of Ada looked shrunken and dissipated. Her hands lay limp and blue; the little finger of the left was in a splint.

Clay found himself swallowing repeatedly at the pitiful sight before him. He clutched Catherine's hand and felt the tremor there. She gave no other sign of the struggle within, but he was smitten with pity for her, knowing how she held her emotions in check. He thought of his own feelings, should this be

Angela, and rubbed the inside of Catherine's elbow and pulled her arm hard against him. After only a brief moment, the doctor ushered them silently out. Catherine walked like a zombie all the way to the car.

When Clay opened the car door, he had to gently urge Catherine to bend, to sit, to turn her legs inside. He wished the doctor could have prescribed a tranquilizer for her, but it would be dangerous in so advanced a pregnancy. Starting the car, Clay felt a double fear now, for both Catherine and the baby. She sat woodenly while he fastened the top button of her coat, tugged at the collar and urged, "You've got to keep warm, Cat." But she only stared straight ahead, dry-eyed, unmoving. There were no trite phrases Clay could bring himself to utter. *Don't worry* or *She'll be all right* were more . . . or less . . . than he wanted to say to the tormented woman beside him. All he could do was find her hand in the dark and lace his fingers through hers as he drove, hoping that the meager offering might help somehow. But her lifeless fingers lay inert within his hold all the way home.

He suffered an agony of helplessness, driving through the night with his thumb brushing against the back of her hand in silent communication to which she did not respond. Their hands lay upon her narrow lap, the back of Clay's resting lightly against her now fully round stomach. He thought of the pain children bear at their parents' expense and hoped his child need never suffer what Catherine now suffered.

At home he helped her with her coat, then watched as she listlessly mounted the steps.

"Catherine, what can I do? Can I fix you something?"

She had stopped, as if she didn't know where she was. He came behind her, his hands in his pockets, wishing she would say, "Make me some cocoa, rub my back, put on some music, hold me . . ." But she shut him out instead, insulated within her carefully guarded solitariness.

"No, there's nothing. I'm very tired, Clay. I just want to go to bed." She walked upstairs with rigid back, directly to the bedroom, and closed the door upon the comfort he sought to offer.

He stood in the middle of the living room looking at nothing for a long time. He shut his eyes. His Adam's apple bobbed up and down convulsively. He pictured Ada, then Catherine's face as she'd looked at her mother's still figure. He sat down on the edge of the davenport with his face in his hands. He did not know how much time had passed before he sighed, rose, and made a phone call to his father. He made up his bed on the davenport and wearily took off his trousers and shirt, but when the light was out he went instead to stand before the sliding glass door, staring out at the ebony night.

He needed the woman upstairs as badly right now as she needed him.

A faint, muffled sound intruded itself into the bruised night, bringing him to turn from the window. He strained to listen and it came again, high, distant, like the wind behind walls—hurt wind, wailing wind—and he knew what it was before he felt his way up the stairs in the dark. He paused at her bedroom door and listened. He laid his palm against the wood, then his forehead too. When he could stand it no longer, he found the doorknob and soundlessly turned it. In the dimness, he made out the blur of the pale blue bedspread, padded silently across to lean and explore it with his hands. He felt her curled beneath the covers, clutching them over her head. He ran his hands along the snail-shaped form, the pity in his heart a choking thing while her high keening came muffled from the womb she had crawled back into. He pulled gently at the covers but she only clung to them the tighter.

"Catherine," he began, but found his throat clotted with emotion.

She gripped the guardian covers fiercely until at last he ebbed them from her fingers to reveal her curled with her head covered with both arms, her elbows tucked between her knees. Gently he lifted the blankets and lay down behind her, then covered them both up again. He tried to pull her into his arms but she only huddled tighter, wailing in that solitary, high syllable that made Clay's eyes sting.

His voice quavered as he whispered, "Cat, oh, Cat, let me help you."

He found her fists clenched in her hair and eased them away, running a palm along her arm, then pressing his chest upon her curved back until he could bear it no longer. Bracing himself on an elbow, he leaned over the curled ball of her, brushing back her hair, assuring her throatily, "I'm here, Cat, I'm here. Don't go through this all alone."

"Mamaaaaaa . . ." she wailed pitifully into the dark, "Mamaaaaa . . ."

"Please, Cat, please," Clay begged, running his hand down her arm to find her hands fiercely knotted between her knees.

"Mama," she wailed again.

He felt her body quaking and sought to calm her by cradling her as best he could with one arm along her thigh, cupping a knee and pulling her back against him.

"Darling, it's Clay. Please don't do this. Let me help you . . . let me hold you, please. Turn around, Cat, just turn around. I'm here."

"Mama, I didn't mean to," she quailed in that same childlike voice that frightened Clay so terribly. He stroked her hair, her shoulder, braced up and rested his cheek on the back of her head, waiting for some sign that she understood.

"Please, Catherine . . . I . . . don't shut me out."

He felt the first soundless spasm, the first sob that was not yet a sob, and gently, gently, pulled at her shoulder, turning her toward him until, like a broken spring, she unwound all at once and burrowed into his arms, while painful sobs wrenched from her throat.

"Hold me, Clay, hold me, hold me," she begged, clinging like a drowning person while her hot tears scalded his neck. Her grip was like iron while she quaked wretchedly and cried into him.

"Catherine, oh, God, I'm so sorry," he said throatily into her hair.

"Mama, mama, it's all my fault."

"No, Cat, no," he murmured, clasping her to him all the more closely, as if to pull her within his very body that he might absorb her pain. "It's not your fault," he soothed, kissing the top of her head while she babbled and cried and blamed herself. All the pent-up tears that Catherine had so long refused to shed for herself came rushing out for her mother while she clung to Clay with arms and hands that could not hold tightly enough. He cradled the back of her head, pulling her cheek against the silken hair of his chest, rocking at times, lost in pity, aching with the feeling of her heaving stomach pressed at last to his, but for the wrong reason. She muttered unintelligible sounds, broken by sobs which Clay welcomed, knowing they were the cure of her.

"It's all my f-fault, all my faul . . ."

He forced her mouth hard against his chest to stop the words. He swallowed convulsively before he could speak.

"No, Cat, you can't blame yourself. I won't let you."

"B-but it's t-true. It's because I'm pre-pregnant. I should've kn-known he wa-wanted the money . . . ba-bad enough. I hate him, I h-hate him. Why did he do it . . . Hold me, Clay . . . I had to get away fr-from him. I had to, but to get a-away I had to b-be those things he c-called me, but I d-didn't care, I didn't care. You're so warm . . . They never hugged m-me, never k-kissed me. I was good, I was al-w-ways good, just that one t-time with you, but he sh-shouldn't take it out on her."

Clay's heart thundered at her pitiful outpouring. She babbled on, almost mindlessly.

"I shouldn't have le-left her. I should have stayed, b-but it was s-so awful there when St-Steve left. He was the only one who ever—"

A deep sob broke from Catherine and she clung more desperately to Clay. Now he softly encouraged her, knowing she must say these things.

"Who ever what?"

"Who ever l-loved me. Not even M-Mama could, but I n-never understood wh-why. They never took me pl-places or bought me th-things like other kids got, or played with m-me. Uncle Fr-Frank used to kiss me and I'd pretend he w-was Daddy. Steve loved me, but af-after he was gone there was nobody and I used to pr-pretend I had a baby who'd love me. I thought if only I had a b-baby I'd never be lonely."

She stopped then, having discovered this truth at last.

Clay squeezed his eyes shut hard. Her heart was hammering against his, her arms clinging tenaciously to his neck. Pity and compassion and the overwhelming need to heal her welled high in Clay. He was deluged by the desire to protect, fulfill, calm her, and to provide the missing years of love that could never be made up for. He fought against tears, holding her long and hard against his body, unable to hold her long enough, hard enough, pressing her so fiercely that at last he opened his legs to let one of hers in, high against him. And hers opened and his knee found shelter against her too. They clung that way, sharing a new bond of warmth and comfort until, pressed between them, the baby objected to all that crowding and moved restlessly within Catherine. A wild exhilaration lifted Clay's stomach, as if he'd just reached the downhill slope of a roller coaster. And everything—the horror Catherine had suffered this day, the first feel of his child's movement in her belly, her own desperate cry for love—made his motions somehow right as his hands skimmed over her body, up her back, down her side, down her warm buttock and leg that lay over his hip. And even as Catherine cried against his chest, Clay found the hollow behind her knee and pulled her more securely into her nestling place. He ran his hand again up her hip, up her side, finding her breast and cradling it, and the side of her stomach with his forearm. She was warm and reaching and unresisting against him, and he whispered raspily against her ear, "Cat, oh, Cat, why did you wait so long? Why did it take all this?"

With a hand, he commanded the back of her head and lowered his mouth into her salt-kiss. Her mouth opened wide and took him in, and it ceased to matter that it was only in desperation she turned to him. It ceased to matter that she might later feel he took advantage of her in her weakness. His hand, warm and soft and seeking, trailed, unchecked, from her full breast to the hard, taut stomach that protruded because of him. He fondled it searchingly, awed by its solidness, by the thought of the life it carried. And as if the baby heard its father's pleas, it moved within. Clay lay stock-still then, stunned, with his palm conforming to the shape of Catherine's flesh, willing the child to move once more. And when it had, and he'd again known the feel of it, Clay reached unhesitatingly to pull Catherine's wide gown up and run his hands over the bare, firm skin beneath. He skimmed his palm again and again over the warm curve of her belly, discovering things that his body had caused in hers: the protruding navel, the engorged breasts, the widened, enlarged nipples, and—yet again—the fluttery motion of life beneath his hand. How often he had wondered. How often he had thought it his right to explore these changes of his making. How often she, too, had longed to share them but had steeled herself against him, shielded in an armor of assumed remoteness.

But what had started out as a journey of pity and compassion became one of sensuality as Clay's caressing hand moved lower, touching the crisp hair that couched the spot where Catherine's burden thrust itself sharply outward from her body. Wordlessly he slipped his hand between her thighs, covering her, swollen there, with the length of his long, closed fingers, pressing gently upward, feeling her pulse throbbing there, learning her. Thoughts of her sexuality, her pregnancy, what he knew he could not do, made him curiously callow in his exploration of her. He moved his hand once more to her stomach.

"Oh, Cat," he whispered, "your stomach's so hard. Does it hurt?"

She moved her head to answer no, amazed by his naïveté.

"I felt the baby move," he whispered almost reverently, yet his breath was warm and labored on her skin. "It moved right there under my hand." He spread his fingers over her stomach again, as if in invitation, but when nothing happened his hand again sought the intimate world between her legs.

And Catherine closed her eyes and let him . . . let him . . . let him, drifting in a myriad of emotions she'd held at bay so long, thinking to her child, It's your father.

And the father's hand filled itself with the mother's body that readied itself for their baby's birth.

"It's too late, Clay," she murmured once.

"I know." But he kissed the hard, warm orb of her stomach anyway, then lay his face in the juncture of her legs as if he must, unable to solace himself and her any other way. The child kicked against his ear.

Catherine was drawn painfully back to reality from the secure place in which she'd allowed herself to drift. The thrum of her heart in odd spots in her body told her she had let Clay go too far to pull away from him unhurt when the time came.

"Stop, Clay," she said in a loving whisper.

"I'm only touching, that's all."

"Stop, it's not right."

"I won't go any further. Just let me touch you," he murmured.

"No, stop," she insisted, stiffening.

"Don't pull away . . . come here."

But now she resisted even more, having come fully to her senses.

He moved and tried to take her in his arms, then asked, "Why do you pull away all of a sudden?"

"Because it doesn't seem right with my mother lying in that hospital."

"I don't believe you. A minute ago you had forgotten all about your mother, hadn't you? Why did you really turn away?"

She didn't know.

Very gently he said, "Catherine, I'm not your father. I won't call you names and make you feel guilty afterward. It's not because of your mother that you turn away, it's because of your father, isn't it?"

She only shivered.

"If you keep pulling away now, he'll have beaten you just as surely as he beat her, only the marks he leaves on you won't go away like hers will, don't you see that?"

"It's my fault he beat her up, because once before I gave in to you. And now here I am again . . . I . . . you . . ." But she stopped, confused, afraid.

"He's making an emotional cripple out of you. Can't you see it, Catherine?"

"I'm not! I'm not! I feel things, I want things, I need things, just like everybody else!"

"Then why don't you let yourself show it?"

"I j-just did."

"But look what it took," he said in a pained whisper.

"Get your hands off me," she quavered. She was crying again but he would not allow her to roll away from him. "Why? What are you afraid of, Catherine?"

"I'm not afraid!" But her voice caught in her throat even as she said it.

He held her flat on her back, silently willing her to admit what it was that had held her emotionally sterile for too long, afraid that what he was doing might backfire and hurt her more.

"Of those names?"

He held her prisoner while her mind raced backward to ugly, unwanted memories which would not set her free. Clay's breath on her face brought her careening back to the present, to this man whom she loved and was so afraid of loving, of losing.

"I-I'm not," she choked, while Clay felt her pulse pounding against him in places where he held her down. The muscles in her forearms tensed beneath his hands as she repeated, "I'm not, I'm not—"

He eased his hold, prompting softly, "What aren't you? Say it, say it, and be free of it. What?" She ceased struggling against him, and when he had freed her arms she flung one across her eyes and sobbed behind it. With infinite tenderness he touched her breasts, her stomach, the swollen world between her legs again, whispering urgently, "What aren't you, Catherine? Say it, say it."

"I'm not—" she tried again, but choked to a halt.

"No, you're not, you're not. Believe me. Say it, Catherine. You're not what?"

It came out in a rush, tumblewords finding voice at last as she covered her face with both hands.

"I'm not bad I'm not a slut I'm not a whore I'm not I'm not I'm not!"

He enfolded her protectively against him, pinching his eyes shut while she flung her arms around his neck and clung. He felt a shudder possess her body and spoke into her hair.

"No, you never were, no matter how many times he said it. You never were any of those things."

"Then why did he say them, Clay, why?"

"I don't know . . . Shh . . . The important thing is that you don't believe him, that you don't let him hurt you anymore."

They rested at last against each other, exhausted, silent. Before she slept, Catherine again pictured her mother and realized she herself had just escaped becoming the same kind of self-contained, undemonstrative being.

And for the first time ever, she felt she had beaten Herb Anderson instead of the other way around.

Chapter 26

ADA OPENED HER eye. It looked like a soft-poached egg. Her mouth tried to wince but couldn't.

"Mom?" Cathy whispered.

"Caffy?" Ada's lips were still grotesquely swollen.

"You've been asleep a long time."

"Have I?"

"Shh, don't move. Try to rest. You have a cracked rib and if you move it'll hurt."

"I'm so tired," the old woman breathed, succumbing, letting her eye slide shut again. But even in her bleary state she'd observed something that startled her eye open again.

"You've veen crying." She couldn't pronounce her *b* 's.

"A little. Don't worry about me, just worry about—" But tears stung her eyes again, burning the swollen lids. Ada saw and fluttered a hand. Catherine took it, feeling the small sparrow-bones and how little strength her mother had. The same helplessness which Clay had felt the night before, now assaulted Catherine.

"I ain't seen you cry since you was a little girl," Ada whispered, trying her hardest to squeeze her daughter's hand.

"I gave it up long ago, Mom, or I would've been doing it all the time."

"It ain't a good fing to give up."

"No—no it isn't." Catherine swallowed. "Mom, you don't have to talk."

"Funny fing, you sayin' I don't hafta talk, me sayin' you don't hafta cry — least not for each other. Vut I guess we gotta do it for ourselves."

"Why don't you wait till you're feeling stronger."

"Veen waiting nineteen years to get stronger."

"Mom, please . . ."

A gentle pressure on Catherine's hand silenced her. Ada spoke with an effort.

"Time it was said. Just listen. I'm a weak woman, always have veen, vut mayve now I faid my dues. Got to tell you. Herv, he was good to me once, when I was first married to him. When Steve was a vavy you shoulda seen Herv with Steve, why you wouldn'ta known him." She closed her eyes, rested momentarily before continuing. "And then all that vusiness started in the Gulf of Tonkin and Herv, he was in the reserves. When his unit got called to active duty, I figured he'd ve vack in no time. Vut it was worse'n we thought, and he was gone two years. He saw a mighty lot in them two years. He saw so much that he come home liking the liquor too much. The drinking he mighta got over, but what he never got over was findin' me expectin' a vavy when he got home."

Catherine wondered if she had understood Ada's distorted words correctly. "A—a baby?"

The room was still. Ada's single, open eye stared at the ceiling.

"Yes, a vavy. That was you, o' course."

"Me?"

"I told you I was a weak woman." Ada's eye teared.

"I'm not his?"

The bruised head moved back and forth weakly on the pillow while a rippling sense of freedom seeped into Catherine.

"So you see, it wasn't all his fault, Caffy. I done that to him, and he could never forgive me, nor you either."

"I never understood till now."

"I was always so scared to tell you."

"But, why didn't you?" Catherine leaned nearer so her mother could see her face better. "Mom, please, I'm not blaming you, I just need to know, that's all. Why didn't you ever stand up for me? I thought you didn't—" Catherine stopped, her eyes flickered away from her mother's.

"Love you? I know that's what you was gonna say. It's no excuse at all, vut Herv, he was just waiting for me to show you some favoritism. Why, he'd use any excuse to vlow up. I was scared of him, Caffy, I was always scared after that."

"Then why didn't you leave him?"

"I figured I owed him to stay. Vesides, where would I go?"

"Where are you going to go now? Surely you aren't going to go back to him?"

"No, I don't need to now that you know. Vesides, it's different now. You and Steve all grown up, all I have to worry avout is myself. Steve, he's made a good life for himself in the service and you got Clay. I don't need to worry avout you no more."

A prickle of guilt traced through Catherine's veins. She rubbed the back of her mother's hand absently, then sat forward to study Ada's face.

"Who was he, Mom?" she asked wistfully.

A contorted smile tried to find its way through the swollen lips.

"It don't matter who, just what. He was a fine man. He was the vest thing that ever happened to me. I'd go through all the years of hell with Herv again if I could live those days once more with your father."

"Then you loved him?"

"I did . . . oh, how I did."

"Then why didn't you leave Da—Herb, and marry him?"

"He was already married."

Hearing all this, Catherine realized that within her mother dwelled an Ada she would never know, except for the glint of remembrance in the bloodshot eye.

"Is he still alive?" Catherine asked, suddenly wanting to know everything about him.

"Lives right here in the city. That's why it's best if I don't tell you who he is."

"Will you tell me someday?"

"I can't make that fromise. See, he went flaces. He's *some*thing now. You'd never have to ve ashamed of having a father like him. My—my mouth is a little dry. Do you think I could have some water?"

Catherine helped her mother drink, listened to her weary sigh as she sank back again.

"Mom, I have a confession to make too."

"You, Caffy?" The surprised way her mother said it made Catherine wonder if Ada might not have always thought her above wrong, only she herself had been too busy looking for outward shows of affection to see the deeper, intrinsic feeling.

"Mom, I did it on purpose—got pregnant, I mean. At least, I think I did. I wanted to get even with Herb for all the times he'd called me names, and I wanted to get away from both of you, from that house where there was never anything but fighting and his drunkenness. I guess subconsciously I believed a baby would get me out and provide me with love. I didn't think he'd take it out on you, but I feel somehow it is part of the reason he beat you, wasn't it?"

"No, no, don't vlame yourself, Caffy. It was a long time coming. He said I shoulda been at his trial, and that it was my fault he never got no money outa Clay. Vut the real reason was because you wasn't his. I don't kid myself that's the real reason, and I don't want you to go vlaming yourself."

"But I've made such a mess of things."

"No, honey. Now you just get that out of your head. You got Clay, and the vavy coming, and with a father like Clay, why, that vavy's vound to ve somevody too."

"Mom, Clay and I—" But Catherine could not tell her mother the truth about her future with Clay.

"What?"

"We were wondering if when the baby is born, if you're strong enough then, you'd come and stay with us and help out for a couple days."

The pathetic excuse for a smile tore at Catherine's heartstrings as her mother sighed contentedly and closed her eye.

It was the day after Clay and Catherine had shared the same bed, but he'd left her asleep that morning. Returning home in the late afternoon, he was eager to see her.

She heard the door slam and her hands grew idle, the water splattering unheeded over the paring knife and the rib of celery she'd been washing. He

came up the stairs, across the kitchen behind her, and laid a hand lightly on her shoulder.

"How was she today?"

A warmth seeped through her blouse at his touch, going beyond skin, beyond muscle, to the core of her. She wanted to turn, take his palm, kiss it and place it on her breast and say, How were you today? How was I? Were we happier for what passed between us last night?

"She hurt a lot, but they gave her painkillers whenever she asked for them. It was very hard for her to talk with her mouth that way."

Clay squeezed her shoulder, waiting for her to turn around, to need him again as she had last night. He could smell her hair, fresh, flower-scented. He watched her hands as water splashed over them and she peeled green, stringy fibers from the celery.

Why doesn't she turn around, he wondered. Can't she read my touch? She must know that I, too, am afraid.

Catherine began to clean another rib of celery she didn't need. She longed to look into his eyes and ask, "What do I mean to you, Clay?" But if he loved her, surely he would have said so by now.

Last night they had been bound together by her vast need for comfort, and by the accident of her pregnancy. At the time that had been justification for the swift siege of intimacy. But he had not said he loved her. Never, during all their months together had he even hinted that he loved her.

Their senses pounded with awareness of each other. Clay saw Catherine's hands fall still. He moved his fingers to the bare skin of her neck, slipping them behind her collar, his thumb brushing her earlobe. The water ran uselessly now, but Catherine's eyes were closed, her wrists dangling against the edge of the sink.

"Catherine . . ." His voice was thick.

"Clay, last night never should have happened," she got out.

Disappointments assaulted him. "Why?" He took the paring knife from her fingers, dropped it into the sink and turned off the water. When he'd forced her to face him he asked again, quietly, "Why?"

"Because we did it for the wrong reasons. It wasn't enough—just my mother's problems and the fact that this baby is yours. Don't you see?"

"But we need each other, Catherine. We're married, I want—"

Suddenly she put her wet hands on his cheeks, interrupting. "Cool off, Clay. It's the easiest way, because we are not going to have a repeat performance of last night."

"Dammit, I don't understand you!" he said angrily, pulling her hands from his face, holding her by the forearms.

"You don't love me, Clay," she said with quiet dignity. "Now do you understand me?"

His eyes pierced hers, steely gray into dusky blue, and he wished he could deny her words. He could easily drown in her tempting eyes, in her smooth skin and beautiful features with which he'd grown so familiar. He could look at her across a room and want to fill his hands with her breasts, lower his mouth to hers, to know the taste and touch of her. But could he say he loved her?

Deliberately now he reached to cup both of her breasts, as if to prove this was all that was necessary. Through the smock and her bra he could tell her nipples were drawn tight. Her breath was heavy and fast.

"You want it too," he said, knowing it was true, for he felt the truth beneath the thumbs that stroked the crests of her breasts.

"You're confusing lust and love."

"I thought last night you finally agreed with me that it's a healthy thing to be touched, to touch back."

"Is this healthy now?"

"You're damn right. Can't you feel what's happening to you?"

Stoically she allowed his hands their freedom, and though she could not prevent her body from responding, she would not give him the satisfaction of moving willfully in any way suggesting acquiescence. "I can feel it. Oh, I can feel it, all right. Does it make you feel macho, knowing what it does to me?"

He dropped his hands suddenly. "Catherine, I can't exist with this coldness of yours. I need more than you put into this relationship."

"And I cannot put more into this relationship without love. And so it's a vicious circle, isn't it, Clay?" She looked straight at his face still glistening with water. She respected him if for nothing more than not lying. "Clay, I'm only being realistic to protect myself. It would have been so easy all these months with you to delude myself every time you turned your eyes on me with that certain look that makes me go all liquid, that you loved me. But I know it's not true."

"To be loved you have to be lovable, Catherine. Don't you understand that? You never try in the least. You carry yourself like you're wearing armor. You don't know how to return a smile or a touch or—"

"Clay, I never learned!" She defended herself. "Do you think things like that come naturally? Do you think it's something you're born with, like you were born with your father's gray eyes and your mother's blond hair? Well, it's not. Love is a learned thing. It's been taught to you since you were in knee pants whether you know it or not. You were one of the lucky ones who had it happening around him all the time. You never questioned it but you always expected it, didn't you? If you fell and got hurt, you were kissed and coddled. If you were gone, then came back, you were hugged and welcomed. If you tried and failed, you were told it didn't matter, they were proud anyway, right? If you misbehaved and were punished, they made you understand it hurt them as badly as it hurt you. None of those lessons were taught to me. Instead, I had the other kind, and I learned to exist without your kind. You take all signs of affection too lightly; you set too little store by them. It's different for me. I can't . . . I can't be—oh, I don't know how to make you understand. When something's in short supply its value goes up. And it's like that with me, Clay. I've never had anyone treat me nice before, so every gesture, every touch, every overture you make toward me is of far greater value to me than it is to you. And I know perfectly well that if I learn to accept them, learn to accept you, I'll be hurt far more than you will when it's time for us to separate. And so I've promised myself I will not grow dependent on you—not emotionally anyway."

"What you're really saying is that we're back where we started, before last night."

"Not exactly." Catherine looked down at her hands; they were fidgeting.

"What's different?"

She looked up, met his gaze directly, then squared her shoulders almost imperceptibly. "My mother told me today that Herb is not my real father. That frees me from him—really frees me—at last. It also gives me even better insight into what happens when people stay in a loveless marriage for all the wrong reasons. I'm never going to end up like her. Never."

During the weeks that followed, Clay mulled over what Catherine had said about love being taught. He had never before dissected the many ways in which his parents had shown him affection. But Catherine was right about one thing: he'd always taken it for granted. He had been so secure in their approval, so certain of their love, he'd never questioned their tactics. He admitted she was right, also, about his placing less value than she upon physical contact. He began to evaluate outward signs of affection by looking at them from Catherine's viewpoint and admitted that he'd taken them too lightly. He began to understand her awful need to remain free of him emotionally, to understand that the idea of loving him loomed like a threat, in light of their agreement to divorce soon after the baby arrived. He analyzed his feelings for her only to find that he honestly did not believe he loved her. He found her physically desirable, but because she had never been demonstrative toward him, it was difficult to imagine he ever would love her. What he wanted was a woman who was capable of impulsively lifting her arms and seeking his kiss. One who could close her eyes against his cheek and make him feel utterly wanted and wanting. He doubted that he could ever achieve with Catherine the kind of free-wheeling spontaneity he needed in a wife.

They bought a spooled crib and matching chest of drawers. He set it up in the second bedroom where the walls still wore that masculine paper of brown designs, totally inappropriate for a nursery.

But when the baby was born, who would stay and who would go?

Her suitcase appeared on the bedroom floor, packed, ready to go at a moment's notice. The first time he came in and saw it, he sank down heavily on the edge of the bed and buried his face in both hands, utterly miserable. He thought about Jill—willing Jill who understood his needs so well, and wished that it were she who was expecting his child. But Jill didn't want babies.

April Fool's Day came, bringing bursting buds and the redolent scent of moist earth that marks spring's arrival. Catherine was given a lavish baby shower by Angela, whose pleasure over the upcoming arrival of her first grandchild was a burning wound to Catherine.

Claiborne surprised Catherine by stopping by one afternoon with "a little something" he'd picked up for the baby: a windup swing Catherine knew the baby wouldn't be big enough to sit in until long after she and Clay were apart.

Ada was back home and called every day to ask how Catherine was. Catherine, grown now to enormous proportions and slothlike slowness, answered, "fine, fine, fine," until finally after hanging up one day, she burst into a torrent of tears, not understanding at all any more what it was she wanted.

* * *

She awakened Clay in the middle of the night, hesitant to touch his sleeping form.

"What?" He braced up on an elbow, hazy yet from sleep.

"The pains have started. They're ten minutes apart."

He flung back the covers and sat up on the davenport, finding her hand in the dark and tugging at it. "Here, sit down."

She got back up immediately, if clumsily. "The doctor said to keep on the move."

"The doctor? You mean you've called him already?"

"Yes, a couple of hours ago."

"But why didn't you wake me?"

"I . . ." But she didn't know why.

"You mean you've been walking around here for two hours in the dark?"

"Clay, I think you should drive me to the hospital, but I don't expect you to stay with me or anything. I'd drive myself, but the doctor said that I shouldn't."

Her words caused a sudden stab of hurt, followed by another of anger.

"You can't keep me out, Catherine; I'm the baby's father."

Surprised, she only answered, "I don't think we'd better waste time arguing now. Do whatever you want when we get there."

They were greeted in the maternity ward by a young nurse whose name tag identified her as Christine Flemming. It did not occur to Ms. Flemming to question Clay's presence. She assumed he would want to stay with Catherine. And so, he was asked to have a seat in a well-lit room with an empty bed in it. When Catherine returned after being blood-typed, she was having a contraction and Ms. Flemming spoke in soothing instructions to her patient, telling her how to breathe properly and how to relax as much as possible. When the contraction ended she turned to Clay and said, "Your job will be to remind her to relax and breathe properly. You can be a big help." So rather than try to explain, Clay listened to her instructions, then stayed in the labor room when the nurse left, holding Catherine's hand, reminding her to keep her breathing quick and shallow, timing the length of contractions and the minutes between.

Soon the gentle-voiced nurse returned and spoke soothingly to Catherine. "Let's see how far along you are now. Try to relax, and tell me if a contraction should start while I'm checking you." It happened so fast that Clay had no time to gracefully withdraw nor to be embarrassed. Neither was he asked to leave, as he thought he'd be at this time. Instead, he stood on the other side of the bed, holding Catherine's hand while her dilation was checked, amazed to find how appropriate it felt to be included in such a natural way. When the nurse finished her examination she pulled Catherine's gown back down, sat on the edge of the bed and lightly stroked the wide base of Catherine's abdomen.

"Here comes another one, Catherine. Now just relax with it and count — one, two, three . . ." Catherine's hand gripped Clay's like the jaws of a trap. Sweat broke out under his arms while beads of perspiration gathered into runnels on Catherine's temples and trailed into her hair. Her eyes were closed and her mouth was tightly shut.

He remembered what he was there for. "Open your mouth, Catherine," he reminded softly. "Pant, pant, little breaths."

And through her pain Catherine knew she was happy Clay was there. His voice seemed to calm her when she was most afraid.

After the pain was over, she opened her eyes and asked Ms. Flemming, "How could you tell it was coming?"

Christine Flemming had a pretty face with a madonnalike smile and a very patient way about her that made both Catherine and Clay feel comfortable in her presence. Her voice was silken, soothing. She was a woman well-suited to her profession.

"Why, I could feel it. Here, give me your hand, Catherine." She took Catherine's hand and curved it low around her stomach. "Mr. Forrester," she instructed, "put your hand here on the other side. Now wait—you'll feel it when it starts. The muscles begin to tighten, starting at the sides, and the stomach arches and changes shape during the height of the contraction. When it ends, the muscles relax and settle down again. Here it comes; it will take half a minute or so until it's at its peak."

Catherine's and Clay's fingertips touched, their hands forming a light cradle around the base of her stomach. Together they shared the exhilaration of discovery as the muscles tensed and changed the contours of Catherine's abdomen. For Clay, it made her pain a palpable thing. He stared, big-eyed, at what was happening beneath his hand. But in the middle of the contraction, Catherine's hand flew above her head and Clay tore his eyes away to her face to find her lips pursed, jaw clenched against the pain. He leaned to soothe her hair back from her forehead, and at the touch of his hand, her lips relaxed and fell open. He spoke his litany again in quiet tones, reminding her, and felt a curious sense of fulfillment that he had the power to ease her, even in the height of her labor.

"That one was longer than the last," Christine Flemming said when it was over. "As they get closer, it's more important for you to relax between them. Sometimes it helps to have your tummy rubbed lightly, like this. I like to think that the baby can feel it, too, and knows you're out here waiting to welcome him." With a gentle palm the nurse stroked the outer perimeter of Catherine's stomach. Catherine's eyes remained closed, one wrist over her forehead, her other hand in Clay's. He felt her grip slacken as the nurse continued those feather-light strokes over her distended abdomen. With a smile, Christine Flemming looked up at Clay and said softly, "You're doing very well, so I'll let you take over for a while. I'll be back in a few minutes." Then on silent white shoes she was gone and Clay was left to stroke Catherine's stomach.

He understood things in that time of closeness with Catherine, things as deep and eternal as the force of life trying to repeat itself in her body. He understood that nature had planned this time of travail to draw man and woman closer than at any other time. Thus the pain had purpose beyond bringing a child into the world.

When they took Catherine to the delivery room, Clay felt suddenly bereft, as if his role was being usurped by strangers. But when they'd asked if he'd taken the classes required for fathers to be in the delivery room, he'd had to answer honestly, "No."

The University of Minnesota Hospital did not use delivery tables any more. Instead, Catherine found herself placed in a birthing chair, which allowed gravity to pull while she pushed. Christine Flemming was there through the delivery, supportive and smiling, and once Catherine even joked with her, saying, "We're not so smart. The Indians knew this secret long ago when they squatted in the woods to have their babies."

The daughter of Catherine and Clay Forrester was born with the fifth contraction in the birthing chair, and Catherine knew before she faded off into blessed sleep—lying flat now—that it was a girl.

Catherine swam upward through a lake of cotton fuzziness. When she surfaced and opened heavy-lidded eyes, she found Clay dozing in a chair, his cheek propped on one hand. His hair was disheveled and he needed a shave. He looks terrific, she thought through a crazy, disoriented fog. Her mind was still moony and wandering as she studied him. The rhythm of his breathing was lengthened by her drug-induced lethargy. Between pains, hazily she thought, I still love him.

"Clay?" The word was a little mumbled.

His eyes flew open and he jumped to his feet. "Cat," he said softly, "you're awake."

Her eyes drifted closed. "Barely. I did the wrong thing again, didn't I, Clay?" She felt him take her hand, felt the back of it pressed against his lips.

"You mean having a girl?"

She nodded her head which felt like it weighed hundreds of pounds.

"You won't think so when you see her."

Catherine smiled a little bit. Her lips were very dry and he wished he had something to put on them for her.

"Clay?"

"I'm here."

"Thanks for helping."

She drifted into oblivion again, her breathing heavy and rhythmic. He sat on the chair beside her bed with his elbows on his knees, holding her hand long after he knew she was asleep again. Then with a heavy sigh he lowered his forehead against her knuckles and closed his eyes as well.

Grandmother Forrester's cane announced her imminent arrival. When she rounded the doorway, the first thing she said was, "Young lady, I am seventy-eight years old. The next one had better be a boy." But she limped to the bed and bestowed an honest-to-goodness kiss upon the consummate perfection of her firstborn great-granddaughter.

Marie came, laughing as ever, with the announcement that she and Joe are going to get married at last, as soon as he graduated from high school in a couple of months. She added that she'd been inspired to "give it a whirl" by Catherine and Clay's success.

Claiborne and Angela came daily, never empty-handed. They brought dresses so absurdly frilly the baby would surely get lost in all those ruffles, stuffed toys so big they would dwarf an infant, a music box that played "Eidelweiss." Although they both fawned over Melissa, Claiborne's reaction to her was heart-touching. He would stand at the nursery window with his fingertips against the glass as if transfixed. Walking away, his head was the last to be turned forward. He even stopped on his way home from work one day, although it was decidedly inconvenient for him to do so. He said things like,

"When she's old enough to ride a trike, Grampa will see that she gets the best one in town." Or, "Wait until she walks—won't that be something?" Or, "You and Clay will have to take a weekend away by yourselves soon and leave the baby with us."

Bobbi came. She stood in front of the window with her thumbs strung up on her rear jeans pockets, her feet rolled over until she was almost standing on the sides of her shoes. "Well, wouldja look at that!" she exclaimed softly. "And to think I had a hand in it."

Ada came with the news that she'd signed up for a course in driver's education so she could come to Catherine and Clay's house to see the baby now and then. Herb had disappeared.

Steve wired an enormous bouquet of pink carnations and baby's breath and followed it with a long-distance phone call in which his main message was that he'd be getting leave again in August, and when he got to Minnesota, he wanted to see Cathy and Clay and Melissa all living under one roof.

And, of course, there was Clay.

Clay, who was just across the river at the law school and popped in at any time of day. Clay, who stood at the end of Catherine's bed when they were alone together and couldn't seem to think of anything to say. Clay, who played the father's role well when other visitors were there, laughing at their jokes about waiting until Melissa was bringing boyfriends home, turning his smile on Catherine, exclaiming over the never-ending stream of gifts, but spending long minutes at the nursery window alone, swallowing at the lump that never disappeared from his throat.

Ada came and helped out for three days after Catherine and Melissa went home. During that time Ada slept on the davenport. It became particularly hellish for Clay, sleeping with Catherine. Each night he would awaken to the tiny sounds of suckling from the other side of the bed and he wanted more than anything to turn the light on and watch them. But he knew Catherine would be bothered by both the light and his watching, so he lay silent, pretending to be asleep. How surprised he'd been at the news that she intended to breast-feed the baby. At first he supposed she made the choice out of a sense of duty, for there was a lot of propaganda on the subject. But as the days wore on, he realized that everything Catherine did for and with Melissa was done instead from a deep sense of mother-love.

Catherine began to change.

There were times when he came upon her with her face buried in Melissa's little tummy, cooing to her, talking in soft expressions of love. Once he saw her lightly suck on Melissa's toes. When she gave the baby a bath, there was a steady stream of talking and light laughter. When the baby slept too long, Catherine actually hounded her bedroom doorway, as if she couldn't wait for Melissa to wake up again and want to be fed. Catherine began singing a lot, at first only to Melissa, but then seeming to forget herself and singing absently when she worked around the house. It seemed she had found her source of smiles, too, and there was always a ready one waiting for Clay when he got home.

But while Catherine's contentment increased, Clay's virtually disappeared. He astutely refrained from getting involved with the baby, though it was beginning to have a growing, adverse effect on him. His temper flared at the slightest provocation while Catherine's seemed as unassailable as Melissa's—for Melissa was truly a satisfied baby with a flowery disposition. As graduation neared, Clay blamed his crossness on the pressure of finals, and the bar exams coming up shortly.

Angela called and asked his permission to plan a little Sunday brunch on the weekend following his graduation. When she said she'd already received Catherine's approval, Clay snapped into the phone, "Since the two of you already have the whole thing planned, why are you bothering to ask me!"

Then he had to do some fancy skirting to get around his mother's demand to know what on earth was eating him.

Clay graduated from the University of Minnesota law school with honors when Melissa was two months old. Now he held a degree, but he had never held his daughter.

Chapter 27

THE DAY OF the brunch would have been well-suited to a June wedding. The sprawling backyard of the Forresters was at its finest. The view over the flaming chafing dishes on the semicircular terrace was lush with color. The terrace itself was delineated by carefully pruned global arborvitae, which in turn were edged with alternating clumps of marigold and ageratum, the purple and gold contrast creating a stunning effect. The yard stretched in falling terraces to the far reaches of the property where a file of blue spruce marked its boundaries. The rose gardens of phalanx symmetry were in full bloom, in full scent. Shapely maples and lindens dotted the grass with vast splashes of shade. It was like a pastoral scene from an impressionist's brush: ladies in filmy dresses drifting from the terrace across the lawn, men sitting on the parapet of the terrace, everyone nibbling on melon and berries.

Catherine was sitting on the grass when a shadow fell over her and she glanced sunward, blinded at first and unable to make out who stood above her.

"All by yourself?" It was Jill Magnusson's rich, lazy voice. "May I join you?"

Catherine held up a forearm to shade her eyes. "Of course, have a chair."

Dropping to the grass, Jill doubled up her Thoroughbred legs and folded them elegantly to the side—like a ballerina in a swan scene, thought Catherine. Jill tossed back her thick mane and smiled directly at Catherine.

"I guess I should apologize for not sending a gift when the baby was born, but you know how it is."

"Do I?" Catherine replied sweetly—a little too sweetly.

Jill's gaze drifted over Catherine before she smiled archly. "Well . . . don't you?"

"I don't know what you're getting at."

"You know precisely what I'm getting at, and I won't be a hypocrite about it. I'm completely jealous of that baby of yours and Clay's. Not that I'd want one, you understand, but it should have been mine."

Catherine controlled the urge to slap her. "Should have been yours? Why, how gauche of you to say so."

"Gauche maybe, but we both know it's true. I've been damning myself ever since last October, but I've finally decided to lay my cards on the table. I want Clay; it's as simple as that."

Some stirring of pride made Catherine answer, "I'm afraid he's already taken."

"Taken for a fool maybe. He's told me what kind of relationship you two have. Why do you want to hold a man you don't love and who doesn't love you?"

"Maybe to give our daughter a father."

"Not the healthiest reason, you'll have to admit."

"I don't have to admit anything to you, Jill."

"Very well—don't. But ask yourself why Clay asked me to wait for him until he could get this mess straightened out." Then Jill's voice became quite purring. "Oh, I see this is news to you, isn't it? You didn't know that Clay asked me to marry him right after he found out you were pregnant? Well, he did. But my silly pride was shattered and I was totally wrong in turning him down. But now I've changed my mind."

"And what does he have to say about it?"

"Actions speak louder than words. Surely you know that while you turned a cold shoulder on him all last winter he knew where to find a warm one."

Catherine's stomach was aquiver. "What do you want from me?" she demanded coldly.

"I want you to do the right thing, turn Clay free before he falls in love with his daughter and stays for the wrong reason."

"He chose me over you. That's hard for you to swallow, isn't it?"

Jill tossed her hair behind a shoulder. "Kiddo, you didn't fool me with that trumped-up wedding of yours. This is Jill you're talking to. I was *there* that night and it's no hallucination that Clay kissed me far more intimately than grooms are supposed to kiss other women." Jill paused for dramatic effect, then finished, "And he told me he still loved me. Strange for a man on his wedding night, huh?"

The memory of that night came back to Catherine, but she hid her chagrin behind a mask of indifference. She turned now to see Clay sitting on the terrace, deep in conversation with Jill's father.

Jill went on. "There's no doubt in my mind that if this . . . mistake"—Jill's pause seemed to denigrate the word further—"hadn't happened between you, Clay and I would be planning our wedding right now. It was always implicitly understood that Clay and I would eventually marry. Why, we've been intimate since the days when our mothers plunked us naked together into our little plastic backyard pools. In October when he asked me to marry him, he admitted you were nothing more than a tragic mistake to him. Why not do him a favor and bow out of the picture?"

It was clear that Jill Magnusson was used to getting what she wanted, by fair means or foul. The woman's manner was insolent and rude. There was no note of appeal in her attitude, only brazen self-assurance.

Oh, she was as cool as Inella's tomato aspic up there on its bed of crushed ice, thought Catherine. But Catherine disliked tomato aspic too.

"You assume a lot, Jill," Catherine said now with a little ice of her own.

"I assume nothing. I know. I know because Clay has confided in me. I know that you've thrown him out of his own bed, that you've encouraged him to live a life of his own, to keep his old friends, his old pursuits. The baby's born now, she has a name, and Clay is financially responsible for her for life. You got what you wanted out of him, so why don't you free him?"

Catherine rose, brushed off her skirt and pointedly raised an arm to wave at Clay, who waved back. Without looking again at Jill, she said, "He's a big boy. If he wants to be free, don't you think he'd ask?"

Catherine headed in the direction of the terrace, but before she could get away, Jill threw one last parting shot, and this one hit its mark: "Where do you think he was while you were in the hospital having his baby?"

Insane thoughts came to Catherine, childlike in their vindictiveness. She wished that Inella's superb tomato aspic was made with Jill's blood. She wanted to shave Jill's head, roll her naked in poison ivy, feed her chocolate laced with laxative. These thoughts didn't strike Catherine as immature. She felt hurt and degraded; she wanted revenge and could think of no way to get it.

And Clay! She felt like taking a handful of melon balls and firing them at him like artillery. Like overturning the chafing dishes, getting everyone's attention, telling everyone here what a liar and a libertine he was! How could he! How could he! It wasn't bad enough that he'd continued his sexual relationship with Jill, but the thought of him confiding the intimate truths about their marriage cut deeper than Catherine ever thought possible. Painful memories came back, bolder than ever: New Year's Eve and Clay kissing Jill with his little finger under her spaghetti strap; the night he hadn't come home at all while she'd fixed supper and waited; and worst of all—four nights while she lay in a maternity ward . . .

It was several days after the brunch.

Catherine had submerged her anger until it lay at the base of her tongue like bile, waiting to be spewed. He'd known for days that she was seething and would soon erupt. What he didn't know was what would trigger it.

All he was doing was standing beside the crib watching Melissa sleep. Suddenly, behind him, Catherine hissed, "What are you doing! Get away from her!"

His hands came halfway out of his pockets and he turned, surprised by her vehemence. "I didn't wake her up," he whispered.

"I know what you're thinking, standing there staring at her all the time, and you can just get it off your mind, Clay Forrester, because it won't work! I'll fight you till my dying day before I let you take her from me!"

With a quick glance to make sure the baby hadn't been disturbed, he moved toward the hall.

"Catherine, you're imagining things. I told you I—"

"You told me a lot of things you wouldn't do, like keep your affair going with Jill Magnusson, but she certainly set me straight about that! Well, if you want her, what's holding you up?"

"What did Jill say to you Sunday anyway?"

"Enough that I know I want to see you gone from this house, and the sooner the better."

"What did she say?"

"Do I need to repeat it? Do you want to rub my nose in it? All right!" Catherine marched into the master bedroom, slammed a hand against the light switch and paraded to his chest of drawers, flinging clothes out to punctuate her words. "You've been sleeping with her all the time you lied to me and said you weren't, so why not move in with her permanently? Do you think everybody doesn't know what's been going on between you when you stood at your own wedding reception and French-kissed her in front of everybody there? Did you tell your mother you'd stepped out for air when you disappeared with Jill on New Year's Eve? How dumb do you think I am, Clay? And why are you hanging around here like a stray dog? I'm not going to take you in and feed you and ask you if you'd like to live with me, because I want this farce to be over. I don't want your phony condescension or your two-bit psychoanalysis about my being emotionally crippled! I don't want you coming in here fawning over *my* daughter—the one I had while you were staying nights at Jill's house. All I want is what you agreed to give me. Child support for Melissa and my college education paid for. And I want you out of here—out!—so I can get on with my life!"

The pile of clothes lay in disarray between them. The air seemed thick, as if her shouting had actually raised dust.

"She told you a pack of lies, Catherine."

Catherine closed her eyes, but the lids quivered. She raised both palms up to Clay.

"Don't . . . just don't. Don't make it worse than it already is." Her voice shook.

"If she said I've been sleeping with her, it's a goddam lie. I've seen her, yes, but I told you I wouldn't sleep with her and I haven't."

"Why are we arguing? This is only what we knew was coming all along. Do you want me to go so you can stay? Okay—" she grew obstinate—"okay, fine." She started dumping armfuls of his things back in the drawers. "Fine, I'll go. I can easily go back home now that Herb is gone." She headed for her own dresser and yanked the drawers open.

"Catherine, you're acting childish. Will you stop it! I don't want you to go! Do you think I'd toss you and Melissa out?"

"Oh, then you want to go."

She marched back to the bureau and stubbornly began to empty it again. He caught her by an arm and swung her around none too gently.

"You're an adult now. Will you start acting like one?"

"I . . . want . . . this . . . over!" she said with emphatic pauses. "I want your parents to know the truth so I don't have to listen to your dad babbling about us leaving Melissa at their house. I'm sick of your mother giving her Polly Flinders dresses that cost forty dollars apiece and making me feel guilty as Judas! I'm sick of you standing over her crib plotting how you can get her away from me! Jill doesn't want her. Don't you understand that,

Clay? All she wants is you! And since you want her, too, why don't we cut through all the crap and give little Jill what she wants?"

Something inside Catherine cringed at her rudeness, her gutter language so like her father's, but she couldn't stop it. The need to hurt Clay like he'd hurt her was too strong.

"I can see Jill really did a number on you. She's very good with words, but did she ever actually say I slept with her, or did she *imply* it? I have no doubt she made me sound totally conniving and guilty."

"You told her!" Catherine raged. "You told her I threw you out of your bed when it was you who chose to sleep on that davenport. You picked out that . . . that damn long davenport, I didn't! And you had no right to tell her such private things about us!"

"I told her we were having problems; she must have guessed the rest."

"It doesn't take much guessing, does it? Not when a man sleeps with one woman while another is in the hospital having his baby!"

Clay's eyebrows lowered ominously. He ran a hand through his hair. "Goddam that Jill." Then he swung around with a palm up entreatingly. "Catherine, it's not true. I saw her the second night you were in the hospital. She was waiting outside in her car when I came home, and she followed me in."

"You had her *here?*" Catherine's voice cracked into a high falsetto. "Here in *my* house?"

"I didn't *have her here,* not the way you put it. I said she followed me in. She said she had to talk to me. We didn't do anything."

But Catherine was done arguing. "If you're leaving, leave. If not, I'm going to start my own packing. Which will it be?"

In the moments during which she stood confronting Clay, waiting for him to make the move, some bereft voice seemed to be calling from within her, beating on the inside of her stomach with tiny fists, "Why are you doing this? Why are you treating him this way when you love him? Why can't you be forgiving? Why can't you reach out and beg him to start over with you? Is that pain in his face? If you don't risk finding out, he'll be gone, and you'll be left to wonder. But then it will be too late." She stood before him, aching for him to love her, knowing she was making herself unlovable again because she loved him so much that the idea of having him—truly having him—as a husband, then losing him, would annihilate her in the end.

"I'll need to know where you'll be so my lawyer can serve the divorce papers" was all he said. Then he went to the closet to get his luggage.

Catherine hid in the kitchen while Clay packed, listening to him making trips out to the car. Her stomach felt queasy. It lifted nauseatingly until she pressed it firmly against the edge of the kitchen counter. She sensed when Clay went in to look at Melissa for the last time. In the silence she pictured him, his blond head bent over the crib, gazing down at the baby's head—blond, too—and she felt heartless and sick with herself. She swallowed back tears, pressing against the counter until her hipbones hurt. The awful need to cry made her throat ache unbearably. It felt like she'd swallowed a tennis ball.

He came quietly to the kitchen doorway, found her standing in the lightless room.

"All of my things wouldn't fit in the car. I'll have to come back for them."

She nodded her head at the wall.

"Good-bye, Catherine," he said softly.

She raised a hand, hoping that from behind, he couldn't tell what a struggle she was having to keep from crying.

A moment later she heard the door shut.

It took him two days to clear out all his belongings for good. It took another two days before a deputy sheriff appeared at her door and served her with divorce papers. It took another week before Angela called, her voice very shaken, obviously grieved by the news. It took a week and a half before Catherine worked up the courage to visit Ada and tell her.

But it took less than an hour for Catherine to begin to miss him.

The days that followed were the most hollow of Catherine's life. She found herself staring listlessly at Clay's favorite things in the house; there were so many earth-tone items he loved so much. The place was more his than hers. She remembered how awed she'd been by its luxury the first day he'd brought her here. Guilt was her constant companion. She ate with it, slept with it, paced the rooms with it, knowing full well that it was she who should have gone, he who should have stayed. And though she had once feared leaving, she now feared staying, for the house seemed to echo Clay's voice, reflect his tastes, and always, always, remind her of his absence. She remembered how much fun it had been to fill the cabinets with wedding gifts, to go grocery shopping together, to work in the bright, well-equipped kitchen. She hated it now. Cooking for one was decidedly the most desolate chore in the world. Even making coffee in the mornings became a miserable task, for it reminded her sharply of all the mornings Clay had sat at the counter with a cup and the early paper, often attempting to tease her out of her morning grouchiness. She admitted now how hard she'd been to get along with, and marveled at how amiable Clay had always remained, no matter how bearish her morning temper. She had the bathroom all to herself whenever she wanted it, but found she missed the occasional trace of whiskers she used to find in the sink, his toothbrush lying wet beside hers, the smell of his after-shave that lingered in the room after he was gone. One day she made popcorn, but after it was buttered, she burst into tears and threw it all down the garbage disposal.

Telling Ada proved to be a terrible ordeal. Ada, whose life was being painfully rebuilt, a day at a time, looked much like she used to when Herb raised his fist at her. She seemed to cower, her shoulders curling, shriveling before Catherine's eyes.

"Mom, please don't act that way. It's not the end of the world."

"But, Cathy, why would you want to go and do a thing like that, divorce a man like Clay? Why he's—he's . . ." But for lack of a better word, Ada finished lamely, "perfect."

"No, Mother, he's not perfect and neither am I."

"But that wedding they give you, and the way Clay give you that beautiful place and everything you wanted—"

"Mother, please understand. It was a mistake for us to get married in the first place."

"But if Melissa is his—" But Ada placed trembling fingertips over her thin lips and whispered, "Oh, she is, isn't she?"

"Yes, Mother, she's his."

"Why, of course, she is," Ada reasoned. "She's got his nose and chin. But if Melissa is his, then why did he leave?"

"We tried it for Melissa's sake, but it just didn't work. You, above all people, should understand that I didn't want to stay with him when he didn't love me."

"No—no, I guess you wouldn't want to do that. But, honey, it breaks my heart to see you give up that good life you had. I was so happy to see you settled that way. Why, you had everything that I never had. Everything I always hoped my little girl would get. And I figured I'd buy myself a little used car soon and come—come over." Then, without changing the hopeless expression on her face, Ada began to cry. She did it silently, sitting in her beaten-up living room chair that she had recently covered with a new slip-cover. The tears rolled down her sad cheeks, and she acted too empty and weary to lift a hand and swipe at them.

"Mom, you can still get a little car, and you can still come to see Melissa. And I'm not coming out of this a total loser. I've got Melissa, haven't I? And Clay is going to pay for me to go back to school in the fall."

"And you'd rather have that than be married to him?" Ada asked sadly.

"Mother, that's not the point. The point is, Clay and I are getting divorced, and we have to accept that. If you're honest with yourself, you'll admit that I never really fit into his class of people anyway."

"Why, I thought you did. The way Angela seemed to love you and—"

"Mother, please." Catherine put a hand to her forehead and turned away. The thought of Angela hurt almost as much as the thought of her son.

"Why, okay, honey, I'm sorry. Only it's so sudden and it takes some getting used to when I've been feeling so good about you being fixed for life."

From then on, whenever Catherine visited her mother, Ada rambled on about all that Catherine would give up in divorcing Clay. It didn't matter how many times Catherine pointed out the ways in which she'd benefited, Ada refused to see it that way.

In late July there came an unannounced visit from Clay's father. Opening the door and finding Claiborne there, Catherine immediately felt her throat swell. He was so strikingly handsome; she knew that Clay would look much like him some day. Missing Clay as she did, there was a swift surge of bitter-sweet joy at seeing his father at the door.

"Hello, Catherine, may I come in?"

"H-hello. Well, certainly."

There was a moment of hesitation during which each assessed the other. And each saw pain. Then Claiborne moved to pull Catherine briefly into his arms and kiss the crest of her cheek. She closed her eyes, fighting the over-whelming sense of déjà vu, fending off the love she felt for this man because he was Clay's father, Melissa's grandfather. She felt suddenly secure and pro-tected in his hold.

When they were seated in the living room, Claiborne stated simply, "An-gela and I were decimated by the news."

"I'm sorry."

It was easier for Catherine if she didn't look at her father-in-law, but she couldn't keep her eyes from his, they were so like Clay's.

"I waited, thinking Clay would come to his senses and come back here, but when we realized he wasn't going to, Angela and I had to know how you are."

"I'm fine, just fine. As you can see, I have everything I need. Clay . . . and you . . . have seen to that."

He leaned forward on the edge of his chair, cupped his palms and seemed to study them.

"Catherine, I'm afraid I must ask your forgiveness. I made such a mistake."

"Please, Mr. Forrester, if you're going to tell me about the ultimatum you issued to Clay, I know all about it. Believe me, we're no less guilty than you. We should have known better than to think marriage would automatically solve our problems. And we weren't truthful with you either."

"He told us about the agreement you two made."

"Oh." Catherine's eyebrows shot up.

"Don't look so guilty about it. None of us is too lily-white, are we?"

"I wanted to tell you long ago, but I just couldn't."

"Angela and I guessed that everything wasn't as calm as it appeared on the surface." He stood up and walked to the sliding door, gazing out much as Clay had often done. "You know, I've only seen this place once since you and Clay moved." He glanced over his shoulder at her. "That was one of the things that made Angela and I wonder. It hurt, the fact that you never invited us here, but I guess we had it coming."

"No . . . oh, no." Catherine followed him to the window, reaching out to touch his elbow. "Oh, God, what good are recriminations? I thought it would be best not to—not to grow to love you, too, under the circumstances, I mean, knowing that Clay and I would be separating soon."

"Too?" he repeated hopefully. She should have remembered, he was a lawyer; he picked up on slips like that.

"You know what I mean. You and Angela were so good to us, you didn't deserve to be hurt."

He sighed, turned his eyes to the summer lawn where sprinklers threw cascades of droplets out across the greens between buildings. It was a warm, lazy afternoon.

"I'm a rich man," he ruminated. "I own all this. But there's very little pleasure in the thought right now."

"Please," she pleaded, "don't blame yourself."

"I thought I could buy Clay and you and my grandchild, but I was wrong."

"I'm not going to deny you the right to see Melissa. I couldn't do that."

"How is she?" The first trace of joy crossed his face at the thought of Melissa.

"She's getting a double chin, but she's healthy and very happy. I never thought a baby could be so good. She's napping now, but due to wake up soon. I could wake her if you like."

Claiborne's smile was answer enough, and she went to get Melissa up, then brought her out to see her grandpa. From his pocket he produced a small teething toy, and his smile was far wider than Melissa's when he gave it to her.

"Listen, Catherine, if there's anything she needs, or anything you need— ever—you must promise to let us know. Is that understood?"

"You've done more for me than you should already. Besides, Clay sends us money regularly." Then she studied Melissa's head, reached to lightly ruffle the feather-fine curls there as she asked, "How is he?"

Claiborne watched Catherine's hand on Melissa's fair head.

"I don't know. We don't see much of him these days." Their eyes met above the baby. There was deep pain in Claiborne's.

"You don't?"

"No. He went to work in the legal department of General Mills as soon as he passed his bar exam."

"But isn't he living with you?"

Claiborne became occupied with the toy, trying to get the baby to hold it in her pudgy hand.

"No, he's not. He's—"

"No need to feel uncomfortable. I think I know where he's living. With Jill, right? But that's really where he belonged all along."

"I thought you knew, Catherine. I didn't mean to spring it on you."

She laughed lightly, got up and spoke over her shoulder while she moved to the kitchen. "Oh, for heaven's sake, don't be silly. He can do whatever he pleases now."

But when Claiborne was gone, it was Catherine who stood staring out the window across the lawns, hollow-eyed, seeing Clay and Jill in the prismatic colors that jetted from the sprayers outside. Without thinking, she clutched Melissa a little too tightly, then kissed her a little too forcefully, and the baby started to cry.

Chapter 28

DURING THAT SUMMER Melissa was Catherine's greatest joy. The love Catherine found so difficult to display toward others she could lavish readily upon her child. Simply touching Melissa seemed to heal Catherine's wounded spirit and bring it back to life. Sometimes she'd flop on her side on the bed, taking Melissa with her, and with five tiny toes against her lips, would tell the child all the hidden feelings she had. In a voice as soft as cotton candy she poured out her feelings.

"Do you know how much I loved your daddy? I loved him so much that I didn't think I'd survive when he left. But there you were and I loved you, too, and you helped me through. It wasn't as bad after a while. Your daddy is handsome, know that? You have his nostrils and pretty hair like his. I'm glad you didn't get my straight hair. It's hard to tell about your mouth yet, whose it is. Why, Melissa, did you smile at me? When did you learn how to do that? Do it again, come on. That's the way. When you smile you look like your Grandma Angela. She's a wonderful lady, and your Grandpa Claiborne is wonderful too. You're a very lucky girl, you know, to come from people like them. They all love you, Grandma Ada too. But I'm the lucky one, I got you, and I love you best. Always remember that, and remember, too, how much I wanted you."

Her soliloquies to Melissa were punctuated by kisses and touches while the baby lay unblinking, her eyes, of yet-undefined color, wide and trusting.

There came a day when Melissa learned to reach. When she first reached for Catherine's face the mother knew a joy of love such as she'd never experienced before. It was pure, unconfounded by conflicts such as other loves she'd experienced. The tremendous outpouring of emotion left Catherine's eyes awash and her heart full. As the baby grew and responded to Catherine's love, there grew within Catherine the realization that she possessed qualities she hadn't known she possessed: patience, kindness, gentleness, an ease of laughter, a modicum of mother-sense and the innate knowledge of how to make a baby feel secure.

They did everything together. Sunbathed on the deck, swam in the pool, took showers—it was during a shower that Melissa first laughed aloud, ate bottled baby food—one spoon for Melissa, one spoon for Mommy—visited Ada, went grocery shopping, and registered Catherine for the next quarter. But Catherine had enough sense not to fall into the habit of taking Melissa to bed with her at night, no matter how comforting it would have been to have the baby there for company. At bedtime, she resolutely tucked Melissa into the crib in her own room, facing the king-size bed alone. She never lay down on it without thinking of Clay and the few nights they'd shared it. She couldn't help wondering if he'd still be here, had she invited him into it from the beginning. Catherine now found recriminations helpful, for she was learning much from them about herself and her shortcomings. And through Melissa she was learning it was far more satisfying to be a warm, loving person than a cold, remote one.

She learned what an abundant harvest love can reap, that the old saying is true: the more love you give away, the more you have.

In late August Steve came home. He was so dismayed to find Catherine and Clay separated that he blew up at his sister, blaming her for not trying harder to hold a man who'd done his damnedest to do right by her.

"I know you, Cathy. I know how godawful stubborn you can be, and how once your mind is made up it sets harder than a plaster cast. You don't have to tell me you didn't love him because I know different. What I want to know is why the hell you wouldn't swallow a little of your pride and fight for him!"

He was the only one who understood all the forces behind Catherine's belligerence and stubbornness, those old millstones which had ultimately alienated Clay. Steve was the first one to come right out and blame her, and Catherine surprised him by admitting he was right. By the time Steve left he realized Catherine had done a vast amount of growing up since her wedding.

In September she went back to school, leaving Melissa with a babysitter. Catherine had to contact Clay to let him know there would be another bill for him to pay. He asked if he could drop by and bring her a check and see Melissa at the same time.

* * *

From the moment the door opened, he could tell that Catherine was different. There was an openness about her, starting with the smile on her face. His attention was torn between it and the wide gaze of curiosity upon the face of his daughter.

"Hi, Clay, come on in."

He couldn't control the size of his smile. "Holy cow! Has she grown!"

Catherine laughed, plopped a loud kiss on the baby's neck and turned to lead the way inside. "She's got lots of chins to nuzzle, haven'tcha, Lissy?" And Catherine did so. "She's kind of getting to that shy stage, so it might take a while for her to warm up to you. But don't feel bad, she's that way with everybody lately."

Following Catherine upstairs, Clay glanced quickly up and down her jean-clad figure. Her old shape was back, and when she turned to face him again he noticed how tan she was. Her hair seemed lighter, bleached into streaks like honey and peanut butter.

"Sit down, you two, and say hello while I bring us a glass of Cola or something."

She put Melissa into the crank-up swing that occupied the center of the living room, then ducked into the kitchen. Melissa immediately realized she'd been left alone with a stranger and stuck out her lip.

"Didn't you warn her I was coming and tell her to put on her best manners?" Clay called.

"I did. I told her you were the fella paying the bills, so she'd better watch her *p*'s and *q*'s."

Melissa began to squall, but quieted as soon as Catherine reappeared. She handed a glass to Clay, cranked up the swing, then sat cross-legged on the floor beside it.

"Oh, before I forget—here." Clay dug a check out of his pocket and handed it to her.

"Oh, thank you. I hated to ask for more."

"You earned it," he said without thinking. But Catherine seemed to take no offense. Instead, she began to describe the babysitter who cared for Melissa, as if to put him at ease about the woman's coming well-recommended.

"You don't have to reassure me about that, Catherine. If there's one thing I don't worry about, it's the kind of care Melissa will get."

"She's a good baby, Clay, really good. She's got your temperament." Then Catherine smiled, shook her head in gay self-deprecation. "Boy, I'm sure glad she didn't get mine or she'd be driving her mother nuts!"

"You had to put up with plenty of temper from me."

"Usually after I started it, though. Oh, well, water over the dam, huh? So, how's everything with you and Jill? Are you happy?"

Clay seemed startled. The last thing he'd expected Catherine to ask about was Jill, especially in that free and easy way.

"Yes, we are. We don't—" But he stopped self-consciously.

"Hey, it's okay. I mean, I didn't mean to pry."

"No, you weren't prying. I was just going to say that Jill and I don't fight like you and I used to, or give each other the silent treatment. We coexist rather peacefully."

"Good for you. So do Melissa and I. Peace is nice, isn't it, Clay?"

He sipped his drink, assessing this changed Catherine who seemed utterly satisfied with herself and her life. She reached over and tucked the baby's collar down, keeping up with the swing while she did it, smiling and saying, "Melissa, this is your daddy. You remember him, don't you? Shame on you for sticking your lip out and crying at him." Again she glanced up at Clay. "Your father came to visit us once. He brought Melissa a toy and asked how we were and said to let him know if we needed anything. But he's been so good to us already I'd feel guilty to take anything from him."

"What is it you need?"

"Nothing. Clay, you've been great about the money part. I really appreciate it. School is going to be great this year, I know. I mean, it's so much easier going to school when you're not pregnant." She flung her arms up and let them flop back down. "I feel like I could conquer the world every day, you know?"

Clay used to feel that way; he didn't anymore. "Are you still sewing and typing?"

"Yes, now that school is in session again it's easy to find jobs. Don't worry, I'll help with the money any way I can. Mostly it goes for groceries. Baby food is kind of expensive." She chuckled and fluffed Melissa's hair as the swing went past. "'Course, I could save a lot on it if I didn't eat so much of it myself. We kind of share stuff, Melissa and I. I share my shower with her and she shares her food with me, huh, Lissy?"

"You take her in the shower!" exclaimed Clay. "At her age?"

"Oh, she loves it. And the pool too. You should have seen her in the pool this summer, just like a baby otter." While she rambled on, she took Melissa out of the swing and sat the baby in her lap facing Clay. He noticed a new contentment in Catherine as she touched Melissa's hair or ear or gently clapped the bottoms of the tiny feet together. There was a naturalness about it that made Clay feel left out. The longer he observed Catherine with the baby the more he sensed how much she'd changed. She was freer than he'd ever seen her, talkative and happy, trying to withhold nothing about Melissa from him. It almost seemed as if she must share everything she could remember. But she did it guilelessly, shifting her attention from the baby to Clay all the while. Finally she said, "I think she's used to you now if you want to hold her."

But when he took Melissa, she immediately complained, so, disappointed, he handed the baby back to her mother.

Catherine shrugged. "Sorry."

He stood up to leave.

"Clay, is there anything you want from the house? I feel awful about taking everything from you. It seems like everything here is yours and I've ended up with it all. If there's anything you want, just say so, it's yours."

He glanced around the neat living room where the only thing out of place was the swing. He thought of the disarray Jill always left in her wake.

"Jill had everything already, thanks."

"Aren't there even any of the wedding gifts you want?"

"No, you keep 'em."

"Not even the popcorn popper?" She looked like a sprite while asking it.

"That wasn't a wedding gift. We bought that together."

"Oh, that's right. Well, I don't make much popcorn, so just say if you want it."

She seemed to have thoroughly adjusted to her life without him. She led the way to the door, opened it and sauntered out to the car with him.

"Thanks for bringing the check over, Clay; we really appreciate it."

"Anytime."

"Clay, one more thing before you go."

He stood beside the open car door, grateful for something that kept him here a little longer. Catherine stared at the ground, kicking a pebble, then looked directly into his eyes.

"Your father mentioned that they don't see much of you anymore. It's none of my business, but he seemed terribly hurt by that. Clay, there's no reason for you to feel like you've failed them or—or whatever." This was the first time she'd acted flustered. Her cheeks were pink. "Oh, you know what I mean. Your parents are really great. Don't sell them short, okay?"

"They don't exactly approve of my living with Jill."

"Give them a chance," she said, her voice gone quite low and musical, persuasive somehow. "How can they approve if they never see you to do it?" Then, quite suddenly, she flashed him a smile. "Oh, forget it. It's none of my business. Say good-bye to your daddy, Melissa." She backed away, manipulating the baby's arm in a wave.

Why was it that Clay, too, felt she was manipulating his heart in some obscure way?

Six weeks after school started a history professor named Frank Barrett asked Catherine to a show at the Orpheum. They returned to her house after an exhilarating live performance of *A Chorus Line,* and Frank Barrett tried to exact payment for the evening. He was handsome enough, in a rugged, dark-whiskered way, and Catherine thought of it as therapy when she let herself be pulled into his arms and kissed. But his beard, which she'd liked earlier, was less likable when his tongue came through it. His body, which had nothing to speak against it, was less appealing when it flattened Catherine's against the entry wall. His hands, which were square-nailed and clean, were too abruptly intimate, and when she pushed them away, it was with a healthy, negative feeling against him that had nothing to do with hang-ups. She simply was not attracted to him, and found it glorious to turn him away for such a reason.

When he apologized, she actually smiled, saying, "Oh, no need to apologize. It was wonderful."

Misreading her reply, he moved in again only to be staved off a second time.

"No, Frank. I meant *saying* no was wonderful!"

The poor, puzzled Frank Barrett left Catherine believing that she was somewhat wacky, not at all like she'd seemed when he'd first noticed her in his classroom.

In late November the law caught up with Herb Anderson and he was returned to Minnesota for trial. When Catherine saw him in the courtroom, she could scarcely believe it was he. His beer belly was gone, his face sallow, his hands shaky; life on the lam had obviously been unkind to him. But the same cynical expression still marred his face, the same droop of lips said Old Herb still thought he deserved a square deal from life and wasn't getting it.

To Catherine's surprise, Clay was in the courtroom, and so were his parents. With an effort, she forced her thoughts back to the proceedings, noting the satisfied smirk that crossed Herb's face when he saw that the Forresters did not seat themselves in the same row with Catherine and Ada.

The trial did not last long, for there was no one to come to Herb Anderson's defense, save two of his booze-buddies from the old days, who looked even more disreputable than Herb, who'd at least been cleaned up and offered fresh clothing, courtesy of the county. Herb Anderson's history of violence was clearly presented in the testimony of Ada, Catherine and even Herb's own sister and brother-in-law, Aunt Ella and Uncle Frank. The past assault on Clay was brought up as evidence and dismissed, yet its impact remained. The doctor who had treated Ada testified, as did the ambulance drivers and Mrs. Sullivan. As the trial proceeded, Herb's usually florid face grew pastier and pastier. There were no verbal outbursts from him this time, only a quivering of his flaccid jowls and a persecuted expression when the judge sentenced Herbert Anderson to two years in the Stillwater State Penitentiary.

Leaving her seat, holding Ada's arm, Catherine saw Clay and his parents' moving, also, toward the center aisle. He wore a stylish cashmere coat of spice brown, its collar flipped up. His eyes sought and held hers as she moved toward him, and wings seemed to flutter within Catherine's chest as she realized he was waiting for her. There was a welcome feeling of security about anticipating his touch upon her arm. Without a word—for the bench had called the next case—it was somehow understood: Angela and Claiborne separated to make room for Ada between them as they left the courtroom, followed by Catherine, with Clay's hand guiding her elbow. Walking beside him, she caught a hint of his familiar cologne. She gave in to the urge to look up at him again, tightening her arm and pulling his hand against her ribs.

"Thank you, Clay," she smiled appreciatively. "We really needed your support today."

He squeezed her elbow. The impact of his smile sent flurries deep into her stomach, and she looked away.

Once again Clay sensed the changes in her. She had gained a new self-assurance that was totally attractive on her, while at the same time, she'd become dulcified. She was no longer skittish nor defensive. He noticed that she'd changed her hairstyle and that the summer's streaks were now blending into its natural gold color. He studied it as she walked a step ahead of him, mentally approving of the appealing way in which it was caught up with combs behind her ears, falling in blithe curls down past her shoulder blades now.

They reached the corridor and found Angela waiting there, gazing at Catherine, fighting tears.

"Oh, Catherine, it's so wonderful to see you."

"I've missed you too," Catherine got out. Then the two were in each other's arms and tears were hovering in the corners of both pairs of eyes.

Observing them, Clay remembered how Catherine had vowed not to let herself grow fond of his parents, but he saw that it hadn't worked, for from Angela's embrace she went to Claiborne's. It was the first time Clay ever remembered Catherine moving unguardedly into a hug, except that time with Steve.

Claiborne's bear hug made Catherine gasp and laugh, breaking the tension, but over his shoulder Catherine's eyes were again drawn to Clay, who was studying her with a faraway expression.

They all seemed to remember Ada then, and the reason for their being there. After they spoke of the case she had just won, the talk moved on to other things, growing a little fast and clipped, as if too much needed crowding into too little time. At last Angela suggested, "Why don't we all go somewhere and have a sandwich or a drink, somewhere we can talk for a while. There's so much I want to hear about Melissa and you, Catherine."

"How about The Mullion?" Claiborne suggested. "It's a favorite place of mine and not far from here."

Catherine glanced sharply at Clay, then at her mother.

Ada's hand fluttered to draw her coat closed. "Why, I don't know. I rode in with Margaret." They now took note of Mrs. Sullivan standing by, waiting with Ella and Frank.

"If you'd like, we'll take you home," Claiborne offered.

"Well, it's up to Cathy."

Catherine heard Clay say, "Catherine can ride with me." She slid him a look then, but he was buttoning up his coat as if it were already decided.

"I have my own car," she said.

"Whatever you'd like. You can ride with me if you like, and I'll bring you back uptown afterward to pick up your car."

The old Catherine intruded, with her impulse to fend off her feelings of attraction for Clay. But the newer Catherine was secure now and decided to go ahead and enjoy him while she could.

"All right," she agreed. "There's no sense in burning up extra gas."

Smiling at the others, Clay said, "We'll see you there then."

And Catherine felt her elbow firmly clasped and snuggled against Clay's warm side.

Outside the wind was howling, eddying in miniature twisters in the valleys between tall buildings. Catherine savored the icy sting upon her cheeks, for they were warm, almost burning. She and Clay got to a corner and stood waiting for a light to change. Catherine kept her eyes on the luminous red circle across the street, but she could feel Clay's eyes on her. She reached to turn up her collar but it caught on the long angora scarf twined around her neck, and Clay reached a gloved hand to help. Through all those layers of wool, his touch could still raise goosebumps up and down Catherine's spine. The light changed then.

"My car's in the parking ramp," Clay said, taking her arm again as they crossed the windy street, then crossing behind her as they turned the corner. Taking the outside, he brushed her shoulder. The touch made her tingle. She searched for something to say, but the only sound came from their heels on the sidewalk. He turned her into the echoing dungeon of a concrete parking ramp, its floor slick with motor oil. The heel of her shoe skittered, dumping her sideways, but she felt herself hoisted upright by that hand so secure on her elbow.

"You okay?"

"Yes, winter is no time for high heels."

He watched her trim ankles, mentally disagreeing with her.

At the elevator he dropped her arm, leaned to push the button, and the silence seemed insurmountable while they waited, shivering, their shoulders hunched against the cold that seemed so much more intense in the concrete dimness. The elevator arrived; Clay stood aside while Catherine boarded. He pushed an orange button. Still they said nothing, and Catherine frantically wished she'd kept up a steady stream of chatter all the way because the privacy of the elevator was unbearable, yet she couldn't think of how to start.

Clay watched the light indicate the floors as they went up. "How's Melissa?" he asked the lights.

"Melissa's fine. She just loves the babysitter's; at least I'm told she's very content and happy there."

The hum of the elevator sounded like a buzz saw.

"How's Jill?"

Clay looked sharply at Catherine, hesitating only a moment before answering, "Jill's fine, at least she tells me she's very content and happy."

"And how about you?" Catherine's heart slammed around inside her. "What do you tell her?"

They had arrived at the correct level. The doors opened. Neither of them moved. The frigid air invaded their cell, but they stood as if unaware of it, gazing into each other's faces.

"My car is off to the right," he said, confused by the confusion in his chest, afraid of making the wrong move with her.

"I'm sorry, Clay, I shouldn't have asked that," she said in a rush, hurrying along beside him. "You have every right to ask about Melissa, but I have none to ask about Jill. I do wonder about you, though, and hope you're happy. I want you to be."

They stopped beside the Corvette. He leaned to unlock the door. He straightened, looked at her. "I'm working on it."

Riding to The Mullion they were both remembering the other time he'd taken her there. Suddenly it seemed childish to Catherine, the way they had grown so ill at ease with each other.

"Are you thinking about it, too, about the last time we went here?" she asked.

"I wasn't going to mention it."

"We're big kids now. We should be able to handle it."

"You know, you've changed, Catherine. Half a year ago you'd have bristled and acted threatened at the idea of going there."

"I felt threatened then."

"And now you don't?"

"I'm not sure of your question. Do you mean threatened by you?"

"It wasn't always against me that you put up your defenses. It was other things, places, circumstances, your own fears. I think you've outgrown a lot of that."

"I think I have too."

"Since you asked me, I'll ask you—are you happy?"

"Yes. And do you know what made the difference?"

"What?" He angled a glance at her and found her watching him in the failing light of late afternoon.

"Melissa," she answered softly. "There have been countless times when I've looked at her and fought the urge to call you and say thank you for giving her to me."

"Why didn't you?"

He'd had his eyes on her for so long she wondered how the car stayed on the road. Catherine moved her head and shoulders in a vague way that said she did not have the answer. He turned back to watch the lane, and the familiarity struck her with a breathtaking blow: his profile there behind the wheel, the wrist draped negligently as he drove with the ease she remembered so well. She let her impulses have their way and suddenly leaned over, putting a hand on his jaw and pulling his cheek briefly against her lips.

"That's for both of us, for Melissa and me. Because I think she's just as grateful to have me as I am to have her." Quickly Catherine centered herself in her own seat and went on. "And you know what, Clay? I'm a fabulous mother. Don't ask me how it happened, but I know I am."

He couldn't help grinning. "And humble too."

She snuggled into her seat contentedly. "There aren't a lot of things I'm good at, but being Melissa's mother is . . . well, it's great. It's a little harder since school started, but I cut a few corners of housework time here and there, let a few things stay dusty, and I still find time for her. But I have to admit, I'll be glad when school is over and I don't have to divide my time so many ways."

The kiss then had been purely a kiss of thanks. It was clearer than ever that Catherine's life was full and happy. She had it all together. Clay listened to her relating stories about it and suffered pangs of regret that she'd been unable to feel this fulfilled when she was living with him. He came from his reverie to realize she'd just said she was dating again. He submerged the twinge of possessiveness to which he no longer had a right, and asked, "How does it feel?"

"Terrific!" She flung up her palms. "Just terrific! I can kiss back without the slightest bit of guilt. Sometimes I can even enjoy it."

She looked at him with an impish grin and they both laughed. But a hundred queries bubbled up in his mind about those kisses, the ones she shared them with, queries which, again, he had no right to ask.

They stayed at The Mullion for over two hours, until Angela had learned about each of Melissa's toys and teeth and vaccinations. Catherine was her new, free, easy self all the while. Clay spoke little, sitting back and studying her, comparing her to the way she used to be. And subconsciously comparing her to Jill. He wondered if she was dating only one man or several. He planned to ask her when he drove her back to her car.

But when the time came to leave, Catherine pointed out that it was actually closer to Claiborne and Angela's route to drop her back uptown, and she rode with them.

Chapter 29

CLAY STOOD IN the window of the high-rise apartment he shared with Jill, staring down at the icy expanse of Lake Minnetonka in the cold, purple dusk below. The lake was a sprawling network of bays, channels and inlets in a western suburb bearing its name. Clay wished it were summer. In summer the lake was a water-lover's paradise, dappled by sails, dotted with skiers, peopled with fishermen, rimmed by intermittent beach and woodland. Its islands emerged like emeralds from sapphire waters. In spots where its shoreline was left to nature's whims, watery fingers erupted in lavender explosions of loosestrife, come August.

But now, in early December, Clay studied the frozen surface in distaste. Winds had whipped it into a froth as it froze, leaving it the pitted texture and color of lava. Rowboats and schooners alike looked bereft, overturned on the shore. Hoisted above the waterline their soiled canvas covers held dirty snow. On a spar below, a trio of dissolute sparrows fluffed their feathers against an arctic wind until they were blown off, trundled sideways as they flew. A small flock of mallards fought a headwind, then disappeared in their search of open water.

Watching the ducks, Clay wondered where the autumn had gone. He had drifted through it listlessly, free this year to enjoy the hunting he so dearly loved, yet somehow never even getting his gun out of its case. In the past he'd hunted with his father more than anyone else. He missed his father. But as winter thickened and intensified, so had his parents' disapproval over his living with Jill. Although they occasionally phoned, Clay sensed their silent chastisement, thus never called them back.

He saw Jill's car curve into the parking lot below and disappear toward the garages. Minutes later he heard her key in the door. Normally he'd have hurried to open it, but today he only continued staring morosely at the chill scene outside.

"Oh, God, it's cold! I hope there's a nice hot toddy waiting for me," Jill said. She crossed to Clay, dropping gloves, scarf, purse and coat across the room like rings from a skipping stone, only—unlike ripples—the articles would not disappear. It aggravated Clay, for he'd just cleaned up the place again when he got home. Jill crooked an arm through his and rubbed her cold nose against his jaw in greeting.

"I like it when you get home first and you're here waiting."

"Jill, do you have to drop your stuff everyplace like that?"

"Oh, did I drop something?" She looked at the trail behind her, then nuzzled Clay again. "Just anxious to get to you, darling, that's all. Besides, you know I always had a maid at home."

"Yes, I know. That's always your excuse." He couldn't help recalling how Catherine used to enjoy keeping the town house clean and neat.

"Irritable tonight, darling?"

"No, I'm just tired of living in a mess."

"You're irritable. In need of some liquid refreshment. What have you been standing here brooding about, your parents again? If it bothers you so much, why don't you go over and see them tonight?"

But it only irritated him further that she simplified it so, as if his problems could be solved by a simple visit. She dropped her shoes in the middle of the room on her way to the liquor cabinet. She picked up a brandy decanter, swung around loosely to face him, and said, "Let's have a drink, then go out and get some supper."

It was Friday night, bleak and cold, and he was tired of running. He wished just for once she'd suggest making dinner at home, doing something cozy and relaxing. The memory of sharing popcorn and studying with Catherine came back, so inviting now. He pictured the town house, Melissa in her swing with Catherine cross-legged beside it in her jeans. Looking out at the cold, icy lake which was receding into dusk's hold, he wondered what Catherine's reaction would be if he showed up at her door. Abruptly, he walked over and closed the draperies. Before he could reach for the lamp switch, Jill moved close in the dark. She wrapped her arms around him, pressed her breasts to his chest and sighed.

"Maybe I can think of a way to coax you out of your bad mood," she whispered huskily against his lips.

He kissed her, waiting for arousal to grip him. Instead, he was gripped only by hunger pangs; he'd skipped lunch that day. It struck him that the state of his stomach overrode his bodily response to Jill. It made him feel emptier, hungrier, but for something that went beyond either food or sex.

"Later," he said, brushing her hair back, guilty now for his lack of desire. "Get your coat and let's go out and eat."

Melissa was teething and fussy and whiny these days. She resisted bedtime, so Catherine often brought her out onto the living room floor until she fell asleep there, then carried her up to her crib.

The doorbell rang and Melissa's eyes flew open again.

Oh, damn, thought Catherine. But she leaned over, kissed Melissa's forehead and whispered, "Mommy'll be right back, punkin."

Melissa started sucking on her bottle again.

Through the door Clay heard her muffled voice.

"Who is it?"

"It's Clay," he said, close to the wood.

Suddenly Catherine forgot her irritation. Her stomach seemed to suspend itself, then drift back into place in an unnervingly tentative way. It's Clay, it's Clay, it's Clay, she thought, deliriously happy.

On the other side of the door Clay wondered what he'd say to her; she'd surely see through his flimsy excuse for coming here.

The door fairly flew open, but when it swung back she stood motionless. First impression made her momentarily mute: his wind-whipped hair in a whorl of inviting imperfection above the turned-up collar of an old letter jacket; faded jeans hugging his slim hips; his hands in his pockets like some uncertain high-school sophomore ringing a girl's bell for the first time. He hesitated as if he didn't know what to say, then his eyes traveled down to her knees, then back up, then seemed not to know where to rest. Everything in her went all loose and jellyish.

"Hi, Catherine."

"Hi, Clay."

Suddenly she realized how long it had been since either of them had moved and remembered that Melissa was on the floor with the cold wafting in.

"I brought Melissa a Christmas gift."

She stepped back, let him in, then closed the door to find herself disarmingly close to him in the rather confined area of the entry.

Clay briefly glanced down at her attire. "Were you in bed already?"

"Oh—oh, no." Self-consciously she tugged the zipper of her robe the remaining two inches up her neck, then jammed her hands into its pockets.

"I guess I should have called first." He stood there feeling graceless and intrusive. The robe was fleecy pink, with a hood, and pockets on the front like a sweatshirt. Her hair was pulled back with a plastic headband and the ends of it were still wet. Her face had that scrubbed, shiny look that he recognized so well. With a start, he realized she'd just gotten out of the shower. He knew perfectly well there was no bra beneath that fuzzy, pink fleece—he remembered that untethered look of hers.

"It doesn't matter, it's okay."

"Next time I'll make sure I call first. I just bought something on impulse, and I was driving past and decided to drop it off."

"I said it was okay. We weren't doing anything special anyway."

"You weren't?" he asked dumbly.

"I was studying and Melissa was teething."

He smiled then, a big, warm, wonderful smile, and she hunched up her shoulders and pushed her hands as far down in her pockets as they'd go because she didn't know how else to contain her happiness at his being here.

Suddenly there was a loud thump and the living room was plunged into darkness, followed by a second of silence before Melissa's wail of panic billowed through the blackness.

"Oh, my God!" Clay heard. He groped, touched the fleecy robe and followed it up the stairs in the direction of the living room.

"Where is she, Catherine?"

"I left her on the floor."

"You get her. I'll get the kitchen light."

Melissa was screaming and Catherine's heart threatened to explode. Fumbling for the light switch, Clay, too, felt a stab of panic. He found the switch, then in five long-legged strides was kneeling behind Catherine who had scooped up the baby and was muffling Melissa's cries against her neck. In the dim light Clay could see the table lamp on the floor, but unbroken. He touched Catherine's shoulder, then Melissa's head.

"Catherine, let's take her into the light and see if she's hurt." He put his hands on Catherine's sides, urging her up and felt through the robe that she was crying too. "Come on," he said sensibly, "let's take her to the bathroom."

They laid Melissa on a fat Turkish towel on the vanity top. They could see right away where the lamp had hit the back of the baby's head. There was a tiny gash there and already it was starting to swell into a goose egg. Catherine was so upset that her distress was conveyed to Melissa, who squalled all the louder. So Clay was the one who swabbed the bruise and calmed them both.

"It's all my fault." Catherine blamed herself. "I've never left her on the floor like that before. I should have known she'd go straight for the lamp cords—she does every chance she gets. But she was asleep when the doorbell rang and I didn't think anything of it. She started sucking on her bottle again and I was just—"

"Hey, it's nothing serious. I'm not blaming you, am I?" Clay's eyes met hers in the mirror.

"But a lamp that size could have killed her."

"But it didn't. And it's not the last bump she'll take. Do you realize that you're more upset than Melissa?"

He was right. Melissa wasn't even crying anymore, just sitting there wet-eyed, watching them. Sheepishly Catherine smiled, sniffled, yanked out a tissue and blew her nose. Clay put his arm around her shoulder and bumped her up against his side a couple of times as if to say, silly girl. At that moment he understood why nature had created a two-parent system. Yes, you're a good mother, Catherine, he thought, but not in emergencies. At times like this, you need me.

"What do you say we show her the Christmas present I bought for her and that'll make her forget she even had an accident."

"All right. But, Clay, do you think this needs stitches? I don't know anything about cuts. She's never had one before."

They fought Melissa's tiny hands and caused her to start complaining again while they inspected the damage.

"I don't know much about it, either, but I don't think so. It's awfully tiny. And anyway, it's in her hair, so if there's a scar it won't show."

Finally, Melissa left the bathroom on her mother's arm, looking back at Clay with a wide-eyed look of inquiry. He set up the lamp and plugged it in again, and they all sat down on the living room floor, the baby in her yellow footed pajamas staring so silently at Clay that he finally laughed at her. Her bottom lip started quivering again, so Clay suggested, "Hurry and open that before I get a complex."

The sight and sound of the bright red, crackly paper captured the baby's attention as Catherine tore it off the white koala bear with its flat nose and lifelike eyes. At the sight of it, Melissa's mouth made a tiny "ooo," then she gurgled. The koala had a music box inside, and it wasn't long before it accompanied Melissa to bed.

Coming back down from Melissa's room, Catherine found Clay waiting at the bottom of the stairs, his green and gold letter jacket slung over one shoulder as if he were going to leave. A throb of disappointment thudded through her. She stopped on the bottom step, curling her toes over the edge, hanging on by her heels only. Her fingertips unconsciously toyed upon the handrails. He stood before her, their eyes nearly on the same level, trying to think of something to say to each other.

"She'll sleep now," Catherine said—not quite an invitation, not quite not.

"Good . . . well . . ." He looked at the carpet while he slowly threaded his arms into his jacket sleeves. Still studying the floor, he straightened the old shapeless collar while Catherine gripped the handrails tightly. He buried his hands in the jacket pockets and cleared his throat.

"I guess I'd better get going." His voice sounded a little raspy, trying to talk soft that way so he wouldn't wake Melissa.

"Yes, I guess so." It took great effort for Catherine to breathe. The banister felt suddenly slippery.

Clay's head came up slowly, his inscrutable eyes meeting hers. He gestured with one of his hidden hands as if waving good-bye—jacket and all.

"So long."

She could barely hear it, he said it so softly.

"So long."

But instead of moving, he stood there studying her, the way she perched on that bottom step like a sparrow on a limb. Her eyes were wide and unsmiling, and he could see the way she forced herself to take shallow, fluttering breaths. His own breath wasn't any too calm. He wished she wouldn't look so stricken, but knew she had good reason to be scared, just as scared as he was at that moment. Her hair was dry now, the ends curling wispily upon her shoulders, upon the folds of the hood that hilled up around her jaw. She stood there all still, arms straight out from her sides, looking almost breastless in her robe. Face shiny, devoid of makeup, hair unstyled, feet bare. He tried not to analyze, not to think either "I should" or "I shouldn't," because he only knew he had to. He took three agonizingly slow footsteps toward her, his eyes roving her face. Then he leaned silently and put his face in the spot where her hair lay, lifted by that hood. He breathed of her remembered fragrance—soft, powdery, feminine scent that he'd always loved. Catherine's lips fell open and she moved her jaw against his temple while deep in her body things went liquid, deep in his things went hard. Her heart scrambled to make sense of this while it seemed to take light-years of time before he straightened and their eyes met. They asked tacit questions, remembered old hurts they'd caused each other. Then, still with his hands in his pockets, Clay leaned and touched her lips softly with his own, seeing her lashes drop just before his own eyes slid shut. He kissed her with a light lingering of flesh upon flesh, letting the past slip into obscurity, yet unable to prevent it from being part of the kiss. He told himself he must go, but when he drew away her lips followed, telling him not to. Their eyelids flickered open to breach that moment of uncertainty before he moved more surely against her lips. There was a timorous, first opening of mouths, warm touch of tongue upon tongue, then Clay wrapped his hands, jacket and all, around her, pulling her inside of it with him. Handlessly they embraced, for she still clutched the rails, and his hands were lost in his pockets behind her, quite afraid to pull them out and start something they certainly should not finish. But it was impossible, unbearable, this handlessness. Then Catherine seemed to lean off the steps, drifting into the warm place he opened up to her, losing her arms deep inside his jacket. He enclosed her in the cocoon of soft, old wool and leather, and hard, young flesh and blood, lifting her off that step, turning, holding her suspended against him while the kiss became reckless and she went sliding down his body. Her bare toes touched canvas and she was standing on his tennis shoes. One hand came out of his pocket and found her hair, cradling the back of her head, pulling her against his mouth. His other hand left the safe confines of its pocket and flattened itself upon the center of her back, then drifted lower, lower, to the shallows of her spine, to bring the length of her body against his. Through her robe she could feel his belt buckle and the hard zipper of his jeans, and she remembered drinking wine from his skin. Ironically, the thought sobered her and she tried to push away. But he pulled her almost violently against the thunder of his heart, crushing her.

"Oh, God, Cat," he whispered in a strangled voice, "this is where we started."

"Not at all," came her shaky reply. "We've come a long way since then."

"You have, Cat, you have. You're so different now."

"I've grown up a little, that's all."

"Then what the hell's the matter with me?"

"Don't you know?"

"Nothing's right in my life anymore. Everything's gone wrong since you and I made that damn agreement. The last year has been miserable. I don't know who I am or where I'm going anymore."

"Is this going to tell you?"

"I don't know. I only know it feels right here with you."

"The first time we met it felt right, and look where it landed us."

"I want you," he half-groaned against her hair, wrapping his arms around her so far she heard old stitches pop up the back of his jacket. She closed her eyes and swam in a warm, wet place of his making, secure enough now to take the plunge, to say that which she'd refused to say during the agonizing months she'd lived with him.

"But I love you, Clay, and there's a difference."

He pulled back to search her face, and she willed him to say it, but he didn't. He read her thoughts and knew what it was she waited for, but found he could not say it unless he was certain. Things had happened so fast he didn't know if he was running on impulse or emotion. He only knew she looked beguiling, and that she was the mother of his child and that they were still husband and wife.

He came back against her hard, and the momentum swept them to the carpeted stairs. All in one motion he pressed her down and lifted his knee, riding it across her stomach, hip and thigh, caressing her with it while he searched the neck of her robe for the zipper, slid it down and plunged his hand inside to slake it with her breast, then run it down her stomach.

"Stop it, Clay, stop it," she implored, dying because she wanted nothing more than to turn her body inside-out for him.

Against her warm neck he said throatily, "You don't want this to stop, not any more than you did the first time."

"Our divorce will be final in less than a month, and you're living with another woman."

"And lately all I do is compare her to you."

"Is that why you're here, Clay, to make comparisons?"

"No, no, I didn't mean it that way." His hand swept down her ribs, down her stomach, heading again for the spot that wept for him. "Oh, Cat, you're under my skin."

"Like an itch you can't reach, Clay?" She grabbed his wrist and stopped it again.

"Don't play games with me."

"I'm not the one playing games, Clay, you are."

He felt her nails now, digging into his wrist. He pushed himself back, leaning on one elbow to see her better.

"I'm not playing games. I want you."

"Why? Because I'm the first thing in your life that you can't have?"

His face changed, grew stormy, then abruptly he sat up on the step beside her and buried his fingers in his hair. God, is she right, he wondered. Is that all it is with me—ego? Am I that kind of a bastard? He heard her zipper go back up but remained as he was, touching his scalp, which tingled at the thought of all that naked skin beneath her robe. He sat that way a long time, then pulled his palms down over his face. But in them he could smell the fragrance of her perfume, gathered from her skin like spring flowers.

She sat beside him, watching him do battle with himself. After a long time, he stretched his frame back against the edges of the steps, lying there at an angle. With his eyes closed he lifted up his hips and tugged at the crotch of his jeans. She could see the telltale bulge there. He rested the back of a wrist over his eyes, let his other hand lie limply down along his groin. He sighed.

Finally she spoke, but her voice was unangry, reasonable. "I think you'd better decide what it is you want, me or her. You can't have us both."

"I know that, I goddam know that," he said tiredly. "I'm sorry, Catherine."

"Yes, you should be, doing this to me again. I'm not as resilient as you are, Clay. When I get hurt it hurts for a long time. And I have no alternate lover to fall back on for support."

"I feel like I'm spinning in circles; nothing's in focus."

"I don't doubt it, living with her, coming here, your parents right in the middle. What about them, Clay? What are you trying to prove by rejecting them the way you have and going to work for someone else?"

She saw his Adam's apple slide up and down, but he didn't answer.

"If you want to punish yourself, Clay, keep me out of it. If you want to go on putting yourself into situations that rub you raw, fine. I don't. I've made a new life with Melissa, and I've proven to myself that I can live without you. When we met, you were the one with direction, the secure one. Now it seems we've changed places. What happened to that direction, that purpose you used to have?"

Maybe it left me when I left you, he thought.

At last he sat up, then pulled himself to his feet and stood with his back to her, staring at the floor.

She said, "I think you'd better go someplace and get sorted out, get your priorities straight. If and when you manage that and think you want to see me again . . ." But instead of finishing the thought, she ended, "Just don't ever come back here asking for me unless it's for keeps."

She heard the snaps of his jacket, like whipcracks in the silence. Clay's shoulders squared, then slumped, then he waved wordlessly, without looking back at her, and left the house, closing the door softly behind him.

Chapter 30

EMOTIONALLY, CATHERINE FOUND herself in that painful, bittersweet state she'd faced and gotten through once before when Clay left her. Again, she suffered reveries from which she emerged to find her hands idle, her thoughts and eyes meandering out the window, across the snowy city to Clay. Clay, whom she'd have on one condition only, thus would probably never have at all. The contentment she'd known from loving Melissa ceased to sustain her. Emptiness crept into her unexpectedly, in the middle of the most everyday activities: studying, folding laundry, walking across campus, giving Melissa a bath, driving in the car. Clay's visage appeared before her constantly, his absence again robbing her of joy, making life seem wan and empty, at times bringing tears to her eyes. And like all lorn loves, she found reminders of him in countless places that were only illusory: in the reddish-gold hair of some stranger on the street; in the cut of a sport coat on a muscular shoulder; in the inflection of someone's laughter; in the way certain men crossed their ankles over their knees, dropped their hands into their pockets or straightened their ties. One of Catherine's professors, when he lectured intensely, had Clay's habit of standing with arms akimbo, holding his sport coat back with his wrists, studying the floor between his outspread feet. His body language was so like Clay's that Catherine became obsessed with the man. It did no good to tell herself she was transferring her feelings for Clay to a veritable stranger. Each time Professor Neuman stood before class that way, Catherine's heart would react.

She counted off the days until Christmas break when she would no longer have to be subjected to Professor Neuman and his similarities to Clay. But Christmas brought its own bittersweet memories of last year. In an effort to stave them off, she called Aunt Ella and wangled an invitation for herself and Ada for Christmas Day. But even having plans didn't help much, for she never turned on the lights of her tiny tree without having to quell the soft, seductive memories of last year at Angela and Claiborne's house. She would walk to the sliding glass door and look out at the snow-laden world and jam her hands into the pockets of her jeans and remember, remember, remember. That magical house with all its love, lights, music and family.

Family. Ah, family. It was so much the root of Catherine's unhappiness, had been all her life. She would look at Melissa and tears would gather, for that family security the child would never know, no matter how much she herself lavished her daughter with love. She fantasized about Clay coming to the door again, only this time it would be different. This time he'd say he loved her, and only her, and they'd bundle Melissa into her little blue snowsuit and when the three of them arrived at the big house it would be just like last year, only better. Catherine closed her eyes, hugging herself, smelling again the tang of newly blown-out candles, remembering soft mistletoe kisses . . .

But that was fantasy. Reality was making it through Christmas alone, as a single parent, with no one to place gifts beneath her lonely tree but herself.

"Let's get a tree and put it up," Clay said.

"What for?" asked Jill.

"Because it's Christmas, that's what for."

"I don't have time. If you want one, put it up yourself."

"You never seem to have time for anything around the house."

"Clay, I work eight hours a day! Besides, why cultivate interests you never intend to use?"

"Never?"

"Oh, Clay, don't start in on me now. I lost my blue cashmere sweater and I wanted to wear it tomorrow. Dammit, where could it be?"

"If you'd muck the place out once a month or so, maybe you wouldn't lose track of your things." The bedroom looked like an explosion in a Chinese laundry.

"Oh, I know!" Jill suddenly brightened. "I'll bet I took it to the cleaners last week. Clay, be a darling and run over and pick it up for me, will you?"

"I'm not your laundry boy. If you want it, go get it yourself."

She picked her way across the littered floor and cooed close to his face, "Don't be cross, darling. I just didn't think you were busy right now." When she would have teasingly inserted her glittering nail into the smile line on his cheek, he jerked his head aside.

"Jill, you never think I'm busy. You always think you're the only one who's busy."

"But, darling, I am. I'm meeting the project engineer for the first time tomorrow and I want to look my best." She tried to put him into good humor with a quick caress. But that was the third time she'd called him *darling,* and lately it had started to bother him. She used the term so loosely it sometimes stung. It reminded him of what Catherine said about the value of affection going up when it was in short supply.

"Jill, why did you want me back?" he asked abruptly.

"Darling, what a question. I was lost without you, you know that."

"Besides being *lost* without me, what else?"

"What is this, the Spanish Inquisition? How do you like this dress?" She held up a pink crepe de chine and swirled in a little side-step, eyeing him provocatively.

"Jill, I'm trying to talk to you; will you forget the damn dress?"

"Sure. It's forgotten." She dropped it negligently on the foot of the bed and turned to grab a brush and begin stroking her hair. "So talk."

"Listen, I—" He hardly knew where to begin. "I thought our life-styles, our backgrounds, our futures were so alike that we were practically made for each other. But, this—this isn't working out for me."

"Isn't working out? Clarify that for me, will you, Clay?" she asked crisply, stroking her hair all the harder.

He gestured at the room. "Jill, we're different, that's all. I have trouble living with the clutter, the meals in the restaurants, and the laundry that's never clean and the kitchen cabinets that are full of magazines!"

"I didn't think you wanted me for my domestic abilities."

"Jill, I'm willing to do my share, but I need some sense of home, do you understand that?"

"No, I'm not sure I do. It sounds to me like you're asking me to give up my career to push dust around."

"I'm not asking you to give up anything, just to give me some straight answers."

"I would if I knew exactly what it is you're asking."

Clay picked up a lace-trimmed violet petticoat from a chair and sat down wearily. He studied the expensive garment, rubbing it between his fingers. Quietly he asked, "What about kids, Jill?"

"Kids?"

Her brush stopped stroking. Clay looked up.

"A family. Do you ever want to have a family?"

She whirled on him angrily. "And you said you're not asking me to give anything up!"

"I'm not, and I'm not even talking about right away, but someday. Do you want a baby someday?"

"I've just put in all these years getting a degree; I have a future ahead of me in one of the fastest-growing fields there is, and you're talking babies?"

Without warning, Clay pictured Catherine crying because Grover's baby had died, then in the labor room with their hands together on her stomach as the contractions built; he thought of her cross-legged on the living room floor clapping Melissa's feet together, and the way she'd cried because Melissa had bumped her head.

Suddenly Jill threw the brush down. It cracked upon the dresser top, went skittering off the mirror and landed on the floor inside an abandoned high-heel pump.

"You've seen her, haven't you?"

"Who?"

"Your . . . wife." The word galled Jill.

Clay didn't even consider lying. "Yes."

"I knew it! As soon as you came in here complaining about the mess, I knew it! Did you take her to bed?"

"For God's sake." Clay stood up, turning away from her.

"Well, did you?"

"That's got nothing to do with this."

"Oh, doesn't it? Well, think again, buster, because I'm not playing second fiddle to any woman, wife or not!" Jill turned back to the mirror, picked up a fat brush and savagely began applying blush to her cheeks.

"That's part of this arrangement we have here, isn't it, Jill?"

She glared at him in the looking glass. "What is?"

"Egos, yours and mine. Part of the reason you wanted me was because you've never had to do without anything you wanted. Part of the reason I left Catherine is because I've never had to do without anything I wanted."

Her eyes glittered dangerously as she swung around to face him. "Well, we're two of a kind then, aren't we, Clay?"

"No, we're not. I thought we were, but we're not. Not anymore."

They stood with eyes locked, hers angry, his sorry, in the meadow of strewn garments, coffee cups, newspapers and makeup.

At last Jill said, "I can compete with Catherine, but I can't compete with Melissa. That's it, isn't it?"

"She's there, Jill. She exists, and I'm her father and I can't forget it. And Catherine has changed so much."

Without warning she flung the makeup brush at him and it hit him on the cheek as she yelled, "Oh, damn you! Damn you! Damn you! How dare you stand there mooning over her! If you want her so bad, what are you doing here? But once you leave, don't think your half of the bed will be cold for long!"

"Jill, please, I never meant to hurt you."

"Hurt? How could you hurt me? You only hurt the one you love, isn't that how the song goes?"

When Clay left Lake Minnetonka, he drove aimlessly for hours. He headed for Minneapolis proper, circled Lake Calhoun, headed east on Lake Street past the quaint little artsy shops at the Lake Hennepin area, farther east where seedy theaters gave way to seedier used-furniture stores. He turned south, caught the strip that cut Bloomington in half and circled west again. The lights of the Radisson South split the night sky with its twenty-two stories of windows as Clay turned onto the Belt Line, unconsciously heading for Golden Valley.

He took the exit of Golden Valley Road without deciding to, and threaded through the streets that once had been his route home, passing Byerly's Supermarket where he and Catherine had first gone grocery shopping. He pulled into the lot beside the town house but let the engine idle, leaving only the parking lights on. He looked up at the sliding glass door and there, shining out onto the snowy balcony were the multi-colored lights from a Christmas tree. As he sat staring at them, they blinked out and the window grew dark. Then he put the car in gear and headed for a motel.

When Clay appeared in the doorway of the study, Claiborne looked up, tried to mask his surprise, but couldn't quite bring it off. He half rose from his chair, then settled down again behind the desk with a bald look of hope.

"Hi, Dad."

"Hello, Clay. We haven't seen you for a long time."

"Yeah, well, don't tell Mother I'm here just yet. I'd like to talk to you alone first."

"Of course, come in, come in." Claiborne removed a pair of silver-rimmed reading glasses from his nose and dropped them on the desk.

"The glasses are new."

"I've had them for a couple of months, can't get used to the damn things, though."

They both looked at the glasses. The room was still. Suddenly, as if inspired, the older man rose.

"How about a brandy?"

"No, thanks, I—"

"A Scotch?" Claiborne asked too anxiously. "Or maybe some white wine. I seem to remember that you liked white."

"Dad, please. We both know white wine isn't going to fix a damn thing."

Claiborne dropped back into his chair. A log hissed in the fire and shot a tongue of blue flame sideways. Clay sighed, wondering as he had so often recently, where to begin. He sat on the edge of the leather loveseat and pressed his thumb knuckles deep into his eyes.

"What the hell went wrong?" he finally asked. His voice was quiet and searching and pained.

"Absolutely nothing that can't be fixed," his father answered. And even before their eyes met again, their hearts seemed to drop burdens which each had borne for too long.

The telephone rang for the fifth time and Clay's hopes waned. He angled the receiver away from his ear, leaning his head back against the headboard and shut his eyes. Traffic roared past on the highway outside. He studied his stocking feet stretched out before him, his suitcases lying open, sighed, and was just about to give up when Catherine said hello.

She stood in the dark bedroom dripping bath water onto the carpet, trying to get a towel wrapped around her without dropping the receiver.

"Hello, Catherine?"

Her heart seemed to flip up into her windpipe and her hands stopped messing with the towel. It slid down off her back and she clutched it to her breast, feeling her battering heart through the terry cloth.

At last she said, "H-hello."

He heard the catch in her voice and swallowed. "It's Clay."

"Yes, I know."

"I didn't think you were home."

"I was in the tub."

The line buzzed for an interminable moment while he wondered which phone she'd picked up and what she was wearing.

"I'm sorry, I can call back."

"No!" Then she calmed herself a little. "No, but . . . can you wait a minute, Clay, while I get a robe on? I'm freezing."

"Sure, I'll hang on." And hang on he did, clutching the receiver in his damp palm while hours seemed to drag past and visions of a pink hooded robe filled his mind.

Catherine flew to the closet, dropping the towel, scrambling for her robe, frantic, impatient, fumbling, thinking, oh, my God, it's Clay, it's Clay! Oh, Lord, oh, damn, where's my robe? He'll hang up . . . Where is it? Wait, Clay, wait! I'm coming!

She tried running back to the phone and stepping into the robe at the same time, but the zipper went only halfway down the front of the thing, and she stumbled, arriving at the phone breathless.

"Clay?" he heard, and the sound of her anxiousness made him smile and feel warm inside.

"I'm here."

She released a pent-up breath, got the zipper up and perched on the edge of the bed in the semidarkness, with only the light from the closet easing around the corner into the room.

"Sorry it took so long."

He figured it had probably taken seven seconds. Still, he was afraid now to ask what he'd called to ask, afraid she'd turn him down, sick at the thought that she might.

"How are you?" he asked instead.

She pictured his face, the face she'd been searching crowds for ever since she'd last seen it, pictured his hair which she'd imagined she'd seen on hundreds of strangers, his eyes, his mouth. Long moments passed before she admitted, "Not so happy since you were here last."

He swallowed, surprised at her answer when he'd expected the usual trite, "Fine."

"Me either."

It was incredible how two such simple words managed to slam the breath out of her. Frantically she searched for something to say, but her mind remained filled only with his face, and she wondered where he was and what he was wearing.

"How's Melissa's head?" he asked.

"Oh, fine. It's all healed up, no worse for the wear."

They both laughed nervously, but the strained sound ended abruptly at both ends of the wire, followed by silence again. Clay raised one knee, propped an elbow on it and kneaded the bridge of his nose, his heart thundering so loud it seemed she must hear it at her end.

"Catherine, I was wondering what you're doing tomorrow night."

She clutched the phone in both hands. "To-tomorrow night? But that's Christmas Eve."

"Yes, I know."

Clay quit kneading his eyes, took up pressing the crease of one trouser leg between his fingers instead. "I was wondering if you and Melissa have plans."

Catherine's eyes slid shut. She raised the mouthpiece up to her forehead so he couldn't hear her jerky breathing. She got control.

"No, not for tomorrow night. We're going to Uncle Frank and Aunt Ella's on Christmas Day, but nothing for tomorrow." Up went the receiver to her forehead again.

"Would you like to come out to the house with me?"

She put her hand on the top of her head to keep it from leaving her body, struggled to sound calm.

"Out to your parents' house?"

"Yes."

He felt physically sick during the interminable moments while she thought, What about Jill? Where is Jill? I told you not to call me unless it was forever.

"Where are you, Clay?" she asked, so quietly he had to strain to hear the words.

"I'm in a motel."

"A motel?"

"Alone."

Joy sluiced through every vein of her body. Her throat and eyes felt flooded while she sat there gripping the phone like some babbling idiot.

"Catherine?" His voice cracked as he said it.

"Yes, I'm here," she got out.

In a stranger's voice he managed, "For Chrissake, answer me, will you?" And she remembered how Clay swore when he was scared.

"Yes," she whispered, and slid down with a thump onto the floor.

"What?"

"Yes," she said, louder, smiling great-big.

The line grew silent for a long, long time, with only the sound of some distant electronic bleeps making music in their ears, then disappearing.

"Where are you?" he asked then, wishing he were with her now.

"I'm in the bedroom, sitting on the floor beside the bed."

"Is Melissa asleep?"

"Yes, for a long time."

"Has she got the koala bear with her?"

"Yes," Catherine whispered, "it's in the crib by her head."

The line went quiet once more. After a long time Clay said, "I'm going back to work with Dad, as soon as possible."

"Oh, Clay . . ."

She heard him laugh, but it was a deeply emotional laugh, as if it were very hard to bring from his throat.

"Oh, Cat, you were right, you were so right."

"I was only guessing."

This time when he laughed it was less strained, then she heard him sigh.

"Listen, I've got to get some sleep. I didn't get much last night or the night before that or the night before that."

"Me either."

"I'll pick you up at five or so?"

"We'll be ready."

Silence roared between them again, a long, quivering silence that said as much as the soft words which followed:

"Good night, Catherine."

"Good night, Clay."

And again, silence, while each waited for the other to hang up first.

"Good night, I said," he said.

"So did I."

"Then let's do it together."

"Do what together?"

She never knew before that you could hear a smile.

"That too. But later. For now, just hang up so I can get some sleep."

"Okay, on three, then?"

"One . . . two . . . three."

This time they hung up together.

But they were both sadly mistaken if they thought they'd get much sleep.

Chapter 31

THE NEXT DAY crawled. Catherine felt light-headed, at times giddy, almost removed from herself. Passing a mirror, she found herself staring at her reflection long and assessingly before covering her cheeks with both hands, closing her eyes and reveling in the heartbeat that seemed to extend into every nerve ending of her body, its cadence fast-tripping. She opened her eyes and warned herself this might be a false alarm. Maybe just Clay's way of seeing Melissa, giving his parents a chance to see her, too, during the holiday. But then Catherine would remember his voice on the phone, and she knew somehow this was what she'd been dreaming of. Her thoughts flew to the oncoming evening. Hurry, hurry!

Finally, to kill time, she bundled Melissa into the car and went out shopping for something new to wear. She moved through the crowds of last-minuters in a thoroughly changed state from the previous day. She smiled at strangers. She hummed along with piped-in carols. She was eminently patient when forced to wait behind slow-moving lines at cash registers. Once she even spoke to an older man whose temper was on edge, whose face was red and quivery and impatient. A new feeling of ebullience lifted Catherine as she saw his impatience dissolve beneath her own good spirits. And she thought, see what love can do?

Back at home she put Melissa down for a nap and took a leisurely bath in an explosion of bubbles. Emerging from the tub, she stood before the wide vanity mirror blotting her skin. She felt giddily gay, childish and womanly all at once. She made a moue at her reflection, then struck a seductive pose with the towel partially shielding her nudity, then tried a different pose, a different facial expression. She leaned nearer the mirror, tugging tendrils of hair out of the hastily secured top-knot, giving herself a kittenish look with loose wisps at her temples and the back of her neck. She wet her lips, allowed them to fall slightly open, lowered her lids to a smoky expression, and breathed, "Hello, Clay." Then she tried standing with her back to the mirror, looking over one shoulder, saying impishly, "Hi, Clay." Next she turned, slung the towel around her neck, its ends covering the rosy peaks of her breasts, put her hands on her bare hips and said sexily, "Whaddya say, Clay-boy?"

But suddenly she dropped the charade; she was none of these characters. She was not a little girl anymore, she was a woman. What was happening in her life was real, and she must present only the genuine Catherine to Clay. The real Catherine dropped the towel at her feet. She stood straight and tall, studying her body, her face, her hair. She took up the bottle of lightly scented lotion she'd splurged on that morning, her eyes never leaving her reflection as she poured some within her palm and began applying it to her long, supple arms, her shoulders, her neck, circling it and reaching as far onto her back as she could. She cupped her hand for another cool, sleek helping, its smell—the scent she knew Clay loved—all around her now in the warm, steamy bathroom. She rubbed it into her stomach, up the cove between her ribs, her eyes sliding closed as her palms slipped over her breasts, feeling the vaguely welcome discomfort at touching the nipples puckered into gem-hard points. Standing there touching herself, she thought of Clay, of the night ahead. I want you, Clay, she thought, I've wanted you for so long. She imagined it was Clay's hands rubbing her breasts. Her eyelids fluttered open and she took more lotion, watched her palms rub slowly together before she raised one foot, resting it on the vanity, pointing her toes as she spread the scented coolness from the arched top of the foot up the calf, behind the knee, thigh, over the buttock, the sheltered spot between her legs. I'm wanton, she thought. Then,

No, I'm a woman, with a woman's needs. The scent Clay loved was all over her now.

Slowly she took the combs from her hair and began brushing it, remembering that night of their blind date, then the night the girls at Horizons had played handmaiden. That was the night of her second date with Clay. She took as much care now with her toilette as the girls had taken that night. She dressed in the minuscule bra and panties that Clay had never seen on their wedding night. She worked over her makeup until it was a subtle work of art. But she kept her hair loose, simple, lightly curled back from her face much as she wore it when she first met Clay.

The new dress was of pale plum crepe de Chine, a wraparound that dropped from lightly gathered shoulders to the hem in an easy looseness. It was collarless, leaving a V of skin exposed at the neck. When she tied the string-belt, the dress gained shape, accenting her hollow-hipped thinness. She buttoned the cuffs at her wrists, then stood back to study herself. She pressed her palms to her dancing stomach, then brushed back a wayward wisp of hair. The movement stirred the scent of Charlie which was trapped now in the fabric of the new dress. Gold loops for her ears, a simple, short chain that fell only to the hollow of her throat, and sling-back shoes of black patent. She chose them because they were the highest she had, knowing how heartily Clay approved of a woman's foot in high heels.

It struck Catherine that she was, without a doubt, trying to be alluring to Clay, and for a moment she felt guilty. But then Melissa called, in her afternap gibberish, and Catherine hurried to get the baby ready.

Clay had gone out and bought a whole new outfit as well. But now, on his way to Catherine's, he wondered for the tenth time whether the silk tie looked too formal. He wondered if he'd appear to be a spit-combed, nervous schoolboy, all trussed up and tightly knotted this way. What the hell was the matter with him anyway? He'd never had the vaguest doubt about choosing his clothing before. But as he sat at a red light, Clay twisted the rearview mirror so he could study the tie once more. He yanked the Windsor knot halfway down, then changed his mind and slipped it back into place. He glanced at his hair, smoothed a palm over it, although not a filament was out of place. Someone behind him honked the horn and he muttered a curse and proceeded through the green light. Suddenly, as if just remembering, he withdrew a tape from the deck, found another and put it in the track, filling the car with the music of The Lettermen. Too obvious! he reprimanded himself, and tucked The Lettermen out of sight again.

With more than a half hour to spare, Catherine was all ready. She pictured Clay, somewhere out there getting prepared to come for her, wondered what he was feeling, what he was thinking. Melissa seemed to pick up her mother's distraction and capitalized on it, getting into things she knew she wasn't supposed to touch: the tree decorations, the knobs of the television, the philodendron on the coffee table. Finally, unnerved further by constantly pulling Melissa away from trouble, Catherine deposited her in the playpen, and continued her pacing without interference.

* * *

The bell rang.

Twice, let him ring twice, she scolded her impatient feet, while outside, Clay crammed his hand into his coat pocket to keep from ringing again too soon.

What should I say, she wondered wildly.

What should I say, he wondered frantically.

The door opened and she stood there in a loosely belted thing that made her look willowy and wonderful.

Snow fell upon the shoulders of Clay's rich, brown leather topcoat.

"Merry Christmas," he said, his eyes on her face while he took in details of her slender feet arched into high-heeled shoes, and the way the dress draped over her hips.

"Merry Christmas," she answered, smiling a small, nervous smile, stepping aside with a hand still on the doorknob to let him pass into the house. He turned around to watch her close the door, letting his eyes travel down to the backs of her calves, then up to the hair on her shoulders. When she met his eyes he said, "Nice dress."

"Thank you. It's new. I . . . well, I spent a little of your money on it."

Why did you say that! she scolded herself, but then he was smiling, saying, "I heartily approve, especially since I did the same thing."

"You did?"

"Christmas present for myself." He opened his topcoat to give her a brief glimpse of herringbone tweed the color of coffee with cream in it.

"In browns, of course."

"Of course."

"But then you always did look your best in browns." The entry suddenly seemed to grow too small, hemming them in, and Catherine moved to lead the way up to the living room, chattering, "Melissa's wearing a new dress, too, one your mother gave her that she just grew into. Come and see her."

"Hey, she'll outshine us both," Clay said right behind her. "Hi, Melissa." And for once Melissa didn't cry at the sight of him.

Catherine stooped and lifted the child, turning with her on her arm, carefully avoiding Clay's eyes as she said, "Can you say hi to Daddy, Melissa?" Their baby only gazed at Clay with bright, unblinking eyes. Catherine whispered something Clay couldn't make out and nudged Melissa's little hand. Still staring, the baby opened and closed her chubby fingers once.

"That's hi," Catherine interpreted, and briefly met Clay's pleased smile. Then she sat down on the davenport and began stuffing Melissa's hands and feet into a blue snowsuit. "Clay, would it be all right if we took my car, then we could take the playpen along."

"We won't need a playpen. Mother had one of the bedrooms redone into a nursery."

Startled, Catherine looked up. "She did?"

Clay nodded.

"When?"

"Last summer."

"She never told me."

"She never had a chance."

"Does she . . . I mean, do they know we're coming tonight, Melissa and I?"

"No. I didn't want to disappoint them if it didn't turn out."

Like a scene from a long-remembered favorite movie, the car moved through the streets while along the way streetlights eased on, signaling the arrival of dark. Catherine was filled with such an odd combination of emotions. The peaceful feeling of being again where she belonged was combined with the breath-halting sense of anticipation leading ever closer to a place where she belonged even more. She counted the hours until the end of the evening.

Clay cast careful glances her way. Christmas did things to a person, he thought, smiling appreciatively at the sight of Melissa reaching for knobs on the dash while Catherine pulled the tiny hands away time and again, and gently scolded. He glanced at Catherine's profile once more, his nostrils almost flaring in the light, powdery fragrance emanating from her, and he wondered how he'd make it till the end of the night when he could get her alone again.

The driveway curved to meet them, and Catherine couldn't control the small gasp. "I've missed it," she said, almost to herself. An expression of pleasure tipped up the corners of her mouth beguilingly.

They swept up in front of the door and Clay was around the car, reaching for Melissa, taking her up and into the crook of his arm, then taking Catherine's elbow as she stepped from the car. They stood for a moment in the mellow glow, splashing their faces from the carriage lanterns. The streamers of a red ribbon made a light tapping sound as they flicked against the bricks in a light, crisp wind. That wind lifted Clay's hair from his forehead, then set it gently back down as Catherine gazed at him. It toyed with the gold hoops at her ears, sending them swinging against her jawline where he wanted to bury his lips. But that would have to wait.

"Let's ring the bell," he said puckishly.

"Let's," she seconded.

When Angela opened the door she was already saying, "I wondered when —" But the words faded and she placed delicate fingers over her lips.

"Do you have room for three more?" Clay asked.

Angela didn't move for the longest time. Her eyes grew too sparkly, going from the smiling face of Catherine, in the shelter of Clay's arm, to that of Melissa, in his other arm.

"Angela," Catherine said softly. And suddenly the older woman in the pale yellow dress moved to encompass all three as best she could, unable to quite contend with everything at once, with the tears threatening to spill over her lids, with getting them all inside, beckoning Claiborne, taking Melissa—blue snowsuit and all—getting kissed by Clay and by Catherine.

When Claiborne saw who it was, he was as excited as Angela. There were more hugs, interrupted by a surprised Inella who stopped short and broke into a pleased smile at the sight of the newest arrivals and was immediately drawn to Melissa who was sitting on her grandmother's lap on the steps, having her snowsuit removed.

The tap of Elizabeth Forrester's cane announced her arrival from the living room. She cast a haughty eye over the assemblage in the foyer, stated to nobody in particular, "High time somebody came to their senses around here," and tapped her way back to the dining room, where she ladled herself a cup of eggnog, added a tot of rum, then mumbled, "Oh, why the bloody heck not," and tipped up the brandy bottle again with a satisfied smile.

The mistletoe was there again, everywhere. Catherine tried neither to avoid it nor seek it, but to ignore it, which was virtually impossible, for each time she looked up she found Clay's eyes seeking her across the room. Those eyes need not stray up to remind her of mistletoe. All evening she felt as if she wore a sprig of it in her hair, so suggestive were the glances they exchanged. It was odd, Clay staying away from her, always eyeing her across the room that way. Time and again she turned from conversation on which she had difficulty concentrating to the tug of his eyes on her back. And always, she would be the first to look away. The food was laid out upon the buffet and they found themselves elbow to elbow moving down the serving line.

"Are you having a good time?" he asked.

"Wonderful. Are you?"

He thought about answering truthfully, No, I'm miserable, but lied instead. "Wonderful, yes."

"Aren't you going to eat anything?"

He glanced at his plate, realized he was halfway past the food and his plate was still empty. She stabbed a Swedish meatball out of the wine sauce and dropped it on his plate.

"A little sustenance," she said, matter-of-factly, never raising her eyes as she moved on to the next chafing dish. He looked at the forlorn piece of meat all alone on the plate and smiled. She knew as well as he did what kind of sustenance he needed tonight.

Melissa let it be known immediately that she resented being left in this strange room, in this strange crib, all alone. Catherine sighed and went back into the room, and immediately her daughter stopped crying.

"Melissa, Mommy's going to be right here all the time. You're so tired, sweetheart, won't you lie down?"

She laid Melissa down, covered her, and hadn't even made it as far as the door before Melissa was standing, clutching the rail and crying pitifully.

"Shame on you, punkin," Catherine said, relenting and picking the baby up again, "you're going to hurt Grandma's feelings after she made this beautiful room all for you." It was beautiful. It had all the charm Angela could so easily bestow on everything she touched: bright patches of gingham checks in pastel pink, blue and yellow, blended skillfully into tiered curtains, patchwork comforter and an adorable padded rocker. Turning around to study the room in the glow of the small night-light, Catherine stopped short at the sight of Clay standing in the doorway.

"Is she giving you trouble?"

"It's a strange room, you know."

"Yes, I know," he said, crossing toward them to stand behind Catherine, talking to Melissa over her shoulder. "How about some music then, Melissa? Would you like that better?" And then, to Catherine, "Mother is starting the carols now. Why not bring her back downstairs? Maybe the music would make her sleepy."

Catherine turned to glance past Melissa's blond head at Clay. The look on his face made her pulse race. She realized they were alone, the sounds of the piano and voices drifted up to them from below. Clay moved, extending a hand to touch her . . .

But it was Melissa he reached for, and in the next instant the weight was gone from Catherine's arm.

"Come on," he said, taking Melissa, but never pulling his eyes away from Catherine's, "I'll take her. You've had her all night."

Melissa fell asleep in Clay's arms during the singing, but when she was returned to the crib, her eyes flew open instantly and she began to whimper.

"It's no use, Clay," Catherine whispered. "She's exhausted, but she won't give up."

"Should we take her home then?"

Something in the way he said the word *home,* something in the beckoning, wistful tone of his voice made the blood clamor in Catherine's head.

"Yes, I think we'd better."

"You get her dressed and I'll make our excuses."

All the way to the town house they didn't utter a word to each other. He switched on the radio and found that every station was playing Christmas carols. To the lull of them, Melissa at last fell soundly asleep in her mother's lap.

It was as if Catherine had played this scene before, putting Melissa to bed, then coming down to find Clay waiting for her. He was sitting on a swivel stool this time, with his coat still on. He had one foot propped on a rung of the opposite stool, an elbow leaning nonchalantly on the edge of the counter. Something caught Catherine's eye, something he twirled between thumb and forefinger, something green. Silently he twirled it—back and forth, back and forth—and it held her gaze like the watch of a hypnotist. Then the thing stopped and she realized it was a sprig of mistletoe he held by its stem.

Staring at it, she stammered, "Th-the baby's . . ."

"Forget the baby," he ordered softly.

"Would you like a drink or something?" she asked stupidly.

"Would you?"

Her eyes were drawn to his, to the level, unsmiling study in gray. The silence hummed, enveloping her momentarily. Then without moving a muscle, he said, "You know what I want, Catherine."

She looked at her feet. "Yes." She felt as if she'd turned into a pillar of salt. Why didn't he move? Why didn't he come and get her then?

"Do you know how many times you've turned me away, though?"

"Yes, eight," she gulped.

The blood leaped wildly to her face as she admitted it. She raised her eyes to him, and he read in them the cost of each of those times. And in the silence the mistletoe again began twirling.

"I wouldn't care to make it nine," he said at last.

"Neither would I."

"Then meet me halfway, Catherine," he invited, stretching out a hand, palm-up, waiting.

"You know what my conditions are."

"Yes, I know." He held the hand as before, in invitation.

"Then—then . . ." She felt like she was choking. Didn't he understand yet?

"Then say it?"

"Yes, say it first," she begged, staring at his long, beautiful fingers, the palm that waited.

"Come here so I can say it up close." It was almost whispered.

Slowly, slowly, she reached to touch the tips of his fingers with her own. But he did not move them until she herself had traveled a share of the distance, telling him what she, too, wanted, as her cold palm slid over his warm one. His fingers closed over hers in slow motion and he pulled her toward him more slowly yet. Her heart slammed against the walls of her chest and her eyes drifted to his as he reeled her close, settling her there against his open legs, his one foot still propped wide onto the rung of that other stool. There was no question then about what it was he wanted. His heat and hardness spoke for itself. He pressed her firmly, securely against his loins, then closed his eyes as his lips opened over hers. The mistletoe grew lost in the long sweep of her hair. She felt his hand, warm and forceful against her buttocks, holding her tight while his warmth and hardness branded her stomach. His kiss became all seeking and fevered, a wild crushing of tongue and lips, and she felt their teeth meet, then tasted blood, but had no thought for whose it was. His hands came one to each side of her face, and he jerked her fiercely away from his lips, looked into her eyes with a tortured expression.

"I love you, Cat, I love you. Why did it take me so long to realize it?"

"Oh, Clay, promise me you won't ever leave me again, so I know what I'm getting into."

"I promise, I promise, I promi—"

She stopped his words by flattening herself against him with such force that he grunted. He pulled the whole long, supple, welcome length of her against him. She felt his raised knee rubbing possessively against her hip and wound her arms around his neck, holding him tenaciously. Then she felt herself hoisted off the floor as he swiveled the stool around and in a single motion half leaned, half fell, pressing her back against the edge of the counter. But it cut into her shoulders, so she pushed him back, turning him, taking him with her on a brief journey together on that swiveling stool until she stood again on the floor between his open knees. They kissed, warm against each other, and somehow while they did it, the stool began twisting back and forth, back and forth, almost like the mistletoe had done twirling earlier in his fingers. And each time the stool moved, Clay's erect body brushed provocatively against hers while she rose up on tiptoe to meet it, brushing harder each time. She felt his hand leave her hair and seek the knot of her belt. Dimly she thought about helping him, but leaned against his loose hold instead, pleasured at the feel of his hand there between them, then at the touch of the belt as it glided down the backs of her legs to the floor. One-handed, he opened the dress, touching the skin of her throat first with his fingers, then with his lips, then moving lower, lower, lower, until his hand lay warm on the lowest part of her stomach. He backed away to look at her while he wrested the dress from her shoulders, and when he saw the brief garments beneath, he groaned and buried his face in the band of bareness between bra and panties, wetting the skin there with his tongue.

"Did you know I wore these on my wedding night?" she asked in a husky voice that sounded strangely unlike her own.

"Did you?" His eyes burned into hers, his hands traced the lotus petals along the top of the bra. "But tonight will be our wedding night." Then both of his arms went around her, and she felt her bra go tight, then loose, then fall away in his hands. His head swooped forward while hers dropped back. His kiss fell upon her bare breast, and a faint growl sounded in her arched throat as his tongue circled the nipple, then the edges of his teeth rode lightly against the cockled point. Strangling in delight, she threaded her fingers in his soft hair, directing him to her other hungering breast. Carried away, his teeth tugged too hard and she flinched, her nostrils distended. With a sound of apology deep in his throat, he suckled more lightly. Deep in her body, sensations sluiced and impatiently she tugged at the shoulders of the leather topcoat he still wore. Without taking his mouth from her flesh, he freed his arms, let her take the coat from his shoulders and drop it, unheeded, behind him, followed by his sport coat. Nuzzling each other, dropping kisses wherever they chose to fall, he worked the knot from his tie while she unbuttoned his shirt. Then it joined the rest on the floor. One-armed, he brought her back where she belonged, with her naked breasts against his bare chest. He eased away from her then, to watch the sight of his hands cupping her breasts. He flattened one hand against her stomach and ran it down inside the front of her bikini until he touched her intimately.

"Do you want me to take the rest off?" he asked, nuzzling her neck, tonguing her skin there, even tasting her perfume now.

"We're in the middle of the kitchen, Clay."

"I don't give a damn. Should I take it off or will you?"

"This was your idea," she whispered coquettishly, smiling against his hair.

"Like hell." But in one swift motion he had her panty hose and bikini down to her knees, then he picked her up effortlessly and set her on the edge of the counter, hooking a stool and sending it out of the way with a foot. He knelt down, raised his eyes to hers as he removed first one high heel, then the other, then with a sweep of both hands had her last two garments lying in a soft heap on the floor. He moved up next to the counter and she raised her arms, looped them around his neck, opened her knees and looped them around his waist and said, "Take me upstairs to our bedroom." He pulled her off the counter until she was astraddle his waist, her ankles locked behind him. Her naked flesh was pressed against his navel and the smell of her perfume was like a cloud about them as they walked that way, kissing, upstairs to the bedroom. He stood by the lamp and said, "Turn it on." She let go of his neck with one hand and reached.

Standing beside the bed he whispered "Let go" into her mouth.

"Never," she whispered back.

"Then how can I get my pants off?"

Without another word she unhooked her ankles and fell backward with a bounce onto the mattress, lying there watching him while he unbuckled his belt, unzipped his trousers, never taking his eyes off her. When he was naked, he knelt above her on one knee, his hands on either side of her head.

"Catherine, I know I'm a year and a half late asking this, but are you going to get pregnant out of this?"

"But if you'd asked that Fourth of July, we wouldn't be here now, would we?"

"Cat, I just don't want you pregnant for a while. I want to enjoy you flat and thirsty for a while first."

"Flat and thirsty?"

He realized he'd given himself away, so he leaned his head down to kiss her and stop her questions. She turned her mouth aside.

"What does that mean, flat and thirsty?"

"Nothing." He nudged around at her lips, trying to get her to stop talking and touch him.

"You answer me and I'll answer you," she said, avoiding another pass of his lips against hers.

If she got mad at him now, he thought, he'd never forgive himself for opening up his big mouth. But he had to answer.

"Okay. I read your diary. All that stuff we did with the wine—that's what I meant by flat and thirsty."

She burned now, but not with anger, with embarrassment and sensuality. "Clay, I feel like I'm dying of thirst right now, and believe me, I won't get pregnant."

She could feel his muscles quivering on each side of her head. His voice was racked as he asked. "Then how long do I have to hang here before you touch me?"

No longer, she thought, no longer, Clay, and reached to touch him lightly with the backs of her fingers, measuring his ardor with feather-strokes that robbed him of breath. The months of want drifted into oblivion at her first caress. The days of searching had their answer. Her hand explored, enclosed, stroked, cupped and thrilled, until Clay's elbows turned to water. He collapsed beside her, reaching, seeking her warm skin. Her stomach was a little softer now, but the old hollows were back below her hipbones. Her thigh was smooth and firm, lifting at his touch to free the spot his hand sought. As he moved toward it, her hand fell still upon his tumescence. Sensing her urgency, her expectancy, he lay his head upon her breast and listened to the thunder of her heart beneath his ear as he touched her depths for the first time. It thundered there in double time, and he could feel it lifting the weight of his head with each beat. Outwardly she lay limp and passive, but her heartbeat told the truth. He moved his fingers once, and she lurched and gulped for air. He rolled half over her, kissing her eyes, her temple, the corner of her mouth, her lips which lay slack, as if what was happening to the inside of her body robbed her of the will to do anything but drift in the grip of pleasure. He aroused her with butterfly touches, bent again to cover her breasts with kisses, sliding his lips over her stomach, feeling it rise with each lift of her hips. Low animal sounds scraped from her throat, then his name, repeated as an accent to each thrust she could no longer control.

He spoke her name—Cat—over and over, letting her soar, experiencing a new high, a sharing of purpose with her as he brought her near climax and sent her shivering. This, he knew, was what he had not given her the first time, and he meant to make it up to her all the other times of their lives.

"Let it happen, Cat," he whispered hoarsely.

But suddenly he knew he had to share the sensation to its fullest. Easing onto her, he sought and found, entered and plunged, murmuring soft sounds; lovesounds that took on their own meaning.

She shuddered and arched first, and he was close behind her, so close that the film of dampness dried from their skins at the same time.

Into her hair he spoke weakly, "Ah, Cat, it was good for me."

"For me too."

He lay his palm on her stomach, then ran it lower, let it rest peacefully upon her body, then just barely inside it. She could feel his jaw move in the hollow of her shoulder as he spoke.

"Cat, remember in the hospital when the nurse showed us the way the contractions build up?"

"Mmm-hmm," she murmured, toying sleepily with his hair.

"It felt the same way inside you a minute ago."

"It did?"

"It made me think of how close pleasure and pain are. It even seems as if the same things happen in your body during the moments of your greatest pleasure and your greatest pain. Isn't that odd?"

"I never thought about it before, but then I never—"

He raised up, leaned on an elbow and looked down into her face. He touched a lock of hair, easing it back from her forehead.

"Was that your first time, Cat?"

Suddenly timid, she surrounded him, hugged him too close for him to see her face.

"Yes," she admitted.

"Hey." Gently he removed her tight grip so he could look at her again. "After all that we've been through, are you getting modest on me?"

"How could I possibly claim modesty now?"

"Just don't ever be afraid to talk to me about anything, okay? If you don't trust me with the things that bother you, how can I help you? All that business about the past and your feelings for Herb, do you see that we seem to have conquered that already, together?"

"Ah, Clay." She sighed and leaned against him, promising herself she'd never withhold her feelings from him again. A short time later she said, "Did you know that I started falling in love with you while you were courting me at Horizons?"

"That long ago?"

"Oh, Clay, how could I help it? All those girls panting after you and telling me how perfect you were, and you coming by in your sexy little Corvette, with your sexy clothes and that sexy smile and all those sterling good manners of yours to offset all that sexiness. God, you drove me crazy."

"Idiot girl," he laughed. "Do you know how much time you could have saved if you'd just once let on what you were feeling?"

"But I was so scared. What if you didn't feel the same way about me? I'd have been shattered."

"Yet every time I made advances I felt like you couldn't stand me."

"Clay, I told you that first night that my dad made me come to your house —marriage had to be for love only. Please, let's always be this way, like we are tonight. Let's be good to each other and promise all those things that we never really promised in that trumped-up marriage ceremony."

Lying naked, with their limbs entwined, secure in each other's love, they sealed those vows at last.

"I promise them, Cat."

"I do, too, Clay."

On Christmas morning Melissa woke them up, babbling and thumping her heels on the crib. Clay came awake groggily, stretched and felt bare skin on the other side of the bed. He turned to study the woman who lay on her stomach, sleeping beneath a swirl of blond hair.

He started to creep from bed noiselessly.

"Where you going?" came a voice from under the hair.

"To get Melissa and bring her in with us, okay?"

"Okay, but don't be gone long, huh?"

They came back together, the one in aqua-blue footed pajamas, the other one in nothing. When Catherine rolled over, Clay plopped Melissa down beside her, then got in too.

"Hi, Lissy-girl. Got a kiss for Mommy?"

Melissa leaned over and sucked her mother's chin, her version of a kiss.

Clay watched with a glad expression on his face.

Catherine looked at his tousled blond hair, his smiling gray eyes and asked, "Hi, Clay-boy, got a kiss for Mommy?"

"More than one," he said, smiling. "This is one child who's going to learn early the value of touching."

He leaned across the baby then, to give his wife what she wanted.

Hummingbird

With love to Mom and Pat

And thanks to Janis Ian,
whose poignant love song
"Jesse" inspired me
to write this story

Chapter 1

WHEN THE 9:50 pulled into Stuart's Junction, it always attracted a crowd, for the train was still a novelty which the whole town anticipated daily. Barefoot children squatted like quail in the sand reed and needlegrass just outside town till the loud, gaseous monstrosity flushed them up and raced them the last quarter-mile toward the gabled depot. Ernie Turner, the town drunk, came each day to meet it, too. Belching and weaving his way out of the saloon, he would settle on a bench by the depot porch and sleep it off till the afternoon train sent him back for his evening round. Down at the smithy, Spud Swedeen laid down his maul, let loose of his bellows, and came to stand in the gaping door with black arms crossed upon blacker apron. And when the ringing of Spud's iron ceased, all the ears of Stuart's Junction, Colorado, perked up. Then along the short expanse of Front Street shopkeepers stepped from their doorways onto the weather-bleached planks of the boardwalk.

That early June morning in 1879 was no different. When Spud stopped his clanging, the barber chair emptied, bank clerks left their cages, and scales in the assay office swung empty while everybody stepped outside to face northeast and watch for the arrival of the 9:50.

But the 9:50 didn't come.

Before long, fingers nervously toyed with watch fobs; timepieces were pulled out, opened, and snapped shut before dubious glances were exchanged. Murmurs of speculation were eventually replaced by restlessness as one by one the townsfolk returned to their shops to peer out occasionally through their windows and wonder at the train's delay.

Time crawled while every ear was cocked for the moan of that whistle, which didn't come and didn't come. An hour, and the stillness over Stuart's Junction became a hush of reverence, as if someone had died, but nobody knew who.

At 11:06 heads lifted, one by one. The first, then the second merchant

425

stepped to his doorsill once again as the livening summer wind lifted the incoming steam whistle on its heated breath.

"That's her! But she's comin' in too fast!"

"If that's Tuck Holloway drivin' her, he's settin' to put 'er right through the depot! Stand back—she might jump the rails!"

The cowcatcher came on in a blur of speed while steam and dust wafted away behind it, and a red plaid arm flailed from the open window of the cab. It was Tuck Holloway, all right, whose words were lost in the slamming of iron and the hiss of steam as the engine overshot the depot by a hundred yards —still miraculously on both tracks. But Tuck's hoarse voice could not be heard above the babbling crowd who'd surged toward the depot. Then a single gunshot made every head turn and every jaw stop as Max Smith, the newly appointed station agent, stood with a pistol still smoking in his hand.

"Where's Doc Dougherty?" Tuck bellowed into the lull. "Better get him fast 'cause the train got held up about twenty miles north of here and we got two injured men aboard. One of 'em's bad shot, for sure."

"Who are they?" Max asked.

"Didn't stop to ask for names. Both of 'em's strangers to me. The one tried to rob my train and the other one saved it. Got hisself shot while he was doin' it, though. I need a couple men to tote 'em off."

Within minutes, two limp bodies were borne from the depths of the train, down its steps, into the waiting arms of bank clerk, hostler, assayer, and blacksmith.

"Someone get a wagon!"

Through the crowd came a buckboard, and onto it the motionless bodies were placed, while from around the saloon corner Doctor Cleveland Dougherty came panting and snorting, his black bag whacking his overweight calves as he ran. A moment later he knelt beside the first stranger, whose face was chalky and unnaturally pacified.

"He's alive," Doc pronounced. "Just barely." The second man was likewise checked. "Can't tell about this one. Get 'em to my place quick, and Spud, you make damn sure you miss every rock and pothole on the street between here and there!"

All who came to town that day lingered. The saloon did a roadhouse business. Down at the livery, Gem Perkins ran out of stalls. The floor beneath the cuspidors in the hotel lobby was well stained long before midafternoon, while underneath the beech trees in Doc's front yard townspeople sat with their eyes trained on his door, waiting now as they'd earlier waited for the arrival of the 9:50. Waiting to hear the fate of the two who'd ridden it in on their backs.

Miss Abigail McKenzie heaved a sigh that lifted her breasts beneath the pleated bodice of her proper Victorian blouse. She ran one small, efficient finger around the inside of the lace-edged choker collar to free it from her sticky skin. She made a quarter-turn to the left, blue eyes glancing askance into the mirror, and placed the back side of one hand beneath her jaw—just so —lifting the skin there to test it for tautness.

Yes, the skin was still firm, still young, she assured herself soberly.

Then she quickly slipped the oversized filigreed hatpin from the crown of her daisy-trimmed hat, placed the hat carefully upon her sternly backswept brown hair, rammed the pin home, and picked up her pristine white gloves from the seat of the huge umbrella stand—a thronelike affair with a mirror on its backrest and umbrellas and canes threaded through holes in its outsized arms.

She considered her gloves a moment, looked out front through the screen door at the shimmering heat ripples radiating skyward, laid the gloves down, hesitated, then resolutely picked them up again, dutifully drawing them over her slim hands. The heat is no excuse to go over town improperly dressed, she scolded herself.

She walked to the rear of her house, rechecking each shade on each south window, assuring herself they were all drawn low against the harsh sun. She glanced in a full circle around her kitchen, but nothing needed straightening, putting away, or taking out. Her house was kept as fastidiously as was her clothing. Indeed, everything in Miss Abigail McKenzie's life was always as orderly and precise and correct as it could possibly be.

She sighed again, crossed the straight shot from kitchen to dining room to front parlor, and stepped onto the porch. But abruptly she reentered, checking the doorstop fussily, in the way of those who manufacture worry because their lives contain too little of the genuine article.

"No sense risking your lovely oval window," she said aloud to the door. That window was her pride and joy. Satisfied that the door was secure, out she went, closing the screen as gently as if it had feelings. She crossed the porch, walked down the path, and nodded hello to her well-tended roses beside the pickets.

She walked erectly, chin parallel to the earth, as a lady of propriety ought. Let it never be said that Miss Abigail stooped, slouched, or slogged when she walked over town. Oh, never! Her carriage was utterly proper at all times. Her sensible shoes scarcely peeked from beneath her skirts, for she never hurried—rushing was most undignified!

She had things on her mind, Miss Abigail did, which didn't rest lightly there. Her errand was not one she relished. But one would never guess from perusing her as she strode down Front Street that there could be the slightest thing amiss with Miss Abigail McKenzie, if indeed one ever could.

Coming along past the houses and yards, her eye was caught by the unusual scene up ahead. Doc Dougherty's lawn was crowded with people, while across the street the benches of the boardwalk were hidden behind solid skirts and men sat on its high ledge while children scuffled in the dirt and horses waited at the hitching rails.

One could always rely upon Miss Abigail to keep her nose out of other people's business. Seeing the crowd, she swung left, walked the short block over to Main, and finished her trek over town along its all but deserted length. Thus Miss Abigail avoided what was probably some sordid spectacle at Doc Dougherty's. That kind of thing attracted riffraff, and she was not about to be one of their number!

Miss Abigail thought it truly lamentable to have to do what she was about to do. Oh, not that there was anything wrong with Louis Culpepper's establishment. He ran a neat and orderly eatery—she'd give him that. But waiting tables was truly a last resort—oh, truly a last! It was not at all the kind of

thing she'd choose to do, had she the choice. But Miss Abigail had no choice. It was either Louis Culpepper's place or starve. And Abigail McKenzie was too ornery to starve.

Sensible black squat heels aclicking, she entered beneath the sign hailing, THE CRITERION—FINE FOOD AND DRINKS, LOUIS CULPEPPER, PROP. As she carefully closed the door, she ran a hand over her blouse front, making sure it was tightly tucked into her skirtband, then, turning, she again sighed. But the place looked deserted. There was a faint odor of yesterday's cabbage adrift in the air, but nothing resembling the aroma of meats stewing for the supper clientele, who wouldn't be long in coming. Why, one would have thought Louis to be better organized than this!

"Hello?" she called, cocking her head, listening.

From somewhere in the rear came a tiny, tinny sound. She walked toward the kitchen to find the alley door open and a hot breeze buffeting the saucepans that hung above the wood range. The place *was* abandoned.

"Well, I declare!" Miss Abigail exclaimed to no one at all. Then, glancing in a circle, repeated, "Well, I *do* declare!"

It had taken her some weeks to finally decide she must speak to Louis. To find his restaurant empty was most disconcerting. Wiping an errant bead of perspiration from her forehead with a single finger of her pristine glove, Miss Abigail chafed at this unexpected turn of events. Inspecting the fingertip, she found it dampened by her own sweat and knew she could not put herself through this a second time. She must find Louis now, today!

Adjusting her already well placed hat, she again took to Main Street, then over one block to Front, on which both she and Doc lived, some two blocks apart. Rounding the corner, she found herself part of the throng that filled Doc Dougherty's yard and the surrounding area. Doc himself was standing under his beech trees, sleeves rolled up, speaking loudly so everyone could hear.

". . . lost a lot of blood and I had to operate to clean up the hole and shut it up. It's too early to tell if he'll make it yet. But you all know it's my duty to do whatever I can to keep him alive, no matter what he's done."

A distracted murmur passed among the townspeople while Miss Abigail glanced around hopefully, looking for Louis Culpepper. Spying a towheaded youth who lived next door to her, she whispered, "Good day, Robert."

"Howdy, Miss Abigail."

"Have you seen Mr. Culpepper, Robert?"

But the boy's neck was stretched and his ears tuned to Doc again as he grunted, "Un-uh."

"Who is Doctor Dougherty talking about?"

"Don't rightly know. Some strangers got themselves shot on the train."

Relieved that it was none of the town's own, Miss Abigail was nonetheless forced to give up her cause as fruitless until the crowd dispersed, so turned her attention to the doctor.

"The other one's not in as bad of a shape, but he'll be out of commission for a few days. Between the two of 'em, I'll have my hands full. You know Gertie's gone off to her cousin's wedding in Fairplay and I'm caught short-handed here. There's plenty of you'll be hollering for me, and I just plain can't be in more than one place at a time. So if there's anybody that'd volunteer to give me a hand looking after these two, well, I'd be obliged."

From somewhere in the crowd a woman's voice spoke what many were thinking. "I'd like to know why we should feel obliged to take care of some outlaw tried his hardest to do us dirt! Robbing our train that way and shooting that innocent young man in there. Why, what if it'd been Tuck he shot?"

Doc raised his hands to quiet the swell of agreement.

"Now, hold on! I got two men in here, and granted, the one done wrong and the other done right, but they're both in need of help. Would you people have me tend the one that's hurt less and turn out the one that's nearly dead?"

Some of them had the grace to drop their eyes, but still they demurred.

Doc continued while he had 'em feeling guilty. "Well, a man can do just so much alone, and that's all he can do. I need help and I'm leaving it up to you to find it for me. The problem isn't just mine—it's all of ours. Now, we all wanted the Rocky Mountain Railroad to put their spur line through here, didn't we? And sure enough we got it! 'Course, we only banked on it hauling our quartz and copper and silver out of here and bringing our conveniences in from the East. But now that we get a little trouble hauled in too, we're not so all-fired anxious to stand up and pay the price, are we?"

Still nobody volunteered.

What Doc said was undeniably true. The railroad was an asset from which they all benefited. Having a spur line run into a hidden mountain town like Stuart's Junction opened it up to both East and West, bringing the town commerce, transportation, and a stable future that it had lacked before the R.M.R. laid tracks up here.

The citizens chose to forget all that now, though, leaving Doc Dougherty to plead his case, and leaving Miss Abigail somehow inexplicably angry at their heartlessness.

"I could pay anyone that took on to help me—the same as I pay Gertie when she's here," Doc offered hopefully.

Miss Abigail glanced around. Her mouth puckered.

"Hell, Doc," someone hollered, "Gertie's the only nurse this town's ever saw or prob'ly ever will. You ain't gonna find nobody to take her place nohow."

"Well, maybe not anybody as qualified as Gertie, but anybody that's willing is qualified enough to suit me. Now what do you say?"

The sweat broke out upon Miss Abigail's upper lip. What she was considering was too sudden, too unprecedented, yet she had no time for rumination. And the smug attitudes surrounding her made her unutterably angry! The thought of tending two injured men in the privacy of her own home seemed far, far preferable to carrying stew and soup to the lot of them. Furthermore, she was almost as skilled as Gertie Burtson. Her pulse thrummed a little behind her proper, tight collar, but her chin was high as ever as she stepped forward, squelching her misgivings, putting those around her in their proper place.

"I believe, Doctor Dougherty, that I would qualify," Miss Abigail stated in her ladylike way. But since a lady does not shout, Doc didn't quite hear her. Nobody believed what they were seeing as Miss Abigail raised a meticulous white glove.

"Miss Abigail, is that you?" he called; somehow the crowd had silenced.

"Yes, Doctor Dougherty, it is. I should like very much to volunteer."

Before he could check his reaction, Doc Dougherty raised his brows, ran a grizzled hand over his balding head, and blurted out, "Well, I'll be damned!"

Excusing herself, Miss Abigail made her way to Doc's side. She parted the crowd almost as Moses parted the Red Sea, still with that level chin and that all-fired dignity she always maintained. As she passed, men actually reached as if to doff hats they weren't wearing.

"G'day, Miss Abigail."

"How do, Miss Abigail."

"Howdy, Miss Abigail."

The ladies greeted her with silent, smiling nods, most of them awed by her cool, flowing presence as she glided toward Doc in her customary, pure-bred way while they fanned themselves and raised their arms to let the breeze at their wet armpits. Moving through their midst, Miss Abigail somehow managed to make them all feel gross and lardy and—worse—small, for the help they'd stubbornly refused.

"Come inside, Miss Abigail," Doc said, then raised his voice to the crowd. "You might as well go home now. I'll leave word up at the station with Max if there's any change." Then, solicitously taking Miss Abigail's elbow, he led her inside.

His widower's house was a mishmash of flotsam, collected and never discarded. The big front room looked like a willful child had messed it up in retaliation for being spanked, except that the strewn articles obviously were an adult's. Doc Dougherty removed a stack of journals and newspapers from an armchair, kicked aside a pair of forlorn house slippers, and said, "Sit down, Miss Abigail, sit down."

"Thank you," she replied, sitting in the cleared spot as if it were the dais in a throne room.

While she gave the impression that none of the debris around her infiltrated her superb hauteur, Miss Abigail noticed all right. Old Doc Dougherty meant well enough, but since his Emma died the place had become slovenly. Doc kept absurd hours, running to anyone who needed him at any hour of the day or night, but leaving himself little time for such refinements as housecleaning. Gertie Burtson was hired as his nurse, not as his housekeeper. That was all too evident by the looks of the room.

Doc Dougherty sat down on the arm of an old lumpy horsehair sofa, spread his old lumpy knees, and covered them with his old lumpy hands. As his rump came into contact with the overstuffed arm, Miss Abigail saw a puff of dust emanate from the horsehair and overcast the air around him. He studied the floor a minute before speaking.

"Miss Abigail, I appreciate your offer." He didn't know exactly how to say this. "But you know, Miss Abigail, I hardly thought you'd be the one to step forward and volunteer. This is probably a job somebody else is better suited for."

Irritation pricked her. Crisply, she asked, "Are you refusing my help, Doctor Dougherty?"

"I . . . I'd hate to say I'm refusing. I'm asking you to consider what you're getting into."

"I believe I have considered it. As a result, I've offered my services. If there is some inexplicable reason why I shan't do, then we are both wasting our time." When Miss Abigail was piqued, her voice became curt and she tended to get eloquently wordy. She rose, looking down her nose as she tugged her gloves more securely on her hands.

He moved quickly to press her back into her chair, his dust cloud swirling with him. She looked up at him from under her hat brim, inwardly gratified that he'd seen her pique. Fine time for him to get choosy!

"Hold on now, don't get yourself all in a huff."

"In a huff, Doctor Dougherty? I hardly would describe myself as being in a huff." She arched one brow and tipped her head.

Doc Dougherty stood above her, smiling, peering at her upturned face under its crisp bonnet of daisies. "No, Miss Abigail, I doubt you've ever been in a huff in your life. What I'm trying to make you see is that you might be if I agree to let you nurse those two."

"Pray tell why, Doctor?"

"Well, the truth is . . . because you're a . . . a maiden lady."

The phrase echoed cruelly through Miss Abigail McKenzie's thirty-three-year-old head, and within her fast-tripping, lonely heart.

"A maiden lady?" she repeated, mouth puckered a little tighter.

"Yes, Miss Abigail."

"And what possible bearing does my being a . . . a maiden lady—as you so kindly put it—have upon my being capable of helping you?"

"You must understand that I hoped for a married woman to volunteer."

"Why?" she asked.

Doc Dougherty turned his back and walked away, searching for a delicate way to phrase it. He cleared his throat. "You'd be exposed to parts of these men that you'd probably rather not be and asked to perform duties that would be—to say the least—unpalatable to a lady of your—" But his words faltered. He found himself unwilling to embarrass her further.

Miss Abigail finished for him. "Tender sensibilities, Doctor?" Then with a little false laugh asked, "Were you about to expound upon my being a lady of tender sensibilities?"

"Yes, you might put it that way." He turned once again to face her.

"Are you forgetting, Doctor, about the years I cared for my father while he was ill?"

"No, Miss Abigail, I'm not. But he was your father, not some gunshot stranger."

"Posh, Mister Dougherty," she said, giving the impression she'd spit out the words when they'd come out with calculated control, along with the word *Mister* instead of *Doctor*. "Give me one good reason why I should not care for these two gentlemen."

He flung his hands out in frustration. "Gentlemen! How do you know they're gentlemen? And what if they're not? What'll you do when I'm fourteen miles out in the country and you're wishing I weren't? One of those *gentlemen* just tried to rob a train and I'm willing to treat him, but that doesn't mean I'll trust him. Suppose he tries to overpower you and escape?"

"A moment ago you advised me not to get into a huff. May I now advise you the same, Doctor? You've been shouting."

"I'm sorry, Miss Abigail. I guess I was. But it's my responsibility to make you see the risk involved."

"You've done your duty then, Doctor Dougherty. But since I see your plea for help did not raise a plethora of willing volunteers, I hardly see that you have a choice but to accept my offer."

Doc shook his head at the threadbare carpet, wondering what her father would have said. Abbie had always been the apple of the old man's eye.

Miss Abigail looked up at him, so prim and erect from her spot on the forlorn old armchair, her mind made up.

"I have a strong stomach, a hand full of common sense, and a nearly empty bank account, Doctor," she stated. "And you have two wounded men who need looking after. I suspect that neither of them is healthy enough right now to either harm me or escape from me, so shall we get on with it?"

She knew she had him with that reference to her bank account.

"You're sure one smooth talker, Miss Abigail, and I'm up a crick, I'll grant you that. But I can't pay you much, you know. Thirty dollars for the week is about it. It's as much as I pay Gertie."

"Thirty dollars will do nicely . . . . oh, and one thing more," she added, easing to the edge of her chair.

"Yes?"

"What do you propose to do with them when your patients arrive tomorrow morning?"

Miss Abigail's eyes had not scanned the room; they didn't have to for Doc to know that his place wasn't exactly her idea of a suitable hospital. He had no delusions regarding the condition of his house. What could be seen from their present vantage point was a sorry mess at best. They both knew what she'd find if she were to peruse the upstairs or—worse—the kitchen. They both knew, too, that she had a penchant for cleanliness. And so when Doc finally finished eyeballing the room, he was totally aware of the place's shortcomings.

"I don't suppose we could put 'em upstairs?" he asked fruitlessly.

"I don't suppose that would be the most convenient place. I propose that we remove them to my house as soon as you think that would be possible. It would be infinitely easier for me to care for them were I to have my own kitchen at my disposal."

"You're right," Doc agreed, and abruptly Miss Abigail got to her feet.

"Now, may I see our patients?"

"Of course. One's on the surgery table and the other on the sofa in the waiting room, but they're both out cold for the time being. Tomorrow'll be time enough for you to take charge of them."

They walked through an archway into Doc Dougherty's waiting room, which was only slightly tidier than the parlor. On a sagging sofa beneath a triple window a man lay unmoving. He wore a city suit, its vest and jacket unbuttoned. One of his feet, brown-stockinged, stuck out from a pant leg while the other sported a bandage covering the forefoot but leaving the heel bare where it rested on a pillow. His face, in repose, was pleasant. His hair was nondescript brown and fell away from his forehead in boyish waves. His ears were flat and his nails clean. And that was good enough for Miss Abigail.

"This is the man who robbed the train?" she asked.

"No. The other one robbed the train. This one—Melcher's his name—

apparently interrupted the proceedings. The way Tuck tells it, Melcher here took a stray bullet from that one's gun." Doc thumbed over his shoulder in the direction of the surgery. "Must've been some kind of scuffle involving a bunch of passengers because by the time Tuck got the train stopped and got back there to see what was going on, everybody was telling the story a different way and these two were lying there bleeding. One of the shots took Melcher's big toe clean off his right foot."

"His big toe!" she exclaimed, pressing her fingers to her lips to hide the smile.

"Could've been worse if the shot had been higher. On the other hand, it could've been little or nothing if he'd had a sensible pair of boots on instead o' them flimsy city shoes he was wearing."

Miss Abigail looked to where Doc Dougherty pointed, and there on the floor sat a single stylish brown shoe of fine, soft leather.

"Had to cut the other one off him," Doc informed her. "Wasn't any good anyway, with the end shot off like it was."

Miss Abigail had to smile in spite of herself. First at Doc's keeping the single shoe, which was no good without its mate, and secondly at the absurdity of the town's first hero saving the day by getting his big toe shot off!

"Is something funny, Miss Abigail?" She sobered at once, chagrined at being caught in a state of levity at this unfortunate man's expense.

"No . . . no, forgive me, Doctor. Tell me, is the loss of a toe a serious injury? I mean, is his life in danger?"

"No, hardly. The toe came off real clean, and there was no lead shavings or powder left on him once the bullet went through that shoe. He was in awful shock and lost some blood, but I put him to sleep and stitched him up and he'll be good as new in no time. When he wakes up, that toe is gonna throb like a bitch in heat, though . . ." Doc suddenly seemed to realize to whom he was talking. "Oh . . . forgive me, Miss Abigail. I forgot myself."

Miss Abigail colored deeply, stammering, "I . . . oh, I shall certainly sympathize with poor Mr. Melcher."

"Yes . . . well . . ." Doctor Dougherty cleared his throat. "Mr. Melcher will undoubtedly find himself walking with a limp from now on, but that should be the worst of it. We'll keep the foot propped up, keep it bandaged for a couple of days, and I'll give you some salve for it. But mostly time and air will have to heal the stitches. You're right—Mr. Melcher will need good old-fashioned sympathy most of all."

"So much for the damage done here. And what about the other?" Miss Abigail asked, relieved that her composure was returning.

Turning toward the surgery door, the doctor walked a step or two toward it. "The other bullet, I fear, did far more damage. This scoundrel will undoubtedly rue the day he set foot on that R.M.R. train . . . if he lives long enough."

They came to the doorway and Miss Abigail preceded him into its cream-colored depths. Here at last was cleanliness, although she devoted not even the quickest glance to it. Her eyes were drawn to the rectangular table where a sheet shrouded an inert figure. The table faced the doorway, so all that was visible was the sole of a left foot—a very long left foot, thought Miss Abigail—and the rise of sheet covering an updrawn right knee and leg.

"This one is lucky to be alive. He lost plenty of blood from the gunshot and more when I had to clean the wound out. He'd have been better off if the bullet had stayed in him. As it was, it came out the other side and blew a hole in him twenty times bigger than the one it made going in. Left a pretty big mess on its way through, too."

"Will he die?" Miss Abigail whispered, staring at that long foot that made her insides jitter. She'd never seen a man's bare foot before, other than her father's.

"No need to whisper. He's dead to the world and he's going to stay that way for a while, or I miss my guess. But as to whether or not the poor son of a b—the poor fool will die, that I can't say yet. Looked to be healthy as a horse before this happened to him." Doc Dougherty had walked farther than Miss Abigail into the room and now stood beside the man on the surgery table. "Come and have a look at him."

Miss Abigail experienced a sudden stab of reluctance but ventured far enough to see bare shoulders with the sheet slicing them at armpit level. Above was a chest shadowed with dark, curled hair, broad, tanned shoulders, and the bottom of a dark-skinned face that sported an evil-looking moustache. She couldn't see any of the features above the moustache from this angle, only the nostrils, which were shaped like half hearts, and the lower lip, which suddenly twitched as she looked at it. His chin wore only a trace of the day's growth of whiskers, and she suddenly found herself thinking that for a train robber he certainly kept himself up, if the clean foot and the recent shave were any indication.

The sheet covered him from biceps to ankle, giving no indication of where he was injured or how seriously. From here he looked as if he might have stretched out for a nap, one knee slung up haphazardly as he serenely dozed.

"He was shot in the groin," Doc said, and Miss Abigail suddenly blanched and felt her stomach go weightless.

"In . . . in the—" she stammered, then halted.

"Not quite . . . but very close. Do you still want the job?"

She didn't know. Frantically she thought of everyone in town hearing the reason she had changed her mind. She stood there considering a man coming to such an end. Whether she still wanted to care for him or not, she felt somehow sorry for the unconscious fellow.

"A train robber might expect to come to a bad end, yet nobody should come to this."

"No, Miss Abigail. It's not a pretty sight, but it could've been worse. A few inches difference and he could've lost . . . well, he could have been dead."

Miss Abigail blushed again but nevertheless looked resolutely at Doc Dougherty. Nobody else had come forward but herself. Even a hapless train robber deserved human consideration.

"I quite understand, Doctor, what the man's dilemma might have been, but don't you agree that even a robber deserves our sympathies, in his present state?"

"My sympathies he's got, Miss Abigail, and plenty of them. He'll get every bit of care I can give him, but I got to warn you, I'm no miracle worker. If he lives it'll be just that—a dad-blamed miracle."

"What am I to do for him, Doctor?" she asked, suddenly deciding that a man this age—he looked to be thirty-five or so—was much too young to die.

"You're sure about this? Very sure?"

"Just tell me what to do." The look in her eyes, just like years ago when she'd taken on the care of her father, told Doc Dougherty she meant business.

"You'll keep the knee raised, keep the thigh up, so the air can get at the underside as well as the top. I managed to staunch the flow of blood, but if it starts up again, you'll have to apply alum to try to stop it. Keep the wound clean—I'll tell you what to disinfect it with. Watch for any putrefaction and if you see any, come runnin' like a cat with her tail on fire the minute you see any sign of it. We'll have to try to keep his fever down. For the pain there's not much we can do. Keep him still. Try to get him to eat. Do you think you can handle that, Miss Abigail?"

"Everything but setting my tail on fire," she replied dryly, surprising Doc with her wit. He smiled.

"Good. You go home now and get a good night's rest because it'll probably be your last for a while. I'm expecting a run on the place in the morning and I'd like to have these two out of here before it starts. I 'spect everyone with so much as an ingrown hair will be in here hoping for a glimpse of either a genuine robber or a genuine hero."

"Ah well, I expect I'm the lucky one then, to have seen them both at close range." A brief smile tugged at the corner of Miss Abigail's mouth.

"I 'spect you are at that. How can I thank you?"

"I'll see you in the morning. Everything shall be in order for their arrival."

"I'm sure it will be, Miss Abigail. Knowing you, I'm sure it will be."

She turned to leave, but at the door turned back.

"What . . . what is his name, the robber's?"

"We don't know. Men in his profession don't carry calling cards like Mr. Melcher did."

"Oh . . . oh, of course not," she replied, then hesitated a moment longer to add, "but it would be a shame if he should die and we should not know whom to inform. He must have someone somewhere."

Doc Dougherty had scarcely had time to think of that yet.

"Only a woman with a heart would think of that at a time like this."

"Nonsense," Miss Abigail said briskly, then turned to leave.

But of course he was right, for her heart was doing monkeyshines as she walked home, remembering a bare long foot; a dark, furred chest; and the prospect of caring for a wound near the man's—

But Miss Abigail McKenzie not only avoided speaking such a word. She could not even think it!

Chapter 2

THE SUN WAS hotter than ever the following day as Doc approached the loiterers on the sagging veranda of Mitch Field's feedstore. They congregated there to drape on the feed sacks, spit and chew, and never give poor Mitch so much as a lick of business.

"All right, which of you lazy no-goods is gonna give me a hand," Doc challenged.

They even laughed lazily, then squinted at the sun, gauging the discomfort of exerting themselves against the chance of getting a gander at them two up at Doc's house. Old Bones Binley scratched his grizzled jaw with the dull edge of a whittling knife and drawled, "Reckon you can count me in, Doc."

It was Doc's turn to laugh. Bones had a yen for Miss Abigail and the whole town knew it. Bones looked just like his name, but along with some help from Mitch and Seth Carter, the transfer of patients was handled without mishap.

Miss Abigail was waiting at her front door and directed Doc and Mitch to place David Melcher in the southeast bedroom upstairs and the other man in the downstairs bedroom, since it was probably inadvisable to carry him up the steps.

The train robber was too long for the mattress, and his feet hung beyond the footrail, so the sheet covered him only up to the waist. Bones and Seth watched Miss Abigail's face as she came around the doorway and saw that bare, hairy chest lying there, but she barely gave it a glance before turning to the pair and dismissing them coolly and unquestionably. "Thank you, gentlemen. I'm sure you have pressing business down at the feedstore."

"Why, uh, yes . . . yes we do, Mizz Abigail." Bones grinned while Seth elbowed him in the ribs to get him moving.

Outside, Seth said, "It might be ninety-nine degrees everywhere else, but a body could freeze to death anywhere within fifteen feet o' Miss Abigail McKenzie."

"Ain't she somethin', though?" Bones gulped, his Adam's apple protruding.

"Whole town knows she can twist you around her finger, but that sugary voice of hers don't fool me none. Underneath that sugar is mostly vinegar!"

"You really think so, Seth?"

"Why, sheee-oot, I know so. Why, lookit how she just excused us, like we was clutterin' up her bedroom or somethin'."

"Yeah, but she took in that there train robber, didn't she?"

"Did it for the money, the way I heard tell. It's prob'ly the only way she could get a man in her bed. And that one that's in it now will be sorry he didn't die when he comes to and finds hisself bein' nursed by the likes of her."

There were those in town, like Seth, who considered Miss Abigail just a touch above herself. Granted, she was always soft-spoken, but she had that way, just the same, of elevating herself and acting lofty.

When Doc had settled the patients and told her to send Rob Nelson if she needed anything, he promised to check in again that evening, then left with Mitch in tow.

She thought Mr. Melcher was asleep when she crept to the door of his room, for his arm lay over his forehead and his eyes were closed. Though his beard had grown overnight, he had a very nice mouth. It reminded her of Grandfather McKenzie's mouth, which had always smiled readily. Mr. Melcher looked to be perhaps in his late twenties—it was hard to tell with his eyes closed. Glancing around, she spied his suitcase under the Phyfe library table near the window and tiptoed across to open it and find his nightshirt. When she turned, she found that Mr. Melcher had been watching her.

"Ah, you're awake," she said gaily, disconcerted at being caught searching through his personal belongings.

"Yes. You must be Miss McKenzie. Doc Dougherty said you'd volunteered. It was very good of you."

"Not really. I live alone and have the time that Doctor Dougherty doesn't." She looked at his foot then, asking, "How does it feel this morning?"

"It's throbbing some," he answered honestly, and she immediately colored and fussed with the nightshirt.

"Yes, well . . . we'll see if we can't relieve it somewhat. But first I believe we'd best get you out of your suit. It looks as if it could stand a flour bath." The brown wool worsted was indeed wrinkled but Miss Abigail had grave misgivings about how to gracefully get him out of it.

"A flour bath?"

"Yes, a dredging in clean flour to absorb the soil and freshen it. I'll take care of it for you."

Although he moved his arm off his forehead and smiled, he was smitten with discomfort at the thought of undressing before a lady.

"Are you able to sit up, Mr. Melcher?"

"I don't know. I think so." He raised his head but grunted, so she crossed the room quickly and touched his lapel, saying, "Save your energy for now. I shall be right back." She returned shortly, bearing pitcher and bowl, towel and washcloth, and a bar of soap balanced across a glass of bubbling water. When she had set things down, she stood beside him, saying, "Now, let's get your jacket off."

The whole thing was done so slickly that David Melcher later wondered how she'd accomplished it. She managed to remove his jacket, vest, and shirt and wash his upper half with a minimum of embarrassment to either of them. She held the bowl while he rinsed his mouth with the soda water, then she helped him don his nightshirt before removing his trousers from beneath it. All the while she chatted, putting them both at ease. She said she would rub flour into his suit jacket and let it sit for a few hours, and by the time she hung it on the line and beat the flour from it with her rug-beater, it would be as fresh as a daisy. He'd never heard of such a thing! Furthermore, he wasn't used to a woman fussing over him this way. Her voice flowed sweetly while she attended him, easing him through what would otherwise have been a sticky situation had she been less talkative or less efficient.

"It seems you have become something of a local hero, Mr. Melcher," she noted, giving him only the beginnings of a smile.

"I don't feel much like a hero. I feel like a fool, ending up stretched out here with a toe shot off."

"The townspeople have a great interest in our new railroad and wouldn't like to see it jeopardized in any way. You've saved it from its first serious mishap. That's nothing to feel foolish about. It is also something which the town won't forget soon, Mr. Melcher."

"My name is David." But when he would have caught her eye she averted hers.

"Well, I'm pleased to meet you, though I regret the circumstances, on your behalf. From where do you hail, Mr. Melcher?"

When she used his surname he felt put in his place and colored slightly. "I'm from back East." He watched her precise movements and suddenly asked, "Are you a nurse, Miss Abigail?"

"No, sir, I'm not."

"Well, you should be. You're very efficient and gentle."

At last she beamed. "Why, thank you, Mr. Melcher. I take that as one of the nicest things you could say, under the circumstances. Are you hungry?"

"Yes, I don't remember when I ate last."

"You've been through an ordeal, I'm sure, that you'll be long in forgetting. Perhaps the right food will make your stay here seem shorter and your bad memories disappear the faster."

Her speech was as refined as her manners, he thought, watching her move about the room gathering his discarded clothing, stacking the toilet articles to carry away. He felt secure and cared for as she saw to his needs, and he wondered if this was how it felt to be a husband.

"I'll see to your suit after I prepare your breakfast. Oh! I forgot to comb your hair." She had stopped halfway out the door.

"I can do that myself."

"Have you a comb?"

"Not that I can reach."

"Then take the one from my apron pocket."

She came back and raised her laden arms so he could get at the comb. His hesitation before reaching to take it told her things about him that a thousand words could not tell. David Melcher, she could see, was a gentleman. Everything about him pleased her, and she later found herself inexplicably buoyant and humming while she worked in the kitchen preparing his meal. Perhaps she even felt the slightest bit wifely as she delivered the tray of bacon, eggs, and coffee, and wished she could stay and visit. But she had yet another patient needing her attention.

At the bedroom doorway downstairs, she hesitated, gazing at the stranger on her bed. Just the fact that he was a criminal was disquieting, though he remained unconscious, unable to harm her in any way. His beard was coal black, as were his moustache and hair, but his skin, since last night, had taken on the color of tallow. Coming fully into the room, she studied him more closely. There was a sheen of sweat on his bare chest and arms, and she reached out tentatively to touch him, finding his body radiating an unhealthy inner heat.

Quickly she fetched a bowl of vinegar water and sponged his face, neck, arms, and chest, as far as his waist, where the sheet stopped, then left the cool compresses on his brow in an effort to bring down his fever. She knew she must check his wound, but at the thought her palms went damp. She held her breath and gingerly lifted a corner of the sheet. Flames shot through her body at the sight of his nakedness. Her years of caring for an incontinent father had done nothing to prepare her for this! With a shaky hand she lay the sheet at an angle across his stomach, his genitals, and left leg, then fetched two firm bolsters to boost up his right knee. She snipped away the gauze bindings, but the bandages stuck to his skin, so next she mixed vinegar water with saltpeter and applied the dripping compresses to loosen the cotton from his wounds. The shot had hit him very high on the inner thigh, which had been firm before the bullet did its dirty work. But now, when the bandage fell free, she saw that the wound had begun bleeding again. One look and she knew she had her work cut out if he wasn't to bleed to death.

Back in the kitchen she spooned alum into an iron frying pan, shaking it over the hot range until it smoked and darkened. She sprinkled the burnt alum liberally onto a fresh piece of gauze, but when she hurried back to the bedroom with the poultice, she stood horrified, gaping at the blood of this nameless train robber as it welled in the bullet hole then ran the short distance into the shallow valley of his groin, where coarse hair caught and held it.

How long she stood staring at the raw wound and the collecting blood she did not know. But suddenly it was as if someone had shot her instead of him. Her body jerked as if from the recoil, and once again she was frantically bathing, staunching, praying. In the hours which followed, she fought against time as a mortal enemy. Realizing that he must soon eat . . . or die . . . she beat a piece of steak with a mallet and put it into salt water to steep into beef tea. But he kept bleeding and she began to doubt that he'd live to drink it. Remembering her Grandmother McKenzie saying they'd packed arrow wounds with dried ergot, she next made a poultice of the powdery rye fungus and applied it. Feeling the man's dark, wide brow, she realized it had not cooled, so she swabbed him with alcohol. But when she stopped sponging, he immediately grew hot again. The fever, she realized, must be fought from within rather than without. She scoured her mind and found yet another possibility.

Wild gingerroot tea!

But when she brought the ginger tea back to him, he lay as still as death, and the first spoonful dribbled from his lips, rolled past his ear, and stained the pillowcase a weak brown. She tried again to force another spoonful into his mouth, succeeding only in making him cough.

"Drink it! Drink it!" she willed the unconscious man almost in an angry whisper. But it was no use; he'd choke if she forced the tea into his mouth this way.

She pressed her knuckles to her teeth, despairing, near tears. Suddenly she had an inspiration and ran through her house like a demented being, flew out the back door, and found Rob Nelson playing in his backyard next door.

"Robert!" she bellowed, and Rob jumped to stand at attention. Never in his life had he seen Miss Abigail look so bedeviled or raise her voice that way.

"Yes, ma'am?" he gulped, wide-eyed.

Miss Abigail grabbed him by the shoulders so tight she like to break his bones. "Robert, run fast up to the livery stable and ask Mr. Perkins for a handful of straw. Clean straw, do you understand? And run like your tail's on fire!" Then she gave Rob a push that nearly put him on his nose.

"Yes, ma'am," the amazed boy called, scuttling away as fast as his legs would carry him.

It seemed to Miss Abigail that hours passed while she paced feverishly, waiting. When Rob returned, she grabbed the straw without so much as a thank you, ran into her house, and slammed the screen in the boy's face.

Leaning over the robber's dark face, she tipped up his chin and forced two fingers into his mouth. His tongue was ominously hot and dry. But the straw was too flimsy, she could see after several unsuccessful attempts to get it down his throat. Harried, she scoured her mind, wasting precious minutes until she found an answer. Cattails! She plucked one from a dried bouquet in the parlor, reamed the pith from its center with a knitting needle, and—hardening her resolve—lifted the dark chin again, pried open his mouth with her fingers, and rammed the cattail down his throat, half gagging herself at what she was doing to him.

But it worked! It was a small success, but it made her hopeful: the ginger tea went down smoothly. With not a thought for delicacy, Miss Abigail filled her mouth again and again, and shot the tea into him, but as she was removing the straw from his mouth, some reflex in him decided to work and he swallowed, clamping down unknowingly upon her two fingers. She yelped and straightened up in a pained, arching snap, pulling her fingers free to find the skin broken between the first and second knuckles of both. Immediately she stuck them in her mouth and sucked, only to find a trace of his saliva on them. An outlaw! she thought, and yanked a clean handkerchief from within her sleeve, fastidiously wiping her tongue and fingers dry. But staring at his unconscious face, she felt her own flood with heat and her heart thrum from something she did not understand.

Realizing it was near noon, she left the man to prepare David Melcher's tray. When she brought it to his doorway, Melcher's jaw dropped.

"Miss Abigail! What's happened to you?"

She looked down to find flecks of blood strewn across her breasts from beating the steak, maybe even some from the body of the man downstairs. Raising a hand to her hair, she found it scattered like wind-whipped grass. As her arm went up, a large wet ring of sweat came into view beneath the underarm of the trim blue blouse which had looked so impeccable this morning. Too, there were those two bloody tooth marks on her fingers, but those she hid in the folds of her skirt.

Gracious! she thought, I hadn't realized! I simply hadn't realized!

"Miss Abigail, are you all right?"

"I'm quite all right, really, Mr. Melcher. I've been trying to save a man's life, and believe me, at this point I think I'd be grateful to see him with enough strength to try to harm me."

Melcher's face went hard. "He's still alive, then?"

"Just barely."

It was all David Melcher could do to refrain from snapping, "Too bad!"

Miss Abigail sensed his disapproval, but saw how he made an effort to submerge his anger, which was altogether justifiable, considering the man downstairs had done Mr. Melcher out of a big toe. "Just don't overdo it. I don't think you're used to such hard work. I shouldn't want you becoming ill over the care of a common thief."

An undeniable warmth came at his words, and she replied, "Don't worry about me, Mr. Melcher. I am here to worry about you."

Which is just what she did when he'd finished eating. She brought his shaving gear and held the mirror for him while he performed the ritual. She studied him surreptitiously, the gentle mouth and straight nose, strong chin with no cleft, no dimples. But it was his eyes she liked best. They were pale brown and very boyish, especially when he smiled. He looked up and she dropped her eyes. But when he tended his chore again, swiveling his head this way and that, his jaw jutting forward and the cords of his neck standing out, it made the pulse beat low in her stomach. Without warning came the memory of the robber's sharper features, thicker neck and longer, darker face. Forbidding countenance, she thought, compared to the inviting face of David Melcher.

"The robber wears a moustache," she observed.

All the gentleness left David Melcher's face. "Typical!" he snapped.

"Is it?"

"It certainly is! The most infamous outlaws in history wore them!"

She lowered the mirror, rose, and twisted her hands together, sorry to have angered him.

"I can see that you don't like to speak of him, so why don't you just forget he's down there and think about getting yourself better? Doctor Dougherty said I should change the bandage on your foot and apply some ointment if it gives you pain."

"It's feeling better all the time. Don't bother."

Rebuffed, she turned quickly to leave, sorry to have riled him by talking about the robber, especially after Mr. Melcher had been so complimentary over the fried steak and potatoes and the fresh linen napkin on the tray. She could see there was going to be friction in this house if the criminal managed to live. Yet she'd taken on the job of nursing him, and she was bound to give it her best.

Returning to the downstairs bedroom, she found he'd moved his right hand —it now lay across his stomach. She studied its long, lean fingers, curled slightly, the shading of hair upon its narrows, and saw what appeared to be a smear of dirt on it. Edging closer, she looked again. What she had taken for dirt was actually a black and blue mark in the distinct shape of a boot heel. Carefully picking up the injured hand by the wrist, she laid it back down at his side. But when it touched the sheet, he rolled slightly, protectively cradling it in his good left hand as if it pained him. Instinctively she pressed him onto his back, her hands seeming ridiculously minuscule upon his powerful chest. But he fell back as before, subdued and still again.

It was hard to tell if the hand was broken, but just in case, she padded a small piece of wood, fit it into his palm, and bound it, winding gauze strips up and around his hairy wrist, crossing them over the thumb until any broken bones could not easily be shifted. She noticed as she worked that his hands were clean, the nails well tended, the palms callused.

Checking his forehead again, she found it somewhat cooled but still hotter than it should be. Thinking back wearily to yesterday when she'd set out for town and a job at Culpepper's, she thought how little she'd suspected she'd end up with a job like this instead. Perhaps Culpepper's would have been preferable after all, she thought tiredly, slogging back to the kitchen for cotton and alcohol again. She looked around in dismay at the room: pieces of torn rags and gauze everywhere; used wet lumps of cotton in bowls; vinegar cruet, salt bowl, herb bags, scissors, dirty dishes everywhere; blood splatters on the wall and the highboy, and the stench of burnt alum hanging sickeningly over everything.

Turning on her heel, she uncharacteristically disregarded it all and returned to her bedroom.

Dear God! He'd turned over . . . and onto his right leg!

Pushing and grunting, struggling with his limp weight, she managed to get him onto his back again, then fell across his stomach, panting. But she knew even before she looked what she'd find: the wound was bleeding profusely again.

So, sighing heavily, almost stumbling now, she fought the entire battle once more: cleansing the wound, burning the alum, staunching the blood, applying ergot, and praying to see the flow stop. He seemed to be rousing more often as the afternoon wore on. Each time he moved a limb, she poured her strength on him, holding him flat if need be, willing him to lie still, badgering him aloud, sweating with the effort, but wiping the sweat from his fevered body rather than from her own. Toward evening when he still hadn't gained consciousness, she gave up hoping for him to awaken fully enough to drink the beef tea and force-fed him again.

Sometime later she was standing staring trancelike at his exposed white hip, counting the minutes since the bleeding had stopped, when Doc Dougherty's knock brought her from her reverie. "Come in." But she barely had the strength left to call out.

Doc had had a tough day himself, but he took one look at her and demanded, "Miss Abigail, what in tarnation did you do to yourself?" She looked ghastly! Her eyes were red-rimmed and for a moment he thought she might start crying.

"I never knew before how hard it is to save a life," she said hoarsely. Doc led her by the arm into her disastrous kitchen. She laughed a little madly as he forced her into a chair. "And now I know why your house looks the way it does, too."

Rather than feel insulted, he snorted laughingly. She'd been initiated then, he thought, as we all must be at first.

"You need a good dose of coffee, Miss Abigail, and a bigger dose of sleep."

"The coffee I'll accept, but the sleep must wait until after he revives and I know he'll make it."

Doc poured her a cup of coffee and left her to check the patients, but as he walked from the kitchen he saw Miss Abigail's back wilt against her chair and knew he was lucky it was she who'd offered to help. Yet, entering the room where the robber lay, he wondered again if she wasn't too delicate to handle wounds like this. At first he'd considered only her sense of propriety, but seeing her so whipped, he wondered if the physical strain wasn't too much for her.

But one look at her handiwork and he marveled at her ingenuity and tenacity. What he found when he checked the wound genuinely surprised him. The man doesn't know how lucky he is that he ended up where he did, Doc thought. The wound looked good, the fever was low, no bleeding, no gangrene. She'd done as much as Doc himself could have.

Upstairs, he said, "Mr. Melcher, I think you're in good hands with Miss Abigail dancing attendance on you. However, I thought I'd lend my meager medical assistance just the same."

"Ah, Doctor Dougherty, I'm happy to see you." Melcher looked fit as a fiddle.

"Foot giving you much pain?"

"No more than I can handle. It throbs now and then, but the salve you gave Miss Abigail helps immensely."

"Laudanum salve, my man. Laudanum salve applied by Miss Abigail—a very effective combination, don't you agree?"

Melcher smiled. "She is wonderful, isn't she? I want to thank you for . . . well, I'm very happy I'm here in her house."

"I didn't have much to do with it, Melcher. She volunteered! And even though she's being paid, I think she puts out more than the money will compensate her for. The two of you are a real handful for her."

At the reminder of the other patient, Melcher's face soured.

"Tell me . . . how is he?"

"He's alive and not bleeding, and both facts seem to be more than believable. I don't know what Miss Abigail did for him, but whatever it was, it worked." Then, noting the expression on Melcher's face, Doc thumped the man's good leg. "Cheer up, my man! You won't need to be here under the same roof with the scoundrel too much longer. This toe is looking up. Shouldn't hold you up here for long at all."

"Thank you," Melcher offered, but his face remained untouched by warmth as he said it.

"My advice to you is to forget he's down there if it bothers you so much," Doc said, preparing to leave.

"How can I forget it when Miss Abigail has to be down there too . . . and caring for him!"

Ah, so that's the way the wind blows, thought Doc. "Sounds like Miss Abigail has made quite an impression on you."

"I dare say she has," admitted Melcher.

Doc laughed shortly, then said, "Don't worry about Miss Abigail. She can take care of herself. I'll be around again soon. Meanwhile, move that foot and use it as much as you want, as long as you feel comfortable doing it. It's doing well." But Doc was smiling at this unexpected turn of events as he headed downstairs.

The coffee had revived Miss Abigail somewhat.

"Got a cup for me?" Doc asked, returning to the kitchen. "Naw, don't get up. Cups in here? I'll pour my own." As he did, he continued visiting. "Miss Abigail, I'm sorry I doubted you yesterday, I can see what kind of fool I was to do so. You've not only done a proper job of nursing those two . . . it seems you've made a devotee of Mr. Melcher."

"A devotee?" She looked up, startled, over her cup.

Doc Dougherty leaned back against the edge of her sideboard as he sipped, his eyes alight.

Flustered, she looked into her cup. "Nonsense, Doctor, he's simply grateful for a clean bed and hot food."

"As you say, Miss Abigail . . . as you say." But still Doc's eyes were

mischievous. Then abruptly he changed the subject. "Word came in by tele-
graph that the railroad wants us to keep that stranger here till they can send
someone up here to question him."

"Ah, if he lives to talk." Once again he could see the weariness in her, could
hear the dread in her voice.

"He'll live. I examined the wounds and they look real good, Miss Abigail,
real good. What in blazes have you got on those poultices?"

"Powdered ergot. It healed the wounds from Indian arrows. I figured it
might heal his."

"Why didn't you call me when he got bad?"

Her eyes looked incredulous. "I didn't think of it, I guess."

He chuckled and shook his head. "You planning to run me a little competi-
tion in the healing business, are you?" he asked, eyes twinkling.

"No, Doctor. It's far too hard on a maiden lady. When these men are fit, I
shall give up my life in medicine, and gladly."

"Well, don't give it up yet, Miss Abigail, please. You're doing one damn fine
job for me."

Too tired to even object to his language, she only answered, "Why, thank
you, Doctor." And he could have sworn she beamed, there in her evening
kitchen amidst the mess and the smell that was so unlike her usual tidiness.
He knew she'd be okay then; she had qualities in her that most women didn't.
Also, she was experiencing the first fledgling joy afforded to those who beat
the odds against death.

On his way to the door, Doc turned. "Oh, I forgot to mention, the railroad
said they'll foot the bill for as long as it takes to get these two healthy. I think
they mean to pacify Melcher and keep him from kicking up a fuss about
getting shot while on board one of the R.M.R. trains. As for the other one
. . . he must be wanted for more than just one holdup for them to be that
interested. I don't mean to scare you, just wanted you to rest easy about the
money. Are you afraid, being here alone with him?"

She almost laughed. "No, I'm not afraid. I've never been afraid of anything
in my life. Not even when I thought I was running out of money. Things have
a way of working out. Yesterday I was facing penury and tonight here I am
with a railroad supporting me. Isn't that handy?"

He patted her arm and chuckled. "That's more like it, Miss Abigail. Now
see that you get some sleep so you can stay this way."

As he opened the screen door, she stopped him momentarily, asking, "Doctor, did the telegram say what that man's name is? It seems strange always
referring to him as 'that man' or 'that . . . robber.' "

"No, it didn't. Just said they want him kept here and no question about it.
They want to get their hands on him pretty bad."

"How can they possibly know if he's wanted for other charges when they
haven't seen him?"

"We sent out a description. Somebody along the line must have recognized
him by it."

"But suppose the man does die? It wouldn't seem proper for a man to die
where not a soul even knew his name."

"It's happened before," Doc stated truthfully.

Her shoulders squared, and a look of pure resolve came over her face. "Yes, but it shan't this time. I will make it my goal, a sort of talisman if you like, to see that he revives sufficiently to state his name. If he can do that, perhaps he can recuperate fully. As you see, Doctor, I intend to be a tenacious healer." She gave Doc a wry grin. "Now hurry along. I have a kitchen to see to and a supper to prepare." Doc was chuckling as she whisked him away. It took more than weariness to defeat Abigail McKenzie!

She hadn't time to worry about her own appearance while she prepared David Melcher's supper tray, yet her heart was light as she pondered Doc's words. A devotee. David Melcher was her devotee. A delicious sense of expectation rippled through Miss Abigail at the thought. She took extra care with his meal and paused to tuck a few stray wisps of hair into place before stepping into his room. He was lying quietly, facing the window with its view of the apricot sky. As she paused in the doorway, he sensed her there and turned with a smile. Her heart flitted gaily, filling her with some new sense of herself.

"I've brought your supper," she said softly.

"Please sit with me while I eat it and keep me company," he invited. She wanted to . . . oh, how she wanted to, but it simply wasn't proper.

"I'm afraid I have things to do downstairs," was her excuse. His face registered disappointment. But he was afraid to be too insistent; she'd done so much already. The room grew silent, and from outside came the wistful cry of a mourning dove. Miss Abigail set the tray on his lap, then offered brightly, "But I've brought you something to read if you'd care to, after you've finished your supper." From her pocket she pulled a book of sonnets.

"Ah, sonnets! Do you enjoy sonnets too? I might have guessed you would."

At his smile of approval she grew flustered and raised her eyes to the cotton candy clouds beyond the window. Again came the call of the mourning dove, singing its question, "Who? Who? Who?" It suddenly seemed to Miss Abigail that the question was being asked of her. It was a question she'd asked herself more times than she cared to remember. Who would there ever be to brighten her life? To give her reason for living?

Lost in reverie, Miss Abigail said rather dreamily, "I find the evening a particularly appropriate time of day for sonnets—rather the softest time of day, don't you think?"

"I couldn't agree more," came his gentle reply. "It seems we have something in common."

"Yes, we do." She became suddenly aware of how she looked, and touched her lower lip with the tips of her fingers. She still wore her stained, sweaty dress that she'd worn all day, and her hair was terribly untidy. Yet even as she fled the room, she realized he'd smiled sweetly and spoken almost tenderly. Was it true, what Doc had said? Abigail McKenzie, you're so tired you're getting fanciful!

But tired or not, her day was not over.

Dusk had fallen and in the gloom of her downstairs bedroom its occupant looked darker than ever. She found herself comparing him to Mr. Melcher. The whiskers on his chin had nearly doubled in length, and she decided that tomorrow she would shave him. She had never liked dark-whiskered men anyway. And moustaches! Well, if dark chin whiskers were sinister, black moustaches were positively forbidding! This one—she stepped closer—bordered his upper lip like thick, drooping bat's wings. She shuddered as she studied it and crossed her arms protectively. Vile! she thought. Why would any man want to wear a bristly, unattractive thing like that on his very face?

But suddenly Miss Abigail's grip on her upper arms loosened. She had a dim recollection of—but no, it couldn't have been, could it? She frowned, remembering the feel of that moustache when she'd fed him, and in her memory it was not bristly, but soft.

Surely I'm mistaken, she thought, shaking herself a little. How could it be soft when it looks so prickly? Yet she was suddenly sure it had been. She glanced warily behind her, but of course nobody was there. It was simply silly to have looked! But she checked again, stealthily, before reaching out a tentative finger to touch the thick black hair beneath the robber's nose. It came as a near shock to find it almost silky! She felt his warm breath on her finger, and quickly, guiltily, recrossed her arms. The softness was disconcerting. Suddenly feeling sheepish, she spoke aloud. "Moustache or not, thief or not, I'm going to make you tell me your name, do you understand? You are not going to die on me, sir, because I simply shan't allow it! We shall take it one step at a time, and the first shall be getting your name out of you. It's best if you understand at the onset that I am not accustomed to being crossed up!"

He didn't move a muscle.

"Oh, just look at you, you're a mess. I'd better comb your hair for you. There's little else I can do right now."

She got her own comb from the dresser and ran it through his thick hair, experiencing a queer thrill at the thought that he was a robber of trains yet she was seeing to his intimate needs. "I can't say I've ever combed the hair of an outlaw before," she told him. "The only reason I'm doing so now is that, just in case you can hear me, you'll know you're not allowed to just . . . just lie there without fighting. This hair is dirty, and if you want it washed, you shall simply have to come around."

Suddenly his arm jerked and a small sound came from him. He tossed his head to one side and would have rolled over, but she prevented it by holding him down with restraining hands. "You've got to lie flat. I insist! Doctor Dougherty says you must!" He seemed to acquiesce then. She felt his forehead and found it cool. But just in case, she brought a sewing rocker from the living room—an armless, tiny thing offering little comfort—and sat down for only a moment, only until she was sure he wouldn't thrash around anymore and hurt himself.

In no time at all her head lolled and her thoughts grew dim as she faded into a dream world where the stranger awakened and smiled at her from behind his soft black moustache. His wide chest moved near and she pressed it with her hands. She avoided his tempting lips, arguing that he was a thief, but he only laughed deep in his throat and agreed that he was, and wanted to steal something from her now. But I don't know your name, she sighed like the night wind. He smiled and teased, Ah, but you know more of me than my name. And she saw again his naked body—soft, curled, intimate—and felt again the wondrous shame of sensuousness. And upon the tiny sewing rocker her sleeping body jerked.

His flailing limbs awakened her and she jumped up and flattened him, using her own body to keep him on his back and still. The strange, forbidden dream was strong in her as she felt the flesh of this man beneath her own. She should not think such thoughts, or touch him so.

Yet she stayed beside him, guarding him through the night. Time and again he tossed, and she ordered, "Stay on your back . . . keep that knee up . . . tell me your name . . ." until she could fight him no longer. In the deep of night she fumbled into the dark kitchen, found a roll of gauze, and tied his left ankle to the brass footboard, his left wrist to the headboard. Blurred by sleep, she again sat on the armless rocker. But sometime during the night she arose insensibly, clambered over the footboard, and fell asleep near the end of the bed with her lips near his hip.

Chapter 3

SLOWLY . . . HAZILY . . . HE became aware of a great, steady heat on his face. And he could tell by its constancy that it was sun.

Mistily . . . lazily . . . he became aware of a soft, lush heat against his side. And he could tell by its curves that it was woman.

Progressively . . . painfully . . . he became aware of raw, gnawing heat in his flesh. But this he could not identify, knew only that it pained in a way nothing ever had before. His eyeballs rolled behind closed lids, refusing yet to give up their private dark, hemming him in with the three heats that melded to scorch his very fiber. He wondered, if he opened his eyes, would he rouse from this dream? Or was it real? Was he alive? Was he in hell? His eyes grated open but he stared up at a ceiling, not the roof of a tent. His body ached in many places. Sweet Jesus, he thought, and his eyes faded closed to leave him wondering where he was and who lay down there near the foot of his bed. He tried to swallow but couldn't, lifted drugged lids again and gritted his teeth till his jaw popped, then raised his head with a painful effort.

A female satyr of some kind was braced on its elbows, gaping at him with wide eyes.

He had only one conscious thought: I must be slipping. This one's a hag and she had to tie me up to get me to stay.

Then he slipped once more into blackness. But he took with him the image of the ugly hag, her hair strewn like vile straw around a face that seemed to have fallen into collapsing folds from her eyes downward. In his insensibility he dreamed she harped at him, commanding him to do feats of which he was incapable. She insisted that he speak, roll over, don't roll over, answer her, be still. Sometimes he dreamed her voice had turned to honey, but then it intruded, thorny-like again, until he finally escaped her altogether and slept dreamlessly.

Miss Abigail despaired when his head fell back and he was lost in oblivion before she could wrest his name from him. All she knew that she hadn't known before was that his near-black eyes held a faint touch of hazel. She'd

expected they'd be jet, hueless, as foreboding as the rest of him. But the hazel flecks saved them from all that.

Groaning, she pulled herself off the bed.

Never in her life had Miss Abigail looked into a morning mirror and seen a sight like that which confronted her today. The night had taken its toll, seemingly having shrunken the skin above her eyes and stretched that below. Plum-colored shadings accentuated her too-wide, distraught eyes while elongated lines parenthesized her lips. Tangled, devastated hair set it all off with cruel truthfulness.

She studied her reflection and felt very old indeed.

The thought of David Melcher brought her out of her maunderings.

She bathed in the kitchen and brushed her hair, coiling it neatly at the base of her neck, then donned a soft, cream-colored blouse much like that she'd worn yesterday and a brown broadcloth skirt. On an impulse she applied the tiniest bit of attar of roses to her wrists.

"Miss Abigail, don't you look lovely this morning!" David Melcher exclaimed appreciatively when she stepped to his doorway with a breakfast tray.

"And aren't you chipper, Mr. Melcher!"

Again he invited her to stay while he ate, and this time she accepted, though propriety demanded she stay only briefly. But he praised her cooking, the coddled eggs, toast, and apple butter, teasing, "Why, Miss Abigail, I'll be plain spoiled by the time you throw me out of here."

His appreciation ruffled her ego in a gentle, stirring way, like a low breeze can lift the fine hair at the back of one's neck and create delicious shivers.

"I would not, as you say, throw you out of here, Mr. Melcher. You are free to stay as long as you need."

"That, Miss Abigail, is truly a dangerous offer. I may take you at your word and never leave." His eyes held just the right amount of mischief to make the comment thoroughly proper. Yet that tickle stirred the back of her neck again. But she'd stayed as long as it was prudent.

"I'd like to visit longer, but I do have work I should like to complete while the morning coolness prevails."

"Why, Miss Abigail, you made that sound just like a sonnet. You have such an eloquent way of speaking." Then he cleared his throat and added, in a more formal manner, "I'd like to read through the sonnets again today, if you don't mind."

"Not at all. Perhaps you'd enjoy some others I have also."

"Yes . . . yes, I'm sure I would."

As she rose from her chair and ran her hands down her sleeves to free them of any nonexistent wrinkles, he thought of how delicate the high collar and long sleeves made her look and of how she smelled like roses and of what a perfect little lady she was.

She fed the robber warm broth through the cattail again. Now, nearing him, her pulse did strange, forbidden things, and as if to get even with him, she scolded the unconscious man, "When will you make up your mind to awaken and tell me your name and take some decent nourishment? You're being an awful lot of trouble, you know, lying there like a great hibernating grizzly! You've put me to the task of feeding you as I did yesterday. I know it seems a vicious method, but it's the only way I can think of . . . and believe me, sir, it's no more palatable to me than it is to you, especially with that moustache."

The feeding finished, she brought out the shaving gear and intrepidly set out to clean him up, not at all sure how well she'd do. She lay thick towels beneath his jaw, lathered him up, and set to work with the blade, all the while puzzling over that moustache.

Should she or shouldn't she?

It truly was a dirty, ominous-looking feature. And maybe if David Melcher hadn't pointed out how typical the moustache was of outlaws, and maybe if it hadn't been so alarmingly soft, and maybe if her heart hadn't betrayed her when she touched it, she wouldn't have shaved it off.

But in the end she did.

When it was half gone she had a pang of guilt. But it was too late now. After she had finished, she stood back to evaluate the face without the moustache and found, to her chagrin, that she'd spoiled it completely! The moustache belonged on him just as surely as did his thick black eyebrows and his swarthy coloring. Suppose when he awoke he thought the same thing? The thought did little to calm her misgivings, and the next task did even less. It was time to give him a bath.

She set about doing so, a section at a time, first lightly soaping an arm, then rinsing it and wiping it dry. His armpit was a bed of straight, thick black hair —unnerving. So she concentrated on his shoulder and tried not to look at it. The far arm presented a problem, for the bed was pushed up into a corner of the room. She tried pulling the bed out to get at him from that side, but he was too heavy and it wouldn't budge. She ended up climbing once again onto the bed with him to facilitate matters.

His upper half was done . . .

She gulped, then remembered he was, after all, unconscious.

Slipping the oilcloth beneath his right leg, she washed it carefully, avoiding the damaged thigh. His foot was long, and it evoked a queer exhilaration as she washed the sole, then between the toes, which were shaded with hair between the knuckles. She admitted now that what Doctor Dougherty said was true: it was infinitely more disconcerting tending the intimate needs of a stranger than those of a father. The sheet still shrouded his private parts. She managed to keep them covered while doing his other leg. *That part* of him she did not wash.

But she had seen it once, and couldn't get the picture from her mind.

As the day progressed, his eyes moved more often, though they remained closed. Now and then she saw muscles flex, and he tossed repeatedly, so she kept him safely tied to the bedrails.

While Miss Abigail freshened up David's room that morning, she learned he was a shoe salesman out of Philadelphia. Then he surprised her by announcing, "When I get back, I'll be sure to send you a pair of our best."

She placed one small hand on the high collar of her blouse, fingers spreading delicately over her neck as if to hide a pulsebeat there.

"Oh, Mr. Melcher . . . it wouldn't do at all, I'm afraid, much as I'd love a fine pair of city-made shoes."

"Wouldn't do? But why?"

Miss Abigail dropped her eyes. "A lady simply does not accept such a personal gift from a gentleman unless he's . . ."

"Unless he's what, Miss Abigail?" he asked softly.

She felt herself color and stared at her hem. "Why, Mr. Melcher, it simply wouldn't be proper." She looked up to find his brown eyes on her. "But I thank you anyway," she added wistfully.

She thought the issue was settled, but at noon Mr. Melcher announced he felt good enough to come downstairs to eat his dinner, but apologized for having nothing to put on his feet.

"I believe I can find a pair of Father's slippers here somewhere."

She brought them and knelt before him.

Such a feeling welled up inside David Melcher, watching her. She was genteel, soft-spoken, refined, and each favor she did for him made David Melcher revere her more. He got up shakily, hopping on one foot to catch his balance, and she whisked an arm around his waist while his came about her shoulder.

"The floor is slippery, so hold the banister," she warned.

They started down, one step at a time, and each time he leaned on her, his face came close to her temple. Again she smelled of roses.

Her free hand was on his shirtfront and she felt his chest muscles flex each time he braced on the banister.

"What color would you like, Miss Abigail?" he asked, between jumps.

"Color?" They stopped and she looked up into his face, only inches from hers.

"What color shoes shall I pick for you?" They took one more step.

"Don't be silly, Mr. Melcher." Again they'd stopped, but now she was afraid to raise her eyes to his.

"How about a pale dun-colored kid leather?" He lightly squeezed her shoulder, sending her heart battering around wildly. "They'd look grand with what you're wearing now. Imagine the leather with this soft lace." He touched the lace of her cuff.

"Come . . . take another step, Mr. Melcher."

"I'd be honored if you'd accept the shoes."

She kept her eyes averted, her hand still upon his chest.

"I'd have no place to wear them."

"That I cannot believe. A fine-looking woman like you."

"No . . . I'd have no place. Please . . . our dinner is ready." She nudged him, but he resisted, and beneath her hand she felt his heart drumming as rapidly as her own.

"Don't be surprised if a pair of shoes arrives one day for you. Then you'll know I've been thinking of you." His voice was scarcely above a whisper as he murmured, "Miss Abigail . . ."

At last she looked up to find a multitude of feelings expressed in his eyes. Then his arm tightened upon her shoulder, he squeezed the soft sleeve, the arm beneath. She saw him swallow, and the breath caught in her throat as his pale brown eyes held hers. As his soft lips touched her she again felt the commotion beneath the palm on his chest. His gentle kiss was as light as a sigh upon her lips before he drew back and looked into her liquid gaze. Her heart thrilled, her knees weakened, and for a moment she feared she might tumble headlong down the stairs, so dizzy was she. But then she dropped her lashes demurely, and they continued on their halting, heart-bound way to the kitchen.

It had been years since David Melcher had lived in a house with a kitchen like this. The tabletop was covered with a starched yellow gingham to match the window curtains that lifted in a whispering wind. Dishes and silver had been precisely laid, and a clean linen napkin lay folded atop his plate. His eyes followed Abigail McKenzie as she brought simple, fragrant foods—three puffed, golden biscuits were dropped on his plate, then she returned with a blue-speckled kettle and spooned thick chunks of chicken and gravy over the top.

"How long has it been since you were home, Mr. Melcher?"

"You might say I have no home. When I go back to Philadelphia, I take a room at the Elysian Club. Believe me, it's nothing at all like this."

"Then you . . . you have no family?"

"None." Their eyes met, then parted. Birds chittered from somewhere in the shade-dappled yard, and the heady scent of nasturtiums drifted in. He thought he never wanted to leave, and wondered if she might be feeling the nesting urge as strongly as he.

The black-haired, clean-shaven man became aware of the smells around him this time much as he'd become aware of the heat once before. With his eyes still closed, he caught the scent of something sweet, like flowers. There was, too, the starchy, agreeable smell of laundry soap in fresh linens. Now and then came the tantalizing aroma of chicken cooking. He opened his eyes and his lashes brushed against some fancy, knotted stitchery on a pillow slip. So . . . this wasn't a dream. The sweet smell came from a bouquet of orange things over there on a low table near a bay window. The window seat had yellow-flowered cushions that matched the curtains.

He shut his eyes, trying to recall whose bedroom it was. Obviously a woman's, for there were more yellow flowers over the papered walls and a dressing table with hinged mirrors.

He had not moved—nothing more than the opening and closing of his eyelids. His left hand was tingling, it prickled as if no blood ran through it. When he flexed the fingers they closed around a cylinder of metal, and he realized with a shock that he was tied onto a bed.

So that hag was no nightmare! Who else could have tied him up? He was no stranger to caution. Stealthily he tested the bindings to see if he could break them. But they were tight on both hand and foot.

He lifted his lids to a brown skirt, smack in front of him, standing beside the bed. He assessed it warily, wondering if he should use his right hand to knock her off her feet with one surprise punch in the gut. He let his eyelids droop shut again, pretending to go back under so he could get a look at her face through a veil of near-closed lashes.

But he couldn't tell much. She had both hands clasped over her face, forming a steeple above her nose as if she was in joy, distress, or praying. From what he could tell, he'd never laid eyes on her before. There wasn't much to her, and from the stark hairdo she wore he knew she was no saloon girl. Her long sleeves and high collar were no dance hall get-up either. At last, surmising he was safe from her, he opened his eyes fully.

Immediately she withdrew her hands and leaned close to lay one—ah, so cool—along his cheek.

She didn't smell like a saloon girl either.

"Your name . . . tell me your name," she said with a note of intense appeal.

He wondered why the hell she wouldn't know his name if she was supposed to, so he didn't say a thing.

"Please," she implored again. "Please, just tell me your name."

But suddenly he writhed, twisted at his bindings, and looked frantically around the room in search of something.

"My camera!" he tried to croak, but his voice was a pathetic, grating thing, and pain assailed him everywhere. At his wild thrashing, she became big-eyed and jumped back a step, her eyes riveted on his lips as he mouthed again, "My camera." The attempt to utter his first words shot a searing pain through his throat. He tried again, but all that came of it was a thick rasp. But she read his lips and that was all she needed to make her suddenly vibrant.

"Cameron," she whispered in disbelief.

He wanted to correct her but couldn't.

"Mike Cameron," she said louder, as if the words were some kind of miracle. "Cameron . . . just imagine that!" Then she beamed and clasped her hands joyfully before her, saying, "Thank God, Mr. Cameron. I knew you could do it!"

Was she zany or what? She resembled the witch he'd imagined in the bed beside him, only she was neat and clean and easy on the eye. Still, she acted as if she didn't exactly have all her marbles, and he thought maybe he *should* have punched her one broadside when he'd had the chance, to bring her out of a spell.

She whirled now, facing the bay window, and from behind it looked like she was wiping her eyes. But why the hell would she be crying over him?

When she faced him again, he tried to say, "My name's not Cameron," but once more the pain shot through his throat, and the sound was unrecognizable.

"Don't try to speak, Mr. Cameron. You've had some foreign objects in your mouth and throat, that's why it hurts so badly. Please lie still."

He attempted to sit up, but she came immediately and pressed those cool hands of hers on his chest to stay him. "Please, Mr. Cameron," she pleaded, "please don't. You're in no condition to move yet. If you promise you won't try to get up, I will remove these gauze bindings." She peered into his stark eyes that were lined with dark suspicion of her.

He had a damn good look at her then, and she looked about as strong as a ten-year-old boy, but her eyes told him she'd give it her best shot at subduing him if need be. So far, every time he'd moved, some muscle pained him like a blue bitch. He felt disinclined to tussle with even such a hummingbird as her. He scowled, gave her the merest nod, then there was a snipping sound above his head and again at his foot and she came away holding the gauze strips, freeing him to move limbs that somehow now refused to do his bidding. "Dear me, Mr. Cameron, you can see what a weakened condition you're in." She lowered his dead arm and began rubbing it deftly, massaging the muscles. "Give the blood a chance to get back. . . . It'll be all right in a minute. You mustn't move, though, please. I have to leave you alone for a bit while I prepare you some food. You've been unconscious for two days."

But suddenly the blood came racing back like a spring cataract, pounding through his arm, shooting needles of hot ice everywhere. He gasped and arched. But gasping hurt his throat and arching hurt everything else. He tried to swear but that hurt worse, so with a drooping of eyelids he subsided, fighting the giddy sensation that his skin was trying to explode. She clasped the inert hand under her armpit while he lay there listening to the deft sound of her beating the blood back into his prickling limb; it sounded like she was making a meat patty for his dinner. He felt nothing of her and a moment later opened his eyes to find his hand again on the sheet at his side, the woman gone from the room.

His right knee was raised. When he flexed its muscles a film of sweat erupted from his forehead and armpits. What the hell! he thought. He looked down his bare torso. A white patch decorated his right thigh. Automatically lifting his right hand to explore the bandage, a new pain gripped him, this time centered in the hand. It felt as if some giant paw were doling out a grisly handshake. He used his left hand instead, exploring damp, clinging cloths that guarded some secret near his groin. It told him nothing. Feeling around, he found a sheet drawn across his left leg, covering his privates, and folded back across his navel. To wake up naked in a woman's bed didn't surprise him at all, but to wake up in one belonging to a woman like this sure as hell did!

His eyes wandered while he listened to clinking, domestic sounds from around the doorway, and he wondered how long it had been since he'd been in a place like this. The room looked like some old maid's flower garden — flowers everywhere! He had no doubt it was her room, that like a humming-bird she'd fit into it. He saw a pair of portraits beside the bouquet, in a hinged, oval frame, and an open book on the bay window seat, with the tail end of a crocheted bookmark trailing from its pages. There was a small rocker with a needlepoint cushion, and a basket of sewing things on the floor beside it. A chifforobe stood against one wall, the dressing table against another.

Through the doorway he saw a green velvet settee in what must be her parlor. A little table beside it, and an oil lamp with globes of opaque white glass painted with roses. God, more flowers! he thought. A corner of a lace-curtained window with fringed, tassled shades. The parlor of a goody twoshoes, he thought, and wondered, as his eyes slid shut, how the hell he had gotten here.

"Here we are, Mr. Cameron." His eyes flew open; he jumped and winced. "I've prepared a light broth and some tea. It's not much, but we'll have to cater to your throat rather than your appetite for a short while." She held a carved wooden tray, white triangles of linen falling over its edges.

Lordy, he thought, would you look at that! Probably handstitched those edges herself. Bracing the tray against her midriff, she cleared a space on the bedside table. He was surprised to see the tray pull her blouse against a pair of healthy, resilient breasts—she dressed like a woman who didn't want the world to suspect she had any! But if there was one thing he knew how to find, it was a pair of healthy breasts. His eyes followed while she crossed to the chifforobe and found a pillow. When she came to mound it up beneath his head, he again caught the drift of that starchy, fresh smell, both from her and the pillow, and he thought of many nights sleeping on the floor of a wet canvas tent with a musty blanket over him as the only comfort. As she cupped the back of his head and lifted it, ripples of pain undulated from muscles far down his body. Automatically his eyes sank shut and he sucked in a sharp breath. When his pain had subsided, her voice came again.

"I've brought something to freshen your mouth. It's just soda water." A cloth pressed his jowl and a glass touched his lips, then he pulled the salty solution into his mouth. "Hold it a minute and let it bubble around. The effervescence is very refreshing." He was too weak to argue, but watched her covertly as she brought the bowl for him to spit into. When dribbles wet his chin, she immediately applied a warm, damp cloth, then proceeded to wash his entire face as if he were a schoolboy. He tried to jerk aside, but it hurt, so he submitted. Next she placed a napkin under his chin and dipped the spoon, cupping her hand beneath it on its way to his mouth.

She wondered why he scowled so, and talked because his near-black eyes were frightening. "You're a lucky man, Mr. Cameron. You were critically shot and nearly bled to death. Luckily Doctor Dougherty . . ."

She rambled on but he heard little beyond the statement that he'd been shot. He tried to lift his right hand, remembered how it hurt, used his left instead to stop the spoon. But he bumped her hand and the soup spilled on his chin, running down his neck. Goddamnit! he thought, and tried to say it — unsuccessfully—while she dabbed, wiped, and sponged fussily.

"Behave yourself, Mr. Cameron. See the mess you've made here!"

She knew perfectly well that any man who'd just found out he'd been shot would want to know who did it! Did he have to ask, with this inflamed throat of his! She dabbed away at the stupid soup, and this time when he grabbed, he got her by the wrist, catching the washcloth, too, under his grip, bringing her startled eyes wide.

"Who shot me?" he tried, but the pain assaulted his throat from every angle, so he mouthed the words broadly, *oooo . . . shawt . . . mee?* She stared at him as if struck dumb, knotted her fist, and twisted it beneath his fingers until he felt the birdlike bones straining to be free.

"It wasn't I, Mr. Cameron," she snapped, "so you've no need to accost me!" His grip loosened and she wrenched free, amazed at how strong he was in his anger. "I fear I untied you too hastily," she said down her nose, rubbing her fingers over the redness where the stiff lace had scratched her wrist.

He could tell from her face that she wasn't used to being manhandled. He really hadn't meant to scare her, but he wanted some answers. She'd had plenty of time to fill him in while flitting around getting that pillow and washing his face. He reached for her wrist again but she flinched away. But he only touched it to make her look at his lips. Who shot me? he mouthed once more.

She stiffened her face and snapped, "I don't know!" then jammed the spoon into his mouth, clacking it against his teeth.

The spoon kept coming faster and faster, barely giving him time to swallow between each thrust. The bitch is going to drown me, damn her! he cursed silently. This time he grabbed the spoon in midair and sent chicken broth spraying all over the front of her spotless blouse. She recoiled, sucked in her belly, and closed her eyes as if beseeching the gods for patience. Her nostrils flared as she glared hatred at him. He jerked his chin at the soup bowl, glowering furiously until she picked it up and held it near his chin. He'd discovered while eating the broth that he was nearly starved. But with his left hand he was clumsy, so after a few inept attempts, he flung the spoon aside, grabbed the bowl, and slurped directly from it, taking perverse pleasure in shocking her.

A barbarian! she thought. I have been fighting to save the life of a barbarian! Like some slobbering beast, he went on till the bowl was empty. But as her thumb curled over it, he jerked it back, mouthing, "Who shot me?" She jerked the bowl stubbornly again, but with a painful lunge he yanked it from her, flung it across the room, where it shattered against the base of the window seat. He pierced her with eyes which knew no end of rage. His face went livid as he was forced to use the voice that cut his throat to ribbons.

"Goddamn you, bitch! Was it you!" he croaked.

Oh, the pain! The pain! He clutched his throat as she jumped back, squeezing both hands before her while two spots of color appeared in her cheeks. Never in her life had anyone spoken to Miss Abigail McKenzie in such a manner. To think she had nursed this . . . this baboon and struggled to get him to awaken, to speak, only to be cursed at, called a bitch, and accused of being the one who shot him! She drew her mouth into a disdainful pucker, but before she could say anything more, the alarmed voice of David Melcher rang through the house.

"Miss Abigail! Miss Abigail! Are you all right down there?"

"Who's that!" the rasping voice demanded.

It gave her immense pleasure to answer him at last. "That, sir, is the man who shot you!"

Before her answer could sink in, the voice came again. "Did that animal try to harm you?"

She scurried out, presumably to the bottom of the steps. "I'm fine, Mr. Melcher, now go back to bed. I just had an accident with a soup bowl."

Melcher? Who the hell was this Melcher to call him an animal? And why did she lie about the soup bowl?

She came back in and knelt to pick up the broken pieces. He longed to hurl questions at her, to jump up and shake her, make her fill in the blanks, but he hurt everywhere now from throwing the damn bowl. All he could do was glare at her while she came to stand beside the bed with a supercilious attitude.

"Cursing, Mr. Cameron, is a crutch for the dim-witted. Furthermore, I am not a bitch, but if I were, perhaps I *would* shoot you to put you out of your own self-inflicted misery and to be rid of you. I, unlike you, am civilized, thus I shall only stand back and hope that you will choke to death!" She punctuated this statement by dropping the broken china on the tray with a clatter. But before she left, she plagued him further by dropping one last morsel, just enough to rouse a thousand unaskable questions.

"You were shot, Mr. Cameron, while attempting to hold up a train . . ." She arched a brow, then added, "As if you didn't know." And with that she was gone.

Chapter 4

HE CLENCHED HIS good fist. Oh, she was some smug bitch! What train? I'm no goddamn train robber! And who is this Melcher anyway? Obviously not her husband. Her protector? Ha! She needs protecting like a tarantula needs protecting.

Miss Abigail stood in her kitchen quaking like an aspen, looking at the broken fragments of china, wondering why she hadn't heeded Doctor Dougherty's warning. Never in her life had she been spoken to this way! She would have him out of here—out!—before this day ended, that much she promised herself. Pressing a hand to her throbbing forehead, she considered running down to Doctor Dougherty's and pleading illness, but if she did that he would certainly remove Mr. Melcher, too. Then she remembered how desperately she needed the money and steeled herself for a long day ahead.

In the bedroom, he longed to raise his voice and bellow like a bull moose until somebody told him what the hell was going on around here. He lay instead sweating profusely, having writhed far more than he should have. His leg, hip, and lower stomach had turned to fire. Resting the back of a hand across his eyes, he gritted his teeth at the pain. That was how she found him.

"It has been two days since . . ."

He jumped and another pain grabbed him. Damn her! Did she have to pussyfoot around like that all the time?

Very collectedly now, she began again, with exaggerated control. "I thought you might have to relieve yourself." But she looked at the knob on the headboard while she said it.

Eyeing her mistrustfully, he knew she had him over a barrel. He did have to relieve himself, but he knew he wasn't going anywhere to do it. So just what did she have in mind?

With a voice like ice, she issued orders. "Don't try to speak or strain your leg in any way. I shall help you roll onto your side first." And coming to the side of the bed, she removed the bolsters from under his knee, lowered it with surprising gentleness, then snapped the ends of the under sheet loose from their moorings and rolled him with it until he faced the wall, still covered by the top sheet. She laid a flat porcelain pan next to him and without another word left the room, closing the door with not so much as a click of the latch.

What kind of woman was she anyway? She sashayed in here carrying that bedpan as if she had no idea that he was the one who'd only minutes before shattered her china soup bowl and called her a bitch. Most women would have refused any further services on spite alone . . . but not her. Why should that aggravate him too? Maybe because she looked frail enough to cow with a savage glare. Maybe because he'd tried it and it didn't work.

She came to collect the bedpan with the same silent poker face as before. They needn't have spoken anyway to tell each other they'd met their matches.

She had the perfect revenge for his insufferable attitude this morning: she left him alone. Miss Abigail knew perfectly well he was lying there with a hundred unasked questions eating him up. Well, good! Let them eat him up! It's no more than he deserves.

In the flowery bedroom that's exactly what was happening. Bitch! he

456

thought time and again, unable to shout, to ask anything he wanted now worse than ever to know. He seethed for the remainder of the day, caught like some damn fool bumblebee in a glass jar, in that insufferable yellow flower garden she'd trapped him in. Once he even heard her humming out there in what seemed to be the kitchen, and it made him all the madder. She was out there humming while he couldn't make so much as a squeak without paying dearly.

Much later he heard her go upstairs, then the two of them come down to supper. Snatches of their conversation drifted through the quiet house, and he heard enough to know they were feeling pretty cozy with each other.

"Oh, Miss Abigail, nasturtiums on the table!"

"Ah, how pleasant it is to find a man who can actually identify a nasturtium."

"How pleasant it is to find a woman who still grows them." The eavesdropper in the bedroom rolled his eyes.

"Perhaps tomorrow you'll feel well enough to sit in the backyard while I do some weeding."

"I'd love that, Miss Abigail, I truly would."

"Then you shall do it, Mr. Melcher," she promised before inquiring, "Do you like fresh lemonade?"

"I wish you'd call me David. Yes, I love lemonade."

"We'll have some, tomorrow . . . in the garden?"

"I'll look forward to it."

She helped him back to bed. The man downstairs heard them go up and a silence that followed and thought to himself, no it couldn't be. But indeed it could be, and David Melcher kissed Miss Abigail adoringly, then watched her go all peach-colored and fluttery.

She came back downstairs from her pleasant interlude to face the horrifying prospect of feeding that black brute again. She'd like to let him starve to death. Furthermore, she was afraid to go near him, and more afraid that it might show. She prepared milk toast for him, and entered the bedroom armed with it, ready to fling it on him and scald him should he make a grab for her again.

"I've brought you milk toast," she informed him. He thought she looked like it had soured in her mouth.

"Bah!" was all he could get out to let her know just what he thought of milk toast. "I'm starving!" he mouthed.

"I wish you were," she said, all honey-voiced, and rammed a napkin under his chin. "Hold still and eat."

The hot milk nearly gagged him, the lumps of slimy bread slithered down his throat, disgustingly. Even so, every swallow was torture. He wondered just what had been in his mouth to make it hurt this way, but it appeared she was still in a snit and wasn't going to tell him anything.

They eyed each other menacingly. He, waiting for the chance to ask questions, she, ready to spring to safety at the first sign of brutality. She could hardly stand the sight of him and thought the only good thing about feeding him was that he couldn't speak. And since he looked in no way ready to carry on a dignified conversation, she left him to stew. She put her kitchen back in order and found herself exhausted. Alas, all of her night things were in her bedroom and the last thing she wanted was to go in there again. So she dreamed up an excuse: a gargle.

Before entering, she tiptoed to the doorway, peeped in, gathering her courage. He faced the window, jaw muscles tensing repeatedly. Ah, so he is still angry, she thought. His beard had grown again, darkening his entire face. Studying the lip, which she had willfully denuded, she trembled to think about what would happen when he discovered his moustache gone. She willed it to please . . . please, hurry up and grow back!

She tread soundlessly across the threshold, her insides ascatter with apprehension.

"Are you ready to act civil?" she asked. His head snapped around and his good fist clenched. Then he grimaced in pain.

Damn that pussyfooting! he thought. "Are you trying to kill me with neglect?" he whispered stridently and pressed a hand to his abdomen, "or just let that slimy milk toast do the job for you?"

The thought of David Melcher's warm compliments made her voice all the more frigid as she replied, "I attempted to teach you a lesson, but apparently I failed." She turned to leave.

"No . . . wait!" he grated hoarsely.

"Wait, Mr. Cameron? For what? To be insulted and cursed at and to have my possessions shattered as repayment for bringing you food?"

"You call that slop food? I'm half starved and you bring me broth and milk toast, then hustle your fanny out of here without so much as a fare-thee-well! I've been laying here waiting for some answers for who the hell knows how long, so just keep your bones where they are, missus!"

Appalled by his rude outburst, she attempted to level him with a little cool, sarcastic superiority.

"My! What an extensive vocabulary you harbor, Mr. Cameron. Slop . . . fanny . . . bones . . . spoken like a true scholar." She threw him a disparaging look, then stiffened her spine and tried to give the impression she was taking command, although she felt far less cocksure than she sounded.

"If you want answers to any questions, quit your cursing, *sir,* treat me with respect, and stop issuing orders! I shall issue orders if any are to be issued, is that understood? You have fallen under my care and—despicable as you are—I am committed to giving it to you. But I do not—repeat, *do not*—have to accept your grossness or your abuse. Now, shall I leave or will you comply?"

He jerked his chin once, gave her a withering look, and whispered something that sounded like, "Sheece!" Then in a guttering voice he obliged, "Enter, Goody Twoshoes, and I'll try to hold my temper."

"You had better do more than try, *sir.*" She could say sir in the most cutting way he's ever heard, considering that sweet little voice she had.

"Yes, *ma'am,*" he countered, giving her a dose of her own hot tongue.

"Very well. I've made a gargle to ease your throat. If you use it, I'm sure it will offer some relief by morning." But she hesitated, just beyond his reach, as if still unsure of him. He considered winking at her just to see her jump, but nodded instead, agreeing to lay off the rough stuff.

She came nearer. "Here, just gargle, don't swallow." She helped him sip sideways. He pulled half the contents into his mouth, but it flew out again in a flume.

"What kind of piss is this!"

"*Missster* Cameron!" she hissed, pulling her blouse from her skin.

He really hadn't meant to spray her that time. After all, he wanted his questions answered, even if he had to toe the line to get his way.

"Sorry," he whispered insincerely.

It seemed to appease her momentarily, for she shoved the cup in his direction and he grimaced, gulped, and gargled while she took vast pleasure in informing him, "It's an old remedy of my grandmother's—vinegar, salt, and red pepper."

This time he hit the bowl, but he couldn't help gagging.

"Rinse!" she ordered imperiously, handing him a glass. He eyed it suspiciously, finally taking it. But it was only water this time.

"What the hell happened to my throat?" he guttered.

"As I said, it had some foreign objects in it while you were unconscious. It should feel better by tomorrow. I'd appreciate it if you would keep your crudities to yourself."

"It's not enough I get shot . . . I have to get choked, too. That would make any man cuss. And what's the matter with this hand?"

"Your gun hand?" she inquired sweetly, intimating a gross guilt upon him with that single arched eyebrow of hers.

He scowled, causing forbidding creases to line his forehead.

"I assume somebody trounced on it in the scuffle, since it has the perfect imprint of a boot heel on its back."

"It hurts like hell."

"Yes, it should, from the looks of it. But then you brought it all on yourself by robbing that train."

"I didn't rob any goddamn train!" he whispered fiercely. Across the room, where she'd been taking things out of a dresser, her back stiffened like a ramrod. It was obvious to Miss Abigail that cursing flowed from his lips more readily than blood from his wound. She would be hard put trying to keep a civil tongue in his head. But there were other barbs with which to admonish him.

"Then why is Mr. Melcher lying upstairs at this very moment, wounded by you, and why has he sworn out a legal complaint against you for the damage you've done?"

"Who is this Melcher anyway?"

"The man you shot . . . and who shot you."

"What!"

"The two of you were carried off the train here at Stuart's Junction, and there was a car full of witnesses to prove you attempted to rob the R.M.R. passengers and he attempted to stop you. In the tussle, the two of you shot each other."

He couldn't believe it, but apparently she did, and a few others in this town, too, by the sound of it. At least he knew where he was now.

"So, I'm in Stuart's Junction."

"Yes."

"And I'm the villain?"

"Of course," she agreed with that uppity look.

"And this Melcher's the town hero, I presume."

This she declined to answer.

"And why did you get the honor of caring for us . . . *Miss* Abigail, is it?"

She disregarded his sarcastic tone to answer, "I volunteered. The R.M.R. is paying me and I need the money."

"The *R.M.R.* is paying *you?*"

"That's right."

"Hasn't this town got a doctor?"

"Yes, Doctor Dougherty. And you'll probably see him again tomorrow. He didn't come by today, so I expect he was called out to the country. You may save the rest of your questions for him. I am extremely fatigued. Good night, Mr. Cameron." She sallied out with her head up like a giraffe, cutting off the rest of his queries, and he got mad all over again. He'd seen some cold-hearted women in his day, but this one beat them all. And stiff! She was so stiff he figured she'd go lean herself in the corner out there someplace and go to sleep for the night. Good night, Mr. Cameron, my eye! My name's not Cameron, but you didn't give me a chance to say so. Just come strutting in here throwing orders around like some pinched-up shrew who takes pleasure from paining a man just because he is one. Oh, I've seen your kind before—bound up so tight with corset stays that you've got permanent indigestion.

Still, from what he'd heard of the conversation between her and this Melcher, he wondered if Melcher had miraculously made some of her juices flow. Then, glancing down at his own bare hip, he wondered what the old shrew's reaction had been to him sprawled out naked in her bed. If it wouldn't have hurt so bad, he would've laughed. No, he decided, she's as cold as frog's blood, that one. He fell to plotting how he might get even with her for shutting him off like this.

In the darkness, a light rustling sounded. He supposed she was changing clothes out in the parlor. He half expected to hear an explosion when those corset stays came undone.

There were spare bedrooms upstairs, of course. But somehow Miss Abigail thought it would be less than appropriate for her to go up there to sleep, now that she and David Melcher were getting along so well. It would be far better for her to stay down here on the parlor settee. True, the formidable Mr. Cameron was just around the other side of the wall, but their antagonism made this arrangement acceptable. After all, by now she had ceased caring whether he lived or died.

She awakened and shivered and stretched her neck taut, aware that something had roused her. It was deep night—no bird sounds came through the windows, only a chill damp, coming in on the dew-laden air.

"Miss Abigail . . ."

She heard her name whispered hoarsely and knew it was he calling her, and unconsciously she checked the buttons up the neck of her nightie.

"Miss Abigail?" he whispered again, and this time she didn't hesitate, not even long enough to light a lamp. She walked surely through the dark, familiar house to the side of the bed.

"Miss Abigail?" he rasped weakly.

"Yes, I'm here, Mr. Cameron."

"It's . . . it's worse. Can you help me?"

"I shall have a look." Something told her he was not feigning, and she lit the lamp quickly to find his eyes closed, the covering sheet kicked completely off him. She flickered it in place and bent to remove the bindings and poultice.

"Oh, dear God," she breathed when the odor assaulted her nostrils. "Dear God, no." The edge of the bullet hole had turned a dirty gray, and the stench of putrefaction all but knocked her from her feet. "I must get Doctor Dougherty," she cried in a choked voice, then hurried out.

Barefoot she ran, the always proper, always fastidious Miss Abigail McKenzie, heedless of the dew that wet the hem of her nightie, made her feet slip on the sharp gravel. Hair flying wildly, she took the length of Front Street to Doc's house. But she knew even as she mauled his front door that he wasn't home. He hadn't come to see the men tonight, which meant he could be sleeping in some forlorn barn with a sick horse or delivering a baby in a country home any number of miles away. Running back home, she alternately cursed herself and prayed, scanning her mind for answers to questions she'd never asked Doc Dougherty, never believing she'd have to know. Never should she have allowed anger to overcome common sense. But that's just what she'd done today. That man had made her so irate that she couldn't bear the thought of checking those poultices to see if they needed repacking. Oh, why hadn't she done it, even in spite of her anger? Her mother had always said, "Anger serves no purpose but its own," and now she knew exactly what that meant.

She leaped the front porch steps, night skirts lifted above the knees, and panted to a halt at the foot of her bed. He lay upon it with eyes closed, breath too shallow and sweet to be healthy. Forgotten now was her anger at him, her fear of him. All she knew was that she must do all she could to save his life. She dropped to her knees to scramble through a cedar chest at the foot of the bed, searching for a much-used book that had crossed the prairies in a conestoga wagon years before with her grandparents. It contained cures for humans and animals alike, and she desperately hoped it held answers for her now.

He moved restlessly as her frantic fingers scanned the pages. "Where's the doc?" he whispered hoarsely. She flew to his side.

"Shh . . ." she soothed. Eyes dark, hair ascatter, she flopped the pages, reading snatches aloud before finally finding the remedy. Then she lurched toward the door, cast the book aside, muttering, "Charcoal and yeast, charcoal and yeast," like a litany.

He drifted for a long time in a kind of peaceful reverie from which he was curiously removed yet somehow aware of his surroundings. He heard the stove lids clang, heard her exclaim, "Ouch!" and he smiled, wondering what she'd done to hurt herself, such a careful woman like her. Some glassy, tinkly sounds, fabric ripping, water being poured. She seemed to float in, arms and hands laden. But he was smacked from his blissful nether state when she began cleaning his wound.

"I'm sorry, Mr. Cameron, but I've got to do this."

He reached down to combat her hands.

"Please don't fight me," she pleaded. "Please. I don't have time to tie you again." He groaned, deep and long and raspy, and she gritted her teeth and bit on her inner cheek. He clasped the sheet with his one good hand while the other tapped listlessly against the mattress. She removed the useless, dead

flesh, swallowing the gorge in the back of her throat, wiping at her forehead with the back of a hand.

Tears formed in her eyes, leaked down the corners while she bathed the wounds with disinfectant, then whispered, "I'm almost done, Mr. Cameron." She felt his hand grope at her chest and thought stupidly how he was using his battered hand and that he shouldn't be. Still, she let him grab a weak handful of the front of her nightgown and pull her up close to his mouth.

"My name's not Cameron. It's Jesse," he croaked.

"Jesse what?" she whispered.

But he drifted into oblivion then, his grip falling slack, his lips grown still, close beneath hers.

It became a personal thing then, refusing to let him die. She mixed warm, damp yeast with the remnants of charcoal, forming the mixture she hoped would keep him alive, all the while feeling for the second time that obdurate will to prevent the death of another human being. What he was and how he had treated her became insignificant against the fact that he was flesh and blood. Stubbornly she vowed that he would live.

If the night before had been difficult, the remainder of this one was a horror.

The book said to keep the poultices warm, so she made two, running to the kitchen to reheat them. The fire flagged and she slogged outside for more wood. Still the poultices cooled too fast, so she topped them with mustard plasters, the only thing she knew that would retain heat. But they needed frequent changing, so rather than bind them, she propped the bottom one and held the top one lightly in place with her hand. He often jerked spasmodically or tossed wildly, and when his moans brought her flying back from the kitchen, she wet his lips with a damp cloth, squeezing a drizzle of water into his mouth, massaging his throat, trying to make him swallow. Sometimes she said his name, the new name—Jesse—encouraging him to fight with her.

"Come on, Jesse," she whispered fiercely. "Come on, help me!"

She knew not if he heard her.

"Don't die on me now, Jesse, not now that we've come this far." He tossed, wild with delirium, and she fought him, throwing what she thought was the last of her strength on him to keep him flat. He muttered insensibly.

She argued with intense urgency, "Fight with me, Jesse. I know what a fighter you are. Fight with me now!"

But she herself could fight just so long. She fought long after she knew what she was saying or who she was or who he was or where they were.

When unconsciousness overtook her she never knew it.

 Chapter 5

MR. MELCHER WAS truly on top of the world the next morning. His toe gave him nearly no pain at all, so he decided to surprise Miss Abigail by going down to breakfast unaided. The house was abnormally quiet as he limped downstairs. From the bottom step he eyed the bedroom doorway leading off the parlor. He was repelled by the thought of that felon sleeping under the same roof as himself and Miss Abigail, but he had an urge to sneak a small peak at the man nevertheless. It would be something to tell the boys back at the Elysian Club just what that robber looked like after he'd laid him low.

But he hadn't expected the shocking sight that greeted him when he stuck his carefully groomed head around the doorframe!

There was the wounded robber all right, but the man had absolutely not a stitch of clothing on, save his bandages. He lay stark naked and hairy, one leg draped over a pair of bolsters, the other sprawled lasciviously sideways, riding the curve of a woman's stomach. She occupied the lower half of the bed, her gown scrunched up to mid-thigh, feet dangling, along with his, between the footrails. Her face was nearly at his hip, but buried beneath a mop of plical-looking hair in which the man's fingers were twined. But most lurid of all: the harlot had one arm stretched out across the brute's hairy thighs, her palm precariously near the man's genitals!

From the looks of her, none of this was surprising. The slut was a mess. The soles of her feet were filthy, her gown the same, smirched with ocher and gray stains; the lace cuffs were grimy. Her hands looked no better than the rest of her, fingernails encrusted, knuckles long in need of scrubbing, those of her left hand wrapped in a piece of dirty gauze, as if she'd been in a saloon brawl.

How the man had managed to get the woman in here was a mystery, but Miss Abigail would be shocked to her very core to witness such a spectacle!

At that moment the man twitched restlessly and mumbled something incoherent. The woman came out of her deep sleep just enough to sigh, grope toward the bandage, and mumble, "Be still, Jesse." Then her hand fell away limply across his knee as she slumbrously snuggled against his long, bare leg, turning her face.

"Is that you, Abbie?" he mumbled, eyes still closed.

"Yes, Jesse, it's me, now go back to sleep."

He sighed, then a gentle snore sounded as his hand relaxed in her hair. And soon her rhythmic breathing joined his while a horrified David Melcher crept soundlessly back to his room.

The scene remained fixed in his memory during the awful days that followed, during the bittersweet afternoons in Miss Abigail's garden, when he longed to ask her for explanations but feared there were no good ones. His jealousy grew, for she spent most of her time with the outlaw, who recovered at a snail's pace. There were times when David paused, passing the room, and looked inside, nursing his hatred for the man who had not only maimed him but stolen the greatest joy from his life. David's limp seemed permanent now, and it undermined his self-esteem, making him believe no woman could possibly find him attractive. He watched the care with which Miss Abigail attended the man, though he was drugged now with laudanum for his own good, and each minute she spent in that downstairs bedroom was a minute of which David felt robbed of her attention.

Miss Abigail puzzled over his withdrawal. She longed for him to kiss her again, to buoy her tired spirits at the end of an arduous day, but he didn't.

David's toe seemed completely healed and she dreaded the thought that he might leave without ever again pressing his suit. When she tried to please him with small favors, he thanked her considerately, but his old compliments were part of the past.

After Doc finally gave the orders to drop the laudanum, Jesse awoke one sunny morning, weak, but hungry as a bear, and amazed to find himself still alive. He flexed his muscles, found them stiff and sore from disuse, but those grinding pains had faded. He heard voices from the kitchen and remembered the man who'd put him here, wondered how many days he'd lain unconscious.

He heard not so much as a footstep, yet somehow knew she was standing there in the doorway. He turned from his study of the trees outside the window to find her watching him with all traces of her former antagonism gone.

She looked as crisp as a spring leaf in a skirt of forest green and a white lawn blouse, her brown hair knotted in its careful coil at the base of her neck, her skin fresh and peachy. And he saw for the first time how a smile could transform her face.

"So you've made it," she said quietly.

He studied her for a moment. "So I have." Softly, he added, "Come over here."

She paused uncertainly, then drifted slowly to the side of the bed.

"You been busy?" He smiled up at her crookedly.

"A little," came her mellow reply.

He flopped an arm out, gathered her in by her forest green skirts, and boldly caressed her buttocks, saying, "I guess I owe you." It was nothing Jesse hadn't done to a hundred women a hundred times, but it was just Miss Abigail's luck he chose that precise moment to do it to her, for the sound of their voices had brought David Melcher to the doorway.

The blood flooded his face before he remarked dryly, "Well, well . . ."

Miss Abigail froze, horrified, helpless. It had happened so fast. She squirmed, but Jesse only held tight and drawled with a lopsided grin, "Mr. Melcher, our avenging hero, I presume?"

"Have you no decency!" David hissed.

Undaunted, Jesse only turned his grin up at Abbie as she struggled to break his hold. "None whatever, have I, Abbie?"

"Abbie, is it?" returned the outraged David while she at last managed to struggle out of Jesse's hold, her eyes on the man in the doorway.

"This . . . this is not what it seems," she implored David.

"Yes it is," Jesse teased, enjoying Melcher's discomfort intensely, but Miss Abigail whirled on Jesse, all her venom returned in full force.

"Shut up!" she spit, little hands clenched into angry balls.

David gave the pair a scathing look. "This is the second time I've found you with him in wh . . . what I'd term a c . . . compromising position," he accused.

"The second time! What are you talking about? Why, I've never—"

"I *saw* you, Miss Abigail, curled up beside him with your hand on—" But he pursed his mouth suddenly, unable to go on.

"You're a liar!" Miss Abigail exclaimed, her hands now on her hips.

"Now, Abbie," put in Jesse, "there were those couple nights—" She whirled on him, sparks seeming to fly from her eyes.

"I'll thank you to shut your despicable mouth, Mr. . . . whatever your name is!"

"You called him Jesse in your sleep," David declared.

"In my—" She didn't understand. Jesse just smiled, enjoying it all.

"I thought you were such a lady. What a fool I was," Melcher disdained.

"I have never done any of what you've intimated. Never!"

"Oh? Then where had you been that night if not out romping in the grass? Your gown, your feet, your hands . . ."

She remembered them all too clearly, the knuckles bound because she'd burned herself on a live coal as she dug for charcoal, her feet and gown soiled by running to Doc's house.

"He was unconscious, and gangrene had set in. I went to fetch Doctor Dougherty."

"Oh? I don't seem to remember the doctor coming that night."

"Well, he didn't . . . I mean, he wasn't home, so I had to treat Jesse—Mr. Cameron, I mean, as best I could."

"You seem to have treated him to more than a mustard poultice," David accused.

"But I—"

"Save your explanations for someone who'll buy them, *Miss* McKenzie."

She was as pale as a sheet by this time and clutching her hands together to stop their trembling.

"I think you had better go, Mr. Melcher," she said quietly. A muscle worked in his jaw as he looked at her standing so still and erect beside the smirking man.

"Yes, I think I had," he agreed, quietly now too, and turned from the room. He went upstairs to gather his things together with a heavy heart. When he returned downstairs she stood clear across the parlor, the pain in her heart well hidden as she faced him.

"I have no shoes," he said forlornly.

"You may wear Father's slippers and have someone return them when they come for your valise." Her hands were clutched as their eyes locked, then parted.

"Miss Abigail, I . . ." He swallowed. "Perhaps I was hasty."

"Yes, perhaps you were," she said in clipped tones, too hurt to soften.

He limped to the screen door and each step crushed a petal of some fragile flower which had blossomed within her since he'd come here. He pushed the door open, and her hand instinctively reached toward him. "You . . ." He turned and she retracted the guilty hand. "You may take one of Father's canes. There's no need to return it."

He took one from the umbrella stand, looked balefully across at her, and said, "I'm ever so sorry." She longed to cross the room, draw an arm through his, and say, "It's all a big mistake. Stay and we'll set it straight. Stay and we'll have lemonade in the garden. I too am sorry." But pride kept her aloof. He turned and limped away.

She watched him until he turned a corner and was lost to her. He was a gentle man and a gentleman, and both attributes had lifted Miss Abigail's waning spinster hopes, but those hopes were firmly dashed now. There would be no lemonade in the garden, no soft, kid city shoes arriving to tell her he was thinking of her. There would be only her quiet afternoons of weeding and her twilights spent with the sonnets. What have I done to deserve this? she thought painfully. I've done nothing but save an outlaw's life.

As if on cue, his voice came, clear and resonant. "Abbie?"

Impossible to believe how a single word could make one so angry.

"There's no one here by that name!" she exploded, swiping at an errant tear.

"Abbie, come on," he wheedled, louder this time.

She wished she could ram a fork down his throat and incapacitate it again! She ignored him and went to do her morning chores in the kitchen.

"Abbie!" he called after several minutes, his voice growing stronger and more impatient. But she went on with her tasks, drawing extreme pleasure now from disregarding him. Hate lodged in her throat like a fishbone.

"Goddamnit, Abbie! Get in here!"

She cringed at the profanity but vowed it would never put her at a disadvantage again. Two could play this wily game, and she wasn't above trying to get even for what he'd done. She calmly ignored his calls until finally, in a voice filled with rage, he bellowed.

"Miss Abigail, if you don't get in here this minute, I'm going to piss all over your lily white bed!"

Appalled, blushing, but believing every word he said, she grabbed the bedpan and ran. "You just try it!" she shouted, and flung the bedpan from the doorway. It came down on his good knee with a resounding *twin-n-n-g,* but she was gone before the reverberations ended. In her wake she heard him hiss something about a vicious asp.

Horrified and shaking, she knew she'd made it worse, for she'd have to go back in there and collect the thing and—oh! he'd been so angry again! Maybe she shouldn't have flung it at him, but he deserved it, and worse. He'd have deserved it had it been full! She pressed her hands to her cheeks. What am I thinking? He's turning me into the same sort of uncouth barbarian he is. I must get control of myself, pull myself together. I'll get rid of him as soon as I can, but until I do, I'll level my temper, like Mother always warned me I must, and somehow squelch this urge for revenge. She was in careful control by the time she reentered his room and spoke with cold disdain.

"I suggest, sir, that for the duration of your convalescence we draw a truce. I should like to see you well and on your way again, but I simply cannot brook your hostility."

"My hostility! I deserve a fit of hostility! First I got shot by that . . . that *fool* for something I didn't do, then tortured by a woman who whacks me in the teeth with her spoon, refused to tell me where I am or why, calls me by somebody else's name, ties me to the bedpost, and holds out on me when I need a bedpan! Lady, you talk about hostility, I've got plenty, and more where that came from!"

His shouting shattered her nerves, but she carefully hid it, purring, "I see you've regained full use of your vocal chords."

Her high and mighty attitude made him bellow all the louder. "You're goddamn right I have!" Her eyes actually twitched.

"I do not allow profanity in this house," she gritted.

"Like hell you say!" he roared.

"How brave you are when you shout like a madman." And finally he started to simmer down. Using her finest diction, her quietest tones, and her explicit vocabulary, she laid down the law while she had him feeling sheepish. "At the onset, sir, you must understand that I shall not accept your calling me by such familiar and disparaging terms as Abigail, Abbie or . . . or *lady*. You shall call me Miss Abigail, and I will call you by your surname if you will kindly give it to me."

"Like hell I will."

How easily he could rout the importance of etiquette and make her feel the one in error.

"What's the matter with calling me Jesse?" he asked now. "It's my name. You were so anxious for me to tell you what it was when you thought I might not make it."

"Yes, for your tombstone," she said smugly.

Unexpectedly, he smirked. "Now I'll never tell you the rest of it." She turned away quickly, fearing she might smile.

"Please, can't we quit this bantering and resolve our dispute?"

"Damn right we can. Just call me Jesse, *Miss* Abigail." Once he'd said it, she wished he hadn't—not that way! He was the most irritating man she'd ever met.

"Very well, if you won't tell me your last name, I'll continue to call you Mr. Cameron. I've grown used to it, in any case. However, if you persist in using crudities as you did earlier, we won't get along at all. I'd appreciate it if you'd temper your tongue."

"My tongue doesn't take to tempering too readily. Most of the places I go it doesn't have to."

"That has become very obvious already. However, I think neither of us likes being cast together this way, but seeing that we are, shall we make the best of it?"

Again he considered her words, analyzing her highfalutin way of speaking and that cocky eyebrow that constantly prickled his desire to irritate her.

"Are you going to poison me with any more of your potions you concoct for naughty gunslingers?" he queried mischievously.

"You have proven this morning, without a doubt, that you don't need it," she replied, her ears still ringing from his tirade.

"In that case, I accept your truce, Miss Abigail." And with that, the tension seemed to ease somewhat.

She went to the bay window and opened it to the morning air. "This room smells foul. It and you need a thorough airing and cleaning. You have grown as rank as your bedclothes," she finished, her back to him as she flung the curtains up over their rods.

"Tut-tut, Miss Abigail, now who's goading?"

That "tut-tut" sounded preposterous coming from a man like him. She wasn't sure if she could handle his newfound sense of humor.

"I only meant to say I thought you might appreciate a bath, sir. If you would rather lie in your own effluvia, I will thankfully let you." By now he knew that she cut loose with her high-class words whenever she got flustered. It was fun seeing her color up that way, so he went on teasing.

"Are you proposing to give me a bath while I lay naked in this bed?" He gasped in mock chagrin and pulled the sheet up like some timid virgin.

Turning, she had all she could do to keep from laughing at him in that ridiculous pose. She cast him a look of pure challenge and stated in no uncertain terms, "I did it before . . . I can do it again."

His thick black eyebrows shot up in surprise. "You did it before!" He pushed the sheet back down, just below his navel. "Well, then . . ." He drawled, relaxing back with his good hand cradling his head.

When she spun from the room he lay there smiling, wondering if she'd really give him a *thorough* cleaning. His smile grew broader. Hell, I'm willing if you are, Abbie, he thought, and lay in the best fit of humor he'd enjoyed since falling into this flower bed of hers.

When she returned, he watched her roll up her sleeves, thinking, ah, the lady bares her wrists to me at last. He knew he had her pegged right. She was virtuous to the point of fanaticism, and he couldn't figure out how she was going to handle this situation and come out as innocent as she went in. He enjoyed himself immensely, potent buck that he was, lying back waiting for her discomfort to begin.

She had very delicate hands that looked incapable of managing the job. But some minutes later she had an oilcloth under him so fast, he didn't remember raising up to have it slid into place. He submitted complacently, raising his chin, turning his head, lifting his arm upon command. He had to hand it to her, she really knew how to give a man a decent bed bath. It felt damn good. He couldn't believe it when she climbed up next to him to get at his left side. But she did it, by Jove! She did it! And raised a new grudging respect in him.

"Now that we've drawn a truce, maybe you'll tell me why you started calling me Cameron," he said while she lathered away.

"I thought you were awake and sensible that first time you spoke. I asked you your name and you said 'Mike Cameron.' I heard it, or rather saw it, distinctly."

He remembered back and suddenly laughed. "I didn't say Mike Cameron, I said 'my camera,' but at the time it felt like somebody was drying their green rawhide around my neck, so it might not have come out too clear." He looked around. "By the way, where is it?"

"Where is what?" She kept on ascrubbing, kneeling there beside him.

"My camera."

"Camera?" She glanced up dubiously. "You've actually lost a camera and you think *I* know where it is?"

He raised a sardonic eyebrow. "Well, don't you?"

She'd been washing his side. The cloth in her hand rested nearly on his hip now, the sheet still covering him from there down. She looked at him and said dryly, "Believe me, Mr. Cameron, I have not come upon a camera on you . . . anyplace." It was out before she could control it, and Miss Abigail was immediately chagrined at what she'd said. Her startled eyes found his, then veered away as she set to work with renewed intensity.

"Why, Miss Abigail, shame on you," he drawled, grinning at the rising color in her cheeks. But he was sincerely worried about his equipment. "A camera and plates take up one hell of a lot of space. What could have happened to them?" he asked. "And my grip was with my photographic gear. Where is it?"

"I'm sure I don't know what you're talking about. You were brought to me just as you are, sir, and nobody said anything about any camera or plates. Do you think I'm hiding them from you? Put your arm up, please."

Up went his arm while she scrubbed the length of it, including his armpit.

"Well, they've got to be someplace. Didn't anybody get them off the train?" She started rinsing the soap off the arm.

"The only things they carried off that train were you, Mr. Melcher, and his valise. I'm sure nobody expected a thief to be carrying a camera." The little upward tilt of her eyebrow told him just how preposterous she thought his little fable. "Tell me, sir, what an outlaw does with a camera." She looked him square in the eye, wondering what lie he'd concoct.

He couldn't resist. "Take pictures of his dead victims for his scrapbook." His evil grin met her appalled look.

"That, Mr. Cameron, isn't even remotely funny!" she snapped, suddenly scrubbing too hard.

"Ouch! Take it easy! I'm a convalescent, you know."

"Please don't remind me," she said sourly.

His tone became conversational. "You wouldn't believe me anyway, about my camera, so I won't bother to tell you. You'd rather think I was merrily robbing trains, then you can feel justified in . . ." his voice raised a few decibals as he yanked away ". . . tanning my hide instead of just scrubbing it! Ouch, I said! Don't you know what ouch means, woman?" He nursed his knuckles. But he could almost hear the bones snap in her neck, she stiffened up so fast.

"Don't call me woman, I said!"

She snatched his hand back and began drying it roughly.

"Why? Aren't you?" Her hands fell still, for he had taken hold of her hand, towel and all, and was holding it prisoner in his long, dark fingers. Panic knifed through her at the flutter of her heart. She looked up at his dark eyes, probing with an intensity that alarmed her.

"Not to you," she answered starchily, and pulled her hand free, then quickly clambered off the bed.

Something indefinable had changed between them in that instant when he grasped her hand. They were now quiet while she proceeded with the washing of his right leg. She soaped the length of it, working gingerly at the area near the wound. Once he arched his chest high and dug his head back into the pillow with a swift sucking breath of pain.

"It's healing, no matter what it might feel like."

But she was still upset about his earlier comments. She was briskly working her way toward his foot with fresh lather when he looked down his chest at her and asked quietly, "Are you to old Melcher?"

Her head snapped up. "What?"

"A woman. Are you a woman to old Melcher?"

But his timing was ill chosen. She had him by the bad leg and was none too gentle about slamming it back down, suds and all. He gritted his teeth and gasped, but she stood there with an outraged expression on her face, hands jammed on the hips of her wet-spotted apron, eyes glaring.

"Haven't you done enough damage where Mr. Melcher is concerned without pushing my nose in it? He's a gentleman . . . but then you wouldn't know anything about gentlemen, would you? Does it satisfy your ego to know you've managed to lose him for me, too?"

His leg hurt like hell now and a white line appeared around his lips, but she had little sympathy. How much more could she take from him?

"If he's such a gentleman, why did you throw him out?" Jesse retorted.

Her mouth puckered and she flung the cloth into the bowl, sending water splattering onto his face, the floor, and pillow. He recoiled, hollering after her retreating figure, "Hey, where are you going? You haven't finished yet!"

"You have one good hand, sir. Use it!" And her skirts disappeared around the door. He looked down at his soapy foot.

"But what'll I do with the soap?"

"Why don't you try washing your mouth out with it, which your mother should have done years ago!"

The soap was beginning to itch. "Don't you leave this soap on me!"

"Feel lucky I've conceded to wash as much of you as I have!"

He drove his good fist into the mattress and shouted at the top of his lungs, "Get back here, you viper!"

But she didn't return, and the soap stayed until the itching became unbearable and he was forced to lean painfully to remove most of it, then dry his foot and calf with the sheets.

As Miss Abigail left the house, she whacked the screen door shut harder than she'd ever done in her life. She pounded down the back steps like a Hessian soldier, thinking, *I have to get out of the same house with that monster!* Nobody she'd ever known had managed to anger her like he had. Standing in the shade of the linden tree, gazing at the garden, she longed for a return of tranquility to her life. But not even the peaceful, nodding heads of her flax flowers could calm her today. She wondered how she would ever endure that odious man until he was well enough to walk out of here on his own. He was the crudest creature she'd ever encountered. She almost had to laugh now at the memory of Doc worrying about her "tender sensibilities." If only he knew how those sensibilities had been outraged by the man she'd freely allowed into her house.

Miss Abigail's mother and father had been people with faultless manners. Cursing and raging had been foreign to her life. She had always been taught to hide anger because it was not a genteel emotion. But Mr. Cameron had managed to elicit more than just her anger. She was smitten by guilt at all she'd done—withheld a bedpan from an invalid, then thrown it at him, then abused his leg, causing him intentional pain, and slamming out of the house like a petulant child. Why, she'd even made one unforgivable ribald comment! The memory of it scalded her cheeks even now.

But the one who had precipitated it all would not allow her escape, not even out here in her garden. His voice riveted through the still summer air, abrading her once more.

"Miss Abigail, what's the railroad paying you for, half a job? Where's my breakfast?" he needled.

Oh, the gall of that man to make demands on her! She wanted nothing so badly as to starve him out of here. Loathsome creature! But she was caught in a trap of her own making. All she could do was gather her ladyhood around her like a mantle while she returned to the kitchen to prepare his meal.

When she came in with the tray, the first thing he noticed was that there was no linen napkin lining it like before.

"What? Don't I get flowers like old Melcher did?"

"How did you know . . ." she said before she could think. He laughed.

"Sounds carry in your house. Is that a real blush I see on the woman's cheek? My, my, I wonder if old Melcher knew he had what it takes to put it there. He certainly didn't look as if he did." The way he said "old Melcher" made her want to smack him!

"Remember our truce, *sir?*" she said stiffly.

"I only wondered why I don't get equal consideration around here," he complained in mock dismay.

"You wanted food, sir. I've brought you food. Do you wish to lie there and blather all morning or to eat it?"

"That depends on what you've chosen to poison me with this time."

It didn't help her temper any to recall all the warm, appreciative comments Mr. Melcher had made about her cooking. She brought a pillow to boost up that black devil's head, wishing she could use it instead to smother him. The thought must have been reflected in her face, for he eyed her warily as she spread a cloth on his chest and picked up the spoon. The glimmer in his eye warned her she'd better look out for those precious, sparkling teeth of his!

"Would you rather do it yourself?" she asked brittlely.

"No, it doesn't work when I have to lie so flat. Besides, I know how you enjoy doing it for me, *Miss* Abigail." A slow grin began at the corner of his mouth. "What is this stuff?"

"This . . . *stuff* . . . is beef broth."

"Are you determined to starve me?" he asked in that horrible, teasing tone she found more offensive than his belligerent one.

"At dinner time tonight you may have something heavier, but for now, it's only broth and a coddled egg."

"Terrific." He grimaced.

"You may consider it terrific when you taste what will follow your breakfast."

"And what's that?"

"I'll prepare a decoction of balm of Gilead, and while you may find it quite bitter, rest assured it's very fortifying for one of your debility." He considered this while she poked a few more spoons of broth into him, carefully avoiding his teeth.

"Do you ever talk like other people, Miss Abigail?" he asked then.

Immediately she knew he was trying to rile her again. "Is there something wrong with the way I speak?"

"There's nothing wrong with it. That's what's wrong with it. Don't you ever talk plain, like—'I mixed up some medicine and it'll make you stronger'?"

She could not help remembering how David Melcher had likened her

speech to a sonnet. A light flush came to her face at this newest unfair criticism. She had always prided herself on her literacy and began to turn away to cover the hurt at being criticized for it now. But he grabbed her wrist.

"Hey, Miss Abigail, why don't you just bend a little sometime?" he asked, and for once the teasing seemed absent from his voice.

"You've seen me as . . . as . . . *bent* as you ever shall, Mr. Cameron. You have managed to anger me, make me lose my patience, shout like a fishwife, and more. I assure you it is not my way at all. I am a civilized person and my manner of speech reflects it, I hope. You have goaded me in countless ways, but I find no reason for this newest assault. Do you intend to wring that spoon from my wrist again?"

"No . . . no, I don't," he answered quietly, but neither did he release it. Instead, he held it loosely, very narrow and fine within the circle of his wide, dark fingers while his hazel-flecked eyes looked from her hand to her eyes and back again. He shook it gently; the hand flopped, telling him that she was not about to try to resist his superior strength. "But you're more believable when you're angry and impatient and shouting. Why don't you get that way more often? I won't mind."

Surprised, she slipped easily from his grasp.

"Eat your eggs." He opened his mouth and she put a spoonful in.

"These things are slimy."

"Yes, aren't they?" she agreed, as if overjoyed. "But they'll build your strength, and the faster you get strong, the sooner I shall be rid of you, so I intend to take excellent care of you from now on. When you've finished your breakfast, I shall walk over town to Mr. Field's feedstore to buy flax seed for a poultice. Flax seed will heal that wound as fast as anything can, but never too fast to suit me."

"How about something for this sore hand, too? Must be something broken in there because it hurts like hell." She gave him a sharp look. "Well, it does. Don't get me wrong, Miss Abigail. I positively glow at your doting, but with two good hands I might have one free for you to hold."

"Save your ill-advised wit for someone who'll appreciate it."

Jesse was beginning to appreciate her more and more. She had a caustic tongue, which he liked, and whether she knew it or not, she didn't have such a bad sense of humor. If he could just get her to bend that ramrod back and those ramrod ideals just a little she might be almost human, he thought. Breakfast really hadn't been so bad after all.

"Oh," he said. "One more thing before you leave. How about a shave?"

She looked like she'd just swallowed a June-bug.

"There's no . . . no hurry, is there?" She acted suddenly fidgety. "I mean, it's been growing ever since you've been unconscious. What will a few more hours matter?" He rubbed his chin and she held her breath, feeling suddenly nauseous. But she was given a temporary reprieve, for his hand stopped its investigation before getting to his upper lip. Suddenly she seemed eager to leave the house. "I'll make you the decoction of balm of Gilead, then go up to the feedstore, and you can . . . well, you can rest while I'm gone . . . and . . ."

"Go . . . go, if you want." He motioned her toward the door, puzzled by her sudden nervousness, which was so unlike her. When she returned a minute later with the balm of Gilead, he opened wide and gulped it down. It was vile.

"Bluhhh . . ." he grunted, closing his eyes, shivering once, sticking out his tongue. Normally his grimace of displeasure would have been all it took to make Miss Abigail happy, but she was too worried about his missing moustache to gloat.

She worried about it all the way over town.

The bay window faced south, with east and west facets. He saw her as she passed along the road, straight and proper, and he couldn't believe she'd donned a hat and gloves on a hot June day like this. She was something, Miss Abigail was. The woman had starch in everything from her bloomers to her backbone, and it was amusing trying to make it crackle. She passed out of his limited range of vision and he thought of other things.

He wondered if they'd found his camera and gear down in Rockwell, at the end of the line. If it had stayed on the train, the crew in Rockwell more than likely had it by now and had let Jim Hudson know it had arrived without Jesse. Jim would get word to him sooner or later.

A knock on the door disturbed Jesse from his thoughts. "Come in!" he called. The man who came was stubby, short of hair and of breath, but long on smiles. He raised his bag by way of introduction.

"Cleveland Dougherty's the name, better known as just plain Doc around here. How you doing, boy? You look more alive than I ever thought to see you again."

Jesse liked him instantly. "That woman's too stubborn to let me die."

Doc howled in laughter, already sensing that the man had sized up Miss Abigail quite accurately. "Abigail? Aw, Abigail's all right. You were damn lucky she took you in. Nobody else in town would, you know."

"So I gathered."

"You were in some shape when we got you off that train. All that's left of your stuff is this shirt and boots. We had to cut the pants off you, o' course. And I guess this belongs to you, too." Doc lifted a pistol, weighing it in his hand while he peered over lowered brows at the man on the bed. " 'Course it's empty," Doc said pointedly. Then, as if that subject were totally cut and dried, Doc tossed the gun onto the bed.

"I guess you can put my boots and shirt under the bed," Jesse said. "That way we won't clutter up Miss Abigail's house."

"Sounds like you already know her ways, eh? Where is she anyway?"

"She went *'over town'* to the feedstore." He managed to say it just like she would have.

"I see you've had the full lash of Miss Abigail's tongue," Doc said, chuckling again. "What in thunderation is she doing there?"

"She said she was going to get flax seed for a poultice."

"That sounds like Miss Abigail all right. Got more cures up her sleeve than a chicken's got lice. Let's see here what she's done to you." He lifted the sheet and found the wound looking surprisingly healthy. "I'd have sworn the best you'd come out of this was losing the leg to gangrene, the way it looked. But she made up a mixture of charcoal and yeast that purified it and kept working the matter to the surface. It seems to have saved your life, boy, or the very least your leg."

"But I hear you did surgery first. I guess I owe you for taking me on when they dragged me off that train. They said I was robbing it and that might've made some men hesitate to patch me up."

"Some men, maybe. Even some men around here. But we're not all that way. Ah . . . what the hell's your name anyway?" Jesse liked the man's down-to-earth language and the fact that he seemed not to care whether it was a train robber or someone else whom he saved.

"Just call me Jesse."

"Well, Jesse, I figure a man's got a right to medical treatment first and a trial second."

"A trial?"

"Well, there's talk around. 'Course, there's bound to be, the way you came in."

"Raised an uproar, did I?"

"Uproar isn't the word for it. Whole damn town congregated on my lawn to raise objections to me taking you on as a patient. Riled me up something fierce, let me tell you! Still, it's natural folks were a mite jumpy about having you under their roofs, considering the circumstances. You can hardly blame them in some ways."

"Still, Miss Abigail braved it?"

"She sure did. Marched right down there in the middle of that crowd, cool as a cucumber salad, and told the whole damn town she was willing to take you in—the pair of you yet! Left everybody feeling a little sheepish, being what she is and all."

"And what's that, Doc?"

"You mean you don't know?"

"Well, I've got a pretty fair idea, but I'd like to hear your version."

"I can tell you, but it's nothing you don't know after spending any time with her at all. I'm sure you've divined she's no floozy. Miss Abigail is more or less the town yardstick." Doc scratched his head thoughtfully, puzzling out a way to describe how everybody felt about her. "I mean, if you want to see just what a proper lady ought to be, you measure her against Miss Abigail, 'cause she's the damnedest most proper lady this town's ever seen. You want to know what a devoted daughter should act like, you measure her up against Miss Abigail, after the way she saw to her old man in his last years. There's a few women in this town could take a lesson from her on keeping their noses out of other folks' business, too. Oh, she's exactly what she appears, make no mistake about that—every inch a lady. I guess that's why the townspeople were pretty surprised that she'd take in a gunslinger like she did." The word might have rankled, but Doc had a way of saying it, offhand, as if it didn't matter to him.

"Has she ever been married?" Jesse asked.

"Miss Abigail? No . . ." Then, recalling back, Doc added, "Now wait a minute. She almost did once. A rounder he was, never could see the two of them together. But, as I recall, he courted her right up until the time her father got bad. Seems he wasn't willing to take on a bedridden old man along with his bride, so he left her high and dry. You know, over the years a person forgets those things. She was different then, of course. But it's hard to think of

Miss Abigail as anything but a maiden lady. Guess that's why we were all so surprised when she took you in." Doc looked up. "How's she bearing up?"

"Staunch as a midwife."

"That'd be typical of her too. She's that way, you know. When she takes on a responsibility she's prepared to see it through, come hell or high water. She gave up the better part of her youth seeing after her father, and by the time he died, we all kind of took for granted that she'd become the town's resident old maid. Some folks thought she got a little uppity, but then you can't blame her. Hell, who wouldn't, being so young when all your neighbors labeled you a spinster? Ah well, in any case, we'd all appreciate it if you gave her her due respect."

"You've got my word on it. Oh, and Doc, could you check this hand of mine?"

Doc pronounced the hand only bruised, then summed up his findings. "Well, you're healing fast, thanks to her, but don't push it. Take 'er slow and easy. Try sitting up tomorrow, but no more than that. I'd say, by the looks of you, you'll be managing a slow shuffle by the end of the week anyway. Just don't overdo it."

Jesse smiled and nodded, liking the man more than ever as Doc prepared to leave.

"Doc?"

"Yup?"

"What's up with that Melcher fellow?"

"Wondered when you'd ask about him." Doc could see the first hard lines in Jesse's face since he'd walked in the room. "Seems he's leaving town today. Went to the depot and bought himself a ticket for Denver on the afternoon train. Did you know you shot his toe off?"

"I heard."

"He probably will limp for the rest of his life. Plenty of grounds for a lawsuit, huh?"

"You'll pardon me if I'm not overcome by guilt," Jesse said with a bitter edge to his voice. "Look what he nearly did to me!"

"Around here that's not going to count for much, I don't think. You see, you're the villain—he's the hero."

Strange, but even at those frank words, Jesse felt no criticism from Doc. As the two eyed each other, it was with mutual silent approval.

"Tell Miss Abigail I'll try to be around if she needs me again, but I don't think she will."

"Thanks, Doc."

Doc stopped in the doorway, turned one last time, saying, "Thank Miss Abigail. She's the one that kept you alive." Then he was gone.

Jesse lay thinking of all Doc had told him, trying to imagine a young and vibrant Miss Abigail courted by an ardent suitor, but the picture wouldn't gel. The image of her taking care of a sickly father seemed far more believable. He wondered just how old she was, guessing her to be thirty or thereabouts. But her bearing and actions made her seem far older, stodgy, and fusty. To picture her with a husband and children seemed ludicrous. She would seem miscast in that role, with a child's sticky fingers pulling at her spotless apron or admiring a mud pie brought for her approval. Neither could he imagine her moaning in ecstasy beneath a man.

But like the change of cards in a stereoscope came the picture of Miss Abigail as she'd been that night fighting for his life, hair and gown and skin a mess, leaning over him, pleading, urging him to fight with her. How intense she'd been then, all fire and dedication, so different from the primness which she usually exuded. The two just didn't go together. But according to Doc Dougherty, he owed his life to her. He felt a prickle of discomfort, thinking about how she'd been jilted by that other man so many years ago just because she'd accepted the responsibility of caring for a sick man, and now the same thing had happened again and it was his fault. Guilt was a new thing to Jesse. Still, he decided he owed her something and would temper his tongue because she'd lost her boyfriend on his account.

But I'll surely miss teasing her, he thought. Yup, I'll surely miss it.

Chapter 6

ALL THE WAY home Miss Abigail knew she couldn't avoid shaving him any longer. He was bound to find out sooner or later that she'd shorn him, if he hadn't already! She'd intended to get the ordeal over with at the same time as his bath, but he'd riled her so that she simply couldn't face it. Oh, if only it were all over. He was simply going to explode when he found that moustache gone, and now that she knew how volatile he was, the thought made her quaver.

"I'm home," she announced from the bedroom doorway, surprising him, as usual. How a woman could move through a house without making a sound that way beat him.

"Aha."

With a half sigh of relief that he still hadn't made the discovery, she came into the room, pulling the white gloves from her hands on her way to the mirror. He was surprised to find himself glad she was back.

"And have you brought your flax seed?" he asked, eyeing her in semiprofile as she raised her arms above her head and removed the ornate, filigreed hatpin. He noticed again that she had generous breasts. Her usual starch-fronted blouses concealed the fact, but from this angle, and with her arms raised that way, they jutted forward, giving themselves away.

"Indeed I have," she said, turning now. "And some fresh lemons for a cool drink."

He bit back a cute remark about Melcher and asked instead, "Did you bring a beer for me?"

She soured up. "Your days of ebriosity are recessed temporarily. Lemonade will have to do while you're here." He understood her now, the way his teasing made her pluck some pretentious word from her ample store of them and use it to bring him down. Ebriosity! But again his newfound agreeability stopped him from teasing, and he agreed pleasantly, "Actually, lemonade will do quite nicely, Miss Abigail."

She stood there in the center of the room, ill at ease for some reason she couldn't define, and the shifting breeze from the open window caught her skirt, billowing it out before her. She took her hat and used it to flatten the skirt down again, the gesture very youthful and enchanting, making him wonder again what she'd been like as a young girl.

"I . . . I'll shave you now, if you like." Her eyes avoided his, and she fussed distractedly with the daisies on her hat. He rubbed his jaw while her heart jumped into her throat.

"I probably look like a grizzly bear," he ventured, smiling.

"Yes," she agreed rather weakly, thinking, and you'll probably act like one in a minute, too. "I'll go heat water and gather the necessary things."

She left the room to stoke up the fire, then found clean cloths and her father's old cup and brush. She was reaching for the basin when his voice roared from the other room.

"Miss Abigail, get your ass in here and fast!" She straightened up as if the toe of his boot had given her a little impetus, then closed her eyes to count to ten, but before she finished, he was yelling again. "Miss Abigail . . . *now!*"

He had completely forgotten his promise to be nice to her. She came in holding the washbasin like a shield before her.

"Yes, Mr. Cameron?" she almost whispered.

"Don't you 'yes Mr. Cameron' me!" he roared. "Where the hell is my moustache?"

"It's gone," she squeaked.

"I've just now discovered the fact. And who is responsible?"

"Responsible? I don't see why you put it that—"

"I'll put it any way I damn well please, you interfering—" He was so angry he didn't trust himself to call her a name, not knowing what might come out. "Who in the hell gave you permission to shave me?"

"I didn't need permission. I am being paid to see after you."

"You call this seeing after me!" His black, piercing eyes held no softening hazel flecks now. "I suppose you figured as long as you were changing everything around here—sheets, bedpans, bandages—you might as well keep right on changing. Well, you changed just one thing too many, do you hear me, woman! Just one thing too many!"

Though she quailed before his wrath, she was unwilling to be spoken to this way. "You're shouting at me and I don't like it. Please lower your voice." But her very control seemed only to raise his temperature and his volume.

"Oh God," he implored the ceiling, "save me from this female!" Then he glared at her. "What did you do, decide the big bad train robber needed his fingers slapped, is that it? I suppose you picked this way to do it. Or did you shave it off just for spite because it's masculine? Oh, I've got you pegged, *Miss* Abigail. I've seen your kind before. Anything male is a threat to you, isn't it? Anything that smacks of virility dries you up till you squeak when you walk. Well, you've picked the wrong man to wreak your puritanical vengeance on, do you hear me, woman? You'll pay for this and dearly!"

Miss Abigail stood red-faced, horrified that he'd struck so near the truth.

"I am paying for this, just standing still for your abuse and your name calling, which I do not deserve."

"You want to talk about deserving? Did I deserve this?" He made a disgusted gesture near his wounded leg. "Or this?" He next pointed to his upper lip. She was again struck by the fact that he looked very naked and unnatural without the facial hair.

"I may have acted hastily," she began, still trembling but willing to compromise now with a sort of apology, if only to silence him. He let out a derisive snort and lay there glaring at the ceiling. "If it makes you feel any better," she said, "I'm sorry I did it."

"Believe it or not, it doesn't make me feel a damn bit better." Then he went on in an injured tone, "Just why the hell did you do it? Was it bothering you?"

"It looked dirty and gave you the appearance of a typical outlaw." Then her voice brightened noticeably. "Why, don't you know that some of the most famous outlaws in history had moustaches?"

"Oh?" He raised his head a little to peer at her. "And how many of us have you met?"

"You're the only one," she answered lamely.

"I'm the only one."

"Yes," she said very meekly.

"And you shaved me so I wouldn't look like the others, huh?"

Miss Abigail, who always had such control, came very close to blubbering. "Actually n . . . no. Well, not . . . I mean, it is very much trouble when . . . well, when you're eating. I mean . . . well, it tickled."

His head came up off the pillow. "It what!"

"Nothing!" she snapped. "Nothing!"

"It tickled?"

Mortified by her traitorous tongue, she was forced to expound. "Yes, when I was feeding you." That brought his head up even further.

"Would you care to explain that, Miss Abigail?" But she had turned so red he could almost smell the starch scorching in her collar as she spun from the room. While she gathered his shaving things, he lay considering. A crazy notion took hold of him, and being very much a ladies' man, it swelled his considerable ego and cooled his anger somewhat. But common sense told him it couldn't be true—not of the ramrod-spined Miss Abigail! Still, the notion gained credence when she returned, for she was skittish as a cat at howling time, fussing around with that shaving stuff, avoiding his eyes, and obviously very uncomfortable.

She felt his eyes following her with a feral glint, but steeled herself and approached, poured some hot water into the cup, and worked up a lather. But when she made a move toward his face, his black eyes snapped warningly.

"I'll do it myself," he protested, and grabbed the soapy brush from her hand. "Just hold the mirror," he ordered. But once he got an eyeful of his naked face in it, he grew disgusted again. "Damnit, Abbie, you might as well have changed the shape of my nose. A moustache is part of a man he doesn't feel the same without." He managed to sound quite wounded now. Looking into the mirror, he shook his head woefully at his own reflection, then started lathering as if to cover up what he saw.

As the black whiskers became covered with white he looked less fearsome, so she admitted, "I knew that as soon as I did it. I'm sorry." She sounded genuinely contrite, so he stopped brushing the soap on his jaws and turned to study her. She kept her eyes on the mirror but said, "I . . . I found that I'd liked you far better with it." Fearing she'd again said the wrong thing and given him ammunition, she ventured a peek at him. But his scowl was gone and, surprisingly, so was much of the anger from his voice.

"It'll grow back."

Something told her that the worst was over, that he was trying, really trying to control himself for her.

Pleased, she offered, "Yes, your beard grows exceedingly fast." They assessed each other for a few seconds, and in that time he realized she'd studied him in his sleep long enough or hard enough to mark the speed with which his beard grew.

"How observant you are, Miss Abigail," he said quietly. And damn if she didn't blush. "Here, you can take over." He handed her the brush. "I'm not too coordinated with my left hand."

"Are you sure you trust me?" Her one fine eyebrow was hoisted higher than the other, but still he smiled.

"No, should I?"

"Mr. Melcher did," she lied, not knowing why she should want this man to think she had shaved David Melcher.

"He didn't look like he had enough man in him to grow a beard. Are you sure there was hair on his face when you started?"

"Hold still or I may cut your nose off yet." She poised the blade above his cheek. "And, unlike your moustache, it shan't grow back."

"Just stay away from my upper lip," he warned, then pulled his mouth muscles to tighten them and could feel the blade as she scraped around none too proficiently. He reached up to stop her so he could talk without getting cut.

"Shape it down around here—"

"I remember the shape well enough, sir," she interrupted, "and you have me by the wrist again." An interminable moment charged past while his brown fingers circled her little wrist.

"So I do," he grinned. "I shall take the razor from you and slit it if you take off one more hair than I think you should." He released her and shut his eyes while she finished. She was getting better at it as she went along. So, he thought, she remembers the shape well enough, does she? For some reason that vastly pleased him.

"Miss Abigail?" She turned from rinsing the razor to find his black eyes filled with wicked amusement as they smiled from his freshly shaved face. "I shall spend time thinking of a way to get even with you for the loss of my moustache."

"I'm sure you shall, sir. Meanwhile, we'll drink lemonade together as if we were the best of friends, shan't we?"

When she brought the lemonade, he had a difficult time drinking from the glass.

"Here, try this," she said, handing him something that looked like a willow twig.

"What's this?"

"A piece of cattail which I reamed out with a knitting needle. You may drink your lemonade through it." He tried it and it worked.

"How ingenious of you. Why didn't you bring it for the broth this morning? Were you so anxious to spoon-feed me?"

"I simply did not think of it."

"Ah," he said knowingly, his expression saying only a fool would believe that.

"I have things to do," she said abruptly, deciding not to stay and drink her lemonade after all, not if he was going to tease again.

"Aren't you having any lemonade? Bring it in here and let's talk a minute."

"I grow weary of your talk. I almost wish your voice hadn't come back."

"How cruel of you to deny me the use of my voice when it's one of the few parts of me that's working right." Before she could decide if he meant the remark to be suggestive, he encouraged, "Don't go. I just want to talk awhile."

She hesitated, then perched on the sewing rocker, wondering why she stayed in the room with him. She sipped daintily while he pulled thirstily at the fresh drink through the piece of cattail, then growled, "Ahhh, that's almost as good as beer."

"I wouldn't know." No, he supposed she wouldn't.

"Doc Dougherty was here while you were gone."

"And how did he find your condition?"

"Much better than expected." She lifted her glass but not her eyes. "He told me I ought to thank you for saving my life."

"And are you?" she challenged.

"I'm not sure yet," he answered. "Just what all did you have to do to save it? I'm curious."

"Not much. A poultice here and a compress there."

"Why so modest, Miss Abigail? I know it took more than a pat on the head to bring me around. I have a natural curiosity about what you did to keep my carcass from rotting."

Unconsciously, Miss Abigail studied her two bitten fingers, rubbing her thumb over the small scabs which had formed, unaware that his eyes followed hers.

"There was very little for me to do. You were strong and healthy and the bullet couldn't do you in, that's all."

"Doc and I are both wondering as to how you fed me. I heard you say I ate —more than once today you referred to it. How can an unconscious man eat?"

"Very well, I'll tell you. I force-fed you, using that piece of cattail you're drinking through. I had to insert it into your throat. That's why it hurt so severely when you first awakened." Again he noted her preoccupation with the marks between her knuckles and began putting two and two together.

"Are you saying you spooned medicine and food through this little hole?" She was growing very uncomfortable under this line of questioning, then suddenly realized his eyes were on the knuckles she'd been nursing and hid them in her skirt.

"I did not spoon it. I blew it," she admitted impatiently.

"With your mouth, Miss Abigail?" he asked in surprise.

"With my mouth, Mr. Cameron." But she would not meet his eyes.

"Well I'll be damned."

"Yes, you probably already are, but please refrain from saying so in my presence."

"Is that how you got tickled by my moustache? By this little bitty short straw here? It sure seems to me like it could have been cut a little longer."

Feeling her face heat up, she shot out of the rocker but he was too quick. He grabbed and got her by the back of her hand. He looked at her exposed fingers, then up at her face, with a mischievous smile creasing one side of his mouth.

"And these . . ." he said, studying the fingers, "what are these?"

"Turn my hand loose, sir!"

"As soon as I'm satisfied about what took place here while I was not coherent. Could these be my tooth marks?"

"Yes!"

He held the hand in a viselike grip while she struggled to pull it free. "What were your fingers doing in my mouth?"

"Holding it open and forcing your tongue down while I inserted the straw into your throat."

"And you call that *nothing much?*"

She glared at him silently, red to the ears now.

"To feed a common thief, mouth to mouth, to put your fingers into his mouth and suffer him to bite them until he broke the skin, and to take broth into your own mouth and blow it into his? That is much more than *nothing much.* That is dedication, Miss Abigail. That is stalwart, admirable dedication, isn't it? It seems I do owe you my gratitude."

"You owe me nothing . . . Let my—"

"I owe you my gratitude. How shall I express it?"

"Just let my hand go and that will be quite enough."

"Ah no, Miss Abigail. Surely that won't do. After all, you've been forced into some unorthodox—not to mention intimate—methods of caring for me. I would be ungrateful to let your generosity pass without notice." With his thumb he gently stroked the tooth marks on her fingers. Their sparring eyes met while a queer thrill grabbed her stomach and she strained to pull free of his grasp. "Since I have no more ticklish moustache to offend you with, allow me . . . by way of apology for this . . ." Then in slow motion he pulled her fingers to his lips and kissed the small scars. He felt the change when she stopped fighting and let him take the fingers to his mouth. Then he turned the hand over, kissed the palm with a light, lingering touch, and lightly ran his tongue out to wet her skin. She jerked then and grabbed the stricken hand with her other.

"I must have been out of my mind to bring you into my house!" she spit.

"I only meant to apologize for biting you. Don't worry, it won't happen again."

"And is this . . . this form of apology your way of getting even for my having shaved your moustache?"

"Oh, that. No, never, Miss Abigail. When I choose the time and the method of getting even, you'll well know it."

His implication was plain, and all Miss Abigail could do was scuttle out, escaping those casually smiling lips and eyes which were so much more of a threat in his newfound good humor than they'd ever been in his anger.

She kept as far away from that bedroom door as she possibly could for the remainder of the day, telling herself that each time she remembered his kiss and her stomach trembled, it was from anger.

At noon she was forced to go to him with his dinner. She made the thickest stew she could manage and unceremoniously plopped the bowl on his chest.

He'd been dozing and awoke with a start. All he had time to say was, "Boy, the service is really going downhill around this place." But she was gone again. She didn't care how he managed or failed to manage eating that stew. Furthermore, she hoped it was thick enough to tear his gut out!

"Got any more of that stew out there?" he hollered a few minutes later.

She should have guessed that a goat like him would eat everything in the house and never be bothered by it at all! She slapped more stew into his bowl and again plopped it wordlessly onto his chest while he lay there grinning as if he knew something she didn't.

In the afternoon she went up to clean Mr. Melcher's room, only to find the book of sonnets lying like a love letter from a lost beau. In a lifetime of much loneliness, she remembered how for those few treasured days he had been a harbinger of something better to come. But he was gone from her life as suddenly as he'd entered it.

A timid knock on the downstairs door brought Miss Abigail from her brown study. Coming down the steps she recognized the fabric of David Melcher's suit sleeve, which was all she could see of him. It brought a flutter to her heart as, crossing the parlor, she paused, put a hand to her breathless lips, then smoothed her blouse front, her waistband, then touched a hand to the coil of hair at the nape of her neck. She didn't realize that from the bedroom Jesse saw it all.

She moved beyond his range of vision, but every word was audible, and even from the bedroom he could detect her breathlessness.

"Why, Mr. Melcher, it's you."

"Yes . . . ahem . . . I came to return your father's slippers."

"Yes . . . yes, of course. Thank you." The screen door spring went twinnng, and a long silence followed.

"I'm afraid I've been a lot of trouble to you."

"No, no, you've been no trouble at all."

Melcher seemed to be having some trouble with his throat. He cleared it several times, followed by a second lengthy silence. When they spoke again, it was simultaneously.

"Miss Abigail, I may have jumped to . . ."

"Mr. Melcher, this morning was . . ."

Silence again while the man in the bedroom cocked his ear.

"You were within your rights to get angry with me this morning."

"No, Mr. Melcher. I don't know what came over me."

"You had good cause, though. I never should have said those things."

"Well, it really doesn't matter, does it, since you're leaving Stuart's Junction on the train within an hour?"

"I want you to know what it meant to me, this time I've spent in your lovely house while you cared for me. You did far more than was expected of you."

"Nonsense, Mr. Melcher . . ." Conscious now of the man in the bedroom, she realized he could hear every word, but there was nowhere else she could take David Melcher. The front porch was too public, the kitchen too private.

"No, it's not, Miss Abigail. Why, your . . . your nasturtiums and the sonnets and your tasteful way of doing things . . . I mean, I'm not used to such treatment. And all that delicious food and your fine care—"

"All in the line of duty."

"Was it?" he asked. "I'd hoped . . ." But this he didn't finish, and Miss Abigail toyed with the lace edging of her high, stiff collar.

"Hopes can be very hurtful things, Mr. Melcher," she said quietly.

"Yes . . . well . . ."

"I see you have purchased yourself a pair of new shoes."

"Yes. Not quite as fine as those I sell, but . . ." Once again his words trailed away.

"Feel welcome to keep Father's cane. I have no use for it since he's gone."

"Are you sure?"

She suddenly wanted very badly for him to take it, for him to carry away some small thing from her house which would always remind him of her.

"I shan't miss it, but you might, if you had to go without it."

"Yes . . . well . . . thank you again, Miss Abigail."

It grew silent again and Jesse pictured the two of them, both probably gaping at the old man's cane. The spring on the screen door sang again.

"If I ever get back through here, I'll return the cane to you."

"You needn't bother."

"Ah . . . I see," he said, rather forlornly.

"I didn't mean . . ." But her words, too, trailed away.

"I will always think of this place when I smell the scent of nasturtiums."

She swallowed, her heart threatening to explode, her eyes to flood.

"Goodbye, Miss Abigail," he said, backing away slowly.

"Goodbye, Mr. Melcher."

It grew so quiet then that Jesse could hear each and every one of Melcher's irregular steps shuffling off down the road. He saw the limping figure through the east facet of the bay window, below the half-drawn shade, and thought, damn fool should've used his head on that train and he wouldn't be limping now. It was the first time Jesse was able to think of Melcher without getting frustrated and angry at his own incapacity. He heard the footsteps of Miss Abigail go back upstairs long, long after Melcher limped away. She must have watched him out of sight, Jesse thought. He couldn't help recalling all that Doc had told him about the other man who'd walked out on her once before, couldn't help comparing now to then. And he could not stop the irritating twitch of conscience that prickled him.

From an upstairs window Miss Abigail watched the puffs of smoke as the afternoon train pulled in. Its whistle swooned through the stillness as she held the lace curtains aside. She pictured Mr. Melcher limping aboard the train. Her heart called to him not to forget her. A puffy cloud lifted above the roof of the depot and the steam whistle cried mournfully once more, bearing David Melcher out of her life. Her eyes stung as she turned to put fresh sheets on his bed.

She fully expected to be teased again after everything the man in her house had overheard. She came to his doorway to find him sound asleep. It gave her a moment of perverse pleasure to disturb him.

"I found some wild weeds that will help your hand," she said loudly, businesslike.

He roused at her words, clenched his good hand, and gave one of those shivering, all-over stretches. It was slow, masculine, and she averted her eyes, remembering how he'd earlier said that anything masculine threatened her. He growled lazily, deep in his throat, twisting and yawing. At last he opened his eyes and drawled, "Howdy, Miss Abigail. Have you been there long?"

"I just . . ." But she had. She'd been watching those muscles twisting and turning.

"Studying my beard grow again?"

"You flatter yourself, sir. I'd as soon watch grass grow."

He smiled, again slowly and lazily.

"I came to put a fomentation on that bruised hand. The sooner it heals, the sooner I'll be excused from wringing out your shaving cloths."

He laughed. He seemed for once to be in a halfway human mood. "Spoken like a true adversary, Miss Abigail. Come on in. I can use the company now that I've been so rudely awakened anyway. I expect you can too, now that Melcher is gone."

"Leave Mr. Melcher out of this, if you please," she said acidly. "Do you want the compress on your hand or not?"

"By all means. After all, it's my gun hand, isn't it?" He extended it toward her and she came to unwrap the old gauze strips and pad. As she unwound the pieces, he added, "And my loving hand, too." She automatically halted all movement, realized her mistake, continued unwrapping while he went on. "Hard for a right-handed man to make love with only one good hand and that his left."

She could already feel the color creeping up behind her choker collar.

"How indelicate of you to say so."

The hand was free now and he flexed it only a little, at the same time moving it toward her face. She jerked back.

"And how indelicate of you to flinch, Miss Abigail, as if I had designs on you. After all, a hand like this is in no shape for loving or shooting, either one. When it is, you'll know it."

Rattled now, she turned her back on him, and her voice was almost pleading. "What do I have to do to keep you from teasing me this way? I am unused to it, thus I have no defense against it. I'm sure the women you've known in the past were quick with rebuttal, but I am simply tongue-tied, time and again, and deeply embarrassed. I realize this is precisely the outcome you hope to achieve with me, so it must pleasure you endlessly to hear me finally admit it. But I lay my soul bare to you and admit that these taunts are disconcerting. I ask you to make my job easier by treating me fairly and honorably."

"Do you want me to beseech you to put fresh nasturtiums in my room?"

When she spoke her voice was exceedingly quiet, almost defeated. "I want absolutely nothing from you except to be treated like a lady, as I was by Mr. Melcher. But then you obviously disdain Mr. Melcher. His qualities of kindness and consideration are foreign to you, I know, but you only make yourself more offensive by making fun of him."

"Old Melcher got to you, did he?"

With an effort she kept her voice calm. "Mr. Melcher knows how to treat a lady, how to make her feel valued and appreciated, how to eke a bit of the sublime out of the everyday tedium. These things may seem soft and weak to you, but it is because you have never learned the strengths to be found in the beautiful and gentle things of this life. Strength to you is only . . . only . . . anger and cursing and goading and making others do what you want by the force of these things. I pity you, Mr. Cameron, for you've somehow been denied the knowledge that such well-worn attributes as politeness, respect, patience, forbearance, even gratitude, have a peculiar strengthening quality all their own."

"And you've practiced these virtues all your life?"

"I've tried." He saw her shoulder blades draw erect proudly as she admitted it.

"And what good did it do you? Here you are, polite and bitter, and left with me and deserted by Melcher."

Still with her back to him, she cried, "You have no right, Mr. Cameron! No right at all! *You* are the reason he is lost to me, you and your teasing tongue. I'm sure you feel supremely self-satisfied that he is gone and that with him went my last chance for . . . for . . ." But at last Miss Abigail broke down, lowered her face into her hands and sobbed, her small shoulders shaking as Jesse had never thought to see them. The last woman he'd caused to cry had been his mother, the last time he'd left New Orleans to come back out West again. Seeing Miss Abigail cry now was equally as disturbing. It made him feel exactly as she had many times said he was: callous and coarse. And this feeling was something new and disturbing. He wanted suddenly to make up for the hurt he'd caused, but before he could say more, she gulped, "Excuse me, sir," and fled the room.

It struck him that even in her discomposure she clung to her impeccable manners as tightly as possible.

Miss Abigail was aghast at her own actions. Never in her life had she cried before a man. Strength came from many sources, but crying, she believed, was not one of them. Still, it was peculiar how purged she felt when she finished. All the bitterness and waste of her life, all the given years, all the unexperienced joys, all the foregone pleasures which she had never before begrudged her father or Richard . . . ah Richard . . . it was a blissful relief to even think his name again . . . welled now in a great, crushing hurt which she allowed herself to explore. All the pent-up frustrations which a lady never shows felt like a blessed release after years in prison.

She stood in her shaded backyard and cried at last for the loss of Richard, of her father, of David Melcher, of children and warmth and companionship. And for the first time ever she rued those years she had sacrificed to her father.

And her breakdown before Jesse made her something which she had never seemed to him before: vulnerable.

And his having caused it made him something she could hardly have suspected him capable of being: contrite.

And so it was that in the late afternoon, when she came to him next, there was a first hint of harmony between them. She came with the same self-assured dignity as before her outburst, as if it had never taken place. The only residual of her tears was a faint puffiness beneath her eyelids. Her face held neither challenge nor rebuke as she stood in the doorway, saying, "It seems I've neglected your hand again."

"My fault," he said simply. He seemed agreeable, no hint of teasing showed in his face.

"I'll take care of it now?" she asked more than stated.

"Come in," he replied. "What have you got this time?"

"The trappings for a fomentation. May I put it on?" What she was really asking was if she could come in without being tortured again by his tongue. He nodded, fully understanding. She entered, took his bruised hand, and began working over it. A grudging admiration once again overtook him. Time and again she came to him, no matter what he did or what he said. There seemed no end to her tenacity in the face of duty.

"How is it feeling?" she asked, studying the hand.

"Not good."

"Do you think any bones are broken?"

"Doc says no, but it hurts every time I move it."

"It would be surprising if none were broken," she said. The bruise was by now a ghastly yellowish-green. She picked up a small, filled cloth bag from a steaming cup.

"What's that?" he asked suspiciously.

"Be still." Holding it gingerly between two fingers, she blew on it.

"Are you punishing me with that thing?" But she only squeezed it against the side of the cup and laid it on the colorful bruise. It didn't quite burn him, but was mighty uncomfortable. "I guess I deserve it," he ventured while she only concentrated on wrapping the hand. "What have you put in that?"

"Something that will take away the aching, heal the bruise."

"Well, is it a secret or what?"

"No, it's no secret. It's just a weed."

"A weed? What weed?"

"A weed called arsesmart."

"Arsesmart! Are you serious?" It was all he could do to keep from making choice remarks about that, but he resolutely refrained.

Meanwhile Miss Abigail thought, Is there nothing we can say to each other that hasn't some ulterior meaning? He was, of course, wearing a grin, which she ignored. To cover her discomfort, she lectured.

"My grandmother taught my mother, and she taught me the value of arsesmart. It can dissolve congealed blood, which is why I'm using it on your hand. My grandmother used it for everything. She even used it on a small mole she had on her chin right here." At last Miss Abigail looked into Jesse's eyes, touching her own chin. Lamely, she finished, "But as far as I can recall, that mole never disappeared. She never . . ." Her words trailed off as she looked into Jesse's dark face, still painfully aware of the tears he had seen her shed earlier, wondering if he would mention them. But he said nothing and now looked deep in thought.

She gathered up the roll of gauze. "I believe that by morning you'll find those muscles noticeably relieved." Her eyes slid to his hand. Now, she thought, now he will taunt me. But instead he only held out the hand, shook his head as if scolding himself.

"Well, that puts one pistol hand out of commission. But it feels much better."

It was not a thank you, but it was close, and Miss Abigail thought about it all the while she fixed his supper tray. An apology was too much to hope for —he had probably never apologized for anything in his life. Still, her outburst of tears had mollified him somewhat, and to let him know she would not be faulted for a genteel life-style, she picked a small nosegay of nasturtiums and put them in a delicate cut glass ewer on his tray, which was again spread with a spotless linen liner.

When he saw the neat tray and fresh flowers, he quirked an eyebrow questioningly but took it all as a peace offering and decided he'd accept.

"Is it these things that smell so sweet?" He flicked a petal.

"It is."

"Nasturtiums, I presume?"

"They are."

They eyed one another like two bighorns deciding whether to butt or back off.

"With this hand I won't be able to handle a knife." And with those words her olive branch was accepted.

"I'll handle the knife," she offered. Then added, "I hope you like liver, Mr. Cameron. It was simply too warm a day to keep the range stoked for long. Liver and onions was the fastest thing I could think of."

At her words he felt a curious swelling at the base of his tongue, warning him not to open his mouth for any liver. But there she sat on the sewing rocker beside his bed, cutting the meat, extending it to his mouth, some sort of unspoken, rocky truce at last between them. So he took it, chewed slowly, and swallowed, willing himself not to gag, not to displease her again as he seemed to do so easily. But oh! how he despised liver!

She kept it coming and coming and finally he had to think of something. "What's in the cup?" he asked.

"Coffee."

"Where's your straw?"

"Right here." She produced it from under the linen napkin on the tray.

"I'll have a drink of that." He was in too much of a hurry and burned his mouth, opened it wide, exclaiming, "Waugh!"

"Oops," she said innocently. "I guess I should have warned you it might be too hot."

But by this time he was too concerned about finishing that liver to ride her about scalding him with coffee. She wanted peace and she would have it, by God! He steeled himself for more liver and never uttered a word, but ate dutifully until the plate was empty.

Meanwhile she rambled on, talking about the many home cures and remedies she'd learned from her mother and grandmother, telling him about the book where she'd found the yeast and charcoal remedy that had saved his life.

And all the while his stomach rebelled.

At last she said, "By morning your hand could be so much improved that you might be slicing your own liver . . . I mean, slicing the liver by yourself."

But he was lying with closed eyes, curiously impassive. Please, no, he was thinking. Anything but liver. Unaware of his roiling stomach, she left with the tray, gratified for the first time at how docile and obedient he had been.

Halfway through the dishes she heard him weakly call, "Miss Abigail?" She cocked an ear, smiled, pleased that he at last was calling her Miss Abigail without his usual annoying tone, yet wondering at the same time what trick he might be up to now.

"Miss Abigail . . . bring me a bucket, please—quick!"

Was that *please* she heard? Then suddenly she realized he'd asked for a bucket. His silence during supper, his closed eyes right afterward, his uncharacteristic passivity . . . oh no! "I'm coming!" she bellowed at the top of her lungs.

The bucket had no more than hit the floor beside the bed when he groaned, struggling to roll over toward it. She whipped the bolsters from under his leg, reached across, and grabbed him—sheet and all—by the buttocks and rolled him to the edge of the bed just in time. He upchucked every bit of her fried liver, onions, coffee, green beans, and even the cherry cobbler. He lay sweating, face down over the edge of the bed, his eyes closed.

At last he took a fortifying gulp of air, then said to the floor, "Has it occurred to you, Miss Abigail, that perhaps we're fated to aggravate each other without even trying?"

"Here, roll over," she ordered. "You must not lie on your wounded leg that way." She helped him onto his back again and saw his chalky complexion beneath the black, black whiskers. "Perhaps I'd better check your wound again."

He flung an arm across his forehead and eyes. "It's got nothing to do with my wound. I just detest liver, that's all."

"What?" she gasped. "And still you ate it all anyway?"

"Well, I tried," he managed with a rueful laugh. "I tried, but it didn't work. I was bound and determined not to antagonize you again, especially when I saw how you'd done up that tray. But it seems I can't keep peace even when I try." He flopped his arm weakly away from his eyes to find Miss Abigail McKenzie in a state of suspended humor, her wide smile hidden behind both hands, and he couldn't help his own sheepish grin from spreading across his face. And then Miss Abigail did the most amazing thing! She collapsed onto the rocker, sending it rolling backward while she laughed and laughed, clutching her waist and letting her merriment fill the room. It was the last thing in the world Jesse had expected her to do. Forward she came, then back again, forgetting herself for once, lifting her feet as a child pumps on a swing, a flash of petticoat lace accompanying her libration. And, oh, how enchanting she looked limp and laughing that way.

"I'm sorry I can't join you," he said, "but it hurts to laugh right after you've just heaved your guts out." But his smile was there just the same while he continued thinking how surprisingly beguiling she looked with her guard down.

"Oh, Mr. Cameron," she sighed at last, "perhaps you're right and we are fated, you and I. Even when you try to do my cooking justice it backfires." She laughed once more, gaily.

"Backfires? For once you've chosen the perfect word," he said, chuckling in spite of his sore stomach muscles. "Oh God, don't make me laugh . . . please." He hugged himself.

"You deserve it after the way you have just insulted my cooking."

"Who insulted whom? You're the one who poked that liver down me without bothering to ask if I liked it or not. It was more than an insult to have to eat it. Believe me, lady, it was a lethal weapon."

By now she was so amused that she forgot to take offense at either his profanity or the way he'd laughingly called her *lady*. She only lolled back in the rocker while he enjoyed just watching her.

"One by one I'm discovering the chinks in your armor," she said, coasting to a stop, with her head tilted back lazily. "And one of them is liver." She was relaxed as he'd never seen her before, hands lying palms-up in her lap. The golden evening sun came through the west window, lighting her hair, her chin, her high collar, the tips of her earlobes and eyelashes, turning them all to gilt.

He wondered again how old she was, for she looked suddenly young, leaning back on the chair that way, and he experienced again a momentary flash of regret for what he'd said earlier about how she'd been deserted by Melcher. He wanted the air cleared of that, thought that maybe now when she was relaxed and affable they might talk about it and exorcise the lingering bad feelings it had caused.

"How old are you?" he asked.

"Too old for it to be any business of yours."

"Too old to let a good prospect like Melcher get away?"

"You're despicable," she said, but without much fight, still easy in that chair. She rolled her head toward him, met his eyes, and a faint smile limned her lips.

"Maybe," he admitted, smiling too. "And you're worried."

"What am I worried about?"

"About getting old and having no man. But there are more where Melcher came from."

"Not in Stuart's Junction there aren't," she said resignedly.

"So . . . I fixed it good between you and Melcher and he was the last prospect around, huh?"

She didn't reply, but then she didn't need to. He studied her appreciatively as she looked into the sun's rays through slitted eyes, as if playing some game with them.

"Should I apologize for that, Miss Abigail?"

She quit playing with the sunbeams and rolled her head his way, quiet for the moment, considering. "If you must ask, it counts for naught," she said softly.

"Does it?" Then after a moment, "Anyway, it would be a bit of a letdown to have apologies between us now, wouldn't it? After all, we started out fighting like alley cats. You'd miss it if I suddenly became meek."

"And it would pain you to apologize, wouldn't it?" she countered.

"Pain me? Why, you do me an injustice, Miss Abigail. I'm as capable of apologies as anyone." But still he didn't say he was sorry.

"I apologized about your moustache, didn't I?"

"Out of fear, I think."

She rolled her head away, back toward the light that poured through the window, and shrugged her shoulders. "An apology is a move denoting strength—not strength of body, which I'm sure you've always had, but strength of character such as Mr. Melcher has."

His mellow mood was suddenly soured by her words. He was getting sick and tired of being compared unfavorably to that man. His ego was definitely singed. He didn't like being found lacking, even by such a sexless woman as her, and certainly not when put up against a milktoast like Melcher. If it took an apology to sate the woman's eternal appetite for mitigation, well she'd have it, by God!

"I'm sorry, Miss Abigail. Does that make you feel better?"

She didn't even turn his way, just sat intent upon that sunlight. But she heard the defensiveness in his voice, making the apology less than sincere.

"No, not really. It's supposed to make *you* feel better. Did it?"

He felt the blood leap to his face, scourged by her refusal to gracefully accept his apology after it had taken much soul-searching to bring it out. Never in his life had he lowered himself to apologize to any woman, and now that he had, look what had come of it. Suddenly angered, he laughed once, harshly and short.

"Tell you what'd make me feel better—if you'd just get out of here and take your liver and all your rosy pictures of Melcher with you!"

Turning, she found his face suffused with irritability. Her amused eyes remained upon his hard ones. She could see that he thought she should have blithely accepted his apology; it did not occur to him that it had been given for all the wrong reasons, making it totally without contrition. The color was back in his face again, and the bite of his words suddenly sowed a seed of suspicion within Miss Abigail. Why, he's jealous of David Melcher! Unbelievable as it was, it had to be true. What other reason could there possibly be for him to react as he had? He glared at her while she, wearing a secret cozening smile, rose and sweetly wished him good night.

It was her smug attitude and that sugary good night that drove him to call after her, "I now owe you two! One for the moustache and one for the liver!"

When she had gone upstairs for the night, he lay awake a long time, puzzling over how she could manage to anger him this way. What was it about Abigail McKenzie that got under his skin? He reviewed all the obvious irritations she'd caused—the moustache and the bedpan and such—but none of these was really the crux of his anger. It stemmed from the way she'd managed to make him feel guilty about scaring Melcher off. Why, he'd had women from New Orleans to the Great Divide, any one of whom would make Abigail McKenzie look like a sorry scarecrow, and here she was, mooning over that pantywaist Melcher, flinching from so much as a finger twitched her way by himself. And when she had finally wheedled an apology out of him, what had she done? Thrown it back in his face, that's what! For a while there tonight, while she sat in that rocker laughing, he wondered if she could be human, with impulses like other women had. Well, he thought, we'll soon find out if that female has impulses or not. If she wants to moon around making me feel guilty about Melcher, always reminding me what a gentleman he is and what a despicable cad I am, even when I'm trying to apologize, I'll give her something to back it up, by God! And maybe next time she forces an apology from me—if that day ever comes—she'll show some of that impeccable breeding she's always throwing in my face and accept it like the lady she claims to be!

Chapter 7

HE HEARD HER creeping softly down the stairs before dawn had fully blossomed in the sky. She flashed past the area he could view from his bed, and he heard the front door open. After a stretch of silence he heard her humming ever so faintly. Off in the unseen distance a rooster crowed. He imagined her standing there at the east door, looking out at the dawn, listening to it. She passed his door on cat feet.

"Taking in the dawn, Miss Abigail?" he asked. And her head popped back around the doorsill. She still had her nightie on, so hid behind the wall.

"Why, Mr. Cameron, you're awake, and you're sitting up!"

"Doc Dougherty said I could."

"And how does it feel?"

"Like I ought to be out there with you watching the sun come up. I'm used to watching it rise over the roughlands, but I haven't seen it for a while. What's it like today?"

She gazed toward the front door, still shielding herself behind the doorframe, but he could see the mere tip of her nose. "It is a myriad of pinks today —striated feathers of color, from deepest murrey to palest primrose, with the spaces between each color as deep and clear as the thoughts of sages."

He laughed, not unpleasantly, and said, "Well put, Miss Abigail. But all I understood was pink."

She felt foolish for having been carried away by the beauty of the dawn, but he would, of course, not be the kind to appreciate it in the same way she did.

"I . . . I need some things for today. May I come in and get them?"

"It's your room. Why the sudden request for permission?"

"I . . . I forgot my robe last night. Would you please look away while I come in?"

From around the doorway came the healthiest laugh she'd ever heard.

"Unless I miss my guess, Miss Abigail, you're swathed in white cotton down to your wrists, up to your ears, and down again to your heels. Am I right?"

"Mr. Cameron!"

"Yes ma'am," he drawled, "yes ma'am, you can come in. You're safe from me." Naturally he sat there leaning against the head of the bed, watching her boldly as she gathered up fresh clothing for the day. She saw his smile from the corner of her eye, and once he had the audacity to ask, "What's that?" She tucked the undergarment out of sight, assuring herself that she would not again forget to get her things out of here while he was sleeping.

"The leg feels fine today," he said conversationally, "and so does the hand. The only thing that hurts is my stomach after the liver you flushed it out with last night. I'm so hungry I could eat a horse and chase the rider!"

She almost laughed out loud. Sometimes it happened so easily that she couldn't control herself, for usually she did not want to be amused by him. But now she replied, "If I see any coming this way, I'll be sure to warn them off. I somehow don't doubt that you'd do it!"

"Feisty this morning, Miss Abigail?"

"I might ask you the same thing, Mr. Cameron," she rejoined, making for the door with her cumulate riggings.

"Abbie?" The shortened name brought her up short.

"*Miss* Abigail," she corrected, raising her chin and turning toward him.

And it was then that she saw the gun.

It was black, oiled, sleek, and he held it loosely in his left hand. She had not the slightest doubt that he could use it accurately at this range, left-handed or not.

All he said was "Abbie" again, reiterating much more than the name. There followed a vast silence while he let the significance of the gun and the short-ened name sink in. Then he said in a casual, mellow voice, "You know, I am feeling a bit feisty this morning after all." A sinister half smile played upon his generous lips, beneath the shadowed skin to which she'd once taken a blade.

She stared at that lip, then back at the gun as he hefted it in his hand carelessly, making her clutch the articles of clothing tightly against her chest.

"Wh . . . where did you get that . . . that thing?" she asked in a quiver-ing voice, her eyes riveted to it.

"I'm a train robber, am I not? How can I rob trains without a gun?"

"B . . . but where did you get it?"

"Never mind that now." But there was little else she could mind. Her eyes were like moons while he took perverse pleasure in the fearful way she gawked at it.

"Abbie?" he repeated. She didn't move, just gaped at the gun while he used the end of it to point at the floor at her feet.

"Drop the duds," he ordered, almost mildly.

"Th . . . the duds?" she choked.

"The ones in your arms." It took some time before the words seemed to get through to her. When they did, she released the clothes in slow motion, letting sleeves, stockings, underwear trail regrettably down to the floor at her bare feet.

"Come here," he ordered quietly. She swallowed but didn't budge. "I said come here," he repeated, lifting the pistol now to point it directly at her, and she began slowly inching around the foot of the bed.

"What did I do?" she managed to squeak.

"Nothing . . . yet." His left eyebrow arched provocatively. "But the day is young."

"Why are you doing this?"

"I'm going to teach you a couple of lessons today." Her eyes, like a cornered rabbit's, didn't even blink. "Do you know what I'm going to teach you?" he asked, and her head moved dumbly on her neck. "Number one . . ." he went on, "I'm going to teach you never to shave the moustache off an unsuspecting outlaw. I said come here and I meant it." She moved nearer but still not near enough for him to reach from where he sat leaning leisurely against the brass headboard. He swung the pistol slowly her way.

"Here," he ordered, pointing with it to the floor directly beside him.

"Wh . . . why are you threatening me?"

"Have I made any threats?"

"The gun is a threat, Mr. Cameron!"

"Jesse!" he spit suddenly, and she jumped. "Call me Jesse!"

"Jesse," she repeated meekly.

"That's better." Once again his voice went quiet, almost silky. "Lesson number two, Abbie, is what happens when you wheedle an apology out of a man then use it to slap him in the face with."

"I did not wheed—"

"You wheedled, Abbie, you wheedled," he wheedled. "You got me to the point where I was actually sorry I'd made old Melcher run off like a scared chipmunk. Did you know you got me to that point, Abbie?"

She shook her head, staring blindly.

"And when I apologized, what did you say?"

"I don't remember."

"I mean to make you remember, Abbie, so you'll never do it again."

"I won't," she promised, "just put your gun away."

"I will . . . after I've taught you your lesson. What you said was that my apology should make *me* feel good, only it didn't . . . because you wouldn't let it. But I aim to feel good—real good, real soon."

She clutched her arms tightly over her breasts, gripping the sleeves of her batiste nightgown.

"Put your arms down, Abbie." She stared into his black, amused eyes, unable to make her muscles move.

"What?" she gulped.

"You heard me." At last she did as ordered, but again in slow motion. "Since I scared Melcher away and you declined to accept my apology for it, I figured the least I could do is make up for what you missed, huh?"

Here it comes, she thought in panic, and her eyes slid closed while she quaked all over.

"But I'm stuck in this bed, so you'll have to come to me, Abbie . . . come on." He made a beckoning motion with the tip of the gun. When she stood directly beside and above him, he pointed the pistol at her, not even looking up as he did so. "You were so all-fired breathless with Melcher, there were times when I heard you heart pitty-patting clear in here. But if old Melcher had any spine, he'd have hung around at least for a little billing and cooing. You know what I mean? Since the big, bad train robber chased him off, the least he can do now is stand in for old Melcher, right?" When she only stood quaking, saying nothing, his silky voice continued. "I know you get the picture, Abbie, so kiss me. I'm waiting."

"No . . . no. I won't," she answered, wondering where she got the air to speak—her chest felt crushed by fear. He moved the pistol then and even through her nightie she could feel the cold metal barrel against her hip. He still didn't even look up, just nudged her hip with the gun. She slowly leaned over and, with eyes wide open, touched his lips quickly with hers.

"You call that a kiss?" he scoffed when she jumped away again. "That felt like some dry, old lizard whipping her tail across my lips. Try it again, like you would if I were Melcher."

"Why are you doing this—" she began, but he cut her off.

"Again, Abbie! And shut your eyes this time. Only a lizard keeps her eyes open while she's kissing."

She lowered her face to his, seeing his black, amused eyes close before her as she dropped her eyelids and kissed him again. The new growth of moustache was like the stem of a wild rose bush.

"Getting better," he said when she again leaped away. "Now give me some tongue."

"Dear God . . ." she moaned, mortified.

"He's not going to help you now, Abbie, so get down here and do as I say."

"Please . . ." she whispered.

"Please, Jesse!" he corrected.

"Please, Jesse . . . I've never . . . I haven't . . ."

"Quit stalling and get to it," he ordered. "And sit down here. I'm getting dizzy watching you bounce up and down."

With her insides trembling, she sat down gingerly on the edge of the bed, hating every black whisker that shadowed his skin, every hair that surrounded his hatefully handsome face.

"What is it you want of me? Please get it over with," she begged.

"I want a responsive, wet female kiss out of you. Haven't you ever kissed a man before, Abbie? I have nothing but time while you practice. What are you afraid of?" When her eyes refused to lower to the gun at her side, he chuckled. "Let's get back to the lesson at hand. You were going to give me some tongue. It's called french kissing and everybody does it that way, probably even lizards." He lounged there insolently, and when she sat stiffly he had to put the gun to her again, this time beneath her right jaw. "Wet!" was all he said, then cocked the gun, making her jump at the metallic click.

She closed her eyes and resigned herself. He didn't quite close his, saw hers pinched tightly shut beneath woven eyebrows, saw her brows twitch as the tip of her tongue touched his upper lip and his tongue came out to meet it. Against her lips he said, "Relax, Abbie," and he lowered the gun and put an arm around her shoulders, pulling her against his bare chest, turning his mouth sideways on hers. "Put your arms around me," he said as he felt her elbows digging against him in resistance. "Come on, Abbie, unless you want to be here all day." And one of her arms crept up around his neck, the other around his bare side. She felt the gun, still in the hand which he used to press the back of her head, forcing their mouths so tightly together. His lips opened farther; the inside of his mouth was hot. He pushed his tongue into the secret crevices of her mouth, withdrew it again, then lightly bit her tongue making her fearfully push against his chest. But he somehow wrestled her arms away, pulling her against him, squashing her breasts flat against his skin, combating her every move while his mouth retained its hold on hers. He broke away then, sliding his lips down, taking her lower lip gently between his teeth. "Jesse!" he ordered in a fierce whisper, ". . . say it."

"Jesse," she whimpered before his mouth slid onto hers again, warm and wet and melting some of her resistance.

"Jesse . . . again," he demanded, feeling her thundering heartbeat through the thin batiste nightgown upon his chest.

"Jesse," she whispered while he rubbed the back of her neck with his fingers and the butt of the gun: warm and cold together. Then he silenced the word again, kissing her with that same intercourse of tongues as before, compounding fear and delight, sensuality and shame, refusal and acceptance all within her confused body.

"Ab . . ." he whispered then, "Ab . . ." Her lips were free to correct him but the thought never entered her head, for some strange languor had befallen her. Then, using his hands and mouth, he pushed her abruptly away, stunning her by asking, "Did it tickle that time?"

She could not look at him. Her head hung down and she felt suddenly filthy, violated in some way she could not comprehend. Not by him but by herself, because she'd stopped fighting him sometime while his tongue moved within her mouth, because she'd begun liking the wet, warm touch of it, the feel of his broad, muscled shoulders beneath her hand, her racing heart upon his chest.

"Today's lesson is over," he said dismissingly, the satisfied smile once again about his eyes. "I told you, when I set out to get even you'd know it."

"And I told you that force is not strength. Gentleness is strength."

"Force is damn effective, though, isn't it, Abbie?"

Once free of him, off the bed, her courage returned. "I want you out of here, do you hear? Immediately!"

"Don't forget who holds the gun, Abbie. Besides, I can't walk yet. What reason will you give all your inquisitive neighbors when they ask why you threw a helpless man out of your house? Will you tell them it was because he taught you how to kiss properly?"

"They won't ask. None of them was willing to take you in in the first place. They won't find fault with me for putting you out now."

"I've been meaning to talk to you about that, Abbie. Doc Dougherty said you were the only who stood up and spoke for me out of this whole town. I've been meaning to thank you for that."

His words brought her blood to the boiling point. Oh, the nerve of the conceited fool to sit there thanking her after what he'd just done! "Your thanks are not essential, nor are they wanted anymore. The railroad is paying me to keep you until they can get their hands on you. It's all the thanks I need!"

He reared back and laughed. "Have you thought of why they want me, Abbie?" he asked, with a knowing look in his eyes.

"What a question from a *train robber!*" She longed to smack the disgusting smirk from his face. "I shall go to the depot today and wire whomever it is that wants you next to come and get you! The railroad can have you, wound, moustache, and all!"

"You'll miss the money you could make off me during my recuperation."

"I will miss nothing of you, you filthy, conceited goat!" she all but shrieked.

"Enough!" he suddenly roared. "Get out of here and get yourself dressed and make me some breakfast before I decide to get even with you for feeding me that liver last night. How long can a man live without decent food?"

She stomped to the pile of clothing at the foot of his bed, flailing the air with each piece before hooking it in the crook of an arm and stamping her way out. Her lips were pursed so tightly that her teeth were dry from sucking wind. When she was gone, Jesse's head arched back and his body bounced with great gasps of silent laughter. Then he dug his dirty shirt out from under the sheet near his feet, wrapped the empty gun in it, and put it back under the mattress.

She had absolutely no intention of cooking him one morsel of food. She made a fire, bathed, dressed, and all the while he periodically bellyached for his breakfast.

"What the hell's taking you so long out there?"

"I'm starving, woman!"

"Where's my food?"

She kept her eye on the clock, anxious for it to reach a proper hour so she could go over town and send the wire. But in the midst of her extreme pleasure in starving the goat in the other room, he informed her, "I don't smell anything cooking out there. I have this gun trained at the wall where I think you are. Should I try for a lucky shot?"

His answer was the loud, tinny whack of a kettle as she smacked it onto the range. She'd fill him up to shut him up, but she'd be blinkered if she'd feed him anything remotely delectable! Cornmeal was the fastest, cheapest, least appetizing thing she could think of. He kept up the needling while she cooked.

"What are you doing now, butchering the hog for bacon? . . . I smell something cooking. What is it? . . . If you're thinking of wasting time bringing me the pitcher and bowl, forget it, unless they're filled with food. A man could starve here and go unnoticed while he's doing it!"

On and on he yammered until by the time she took his tray in she was livid.

"Ah, I see you heard me at last," he said, with a stupid grin on his face. She looked for the gun but it was nowhere in sight.

"The people clear over town heard, I'm sure."

"Good! Maybe somebody will take pity on me and bring me some hardtack and jerky to store under my mattress. It would sure beat the cooking around here—not to mention the service. You didn't bring me any more of your slimy eggs, did you?"

"You are insufferable! Despicable!" she spit venomously.

He only smiled broader than before. "You too, Miss Abigail, you too." He sounded downright jovial. "Now stand back and let me at this Epicurean delight of the week. Ahhh, cornmeal. Takes a skilled hand to make cornmeal."

The only thing she could think of at the moment was, "Even animals wash before they eat."

"Oh yeah? Name me one," he said through a mouthful of cornmeal. She looked aside in distaste.

"A raccoon."

"Coons wash their food, not their faces. Besides, they can afford the time. Nobody makes them throw up then leaves them to starve all night."

It was beyond her why she spoke to him at all. But just once she'd like to get the best of him. But there was no dealing with a swine. Irritated, she flounced out. In a ridiculously short time he called for more cornmeal mush.

"I could use another bowl of that Epicurean cornmeal," he informed her loudly. She took the kettle right in there and plopped a now-cold gob of the stuff in his bowl. It had, in the ensuing time, acquired the look and texture of dried adobe.

"When you get rid of me, why don't you get a job slinging hash?" He grinned devilishly. "You've got a real knack for it." He chopped the cornmeal brick into smaller pellets that sat like islands sticking out of the lake of cream he poured over them. As she turned on her heel, he was smiling crookedly and digging in again.

Why in the world did I ever think that taking care of him would be preferable to "slinging hash" at Louis Culpepper's, she wondered. I would work for Louis now . . . and gladly . . . if only I could!

By the time he'd filled that empty leg of his he'd cleaned up enough cornmeal to stuff a flock of geese. All he said by way of appreciation was, "We could use you in camp, Abbie." It crossed her mind that any woman foolish enough to be found in a bandit's camp would undoubtedly find herself used, all right!

Next he raised his voice and shouted, "What does a man have to do to get a pot of hot water around here? I need to wash up and shave. Do you hear me, Abbie?"

She had no source of comparison by which to measure the man's capacity for being overbearing and rude, but surely he must set the world's record, she thought. She delivered the water and as stinging an insult as she could manage. "Wash yourself . . . if you've ever learned how!"

He only laughed and observed, "Witty little chit this morning, aren't you?"

He made a real sideshow out of his washing. Even from the kitchen she knew every single thing he was doing. He sang out loud, splashed, exclaimed how good this felt, and that felt. It was disgusting. She had no idea how he was coping with one hand, but she didn't care. Several times she became angrier because he almost made her smile. Finally he called, "I'm as fresh as a blinkin' nasturtium. Come and smell!"

Even in the kitchen she blushed. Never in her life had she been so worked up. He had to threaten her with the gun again to get her to bring the shaving gear. When she carried it in, she cast her eyes down her nose at an angle suggesting that perhaps she was trying to outstare a fly on its end. "Shall we proceed?" she asked acidly. Half expecting him to be buck naked, she was at least relieved to see he'd covered himself with the sheet.

"We?"

She stood with strained patience, awaiting his newest objection, wishing she could take the blade and scrape every hair off his entire head.

Maybe the look in her eye told him to beware, for he finally said, "Keep away from my beard, woman. You made me wash up by myself—just why so anxious to help me shave? As if I didn't know. I've got one and a half good hands and I can sit up now. I'll manage without your help." Then, as she turned to leave, he added, ". . . Delila."

Her back stiffened, and he began his shave. He was damned if he was going to let her near his moustache again after what he'd done to her this morning. He smiled, remembering it. But shaving turned out to be more difficult than he'd planned, being only slightly better than one-handed. The mirror was one of hers. Damn female gizmo! he thought. He tried to hold the long handle between his knees while he pulled at one cheek, used the other hand to work the blade, but the useless thing slipped down or turned sideways, refusing to stay where he wanted it. He finally gave up in frustration and called, "Miss Abigail, I can't manage the mirror. Come and hold it for me." She only began singing as if she hadn't heard a word he said. But his voice was deep and strong again, and there was no way it could be missed. "Did somebody step on a cat's tail out there? Seems I have to shout to be heard above the caterwauling! Come and hold the mirror!"

"You have one and a half good hands and can sit up again. Hold it yourself!" She listened, heard him sigh disgustedly. Then—lo and behold!—out came the magic word.

"Please?" That brought an enormous smile to Miss Abigail's lips.

"I'm sorry, did you say something, Mr. Cameron?" she called, the smile growing wider.

"I said please, and you know damn well I did, so quit basking in self-righteousness and get in here."

"I'm coming," she sang. She was fast learning what exquisite joy it could be to be snide. From the doorway she said pleasantly, "How can I refuse a man with such sterling manners?" She eyed his foamy face, which spoke for itself. "What would you have me do?" His eyes, like chunks of coal in a snowman, were stark and snapping.

"Just hold the damn mirror, Your Highness!"

Taking it, she noted, "You're obviously in more than one kind of a lather. If you'd like, I'll shave it for you. My hand is undoubtedly steadier anyway—see the way you're shaking?" He ignored her and peered at himself sideways in the mirror, scraping a cheek, circumscribing a black, thick sideburn, outlining one side of his precious moustache.

She raised a little finger. "Ah, be careful of the moustache," she warned, watching the lather come away black-speckled while his scowl was revealed beneath it.

"Just hold the thing still so I can see." He drew his top lip down, curling it against his teeth, shaping the moustache. "It's damn hard to follow . . . a shape . . . that isn't there anymore."

"I think you should have etched it a bit more deeply along this side," she advised, lowering her brows as if seriously studying the fault.

"Damnit, Abigail, shut up! You were easier to put up with before you found your sense of humor. You moved the mirror again!"

"Oops, sorry." She settled back and watched him finish. It was surprisingly enjoyable. Amazing, she thought, how fast the man's beard grows. When he finished his shave, the moustache stood out blackly again. Funny thing, she thought, but the fool actually looks better with it.

"Intriguing?" he asked. She jumped, abashed at being caught regarding him that way. "You can feel it any time you want. The pleasure will be mine."

"I'd as soon feel the whiskers of a billy goat!" she snapped.

"You're excused," he laughed, as she headed for the door. On second thought, added, "But just be good."

It seemed to take forever until it was late enough to go over town while she wondered just what "be good" meant. Would he try to stop her with that gun again? She tiptoed to the back door, knowing she could not cross the open bedroom doorway without being seen. But the spring gave her away, and his voice told her he knew exactly what she was up to.

"While you're gone, see if they have any meat in this town besides liver, will you? Nobody's going to come for me tomorrow. It's Sunday."

She gave into some deep, deep need and slammed the screen door until it whacked against the frame and bounced halfway open again before settling shut. Naturally he laughed.

Chapter 8

"I CAN'T SEND no such wire on your say-so," Max insisted.

"Why ever not?" Miss Abigail bristled.

"Got to be the sheriff does 'at," Max said importantly. "You go over and see Sam about it, then he'll send the wire. He knows who's the right person to send it to anyways. I don't."

Stymied, Miss Abigail stood, stiff-backed and upset, at a loss now. She didn't want to traipse all over town letting the entire citizenry know she was anxious to have that man out of her house. What rankled was that he was partially right. She was afraid that if she ran all over saying "I want him out," people would wonder why. And then what would she say? That he'd drawn a gun on her and made her kiss him? No power on earth could make her confess such a thing. Could she say he drew a gun on her to make her fix him his breakfast? Hardly. After all, she was being paid by the railroad to do those things for him. How would it look if she admitted she'd tried to starve him out of her house? What if she said he'd forced her at gunpoint to help him shave? The implications became worse all the time. Oh, why did that fool Maxwell Smith have to get all uppity with her? One quiet telegram is all it would have taken. Against her better judgment she went to Sheriff Samuel Harris next.

"Sorry, Miss Abigail," Sheriff Harris said. "Got to have a release from Doc Dougherty first. It's the law. Any prisoner under a doctor's care has got to be released officially by the doc before he can be transferred from one jail to the next—oh, begging your pardon ma'am, that's not to say your house is a jail. You know what I mean, Miss Abigail."

"Yes, of course, Mr. Harris," she condescended. "I shall speak to Doctor Dougherty then."

But Doc Dougherty wasn't home, so she went back to Main Street again, headed for the butcher shop, thoroughly disgusted now.

"Howdy, Miss Abigail," Bill Tilden greeted, coming out of his barbershop.

"Good day, Mr. Tilden."

"Hot, ain't it?" he observed, glancing at her unhatted hair. She nodded briskly, moving on. "Going over to Culpepper's for dinner," he called after her conversationally just as Frank Adney hung up his sign next door that said OUT TO LUNCH.

"How do, Miss Abigail," he greeted.

"Mr. Adney," she acknowledged.

"Some scorcher, huh?

"Indeed." She headed on up the boardwalk thinking how limited the range of conversation was in Stuart's Junction. Behind her, Bill Tilden asked Frank Adney, "You ever seen Miss Abigail uptown without her hat and gloves before?"

"Come to think of it, I ain't."

"Well, wonders never cease!" they turned to watch Miss Abigail as she entered the door of Porter's Meat Market, shaking their heads in disbelief.

"Howdy, Miss Abigail," Gabe Porter said.

"Good day, Mr. Porter."

"Heard tell you took in that train robber up to your house."

"Indeed?"

Gabe stood with his ham-sized arms crossed over his mammoth, aproned stomach, the flies buzzing around the blood stains there, one occasionally landing on the fly paper that hung coiled from the ceiling. "Shucks, everybody knows about it. He ain't giving you no trouble, now, is he?"

"No, he's not, Mr. Porter."

"Heard 'at other city dude cleared out on the train yesterday, huh?"

"Yes, he did."

"Ain't it a little risky, you bein' up there all alone with 'at other one?"

"Do I look as if I'm in jeopardy, Mr. Porter?"

"No, no indeed you don't, Miss Abigail. Folks is just wonderin' is all."

"Well, folks may cease their wondering, Mr. Porter. The gravest danger I'm in is that of being eaten out of house and home."

Then Gabe jumped, realizing she was waiting to buy some meat. "Ah . . . right! And what'll it be today?"

"How are your pork chops today? Are they fresh and lean?"

"Oh both, ma'am. Fresh cut today and kept on ice for as long as I can keep it from melting."

"Very well, Mr. Porter. I shall have three of them."

"Yup, coming right up!"

"On second thought, perhaps I shall need four—no, five."

"Five? These ain't gonna keep till tomorrow, Miss Abigail, even down the well."

"I nevertheless shall take five, and a length of smoked sausage, oh, say— this long." She held up her palms six inches apart, then lengthened the span to ten or so and said, "No, this long."

"What in Hades you feedin' up there, Miss Abigail, a gorilla?"

It was all she could do to keep from replying, "Exactly!" Instead she thrust poor Gabe into total dismay by requesting, "I should like one pig's bladder added to my order."

"One . . . pig's bladder, Miss Abigail?" Gabe asked, bug-eyed.

"You just butchered, did you not? Where are the entrails?"

"Oh, I got 'em. I mean, they ain't been buried yet, but what—"

"Just wrap up one bladder, if you please," she ordered imperiously, and he finally gave up and did as she requested. When she was gone Gabe muttered to the flies, ". . . a pig's bladder . . . now what in the hell is she gonna do with that?"

When Miss Abigail reached her house again there were fresh buggy tracks in the fine, dry dust out front, and she realized she'd missed Doctor Dougherty again. What dismal luck to have missed him when she needed his help to get that man out of here.

In her customary way, she stopped to peak at her reflection in the mirror of the umbrella stand. There was no hat to remove, so she smoothed her hair, her sleeves, her waistband, then quickly tested the tautness of the skin beneath her chin with the back of her hand.

"Is it firm?" a deep voice asked, and she whirled and jumped a foot off the floor, pressing a hand to her heart.

"What are you doing up?" He was standing just this side of the kitchen archway, leaning on crutches, his dark chest, calves, and feet sticking out of a sheet he had wound around himself.

"I asked first," he said.

"What?" All she could think of was, what if that sheet dropped off!

"Is it firm? It should be, the way you point that saucy little chin at the ceiling all the time." As if to verify it, up went her chin.

"If you are up, you are strong enough to get out of here. How heartening!"

"Doc brought me the crutches and I needed to go out back after he left, so I decided to give it a go. But I'm not as strong as I thought."

"You traipsed clear across the backyard dressed in that sheet?" she gasped. "What if someone saw you?"

"What if they did?"

"I have a reputation to uphold, sir!"

"Don't flatter yourself, Miss Abigail," he smirked. She stood there with the blood cascading into her face, until even her ears felt hot. "You know, I'm getting a bit lightheaded," he said.

"Lightheaded? Don't you dare pass out wrapped in that sheet! Get back into bed, do you hear? I should never be able to budge you if you collapsed on the floor!"

He stumped his way across the far end of the parlor and all went well until he came to a hooked rug that lay in the bedroom doorway. One crutch caught in it and he began to waver. She hurried across, grabbed him around his middle to keep him from tipping over, and when he was steadied, went down on one knee to remove the rug. But the crutch was still planted on it, holding it down. "I can't pick it up. Can you move the crutch?" she asked, looking up the long length of him. It was a long, long way indeed to the top of that length, and she warned, "Mr. Cameron, if you tip over on top of me I'll never forgive you."

"There'd be nothing left to forgive with. You'd be one . . . squashed . . . hummingbird." He swayed against the doorjamb as one crutch crashed to the floor.

"Quickly, get to bed," she ordered, taking his arm over her shoulders. He was as tall as a barn door and nearly as broad at the shoulders, but they made it to the bed all right and sat down on the edge side by side. She quickly unwound his arm from her shoulder and rose.

"I'll thank you to use some common sense from now on. First of all, if you intend to parade around, you shall do so in pajamas and a robe. Secondly, you shall tend to necessities and not stand around yammering while you make a hazard of your big self in my house. If a . . . a gorilla like you ever fell, how would I ever get you up?"

In spite of his haziness, he asked, "Did you send your telegram, Miss Abigail?"

"Yes!" she lied, "and they cannot come too soon to get you off my hands."

"If you want to get rid of me, you'd better start feeding me better. I'm as weak as a mosquito. Did you buy some decent meat?"

"Yes! I bought something perfectly suited to you!"

He awakened from a dream that there was rain spattering on the canvas of his tent, but it was the pork chops splattering away on top of Miss Abigail's kitchen range. He stretched, feeling the skin of his right leg tight but healing and hurting less all the time. Something smelled so good his stomach lurched over, his mouth salivated, and a rumble sounded somewhere deep inside of him. By the time she brought the tray in he was ravenous.

"Mmm . . . it smells like pork chops. Is it some real meat at last?" He brightened as she set the tray on his lap. She had even considerately covered the plate with an upturned bowl to keep it hot.

"Yes, real meat," she confirmed, all smiles.

"Could it be you have a heart after all?"

"Decide for yourself," she replied saucily as the bowl came up in her hands, revealing the raw pig's bladder. She simply had to stay long enough to see the expression on his face. It was a black, shaking visage of anger while a spate of filth poured from him. At some time while he cursed, he asked what the hell it was on the plate.

"Real meat. Isn't that what you wanted?" she asked innocently, enjoying every minute of this. "As a matter of fact, it is pork. A pig's bladder . . . simply perfect for a goat like you."

He glared at her venomously and roared, "I smell pork chops, Abbie! Don't tell me I don't! Now do I get some or do I walk uptown in my sheet and tell them that the hussy Abigail McKenzie refuses to feed me as she's being paid to?"

She was in a fine fury, little fists clenched into tight balls, eyes bright with vindication as she stamped her foot.

"It is *my* turn to teach *you* a lesson, *sir!* I have pork chops, potatoes, gravy, vegetables, everything to sate your fool appetite and get you strong and out of here. All I want from you in return is some decent treatment. You give me that filthy gun!"

"Bring me my pork chops!" he shouted, glowering at her.

"Give me the gun!"

"Like hell I will!"

"Then you shan't have pork chops!" But the gun appeared so quickly she'd have sworn it was there in his hand all the time. It shut her up like a sprung trap.

"Give . . . me . . . my . . . pork . . . chops," he growled.

She stammered, "Keep th . . . that filthy thing out of m . . . my sight!"

"I'll put it away when you bring me the pork chops you're being paid to give me!"

"Please!" she bellowed now.

"PLEASE!" he bellowed back.

Then silence crashed around them, and for one self-conscious moment they both felt foolish, glaring at each other that way.

He got his pork chops all right. And by that time, Miss Abigail was in a state! She admitted that it was a blame good thing tomorrow was Sunday. She was definitely in need of divine guidance after all the transgressions she'd been committing lately. Anger, spite, vengeance, lying, even promiscuity. Yes, she even admitted that what had happened during that kiss had been undeniably promiscuous—well, it had ended that way, anyway. But if she was guilty of all this, think of what he had to ask forgiveness for—not that he ever would. Besides his own, he'd caused every single one of her sins!

The pig's bladder had mysteriously disappeared. She didn't know where it had gone and didn't ask. Being the goat that he is, she thought, he probably ate the thing and enjoyed every bite!

"I've brought you some bed clothes of my father's. Put them on and leave them on. I'm sick and tired of looking at your hairy legs and chest."

"So you say." He puffed out the chest in question and rubbed its furred surface as if it were spun gold. She ignored his conceit, moving away, but then she spied the bladder soaking in the water bowl. She reached two fingers in to pick up the smelly thing and take it away, but he ordered, "Leave it where it is."

"What!"

"I said leave it where is it."

"But it stinks!" She made a face at the offensive innard which had left a residue of scum on the surface of the water.

"Leave it!" he repeated, "and leave the pajamas and get out."

She dropped the gut back in its swampy water and left, thankfully.

It was Saturday afternoon and she spent it cleaning the house for Sunday, as she'd done all her life. When she had cleaned everything else, she came near the door to his room, calling first, "Are you decent now, Mr. Cameron?"

"Does a snake have armpits?" came the reply.

She grabbed her cheeks to keep from laughing. How could that infernal man make her laugh so easily when she was thoroughly disgusted with him?

"I'm covered, if that's what you're asking, but I'll never be decent, hopefully."

She took one look at him and had to work diligently to prevent her face from smiling again. He looked utterly ridiculous. The pajama legs stopped halfway down his hairy calves.

"Well, what are you smirking at?" he grumbled.

"Nothing."

"The hell you say. Keep it up and I'll take these idiotic things off. I feel like a damn coolie in them anyway . . . or at least I would if they were long enough. Your old man must've been a midget!"

"They'll just have to do. I have none that are longer." But in spite of herself she stood there smiling openly now at the hairy calves and feet sticking out of the drawers.

"All right! Get to your cleaning if that's what you came in here for because if you stand there smirking one minute longer I'll take these damn things off!"

"You have the vilest tongue of any man I've ever known. I'm tempted to fix it with the cattail again."

"Just get on with the cleaning and quit hassling me."

Their constant bickering had come to have a pattern. When they were angry their tongues cut sharp and deep with words they seldom meant. And when it went too far they reverted to sarcasm or teasing, scrimmaging verbally in a way which even Miss Abigail had come to enjoy. Cleaning the room, she felt his eyes on her all the while. He moved to the window seat while she changed his sheets and dustmopped under the bed. Kneeling, she saw his boots pushed deeply beneath it, and the lump of what must be his shirt with the gun wrapped in it, between the mattress and the open wire spring. The only way it could have gotten there was if Doc Dougherty had brought it to him, but she couldn't believe the man's idiocy to do such a thing. She didn't mention the gun again, but made as if she hadn't seen it there, then went on to her featherdusting, and finally to clean the tabletop where the pitcher and bowl sat.

"May I ask what you propose to keep this filthy thing for?" She looked distastefully at the bladder.

"Never mind," was all he'd say. "Just leave it."

Supper passed uneventfully, except that he let her know he hated those bloody-looking beets.

The bladder still lay in the bowl. And a plan was forming in Miss Abigail's head.

Evening came and Jesse grew bored and listless. It was funny how he'd grown used to her coming and going. The minute it grew quiet and he was left alone, he almost wished she'd come in, even if only to argue. Like a child who's fought with a playmate, he found he preferred her aggravation to her absence. He heard her making a lot of watery noises and got up with the crutches and came to find her leaning over the back step, washing her hair. He opened the screen door and tapped it against her head twice, softly, just enough to vex her. "This is a hell of a place to wash your hair. You're directly in the path between bedroom and outhouse."

"Get that screen door off my head!" she exclaimed from under her sopping hair. "I'll wash my hair anywhere I like. It just so happens I do it here because it makes less mess to clean up than in the kitchen."

He stood looking down at her, kneeling on the earth with her head over the basin. The hollow at the nape of her neck held some soap suds, and he found it hard to take his eyes off it. He opened the screen door enough to get out, causing her to sidestep on her knees. She felt vulnerable, knowing he stood above her, watching her.

The way he stood, right foot hanging conveniently before him, it was easy to reach out and put his big toe right there in that little hollow that held the shampoo captive at the back of her neck.

"Getting rid of all the nasty *effuvia* so you're all polished and shined for church tomorrow?" he teased, using the pretentious word she'd once used on him. She swatted blindly at the foot, but he'd swung on down the yard, wearing only those short pajama pants, calling back, "Whose redemption are you going to pray for, Miss Abigail, yours or mine?"

And from the yard next door Rob Nelson heard and saw it all and ran into his house, hollering, "Maw! Maw! Guess what I just seen!"

She was gone, pan and all, when he came back to the house. He felt weak again and went straight to his bed, making up his mind that he must continue to work up his strength by staying up longer each time with the crutches. He sank down on the edge of the bed and ran a hand through his hair. It itched. In spite of his teasing, that shampoo had looked mighty inviting.

"Miss Abigail?" he called, but the house was quiet. "Can you hear me?" No answer.

"Don't I get a shampoo?"

There still was no answer but he heard a floorboard creak above him.

"Hey, I could use one myself, you know." He didn't really expect an answer, neither was she about to give one. To himself, he said, "She keeps typical old maid's hours. Closeted in her bedroom before eight o'clock on a Saturday night." He was bored to death and wished she'd come down and keep him company. If she could just hold that sharp tongue of hers, he'd try to do the same, just for somebody to talk to for a while. The sounds of light revelry drifted from the direction of town, and he longed for a beer and a little company, maybe even a woman on his knee.

Miss Abigail was drying her hair at an open upstairs window, fluffing it with a thick towel, wondering when she would find her first gray hair. He called something again, but she ignored him, thinking of how he'd touched the back of her neck with his toe, secretly smiling. He could be so exasperating and so funny at the same time. She thought of what she'd wear for church in the morning; this time she'd gathered all her things from his room. She thought of the gun beneath his bed. She thought of his kiss, but pushed the thought aside because it did funny things to her stomach. The air was so still you could hear every sound from the saloon, but then it was nearly July and the summer heat did that. How many Saturday nights had she washed her hair and combed it dry, gone to bed early, and wished to be doing something else? Something with a man. Now she was thrown together with a man who might have been company had he not turned out to be the height of loath-someness. How much longer would she be stuck with him? She heard him call, saying he wanted a shampoo too. Nonsense! He couldn't stand up long enough to have his hair washed. How many days had it been since he'd had his hair washed? Nine? Ten? She remembered how she'd promised when he was unconscious that she'd wash it for him. She was stuck with him until the railroad took him off her hands. At least if he was clean he would be that much less offensive, she told herself, not wanting to admit that she was lonely, that even his company was preferable to none.

When she stepped into his room and saw what he held, she asked in disgust, "Whatever are you doing with that vile thing?"

The pig bladder was scraped clean, blown up, and tied with yarn from her sewing basket. He clenched it in his right hand, squeezing repeatedly, then relaxing time and again. The action was as suggestive as the licking of lips, and he smiled as he drawled, "Exercising my *gun* hand."

Mortified, her eyes could not seem to leave the dark, supple fingers as they squeezed, squeezed, squeezed. Her lips fell open and her stomach went light and fluttery. Should she turn and escape? And let him have the satisfaction of humiliating her once again? Though her cheeks blazed, she ordered, "Put that horrible thing away if you want me to help you with your hair."

He gave it several more slow, suggestive squeezes before tossing it aside negligently, with that same knowing smile on his lips. Well, well, he thought, the queen descendeth! And in her nightie and wrapper, no less!

"You're too weak to stand or lean over long enough to shampoo your hair with water, so I'll give you the next best thing, an oatmeal shampoo. It's not as fragrant, but it works."

"No offense, Abbie, but do you know what you're doing?"

"Precisely, but you'll have to lie down."

"Oatmeal?" he asked skeptically, making no move to lie down yet.

"Exactly," she said crisply. "Do you want the dry treatment or none at all?" Too late she realized what she'd said. The smile was already sneaking around the outer edges of his eyes, and by the time it made it to his lips she was the color of cinnamon.

He stretched out full length and drawled, "By all means, give it to me dry."

Flustered beyond belief, she fussed with her bowl of dry oatmeal, a towel, and three clothespins while he eyed them inquisitively. "The towel goes *under* your head," she said testily, as if he were truly a dolt.

"Oh yes, how stupid of me." He grinned, lifting his head while she arranged the towel under it. Then, to his amazement, she dumped half of the bowl of oatmeal on his hair and started working it in as if it were soap and water.

"Serves double duty, huh?" he quipped. "Tomorrow you can cook it for my breakfast instead of cornmeal." She was caught unaware and let out a huff of laughter while he peeked up at her prankishly. Finally he shut his eyes and let himself enjoy the feeling of her hands in his hair—a Saturday night feeling remembered from childhood. He believed he could nearly smell the fresh shoe blacking on all the shoes of his sisters and brothers, lined up at the bottom of the stairs awaiting Sunday morning. How long since he'd been in a house where Saturday was set aside for those get-ready things?

"Up!" she ordered, interrupting his reverie. "I must shake this. Hold still till I come back." She took the towel gingerly by its four corners and went away with the soiled oatmeal. She repeated the process once again, only this time when she had the clean oatmeal in his hair, she bound the towel up turban-style and secured it with the clothespins. "The oatmeal will absorb the oils. We'll leave it on for a while," she said, and went to the bowl to wash her own hands. But the water was still there from the pig bladder. With a grimace she took it away to dump.

When she returned, he was exercising his hand with that *thing* again, but he invited, "Stay while I soak."

She glanced at the flexing hand, back up at him skeptically.

"What can I do bound up like a sheik with the fleas?" he asked, rolling his eyes upward. Unconsciously she tightened the ends of her tie belt that held the wrapper. Finally, he tossed the thing aside and said cajolingly, "Hey, it's Saturday night, Abbie, the social hour . . . remember? I've been in this bed for almost two weeks now and, truthfully, I'm getting a little stir crazy. All I want is a little talk."

She sighed and perched on the trunk at the foot of the bed. "If you're growing restless you must be healing."

"I'm not used to sitting still for so long."

"What are you used to?" She wasn't really sure if she wanted any sordid details about his robber's life, yet the prospect of hearing about it was strangely alluring. He, meanwhile, was wondering whether she'd believe him if he told her the truth.

"I'm not used to a place like this, that's for sure, or spending time with a woman like you. I travel around a lot."

"Yes, I supposed you did, in your occupation. Doesn't it grow tiresome?"

"Sometimes, but I have to do it, so I do."

She looked him dead in the eye—Miss Goody Twoshoes giving her reformer's pitch. "Nobody has to live that kind of life. Why don't you give it up and find a wholesome occupation?"

"Believe it or not, being a photographer isn't far from wholesome."

"Oh, come now, you can't think I believed your story about the camera you left on the train?"

"No, a woman like you wouldn't believe it, I guess."

"What is it that you claim you photograph?" she asked, making it clear that this was all too farfetched.

"The building of the railroads," he said, with that half smile on his face. "The grandeur of history in the making," he emoted, raising his arms dramatically. "The spanning of our land by twin iron rails, capturing it forever for our posterity to share." But then he dropped his arms and his dramatizing and fell thoughtful, introspective. "You know, it'll never happen again just like it's happening now. It's been something to see, Abbie." He sighed, entwined his fingers behind his head, and studied the ceiling. And for a moment she almost believed him, he sounded so sincere.

"I'm sure you would like me to believe you, Mr. Cameron."

"Would it hurt you to call me Jesse? It would make it more pleasant while we talk this way."

"I thought I'd made you understand that I live by rules of propriety."

"There's nobody here but you and me. I won't tell," he teased mischievously.

"No, you won't, because I shan't call you Jesse . . . ever. Now quit changing the subject and tell me about your occupation. Try to convince me that you are not a robber of trains."

He laughed, then said, "All right. I work for the railroad, photographing every phase of its construction, just like I said. I have free passage as long as I work for them, and I travel to the railhead—wherever that may be—to take most of my photographs. I live in camps and on trains most of the time. There's not much more to tell."

"Except why, if you have a decent job, you chose to steal from the very hand that feeds you."

"That was a mistake, Abbie."

"Miss Abigail," she corrected.

"Very well, Miss Abigail, then. Have you ever seen a railroad camp?"

"Hardly."

"No, you wouldn't have. Well, it's no Abigail McKenzie's house, I'll tell you that. It's wild out in the middle of nowhere, and the men who work there are not exactly parlor fare."

"Like you?" she couldn't resist saying. Again he laughed lightly, letting her think what she would.

"I'm a veritable goldmine of manners compared to the navvies who build the railroads. Their life is rough, their language is rougher, and anybody who crosses anybody else can expect a bullet between the eyes. There's no law where they live, none at all. They settle their disputes with guns and fists and sometimes even with hammers—anything that's convenient. There not only is no law at the end of a railroad line, there's no town. No houses, stores, churches, depots—in other words, no shelter of any kind. A man who lives in the wilds like that won't survive long without a gun. There are bobcats in the mountains, wolves on the prairies, and everything that grows teeth in between. Naturally they all go to water, which is usually where bridges and trestles go up. About this time of day the animals always come to drink."

"What's your point, Mr. Cameron?"

"My point is that I carry a gun like every other smart fellow who expects to tame the West and live to see it. I'm not denying I had a gun on me on that train. I am denying I used it to pull a holdup."

"You're forgetting you were caught red-handed."

"Doing what? I had just taken it out, thinking I'd clean it, but before I got it unloaded, some nervous old biddy was screaming, and I found myself on the floor, shot, and the next thing I knew I woke up here in your house. That's all I know."

"A likely story. You would make a fine actor, Mr. Cameron."

"I don't need to be a fine actor—I'm a fine photographer. When I get my plates back, you'll see."

"You seem very confident about that."

"I am, wait and see."

"Oh, I shall wait, but I doubt that there will be anything to see."

"You're a hard woman to convince."

"I'm a woman who recognizes the truth when it's staring her in the face."

"But that's what I do as a photographer. Recognize the truth and record it permanently in pictures."

"The truth?"

He considered for a moment, then cocked his head to the side as if studying her. "Well, take last night for instance. You'd have made a very fetching subject last night when you sat in that rocker there, laughing. The light fell on you at precisely the right angle to take all of the affected hardness away from your face and lend it a natural quality it was meant to reflect. Call it unpretentiousness, if you will. In that brief moment, if I'd had my camera I might have captured you as you really are, not as you pretend to be. I might have exposed you as a charlatan."

Faintly smarting at his words, denial sprang instantly to her lips. "I am no charlatan." Rather than argue, he studied her with cocked head, as if he could see into her depths and knew exactly what he was talking about. "If there is any charlatan here it is you. You have proven it by your own words. Any photographer knows that a subject could not be photographed rocking in a rocking chair. Even I know that subjects must be stiff, sometimes even braced into place in order to take successful photographs."

"You've missed my point completely, but on purpose, I think. However, if that's how you want it, it's all right with me. Let me only say that if you want stiff, braced-looking results, they're easy to obtain. My photographs lack such artifice. It's why I do what I do for the railroad. They want their history photographed as it happens, not as some fools see fit to pose and posture the real thing. It can be the same with people. Someday I'll take your picture and it will prove to you what I meant. It will show you what the real Abbie is like."

It was easy to tell from her expression that she had censured out of his words all she chose to disbelieve. "The real me is inutterably weary," she said, rising from the trunk. "But not weary enough to fall for such a story as yours. I still believe you're a finer actor than either train robber or photographer."

"Have it your way, Miss Abigail," he said. "Charlatans usually do."

"You should know," she replied, but his eyes caught and held hers, making her wonder just what he'd meant by all he'd said. At last she glanced at his turbaned head and said, "I believe we can remove the oatmeal now." She went to the dressing table to get her brush.

"I can brush it myself," he offered, but she waved away his hand, removed the clothespins, stretched out the towel, and began brushing.

"You'd have it all over everything and oatmeal attracts mice," she said. "They are not as opposed to eating it secondhand as you are."

He closed his eyes and rolled his head this way and that when she told him to. What a Saturday night, he thought, getting oatmeal brushed out of my hair by a woman who dislikes me and mice. "I can't reach the back. Could you sit up and lean over the edge of the bed?" He sat up, hunched forward, elbows to knees, and she spread the towel carefully on the floor between his feet. He watched the oatmeal dust drifting down as she brushed from the nape of his neck forward in deft strokes. There were times when she could be quite appealing, like last night in the rocker, and now, doing a common thing like brushing his hair. It was seldom, though, that she did anything in a common way. She preferred, for some reason, to pose herself, taut, rigid, as inflexible as the everlasting restrictions she put upon her behavior. It was beyond him why he should try to make her see herself truthfully. If she was happy with the artifice, let her be, he thought. Still, it was hard for him to understand why anyone would set such a mold for themselves.

The brushing made goose pimples shiver up his arms. It was deliciously relaxing. In his drowsy thoughts he wondered about Abigail McKenzie, thought of other things he might say to her, but then he realized the brushing had stopped; she had gone as silently as she'd come, leaving the brush lying bristles-down on the back of his neck.

Chapter 9

SHE HAD LEFT him relaxed and drowsy and lay now listening to the muffled sounds below. She heard the bedsprings twang beneath his weight, then the muted chiming of the brass headboard as he pulled against it. She visualized him turning on his side, sighing and falling asleep while she waited patiently. She fought drowsiness, listening to the occasional sounds from town petering out until all was as still as eternity. A dog barked, once, far away and lonely, but it made her flinch awake and sit up straighter, resisting slumber.

After an interminably long time she arose, quickly and lightly, creating only one little twank that was then gone. Again she waited, patient as a cat on the stalk, and when she moved, it was to the accompaniment of sheer soundlessness. She took the stairs barefoot, in a swift, gliding descent, knowing she risked less sound going that way than if she hesitated on each step. But once at the bottom, she waited again. She could hear his breathing in the stillness—long, rhythmic, somnolent. And she moved again, stopping not at the bedroom door, or the foot of his bed or to peer down to make sure he was sleeping; any of these hesitations, especially the last, might key some instinctual reaction and arouse him. Instead, surefooted and silent, she glided to the side of the bed and lay down on the floor half under it.

He breathed on as before while her breath came in short, scared spurts.

The shirt-wrapped gun was close to the outer edge of the mattress, where he could get at it without having to reach too far underneath. She touched it, exploring the fabric of the shirt, the hard lump inside, the ridges of the cartridge chamber, the sharp, crooked hammer, the butt, the barrel. She shivered. If she were to try to pull it through the rectangular spaces between the wires of the spring, it would undoubtedly get caught, for the gun was bigger than the holes. Instead, she studied the shape as a blind person might: using her fingertips, determining that it was so near the edge that no more than the slightest upward pressure on the mattress would free the gun so she could slip it out sideways.

The problem was raising the mattress an inch or so.

She would simply have to wait until he decided to roll over. Maybe when the springs squeaked she could yank the gun out quickly and he'd never know the difference. The floor grew as hard as an anvil. She grew chilled and needed badly to fidget, and still he slept on peacefully. She heard the dog again, far off, and the answering call of a wolf even farther, and in spite of the hard floor, began to get sleepy. To keep awake she reached out a hand and it touched something cold and fleshy. She recoiled in fear, then realized it was only the pig bladder. The memory of his long, strong fingers squeezing it came back to haunt her, and she pinched her eyes shut to blot out the picture. But just then Jesse snuffled, sighed, and shifted onto his side, causing the bedsprings to creak. At that exact moment, she pushed with one hand through the open spaces of the bedspring while with her other she pulled the shirt free, gun and all. It landed in the small of her chest, thudding heavily, and she checked the impulse to gasp at the weight of it.

She lay absolutely motionless, repulsed by the thing weighing her down. But she had the ominous weapon at last! Slowly she unwrapped it. The shirt lay upon her stomach and breasts and she could smell the smell of him in it. She shuddered. Then she slowly rolled the shirt into a tight ball, making sure not so much as a button clicked on the floor. While she waited with the cold steel upon her chest, she imagined what kind of a person it took to draw it, raise it, and aim it at another human being. She saw herself at the other end of it as she'd been this morning, and once again told herself it would take an animal to do such a thing.

He was breathing evenly again. She held her breath, shivering at the thought of getting caught. But the hardest part was done—the rest was easy. Be patient, be patient, she admonished herself. He was snoring lightly now. With the gun in one hand and his shirt in the other she sat up, alert, poised to spring should he move, almost startled to see how near she'd actually been to his head all this time. He faced the wall so she raised herself further, sound-lessly as ever, and the moment her soles touched the floor she hit for safety.

She had taken less than one full step when an arm lashed out, caught her, and flipped her over backward, somersaulting her across a lumpy hipbone till her toes cracked high against the wall. As she slithered down into a heap, a horrible weight settled upon her chest. In the next moment she was sure she was dying, for he'd knocked the wind out of her. The small of her back where it had bumped across him felt like there were two boulders beneath it and she reached to knead the pain, but just that fast he pinned the arm beneath him and pinioned the other one against the mattress over her head, the gun still tight in her grasp.

"All right, lady, you want to sneak around under my bed, this is what you get!" he snarled. "Give me the goddamn gun! Now!" He pushed her wrist into the mattress, trying to wrest the pistol from her fingers. But it was useless. They were clenched in a death-grip, locked in mid-motion when he'd flattened the breath from her. The pain in her chest grew to a choking, hammering, crushing insistence while she struggled for air that refused her. He pummeled her wrist against the bed, leaning on her, adding stress to her lungs until she felt her eyes would pop from their sockets.

"Give me the gun, you asinine woman! Did you think I was fool enough to let you get away with it?" Still no breath came and her fear swelled and swelled and she panicked, unable to tell him what was wrong. And just when she knew more certainly than ever that she was starting to die, a rattling issued from her throat and her hand went lax, loosing the gun. He heard the hissing and gasping as she fought for breath. Then suddenly her knees pulled up fetally.

He jumped off her chest, exclaiming, "Christ, Abbie!" She curled up like an armadillo, half crying, half gasping, and rolled from side to side, grasping her knees. He tried to make her straighten out so the air could get in, but she only curled tighter.

Finally he flung her onto her belly like a rag doll, the gun flying to the wall, then clunking to the floor in the corner behind the bed. With her forehead now screwing itself into the mattress, she clutched her stomach, writhing, her hind side hoisted up by nature trying to renew her life force. Jesse got her by the hips, his giant hands holding her up, trying to help her breathe again.

"I didn't mean to knock the wind out of you." Still her breath came hoarse and rasping. She could feel her posterior shimmed up against something warm. "Abbie, are you okay?" But his thumb pressed a spot that had been bruised by his hipbone. Heaving, gasping, crying all at once, she tried to break free.

"Put me . . ." But her voice wasn't working yet and he held her in that ignominious position against his pajama-clad body.

"Don't try to talk yet," he ordered, "let your breath come back first."

Then finally it came. Blessed, pure, giant puffs of air, flowing into her lungs and fortifying her. "Put . . . me . . . down," she managed while her fists still gripped the sheet and she flailed one foot dissolutely. He released her at last and she slumped flat. She felt her weight roll as he moved to kneel beside her.

"Hurt?" he asked, and she felt his hand rubbing the small of her back while she lay there limp, panting, waiting for her near-bursting heart to ease.

"Get . . . your . . . filthy . . . hands . . . off . . . me," she sputtered into the mattress between gasps of air.

"It's your own fault," he said, ignoring her order, still rubbing, warmer now and in longer sweeps. "Just what were you trying to do, shoot me?"

"Nothing would pleasure me more," she puffed.

"That goes to show what you know," he said, and purposely ran his long, lean fingers—one swipe—down her spine where its hollow widened, then narrowed. She jumped like a jackrabbit in a desperate leap toward the corner of the bed, lunging for the gun. But her head hit the corner wall with a resounding crack! The bedsprings twanged and he grabbed her by the calves and dragged her backward, her fingers never touching the pistol, her nightgown shinnying up in a roll beneath her. She reached for it desperately, but just then he flew and landed full-length on top of her, reaching easily with one long arm to retrieve the gun from the floor. His chest pushed her face into the bed, then the weight was gone, settled farther down as he straddled her like a cowboy on a bronc, holding her arms pinned to her sides by his knees.

But now he was panting too, gritting his teeth while he pressed a hand to his throbbing wound. He rocked a time or two, suddenly angry because of the pain.

"All right, Miss High-And-Mighty, so you want to play guns, do you? Okay, I'll play." Through the ringing in her head she heard his ragged breathing. Then he swung off her hips and she heard the gun click by her ear. "Roll over," he ordered.

She struggled with the nightgown, but as she tugged, the gun barrel skewered it to the center of her back, holding it where it was.

"Roll over," he repeated, tight and hard now, and nudged her a little harder with the barrel. She rolled fearfully away from him, shivering near the wall. "Why is it that every time I wake up you seem to be in my bed?" he accused.

She clutched her head, which was aching uncontrollably now, closed her eyes while his unctuous voice flowed. "Is this why you took me into your house, Abbie? So you could weasel your way into a gunslinger's bed? Why didn't you just say so instead of pretending to be the gracious nurse? Nurse . . . ha! Do you know what all you've done to me under the guise of nursing? Let me recount every one so you'll know what I'm about to get even with here. First you shaved off my moustache for no apparent reason at all. You made me lie in need until I thought my bladder would burst. Then you threw the bedpan at me. Then you pushed branches down my throat until it was practically useless to me, then claimed afterward that it was for my own good you had to starve me. Next, you proceeded to calmly poison me with liver until I puked like a buzzard. Then, you presented me with a raw pig's bladder while I groaned for a square meal. And now—last but not least—you try to shoot me!"

"I did not try to shoot you!"

"You, Miss Abigail, were caught red-handed. Are those familiar words? Do you remember hearing them recently?"

"You shot Mr. Melcher and he has a toe gone to prove it. I shot nobody. I was only after the gun."

"You shot nobody because I was faster than you. What's the matter, your head hurt now?"

"I hit it on the wall."

"As you also said to me once, it's your own fault. You brought it on yourself when you came sneaking in here. You pulled your pussyfooting act just once too often."

"I saved your life, you ingrate!" she spit, and was going to call his bluff, thinking he wouldn't really harm her. But her shoulders got no more than a hand's width off the mattress before she found herself pushed flat again, his knuckles prying into the bones of her chest.

"Ingrate?" he chuckled wickedly. "Yes, perhaps I have been an ingrate. Perhaps I haven't shown the proper gratitude for all you've done for me. Maybe I'd better do it now . . . in kind. Pay you back for all you've done to me, is that what you want?"

"N . . . no, I didn't mean it."

"But of course you meant it. Let's just call it payment for services rendered."

"Don't . . ." She crossed her arms protectively over her chest.

"Let's see how you like having your mouth invaded, Abbie." He moved so swiftly she had no chance to fight. The next moment one of her arms was imprisoned between the mattress and his body, the other wrist pressed against a rail of the brass headboard while he held it there with a powerful hand. His mouth swooped down but she rolled her face aside and he missed. He tried again but she rolled the other way.

"So you still want to play games, huh?" She struggled while he yanked her arm down. But he rolled her easily to her side, forcing the arm up behind her back before her own weight and his rendered it useless. His newly freed hand came to the back of her neck, long fingers trailing up through her freshly washed hair, controlling her as he lowered his mouth to hers again and ran his tongue across her bared teeth. She gasped and bucked, but pain shot into her arm so she fell still, realizing she was no match for his strength. He lightened his hold on her lips, teasing now with his tongue, running it to the corners of her mouth, torturing her with its sleek, wet insinuation. Unable to combat him, her only recourse was to lay limp and submissive, determined to show neither fight nor fear.

He sensed what she was doing and slid his lips down to the hollow beneath her jaw, whispered near her ear, "I'm going to pay you back for every single thing you did to me, Abbie." Then he nuzzled his way back to the corner of her mouth, his full lips closing upon it leisurely while she resolutely kept her jaws clamped shut. He chuckled low in his throat and she felt him smile against her lips. "How do you like it, Abbie?" Her heart danced to her throat and her eyelids trembled as she held them tightly shut. He moved to catch the side of one nostril as a stallion nips a mare, leaving her skin damp as he moved on, bending lower. He took her small pointed chin in his mouth, sucking gently, sending shafts of heat darting through her body. And far down the bed she felt him grow harder and harder against the back of her captured hand. Wanting to die, yet feeling more alive than ever before in her life, Abbie absorbed the feeling of it all. Held prisoner, she suddenly felt as if she soared free.

His hand slid away from her hair and he ran only the outer edges of its little finger down the valley between her breasts, to her waist. Then, hooking each button with that single finger, he flicked them open on his leisurely way back up. "Hey," he whispered against her neck, "did you think you were going to get away with my shirt tonight? You steal mine . . . I steal yours." Then slowly he pushed aside the bodice of her gown, opening first the left side, then the right, still using only that little finger, but sailing its back side against the surface of her breasts, over each smooth mound to each erect nipple, skimming them like warm wind and creating uninvited goose bumps upon her skin.

"You know what you do to me, Abbie? You rub me in a hundred wrong ways. Let me show you the one right way." His palm cupped her bare breast and her eyes flew open. She saw his dark moustache so close to her face, felt his breath on her mouth, his hot hardness against the back of her hand. And all the while he kneaded her breast with its unforgivable taut nipple, he caressed her ribs and stomach with his forearm. Her eyelids slid closed, the breath which he'd earlier knocked from her caught now in her helpless throat.

"How about a bed bath, Abbie? I owe you one." Her senses fled to one central spot as he fondled one breast while leaning to circle the other with his warm, wet tongue, slowly and painstakingly bathing it, from rigid crest to softest perimeter. She felt the forbidden lick of grain upon smoothness, made sleek by moisture. His teeth, open, gently sliced, their edges unhurting, knowing. Between tongue and upper teeth he took the ruby crown of her breast, lightly, lightly, stroking, tugging until her shoulder strained off the mattress. He lowered his mouth to the soft cay where breast met rib and there washed her with warmth before continuing downward while her body reached its dewpoint. He dipped his tongue into the cupule of her navel as a bee dips into the chalice of a flower for honey. His warm tongue disappeared, then he kissed her lightly a little lower, raised his face to ask, "Should I do a thorough job or leave you half-finished like you did me?"

"Please . . ." she begged in a ragged whisper.

"Please what? Please finish or please stop?"

"Please stop." Tears seemed to have gathered in her eyes, her throat, and between her legs.

"Not yet. Not till I bring some life to these limbs like you did to mine. Remember, Abbie? Remember how you massaged the life back into me and made my blood beat again after you tied me up?" She could no longer tell if this was torture or treat. It seemed her heart beat in every pore of her body as once again, in that slow, slow motion, he did what he wanted with her, sliding his arms along the lengths of her own, catching one up high above her head, sealing the other beneath them. He stretched his length out upon her, holding her now from behind while her wrist was clamped against brass which chimed a muted knell each time he pulled, grinding his tumescent body against her aroused one. Her lips fell open as her traitorous body responded. Her breath beat fast and warm upon his face. She'd made no sound, yet he heard her whimper all the same. Whimper for all the fear mingled with this new sensual turbulence so suddenly awakened in her, the pulsing void that seemed to cry for fulfillment.

Suddenly he stilled, looking down into her shadowed face with its closed, trembling eyes, its open, trembling lips. He touched the crest of her cheek softly. "How old are you, Abbie? You lied to me, didn't you? You said you're old because it's a shield you hide behind, afraid of what life is all about. But what do you fear now, living with this or without this?"

A sob caught in her throat. "I am thirty-three and I hate you," she whispered. "I shall hate you till my dying day." Her fear of him was gone, replaced by fear of a new and different kind: a fear of herself. A fear of the muscle and blood that had responded too plainly to all he'd said and done.

How long had her hands been free? They rested inanimately, curled in limp abandon, commanded now only by the air, for he was smoothing the hair back from her brow—too gently, too gently. He had claimed his victory over her, true, but somehow it left him hollow and beaten himself. As she lay beneath him, disheveled and defeated, he suddenly wished he had the old Abbie back, all starch and spitfire.

"Hey, what started this anyway?" She heard the change in his voice and it did nothing to calm the riotous vibrations of her flesh. She swallowed the tears in her throat, but her voice was thick, the back of her wrist falling across her eyes.

"If I remember correctly, somebody brought a train robber into my house and he wore a moustache."

"Abbie . . ." he said tentatively, as if there were so much more unsaid. But she pushed him off her and struggled to the edge of the bed, leaving him sorry he'd done as much as he had, sorrier still that he hadn't done more. But as she slid across the rumpled sheets her hand touched cold steel, abandoned in their struggle which had ceased to be a struggle. Her fingers closed over it as she moved off silently in the dark.

Chapter 10

IT WAS A fine Sunday, bright and fresh, the sky as blue as a robin's egg. But all through services Miss Abigail found it difficult to pay attention. Even while praying to be forgiven for the responses she'd been unable to control last night, she felt her skin ripple sweetly in remembrance. Standing to join in a hymn, her lips parted to form the words, but the memory of his tongue between them scorched her with shame and a tingling, forbidden want. Putting a hand to the nape of her neck to smooth her hair, the memory of his hand there made her hang her head in shame. But as she did she looked down the lace-covered bodice of her proper, high-necked dress only to know that within it her nipples were puckered up like gumdrops. And within her pristine soul Abigail McKenzie knew that she was truly damned now, yet all through no real fault of her own. She had lived a demure life, one in which—granted—little temptation of last night's sort had been put in her way. But she had not deserved to be treated so ruthlessly.

While Miss Abigail contemplated all this she occasionally caught herself eyeing the back of Doc Dougherty's bald head, wishing she could take the butt of that gun and rap some sense into it!

When the service was over she lost track of how many times she was asked how everything was going up at her house, how many times she was forced to lie and answer, "Fine, fine." She was asked everything from how the outlaw's wounds were healing to what in the world she wanted with that pig bladder! To the latter she again replied with the half lie that the train robber used it to strengthen his bruised hand—true enough, but hardly the reason she'd bought it. When she finally got Doc Dougherty off to one side, she was upset not only with him but with everyone who'd asked her what was none of their business.

Doc was his usual congenial self as he greeted, "How-do, Miss Abigail."

"Doctor, I must talk to you."

"Something wrong with our patient? What's his name again? Jesse, isn't it? Has he been up getting some exercise?"

"Yes he has, but—"

"Fine! Fine! That limb will stiffen up like an uncured pelt if he doesn't move it. Feed him good and see that he gets up and around, maybe even out of the house."

"Out of the house! Why the man has no clothes. He went to the outhouse yesterday wrapped in nothing more than a sheet!"

Doc laughed, his belly hefting jovially. "Never thought about that when I brought his stuff back the other day. Guess we'll have to buy him some clothes, eh? The railroad'll pay for—"

Impatiently, she interrupted, "Doctor, whatever were you thinking to return his gun to him? He . . . he threatened me with it, after all I've done for him."

Doc scowled worriedly. "Threatened you?"

"Shh!" She looked quickly around, then lied again. "It was nothing too serious. He just wanted some fried pork chops for his dinner."

Suddenly Doc suspected just what sort of rivalry might have sprung up

516

between two such willful people, and a telltale sparkle lit his eyes as he inquired, "And did he get them?"

She colored, fussed about pulling her glove on tighter, and stammered, "Why . . . I . . . he . . . yes, he did."

Doc reached into a breast pocket, found a cigar, bit off the end, and gazed off across the distance reflectively. Then he spit the cigar end into the dirt and smiled. "Pretty crafty of him, considering the gun had no bullets."

Miss Abigail felt like somebody had just opened her chemise and poured ice water inside.

"Bullets?" she snapped, her jaw so tight she could have bitten one in half just then.

"Bullets, Miss Abigail. You didn't think I'd turn his gun over to him with a cylinder full of bullets, did you?"

"I . . . I . . ." But she realized how very stupid she must appear to Doc Dougherty, admitting that she'd been duped by a felon with an empty pistol. "I had not thought the gun might be empty. I . . . I . . . should have known."

"Of course you should have. But I'm sorry he pulled it on you anyway. Sounds like you've had your trials with him. Is everything else all right?"

Miss Abigail could not, would not admit to a living soul how extremely unright everything was. She could never again face a person in this town if people found out what she had suffered at the hands of that scoundrel up at her house. She prided herself on control, good breeding, fine manners, and the town respected her for those things. She would not give them any reason to raise eyebrows at her now. Not at this late date!

"I assure you that everything is all right, Doctor Dougherty. The man has harmed me in no way whatsoever. But he is a loutish brute, crude-mannered and vain, and I have grown thoroughly sick of having him in my house. The sooner he gets out, the better. I should like it if you would sign a release immediately so that Sheriff Harris may wire the railroad authorities to come and get him."

"Sure enough! I'll do it first thing in the morning. He should be well enough to travel soon."

"Just how long do you think it will be before they come and get him?"

Doc scratched his chin. "That's hard to say, but it shouldn't be too long, and I'll be up every day. You can count on that, Miss Abigail. As soon as I see he's able to travel, we'll have him out of there and off your hands for you. Anything else I can do for you?"

"Yes. You may purchase some britches for him. If he is to be traipsing around on those crutches I insist he dress properly."

"Sure thing. I'll have 'em up there first thing."

"The earlier the better," she suggested, none too placatingly. Then with that little upward nudge of chin she wished him good day and turned toward home, angrier than she ever remembered being in her life. To think that she'd been duped, gulled, toyed with in such a manner by that . . . that *dog* she'd taken in off the streets when nobody else in town would so much as throw their table scraps to him! He had victimized her not once, but *twice* . . . and with an empty gun yet! The thought had her positively sizzling by the time she reached the house.

Jesse heard the loud Clack! Clack! Clack! of her heels on the steps as she went noisily upstairs. A moment later she came down again, marching loudly, regularly, as if some band accompanied her parade. The uncharacteristic noise surprised him; before church she'd been pussyfooting again. She flashed past his door, went to the kitchen, and opened the pantry door. He heard her pouring something, then here she came again, still marching. Around the bedroom doorway she swished. Up to the bed she hiked, and before he could say a word, wound up, hauled off, and smacked him across the face so hard that his cheek reverberated off the headboard. The brass sang out like she'd slammed it with a ball peen hammer. While he was still stunned senseless, she crossed calmly to the water pitcher, dumped a cupful of something into it, then held his pistol over it, using thumb and forefinger only.

"Never again will you threaten me with this distasteful object you once called a gun," she said, all eloquent and self-righteous, before releasing the gun with a plop! into the water. "Neither *with* nor *without* bullets!" Still too surprised to move, he heard burbles from within the pitcher as water gurgled its way into the barrel. When it finally struck him what she'd done, he leaped from the bed and hobbled to the pitcher. He was about to plunge his hand in after the gun when she coolly advised, "I wouldn't try dunking for it unless you want your hand dissolved, too, by the lye." She had retreated a safe distance.

He hopped around, swinging awkwardly to face her, but jostling the table in the process. "You daughter of a snake! Get that gun out of there or I'll dump the whole thing on the floor, I swear!"

"My tabletop!" she exclaimed, as the lye water puddled on the varnish. She lurched a few steps toward it, but stopped uncertainly.

"Get it out!" he roared. They glowered at each other, his jaws grinding, her mouth pinched and quivering. Like feral animals they poised, wary, tensile, cautious. In a scarcely controlled fit, from between clenched teeth he spoke, punctuating his words with grand, empty gaps: "Get . . . it . . . out!"

And she knew she'd better get it out.

With a toss of shoulders and thrusting out of ribs, she carried the pitcher away, out the back screen door. He heard it slam, then the slosh as she emptied the whole mess into the yard. She came running back with a rag to wipe off her precious tabletop. While she dabbed at it, Jesse collapsed into the rocker, burying his face in his hands, muttering disgustedly, "What did you do a goddamn thing like that for?"

In a voice oozing sarcasm, she began, "Your foray into the prolix is truly impressive—"

"Just don't start in on me with your three-dollar words," he barked, "because we both know that every damn time you do it, it's because you're running scared! I'll say anything I want, any way I want to!"

"So will I! You may have thought you bested me last night, but Miss Abigail McKenzie shall not be bested, do you hear!" She scrubbed at the tabletop with violent motions. "I take you into my house—You! A common train robber!—and keep your rotting hulk alive, and for what! To be criticized for my cooking, my language, my manners, even the flowers I grow in my garden! To be pawed and degraded in repayment for my care!"

"Care?" He laughed harshly. "You never cared about anything in your entire, dismal life! Your blood is as cold as a frog's. And just like a frog, you live on your lonely lily pad, jumping in and hiding whenever anything resembling life comes anywhere near you! So you found out the gun wasn't loaded, huh? And that's why you marched in here and smacked me clear into next week, then dropped my gun into lye? Is it?"

"Yes!" she screeched, whirling on him, tears seeping to her eyes now.

"Like hell it is *Miss* Abigail McKenzie! The reason you did it is because you knew that gun wasn't even pointed at you anymore when you turned to jelly beneath me, isn't it? Because what you felt last night had absolutely nothing to do with a gun. You've lived your whole life in this godforsaken old maid's house, scared to death to show any emotion whatever, until I came along. Me! A common train robber! A man your warped sense of decency has told you to beware of since the first minute I was hauled in here. Only you can't admit to yourself that you're human, that you could be lit up by the likes of me, that you could lie there on that bed and find that bare skin can be something less than sordid, in spite of who it's touching, in spite of what you've forced yourself to believe all these years. You've also learned that a little fight now and then can be pretty invigorating, not to mention downright sexually stimulating. Only it's not supposed to be, is it? Since I've been here you've experienced every emotion that's been forbidden to you your entire life. And the truth is, you blame me because you like them all and you don't think you're supposed to."

"Lies!" she argued. "You lie to defend yourself when you know that what you did last night was low and cruel and immoral!"

"Low? Cruel? Immoral?" Again he laughed harshly. "Why, if you had any sense, Abbie, you'd be thanking me for showing you last night that there's hope for you after all. The way you've been pussyfooting your life away with your clean white gloves and your fastidiously clean thoughts, I'm surprised you didn't ask the congregation to stone you as a martyr this morning. Admit it, Abbie. You're sore because you enjoyed rolling around on that bed with me last night!"

"Stop it! Stop it!" she shrieked. Then she whirled and threw the lye-soaked rag at him. It landed across his lower face, a sodden end cloying like a rat's tail around his jaw and neck. Instantly his skin began to burn and his eyes grew wide. He clawed at the rag wildly as she realized, horrified, what she'd done. The next moment she was reacting as her life had programmed her to react, grabbing a dry towel from the washstand, lunging to wrap his face. Their hands worked together frantically to dry his skin before any damage was done. He saw her eyes widen with fear, telling him she knew she'd gone one step too far.

"You . . ." she choked out, scrubbing at his skin harder than she had at the tabletop. "You laugh at all I do for you and de . . . deride me for everything that is your fault. Never once since you've been here have you ap . . . appreciated a single thing I've done for you. Instead, you criticize and berate and slander. Well, if I'm so cold-blooded and straight-laced and undesirable, why did you start what you did on that bed last night? Why?" Stricken, on the verge of breaking down, she met his eyes nevertheless. "Do you think that I don't know the reason you turned me loose? Do you think I'm so naive that I couldn't tell you ended up in self-defeat by liking it yourself?" Her hands had

fallen still on the towel, which trailed away behind his shoulders. It covered his mouth, but his moustache appeared blacker than ever, contrasted against its whiteness. They faced each other now in silent standoff. His black eyes bored into hers, which dropped to his bronze chest. Her hands fluttered from the towel as her eyes had from his relentless, knowing gaze. She suddenly wished she could reclaim her words. In slowest motion his swarthy fingers pulled the towel free from his mouth. His words, when at last they came, were the most fearsome yet, for they were spoken in a hushed, confused voice.

"And what if I did, Abbie? What if I did?"

Stricken anew, she felt her nerves gathering into wary knots, the skin at the back of her neck prickle, while confusion sluiced through her. He was a player of games, a lawbreaker, her enemy. He could not be trusted. Still she looked up at his disconcerting train robber's eyes and they skewered her to the spot as no gun ever could. He neither smiled nor frowned, but looked at her with an expression of intense sincerity.

"I did not ask for it," she managed in a choked whisper.

"Neither did I," he said low.

Quickly she turned from him, asking, "Is your skin burned?" But his strong hand came out to stay her in a firm grip just above her elbow.

"Did you really want to burn me?" he asked, studying the taut cords of her neck as she arched sharply away from him and swallowed.

"I . . . no . . . I don't know what I wanted." Her voice was timorous and uncertain. "I don't know how to survive around you. You make me so angry when I don't want to be. I want . . ." But she sighed to a halt, unable to finish. All she wanted was peace, not this hammering heart, this threatening desire for a person like him.

"You make me angry too," he said most gently, squeezing the flesh beneath his sinewed fingers.

He watched the profile of her right breast lift as she drew in a great, shuddering breath. He saw her eyelashes drift down upon her pinkened cheek.

"Let my arm go," she begged shakily. "I don't want to be touched by you."

"I think you're too late, Abbie," he said. "I think you already are." He shook her arm gently. "Hey, look at me."

When she wouldn't, he gripped her narrow shoulders and forced her to face him. She studied the floor at his feet while his hands burned a trail down her limp arms to her elbows and on to her wrists. He took her hands loosely in his while she fought the compulsion to raise her gaze to those dark, dark eyes.

"It's Sunday, Abbie. Should we just be friends for one day and see how it works?"

"I'd . . ." She swallowed. Her heart clamored in her throat and she braved raising her eyes as far as his chin. He had shaved while she was gone, and he smelled of soap. His moustache was thick and black, but she would not raise her eyes farther. Suddenly he sighed and dropped back down into the rocker again, still holding her hands, doing something soft and wonderful to the backs of them, rubbing them slowly with his thumbs, from cuff to knuckle, while she stood in confusion, telling herself to pull her hands free from his, yet absorbing the very niceness of the touch, so different from how he'd ever touched her before. This was gentle, tender in a way she would have sworn this man could never be. She stared at their joined hands and knew fully what he was doing, but she let him go about it.

Slowly he turned a palm to his mouth, and his eyes closed as warm lips and soft moustache grew lost in it. Her fingers lay curled beneath his chin and she stood like a statue feeling the touch of a magic wand, suddenly imbued with life-giving current while his kiss lingered in her cupped hand. Then his hand stole up to her waist and he tugged her toward his lap.

"No, don't—not again," she begged even as he eased her down expertly.

"Why not?" he whispered as strong hands closed over her shoulders and turned her inexorably toward his chest.

"Because we hate each—" He stopped her words with his open lips while his hands went aroving up and down her back. His moustache was soft now, almost as soft as before she'd shaved it, and his warm tongue came seeking, thrilling, inviting with supple sensuousness before she broke away, claiming, "This is crazy, we must not—" But his long palms spanned her cheeks and he had his way with her again. He pulled her mouth to his, then found her arms and placed them behind his neck, holding them in place until he felt her acquiesce and curl them around his head.

And she thought, I am crazy, and let him go on kissing her until his hands were on her back again, running up and down, up and down. Then at her waist, pressing firmly at her sides, down low, just above her belt line.

He whispered things into her mouth. "Don't fight it, Abbie . . . for once, don't fight it," and the words were blurred from his tongue moving against hers as he spoke. His hands moved lower, to her hips, swiveling them around until she half lay, half sat on his lap. He stiffened his body in the very small chair, lifting and shifting her until she no longer controlled where she was or how she rested upon him. With chest and waist arched away from the chair, Jesse manipulated her until she lay upon him. He was one smooth, hard plane of flesh upon which she settled while both of his arms circled her waist, holding her very still, allowing her to know the feel of him through flounced petticoats.

And he was long . . . and hard . . . and somehow very good.

Sense intruded and she broke away, resisting. "No . . . you are a thief. You are my enemy."

"You are your own enemy, Abbie," he whispered. Then she felt his hands cup her beneath her arms while he raised her whole body, sliding it effortlessly upward until her breasts were over his face and he held her that way, breathing through the starched front of her proper dress, blowing hot life into her who fought against wanting it.

"Oh, please . . . please, put me down." She was almost in tears now, pain and pleasure intermingling in her breasts, her heart, her hands upon his hard shoulders . . . and the part of her that now rested against his chest.

"Abbie, let me," he said into her breasts, "let me."

"No, oh, no, please," she begged, her lips brushing against his soft hair as she spoke into it.

"Let me make a woman of you, Ab."

"No, don't," she gasped. "I . . . I won't touch your gun or your moustache again. I promise. I'll feed you anything you want, only let me go, please."

"You don't want me to," he said, letting her slide back down the length of him until her lips were at his again. But the towel had worked its way between their mouths somehow.

"Take the towel away, Abbie," he entreated, his arms firm and solid about her waist.

"No, Jesse, no," she breathed tremulously.

And hearing her utter his name, Jesse knew that she wanted him, too. He raised his chin, nudging the towel down with it, nuzzling her neck. "Let's be friends," he said against her high, stiff collar.

"Never," she denied as his lips eased back to hers. He pushed the rocker back and lay further horizontally, his hips plying hers, rocking a little bit, a little bit, each movement of the chair driving his hard body against hers. He knew it was truly beyond her to say yes to him, that the only way he'd ever have her would be nothing short of rape, for even if she gave in, she'd be doing so against her will. He had to hear her say yes or turn her loose. But he understood, too, that that one word—*yes*—was impossible for her to utter. When he released her, she'd be shamed even by what she'd done so far. But release her he must, and so, to make it easier on her, he quipped, "Say yes quick, Abbie, because my leg hurts like a bitch."

At his teasing she jumped back, too peeved for shame. "Oh, you! You are egotistical and insufferable!" To her dismay, he laughed, holding her down just a moment longer.

"But let's still be friends, for today anyway. I'm sick of the fighting too."

She struggled up from his lap, adjusting her clothing. "If you promise not to do anything like this again."

"Well, could I maybe just think about it?" His dark moustache curled above a teasing smile while Abby scarcely knew where to let her eyes light, she was so flustered. She headed for the kitchen and he followed on his crutches.

"Mind if I sit out here awhile?" he asked. "I'm getting pretty sick of that bedroom."

She wouldn't look at him, but allowed, "Do whatever you like as long as you stay out of my way."

He sat down nonchalantly beside the table, leaning the crutches on the floor beneath his legs. "I won't be any bother," he promised. However, it bothered her already, the way he sat there with his legs sprawled and those walking sticks resting against his crotch. It took a supreme effort to keep her eyes from straying to it, and she had no doubt he knew exactly what he was doing to her. But before he could fluster her further, Doc Dougherty's voice came from the front door.

"Hello in there. Can I come in?" And in he came, for the way Miss Abigail's house was designed he could see down the straight shot from front to back that they were both in the kitchen. "W-e-e-ll," he drawled at the sight of Jesse, "you're looking fit as a fiddle, sitting up on that kitchen chair. How do you feel?"

"Stronger every day, thanks to Miss Abigail," Jesse answered, pleased, as usual, to see the doc.

"So she told me at church earlier. Oh, Miss Abigail, I got those britches you asked me to get. Avery opened his store special. We figured pants for a real necessity, so he obliged. If they don't fit, it'll be too bad, because Avery already locked up again."

Miss Abigail gave the denims a scant glance, then continued with her dinner preparations again as Doc and Jesse retired to the bedroom to have a look at his leg. She could hear their muffled voices before Doc came back to repeat his order of earlier. "He's long past any danger and he can do whatever he feels strong enough to do—inside, outside, doesn't matter. A little fresh air and sunshine might do him good. Now that he's got decent clothes, it wouldn't hurt to take a ride in the country or sit in that garden of yours."

"I doubt that he'd enjoy either of those things."

"I already suggested it and he seemed real anxious to get out. Might not do you any harm either. Well, I better be off now. You need anything else, just holler."

She showed him to the front door, but halfway there Jesse came out of the bedroom, dressed now in blue denims and a pale blue cotton shirt, which hung open.

"Thanks for stopping, Doc, and for the clothes," he said, and went along to the front door as if the house were his own.

"It was Miss Abigail's idea," Doc informed him.

"Then maybe I should thank Miss Abigail," Jesse said, casting a brief grin her way. But Doc was away, out the door, down the porch steps, calling as he went, "See you tomorrow, you two!" The way he said it, lumping the two of them together that way, left a curious warm feeling almost like security in Abbie, standing there beside Jesse at the front door after having ushered Doc out together.

Unexpectedly, Jesse's voice beside her was polite and sincere as he said, "It feels good to have some clothes on that fit me again. Thanks, Abbie." It took her aback because she had grown so used to his teasing and criticism, she hardly knew how to handle politeness from him. She was acutely aware of the fact that while Doc was here Jesse had politely called her Miss Abigail, but as soon as he left, he reverted to the familiar Abbie again. She could feel him looking down at her, caught sight of that bare, black-haired chest, those long naked feet, and wondered what to say to him. But he turned then, lifted a crutch, and gestured politely for her to move ahead of him back to the kitchen. She felt his eyes branding her back as he thumped along behind her.

She returned to her cooking and he to his chair, but the room remained strained with silence until Jesse commented, "Doc gave me hell for pulling that gun on you."

She could not conceal her surprise. Out of the clear blue sky he said a thing like that. Then he added, "I was surprised you admitted it to him."

Sheepishly, she said, "I only told him you made demands regarding pork chops, nothing more."

"Ah," he returned, "is that all?"

She was disconcerted by his sitting behind her, probably staring at every move she made. At last she ventured a peek over her shoulder. The crutches were resting against the same distracting spot as before as he leaned an elbow on the table, scowling, running a forefinger repeatedly over his moustache as if deep in thought.

She turned her back on him before inquiring innocently, "Did he say anything else?"

Silence for a long moment, then, "He wanted to know why my chin and neck were red. I told him I'd been eating fresh strawberries from your garden and they make me break out. You'd better have some strawberries in that garden of yours . . ." From behind, he saw her hands fall idle.

Abbie could feel the coloring working its way up her neck. "You . . . you mean . . . you didn't tell him about the lye in the rag?"

"No." He watched her shoulders slump slightly in relief.

To the top of the range, she said, "Yes, I do have strawberries in my garden."

Behind her, he sat watching as she started whipping something with a spoon. The motion stirred her skirts until they swayed about her narrow hips. Suddenly she stood very still, and said quietly, "Thank you."

A strange feeling gripped him. She had never spoken so nicely to him before. He cleared his throat and it sounded like thunder in the quiet room. "Have you got anything to put on it, though, Abbie? It's starting to sting pretty bad."

She whirled quickly, and he caught an unguarded look of concern on her face as she crossed the room to him. Her hand reached tentatively for his chin, withdrew, and their eyes met, each wondering why the other had softened the truth when Doc Dougherty had asked his questions.

"Buttermilk should help it." Her eyes dropped to the crutches.

"Have you got any?" he asked.

"Yes, outside in the well. I'll get it."

He watched her walk down the yard and draw the bucket up and bring a fruit jar back into the house. All the while the frown stayed on his face. "I'll get some gauze to apply it with," she said when she returned. Bringing it, she stood hesitantly, somehow afraid to touch him now.

He reached out a hand, palm-up, saying, "I can do it myself. You're busy." When she was back at the stove he surprised her once more by asking, "Are your hands okay?"

"My hands?"

"From the lye. Are they okay, or do you need some buttermilk too?"

"Oh, they're all right. I barely got them damp."

When she collected the buttermilk and wet gauze to begin setting the table for their dinner, she stopped in the pantry door, looked across the room at him. "Do you like buttermilk?" she asked.

"Yes, I do."

"Do you want some with your dinner?"

"Sounds good."

She disappeared, returned with a glass of frothy white, and handed it to him. His fingers looked tawnier than ever against the milk.

"Thank you," he said to her for the second time that day.

At last she joined him at the table, extended a platter his way, asking politely, "Chicken?"

"Help yourself first," he suggested. And pretty soon—unbelievably—their plates were filled and they were eating dinner across from each other without so much as one cross word between them.

"We used to have chicken every single Sunday when I was little," he recalled.

"Who is we?"

"We," he repeated. "My mom and dad and Rafe and June and Clare and Tommy Joe. My family."

"And where was that?"

"New Orleans."

Somehow the picture of him in a circle of brothers and sisters and parents seemed ludicrous. He was—she reminded herself—a consummate liar.

"You don't believe me, do you?" He smiled and took a bite of chicken.

"I don't know."

"Even train robbers have mothers and fathers. Some of us even have siblings." He was back to his customary teasing again, but somehow she didn't mind this time. The word *siblings* was a surprise, too, the kind he now and then tossed out unexpectedly. It was her kind of word, not his.

"And how many *siblings* did you have?"

"I had . . . *have* . . . four. Two brothers and two sisters."

"Indeed?" She raised an eyebrow dubiously.

He raised his buttermilked chin a little and laughed enjoyably. "I can hear the skepticism in your voice and I know why. Sorry if I don't fit your notion of where I should or shouldn't have come from, but I have two parents, still living in New Orleans, in a real house, still eating real chicken on Sundays— only Creole-style—and I have two older brothers and two younger sisters and last night when you washed my hair it reminded me of Saturday nights back there at home. We all washed our hair on Saturday nights, and Mom polished our shoes for Sunday."

She was unabashedly staring at him now. The truth was, she wanted to be convinced that it was all true. Could it possibly be? She reminded herself again that he was an accused felon, that the last thing she should do was believe him.

"Surprised?" he asked, smiling at her amazed expression. But she wasn't ready to believe it yet.

"If you had such a nice home, why did you leave it?"

"Oh, I didn't leave it permanently. I go back regularly and visit. I left my family because I was young and had my fortune to seek, and a good and loyal friend who wanted to seek his along with me. But I miss them sometimes."

"And so you left New Orleans together?"

"We did."

"And did you find your fortunes?"

"We did. On the railroads—together."

"Ahhh, the railroads again," she crooned knowingly.

"What can I say?" He threw his hands out guiltily. "I was caught redhanded."

His blithe, devil-may-care attitude puzzled her, but she smiled at his affability, wondering if it was all true about New Orleans and his family.

"And what about you?" He had finished eating and leaned back relaxedly in his chair, one elbow slung on the table. "Any brothers or sisters?"

She immediately gazed out the screen door, faraway things in her expression as she answered, "None."

"I gathered as much from Doc. I left my family when I was twenty. He said you stayed with yours."

"Yes." She picked away a nonexistent thread from her skirt.

"Not by choice?"

She looked up sharply. It would not do to admit such a thing, no matter what the truth. A good daughter simply would not begrudge a father anything, would she? Jesse was absently toying with his moustache again, resting his forefinger beneath his nose as he continued. "Doc told me once that you gave up your youth to care for an ailing father. I find that commendable." She glanced to his eyes to see if he was teasing again, but they were serious. "How long ago was that?"

She swallowed, weighing the risks of telling him things she never talked about. Finally she admitted, "Thirteen years."

"When you were twenty?"

"Yes." Her eyes dropped to her lap again.

"What a waste," he commented quietly, making the skin at the back of her neck prickle. She didn't know what to reply or where to look or what to do with her hands. "It's not everyone who'd do a thing like that, Abbie. Do you regret it now?"

The fact that she did not deny her regret was the closest she had ever come to admitting it.

"When did he die?" Jesse went on.

"A year ago."

"Twelve years you gave him?" Only silence answered him while she demurely looked at her hands. "Twelve years, and all that time you learned how to do all the things you do so well, all the things it takes to make a house run smoothly, and a family . . . yet you never had one. Why?"

She was startled and embarrassed by his question. She'd thought they had come to a silent agreement not to intentionally hurt each other anymore. But some shred of pride kept her eyes from tearing as she replied, "I believe that's obvious, isn't it?"

"You mean you had little choice in the matter?"

She swallowed, and her face became mottled. I should have known better than to confide in him, she thought, her heart near bursting with bitter pain.

"Until Melcher came along and I took the choice away from you by scaring him away."

She could not tolerate his barbs anymore. She flew from her chair to run, but he stopped her with a hand on her arm. "I see now I was wrong," he said quietly, making her eyes fly to his. It was the last thing she had expected him to say. It wilted her resolve to hate him, yet she was now afraid of what would take hate's place should she relinquish it.

"Do we have to talk about this?" she asked the tan hand upon her sleeve.

"I'm trying to apologize, Abbie," he said. "I haven't done it many times in my life." She looked up, startled, to find utter sincerity in his eyes, and her heart set up a flurry of wingbeats at the somber look he wore.

Knowing that once she said it she would be on even more precarious footing, she said anyway, "Apology accepted." His dark fingers squeezed her arm once, then slid away. But it felt as if he had branded her with that touch while he spoke the words she had never thought to hear from him.

Chapter 11

MISS ABIGAIL KEPT her gardens just as fastidiously as she kept everything else, Jesse thought as he lounged against a tree, hands laced on his stomach, watching her. There was a predominance of blues, but being a man, he could not identify bachelor buttons, canterbury bells, or forget-me-nots, though he did know a morning glory. He squinted as Abbie flitted to explore them where they climbed a white trellis against the wall of the house. He almost expected her to dip and sip from one, he had thought of her as a hummingbird for so long. Lazy and sated, he watched her move from flower to flower. She leaned to pull an errant weed and he smiled privately as her derriere pointed his way. The backs of her calves came into view beneath her skirt. He closed one eye, leaving the other open as if taking a bead on her. When she seemed about to turn around, he pretended to be asleep. Then, in a moment, he carefully peered out at her again. Once more he assessed her slim ankles, realizing that she was a damn fine-looking woman. Let that tight knot of hair down, unbutton a couple buttons, teach her it's all right to laugh, and she'd make some man sit up and take notice. Realizing what he was thinking, he shut his eyes completely and thought, *That hummingbird's not for you, Jess.* But then why had they goaded and fought with each other like they had? It had all the earmarks of a mating ritual and he knew it. Didn't the stallion bite the mare before mounting her? And the she-cat—how she screamed and growled and spit at the tom before he jumped her. Even the gentle rabbits became vicious beforehand, the doe using her powerful back legs to box and kick the buck as if repulsed by him.

He studied Abigail McKenzie through scarcely opened eyelids. She picked some yellow thing and raised it to her nose. She had a cute little turned up nose.

He considered the hummingbird. Even its disposition turned pugnacious at mating time, both male and female becoming quarrelsome and snappish in their own avian way. He'd seen hummingbirds countless times in the woods, feeding from honey trees sweet with blossoms. Each male marked his feeding territory, defending it against all comers who sought to sip the nectar of his chosen flowers. He fought off all invaders until one special female arrived to tempt him. Together they would flit through the air flirting, toward and away from the prized flowers. Then, at the last, the female stilled her wings and hesitated just long enough for the male to mate with her, thus paying for the taste of his flowers before sipping quickly and caroming away too fast for the eye to follow.

He recalled how Abbie had withheld food from him, trying to starve him out of her house. He remembered all the teasing, the fighting, the baiting they'd each done.

She straightened and wiped her forehead with the back of a hand, her breast thrown into sharp relief against the mass of blue flowers behind her.

Damnit, Jess, get your carcass healed and out of here! he thought, and sat up quickly.

"What do you say we go for that ride?" he asked, needing some distraction.

She turned. "I thought you were asleep."

"I've slept so much in the last couple of weeks I don't care if I never do again." He wore a faint scowl as he looked away at the mountains.

"How is your skin?" she asked.

"Sour, I think. This buttermilk was soothing but I think it'd better come off before the neighbors start complaining." An amused smile lifted her lips and she wiped the back of her forehead again.

"I'll get some water." Soon she returned with a basin of cold water, a cloth, and a bar of soap, placing them on the ground near him.

"Pew! You do stink!" she exclaimed, backing away.

"If you think it smells bad from over there, you should smell it from over here." Again she laughed, then sat down a proper distance away, tucking both feet to one side beneath her skirts, watching him draw the basin between his legs and lean over to bathe his face. He lathered his hands instead of the cloth, raised his chin, running the soap back around his jaw and neck. He rinsed, opened his eyes, and caught her watching him, and she quickly glanced off across the flats to where the mountains rose, blue-hued and hazy, even in the high daytime sun.

"It'd be nice to take a buggy ride out there," he said.

"But I don't own a buggy or a horse," she explained.

"Hasn't this town got a livery stable?"

"Yes. Mr. Perkins runs it, but I don't think it's a good idea."

"But Doc said it's okay. I've been up a lot. I was up all the while you were gone. I even washed my hair with soap and water, didn't you notice?"

Oh, she'd noticed all right. She could still remember the smell of it while he breathed into her breasts on the rocker this morning.

"Being up is different than riding along in a bumpy buggy." But she looked wistfully at the road, lifting smoothly out of the valley into the foothills that gently inclined toward the ridges above the town.

"Are you afraid to go for a ride with me?"

Startled because he'd guessed the truth, she was forced to lie. "Why . . . why no. No, why should I be?"

"I'm a wanted man."

"You're an injured man, and in spite of what Doc Dougherty says, I refuse to believe it could do you any good to go riding on a hard buggy seat."

"When's the last time you saw my wound, Abbie? Doc's been the one looking at it and he says buggy riding's okay."

"It's not a good idea," she repeated lamely, picking a blade of grass.

"It's not me you don't think should go off in a buggy, it's you. Admit it."

"Me!"

He squinted up at the mountains, while her eyes strayed to the black hairs on the tops of his bare toes. "I mean," he drawled, biting on a piece of grass now himself, "it would probably look pretty queer, Miss Abigail McKenzie renting a rig to take her train robber off to who knows where on a Sunday afternoon."

"You are not *my* train robber, Mr. Cameron, and I'd appreciate it if you'd not refer to yourself as such."

"Oh, pardon," he said with a lopsided smile, "then the town's train robber." He could see her weakening—damnit, but she was getting to look more appealing by the minute—and he wondered if he should stay put.

"Why are you after me like this again? You promised you would behave."

"I'm behaving, aren't I? All I want to do is get out of here for awhile. Furthermore, I promised Doc I wouldn't harm you or try to escape. It's Sunday, everybody in town's relaxing and doing exactly as they please, and here you sit, gazing at the mountains from your hot backyard while we could be up where it's cooler, riding along and enjoying the day."

"I'm enjoying it right here—at least I was until you started with this preposterous idea." But she tucked a slim forefinger into the high, tight band of her collar and worked it back and forth.

He wondered if ever in her life she'd taken a buggy ride with a man. Maybe with that one thirteen years ago, she had. He found himself again trying to picture how she'd looked and acted when being courted.

"I wouldn't bite you, Abbie. What do you say?"

Her blue eyes seemed to appeal to him not to convince her this way, yet as her finger slid out of her collar her lips parted expectantly and she glanced once more at the mountains. Her cheeks took on a delicate pink color of her own primroses. Then she dropped her eyes to her lap as she spoke. "You would have to button up your shirt and put your boots on."

All was silent but for the chirp of a katydid. She raised her eyes to his and he thought, what the hell are you up to, Jess? He suddenly felt like some damn fool bumblebee sitting in her garden while she poised a glass jar above him, ready to slam it down and clap the cover on. But, against his better judgment, he smiled and said, "Agreed."

"Why, howdy, Miss Abigail," Gem Perkins said, answering her knock, trying hard not to show his surprise. Never before had she come to his door, but here she was, decked out flawlessly in white hat and gloves.

"Good afternoon, Mr. Perkins. I should like to rent a horse and buggy with a well-sprung seat. One that will jostle as little as possible."

"A buggy, Miss Abigail?" Gem asked, as if she'd requested instead a saddled gila monster.

"Do you or do you not rent buggies, Mr. Perkins?" she asked dryly.

"Why, o' course I do, you know that, Miss Abigail. I just never knew you to take one out before."

"And I wouldn't be now, except that Dr. Dougherty wants that invalid up at my place to grow accustomed to riding again so that he may be packed off on the train as soon as possible. However, we shall need an upholstered seat with lithe springs."

"Why, sure thing, Miss Abigail, upholstered seat and what was that other again?" He led the way to the livery, still surprised at her showing up here this way.

"Springy springs, Mr. Perkins," she stated again, wondering how long it would take for the news to spread to every resident of town what she was doing.

Jesse chuckled, watching her drive the rig up the street. He could see she didn't know the first thing about handling a horse. The mare threw her head and nickered in objection to the cut of the bit in Abbie's too-cautious hands. She pulled up in front of the pickets and he watched her carefully dismount, then swish up the walk. No, he decided, she'd never done anything like this before in her life.

By the time she entered the parlor, he was waiting on her graceful settee. Miss Abigail resisted the urge to laugh at how ridiculous he looked there—the only discrepancy in her otherwise tidy room. No, she thought, he'll never make *parlor fare.*

"The leg's a little stiff," he said, "and so is the new denim. Could you help me with my boots?" She looked down at his bare toes, chagrined to feel a peculiar thrill at the sight of them, then quickly she knelt and held first his socks, then his boots. They were fine boots, she noticed for the first time, well oiled and made of heavy, expensive cowhide. She wondered if he'd robbed a train to pay for them and was again surprised that the thought did nothing to deter her from wanting to ride out with him.

When the boots were on she rose, carefully avoiding looking at his dark-skinned chest behind the gaping garment. "You promised you'd button up your shirt," she reminded him.

He looked down at himself. "Oh, yeah." Then he struggled to stand clumsily on one foot, buttoned the shirt, then turned his back to her and unceremoniously unbuttoned his fly and began stuffing his shirttails in. Her cheeks flared red yet she stood and watched the play of his shoulder muscles while he made the necessary adjustments. Finally realizing what she was doing, she spun from the room and went to wait for him on the porch.

He stumped his way out on his crutches and moved to the side of the buggy. The denims were indeed very stiff. It immediately became apparent that he'd have trouble boarding. There was only a single, small footrest high on the buggy, and after three attempts to lift his foot to it, she ordered, "Wait on the steps and I'll pull up near them."

He withdrew to the porch steps to watch her inexpertly drive the rig around the end of the picket fence.

"You're pulling too sharp!" he warned. "Ease off!" He held his breath for fear she'd overturn the thing before the mission even got under way. But the rig arrived safely at the porch and he poised on his crutches on the second step.

"Can you make it?" she asked, measuring the distance visually.

He grinned, quipping, "If I don't, just ship my bones back to New Orleans." Then he swung both feet toward the floor of the rig, dangling momentarily by his armpits on the crutches. But the rest of his body didn't come along with his feet, and he teetered precariously, on the verge of going over backward.

"No!" Miss Abigail exclaimed, reacting automatically, reaching to grab the only thing she could see to grab: the waistband of his new denims. It did the trick, all right, but she yanked a little too hard and he came plummeting like a felled tree, nearly wiping her clean out the other side of the buggy. The next moment she found herself squashed beneath him, one hand splayed on his hard chest, the other still delving into his waistband. Suddenly realizing where that hand was buried, she jerked it out. But not before his suggestive smile made her face flame. She pushed him away and fussily adjusted her hat, whisked at her skirt, and refused to look at him. But his smirk remained in her peripheral vision. He was up to his cute tricks again, naturally! Red to the ears and trying to pretend she wasn't, she stiffened her back while he took the reins, clicked, whistled, and the mare set off while Abbie sat like a lump of her own cornmeal being taken for a ride.

"Are you all right?" he asked. But she could hear that smirk still coloring his words.

"I'm perfectly fine!" she snapped.

"Then what are you snapping at me for?"

"You know perfectly well why I'm snapping at you!"

"What did I do now?" All innocence and light.

"You know perfectly well what you did! You and your shifty, suggestive eyes!"

He smiled sideways at her starchy, affronted pose. "Well, I wasn't going to mention it, but as long as you did, what's a man supposed to do when a woman's got her hand in his pants?"

"My hand was not in your pants!" she spit, really puckered now.

He laughed boldly. "Oh, a thousand pardons, Miss Abigail. I guess I was mistaken. It must have been some other woman's hand in my pants just now." He looked around as if searching for the culprit. He chuckled low in his throat once, assessing her mirthfully. She wasn't taking his teasing too well today. He liked it best when she gave him tit for tat. He grinned, casting sideward glances at her stern face, and relaxed back and started whistling some little ditty softly between his teeth, deciding he'd be nice for a while and see if he couldn't sweeten her up some.

They headed north on a double track that paralleled the railroad tracks toward the foothills. It was scorching, and Miss Abigail was grateful for even the sliver of shade afforded by her narrow hatbrim. The leg space was inadequate for his long limbs, so his knees sprawled sideways, brushing against her skirts, though she kept her feet primly together and her hands in her lap. She inched away as far as possible, but they hit a bump and his knee lolled over and thumped against her and his smiling eyes leisurely roved her way. When she sat stiff and silent, he finally glanced off at the scenery without saying a word.

As they neared the foothills the undergrowth thickened and Jesse raised an arm, silently pointing. She followed his finger to where a cottontail hit for cover, and without knowing it, she smiled. Her eyes stayed riveted to the spot until they reached and passed it, and Jesse furtively watched her search for more animal life. A hawk appeared, circling above him, and she lifted her face to follow it. The greenery hedged closer to the road, and she seemed enchanted by a flock of lark buntings flitting in and out, feeding upon piñon nuts. The rails swung right while the wagon track bore left, and once again they broke into an open space where spikes of blue lupines created a moving sea all about them, as if part of the sky had fallen into the peaceful mountainside. Her lips formed a silent "Ohhh," and he smiled appreciatively. Silently they swayed along, climbing higher and higher until the terrain became rockier, with outcroppings here and there holding a strangling yew. They passed a cluster of bright orange painted cups, and again her eyes strayed behind to linger on the flowers as long as possible.

He turned his slow gaze upon her. "Where does this go?"

She perched like a little chipping sparrow, on the edge of her seat, alert and taking everything in. "To Eagle Butte, then along the Cascade Creek to Great Pine Rock and over the ridge to Hicksville."

Again they fell silent, he smiling and she taking in everything, while the mare trotted along. Once Jesse wiped his forehead on his shirtsleeve. They entered a patch of quaking aspen and the trembling, dappled shade the trees created. Here and there was a fragrant evergreen—juniper or spruce—vying for sky as the branches formed a tunnel overhead. Soon they came to a flat, shapeless gray rock precipice.

"Is this Eagle Butte?"

She looked around in a full circle. "I think so. It's been a long time since I was up here."

He stopped the horse and they sat with the sun pelting them mercilessly as they gazed beyond the enormity of Eagle Butte to a similar ridge that rose across a chasm along which they'd been riding for some distance. Over there the firs were in deep shadow—a rich, lush haven of coolness, while on this side the afternoon sun still blazed. Studying the scene opposite, Jesse absently unbuttoned two buttons of his shirt and ran a hand inside. Mingling with the scent of pine was that of ripe grass and the pleasantly fecund scent of the sweating horse.

"If you continue on, we should soon reach Cascade Creek and it should be much cooler there."

He clucked to the mare and they moved on. When they reached Cascade Creek it was, indeed, cool and inviting, brattling its way shallowly down a rocky bed between shady willows and alders.

The horse plodded to the water, dipped her head, and drank, then stood blinking slowly. Both of the riders watched the animal for several long, silent minutes.

At last Jesse asked, "Would you like to get down for a while?"

She knew it would be best to keep this outing strictly to riding, but she cast a wishful glance at the water. Instead of waiting for an answer, Jesse flicked the reins and turned the horse, nudging her toward a low-hanging branch on a gnarled pine tree. He stood, grabbed the sturdy branch, and swung easily to the ground. He retrieved his crutches from the buggy while she concealed her surprise at his lithe agility—for someone as big as he was, he moved like a puma. He reached up a brown hand to help her down, and she glanced, startled, at it, quite unprepared for this civility.

"Don't bump your head," he said, indicating the branch above her.

His palm waited, callused and hard, becoming more of an issue the longer she delayed placing her own in it. But she recalled that she was wearing her white gloves, and at last placed one in his firm grip as he helped her jump to the ground. She moved ahead of him toward the inviting water, but she had those gloves on, and he was on crutches so neither of them touched it. Instead they watched it bubble away at their feet. After some time he pulled his shirttails completely free of his pants again and unbuttoned the shirt the rest of the way. She stood stiff and formal, yet. Jesse glanced around, and spied a comfortable-looking spot where the water had scooped away the bank to form a rude, but natural chair. He hobbled over, threw his crutches down, then settled himself with a sigh. The creek burbled. The birds spoke. The woods were redolent with pine spice and leaf mold. Jesse crossed his arms behind his head and leaned back, watching the woman who stood on the creek bank.

Her back was as straight as a ramrod: she never allowed herself to relax those infernal gentilities of hers. Now she stood as stiffly as the boles of the pine trees, although he knew she was hot, too, for she'd raised a white glove to touch her forehead, then again to brush at the nape of her neck. What was she thinking as she looked at the creek? What did she want to do that her silly manners would not allow? He wondered if she'd even sit down, if she'd touch the water, if she'd condescend to talk to him.

"The water looks nice and cool," he commented finally, watching her carefully to see what she'd do. When she neither replied nor moved, he added, "Tell me if it is. I can't reach."

Her hands remained as motionless as a watched clock for a long, long time. Finally she drew her gloves off. He could tell by the hesitant way she leaned to touch the water that she wished he weren't watching her. Even a simple, sensual gesture like that caused her second thoughts. For a moment he pitied her. The hem of her dress slipped a little bit and she hurriedly clutched it up, away from the surface of the stream.

And he thought, let if fall, Abbie, let it fall, then wallow in behind it and see how great it feels. But he knew, of course, that she never would.

"Bring me some," he called anyway, just to see what she'd do.

She turned a brief, quizzical glance over her shoulder. "But I have nothing to carry it in."

"So carry it in your hands."

Abruptly she stood up. "There is a ridiculous suggestion if I ever heard one."

"Not to a thirsty man."

"Don't be foolish, you can't drink from my hands."

"Why not?" he asked casually.

He could hear her thinking, as clearly as if she'd spoken the words aloud, "It is just not done!"

"If I could drink from your mouth while I was unconscious, why can't I drink from your hands now?"

Her shoulder blades snapped closer together and she said, still facing away from him, "You take very great pleasure in persecuting me, don't you?"

"All I want is some water," he said reasonably, still with his head hanging backward in the cradle of his two hands. Then he sighed, looked upstream, and muttered, "Aw, what the hell, just forget it then," and laid his head back on the creekbank and closed his eyes.

He looked very harmless that way when she ventured to peek at him. Funny, but she really did not like being on the bad side of him, yet she never quite knew what he was up to. She glanced at his moustache—it was almost as thick as when she first saw him—then to the water, then back at him again. She looked around for something she could shape into a cone or vessel, but there was nothing. Never in her life had she done such a thing, but the thought of doing it caused an earthy sensation in the pit of her stomach. The water had felt deliciously cool. Even the horse had needed a long drink. And Jesse was obviously very hot. He'd unbuttoned that shirt again, and she remembered how he'd run his hand inside it earlier. She looked at him dozing peacefully. She looked at the water.

Jesse's eyes flew open as two large splats of water hit his bare chest. He jumped but then grinned: she was standing over him with cupped hands.

"Open up," she ordered.

Well I'll be damned, he thought, and opened his mouth like a communicant. She lowered her palms, created a split in their seam, but the water trailed away, down inside her cuffs, some hitting his chest and chin, but none reaching his lips. She half expected him to jump up and smack her hands aside, remembering the time she'd clacked the spoon against his teeth, but he surprised her by rubbing a hand over his dark chest, spreading the water wide.

"Ah, that's cool," he said appreciatively, then his eyes twinkled. "But I'd like a little in my mouth, too."

"Oh, I got my cuffs wet," she complained, pulling at them. But they stuck to her wrists and would not even slide on her skin.

"As long as they're already wet, may as well try again."

This time it worked better, for he reached to cup the backs of her hands and pour the water into his mouth from her fingertips as if they were the lip of a pitcher.

It was a decidedly sensuous thing, watching him drink from her fingertips. It made queer quivers start way down low in her stomach. After he swallowed, droplets were left upon his moustache. Fascinated, she watched his tongue run along its edge and lap them up. She realized suddenly that she'd been staring. Immediately her eyes flitted to some distant bush.

"Why don't you have some?"

She touched her throat just below her jaw. "N . . . No, I don't want any."

He knew it was not true, but understood—she'd already gone too far.

"Come on, sit down awhile. It's nice and cool here and really quite comfortable."

She glanced around as if someone might catch her at it if she dared. Reaching some sort of compromise with herself, she said, "I'll sit here," and perched on a rock near his feet.

"You've never been up here before?" he asked, studying her back as she faced the creek.

"When I was a girl, I was."

"Who brought you?"

"My father. He came to cut wood and I helped him load it."

"If I lived around here I'd come up here all the time. It's too flat and hot down in the valley to suit me." He laced his hands behind his head and looked up into the trees. "When my brothers and I were small, we spent hours and hours by the Gulf, catching sand crabs, playing in the surf, shell hunting. I miss the ocean."

"I've never seen the ocean," she said plaintively.

"It's no prettier than this, just pretty in a different way. Do you want to?"

"Want to?" She glanced back at him.

"See the ocean?"

"I don't know. Richard was—" But she stopped dead and quickly faced the creek.

"Richard? Who is Richard?"

"Nothing . . . nobody . . . I don't even know why I brought him up."

"He must be *somebody,* or you wouldn't have."

"Oh . . ." She circled her knees with her hands. "He was just someone I knew once who always said he wanted to live by the ocean."

"Did he make it?"

"I don't know."

"You lost touch with him?"

She sighed and shrugged. "What does it matter? It was a long time ago."

"How long ago?"

But she didn't answer. She was afraid to confide in him. Yet he urged her to speak of things which no other person had ever cared enough to ask about.

"Thirteen years ago?" he prompted. Still she didn't reply, and he thought long and hard before finally admitting, "I know about Richard, Abbie."

He heard her breath catch in her throat before she turned startled eyes to him. "How could you know about Richard?"

"Doc Dougherty told me."

Her nostrils distended and her lips tightened. "Doctor Dougherty talks too much for his own good."

"And you talk too little for yours."

She hugged herself and turned away. "I keep my private affairs to myself. That is exactly how it should be."

"Is it? Then why did you bring up Richard?"

"I don't know. His name slipped out inadvertently. I've never talked about him since he left and I assure you I am not about to start now."

"Why? Is he taboo, just like everything else?"

"You talk like a fool."

"No, I suspect somebody did that long before I came along, or you wouldn't be so tied up in knots over letting go a little bit."

"I don't even know why I listen to you—a completely impulsive person like you. You have no notion of restraint or self-control of any kind. You . . . you charge through life as if to give it a shock so it will remember you've been there. That may work well for you, but I assure you it is not my way. I live by strict standards."

"Has it occurred to you, Abbie, that maybe you set your standards too high, or that somebody else may have done it for you?"

"That is impossible for any living person to do."

"Then tell me why you're sitting out here five miles from civilization yet you wouldn't take your hat off if it grew tentacles or even unbutton the cuffs that are probably chafing you raw right now. But worst of all you won't talk about something that caused you pain, because some fool said a lady shouldn't? Nor does she show regret or anger, is that right? A lady just doesn't spill her guts. She sits instead with them all tied in neat, prim knots. Of course talking would make you human, and maybe you prefer to think you're above being human." He knew he was making her angry, but knew too that was the only time she truly opened up.

"I was taught, sir, that it is both ill-mannered and—yes—unladylike to wail out one's dissatisfactions with life. It simply is not done."

"Who said so, your mother?"

"Yes, if you must know!"

"Humph!" He could just about picture her mother. "The best thing in the world for you would be to come right out and say, 'I loved a man named Richard once but he jilted me and it makes me mad as hell.' "

Her fists knotted and she spun to face him, eyes dangerously glistening. "You have no right!"

"No, but you do, Abbie, don't you see?" He sat straighter, intense now.

"All I see is that I should never have come up here with you today. You have succeeded again in making me so angry that I should like to . . . to slap your hateful face!"

"It'd be the second time today you slapped my face for making you feel something. Is it that frightful to you to feel? If slapping me would make you feel good, why don't you come over here and do it? How mad do I have to make you before you'll break out? Why can't you just cuss or laugh or cry when something inside Abbie says she should?"

"What is it you want of me!"

"Just to teach you that what comes natural shouldn't be forbidden."

"Oh, certainly! Slapping, crying . . . and . . . and that . . . that little scene on the rocker this morning! Why, if you had your way you would turn me into a wanton!" Tears brimmed at the rims of her eyes.

"Those things aren't wanton, but you can't see it because of all the silly rules your mother made you live by."

"You leave my mother out of this! Ever since you came to my house you've been contrary and fault-finding. I will not let you attack my mother when your own could have taught you a few manners!"

"Listen to yourself, Abbie. Why is it you can call me names and get angry with me when the ones you really blame are your mother and father and Richard for what they did to you?"

"I said leave them out of this! What they were to me is none of your business!" Her eyes blazed as she jumped to her feet.

"Why so belligerent, Abbie? Because I hit on the truth? Because it's them you blame when you think you're not supposed to? Doc Dougherty didn't have to tell me much to fit the pieces together. Correct me if I'm wrong. Your mother taught you that a good daughter honors her father and mother, even if it means sacrificing her own joy. She taught you that virtue is natural and carnality isn't, when actually it's the other way around."

"How dare you sit there and pour acerbations on innocent people who wanted only the best for me?"

"They had no idea of what was best for you—all except Richard, I suspect, and he was smart enough to know he couldn't fight your dead mother's code of ethics, so he got out!"

"Oh! And you know what's best for me, I suppose!"

He assessed her dispassionately. "Maybe."

She assessed him passionately. "And maybe you'll sprout wings and fly away from the law when they come to get you!" She waggled a finger in the direction of town.

Comprehension dawned in his eyes. "Ah, now we're getting down to the truth here, aren't we?" He reached for his crutches without taking his menacing eyes from her. "It baffles you how some common, no-good train robber like me could possibly hit on the truth about you, doesn't it?"

"Exactly!" she spit, facing him, fists clenched angrily at her sides. "A common, no-good train robber!"

"Well, let this common, no-good train robber tell you a few things about yourself, Miss Abigail McKenzie, that you've been denying ever since you laid eyes on me." He struggled to his feet, advancing upon her. "It is precisely *because* I'm an outlaw that you have, on several occasions, ventured forth from your righteous ways and lost control. With me you did things you never dared do before—you sneaked a peek at life. And do you know why you tried it? Because afterward you could wipe your conscience clean and blame me for goading you into it. After all, I'm the bad one anyway, right?"

"You talk in circles!" she scoffed, quaking now because he'd hit upon the truth and that truth was too awful for her to admit.

"Are you denying that it's because I'm a . . . a criminal that you dared to bend your holy bylaws around me a little?" They were nose to nose now.

"I don't know what you're talking about," she said prissily, and turned away, crossing her arms tightly across her breasts.

He reached out to grab her upper arm and try to make her turn to face him. "Oh, pull your head out of the sand, Miss Abigail Ostrich, and admit it!" She yanked herself free of his grip, but he moved in close behind her, pursuing her with his relentless accusations. "You slammed doors and threw bedpans and kissed me and hollered at me and even got yourself a little sexually excited, and you found out it all felt pretty damn fun at times. But you could blame all those forbidden things on me, right? Because I'm the nasty one here, not you. But what would happen to all your grand illusions if I turned out to be something other than the brigand you think I am?" Again he got her by the arm. "Come on, talk to me. Tell me all your well-guarded secret guilts! You can tell me—what the hell, I'll be gone soon enough and take them all with me!"

At last she spun on him, whacking his hand off her arm. "I have no secret guilts!" she shouted angrily.

His eyes bored into hers as he shouted back, with ferocity equal to hers, "Now *that's* what I've been trying to make you see all this time!"

Silence fell like a hundred-year oak. Their eyes locked. She struggled to understand what it was he was saying, and when the truth came to her at last, she was stricken by her own comprehension, and she turned away.

"Don't keep turning away from me, Abbie," he said, making his way to her on the clumsy crutches, touching her arm more gently now, trying to make her face him willingly, which she stubbornly refused to do. "Do I have to say it for you, Abbie?" he asked softly.

Tears began gathering in her throat.

"I . . . I don't know what it is you want me to . . . to say."

In the quietest tones he had ever used with her, Jesse spoke. "Why not start by admitting that Richard was a randy youth, that something happened between you and him that made him leave." Jesse paused a long moment, then added even softer, while with his thumb he stroked the arm he still held, "That it had nothing to do with your father."

"No, no . . . it's not true!" She covered her face with her palms. "Why do you goad me like this?"

"Because I think Richard was exactly like me and it's got you scared to death."

She whirled then and hit him once with her pathetic little fist in the center of his bare chest. It send him hobbling backward, but he didn't quite fall. "Wasn't he?" Jesse persisted.

She looked into his relentless eyes like a demented woodland nymph, shaken, tears now streaming down her cheeks. "Leave me alone!" she begged miserably.

"Admit it, Abbie," he said softly.

"Damn you!" she cried, sobbing now, and raised a hand to strike him again. He did not cringe or back away as the blow, and another and another rained upon his shoulders and chest. "Damn you . . . R . . . Richard!" she choked, but Jesse stood sturdy as she hit the side of his neck and her nails scraped two red welts upon it.

He did not fight her, did not block her swing, only said very gently, "I'm not Richard, Abbie. I'm Jesse."

"I know . . . I kn . . . I know," she sobbed into her hands, ashamed now of having sunk to such depths.

He reached out and encircled her shaking shoulders, gathering her near, pulling her forehead against his hard chest. Her tears scalded his bare skin and brought some wholly new and disturbing stinging behind his eyes. A crutch dropped to the ground, but he steadied himself and let it fall. Her hat had gone askew and he reached to pull the pin from it.

Her hands flew up and she choked, "Wh . . . what are y . . . you doing?"

"Just something you wouldn't do for yourself—taking your hat off. Nothing more, okay?" He stuck the filigreed pin through the straw, tossed it behind him onto the creek bank, then pulled her again into his arms, circling her neck with one large hand, rubbing a thumb across the hair pulled so prudishly taut behind her ear.

She cried against him with her elbows folded tightly between them, comforted more than she'd thought possible by the feel of his forearm spanning her narrow shoulders and his palm stroking her sleeve. He touched her soft earlobe. He laid his cheek against her hair, and she felt a queer sense of security, staying within his arms that way.

Abbie, Abbie, he thought, *my little hummingbird, what are you doing to me?*

He smelled different than her father—better. He felt different than David—harder. She reminded herself who he was, what he was, but for the moment it didn't matter. He was here, and warm, and real, and the beat of his heart was firm and sure beneath her cheek upon his chest. And she needed so terribly badly to talk about everything at last.

When her crying eased, he leaned back, taking her face in both hands, wiping at the wetness beneath her eyes with his thumbs.

"Come on, Abbie, let's sit down and talk. Don't you see you've got to talk about it?"

She nodded limply, then he drew her by the hand toward the creek bank, and she followed docilely, exhausted now from her fit of tears.

A blackbird sang in the willows. The creek rushed past with its whispered accompaniment as Abbie began to speak. Jesse did not touch her again, but let her talk it all out, drawing from her the truths which he'd guessed days ago. He pieced together the picture of a pathetic, retiring husband and the single child, both of whom the mother had wronged with her narrow version of love. A rigid woman of stern discipline who taught her daughter that duty was more important than the urgings of her own body. And Richard, the man who made Abbie aware of those urgings, but could not free her from the stringent laws laid down by her mother. And Abbie, hiding all these years behind the delusion that Richard had deserted her because of the invalid father.

But Jesse now saw the imprisoned Abbie escape, as the bullfrogs set up their late-day chorus. He watched the woman on the creek bank change into a mellow, human entity, with fears, misgivings, frailties, and regrets. And it was this transformed Abbie of whom Jesse knew he'd best be careful.

Things were infinitely different between them by the time they started back to town. The myths were shattered. The truth now rode like a passenger on the seat, intimately, between them. There was a disturbing ease, born of a deeper understanding, and far more threatening than the animosities which had earlier riddled their relationship.

For she had learned he could be kind.

And he had learned she could be human.

They rode in silence, aware of each brush of elbow and knee. White moths of evening came out and the song of the cicada ceased. The shadows of the trees grew to longstretching tendrils then disappeared in the cease of sun. The leaves whispered their last hushed vespers. The mare quickened her step toward home, her voice the only one heard as she nickered to the growing twilight. Abbie's sleeve brushed Jesse's shoulder and he leaned forward, away from it, staring straight ahead, elbows to knees and the reins limp in his hands. He had helped her break down many barriers today, but she was still bound by propriety. She was not at all his kind of woman. Yet he looked back over his shoulder and caught her watching him, her eyes quite the color of the evening sky, her piquant little face showing signs of confusion, but her hands again in white gloves, glowing almost purple now as dusk came on.

Her eyes strayed, then came back to meet his, and she knew the swift, intimidating yearning of the woman who feels herself drawn to the wrong man. The wheels hushed along, the riders rocked in unison, their eyes locked. At last her troubled gaze drifted aside, as did his. She thought of a gun in his hand on that train and her eyes slid shut, not wanting to picture it yet unable to keep the image at bay. She opened her eyes again and studied his broad shoulders with blue cotton pulled taut against rippling muscle, black hair curling down over his collar, thick sideburns curving low on a crisp jaw, sleeves rolled to elbows upon arms limned with dark hair, the limp wrist, those long fingers. She remembered them upon her, then looked away, distracted.

God help me, she thought, I want him.

Town approached. Jesse shifted the reins to one hand and, without saying a word, considerately buttoned up his shirt. In the gathering dusk she felt herself blush. He leaned back, their shoulders touched again, then her familiar white picket fence was beside them and he pulled up before the porch steps.

He handed her the reins. They were warm from his hands.

He spoke gently. "Don't turn her so sharp this time. I don't want you tipping over."

Something too good happened within her at his quiet admonition.

He stood in the twilight watching her again cut too sharply around the pickets, holding his breath, releasing it only when she'd straightened the rig and was heading up the street. Then he clumped to the swing at the north end of the porch to wait for her. He braced his crutches in the corner and swung idly, surveying the porch, which was so typical of her. It was tidy, freshly painted, surrounded by a spooled rail that quit only where the wide steps gave onto the yard. At the opposite end was a pair of white wicker chairs with a matching table between them holding a sprawling fern. He thought of her while he swung, accompanied by the soft, jerking squeak of the ropes.

She rounded a corner down the street and he watched her come on, small and straight, and felt the strength of his healing muscles and knew he'd damn well better leave this place soon.

She started slightly when she saw him there in the shadows, one arm stretched carelessly along the back of the double seat. She wondered how it would feel to simply settle down in the lea of that arm and lean her head back against him and swing away companiably until full darkness fell and he should say, "It's time for bed now, Abbie."

But he was Jesse the ominous train robber, so she stood uncertainly at the top of the steps. Only, he did not look very ominous swinging away idly there. The ropes spoke a creaky complaint about his weight, and for a moment she remembered the awesomeness of it upon her. She dropped her eyes guiltily.

"Are you hungry?" she asked, unable to think of anything else to say.

"A little," he replied. He realized only too clearly what it was he was hungry for.

"Would cold chicken and bread be all right?"

"Sure. Why don't we eat it out here?"

"I don't think—" She cast a glance at the house next door, then seemed to change her mind. "All right. I'll get it." She left him swinging there, and when she returned with the tray he sensed her hesitation to approach him.

"Put it on the floor at our feet and come sit with me," he invited. "It's getting dark—nobody will see us." But her eyes skittered to the elbow slung along the back of the swing, and only when he lowered it did she set the tray down and perch beside him.

They nibbled silently, caught up by awareness, lashed into silence by the new tension which had sprung up between them. They ate little. She told herself to take the tray back inside, but sat instead as if her legs had wills of their own.

He crossed his near ankle over his knee, dropped a dark hand over the boot to hold it there while each stroke of the swing now whispered his knee across Abbie's skirts. Her eyes were drawn to the sturdy thigh tight-wrapped in straining denim. She clenched her hand in the folds of her skirts to keep it from reaching out and resting upon that firm muscle which flexed repeatedly with each nudge of his heel upon the floor. She could almost feel how warm and hard that thigh would be, how sensual it would feel to run her palm along its long, inner side, to know the intimate shift of muscle as it moved with the swing. But she only stared at it while her unwieldy imagination did strange things to the low reaches of her stomach. A tightness tugged there, and queer trembles afflicted her most intimate parts. She sat there coveting that masculine thigh and becoming enamored with the mere touch of her own clothing against her skin.

He draped his wrist lazily over the back of the swing, never touching her, yet making her heart careen when she realized how close it hung to her shoulder.

"Well, I guess it's bedtime," he said quietly at last. Her pulses pounded and the blood beat its way up her cheeks. But he only removed his hand from the back of the swing and craned around for his crutches in the corner, then rose and positioned them, politely waiting for her to precede him.

He managed the screen door, and when she passed before him into the parlor, asked behind her, "Do you want the inside door closed?"

She was afraid to look back at him, so continued toward the kitchen, answering, "No. It's a warm night, just hook the screen."

Jesse felt a sense of home, coming in with her this way, putting things in order for the night, and knew more than ever that it was time to move on. He shuffled through the dark in the direction of the kitchen.

"Where are the matches?" he asked.

Her voice came from someplace near the pantry door. "In the matchbox on the wall to the left of the stove."

He groped, found, struck a wooden tip and held it high. Abbie sprang into light, hovering in the pantryway with the tray pressed against her waist, and her eyes big and luminous in the lamplight. He put the chimney back on the lamp and looked across at her, tempted . . . oh so tempted.

For a minute neither knew what to say.

"I'll . . . I'll just set these dirty dishes in the pantry."

"Oh . . . oh, sure," he shrugged, looked around as if he'd lost something. "Guess I'll go out back then before bed." Resolutely, Jesse headed for the door, knowing he was doing the right thing. But as he was negotiating the dark steps he found her behind him holding the lantern aloft to illuminate his way. He swung around and looked up at her.

Unsmiling, she studied his face glowing red-gold below her, his hair blending with the backdrop of the night. The lantern caught the measureless depths of his eyes, like those of a cat impaled by a ray of direct light.

"Thanks, Abbie," he said quietly, ". . . good night." Then his arms flexed upon the crutches and he was gone, downyard, swallowed by the dark.

She put the pantry in order for the night, and still he hadn't come in. She went to the back screen and peered out. The moon had risen and she made out his shape by its pale white light, sitting in the backyard under the linden tree. His face was in lacy night shadow, but she made out his boots and the way one knee was raised with an arm slung over it.

"Jesse?" she called softly.

"Aha."

"Are you all right?"

"I'm fine. Go to bed, Abbie."

When she did, she lay a long time listening, but never did hear him come back inside.

Chapter 12

THE FOLLOWING MORNING a grinning Bones Binley stood on Miss Abigail's front porch, looking like a jack-o'-lantern atop a knobby fence post, with his overlarge head, gap-teeth, and protruding Adam's apple.

"Mornin', Mizz Abigail. Fine mornin'. Fine mornin'. This package . . . ah . . . come for you at the depot on yesterday's train, Mizz Abigail, but there wasn't nobody around to bring it on up, so Max he ast me to this mornin'."

"Thank you, Mr. Binley," she answered, opening the screen only enough to slip the package through, disappointing old Bones, who'd have given a half plug of tobacco to see just what was inside that box and the other half to see what that train robber was doing inside her house. But when Bones continued to grin at her through the screen, she added, "It was very obliging of you to deliver it to me, Mr. Binley."

She was the only person ever called him Mister that way.

"Sure thing, Mizz Abigail," Bones said almost reverently, nodding and shifting enormous feet while she wondered if she'd have to swat him off her porch with the screen door, like some pesky fly.

Once when they were younger Bones had bought Miss Abigail's basket at a Fourth of July picnic, and he'd never forgotten the taste of her sour cream cake and fried chicken, or her ladylike ways and the time she had him up to do a little repair work on the shingles and how she'd asked him in afterward for cake and coffee. But he could see now that he was no more going to get inside her house than any train robber was going to get inside her pants, which was after all what the whole town was buzzing about.

"How's that there robber feller doing?" he asked, lifting his battered hat and scratching his forehead.

"I'm not qualified to give a medical opinion on his state of health, Mr. Binley. If you want that information to pass around with your snuff down at the feedstore, I suggest you ask Doctor Dougherty."

Bones had just then worked up a good hock and was about to let 'er fly when Miss Abigail warned from her front door, "Do not leave your residue on my property, if you please, Mr. Binley!"

Well, by damn! thought old Bones, if she was talking about spit, why in tarnal didn't she just come right out and say spit? Maybe folks was right when they said she got a little uppity at times. But anyways, Bones waited till he got to the road before he laid a good gob. He wasn't gonna go messin' with her—nossir!—not old Bones. And unless he missed his guess, wasn't no man ever gonna mess with her, train robber or not!

The package was unmarked, except for a Denver postmark and her name and Stuart's Junction, Colorado. She did not recognize the handwriting. It was angular, tall, and made her heart race. In her entire life she might have gotten maybe three packages. There was one a long time ago that had brought the small picture frame she'd sent for, to hold her mother's and father's tintypes. Then there was the time she'd sent away for the bedpan when her father could no longer execute the walk to the backyard. This package now was Miss Abigail's third, and she wanted to savor its mystery as long as possible.

She shook it and it clunked like dried muffins in a pie safe. She saw Bones disappear down the street and on an impulse took the box back outside to the porch swing. She savored it for a long while before finally carefully removing the outside wrapper, keeping the paper in one piece to save away and treasure later. She shook the box again and even sniffed at it. But all it smelled like was the pages of an old book, papery and dry. She set it on her knees and ran a bemused hand over the lid and swung idly upon the swing, drawing out the delicious wonderment while curiosity welled beautifully in her throat. She took some moments to cherish the anticipatory feeling and file it away for future memory. Finally she lifted the lid and her breath caught in her throat. Nestled within, like two pieces of a jigsaw puzzle, was a pair of the most beautiful shoes she had ever seen. There was a folded note, but she reached for neither note nor shoes immediately, sat instead with her hand over her opened lips, remembering David Melcher's face as she had last seen it, stricken with regret.

At last she lifted the note in one hand and a single shoe in the other.

Oh my! she thought. Red! They are red! Whatever shall I do with a pair of red shoes?

But she examined the exquisite leather, soft as a gentian petal, so soft that she wondered how such supple stuff could possibly support a person's weight. They were buskin styled, with delicate lacets running from ankle to top and sporting heels shaped like the waists of fairies, concave and chic. Touching the chamois-soft texture, she knew without needing to be told that they were indeed made of kidskin, the finest money could buy. David, she thought, oh, David, thank you. And she pressed a shoe to her cheek, suddenly missing him and wishing he were here. She would have liked to put the shoes on while she read his note, but she could never put these scarlet shoes on where they might be seen. Oh, perhaps sometime in the privacy of her bedroom. But for now she laid the shoe back in the box beside its mate and read his note:

My Dear Miss Abigail,

I take the liberty—no, the honor—of sending the finest and newest pair of shoes from the shipment awaiting me when I arrived in Denver. It will please me to imagine them on your dainty feet as you snip nasturtiums and take them into your gracious home. I think of you in that setting and even now rue my rashness in speaking to you as I did. If you can find it in your heart to forgive me, know that I would have willed things to take a different course than they've taken.

Yours in humility and gratitude,
David Melcher

She'd thought thirteen years ago that she'd realized what a broken heart felt like, when she was spurned by the man she'd grown to love through all her growing years. But it felt now as if this sense of a thing lost before it was ever gained was sorrier than anything she'd suffered back then. Her heart stung at the thought that David Melcher pined for her—impossible as it seemed, herself being the age she was. Such a refined man, who was just what she'd been looking for for so many years, ever since Richard ran away. And now she had no way to reach him, to say, "Come back . . . I forgive you . . . let us begin from here." The shoebox told her nothing. It held no company name, no color or style markings. There was no clue as to whom he worked for. All she knew was that he'd mentioned Philadelphia and that this package had been posted in Denver. But they were big cities, Denver and Philadelphia, cities in which there were undoubtedly many shoe manufacturers, many hawkers. It would be impossible to find a man who did not even possess a permanent address. But at the thought of his lack of a residence, the words *Elysian Club* came back to her.

The Elysian Club! Philadelphia!

That was where he stayed when he went back there. With a leaping heart she knew she would write a thank-you to him in care of the Elysian Club, Philadelphia, and just hope he would somehow receive it on one of his return trips, and maybe—just maybe—he would come back to Stuart's Junction some day and look her up.

"Abbie? What're you doing out there?" A tousled Jesse, fresh up, stood barefoot, bare-chested in the front door.

Excitement animated her voice as she bubbled, "Oh, Mr. Cameron, look at what has just arrived for me." She had eyes for nothing but the shoes, which he could not see yet. She brought the package into the front parlor, crossed, and laid it on the dining room table at the far end, the wrapping paper address-side-up so there could be no mistaking the shoes were meant for her.

Jesse hobbled over to see what it was. "Where did you order those from?" he asked, surprised when he saw the scarlet shoes, for they didn't seem at all the kind of thing she'd choose.

"I didn't order them. They are a gift from David Melcher."

Suddenly Jesse needed a second look, and after taking it, decided he disliked the shoes wholeheartedly. *"David* Melcher? My, my, aren't we becoming informal all of a sudden? And shoes yet! How shocking, Miss Abigail."

"I find it rather endearing myself," she said, fingering the leather, her mind scarcely on what she was doing. "Not the kind of gift that just any man would choose."

Jesse could sense her excitement as she let her fingers flutter over the red leather, butterflylike, touching the laces, the tongue, the toes, almost reverently.

"You can wear 'em over town every time you need a pig's bladder from the butcher shop," he said testily, "or whenever you need to send a wire asking somebody to get rid of a gunslinger for you."

She was too happy to heed his attempt to snub the gift.

"Oh my, I fear I cannot wear them anyplace at all. They simply aren't — well, they're much too fine and elegant for Stuart's Junction."

A black scowl drew his eyebrows down. She was damn near fondling the red leather now, and her face wore a beatific expression while she raved on about the exquisite workmanship and the quality of the leather. He'd never seen her glow so before, or bubble this way. Her eyes were as blue and bright as her morning glories, and her lips were parted in a rare, pliant smile. Watching it, he wanted to smack those damn red shoes from her hands.

But suddenly Jesse realized that Abbie's hair was less than tidy and she was wearing an old, shapeless, dark floral shirt with sleeves rolled up to her elbows and a dishtowel tied triangularly around her belly. She looked as ordinary as a scullery maid, and the effect was devastating. He found himself studying the knot of the dishtowel which rode the shallows of her spine.

"Oh, my heavens!" she said gaily, "you slept so late and here I stand gaping at these things while you're probably fit to starve." She plopped the cover back over the shoes and looked up to catch the dark frown on his face.

For a moment it seemed to Abbie that he'd grown taller overnight, but she suddenly realized why.

"Why, you're walking without crutches!" she exclaimed gladly. Then she thought, gracious, but he is tall! And immediately afterward, gracious, but he is only half-dressed! He was shirtless and barefoot, as usual, wearing nothing but the new dungarees. "Now, Doctor Dougherty said you must take it a little at a time," she scolded, to cover her flustration at the sight of his bare skin.

Her concern assuaged some of the nettlesome annoyance he'd felt over the shoes, and his anger faded.

"I'm starved. What time is it?" He rubbed his hard, flat belly, pleased to see her eyes skitter away.

"Approaching noon. You slept very late." She turned toward the kitchen and he followed.

"Did you miss me?" He gave the shoebox a last scathing look and eyed that knotted dishtowel as it lifted perkily, bustlelike, with each step she took. She had one of the trimmest backsides he'd ever seen.

"I hardly had time. I was busy doing the washing."

"Oh, so that's why you're dressed like a scullery maid. I don't mind saying it's a pleasant change."

Suddenly she became self-conscious and began unrolling one of her shirtsleeves, flicking the folds down to cover her exposed arms, and he wondered if she'd have left them rolled up were he David Melcher. The thought irritated him further.

"Dirty jobs do not magically get done," she said, all business again, efficiently buttoning up her cuffs, then reaching behind to untie her dishtowel. He was sorry to see it go as she set about preparing their noon dinner. There was no evidence of her having washed clothes in the kitchen, but outside he found lines strung now, holding bedding, dishtowels, and some skirts and blouses. Limping his way to the privy, he caught sight, too, of pantalets and chemises trimmed with eyelet, hidden as inconspicuously as possible behind the larger, more mundane pieces of laundry. The corset he'd imagined her in, giving her chronic gastric and emotional indigestion, was nowhere in evidence.

However, when he got back to the house he figured the reason it was not on the line was because it must be busily binding her up in knots! Her waspish temperament had inexplicably returned. She started in on him the minute he walked in the door.

"I've asked you not to go about undressed that way, *sir!*" she stated tartly, obviously in a snit over a damn fool thing like that.

"Undressed!" He looked down at himself. "I'm not undressed!"

"Where is your shirt!"

"It's in the bedroom, for God's sake!"

"Mister Cameron, would you set aside your own offensive vernacular until you are once again in the sort of company that will appreciate it?"

"All right, all right, what bit you all of a sudden?"

"Nothing *bit* me, I just—" But she turned away without finishing.

"A minute ago you were all sloe-eyed over old Melcher's shoes and now—"

"I was *not* sloe-eyed!" She spun, eyes snapping, hands on hips.

"Huh!" he snorted, gripping the edge of the highboy behind him, tapping out a vexed rhythm with his fingertips. "He lit you up like a ball of swamp gas with those . . . those pieces of frippery!" He flung a disparaging hand toward the dining room.

Her eyebrows shot up. "Yesterday you were telling me to throw caution to the wind and feel things. Today you disparage me for a simple show of appreciation."

They stared at each other for a few crackling seconds before Jesse said the most absurd thing.

"But they're red!"

"They're what?" she asked, baffled.

"I said, they're red!" he roared. "The goddamn shoes are red!"

"Well, so what?"

"So . . . so they're red, that's all." He started pacing around in the corner by the pantry door, feeling silly. "What the hell kind of woman wears red shoes?" he squawked, forgetting that he'd just been admiring the way that dishtowel made her look like precisely the kind of woman who might wear red shoes.

"Did I say I wanted to wear them?"

"You didn't have to say it. The look on your face said it for you."

She pointed out the back door. "While I am trying to preserve some decorum around here, you limp out to the outhouse, naked as a savage, then have the audacity to scold me for thinking I should like to wear red shoes!"

"Let's get the issue straight here, *Miss* Abigail. You're not mad about me going out in the open without a shirt and shoes. You're mad because I caught you looking sloe-eyed over those insufferable shoes!"

"And you're not mad because the shoes are red, you're mad because they're from David Melcher!"

"David Melcher!" he squawked disbelievingly, almost in her ear as she thundered past him into the pantry. "Don't make me laugh!" He followed right behind her, nose first, like a bloodhound. "If you think I'm jealous of a pantywaist like that—" But just then she swung around and stepped on his bare toe. "Ouch!" he yelped, while she didn't even slow down or say excuse me.

"You wouldn't get stepped on if you'd dress properly." She clapped some dishes on the table.

"The hell you say! You did that on purpose!"

"Maybe I did." She sounded pleased.

He nursed his toe against his calf. "Over nothing. I didn't do a damn thing this time!"

But she whirled on him, pointing an outraged finger at the backyard. "Nothing, you say? How dare you, sir, walk across my yard dressed like *that* and gape at my underthings in front of the whole town!"

His eyebrows shot up and a slow smile crept across his countenance, lifting one corner of his moustache before it lit up his mischievous eyes and he started laughing deep in his throat, then louder and louder until at last he collapsed onto a chair.

"Oh you . . . you . . . just . . . just shut up!" she spluttered. "Do you want the whole town to hear you?" She clapped herself down on the chair opposite and created a gross breach of etiquette for Miss Abigail McKenzie, serving herself without waiting for him. She whacked the serving spoon against her plate, splatting potatoes onto it while he sat there snickering. Finally she shoved a bowl in his direction and grunted, "Eat!"

He loaded his plate in between maddening chuckles while she felt like kicking his bad leg under the table. Finally he braced an elbow on the corner of the table, leaned near, and whispered very loudly, "Is it better if I whisper? This way the neighbors won't hear me." Even staring at her plate she could see that insufferable moustache right by her cheek. "Hey, Abbie, you know what I was looking for out there? Corsets. I wanted to see just how much rigging I'd have to get through before I hit skin."

She dropped her fork and knife with a clatter and left her chair as if ejected from it, but he made a grab and caught her by the back of her skirt.

"Let me go!" She yanked at the skirt, but he hauled away and pulled her back between his spraddled thighs while her arms flailed ineffectually.

"How many layers are under there, Abbie?" he teased, trying to get an arm around her waist and pull her down to his lap. She yanked and slapped and tried to free her skirt but he hauled it in like lanyard, all the while chortling deep in his throat.

"Get away!" she barked while he got her up against his lap like a schooner against a piling. She battled frantically, then luffed around till she could push against his shoulder, still trying to control her skirt with the other hand.

His smile was wicked, his hands deadly, as he breathed hard in her ear, "Don't you wear petticoats, Abbie? Come on, let's see." They were a dervish of arms and hands and elbows and petticoats and knees by this time. He gained and she struggled. He captured and she flapped. He fended off a misaimed slap, feinting back expertly while she rapidly lost ground.

"You maniac!" she bellowed, clawing his fingers loose from her wrist.

"Come on, Ab, quit teasin'." He got her wrist again, tighter than before.

"Me! Let me go!" she squawked. But somehow he had her turned around facing him. He pulled her up against his crotch, her thigh against his vitals while she fell upon his stone-hard chest. But once more she yanked loose, spun in a half turn till his hands got her by the hips and took her into port again.

"God, can you scrap for such a hummingbird," he puffed. And as if to prove it she almost got away. But his powerful arm caught her waist and she felt her backside hauled unceremoniously against his lap. "Ugh!" he grunted when she hit his sore leg, but his grip held at her waist.

"Good!" she spit, "I hope I hurt you! Get your hand down! Leave my buttons alone!"

He had her from behind, cinched the arm tight around her little middle, grappling for the buttons at her throat with his other hand. He managed to get one undone while she struggled to snatch his hand away and contend with the other that snaked up her midriff to her breast.

"Come on, Abbie, I won't hurt you." Her struggle only seemed to amuse him further while the skirmish at her blouse front went on.

"I'll hurt you any way I can!" she vowed—a mosquito threatening a rhinocerous. "I warn you!" She struggled valiantly, breathless now, but he kept her pinned so tightly she couldn't get far enough away to do any damage.

"God, how I like you in this old faded shirt," he panted, and somehow managed to spirit a second button free while she tried to seize both of his hands and gain her freedom at the same time.

"You filthy louse . . . I hope they . . . hang you!" she grunted.

"If I hang . . ." he grunted back, "at least give me . . . one last . . . sweet memory to take al . . . along." He had one breast now and she twisted around violently while he ducked to avoid a flying elbow.

"Atta girl, Abbie, turn around here where I can get at you." His black moustache came swooping for her mouth, but she clutched a hank of hair at his temple and pulled with all her might.

"Ouch!" he yelped, and she yanked harder until suddenly, unexpectedly, he released her. Sprawled as she was, she went down at a full slide, landing on her knees with her mouth just above his navel. But her elbow caught him precisely in the spot where he'd been shot, and he gasped and stiffened back, arms outflung, as if she'd just crucified him to that chair. His throaty groan told her the battle was over.

She scrambled up out of his thighs, fastening her two neck buttons while his eyes remained closed, the lids flinching. His lips had fallen open, his tongue tip came out to ride the lower edges of his even, upper teeth, then he sucked in a long, pained breath and looked up at the ceiling, with his head still hanging backward. Limply he touched the hair at his temple, massaging it gingerly while she watched, quivering and wary. His arm flopped back down and he finally grunted, pulling himself up by degrees until he was L-shaped again. The silence in the room was rife as he leaned an elbow on either side of his plate and stared down at it as if some piece of food there had moved. She eased to her chair, sat with her hands in her lap, then listlessly picked up a knife that was stuck at a precarious angle into a mound of mashed potatoes. She cleaned it off against the edge of her plate and laid it down very carefully and still neither of them said anything. She tried a bite, but it seemed to stick in her throat. He raised his head and stared past her down the length of the house, out the front door. There was no use pretending to eat, so she carefully wiped her mouth, folded her napkin, laid it down precisely, as if awaiting her penance.

He knew now why he'd done it. It really came as no surprise to him to find that he was jealous, just that he should be so over a woman like her. Yet, never had he been able to make her smile, laugh, or twinkle as that pair of shoes from Melcher had done.

Her chair scraped back into the silence at the same moment he finally decided to speak.

"Abbie, I think—"

"What?" She halted, half up, plate in hand.

He stared out the far front door, not trusting himself to look at her. "I think I'd better get out of here before we do hurt each other."

She stared at the plate in her hand, suddenly very sorry she'd hurt him.

"Yes," she said meekly. "I think you had better."

"Would you get my crutches from the bedroom please?" he asked, very politely.

"Of course," she agreed, equally as polite, and went to get them. She wanted to say she was sorry, but thought he should say it first. He had started it. Silently, she handed him the sticks.

"Thank you," he said, again too politely, pulling himself to his feet, then stumping off toward his room, gingerly favoring the right leg again. There followed a long, deep sigh as he lowered himself to the bedsprings.

Abbie stared out the back door for the longest time, seeing nothing. Finally, she sighed and put the room in order, then crept off to her upstairs room to discard the floral blouse.

But she slumped to the edge of the bed disconsolately, burying her face in her hands. Oh, she was so confused by everything. Nothing seemed simple like it had before the two men had entered her life. She could no longer deny her attraction for Jesse. At times he could be so warm and sympathetic. Like yesterday, when she'd told him things she'd never told another living soul and had begun to trust him, only to have him do what he'd just done. Why couldn't he be like David? David—so much more like her. David—a gentleman whose values ran parallel to hers. David—who had kissed her so sweetly on the stairs but would never have tried anything like Jesse had just pulled on that chair downstairs. But thinking of it, she felt that odd, forbidden exhilaration that would not be quelled. Why was she unable to resist the dark, foreboding charms that drew her into Jesse's web time and time again?

She tried to imagine her father ever carrying on with her mother in that fashion but simply could not. Why, her mother would have left home. Yet Abbie wondered now why her father and mother never touched or kissed. She had always assumed that their polite way was the way all well-bred married couples acted.

Abbie pressed her hands to her heated face, remembering her mother saying that all men were beasts. She remembered Richard tackling her in the livery stable one time and how she'd slapped him. She remembered Jesse grappling with her on that chair, and that night in the bed with his tongue all over her breasts and belly. She shivered, there in the heat of the upstairs bedroom, assuring herself that what she'd felt that night and today was fear and nothing more. For anything else would be sinful.

She pulled herself up sharply, changed into proper clothing, and made up her mind she must offer him some apology for hurting him and would go down and make lemonade, which would suffice if she could not bring herself to utter the words.

Chapter 13

SHE WAS JUST about ready to pour the lemonade when there was a knock at the front door. There, on the porch, stood a swarthy, well-dressed man of perhaps forty-five years. Everything from his cordoban shoes to his Stetson hat was impeccably crisp, clean, and correct. He doffed his hat with a flawlessly groomed hand and bowed slightly, adjusting a package he held beneath an arm.

"Good day. Miss Abigail McKenzie?"

"Yes."

"I was told in town that you have a Mr. DuFrayne here."

"DuFrayne?" she repeated, confused.

"Jesse DuFrayne," he clarified.

She was momentarily taken aback by the name. Jesse *DuFrayne?* Jesse DuFrayne. It rhymed with train and had a rhythmic, beat-of-the-rails motion to it. Of its own accord, the name repeated itself in her mind, as if steel drivers churned out the message:

> *Jesse DuFrayne*
> *Rode in on a train . . .*
> *Jesse DuFrayne*
> *Rode in on a train . . .*

Still, somehow she thought the name could not belong to the Jesse she knew. To lend him a genuine surname would be to afford him unwarranted validity.

"Is he here, Miss McKenzie?"

Abruptly she twitched from her musings.

"Oh, I'm sorry, Mr—?"

"Hudson. James Hudson, of the Rocky Mountain Railroad. We have, Miss McKenzie, as you've probably already guessed, a vested interest in Jesse DuFrayne."

So, she thought, Mr. Jesse DuFrayne is no train robber, is he not? This was the moment she had waited for; vengeance was hers. But it somehow lost its savor.

"Come in, Mr. Hudson, please do come in," she said, opening the screen and gesturing him inside. "I believe the man you're looking for is here. He refused to tell—"

But at that moment his voice came from the bedroom. "Hey, Doc, is that you out there? Come on in here."

A smile suddenly covered Mr. Hudson's face, and he made a move toward the voice, then halted—properly if impatiently—asking, "May I?"

She nodded and pointed to the bedroom door. "He's in there."

James Hudson did not conceal the fact that he was in an overjoyed hurry to hit that bedroom doorway. Six or seven long strides across the living room and their voices were booming.

"Jesse, Gol-damnit, how did you end up here?"

"Jim! Am I glad to see you!"

550

Abbie tiptoed timidly to the door. Jesse'd been shaving, but even through the suds she could tell that he had absolutely no fear of Jim Hudson, was instead elated to see him. To her amazement the two bear-hugged and affably pounded each other's backs.

"Goddamn if you aren't a sight for sore eyes!" DuFrayne exclaimed, pulling back.

"Look at yourself! I could say the same thing. Word came along the line that you'd been shot. What happened? Somebody take your moustache off with a stray bullet? It looks kind of ragged."

DuFrayne's laughter, genuine, spontaneous, filled the room while he glanced in the mirror he held. "I wish that was all a stray bullet had bothered."

"Yeah? What else got hit?"

"My right leg, but it's doing fine, thanks to Miss Abigail here. They hauled me off the R.M.R. coach and plunked me down here and she's been stuck with me ever since."

"Miss McKenzie, how can we thank you?" Jim Hudson asked, but as if to answer his own question lifted the package he'd brought and came to her, extending it. It was wrapped, but even so the shape of a bottle was evident. "This isn't much, but please accept it with my heartfelt thanks."

She stood in startled confusion, reached for his proffered gift with the hands of an automaton, quite stunned by what all this seemed to mean, but Hudson immediately turned back to DuFrayne.

"What happened, Jesse? We were worried as hell. You turned up missing and the boys down at Rockwell found your gear on the train, and no Jesse! Then somebody from the depot in Stuart's Junction wired down a description of an alleged robber they pulled off a train up here and it sounded like you: coal black moustache and tall as a barn door. I said to myself, if that's not Jess I'll eat my fifteen-dollar Stetson."

Jesse laughed again from behind the lather and sank back onto the bed where he'd been when Hudson came in. "Well, you can wear your fifteen-dollar Stetson out of here because I'm all right." He cast a cautious glance at Abbie. "Leg's been acting up a little this afternoon so I thought I'd sit down while I shave is all."

"So . . . what happened? Are you going to keep me in suspense all day?"

"No, not all day, but just a little longer. This shaving soap is drying up and starting to itch. Mind if I finish this first?"

"No, no, go ahead."

"Come on in, Abbie. No need to hover in the door. Jim, this is Abbie. She's done a damn fine job of keeping my carcass from rotting for nearly three weeks now. If it hadn't been for her, I'd be crow bait by this time. Miss Abigail McKenzie, meet Jim Hudson."

"Mr. Hudson and I met at the door. Won't you have a seat, Mr. Hudson?" she invited, pulling the rocker forward. "I'll leave you two alone."

"Wait a minute, will you, Abbie?" Jesse had again taken up razor and hand mirror but was having trouble executing everything at once, needing both hands for the straightedge. "Hold this damn thing, so I can finish." The request was made so amiably that she forgot to take offense and came to do his bidding.

Watching the two of them, Jim Hudson thought this little domestic scene quite unlike his friend Jesse and wondered what had taken place around here during the last few weeks.

"Jess, what in the heck happened to your moustache? Looks like you took the blade to it," he observed. "I never thought I'd live to see the day."

Jesse's and Abbie's eyes met briefly over the mirror before he replied, "Neither did I. I just decided I'd see what I looked like plain-faced. I guess you can tell what I thought of myself. One day without it and I was growing it back as fast as possible. Abbie agrees I look best with a moustache too."

She felt her face flush and was grateful that her back was to Jim Hudson. Jesse swabbed off his face, then his eyes merrily met hers again while she knew a profound confusion at the very different way he always treated her before others, always respectful, hiding any trace of her transgressions, blaming only himself. What manner of man is this, she wondered, while his eyes danced away again.

Shaving done, Jesse stayed on the bed while the men continued talking.

"What's wrong with your hand, Jess?"

"It got jimmied up somehow on that train."

"Come on, I've waited long enough. Tell me what happened here."

"There's nothing much to tell. It was a damn fool mistake is all. I was headed up to Rockwell, as you know . . ." While Jesse told his account of the incident on the train, Abbie leaned over the bed to collect his shaving equipage. As she did, he absently laid a hand on her waist, then gave it a light pat as she straightened and moved away. Jim Hudson noted the touch with interest. The heedless gesture was as intimate as a caress might have been, for while he did it, Jess kept right on talking, and Jim was certain he was oblivious of the fact that he'd touched the woman at all. Hudson did a good job of concealing his surprise. Miss McKenzie wasn't Jess's type at all. It hadn't taken more than thirty seconds at her front door for Hudson to recognize that fact. He watched her leave the room, puzzled by what he'd just witnessed.

While Jesse was unconscious of what he'd done, Abbie was not. The spot on her spine where his palm had rested seemed afire. In her entire life no man had ever laid a hand upon Abigail McKenzie in so casual a fashion. It was totally different from the many ways in which Jesse DuFrayne had touched her before: sometimes teasing, sometimes daring, sometimes angry, but always for a reason. No, this touch was different. It was the kind she'd wondered about between her parents, the kind she'd never seen between them, and it raised her bloodbeat by its very offhandedness.

All the while she prepared more lemonade in the kitchen, the thought rang through her mind—Jesse DuFrayne has just touched the small of my back before his friend . . .

In the bedroom, Jim Hudson said, "Now listen, Jess, we'll have all of this straightened out in no time. You know there's no beef with the railroad." He laughed, shook his head goodnaturedly, and continued. "Why, hell, we know you weren't robbing any train. But this Melcher fellow is raising a stink. He's up in arms and out to sue us for everything he can get, because of his permanent disability."

"Just what do you think he'll get?"

"We'll find out tomorrow. I've got a meeting set up right here in town for noon and we'll settle it then if we can. Melcher will be coming in, but I'll be there to represent the railroad, so you don't need to come unless you want to, of course, and only if you're feeling up to it. Melcher will have his lawyer present, I'm sure. It'll be best to settle this thing with as little publicity as possible, don't you agree?"

"I agree, Jim, but it still riles me to think what that little shrimp can get by pointing an accusing finger at the railroad and walk away two days later while I lie here with a hole as big as a goose egg blown in me."

"And that's the main thing you should be concerned with. Let me handle the legal stuff. Hell, everybody's more worried about you than about what Melcher plans to ask for as a payoff. He'll probably turn out to be more bluff than threat anyway. But how about you? Just how is that leg healing?"

"Oh, it's stiff as hell, so's the hand, but I couldn't have been luckier if the shot had blown me straight into the arms of Doc Dougherty—he's the local medic. Abbie's got remedies up her sleeve that Doc Dougherty never dreamed of. He fixed me up that first day, but it was Abbie who kept me alive afterward."

"Which reminds me," Hudson put in, "did she get our message saying we'd compensate her for putting up you and Melcher?"

"She got it . . . and Jim?" He lowered his voice, even though they'd been talking in low tones already. "See that she gets plenty. I've been a regular son of a bitch to her."

In the kitchen Miss Abigail heard a burst of laughter, though she didn't hear what prompted it.

"I take it you're impressed with the lady?" Jim Hudson asked quietly, with one eyebrow raised.

"Have you ever seen a lady that didn't impress me, Jim?"

"Hell, I don't think I've ever seen you with a *lady* before, Jess." There was good humor written all over both of their faces.

"I admit she's something of an oddity for me, but all in all I'm not having a half bad time of it here, other than the fact that she considers me a robber of trains, a defiler of women, a teller of lies, and the blackest of blackguards. And she's doing her damnedest to reform me. I put up with it because I like her cooking—watery broth, slimy eggs, and lethal liver." Jesse laughed, remembering it all.

"Sounds like she's just what you've always avoided, Jess—a straight woman. Maybe she's just what you need."

"What I need, James-Smart-Boy-Hudson, is a train out of here, and the sooner the better. I'll be at that meeting tomorrow whether Doc turns me loose or not. I thought you were Doc when you came in. He's supposed to give me my walking papers, so to speak. I'm already pretty handy on those crutches, though."

"Well, don't rush it, Jess. I'll have to look up this man Dougherty, too, while I'm in town. I expect you ran up a bill with him too, huh?"

"I'm still running it, but I knew you'd come along after me and pick up the bill."

Hudson laughed. "Say, the boys up in Rockwell want to know what to do with your gear."

"Is it okay, Jim?"

"Intact, I assure you. Everything. They stored it all in the line shack up there."

"In the line shack! Hell, those galoots will have every one of my plates shattered. I want them out of there. Are you going up that way?"

"No, I'm headed back to Denver again after the meeting tomorrow. You know we're listening to every mayor of every mining town in this state beg for a spur line to get their ore out. We can't build 'em fast enough, so hurry and get well."

"I'll trust your judgment on that, Jim. Just let me know what's up because I'm already tired of this leisure life. As soon as Doc even relaxes his grizzled old eyebrows my way, I'll be up and gone from here back to the railhead. I just want to make damn sure my gear is safe in the meantime."

"I could have Stoker bring it down on the supply train," Hudson suggested with a knowing grin.

"God, no! Save me from Stoker!" They both laughed. "He does all right with steel and wood, but I'd just as soon have my gear rolled down the side of the mountain as brought down in Stoker's engine. Just leave it there for the time being. Maybe I'll think of something. I might even make it out of here with you tomorrow. Who knows?"

"Well, rest up, boy. I have this Doc Dougherty to see yet, and as long as I'm up here, I may as well see if the depot agent has any complaints on this new spur. I guess I'd better be going, Jess. One way or another, I'll see you before I leave town."

As Hudson prepared to take his leave, Miss Abigail appeared in the doorway with a tray. "May I offer you a glass of lemonade before you leave, Mr. Hudson?"

"I think we've been enough trouble to you already, Miss McKenzie. I'm the one who must offer you something before I leave. How much do I owe you for your care of the two men?"

Regardless of how many times she had reminded Jesse that she'd taken him in only for the money, when offered payment now she became disconcerted.

Jesse could read her discomfiture over Jim's question, saw her reluctance to put a dollar value on what she'd done. Like many other subjects, money was an indelicate subject for a lady to discuss. "Give the lady a fair price, Jim."

"Just what do you think your hide is worth, DuFrayne?"

The two of them exchanged a look of amused conspiracy before Jess answered, "I don't know what my hide is worth, but a glass of Abbie's lemonade is worth a thousand bucks any day."

"In that case, I'll have to try a glass before I leave," Jim Hudson said, smiling now at Abbie.

"I shall pour one for you then," Abbie offered, uncomfortable before their obvious teasing.

"Where will you take it, Mr. Hudson?" she asked.

"How about on your front porch, Miss McKenzie? Will you join me?"

Why did she glance at Jesse first before answering, as if she needed his permission to sit on the porch with another man?

"Go ahead, Abbie, you deserve a rest," he said, noting the pink in her cheeks. "Jim, you big galoot, thanks a hulluva lot for coming."

Hudson approached the bed and the two shook hands again, Hudson squeezing the back of Jess's as he said, "Get your bones out of here and back on those tracks, do you hear? And don't give the lady any fuss while you're doing it. That's an order!"

"Get the hell out of here before that lemonade evaporates in this heat." Then as the two left the room, he called after them, "See that you use your best manners out on the front porch, Jim. Miss Abigail is a lady of utmost propriety."

The north end of Miss Abigail's porch was in cool shadow now in midafternoon. Hudson saw the slatted wooden swing there but gestured Abbie instead to the opposite end, where the wicker chairs were. His manners showed in everything he did, she thought, even in his choosing separate chairs in the beating sun rather than the more intimate double swing in the inviting shade. He remained on his feet until she was seated. She noted how he pulled his sharply creased trousers up at the knees as he took the opposite chair.

"I take it Jesse has been less than a model patient," he opened.

"He was gravely wounded, Mr. Hudson, hardly expected to live. It would be difficult for anyone to be a model patient under those circumstances." Once said, she didn't know why she had defended Jesse that way, just as he had her.

"I think you're tiptoeing around the mulberry bush, Miss McKenzie, but I know Jess better than that. You've earned every penny you get. I fear he's not one who takes to coddling and being cooped up too gracefully. In his own element he's a damn fine man, the best there is."

"Just what is his element, Mr. Hudson?"

"The railroad, of course."

"So he does work for the railroad?"

"Yes, and a damn fine job he does."

Hearing it, Abbie's senses whirled. So it was true after all. With an effort she kept her hand from fluttering to her throat.

"Your loyalty does him credit, Mr. Hudson, since you yourself seem to be a respectable sort." Taking in his flawless elegance, his politeness, his obvious admiration of Jesse DuFrayne, she felt overcome by the swift shift of her patient's status.

"Men earn respect in different ways, Miss McKenzie. If I'm respected, it's for different reasons than he is. Take my word for it, Jess DuFrayne is a gem in the rough, and there's not a man on the R.M.R. line that'll say different."

"Just what has he done to earn that respect?" She wondered if he could see the glass trembling in her hand.

"I hear rebuttal in your tone, Miss McKenzie, and I'm thinking he's given you little reason to see good in him. I'd do him an injustice to list his merits. You'll only believe them if you discover them yourself. If you ever get a chance to see his photographs, study them well. You'll see more than sepia images . . . you'll see where his heart lies."

Funny, she had never thought of Jesse as having a heart before.

"Yes, I shall, Mr. Hudson, if I ever see them." He *is* a photographer, she was thinking as wings seemed to beat about her temples, he really is!

"Jess was right," Jim Hudson said, placing his empty glass on the wicker table between them. "This lemonade is worth a thousand dollars a glass on a day like today."

"I'm glad you enjoyed it."

"If there's anything you need while he's here, you have only to say the word and it's yours."

"How very gracious of you, sir."

"I'm sure if our graces were held up for comparison, mine should be found sadly lacking beside yours. Good day, Miss McKenzie. Take care of him for me." Jim Hudson looked at the front door as he said it.

That curiously heartfelt remark put the final touch of confusion upon Miss Abigail's already confounded emotions. She had thought Jim Hudson had come to her door to mete out justice, but instead he had vindicated the man she had repeatedly called "robber." Watching Hudson's trouser legs as he walked off down the dusty road, she was shaken anew by the revelations regarding Jesse Cameron-DuFrayne.

Once again, the ironic rhyme came to her out of nowhere:

> *Jesse DuFrayne*
> *Rode in on a train . . .*

She could not stand out here on the porch indefinitely. She had to go in and face him. But what could she say? She seemed to be having great difficulty breathing and could feel the blood welled up to her hairline, her pulse clicking off the passing seconds as memories came hurtling back, memories of the countless times she'd taunted him because he was a train robber. She tried to compose herself but found that she was feeling inexplicably feminine, and somehow very vulnerable. How he must have laughed to himself all these days, she thought. And what is he thinking now?

She opened the door silently, stepped before the umbrella stand to check her reflection, but her hand paused before it reached her hair. There on the seat lay a rectangular piece of paper. Something seemed to warn her, for her hand hesitated, then finally picked it up.

There followed an audible gasp.

It was a check boasting the payer's name across the top in block letters: ROCKY MOUNTAIN RAILROAD, DENVER, COLORADO. It was made out to Abigail McKenzie in the amount of one thousand dollars!

Her stomach began to tremble and the paper quivered in her fingers. She looked up at the bedroom doorway, suddenly more afraid than ever to face him again.

One thousand dollars! Why, it would take her two years or more of waiting tables at Louis Culpepper's to earn such a sum. Just what was this Jesse DuFrayne that the railroad would put out money like this for his safekeeping? Utterly befuddled, she gaped at the check, knowing she'd earned not even a quarter of this amount. She remembered the knowing looks exchanged by Jesse and Jim Hudson and the words, "A glass of Abbie's lemonade is worth a thousand bucks any day." More confused than ever, she swallowed back the lump in her throat.

"Abbie, is Jim gone?" he called.

"Yes, he is, Mr.—" But what should she call him now? She could still not connect him with his new name, or with his old. Everything had suddenly changed. She looked at herself in the mirror, saw her flushed face, the paper in her hand, the confusion in her eyes, and stood rooted, not knowing, suddenly, how to act before the man on the other side of the wall. He had a real name and a very respectable job and a very impressive friend, plus a whole railroad full of cohorts who apparently respected him immensely. But all that seemed secondary to the fact that his being shot had had enough impact to cause the railroad to pay her grandly for his care.

How should she act?

She had called him Mr. Cameron, train robber for so long that it was perplexing to suddenly have to change her opinion, which—she admitted now —had been largely based upon the supposition that he was guilty as accused. But then, how many times had he himself implied he was an outlaw? Why, just yesterday he'd said he wouldn't be around long enough for it to matter what she told him about herself and . . . and Richard. She understood now that he'd been toying with her, implying that it was justice which would come to take him, when he'd known all along it was Jim Hudson.

With a sinking feeling, she recalled all those other things—the fighting and kissing and pulling the gun on each other and the terrible ways they'd goaded and hazed. Was he right about all that? Had she lost her sense of decency thinking he, the train robber, was the indecent one responsible?

Only he was no robber.

But she suddenly came to her senses, realizing she could treat him no differently than she had before James Hudson's visit. He was not instantly exonerated of all he'd put her through! But she held a thousand dollars in her unsteady hand, and deny it though she might, it *did* exonerate him in some way.

Her heart thumped crazily as she approached his room and found Jesse sitting on the floral cushions of the window seat, looking so black and brown against all those yellows and greens, so masculinely out of place in his dungarees and unbuttoned shirt. He was watching Jim Hudson walk back uptown and didn't know she stood there observing him. She swallowed thickly, for he looked too handsome and excusable and she wanted him to look neither. He dropped the curtain, absently scratched his bare chest, and her eyes followed the lean fingers that tracked across his skin. At last she cleared her throat.

He looked up, surprised. "Oh, I probably shouldn't sit here, huh?" He moved as if to rise.

"No, you're fine. It's cool there between the windows, stay where you are."

He settled back down. "Well, come on in. Maybe you're not afraid to now." But all traces of teasing were gone from his voice and eyes, and she suddenly wished they would return and ease this dread fascination she felt for him.

"I . . . I still am," she admitted. But neither of them smiled. "I want to say 'Why didn't you tell me,' only—silly as it seems—you did."

He was gracious enough not to rub it in, and now all she wished was that he would. It would be far preferable to this strained seriousness. All he said was, "I could use a glass of lemonade too, Abbie. Would you mind getting me one, please?"

"How can I mind? After all, it *is* paid for now." She felt his eyes upon her, and her hands shook as she poured the drink. Who are you? her mind cried out. And why? She was totally disturbed by the change she sensed in him since Jim Hudson left. He accepted the glass, thanked her, took a swallow, and leaned forward, bracing his elbows on his knees, staring at her in silence.

"Before I say anything else," she began nervously, "I want to make it explicitly clear that I did not hurt you intentionally in the kitchen before, and . . . and the reason I say so now has nothing whatever to do with whether or not you hold up trains for a living."

"That's nice to know. And of course I believe you. You're a most honorable person, Abbie." His eyes seemed to delve into her very depths.

"And how about yourself?"

"Sit down, Abbie, for God's sake . . . there in your little rocker, where I can talk to you." She hesitated, then sat, but hardly relaxed. "Every damn thing I ever told you about myself is true. I never lied to you."

"Jim Hudson is the friend of whom you spoke? The one who left New Orleans with you when you were twenty?"

He nodded, then stared out the window, disturbed anew by this woman and wishing he were not.

"He's very personable," she admitted, looking down into her glass, then added in the quietest of tones, "and very rich."

He turned his hazel-flecked eyes on her again but said nothing.

"I simply cannot accept a thousand dollars. It's far too much."

"Jim doesn't seem to think so." Her eyes met his directly.

"I don't think Jim alone decided."

"No?" His expression was noncommittal. He raised the glass to his lips as if it really didn't matter to him. She caught herself watching his full mouth upon the rim of the glass, his dark, dark moustache, which he brushed with a forefinger after he drank.

"Who are you?" she asked when she could stand it no longer.

"Jesse DuFrayne at your service, ma'am," he returned, raising the glass as if toasting her in introduction.

"That's not what I meant and you know it."

"I know." He now made a deep study of the lemonade. "But I don't want you to have to reestablish your commitment to me in any way, which may happen if I suddenly become a real person to you."

She drew a deep, ragged breath. "You are a real person to me and you know it, so I may as well have it all."

He continued studying the glass intently, swirling it so the liquid eddied into a whirlpool, leaving transparent bits of lemon meat on its sides. "I don't want to be a real person to you. Let me put it that way then." His disturbing eyes challenged as he at last raised them and looked directly into hers. "But nevertheless, you already know what I am. I'm a photographer, just like I said."

"Hired by James Hudson?"

He took a long pull while looking over the rim of the glass, then dropped his eyes as he swallowed, and said, "Yup."

"Why should the railroad protect you if all you are is a picture taker?"

"I guess they must like my stuff."

"Yes, they certainly must. I'll be anxious to see it, if I'm allowed. Your photos must be something really extraordinary."

"Not at all. They're graphic, but the only thing about them that might be considered extraordinary is the fact that they depict railroad life as it really is."

"That's not what you said the other night."

He smiled for the first time, a little crookedly. "Oh well . . . that's the one time I may have lied just a little. But you can judge for yourself if you ever see them."

"And will I?" she dared, her heart in her throat.

"It's hard to say. Jim and I are going to tie up some loose ends around here tomorrow." He braced a dark arm upon the window frame and studied the road beyond it. "Then I'll be leaving town."

No, not yet! her thoughts cried silently. Already she felt an emptiness, realizing this was unwarranted after all the times she'd wished him gone. Sober eyes still on the road, he added, "If I ever get the chance to drop back in and show you my photographs, I'll be sure to do it."

Sadly she knew he never would. "Are you sure you're well enough to travel?"

He flicked a glance her way. "Well, you want me out of here, don't you?"

"Yes, I do," she lied, then finished truthfully, "but not hurting."

His eyes moved to her face and their expression grew momentarily soft. "Don't worry your head over me, Abbie. You've done all the worrying about me that you'll have to."

"But you've paid me too highly for it," she claimed. He noted her stiff posture on the rocker, the hands clutched around her glass as if still scared to death of him. He supposed she suspected the real truth about him, but leaving would be easier if he never verified it.

"It was the railroad who paid you, not Jim or me," he said convincingly.

"I know. It was just a figure of speech. I only meant it was too much."

"How much would you say my life is worth?" he asked, just to see what she'd say, knowing now how much it mattered that she value him in some way.

Her eyes skimmed the room in a semicircle, ended up studying the glass in his hand. "More than a glass of lemonade . . ." But at last her composure slipped. "Oh, I don't know," she sighed and slumped, resting her forehead on a hand, studying her lap.

"How much would you say it was all worth—all the things you had to do to save my life? I never really did find out for sure everything you did. Some of it I knew that night when I had you—" His eyes went to the bed, then he abruptly looked out the window again. Damn, but the woman did things to his head! Staring out unseeingly at the summer afternoon he said gruffly, "Abbie, I'm damn sorry about it all."

Her head snapped up to study his profile. She saw him swallow, his Adam's apple rising, settling back down. He seemed intrigued by that yard out there, which was fine, for her face was burning and her own mouth and eyes seemed suddenly filled with salt.

"I . . . I'm sorry too, Mr. D . . . DuFrayne," she got out.

Palm braced against the window frame, he turned his head to look across his biceps, resting his lips there against his own skin while studying her. Then he said one last, quiet time, from behind that tan arm, "Jesse . . . the name is Jesse." He wanted somehow to hear her say it, just once, now that she knew he was no criminal.

She lifted her eyes to his face, searching for a trace of humor, finding none this time, finding only that quiet intensity which threatened to undo her. The name hung in the air between them, and she wanted to echo it, but had she done so they'd both have been lost, and in that poignant moment they knew it. Her eyes traveled the length of that muscular arm, lingering at the point where his lips must be. His moustache glanced darkly back at her from behind the arm. It took a perceptive eye by now to tell that it had ever been shaved: Mr. Hudson knew this man very well to discern it. So, must he now know equally as well all those inner qualities he'd hinted at? Abbie wondered.

Minutes ago, studying Jesse from the doorway, it had been obvious that he followed his friend's progress down the street as if anxious to follow him out of here, back to the brawling, tough railroad life the two had shared for many years. She had absolutely no business wishing he didn't have to go quite yet.

The silence grew long and strained, but at last he dropped his arm from the window frame and glanced around the room, surveying it fully as if for the final time. "I want to thank you for the use of your room, Abbie. It's pretty. A real lady's room. I imagine you'll be glad to get back into it again."

"I haven't been uncomfortable upstairs," she said inanely.

"It must be a lot hotter up there these nights than down here. Sorry I put you out." Then he looked at the small double oval picture frame. He reached to pick it up. "Are these your parents?"

"Yes," she answered, following the frame with her eyes, watching a tan finger curve and tap it thoughtfully.

"You don't look much like her. More like him."

"People always said I looked like him and acted like her." It was out before she realized what she'd said. The room grew quiet. Jesse cleared his throat, studied the picture, bounced it on his palm a time or two, then it hung forgotten in his fingers as he leaned forward and spoke to the floor between his feet, his tone as near emotional as she'd ever heard it.

"Abbie, forget what I said about your mother. What the hell—I mean . . . I didn't even know her."

She stared at the tintype and the familiar hand which held it. A lump lodged in her throat and tears formed on her lids. "Yes . . . yes you did. You knew her better than I did, I think."

He raised his startled eyes while his elbows came off his knees in slow motion and his muscles seemed to strain toward her even though he never left the edge of the window seat. For a heart-stopping moment she thought he would. She saw the battle going on in him while he sat poised in indecision. He uttered then the familiar name he'd spoken so often to tease her, but it came out now with gruff emotion.

"Abbie?"

The way he said it made her want to impress the word into a solid lump to carry in a locket maybe, or to press between the pages of a sonnet book. She should correct him, but those days when she'd chided him seemed part of a misty forever ago, for light years seemed to have passed during this conversation. Here, now, with her name fresh on his lips, with his dark troubled eyes seeming to ask her questions best left unanswered, with his black moustache unbroken by smile, she silently begged him not to look as if he too hurt.

"Abbie?" he said again, soft as before: too beautifully threatening. And she shivered once, then broke the spell which should not have been cast in the first place.

"I have at least two more meals to feed you, Mr. DuFrayne, and not a thing in the house resembling meat. I'd best walk over town before the butcher shop closes. What would you like?"

His eyes pored over her face, then slowly, thankfully, the old hint of humor returned to his lips. "Since when have you bothered to ask?"

"Since the buttermilk," she answered, knowing the exact moment.

He laughed lightly, enjoying her immensely, as he so often could. She was a pretty little thing, he had to admit as he scanned her crisp, high collar and swept-back hair. She, in turn, enjoyed his swarthy handsomeness and the imposing breadth of partially exposed muscle before her.

"Ah yes, the buttermilk," he remembered, shaking his head in amusement. They both realized the buttermilk had been a turning point.

"And for your supper?" she asked.

He allowed his warm smile to linger upon her bewitching eyes. His glance, of its own accord, lowered to her breasts, then raised again.

"I'll let you choose," he said, very unlike the Jesse she'd grown used to.

"Very well," she returned, very like the Miss Abigail he'd grown used to.

When she rose, her knees felt curiously watery, as if she'd run a long way. Yet she ran again, though her steps were slow and measured as ever. She ran from the smile in Jesse's eyes . . . to the umbrella stand, to arm herself with a daisy-trimmed hat and a pair of gloves that bore smudges of dirt from leather reins and a creek bank.

Chapter 14

THE TOWN WAS buzzing with the news. Miss Abigail knew it. She sensed eyes peering at her from behind every window of the boardwalk. But she carried herself proudly, flouncing into the meat market as if unaware of all the curious stares following her.

"Why, Mizz Abigail," Gabe Porter plunged right in. "What do you think about that man up to your house turning out not to be a train robber atall? Isn't that something? Whole town's talking about this railroad feller that come in today to pay off your patient's debts. Seems we had him all wrong. Seems he works for the railroad after all. What do you think of that!"

"It's of little interest to me, Mr. Porter. What he is has no bearing on how he is. He is not fully healed and shall be under my care for one more day before he's ready to leave Stuart's Junction."

"You mean you're gonna keep him up there even though he ain't got to stay if he don't want to now?"

Miss Abigail's eyes snapped fire enough to precook the meats hanging on the hooks of the huge tooled iron rack on Gabe's wall. "What exactly are you implying, Mr. Porter? That I was safe with him as long as he was a felon but that I'm not now that he's a photographer?"

That didn't make much sense, even to Gabe Porter. "Why, I didn't mean nothin' by it, Miss Abigail. Just lookin' out for a maiden lady's welfare is all." Gabe Porter couldn't have cut her any deeper had he chopped her a good one with his greasy meat cleaver, but Miss Abigail's face showed no trace of the stark ache his words struck in her heart.

"You may best look after my welfare by cutting two especially thick beef steaks, Mr. Porter," she ordered. "Meat is what builds one up when one has been weakened. We owe that man some good red meat after the blood he lost because of this unfortunate incident, wouldn't you agree?"

Gabe did as ordered, all the while remembering how Bones Binley had said that Gem Perkins had said that Miss Abigail had been out in a trap with that photographer, riding in the hills, and right after young Rob Nelson had seen the man prancing around Miss Abigail's backyard dressed in nothing but pajama pants, mind you. And from the sound of it, he had took to having presents shipped in to her by railroad express from Denver. It had to be from him. Hell, she didn't know nobody else from Denver!

But if Gabe Porter was white-faced at all that, he had the jolt of his life still coming. For on his way home Gabe heard that on her way home Miss Abigail had stopped over to the bank and deposited a check for no less than one thousand dollars, and it drawn against the Rocky Mountain Railroad Company, which, everyone in town knew by that time, the man up at her house took "pitchers" for.

Coming around the corner between the buildings, Miss Abigail was disconcerted to see Jesse waiting for her on the porch swing again. She controlled the urge to glance up and down the street and see if anyone else had seen him there. Ah, at least he has his shirt on, she thought, and coming nearer saw that it was buttoned nearly to the point of decency. But when she mounted the steps she saw that his feet were bare and one of his legs half slung across the swing seat, causing it to go all crooked when he set it on the move.

"Hi," he greeted. "What did you decide on?"

Sheepishly remembering the bugging eyes of Blair Simmons as she slid the check under his cage at the bank only minutes ago, she answered, "I kept it."

Confused, he asked, "What?"

"I kept it," she repeated. "I deposited it at the bank. Thank you."

He laughed and shook his head. "No, that's not what I meant. I meant what did you decide on for supper." The thousand dollars didn't seem to faze him at all. He scarcely seemed to give it a second thought, as if he really thought it was her due, and that was the end of that.

"Steak," she answered, pleased now at how he played down that thousand.

"Goddamn, but that sounds good!" he exclaimed, slapping his stomach, rubbing it, rumpling his shirt and stretching all at once.

All of a sudden she found it impossible to grow peeved with him for his coarse language, and harder yet to keep from smiling. "You are incorrigible, sir. I think that if you stayed around here any longer I might be in danger of failing to note your crassness."

"If I stayed here any longer, you'd either have to convert me or run me out on a rail—probably right beside you, though. I am what I am, Miss Abigail, and steak sounds goddamn good right now."

"If you said it in any other way, I'm not sure I would believe you any more, Mr. Came—Mr. DuFrayne." Her smile was broad now, and charmed him fully.

It was infinitely easier exchanging light badinage with him again. This, she knew, would get them safely through the evening ahead. But just then he swung his foot to the floor, leaned his dark, square palms on the edge of the seat, and with the now familiar grin all over one side of his face, said quietly, "Go fry the steak, woman."

And after all they'd been through, it was the last thing in the world that should have made her blush.

The sun fell behind the mountains while the steak was frying, and the front porch was cool and lavender-shadowed. Jesse DuFrayne sat there listening to the sounds of children playing "Run Sheep Run," drifting in on the wings of twilight. From the shrill babble he could hear occasional childish arguments: "No he didn't! . . . Yes, he did. . . . He didn't neither! . . ." Then a swell of argument again before the squabble was apparently settled and the sheep ran again in a peaceful fold. The smell of meat drifted out to him, augmented by an iron clank every now and then and an occasional tinkle of glassware. He got up lazily and limped inside and there she was, coming out of the pantry with a heap of plates and glasses and cups balanced against her midriff. They pulled her blouse tight against her breasts and he admired the sight, then raised his eyes to find she'd caught him at it. He grinned and shrugged.

"Can I help?" he asked.

Oh, he was just full of surprises tonight, she thought. But she handed him the stack of dishes anyway. When he turned toward the kitchen table she surprised him.

"No, not there. Put them in the dining room. That table is never used anymore. I thought we might tonight."

His moustache teased. "Is it going to be a little going-away party then?"

"Rather."

"Whatever you say, Abbie." He moved off toward the dining room.

"Just a minute, I'll get the linen."

"Oh? It's a linen occasion too?"

She came with a spotless, stiff cloth and asked, "Can you pick up those candlesticks too?"

"Sure." He got the pair off the table, along with his other burden, and held everything while she snapped the cloth out in the air. He watched it billow and balloon and fall precisely where she wanted it to.

"Why, that's the damnedest thing I've ever seen!"

"What is?" she asked, leaning over to smooth the already perfect surface of the cloth.

"Well if I tried that, the thing would probably go in the opposite direction and carry me off with it." He cocked his head and hung on to his stack of dishes and watched her little butt as she leaned over the table edge that way, ironing wrinkles with her hands. He snapped back up straight when she turned around.

"Do you want to finish this or stand holding those things all night?"

"I want to see you do that once more," he said.

"What?"

"Flip that thing up and get it to land exactly centered like that. I'll make you a bet that you can't do it again."

"You're insane. And you're going to smash the rest of my dishes if you don't set them down."

"What do you wanna bet?"

"Now you want me to take up gambling on top of everything else?"

"Come on, Abbie, what will you put up? One throw of the cloth."

"I've put up with you, that's enough!" She smiled engagingly.

"How about one photographic portrait against one good home-cooked meal?" he suggested, thinking it would bring him back to Stuart's Junction again with a plausible excuse for coming.

What in the sam scratch got into Abigail McKenzie she couldn't say, but the next thing she knew, she was taking that tablecloth back off the table, flapping it high again while he watched. Of course, the cloth landed crooked this time . . . and the next . . . and the next . . . and by then they were both laughing like loons when it really wasn't *that* hilarious!

The dishes clinked against Jesse's chest as he mirthfully teased, "See, I told you you'd never be able to do it again with one toss. I win."

"But I did it the first time, so it doesn't matter. It was hardly fair after all the air currents were stirred up. Anyway, what am I doing here flapping a tablecloth like a fool?"

"Damned if I know, Abbie," he quipped, and finally set his stack down.

And for the first time in her life she thought, damned if I know either.

"I'd better turn those steaks," she said, and went back to the kitchen.

He followed in a moment with the flat-bottomed glasses she'd given him. "Hey, if this is a party, shouldn't we use champagne glasses and drink the champagne Jim brought?"

"Champagne?"

"I opened the bag while you were gone, and good old Jim brought you champagne. Just in time for my going away party. What do you say we pop it open?"

"I'm afraid I don't drink spirits, and I don't think you—" But things were different now. He was respectable. "You may have champagne if you wish."

"Where are the glasses?"

"Those are all I have."

"Okay, what's the difference?" And he went off to put them back on the table.

He opened the bottle out in the backyard, using a knife blade, and she was sure that the whole blasted town could hear that cork pop—not that too many of them would recognize the sound.

"All set?" he asked, coming back in. She took off her apron, preceded him into the dining room carrying the beef steaks and vegetables on a wide, ivory-colored platter. But all that was there for light were the candles.

"Bring the lantern, too," she said over her shoulder, "it's growing dark." He grabbed it off the kitchen table and came behind her, swinging none too jauntily on his impaired leg, oil sloshing in one container, champagne in the other.

"The matches . . ." she said.

"Coming up."

It struck her that by now he knew where many things were kept in her house and that she liked having him know. She suffered a sudden, wistful pride, watching while he fetched the matches as if he were lord of the manor come to light its fires.

"Sit down, Abbie, I'll do the honors. I'm in charge of the table anyway tonight." He lit not only the lantern but the two candles also, casting the room into blushing rosiness around them. His hand captivated her with its long fingers curled around the match, the dark hairs sweeping down from his forearm and wrist as he blew out the match. The table was twice the size of that in the kitchen, but he had set their two places cozily at right angles. "You'll have to forgive me, Abbie, I'm not dressed for the occasion," he said, checking his buttons as he sat down.

She smiled. "Mr. DuFrayne, for you that *is* dressed."

He patted his ribs and laughed. "I guess you're right."

On his plate she put steak and round, browned potatoes and old gold carrots, and he eyed them all while she served, then began eating with obvious relish, groaning, "God, I'm hungry. Dinner wasn't—" But they weren't going to bring up dinner. He shrugged and went on eating.

"Dinner was interrupted," she finished for him, raising an eyebrow. She'd never in her life seen anyone who enjoyed eating quite like he. Surprisingly, he did it quietly, using the proper moves, using the knife for cutting only, not for stabbing with and eating from. He used his linen napkin instead of his sleeve, relaxed back in his chair when he drank. Abbie could not help comparing this pleasant, polite man to the scoundrel who'd criticized her during those first meals she'd served him. Why couldn't he have been this smiling and amenable right from the first?

"I'll miss this good food when it's not available anymore," he said, as if reading her mind and reinforcing her newly formed opinions of him.

"Like most things, once beyond reach, my cooking will seem better than it truly was."

"Oh, I doubt that, Abbie. Once we stopped fighting at mealtime, I really enjoyed your food."

"I didn't know that before. I thought there was nothing you enjoyed so much as a good . . . or should I say a *bad* fight."

"You're partially right. I do enjoy a good fight. I find it invigorating, good for the emotional system. A good fight purges and leaves you clean to start over again." He peered up impishly at her, adding, "Kind of like liver."

She laughed and had to snatch the napkin to her lips quickly to keep the food from flying out. Ah, she would miss his wit after all. When she could swallow and speak once more, she did so with a bedeviling smile for him.

"But does your emotional system need purging quite so often, Mr. DuFrayne?"

He laughed openly, leaning back in his chair in pure enjoyment. He loved her this way, at her witty best, and took his turn at thinking he would miss this lively banter they'd grown so skilled at tossing back and forth. "Your wry wit is showing, Abbie, but I've come to love it. It has spiced up the days as much as the little fights we had now and then." Behind his glass his eyes looked all black, the night light not bright enough for her to make out those hazel flecks she knew so well by now.

"*Little* fights?" she returned. *"Now and then?"*

He stabbed a chunk of meat, eyeing her amusedly across the table. "I guess you got more than your share of my bad temper . . ." Here he brandished his fork almost under her nose. "But you deserved it, you know, woman."

She leveled him with a look of mock severity and pushed the fork aside with a tiny forefinger. "Quit pointing your meat at me, Jesse."

Too late she realized what she'd said. His expression turned to a suggestive smirk while her face grew scorching. Amused, he watched the blood rise from her chin to her hairline. He hadn't the decency to say something diverting, which would have been the chivalrous thing to do. But when had Jesse ever been chivalrous? He only sat back and used her ill-advised remark to his advantage, his teeth sparkling in a broad smile while she patted the napkin again to her lips and dropped her eyes to her plate, stammering for something to say. "I . . . I . . . did not deserve to . . . to have my best china thrown across my c . . . clean bedroom, and . . . and soup and glass all over everything."

He drew circles on his plate with the chunk of meat which had started all this, finally deciding to let her off the hook. He popped the meat into his mouth, studied the ceiling thoughtfully, and mused, "Now why the hell did I do that again, do you remember?"

This time his ridiculous innocent act caught her unaware. She laughed without warning and spit out a chunk of meat. It sailed clear across the way and landed on her clean linen tablecloth while she clasped her mouth with both palms and laughed until her shoulders shook.

He picked up the errant meat, laughing now too, and scolded, "Why, Miss Abigail McKenzie, you put this right back where it belongs!" Then he held it over her nose. Not quite believing it was herself acting so giddy, she obliged, finding it very hard to open one's mouth when one is laughing so hard.

She listened to a humorous recap of all the indignities he'd suffered at her hands, ending with his accusation that she'd tried to drown him with soup.

"So you grabbed the bowl and slurped like a hog at a trough," she finished.

"Aw, there's a new one—a hog at a trough. I'm a regular menagerie all rolled into one. Do you realize, Miss McKenzie, that you have called me by the names of more animals than Noah had on his ark?"

"I have?" She sounded surprised.

"You have."

"I have not!" But as she smirked, he started naming them.

"Goat, swine, baboon, hog . . . even louse. He held knife and fork very correctly, feigning a sterling table etiquette. "Now I ask you, Abbie, do I have the manners of a goat?"

"What about the liver?"

"Oh, that. Well, that night, as many others, just when I was ready to make peace with you, you brought that lethal liver. It's true, Ab, every time I made up my mind to be nice to you, you came charging in with some new scheme to make me miserable and mad at you." He wiped his mouth, hiding a smile behind the napkin while she realized how enjoyable it was to laugh at all of it now with him.

"But you know what, Abbie?" he asked, reaching for the champagne bottle. "You were a worthy adversary. I don't know how we put up with each other all this time, but I think we both deserved everything we got." He filled both of their glasses and said, "I propose a toast." He handed her a glass and looked steadily into her pansy-colored eyes. "To Abigail McKenzie, the woman who saved my life and nearly killed me, all at the same time."

His glass touched hers, and the dark knuckle of his second finger grazed her fairer one. She looked away. "I don't drink," she reiterated as the room grew hushed.

"Oh, no, of course you don't. You only try to kill wayward gunslingers." He still held his glass aloft, waiting for her. She felt silly denying him the right to end this all gracefully, which he'd been managing nicely all through their pleasant supper so far. And so she touched his glass and took a small, wicked sip and found it did not hurt her at all, only made her want to sneeze. So she took another, and did sneeze. And they laughed together and he drained his glass and refilled it, and hers.

"You must return a toast of your own," he insisted, leaning back nonchalantly in his chair, "it's the only acceptable way."

Her eyes, meeting his, were violet in the soft light, registering deep thought. He wondered if she was remembering . . . as he was . . . the good times they'd shared since he'd been here. He wished that he could see what images went through her mind, for she looked thoroughly adorable tonight.

Abbie sat with her elbow resting on the table, the unfamiliar champagne bubbling before her eyes.

"Very well," she agreed at last, then sat a moment longer peering at him through the pale gold liquid, puzzling over how to say it. At last she lowered her glass enough to see his face above it and intoned quietly, "To Jesse DuFrayne, who actually admires my morals all the while he tries to sully them."

But this time after their glasses touched it was he who did not drink from his. Instead his brow furrowed and he scowled slightly.

"What did you say?"

"I said, 'To Jesse DuFrayne who—'"

"I know what you said, Abbie, I want to know why you said it."

Do you, Jesse, she thought. Do you? Or do you understand perfectly, just as I do, that you could have forced yourself on me any one of countless times, yet you always backed off. Must I tell you why? Do you understand so little of yourself? Abbie drew a deep breath and met his eyes.

"Because it's true. Perhaps because I have noted that when others are around you refer to me respectfully as Miss Abigail, no matter what you might call me when we're alone together. Maybe too because you—Oh, never mind." She didn't think she could go through with it and tell him what he couldn't see for himself.

"No, I want to know what you were going to say." He leaned forward now, bracing his forearms against the edge of the table, rolling the glass between his palms, the frown lingering about his eyes.

She considered a moment, sipped a little, then looked away from his mouth:

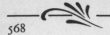

he was chewing somehow on the fringe of his moustache, and she thought it might be a danger sign. "The truth as I see it would sound blatantly conceited were I to say it. I don't want you to leave here thinking of me in that light."

"You of all people are the farthest thing from conceited I've ever met. Self-righteous maybe, but not conceited."

"I'm not sure whether I should say thank you or spit in your eye."

"Neither. Just explain what you meant about me and your morals."

She sipped again for false courage, her eyes picking up some of the champagne bubbles and refracting the lamplight off them. "Very well," she agreed at last, looking into her glass to find it surprisingly empty. He refilled it as she began. "I think that you find me . . . let us say, not totally unattractive. I also, however, think that my feminine gender in itself would serve that purpose for you, because you just plain *like women.* But that's beside the point. I only mentioned it to point out that I do not say this in a vain way. I think you are attracted to me by the very thing that you seek to change in me. Unless I miss my guess, I am the first woman you've encountered in a good long time who possesses any of the qualities that the old beatitudes praise. And all the time you berate me for my inability to bend, you are hoping I will not do so. In other words, Mr. DuFrayne, I think that for perhaps the first time in your life you have found something besides flesh to admire in a woman, but you've never learned how to handle admiration of that sort, so you resort to breaking down my morals in order to feel at ease in your relationship with me."

He sat there with his shoulders lounging at a slant against the back of his chair, but the scowl on his lips belied the lax attitude of his body. He had an elbow propped on the arm of his chair and ran an index finger repeatedly along the lower fringe of his moustache.

"Perhaps you're right, Abbie." He took a sip, measuring her over the glass. "And if you are, why do you blush like a schoolgirl? Your beatific nature is all intact—everything right where it was when I first found you." Lazily he leaned and reached out that bronze finger that had been stroking his moustache, touched her lightly beneath the chin, and made her look up at him. But she stiffened, drawing her eyes away again, turning her chin aside to avoid the finger that seemed too, too warm and exciting. When she would not look up again he ran the callused finger lightly along her delicate jawbone. That at last made her eyes fly to his.

"Don't!" She jerked back, but something strange happened inside her head. For a moment things looked like they had fuzzy edges.

His eyes traveled over her open lips, noted her quick breath, the distended nostrils, then lazily eased back to the blue threatened depths of her wide eyes.

"All right," he agreed softly, "and this time I won't even ask why."

Panicked by the sudden change in him, she lurched up from her chair, but a tornado seemed to be whirling inside her. She fell forward, hands pressed flat on the tabletop on either side of her plate. Her head reverberated. Her neck felt limp, and a lock of damp hair hung down across her collar.

"You've duped me again, have you, Mr. DuFrayne? This time with your innocent toasts." Her head hung down disgracefully but she couldn't seem to raise it, not even to look daggers at him for doing this to her.

"No I haven't. If so, I didn't mean to. Why, you hardly had enough wine to inebriate a hummingbird." He picked up the bottle and tipped it, looking at the lantern light through it. It was still half full.

"Well, this hum . . . hummingbird is in . . . inebriated just the same," she said to the slanting tabletop, her head sinking lower between her shoulder blades all the time.

He smiled down at the part in her hair, thinking how appalled she'd be in the morning and how they weren't going to get out of this without another fight after all. Abbie drunk, imagine that, he thought, unable to keep from smiling at her.

"It must be the altitude," he said now. "Up this high it doesn't take much, especially if you've never drunk before." He came to put an arm around her and lead her toward the back door. "Come on, Abbie, let's get you some fresh air." She stumbled. "Be careful, Abbie, the steps are here." He took one floppy hand and put it around his waist and it grabbed a handful of shirt obediently. "Come on, Ab, let's walk, or you'll find your bed spinning when you lie down."

"I'm sure you kn . . . know all about . . . sp . . . spinning b . . . beds," she mumbled, then pulled herself up and slapped lamely at his helping hands. "I'm fine. I'm fine," she repeated drunkenly, thinking she was regaining a little decorum. But she started humming next and knew perfectly well that she wouldn't be humming if she were truly fine.

"Shhh!" he whispered, forcing her to walk.

She flung a palm up. "But I'm a . . . a hummingbird, am I not?" She actually giggled, then swayed around and fell against him, tapping him on the chest. "Am I not a hummingbird, Jesse? Hmm? Hmmm?" Her forefinger drilled teasingly into his chin, and he lifted it aside.

"Yes, you are. Now shut up and keep walking and breathe deeply, all right?"

She tried to take careful steps, but the ground seemed so far away from her soles, and so evasive and tipsy. They walked and walked, all around the backyard. And once more she giggled. And more than once stumbled so he'd grab her more tightly around the waist to set her aright. "Keep walking," he insisted again and again. "Damnit, Abbie, I did *not* do this to you on purpose. I never in my life saw anybody get tight on a thimbleful of champagne. Do you believe me?"

"Who cares if *I* believe *you.* Do *you* believe *me?*"

"Keep walking."

"I said *do you believe me!*" she suddenly demanded, her words ringing out through the still air. "Do you believe what I said in there about you and me!" She got belligerent and tried to yank away, but he steadied her close against his hip and she submitted to his strong, forceful arm.

"Don't raise your voice, Abbie. The neighbors might still be up."

"Ha!" she all but bellowed. "Carve that one on marble! *You* worried about what *my* neighbors might think!" She lurched and grabbed his shirtfront in both fists, shaking it, tugging till it pulled against his neck.

"Shh! You're drunk."

"I'm as sober as a judge now. Why won't you answer me?"

Was she drunk or sober when she reared back and began trumpeting in the most unladylike way, "Jesse DuFrayne loves Abbie Mc—" and he plastered his mouth over hers to shut her up? Her arms came around his neck and he lifted her clean up off the ground, her breasts flattened mercilessly against his rigid chest. But once his mouth covered hers, he forgot he was only trying to shut her up. He took her mouth wholly, and there was nothing dry about it. She had both of her arms folded behind his strong neck, her toes dangling half a foot off the earth, and they stood that way in the silver moonlight, kissing and kissing, and forgetting they had vowed to be enemies, all tongue and tooth and lip and a soft, thick moustache. Her mouth was hot and sweet and tasted of champagne. The smell of roses came from the fabric of her starched blouse and she made a small groaning whimper deep in her throat, her breath coming warm against his cheek. And in no time at all his body grew uncomfortably hard, so he set her down on her feet none too gently, pulled her arms away from his neck, and ordered fiercely, "Get the hell up to bed, Abbie. Do you hear me!"

She stood there drooping, conquered.

"Can you walk by yourself?" His warm hand still gripped her elbow.

"I told you I'm not drunk," she muttered to the earth at her feet.

"Then prove it and get inside where you belong."

"I, Mr. DuFrayne, am as sober as a veritable judge!" she boasted, still to the night earth, for she could not raise her head. He carefully released her elbow, and she swayed a little but remained upright.

"Don't judge me for this, Abbie, just get the hell out of here!"

"Well, you don't have to sound so mad about it," she said childishly, and knew somewhere in her bleary head just how drunk she really was to be talking that way, almost whining. Ashamed now of what she'd done, she turned and weaved her way to the house, gulping deep draughts of the stringent night air. On her way past the dining room table she gulped a whole cup of cold coffee. And by the time she made her way upstairs it was herself she was judging, not him. Champagne was no excuse, none at all. The pure, unadulterated truth was that she'd been wanting him to kiss her all night. Worse, she'd been wanting to kiss him back. Worse yet, she didn't think that was all she wanted anymore.

Upstairs, she flopped backward onto the bed, arms as limp as the excuses she tried to think up. Heavens, that man can kiss! One finger wound around a tendril of hair until she'd curled it all the way to her scalp. She closed her eyes and groaned, then hugged her belly and curled up, suddenly tragically sure her mother had been dead wrong. Here she was, Abigail McKenzie, spinster, thirty-three and heading upward, never to know just what it was that her mother had so warned her against. Certainly it couldn't be kissing. It had been nothing short of a swift, sweet miracle, the way that kiss had felt. It had been so long ago with Richard that it was impossible to recall if it had been this good. And certainly David's kiss had not started such a volcanic throbbing in her. But always before she had held back, afraid of what her mother had said. But when you loosen your reserve and put everything into it, kissing was a different matter entirely. It started such strange and pleasant rippling sensations shimmying downward through one's body.

Lying in the darkness above Jesse, she again pictured his body. Ah, she knew it so well. She knew the shape and hue and texture of each part of it, the valleys of his shoulder blades where strong muscles welled up to leave inviting hollows. His dark arms, long, strong, etched with veins at the inner bend of elbow. His legs and feet, how often she'd seen them, washed them. She knew his hands, large, square, with equal capacity for teasing and gentling. His eyes seemed to seek her out in the darkness, from beneath brows whose outline she traced on her stomach now from memory. Those eyes crinkled at the corners in the instant before his soft, soft moustache lifted with a lazy smile. She knew the spot where the skin grew smooth, down low where the hair of his broad chest narrowed and dove in a thinner line, narrowing, narrowing along his hard belly to his groin.

She rolled onto her stomach because her breasts hurt. She clamped her arms against the swelling sides of those breasts and squeezed her thighs together, locking her ankles, holding them tightly, tightly, trying to forget the image of the naked Jesse. But forgetfulness refused her. She opened her mouth, waiting for the heat of his imaginary kiss. But she touched only the pillow, not warm, soft lips. She rolled to her side clutching a knob of nightgown between her legs, feeling what was happening there, this awful aching need to be filled.

Was this then how it was? How it ought to be? What her mother had known? What her mother had never known? It was fullness and emptiness, acceptance and denial, hot and cold, shiver and sweat, yes and no. It was the coming apart of scruples, ethics, codes, standards, and virtues and not caring in the slightest, because your body spoke louder than your conscience.

Jesse had been right all along, and her mother had been wrong. How could such compulsion be wrong? Senses Abbie had never realized she possessed were now expanded to their fullest. Her body throbbed and beat and begged. How right . . . how utterly right . . . it would be to simply go to him and say, "Show me, for I want to see. Give me, for I deserve. Let me, for I feel the right."

The question no longer was could she do that and live with it afterward. The question now was could she not do that and watch her one chance walk out the door tomorrow to leave her ignorant and unfulfilled.

Chapter 15

THE MOON WAS rich cream, high, melting down through the wide bay window, running all over him as he lay, sprawled carelessly, naked on the bed. His head and chin were screwed around at an odd angle, as if trying to see the headboard backward. She had listened to his restless movements for what seemed like hours, working up the courage to creep downstairs. But now he slept, she could tell by his measured breath and the one dark foot that dangled off the end of the bed where he had never fit and never would. She came trembling to the bedroom doorway, afraid to enter, afraid not to. What if he turned her away?

Little tight fists pressed against chin and teeth, she eased closer. Her chest felt as if it were in a vise. How should she awaken him? What should she say? Should she touch him? Maybe say, "Mr. DuFrayne, wake up and make love to me"? How absurd that she didn't even know what to call him anymore. Suddenly she felt awkward and sexless and knew for sure he'd tell her to get back upstairs and she would die of humiliation.

Yet she whispered his name anyway. Or did she whimper it?

"J . . . Jesse?"

It might have been the brush of curtain upon sill, so tentative was the sound.

"Jesse?" she asked again of his moon-clad body.

He straightened his head around on the pillow drowsily. Although she couldn't make out his eyes, she saw the moon's reflection on the bolder lines of his face. His moustache made a darker, beckoning shadow. His chin lowered and he looked across his chest and saw her, and pulled a hank of sheet over to cover himself.

"Abbie? What is it?" he asked sleepily, disoriented, braced up on his elbows now.

"J . . . Jesse?" She quavered, suddenly not knowing what else to say. This was awful. This was so awful. It was worse than any of the insults she'd suffered at his hands, yet she stood as she was, her two hands, fisted tight, bound together against her chin.

But he knew. He knew by the tremulous way she spoke his name at last. He sat up, taking more of the sheet across his lap, dropping a single leg over the edge of the bed for equilibrium.

"What are you doing down here?"

"Don't ask . . . please," she pleaded.

The silent night surrounded them and time seemed to cease its coursing until out of the creamy night quiet came his voice, low and knowing.

"I don't need to ask, do I?"

She gulped, shook her head no, unable to speak.

He didn't know what to do; he knew what he must do.

"Go back upstairs, Abbie. For God's sake, go. You don't know what you're doing. I shouldn't have let you have that champagne."

"I'm not drunk, Jesse. I . . . I'm not. And I do not want to go back upstairs."

"You don't need this in your life."

"What life?" she asked chokily, and his heart was clutched with remorse for having made her question the blandness that had always been enough before.

"The life you've always prided yourself on, the one I don't want to ruin for you."

"There have been so many times I thought I knew what would ruin my life. My mother always warned me that men like Richard would ruin it. Then she died and he ran away and I wondered how to exist from one day to the next with all that nothingness. Then a man named David Melcher came into my house and made me hope again, but—"

"Abbie, I tried to apologize for that. I know I shouldn't have done that to you. I'm sorry."

"No, you shouldn't have, but you did, and he's gone and shall never be back. And I need . . . I . . ." She stood as still as a mannequin, the moonlight limning her in ivory, her hands pressed to her throbbing throat.

"Abbie, don't say it. You were right at the supper table tonight. I do value all your old-fashioned morals or I'd have taken you long ago. I don't want to be the one to make them come crashing down now, so just go back upstairs and tomorrow I'll be gone."

"Don't you think I *know* that!" she cried desperately. "You are the one who made me realize the truth about Richard and me. You are the one who accused me of stagnating, so who better shall I ask? Don't change on me now, Jesse, not now that I've come this far. You . . . you are my last chance, Jesse. I want what every other woman has known long before she's thirty-three."

He jumped off the bed, twisting the sheet around him, holding it low against one hip. "Goddamnit, that's not fair! I will not be the one to aid in your undoing!" He tugged the sheet viciously but it was anchored beneath the mattress, tethering him before her. "I lay there thinking about you for hours after I went to bed and I found you were a hundred percent right about my motives. I don't know what it is about you that mixes me up so, but one minute I want to bend you and the next I'm cussing because you're so godalmighty moral that if you bend, I'm the one who breaks. But you know that and you're using it against me!"

She was. She knew it. But she swallowed her pride and spoke in a strained whisper. "You're sending me away then?"

Oh, God, he thought. God, Abbie, don't do this to me when I'm trying to be noble for the first time in my life! "Abbie, I couldn't live with myself afterward. You're not some . . . some two-bit whore following the railroad camps."

"If I were, could I stay?" Her plaintive plea made him ache with want.

Why the hell did I push her so far, he berated himself, wondering how to get them both out of this without lasting hurt to either. This was the moment when her morals and her mother's morals faced off. How ironic that he should now be the spokesman for the mother he had criticized.

"Abbie," he reasoned, "it's because you're not that you can't. Do you understand the difference?" Had she no idea what she did to him, standing there hugging herself, swathed in moonlight and trembles? "You'll hate me afterward, just like you hate Richard. Because I'm going, Abbie. I'm going and you know it."

"The difference is that I know it beforehand."

Sweat broke out across his chest and he tightened the twist of sheet at his hip until it dug into his skin. "But you know what I am, Abbie."

She raised her chin proudly, though her body quaked. "Yes, you are Jesse DuFrayne, photographer, seer of life as it really is. But you are the one running from reality now, not I."

"You're damn right I'm running." His labored breath sounded like he actually had been. "But the reason is you. Tomorrow you'd look at this differently and you'd hate me."

"And would you mind?" she braved, her chin lifting defensively.

"You're damn right I'd mind, or I wouldn't be standing here arguing, wrapped in these sheets like some timid schoolboy!"

"But you know that if you send me back upstairs, I shall hate you anyway."

The moonlight scintillated off their outlined bodies as they strained to see each other's faces. He thought he could smell roses clear across the room. Her shoulders were so small, and she looked all vulnerable and scared with her arms folded up the center of her chest that way. But her hair was loose, lit by moonglow, like a nimbus about her shadowed face.

"Abbie . . ." His voice sounded tortured. "I'm not for you. I've had too damn many quick women." But his conviction somehow faded into appeal and he took a halting step toward her. She too took one tremulous step, then another, until he could make out the quick rise and fall of her breathing.

"All the better that it be you, Jesse, my one and only time—you who know so well." Her words were soft, breathy, and raised the hair along his arms. They were so close that Jesse's shadow blocked the moonlight from her upraised face. Tension tugged at their hovering, unsure bodies. The whisper of curtains in the night breeze was now the only sound in the room. Jesse's nostrils flared while he clutched the sheet tighter, tighter. He thought of tomorrow and knew she had no idea that David Melcher would be back in town. All he had to do was tell her so and she would turn back upstairs obediently. But the thought of leaving her to Melcher flooded him with livid jealousy. He could take her now, but how she'd hate him afterward, when she found out he'd known all along of Melcher's return.

She knew absolutely nothing about what he could do to her, he was sure. There she stood, imploring him for that of which she was ignorant—his tiny little hummingbird Abbie, who'd fought for his life and defied death right here in this very room. And in return she asked just one thing of him now . . . and he wanted to give it to her so badly that it physically hurt. She was a scant four feet in front of him now. All he had to do was take one step more. Standing there, fighting desire, smelling the aura of roses drifting from her, Jesse floundered, became lost in her. "Abbie," he uttered, the name strained, deep in his throat, "you're so damn small." And the sheet, like a puddle of rippling milk, moved with him as he leaned to whisper in her ear, "Don't hate me, Abbie, promise you won't hate me." His gruff words moved the hair behind her ear and trapped her heart in her throat. A sinewy hand reached through the moonlight to close itself about her upper arm.

Her lips fell open. She raised her face and her nose touched his firm shoulder. His skin smelled of night warmth and sleep and held a faint trace of dampness, not wholly unpleasant. She raised a hesitant hand to brush it with her fingertips. He was so hard, so warm, and she so unsure. He poised, his breath beating upon her ear, and she wondered what he would have her do. She knew so little, only that to kiss as they'd kissed in the yard had turned her body to sweet, shaking jelly. So she raised her lips and asked near his, "Would you kiss me first, like you did in the yard, Jesse?"

His grip on her arm grew painful. "Oh, God, Abbie," he groaned, and let the sheet spill from him as he scooped her up in powerful arms and held her against the heart that hammered wildly in his breast. He buried his face in her hair, knowing he should not do this, but was unable to deny himself any longer.

She rubbed her temple against his lips, eager for the touch of them on her own. Then slowly, timidly, her face turned up, seeking that remembered rapture.

"Abbie, this is wrong," he reiterated one last, useless time.

"Just once, like in the yard," she whispered. "Oh, Jess, please . . . I liked it so much."

Sanity fled. Her childlike plea threw his heart cracking against his ribs. He lowered open lips to her warm, waiting ones. As she met his kiss her arms went twining around his neck, fingers delving the mysteries of thick, black hair at the back of his head. His tongue, once dry with fever, was now wet with fervor, dipping against hers, slipping to explore her mouth greedily. She responded timidly at first, but imitating his actions, her pleasure grew and her tongue became bolder within his mouth. He released her suddenly and her knees and legs went sliding down along his until her feet touched the floor. He cinched powerful arms about her ribs, lifting her untutored body up and in against him. His mouth slanted demandingly across hers and his tongue delved deeper, plying, playing, melting her insides like sugar candy until she felt it drizzle, sweet and warm, far down from the depths of her.

For Abbie it was the wonder of the first kiss magnified a hundred times as her body pressed willingly against his. He made a faint growling sound in his throat, then threaded his long fingers back through the hair at her temples, cradling her head in his palms while he scattered little kisses everywhere. He seemed to be eating her up by nibbles, making her feel delicious as he took a piece of her chin, then her lip, her nose, her eyebrow, ear, neck, settling back upon her mouth again, biting her tongue lightly as if finding it the tastiest. She forgot everything but the slow, sweet yearning inside her body. She let it control her, leaving her with the wonder of this man whom she had so long feared, but whom she wanted now with a desire that shut out all thoughts of wrong. She forgot that his was a practiced kiss, knew only that it was the prelude to all she was so eager to learn from him, of him. He buried his face in her neck, his breath summer warm on her skin.

"Abbie, I have to know, so I don't hurt you," he said in a hoarse, stranger's voice, "did you and Richard ever do this?"

Her hands fell still upon his neck.

"No . . . no!" she answered in a startled whisper, straining away suddenly. "I told you—" She would have turned aside, abashed, but he took her jaw in both of his warm hands, tipping her face up as if it were a chalice from which he would sip, forcing her to look at him.

"Abbie, it doesn't matter," he said low, brushing his thumbs lightly, lightly upon the crests of her cheeks. "I don't want to hurt you is all. I had to ask."

"I . . . I don't understand," she said tremulously, her eyes wide on his, lips fallen open in dismay.

She swallowed hard; he felt it beneath the heels of his hands, and thought, Lord, she's so small, I'll kill her. Yet he brushed her cheek with his lips and hushed, "Shhh . . . it's all right," and lifted her face to meet his kiss again, making them both forget all but the turbulent senses aroused now beyond recall. With his tongue in her mouth, he picked her up again and carried her to the edge of the bed, where he sat with her upon his lap. Silently he vowed to go slow with her, to make it good, right, memorable if he could. He lifted her bashful arms and looped them around his neck. She was ever aware that he was naked, that his skin burned warmly through her wrapper and gown. His lips slid to the warm cay of her collarbone, and he murmured, "You smell like roses . . . so good." She twisted her head sensuously, rubbing a jaw against his temple. He touched her neck with his tongue, and she shuddered with some new, vital want. "Can I take your wrapper off, Abbie?" he asked, trailing brief kisses to a soft spot on the underside of her chin.

"Is that how it's done?" she asked rather dreamily.

"Only if you want."

"I want," she confessed simply, sending his senses thrumming. So he found the twist of belt at her waist and tugged it free and brushed the garment away until it lay tumbling across his bare knees.

He kissed her once more, then said into her mouth, "Abbie, I'm shaking as if it's my first time."

"That's good," she whispered.

Yes, he thought, it's good.

Then she added, "So am I," and he heard the smile in her words. He smiled too, against her cheek, then bit the tip of her ear.

"Remember when we were sitting on the swing? I really wanted to do this then, but I was afraid to put my arm around you all of a sudden."

"You've never been afraid, I don't think. Not of this." But still it pleased her that he said so. His hand slid to her ribs, rubbing sideways, abrading her skin softly through the thin cloth of her nightgown.

"I'm afraid now, Ab, afraid this might melt away beneath my hand."

She held her breath, her skin tingling with anticipation until at last his palm filled itself with her breast, warm and peaked and generous. The pressure of his other hand grew insistent at the back of her neck until she obeyed its command and turned her mouth again to his. But this time his kiss was no heavier than the touch of a moth's wing, more a kiss of breath than of lips. But it made shivers ride outward from every pore of her body. His caresses were loving, gentle, as he took a nipple, hard and expectant, between his thumb and the edge of his palm, squeezing it gently until she sighed against his lips. His hands roamed her shoulders and the nightgown fell down about her hips, letting first the warm fingers of night air ripple over her bare skin . . . then the warm fingers of Jesse DuFrayne. When his hand at last cupped her bare breast, she laid her forehead against his chin, lost in the magic of his touch. He brushed the erect nipple with the backs of his fingers while her wrists went limp, hanging across his shoulders. Drifting in sensation, she unconsciously pulled back to free a space so he could explore further. Finding her other breast as aroused as the first, he made a satisfied sound in his throat. "Ahhh, they're so hard," he said thickly.

She murmured some wordless reply, adrift in pleasure, wanting this to go on forever. She seemed to be floating above herself, looking down at a strange, lucky woman being pleasured by her man. She'd never imagined people talking when they did things like this, yet his soothing tones freed her from the bonds of restraint, and the lover she watched from above answered her consort, "Sometimes all I have to do is think of you and they get that way. Once it even happened in church."

He chuckled softly against her neck, but it was all he could do to keep from tumbling her backward and delving into her, deep and hard and now. He felt like he would burst from his skin! He wanted to taste her, smell her, hear her whimper, feel her flesh surround his. But he restrained himself, knowing it best to make it last long and good for both of them. He plied her with more kisses, running a hand up her back, then low along her spine. His fingers slid to her waist and pulled her bare hip up hard against the erect evidence of his desire, giving her time to learn the newness of a man, teaching her the difference between himself and her. He eased a hand onto her stomach, the other to the base of her spine, and sat as if praying, with her between his folded hands. Then his large palm swallowed up her breast as he took her with him, back, back, onto the softness of rumpled sheets. She fell atop his hard chest, but he rolled her onto her back, dipping his head down to kiss her shoulder, her collarbone, then the warm swell of skin below it. She felt his soft moustache, pictured it vividly as his hot, wet tongue trailed nearer and nearer a nipple until at last he was upon it, receiving the cockled tip beneath his stroking tongue, making her gasp, arch her ribs, and reach blindly for his hair. He tugged and sucked, sending billows of feeling flowing outward, downward from where he taught her skin to crave the moistness of his loving. He left one nipple wet, and she shivered as he moved to the other, her palm now guiding his jaw. With his ardent kiss upon her breast, all of her long-unused senses came to life, sluicing downward in a grand, liquid rush. Her nipples ached sweetly for more, but he stretched out beside her then, bending an arm beneath his ear, tickling her chest with a single playful fingertip. Goose bumps erupted all over her body, then she laughed girlishly and rolled a little bit, pushing the teasing finger away.

"I want to touch you all over," he said. But, curiously, he had removed his touch from her altogether, making her long greedily for its return. They stared into each other's eyes for a long, intense minute, neither of them speaking or moving. She sent him a tacit invitation to come back and try again, unable to say it in words. His hand lay down along his hip. He lifted it slowly and saw her eyelids flinch and widen as he touched her stomach lightly with the tip of an index finger, drawing tendrils and grapevines around her navel, up her ribs, around her nipples, up to her throat. Then, still with that single fingertip, he surveyed the line along which the fine hairs of her body met, joined, and pointed like nature's arrows, to the place which wept for want of him. He pressed her stomach, letting his fingertips trail into Spanish moss, lingering there while she lay with the breath caught in her pleasured throat. But as his fingers moved lower she recoiled, instinctively protecting herself against intrusion.

Realizing what she'd done, she felt awkward and stupid, covering herself that way, but she was suddenly, inexplicably afraid. Surely he would get disgusted now and think her utterly childish and realize he'd been wasting his time with her.

But instead, he whispered near her ear, "It's all right, Abbie, it's all right." He looped an arm loosely about her waist and kissed her again, exploring her back, shoulders, and the firm rises at the base of her spine. He lifted his head, looking down into her face. "Abbie, have you changed your mind?" he whispered, husky and strained. Her wide, uncertain eyes looked up at him, but she could not speak. Sensing her last-minute fear, he soothed her with whispered words, running the backs of his knuckles down her shoulder and around the outer perimeter of a breast. "Your skin, Ab, I never felt such skin. It's like warm custard pudding . . . smooth . . . and soft . . . and sweet." And as if to prove it, he leaned to take a taste, just inside her elbow where the soft pulse throbbed. He took the velvety skin gently between his teeth, tugging at it tenderly, then buried his face in the hollow of her abdomen. Her spine went taut, so he eased up to whisper into her mouth, "Don't be afraid, Abbie."

Then gently, insistently, his hand flowed downward, warm, slow, but sure. She squeezed her eyes shut, took a deep breath and held it tightly, envisioning the exact length and strength of his fingers before they sought, found, and entered.

She was sweetly swollen and wholly aroused, all sleek, wet satin. He braced up on an elbow, the better to see her. He moved his finger, watching her face all the while—the eyelids that trembled, the lips that fell open, the cheeks that grew hollow. She arched and gasped at what was happening within her. He plied her with the certain knowledge that she was ripe with the need for this. He teased her knowingly until, in abandon, she flung an arm over her head, eyes hidden now behind her elbow, her breath fast, hot and urgent.

He smiled, watching her go all sensuous and stretching.

Then his touch slipped away.

She opened her startled eyes to his smiling face above her.

"Jesse . . ." she choked, dying of need.

"Shhh . . . we have all night." He circled her with a strong arm and turned them onto their sides, pulling her up tightly against his hot length. His knee slid silkily between her legs, rode up high against the place his hand had abandoned. With the sole of his foot he caressed the back of her calf and the softness behind her knee. Even in the vague light he could see the look of longing in her eyes. He kissed her just enough to keep the fever high, then pressed her shoulder blades back against the sheets again. With agonizing slowness he slid his hand along her belly, her ribs, her breast, her armpit, then on up, up, up the length of her loose-flung arm, finally closing over her palm, carrying it down between their two bodies. He felt her tense as she sensed where he was taking that hand.

"No . . ." she uttered before she could stop herself. Her fingers strained against his grip, leaving him doubtful of how to proceed with her. At last he laid her hand upon his ribs, leaving the choice up to her. But to tip the scales in his favor he used ardent words and a timeless language of body to tempt her.

"Touch me, Abbie," he encouraged, "touch me like I just touched you." His voice was a racked whisper, his kisses trailed fire paths across her face, his knees and hips spoke intimate promises against her. The hand remained on his ribs, trembling there, warm and slightly damp. "That's how it's done, Ab, we touch each other first. Did you like it when I touched you?" He heard her swallow convulsively. "It was good, wasn't it? Men like it just as much as women do."

A fearful timidity swelled her throat but the hand would not move. Do it! Do it! she told herself, her heart leaping and lunging within her breast. But nothing had prepared her for this. She had thought to lie passively and let him do what he would with her. The thought of fondling him made her palm burn to know him, but she was afraid once she reached, touched, her mother's spirit would somehow know what she was doing.

"Just a touch, then you'll know." He reached to titillate her again, hinting at bestowing the fire that had driven her wanton before, and she found herself thrusting up in welcome. But his teasing fingers left again, and she understood frustration as she never had before. She swallowed and made her hand move. He fell dead still, waiting. But when at last her fingertips came into contact with his tumescence they retracted into a quick clinch: he was so unexpectedly hot!

He lost all sense of caution then and moved swiftly, capturing her wrist between their bellies. "Just take it, Ab, just touch," he begged in a strident whisper. Fear lodged in her throat. The back of her hand now rested against that soft-hard heat, but timidity crushed her will to do what he asked. She pinched her eyes shut as he relentlessly forced her fingers to close around his engorged flesh and showed her how he would have her please him. A racked sound fell into the night and her eyes flashed open to find him raised on an elbow, his head flung back, mouth open almost as if in the throes of pain. He groaned raggedly and she jerked her hand away guiltily.

"Jesse, what is it! Did I hurt you?"

He swooped over her in a rough, swift enveloping turn, clutching her hand back where it had been.

"Lord . . . no, no, you didn't hurt me. You can do anything you want. . . . Do it . . . please." His lips smothered hers, almost violently, his tongue and hips thrusting rhythmically while his hand slid over her stomach in a frantic search now.

Her senses were torn between the sinuous ebb and flow within her grasp and the warm hand sliding up her thigh, the faint feather strokes with which he again quickened her, his knowing fingertips never faltering. Femininity had lain fallow within her for thirty-three years, planted by nature, nourished by time, until it took now but a kiss-breadth to make it erupt and flower.

She was dimly aware that he roughly jerked her hand off his flesh, but her eyes could no more open than could her body control the volcanic climax which he brought to it so effortlessly. And all the while he chanted murmurously, leaning on an elbow above her, kissing her eyes, stroking her flesh. "Let it come, Ab . . . let yourself fly . . . fly, Abbie . . . fly with me . . ."

His name escaped her throat as spasms of heat pulsated from deep in her stomach downward, downward, and her hips reached high, yearning. When the final seizure gripped her, she was unprepared for its force. She had never, never guessed . . . aaah, the power of it, the rapture . . . Jesse, she thought, ah, Jess, it's so good. . . . Jess, you were right. . . . Mother, why did you warn me against this?

Her nails cut into his arm. A rasping cry of ecstasy was wrenched from her throat and even as she shuddered his body covered hers. He spoke her name as the silken hair of his chest pressed upon her bare breasts, absorbing the faint sheen of moisture there. His tumescent body searched, probed, and found its home. He flanked her narrow shoulders with his hands, bracing away.

"Abbie, it's going to hurt, love, but just once, I promise."

Hot flesh entered her; her own resisted. She started to struggle, pushing against his chest. "Relax, Abbie, relax and it'll be better. Don't fight me,

Abbie." But her fists pummeled him, so he captured them and pinned them to the mattress. "I want to make it good for you," he intoned as his weight pressed heavily and he plunged. She gasped and a cry of appeal tore from her throat, but he smothered it with his kiss, then spoke her name in loving apology.

From the ecstasy of a moment ago she was seared by pain. Her shoulders strained up off the mattress, but he held her helpless, moving within her. Delicate membrane tore and sent stabbing anguish through her recently pleasured limbs. She struggled uselessly, for her every resistance was controlled by his awesome strength and size. His breath scraped harshly with each thrust until at last she gave up, throwing her face aside, waiting passively for the torment to end.

As Jesse moved, each stroke brought shards of glassy pain to him, too. The long-unused muscles of his leg flamed as if a hot poker had been thrust into his wound. He gritted his teeth, his hands clinching her wrists like talons, thinking of how small she was, causing himself more misery by shimming his weight high to keep from hurting her. He fought pain in an effort to derive the most from his pleasure, but the faster he moved, the more it hurt. Sweat broke out on his brow as pain slowly but surely got the upper hand. His head sagged down, and his efforts at release grew grim. His arms shook mightily and a deep groan escaped him when finally he collapsed upon her, burning jets of white-hot fire searing his loins. He sighed, but it was not a replete sound, it was filled rather with relief.

He fell half off her, one leg still sprawled across her thighs, and she knew even in the depth of her naiveté that something was wrong. It had not been good for him as it had been earlier for her. He groaned into the pillow beside her ear and rolled himself away, limb by limb. But she could hear him gritting his teeth, and could feel his tensile muscles still shaking. She reviewed it all and knew exactly whose fault it was. His sudden withdrawal could only have been caused by her lack of prowess. Unsure of what she'd done wrong, she knew beyond doubt it was something, for it came back to her how he'd roughly jerked her hand off his body. He lay now with the back of a wrist over his eyes, obviously greatly relieved that it was over. Chagrined, she rolled away, cursing herself for being a stupid virgin of thirty-three, unable to perform even the simplest act to his satisfaction.

"Where are you going?"

"Upstairs." She began to sit up, but a long arm pinned her flat.

"What's the matter?"

"Let me go." She could already feel tears gathering in her throat.

"Not until you tell me what's wrong."

Her eyelids stung. She bit the inside of her lip, disappointment, anger, and guilt settling in with a sudden, deflating whump.

"Thank you, Mr. DuFrayne, for a heartfelt performance," she said stingingly.

"For *what!*" His neck crimped up, his fingers bit into her arm.

"What else shall I call such a sham?"

"What's wrong, Abbie, didn't I do it to suit you?" he asked sarcastically.

"Oh, you suited me fine. I fear I'm the one who did not suit."

He instantly softened. "Hey, it's your first time. It takes time to learn, all right?"

She pried his fingers from her arm and rolled away from him, thoroughly ashamed now of all the moaning and groaning she'd done when he had, in his turn, acted as if he couldn't wait to be done with her. He'd rolled off and out of her as fast as he could, then just lay there like a big, silent lump, saying nothing. All right then! If he had nothing to say, neither did she! She stared at the moonlit window, battling tears, remembering how he hadn't wanted to make love to her in the first place, how she'd practically had to beg him. Mortified, she lurched up as if to leave, but he got her by the shoulders and toppled her back down.

"Oh, no you don't! You're not running out of this bed and leaving this unsettled, because I'm not about to let you! You're going to stay right here until I find out what's got you prickled up, then you're going to give me a chance to put it right!"

"I am not prickled up!"

"Like hell you aren't! Can't we even do *this* without a fight! Not even this!" She bit her lip to keep from bawling out loud. He went on, "I thought we did rather well, myself, considering it was our first time together. So what's your gripe?"

"Let me up. You're all done with me anyway." Martyrdom felt blessedly sweet. But one hard arm pressed her shoulders relentlessly, allowing no escape.

"I'm *what!*" he barked, growing angrier by the minute at her sudden, unexplained peevishness. "Don't you use that tone of voice on me, as if I'd slung you here against your will and raped you!"

"I didn't mean it that way. I only meant that it was obvious I was nothing."

"Abbie, don't say that." His voice lost its harshness. "This shouldn't happen between a man and a woman and leave them as nothing. It should always leave them as more."

"But I was nothing. You said so."

"I never said any such thing!"

"You said it takes s . . . some time t . . . to learn." The tears were growing plumper on her lids.

"Well, damnit, it does! But that's nothing against you."

"Don't you dare lie there over me, swearing right into my face, Jesse DuFrayne!"

"I'll lie here and do any damn thing I please, Miss Abigail McKenzie! You've got the story all wrong anyway. Look at you! Why, you're half the size of me. Just what do you think would happen if I laid into you with all I've got?" She turned her face aside. He grabbed her cheeks and made her look him in the eyes. "Abbie, I didn't want to hurt you so I held back . . . and there's not as much in it, is all, when a man does that. And yes, you're inexperienced, and no, you don't know all the moves, but I didn't care. By the time we got to the end I knew exactly how painful it was for you—the first time is always like that for a woman. I just wanted to end it quick for you."

"I am not made of china like the soup bowl you shattered once in this room!" she pouted.

"I don't think I know exactly what you're bitching about! Just what is it!"

Her chin trembled and a tear spilled. She looked at the moonlight streaming across the windowseat. "I . . . I don't kn . . . know either. You just . . . you acted like you were glad it was ov . . . over, that's all."

He sighed, tired and disgusted now. "Abbie, my leg hurt like hell and I was worried about hurting you any more and . . . and . . . *oh, goddamnit!*" he exclaimed, pounding a fist into the mattress and flopping onto his back to stare at the ceiling.

She knew he was done with her for sure then, so sat up. But he touched her arm, gently though. "Stay a minute," he placated. "Will you stay?" There was a new note of sincerity in his voice as he dropped his hand from her arm. She pushed her hair back and wiped her eyes, so sorry now that she'd ever started this. "Don't go, Abbie, not like this," he pleaded, raising up on an elbow.

"I'm just getting the sheet." She found it on the floor and wiped her eyes with it before lying down and flinging it over her. It fell across him too, and they lay there like a pair of scarecrows under the sheet and the silence and the misunderstanding. Finally he rolled onto his side facing her and folded an elbow beneath his ear, studying her stiff profile against the square of milk-white window. His voice came again, soft and disarming. "Abbie, do you think it's always so easy for a man? Well, it's not. A man is expected to lead the way and a woman relies on him to do the right thing. But being the leader doesn't make him either infallible or fearless." She stared at the ceiling, the sheet clinched tightly beneath her armpits as tears dripped down into her ears. He ran an absent finger back and forth along the taut edge of the sheet while he went on quietly. "I took a virgin tonight. Do you know what goes through a man's mind when he does that? Do you think I didn't fear you'd push me away or think I went too fast or too hard or too far? Do you think I didn't know how you recoiled from touching me, Abbie? What was I supposed to do then? Stop, for God's sake?" Back and forth, back and forth went his finger, lightly whisking her skin and the edge of the sheet. "I promised to make it good for you, as good as I could, but the first time is never too good for a woman. Abbie, can you believe that I was afraid after that? Every step of the way I had doubts just like you, just like all lovers do the first time. The farther I went, the more afraid I was that you'd get up and run out of here in the middle of it all. Abbie, look at me."

She did, because he sounded very hurt and sincere.

"Abbie, what did I do wrong?" he asked softly. His hand had stopped toying with the sheet and lay unmoving between her breasts, his elbow resting lightly along the shallows of her ribcage.

"Nothing . . . nothing. It was m . . . me. I was terribly noisy, and afraid to do what I knew you wanted me to do, and I blamed you because it hurt at the end, and . . . and . . . oh, everything." Chagrined, she turned her face against his biceps. Tears were coming fast now. "It . . . it's just easier to get m . . . mad at you than it is t . . . to get mad at mys . . . self."

"Shhh, Abbie," he hushed, "you were fine."

"N . . . no, I was not f . . . fine. I was sc . . . scared and childish, but I d . . . didn't expect—"

A big hand found her cheek, its thumb brushed near a lower eyelid. "I know, Ab, I know. It's all new to you. Don't cry, though, and don't think you didn't give me pleasure, because you did."

She was horrified that she could not stem the flow of tears. His thumb grew sleek upon the hot puddle in the hollow beneath her eye. Her chest felt like it was near bursting from holding the sobs back.

"Th . . . then why were you in such a hurry to have it over with? I even h . . . heard you gritting your t . . . teeth."

"I told you why I hurried. My leg hurt and I thought I'd crush you. Besides, my own performance was none too great at the end either." He lifted his head off its cradling arm to look down into her face and find her eyes tightly jammed shut. In all his life he'd never faced a situation such as this after lovemaking. He too felt inept and wanting, dissatisfied in spite of what had passed. But at the same time he felt singularly protective toward this woman: the first he'd ever encountered who was as much concerned with fulfilling his needs as her own. He leaned to kiss the river of salt that streamed from her eyes, and she suddenly choked and clutched his neck, sobbing pitifully, her arms tenaciously trapping him too close for him to watch her misery. Her chest heaved with wrenching sobs that shook his own and made his stomach cinch tight with the need to comfort her and make things right.

"Abbie, Abbie, don't cry," he whispered throatily against her hair. "We'll try it again and it'll be better." But he understood what she really cried about. He understood how far she'd come from propriety to this. So he held her tenderly, cooing soft endearments as he smoothed the hair up from the nape of her neck and back from her temples, wondering miserably how things could have gone so wrong.

"Oh, Jess, I w . . . wanted my memories of this n . . . night to be good. I didn't w . . . want us to f . . . fight tonight. I wanted us to pl . . . please each other."

"Shhh, Abbie, there are lots of ways." He dried her cheeks with the tail of a sheet. "Lots of ways and lots of time."

"Then show me, Jess, show me," she pleaded, desperate now to see that this night not end in desolation. His hand stopped moving. He kissed her forehead. She heard him swallow.

"I can't right now. A man needs time in between, Abbie, and my leg needs a rest too. But in a while . . . all right?"

But she didn't believe him. She was sure now that he was only placating her because she'd done such a miserable job the first time. He rolled to his back again, swallowing the sigh which formed as he fully rested his leg. She lay very still, staring at the ceiling, going over it all in her memory, recategorizing Jesse DuFrayne once again according to what this night had taught her about him. No longer could she consider him a defiler of women, but a tender, considerate lover instead. Not fearless, as she'd thought, but human, with misgivings not unlike her own. He'd always seemed so bold and doubtless in his teasing. What a revelation to think that there lurked trepidation behind his bravado. Yet even in his disappointment he eased her with kind, sweet words and assuaged her feelings of inadequacy by taking the blame upon himself.

But how could she face him come morning? How could she awaken here and look into his dark eyes when neither would be able to deny that their lovemaking had been disastrous? As she had once before in this room, she lay falsely still, waiting for sleep to overtake him so she could slip away. But a large, heavy hand sought and found her hair, smoothed it, then drew her to her side and pulled her up against his chest. He rested his chin upon the top of her head and her eyelashes fluttered shut as she sighed and stayed, unwilling to deny herself the comfort of being cradled that way. After some minutes his hand moved lazily against her hair. His brawny chest had a silken texture beneath her cheek. She told herself she must get up and go—what would she say to him in the morning? But like a bridling in its nesting place, she felt secure. His hand grew weighted upon her skull, then fell still. His other hand, which lay flung across her hip, twitched once spasmodically. His breathing became heavy and buffeted the top of her hair. A lethargy unlike any she'd known before came to lower her lids and sap her limbs. She knew she was falling asleep in the arms of Jesse DuFrayne. She knew he'd been a gentle and considerate lover. She knew she must awaken tomorrow to the fact that he was leaving. But it all ceased to matter.

And they slept, unaware.

The Colorado Rockies spread protective arms about the lovers. The moon pulled the earth around, climbed the clouds, and slid down the other side, to the west. The dawn peepings of birds stirred upon the pinkening air. A sleeping man rolled over and settled his face against a fair, warm arm. A sleeping woman pulled her pillow into the deep curve of her shoulder, bent a bare knee toward her nose. The man snored lightly and shifted onto his stomach, and a lock of hair caught in his moustache, fluttering as he breathed, tickling him distractingly. The edge of a long, dark hand scratched the nose, tried to brush the nuisance away. But his breath fluttered it again, still caught, still tickling. He snuffled, roused, felt something warm covering his fingers, and opened his eyes groggily to see what it was.

Abbie.

He grinned at the sight of a single rose-tipped breast half covering the back of his hand. Her other breast was buried beneath her someplace, for she too was half on her belly, one knee drawn up high, presenting a beautifully turned hip, but hiding her feminine secrets. He smiled crookedly. She likes to hog the bed, he thought. The smile dissolved as he remembered how she'd cried last night. He carefully extracted his hand, rolled onto his side, and braced his jaw on a palm. His eyes leisurely traveled the length of her, several times. Tiny toes, delicate ankles, shapely calves. He remembered glimpsing them before, but never as freely as this. Her hip was as round as the swell of a sea wave, and her waist as sharp as the trough created by tides. The deep crevice carved an enticing angle, buttressed by the knee she'd cast upward toward her chest. Myriad memories flitted through his mind. Abbie, you saved my life. Abbie, I made you cry. Abbie, I must leave soon. He looked at the window where pink-gray light crept over the sill and knew an emptiness unlike any he'd ever faced upon leaving a woman's bed. No, last night's pleasures, for him, had been minimal at best, yet his body sprang to life now at the sight of her. He leaned to drop a light kiss upon her ribs, then on that pale hip. He placed a much more lingering one in the trough of her waist. A small hand came down and swatted unconsciously at him. Then she flopped over, facing away from him, with her top leg pulled up high as before.

His heart went crazy and moisture erupted on his brow. She was small and exquisite and—yes, it was still true—innocent, for she knew nothing of the ways in which he yet desired her. He released a pent-up breath and eased down low on the bed, touched his tongue to the soft place behind her knee, closed his eyes and breathed against her skin, knowing he was taking unfair advantage while she slept, yet he was aroused so ardently that his body felt it would burst its bounds. He tasted salt and roses and maybe a little of himself. He followed the contour of her leg, his hair brushing against her thigh, recalling how very familiar she had long ago become with his own body.

What he did seemed inevitable; the weeks of intimacy they had shared made it almost preordained. He kissed her everywhere but the one spot he wanted most to taste, waiting for her to awaken that he might kiss it, too. He learned the ridges of her vertebrae, the firmness of her hip, the resilience of her thighs, buttocks, calves. He memorized even her half-flattened breast. She awakened when he lightly bit the arch of her updrawn foot, and with a start she looked back over her shoulder at the man behind her. Vague, predawn light caught in his black, aroused eyes as he braced up and searched her face for permission. Above his open lips his moustache was a dark, trembling shadow. Her eyes were drawn to it, sensing that it had just explored her skin. Her startled eyes again fled to his, and she read in that gaze a kind of ardent agony which she'd not suspected a man could harbor. It brought her heart and blood alive with a leap of sensuality and expectation.

"J . . . Jesse?" she stammered croakily. Slowly she eased her leg down, realizing how immodest her pose had been and that he'd undoubtedly been awake for some time. "Y . . . you woke me up."

"I meant to, love," he whispered, holding her captive by only the strong, sensuous tether of his gaze. She rolled backward slightly, twisting at the waist, bracing up on an elbow now and watching his eyes drop to the peak of her other breast, which curved into view, then return to her face. She felt his warm palm travel from the small of her back, around one buttock, along the back side of her calf, gently tucking her knee back up as it had been before. And all the while his eyes never left hers.

"It's my turn to know your body like you've known mine all these weeks, Abbie." She became aware of all the places where her body was wet, where his tongue had trailed as she slept, where her skin now cooled as it dried. Naiveté vanished as she read his eyes and understood his intention. Involuntarily she shivered, then slowly hid her breast behind her upper arm, not quite knowing how to hide the rest of her. Mesmerized by the hunger in his gaze, she watched in fascination as he dipped his head again to her white hip, his eyes sliding closed while a sound of deep passion rumbled from his throat. He braced up on one hand, twisted now at the waist, and with a warm, caressing palm, pushed her back down onto her stomach. Her cheek grew lost in a pillow and her heart thrust wildly against the mattress as his warm lips brushed up and down her back and he began uttering her name against her skin. "Abbie . . . Abbie . . . Abbie . . ." Over and over, roaming her body with his soft moustache and his softer mouth until everything inside her grew yearning and outreaching. He turned her gently onto her back, moving her limbs where he would have them, trailing wetness and love words as his kisses tracked across her flesh. His gravelly voice whispered that the second time was better, begged her to be still, to let him. "Don't fight me, Abbie, I'll show you . . . Abbie, you're so tiny . . . God, you're beautiful . . . Shhhh, don't hide from me . . . there's more. . . . Trust me, Ab." When she reached instinctively to cover herself, he nudged her hand aside with his nose. Then his teeth gently closed upon the side of her thumb and he carried it to the hollow of her hip.

"Jesse . . ." she rasped once, beseeching him for she knew not what.

"Nothing's going to hurt this time, Abbie, I promise."

No, she thought, people don't do this! But people did, she learned, for his mouth possessed her everywhere, sent her spinning into mindless wonder while she lost all will to resist. He sailed her high and writhing until heat exploded like a skyrocket inside her, sending sparks sizzling from the core of her stomach to the tips of her toes and fingers in a gigantic burning burst of sensation. She opened her eyes to the sight of him gazing in undisguised need up her stomach, into her dazed, glazed eyes. She groaned and rolled a shoulder languorously away from the mattress, then let it sag back again. She pulled her senses up from their debilitated depths and opened her eyes, realizing that he needed fulfillment equally as much as she had a moment ago. So she raised her drugged arms in welcome.

He lunged up, rasping instructions in her ear, encompassing her with powerful brown arms that lifted her, turned her, and set her on top of his stomach, then brought her down until her breasts were crushed against the mat of hair on his chest. Words became unnecessary, for her body and his hands told her what to do. Innocence, timidity, naiveté all fled as she started to move, watching his pleasured face as his eyes slid closed and his head arched back against the jumbled pillows. As his lips fell open and his breath scraped harshly, she saw in his face the plenary abandon which he'd earlier brought to her. Her heart soared. Her eyes stung. This, this, this, is how it should be for both man and woman, she realized. The one giving to the other, the one taking from the other, with as much joy derived from the giving as from the taking. She faltered and his eyelids flickered opened momentarily, then closed again and his temple turned sharply against the pillow as she regained the rhythm. Unbelievably, when he reached his climax he cried out—was it her name or some mindless profanity or both? It mattered not, for it made her smile, made her feel skilled and agile, and bursting with joy.

She collapsed onto his broad chest, her forehead nestling beneath his jaw. One of his hands fell tiredly onto her shoulder, rubbed it in a light, caressing circle of satisfaction before flopping weakly onto the pillow again. Then, surprisingly, beneath her ear, a slow, quiet, wonderful chuckle began. It rumbled there like sweet thunder until, puzzled, she raised her head to study him. But his eyes remained closed while his chest rose and fell beneath her own, with silent laughter. And suddenly she understood why he laughed—it was a laugh of elemental satisfaction. A smile blossomed upon her lips, and a slow glow began deep down in her belly, in answering gladness. He slung his tired arms about her, hugged her tightly, and smiled against her hair as he rolled them both from side to side several times.

"Ahh, Abbie, you're good," came his lover's hosannah, "you're so damn good."

Nothing he might have said could have pleased Abbie more at that moment. She smiled against his chest. Then his hands flopped back, palms-up, on either side of his head. She sat up, peered at him, but his eyes remained peacefully closed, and while she watched in astonishment, he fell asleep, with her sitting yet astride him—stunned, naked, and new.

Chapter 16

WITH HER FIRST rising movement, Abbie knew she'd overdone it. She was thirty-three years old and some of the muscles she'd stretched last night hadn't been stretched for years. Suppressing a groan, she rolled to the edge of the bed.

"Good morning, Miss Abigail," drawled a pleasant, raspy voice behind her. But she couldn't endure the thought of facing him, knowing that in a few short hours he would simply be walking out of her life. Two strong brown hands circled her white hips, and he kissed her down low, almost where she sat, laying behind her, strewn all over the bed hazardly, like the tumbled sheets.

"Where you going?" he inquired lazily, giving her a fond squeeze.

She sucked in her breath and her back went rigid. "Don't do that, it hurts!"

His hands slipped away and he watched her get up slowly with one hand bracing the small of her back. Two or three steps told them both that her back wasn't the only thing that hurt. But she eased her way to the pile of discarded clothing on the floor, bent over painfully to pick up her wrapper.

Ooooo, did he enjoy that!

He'd planned on a little morning morsel of her but could see that was definitely off. She straightened up just fine, but wasn't moving any too spryly. She shuffled out wiltedly while he felt like the first rose of summer—no doubt about it! He flexed, yawned, scratched his chest, and popped up happily to slip into his pants.

Abbie stood looking at the greasy, ivory-colored platter, the bones and hardened fat with dry, curling edges. She surveyed the coffee cups with brown rings and residue in their bottoms, the plain everyday glasses with now-flat champagne lying lifeless in their depths, the spot on the linen where the laughing piece of steak had hit when it flew from her mouth. Miserably she remembered their gay laughter while she'd tried in vain to settle the tablecloth perfectly all those times. She studied it all and it sickened her, standing in the middle of the room, gripping both ends of her tie-belt as if considering pulling, pulling, pulling, until it cut her in half. She told herself she would *not* think of last night as sordid! *She could not!* But eyeing the mess on the table, she wondered sadly which she wanted to wash up first, the dishes or herself.

Behind her, Jesse crossed his brown arms and leaned a shoulder against the doorframe. He could read her as accurately as if the old beatitudes were suddenly running ticker-tape fashion across the back of her sensible, sexless wrapper.

He wondered what to do or say. If he made a joke, it would fall flat. If he tried to take her in his arms, he was sure she'd push him away. If he conferred upon her the right to place the blame on him, it would only make matters worse. Still, he could not let her stand there interminably, being her own censor.

He came up behind her, placed both hands on her shoulders, and decided to simply say the truth. "In the morning sometimes a person needs reassurance, sometimes both people need reassurance." Her neck was very stiff and he slowly rubbed his long thumbs along its taut cords. He felt her swallow and went on soothingly, "It always seems different in the morning, so the best thing to do is wait until later in the day to decide just how you feel about it. In the meantime, it's customary to at least acknowledge one's partner. That is usually done in a very charming and old-fashioned way—like this."

Abbie felt herself being turned by her shoulders. She knew her hair and face were a fright, that this whole situation was frightful. But he made all that seem petty by lowering her hands when she sought to hide her hair and eyes, by kissing her ever so lightly while softly kneading her neck. She wanted to respond, but was afraid and guilty, thus Jesse had to settle for no reassurance at all, nothing more than the closing of her eyelids. Yet he understood that self-retribution already had her in its clutches, so he kissed her tenderly again, touching her fleetingly on each corner of her mouth.

His kiss was a new surprise, a unique, nice sensation which threatened her only with gentleness. But in the middle of it, with his warm lips wishing her the first lover's good morning of her life, she remembered that before the day wore out he'd be gone. Stricken, she controlled the urge to cling to him. She bit her lip as he rested his chin on top of her head. His hands rubbed her lower spine in heartrending consideration while he murmured, "The soreness will go away in no time."

And her thoughts cried, Oh, but so will you, Jesse, so will you!

She was shaken by his sensitivity, his depth of understanding. Both last night and this morning he had been tenderhearted in his treatment of her, and she now wished this weren't true. It made his imminent departure too abrupt and harsh to quite accept. Were he to turn again to his former ways, teasing, needling, or irritating her in some fashion, it would suit her far better, for she told herself rigidly that she would not—would not!—beg him to stay.

He patted her then, back there low, and said, "Why don't you take a nice hot bath and don't worry about breakfast? We ate late last night anyway."

She turned stiffly from his embrace, his consideration ripping some new wound in her with each passing moment. But still it went on, for when she was laying the fire and he saw her wince as she lifted a heavy chunk of wood, he came to take it from her, saying, "Here, let me do that. You go gather up your clothes or those dishes or something while I get a fire going and bring in some water."

As she turned away, burdened by his sweetness, he stopped her, calling quietly, "Abbie?"

She craned around, meeting his eyes directly for the first time across the morning expanse of kitchen. He looked as engagingly natural as ever: nothing on but his jeans, standing there barefoot, with that hunk of wood in his long brown fingers, his hair tousled and dark, his moustache and eyes as unsettlingly attractive as ever.

"What?" she got out.

"You haven't said anything to me yet this morning except 'Don't do that, it hurts.' "

She thought, damn you, Jesse, don't do this to me! I don't deserve it—not all this!

Why did he have to stand there looking so damn handsome and considerate and warm and likeable only now when he was on the very brink of leaving?

"I'm all right," she said evenly, disguising her turmoil. "Don't worry about last night. I can live with it."

"That's better," he said, putting the chunk of wood down, brushing bark bits off his palms. "Abbie, I have to ask you for a favor."

"Yes?"

"Are the stores open in town yet?"

"Yes."

"Well, all my stuff went on the train with my photographic gear. It was all packed together. I want to go buy a set of clothes, but I don't have any money. I never thought to ask Jim for some. If you could lend me some out of that thousand, I'll see that you get it back."

"Don't be silly. You do not need to pay it back. The money was for anything you need, and if you need clothes, of course you may have as much as you wish."

"I thought I'd just wash my face quick and run a comb through my hair and go on up to buy what I need, then come back here and get cleaned up and changed before I leave. Is that all right with you?"

"You're leaving on the morning train, then?"

"No. I'm meeting some people at noon to discuss . . . some business, then I'll take the three-twenty out this afternoon."

"Meeting some people?" she asked, puzzled, but he looked away, busying himself at his firebuilding.

"Yeah, Jim set up a meeting here and told me about it yesterday. He said I don't have to be there, but I want to since it's . . . well, it's railroad business and I'm involved in it."

She couldn't help but wonder what kind of meeting a railroad photographer would be attending in a town as remote and insignificant as Stuart's Junction, but decided it was none of her business whatsoever. She was acting like a presuming lover on the basis of a one-night consortion. He had no obligation to explain his business dealings to her at all.

"Of course," she agreed, watching him poke at the fire. He looked so natural, bare-chested and barefoot that way. It was hard to imagine him in a full set of clothes. She'd never thought to see the day he'd actually buy and wear them, railroad meeting or not. It struck her that he must be inordinately eager to leave, for he had memorized the exact time of the train whistles.

Some minutes later she was sitting at the secretary in the parlor when he came out of the bedroom, shirt buttoned, all tucked in neat and proper, boots on, hair combed.

"I hope it's all right if I used your brush, Abbie, since I don't have one of my own."

She didn't know whether to laugh or cry at that remark after what the two of them had shared last night. She handed him a bank draft she'd written out, saying, "Yes, of course it's all right. Here. I hope this will do. I haven't much cash in the house."

He reached out slowly, his eyes never leaving her downcast face while he scissored the check between two lean fingers.

"I'll be back soon." He hesitated, wishing she'd look at him, but finally swung away, seeing she would not.

As he went out, limping slightly, she called, "It's Holmes's Dry Goods Store, on the left side of the street about half a block down."

Her eyes devoured his broad back. But suddenly he stopped, braced a palm against the porch column, and studied his boots. Then he slapped the column, muttered, "Damn," and pivoted.

The screen door squeaked like her love-sprung bones, and her heart careened while she wished desperately that he'd just go, get out fast. But he came instead to stand dejectedly beside the desk, his weight slung on one hip, a thumb hanging from the waist of his denims. He slumped one shoulder, leaning his half of the way, but she refused to look up from the pigeonholes of the desk. The thumb left the waistband and came to her chin, but she jerked aside, snapping, "Don't!" He hesitated a moment longer, then leaned the rest of the way, and dropped a kiss on her nose.

"I'll be back." His voice sounded a little shaky, and her chin quivered. He straightened, touched her lips with the back of a forefinger, then left the house as fast as he should have the first time. The screen door slammed and she leaned both elbows onto the desktop, then dropped her face into her hands. She sat that way a long time, miserable, knowing she would get far more miserable before she managed to get over him. Yet get over him she must.

At last she rose, bathed, and went upstairs to dress for the day. She donned a black skirt and a pastel blue organdy blouse. She closed the loops over the many buttons of the deep cuffs, then stretched her neck high and smoothed the tight lace up her throat until it nearly grazed her ears. All the evidence of last night's tryst had been erased, but as she studied her reflection in the oval dresser mirror, she looked ten years older than she had yesterday morning. Behind her, reflected in the glass, she saw the red shoes. She raised her own castigating eyes once more, wondering if after last night those red shoes might fit. She turned, picked one up, studied it, closed her eyes, judging herself. Finally she sat down on the bed and drew a red shoe on.

From downstairs she heard the screen door slam, then Jesse, call, "Abbie? I'm back. Hey, where are you?"

"I'm upstairs," she called, casting a baleful look at the shoe.

He came to the foot of the steps and called up, "Is it all right if I take a bath?"

"Yes. There's hot water left in the reservoir, and clean linens in the bureau drawer across from the pantry."

"I know where you keep them." His footsteps moved away.

She closed her eyes against the onslaught of welcome she felt at his returning, calling up the stairs in that familiar way.

Oh, God, God, she didn't want him to go, not so soon.

The red shoe still dangled from her toe, and she leaned to lace it up. She stuck her foot out, rotated the ankle this way and that, admiring the look and feel of David Melcher's gift.

And somehow Miss Abigail felt reassured, so she put on the second shoe.

She examined them again and the red color seemed to fade into a less offensive, less improper shade. She stood up, balanced on the comfortable shoes, and found they had a heavenly fit. They made her feel petite and feminine. It was the first brief wisp of vanity Abigail McKenzie had allowed herself in her entire life. By the time she'd paced off four trial steps, the shoes had lost all garishness and were actually now quite appealing. It did not concern her that this was true only because she wanted it to be. Pacing back and forth across the bedroom floor, hearing the baby french heels click on the floorboards, there was nothing within Miss Abigail's conscience to suggest that the reason she was going to wear these shoes downstairs was to show Jesse DuFrayne that even though he was about to walk out of her life forever, he could just bear in mind that he wasn't the only fish in the sea.

"Where the hell do you keep the razor anyway?" Jesse called from downstairs, sounding like his old self again. "Abbie? I've got to hurry."

"Just a moment, I'm coming," she answered, hustling down the steps, the red shoes forgotten. She produced the razor from its kitchen hiding place and turned to find Jesse standing behind her in a pair of greenish-blue stovepipe pants—that's all. Her eyes traveled from his waist to his long toes, then back to his face as he reached for the razor.

"Could you fetch me the strop too, Abbie?" he asked, seemingly unaware of anything that might be happening inside of her.

And something was definitely happening.

Here was a bittersweet pang of a new kind. Here was her house filled with the sight and sound and smell of a man's toilette, something she'd long thought it would never again see. Oh, he had shaved and bathed and dressed here before, but now he did it in preparation to desert her. Now she was intimate with the muscle beneath the trouser, the ridges beneath the razor, the texture beneath the comb, the warmth beneath the smell. Now she wanted to call back time, forbid him to beautify his body for any cause other than her. But she had no right.

So she tried to keep from watching his bare shoulders curl toward the mirror, his head angle away, his eyes strain askance as he shaved near an ear. She tried not to dote upon the scent of shaving soap drifting through her old maid's kitchen. She tried to keep her eyes from coveting the rich fabric of the new pants he was wearing. She tried to ignore the whistle of the 9:50 from Denver when it keened through the house, the same train that had brought him here initially. She pretended that there would be no afternoon train to take him away.

"I left the change on the secretary in the parlor," he said, drying his face, leaning to comb his moustache. She'd never seen him do that before. She tore her greedy eyes away and moved into the parlor to sit before the secretary in an effort to appear busy, rummaging through some papers officiously. But all the time her heart grew heavier. He went into the bedroom and from around the doorway came the rustle of clothing, clunk of boot, chink of buckle, soft whistle through teeth, all punctuated by proclamations of silence during which her imagination took fire with images too familiar and forbidden.

And then out he came.

He stepped through the bedroom doorway and it was all she could do to keep from gasping and letting her jaw drop slack. He might have been a stranger, some striking dandy come to call as he paused, smoothing his vest almost self-consciously with a queer look on his face. His bronze skin beneath the slash of moustache was foiled against a high, stiff wing collar of pristine white, its corners turned back to create a 'V' at his Adam's apple. A four-in-hand tie was meticulously knotted and boasted a scarf pin against its bedeviling silken stripes. The rolled collar of a double-breasted waistcoat peeped from beneath impeccable lapels of a faultless cutaway jacket shorter and more contouring than the frock coats she saw in church on Sundays. The sight of him was breath-stopping, especially in this town, where miners trudged in dirt-grimed britches held by weary suspenders over grayed union suits. Jesse's entire suit was made of that startling color that reminded Abbie of the head of a drake mallard.

She suddenly knew a stab of jealousy so great that she dropped her eyes to keep him from reading them, jealousy for a cause which could make him dress like a peacock only as he left her, when all this time she could scarcely get him to don boots or shirt.

She spoke to her desktop. "You found all these . . . *habiliments* in Stuart's Junction?"

He'd thought she'd be pleased to see him dressed civilly at last, but the three-dollar word was definitely irritated and faultfinding.

"You seem surprised, but you shouldn't be." He moved gracefully to the side of the secretary, touched its writing surface lightly with three fingertips. "The railroads bring in everything they have in the East these days. The Yankees no longer have a monopoly on the up-to-date."

"Hmph," she snorted, "I should think you'd have chosen a less obtrusive color at least."

"What's the matter with this? It's called verdigris, I'm told, and it's all the rage in the East and Europe."

"Verdigris indeed?" she disdained, cocking an eyebrow at the fingers that haunted her, no matter how she tried to ignore them. "Peacock would have been more apropos."

"Peacock?" At last he withdrew his hand to tug his new lapels. "Why, this is no more peacock than . . . than the shoes old Melcher sent you."

Reflexively, she tucked her feet behind the gambriole legs of the desk chair while silently admitting the verdigris was not a bit offensive. It was deep, masculine, and utterly proper. But none of that mattered, for it wasn't really the color which riled her, and by now they both knew it.

"Perhaps it is not the suit that is peacock but only its wearer," she said stringently, and could sense Jesse bristling now.

"Why don't you make up your mind what you want out of me, Miss Abigail?" he asked hotly, referring of course to the clothing, but making her color at the memory of last night's request. Her mouth grew pinched.

"It must be a vital assignation you are going to, to bring about such a transformation when I could scarcely get a shirt on you for love or money!"

Their eyes at last met in a clash of wills, but her dubious, ill-chosen phrase became poignant with unintended meaning.

"Not for love or money?" he repeated, slowly, precisely. She realized she had employed both in the last ten hours.

"Do not dare take those words figuratively, sir!" she snapped. "Just go! Be off to your *tête-à-tête*—whatever it is—in your *verdigris* suit. But don't forget to take your everyday britches along. You never can tell when you'll get these shot off for you!"

They glared at each other while Jesse wondered how to get out of here gracefully without further recriminations on either side. At last he placed his hands on his hips, his stance wilted, and he shook his head at the floor. "Abbie," he asked entreateningly, "for God's sake, can't we at least say goodbye without all this again?"

"Why? It makes it far more familiar to see you leave with anger in your eyes."

He realized that this was true, that wrapped in the security blanket of anger she needn't make appeals or excuses. He squatted beside her chair as she stared unblinkingly into the pigeonholed depths of the desktop.

"Abbie," he said quietly, taking one of her small, clenched hands, which refused to open, "I don't want to leave you in anger. I want to see you smiling and I want to be smiling myself."

"If you'll pardon me, I don't seem to have a lot to smile about this morning."

He sighed, stared at her hem, and absently rubbed his fingers over her tightly knotted fist that he had placed on his upraised knee.

Damn! Damn! she thought, why does he have to smell so good and be so nice? Why now?

"I knew you'd be bitter this morning," he went on. "I tried to warn you but you wouldn't listen. Abbie, I don't have time to stay here and help you straighten out your conscience. Just believe me. What happened happened, and you have nothing to be ashamed of. Tell me you won't go on feeling guilty."

But she would not say any such thing, or loosen her fist, or even look at him. Had she done any of those things she would end up in his arms again, and already she was bound for a long stint in hell, she was sure. Jesse realized it was getting late, that he must soon leave. "Abbie, there's one thing that's. . . . Listen, Abbie, what we did might not be over yet, you know. If anything happens, I mean if you should be pregnant, will you let me know?"

It had never, never entered her mind. Not before, during, or after making love with him, but his considering the possibility gave her the final, unforgivable cut, for she knew he would never come back and marry her if it did turn out that way.

He was saying, "You can reach me any time by wiring the central R.M.R. office in Denver," when she slowly pivoted toward him and slipped two scarlet kidskin toes from beneath her skirt, right next to that verdigris knee on the floor. He saw the red toes peep slowly from beneath her skirt, like two insolent, protruding tongues, and jumped to his feet, fists clenched at his sides, two small horizontal creases now behind the knee of the very pant leg which he had bent to her with the kindest of intentions.

"Goddammit, Abbie, what do you expect of me! he shouted. "I told you last night I was going, and I am! Don't think I don't know why you're wearing those . . . those strumpet's shoes! But it's not going to work. You're not going to beat me over the head with the kidskin fact that you are now a scarlet woman, because it takes more than one night in bed with a man to make you one! You wanted what you got and so did I, so don't make me the fall guy. Grow up, Abbie. Grow up and realize that we're both a little right and both a little wrong and that you do not have the corner on guilt in this world!"

She kept her eyes trained on his knee and innocently intoned, "My, my, what a shame, Mr. DuFrayne, to have crimped your faultless peacock pant leg that way."

"All right, Abbie, have it your way, but don't make a fool of yourself by parading down Main Street in those goddamn red shoes!"

At that moment a querulous voice spoke from the front door. "Miss . . . Miss Abigail, are you all right?" David Melcher peered in, suffering the unsettling feeling of *déjà vu,* for it seemed he'd lived through this scene once before.

Miss Abigail shot to her feet, gaping. You could easily have stuffed both red shoes into the cavern of her mouth just then before she gathered her scattered wits enough to stammer, "M . . . Mr. Melcher . . . how . . . how long have you b . . . been standing there?" Frantically she heard the echo of Jesse's comments about scarlet women and pregnancy.

"I only just got here this minute. How long has *he* been here?"

But Jesse DuFrayne would not be talked past as if he were some cigar store Indian. His tone was icy and challenging as he faced the door. "I've been here since before you left, Melcher, so what of it!"

David pierced him with a look of pure hate. "I'll speak with you across a bargaining table at high noon and not a minute before. I am here to see Miss Abigail. I assumed you would have relieved her of your presence long before this, especially since you are obviously well enough to be arranging arbitration discussion these days."

DuFrayne angrily jerked a cuff into place, confirming flatly, "As you say, at noon then." He spun toward the bedroom to get his few things, leaving Abbie to seethe with shock yet unable to show it.

He knew! He knew! All the time he knew! He knew since Jim Hudson came that David would be returning to Stuart's Junction. He knew because the meeting today was between the two of them, apparently to settle the liability over the shootings on the train. The pompous, conceited bag of arrogance knew that he was not her last chance, yet he stole her virginity anyway, knowing she'd never have given it had she known of Melcher's imminent return. Neither did it take much perception to guess that a man like David Melcher would never accept a soiled bride. Miss Abigail wanted to fly at Jesse DuFrayne and pummel him to a pulp, scream out her rage at how she'd been taken advantage of when he could simply have told her the truth and David might have been hers!

Melcher saw the anger blotch her face, but could not guess at what the foul-mouthed DuFrayne had said this time to place it there. Miss Abigail seemed to gather her equilibrium again, for she turned and invited sweetly, "Please come in, Mr. Melcher," and even opened the screen for him.

"Thank you." He came in bearing her father's cane, but just then Jesse shouldered his way around the bedroom doorway, gripping his wadded-up britches and gun in one hand as he clomped through the parlor.

"Your man has arrived in town then?" Melcher inquired expressionlessly.

"He got here yesterday," DuFrayne answered, the quivers of anger scarcely held in check. "And yours?"

"He's waiting at the depot as the wire stated he should."

DuFrayne nodded once sharply, feeling Abbie's eyes boring into the back of his head in cold, suppressed wrath. He turned, relaxed his jaw long enough to say stiffly, "Goodbye, Miss Abigail."

She was suddenly revisited by all the hate she'd felt for Jesse DuFrayne that other morning when his insinuations had lost David to her. Now it scarcely mattered that it was DuFrayne going and Melcher staying, for the mild-mannered man was again lost to her as surely as if Jesse DuFrayne had raised his gun, pointed, and shot David Melcher square between the eyes.

Jesse read before him the face of woman spurned, and his insides twisted with guilt.

"The same to you . . . *Mister* DuFrayne!"

His eyes bored into hers for a moment before he turned on his heel, banked past David Melcher, and hit for the door. In his wake, Abbie's nostrils were filled with the distressing scent of his shaving soap.

"Well, at least he's learned to address you in terms of respect," David noted stiffly.

Watching Jesse limp away down the street, she murmured, "Yes . . . yes, he has," though she longed to shriek a last démenti at the sarcasm now reflected by the term.

David cleared his throat. "I . . . I've returned your fa . . . father's cane, Miss Abigail." When she did not respond, he repeated, "Miss Abigail?"

She turned absently, forcing her mind away from Jesse DuFrayne. "I'm happy you did, Mr. Melcher, I really am. Not because I wanted it back, but because it gives me a chance to see you again."

He colored slightly, rather surprised by her directness, so different than the last time he'd spoken to her. He thought that he detected a brittle edge to her voice that he didn't remember from before either.

"Yes, well . . . I . . . I had to return to Stuart's Junction to attend a meeting at which we will attempt to ascertain who was to blame for the entire fiasco aboard the train."

"Yes, I only heard of the meeting this morning. How *is* your foot?"

He looked down at it, then back up. "The discomfort is gone. The limp is not."

At last the old solicitude returned to her voice. "Ah, I am so sorry. Perhaps in time it too will disappear." But she recalled how Doc said he would walk with a limp for the rest of his life.

"I see you . . . ahum . . . got the gift I sent," he stammered.

Now it was Miss Abigail's turn to glance at her feet. Gracious! she thought, I would have to have these things on just when he arrived!

"They're even lovelier on your feet than off," Melcher said, completely unaware of the shoe's unacceptability, and she hadn't the heart to crush his pride.

"They're a perfect fit," she said, truthfully enough, raising her skirt a few inches and flexing her toes within the supple kidskin. "I wanted to thank you but I had no address where I might reach you." Looking up then, she saw that David Melcher was embarrassed by how much of her ankle she'd revealed. Quickly she dropped her skirts. How rapidly one forgot propriety before a true gentleman after even a brief sojourn with a rounder like Jesse.

"You must forgive my rude manners, Mr. Melcher. Please sit down," she insisted, indicating the settee and taking a side chair. "I've had a somewhat trying morning and I'm afraid I've allowed my manners to lapse because of it. Please . . . please sit. Enough about me. What about you? Will you be on your way again selling shoes as soon as this meeting today is concluded?"

"I'd hoped . . . that is to say . . . I had considered spending . . . ah well, a couple of days right . . . right here in Stuart's Junction. I've taken a room at the ah, hotel, and deposited my gear there. I have the largest shipment of shoes ever—it was waiting for me in Denver. I thought I would see about finding some new markets for them right here and in the towns close around."

"Well in that case, perhaps you'll be free this evening to pay a call on me and tell me the outcome of today's meeting. I am most interested, of course, since both you and—" she found it difficult to say his name now "—Mr. DuFrayne were both under my care."

"Yes," David said a little breathlessly. "I . . . I'd like that ev . . . ever so much. Of course I realize you'll be anxious for the . . . the news."

"The whole town will be, Mr. Melcher. Nothing quite like this has ever happened in Stuart's Junction before and I'm sure tongues have been wagging fit to kill. When the meeting commences, the townspeople will be even more curious, I'm sure."

He fiddled with his vest buttons nervously before finally asking, with countless clearings of his throat, "Miss . . . Miss Abigail, did . . . agh . . . did you, or rather . . . has your . . . agh . . . has your repu—that is to say, have the townspeople . . . agh, said anything . . ."

She finally took pity on his overstrained sense of delicacy. "No, Mr. Melcher. My reputation has not suffered because of either you or Mr. DuFrayne being here at my house. I believe it's fair to say the people of this town know me better than that."

"Oh, of course," he quickly put in, "I didn't mean—"

"Please," she extended one delicate hand toward him, "let's not speak in parables. It brings only misunderstandings. Let us agree to start over as the best of friends and forget anything which has passed."

Again her directness befuddled him, but he reached out and took the proferred fingertips in his own for a fraction of a second while his raddled face told her again how very, very different this man was from Jesse DuFrayne.

"Until this evening then," she said softly.

"Yes . . . agh . . . until this evening."

He cleared his throat for perhaps the fiftieth time since entering her house, and suddenly it irritated Miss Abigail profoundly.

The inquisitive citizens of Stuart's Junction knew something was up when Max kicked Ernie off his customary bench on the depot porch long before the

3:20 was due, declaring the station was closed for official railroad business until further notice.

All up and down the boardwalk the news spread that that Melcher fellow with the shot off toe had checked in up at Albert's Hotel, along with some dandy in a yellow-checkered suit. They knew, too, that some fancy-dressed railroad bigwig had been in town since yesterday. And it was no secret that the one from up't Miss Abigail's house came uptown this morning and bought that fancy suit they'd all been starin' at in the window of Holmes's Dry Goods Store. When they saw him limp down the street wearing it, speculation grew heavy.

"Well, if he ain't no train robber, what do you reckon he is, and what do you reckon's goin' on up to the depot?"

But all they could get out of Max was that a representative of the R.M.R. had called a meeting here.

Max dusted the runged oak chairs and gathered them around a makeshift conference table made of a couple of raw planks balanced on two nail kegs, since the station was too new to boast a real table yet. Word had it the men were gussied up fit to kill. Max picked a sliver off a raw-edged plank, anxious to please. Yessir, he thought, looks like this is real important, whatever it is. So he rounded up a pitcher and four glasses, and filled it with water from the giant holding tank looming above the tracks outside where the steam engines drank their fill.

The four of them converged on the depot at the same time, the quartet looking altogether like a rainbow trout. There was James Hudson, in a wine-colored business suit. He shook Max's hand. "Nice clean depot you keep here, Smith." Instantly he gained Max's sympathy. Jesse DuFrayne appeared in the teal blue suit which even Max had been eyeballing at Holmes's Dry Goods. When Hudson introduced Maxwell Smith, he said, "Smith is our station agent here in Stuart's Junction."

DuFrayne, extending his hand, noted congenially, "Mr. Smith, the man who refused to deport me without a release from Doc Dougherty? I want to thank you for that, sir."

Though Max said, "Aw, think nuthin' of it," he was enormously pleased and proud.

Hudson seemed to take the lead in all the introductions and Max kept his ears open, learning that the man in the yellow-checkered suit was Peter Crowley, Melcher's lawyer. By the time Hudson suggested, "Gentlemen, shall we all be seated?" Max was relieved. All this commotion and color during the hand shaking was getting him dizzy. He'd never seen such a bunch of dandies in his life!

James Hudson took a seat at the makeshift table as if it were polished mahogany. There was an air of leadership about him that stood out among the four. "Now, Crowley," he began, "I suggest we forego accusations and stick to the straight facts regarding the circumstances surrounding the shootings. Both Mr. Melcher and Mr. DuFrayne have obviously undergone some incapacitation due to the incident on the train."

"Mr. Melcher has come here to discuss liability," Crowley replied. Melcher nodded. DuFrayne sat like a statue, glowering at him while verdigris arms remained folded tightly across his chest. Hudson and Crowley went on.

"Do you mean liability on both sides or just one?" Hudson asked.

"By that I take you to mean that DuFrayne sees Mr. Melcher as liable in some way?"

"Well, isn't he?"

"He doesn't think so."

"He is the one who precipitated the scuffle in which Mr. DuFrayne was shot."

"He did not precipitate it. He came in in the middle of it."

"Causing DuFrayne to receive a nearly fatal gunshot."

"From which your client has obviously recovered, according to reports I have here from one . . ." Crowley examined a sheaf of papers before him ". . . Dr. Cleveland Dougherty, who states that DuFrayne will, in all likelihood, recover full use of the leg, while Mr. Melcher will undoubtedly walk with a limp for the remainder of his life."

"For which Mr. Melcher presumably feels he is entitled to a settlement of some sort?"

"Indeed." Crowley leaned back in his chair.

"To the tune of what?" Hudson asked, steepling his fingertips.

"Mr. Melcher was riding aboard an R.M.R. coach when he was shot. Should not the owners of the railway be liable?"

More sharply this time, Hudson asked, "To the tune of what, I asked, Mr. Crowley?"

"Shall we say ten thousand dollars?"

Then all hell broke loose. DuFrayne leaped to his feet like a springing panther, glaring at Melcher with feral eyes. "Shall we *not* say ten thousand, you scheming little parasite!" he shouted.

"Parasite!" the shaken Melcher braved in his angriest tone while Hudson and Crowley tried to settle the pair down. "Just who is the parasite here, I ask!"

"Well, it sure as hell isn't me!" DuFrayne stormed. "You're the one looking for a handout, thinking that the railroad can afford it. After all, railroads are rich, aren't they? Why not milk this one for as much as you can get?"

"Any railroad can well afford that amount, it's true."

"Why, you little—"

"Jess, settle down!" Hudson got him by an arm and pushed him back toward his chair.

"Gentlemen, control yourselves," Crowley interjected.

"DuFrayne obviously doesn't know the meaning of the word. He never has!" Melcher claimed irately.

Crowley took his client in hand. "Mr. Melcher, we're here to discuss liability."

"And so we shall. He is liable, all right, for far more than a physical wound to me. What about the wounds he caused Miss Abigail?"

A fine white line appeared around the entire circumferance of DuFrayne's lips, but hidden on the upper one by his moustache, which outlined his formidable scowl. Rage bubbled in him, spawned by Melcher's accusation, but swelled by his own secret guilt over Abbie. Having Melcher unwittingly remind him of it only increased his hatred of the man.

"You leave Miss Abigail out of this!" DuFrayne barked.

"Yes, you'd like that, I'm sure. You were insufferable to her and would probably like not to be reminded of just exactly how insufferable!"

Confused, James Hudson spoke. "Miss Abigail? Do you mean Miss Abigail McKenzie? I cannot see what possible bearing she could have on any of this."

"Nor I," agreed Crowley. "Mr. Melcher, please—"

"No amount of money can atone for his treatment of her," Melcher said.

"Miss Abigail has already been recompensed for her help," Hudson assured him. "Mr. DuFrayne saw to that."

"Oh, yes, I've seen just how DuFrayne pays her back for everything she does. He forces her—"

Again DuFrayne flew to his feet. "You leave Abbie out of this, you little pipsqueak, or so help me—"

"Damnit, Jess, sit down!" Hudson at last lost patience. But in his anger, Jesse had used the familiar first name of the woman. Max noted it with great interest. When things cooled down a little, Hudson placed ten fingertips on the pine plank and spoke carefully. "It seems you two are picking bones that have nothing to do with the issue at hand. Now, you have asked Mr. Crowley and myself here as your arbiters. Will you allow us to arbitrate or shall we leave the two of you to haggle by yourselves?" A pause, then, "Mr. Crowley, suppose that Mr. DuFrayne agrees to a settlement on Mr. Melcher, what consideration would he receive in return?"

"I'm afraid you confuse me, sir. I didn't think it was DuFrayne's decision. I thought that you spoke for the railroad in this matter."

Hudson cleared the tabletop of his fingers, glanced at Jesse.

"Jess?" he asked quietly. All eyes in the room trained on DuFrayne.

"No."

"It's time, Jess. Do you want to pay out ten thousand for nothing?"

But DuFrayne clamped his lips tightly and brooded while the two arbiters went on discussing. Jesse's dark face was unreadable, although Melcher pierced him with hating eyes. Fraught by guilt over the night before, and by anger that Melcher should be squeezing for every penny he could get, Jesse was plagued by an idea that would not desist. Suppose they settled enough money on the vulture to set him up for life? Suppose they made the damn fool so rich that he could settle down in one place and sell shoes till hell froze over? Suppose they fixed him up comfy and cozy right here where all he'd need next was a woman to settle with? As distasteful as it was, it would at least salve Jesse DuFrayne's conscience over last night. If he could arrange it, Abbie would end up with everything she'd ever need or want—that sheep-faced shoe peddler, the means to set up a substantial business, and enough money to keep the two of them in red kidskin for the rest of their lackluster lives! DuFrayne again pictured Abbie's face as she'd come to him last night, saying, "David Melcher is gone and he shall never return. You're my last chance, Jesse." Glimmers of what had followed painted Jesse's mind. She was a woman with too much fire to be wasted on the likes of Melcher, but she was probably right in assuming that Stuart's Junction offered no better alternatives. Better she should have Melcher to shower a few sparks on than burn for nobody at all.

He came out of his ruminations and picked up the thread of argument still going on.

". . . hardly think the sentence of life as a partial cripple would be considered nothing if this were taken to court, do you? You must consider the fact also that Mr. Melcher thought he was *defending* the railroad against what he considered an armed thief." Crowley's tone sounded slightly smug, and at last Hudson lost patience.

"Mr. Crowley," he rebutted testily, "I want to get something straight for the record. I'm tired of DuFrayne's name being bandied about as a train robber when it's the most preposterous accusation in the world! Now I ask you, why would any man want to rob his own train?"

"Jim!" barked DuFrayne, but his friend paid him little mind.

"Yes, you heard me correctly. You see, gentlemen, Jesse DuFrayne is a major shareholder of stock in the R.M.R. In other words, he owns the railroad—which he is accused of robbing."

In his corner, Max sat like a katydid with stilled wings. Crowley looked like he was trying to spit up a goose egg caught in his throat. Melcher looked like he was trying to swallow one. DuFrayne sat like a stone, facing the window, staring at the blue sky beyond, where a tip of the water tank showed. Hudson waited for the spell to take full effect. Melcher was the first to speak.

"If you think that this changes what you owe Miss Abigail, it doesn't. Your being a big railroad owner in no way excuses your actions toward her. You may be innocent of robbing that train, but where she is concerned, you are guilty of the most grossly unforgivable breaches of con—"

"Pay him!" Jesse snapped with agate hardness, attempting to shut the man up, for by now Jesse had become aware of the station agent, gawking like a hawk from his corner. The man had ears, and it didn't take much straining to hear everything being said in the room.

"Now wait a minute, Jess—"

"I said pay him, Jim, and I mean it," barked DuFrayne.

Melcher couldn't believe his ears. Only a moment ago he'd have sworn all chance for monetary gain was nil, realizing how thoroughly he'd misjudged DuFrayne's intentions aboard that train. Still, he could not hold his tongue.

"Conscience money is just as sp—"

"And you shut up, little man, if you want so much as a penny out of me!" Jesse spit, jumping to his feet, pointing a finger. "Jim, just do as I say."

"Now wait a minute, Jess, the railroad is partly mine. I want some satisfaction out of this before we just hand him what he wants."

Suddenly DuFrayne lurched around. The scrape of chair legs made Melcher twitch back from the table. "I want to talk to you outside, Jim." DuFrayne was oblivious to the curious stares from across the street. He stood steely, furious, on the depot porch, his thumbs hooked into his waistcoat pockets, eyes narrowed vacantly at the gold pans hanging on display before a store across the way.

"Jess, I had to tell them about your ownership," Hudson reasoned.

"That's all right, Jim, it was bound to come out sooner or later. I just didn't want Abbie to find out about it before I left town, that's all."

"There's something going on here that I don't understand and maybe it's none of my business, but I just want you to think of what you're doing before you make any rash decisions about handing over what that leech wants."

"I've been considering it and my mind is made up."

"You're sure?"

"With several stipulations, and with the understanding that the money paid to Melcher is from my profits only, not yours."

They spoke quietly for several minutes, then reentered the station and took their places at the makeshift table.

"Mr. Crowley," Hudson addressed the man rather than his client, "if the railroad agrees to imburse Mr. Melcher ten thousand for damages, we will in turn demand that certain stipulations be fulfilled by him. First, Melcher will issue a statement to the local newspaper to the effect the railroad was in no way liable for this incident due to the fact that Mr. DuFrayne was carrying a gun, but only to the extent that your client was aboard one of our coaches when he was shot. The statement must in no way denigrate Mr. DuFrayne's name or that of Miss Abigail McKenzie but shall instead make it explicitly clear that Mr. DuFrayne was indeed not robbing the train, but that Mr. Melcher misjudged DuFrayne's intentions at the time. He may indicate that he acted for what he thought was the good of the passengers if he wishes, but that is the only defense he must give for his actions.

"Our second stipulation is that Mr. Melcher invest no less than two-thirds of this settlement money in a business or livelihood based in Stuart's Junction. He may choose whatever type of venture he wishes, but it must be in this town and it cannot be sold within the next five years.

"The third stipulation is that Mr. Melcher, personally, never again ride aboard an R.M.R. train. He may, of course, use the railroad to further his business venture by transporting goods, but he himself shall never again set foot on one of our coaches.

"We shall want these terms validated in writing and notarized, and of course there shall be an inclusion stating that if any of these terms are not fulfilled Mr. Melcher shall be liable to repay the R.M.R. the full amount of ten thousand dollars upon demand."

Crowley raised a silent, inquiring eyebrow at Melcher, who still floundered in the backwash of shock. Not only was DuFrayne vindicated of attempted robbery, he was rich enough and powerful enough to put the final nod to a settlement of ten thousand dollars of what, in retrospect, was his own capital anyway! The fact made Melcher's face flame and his hands shake. He clearly did not understand the man's reasons for stipulating that the money be reinvested in Stuart's Junction, but he was certainly not about to inquire. It was appalling enough to be subjected to the man's self-satisfied supremacy without being subjected to his reasoning, which might be as galling as the fact that he was issuing ultimatums in the first place.

"I will agree," Melcher stated flatly, "but with one condition of my own."

"And that?" Hudson asked.

"That DuFrayne pr . . . privately apologize to Miss Mc . . . McKenzie."

"You go too far, Melcher!" DuFrayne warned stormily, his face now livid. "Any animosity between Miss McKenzie and myself has no bearing on this bargaining session and, furthermore, is none of your business!"

"You made it my business, sir, one morning when you took gross liberties in her bedroom right before my eyes!"

"Enough!" roared DuFrayne, while Max nearly swallowed his tongue. The big man took to his feet, bumping the table and nearly upsetting it, sending the water pitcher careening precariously, glasses teetering. One circled and finally tipped, sending a splash of water over the table edge onto Melcher's lap while DeFrayne, with feet aspraddle, glared venomously, clenching his fists. "Our differences are settled, Abbie's and mine, so say no more of her, do you hear? You can take your ten thousand in blood money or toe money or whatever you choose to call it and live in splendor the rest of your days, or you can watch me walk out of here with the control of it still in my pocket and never see me again! Now which will it be?"

Melcher glared at the black moustache, envisioning again that bold, bare body that had taunted both him and Miss Abigail, wishing fervently that the bullet had struck DuFrayne's anatomy about four inches to the left of where it had! But were he to voice his thought, he stood to lose ten thousand dollars of this devil's own lucre. Neither did he doubt that DuFrayne meant it when he said one more word and David would see his back but not his money. And so David bit his tongue, daring not to insist again on the apology he so badly wanted for Miss Abigail. His Adam's apple bulged where his pride was stuck in his throat. But he only nodded woodenly.

"Very well. I'll give the newspapers only the answers you want, but don't you ever come back to Stuart's Junction again, DuFrayne. You have no reason to." They both knew he eluded to Abigail McKenzie, but DuFrayne carefully thrust one last riposte at Melcher.

"You're forgetting, Melcher, that I own property here, some of which you are standing upon at this very minute. Don't dictate to me where I can and cannot go . . . in business interests, of course," he finished sarcastically, with one eyebrow quirked.

Hudson interjected, "There seems little more to be said here," attempting to dull the animosity between the two and draw an end to the proceeding before they came to blows. "Mr. Crowley, if you will remain, we can draw up the agreement, have it verified before I leave town, and we will see about getting a bank draft to Mr. Melcher within three days at whatever destination he signifies. You understand that Mr. DuFrayne will have to free that amount personally from his accounts in Denver."

"Yes, I understand. If that is agreeable to Mr. Melcher, that is agreeable to me."

Melcher stood stiffly.

When things broke up, Hudson and DuFrayne stepped outside into the arid midday heat, which didn't help Jesse's temper any.

"What the hell's wrong with you anyway, Jess?" Hudson took his friend's elbow as if to cool his temper. "I've never seen you quite this defensive and belligerent over a woman before."

"Woman, hell! I just signed over ten thousand of my hardearned bucks to that pipsqueak in there! How the hell would you feel?"

"Now hold on, Jess. You're the one who said give it to him, and I gathered at the time it was as much to shut him up as for any other reason. Just what did go on up there at Miss McKenzie's house anyway?"

Jesse's eyes moved to the gable of Abbie's house, visible beyond the false-fronted saddlery and harness shop. His stare was mechanical, his lips taut as he replied, "You have an inquisitive mind, Jim, and I have a temper. And that's why you do the business and I do the field work. Let's just keep it that way, only reserve your inquisitions for the likes of Melcher there, old buddy, huh?"

"All right . . . as you like it. But if you're after preserving Miss McKenzie's reputation, how about that station agent with his cocked ear and bulging eyes? I don't know what that remark meant, about your taking liberties in the bedroom of the lady in question, but it could come to have all kinds of unexpected ramifications once it rolls off the tongue of our station agent. Shall I go inside and bribe him or will you?"

"Goddamnit, Jim, didn't I take enough abuse from Melcher without you adding to it?"

But Hudson understood his friend's frustration, thus his scolding was taken with a grain of salt. But there was something eating Jess that he wasn't letting on about. Hudson couldn't help but wonder exactly what it was.

"Just trying to be practical," Hudson added.

"Well, you go on inside and be practical any way you see fit. I've already lost enough . . . *practicality* for one day."

They made arrangements to meet back at the hotel just before train time, then Hudson went back into the depot while DuFrayne made for the local saloon, to be stared at by everybody in the place except Ernie Turner, who was sound asleep with his head in a puddle of sweat from his beer glass.

⚛ Chapter 17

FROM THE SECOND-STORY window in his hotel room on Main Street, David Melcher watched Hudson and DuFrayne board the 3:20. He had done as promised, had given the newspaper only the information agreed upon, yet it vexed Melcher mercilessly to have had to gild DuFrayne in any way whatsoever. It would vex him even more to accidentally run into DuFrayne at Miss Abigail's house again, thus he waited until DuFrayne was safely aboard the train and it had ground its way out of town.

Then and only then did David Melcher allow his victory to overwhelm him, to make him smile at its limitless possibilities. The thought of owning ten thousand dollars elated him, and he hummed as he changed clothes and brushed his hair, thinking of the sudden rosy future ahead of him. By the time he arrived at Miss Abigail's doorstep, he was beaming like the headlamp of an R.M.R. engine.

"Why, Mr. Melcher, you're early!" she said when she saw him there. But she was relieved to have his company, for the past five hours had been the longest of her life. Not only had her imagination run rife with scenes from the meeting at the depot, she had had to allow it to run its course with visions of Jesse boarding the 3:20, which she could not see from her place, and riding out of Stuart's Junction in that stunning suit, with his likable friend, James Hudson, the two of them never to return again. When the steam whistle raised its billow of white above the rooftops and sighed its departing scream, she had crossed her arms tightly across her chest and thought, Good. He is getting out of my life forever. But when the last clack of wheels had died away into summer silence, she had felt suddenly bereft and lonely.

Having David Melcher arrive, with his cheerful expression, was exactly what she needed to chase away lingering thoughts of Jesse DuFrayne. Standing now on her porch step, David wore an almost cherubic look, his pink cheeks blossoming into a little boy smile, almost as if he wanted to flatten his nose against the screen in delight. She knew immediately that the decision at the depot must have gone in his favor.

"And what has brought such a look of jubilation to your face?" Miss Abigail asked.

For once he forgot himself and asked, "Can I come in?" He had the door open before she could give him permission or open it for him. "Yes, I'm early, and yes, I'm jubilant, and can you guess why, Miss Abigail?"

She could not help but smile with him. "Well, I guess the meeting's results met with your approval, but—my goodness, Mr. Melcher—you're almost dancing. Do sit down."

He perched on the edge of the settee, then popped back up like a jack-in-the-box.

"Miss Abigail, I hope you're still wearing those red shoes, because I want to take you out for supper to celebrate."

"To celebrate? . . . Out to supper? . . . Why . . . why, Mr. Melcher!" She'd never been taken out to supper in her life.

He forgot himself even further and clasped both of her hands in his and, looking down into her amazed face, said, "Why, our victory of course. The railroad has agreed to settle ten thousand dollars on me for damages."

For a moment she couldn't speak, she was so stunned. Her jaw dropped down so far that her high collar bit into her neck. "Ten . . . thousand . . . dollars?" she repeated incredulously, then dropped off her feet into a side chair.

"Exactly!" He beamed at her a moment longer, then seemed to remember himself and dropped her hands to take his seat over on the settee again.

"My, how admirably generous," she said lamely, picturing James Hudson again, and the check for the thousand dollars he'd left on the seat of the umbrella stand.

David Melcher knew he should tell her now about DuFrayne being part-owner of the railroad, but he did not want anything putting a damper on their evening together.

"Do say you'll allow me to take you out this evening to celebrate with me. I consider it our victory, yours and mine together. It seems only right that we should commemorate it with an evening on the town."

"But it's your compensation, not mine."

"Miss Abigail, I don't care to cast shadows over the bright joy of the moment, but considering the circumstances under which we met, I feel —

shall we say—rather liable to you for the indignities you suffered at the hands of that vile man DuFrayne. I have felt helpless to make up in any way for all that. Now, coming out the winner in this dispute seems like we've somehow brought him to bay at last. Not only for what he did to me, but what he did to you, too."

She studied the man perched on the edge of her settee. He spoke with such earnestness, wanting to be her champion, that she was suddenly swept by guilt that he should still consider her a flawless lady, worthy of his chivalry. She felt, too, an utter hopelessness, because she could not undo what she and Jesse DuFrayne had done together. How she wished that it had never happened, that she could honestly deserve David Melcher's advocation and admiration. She touched a hand to her high collar and looked away.

"Oh, Mr. Melcher, I'm truly touched, but I think it would be best for me not to celebrate your victory. Let me just congratulate you and keep the shoes as your thank you."

Disappointment covered his face. "You won't even let me buy you dinner?"

But their relationship had no future now. She got up from the side chair and walked over to the secretary and pretended that a cluster of papers there needed straightening. With her back to him, she answered, "I simply think it's best if you don't."

David Melcher swallowed, flushed, then stammered, "Is . . . is it that you c . . . cannot forgive me for what I ac . . . accused you of, that awf . . . f . . . ful morning when I left here?"

"Oh, no!" She swung to face him, an imploring look upon her face. "That's all forgotten, please believe me, Dav—Mr. Melcher."

But he'd heard her slip. He stood up, gathered his courage, and approached her. Flustered, she turned toward the desk again.

"Then pr . . . pr . . . prove it," he got out finally.

She turned to look over her shoulder at him, one hand still trailing on the desktop.

"Prove it?" she repeated.

"C . . . come to dinner with m . . . me and pr . . . prove that everything up t . . . till now is f . . . f . . . forgotten."

Again she touched the lace at her throat, a winsome expression softening her features. Oh, how she wanted to go to dinner with a fine gentleman like him, for the first time in her life. She wanted the gaiety and carelessness that her youth had never tasted, the charm and companionship of a man at her elbow. She wanted to share the mutual interests which she knew the two of them were capable of sharing.

He still waited for her answer, the invitation alight in his brown eyes.

Recriminations jangled through her mind. If only it were yesterday. If only I had not done what I did with Jesse. If only . . . if only. Anger touched her, too. Damn you, Jesse, why didn't you tell me he was coming back?

She knew she must refuse, but in the end David's invitation was too tempting. What will it hurt if I spend one evening with him—just one? He, too, is here today and gone tomorrow, so what harm can come of a single evening in his company?

"Dinner sounds nice," she understated, already feeling guilty for accepting.

"Then you'll come?" He again looked jubilant.

"I'll come."

"And you'll wear the red shoes?"

Oh, dear! she thought, feeling herself flush. But there was no graceful way to get out of it now, for he was totally unaware of the shoes' flamboyance. But then, as if in answer to her discomfort, came Jesse's belittling voice, as she remembered him warning, "Just don't make a fool of yourself by parading down Main Street in those goddamn red shoes!" And so, diffidently, she left them on, praying all the way that none of the townspeople noticed them on her feet. But she'd have given that thousand-dollar bank deposit if Jesse DuFrayne himself could have seen her wearing them uptown to have dinner with David Melcher, her gloved hand in the crook of his arm as they walked along the boardwalk.

Not a soul in town could find fault with their demeanor.

By the next morning everyone in Stuart's Junction knew exactly how polite David Melcher had been and just how proper and prim Miss Abigail had been. They also knew what the couple had ordered and exactly how long they'd stayed and how many times they'd smiled at each other. But they had it straight from Louis Culpepper's mouth how Miss Abigail showed up wearing *red* shoes, of all things. Red! They must've been a gift from Melcher, 'cause it seemed he was a shoe peddler out of the East somewhere.

Imagine that! they all said, Miss Abigail taking up with a shoe peddler, and an easterner no less. And doing it decked out like December twenty-fifth in red shoes the man had given her after sleeping in her house!

"What a memorable evening," Miss Abigail said as they walked idly back to her house after supper. It was the slowest she had ever walked home from town. "How can I thank you?"

He limped along beside her. With each step he took, she could feel the hitch of his stride pull lightly at the hand with which she held his elbow.

"By not refusing me the next time I ask you."

She controlled the urge to turn her startled eyes up at him. "The next time? Why, aren't you leaving Stuart's Junction soon?"

"No, I'm not. As I said earlier, I have a large stock of shoes to sell and I intend to approach some local merchants in hopes that they'll act as outlets for us. Also, the railroad will be sending my settlement money to Stuart's Junction, so I'll have to wait here till it arrives."

Again she controlled the urge to ask how many days it would take.

He refrained from telling her that he was being forced to invest the major portion of the settlement money right here, for it made him look like DuFrayne's puppet, and the fact that David was galled him. David wanted her to believe that the decision to stay and settle here had been his own, which it probably would have been if it had been left up to him.

"How . . . how many days do you think it will take?" she finally asked.

"Three days maybe."

Three days, she thought. Oh, glorious three days! What harm can come of enjoying his company for three days? They're all I'll have, and then he'll be gone for good.

"In that case, I shall not refuse you anything while you're here," she said, and felt him tighten his elbow around her gloved hand and pull it against his ribs.

"Miss Abigail, you won't be sorry," he promised.

But deep inside Miss Abigail already was, for tonight had been so wonderful. And because her heart had jumped when he pulled her hand against his ribs.

"Tell me what grand things you intend to do with that money once it comes," she said, to distract her thoughts.

"I hadn't thought about it much. It's enough for now just to feel the sense of freedom it brings. I've never been wanting, but I've never had security such as this either."

They were nearly at her house, their steps slower than ever.

"It's strange, isn't it," she asked, "that much the same sort of thing has happened to me because of all this? Did I tell you that the railroad paid me a thousand dollars for my care of you and . . . and Mr. DuFrayne?" It was dreadfully hard to say his name now, and when she did, she felt David's arm tense, but she went on. "It brings me a sense of security too. Temporary, of course, but security nevertheless."

David Melcher certainly did not begrudge her the thousand dollars, only the fact that DuFrayne was the one who'd paid her off and was rich enough to do it so easily.

But he submerged his irritation and asked, "How did that come about?"

"Mr. Hudson came here and left a bank draft for me. He seems to be in a position of authority on the railroad. Is he the owner?"

David swallowed, still reluctant to tell her that DuFrayne was the other owner. "Yes," he answered tightly. "You deserved every penny he paid you, I'm sure."

They reached her porch then, and she asked, "Would you care to sit for a while? Your foot is probably tired."

"No . . . I mean yes . . . I mean, my f . . . foot is f . . . fine, but I'd like to sit awhile anyway."

She glanced at the pair of wicker chairs but led the way to the swing instead, justifying her choice by reiterating silently how little time they had together.

When she had seated herself, David asked politely before sitting, "May I?"

She pulled her skirt aside and made room while he settled quite stiffly and formally beside her, making sure that his coat sleeve did not touch her. There were restless night sounds all around them—insects, the saloon piano, leaves astir in the faint breeze.

He cleared his throat.

She sighed.

"Is something wrong?" he asked.

"Wrong? No . . . no, everything is . . . is wonderful." And indeed it should have been. He had his money, she had hers, he'd taken her to dinner, she was at last rid of Jesse DuFrayne.

He cleared his throat. "You seem . . . dif . . . different some . . . sometimes."

She hadn't realized it showed. She would have to be more careful.

"It's just that I'm not used to everything turning out so well. It all happened so fast. And I'm sure you've guessed that I don't get dinner invitations just every night. I was still thinking about how enjoyable it was."

"It—" He cleared his throat once more. "It was for me, too. I thought of it all the t . . . time after I left St . . . Stuart's Junction, about how I w . . . wanted to come back and take you to dinner." Here he cleared his throat yet again. "And now here we are."

Yes, like two pokers, she thought, surprising herself, wishing that he would put his arm along the back of the swing like Jesse had done. But he was no Jesse, and she had no business wishing David would act even remotely like him! Still she grew more disappointed as the minutes passed and David sat sticklike beside her. His attitude seemed suddenly puerile. She wondered if she could soften him up somewhat.

"This was where I was when I opened the package with the shoes."

"Right here? On the swing?"

"Yes. Mr. Binley brought them up from the station. Remember Mr. Binley —the one who helped carry you to my house that first morning?"

"Would he be the tall, skinny one they called Bones?"

"The same. He seemed fascinated by the fact that I'd received a package. I'm sure he was hoping I'd open it before him."

"But you didn't?"

"Gracious no. I sat down and took the package here on the swing after he was gone and opened it all alone."

"And what did you . . . ahem!"—that was his throat again—"think?"

"Why, I was amazed, Mr. Melcher, simply amazed. I don't think another woman in this town owns a pair of red shoes." That was the truth!

"Well they will before long, because I have others in my stock. Red is the coming thing, you know."

She simply hadn't the heart to tell him her true feelings about the shoes. He would just have to find out for himself when his stock of reds didn't sell. Out here in the West, the staid, hard-working woman wanted sturdy browns and blacks, but he, like so many people in sales, was convinced that what he sold was the best, and could not see any fault with it.

"Would you have preferred another color?" he asked now.

She lied. "Oh, no! Of course not! I love these!" When had she become so glib at lying?

He once more cleared his throat. He placed his hands over his kneecaps and stared straight ahead. "Miss Abigail, when I approached your door today, I distinctly heard you and DuFrayne arguing about the shoes."

"We were," she admitted candidly.

"Why?" he asked, surprising himself at his own temerity. But where his products were concerned, he had backbone.

"He disliked them."

"Good!" he exclaimed, suddenly feeling very self-satisfied. It was perhaps the most romantic thing he had said that night, but she was too busy worrying about what else he'd overheard this morning to note David's pleased expression.

Her heart thudded as she worked up her courage and asked, "What else did you hear?"

"Nothing. Only his remark about the shoes."

She concealed a sigh but was greatly relieved.

David looked at her entreatingly and said, "He's gone now and we can both forget him."

"Yes," she agreed. But there was a sick feeling in the pit of her stomach and she could not meet David's eyes, knowing that for as long as she lived she would never forget Jesse DuFrayne. She attempted to lighten the atmosphere by suggesting, "Let's talk of more pleasant things. Tell me what it's like in the East."

"Have you never been there?"

"No. I've never been farther than Denver, and I was there only twice, both times as a child."

"The East . . ." He stopped momentarily and ruminated. "Well, the East has absolutely everything one could want to buy. Factories everywhere producing everything, especially since the war is over. The newest innovations and the grandest inventions. Did you know that a man named Lyman Blake in Massachusetts invented a machine for sewing soles onto shoes?"

"No, no I didn't, but I guess I must thank him for his glorious invention." Miss Abigail realized she was bored to death by this conversation.

"The East has all the up-and-coming modern advancements, including women's suffragettes voicing their absurd ideas and encouraging such outlandish activities as the game of tennis for females. Not everything in the East is proper," he finished, making it clear what he thought of women playing tennis.

"I've heard of Mrs. Stanton's Suffrage Association, of course, but what is tennis?"

"Nothing at all for you, Miss Abigail, I assure you," he said distastefully. "Why, it's the most . . . the most unladylike romp that France ever invented! Women actually running and . . . and sweating and swatting at balls with these gutstring rackets."

"It sounds like the Indian game of lacrosse."

"One might expect such behavior out of an uncivilized savage, but the women of the East should know better than to wear shortened hems and shortened sleeves and carry on like . . . well, it's disgraceful! They have lost their sense of decency. Some of them even drink spirits! I much prefer you women out West, who still conform to the old social graces, and for my money I want to see it left that way. Leave the upstart ideas out East where they belong."

He had scarcely stammered at all during that long diatribe. She realized he was very incensed about the subject. Miss Abigail sat on the porch swing, rocking quietly, and suddenly found herself comparing David Melcher's opinions to those of Jesse DuFrayne on the many occasions he'd encouraged her to set aside her prim and proper ways. She remembered that day up in the hills when he'd taken her hat off for her and teased her about not unbuttoning her wet cuffs. She pictured his dark hand pouring champagne and recalled the loose, easy feeling as it ran through her blood. And then there was that untidy scrap they'd had on that kitchen chair and somehow in the middle of it he'd said he liked her in that old faded shirt . . ."

". . . don't you agree, Miss Abigail?"

She came out of her reverie to realize David had been expounding upon the virtues of a western woman while she'd been wool-gathering about Jesse, comparing him—and unfavorably yet!—to David.

"Oh, yes," she sat up straight. "I quite agree, I'm sure." But she wasn't even sure what she was agreeing with. Would Jesse's memory always distract her so?

Apparently she had agreed that one o'clock would be a good time for them to meet tomorrow, for he was rising from the swing and making his way across the porch while she followed.

He went down one step, turned, cleared his throat volubly, came back up the same step, fumbled for her hand, and kissed it quickly, then retreated down the step hurriedly.

"Good night, Miss Abigail."

"Thank you for dinner, Mr. Melcher."

For some reason, watching him disappear up the street, she found herself wishing he had not cleared his throat that way or fumbled as he reached for her hand or even kissed *it!* She wished that he might have kissed her mouth instead, and that when he had, she'd have found it preferable to the kisses of Jesse DuFrayne.

Inside, the house was beastly quiet. She wandered in without even lighting a lamp, listless and dissatisfied. She raised the back of the kissed hand to her lips, trying to draw some feeling from the memory. David Melcher approved of her wholeheartedly, she was sure. She willed that to be enough for now, but the memory of Jesse DuFrayne contraposed every action and mannerism that David had displayed tonight. Why should it be that even though he was gone Jesse had the power to impose himself on her this way? And at the most inopportune times possible? Instead of reveling in David's seeming attraction for her, her joy was blighted by her endless contrasting of the two men in which Jesse invariably came out the winner. With these couple of days so precious, while David remained, she wanted to find him perfect, flawless, incontestable. But Jesse wouldn't let her. Jesse dominated in every way.

Even here in her house, from which he was gone, she found herself listening for his breathing, his yawning, the squeak of the bedsprings as he turned. Perhaps by taking over her old room she could exorcise him. But wandering into it she was smitten by a sense of emptiness for her "gunslinger." The bed was dark and vacant. The pall of silence grew awesome. She dropped down onto the edge of the bed, feeling his absence keenly, knowing a bleakness more complete and sad than that which she had felt at the death of her father.

Twisting at the waist, she suddenly punched one small fist into the pillow he'd occupied so lately, demanding angrily, "Get out of my house, Jesse DuFrayne!"

Only he was out.

She punched the pillow again, her delicate fist creating a thick, muffled sound of loneliness. He's gone, she despaired. He's gone. How could she have grown so used to him that his absence assaulted her by its mere vacuity? She wanted her life back the way it had been before he'd come into it. She wanted to take a man like David Melcher into that old life and forge a relationship of genteel, sensible normalcy, instead she sank both hands into the soft feathers of Jesse's pillow, taking great fistfuls of his absence, her head slung low between her sagging shoulders as she braced there in the gloom.

"Damn you, Jesse!" she shouted at the dark ceiling. "Damn you for ever coming here!"

Then she fell lonely upon his bed, rolling onto her side and hugging his pillow to her stomach while she cried.

Chapter 18

AWAKENING THE FOLLOWING morning, Abbie forgot she was in the house alone. She stretched and rolled over, wondering what to fix Jesse for breakfast. Realizing her mistake, she sat up abruptly and looked around. She was back in her own bedroom—alone.

She flopped back down, studied the ceiling, closed her eyes and admonished herself to be sensible. Life must go on. She could and she would get over Jesse DuFrayne. But she opened her eyes and felt empty. The day had nothing to inspire her to get out of bed.

She spent it trying to scrub every last vestige of Jesse from her bedroom. She washed the smell of him from her sheets, polished his fingerprints from the brass headboard, and fluffed his imprint from the cushions of the window seat. But even so, she could not reclaim the room as her own. He remained present in its memory, possessing each article he'd touched, lingering in each place he'd rested, an unwanted reminder of what he'd been to her.

When her cleaning was done, she had an hour to spare before David would arrive. But the *Junction County Courier* arrived before he did. She heard it thwack upon the porch floor and retrieved it, grateful for any diversion that would keep her mind off Jesse.

Idly, she went back inside, pausing before the umbrella stand and using the folded up newspaper to check the tautness of her chin. But even that longtime, private habit now reminded her of Jesse, standing half-naked in the doorway, teasing, "Is it firm?" Abruptly she turned away from the mirror and snapped the newspaper open, seeking to scatter his memory.

Lotta Crabtree was appearing at the famed Teller Opera House in Central City and would be followed by the great Madjeska.

Another railroad baron had chosen to build his mansion in the vastly popular Colorado Springs, playground of the rich, who flocked there to soak away their ailments in the famous mineral springs.

Some accused train robber . . .

Miss Abigail's eyes widened and her tongue seemed to grow thick in her throat.

ACCUSED TRAIN ROBBER PROVES TO BE
OWNER OF RAILROAD

At a meeting Tuesday afternoon in the Stuart's
Junction Depot, arbiters debated . . .

It was all there, including the truth about Jesse DuFrayne, which she
should have guessed long ago. Standing in the middle of her proper Victorian
parlor, Miss Abigail placed the back of a lacy wrist to her throat. *Jesse owns
the railroad! The man I called train robber* owns *the railroad! And so he has
the last laugh after all. But then, didn't he always?*

With a mixture of horror and dismay she recalled the awful things she had
done to him—the owner of a railroad!

And suddenly she was laughing, raising her delicate chin high, covering her
forehead with a palm. The daft, sad sound cracked pitifully into the silence.
And when at last it faded away, she was left staring at the article like a glassy-
eyed statue, while its significance sank in, while she absorbed what she should
have guessed that day Jim Hudson had come. Maybe she had guessed but
simply hadn't wanted to admit it could be true. What she read again pounded
home the facts in black and white. The article described the meeting right
down to the clothing the four men had worn. It described James Hudson as
the business agent-co-owner of the railroad, while Jesse DuFrayne was called
the hidden partner who oversaw his enterprise from behind the hood of a
photographic camera. The meeting itself was described as a "sometimes placid
discussion of terms, sparked at times by fiery clashes of animosity between
DuFrayne and Melcher over the seemingly alien subject of one Miss Abigail
McKenzie, a longtime resident of Stuart's Junction, who had nursed both
DuFrayne and Melcher during their convalescence."

As she finished, she stood mortified! By this time she was in a state of anger
that would have delighted Jesse DuFrayne.

David Melcher, however, who happened to the door at that precise moment
was dismayed when he stepped inside and she gave him a flat slap across his
chest with the folded newspaper.

"Mi . . . Miss Abigail, what's wr . . . wrong?" he stammered.

"What's wrong?" she repeated, barely controlling the volume of her voice.
"Read this and then ask me what's wrong! I am a respectable woman who
must live in this town after you and Mr. DuFrayne have long left it. I do not
care to have my name spewed from the lips of every gossipmonger in Stuart's
Junction after the two of you saw to it that I made the front page of the
newspaper in the most intriguing way possible!"

Perplexed, he glanced at the article, back at her, then silently started reading, finding more in the paper than he had told the newspaper editor.

"Whatever possessed you to argue about me in a meeting with the press
present?"

"There was n . . . no press . . . pre . . . present. It was strictly pr . . .
private. I . . . he . . . DuFrayne even made me pr . . . promise that no
word would l . . . leak out about you."

That surprised her. "Then how did it?" she demanded.

"I . . . I don't know."

"Just what brought my name into a discussion of liability settlements?"

He'd only meant the best for her yesterday and quavered now at the
thought that he'd messed everything up so badly.

"I thought he sh . . . should apologize to you for . . . for all he put you through."

She turned her back on him and plucked at her blouse front. "Had it occurred to you that perhaps he might already have done so?"

"Miss Abigail! Are you defending him against me, when it is I who set out to d . . . defend you against him?"

"I am defending no one. I am simply chagrined at finding myself the object of two men's animosity and having it appear in newsprint. I—What will it look like to the people of this town? And why didn't you tell me last night that he is part owner of the railroad?"

He considered her question a moment, then asked, "Does that change your opinion of him now?"

Realizing that if it did she was nothing but a hypocrite, she turned to show David she was sincere.

"No, it doesn't. I simply think you would have told me that the money was coming from him, that's all."

"It's only right that he should pay me. He's the one who shot me."

"But he was *not* robbing that train when he did it. There lies the difference."

"You *are* defending him!" David Melcher accused.

"I am not! I'm defending myself!" Her voice had risen until she was shouting like a fishwife, and when she realized it she suddenly put her fingertips over her lips. She found she'd been haranguing him in the same way she'd done countless times with Jesse. Angry now at Jesse too, she'd attacked David as if he were both of them. To her horror, she found herself anticipating the exhilaration of the fight, welcoming the kind of verbiage Jesse had taught her to enjoy with him.

But David was no Jesse DuFrayne. In fact, David was stunned by her almost baiting attitude and unladylike shouting. His face grew mottled, and he stared at her as if he'd never seen her before. Indeed he hadn't—not like this. In a calm voice, he said, "We are having a fight."

His words brought her to her senses. Chagrined at what she had just caught herself doing, she felt suddenly small and completely in the wrong. She sat down properly on the edge of the settee, looking at the hands she'd clasped tightly in her lap.

"I'm sorry," she said contritely.

He sat down beside her, pleasantly surprised by her change back to the Miss Abigail he knew.

"So am I."

"No, it was my fault. I don't know what came over me to speak to you in such tones. I . . ." But she stumbled to a halt, for it was a lie. She was not sorry, and she did know what had come over her. The ways of Jesse DuFrayne had come over her, for it was as he'd said, fighting was like an emetic. It felt good. It purged.

David spoke softly beside her. "Maybe we wouldn't fight if we didn't . . ." He was going to say "care for each other," but stopped himself in time. It was too soon to say a thing like that, so he finished, ". . . didn't talk about . . . him."

The tension remained between them, each displeased with the other as they sat silently.

After a moment David said, "You know I would not do or say anything to jeopardize your reputation. Why, it would be as good as ruining my own now, don't you see?"

She looked up at him, perched beside her on the settee.

"No, of course you don't see," he continued. "I haven't told you yet. I was going to tell you when I c . . . came to the door, but you were there with that . . . that newspaper and didn't give me a chance."

"Tell me what?"

He smiled boyishly, the soft, brown eyes locked with hers. "That I am going to stay in Stuart's Junction and open a shoe store right here with the money I have coming from the railroad."

Her heart hit the roof of her mouth. Remorse and fear welled in her throat, then drifted through her veins. His words sieved their way downward and dropped hollowly at last into the womb she had begged Jesse DuFrayne to unseal. She'd been so sure no other man would come along in her lifetime to do it. It was all too, too ironic to think that not only had Jesse done her bidding on the very eve of David's return, but had then given David the fistful of money that would enable him to establish himself right here under her nose and court her, when that was now out of the question. What was she supposed to do? Abet the situation when she knew that under no circumstances must she encourage David Melcher now? Furthermore, it was becoming increasingly obvious that he intended to actively court her.

She had been hazed by Jesse DuFrayne for the final, most humiliating time of all: he had given David the means for marriage while robbing her of the same.

David Melcher watched myriad expressions drift across Miss Abigail's face. At first she looked surprised, then happy, then perplexed, quizzical, stunned, and lastly, he could have sworn that she looked guilty. At what he had no idea. But after watching that parade of emotions, he certainly did not expect her final reaction, which was the placing of her tiny fingers upon her lips as she whispered, "Oh no!"

He was stricken with disappointment at her words. "I thought you'd be happy, Miss Abigail."

"Oh, I am, I am," she said quickly, touching his sleeve. "Oh, how wonderful for you. I know that you're not a man who likes wandering ways." But she did not look at all happy.

"No, I don't. I've wanted to settle in one spot for the longest time. It's just that I never had the means and I never found the right spot." Timidly he took one of her hands. "Now I think I've found both. Will you come with me this afternoon? You could be such a big help. I must arrange to find a place to rent or find some land to put up a place on. There's a corner at the far end of Main Street that I like. You know who to see and where to find people I'd need to talk to, and of course you could introduce me to those I might need to look up. Oh, Miss Abigail," he implored, "come with me. We'll look them all in the eye and make them take back any gossip the paper might have started."

Sensibly, she withdrew her hand and dropped her eyes. "I'm afraid you don't know the people of this town too well. If we show up arranging business agreements together after what was printed in the paper, they'll take nothing back. I'm afraid we would start more gossip than we'll stop."

"I hadn't thought of that, and of course you're right."

She had quite decided to end any budding relationship with him here and now. It would be the best way. But he looked so depressed at her refusal to help him that she felt mean denying him her help. It was true that she could expedite matters for him, for he was a stranger here.

"On the other hand," she procrastinated, "if we were to face the town and show them we are associating solely on a business basis, we might just put the gossip to rout, mightn't we?"

He looked up hopefully, his face suddenly youthfully attractive, like that first day he'd been carried into her house.

"Then you'll come? You'll help me today?"

She controlled the urge to sigh. Whatever was she doing?

"Yes, I'll come. But only as an ambassador, you must understand."

"Oh, of course, of course," he agreed.

David Melcher was a man who left good impressions in his wake. While he and Miss Abigail made business contacts that day, his soft-spoken, likable approach made people realize he was no "slick talker" from the East, as they considered most peddlers to be. Indeed, there were those who said that were it not for Miss Abigail's effrontery Melcher would have gotten nowhere, for he was unpushy and retiring. She, however, opened the way for him in the businesslike manner she always used on the townspeople. If any of them objected to her briskness, they didn't say so. As usual, they treated her—and thus him—with deference. Perhaps it was because they'd grown used to granting her wide berth, perhaps because she had not had an easy life and they all knew it, or perhaps because they were just plain nosy about her relationship to the two men who'd had words over her. For whatever reason, while she and David traversed the town that day they seemed to gain the town's approval and along with it many invitations to attend the following day's Fourth of July celebrations. Indeed, some businessmen seemed more intent upon making sure the two appeared at the morrow's festivities than they were about selling land, leasing property, or discussing lumber prices.

But behind them speculation was rife. That settlement money raised questions they all wished they had answers for. It's no wonder they all said, "Now don't forget to join the fun over in Hake's Meadow tomorrow," or "You're coming, aren't you, Miss Abigail?" or "You're both coming, aren't you?"

Someone else put it more bluntly: "There's to be a basket social and a greased pig contest and log rolling and sack races and what not. Good way for you to get acquainted with all the folks you'll be calling customers afore long, Melcher."

Someone else bid them goodbye by saying, "Bring her over and help us all celebrate. Wagons'll be loading up in front of Avery's store at a quarter to ten or so."

They were also bribed. "It's the only time of the summer you'll find ice cream in Stuart's Junction. You wouldn't want to miss that now, would you?"

But what *they* all really didn't want to miss was a chance to observe Miss Abigail with that new beau she'd apparently taken up with the minute the old one left town. Of course they all knew Melcher was going to be filthy rich on the other guy's money yet. Now who'd've dreamed Miss Abigail would ever become a pants-chaser, and furthermore that she'd make sure those pants had full pockets? 'Course, they all said, it was a fact she was almost clean out of money since her pa died. You couldn't hardly blame the woman. There was that thousand the railroad had paid her, but how long would that last? She was probably just investing in her future, hooking up with Melcher this way. Not a soul in town but couldn't wait to see if the two of them'd show up tomorrow and if she'd seem sweet on him. Nobody could really tell from her businessy attitude today. But tomorrow would be another story!

When he saw her home it was with a mutual feeling of satisfaction. They'd accomplished much in one day. They'd checked out some rental property, found out Nels Nordquist owned the vacant lot next to his saddlery and leather shop, spoken to him about a selling price, checked on the deed at the land office, arranged for blueprints to be drawn up for a simple, single-story frame building with storage at the rear, sales area at the center, and display windows at the fore, and found out whom to see about lumber prices and delivery.

Back at her house now, she led the way to the wicker chairs on the porch.

"I can't thank you enough," he said.

"Nonsense, you were right. I do know everyone in this town and it would have been foolish for you to try to make the necessary contacts alone."

"But you were marvelous. People just seem to . . . to bend to your will."

Before the advent of Jesse DuFrayne in her life she would not have dreamed of replying as she did now. "I tend to cow people and make them afraid of me." She knew it was a graceless, unfeminine admission, and she could see it made David uncomfortable. But she herself felt oddly free after admitting it.

"Nonsense," David said, "a lady like you? Why, you're not . . . pushy."

But she suddenly knew she was and that he did not want to admit it. Pushiness was unfeminine. Ladies should be shyly retiring. But Jesse had taught her much about self-delusion, and she was getting better and better at ridding herself of it.

"It's not nonsense. I'm afraid it's true. However, today it served our purpose, so I shan't complain." Yet it hurt her a little that people opened doors for her because she cowed them while they'd opened doors for David because they instantly liked him.

"There's still so much to be done besides making building decisions. I'll have to take inventory of my stock and put in an order for a much larger number of shoes than I've ever been able to carry with me on the road. And there's the furnishings to order and the awning and the window glass. I'll have to drive out to see about a winter wood supply somewhere—And, oh! I'll need to order a stove from the East and—"

He stopped abruptly, breathlessly, realizing he'd been running on.

But she suddenly looked at him differently and found herself laughing, enjoying his enthusiasm.

"I guess I got carried away by my plans," he admitted sheepishly.

"Yes, you did," she said agreeably, "but you have every right. It's such a big step you're taking. It will take a lot of planning and enthusiasm."

His face suddenly looked worried. "Oh, I didn't mean that I expected you to be running along beside me each step of the way. I wouldn't expect that of you. You've done more than your share today."

But they went on making plans for the store, its furnishing, accoutrements and prospects. He was very animated, but forced himself to sit still and contain his excitement.

Time and again she compared him to Jesse. Jesse with his boundless ego and limited crassness. Never would he sit there like he'd gotten himself caned into that chair seat the way David did. He'd be pacing up and down, probably bellowing, "Goddamnit, Abbie, I know this business can go, and you're going to help it!" Abigail McKenzie! she scolded herself, stop making these unjustifiable comparisons and pay attention to what David is saying!

"It seems we've g . . . gotten ourselves almost . . . ah . . . expected at the fes . . . festivities tomorrow," he stammered. "Do you mind?"

She tried not to be annoyed by his lack of assertiveness, but guilty for having compared him to Jesse all afternoon, she made up for it by answering, "It's almost a matter of good business by now, isn't it? No, I don't mind. I attend the festivities annually anyway. Everybody in town does."

"I . . . ahem . . . we could . . . ah . . . go out together then," he stammered.

It was not at all the way Miss Abigail would like to have been invited. She was reminded that Jesse had once called David a milktoast, then kicked herself mentally for being unfair to him.

"Well . . . if . . . if you'd rather not."

"Oh, I didn't mean—Of course I'll go out with you."

He stood to leave, and she found herself actually quite glad he was going. "Where is Hake's Meadow?" he asked.

"It's out northeast of town where Rum Creek broadens. As you heard earlier, several wagons leave from Avery Holmes's Dry Goods Store and anyone who wants may ride out from there."

"At qu . . . quarter to ten?"

"Yes."

"Then I'll come. . . . Should I . . . well, come for you a little before then?"

"I'll be ready," she replied, growing irritated by his stammering.

"I'd better be leaving now . . ." His voice had a way of trailing off uncertainly at the end of phrases, which was beginning to make her nerves jangle. It seemed that only the subject of business could wring a positive, assured note from him. Personal subjects made him stutter and stammer. At the steps he did it again.

"I . . . I . . . could I . . ."

But he seemed unable to finish, and only looked down at her with spaniel eyes. She was suddenly very sure that he wanted to kiss her but didn't dare. Even though she had no business thinking it, she wondered, Why doesn't he just grab me and do it? She need not add, like Jesse would. By now she was comparing every action, every inflection, every mannerism of the two men. And unbelievably, in each instance she'd found David lacking. It stunned her to realize, while she watched him walk away, that though David's manners were impeccable, she now preferred Jesse's boorishness.

Chapter 19

MISS ABIGAIL DID not approve of everything that went on out at Hake's Meadow on the Fourth of July, but she was always in attendance nevertheless. She had a feeling for patriotism, and this was a patriotic holiday, though somehow it always seemed to turn into one sprawling, noisy beer-soaked melee. Each year it started with the mayor's inept speech while children held flags, but before long the politicians lost ground to beer and the ribaldry that inevitably followed. For the beer flowed as freely as did the baked beans tended by the D.A.R. members, who cooked them in an open fifty-gallon drum. It was, too, a perennial joke that had those D.A.R.s stirred up a few drums of their infamous beans back in 1776 and fed them to the British, they might have cut the war short by seven years. And when those beans merged with beer . . . well, rumor had it that Royal Gorge was no natural wonder; it was ripped out one Fourth of July when the picnic was held down there instead of at Hake's Meadow.

There were battles of every sort imaginable—some scheduled, some not. Rum Creek slid coolly out of the mountains and slithered to a halt above a beaver dam, creating Hake's Pond, where loggers from up mountain whupped the hell out of every aspiring log roller and tree skinner from Stuart's Junction, who later returned the favor at horseshoes and chasing a greased pig.

Then, too, there was the kissing, which grew more uninhibited as the day wore on and people just seemed to do it whenever and with whomever they could manage. Of course, the darker it got, the easier it was to manage.

The whole affair started at ten A.M. and officially ended with the ten P.M. fireworks display, unofficially when the last roaring drunk was hauled home by his wife, still singing loudly and probably more amorous than he'd been since last Fourth of July.

Miss Abigail had brought a basket for the basket social—her way of joining wholeheartedly in the festivities. She deposited it with all the others under a huge oak tree where the bidding was always done. She wore her daisy-trimmed hat, as usual, and a dove gray dress with matching overjacket of simple lines, which fairly clung to her skin by eleven o'clock. David Melcher, in a brown day suit, white shirt, and string tie, grew equally as hot as the sun rose toward its apex.

The two of them were sitting in the shade sipping sarsaparilla.

"Don't you drink beer?" she asked.

"I never developed a taste for it, I guess."

"Beer, as you've probably already guessed, is the drink of the day here, though I've never been able to understand why these men don't stop at their quota. On the Fourth of July they just don't seem to. Look! Look at Mr. Diggens. He's the one in the blue shirt who is challenging that logger twice his size. Is it the beer that makes him believe he can actually beat that logger at arm wrestling?"

They watched the mismatched contestants across the way as the pair knelt on either side of a stump, and of course the smaller Mr. Diggens lost, though he came up laughing and gamely warned the huge, strapping logger, "A few more beers and I beat you good!"

"Is that so!" the logger bellowed. "Well, let's get 'em into you then!" And before Diggens could protest, the logger lifted him bodily as if he were a bride being carried across a threshhold and carried him to the beer kegs, ballyhooing, "Feed my friend here some beer, Ivan. I want to see him beat me!"

A shout of laughter went up from the crowd and the logger took off his shirt, tied it by its sleeves around his waist, and stood like Paul Bunyan himself, drinking beer beside the dwarfed Diggens, as if waiting for him to suddenly sprout up and grow bigger.

Looking on, Miss Abigail and David joined in the laughter.

"As you can see, these little duels enhance the real contest which will all take place this afternoon," Miss Abigail explained.

David's eyes scanned the area. "I've never been much at physical things," he admitted unabashedly.

"Neither has Diggens, I'm afraid."

Then, as their eyes met, they both burst into laughter again.

"I think the speech makers are losing their audience," he noted some time later. Most of the listeners had drifted away from the pondside as soon as the mayor had finished his windy oratory.

"They'd rather listen to the nonsense at the beer kegs."

Another bit of revelry had started up there. Now the hairy-chested logger who'd tied his shirt around his waist was curtseying with that same shirt to Diggens before the two embraced and began a ridiculous impromptu dance while a fiddle scraped in the background. As they spun, beer flew out of their mugs, splattering two young women, who jumped back and shrieked joyously, only to be profusely apologized to by the men. The girls giggled as the logger again made his ridiculous curtsey to them.

"Something just seems to come over people out here on the Fourth of July," Miss Abigail said, unbuttoning her overjacket, which was becoming unbearable in the heat.

"It's a beautiful spot. It makes me happy all over again that I decided to stay in Stuart's Junction. These people . . . they were all so nice to me yesterday. I can't help but feel like I'm welcome here."

"Why shouldn't you be? Don't you think they know that your new business is going to be an asset to this town?"

"Do you think so? Do you really think it will succeed?"

He was very transparent. At times he displayed an almost childish need of her support and encouragement.

"Can you think of a thing more necessary than shoes? Why, just look at all those feet out there." She turned to survey the picnic grounds. A bunch of little boys scuffled under a nearby tree, playing some sort of rugby game they had improvised, kicking at a stuffed bag with curled-toed boots; a mother passed by, leading a little girl who was wailing over a stubbed, bare toe; the mother herself wore down-at-the-heel oxfords, long in need of replacing. "Look at the beating all those shoes are taking. Chances are that later every one of these people will come directly to your store to buy new ones."

He beamed at the thought, spinning visions of the future, but at that moment they were approached by a giant of a man wearing the familiar logger's uniform of loose-slung britches, black suspenders, and a red plaid shirt.

"Hey there, Melcher, you're the man I'm looking for!" A huge, hairy,

friendly paw was extended. "Michael Morneau's the name. I hear you'll be needing some timber for a building you aim to put up. I'm the man's got just what you need. I brung you a beer so we can talk about it friendly like."

David Melcher found himself pulled to his feet and a beer slapped into his hand.

To Miss Abigail, the amiable logger said, "Hope you don't mind, lady, if we mix a little business with pleasure. I'll bring him right back." A big arm circled David's shoulders and herded him away. "Come on over here, Melcher. Got some people I want you to meet."

Miss Abigail saw how David was rather bulldozed into drinking that beer. It was more than a drink—it was the symbol of goodwill among those men who swilled together in great camaraderie. Even from this distance she could tell when they talked business, from the forgotten way the mugs hung in their hands. But when some point was agreed upon, up in the air went the beers before everyone, including David, drank.

She watched his brown shoulders buffeted along among the mixture of shirts: red plaids, white businesses, even some yellowed union suits, and into each new group came fresh beer. Once he caught her eye across the expanse of meadow and made a gesture of helpless apology for abandoning her, but she shrugged and smiled and swished her hand to tell him not to worry. She was fine. She sat contentedly watching all the commotion around her. David was concluding more business arrangements and gathering more goodwill among the beer swillers than he could garner in a fortnight of selling quality shoes or beating the boardwalks downtown.

So Miss Abigail wandered off to watch the children's sack races.

Rob Nelson came running past but shied to a halt when he saw her.

"Howdy, Miss Abigail."

"Hello, Robert. Are you entering the sack race?"

"Sure am."

"Well, good luck to you then."

There was something different about Miss Abigail today. She didn't look like she just ate a pickle.

"Thank y', ma'am," the boy said, spinning away only to screech to a halt and return, squinting up at her, scratching his head, something obviously on his mind.

"What is it, Robert?"

"Well, y' know them there straws I brung you that time for that train robber?" He watched for danger signs, but she looked kind of young and pretty and her mouth kind of fell open and she touched her blouse where her heart was.

"Yes?"

"Did they work?"

"Why, yes they did, Robert, and I want to thank you very much for getting them."

"What'd you do with 'em?"

To Rob's surprise, Miss Abigail smiled and leaned down conspiratorially. "I blew soup into him," she whispered near his ear. She straightened then. "Now run along to your race."

But Rob didn't move. Just stood there slack-mouthed, in wonder. *"You blew soup into a train robber,* Miss Abigail?" he asked incredulously.

"He wasn't a train robber after all."

"Oh," Robert said shortly, then looked thoughtful before stuffing his hands into his pants pockets and saying, "You know, he really didn't look much like a train robber in those pajama pants."

Now it was Miss Abigail's turn to go slack-jawed. Horrified, she spun Rob about by the shoulders, controlling the urge to paddle his little backside. "Robert Nelson, don't you dare repeat that to a single living soul, do you hear? Now git!"

And the impetuous child ran off toward the sack race, trailing a burlap bag as he ran.

But when he was gone she crossed an arm upon her waist, rested her elbow upon it, and lightly covered her smiling mouth. Her shoulders shook mirthfully as she recaptured the picture of Jesse stumping around in pajama pants much too short for him.

"Is something funny, Miss Abigail?"

"Oh, Doctor Dougherty, hello. I was just enjoying the children's sack races."

"I've been meaning to get up to your place and thank you for all you did. You sure helped me out of a pickle."

"I was only too happy to help."

"Did that man behave himself and put that gun away? I sure didn't mean to put you in any ticklish spots by returning it to him."

"Oh, it's all over and done with now, water under the bridge." But she refused to meet his eyes, squinted into the sun instead to watch the races now in full swing.

"Yup!" he agreed, following her eyes to the jumping, writhing boys, some now sprawled out on their stomachs, struggling to regain their feet. "I heard you got paid real well."

Her eyes snapped to him. Only the doc would have the temerity to come right out with a thing like that. "Everybody in this town hears everything," she said.

"Yup," he agreed, "and what they don't hear, they damn well guess at."

"I hear Gertie got back from Fairplay," she said quickly, changing the subject.

"Yeah, she's got my office running slicker'n a greased pig again. And I heard you were all over town yesterday introducing that Melcher around and blazing trails for him to open up a new business."

"That's right. This town owes him that much, I think."

"Why so?"

It was an odd question. She gave him a puzzled look. But Doc had drawn a penknife from his pocket and was calmly cleaning his nails as he went on. "Seems to me we owe Jesse something if we owe anybody. Folks around here were mighty nasty about even letting him off his own train in our midst. If it weren't for you he could've rotted right there on it, for all they cared. And all the time it's his railroad that's brought new prosperity to Stuart's Junction. Just goes to show how wrong about a person you can be."

Doc didn't so much as glance at Miss Abigail, just snapped his penknife shut, tucked it away in a baggy pocket, and glanced out toward the sack races, where a lad lay humped up on the ground clutching his stomach. "Well," Doc murmured, as if ruminating to himself, "guess I'd better go see if I can get the scare out of him and the wind back in." And he shambled off to the rescue, leaving Miss Abigail to wonder just how much he guessed about her relationship with Jesse.

As she watched Doc moving toward the boy, she remembered the night she'd had the wind knocked out of her, and of the things which had followed, and she thought about Doc's words, "Just goes to show how wrong about a person you can be."

"Miss Abigail, I've been looking all over for you," David said, making her jump. She gasped and put a hand to her heart. "I'm sorry, I didn't mean to scare you."

"Oh, I was just daydreaming, that's all."

"Come. They're going to auction off the baskets now. You've been standing here in the sun too long. Your face is all red."

But it was memories of Jesse which had heightened her color, and she was grateful that David could not read her mind. He took her by the arm to where the crowd had gathered under the huge, sprawling oak for the pairing off and picnicking. He continued to hold her elbow as the auctioning began, and she could smell the yeastiness about him from the beer he'd drunk. Now and then he'd weave a bit unsteadily, but he was apparently sober enough to recognize the napkin that matched her kitchen curtains peeking out from under the lid of her picnic basket. When it came up for bids, he raised a looping arm and called out, "Seventy-five cents!"

"Way to go!" Someone slapped him on the back and he barely retained his stance. Then some unseen voice hollered, "That's Miss Abigail's basket, Melcher. Bid 'em up!"

Laughter, good-natured and teasing, went up, and her cheeks grew pinker.

"A dollar!" came the second bid.

"A dollar ten!" called David.

"Hell, that ain't no way to pay back a lady that saved your life! A dollar twenty!"

David rocked back on his heels, grinning quite drunkenly.

From the crowd someone hollered, "Melcher, you ain't too drunk to see Miss Abigail's colors flying from under that there basket lid, are you?"

"A dollar and a quarter!" Melcher thought he shouted, only he hiccuped in the middle and it came out, "A dollar and a quor-horter!" raising a whoop of laughter.

The auctioneer bawled, "Anybody got more'n a dollar and a *quor-horter* for this here basket?" Laughter billowed and so did Miss Abigail's blush.

"Sold!"

The gavel smacked down, and from all around rose catcalls, whistles, and hoots. David just grinned.

"Give 'er hell, David!" someone encouraged as David made his unsteady way forward to get the basket. As he passed Michael Morneau, a hand steered David and steadied him while the lumberman laughed, "We got all that business taken care of. Time for a little fun now, eh, Melcher?"

Miss Abigail thought David would never make it to that basket and back again, but soon he returned, offering an arm, leading her proudly. She was as red as a raspberry by now, moving through the crowd, being watched by the entire town while he plunked the basket down in the shade of a nearby tree. Finally the bidding resumed and drew people's attention away from them for the time being.

She knelt and opened the lid of the basket and began taking food out while he dropped to his knees, bracing his hands onto his thighs.

"Miss Abigail, I have to beg your forgi-hiveness," he hiccuped. "I said I-hime no beer drinker, but the bo-hoys took me in hand. I thought it'd be good business to mingle with the boys a li-hittle."

She was embarrassed by the entire scene, but still there was something unblamable about his tipsy state. She remembered all too well how easily she herself had gotten that way on a "thimbleful of champagne." She suddenly couldn't find it in her heart to be angry with him.

He sat with head hung low, hands still grasping thighs—a disconsolate drunk having a staring contest with the ground between his knees. Now and then he would quietly hiccup behind closed lips. She went about calmly laying out their food.

"I'm really sorry. I shouldn't have left you alone like tha-hat."

"Here. If you eat a little something, those hiccups will stop."

He looked at the piece of fried chicken she extended as if trying to identify what it was.

"Here," she repeated, gesturing with the drumstick as if to wake him up. "I'm not angry."

He looked up dumbly. "You're naw-hot?"

"No, but I will be if you don't take this thing and begin eating so people will stop staring at us."

"Oh . . . oh, sure," he said, taking the drumstick very carefully, as if it were porcelain. He bit into it, looked around, then stupidly waved the piece of meat toward a clump of gawking people as if signaling, "Hey there . . . how's it goin'?"

"You know, I really don't like beer," he mumbled to the chicken.

"Yes, so you told me. And as I told you, something just seems to come over people out here on the Fourth of July."

"But I shouldn't have drunk so much."

"Something good seems to have come of it though, hasn't it? I believe you've had your initiation today and now you truly are an accepted member of the community."

"Do you really think so?" He looked up, surprised.

"When you sat down here do you remember what you said? You said something about *the boys* insisting you have another beer."

"Did I say that?"

"Yes you did, just as if you were one of them."

He raised his eyebrows foolishly and grinned. "Well now, maybe I am, maybe I am." Then after a long pause, "Wouldn't that be somethin'?"

"I have a feeling that at first some of the men around here took you for the usual high and mighty easterner . . . and a peddler to boot. That combination doesn't always meet with the approval of Stuart's Junction's businessmen.

I wouldn't be surprised if they actually set you up to see if you'd pass their rites."

"Do you think so?" He continued to ask dumb, rhetorical questions but she could not help smiling because he was obviously abashed at his state . . . and it was funny in its own way.

"Oh, I'm only guessing. Don't be alarmed. If they did set you up, it'll be for this once only, and my guess is you already passed muster."

"Do you think so?" he asked again, in the exact dumb tone he'd used all the other times.

"Well, you got some business handled in between beers, didn't you? Or wasn't that what all those raised glasses were all about?"

"Come to think of it, I did." He looked astounded.

"Well then, where's the loss?"

Even in his drunkenness he was touched by her magnanimity. "You're being awfully understanding, Miss Abigail, considering how embarrassed you must have been during the bidding."

"Would you like to know a secret?" she asked.

"A secret?"

"Mm-hmm." She tilted her head sideways, a mischievous look in her eye. "Today was nothing compared to the year that Mr. Binley bought my picnic basket."

"Bones Binley?" he asked, amazed. His mouth hung open, displaying a bite of chicken.

"Yes . . . one and the same."

"Bones Binley bought your basket?" The chicken fell out and she hid her laughter behind her hand and came up smiling.

"Aha. It sounds like a tongue twister, doesn't it?" There was no artful coyness in her admission whatsoever. It simply seemed easier for her to erase his discomfiture and have a pleasant day than to hold him responsible for the teasing of the townspeople and the fact that they'd coerced him into getting drunk.

"Bones Binley with the tobacco and the brown teeth at the feedstore all day long spitting?"

It *was* funny, although she'd never seen it as funny before. She rocked forward on her knees, smiling, chuckling as she remembered. "It's funny, isn't it? But it wasn't then. He . . . he bought my basket and nobody teased him at all. It was horrible, just horrible, walking through the crowd with him. And he's looked at me with cow eyes ever since."

"Musta been your fried chicken that did it." He was sobering up a little bit by now, but was still elevated enough to laugh at his joke. Then he sucked at his greasy fingers and they happened to be both laughing when another contingent came past with a basket of their own. Frank Adney waved to David as he passed, calling, "Sounds like she's not too mad after all, eh, David?" Then he tipped the brim of his hat up briefly at her. "No hard feelings, Miss Abigail?"

"None at all, Mr. Adney." She smiled back. Frank was surprised to see what a pretty woman Miss Abigail actually was with that smile on her face and laughing the way she was. He mentioned so to his wife, and she agreed as they moved away.

Miss Abigail, watching the Adneys move on, felt suddenly more a part of the town than ever before. David, watching her, felt expansive and wonderful. In two short days he'd melded into both the social and business environment of Stuart's Junction with an almost magical smoothness, and it was all due to her support.

"Miss Abigail?"

"Yes?" She looked up.

"I love this chicken, and the deviled eggs too." What he really thought he loved was her.

Suddenly she realized that all of this was simply too, too enjoyable and that she should not be encouraging him with smiles and laughter this way.

"You've lost your suit jacket somewhere," she observed.

Looking down at his chest he acted surprised to find it clad only in shirt and tie. "It's out there somewhere." He waved the chicken at the world at large. "It'll be around when I need it. It's too hot anyway for all that. Don't you want to take your jacket off?"

Informality breeding familiarity, she knew she shouldn't. But it was ghastly hot, and she'd been schooled by Jesse to rid herself of her too-rigid proprieties. She tried not to think of how pleased he'd be if he could see the change in her today. "It is awfully hot," she said, beginning to shrug the garment off.

David quickly used his napkin and walked on his knees, coming to help her out of it.

"Yes, that's much better," she said, laying it across the top of the picnic basket, swiping a hand upward from the nape of her neck to tuck up absolutely nothing; her hair was perfectly in place.

He had finished eating but still felt very mellow from the beer and stretched out on the grass, relaxed. He wondered how it would feel to lay his head in her lap. Instead, he said, "Tomorrow I'm supposed to go up to the logging camp and put in an order with Morneau for some lumber at the mill. But I don't know where it is for sure."

"It's about halfway up that ridge over there," she said, pointing and squinting, conscious of his eyes on her.

He liked the way the shade dappled her forehead when she raised her head to look at the ridge.

"Would you . . ." he began, but stopped. Should he simply invite her out for a ride or tell her he needed her help to find the place? She seemed to shy away from anything personal, but as long as he kept things on a business basis, she was more amenable. "Could you come along and show me where to find it?"

She wanted to say yes, but said instead, "Tomorrow I must do the ironing."

"Oh," he replied flatly. He lay there considering her while she began to pack up the remnants of their meal. Finally he said, "If it didn't take you all day maybe you could make it in the afternoon?"

She was pleased about one thing regarding the beer: since he'd been under its influence he'd stopped stammering. It almost made her break down and say yes, but again she realized she had no right to involve herself with him, not anymore.

"No. I simply can't make it at all," she said crisply, continuing to fuss with the picnic basket.

Rebuffed, he immediately sat up. Her abrupt changes of mood confused him. A minute ago she'd been very amiable, but suddenly she became cold and terse, refusing to look at him.

"I said before that I didn't expect you to follow me hand and foot through this entire opening up of the business, and now here I am, asking you again, the first thing. I shouldn't have asked."

Once again she felt irritated by the way David extended his invitation. Even though she knew better than to encourage him, she wished he would not always dream up an excuse to be with her. Female vanity, she chided herself, remembering the way Jesse had goaded and teased her into taking her for a ride. She put Jesse firmly from her mind, wishing he'd stay away.

As if to make up for his transgression, David asked, "Do you want some ice cream?"

But she was preoccupied, irritated with herself for leading David on, and at David for not being manly enough to lead her on. It was all very confusing. "Do you?"

She came out of her maunderings to find him standing beside her. She blinked once, hypnotically. "What?"

"I asked, do you want some ice cream," he repeated. "It's ready." He was handsome and polite and unassuming, and she stared up his body for a moment, confused by the sharp comings and goings of feelings she experienced for him.

"Yes, please," she said, sorry that she'd snapped at him.

The smile was gone from his face as he turned and limped away, only to remind her again of Jesse limping away from her down the street the last time she saw him.

David was thoroughly confused by Miss Abigail since he'd come back to Stuart's Junction. Her quicksilver mood changes were totally different from the steady, sweet woman she had been before. There were times when he swore she liked him—more than liked him—and other times that cold light would come into her gaze, making him sure that she cared nothing at all for him.

But he was reminded again of what she could mean to him when he was served ahead of the children who'd been waiting their turns around the ice cream churn. The whole town seemed to treat him solicitously! Even the fat woman who scooped out ice cream and served him out of turn.

"You tell Mizz Abigail I picked them peaches myself last fall. Tell her Fanny Hastings says she brought a real swell feller here when she brung you," the ingratiating woman said, her dimples disappearing into her plump cheeks.

He thanked the woman and picked his way back to Miss Abigail, wondering what mood she would be in now.

He stood above her, smitten all over again with her cool, calm ladylike demeanor, studying her breasts beneath the high-necked blouse.

"Fanny Hastings says to tell you she picked the peaches for the ice cream herself."

Abbie looked up and reached for his peace offering, knowing by the look in his face that he thought he'd done something wrong, something to upset her, when it was she who continuously upset herself these days. And because he truly had done nothing wrong, and because Jesse DuFrayne refused to free her from the grip of memory, and because there was such a whipped-pup look in David's eyes as he offered her the streaming ice cream, she said, "Mr. Melcher, I believe I'll have time to show you the way to the mill tomorrow after all."

His face was immediately transformed into cherubic radiance. She realized when he smiled so quickly, so joyfully, how little it took for her to make him happy. Gratitude and admiration shone from his eyes at each little bit of attention she showed him.

This man, she realized, could be manipulated by nothing more than a smile. It should have been a heady thought, but it left her inexplicably unexcited. Still, she made up her mind she would be nice to him for the rest of the day, because he did not deserve to suffer the consequences of her constant thoughts of Jesse DuFrayne.

"Let's go watch the tree skinners choose up sides," she suggested, reaching a hand up to him. Like a grateful puppy, he helped her to her feet, his expression one of devotion.

David Melcher's initiation had only begun with the morning draught session and the subsequent bidding on the picnic baskets. Being the subject of much conjecture, he was greeted profusely wherever he and Miss Abigail went. Each greeting was enhanced in cordiality by the offer of a mug of beer, and just like that morning, David found his hand filled with a sweating glass through the entire afternoon, through no wish of his own. It was understood that Miss Abigail would not drink beer, but the mere fact that she accompanied David while he did seemed to make Miss Abigail more human in the eyes of the citizens of Stuart's Junction. At times she was actually seen smiling and laughing, and the townswomen took note of this, poking their elbows into one another's ribs, winking. And hour by hour, David became increasingly inebriated, and more thoroughly accepted.

Before the end of the day, Miss Abigail too felt herself accepted in a way she'd never been before. The women included her in their plans for the next meeting of the Ladies of Diligence Sewing Circle, gave her an apron and a spatula when the pie eating contest took place, kept her in their cheering circle when David participated with their men, and took her by the elbow as they moved to the more rowdy contests. David participated in everything—the sack jousting, pole climbing, Indian wrestling, and even the tobacco spitting contest. And he was a miserable failure at everything he tried. But only if success was measured by the official contest results, for in goodwill he was the greatest achiever of the day. The fact that he tried all the contests, in spite of his lost toe, in spite of his limp, in spite of the fact that he was assured of a loss even before he started, endeared him to the men. And the fact that he had wrought such a change in Miss Abigail endeared both of them to the women.

David was finally forced to desist at the final event of the day, the log rolling contest. It took the nimblest of feet and a perfection of balance to even enter the event—obviously he lacked both. He had been slapped on the back and hugged by more than one of the log rollers, though, as they slogged out of the pond, defeated, dripping, laughing. Thus, by the time he at last returned to Miss Abigail he was as wet as if he'd participated himself. He was roaring drunk too, stained with tobacco and pie, reeking to high heaven of beer—an

unequivocal mess. In this deplorable state he was carried to Miss Abigail's side, to where she was working with the women who were putting away pie tins, picking up forks and glasses, and distributing picnic baskets to their rightful owners.

"Miss Abigail," roared Michael Morneau, "this man is the best goddamn sport that ever got a toe shot off!"

The women noticed how she didn't so much as bat an eyelash at the word *goddamn*. Instead she turned to find the disheveled David actually borne to her on the shoulders of the well-oiled men who were to be his cohorts for as long as he chose to live in this town. They were all laughing, staggering, singing, swaggering, arms around each other so that if one of them leaned to the left, the lot of them leaned. Swaying back to the right, the lot of them swayed.

"Town's got a helluva wunnerful newcomer here, ain't that right, Jim?"

Whomever Jim was, he roared even louder than his companions and drunkenly doubled the motion. "Damn right, and we got Miss Abigail here to thank for bringin' him in! Ain't that right, boys?"

More amiable cussing and approval followed, and Miss Abigail looked up to where David swayed on their shoulders.

"See? We brung him back to you, Miss Abigail." But the inebriated speaker seemed unable to locate David all of a sudden and looked around searchingly. "Didn't we?" he asked, raising another hullabaloo. "Where the hell'd we put 'im?"

"I'm up here!" called a grinning David from his perch on the men's shoulders.

The one who'd been searching looked up. "There you are! Well, how the hell'd you git up there?"

"Why, you dummy, we was bringin' him back to Miss Abigail, remember?" another voice slurred while somebody stumbled and the gleeful band swayed, *en masse,* in the other direction.

"Well, put 'im down then, 'cause here she is!"

She could see it happening even before it actually did. One minute David was up there smiling like a besotted walleyed pike, the next minute the shoulders separated almost as if choreographed—half in one direction, half in another. Like the Red Sea they parted, dropping David Melcher, still smiling and waving, down the chasm. Miss Abigail saw him coming and gasped, then lurched futilely to save him. He fell, octopuslike, a tangle of jellied arms and legs, but just as he plummeted, she gained the cleft in the human sea and David's disappearing shoulder caught her on the side of the neck and down she went with him! She landed flat on top of him, arms and legs splayed in the most unladylike fashion imaginable.

As soon as the crowd realized what had happened, solicitous hands reached toward the pair of casualties piled up in their midst. The men "ooh-ed." The women clucked. But David, with that pikey grin still all over his face, opened his eyes to find Miss Abigail McKenzie's face smack in front of him—and Lord! if she wasn't lying on top of him! Her hair was falling sideways out of its knot, her breasts were smashed against his damp, beery shirtfront, her blue eyes were startled, and her cheeks were a darling pink. He didn't care how she got there, or when. This was just too good a chance to miss.

He threw two very loose-jointed arms around her and kissed her so long and hard he thought he'd throw up for lack of wind and dizziness and the bump his head had just suffered.

Miss Abigail felt his arms tighten and saw his lopsided grin become even more lopsided, and she knew beyond a doubt what he was going to do, but she could not scramble off of him in time to prevent it. She felt her hair go sliding to hang over their two cheeks as he kissed her with the smell of tobacco juice and beer and sweat and cherry pies all around them.

And suddenly she was aware that a great, pulsing roar of applause had burst out. Even the ladies were clapping and cheering. Men whistled through their teeth and kids came scrambling among long legs and petticoats to see what was going on within the circle.

"Atta boy, David, give it to 'er!" somebody yelled.

Miss Abigail pushed and rolled and finally broke free, tumbled to the dirt, and sat beside him. She was positively scorching! But what made the final difference, what everyone could not quite believe they were seeing, was the way she burst out laughing, trying to hide her blushing cheeks behind a small, uncharacteristically grimy hand. Sitting there in the dirt, she reached both hands toward the hovering men and said, "Well, are you going to stand there applauding all day or is somebody going to help me up?"

Everyone was laughing with her as they tugged her to her feet, followed by David. The ladies fussily dusted off her skirts and scolded their foolish husbands. But secretly they were all well pleased. Miss Abigail, it seemed, wasn't the stick-in-the-mud she'd seemed all these years, and David—why, he was perfect for her. Every citizen of the town congratulated himself on what a tidy bit of matchmaking had been accomplished here today. From that moment on David Melcher and Abigail McKenzie were accepted not individually, but as a pair.

She felt it happening all day long, the curious tide of that acceptance. It was a new feeling to her, one that had been denied to Abigail McKenzie all her single life. The subtle change that had started that morning had grown more palpable as the day wore on. If she were to try to define it she could not, in her vast store of words, find just the right ones to describe the exclusion of the single person from the immutable charmed circle of those who live life two by two. Only in retrospect did she feel it fully. Not until the end of this day during which she had felt so much included did she realize how much she had been excluded until now.

Basking in the glow of the feeling she found herself again beside David Melcher, seated on the ground beneath the deep blue night sky of Hake's Meadow. Legs stretched out before them, faces raised, they watched the intermittent bursts of fireworks that illuminated both them and the sky.

From the corner of her eye she could see that David was watching her.

"I ought not to have . . . have kissed you that way," he stammered, sobering for the second time that day, admiring her chin, nose, and cheeks as explosions came and went. She kept her face raised, but said nothing. "I . . . I didn't exactly know . . . what I was doing."

"Didn't you?" she asked.

He looked up as a skyrocket exploded. "I mean, I had too much beer."

"Like everyone else."

He took heart. "You're not . . . you're not angry?"

"No."

The two of them leaned back, elbows stiff, palms on the grass behind them. He edged one hand sideways until his fingers touched hers, and when the next firefall burst, he saw that she was smiling up at the sky.

David's fingers were warm, his eyes upon her admiring. She was filled with a sense of well-being from the day they'd shared and wondered, when they reached the doorstep would he kiss her?

On the ride back to town aboard the crowded wagon, David held her hand as they sat side by side on a bundle of hay, their hands concealed beneath the folds of her skirt. Their hands grew very damp and once he released hers and wiped his palm on his pant leg, then found her fingers again beneath the skirt of dove gray. She thought of Jesse, of his straightforward moves so unlike David's unsure ones. Guiltily, then, as David's hand returned to hers she squeezed it.

He walked her home when the buckboard unloaded, but there were others walking their way so he kept his distance. At her door, with hammering heart, he took her hand once again in his damp one.

"I . . ." he began, but stopped, as usual.

She wished he would simply say what he was thinking, without these false starts. He's not Jesse, she reminded herself, give him time.

"Thank you," he said in the end, and dropped her hand, stepping back as the Nelsons came home next door.

"I didn't do anything deserving thanks," she said quietly, disappointed that he'd dropped her hand.

"Yes you did."

"What?"

"Well . . ." He seemed to search his mind a moment. "How about the picnic?" He spied the basket on the porch floor.

She said nothing.

"You . . . you did more, Miss Abigail, you know you did. You m . . . made . . . m . . . me accepted in Stuart's Junction today."

The night was quiet, contentment seemed to spread around Abbie like a comfortable warm wind. "No, you made me accepted."

"I . . . I . . . what?"

She looked down at her hands and joined them together. "I've lived here all my life and have never felt as much a part of this town as I do right now. You did that for me today, Mr. Melcher."

He suddenly took both of her hands again. "Why, that's what I feel like. Like . . . like I've found my home at last."

"You have," she assured him, "one where you are liked by everyone."

"Everyone?" he swallowed as he asked.

"Yes, everyone."

He stood squeezing her hands a long time and she heard him swallow again. His hands were much smaller than Jesse's. She tried not to compare them. Kiss me, she thought. Kiss me and chase him from my mind.

But he could not gather the courage, sober as he was now. And he knew he was in a sorry state, smelling of beer and tobacco, clothing soiled and damp.

"You'll show me the way to the mill tomorrow?" he asked.

"Certainly. The sooner the building goes up, the sooner you'll be open for business."

"Yes."

He let her hands go, disappointing her immensely, for she knew by the way he did it that he'd rather have continued holding them.

Jesse would have held them.

Damn you, Jesse, leave us alone.

"I had a marvelous day," she urged, finding an almost compulsive need within her to be kissed by this man, although perhaps not solely for the right reasons.

But David only said, "So did I," then wished her good night and turned to go.

Her heart fell. She was doomed to another night of thoughts of Jesse after all. Wearily, she went to the swing and sat there in the dark, listening to the sound of David's irregular footsteps retreating up the gravel street. Soon he moved beyond earshot and the sound of his steps was replaced by the gentle creaking of ropes as she nudged the swing. A cricket answered the ropes. She stared hypnotically up the dark street, saw not dark street but dark moustache instead.

David . . . Jesse . . . David . . . Jesse . . .

David, why didn't you kiss me?

Jesse, why did you?

David, would I have let you?

Jesse, why did I let you?

David, what if you knew about Jesse?

Jesse, if it weren't for you there'd be nothing for David to know. Why didn't you force me to leave your room that night as any gentleman should have? Why did I force my way in as a lady should not have? All it has brought me is pain. No, that's not true, it brought me David, who is all the gentle, refined and likable things I ever wanted in my life. Why must I compare him to you, Jesse DuFrayne? Why should he have to measure up to you, who did everything wrong from start to finish? David, David, I'm sorry . . . believe me. How could I know that you would come back? What would it do to you, with your gentle nature, if you learned the truth about me? Why do I find fault with you for being hesitant and polite and being a gentleman? Jesse was fast and rude and nothing gentlemanly whatsoever and I hated it . . .

Ah, but not at the last . . . not at the last, her disloyal body claimed.

She crossed an arm over her stomach, rested an elbow on it, and cradled her forehead tiredly, trying to forget.

The swing ropes squeaked rhythmically, and memory descended mercilessly. A bare chest showing behind the open buttons of a shirt, an arm slung along the back of a swing, a smile that began slowly at the corner of a moustache, hands upon her skin, lips and tongue upon her skin.

At the instant tears gathered in the corners of her eyes, she realized that her breasts were puckered up like tight little rosebuds.

Get out of my life, Jesse DuFrayne! Do you hear me! Get off my swing and out of my bed so I may go to it in peace again.

Chapter 20

THE TOWNSPEOPLE GREW accustomed to seeing Miss Abigail and David together in the days that followed. The two of them spent long hours making the many decisions necessary for establishing a new business from the ground up. The day after the picnic, when they showed up at Silver Pine Mill, Miss Abigail was right beside David as the arrangements for the sale of lumber were handled. Demonstrating her keen business acumen, she secured his lumber at a better price than he'd have gotten on his own by insisting that they be shown the less desirable knotted pine, which brought the price down. These, she wisely noted, were good enough for building storage shelves at the rear of the building.

The plate glass for the windows, which would be shipped by train from Ohio, would have been one of their most expensive commodities had they purchased plates of the large size he envisioned. She suggested instead that they order numerous small panes that could be shipped at a far smaller price due to the fact that they were far less liable to break in transit. Thus the plan for a flat, cold, indifferent storefront was scrapped in favor of a warm, inviting Cape Cod bow window, the first Main Street was to boast. In the words of Miss Abigail, why not let women ogle the shoes from three directions instead of just one? Perhaps they could sell three times as many that way.

While the store's first studs began rising she marched one day down to the feedstore and presented Bones Binley with a proposition he found impossible to refuse: she would furnish him and his cronies with a picnic basket each day for seven days if during that time they could whittle a set of twenty-eight matched spools of which a railing would be made for the back of the display window. The railing, rather than a wall, would allow the window display items to be seen from inside the store while at the same time creating a warm, inviting atmosphere when viewed from outside.

When it was announced at services one Sunday that pews had finally been ordered for the church, she suggested to David that they see about purchasing the old wooden benches at a fraction of what new chairs would have cost. This done, she next raided Avery Holmes's back room and came up with a dusty bolt of sturdy rep that had been lying there untouched for years simply because it was bright scarlet. She considered scarlet the perfect color to lend the shoe store the interior warmth she was striving for. She talked Avery into selling her the entire bolt at a ridiculously low price and left him feeling only too glad that he'd unloaded it at last. Afterward, she talked the ladies of the sewing circle into experimenting with upholstering, which none of them had ever tried before. They padded and covered the old church benches with the red rep, all the while thanking Miss Abigail for giving them a chance to try their hand at this new craft.

The bolt of rep seemed to have no end. When the benches were completed, there were still yards and yards left. Abbie fashioned simple, flat curtain panels with which to frame the bow window, to be tied back, giving the whole display a stagelike affect. Still she hadn't run out of the red fabric, so the remainder of the bolt she began tearing into strips whenever she found time, to be used later in braided rugs for in front of the door and before the iron stove at the rear of the store.

As August neared and the building took shape, Abbie and David worked together on the massive order that needed placing with the factory in Philadelphia for the first stocking of the shelves. The heat remained intense, the air seeming always to carry its low haze of dust motes. One such late afternoon the two of them were in the coolest spot they could find: on the grass out under the linden tree in Abbie's backyard, with ledgers, lists, and catalogues spread all about them.

"But you have to think about winter coming!" Abbie was insisting. "Be practical, David. If you were to place an order from your company only, for nothing but high-fashion shoes, you'll lose out on the far greater share of your potential business."

"I've always sold fine, up-to-date shoes," he argued. "People can buy boots in a dry goods store—so let them."

"But why lose their business?"

"Because I don't think I'll need it. I'll have all the business I need selling the more fashionable styles I've always handled."

"Maybe in the East you would, and maybe traveling in a circuit like you did in the past, because what you carried was a novelty and those who saw them thought they'd lose the chance to buy such shoes once you moved on. But out here, in one place, you'll need to suit all needs. Work boots would be your best seller of all."

"But how will work boots look in that lovely little Cape Cod window you talked me into?"

"Horrible!"

He blinked at her questioningly. "Well?"

Immediately she was planning: she was always filled with fresh ideas. "Well . . . we'll put them in the back of the store, in a spot more suited to them. We'll display them where the men will feel more comfortable looking at them. That's it!" she exclaimed, the idea suddenly gelling. "We'll make a spot exclusively for the men! Men are so funny that way, they like to have a spot of their own. We'll get a few captain's chairs like the ones out in front of Mitch's feedstore and we'll circle them around the stove and . . . and . . . let's see . . ." She pondered again, placing a finger against her teeth. "We'll make it homey and masculine both at once—a red rug in the middle of the circle of chairs, and maybe we can display the boots in a masculine way that's attractive and takes a little of the dullness away."

"I don't know," David said doubtfully.

She became impatient with him and jumped up, spilling ledgers and scattering notes and papers. "Oh, David, be sensible!"

"I am being sensible. This town already has an outlet for work boots and everyday shoes. I specialize in fashionable shoes and they are what I know how to sell. It's the ladies I want to appeal to. When they see what is in the front window, I want them to run straight home and exclaim to their husbands, 'Guess what I saw today!' "

Abbie stood very still now, hands on her hips, challenging him. "And what exactly will they describe?"

"Well, the window display, of course, filled with the kind of shoes that appeal to their vanity or maybe their husband's vanities. Heavenly shoes the likes of which they've never seen in their lives, straight from the East."

Whether or not it was wise, she asked, "Red shoes?"

"What?" He blinked up at her.

"Red shoes, I said. Will they be describing red shoes?"

"Why . . . why, yes, some of them. Red shoes just like yours."

But they both knew she'd never worn those red shoes since that one and only night when he'd taken her out to dinner.

"You . . . you like the red shoes, d . . . don't you, Abigail?"

She came near him and squatted down, her skirt forming a billowy mushroom about her as she reached to lay an arm upon his sleeve. "Please understand, David. I like them because they are from you, but I . . . ."

When she hesitated, he insisted, "Go on."

She looked into his face, then away, then nervously stood up and turned her back on him. "Do you know what . . . what Mr. DuFrayne said when he saw them?"

David instantly bristled at the mention of DuFrayne. "What does DuFrayne have to do with it?"

"He was here the day they arrived, as you know." Resolutely she turned to face David before adding, "He called them strumpet's shoes." David's face burned and his lips pursed.

"Why do you bring him up? What does it matter what he thinks?"

Her tone became imploring. "Because I want your business to succeed. I want you to realize that here in Stuart's Junction people don't wear red shoes, but they wear a lot of work boots and sensible utility shoes. If you are going to succeed, it is imperative that you understand. In the East, where bright colors are all the rage, it is perfectly acceptable to sell them and to wear them. It's different here. You look at those colors from the salesman's point of view. People here, particularly women, are far more conservative. No matter how much they might even secretly admire them, most of these women would not dream of purchasing them. That is the only reason I repeated Mr. DuFrayne's comment, because it symbolizes the views of the town."

"Abigail." His mouth was pinched, his jaw rigid. He had completely forgotten the reason for her soliloquy. Only one thing now possessed his thoughts. "Are you saying he called you a strumpet?"

Without thinking, she replied, "Oh, no, he was just jealous, that's all."

David jumped to his feet, snapping, "What?"

She tried to make light of it, realizing her mistake. "We're getting off the subject. We were speaking of the most sensible shoes for you to order."

"*You* were speaking of the most sensible shoes for me to order. *I* was speaking of why DuFrayne should have cause to feel jealous. Was there something between you two after all?" David Melcher became strangely self-assured and glib-tongued whenever DuFrayne's name came up. He possessed a firm authority which was missing at other times.

"No!" she exclaimed—too fast—then, calming herself, repeated more quietly, "No . . . there was nothing between us. He was hateful and inconsiderate and insulting whenever he got the chance to be." But she knew that wasn't entirely true, and she could not meet David's eyes.

"Then why should he care one way or another if I sent you a pair of strumpet's shoes? After that scene on the bed the morning I left, I should think he'd be the type to applaud red shoes, if what you say is true and they really are considered inappropriate."

Unwittingly, David had hit on one of those inconsistencies about Jesse DuFrayne that rankled her still, all these weeks after he had left. It was disconcerting to have it put into words by someone else when it was in her thoughts so often, seemingly inexpressible.

"I cannot answer for him," she said, "and I don't think it's your place to upbraid me. After all, you and I are nothing more than—" But she suddenly came up short, chagrined at herself. She dropped her eyes and fidgeted with the button on her cuff. She really did not know what she and David were to each other. He had been the epitome of politeness in the weeks they'd been working together on plans for the store. The only change—and it was natural —was that they'd begun using each other's first names. He'd made no further attempt to kiss her or even hold her hand. In no other way did he indicate that he was wooing her. She supposed that he thought he'd offended her by getting drunk and kissing her that way before the entire populace of Stuart's Junction on the Fourth of July and was making amends by his extreme politeness since then.

Again with that aura of authority, he said unequivocally, "I don't want that man's name mentioned between us again, Abigail."

Her eyes came up sharply to meet his. By what right did he give her orders? They were not betrothed.

Suddenly David softened. The wind lifted the brown hair from his forehead, and the expression about his eyes grew wistful. He stood with his weight on his good leg—he often did that, perhaps because his other foot gave him discomfort—and it lent him a relaxed look, especially when he had the thumb and forefinger of one hand hidden inside his vest pocket, where he carried his watch.

"Abigail, what were you going to say just then? That you and I are no more than what? You didn't finish."

But how could she finish? It had been a slip of the tongue. He should be the one to finish, to understand what it was she had meant. She had grown so used to being with him, and she enjoyed him most of the time. Now and then she thought of her lost virginity and the fact that she should cease encouraging David, but as time went on she thought of it less and less. Still, he never made any advances toward her or even acted as if he thought about doing so. They shared a platonic relationship at most. And so Abbie thought up a likely answer for him.

"I was going to say business partners, but I guess we're not even that. The business is yours." She could not quite meet his eyes.

"I feel like it's half yours too. You've done as much or m . . . more than I." He began to stammer as soon as the subject broached anything personal. While speaking of the store his enthusiasm kept his voice steady. But now, perilously close to clarifying his relationship with Abigail, he grew timorous again.

"I've done no more than any friend would do," she said humbly, hoping he would deny it.

"No, Abigail, you've done much more. I don't know how I could have done it all without you. You . . . your judgments are m . . . much better than mine."

She waited with her heart in her throat, wondering if he'd go on to more personal things, but she could sense his shyness—for some men it is not easy to be the man in a situation like this. The silence lengthened between them and became uncomfortable and she could see he'd lost his nerve.

"We still haven't agreed on the ordering of the stock," she said, and the moment of discomfort passed.

"Something tells me I should trust your judgment again on this."

"There is room at the rear of the store for boots. I am also very sure that we'll sell more of them if we do it the way I've envisioned it. Come to the store and we'll look around and I'll show you just where we could put the boot section and how we'll plan it."

"Now?"

"Why not?"

"But it's Sunday."

"So it is, and there'll be no noisy hammering and banging and we should be able to talk in peace and study the possibilities."

He smiled, conceding. "You're right. Let's go."

She no longer wore her hat and gloves when the weather was too hot for them. They walked uptown in the late-day sun, nodding hello to an occasional neighbor who now called an amiable greeting to both of them. "Afternoon, David, Miss Abigail. How you doin'?" There were times when Miss Abigail already felt married to him.

The skeleton of the building was up. It had walls and part of a roof, but inside the studs showed. The framework of the bow window lay in wait of panes, and there was no front door yet. The interior walls were to be of tin wainscot above the shelves—the stacks of wainscot lay amid sawhorses and planks.

Abigail picked her way among pails of nails, stacks of shelving, the carved posts Bones and the boys had already completed. "See here?" At the rear of the building she pointed to a spot where a hole had been left for the chimney pipe. "Now here's where the stove will be. Suppose we cut some giant rounds of oak and leave them, bark and all, just as they come from the woods. We'll put them here near the stove and set the rugged work boots on the wood to add just the right touch of masculinity. A basket of nuts here, the ring of sturdy chairs around the stove, or leaning up against the wall behind it, almost as if reserved for each man. Why, they'll love it! Men love it near a stove. Women get enough of stoves working in their kitchens, so we'll put their shoes up front where it's cool, in the display window surrounded by the spooled railing. And while it might be true that no woman around here might like the color red on her shoes, they will find it cheerful and gay when it is brightening up the store as a background for displays. Imagine it at Christmas with the fire snapping and a hot pot of coffee back here on the stove for the men. We could invite them to leave their mugs right here, hanging on the wall on pegs. We'll sell boots all right, and plenty of them. At the same time the ladies will be up front oohing and aahing over your fancy shoes, and gossiping, away from their husbands."

Abigail didn't know it, but carried away as she was by her plans for the store, her face had taken on the same lovely look that Jesse had discovered upon it the day the red shoes came. Neither did she realize she had said *"we'll* sell boots all right." Her face was animated, bright-eyed and radiant. And just as Jesse DuFrayne had been moved by it weeks ago, David Melcher was moved by it now. The hem of Abigail's skirt had stirred up sawdust in the air, and the sun, glinting down through the chimney hole and half-finished roof, caught it in hovering cantles as she gestured, moved, turned, and spoke. She raised a hand to point at where the coffee pot would be, bubbling away on a winter stove . . . and David forgot the summer heat, imagined her here then, helping the ladies select shoes, bringing her enthusiasm along with her good business sense. He imagined helping the husbands while he told their ladies, "My wife will help you up front."

And suddenly he knew it could not possibly be any other way.

She swung around and he surprised her hand by capturing it in midair. For a moment the words stuck in his timid throat. The sawdust drifted around them like summer snow, settling here and there on their shoulders. It was silent and woodscented and private. And he loved her very much.

"Abigail . . ." he said, then swallowed.

"Yes, David?"

"Abigail, may I . . . k . . . kiss you?" He had made so many blunders with her already that he thought it best to ask first.

She wished he had not asked. Jesse would not have asked. Afraid David might have read the unwanted thought, she lowered her lashes. Instead, he took it for her demure refusal and dropped her hand.

"I'm sorry . . ." he began.

Her eyes flew back up. "How can you be sorry?" she asked quickly. "You haven't done anything." It was unreasonable for her to feel piqued when all he meant to do was be polite, but enough was enough!

"I . . . do . . . don't . . ." he stammered, but her reply had confused him so, he didn't know what to do.

"Yes, you may kiss me, David."

But by now the situation had lost the grace that a spontaneous kiss would have lent. In spite of this, he took both of her hands and leaned toward her. There was a short piece of planking between their feet, but rather than move around it or step over it to take her in his arms, he leaned over the barrier and, with closed eyes, gently placed his lips over hers.

He had fine, soft, warm, shapely lips. And she thought, what a shame he does not know how to use them.

He laid them over hers for a wasting flight of seconds while Abigail felt absolutely nothing. The talk about how they should display the shoes had excited her more than his kiss. He straightened then and remained perfectly silent, as silent as his kiss had been. She gazed down at the sawdust beneath their feet, at the plank which separated them, thinking it might as well have been between their torsos as well as there on the floor for all the contact there'd been during that kiss. A kiss of the lips only, she determined, was a decidedly unsatisfying thing. So she raised her lips to David's again and dared to put her hand behind his neck for a brief moment. But the kiss was brief, and immediately afterward David said the appropriate thing.

"Shall we go?"

She wanted to say, "No, let's try that again without the plank between us. Let's try that again with a little tongue." But he finally came around the plank and took her elbow, leading her toward the nonexistent door. She could tell, though, that the kiss had flustered him, for he talked nervously all the way home, about how she was right and he'd immediately put in an order for boots so they would arrive in time for the planned October opening, about how there might even be snow by then and he'd better get his wood stacked in the back, and how they would plan a special announcement in the paper, even though everyone in town knew the store would open and when.

He refused to stay for supper, which he'd done quite often recently— indeed, suppers together had become the rule rather than the exception —but collected his materials and left, insisting that he'd better get started putting the order on paper.

That night she tried to analyze her feelings toward David Melcher, to sort out her reasons for encouraging him as she had today. By now she was sure that she was not pregnant, so the biggest potential obstacle to their relationship had been removed. Oddly enough, the overwhelming guilt she had once felt no longer riddled her. She had performed an immoral act, but she did not think she had to pay for it for the rest of her life. She did deserve some happiness, and if David Melcher offered it to her, she no longer believed she'd be deceiving him to take him up on it.

No, her problem with David was no longer a problem of morality, it was one of sexuality. She simply was not stimulated by him. She tried not to think of Jesse . . . oh, she really, really tried. But it did not work. Being kissed as she had been by David, it was impossible not to contrast his kisses with that of the practiced, the fiery, the tempting Jesse. Vivid memories came flooding back until they swept everything from her mind except her intimate knowledge of him. She knew every part of his body as well as she did her own, and it no longer seemed shameful to admit it. She thought of each part of it, wondering if the importance of sexual attraction would wane in time if she married David. Ah, but David had not asked her. Ah, but David would. It would take a little more time, but she was sure he would. And when he did, what would she say? No—I won't marry you because you don't make my blood run high like Jesse? Or yes—because in every other way we are compatible. She thought, as she lay awake into the wee hours, that if she could entice David into displaying more ardor, she might at least have a larger basis of comparison between him and Jesse DuFrayne.

The following evening David accepted her invitation to supper. It was a pleasant meal, shared at her kitchen table in the familiar way they had so often shared such meals. Over coffee, David was hugely complimentary, as he always was.

"What a delicious meal. Everything you make is always delicious. It warms more than a man's stomach."

If she was going to contrast the two men, then let her do it truthfully, and garner for herself an honest choice about them. She let the voice of Jesse echo back, with its infernal teasing, which at the time had so galled her but which now only tempted. "And what are you planning to poison me with this time,

Abbie?" She was unaware of the lingering smile the memory brought to her lips.

"Did I say something funny?" David asked, noting it.

"What?" She brought herself back to the present—regretfully.

"You were laughing just then. What were you thinking?"

"I wasn't laughing."

"Well, your shoulders were moving as if you were laughing inside."

She shook her head. "It was nothing. I'm just glad you enjoyed your supper."

Her answer appeased him. He pushed his chair back from the table, suggesting, "I thought maybe we'd read some of your sonnets after supper. That's all it would take to make the evening perfect."

Why all of a sudden did sonnets sound as dry as his kisses had been?

"You always say the nicest things," she said to atone for the errant thought. I really must be more fair to him, she promised herself, for it was not he who had changed. It was she.

They read sonnets, he sitting on the settee and she sitting on a stiff side chair. The lamps were lit, they had nothing to do but enjoy the verses together. But he sensed an impatience, almost a relief, in her when they finally put the book aside. He puzzled once again at the change he sometimes sensed in her, a restlessness that continued to intrude upon the tranquility he loved and sought.

He kissed her good night. A chaste kiss, David thought. A dry kiss, Abbie thought.

Several days later they sat on the swing in the early evening. September was upon them, the hint of winter not far behind it.

"Something has been . . . bo . . . bothering you, has . . . hasn't it?"

"Bothering me?" But her tone was sharp. She was working on the strips for the rugs, and her hands tore and rolled the rags almost frantically.

"I can tell that I displease you, but I d . . . don't know what it is that br . . . brings it on."

"Don't be silly, David," she said reprovingly. "You don't displease me at all. Quite the contrary."

She ripped a long strip of the cloth, her eyes never leaving it, and the harsh sound scraped on his nerves. He wished that she would stop the rag work while they talked.

"There's no need for you to . . . t . . . try to be kind by disguising it. I would only like t . . . to know what it is that bothers you."

"Nothing, I said!" Her hands were a blur, winding the strips up into a ball. How could she say that everyone in town was expecting the two of them to get married and that she'd give anything if only he would ask her, yet feared more each day that he would? Just how could she explain such a confusion of thoughts to him when she couldn't straighten it out for herself.

Quietly he reached out to lay a hand over hers, which were furiously rolling those rag strips into a tight, tight ball.

"Whatever it is that you call nothing is a very large lump of something. Much larger than I thought. You're winding those rags like you wish they were choking somebody. Is it me?"

She dropped the rag ball into her lap and her forehead onto the heel of her hand, but said not one word.

He sat staring down at the tattered red threads that lay all over her lap like a web. "It started that d . . . day I asked if I could k . . . k . . . kiss you. I could tell you were disgusted w . . . with me. Is that it, Abigail? Are you angry b . . . because I k . . . kissed you?"

She tapped her fingers against her forehead and looked at her lap, not knowing what to say. She didn't know if she wanted him to pursue this subject or not. How could she tell after those two lackluster kisses?

"Oh, David . . ." She sighed heavily and looked away, across the yard.

"What is it? What have I done?" he asked pleadingly.

"You haven't done anything," she said, now wishing fervently that he would so she could know once and for all what she felt for him.

"Abigail, when I first came here I sensed a . . . a rapport between us. I thought you felt it too. I thought how we were the same k . . . kind of people, but . . . well, since I've been back you seem d . . . different."

It was time she admitted the truth.

"I am," she said tiredly.

"How?" he braved.

The tiredness left her and she jumped to her feet, snapping in irritation, "I don't like sonnets anymore." The rag ball rolled onto the porch floor, untwining, but she paid it not the scantest attention. She crossed her arms over her ribs and left him to contemplate her erect shoulder blades.

He sat staring at them, thoroughly befuddled. In a moment she entered the parlor, slamming the screen door shut behind her. He remained on the swing for some time, wondering just what she wanted out of him, wondering what sonnets had to do with anything. Finally he sighed, rose, and limped to the door. He opened it quietly and entered to find her standing before the monstrous throne-shaped umbrella stand, gazing at her reflection in the mirror. As he watched she did a most curious thing. She raised a hand and pressed the backs of her fingers upward against the skin on her jaw, studying the movement in the glass.

"What are you doing?" he asked.

She did not answer immediately, but continued pressing her chin. At last she dropped the hand as if she were very weary, then turned to him with a sad expression on her face, and answered almost dolefully, "Wishing you might kiss me again."

His lips opened slightly and she could almost see his thoughts drift across his transparent face: he'd been worried for so long that he'd gone too far, kissing her in the store that day. He was relieved yet timid, perhaps a tiny bit shocked that she should ask him. But at last he moved toward her, and she read one last look in his face—awe that she should really, really want him.

This time there was no plank between them, but when he kissed her he still held her undemandingly, fragilely. It was like before, only worse, because now, without hindrance, he could have pulled her flush against him, but he didn't. He held her instead in a wan imitation of an embrace, afraid to believe his lips were on hers at last, and with her full consent.

Suddenly she needed to know about David Melcher, about herself. She lifted her arms and they swirled onto his shoulders as she raised up on tiptoe and offered her lips to him with feigned passion. She pressed her breasts against his vested chest, but rather than accepting her invitation he sucked in his breath, taking himself away from the touch of her, afraid the contact was too intimate yet.

"Abigail, I've thought about this for so long," he said, looking into her eyes. "I thought about you and the house and the store and everything, and it just seemed too good to be true to think that you might feel the same about me as I do about you."

"How do you feel, David?" she asked, trying to force the words from him.

He released her fully, properly, stepping back and holding her only by her upper arms. "I want to marry you and live here in this house and work in the store with you by my side."

She had the sinking feeling that he desired all three equally. She had the even more sinking feeling that she did, too.

"I love you," he said then, and added, "I guess I should have said that first."

What could she say to that? Yes, you should have? Tell me again and kiss me and pull me against you and touch my body here and here and inspire me to love you also? Touch my skin, touch my hair, touch my heart and make it race and touch my breast and make my blood pound and touch me beneath my skirt and show me you're as good at it as another man was before you?

But the cool fact was, none of these things happened. He did not kiss her passionately or pull her against him or touch her hair or heart or breast or any other part of her as Jesse had done. Instead, he drew back, gave her shoulders a loving squeeze, controlling all his body's urges with a will that she suddenly detested. He waited for her reply. She moved to him and kissed him, allowing her lips to grow lax, to be opened by his tongue should he choose. But his soft lips remained together, guarded by discretion.

But discretion was the last thing she yearned for. She longed to be reduced —no, heightened—by the ecstasy she knew could sluice through her body should he wield it in just the right way. But standing in David's hands she thought, He's not Jesse. He'll never be Jesse.

But might that not cease to matter? Here he was, offering her safe keeping for life. One did not decline an offer of marriage simply because of the way a man kissed or didn't kiss. She ought to be flattered by his courtliness, not be insulted by it. But Jesse had managed to change her sense of values somewhere along the line.

"There's time enough for you to decide," David was saying. "You don't have to answer me tonight. After all, I know this is a bit sudden."

She had the awful urge to laugh aloud. She had known him over three months and her blouse buttons had never touched his vest, yet he thought his chaste kiss and this invitation sudden.

What would he think if he knew that in three weeks she'd touched every part of Jesse DuFrayne's body and had pleaded with him to take her to the limits?

"Are you sure you want to marry me?" Abigail asked David, knowing it was not him but herself she should be asking.

"I've been quite sure since the day you threw me out after I accused—" But there he stopped, not wanting to bring DuFrayne's name into it, not realizing it had been in it all the time. "Can you forgive me for what I accused you of? I was very foolish and very jealous myself that morning. I know now that you're not at all that kind of woman. You're pure and fine and good . . . and that's why I love you."

If ever there was a point of no return, it was now. Now, when his words could easily be denied if they were going to be. But deny them she did not. She kept her silence, knowing that even it was a lie.

David gave her shoulders one last squeeze. "Besides," he said in a light attempt at gaiety, "what would my store be without you?"

But again she wondered if he did not value her more because she could help in his store, and because he could live in her house, than he did because she could be his wife.

"David, I'm very proud to have been asked. I'd like to think about it, though, at least overnight."

He nodded understandingly, then pulled her toward him by her shoulders and kissed her on the forehead before leaving. He left her standing next to the umbrella stand. For a long moment she stared disconsolately at nothing. Finally she turned her head and confronted her reflection, admitting once and for all how old she was getting. She sighed deeply, rubbed the small of her back, and went out onto the porch to collect the rag ball and rewind it mechanically as she wandered aimlessly into her bedroom. She stood beside the window seat winding, winding, remembering Jesse sitting here that afternoon after Jim Hudson left. She dropped the ball into the sewing basket on the floor, remembering how Jesse had taken a hank of yarn from it to tie up that pig bladder with which he had so mercilessly teased her. She pictured his long-fingered hands, dark of skin, gentle of touch, flexing on that inflated bladder, flexing upon her own breast. She thought of David, afraid to pull her against him as he kissed her on the eve of his marriage proposal to her.

She sighed, dropped down onto the window seat, leaned her elbows to her knees, cupped her face in both hands, and cried.

Fortunately, during that night good common sense took over and made Abigail realize that David Melcher was a decent, honest man who would treat her decently, honestly for the rest of her life. She, too, could offer the same, from here on out. Whether it was scheming or not to consider it, she admitted that David, in his naiveté, would probably not know whether or not she was a virgin anyway. If she were mistaken about that, she would tell him it was Richard, those many years ago. If her marriage had to begin with that one, last lie, it was a necessary lie—necessary to prevent David's being hurt any further. And since there was no chance of her ever falling into promiscuity again, her decision was made.

David kissed her tenderly, if dryly, when she told him that she was accepting his proposal. Standing in his light embrace, she felt a sense of relief that the decision was made. This time he did hug her to his chest, but his eyes were scanning her front parlor.

"Abigail, we're going to be so happy here," he said near her temple. A deep sense of peace overcame him here in her house.

"You'll have roots at last," she returned.

"Yes, thanks to you."

And to Jesse DuFrayne, she thought, but she said, "And the citizens of Stuart's Junction."

"I think they were half expecting us to get married."

"I know they were, especially after the Fourth of July."

He released her, smiling his very youngish smile. "When shall we announce it?"

She looked thoughtful for a moment, then quirked an eyebrow. "How about in Thursday's paper? Mr. Riley started all this when he linked my name with yours in June. Shall we give him the opportunity to print the ensuing chapter?"

The announcement in Thursday's paper read:

> Miss Abigail McKenzie and Mr. David Melcher happily announce their intentions to be married on October 20, 1879, in Christ Church, Stuart's Junction. Miss McKenzie, a lifetime resident of this town, is the daughter of the late Andrew and Martha McKenzie. Mr. Melcher, formerly of Philadelphia, Pennsylvania, has traveled for several years in this area as a circuit salesman for the Hi-Style Shoe Company of that city. Upon marriage to Miss McKenzie, Melcher will open for business in the Melcher Shoe Salon, the edifice currently under construction at the south end of Main Street directly adjacent to Perkins' Livery Stable. The business is slated to open its doors immediately upon the couple's return from a two-week honeymoon in Colorado Springs.

The first frosts came. The quaking aspens blanketed the hills with brilliant splashes of amber. Mornings, even the cart ruts were beautiful, trimmed in rime, glistening in the touch of new light. Sunsets turned the color of melons and became jaggedly streaked with purple, presaging the cold breath of winter soon to follow. The mourning doves left; the nuthatches stayed. Weather eyes were cast at the mountains as the first leaves tumbled like golden gems to the earth.

A flood of good wishes poured into Miss Abigail's house and David's store, which was fast nearing completion. Neighbors and townsfolk could not resist stopping at one place or the other when passing by. Their good wishes reaffirmed to Abigail that she had done the right thing in accepting David's proposal.

It was easy and natural now to be with David, and daily they reaffirmed the fact that they were very much alike in ideals, likes, dislikes, goals. He was a totally adoring suitor, ever ready with a compliment, a smile, a look which told her he approved of her in every way. His kisses became more ardent, which pleased her, but his immense respect for her kept improper advances at bay. He stammered less and less as they became more familiar with each other. This newfound ease pleased her immeasurably.

Often as not, David and Abigail could be found at the shoe store, stacking a winter supply of wood at the rear, staining the lovely spooled rail, building shelves, hanging red draperies in the bow window, carrying in the huge oak rounds, or unpacking a partial shipment of stock, which had finally arrived. They worked together constantly, becoming a fixture of the small town's society even before their wedding took place. Those who stopped by to say hello or to ask if they needed a hand with anything went their way again thinking they'd never seen a pair more suited to each other; it really was a match made in heaven. Some chuckled, patting themselves on the back, thinking, well, if not in heaven, then at Hake's Meadow.

Abigail was a mistress of efficiency as the wedding day neared. Besides helping David make preparations for the opening of the store, there were countless personal details demanding her attention. She had decided to wear her mother's wedding gown of ivory silk, but it needed alterations. The lace veil was in excellent condition. However, some of the seed pearls had come loose from the headpiece and needed replacing, thus it had been sent to a jeweler in Denver for renovation. David had ordered a special pair of white satin pumps for her and she anxiously awaited both headpiece and shoes. Once the entire bridal ensemble was in her possession, she would pose for a photograph—her bridal gift to David. She contracted a Denver photographer, Damon Smith, to come out to do the portrait. They'd planned to have a wedding reception at the house, and Abbie began baking cookies and *petits fours,* freezing them now that frosts had come to stay. The garden was cleaned out until spring. The little iron stove was installed in the store, and the coffee pot there was already a fixture. She was often happy to have it, for between the store and the house, her duties kept her juggling her precious time and attention between wedding and grand opening preparations.

The store was turning out beautifully. There, it seemed, was where Abigail and David shared their closest intimacies. Times when they found themselves alone, stocking shelves in the storeroom, he would steal kisses, making her impatient for their wedding day to arrive . . . and, more importantly, their honeymoon. There were times when she knew he was on the brink of breaking down his own self-imposed restrictions, but either he would back away or they would be interrupted, for people came in and out of the store as if it were already open for business.

The interior was as bright, warm, and cheerful as she'd imagined it, with its red curtains, braided rugs, and upholstered benches. The circle of comfortable chairs wreathed the fireplace where a cheering blaze beckoned. The smell of fresh wood and bark permeated the air, combined with coffee, leather, and the clean smell of shoe wax. People loved it and there were always friends gathered around the stove. There was not a doubt in the world that the business would thrive, or the marriage either.

Chapter 21

IT WAS ONE of those dark, steely late afternoons when the thought of supper in a toasty kitchen made footsteps hurry homeward. The murky clouds played games with the top of the mountain, gathering, scattering—wind-whipped shreds scudding in a darksome sky, making all mortals feel lowly indeed.

The bell and the pearl headpiece had arrived from Denver. Bones Binley had walked the packages up from the depot after the late train pulled through. Pleased, Abigail now donned her new green coat, wrapped a matching scarf about her head, and flung its tails back over her shoulders. Smiling, she left the house with the small brass bell tucked warmly in her white fur muff.

Snow flecks stung her forehead and the wind sent the scarf tails slapping about her cheeks. She shivered. David would already have the lanterns lit at the store. The stove would be warm, and she pictured David standing with one foot braced on its fender, a cup of coffee in his hand. Oh, he would be pleased that she'd thought of the bell. She skipped once and hurried on.

Coming around the corner of the saloon, she stepped up onto the boardwalk and the wind shifted, hitting her full in the face, driving icy needles of snow against her skin. She glanced down the street at the welcome orange lantern-light spilling from the bow window. A man was standing looking in through the small panes, a big man in a heavy sheepskin jacket with its collar turned up and his hands plunged deep into its pockets. He stood motionless, bare-headed, with his back to her, while for some inexplicable reason her footsteps slowed. Then he hung his head low, stared at his boots a moment before turning toward the livery stable next door and disappearing inside. He was very tall, very broad. From behind he'd reminded her of Jesse, except that he had no limp. Once more she hurried, keeping her eyes on the door of the livery stable, but no one came out as she advanced toward the door of the store, above which hung a fresh, new sign, swinging wildly in the wind.

MELCHER'S SHOE SALON, it said, DAVID AND ABIGAIL MELCHER, PROPS.

It was lusciously warm in the store. As usual, there was a circle of men around the stove, David among them, sipping coffee.

He came forward immediately to greet her. "Hello, Abigail. You should have stayed at the house. There's weather brewing out there."

She radiated toward the stove, removing her coat, scarf, and muff, tossing them onto a red-padded bench along the way.

"I had to come to tell you the good news. My headpiece came back from Denver this afternoon, all repaired at last."

"Good!" David exclaimed, then winking at his cronies around the stove, added, "Now maybe I won't have to listen to her fretting about that photograph anymore." The men chuckled and sipped.

"And look what else came." She held up the tinkling, brass bell. "It's for your door—a good luck charm. Every new store must have a bell to announce its first customer."

David smiled in genuine delight and set his coffee cup down, coming to squeeze and chafe her upper arms affectionately. "It's just the right touch. Thank you, Abigail." The smile on his face made her feel treasured and precious. "Here," he said, "let me hang it."

645

"Oh, no," she said pertly, lifting the bell out of his reach, "it's my gift. I shall do the hanging."

David laughed, turning back to the men. "Never saw such a nuisance of a woman—always wants her own way."

"Well, David, you just gotta learn to step on 'er a little bit when she gets outta line." Then the men all laughed in easy camaraderie. They could do that now, laugh at Miss Abigail this way—she had changed so much since David Melcher came around.

She got a hammer and tacks from the back room and hauled one of the chairs up near the front door. The bell tinkled as she climbed up, reaching toward the sill above the door to find the perfect spot for the bracket. But even on the chair she couldn't quite reach, so she put one foot up on the spooled railing beside her and stepped onto it.

That was how Jesse DuFrayne saw her when he came out of the livery stable and stopped again before the shop with the sign reading, . . . DAVID AND ABIGAIL MELCHER . . .

She had two tacks in her mouth and was holding the brass bracket against the doorframe, hammer poised, when she saw a man's legs stop outside the Cape Cod window. With her arms raised that way she could not see his face, but she saw cowboy boots, dark-clad legs spraddled wide against the wind, and the bottom half of a thick, old sheepskin jacket. Something made her duck down to peer beneath her sleeve at the face above those wide-braced legs.

Her eyes widened and one of the nails fell from her lips. An agonizing, wonderful, horrible terror filled her heart.

Jesse! My God, no . . . Jesse.

He was gazing up at her with that big sheepskin collar turned high around his jaw while the wind caught at his thick black hair, whipping it like the dark clouds above the mountain. The lantern glow coming through the window illuminated his face and kindled his dark, intense eyes that were raised in an unsmiling study of her. It lit, too, his forehead, cheeks, and chin, making them stand out starkly against the stormy darkness behind him. His moustache was as black as a crow's wing, and as she stared, hammer forgotten in hand, he smiled just a little and lifted one bare hand from his pocket in silent hello. But still she seemed unable to move, to do anything more than gape as if struck dumb, filled with pounding emotions, all at odds with each other.

Then one of the men behind her asked how she was doing up there, and she came back to life, turning to look over her shoulder at the stove and mutter something. When she looked outside again, Jesse had stepped back beyond the circle of window light, but she could still see his boots and knew he stood there watching her with those jet black eyes and his old familiar half grin.

She scuttled down to search for the tack on the floor, but couldn't find it, so clambered back up again and started hammering the one she had, ever conscious now of the angle from which he studied her, the way her breasts thrust out against her dress front and jiggled with each fall of the hammer.

The other tack winked at her from inside the spooled railing and she climbed down to retrieve it, unable to keep her eyes from seeking the waiting figure beyond the window. For a moment she stood framed by red curtains, like a dumbstruck mannequin on display, quite unable to move her limbs or draw her eyes away from the dim figure who watched from the street, frowning as the wind tried to blow him over.

Jesse, go away, she pleaded silently, terrified of his pull on her.

Somehow her limbs found their ability to move, and she climbed up on the railing again and pounded in the second nail, her heart cracking against her ribs in rhythm with the hammer.

David came from the rear of the store then, admiring her handiwork.

"Should we hang the bell together?" he asked.

"Yes, let's," she choked, hoping he would not note the hysteria in her voice. "That way it will bring good luck to both of us." She could see now that Jesse's legs were gone and wondered if David had spied them out there.

When the bell was on the bracket, David brought her coat and helped her into it. "You'd better get back home before the weather gets worse."

"You're coming up for supper, aren't you?" she asked, trying to keep the desperation from reverberating in her tone.

"What do you think?" he answered, then pulled her scarf protectively around her neck and turned her by the shoulders toward the door before he opened it for her and smiled her away.

The bell tinkled.

Two steps outside she turned, imploring, "Hurry home, David."

"I will."

She lowered her head to hold the scarf more tightly around her neck, but the wind lifted its fringed end and threw it back at her face. She scanned the dark street ahead.

He was gone!

The snow was fine and stinging and had glazed the streets with dangerous ice, which left no tracks for her to either follow or avoid. The wind slashed at her back, buffeting her along the slick boardwalks while her skirts luffed like a mainsail in a gale. She looked into each lighted store as she passed but he was in none of them. Turning at the saloon corner, the wind eddied into a whirl-pool and twisted her skirts about her with renewed mastery. She ducked her head, hanging on to her scarf to keep it on her head, pulling her chin down low into her coat collar.

"Hello, Abbie."

Her head snapped up as if the trap door of a gallows had opened beneath her feet. His voice came out of the wild darkness, so near that she realized she'd nearly bumped into him rounding the corner. He stood with feet spread wide, hands in pockets, the swirling wind lifting his white, misty breath up and away.

"Jesse," she got out, "I thought it was you." She had come to a stop and could not help staring.

"It was."

The way they stood, the wind pelted his back but riveted the icy snow into her face, stinging it. She had forgotten how big he was, strapping wide and so tall that she had to look up sharply to see his face.

"What are you doing here?" she asked, but her teeth had begun to chatter, the cold having little to do with it.

"I heard there's going to be a wedding in town," he said, as conversationally as if they were still in her summer garden on a mellow, floral afternoon.

Without asking, he withdrew a bare hand from his pocket and turned her by an elbow so that her back was to the wind, his face into it. He moved her nearer the clapboard wall, stood close before her, and jammed his hand back into his pocket again.

"How did you know I was getting married?"

"I figured it before I left, so I kept my eye on the papers."

"Then why didn't you just stay away and leave us in peace?"

His smileless face looked as ominous as the roiling clouds that had brought on the early dark. He scowled, black brows curling together as he ignored her question and asked one of his own.

"Are you pregnant?"

He couldn't have stunned her more had he kicked her in the side of the head with his slant-heeled cowboy boot.

"Why, you insufferable—" But the wind stole the rest of her lashing epithet, muffling her voice as the scarf flapped at her lips.

"Are you pregnant!" he repeated, hard, demanding, standing like a barrier before her. She moved as if to lurch around him, but he blocked her way simply by taking a step sideways, with his hands still buried in his pockets, keeping her between his bulk and the saloon wall.

"Let me past," she said coldly, glaring up at him.

"Like hell I will, woman! I asked you a question and I deserve an answer."

"You deserve nothing and that is precisely what you shall get!"

In an injured tone he went on, "Damnit, Abbie, I left him enough money to set the two of you up in high style for life. All I want in return is to know if the baby is mine."

Rage swooped over her. How dare he sashay into town and imply such a thing—that she had allowed David to make love to her to disguise the mistake she'd made with him, Jesse. At that moment she hated him. She wound up and swung, forgetting that the muff was on her hand. It caught him on the side of the face, doing no damage whatsoever with the soft white rabbit's fur, the pathetic attempt at violence made all the more pitiful by its ineffectuality.

With his hands in his pockets he couldn't block her swing in time, but shrugged and feinted to one side and the muff glanced off his cheek and rolled away onto the icy street behind him.

She made a move toward it, but he caught her by the shoulders, swinging her in a half circle to face him.

"Listen to me, you! I came back here to get the truth out of you and—by God!—I'll have it!"

She skewered him with her eyes and moved again as if to pick up the muff. But he pushed her back against the wall, his eyes warning her not to move, then he knelt and retrieved the muff, but when he handed it to her she had forgotten all about it.

"You despicable goat!" she cried, tears now freezing paths down her cheeks. "If you think I'm going to stand here in the middle of a blizzard and be insulted by you again, you are sadly mistaken!"

"All it takes is a simple yes or no," he argued, holding her in place while the wind threatened to rip them both off their feet. "Are you pregnant, damnit!"

Again she tried to jerk away, but his fingers closed over her coat sleeves like talons. "Are you?" he demanded, giving her a little shake.

"No!" she shouted into his face, stamping her foot and at last spinning free, running away from him. But the ground was glare ice now and a little foot flew sideways, and the next thing she knew she was sprawled at his feet. Immediately he went down on one knee and reached for her elbow, still holding the white muff in his massive, dark hand.

"Abbie, I'm sorry," he said, but she shook his hand off, sat up and whisked at her skirts, fighting back tears of mortification. "Damnit, Abbie, we can't talk here," he said, reaching as if to aid her once more, but she slapped his hand away.

"We cannot talk anywhere!" she exploded, still sitting on the street, glaring up at him. "We never could! All we could ever do was *fight,* and here you are, back for more. Well, what's the matter, Mr. DuFrayne, couldn't you find any other woman to force yourself on?"

All traces of temper left his voice as he looked into her angry eyes, kneeling there on one knee, engulfed in that dreadfully masculine sheepskin jacket, and said simply, "I haven't been looking for one."

God help me, she thought, and gathered her outrage about her like armor, struggling to her feet while he held her elbow solicitously and offered her the muff, which she yanked out of his hand. As she swung away and stalked up the street again, everything in her stomach threatened to erupt.

He watched her retreating back a moment, then called out to her, "Abbie, are you happy?"

Don't! Don't! Don't! she wanted to scream at him. Not again! Instead, she whirled into the banshee wind and yelled, "What do you care! Leave me alone. Do you hear! I've been screaming it to an empty house for three months now, but at last I can scream it to you in person. *Get out of my life, Jesse DuFrayne!*"

Then she spun again toward home, running as best she could on the precarious ice.

For some minutes after she rounded Doc's corner and disappeared, Jesse stared at the empty street, then he stamped the gathering snow off his boots and turned back toward the corner saloon. Inside, he ordered a drink, sat brooding until it arrived, then downed it in a single gulp, his mind made up. He'd damn well go back up to her place and get some answers out of that woman!

The roses were gone now from beside her white pickets, which looked forlorn in the wintry gale. Walking up the path he studied the porch. The wicker furniture was gone now. The swing hung disconsolately, shivering in the wind as if a ghost had just risen from it—maybe two. He took the steps and peered through the long oval window of her front door. He could see her rump and the back of her skirts at the far end of the house. It looked like she was bending over, putting wood into the kitchen range.

Hitching his collar up, he rapped on the door, watching her hurry toward him down the length of the house. He stepped back into the shadows.

As she opened the door, she began, "Supper's not ready yet, David, but it —" The words died upon her lips as Jesse stepped into the light. She lurched to slam the door, but his long fingers curled around the edge of it and a boot wedged it open at the floor.

"Abbie, can we talk a minute?"

Her cheeks made up for the missing roses outside.

"You get off my front porch! Do you hear me, *sir.* That is all I need right now, for you to be seen here." She darted a look beyond him, but the yard and street were empty.

"It won't take a minute, and shouldn't an old friend be allowed to wish the bride well?"

"Go away before David comes and sees you here. He is coming for supper any minute."

"Then I can congratulate the groom too."

Her eyes quickly assessed the hand and boot holding the door open; there was no possible way she could force him to leave.

"Neither David nor I wish anything from you except that you be gone from our lives." The cold air swirled into the house causing the flames to flicker in the lanterns. Jesse's hand was nearly frozen to that door.

"Very well. I'll leave now, but I'll be seeing you again, *Miss Abigail.* I still owe you one photograph and that twenty-three dollars I borrowed from you."

Then, before she could harp once more about wanting absolutely nothing from him, he released the door, bounded down the porch steps, hit the path at a run, and jogged off toward town, kicking up snow behind him.

His limp was completely gone.

When David arrived for supper, Abigail's greeting was far warmer than usual. She took his arm and squeezed his hand, saying, "Oh, David, I'm so glad you're here."

"Where else would I be three days before my wedding?" he asked, smiling.

But she squeezed his arm harder, then helped him out of his coat. "David, you're so good for me," she said, holding his coat in both arms against her body, hoping, hoping, that it was true.

"Why, Abigail, what is it?" he asked, noting the glitter of tears in her eyes, moving to take her in his arms.

"Oh, I don't know," she said chokily. "I guess it's all the plans and jitters and getting everything done in time. I've been so worried about the headpiece not arriving in time for the photograph, and now this storm is starting and what if the photographer can't make it in from Denver?" She backed away, swiped at a single tear which had spilled over, and said to the floor between them, "I guess I'm just having what I've heard most brides have sooner or later—an attack of last-minute nerves."

"You've done too much, that's all," he sympathized. "What with the store and the preparations for the reception and getting all your clothes ready for the ceremony and our trip. It isn't *all* necessary, you know. I've told you that before."

"I know you did," she said plaintively, feeling foolish now at her display of jangling nerves, "but a woman has only one wedding in her lifetime and she wants it perfect, with all the amenities."

He circled her shoulders with an arm and herded her toward the kitchen. "But most women have mothers and sisters and aunts to help carry the load. You're doing too much. Just make sure you don't overdo it, Abigail. I want you well and happy on Saturday."

His concern made her feel somewhat better, but it was extremely difficult to forget that somewhere out there Jesse DuFrayne was spending the night, and should David encounter him between now and Saturday and stir up old animosities, there was no telling what might happen. The results could be unpleasant, to say the least, disastrous, to say the most. For she wouldn't put anything past Jesse.

All through supper she found her thoughts returning time and again to one plaguing question: would Jesse stoop so low that he'd tell David about what they'd done together?

An instinct for preservation made her broach the subject of Richard. David was relaxed and lethargic, sitting back on the settee with his hands laced over his full stomach, feet outstretched and crossed at the ankle.

"David?"

"Yes, Abigail?" He had never taken to using any shortened form of her name like Jesse had. It had always disappointed her just a little.

"Did I ever tell you I was engaged once?" She knew perfectly well she'd never told him before. He suddenly sat up and took interest. "It was long ago —when I was twenty."

She could tell by the stunned look on his face that there were a hundred questions he wanted to ask, but he just sat there waiting for her to go on.

"His name was Richard and he grew up here in Stuart's Junction. We . . . we used to play hopscotch together. I'm actually surprised that nobody has mentioned his name to you because people around here have long memories."

"No, nobody has," he said, red around the collar.

"I just thought that you should know, David, before we got married. We've never spoken much about our pasts. We've had such a mutual interest in our future, with the store to plan and everything, that it has rather superseded other topics, hasn't it?"

"Perhaps it has—you're right. But if you don't want to tell me about Richard you don't have to. It doesn't matter, Abigail."

"I want to," she said gazing at him directly, "so that perhaps you'll understand my sudden jitters." Then she looked at her lap again as she went on. "There had never been anyone except Richard, and we more or less grew up suspecting that one day we'd marry. My mother died when I was nineteen, and within a short time Richard and I became engaged. I was very young and naive and believed in such things as destiny then." She paused, creating the effect of the passage of time in her narrative. Then she sighed. "Richard apparently believed differently, though, for when my father fell ill and became a total invalid within a year of my mother's death, it seems Richard found me less desirable as a future wife. I guess you might say he considered my father excess baggage. At any rate, my . . . my fiancé disappeared scarcely a week before the wedding. His family moved too, shortly afterward, and I have never seen them or him since."

David's face wore a caring expression. He reached for her hand. "I'm sorry, Abigail. I truly am."

She looked up at his gentle, unassuming face, knowing at that instant just what a good, moral man he was and knowing also that she was very lucky to have found someone like him so late in her life.

"I understand your jitters now," he said into her eyes, "but I would never leave you like he did. Surely you know that."

"Yes, I do," she assured him. But she felt small and guilty, for she knew he was too good to read into her story the possibility that she and Richard had been intimate. "David," she said, really meaning what she was about to say, "I do so want everything to be perfect in our lives together, that's all."

"It will be," he promised. But he promised it holding nothing more than her hand, and she could not help thinking that this was the kind of thing which two people in love should be sharing wrapped up tightly in each other's arms. "I'm glad you told me, Abigail. I could see that something had you upset tonight, and now that the story is out, consider it forgotten."

At last he kissed her, and she clung to him with a sudden desperation very much unlike her. Taking his lips away, he said, "I think it's best if I go now, Abigail."

But she clung harder, willing him to stay a little longer, to keep the threat of Jesse DuFrayne at bay. "Do you have to go so soon?"

He put her firmly away from him. "You can use a good night's rest, you said so yourself a while ago. I'll see you tomorrow evening, like we agreed."

He kissed her at the door before leaving, but he had put on his overcoat first, so all of the warm contact of hugging was lost in the bulk of woolen coat and muslin skirt.

Chapter 22

IMMEDIATELY AFTER DAVID left, Abbie dressed for bed and retired, wanting to get the lanterns blown out as quickly as possible. The wind buffeted the house, rattling shingles, tapping barren branches against eaves, promising a full night of its wrath. The storm sounds only multiplied her trepidation. Resolutely she closed her eyes and recounted the needs David effectively fulfilled in her life: security, companionship, admiration, love. She spent time analyzing each. He was paving the way to the most secure life she had ever known. Companionship was unquestionable—they had recognized it between themselves from the first. And when it came to admiration—out of all the people she'd known in her entire life none had been more complimentary, appreciative, or admiring. And love—

Her thoughts were hammered to an abrupt halt by the loudest beating her back door had ever suffered. Nobody ever came to her back door. She knew before her feet hit the icy floor who it would be and realized she'd been lying there riddling herself with thoughts of David to keep them off of Jesse DuFrayne.

For a moment she considered letting him bang away until he gave up, but then he shouted at the top of his lungs, and even above the howling storm, she was afraid someone next door would hear.

She found her wrapper and hurried to the back door, listening, her toes curled against the drafty floorboards. He banged and hollered again so she lit a lantern but left the wick low, almost guttering, still afraid of anyone seeing him through the windows.

"Abbie, open up!"

She did, but only partway, refusing to step back and let him in.

He was standing in the wind and snow, hair, eyebrows, and moustache laced with the stuff, determination boring into her from eyes as black as the night.

"I told you to keep away from me. Do you realize what time of the night it is?"

"I don't give a damn."

"No, you never did."

"Are you going to let me in or not? Nobody saw me, but they sure as hell will hear me beat the door down if you slam it in my face again." The wind invaded the house while she clutched her wrapper together over her breast-bone. Her feet were freezing and the wrapper did little to protect her against the shudders that overtook her.

Suddenly he ordered, "Get in there before you freeze to death along with me," and in he came, filling the kitchen with ten pounds of sheepskin jacket, three inches of wet moustache, and nearly two hundred pounds of stubbornness.

She lit into him before he even got the door shut. "How dare you come barging in here as if you owned the place! Get out!"

He just gave a large, exaggerated shiver, rubbed his palms together, and exclaimed, "God, but it's cold out there!" completely ignoring her order, shrugging out of his jacket without so much as a by-your-leave. "We're going to need some wood on that fire to keep us from freezing solid." He jerked a chair from the kitchen table, clapped it down right in front of the stove, hung his jacket on the back of it, then opened a stove lid and reached for a log from the woodbox—all this time he hardly looked at her.

"This is my house and you are not welcome in it. Put that wood back in my woodbox!"

Again he paid no heed but stuffed the wood into the stove, replaced the lid, then turned and bent over at the waist, brushing snow curds from his hair. He spied her bare toes peeking from beneath the hem of her wrapper, pointed at them, and said, "You'd better get something on those tootsies, tootsie, because this is going to take a while."

By this time she was livid. "This will take no time at all because you are leaving. And don't call me tootsie!"

"I'm not leaving," he said matter-of-factly.

She knew he meant it. What was she supposed to do with a bull-headed fool like him? She clenched her fists and grunted in exasperation while he took another chair and clapped it down beside the first, then stood back with a thumb hooked in his waistband.

"We've got some talking to do, Abbie."

The frost was melting from his moustache now and a drop fell from it as he stood patiently waiting for her to give in and sit down. His nose was red from the cold, hair glistening and tousled from its recent whisking. He looked more like a gunslinger than ever in those boots and denims, dark shirt and rough leather vest. His skin was swarthy, the perfect foil for his black hair, moustache, and swooping sideburns. He might have ridden in from the range just now after rounding up cattle in the blizzard or outrunning a posse. His appearance was totally masculine, from the clothing to the ruddy cheeks, the wind-reddened nose to the untidy hair. Her eyes fell to his hip—no gun.

"You don't have to be afraid of me, Abbie," he assured her, following the direction of her eyes. Then he drew a handkerchief from his hip pocket and blew his nose, all the while studying her above the hankie, his eyes refusing to let her go.

How could her feelings betray her like this? How could she stand here thinking that even the way he blew his nose was attractive? Yet it was. Oh, Lord, Lord, it was because Jesse DuFrayne was undeniably all man. Angry with herself for these thoughts, she lashed out at him.

"Why did you come here again? You know that if David finds out, he'll be terribly angry, but I suppose you're planning on that. You haven't done enough to me, have you?"

He bent forward at the waist, reaching behind to stuff the hankie away in his pocket, and said calmly, "Come on, Abbie, sit down. I'm half-frozen from standing out there waiting for him to leave." Then he sat down himself and held his palms toward the heat.

"You've been standing out in the street watching my house? How dare you!"

He continued leaning toward the stove, not even bothering to turn around as he said, "You're forgetting that I'm financing this setup. I figure that gives me plenty of rights around here."

"Rights!" She came one angry step closer behind him. "You come in here spouting rights to me in my own house and put wood in my stove and . . . and sit on my chair and say you have rights? What about my rights!"

He slowly brought his elbows off his knees, straightened his shoulders almost one muscle at a time, sighed deeply, then got up from the chair with exaggerated patience, and swaggered across the room to her with deliberate, slow clunking bootsteps. His eyes told her he'd put up with no more of her defiance. And he took her upper arm in one hand, the back of her neck in the other, then steered her toward the pair of chairs. This time when he ordered, "Sit down," she did.

But stiffly, on the very edge of the chair, her arms crossed tightly over her chest while she poised like a ramrod. "If David finds out about this and I lose him I'll . . . I'll . . ." But she spluttered to a stop, unable to find harsh enough words, he infuriated her so.

Jesse just stretched his long legs out and leaned back, relaxed, fingers laced over his stomach. "So are you happy with him then?" he asked, studying her stiff profile.

"When you left here that was the last thing on your mind!"

"Don't make assumptions, Abbie. When I left here things were in a jumble and I don't like leaving things in a jumble, so I came back. When I didn't hear from you but I read that you were getting married, I had to know for sure if you might be in a family way."

She pierced him with a malevolent look. "Oh, that's big of you—really big!" she spit. "I suppose I should get all fluttery at your tardy concern."

"I hadn't thought you might, not after the iceberg treatment I got on my way out of here that morning." He grinned crookedly, and out of nowhere there came to Abbie the memory of Jesse in that stunning verdigris suit, bending to her on one knee.

"Well, you deserved it," she said petulantly, but with a little less venom.

"Yes, I guess I did," he admitted good-naturedly, an amiable expression about his eyes.

Behind them the low-burning lantern guttered, sending their shadows dancing on the wall behind the stove. Before them the fire grew, licking against the isinglass window in the cast-iron door of the stove. Outside the wind keened, and for a moment they looked at each other, thinking back.

Then Jesse asked softly, "You're not, are you, Abbie?"

"Not what?"

"Pregnant."

Beleaguered once again by those conflicting emotions that this infernal man could always rouse in her, she turned to stare at the isinglass window. She was so confused. All he had to do was walk in here and start being nice and it started all over again. She pulled her feet up off the drafty floor, hooked her heels over the edge of the chairseat, and hugged her knees up tight, laying her forehead on her arms.

"Oh, Jesse, how could you?" she asked, the words coming muffled into the cacoon of her lap. "Out there in the street you practically accused me of . . . of consorting with David to confuse the issue of . . . of this nonexistent paternity."

"I didn't mean it to sound that way, Abbie." He touched her elbow, but she jerked it away, still keeping her head buried in her arms.

"Don't touch me, Jesse." Now she looked up, accusingly, "Not after that."

"All right . . . all right." He put his hands up as if a gun were pointed at him, then slowly lowered them as he saw the fierce, hurt expression on her face.

"Just why did you have to come back here? Didn't you do enough the first time without coming back to haunt me?"

Their eyes locked, held for a moment, while he asked softly, "Do I haunt you, Abbie?"

She looked away. "No, not in the way you mean."

He looked down at her bare toes curling over the edge of the chair, then sprawled back lazily, studying her while he slung a wrist over the back of her chair. "Well, you haunt me," he admitted. "I guess that's why I came back, to settle all the misunderstandings between us that still haunt me." Without removing his wrist from the chair back, he took a lock of her hair between index and middle fingers, rubbing the silky skein back and forth a couple of times. At the fluttering touch she worked her shoulder muscles in an irritated gesture and pulled her head forward to free the hair.

"I thought we understood each other fully that last day," she said, hugging her knees tighter.

"Not hardly."

Memories of that last day came hurtling back as they sat side by side, warming by the stove, warming to each other again, anger dissipating with the cold. Something unwanted seemed to seep into their pores along with the radiating warmth from the stove. After some time her voice came again, small and injured.

"Why didn't you tell me you knew David was coming back before we . . ." But she was afraid to finish. He was too near to put that into words.

He considered her for a long moment before asking quietly, "Why didn't you go back upstairs when I told you to?"

But neither of them had the answers to these questions that echoed through the windswept night. Abbie lowered her forehead onto her crossed arms again and silently shook her head. She heard Jesse move, sitting forward on the edge of his chair, leaning his elbows on his knees again.

"Is there any coffee in that pot?"

She got up, lifted the blue-speckled pot, found it full, then placed both palms around it. He watched from under lowered brows, reminded of those hands upon him, feeling for fever. She disappeared into the dark pantry.

There, alone, she pressed her hands to her open mouth as if it might help her control this urge to cry when she got back out there where he could see her.

His eyes followed her as she came back out with cups, filled them, then turned to find he had removed his boots and braced his feet up on the fender of the range to warm them. Wordlessly she handed him his cup, their eyes locked while he lowered his feet so she could step past to her chair.

Side by side they sipped, not talking, both of them staring introspectively at the little patch of fire visible through the stove window. He rested his feet once more against the fender while she wound her toes around each other. There was something about sitting barefoot together before a snapping fire that was disconcertingly calming. Animosity ebbed away, leaving them almost at peace with each other.

"Did you think that I knew Melcher was coming back to stay?" he asked without turning to look at her.

"Well, didn't you?" she asked his toes. She remembered what his feet looked like bare and was conscious of how bare her own were right now.

"I know that's what you've been thinking all these months, but it's not true. I knew he was coming for the meeting the next day, but I had no idea he'd end up staying."

She turned to study his profile, following the line of his forehead, nose, moustache, and lips that were lit to a burning, glowing yellow-red. He lifted his cup, took a swallow, and she watched his Adam's apple lift and settle back down. He was, she admitted, a decidedly handsome man.

Almost tiredly she said, "Don't lie to me anymore, Jesse. At least don't lie."

He lifted his eyes to hers, to the firelight dancing away on her smileless face. "I never lied to you. When did I lie?"

"Silence can be a lie."

He knew she was right. He had deceived her by his silence many times, not only about Melcher coming back, but about owning the railroad and being the one who paid her for his keep. She took a drink of coffee, then held the cup carefully in both palms, looking down into it.

"You knew what hopes I'd pinned on him, Jesse, you knew it all the time.

How could you not tell me?" She looked perhaps seventeen, and broken-hearted and all golden-skinned in the blush of the dancing firelight. It was all he could do to keep both of his hands around his cup.

"Because if I'd told you he was coming back I couldn't have had you that night, isn't that right?"

Startled, she found his eyes. She didn't know what to say. All this time she had thought . . .

"B . . . but Jesse," she said, eyes gone wide, "it was I who came to you that night. it was I doing the asking."

"No it wasn't." He scanned her face, those wide eyes which looked black in the shadowy kitchen, then forced himself to look away. "Not from the first day it wasn't. It was me, always me, right up to the very end, trying to break you down until I finally succeeded. But you know something, Abbie?" He pulled his stocking feet off the fender, leaned elbows to knees and spoke into the depths of his coffee cup. "When it was over, I didn't like myself for what I'd done."

At that moment the lantern on the table behind them guttered, spluttered, and went out. Shaken, she studied the back of his neck, the hair that grew thick and curling about his ear. "I don't understand you at all."

He glanced back over his shoulder. "I want you to be happy, Abbie. Is that so hard to understand?"

"I just . . . it doesn't . . . well, it doesn't fit the Jesse I know, that's all."

He eyed her over his shoulder for a moment longer, then turned his eyes to the fire again and took a drink of coffee. "What fits me then? The image of a train robber? You're having trouble untangling me from that image. That's part of the reason I came back here. Because I cared what you thought of me afterward, and that's never happened to me before with a woman. You're different. The way we started out was different. We started so . . ." But he stopped, going back to the beginning in his thoughts, enjoying some memories, sorry about some others, but unable to encapsulate his feelings into words.

"How did we start?" she encouraged, wondering what he'd been about to say.

"Oh, all the fighting and baiting and getting even. When I woke up the first time in this house and found out how I got here, you know how mad I was, and you were convenient so I took it out on you. But I just didn't want you to go on thinking that I was still getting even that last night when we made love. That had nothing to do with getting even."

She realized there had been countless times since when she'd thought exactly that. It was part of what haunted her. He looked back over his shoulder, but she was afraid to meet the disturbing eyes of this new, sincere Jesse.

"Is that what you thought, Abbie? That I made love to you so I could hand Melcher the money with one hand and a soiled bride with the other and watch him squirm while he decided what to do with them?" He still sat a little forward of her, coffee cup slung on a single finger, empty, forgotten, looking back, waiting for the answer she was afraid to give. "Did you?" he quietly insisted.

And at last her eyes could not resist. They trembled to find him as she managed to choke out, "I . . . d . . . didn't want to."

Her words were greeted by a long silence before Jesse sat back in his chair, crossing an ankle over a knee so his stockinged foot brushed her gown, almost touching her knee. One dark hand fell over his anklebone, the other dangled the cup over his upraised knee.

"Abbie, I'm going to tell you the truth, whether you believe it or not. It *was* conscience money I gave Melcher, but not because I'd shot him. It wasn't him I was paying off, it was you, because I felt guilty about the night before. But I swear to you, the idea came to me in the middle of that arbitration meeting. I figured if I gave him that much money he *could* settle here and probably *would.* Oh, I admit I forced his hand a little bit, but I didn't do it to put you on the spot, Abbie. Not at all. I thought if I could fix it so you could have him and a nice cozy marriage and a nice cozy business and a secure financial future, I'd have you off my conscience."

She looked at the side of his face. He was watching the coffee cup as he tapped it on his knee.

"And am I?"

The cup fell still. He looked into her eyes.

"No."

She picked at a thread on her lap. "Are you always so generous with your mistresses?" she asked, seeking to break this spell of madness that was weaving itself about them like some silken, seductive web.

He surprised her by simply answering, "No."

She realized she'd been expecting him to deny the others, and that it suddenly hurt when he didn't. What did it matter that there had been others? Yet she could not look him in the eye for fear he'd understand more about her feelings for him than was prudent at the moment.

"Wouldn't it have been much easier to just turn me away when I came to you?"

His foot came off his knee and hit the floor and he was on his feet, suddenly absorbed in refilling his cup. With his back to her, he answered, "Hardly." Then he took a long pull of coffee while, stunned, she stared at the thick hair on the back of his neck. He stood there for a long time before finally asking, "Did you know you were the first woman who ever said no to me, Abbie?"

Again he had managed to surprise her; what he said made no sense.

"But I—"

He turned to face her suddenly, interrupting. "Don't blame yourself, Abbie, not one more time. It was me who did the asking, no matter who came to whose room, and you know it. But you were different from the rest."

"I should think that in bed one woman is no different from the rest."

His hand shot out, grabbed her by the chin, and lifted her face roughly. He looked for a moment like he might strike her. "You cut it out, Abbie! You know damn well you were different and that it was more than your just being a virgin. It was all we'd been through together that made you different. That and the fact that you'd saved my life."

Suddenly, at his angry touch, at the intensity in his eyes, she felt her own sting with tears. She twisted her chin out of his grip, her eyes never leaving his as at last she unburdened herself.

"Do you know how low I thought you were for using what I didn't know against me? For not telling me David was coming back? For not telling me you owned the railroad? For not telling me it was your money that was . . . was paying me off like . . . like some whore?"

"Abbie—"

"No, let me finish. I've been angry at how you sashayed out of here and thought a little tumble in the hay didn't matter to a woman like me, who—"

"I never thought—" He sat down, putting one hand on the back of her chair again.

"Be quiet!" she ordered. "I want you to know what hell you put me through, Jesse DuFrayne, because you did . . . you did. You made me feel unworthy of David's love, like I had no right to marry him even if he asked. You cannot imagine what that did to me, Jesse. I don't want you to leave here with a clear conscience. I want it to hurt you like it did me, because even after you were gone all I had to do was walk through this house to be reminded of what I'd done with you, or to walk into David's store to be reminded that you'd paid for it all. Even there you seemed to be laughing at me from the very walls you'd financed. I wanted to strike back at you, but there was no way, and I'd begun to think I couldn't be free of you."

"Do you want to be?"

"I want it more than anything in the world," she said in utter sincerity.

"Meaning you're not?" He looked up at her hair, down at her trembling lips.

"No, I'm not. Maybe I'll never be, and that's why I'm glad I'm on your conscience. Because all it would have taken was one single statement of fact that night and none of this guilt would have been necessary. Now I face a wedding night of . . ." She looked down at her lap. ". . . of questionable outcome, to say the least. And you say *you* want a clear conscience?"

"Abbie," he pleaded, moving nearer, turning to face her, with his hand still on the back of her chair. "I told you, I didn't know he'd stay—"

But she cut him off. "You realize, don't you, that I still stand to lose it all. Now, when I am on the very brink of everything I ever hoped for—a husband who thinks the sun rises and sets on me, a business that will mean security for as long as we live." She looked up at him squarely. He was very close, leaning toward her. "Why, I've even acquired an acceptance from this community that I never had before I knew David. As his wife I will at last fit in, where before I was nothing more than 'that . . . that *maiden lady* up the street.'"

It grew quiet, all but for the wind and the fire. He studied her, sitting there in her nightgown and wrapper, looking down at her lap. And he suddenly knew that to stay here was to hurt her further.

"What do you want me to say?" he asked miserably. "That I'm sorry?" His fingers touched the back of her hair again, but she did not flinch away this time. "I am. You know it. I'm sorry, Abbie." She looked up and found his face filled with sincerity, all hint of smile or teasing erased.

"I've gone through hell because of you, Jesse. Maybe sorry isn't enough. I knew from the first day David told me he was going to settle in Stuart's Junction that he was settling here because of me. I knew he had me on a pedestal, but I couldn't tell him differently. He would never, never understand why I did what I did with you. But do you know what my deception is doing to me, inside?"

It was clear to Jesse what it was doing to her. He could see the pain in her face and wished he had not been the cause of it. He moved back a little bit.

"What will you say on your wedding night if he suspects?"

Her eyes moved to the isinglass door. "That it was Richard."

"You've told him about Richard?" he asked, surprised.

"Not all that I've told you, but enough."

"Will he believe you?"

She smiled, somewhat ruefully. "He's not like you, Jesse. He hasn't had every woman who came along the pike."

Repeatedly he lifted the hair from the back of her neck, letting it drop back down. Very quietly he said to her ear, "There've been no women along my pike since I left here."

Shivers tingled up her spine and down her arms. But he was what he was. "I'm going to marry David, Jesse. He's very good for me."

"So was I once."

"Not in that way."

"In lots of ways. We could always talk, and laugh and—"

"And fight?"

His hand stopped toying with her hair for a second. "Yes, and fight," he admitted unabashedly, with a smile in his voice.

"Even after you left I was still fighting you. When I read the truth in that newspaper the day after the meeting I smoldered for days."

He grinned. "You were always good at smoldering," he said, low in his throat.

"Remove your arm from the back of my chair, Mr. DuFrayne, or I shall smolder all over again."

"The name's Jesse," he said, leaving the arm where it was.

"Oh, spare me from all that again. The next thing I know you'll be claiming you're a train robber with a bullet in your hip."

He laughed and squeezed the back of her neck, then gave it a gentle shake and rubbed her earlobe with his thumb. "Let's see you smolder a little bit, huh, Abbie? For old times' sake?" His hand left her neck and he got her by a little piece of hair and yanked it lightly.

But she calmly faced him, repeating, "I'm going to marry David Melcher and until I do you're going to get out of my house and out of my life."

He finally faced the stove again, stretched out with his hands on his stomach, slung down low with the nape of his neck hooked on the chair back.

"Did you really have to scream that to the empty rooms when I was gone?"

"Oh, don't let your ego swell up so," she said testily. "I hated you every time I did it."

He rolled his face her way.

"You never hated me."

"Yes I did."

"You hate me now?"

But instead of answering, she stretched out on her chair too, putting her feet up on the fender beside his.

"Tell me now that you hate me," he challenged, moving his foot to cover the top of hers.

"I will if you don't get your foot off mine and leave here this very minute."
He got her foot now between both of his, rubbed it sensuously.

"Make me."

She looked at him to find the old teasing smile back on his lips, certain at
that moment that if she could make him believe her, she would at last be free
of him. She lounged there on her chair, just as indolently as he, and said
without a qualm, "You are still convinced that forcefulness is strength, aren't
you? I can't make you go and you know it. But I can repeat what I said long
ago, that David Melcher has all the beautiful and gentle strengths which I
admire in a man, and I'm going to marry him for them."

Jesse perused her silently for a moment, then reached out and took her
hand. Her heart did crazy things, but she watched his thumb stroke hers and
kept outward appearances unruffled.

"You know, I think you really mean it."

"I do," she said, letting him have his way with her hand to prove that she
was no longer affected by him.

"Is he good to you?" Jesse asked, and she suddenly wanted to lace her
fingers with his and pull that hand against her stomach. This was the hardest
of all—it always was—when Jesse became concerned and caring and let it
show in his voice and his touch.

"Always . . . and in all ways," she answered softly.

The wind moaned about something that hurt.

"And is he good *for* you?"

The snow tittered its secrets against the house.

"Abbie?" he persisted when she didn't answer.

"They're one and the same."

"No they're not."

"Then perhaps the question is, am I good for him."

"That goes without saying," came Jesse's gentle words.

To their joined hands she said, "Don't be kind. It's when you've been kind
that we've traditionally made fools of ourselves."

That broke the spell and he released her hand with a light laugh, saying,
"Tell me all about your plans. I really want to hear them."

Funny, she thought, but here she was two days away from her wedding and
she'd never had a friend with whom to discuss it. How ironic that it should be
Jesse who drew her out. But he was right about one thing—they could always
talk, and by now she was feeling very comfortable with him. And for some
reason she was telling him everything. All about the wedding plans, the
reception plans, and about how hard she and David had worked setting up the
store. She told him they were going to Colorado Springs on their honeymoon.

He quirked a cute sideways smile at her and teased, "Oh, so I'm paying for
a honeymoon too?" But then he told her that the store was nicely done. He
could see her hand in it.

And she told how her mother's seed-pearl headpiece had worried her by not
arriving until today for the photograph tomorrow. He asked who she'd hired
to take it and told her he knew Damon Smith. Smith did good work and she'd
be pleased. Then she made him laugh by asking him if he really was a photographer then, and when he smiled at her and said, "You mean you still don't
believe me," they ended up laughing together.

They were getting very lazy and woozy-tired by now, and the conversation was becoming a little punchy and lethargic. She told him he looked more like an outlaw than a photographer in those clothes of his, and he asked if she preferred him in that verdigris suit and she admitted no, these clothes suited him better. From time to time during this lazy exchange, he'd cast that damnably sleepy grin her way before they'd both stare at the isinglass window again, all natural and relaxed and getting sleepier and looser by the minute. The hour ceased to matter as they talked on into the stormy night.

He told her about how he and Jim had started out surveying on a railroad crew and had gone from there to blasting tunnels, building trestles, and even laying tracks before they'd finally started laying down rails of their own, beginning with one little spur line, because by that time they could see the money was not in laying down rails but in owning them. She'd see, he said, when she got to Colorado Springs where all the railroad barons built their mansions.

"You too?" she asked indolently.

"No," he laughed, he didn't go for that stuff. Besides, his railroad wasn't really that big. But he talked more about how photography had started as a diversion for him, then how he'd come to love it.

By this time he was slung low upon his chair, feet crossed on the fender, contented, half-asleep. Still he asked, "And you believe me now?"

"Yes, I guess I do."

It had taken a long time to hear her say that, a long time and a lot of misunderstandings.

The howling night sounds came and went as they sat, listening in companionable silence now.

"It's very late," Abbie finally said. "I think you should be going or my photograph will be of one very wrinkled looking bride tomorrow."

He chuckled, hands rising and falling on his stomach, remembering. "Just like the first time I ever saw you. God, you were a mess, Abbie."

"You certainly have a way with words." But they were both too lazy to care anymore. They rolled their heads to look at each other.

"Don't let me fool you, though, Abbie," he said quietly.

He'd never change, she realized. He'd always be the same teasing Jesse. But he was not for her.

"I'm glad we talked," he said, sitting up at last, stretching, then yawning widely.

She followed suit, stiff and tired. "So am I. But Jesse?"

"Mmm?" he said, blinking slow at her, his hands hanging limp between his knees.

"Could you sneak back into your room without being seen, or will I have to think up quick excuses for David again?"

"Only a fool would be up this late. I'd be sneaking for nothing."

"You will try not to be seen, though, won't you?"

"Yes, Abbie." And for once he didn't tease.

He tensed every muscle in his body then, grasping the back of one hand, stretching them both out before him while he perched on the very edge of his chair in one of those quivering, shivering, all-over stretches that involves legs, stomach, neck, arms, even head. She'd seen him do it a hundred times before.

Memories.

Then he doubled up and began slowly pulling his boots on. Watching, she recalled once when she'd helped him do that.

He stood. He stretched again. He tucked his shirttails in and she got to her feet, standing uncertainly beside him.

He hooked a thumb in his belt and stood there looking at her.

"I guess I'm not invited to the wedding, huh?"

She stilled the wild thrumming of her heart and smiled. "Mr. DuFrayne, you are incorrigible."

Without taking his eyes off her, he reached for his jacket from the back of the chair and shrugged it on. She stood watching every movement, hugging her arms.

The jacket was on. But instead of buttoning it up, he used the front panels to hang his hands on, then just stood there that way, making no move toward the door.

"Well . . ." he said, relative to nothing. She smiled shakily, then shrugged.

"Well . . ." she repeated stupidly.

Then their eyes met. Neither of them smiled.

"Do I get to kiss the bride before I go?" he asked, but there was a husky note of emotion in his voice.

"No!" she exclaimed too quickly, and backed a step away from him, but tripped on the chair rung behind her. He reached for her elbow to keep her from falling, then pulled her slowly, slowly, inexorably into the deep, fuzzy pile of his jacket front. His eyes slid shut while he cupped the back of her head to keep her there against him.

Abbie, he thought, my little hummingbird.

And like the heart of the hummingbird, which beats faster than all others in creation, the heart of Abigail McKenzie felt as if it would beat its way out of her body.

Standing against Jesse felt nothing whatever like standing against David earlier. Jesse's coat was more bulky but through all these thick, thick layers of sheepskin she could feel the thrum of his heart.

"Be happy, Abbie," he said against her hair, and kissed it.

She squeezed her eyes shut tight while a button impressed itself into the soft skin of her cheek.

"I will," she said against the sheepskin and his hammering heart. The big hand moved in her hair, petting it, smoothing it down against her neck, tightening almost painfully as he held her tightly against him for one last second.

Then he stepped back, his hands trailing down her arms until he captured her hands. With a last searching look into her startled eyes, he took her palms to his cheeks and placed them there for a moment, her thumbs resting at the outer corners of his black moustache. His eyelids slid closed and trembled for just a moment. Then he opened them again and said so softly she scarcely heard, " 'Bye, Ab."

Her hands wanted suddenly to linger upon his dark, warm face, to stroke his moustache, touch his eyes, and move from there down his well remembered body. But he squeezed them painfully, and she swallowed and said into his eyes. " 'Bye, Jess."

Then he backed away and stood looking at her all the while he slowly buttoned up his jacket and turned the collar up around his ears.

He turned. The door opened and the snow swirled in about her feet.

And in the silence after the door closed, slicing off a quick chunk of cold, she whispered to the emptiness, " 'Bye, Jess."

⟶ Chapter 23

WHEN ABBIE AWAKENED the following morning and saw her haggard face in the mirror, she was relieved that David wouldn't have a chance to see her this way. They had agreed she would not go down to the store at all today, so she wouldn't see him until seven this evening, when he came by to walk her over to church for their wedding rehearsal.

Assessing herself in the mirror, she found her face a disaster and her nerves ruined. Both needed immediate help.

The best she could do for her face was to give it the astringent benefits of a freshly sliced lemon. The results were an infinite improvement over the perdition which had shown in every pore when she first woke up. She managed to dim the telltale puffiness and shadows beneath her eyes by using handfuls of snow to soothe and invigorate them. After a bath and hair wash, she began to feel even more human. The visible devastation was repaired.

But what about the invisible?

It certainly didn't help her quivering stomach at all to think about Jesse, but she couldn't help it. She paused in putting the finishing touches to her hair. How different Jesse had seemed last night.

Forget him, Abigail McKenzie!

She forced herself to think of David, of the store, the photograph, the practice tonight, the ceremony tomorrow, the reception. The honeymoon. For a moment her thoughts strayed back to Jesse, but she brought them up short.

Go through the list of things that need doing for the reception! Get out the lace tablecloth, lay out the plates, forks, cups. Frost the tea cakes, slice the breads and set them aside. Press Mama's gown. Worry about the snow.

She glanced out the window but the blizzard had blown itself out toward dawn. Still, snow in the mountains often meant delayed trains, since not all lines had adequate snow sheds so trains were forced to wait while crews cleared the tracks after a blizzard like they'd had last night. Suppose the train was late or never came at all. The photograph was no life and death matter, she told herself one minute. Then the next, watched the clock, listening for the whistle, railing, oh, why did it have to snow!

Jesse—with snow melting off his hair, his moustache . . .

Forget him! Think of David. Get your clothing ready to carry to the hotel.

The 9:50 whistle! At last! That meant Damon Smith had arrived and would be setting up his photographic equipment at the hotel.

Did it mean, too, that Jesse was boarding the train to leave town?

Oh yes, yes, please be gone, Jesse.

Would David find out Jesse had been in town, even for such a short time? Did anyone see Jesse returning to the hotel at three o'clock in the morning?

Don't think about it! Pack the pearl headpiece and veil in tissue, cover the wedding dress on its hanger, get shoes ready to take. Your face looks fine, Abbie, quit looking in the mirror! Your dress is beautiful, everything will turn out fine if you simply forget Jesse DuFrayne.

With fifteen minutes to spare, Miss Abigail McKenzie stood before her umbrella stand beside the front door with its lovely oval window. She glanced outside at the windless, dazzling day, dressed as it was in white, in honor of her wedding. On the seat of the umbrella stand were her garments, stacked all neatly. On top of the stack was a pair of delicate white satin slippers of tapering heel and pointed toe—her wedding gift from David.

In the mirror determined eyes stared back at her, chastising Abbie for her foolish, tremulous misgivings. She watched herself draw arms into a new jade green coat with capelet and hood, purchased for her honeymoon trip. She forced herself to refrain from thinking it was Jesse's money that had bought it. She drew her hands into her muff. He'd bought it, too.

Lifting her eyes, she thought, pick up your wedding garments, Abigail McKenzie, and carry them over town and get this photograph taken and get yourself married to David Melcher and quit being a simpering schoolgirl. She thought of how long it had been since she'd checked the tautness of her chin. She need not do that anymore; she was not old. Yet neither was she young. She was in between, and it was a blessed relief not to have to worry about it anymore. David accepted middle age with total unconcern, which made her do the same. She need not fear life passing her by again. From now on there'd be David.

Edwin Young was behind his front desk when Miss Abigail came into the hotel lobby, lightly stamping snow from her feet as she closed the door behind her.

"Here, let me help you with those things, Miss Abigail," he offered, coming across the lobby.

"Thank you, Edwin, but I've got them in hand."

"These're your wedding things, I suspect."

"They certainly are."

"Too bad the weather had to turn nasty right before your wedding."

"I really don't mind the snow," she said. "I had the thought this morning that it makes the entire mountain look as if it dressed up for David's and my wedding."

Miss Abigail sure has changed, Edwin thought, since David Melcher came to town. She was just as nice and common and friendly as could be. A person felt comfortable around her now. Edwin even dared to touch her chin lightly.

"You just keep that smile on your face, Miss Abigail, and—if you'll pardon my saying so—your photograph will be pretty as a picture."

They laughed and Edwin noted how Miss Abigail had lost her loftiness which used to make him think she considered herself a cut above the others in this town.

"I take it Damon Smith has arrived on the morning train as expected?"

"Oh, he sure did, Miss Abigail. Drug in enough gear to photograph the entire population of Colorado, the way it looked."

"I worried about the snow blocking the tracks. I was relieved to hear the whistle."

"Nope. He's here, all right, and if you'll follow me I'll be happy to show you to his room and help you carry these things."

"You don't need to do that, but thank you anyway. As long as I have everything in hand I'll just go up if you'll tell me what room he's in."

"He's in number eight. You sure I can't help you?"

But she was halfway up the stairs by that time.

The long, narrow upstairs hall dissected the building down the middle, with four rooms on either side. Number eight was the last one on the left, where a long window lit the hall, sun glancing in off brilliant snow, giving life to the faded moss roses on the carpet.

Juggling the garments in one arm and holding the ivory dress folded over the other, she knocked on the door with its centered brass numeral eight. She had never been in a hotel room in her life and was rather discomfited at being here now. She intended to make sure the door remained open during the session.

Footsteps came across the floor on the other side of the door and she wondered what Damon Smith would be like. David had met him and thought highly of his work. The doorknob turned and the door was opened by Jesse DuFrayne.

She gaped at him as if she'd gone snowblind. She blinked exaggeratedly, but, no, it was Jesse all right, gesturing with a sweep of hand for her to enter.

"I must have the wrong room," she said, standing rooted to the spot, the eight on the open door seeming to wink at her.

"No, it's the right one," he said, unperturbed.

"But it's supposed to be Damon Smith's room."

"It is."

"Then where is he?"

"In my room, right there." He pointed to the closed door of number seven. "I persuaded him to trade rooms with me for a while."

"You persuaded him?"

"Yes, rather. A favor between fellow photographers, you might say."

"I don't believe you. What have you done to him?" She turned toward number seven, half expecting Jesse to try to stop her. But he leaned against the doorframe, arms folded, and said—oh so casually, "I paid him off. He won't be taking your photograph. I will."

Angry already, she flung at him, "You are just as pompous as always!"

He grinned charmingly. "Just paying my debts is all. I got that free dinner, but I still owe you one portrait, just like we wagered. I'll take it for you today."

"You will not!" And Abigail rapped soundly at the door of number seven. While she waited for an answer, behind her Jesse said, "I told him you and I are old friends, that you'd even saved my life once and by a lucky coincidence I'm here in town to do you a favor in return."

Just as she raised her knuckles to rap again, the door was opened by a blond, blinking man who was buttoning his vest and suppressing a yawn. It was apparent he'd been sleeping. He ran a hand through his tousled hair, grinned in a friendly manner, and glanced from one to the other. "What's up, Jesse? Is this Miss McKenzie?"

"Yes, this is Miss McKenzie!" snapped Miss McKenzie herself.

"Is something wrong?" he asked, surprised.

"Are you Damon Smith?"

"Yes . . . sorry, I should have intro—"

"And were you commissioned to take a wedding portrait of me?"

"Why, yes, but Jesse explained how he just happened to be in town at the right time to do it instead, and since the two of you are such close friends I have no objection to stepping aside. As long as he paid me for my trouble, there are no hard feelings. No need to apologize, Miss McKenzie."

"I am not knocking on your door to apologize, Mr. Smith. I am knocking to get my photograph taken as we agreed!"

Smith scowled. "Hey, Jesse, what the hell is this anyway?"

"A lovers' quarrel," Jesse answered easily, in a stage whisper. "If you'll just bow out, we'll get it settled. See, she's marrying this guy on the rebound." Jesse continued lounging against the doorframe.

Smith grunted while Abbie, outraged, swung first to one man, then to the other, claiming to deaf ears, "He's lying! I hired you to do my picture, not him. Now will you do it or not?"

"Listen, I didn't even set up my equipment, and besides, I don't want anything to do with whatever bones you two are picking. Just leave me out of it. Jesse already paid me twice what you would have, so why should I go through the trouble of setting up my gear? If you want your picture taken, let him do it. He's all set up for it anyway."

And before her astonished eyes, Damon Smith withdrew, mumbling about how in the hell he'd got into the middle of this in the first place, and slammed the door.

Immediately Abbie whirled on Jesse, incensed. "How dare you—" But he came away from that door, propelled her toward number eight, looking back over his shoulder down the hall with a conspiratorial grin.

"Shh," he teased. "If you want to pull your fishwife act, wait until the door is closed or the whole town will know about it."

She balked, outraged, jerking her elbow out of his grasp and taking root.

Rather than force her, he again made a gallant, sweeping gesture, saying politely, "Step into my parlor . . ."

Venomously, she added, ". . . said the spider to the fly!"

"Touché!" he saluted, smiling at her clever riposte. "But all I want to do is take your photograph, and you really don't have much choice in the matter now, do you?"

"I have the choice of having no photograph taken at all."

"Do you?" he asked, quirking one eyebrow.

"Haven't I?"

"Not if you want Melcher to remain blissfully ignorant of your midnight

tête-á-tête last night with a caller who crept out of your house at three in the morning. Then, too, there's that clerk downstairs who knows perfectly well that you're up here at this very minute, having Damon take your photograph. Just how are you going to explain away your time spent with him if you can't produce a picture?"

She glared at the closed door of number seven and knew the spider had trapped her even before she entered his parlor. She could see that he did indeed have a hooded camera set up on a tripod, but it was little consolation. She thoroughly mistrusted him.

"Having created such a sensation the first time you entered this town," she reasoned, "you're certain not to have been missed this second time. The clerk knows you are up here too. One way or another David is bound to learn that you've been in town."

"But I have a perfectly legitimate business holding in this town, which he probably also knows I came to check on. So far nobody knows that you and I were together last night, or today for that matter, except Smith and he's been taken care of."

The man totally frustrated her. How could he change from the understanding warm person of last night to this conniving sneak?

"Ohhh! You and your railroad and your money! You think you can buy your way into or out of anything, don't you—that you can manipulate people's lives with the flash of your money."

"What good is my money if I don't use it to make me happy?" he asked innocently, once more indicating the open door.

She was licked and she knew it. She entered huffily while he began closing the door.

"Leave it open, if you please," she snapped, thinking, what can he do with the door wide open?

"Whatever you say," he agreed amiably, leaving the door as it happened to be, nearly closed, but unlatched. He advanced toward her, reaching politely for the things she held. She was now so leery of him that when he would have taken the garments, she refused to relinquish them.

Glancing at her hand clutching the ivory satin, he warned, "You'll wrinkle your wedding dress before you pose. What will David say?"

He took the garments and placed them on the bed, then came back to her. "Let me help you with your coat," he said, standing behind her while she unbuttoned it and let him remove it. "Nice coat," he noted as she shrugged it off. "Is it new?" She didn't have to see his face to recognize the knowing gleam in his eye. The coat was obviously part of her trousseau: it was obvious whose money had paid for it.

He laid it on the bed along with the other things, then turned to face her. They said nothing for a moment, and Abbie began to feel uneasy. What was she supposed to do, change clothes now?

"Isn't this where you're supposed to ask me if I'd like to see your etchings?" she asked sarcastically.

He surprised her by exclaiming, "Good idea!" with a single clap of his hands. "They're right over here."

Impossible as it was to believe, he meant it, for he squatted down by three large black cases and began unbuckling the straps on one of them. She knew immediately that these must be his photographs he'd mentioned so often.

"I was being facetious," she said, more mellowly.

"I know. Come and have a look anyway. I've wanted you to see these for a long time and maybe once you do you'll feel better about posing for me."

"You said you don't do portraits."

"I don't," he said, glancing up, sitting on his haunches with his hands resting on his thighs, "just yours."

He opened the first case and began removing layers of velvet padding from around the many heavy glass photographic plates, then the plates themselves.

"Come on, Abbie, don't be so skeptical and stubborn. I'll show you what it takes to build a railroad."

She was curious to see what kind of photographs he took, but still hesitated uncertainly. She'd been disarmed by him many times before.

"C'mon." He reached a hand up as if to pull her down beside him where he sat, encircled by glass squares. He looked very appealing and even a little proud as he waited for her to join him. She ignored the hand but picked her way to the clear spot on the floor beside him and knelt in a puff of skirts, her eyes moving immediately to the photographs. The first one she saw was not of a train but of a square-sailed windjammer.

"I think this vessel would have a little trouble negotiating the rails," she observed.

He laughed and picked up the photograph, dusted it with his sleeve, and smiled down at it. "She's the *Nantucket,* and she made it around the Cape, from Philadelphia to San Francisco in just one hundred twelve days in eighteen sixty-three. The *Nantucket* brought the first two engines."

"Railroad engines?" she asked, surprised and interested in spite of herself. He gave her a brief smile, but his interest was mainly for the photographs.

"Everything came by ship then and everything rounded the Horn—engines, rails, spikes, fishplates, frogs—everything but wood for the ties and trestles."

Fishplates? Frogs? He sounded like he knew what he was talking about. Furthermore, while he talked, a delight shone from his eyes like none she'd ever seen there before. Next, he pointed to a picture of a locomotive riding aboard a lithe, graceful river schooner whose stern wheel churned the waters of the Sacramento levee.

"The railroads had to rely on the river steamers," he explained. "Did you know that the levee was built especially to transport supplies for the railroad, only to lose its own lifeblood to the railroads after doing so?"

He studied the picture, and she could not help being touched by the sadness that came into his eyes. He might have forgotten she was in the room, so absorbed was he. He reached to dust the picture with his fingers and she saw things about him she had never seen before.

Without taking his eyes from the picture, he reminisced, "I rode on a riverboat several times when I was a boy. New Orleans will never be the same without them." In his voice, in his touch of fingertips to glass plate, were both passion and compassion, and they moved Abbie deeply.

Next came pictures of trestles, their diamond girders snaking away into the hearts of mountains or the abysses of canyons.

"Sometimes the cinders set them on fire," he ruminated, frowning as if unable to forget a bad memory.

Next was a picture showing hundreds of antlike coolies pushing minute wooden barrows toward those endlessly stretching trestles, ballasting them by hand against the threat of fire. Jesse explained each photo, often smiling, sometimes frowning, but always, always with a concentrated emotion which struck Abbie deeper and deeper.

"That's Chen," he said of a wrinkled, sweating Chinese man.

She looked at the ugly, leathery looking face, then up at Jesse, who smiled down at some good memory.

"Was Chen's skin really yellow like I've heard?" she asked, mystified.

Jesse laughed softly and said, almost as if to himself, "No, more like the color of the earth he carried in his barrow, never complaining, always smiling." Again he dusted the picture with his sleeve. "I wonder where old Chen is now."

There were tunnels that stretched into black nothingness, their domed tops cavernous and foreboding. Even they made Abbie shiver. There were tent towns Jesse had once described to her, pictured in sun, in mud, at dinnertime, at fight time, even at dancing time—men dancing with men at the end of a dirty day. At these Jesse laughed, as if he remembered those good times vividly and had shared them. There were faces seamed with silt, backs bent bare over hammers, pot-bellied dignitaries in faultless silk suits with gold watch chains stretched across their bellies, contrasted against the sweat-streaked stomachs of soiled, tired navvies. There were two well-groomed hands clasped above the golden spike. There was a single stiff, gnarled hand sticking out of a mountain of rubble at which men frantically clawed.

"That was Will Fenton," Jesse said quietly. "He was a good old boy."

But this picture he did not dust. He just stared at it while Abbie watched pain drift across his face, and swallowed at a thick lump in her throat. She had the compulsion to reach out and lay a hand on his arm, soothe the tight, sad expression from his brow. Jesse, she thought, what else is inside you that I've never guessed? She looked at his long fingers resting along his thighs and again at Will Fenton's hand in the photograph.

What Abbie saw round her was a gallery of contrasts, a conscientious account of what it had cost to connect America's two shores with iron rails, of what some had paid while others profited, a pictorial statement from a man who'd done some of each—some paying and some profiting—and who knew the value of both.

James Hudson had been right.

"Well, do I pass muster?" Jesse asked, breaking into her reverie.

"Impressively," she answered, quite humbled by what lay around her, no longer sorry he'd tricked her into this room.

"Then why don't you get on all that wedding finery while I put these away?"

He bent to his task as if forgetting that she was there, and she glanced at the clothing still lying on the bed, then at the hinged screen in the far corner of the room and hoped she was doing the right thing as she went to collect her garments.

Behind the screen, she told herself that although she was very impressed by his photographs, she was not imbecile enough not to realize she'd just been soft-soaped by Jesse.

Step into my parlor, said the spider to the fly . . .

But all the while she was getting into her wedding gown, she kept remembering those photographs and the expression on Jesse's face. She hurried, telling herself to be wary of him, whether he'd won her respect as a photographer or not. He was still the wily Jesse DuFrayne.

He was clattering around out there, putting away his plates, whistling, then it sounded like he was shoving a piece of furniture about. When she stepped from behind the screen, his back was to her. He was kneeling down, taking something from the floor beside his camera. While she watched, he put it beneath the rockers of a chair he'd set before the camera. She caught his eyes while he knelt beside the rocking chair, but he continued that nonchalant whistling, obviously enjoying his trade.

"I need to see in your mirror," she said, noting that he'd rolled his shirt-sleeves up as if he meant to do business.

"Fine," he said, rising and stepping aside so she could get between him and his camera to the dresser. He watched out of the corner of his eye while she smoothed back her hair and tightened the hairpins holding the severe french knot pulled back. In the mirror she watched him pull a pedestal table and fern over beside the rocking chair, obviously as a backdrop. Surely he wasn't planning to photograph her sitting in a rocking chair! What about her headpiece and the trailing veil? But she didn't question him yet, just lifted the seed-pearl circle. But when she was about to place it on her head, he ordered, "No, don't put that on!"

"But it's my bridal veil. I want it in the picture."

"It will be. Bring it here," he said, gesturing her toward the rocker.

"Surely you don't intend to have me sitting in a rocking chair in my wedding picture. I'm not *that* old, Jesse."

He laughed, a full-throated, wonderful laugh. He'd never known another woman with her great sense of humor. He stood loose, relaxed, hands on hips, letting his eyes take in the sight of Abbie in her mother's wedding dress. "I'm glad I've taught you that fact anyway, but yes, you're sitting in the rocker."

"Jesse . . ." she started to argue.

"I think I know a little more about this than you, so get over here." When she didn't move, he said, "Trust me."

She thought, look what happened last time I trusted you, but she did as he asked and neared the chair. He had propped it back at a sharp angle, shimming a block of wood beneath the rockers, and she suddenly realized what he was up to.

"This is supposed to be a picture of a bride, not a boudoir," she noted caustically.

"Don't be so suspicious, Ab, I know what I'm doing. David will love it when he sees it."

That made her more suspicious than ever.

"I want you to take my picture standing up."

"I'll be standing up. Don't worry."

"Don't be ridiculous, you know what I mean."

"Yes, of course I do. Just some facetiae of my own. But either we do this my

way or David wonders why there's no picture to show for all your time up here today."

He reached out a palm, stood waiting to hand her into the chair. Stymied, she had to do as he wanted. With grave misgivings she let him take her hand and help her into the tilted rocker. His hand was hard and warm and somehow very secure-feeling as he squeezed hers, lending some balance while she lowered herself into the propped-back chair. This rocker was larger than her little sewing one, and had arms and a high back decorated with turned finials on each side of the curved backrest. The way he had the thing listing at such a severe angle, once she fell back into it she was quite helpless to get back out again. She felt positively adrift with her feet dangling free, and tried to hold her head away from the back of the chair.

Jesse took the veil from her hand and moved around behind her to lay it on the bed. He stepped to the back of the chair and looked down at her hair. Laying a hand on her forehead, he pulled her head back against the carved oak which caught her just above the nape of the neck.

"Like this," he said, "relaxed and natural."

At the touch of his hand, her heartbeat became pronounced within the high, tight collar of Mechlin lace. As her french knot touched the back of the chair, she found herself looking at Jesse upside down. They stared at each other for a moment and she wondered frantically what he was going to do to her.

In a velvety voice he began speaking as he slowly moved around the chair, never taking his eyes off hers. "What we have here is the bride not before the ceremony, but after—the way every groom wants to remember his bride. When her hair is a little less than perfect and she doesn't know it."

He seemed to be moving in slow motion, reaching toward a pocket, producing a small comb while her eyes never left his, but she saw the comb coming toward her temple, where it bit lightly, loosing some strands from their moorings while she failed, for once, to protest. She knew she should put her hands up to stop him from this madness, but he seemed to have hypnotized her with those dark, probing eyes and that low, crooning voice.

"There is a look a man likes about his bride," came that voice again. "Call it tousled maybe . . . less than perfect after all the cheeks that have pressed hers that day and all the arms that have hugged her, all the losers that have danced with her and touched her temple with theirs." He leaned toward her slowly, reaching a dark hand again to hook a wisp of hair in front of the opposite ear, not smiling, but studying, studying. She knew her french knot was being annihilated, but sat entranced while he freed the fine strand, then moved around the rocking chair while she followed him with her eyes.

"He likes tendrils that cling here and there and stick to her damp skin."

No, Jesse, no, she thought, yet sat mesmerized while he wet the tip of his own finger with his tongue, touched it to the crest of her cheek, then stuck the curl onto it. She saw and felt it all as if only an observer at a distance—the tip of his tongue, his long finger, the wet, cold spot of his saliva on her cheek. She tried not to think of how many places on her body he had touched with his tongue, but his finger went to his mouth again and he did the same on her other cheek, then backed away a little, approving, "Oh, much better, Abbie. David will love this."

She gripped the arms of the chair and stared up at him, her errant pulse skipping to every part of her he had touched and many he had not.

"Oh, but you're so tense. No bride should clutch the arms of her chair as if she's scared to death." His hair came very close to her face as he took both of her hands from the arms of the chair and ordered in that same dreamlike voice, "Loosen up," then shook them lightly until her wrists acquiesced and grew limp. "Just like in your bedroom that night when you first laughed," he reminded her. "Remember?" She let him do what he would with those lacebound wrists. He turned one over and laid it palm-up on her thigh. "That's right," he murmured, then ran one of his fingertips from its wrist to the end of her middle finger, flicking it, finding it relaxed. Shivers ran across her belly. He rose and disappeared momentarily, and her wide eyes only waited for the return of his dark face before her.

"Now the veil . . ." He brought it, a cloud of white in his swarthy, masculine hands, "the symbol of purity, about to be discarded." Her heart leaped wildly as his arm came toward her, but he only hung the headpiece on a spooled finial beside her temple and brought the lace train over one arm to lay in a flowing heap cascading from her lap. "Palm-up, okay, Ab?" The texture of netting crossed her palm as he placed it there, as if she had just tiredly removed it from her head. Then he lifted her other arm and draped its wrist like a willow branch over the chair arm. He knelt on one knee before her.

"It's the end of the day, right? Far too late for tight shoes and stiff collars." And before she realized what was happening, he had swept David's satin gift from her feet, his palm sliding over her sole in a sensuous fleeting touch. She gazed, awestruck, into silence as he rose and moved behind her again, hypnotizing her with his dark eyes above the slash of moustache which curved in the direction of a smile as she once again viewed it upside down. She knew he was reaching for the buttons at her throat but was powerless to stop him. His fingers slowly freed the first one, relieving some of the pressure where her heartbeat threatened to shut off her breath. He freed a second button, then a third—tiny buttons, close together, held by delicate loops that took time, time, time before he had finally exposed the hollow of her throat. She stared up into his black eyes. His hands slid from her throat to the finials of the chair and tipped it farther back, holding it as he looked down into her tortured eyes and asked throatily, "What man would not like to remember his bride this way?"

His eyes, even upside down, burned like firebrands, scorching her cheeks, making her want to cover her face with the inverted palm that lay instead lax upon her lap. Had she wanted to get up and run from him she could not. She had no recourse now but to submit to his narcotic voice and eyes.

Looking down at her, Jesse could see a tricky sunshaft emphasize the heartbeat in the hollow of her throat behind the filigreed lace which lay open and inviting. He released the chair slowly until it rested against its shim again, then equally as slowly moved to its side, never taking his eyes from Abbie's face, trailing one hand on the finial very close to her cheek.

"Wet your lips, Abbie," he said softly. "They should be wet when the picture is snapped." But he made no move toward the camera, neither did she wet her lips.

"Wet them," he urged, "as if David has just now kissed them and said . . .

I love you, Abbie." Jesse stared down at her soft, parted lips, his eyes roved up to hers, then back down to her mouth again, waiting. The tip of her tongue crept out and slipped across her lips, leaving them glistening, opened yet as the breath came labored between them.

He leaned down, placing one hand on each arm of the chair, his face only inches from hers, his voice like warm honey. "Your eyes are opened too wide, Abbie. When a man tells his wife he loves her, don't her eyelids flutter closed?" She fought for breath, staring at his handsome, handsome face, so near that when he spoke, she felt the words against her skin. "Let's try it once more and see," he whispered, still leaning above her.

"I love you, Abbie." And her eyelids lost their moorings.

"I love you, Abbie," she heard again . . . and they were at half mast.

"I love you, Abbie." And they closed against his cheek as his mouth came hungering. She no longer wanted to get up from the chair, for his open lips claimed hers and his long hands cinched her shoulders, thumbs reaching to stroke the spot where he'd seen her heart fluttering in her throat. He knelt on one knee at the side of the rocker while he kissed her back against it, his tongue dancing and stroking upon hers while everything in her reached and yearned for more.

But suddenly she felt panic rise within, tightening her lungs, her throat, her scalp. "No, I'm being married tomorrow," she choked, turning her head aside from his kiss which taunted her to forget.

"Exactly—tomorrow," he murmured softly into her neck.

Her eyes slid closed, and she turned sharply away from him in a vain attempt to combat the feelings he unleashed in her. "Let me up from this chair," she pleaded, close to tears.

"Not until I get a proper kiss from the bride," he said, kissing the underside of her jaw. "Ab, you're not his wife yet, but when you are, I won't be here to kiss the bride. Just one day early, that's all . . ."

When she still refused to turn toward him, he said, "Why not, Ab? Let's make you look like a kissed woman for David's photograph. That's how a woman looks on her wedding night, isn't it?" Then a strong hand spanned her chin and turned her mouth to his. But when he swooped to kiss her again, she began struggling against him, using arms, hands, and elbows. But he captured her arms effortlessly and lifted them around his neck, holding them there forcibly until he felt her struggling begin to quell.

Those arms had been denied for so long. Now at last they curled around the dark hair at the back of his neck while she arched up and opened the lips she had wet at his command, for David.

Jesse's mouth twisted hungrily across hers, then suddenly jerked away as he knocked the block of wood from beneath the rocker with a thrust of his knee. The chair came reeling forward and he was there to meet her as she came with it. Their mouths met almost desperately and he pulled Abbie from the chair onto her knees before him. He wrapped a powerful arm about her waist, forcing her against his hard, bulging loins, which moved in slow, sensuous circles against her satin wedding dress. His hands moved down to hold her tightly against him while their tongues spoke messages of want into each other's mouths and their lips spoke like messages against flesh that arched and pressed until both ached sweetly.

Tearing his lips from hers, he uttered against her temple, "You can't marry him, Ab. Say you can't." But before she could make a sound his impatient mouth sought hers once more, delving into its warmth and wetness with his seeking tongue. "Say it," he demanded in a voice gruff with passion as he lowered his lips to her jaw, then down, down to the open neck of her wedding dress. But she was adrift in splendor, could think of nothing but the pleasured sound which his touch brought from her throat. She leaned her face into his hair, kissing the top of his head while her hands caressed his face. His mouth moved beneath her palms, opening wide as he tasted her skin and buttons sprayed like sundrops around them, glancing off his face as he lowered it to the newly cloven garment where her breasts waited for his lips.

She recaptured enough sanity to murmur, "Jess . . . my wedding dress . . ."

Into her breasts he answered, "I'll buy you a new one." Then his head came up and his palms slid within the torn garment, touching a taut nipple, flattening it, then stroking it to an erect, pink peak.

"But it's my mother's," she said senselessly.

"Good," he grunted, running both of his palms upward past her breasts, onto her shoulders, then peeling the garment away with an outward thrust of wrists. He forced it down in back until it lay tight just above her elbows, imprisoning them within the long, lace sleeves but freeing her breasts to his hands, his tongue, his teeth, while her throat arched backward in abandon. He tugged at a nipple, groaned deep in his throat, then released it to rub the soft hair of his moustache back and forth across it as he admitted, "God, Abbie, I couldn't get you out of my mind."

"Please, Jess, we've got to stop."

But he didn't, only moved to her other breast.

"Did you think about me too?" he asked in a choked voice.

She tried halfheartedly to pull his head away from her breasts, but he continued kissing and suckling while her arms remained pinioned by the garment, useless.

"I tried not to. Oh, Jess, I tried."

"I did too . . ."

"Stop, Jess . . ."

"I love it when you call me Jess that way. What do you call him when he does this to you?" He knelt up straight again and held the back of her head in his two wide hands, searching her eyes before pulling her to him to kiss her with an almost savage anguish. Breaking away, he touched her very deliberately in her most sensitive spots—breast, belly, down her ivory skirts that remained between his hand and the warm, weeping female flesh within. "Can David make you quiver like this, want like this? Can he make your breasts get hard and your body go dewy like I can?"

And he knew from the tortured look upon her face what the answer was before she touched his face and kissed his chin, moving close.

"No . . . not like you, Jess, never like you . . ."

And she knew if she lived with David a thousand years the answer would remain the same.

Chapter 24

THE BELL TINKLED and David looked up to find Bones Binley shambling toward him between the red benches. Now that the cold weather was here, Bones had taken to loitering in the store, which was far more comfortable than Mitch's veranda, and where the coffee was hot. Then, too, it gave him a chance to eye Mizz Abigail now and again.

She wasn't here today . . . but Bones knew that before he came in.

"Howdy, Bones," David greeted the gangly stalk, experiencing the peculiar momentary twinge of ego he always felt in Bones's presence ever since he'd heard Bones had eyes for his woman. As Abbie's "chosen one," David often patronized Bones just the smallest bit. As the "non-chosen," Bones sensed this and bridled inwardly. He couldn't figure out what Mizz Abigail saw in Melcher anyway.

"What say, David?" Bones returned.

"Thanks for taking Abigail's packages up from the depot yesterday. She was really happy to see them. She'd been waiting for the headpiece for days and was worried it might not get here in time."

Bones nodded at the floor. "Yup."

"She said to thank you again when I saw you."

"Yup."

"She's up at the hotel having her picture taken."

"Yup."

David laughed. "I don't know why I bother telling you anything. There's not a thing happens in this town you don't know about before it does."

Bones again laughed at the floor—a soundless shake of shoulders.

"Yup, that's a fact. Now y' take like yesterday, with that blizzard brewin', I musta been the only one out when the two-twenty come in and that DuFrayne feller gits off carryin' all that pitcher-takin' gear and checks in up at Edwin's." Bones found his twist of tobacco and bit off a good-size chew.

David went white as the new snow.

"D . . . D . . . DuFrayne?"

"Yup."

"Y . . . you . . . m . . . must be mistaken, Bones. That wasn't D . . . DuFrayne, it was D . . . Damon Smith with the picture-taking gear."

"Him? He the blond one? Short? About so-high? Naw, he din't come in till the nine-fifty this morning. No, that other one, he come in on the late train yesterday and checks in at Edwin's just like I said. Far as I know he's still right there." Bones lifted the lid off the pot-bellied stove, took deadly aim, and let fly with a brown streak of tobacco juice that sizzled into the lull that had suddenly fallen. Then he wiped the side of his mouth with the edge of his hand, keeping the corner of his eye on David.

"I . . . I see it's time for me to go m . . . meet Abigail, Bones. I t . . . told her I w . . . would, after she was d . . . done with the ph . . . photograph. If you'll excuse me . . ."

"Sure thing, sure thing," returned the pleased Bones as David hurried to the back room for his coat.

Three and a half minutes later, David entered the hotel lobby.

"Well, David, my man, how's business?"

"All s . . . set to go, right af . . . after the w . . . wedding."

Edwin chuckled amiably, noting David's nervousness. He gave David a conspiratorial grin. "Last twenty-four hours before a wedding are the toughest, eh, David?"

David swallowed.

"Don't you worry now, with that store and that wife, you're gonna be as happy as a hog in slop."

Normally David would have laughed heartily with Edwin, but he only asked now, with a worried look upon his face, "Is she here, Ed?"

"Sure is." Ed thumbed toward the ceiling. "Been up there an hour already. Should have a dandy photograph by this time."

"I . . . I n . . . need to talk to her a m . . . minute."

"Sure thing, go right on up. Smith's in number eight, end o' the hall on your left."

"Thanks, Ed. I'll find it."

Upstairs the sunlight streamed through sheer lace on the long, narrow window at the end of the hall as David strode silently upon the long runner strewn with faded moss roses. His toe had begun to hurt, and his heart felt swollen, as if it were choking him. An hour? She had been here an hour? Did it take an hour to have a photograph made? But it *was* Damon Smith she was with, It was! Yes, it surely must take at least an hour for the posing and the developing, which was done on the spot.

As he approached number eight, he saw that the door was closed but not latched.

A murmur of voices came from inside—a man's, husky and low, a woman's, strained and throaty. David felt suddenly weak and placed his palm against the wall for support. The voices were muffled, and David strained to hear.

"Stop, Jess . . ."

Oh, God, that was Abigail's voice. David's eyes slid closed. He willed his feet to move, to take him away, but it felt as if those moss roses had suddenly sent up tendrils to hold his ankles to the carpet. Tortured, he listened to the husky words that followed.

"I love it when you call me Jess that way. What do you call him when he does this to you?"

David's mind filled with terrible moving pictures as a long, long silence followed and sweat broke out on his brow. Move! he told himself. Get out! But before he could, DuFrayne's voice, fierce, passionate, asked, "Can David make you quiver like this, want like this? Can he make your breasts get hard and your body go dewy like I can?"

And Abigail's shaken reply, "No . . . not like you, Jess, never like you . . ."

David hesitated a moment longer, nausea and fear plummeting through him while from within the room came the sounds of lovers who forget themselves, and the temptation became too great.

Stepping to the door, he pushed it open, then gulped down the gorge that threatened to erupt from his throat.

Abigail knelt on the floor, eyes closed, head slung back as hair tumbled in wanton disarray down her bared back. The bodice of her wedding gown was lowered, pinning her elbows to her sides, baring her breasts to Jesse DuFrayne, who knelt on one knee before her, his mouth upon her skin. Abigail's bridal veil was crushed beneath their knees, its headpiece lay in a misshapen gnarl under the rocking chair behind her. Pearl buttons lay ascatter amid hairpins, a comb, the satin shoes he'd given Abigail as a wedding gift. Sickened yet unable to tear his eyes away, David watched as the woman he was supposed to marry tomorrow reached blindly to cup the jaw of the dark man before her, guiding his mouth from one breast to the other as a soft moan escaped her lips.

The shamed blood came surging to David's face as he bleated out a single word. "Abigail!"

She jerked back. "David! Oh, my God!"

"Well, you certainly had me fooled!"

The blood drained from her face, but as quickly as she pulled back, Jesse instinctively pulled her against his chest, shielding her bare breasts from intruding eyes, cupping the back of her head protectively, even his raised knee tightening against her hip as he settled her safely against the lee of his loins.

"You'd better watch what you say, Melcher, because this time it will be me who answers, not her," Jesse warned, his voice resounding mightily against Abigail's ear which lay against his chest.

"You . . . you scum!" David hissed. "I was right all along. You're two of a kind!"

"It seems we are, which makes me wonder why in the living hell she'd want to marry you."

"She won't be! You can have her!"

"Sold!" barked Jesse, piercing Melcher with an ominous glare while he reached blindly to pull the shoulders of Abigail's dress back up.

"An apt word, I'd say, considering the money she's already taken from you, you son of a bitch!"

Abigail felt Jesse's muscles tense as he put her away from him and made as if to rise.

"Stop it! Stop it, both of you!" Abbie cried, clutching her dress front and struggling to her feet, followed by Jesse, who kept a shoulder between her and the door. The torn garment, their compromising pose, and what David had overheard made denial impossible. She felt as if she were freefalling through endless space into the horrifying noplace of *déjà vu.* She lurched around to move toward David, but he backed away in distaste.

"David, I'm sorry . . . I'm sorry, David, please forgive me. I didn't intend for this to happen." She reached a supplicating hand toward him even as the other continued to hold her bodice together. But apologies and excuses were so pitifully inadequate they only added to her shame.

"You lying harlot," he ground out venomously, all signs of stammering somehow surprisingly gone from his voice. "Did you think I wouldn't find out? Just one more time before you married me, is that it? Just one more time with this son of a bitch you'd rather have than me? Well, fine—keep him!"

Today was the first time she'd ever heard David swear. She reached to clutch his sleeve, horrified at what he'd witnessed, at herself for having fallen so low.

"David, please . . ."

But he jerked free, as if her touch were poison.

"Don't touch me. Don't you ever touch me again," he said in cold, hard hate. Then he tugged his coat squarely onto his shoulders, turned on his good foot, and limped away without a backward glance.

Standing there staring at the empty doorway the enormity of her offense washed over her. Tears formed in her eyes and her hands came to cover her open mouth, from which no sound issued for a long time. She felt sickened by herself and her eyes slid shut as she started quaking uncontrollably.

"He'll never marry me now. Oh God, the whole town will know within an hour. What am I going to do?" She covered her temples with her fingertips and rubbed them, then clutched her arms tightly and rocked back and forth as if nearing hysteria.

Jesse stood several feet behind her, did not approach or try to touch her as he said quietly, "It's simple. . . . Marry me."

"What!" She spun to face him, staring for a moment as if he'd gone mad. But she was the one suddenly laughing, crying, shaking all at once in a queer fit tinged by frenzy. "Oh, wouldn't that be jolly. Marry you and we could spend the rest of our lives screaming and biting and scratching and trying to get the better of each other. Oh . . ." She laughed again hysterically, "Oh, that's very funny, Mr. DuFrayne," she ended, tears streaming down her face.

But Jesse was not laughing. He was stone serious, his face an unmoving mask as he said intensely, "Yes, sometimes it is very funny, Miss McKenzie — funny and exhilarating and wonderful, because that's our way of courting each other. I found I missed it so much when I was away from you that I had to come back here to see if you were as good as I remembered."

"You purposely came back to cause trouble between David and me, don't deny it."

"I'm not denying it. But I changed my mind last night while we talked. What happened here today was not planned. It just happened."

"But you . . . you tricked me into this room, into . . . into sitting in that rocking chair and . . . and . . ."

"But you wanted it just as bad as I did."

The truth was still too frightening for her to face, and she was, as always, confounded by his changeability. She could not help wondering what his motives were today. She swung around him and swooped toward the screen in the corner, accusing, "It's all a big game to you, manipulating people so th—"

"This is not a game, Abbie," he argued, following her right around the screen, talking to her shoulder as she turned her back on him. "I'm asking you to marry me."

She unbuttoned her cuffs as if they were made of itchweed. "Oh, wouldn't we be the laughingstock of Stuart's Junction—Miss Abigail and her train robber!" She turned to him, yanking at the sleeves, affecting the sugary tone of a gossip. "Oh, you remember, don't you? The couple who were caught in the act the day before her impending marriage to another man?" She yanked the bodice down, fuming. He moved up close behind her.

"That in itself should tell you that we're right for each other. You know damn well you enjoy it more with me than with him or you never would have let me get as far as I did today."

She whirled on him, holding some garment over her breasts. "How dare you insinuate that I did anything with David! We did nothing—absolutely nothing! We were as pure as the driven snow and this town knew it!"

They stood nose to nose, each of them glaring.

"Who gives a damn about what this town thinks? What has this town ever done for you besides label you a spinster when you were only twenty years old?"

"Get out of here when I'm changing my clothes!" she shouted, and presented her back to step out of the wedding dress, bending forward and giving him a rear view of white pantalets more ruffled than any he'd seen on her clothesline. His eyes traveled down her skin, down the shadowed hollow that receded into the white cotton waistband.

"When I get out of here, it will be with you on my arm, wearing that expensive green coat I paid for, telling this town to kiss off as we board my train!"

She yanked a camisole over her head and he watched the fine hair at the back of her neck as she looked down and tied the string at her waist.

"You're still not done flaunting your money, are you?" She threw a brief, disparaging look over her shoulder. "Well, you've come up against the one thing you can't buy!" She pulled a petticoat and skirt on and buttoned them at her waist.

"Buy you!" he shouted, "I don't want to buy you. I want you free! You have to give yourself to me freely if we get married, because you want to."

"You planned this seduction today, don't tell me you didn't." She pulled a blouse off the top of the screen and slipped her arms into it.

He reached out and got her from behind by both breasts, pulling her back against his hardness. She purposely remained aloof, acting as if his touch went thoroughly unnoticed except when she had to push his hands aside to close the buttons of her blouse.

"So we're even then, aren't we, Ab?" he asked, pressing the side of his mouth against the hair behind her ear. "Didn't you plan my seduction once? Only you succeeded where I haven't . . . so far." As he nuzzled her rose-scented neck, he fervently began caressing her breasts, at last awakening the fight in her. She fought his hands, but he only held her tighter, slipping his palm inside her partially opened blouse, leaning to kiss the nape of her neck, sliding his other hand down her stomach, then lower. They grappled together, elbows flying, sending the screen crashing to the floor.

"You have the most unscrupulous courting methods I've ever seen!" she bawled, pulling at his wrists, but just then he got one powerful arm cinched around her stomach, his other hand once more finding its way to her breast and forcing her back against his tumescent body.

"Feel that. Tell me you don't want it. Tell me I don't know what's best for you."

For a moment she wilted and his grip slackened, giving her enough advantage to break free and spin to face him.

"How can you know what's best for me when I don't even know myself?" Her eyes flicked to the door David had left open.

"Then I think it's time I showed you again," he threatened with honey in his voice, taking a step nearer.

Her heart was hammering wildly now, confused by the mixture of emotions Jesse could always stir up in her. They eyed each other like a pair of cats at howling time, beginning slowly, slowly to circle until she gained the side of the room closest to the hall. Suddenly she turned and hit for the door, but he had it slammed so fast the wind dried her eyeballs. She backed away, big-eyed, panting, feeling the throb of her pulse in every wary nerve of her body.

He leaned back casually, holding the doorknob behind his back. One foot was flat on the floor, the other crossed in front of it with only the toe of his boot on the floor. He wasn't even breathing heavily. He lounged there as if he had all the time in the world, the ghost of a grin crawling up one side of his mouth while those hazel-flecked eyes assessed her with a tinge of knowing mirth. His voice was soft, cajoling, seductive.

"You know we're doing it again, don't you? The old courting dance we both love so much. This is the way we always start out, Abbie—me pursuing, you fighting me off. But this is no fight and you know it, because in the end we both win." He brought his shoulders away from the door in slow motion. "So come here you little hell-cat," he ended with a hoarse whisper, "because I'll only stalk you so long before I pounce."

She loved it, she'd missed it, she wanted it, this hammering of the senses that exhilarated like nothing else she'd ever experienced as she waited, waited, knowing what he'd do. Her breasts were heaving and her eyes sparkled, but like a true hellcat she spit one more time. "Come here! Do this! Do that! Marry me! And then what? Go through this for the rest of our lives!"

His grin grew bolder. "You're goddamn right," he said, low.

"Oh, you . . . you . . ."

But he was done waiting.

"Damn . . ." he muttered, and sprang! He grabbed her wrists and swung her adeptly until her back slammed flat against the closed door. His hands grasped her beneath the armpits and she felt her feet leave the floor as he lifted her bodily, holding her plastered against the mahogany panel, kissing her. His wide palms bracketed the sides of her breasts while his lips, too, held her prisoner, controlling hers, sending spasms of desire rippling through her body, directed each to its own nerve by his mastering tongue. Emotions stormed her senses while Jesse stormed her body, breathing now like a hurricane while he besieged her with deep kisses, his tongue fierce and probing, impaling her against the door.

At last he freed her mouth, gazing with dark, tempestuous eyes into hers.

"Damnit, Abbie, I love you. It was me saying I love you before, for myself, not for David."

She seemed unable to speak, and they both suddenly realized he still had her up against that door. He let her slide slowly down, a last hairpin dropping unnoticed from her hair. When her toes touched the floor, he continued holding her lightly by both breasts, searching her eyes for some sign of entente.

"What do you say, Abbie?"

Her eyes, kindled yet confused, sparkled within the shock of loosened hair framing her face.

"How can I marry a man I'm afraid of half the time, who just flung me against a door?"

A pained expression crossed his face and he dropped his hands from her breasts to her ribs, touching her gently, caringly.

"Oh, God, did I hurt you, Abbie? I didn't mean to hurt you." He kissed one of her eyelids, then the other, then backed away to look into her blue eyes, his voice as close to tortured as she'd ever heard it. "Are you really afraid of me, Abbie? You don't ever have to be afraid of me. All I want to do is make you happy, make you laugh, maybe moan . . . but not from hurt. From this . . ."

He closed her eyes once again with his lips, then trailed them down her nose to her cheek, along her delicate jaw to her chin, then finally up to her lips, which had fallen open by the time he reached them. His hands went to the shoulders of her unbuttoned blouse, squeezing until she thought her bones would crack. But his mouth upon hers was a direct contrast to the pressure of his hands—soft, gentle, convincing, while his warm tongue skimmed lightly, lightly over her lips, then over her teeth before he moved to her ear and said into it. "Admit it, Abbie, it's what you want too. Be honest with me and with yourself."

"How can I be honest when you've got a hold on me this way? Jesse, I can't think."

He cautiously dropped his hands, but only to her ribs, riding them lightly as if afraid she might escape him yet. And there they lay, warm, large, spanning her torso, one of his thumbs reaching up to brush the underside of her breast while he searched her face.

"Abbie, you said you had to shout to the empty rooms when I was gone, trying to be free of me. Doesn't that tell you something?"

Her eyes pleaded but he did not relinquish his hold on her. Instead, the warmth from his palms seeped through the layer of cotton over her skin, his hands now inside the blouse, on her ribs, that long thumb still arousing her to shivery sensuality as it slid slowly back and forth.

"I'm so mixed up," she said in a trembling voice, eyes sliding closed, head resting back wearily against the door.

"You have a right to be. I'm exactly the opposite of what you've been told all your life was right for you. But I am right, Ab, I am."

She rolled her head from side to side, swallowing. "I don't know . . . I don't know."

"Yes, you do, Abbie. You know what kind of life we'd have. We're good together at everything we do. Talking, arguing, making love, making sense . . . and nonsense. What are you afraid of, Abbie, that you'll get hurt again? Or of what this town will say? Or what David will say?"

She opened her eyes but looked over his shoulder at the lacy window curtain and the snow beyond.

"I've hurt David so badly." Her nostrils flared and her eyes slid shut.

"Maybe you had to, for your own salvation."

"No, nobody deserves to be hurt like that."

"Did you, thirteen years ago?"

She looked into his eyes again.

"I refuse to appease my conscience by saying two wrongs make a right."

"Then let me share part of the blame for hurting him. Hell, I'll even march up the street and apologize to him if that's what it takes to win you. Is that what you want me to do, Abbie?"

Tears suddenly stung her nose, for the loss of David, for this man's devotion. She somehow believed Jesse meant it and would actually face David and apologize. After all, Jesse was a man who'd go to any lengths to get what he wanted. It struck her just how badly he wanted her. Still, she leaned against that door and let him go on convincing her, for it was heavenly standing there with his dark face so close to hers as he leaned both forearms now on either side of her head.

"There's a whole country out there, Abbie. You can pick any city you want to live in. I'll take you anyplace. You want to live like the wife of a railroad baron in some mansion in Colorado Springs, all right. It's yours. You name the place and we'll go. How about starting in New Orleans? I'll take you to see the ocean, Abbie, and to meet my family. You've always wanted to see the ocean, you told me so. You even tried to bring a little of it here by designing that Cape Cod window in that shoe store, but I'll take you to Cape Cod to see the real thing if you want." His eyes were filled with sincerity as he went on. "Abbie, I don't want to buy you, but I would if I had to. I'm rich, Abbie, so what's wrong with that? What's wrong with me wanting to spend my money making you happy? I owe you my life, Abbie, let me give it to you . . ."

This, this, this, she thought, was what she had always dreamed of, the Jesse she'd always dreamed of, whispering love words in her ear, making her blood pound and her senses soar. Her eyes drifted open and found his, dark, intense, promising her the world. She floated in the warm security of the knowledge of his love for her, quite unable to speak at the moment.

Is this me, she thought, Abigail McKenzie? Is this really happening? This startlingly handsome man, with his elbows leanings beside my ears, convincing me with utter sincerity in his every word that he loves me? Her heart felt ready to explode.

He leaned to nuzzle her neck, to nip her earlobe, then touch the inside of it with the tip of his damp tongue.

"That's what I want, Ab, but what about what you want right now?"

She felt his breath—warm, fast—beating upon her ear, then his voice came again, strangled and strange, making things melt within her body. "Don't discount it as unimportant. If I slipped my hand beneath your skirt and touched your body, I know what I'd find. Don't deny that it's important, Ab. I've felt it there before because you wanted me, and I know it's there again."

And deep inside Abbie felt a welcome liquid rush of femininity, accompanied by the sensual swelling of that part of her which no man except Jesse had ever touched.

Her eyes slid closed. Her chest tightened. Her breath came jerky. Even the hair at the back of her neck felt like it had nerves, each of them aroused, ready for response.

Across the fullest part of her stomach, she felt him press his aroused body, lightly, lightly brushing from left to right, right to left, making circles on her while his palms remained pressed flat against the door above her head. Her own palms tingled, eager to be released and to touch him, yet she kept them pressed flat against the door behind her hips, drawing out this sensual mating dance to its fullest, wanting it to build slowly, slowly, slowly in tempo and heat while he rubbed against her, his shirt buttons now lightly grazing the tips of her nipples, which were drawn up tight like tiny, hard bells beneath the flimsy cotton camisole.

She trembled with sensation. Jesse, Jesse, she thought, you are so good at this . . . so good . . .

He looked down to find a faint smile upon her lips, her eyes still closed, her breasts now straining as far forward as she could manage and still keep her shoulder blades against the door. He smiled slowly, understanding her well, letting his elbows slide several inches lower, bringing his midsection away from hers, then flicking his tongue out to touch the very corner of her eye.

She's had so little love, he thought, I will drown her in it for the rest of her life.

No word was said. Her hands came from behind her to blindly find his hips and pull them back against her, bringing his heat and hardness where she wanted them, making him smile against her hair and slip one arm between her shoulder blades and the door, down to her waist. His other hand grasped the doorknob for leverage as he ground himself against her, a hand clapped tight now upon the seat of her petticoats, quite unable to feel much more through all those layers.

Her hips began to move with his, while her palms remained just below his belt as if she must know fully his every motion—she must, she must, she had waited so long. She opened her eyes as if drugged, pleading silently until his mouth came down to find hers open, waiting, yearning. And together their tongues dove deep while their flesh pressed so tightly together that pulses seemed inseparable.

She writhed between him and the door and he moved his mouth to her ear, whispering hoarsely, "Abbie, I'm going to take you to that bed and make love to you like you never imagined you'd be made love to again."

He felt her shudder and understood what was happening inside her. His own body was straining against the confines of clothing. Still, he leaned low and lightly bit one of her nipples—as if in passing—through the cloth and all, making her twist and suck her breath in sharply and open her eyes.

He slipped an arm around her shoulder, the other beneath her knees, and lifted her effortlessly from her feet, her arms twining up and about his broad shoulders, fingers twining into the hair at the back of his neck while he turned slowly, slowly toward the bed.

"And I'm going to keep it up . . . and keep it up . . . and keep it up . . . until you admit that you love me and say you'll marry me," he said throatily.

They stared into each other's eyes as he strode toward the bed, the muscles of his chest hard and warm against her breast.

She heard the springs sing out as he knelt with one knee and leaned to lay her down. With a hand on either side of her head, he hung above her, and said into her eyes, "And I don't intend to be hindered by the petticoats you chose to wear for any wedding to another man—whether I paid for them or not." Then without watching what he was doing, he found the buttons at her waist and she felt them come free. Tingles shafted through her and she smiled, a glitter of eagerness now playing up at him from behind fringed lashes.

"But, Jesse, you paid so dearly to arrange that wedding," she said softly, seductively.

"Well, I'm unarranging it," he said gruffly, and he stripped the petticoats away down her calves, then grabbed her hand and pulled her to a sitting position.

"And neither will I contend with Victorian collars that signify nothing."

With agonizing slowness he removed her blouse. She obediently complied, but when his dark head dipped near hers as he slid the garment away she informed him, "Whether I marry you or not, I will dress as I see fit—like a lady."

"Fine," he returned as the blouse came off. "You do that. In our parlor when you have the ladies of the other railroad barons to tea." He tossed the blouse over his shoulder. "In our bedroom you leave them hanging in the chiffonier along with your camisole and these." He inserted a single finger into the waistband of her pantaloons, tugging.

She fell back languidly, arms flung loosely above her head, and lay there in wait, loving him more with each passing word.

"You paid for these too. I suppose that gives you the right to do what you will with them."

He knelt beside her and without taking his eyes from her face, removed his vest and shirt, flinging them over his shoulder to join her petticoat and skirt on the floor.

"Exactly. Just like I paid for that green coat you were going to wear on your honeymoon. And if you weren't proud of the fact that I'm rich you wouldn't keep pointing it out time and again." And off came his belt.

"I would have been content to run a simple shoe store," she purred, reaching out to brush the backs of her fingers against the part of him she'd first seen when he was dying upon her bed, making his eyes burn bright before her fingers trailed away from his trousers.

Then slowly, tantalizingly, he freed the buttons up the front of his pants, while his voice poured over her like liquid silk.

"When I'm done here, I'm going to shoot down that goddamn sign that's got your name on it with his." The ardor in his tone made the word *goddamn* almost an endearment. Then his pants, too, were gone.

"Signifying nothing," she murmured with a slow smile.

"Like hell," he said gruffly, reaching to untie the string at the waist of her camisole, then sliding a hand inside, up, up, over her ribs as he sat on the bed and stretched his long, dark limbs toward Abbie.

Her nostrils widened and her breath came jagged.

"You don't think it's significant that I'm taking back what I once gave away so foolishly?" he asked possessively, pushing the camisole up by increments, leaning his dark head to kiss the hollow between her ribs, then that beneath her left breast.

Eyes closing, she whispered, "This whole town probably knows what we're doing right now," caring not the least, loving it anyway.

He moved his tongue to the hollow beneath her other breast, chuckling deep in his throat, his lips nuzzling against her skin.

"And they'll probably run home and do a little of it themselves, just at the thought."

"Not everyone's like you, Jess," she said, smiling behind closed lids, wishing he would hurry up.

But he moved like a seductive snail, unbuttoning the waist of her pantaloons and slipping them only to her hips, exposing their hollows provocatively.

"No, but you are, and that's all that counts." Again his mouth found her hollows, these just inside her hipbones, while she stirred sinuously. And after some moments the last garment moved slowly, slowly downward while he kissed a path in its wake and she lay with a wrist across her forehead, all resistance gone, her lips parted as his tongue danced upon her.

"I remember this best," he whispered hoarsely before delving into her, following as she arched, stroking until she moaned and fell back, shuddering beneath him.

"I did too . . . I did too," came her strangled voice.

He knew her well, he loved her well, he drew his head back just at her breaking point, moving up her body to thread his fingers back through her hair and lay his hot, hard length upon her, not in her.

"Say it, Abbie," he begged, kissing her beneath the jaw as her head arched back. "Say it now while I come into you."

She opened her eyes and found his filled with love as they probed hers. His elbows quivered beside her as he braced away, waiting to hear the words.

She reached between them and found him, guided him home, her eyes never leaving his as he came into her, moving strong and sure to the rhythm of her repeated words,

"I love you, Jesse . . . love you . . . love you . . . love you . . ." over and over again in accompaniment to his long, slow strokes. He saw tears well and slip from the corners of her eyes as her lips formed and reformed the words, faster and faster, until her lips fell open. And shortly, he followed the way she had gone, through that plunging ride of ecstasy.

The room grew quiet, the afternoon light reflecting in off the snow as her hand lay on the damp nape of his neck. She toyed with his hair absently. Then, closing her eyes tightly, she suddenly grasped him to her, holding him, possessing him, lying perfectly still for that moment, recording it in her memory to carry with her into the length of their days together.

"Jesse . . . oh, Jesse."

Lost in love, he rocked her, rolling wordlessly from side to side, and finally falling still beside her, looking into her serene face.

"The train is coming," he said softly.

She smiled and touched his lower lip, then trailed a fingertip from the center of his moustache to its outer tip. "Even the train schedule accommodates you, doesn't it?"

"And what about Miss Abigail McKenzie?" he asked, holding his breath.

She gazed into his beloved eyes. "She too," she said softly, "she too."

His eyes slid shut and he sighed, content.

But she made them open again when she asked, "But what shall she do with her houseful of wedding cakes and sandwiches?"

"Leave them to the mice. They'll like them better than oatmeal."

"Leave them?" she asked, puzzled.

He braced up on one elbow, all trace of smile gone from his face as he gazed at her intently.

"I'm asking you to get up off this bed and put on your clothes and walk to the train depot with me, holding my arm, never looking back. Everything starts with now."

"Leave my house, my possessions, everything—just like that?"

"Just like that."

"But the whole town is probably out there waiting for us to come out of this hotel. If we go straight to the depot, they'll know."

"Yes, they will. Won't we create a sensation walking out right under their noses, boarding the executive coach—Miss Abigail and her train robber?"

She eyed him, considering it.

"Why, Jesse, you want to shock them, don't you?"

"I think we already have, so why not finish it off with aplomb?"

She couldn't help laughing. At least she tried to, but he hugged her again, pressing his chest across hers, and he was very, very heavy. All that came out was a soundless bouncing, which made him relieve her of some of his weight, but not quite all—not until she said yes.

"We are so very different, Jesse," she said, serious again, touching him upon his temples. "In spite of what we have in common, we are still opposites. I could not change for you."

"I don't want you to. Do you want me to?" For a moment he was afraid of what she might answer. Instead she said nothing, so he sat up on the edge of the bed, turning his back on her.

But she knew him well enough by now to recognize the tensing of his jaw muscle for what it was. She sat up behind him and ran a hand over one of his shoulders, then kissed his back.

"No," she said quietly against his skin, "just as you are, Jess. I love you just as you are."

He turned to her with a smile aslant his lips, the bedeviling moustache inviting as he reached out a single hand, palm-up.

"Then let's go."

She placed her hand in his and let him tug her off the bed, almost catapulting into his arms, laughing.

He hugged her naked body long against his, running his hand down her spine while her bare toes dangled above the floor.

"Back off, woman," he warned with a chuckle, "or we're going to miss that three-twenty to Denver."

Then he let her slip down and slapped her lightly on her naked rump.

They dressed, their eyes on each other instead of what they were doing. But when she began gathering up the torn wedding gown and the buttons and satin shoes, he ordered gently, "Leave them."

"But—"

"Leave them."

She looked down at the dress. The touch of its satin beneath her fingers reminded her again of David, and she knew what she must do. "Jesse, I can leave everything else, but I must . . ." She looked up entreatingly. "I must not leave David—not this way." Jesse did not move a muscle or smile. "Not hurting him as I have. May I just go back to the store and try to make him understand I never meant to hurt him?"

Jesse's eyes were dark, inscrutable, as he knelt before her, buckling the straps on one of his photograph cases.

"Yes. If it'll mean not having him between us for the rest of our lives, yes." They were the hardest words Jesse DuFrayne had ever spoken.

A few moments later he held the new green coat as she slipped her arms into it. Then they turned at the door to survey the room for a moment —the overturned screen still lying on its side, wedding gown in a heap, torn and wrinkled, its buttons strewn around the room along with her crushed veil and the discarded satin pumps.

Hoping he'd understand, she went back in and retrieved the shoes, tucking them into her coat as they left the hotel and stepped into the cold, sparkling sunlit afternoon.

He held her arm as they walked along the boardwalks to the shoe store at the end of the street, and he stood outside stoically, his hands buried in his pockets, waiting, while she went inside to return the white satin pumps to David Melcher. It seemed to take forever, though it was a matter of only several minutes.

The bell tinkled and Jesse looked up, searching her face as she came back out and took his arm to walk back toward the depot.

There was an odd, sick feeling in the pit of his stomach. He looked down at her gravely.

She smiled up at him. "I love you, Jesse."

And he breathed again.

They walked the length of Main Street, feeling eyes upon them every step of the way. At the station the train waited, chugging and puffing impatiently, its breath white upon the cold Colorado air.

On the side of the second to the last car glittered an ornate crest bearing an R.M.R. insignia done in gold leaf, intertwined with a design of dogwood petals.

Puzzled, Abbie looked at it, then up at Jesse, but before she could ask, he scooped her up in his arms and mounted the steps of the executive coach.

But suddenly he stopped, turned, looked thoughtfully out at the deserted street, deposited her on her feet again, and said, "Just a minute. Don't go away." Then he swung down the steps again.

And cool as you please, Jesse DuFrayne drew a gun, took a bead on the sign down the street that bore the names of David and Abigail Melcher, and popped off two shots that brought every person out of the shops from one end of Main Street to the other to see what in tarnation was going on.

But all they saw was that sign lying in the snow down there in front of the shoe store and the back of Jesse DuFrayne disappearing up the steps into the train.

Inside, he again scooped Abbie into his arms, closing her surprised lips with his own.

"There's no place like home," he said when he had kissed her thoroughly, kicking the door shut behind them.

"Home?" she repeated, glancing around at the lush emerald green velvet interior of the car. "What is this?"

She strained to see around his head. As she turned this way and that he nuzzled her neck, for she was still in his arms and he had no intention of putting her down just yet.

"This, my darling Ab, is your honeymoon suite, especially ordered for the occasion."

What Abbie saw was no common steerage. She had never seen such luxury in her life—a massive bed covered in green velvet, an intimate dinner table set for two, a magnum of champagne in a loving cup, an ornate copper tub off to one side near an ornate pot-bellied stove, where a fire crackled, deep chairs, thick rugs.

"Jesse DuFrayne, you conniving devil! How did you get this coach to Stuart's Junction at the exact time we needed it? And quit kissing my neck as if you don't hear a word of what I'm accusing you of." But in spite of her scolding, she was giggling.

"It'll be a cold day in hell before I quit kissing your neck, Miss Abigail McKenzie, just because you order me to."

"But this *is* an executive coach. You ordered this car to be here. You *did* plan my seduction right down to the last minute!"

"Shut your precious mouth," he said, shutting it for her as the train started moving, and he strode to the oversized bed at the far end of the car, the kiss actually becoming quite slippery and misguided as the coach rocked and gained speed.

They laughed into each other's mouths, then he tossed her onto the bed, stood back, and asked, "What's first? A bath, dinner, champagne . . . or me?"

"How much time do we have?" she asked, already undoing her coat buttons.

"We can go all the way to New Orleans without coming up for air," he replied, that roguish grin tempting her while his eyes danced wickedly.

Taking her coat off she eyed the copper tub, the magnum of champagne, the table set for two, the window beside it where the world raced past. And the man . . . unbuttoning his cuffs.

"Well then, how about all four at once?" Abigail McKenzie suggested.

His eyebrows flew up, and his hands fell still momentarily before starting down the buttons on his chest.

"Well, goddamn . . ." muttered Jesse DuFrayne deliciously, his moustache coming at her in the most tantalizingly menacing way.

About The Author

LAVYRLE SPENCER published her first novel in 1979 and has since gone on to become a major *New York Times* bestselling author with over thirteen million copies of her novels in print. She is the winner of numerous writing awards for her unique, heartwarming novels of life and love. In addition to the three novels in this collection, LaVyrle Spencer's recent bestsellers include *Morning Glory, Bitter Sweet,* and *Forgiving.* She lives with her family in Minnesota.